The New
Encyclopedia of
Science Fiction

A PROMISED LAND PRODUCTION

The New
——Encyclopedia of——
Science Fiction

Edited by James Gunn

VIKING

VIKING

Published by the Penguin Group
Viking Penguin Inc., 40 West 23rd Street,
New York, New York 10010, U.S.A.
Penguin Books Ltd, 27 Wrights Lane,
London W8 5TZ, England
Penguin Books Australia Ltd, Ringwood,
Victoria, Australia
Penguin Books Canada Ltd, 2801 John Street,
Markham, Ontario, Canada L3R 1B4
Penguin Books (N.Z.) Ltd, 182–190 Wairau Road,
Auckland 10, New Zealand

Penguin Books Ltd, Registered Offices:
Harmondsworth, Middlesex, England

First published in 1988 by Viking Penguin Inc.
Published simultaneously in Canada

Page 523 constitutes an extension of this copyright page.

ISBN 0-670-81041-X

Library of Congress Catalog Card Number 87-40637
(CIP data available)

Printed in the United States of America by Arcata Graphics,
Halliday, West Hanover, Massachusetts
Set in Optima and Garamond Book
Designed by Jack Eckstein
Associate Editor: Stephen Goldman

EDITOR'S FOREWORD

For most of its existence as an identifiable genre—since the publication of the first science-fiction magazine, *Amazing Stories,* in 1926—science fiction has been a popular literature enjoyed by a relatively few intensely involved readers. These readers created fandom and supported new writers, some of whom emerged from their midst, and even early collections of books and magazines; from their interest sprang an entire publishing industry, and the beginnings of criticism and scholarship, as well as the tools, the reference works, to make them possible. While they provided an environment in which the genre could develop and evolve, it was one which could exist only on the margins of the literary and economic worlds. Over sixty years later, science fiction occupies a new place, and the way in which it was born, grew, and changed is one of the dramatic stories described in this Encyclopedia.

How has science fiction changed? From what Dale Mullen called "the science-fiction ghetto" and Damon Knight referred to as "the mass medium for the few," science fiction has become a majority literature that has outlasted, and surpassed, all the other popular magazine genres—western, detective, sports, romance—that had their start in the U.S. between 1915 and 1930. Everybody, not just an isolated malcontent here and there, reads science fiction. Today 1500 books of science fiction and fantasy—one out of every four or five books of fiction—are published every year. Science-fiction novels appear regularly on the bestseller lists. The most popular and biggest moneymaking films of all time are science fiction.

The reasons for this remarkable development are discussed in the entries in this Encyclopedia, but perhaps they boil down to a general recognition, at least in industrialized and post-industrialized countries, that the most important fact about the times we live in is that they are going to be different soon. We live in a world of change—what Isaac Asimov has called "a science-fiction world"—and anyone who wants to read a "realistic" fiction turns naturally to science fiction, the literature of change.

What, finally, *is* science fiction? Definitions of SF have ranged all the way from the intuitive (Damon Knight's "science fiction is what I mean when I point at it") and the pragmatic (John Campbell's "science fiction is what science-fiction editors publish" and Norman Spinrad's "science fiction is anything published as science fiction") to the elaborately restrictive (Kingsley Amis's "science fiction is that class of prose narrative treating a situation that could not arise in the world we know, but which is hypothesized on the basis of some innovation in science or technology, or pseudo-science or pseudo-technology, whether human or extraterrestrial in origin") and the formalist (Darko Suvin's "cognitive estrangement" and Robert Scholes's "structural fabulation").

This book identifies it as a genre, which places the emphasis on the reader and the clues ("instructions") given the reader by the author on how to read a particular work. The problem with defining SF is complicated by the fact that it differs from almost every other popular genre of fiction in that it has no characteristic setting (like the western or the gothic) or characteristic action (like the detective story), but is more, as Frederik Pohl has said, "a characteristic way of thinking about things."

At its simplest level, genre identification is, after all, part of the long process that turns an idea in the author's mind into an image in the reader's head—creation, acceptance, publication, sale, and consumption. The SF label is, in the end, a bookseller's and book purchaser's convenience: it tells the bookseller where to place the book in his shop, and the book buyer where to look for it. Authors may not care into what category their books are placed (although some do: Isaac Asimov wants to be identified as writing SF; Kurt Vonnegut does not), but editors and publishers do so as to call the books they publish to the attention of the appropriate readers and largest number of potential purchasers.

But, on a more profound level, once readers have the book in their hands, as Samuel R. Delany has pointed out, they have to know how to read it. All genres have reading protocols, including SF.

Unlike traditional fiction, which can be seen as the literature of continuity, SF is the literature of discontinuity: it deals with a world that is not the same as our familiar world of everyday reality because of some significant alteration in that world. While fantasy is also part of the literature of discontinuity, science fiction is "the literature of change"; fantasy is simply "the literature of difference." "Change" implies an alteration in present reality whose origins can be traced through plausible cause and effect; "difference" implies an arbitrary alteration in present reality. At the simplest level, fantasy asks to be read with a suspension of disbelief, while SF offers plausible arguments for suspending disbelief. One cannot read the SF that is at the heart of the genre without asking it hard questions: How did we get there from here? How is the world of the story like and unlike the real world? What do those similarities and differences mean to life in those times and our attitudes toward it? Those kinds of questions destroy fantasy. The knowledgeable author understands this and instructs the reader how to exercise the appropriate reading protocols by various devices, including the method by which the characters arrive at the "discontinuous world": the SF character travels by spaceship, say, or by time machine; the fantasy character falls down a rabbit hole or passes through a door in a cupboard.

Science fiction is the focus of this Encyclopedia, and we have attempted to cover it in all its aspects. The novel, for instance, may be SF's best known and most popular format, but the short story, the novelette, and the short novel are perhaps its ideal length, and we have dealt with these as well. Similarly, science fiction can be found in film, in illustration, in poetry, in theater, and in music, and we have given coverage to them all, along with their particular qualities and standards of excellence. Fantasy, for reasons of definition and space, has been excluded.

Like all writing, encyclopedias are the consequences of a long series of decisions. Our first decision was how to limit the subject to entries and the entries to lengths that could be published in a single volume. All encyclopedias, even the most comprehensive, use some principles of exclusion, and modern, one-volume encyclopedias have an even greater need to circumscribe the universes they include within their covers.

We also have had to make some choices, sometimes hard choices. We had, for instance, to decide whether to include entries on everybody who had ever written in the field; our conclusion was to include only authors who had a body of work or who promised, at this early stage in their careers, to develop a body of work. We had to decide whether entries deserved individual mention or could be brought together fruitfully; that led to the commissioning of essays on SF in foreign countries where SF was significant and coverage of most foreign authors in those essays. We included individual entries only on major magazines; the rest are rounded up under "Magazines, Limited Run." Similarly, we have entries on Agents, Business, Publishers, Scholarship, and so forth.

The creation of this Encyclopedia, at this point in the history of technological civilization and the history of science fiction, is understandable. It could not have happened without the vision and untiring efforts of two dedicated women, Peg Streep and Leslie Garisto of Promised Land Productions, nor without the planning, assistance, insight, and unstinting contributions of my associate editor, Stephen H. Goldman, nor the work of the more than 100 contributors whose initials identify the entries they have authored for this book and whose qualifications are listed under "Contributors." From the beginning we wanted this book to utilize the best ideas of the best writers and scholars we could induce to work on it. To them goes most of the credit: fortunately, and perhaps understandably, along with the growth of science fiction has come the growth in scholars of all kinds and scholarship of all kinds.

We also owe a debt to all the bibliographical and biographical work that has preceded this book, from the enlightened efforts of fans such as Bradford M. Day and Donald H. Tuck through the work, early and late, of Everett F. Bleiler, up to the work of Neil Barron, Thomas D. Clareson, Robert Reginald, Curtis C. Smith, William Contento, Charles N. Brown, Marshall B. Tymn, Mike Ashley, Hal Hall, the science-fiction news magazines *Locus* and *Science Fiction Chronicle,* and Peter Nicholls and *The Science Fiction Encyclopedia.* Because of their efforts, this Encyclopedia did not have to start its work from the ground floor but could build on their foundations. These authors and their earlier works can be recommended to the interested reader not only for their still useful information, some of which may not be duplicated in this Encyclopedia, but for their insights and for the perspectives they offer on their historic times. It is illustrative, however, of the rapidity of change in the field that the decade since the publication of *The Science Fiction Encyclopedia* has seen science fiction's greatest growth, in readership, in general popularity, in financial returns, in scholarship, in new authors—in practically every aspect by which changes in a genre can be measured.

What we set out to create—beginning with Ned Huston, my graduate assistant, and Johan Heje, my Danish Fulbright scholar, and proceeding through the contributors, the encyclopedia editors, the copy editors, the designer, up to the publishing house and its editor—was a concise, wide-ranging, affordable, handsome encyclopedia. The result is in your hands.

James E. Gunn

——— HOW TO USE THIS BOOK———

The articles in this volume fall into three general categories: author entries (writers, artists and illustrators, actors, directors, and the like), film entries by title, and essays, as well as a number of entries on important publications and organizations. All the entries are arranged alphabetically. All the essays—which range from broad discussions of themes, topics, and the historical development of science fiction to the literary aspects of SF and SF in specific countries—are listed in the table of contents ("Essays"). They are also set off typographically from entries.

Film and television entries begin with credit and technical information, set in italics. A checklist of all the entries pertaining to film and television can be found on page 521 at the back of the book.

Within an article, references to other entries and essays are given in small capital letters at their first mention. Articles of related interest appear at the end of the entry after the words *See also.* Writers are listed under the name by which they are best known; in some cases, these are, in fact, pseudonyms. All entries are signed with the contributor's initials, a key to which is contained on page *ix.*

Biographical Data

Dates: All dates for literary works represent first publication in book form unless otherwise indicated. When two dates appear separated by a slash (1945/1968), the first represents magazine publication, the second, book publication. Hyphenated dates (1955–56) indicate that magazine publication covered at least part of two or more calendar years. Dates separated by commas (1964, 1965, 1967) indicate that parts of the work appeared separately in those years. Films are dated by the year of their release. Every effort has been made to supply birth and death dates for author entries; when no dates are available, the omission is indicated by a question mark.

Film titles: Films are listed by their American release title. When a film has been released under an alternative title, that title follows the original in parentheses (after *Also known as*). When there are a number of alternative titles, they are listed after the credits. Foreign films are listed by their American release title; the original foreign title follows in parentheses.

Works: This book uses three different kinds of listings for works by authors. (Only works in the SF genre are included.) "Works" lists the complete body of work by a given author. "Other Works" contains a partial list which, when combined with the works mentioned in the article, constitutes the writer's complete body of work in the genre. "Notable Other Works" is a selective list of works in the genre, used primarily for very prolific authors.

Translations: When a work has been translated into the English language, it is referred to by its translated title, with the original-language title in parentheses and italics. Where a work has not been translated into English, the original title is given first, with a literal translation following in parentheses and quotation marks.

CONTRIBUTORS

F.J.A. **Forrest J Ackerman** has been an author, agent, editor, and number-one SF fan since 1926; he is the author of over 2000 articles about SF and fantasy fiction and films, as well as many books, including *Fantastic Movie Memories, Sense of Wonder Science Fiction*, and *The Frankenscience Monster*.

B.W.A. **Brian W. Aldiss**, a renowned English novelist and short story writer, is the author of several books of science-fiction criticism, including *The Shape of Further Things, SF Art, The Pale Shadow of Science*, and *Trillion Year Spree*, as well as many novels and collections, including the Helliconia trilogy.

P.A. **Poul Anderson**, a major author of SF and fantasy since 1947, has written more than eighty books, including *Brain Wave, The High Crusade, Three Hearts and Three Lions*, and *The Man Who Counts*; he has also contributed articles about SF writing to books and journals.

M.A. **Mike Ashley**, an English editor, scholar, and anthologist and one of the field's leading experts on magazines and magazine SF, has written or edited some twenty books, including *The History of the Science Fiction Magazines* and (with Marshall Tymn) *Science Fiction, Fantasy, and Weird Fiction Magazines*.

D.B. **Douglas Barbour** is professor of English at the University of Alberta, poetry editor of *Canadian Forum*, the author of *Worlds out of Words: The SF Novels of Samuel R. Delany*, and a contributor of articles on SF authors to a variety of publications.

C.B. **Craig Barrow**, a professor at the University of Tennessee (Chattanooga), is a frequent contributor of essays and reviews, and is the author of *Montage in James Joyce's Ulysses* and co-editor of *Politics, Society and the Humanities*.

G. Bear **Greg Bear** sold his first science-fiction short story at the age of fifteen; since then, he has continued to write both short and longer fiction, including *Hegvia, Psychlone, Beyond Heaven's River, Strength of Stones*, and *The Infinity Concerto*.

G.B. **Gregory Benford** is professor of physics at the University of California, Irvine; he is internationally known for his short stories and novels, among them *Timescape, Across the Sea of Suns, Against Infinity, In the Ocean of Night*, and *If the Stars Are Gods*.

E.F.B. **Everett F. Bleiler**, a long-time editor (at Dover Books), bibliographer, and scholar, edited the first important SF bibliography, *The Checklist of Fantastic Literature*, in 1948 and the first Best of the Year anthology (with T. E. Dikty) beginning in 1949; he has continued his work into the 1980s with *Science Fiction Writers* and other reference works.

J.E.B. **Judith E. Boss**, associate professor of English at the University of Nebraska at Omaha, is a contributor to *Extrapolation, Science-Fiction Studies*, and other periodicals.

E.N.B. **E. Nelson Bridwell**, a writer of comics and an expert on comics history, worked for DC Comics and wrote for *Mad* magazine for more than twenty years; he served as associate editor of the Superman line and was considered a major figure in the "Silver Age of Comics." He died in 1987.

P.B. **Peter Brigg** is a professor at the University of Guelph (Ontario) and is the author of *J. G. Ballard* and a contributor to *Twentieth-Century Science Fiction Writers*.

| R.D. | **Richard Dalby** is a British freelance writer, bibliographer, literary researcher, and editor of several fantasy anthologies; he has also contributed to *The Penguin Encyclopedia of Horror and the Supernatural* and *The Biographical Dictionary of Science Fiction and Fantasy Artists*. |

K.R.D. **Kevin R. Danzey** is an independent filmmaker with over fifty short SF films to his credit. He has written for *Amazing Cinema* and *Magick Theater* and published his own SF fanzine, *Xenomorph*.

E.L.D. **Eric Leif Davin**, a former teacher of nonfiction writing at the University of Pittsburgh, is a frequent contributor to *Fantasy Commentator* and *Radical History Review*, among other periodicals.

J.R.D. **John R. Dean**, professor at the University of Paris, is the author of *Restless Wanderers: Shakespeare and the Pattern of Romance* and *Foreign: Poems and Short Stories*, as well as articles for journals and periodicals.

L.S.d.C. **L. Sprague de Camp** has been a distinguished author of science fiction, fantasy, and heroic fantasy since 1937. Among his credits are *Lest Darkness Fall*, *The Compleat Enchanter* (with Fletcher Pratt), and contributions to the Conan series, as well as nonfiction books about science, archeology, and ancient history, and the writing of science fiction.

C.C.d.C. **Catherine C. de Camp** has collaborated frequently on a variety of subjects with her husband, L. Sprague de Camp.

B.D. **Bradley Denton** has been a full-time writer since his graduation with a master's degree from the University of Kansas; his short fiction, most of it published in *Fantasy and Science Fiction*, earned him a Campbell Award best-new-writer nomination. His first novel was *Wrack and Roll*.

H.D. **Howard DeVore**, a member of First Fandom and a book dealer with a substantial private collection, publishes *A History of the Hugo, Nebula, and International Fantasy Awards*, a reference work co-authored by Donald Franson.

G.R.D. **Gordon R. Dickson**, a former president of the Science Fiction Writers of America, has written over sixty novels including *Dorsai!* and other titles in his long epic of human evolution, the Childe Cycle.

V.D.F. **Vincent Di Fate** began his freelance art career in 1969 and has worked almost exclusively in the science-fiction, astronomical, and aerospace art markets ever since. In addition to his art activities, he wrote a column on SF art for *Starship Magazine* and lectures extensively; a book of his work, *Di Fate's Catalogue of Science Fiction Hardware*, has been published.

T.D. **Terry Dowling**, an SF author and critic, is a frequent contributor to *Science Fiction: A Review of Speculative Literature* and other journals and co-editor of *The Essential Ellison*. He received the William Atheling Award for criticism.

T.P.D. **Thomas P. Dunn** teaches at Miami University in Ohio. A frequent contributor to *Extrapolation* and *Fantasy Review*, he is also co-editor (with Richard Erlich) of *The Mechanical God: Machines in Science Fiction* and *Clockwork Worlds: Mechanized Environments in SF*.

J.M.E. **Jeffrey M. Elliot** is professor of political science at North Carolina Central University and the author of over fifty-seven books, including *Science Fiction Voices #2*, *Science Fiction Voices #3*, *The Future of the Space Program*, *If J.F.K. Had Lived*, and *Kindred Spirits*.

A.C.E. **Alan C. Elms** is professor of psychology at the University of California at Davis, and a frequent contributor to *Psychology Today*; he is working on a book about Cordwainer Smith.

P.J.F.	**Philip José Farmer,** a major science-fiction author since 1952, has produced more than sixty novels and collections of short fiction; he is best known for his five-volume Riverworld series beginning with the Hugo Award–winning novel *To Your Scattered Bodies Go.*
H.B.F.	**H. Bruce Franklin** is professor of English and American literature at Rutgers and the author and editor of thirteen books, including *Future Perfect: American Science Fiction of the Nineteenth Century, Robert A. Heinlein: America as Science Fiction, The Wake of the Gods,* and *The Superweapon in American Culture.*
A.J.F.	**Adam J. Frisch** is professor of English at Briar Cliff College (Iowa).
V.G.	**Vladimir Gakov** is a pseudonym of Michael A. Kovalchuk, a Soviet critic and reviewer specializing in science fiction. He has contributed numerous articles to Soviet publications.
R.G.	**Robert Galbreath** is a bibliographer at Northwestern University Library and a frequent contributor to *The Journal of Religion, Science-Fiction Studies,* and *Extrapolation,* among other periodicals.
S.H.G.	**Stephen H. Goldman,** associate professor of English at the University of Kansas, has written articles in SF journals and entries in reference works; he is at work on a book about the fiction of Frederik Pohl.
J. Gordon	**Joan Gordon** has a Ph.D. in English from the University of Iowa, where she wrote her dissertation on science fiction. She wrote two books for the Starmont series, on Joe Haldeman and Gene Wolfe.
R. Goulart	**Ron Goulart,** a prolific long-time author of popular books in several genres as well as comics magazines, also has written books about the popular media, such as *Cheap Thrills: An Informal History of the Pulp Magazines.*
B.K.G.	**Barry Keith Grant** is associate professor of film and popular culture at Brock University (Ontario). He is the author of *Planks of Reason: Essays on the Horror Film, Film Study in the Undergraduate Curriculum,* and *Film Genre: Theory and Criticism,* as well as many articles.
S.E.G.	**Scott E. Green** is a poet in the fields of science fiction, fantasy, and horror; he has been published in *Amazing* and *American Fantasy* and is currently compiling a directory of SF, fantasy, and horror poets.
M.H.G.	**Martin H. Greenberg,** professor of regional analysis at the University of Wisconsin, Green Bay, is best known as the field's most prolific anthologist, with more than 100 anthologies and single-author collections to his credit.
J.E.G.	**James E. Gunn,** professor of English at the University of Kansas, former president of both the Science Fiction Writers of America and the Science Fiction Research Association, and a well-known author of SF since 1948, including *The Immortals, The Listeners,* and *The Dreamers,* is equally known for his books about SF, including *Alternate Worlds: The Illustrated History of Science Fiction* and his four-volume critical anthology, *The Road to Science Fiction.*
J.G.	**Jon M. Gustafson** has contributed to *The Visual Encyclopedia of Science Fiction, The Science Fiction Encyclopedia,* and *The Starlog SF Book;* he is the author of *Chroma: The Art of Alex Schomburg.*
R.M.H.	**Ronald M. Hahn,** a German SF writer, editor, translator, and literary agent, has edited *SF Nova,* written more than half a dozen SF novels, and edited several anthologies, including *Science Fiction aus Deutschland.*

H.W.H.   **Hal W. Hall,** head of the Special Formats division of the Texas A & M University library, is best known for his *Science Fiction Book Review Index* and *The Science Fiction Magazines: A Checklist of Titles and Issues through 1982.*

D.M.H.   **Donald M. Hassler** is professor of English at Kent State University, managing editor of *Extrapolation*, and a former president of the Science Fiction Research Association. He is the author and editor of numerous studies in SF, including *Comic Tones in Science Fiction, Hal Clement,* and *Isaac Asimov.*

J.H.   **Johan Heje,** a teacher of English in a gymnasium near Copenhagen and at the University of Copenhagen, has studied science fiction at the University of Kansas with a Fulbright grant and has been involved with the production of Danish radio programs about SF.

E.A.H.   **Elizabeth Ann Hull** is an associate professor of English at William Rainey Harper College; she is a frequent contributor to *Extrapolation, Locus, Science Fiction Chronicle,* and *Fantasy Review,* among other periodicals.

N.H.   **Ned Huston,** a published SF writer, is working on a Ph.D. in English at the University of Kansas.

M.J.   **Maxim Jakubowski,** a British writer, critic, editor, translator, and anthologist, has written SF stories and edited numerous anthologies of French SF.

E.J.   **Edward James** is a senior lecturer in history at the University of York (U.K.) and the editor of *Foundation: The Review of Science Fiction;* he is also the author of numerous articles on SF and six books on medieval history and archeology.

L.A.J.   **Lethonee A. Jones** teaches in the School of Social Work at Western Michigan University.

S.T.J.   **S. T. Joshi** is editor of *Lovecraft Studies* and *Studies in Weird Fiction;* he has edited *H. P. Lovecraft: Four Decades of Criticism* and a corrected edition of Lovecraft's collected fiction.

J.K.   **John Kessel,** assistant professor of American literature and creative writing at North Carolina State University, won the 1982 Nebula Award for his novella "Another Orphan." He is a frequent contributor to *Isaac Asimov's Science Fiction Magazine* and *Fantasy and Science Fiction* and the author of the novel *Freedom Beach* (with James Patrick Kelly).

B.L.   **Brooks Landon,** a professor of English at the University of Iowa with a special interest in science-fiction film, produced a series on the American science-fiction movie for Iowa Public Television.

W.L.   **Walt Lee,** an American film writer, consultant, and editor, wrote the three-volume *Reference Guide to Fantastic Films* and an SF-horror novel, *Shapes,* with Richard Delap.

R.F.L.   **Russell F. Letson,** a microcomputer consultant and writer, is a contributor to *Fantasy Review, Foundation, Extrapolation,* and *Science-Fiction,* among other periodicals, and has written introductions and entries for a great many works in the field.

M.M.L.   **Michael M. Levy** teaches at the University of Wisconsin (Stout); he is a frequent contributor to *Fantasy Review* and is the author of the forthcoming book *Natalie Babbitt.*

R.A.L.   **Richard A. Lupoff** is a frequent contributor to periodicals, among them the *San Francisco Chronicle*, the *Washington Post*, and *Ramparts*. He is also the author of *Edgar Rice Burroughs: Master of Adventure*, *All in Color for a Dime, Countersolar Galaxy's End*, and *Lovecraft's Book*, among other titles.

F.L.   **Francis Lyall** is professor of public law at the University of Aberdeen (Scotland) and is a frequent contributor to legal periodicals. He is the author of *Of Presbyters and Kings: Church and State in the Law of Scotland*, among other titles, and he is the editor of *The Marathon Photograph and Other Stories* and *Brother and Other Stories*, both by Clifford D. Simak.

B.M.   **Barry McGhan** has a Ph.D. in educational sociology and works as the instructional computer specialist for a Michigan school district; he has written articles on SF for *Extrapolation, The English Journal*, and other publications, and is the author of *Science Fiction and Fantasy Pseudonyms.*

B.N.M.   **Barry N. Malzberg** is the author of some twenty-five SF novels and 300 short stories, among them *Beyond Apollo, Tactics of Conquest, Herovit's World*, and *Galaxies*, as well as a collection of critical essays about SF, *The Engines of the Night.*

W.E.M.   **Willis E. McNelly** is professor of English at California State University and the editor of *The Dune Encyclopedia, Mars, We Love You, Above the Human Landscape*, and *Science Fiction Novellas*, in addition to dozens of articles.

R.M.   **Richard B. Mathews,** associate professor of English at the University of Tampa, is a frequent contributor to *Fantasy Review, Konglomerati*, and the *Southern Poetry Review*. He is the author of *The Clockwork Universe of Anthony Burgess, Worlds Beyond the World: The Fantastic Vision of William Morris*, and *Lightning from a Clear Sky: Tolkien, The Trilogy, and the Silmarillion.*

S.L.M.   **Sandra L. Miesel** is the author of some fifty articles about science fiction and SF art which have appeared in books and periodicals, among them *Amazing, Asimov's Galileo, SF Monthly, Destinies*, and *Extrapolation.* She is the author of *Dreamrider.*

F.J.M.   **Francis J. Molson,** professor of English at Central Michigan University, is a frequent contributor to *Children's Literature Quarterly.*

C.M.   **Chris Morgan** is a contributor to *Fantasy Review* and *Vector* and is the author of *Future Man, The Shape of Futures Past*, and *Fritz Leiber: A Bibliography.*

S.M.   **Sam Moskowitz,** a long-time fan and chronicler of the fan movement, was one of the earliest teachers and scholars of SF, producing important early studies of SF writers in *Explorers of the Infinite* and *Seekers of Tomorrow* as well as anthologies such as *Science Fiction by Gaslight* and *Under the Moons of Mars.*

P.N.H.   **Patrick Nielsen Hayden** has edited literary criticism for a New York publisher of reference books, and co-edits the Hugo-nominated SF fanzine *Izzard.* He has also been twice nominated for the Hugo Award in the Best Fan Writer category.

D.P.-S.   **Diane Parkin-Speer** teaches English at Southwest Texas State University and is a frequent contributor to *Extrapolation* and *Fantasy Review.*

J.J.P.   **John J. Pierce,** associate editor of *Private Label* magazine and former editor of *Galaxy,* is a frequent contributor of essays about SF authors to journals and reference volumes, and is the author of a three-volume study of SF beginning with *Foundations of Science Fiction.*

F.P.   **Frederik Pohl** is a writer who has also been an agent and an editor; he is a five-time Hugo winner and has won most of the other awards the field has to offer. His best known novels are *The Space Merchants* (with C. M. Kornbluth), *Man Plus*, *Gateway*, and *JEM.*

H.L.P.   **Harold Lee Prosser** is a former sociology teacher; now a freelance writer, he is the author of over 800 articles and works of fiction and nonfiction, among them *Dandelion Seeds: Eighteen Stories, The Capricorn and Other Fantasy Stories, Goodbye, Lon Chaney, Jr., Goodbye, Summer Wine, Frank Herbert: The Prophet of Dune,* and *Robert Bloch: The Man Who Walked through Mirrors.*

M.R.   **Mike Resnick** is the author of eighteen science-fiction novels, including *Santiago, Walpurgis III, Tales of the Velvet Comet,* and *The Branch.*

J.S.   **Joseph L. Sanders** is professor of English at Lakeland Community College and the author of *Roger Zelazny: A Primary and Secondary Bibliography* and *E. E. "Doc" Smith,* as well as numerous articles and essays.

P.S.   **Pamela Sargent** is the author of *Cloned Lives, Starshadows, The Sudden Star, Watchstar, The Alien Upstairs, Eye of the Comet, Venus of Dreams,* and *The Shore of Women.* She has also edited five antholoilgies.

S.S.   **Stanley Schmidt** is editor of *Analog Science Fiction/Science Fact,* and a frequent contributor to periodicals. He is the author of the novels *Newton and the Quasi-Apple, The Sins of the Fathers, Lifeboat,* and *Tweedlioop.*

D.J.S.   **David J. Schow** is the author of *The Outer Limits: The Official Companion* and a novel, *The Kill Riff,* in addition to sixteen psuedonymous series novels and TV/film novelizations. He recently edited *Silver Scream,* an anthology of cinema horror stories, and assembled his first collection of short fiction, *Seeing Red.*

D.S.   **Darrell Schweitzer** is a frequent contributor to *Night Cry, Twilight Zone, Science Fiction Review,* and *Aboriginal SF,* and is the author of *The Shattered Goddess, We Are All Legends,* and *Tom O'Bedlam's Night Out,* among other titles.

S.M.S.   **Susan M. Shwartz** is a contributor to *Amazing, Analog,* the *Washington Post,* and *The New York Times,* among other periodicals, and is the author of *Silk Roads and Shadows, Byzantine Trilogy,* and *Heritage of Flight,* along with short fiction. She has also edited several anthologies.

N.S.   **Norman Spinrad** is a major SF writer best known for his novels *Bug Jack Barron, The Iron Dream, Riding the Torch, Child of Fortune,* and *Little Heroes;* he also contributes columns of criticism to *Isaac Asimov's Science Fiction Magazine,* has edited *Modern Science Fiction,* and has written about SF for several books and journals.

B.S.   **Brian Stableford** is an SF writer and scholar, lecturer in sociology at the University of Reading (U.K.), and the author of, among other titles, *Scientific Romance in Britain 1890–1950, The Third Millennium: A History of the World A.D. 2000–3000* (with David Langford), and *Future Man.*

W.D.S.   **W. D. Stevens** is the author of *Double, Double, Toil and Trouble, The Perils of Pauline Programmer,* and *The Care and Feeding of Data Base Systems.*

R.H.T.   **Raymond H. Thompson** is a professor of English at Acadia University, Nova Scotia, specializing in medieval literature and science fiction and fantasy. He has published a bibliography of Gordon R. Dickson and has a special interest in the work of Doris Piserchia.

A.E. van V.   **A. E. van Vogt** is the author of some fifty SF novels and collections, among them *The Mixed Men*, *The War against the Rull*, *Rogue Ship*, *Children of Tomorrow*, *The Battle of Forever*, *The Anarchistic Colossus*, *Pendulum*, *Cosmic Encounter*, and *Computerworld*.

D.P.V.   **Dianne P. Varnon** is a graduate student at the University of Nevada (Reno).

B.W.   **Bill Warren** is a major authority on SF and fantasy film who is best known for his two-volume survey of SF films between 1950 and 1962, *Keep Watching the Skies!*.

P.W.   **Patricia S. Warrick,** a former president of the Science Fiction Research Association, teaches at the University of Wisconsin Center (Menasha) and is the author of *The Cybernetic Imagination in Science Fiction* and *Mind in Motion: The Fiction of Philip K. Dick,* as well as the co-editor of several anthologies.

I.W.   **Ian Watson** is senior lecturer in futures studies at Birmingham Polytechnic (U.K.) and is a frequent contributor to *Fantasy and Science Fiction*, *Interzone*, *Foundation*, and the *Review of Science Fiction*. He is the author of fourteen novels, among them *The Embedding*, *Miracle Visitors*, *Chekhov's Journey*, *Deathhunter*, and *Slow Birds*.

R.H.W.   **Robert H. Wilcox** is a retired professor of English at Glendale College (Arizona) and has been a consulting editor for *Amazing Stories,* as well as the author of numerous articles.

J.W.   **Jack Williamson** is a world renowned science-fiction writer, recognized with the Grand Master Award by the Science Fiction Writers of America, and a retired professor of English at Eastern New Mexico University; his published works, beginning in 1928 and continuing through 1988, include *The Legion of Space*, *The Humanoids*, and *Firechild*, as well as *H. G. Wells: Critic of Progress* and *Teaching SF: Education for Tomorrow*.

D.W.   **Don Willis** is a frequent contributor to *Film Quarterly* and is the author of numerous articles on film. He is also the author of *Horror and Science Fiction Films* (volumes I, II, and III) and *The Films of Frank Capra,* and the editor of *Variety's Complete Science Fiction Reviews*.

M.T.W.   **Milton T. Wolf** is collection-development librarian at the University of Nevada (Reno) and the author of numerous articles.

G.K.W.   **Gary K. Wolfe,** Dean of the Evelyn T. Stone College at Roosevelt University, is a prominent SF scholar and author of *The Known and the Unknown: The Iconography of Science Fiction* and *Critical Terms for Science Fiction and Fantasy: A Glossary and Guide to Scholarship*.

M.M.W.   **Martin Morse Wooster,** formerly Washington editor of *Harper's Magazine* and currently associate editor of the *Wilson Quarterly,* has contributed articles and reviews to *Esquire*, *Reader's Digest*, *The Wall Street Journal*, *The Washington Post*, and *Twentieth-Century Science Fiction Writers*.

J.R.W.   **Jacqueline R. Wytenbroek** has taught in the department of English at the University of British Columbia; she has a special interest in the work of Madeleine L'Engle.

H.M.Z.   **Hoda M. Zaki** teaches at Hampton University (Virginia) and is the author of *Phoenix Renewed: The Survival and Mutation of Utopian Thought in North American Science Fiction, 1965–1982*.

G.Z.   **George Zebrowski** is an editor, author, and expert on SF film; he has edited several anthologies including three volumes of *Nebula Awards*, *The SFWA Bulletin*, an SF reprint series, and the quarterly magazine *Synergy;* his best known novels are *Macrolife*, *The Omega Point*, and *Sunspacers*.

ESSAYS

A

ABBOTT, EDWIN A[BBOTT] (1838–1926).

British clergyman and educator. Abbott was the author of *Flatland: A Romance of Many Dimensions* (published under the pseudonym A. Square, 1884). A satiric exploration of mathematical concepts and the limits of perception, *Flatland* describes a two-dimensional world whose inhabitants appear in the shape of squares, triangles, circles, and so on.

J.H.

ABE, KOBO (1924–).

Japanese author and playwright whose singular literary style draws on both twentieth-century European and traditional Japanese culture and myth. This synthesis frequently produces haunting, poetic works (even in translation) such as the non-science-fiction novel *The Woman in the Dunes* (1960, translated into English 1964) whose fantasylike, enigmatic world defies any national label. This novel reminds readers of the work of Kafka, but there is a delicacy to the setting and characters that sets it apart. In the same way, *The Ruined Map* (1969) and *The Box Man* (1973, translated 1974) are better defined by their absurdist features (used to highlight the alienation of individuals) than by the minor traces of science fiction each contains.

With *Inter Ice Age 4* (1959, translated 1970), however, Abé produced a novel that is indisputably science fiction. Set in the near future, it describes humanity's attempt to adapt the race to the coming inundation of the Earth by the melting of the polar ice caps. The Japanese have developed a technique whereby human embryos can be modified to produce gill-breathers capable of living on the future ocean planet. At the same time, computer technology can create complete human analogues, with which computers can both predict future human behavior and store doppelgängers of living people. Abé used this complex plot to question the relation of the present to the future. Should people presume to shape the future so as to continue the present? Or must the future be allowed to develop without being limited by the shortsightedness of contemporary self-interest? In *Inter Ice Age 4* Abé took a major SF theme, complete with a credible technology, and created an original, enduring work.

S.H.G.

ABERNATHY, ROBERT (1924–).

American linguist and short story writer. Abernathy contributed about forty short stories to *Planet Stories*, THE MAGAZINE OF FANTASY AND SCIENCE FICTION, and other science-fiction magazines during the 1940s and 1950s. He is a Slavic scholar and has translated articles by Stanislaw LEM.

J.H.

THE ABOMINABLE SNOWMAN OF THE HIMALAYAS (1957).

Directed by Val Guest; screenplay by Nigel Kneale; adapted from the teleplay "The Creature" by Nigel Kneale; photographed by Arthur Grant; music by Humphrey Searle. With Forrest Tucker, Peter Cushing, Maureen Connell, Richard Wattis, Robert Brown, Michael Brill, Wolfe Morris, Arnold Marle, Anthony Chin. 85 minutes. Black and white. Alternate title: The Abominable Snowman.

The yeti of Central Asia have provided material for few films, perhaps because of the limited nature of the necessary setting. In this Hammer Films adaptation of Nigel Kneale's teleplay, sensationalism is played down in favor of mystery, tension, and the clash between characters. An American entrepreneur (Forrest Tucker), ironically named Friend, convinces reluctant botanist Rollason (Peter Cushing) to help him search for the mysterious yeti. Friend kills one of the creatures and steals its corpse; the other yeti dog the trail of the expedition. After a series of desertions and fatal accidents, only Rollason survives. In a cave he is confronted by the briefly glimpsed yeti, who are intelligent and reclusive, a gentle race hiding from humans. Though handsome and well acted, the film lacks excitement; even so, it is easily the best movie on the subject.

B.W.

THE ABSENT-MINDED PROFESSOR (1961).

Directed by Robert Stevenson; screenplay by Bill Walsh; adapted from the short story "A Situation of Gravity" by Samuel W. Taylor; photographed by Edward Colman; music by George Bruns. With Fred MacMurray, Nancy Olson, Keenan Wynn, Tommy Kirk, Elliott Reid, Leon Ames, Ed Wynn. 97 minutes. Black and white.

After the success of the fantasy *The Shaggy Dog*, Walt Disney made this similar, also successful film; a sequel, *Son of Flubber*, followed. *The Absent-minded Professor* renewed Fred MacMurray's lagging career; after it he made several more films for Disney. Eccentric professor MacMurray invents an antigravity goo that he dubs *flubber*. He uses it to make his Model T fly and thereby accomplishes his romantic and financial goals. This is a silly, amusing family movie, directed as a farce; although not to everyone's taste, the film is a good example of its genre. Surprisingly, although the science is fantastic, it is treated with stringent logic.

B.W.

ACKERMAN, FORREST J[AMES] (1916–).

American writer, editor, and literary agent, best known as "Mr. Science Fiction," SF's number-one fan, whom Ray Bradbury called "the most important fan/collector/human being in the history of science-fantasy fiction." Ackerman discovered science fiction with the October 1926 issue of AMAZING STORIES and became both an avid fan and a collector. He assembled one of the most complete collections of science fiction and fantasy; now called the Fantasy Foundation and housed in a four-story, seventeen-room mansion, it includes not only almost all the SF books and magazines ever published but also masses of other memorabilia, including over 125,000 movie stills, scripts, posters, record albums, correspondence, and autographs. As a fan Ackerman was associate editor of the first true SF fanzine, *The Time Traveller* (1932) and produced his own fanzine, *Voice of the Imagi-Nation* (1939–1947); for these efforts he received the first Hugo Award in 1953 as No. 1 Fan Personality.

As a writer Ackerman first appeared in print with "A Trip to Mars" (1929), winner of a contest run by the *San Francisco Chronicle* for best short story by a teenager. He has published stories, many of them collaborations, sporadically ever since; a selection appears in *Science Fiction Worlds of Forrest J Ackerman and Friends* (1969). Much of Ackerman's fiction reflects his schoolboyish sense of humor and love for words. He is a devoted Esperantist, a frightful punster, and the coiner of many fannish expressions, including the notorious term *sci-fi*.

As an editor Ackerman is best known for *Famous Monsters of Filmland*, which he edited from 1958 to 1982, along with its companion magazines (*Spacemen* and *Monster World*) and many spin-off books. He also edited the American edition of *Perry Rhodan* (1969–1977). Strictly within the SF field Ackerman has edited the anthologies *Best Science Fiction for 1973* (1973), *The Gernsback Awards, volume 1, 1926* (1982) and *Gosh! Wow! (Sense of Wonder) Science Fiction* (1982).

Although as a writer and an editor Ackerman has made only a peripheral impression on the SF world, his role as curator and savior of science fiction's legacy is of considerable importance.

M.A.

ADAMS, DOUGLAS [NOEL] (1952–).

British author. Born in Cambridge and educated at Cambridge University, Adams graduated from free-lance writing to a position as script editor of the DOCTOR WHO television series (1978–1980) and his own 1978 BBC radio show, THE HITCH-HIKER'S GUIDE TO THE GALAXY, which the following year was turned into a mini–TV series and a best-selling book. The success of the book and the series was perhaps surprising, particularly because they were comic spoofs of science-fiction conventions such as aliens, tourism, universal translators, faster-than-light travel, robots, galactic empires, and the meaning of life.

The good fun, and the best-seller tradition, continued through three sequels: *The Restaurant at the End of the Universe* (1980), *Life, the Universe, and Everything* (1982), and *So Long, and Thanks for All the Fish* (1985), although the comic invention tends to dwindle through the last two. The basic story—Arthur Dent, the only human survivor of the destruction of Earth to make way for an interstellar bypass, takes off, with galactic tour-guide writer Ford Prefect, on a hitchhiking tour of the galaxy—allows Adams to indulge in comic characterizations and improbably hilarious situations capitalizing on puns, clichés, and shaggy-dog endings.

In 1987 Adams switched to the SF mystery genre with *Dirk Gently's Holistic Detective Agency*; Gently specializes in solving "the *whole* crime; we find the *whole* person." He encounters time travel, quantum mechanics, possession, and Electric Monks from another galaxy (who "believed things for you, thus saving you what was becoming an increasingly onerous task, that of believing all the things the world expected you to believe") while helping a Cambridge classmate wanted for murder and saving the human race from extinction.

J.E.G.

THE ADVENTURES OF BUCKAROO BANZAI (1984).

Directed by W. D. Richter; screenplay by Earl MacRauch; photographed by Fred J. Koenenkamp; music by Michael Boddicker. With Peter Weller, John Lithgow, Ellen Barkin, Jeff Goldblum, Christopher Lloyd. 100 minutes. Color.

Buckaroo Banzai is a CYBERPUNK Doc Savage film. Peter Weller plays Buckaroo Banzai, head of a group of crime fighters (as well as neurosurgeon, physicist, rocket-car driver, and rock singer) pitted against John Lithgow as the sinister Dr. Lizardo. The plot makes absolutely no sense, but knowing that Martians really *did* land in Grovers Corners, New Jersey, during Orson Welles's *War of the Worlds* broadcast will make things clearer. There's a great deal of manic energy in the film, and Weller is certainly a likable hero (and Lithgow a fascinating villain), but Earl MacRauch's screenplay is so dense that it might have worked better as a novel. All things considered the film is a satisfying, if puzzling, entertainment.

M.M.W.

AELITA (Silent, 1924).

Directed by Jakov Protazanov; screenplay by Fedor Ozep and Aleksey Fajko; adapted from the novel by Alexei Tolstoy; photographed by Yuri Zheliabovsky and Emil Schoenemann. With Yulia Solntseva, Nikolai Tseretelli, Nikolai Batalov, Igor Illinski. 120 minutes. Black and white. Alternate title: The Revolt of the Robots.

Based on a novel by Soviet engineer Alexei Tolstoy and made in the USSR, *Aelita* is noteworthy primarily for its influential futuristic look. Its comic story—of three Russian men who fly to a Mars ruled by the beautiful but oppressive queen Aelita and the subsequent failure of a revolution against her rule—turns out to be a dream. But the sharp-edged cubist angularity of this film's sets and costumes became the visual norm for FLASH GORDON, BUCK ROGERS, and many subsequent SF films.

B.L.

———— AGENTS ————

In most fields of fiction literary agents are best remembered for the spectacular advances or contracts they obtain for their clients, but, in keeping with its collaborative nature, science fiction is unusual for the number of agents who have contributed to the development of individual authors or to the field itself.

An agent's basic function is to sell to a publisher on terms most advantageous to the author the work an author sends him (until the 1970s the male pronoun was almost universally appropriate). An agent also finds new markets in which to sell work again and again. But informally the agent may serve as critic, cheerleader, hand holder, friend, even banker. Some agents are known actually to contribute to the writing or editing of their authors' work. For these services an agent traditionally keeps 10 percent of the income he earns for the author, although more recently some agents have increased their proportion to 15 percent, with other costs added on.

H. G. WELLS, as always a breaker of traditions, was one of the first authors to employ an agent to maximize his earning potential and even to act as a business manager. He eventually settled on London agent A. P. Watt, who also represented G. K. Chesterton and Rudyard Kipling. The agency that bears Watt's name, one of the oldest in the world (Curtis Brown is of comparable age), still functions and, under the direction of Hilary Rubinstein, continues to handle many SF authors of note.

Literary agents in science fiction truly came into their own only when SF broke out of the pulp ghetto in America, bridging the gap between author and, in most cases, New York publisher and finally leading some authors into the Promised Land of million-dollar contracts. Early-twentieth-century British agents were intimately part of the literary establishment, but the new American breed had more diverse origins: they might be ex-editors, hustlers with Hollywood connections, and, in science fiction, fans or writers. One such was Julius Schwartz, who represented many of the leading practitioners in the 1930s and early 1940s and went on to become a major figure in comics publishing. Forrest J ACKERMAN was another enthusiast whose agenting activities began more as a service to friends in fandom and writers in southern California who lacked the necessary contacts in publishing.

The business of literary agenting intensified with the paperback revolution that followed World War II and saw the rise of onetime fan Scott Meredith, who handled a significant number of paperback original writers toiling in both the SF and crime fields. Built on sheer volume of transaction, the Scott Meredith Agency has since grown into one of the world's largest, representing such leading literati as Norman Mailer, prominent politicians and film stars, as well as SF luminaries such as Arthur C. CLARKE, Fredric BROWN, John WYNDHAM, and Philip K. DICK. In addition to perfecting the reading-fee business, Meredith is credited with having invented the concept of the literary auction, in which publishing houses bid against one another for the right to publish a manuscript. He has had several major assistants, many of whom have gone on or back to writing or have started their own agencies; in the 1980s the most important figure in the SF involvement of the Meredith agency is Russell Galen, who controls a formidable array of talent, both inherited and developed.

Frederik POHL, a fan who went on to be an influential editor and one of the most distinguished SF writers of several decades, became an agent in 1947 when he encouraged a friend, Dirk Wylie, to set up an agency with himself as silent partner. When Wylie died Pohl took over the business. Science fiction was growing swiftly after World War II: new SF magazines were springing up, mainstream magazines were beginning to publish SF, fan publishers were setting up to publish several titles, and even mainstream publishers, such as Doubleday, were creating SF lines. Fanzines and conventions were no longer sufficient to spread the news. Agents became not only scouts but missionaries, in some cases creating markets and trying manuscripts in markets their authors would not have considered.

Pohl cornered most of the SF authors and most of the markets, increased top SF magazine fees from two to three cents a word, and created markets such as the paperback anthology and *Star Science Fiction,* an original anthology, for Ballantine. But his practice of advancing money to his authors put him $30,000 in the red, and he quit the business in 1953.

Harry Altshuler, a part-timer who worked as a newspaper editor, took over many names from Pohl's list. Lurton Blassingame was notable chiefly for representing Robert A. HEINLEIN (and getting his stories into the slicks as well as securing for him a profitable contract with Scribner's for a series of juveniles). In the late 1970s Blassingame became Blassingame-McCauley-Wood. The Wood is Eleanor Wood, and the McCauley, one of the more aggressive younger agents of the 1980s, is Kirby McCauley (best known for his multi-million-dollar deals for Stephen KING), who came up the familiar way, from horror and fantasy fandom.

Henry Morrison, the late Robert P. Mills (an ex-editor

of THE MAGAZINE OF FANTASY AND SF who inherited some of Pohl's clients and later took over many of Altshuler's), Harold Matson, and Don Congdon also have played important roles for authors with substantial SF involvement.

In Great Britain, E. J. (Ted) Carnell, founding editor of NEW WORLDS and *Science Fantasy,* also built up a substantial agency, representing at one time or another most of the major homegrown British authors as well as subagenting in the United Kingdom and the Commonwealth for many U.S. agencies. On Carnell's death the agency was continued with much flair by bookseller and fan Leslie Flood. On Flood's retirement in 1986, Pamela Bulmer, ex-wife of British writer Ken BULMER, took over. Other British agents include Maggie Noach (an A. P. Watt alumnus) and Christopher PRIEST, a prominent writer who handles many young U.S. counterparts.

Literary agents have never been as prominent or influential in Europe, where most agencies subcontract material from U.S. agents and publishing houses, but a trend toward representing local authors is growing. Franz Rottensteiner in Austria has been instrumental in spreading the works of Stanislaw LEM, and Thomas Schlück in Germany has strong SF links (Schlück began as an SF fan at the age of thirteen).

Prominent contemporary SF agents include Virginia KIDD, ex-wife of the late James BLISH, who lives in Milford, Pennsylvania, a bit remote from New York but famous during the 1950s for its Milford Writers Conferences, which have been duplicated in other locations since; Richard Curtis, previously an author and publisher, who writes insightful articles on the craft of agenting for a variety of publications, including the SF fan magazine *Locus;* Merrilee Heifetz of Writer's House; Martha Millard; Diana Price; Sharon Jarvis; Adele Leone; Joseph Elder; Ellen Levine; and Patrick Delahunt.

Literary agents are now an integral part of the book and SF landscape. The reader seldom sees them, but publishers and authors know their importance. No longer does any single agent wield the influence of a Meredith or a Pohl, or even of an Altshuler or a Mills—authors are scattered among too many agents for that to happen. Still, after How can I get my story published?, the question every aspiring author asks a successful one is How can I get an agent? As a rule, the answer is You can't until you get published on your own. Aspiring authors may find some consolation in the fact that a number of their role models, the most prominent and prolific being Isaac ASIMOV, do not even feel the need for an agent.

M.J.

ALDISS, BRIAN W[ILSON] (1926–   ). British novelist, essayist, poet, editor, and historian of science fiction. Aldiss has achieved acclaim from SF fans and mainstream literary critics alike. His works have ranged from deliberate evocations of models such as H. G. WELLS, Thomas Hardy, James Joyce, and Alain Robbe-Grillet to the thoughtful, detailed creation of an entire solar system and its ever-changing cyclic civilizations in his masterpiece, the epic series consisting of *Helliconia Spring* (1982), *Helliconia Summer* (1983), and *Helliconia Winter* (1985).

Aldiss's parents were shopkeepers in East Anglia, a location he revisited with considerable nostalgia in *Life in the West* (1980). His education at a minor public school and his service in the British Army from 1944 to 1948 provided him with basic material for the mainstream novels in the Horatio Stubbs series: *The Hand-reared Boy* (1969), *A Soldier Erect* (1971), and *A Rude Awakening* (1978), all controversial but popular. After military service he settled in Oxford (where he has lived ever since) and began working as an assistant in a bookstore, an experience that later supplied him with the skeleton for *The Brightfount Diaries* (1954), his first book-length work. Semiautobiographical, this loosely connected series of vignettes was both a popular and a critical success. Since that time Aldiss has published a new book almost every year.

His first SF stories were followed by dozens more as he learned his trade. In his first novel, *Non-stop* (1958), he boldly attempted a new version of the hackneyed theme that had haunted science fiction writers for years—the creation of a closed universe aboard a spaceship whose voyage has lasted for generations (in this case, twenty-three) and has no apparent end. In this book and in many of his early short stories (later published as *Space, Time, and Nathaniel,* 1957, a book that has been reprinted in each succeeding decade), he sketched a number of the themes to which he would return again and again in his later works. These concerns—change and stasis, reality and illusion, contemplation and action, intellect and feeling, art and artifice (to name only a few)—have provided Aldiss with much of the material for such novels as *Life in the West* (1964), *Greybeard* (1964), *Report on Probability A* (1968), *Barefoot in the Head* (1969), and *The Malacia Tapestry* (1976).

Yet as he examines and reexamines these themes, Aldiss never seems to repeat himself. Instead he concentrates on one specific aspect of a topic in each of his books. For example, *Report on Probability A* focuses on the art of the antinovel in the French sense as several characters, known only as C, S, and G, do nothing for several hundred pages. An enigma to be sure, *Report on Probability A* may infuriate readers with its repeated, harrowingly detailed descriptions. However, most people who approach the novel with respect for art and form will never forget its combination of specificity and unsolved mystery. By contrast, *The Malacia Tapestry* is rife with action, almost ironically so, for the city-state of Malacia is an "ever-ever" land, doomed by its creator to remain unchanged forever.

Brian Aldiss

Aldiss has been one of SF's preeminent critics for nearly three decades. His early essays in British journals both explained and defined the New Wave of the 1960s and 1970s. They also helped make the general British reading public aware of the fact that science fiction is considerably more than pulp writing—a genre with style, rules, substance, and form. In 1978 he received the coveted Pilgrim Award for distinction in SF criticism given by the SCIENCE FICTION RESEARCH ASSOCIATION. His *Billion Year Spree* (1973, revised as *Trillion Year Spree*) remains one of the best histories of the genre, and Aldiss's collections of critical essays, such as *This World and Nearer Ones* (1979), *The Pale Shadow of Science* (1985), and *. . . And the Lurid Glare of the Comet* (1986), can be studied not only for their penetrating insights into science fiction but also for their views of the mind of the creative artist at work.

OTHER WORKS: *Hothouse* (1962); *The Airs of Earth* (1963); *The Dark-Light Years* (1964); *Earthworks* (1965); *An Age* (1967); *The Moment of Eclipse* (1970); *The Shape of Further Things* (1970); *The Eighty-Minute Hour* (1974); *Enemies of the System* (1978); *New Arrivals, Old Encounters* (1979); *Moreau's Other Island* (1980); *Seasons in Flight* (1984); *The Year Before Yesterday* (1987, combining *The Equator*, 1958, and "The Impossible Smile," 1965).

W.E.M.

The clash of continual events within an unchanging or glacially changing world also infuses the Helliconia series, wherein a single planet circles twin suns; this astronomical oddity results in a planetary climate whose seasons last for centuries. The planet's inhabitants survive only by adjusting to this creeping change. As Aldiss's further commentary on the interaction between art and reality, the rising and falling Helliconian civilizations are constantly observed by the peoples of the Earth, who view the reality of Helliconia as merely a vast art form. The relation between art and reality also lies at the heart of *Frankenstein Unbound* (1973). Here Mary SHELLEY is a major character who has a brief but passionate affair with Aldiss's hero, Joseph Bodenland. The novel celebrates Aldiss's own view of Shelley's crucial importance to science fiction.

Few SF writers possess as fine a prose style as Aldiss. In some of his earlier works he honored H. G. Wells, James Joyce, and Thomas Hardy not only by suggesting their styles or techniques but also by penetrating their insights and general method of approach. This homage is evident in such works as "The Saliva Tree" (1965), for which he won the Nebula Award; *Barefoot in the Head;* and *Greybeard.* Nonetheless, Aldiss's voice is assuredly his own, and his style is elegant, sometimes elegiac, always carefully honed, never affected.

ALIEN (1979). *Directed by Ridley Scott; screenplay by Dan O'Bannon; photographed by Derek Vanlint; music by Jerry Goldsmith. With Sigourney Weaver, Tom Skerritt, Veronica Cartwright, Harry Dean Stanton, John Hurt, Ian Holm, Yaphet Kotto, Bolaji Badejo. 117 minutes. Color.*
ALIENS (1986). *Directed by James Cameron; screenplay by James Cameron; photographed by Adrian Biddle; music by James Horner. With Sigourney Weaver, Michael Biehn, Paul Reiser, Carrie Henn, Lance Henriksen, Bill Paxton, William Hope, Jenette Goldstein. 137 minutes. Color.*

The original *Alien* is essentially a B movie writ large, a film whose superlative production values enhance an ordinary story of an alien loose in a spaceship who kills the ship's crew one by one. But it is also one of the strongest terror films of recent years: dramatic lighting, quick cutting, striking set design, bloody shock effects, relentless pacing, a throbbing soundtrack, and false endings all contribute to the film's impact.

The alien itself, a sexually murderous, insectoid-humanoid creature, exerts a hideous fascination, and its graphically depicted reproductive cycle entails some of the most imaginative biology ever concocted for a science-fiction film. The look of the film too is extraordinary, thanks to the brilliant design, both of the creature and the derelict alien spaceship, by the Swiss surrealist

painter H. R. Giger. Special effects were by Brian John-
ston, Nick Allder, and Roger Dicken. All the actors put
in creditable performances, but Sigourney Weaver, as
the take-charge heroine, is the film's most believable
and sympathetic character. The visual and emotional
force of the movie carries the viewer right past the occasional blunders in science, lapses of logic, and routine
plot.

Aliens, the sequel, directed by the writer-director of
THE TERMINATOR and coauthor of *Rambo*, is in essence
a combat film, again superlatively manipulative but suffering somewhat from a tendency to rehash every successful element in the original. Nevertheless, this tale of
space marines (with Weaver along as a civilian "consultant" who soon finds she must replace the squad's
inept commander) remains gripping, and by appealing
to the same power-and-frustration fantasies as *Rambo*,
Rocky, and so on, it touched a popular nerve and became, even more than the first film, a smash hit.

D.S.

——————— ALIEN WORLDS ———————

Since its beginnings as a genre, science fiction has displayed a fascination with other worlds. In some instances, such as the many prototypical stories of lunar
voyages or the Mars novels of Edgar Rice BURROUGHS,
those worlds have been based on the relatively familiar
and undeniably existent worlds of the Earth's own solar
system. In other cases, such as the novels and stories of
Hal CLEMENT, the planetary settings have been entirely
speculative. In either case, however, authors have been
confronted with a unique literary task: "building" an
entire world, as it were, from the ground up.

Early stories placed on the planets and satellites of
Earth's solar system had the advantage of existing astronomical knowledge about their settings, from the extremely hot planet of Mercury through the "Earthlike"
planets of Venus and Mars and the gas giants Jupiter,
Saturn, Uranus, and Neptune to the extremely cold world
of Pluto. Each has distinctive features, such as Venus's
clouds, Mars's deserts, Jupiter's moons and "red spot,"
and Saturn's moons and rings, and these, together with
data on such matters as orbit, size, mass, gravity, atmosphere, and temperature—the last two uncertain—
gave writers a few starting points.

Except for clear violations of what was known—most
of which has proven illusory—authors were free to invent details as they wished, and the memorable stories
were those whose authors took the trouble to be imaginative rather than borrowing the clichés of desert Mars
and jungle-covered Venus, with the implication that a
planet was the same over its entire surface. Burroughs's
tales of Mars (beginning in 1912) may seem primitive
today, but they make vivid the planet's dying civilization

in addition to a colorful assortment of outside peoples
and places. Stanley WEINBAUM, in his 1934 "A Martian
Odyssey" and "Valley of Dreams," took inspiration from
H. G. WELLS and offered a Mars that has similarly fallen
from greatness but is populated by nonhuman beings.
Robert A. HEINLEIN's interplanetary stories, up to and
including *Stranger in a Strange Land* (1961), clearly
show Weinbaum's influence.

Even before spaceflight began in reality, science fiction was looking beyond Earth's neighboring planets,
none of which, astronomy was showing, could be hu-
manly habitable. Moreover, because nothing was known
about worlds outside the solar system, writers seemed
to have a free hand. That hand, however, has been
limited by SF's need to be scientifically plausible. Limitations often improve art, and the need for plausibility
has led to the development of a craft: the designing of
alien worlds. Masters of that craft have generated fascinating, exotic locales from which have emerged stories
that would not have existed without that limitation.

A number of authors started simply, with planets that
are much like Earth except for differences in geography,
life-forms, history, and so forth, under the assumption
that thousands of planets similar to Earth exist in this
galaxy. In addition, Earthlike planets may be the only
kind where humans can survive without artificial means,
as stories often demand.

Most of the better writers accept the fact that no matter
how alike these worlds are, life on them cannot have
followed the same evolutionary paths. Study of the fossil
record on Earth reveals how frequently sheer chance
determined the origin, development, and sometimes ter-
mination of species. Although basic biochemistries may
be akin (no one knows how much latitude nature permits), and form may follow function to produce some
plants and animals that may resemble species on Earth,
in general the differences will be enormous. This realization is more liberating than confining, since it gives
imagination a correspondingly wide scope. Thus, C. J.
CHERRYH's carefully thought out intelligent nonhumans
all stem from environments in which a human could
work in shirtsleeves.

To be sure, any Earthlike planet is likely to differ from
Earth in more than its continental outlines. L. Sprague
DE CAMP's alien planet Krishna, on which he placed a
number of stories and novels, has two moons, which
must affect tides, currents, and weather, although he has
not gone into this matter in any detail. As simple a factor
as a planet's rate of rotation or inclination of axis will
have profound consequences, providing the writer with
interesting phenomena and plot possibilities.

In his vast Robots, Empire, Foundation cycle of stories
and novels, Isaac ASIMOV avoided the problem of world
creation by postulating humanity as the only sentient
race in the galaxy: Earth alone happens to have the right
conditions for producing advanced life-forms. Every-

A Rescue from Jupiter
by
Gawain Edwards

Jupiter as envisioned by Frank R. Paul

where else they are of a low order, and expanding humanity settles only Earthlike planets.

Other authors assume that intelligent life may develop under wide variations in conditions. For *The Rebel Worlds* (1969) Poul ANDERSON gave the imaginary planets Dido and Aeneas the traditional characteristics of fictional, marginally livable Venus and Mars, even giving Aeneas the two hurtling moons of Mars. He adjusted the planetary parameters, mostly mass and insolation (exposure to the sun), to make such planets possible. In Larry NIVEN's Known Space series mass and insolation have a broad range on planets where humans nevertheless can flourish. The surface gravity of Niven's planet Jinx, for instance, equals 1.78 times that of Earth, while the pull of We Made It is merely 0.59; conditions on Plateau are lethal except on an immensely high tableland.

Ursula K. LE GUIN's Winter, scene of *The Left Hand of Darkness* (1969), contrasts with Earth in several ways, most conspicuously temperature. The planet is in an ice age, and the reader gets the impression that it never had any especially warm periods. In "The Storm" (1943) A.

E. VAN VOGT gave a planet to the blue-giant star S Doradus. To avoid searing heat, it moves in so huge an orbit that the year is as long as 4,000 of Earth's; seen from the ground, the sun is a spark lost in the fluorescence its radiation excites in the upper atmosphere. Anne MCCAFFREY's Dragonrider series is set on Pern, whose sun periodically swings close to a red-dwarf companion, allowing destructive "threads" to cross the space between. Tiamat, of Joan VINGE's *The Snow Queen* (1980), circles a sun with two companions, one of them a black hole, which causes its own year to be just part of a cycle 200 times as long. Lagash, of Asimov's "Nightfall," is in a six-sun system; once in 2,000 years all the suns are close together in the sky or eclipsed, and the farther stars become visible from the opposite hemisphere.

Frank HERBERT's Arrakis, of *Dune* (1965) and its sequels, is doubtless the most famous variant of Earth, a global desert where water is scarce. The reader may wonder how such a situation developed, because hydrogen and oxygen are cosmically abundant, how life got started and maintains itself, and why the air is not always full of dust. But nobody can deny that the planet and its dwellers are visualized in dazzling detail; and technical arguments are among the pleasures granted readers of such stories.

Planetary composition figures in Jack VANCE's *Big Planet* (1957), which presents a world much larger than Earth but with the same surface gravity and a breathable atmosphere. Almost devoid of the heavier elements, Big Planet has a low mean density. The shortage of metals has affected colonists in many ways; their inability to build fast vehicles and the planet's enormous area have brought about a proliferation of different societies. Diomedes in Poul Anderson's *The Man Who Counts* (1958) is like Big Planet in its composition, but Anderson used its gravitational potential to keep a far denser atmosphere in order to allow winged intelligent beings. He added an extreme axial tilt that forces long annual migrations. Such metal-poor worlds must have formed freakishly, presumably because of fluctuations in the clouds from which they condensed.

In a chapter by Anderson, "The Creation of Imaginary Worlds," in *Science Fiction, Today and Tomorrow* (1974), the principles of world building are described in greater detail, and two excellent books, *Intelligent Life in the Universe* by I. S. Shklovskii and Carl SAGAN and *Habitable Planets for Man* by Stephen H. Dole, go into the subject in depth.

Today's astrophysicists would deny that van Vogt's life-bearing planet of S Doradus can exist. The big stars shine at their prodigal brilliance for a mere few million years and then explode as supernovae or balloon into red giants before sinking into darkness. The spectral range from about middle F through G is reasonably Sol-like in brightness and longevity and has many more representatives. Still more common are the red dwarfs, but a planet would have to be quite near one of them to be warm, and this proximity might lead to gravitational complications. Similarly debatable is the stability of planetary orbits, such as that of Asimov's Lagash, in multiple-star systems.

The creation of non-Earthlike worlds, and life-forms to live on them, must be consistent with current scientific knowledge. The luminosity of a star is closely dependent on its mass and age. From these the light and heat energy a planet receives in any orbit can be calculated, and from the size of the orbit the length of the year can be determined. From the mass of a planet and the orbits of any moons, the behavior of the moons can be deduced, and, figuring in their masses, what tidal effects they may have on their primary. The mass of the planet also settles many questions about its nature. If it is quite large, it will retain its primordial atmosphere, mostly hydrogen and helium; if it is quite small, it will keep little or no gas. Surface gravity is a function of mass and diameter. These considerations, together with others such as rotation period and axial tilt, are important to weather patterns and hence in the long run to geology, topography, and so on for a lengthy list.

Biology is another question: on Earth, for instance, life is a potent geologic force. Along with much else, it is responsible for our atmosphere of free nitrogen and oxygen. Life on planets very different from Earth is presumably very different in both its nature and its effects.

Although the universe as it is presently understood offers writers a tremendous choice of parameters with which to work, they should avoid absurdities. For instance, a fair-sized moon cannot orbit too close to its planet; tidal forces would break it up. An atmosphere of oxygen and hydrogen could not last; they combine too readily. Such principles, and others, are fundamental, but special conditions can produce unique results. Every mission to a member of our solar system has harvested surprises. Nature probably has many more in store for humanity throughout the galaxy, and science fiction can try to anticipate some of them. For *A Stone in Heaven* (1979) Anderson invented a way for a planet with a mass like Jupiter's to have an atmosphere like Earth's. For his novels about Helliconia, Brian W. ALDISS considered how a giant star might have a habitable planet in spite of astrophysics.

One job of world building is made explicit in *Medea* (1985), edited by Harlan ELLISON. At his instigation four successive people worked up an alien world. Hal Clement made it a satellite of a supergiant planet that, red hot from self-compression, furnishes most of the heat energy; Anderson developed the globe itself; Larry Niven did the life-forms; and Frederik POHL went into the sociology. A panel of fellow writers discussed these papers, generating more ideas, and finally everyone concerned contributed a story set on the world.

Scientific knowledge is not so complete that the con-

Gold mining on the moon as forecast in 1895

clusions to be drawn from a number of premises are cut and dried. Thus, a conference once studied some specifications without knowing that they were those of the large planet Starkad in Anderson's *Ensign Flandry* (1966). The picture that emerged was quite different from what the author had had in mind. This kind of thinking leads to what Clement has called "the game," wherein readers try to catch an author on matters of fact or logic.

Clement is the unquestioned dean of world builders. His *Mission of Gravity* (1954) is a guided tour of the planet Mesklin, enormous, flattened to a discus by its furious rotation, so cold beneath its dim red sun that water is a mineral and the seas are liquid methane, while weight depends on latitude. The related *Star Light* (1971) and *Close to Critical* (1964) ring equally brilliant changes on the giant-planet theme; *Iceworld* (1953) makes Earth a frozen hell, as experienced by a visitor from a planet humans would regard as an inferno; *Cycle of Fire* (1957) explores the consequences of being in an unusual orbit—and these are only the more obvious products of Clement's imaginative and meticulous mind.

Some of Clement's colleagues have taken similar care and sometimes grow still more audacious. Four memorable creations are the living oceanic surface of Stanislaw LEM's *Solaris* (1961; in English, 1971), the sentient nebula of Fred HOYLE's *The Black Cloud* (1957), the moon-sized organism of John VARLEY's *Titan* (1979) and its sequels, and the sun whose ring of gas and solid material has brought forth life in Niven's *The Integral Trees* (1984).

In some stories mortals rather than the Almighty have made or decisively remade worlds. Among these bodies are the kaleidoscopic pleasure moon Cyrille in C. L. MOORE's *Judgment Night* (1952); Niven's variously transformed asteroids in his Known Space series; the same author's annular structure the size of Earth's orbit in *Ringworld* (1970), and its sequel; the Dyson shell entirely enclosing its sun in Bob SHAW's *Orbitsville* (1975) and its sequel; and the setting of Philip José FARMER's Riverworld tales, where the great stream loops and reloops over the entire surface of its planet, and its mouth flows into its source.

Farmer's World of Tiers is no spheroid or cluster of spheroids but is layered like a wedding cake. To escape any restrictions set by established natural law, Farmer put his planet entirely out of this universe. The same device has enabled a number of writers to show alternate versions of Earth or, sometimes, other worlds that are truly bizarre. It can even be assumed that in these foreign space-time continua the forces of magic are real and controllable. An early and delightful example of this type of setting is *The Incomplete Enchanter* (1941) by L. Sprague de Camp and Fletcher PRATT. Here, though, stories cross the border into fantasy.

P.A.

ALIENS

The idea of aliens as genuinely different from ourselves arose only in the late nineteenth century. Until then authors depicted other worlds in which humans or odd animals played a satiric role. Camille Flammarion's *Real and Imaginary Worlds* (1865) envisioned aliens as vessels for storing human souls after death, beginning a long association of aliens with theological concepts. The reverse image of alien as fierce competitor stemmed from Darwinian ideas and found its first major expression in H. G. WELLS's *War of the Worlds* (1898).

This notion proved remarkably useful in powering plots of the pulp age. Aliens were invented by adapting earthly forms. Often those in the semblance of the lower orders

(reptiles, spiders) were evil and wished either to eat or to mate with human females; Edmond HAMILTON's Captain Future (published 1940–1950 by Standard Magazines) was one of the better examples of this approach. Good aliens (usually sidekick allies) were mammalian or birdlike; as these palled authors turned to intelligent plants or beings of pure energy that sometimes resembled angels.

The repulsive alien invader remained a staple into the 1950s. Robert A. HEINLEIN's *The Puppet Masters* (1951) and *Starship Troopers* (1959) both depict beings of intelligence but implacable animosity. Robert Plank analyzed the long history of this view of the alien in *The Emotional Significance of Imaginary Beings* (1968). Heinlein clearly had specific political analogies in mind, but most earlier writers simply used aliens as conveniently motivated baddies.

Stanley WEINBAUM's "A Martian Odyssey" (1934) began the trend away from aggressive monsters by detailing a plausible biosphere with diverse life-forms, all interacting peacefully. His oddities, such as silicon-based life presented sympathetically, evoked great reader response. Weinbaum also contributed significantly to a growing depiction of the necessary complexity of alien biospheres. Although Wells had already presented a socially detailed alien society in *The First Men in the Moon* (1901), such complexity in the physical and biological realm did not become standard until the 1950s, when Hal CLEMENT's *Mission of Gravity* (1954) made the entire landscape of a vast, high-gravity planet the center of interest. Clement's aliens were physically products of their bizarre surroundings, but mentally they seemed easily understandable. Since the appearance of that book authors have created increasingly odd societies implied by their environments, as in Frank HERBERT's *Dune* (1963–1965) and Donald Kingsbury's *Courtship Rite* (1982).

Science fiction writers have often portrayed aliens as not anthropomorphic but anthropocentric. Poul ANDERSON's *The People of the Wind* (1973) treats birdlike aliens in detail, but they have very human motivations. A variant on this depiction is Larry NIVEN's Known Space series (1966–1970), which features aliens as animals: kzinti are carnivores, Puppeteers are herd animals whose cities stink like a corral. Such effects quickly wear off, as in *The Mote in God's Eye* (1974) by Niven and Jerry POURNELLE, in which aliens are not bilaterally symmetrical but have relatively simple behavior patterns. Even highly idealistic works, such as the visionary *Star Maker* (1937) by Olaf STAPLEDON, give aliens biological variations that ultimately have no impact whatever on the gross socioeconomic forces at work. Stapledon followed a familiar tactic in projecting the politics of his era into space, depicting a clockwork Marxism that drives species after species into a tired and implausible confrontation of labor with capital.

Aliens were similarly used as foils in stories that equated planet with colony and aliens with Indians, as in the anthology *Galactic Empires,* edited in 1976 by Brian W. ALDISS. Political projection often dominated, as in Murray LEINSTER's famous "First Contact" (1945): when humans meet aliens, they eventually trade ships as the only way to give away equally implicating information about themselves and to destroy information about the location of their home planets. In "Cor Serpentis" (1962), Soviet author Ivan Yfremov responded to this view by proposing that aliens would be so advanced into socialist perfection that they would see suspicion as childish.

Communication among alien species was a knotty problem often sidestepped in early SF. The "universal translator" conveniently made every alien speak midwestern English so that the slam-bang pulp plot could get on with more important matters. The difficulty and perhaps impossibility of finding a common language was confronted by H. Beam PIPER's "Omnilingual" (1957), in which a woman tries to find a Rosetta stone to decipher a dead Martian language; she discovers common ground in the periodic table. This argument was adapted by scientists themselves in their proposals to listen for extraterrestrial radio broadcasts. They believed that certain "natural" frequencies and methods of encoding emerge from the sciences themselves and would provide a foundation for building a mutual language. This remains general doctrine in the field, making alien contact an experience of rarefied mathematics, as in James GUNN's *The Listeners* (1972) and Carl SAGAN's *Contact* (1985).

Only slowly has the notion of aliens as genuinely strange and perhaps impossible for us to contact come to the fore. Stanislaw LEM's *Solaris* (1961, translated 1971) resolutely refuses to explain the awesomely intelligent ocean that covers an entire planet. Instead the novel insists that humans will never truly know the genuinely alien and will instead resort to scientific-style models and oversimplifications that fail to grasp the essence or even make real contact. A less dogmatic view suffuses Arthur C. CLARKE's *Rendezvous with Rama* (1973), in which a huge alien ship arcs through the solar system, leaving mystery behind while making no attempt at contact. There has been a tendency to use giganticism as an easy signifier of alienness, as in Larry Niven's *Ringworld* (1970), Bob Shaw's *Orbitsville* (1975), and John VARLEY's Titan trilogy (1979–1984).

Still one of the emerging themes in modern science fiction is the irreducible strangeness of the alien. Whereas science in SF represents the knowable, there is a tension between such hard certainties and the fundamental unknowability of the truly alien. The simple evocation of this mystery can fill narrative with suspense, as in Chad OLIVER's *The Shores of Another Sea* (1971), which treats an extraterrestrial form that is never described but operates through the baboons near a field station in Africa. The contrast between the primitive and natural surround-

ings and the looming alien is telling. More directly, Damon KNIGHT's "Stranger Station" (first magazine publication 1956) captures the anguish of a man trying to enter into an alien's way of perceiving and thinking. He emerges with a provisional sense of the alien form of cognition, but there is also a strong hint that he has projected his own childhood traumas onto the huge creature.

Although aliens figure as emblems of many kinds, some of the most effective writing about them tries to induce the *experience* of confrontation. Wells's *War of the Worlds* and Clarke's *2001: A Space Odyssey* (1968) are not read for their views on Martian biology or possible explanations for the enigmatic monolith but for their sensations of encounter. Much of Terry CARR's "The Dance of the Changer and the Three" (1968) lulls the reader into accepting the unremarkable aliens as predictable, with interesting folklore. The sudden murder of nearly all the human expedition comes as a shock, yet in the end there is no possibility of explaining why the aliens did it. The wrenching experience is the story's point, after which it states, "Their reason for wiping out the mining expedition was untranslatable."

A different modern approach to the experience of alien encounter appears in Robert SILVERBERG's "Sundance" (1969). It tells of an American Indian who takes part in a "corrective" program of slaughtering alien herd animals on a distant planet. But are the aliens mere animals? The text moves among points of view and tense changes, and ricochets between objective description and intense personal vision. It achieves a sense of dislocation, a distortion of reality, and confusion of subject and object, undermining all human categories of perception. The goal is to convey not an intellectual point about aliens but the sensation of a brush with them.

The assumption that humans would be overwhelmed by the genuinely alien runs throughout science fiction. Fred HOYLE's *The Black Cloud* (1957) describes scientists trying to cope with an immense, superintelligent cloud of plasma that enters the solar system. The protagonist attempts direct mental contact with it, deciding "to accept the rule that the new should always supersede the old whenever there was trouble between them"— this rule is close to an SF article of faith. But the attempt to integrate mentally with the alien leads to death from inability to reconcile concepts. This sense of oblivion through immersion appears in works as diverse as Clarke's *2001,* Silverberg's *Downward to the Earth* (1970), Gregory BENFORD's *In the Ocean of Night* (1977), and George R. R. MARTIN's "A Song for Lya" (1974).

Perhaps the most comprehensible immersion is sexual. Philip José FARMER's novella *The Lovers* (1952) electrically merges aliens, parasitism, and sex, demolishing a long-standing taboo. James TIPTREE, Jr.'s, short story "And I Awoke and Found Me Here on the Cold Hill's Side" (1972) goes further, supposing that we might be relentlessly attracted to aliens but end up mere one-night

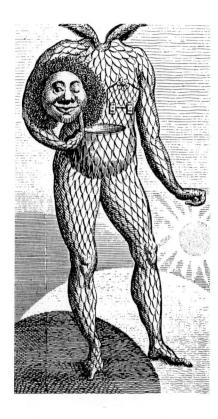

Eighteenth-century images of aliens

stands and pine away forever after. Gardner DOZOIS's *Strangers* (1978) explores the bittersweet aspects of actual marriage to an alien, and Octavia E. BUTLER's "Bloodchild" (1985) paints a horrific picture of aliens who use humans as living carriers of their eggs, from which the creatures are born through the body wall. Often SF gains power and suspense by toying with the boundary between the yearning for connection and the terror of being dominated, used, or either physically or mentally inhabited.

An opposite strategy lies in treating aliens as metaphor. We can never truly imagine something utterly alien but only conceive of alienness by contrast or analogy with the already known. Acknowledging that an alien cannot possibly be actualized in a text, authors gesture toward the known, sometimes in an obvious and even self-conscious way. Robert SHECKLEY's "Specialist" (1953) deliberately shows aliens as biologically specialized for various tasks in an immense starship. Humans on Earth are unhappy because they have been denied the chance to act out their ordained jobs as "Pushers," who boost the ship to faster-than-light speeds. By conspicuously anthropomorphizing the alien, Sheckley made sure we would read his work not as ludicrously inept scientifically but as satire.

At the opposite pole, Clarke's *Childhood's End* (1953)

describes an alien visit that precipitates events following the schema of the Jesuit Pierre Teilhard de Chardin. Although Clarke has said that such symbolism is "entirely accidental," his aliens have obvious theological roles and in fact resemble the Devil.

The alien is still primarily used as a template on which we can project our hopes and fears. The truly alien remains a kind of holy grail in science fiction, forever approached but never reached.

G.B.

ALLEN, IRWIN (1916–). American film and television producer, responsible for numerous science-fiction and borderline SF productions, who has been described as "the Jules Verne of SF television." Allen carefully oversees all his ventures, always leaving his unmistakable imprint—flashy sets, big-name stars, and impressive special effects; indeed, he is considered one of Hollywood's last great "showmen." His unabashed commercialism has often generated controversy: as the so-called Master of Disaster in the 1970s with films such as *The Poseidon Adventure* (1972) and *The Towering Inferno* (1974), he received a good deal of flak from the critics, who ignored the films' mass appeal. Two of Allen's television series remain very popular in reruns: LOST IN SPACE (1965–1968), the adventures of a castaway space family, and VOYAGE TO THE BOTTOM OF THE SEA (1964–1968), featuring the missions of the submarine *Seaview.* Both series reflect Allen's love for the classics of adventure and SF literature.

His other SF films and TV series include *The Lost World* (1960), *Voyage to the Bottom of the Sea* (1961), *The Time Tunnel* (TV series, 1966–1967), LAND OF THE GIANTS (TV series, 1968–1970), *City beneath the Sea* (TV movie, 1970; also known as *One Hour to Doomsday*), *The Time Travelers* (TV movie, 1976), *The Return of Captain Nemo* (TV miniseries, 1978; also known as *The Amazing Captain Nemo*), *The Swarm* (1978), and *Alice in Wonderland* (TV miniseries, 1985).

K.R.D.

ALPHAVILLE (*Une Etrange Aventure de Lemmy Caution,* 1965). Directed by Jean-Luc Godard; screenplay by Jean-Luc Godard; photographed by Raoul Coutard; music by Paul Misraki. With Eddie Constantine, Anna Karina, Akim Tamiroff, Howard Vernon, Laszlo Szabo, Michel Delahaye, Jean André Fieschi, Jean-Louis Comolli, Christa Lang, Jean-Pierre Léaud. 98 minutes. Black and white.

Jean-Luc Godard's sole venture into science-fiction film is a highly original, heady mixture of pop culture and modern philosophy. As a narrative it is actually relatively formulaic, combining a series of conventions from a number of film genres with elements of classical myth, particularly the descent of Orpheus. An "intergalactic agent," Lemmy Caution, arrives in Alphaville, a city in an unspecified future time and place, to find the evil scientist von Braun. Von Braun is the mastermind behind the giant computer Alpha 60, which controls the life of the city's inhabitants, and Caution manages to defeat his machine by providing poetic answers to the computer's factual questions. He kills von Braun and escapes with his daughter, who, as the pair are leaving the city, begins to rediscover words that had fallen into disuse in that computerized environment.

As is typical of Godard's early work, this story is merely a pretext for an investigation of a variety of artistic and philosophical issues, including the nature and function of art, the power of language, and the relation of ideology and culture—issues that came increasingly to the fore as Godard's career grew more overtly political in the late 1960s. The film also anticipates Godard's subsequent abandonment of narrative in favor of a more experimental and often highly metaphorical style. (For example, Caution arrives in Alphaville in a Ford Galaxy—a bit of obligatory narrative "exposition" that clearly reveals Godard's preference for cultural politics over verisimilitude.)

As Godard himself once remarked, he is interested not in images of reality but in the reality of images.

B.K.G.

ALRAUNE (Silent, 1928). Directed by Henrik Galeen; screenplay by Henrik Galeen; adapted from the novel by Hans Heinz Ewers; photographed by Frank Good. With Brigitte Helm, Paul Wegener, Ivan Petrovich, Mia Pankau. 125 minutes. Black and white. *Alternate titles:* Daughter of Destiny, Unholy Love.

There are no fewer than five film versions of Hans Heinz Ewers's story of a girl born when a hanged murderer's semen is used by a scientist to artificially inseminate a prostitute. But the 1928 version, starring Brigitte Helm and directed by Henrik Galeen, is the best known. The "soulless" Alraune eventually turns in revenge on her scientist-father, thus joining a long line of female science-fiction characters whose enchanting external form masks an artificial and destructive "otherness," an SF updating of the half-human, half-animal mermaids, nixies, and swan maidens of legends and fairy tales.

B.L.

ALTERED STATES (1980). Directed by Ken Russell; screenplay by Paddy Chayefsky as Sidney Aaron; adapted from the novel by Chayefsky; photographed by Jordan Cronenweth; music by John Corigliano. With William Hurt, Blair Brown, Bob Balaban, Charles Haid, Thaao Penghlis, Miguel Godreau, Charles White Eagle. 102 minutes. Color.

One of the few science-fiction films to explore psychological mysteries, *Altered States* is dazzling visually but hard to follow, even trivial. Director Ken Russell emphasized the visual elements so much that the film resembles a 1960s "acid trip" movie; this approach is in keeping with the content, however, because the film focuses on the use of mind-altering drugs to explore humankind's primitive beginnings.

A young researcher (William Hurt) combines sensory deprivation and psychedelic drugs, finally regressing physically and turning into a frenetic little ape-man. Going further, he is in danger of losing form altogether, but his wife's love saves him.

Paddy Chayefsky insisted on the use of a pseudonym for this screenplay credit, although the film follows his novel closely, including much of the dizzying technical chatter that makes the book difficult to read. Russell probably felt he was blazing new trails, but the story line resembles a combination of *Dr. Jekyll and Mr. Hyde* and *Monster on the Campus* (1958). Technically the film is outstanding, with superb special effects (makeup by Dick Smith), fine acting, and a driving pace. However, even with all its vivid trappings and religious imagery, it seems superfluous.

B.W.

ALTERNATE WORLDS AND ALTERNATE HISTORIES

Alternate worlds or histories remains a rather limited but appealing subgenre of science fiction, the essence of which is the supposition that one vital factor of our past is changed so as to alter radically our present. Frequently this crucial change revolves around an eminent personage. The seed for this subgenre was sown in a once-famous pamphlet, "Historic Doubts respecting Napoleon Buonaparte," by Richard Whately, tutor at Oriel College, Oxford, who later became archbishop of Dublin. Published in 1819, only three years after the Battle of Waterloo, this pamphlet purports to consider seriously the question of whether Napoleon existed and prove that he was, at the least, unlikely.

This witty pamphlet probably inspired a better-known essay by the historian Sir George Trevelyan, "If Napoleon Had Won the Battle of Waterloo," which gained a prize when it was published in 1907. Trevelyan gave a glimpse of a fatigued and peaceful Napoleon ruling over a stabilized Europe until his death in 1836. In England, Lord Byron leads a revolt of the peasantry and is executed, while Percy Bysshe Shelley is imprisoned.

The hinge of an alternate-world tale may be a seemingly small matter. Such was the device of the historian A. J. P. Taylor in his "If Archduke Ferdinand Had Not Loved His Wife" (in which case, he would not have been shot at Sarajevo, and World War I would not have happened). Taylor's argument relies on the remorselessness of railroad schedules and reaches this conclusion: "The First World War had begun—imposed on the statesmen of Europe by railway timetables. It was an unexpected climax to the railway age."

Obviously this strategy was too interesting to be left to historians, although their fingerprints, rather than those of scientists, remain on the subgenre to this day. In 1932 a collection of essays entitled *If: Or, History Rewritten*, edited by J. C. Squire, was published in Britain; it was reprinted later as *If It Had Happened Otherwise*. The book includes Trevelyan's and Taylor's essays, along with an ingenious piece of event reversal by Sir Winston Churchill, "If Lee Had Not Won the Battle of Gettysburg." With this essay American history entered the arena and a consideration of American history led to possibly the best and best-loved alternate-world novel, Ward Moore's *Bring the Jubilee* (1953).

Bring the Jubilee is set in an America where the South has won the Civil War. As a result the present is rather antiquated and slow. A historian named McCormick invents a time machine in which to travel back to witness the Battle of Gettysburg and Lee's glorious victory for himself. His unwitting intervention alters the outcome of the battle so that history changes, to become the present we know and love. *If the South Had Won the Civil War* (1961) by MacKinlay Kantor, the author of *Ander-*

sonville, is a somewhat similar exercise in which the United States, following the victory of the South, is divided into three nations.

Obviously such crucial events as the Civil War attracted fantasists and satirists. It is thus not surprising that World War II should also provide a hinge subject for an excellent crop of novels.

The Sound of His Horn (1952), by John W. Wall writing as "Sarban," is remarkable for its dark, Teutonic mood. Hitler has triumphed over Europe, and his gauléiters have turned their vast territories into hunting estates. The cream of the hunt is woman. This is a notable rural hell, the mirror image of multitudinous urban dystopias. The sadistic strain in the book is compelling, the donnée totally convincing.

A little later came *The Occupation* (1960), published with no author's name, in which the Germans invade and occupy Britain in 1940. There are concentration camps in Bangor and Welwyn Garden City. As with Sarban's novel, a strong, rather sadistic sexual interest is in evidence; a German Gestapo chief falls in love with a Jewish girl and shelters her.

By overwhelming agreement the great classic in which the Allies lose World War II is Philip K. DICK's *The Man in the High Castle* (1962). The Axis powers divide America into three areas: the East going to the Nazis, the Pacific coastal region being held by the Japanese, and a neutral buffer zone, the Rocky Mountain states, separating the other two. Franklin D. Roosevelt has been assassinated in the mid-1930s, and America has never pulled out of the Depression. Dick complicates his narrative by introducing a banned book, *The Grasshopper Lies Heavy*, by Hawthorne Abendsen, which postulates a world resembling ours, in which the Axis powers were defeated. The Japanese characters Betty and Paul Kasoura explain the nature of the banned book to Robert Childan:

> "Not a mystery," Paul said. "On contrary, interesting form of fiction possibly within genre of science fiction."
> "Oh, no," Betty disagreed. "No science in it. Not set in future. Science fiction deals with future, in particular future where science has advanced over now. Book fits neither premise."
> "But," Paul said, "it deals with alternate present. Many well-known science fiction novels of that sort."

In this way Dick made it clear that he knew exactly what he was doing and where his novel was to be placed in the complex pigeonholing systems of science fiction.

Another author who understood well what he was doing is Kingsley AMIS in his novel *The Alteration* (1976). His ten-year-old choristers are fond of reading TR, or Time Romance. One form of TR is CW, or Counterfeit World, "a class of tale set more or less at the present date, but portraying the results of some momentous change in historical fact." The CW currently being enjoyed by the choristers is Philip K. Dick's *The Man in the High Castle*, although in Amis's counterfeit world Dick's novel is not the one with which we are familiar. (*The Alteration* also contains a covert reference to John Wyndham; Hubert, one of the choirboys, buys a copy of *The Orc Awakes*, by J. B. Harris.)

The hinge in Amis's novel is religious. The Reformation never happened; Martin Luther went over to Rome and became Germanian I; England in consequence is under the pope, while the United States remains "a mean little den of thieves" in New England, according to one account. The plot turns ingeniously on Hubert's testicles. Are they to be removed so that he can become one of the famous castrati of his time? Throughout this poignant, amusing, and well-plotted story, Amis conducts a vendetta against God, represented here as the same peevish and sadistic individual he was in *The Anti-death League* (1966).

The heavy hand of the Roman Catholic church is also felt in the stories by Keith ROBERTS that became *Pavane* (1968). The premise here is the assassination of Elizabeth I of England and the subsequent conquest of the country by the Spanish Armada. The world is, in consequence, backward and oppressive. Amis pays tribute to Roberts's book, but his novel displays a much stronger grip on present-day reality than does *Pavane*. We never have any doubt that the world of *The Alteration* is a nasty one, whereas Roberts seems to relish every detail of his rural, law-ridden Britain. However, Roberts writes well: each of the six long stories that make up his book is "a masterpiece in miniature," according to David Pringle in *Science Fiction: The 100 Best Novels*. Where Roberts certainly scores is in the chilling and finely detailed novella "Weihnachtsabend" (1972), depicting a ruralized world in which the Nazis (once more) have won World War II. This is perhaps his most successful story.

An interesting variant on the World War II theme is Norman SPINRAD's celebrated *The Iron Dream* (1972), an alternate world in which Adolf Hitler emigrates to the United States and becomes a pulp writer; Hitler's sword-and-sorcery novel *Lords of the Swastika* (almost as famous an imaginary book as H. P. LOVECRAFT's *Necronomicon* or Dick's *Grasshopper Lies Heavy*), loaded with thud and blunder, takes up most of *The Iron Dream* and supposedly reveals something of Hitler's repugnant inner life.

The "counterfeit worlds"—to borrow Amis's excellent term—so far mentioned use a limited range of hinges and do not particularly seek to convince us that our present is much better or worse than the alternative depicted. Ingenuity rather than didacticism is the name of the game. This priority is shown by the way in which the hinge is generally revealed early on. Counterfeit worlds may be regarded as conceits in the old meaning of the word, something witty and farfetched.

The rules of the game were changed slightly in Harry HARRISON's *A Transatlantic Tunnel, Hurrah!* (1972, also known as *Tunnel through the Deeps*), in which there are two hinges and revelation of the second and more vital one is delayed until fourteen pages from the end. The first hinge concerns the shooting of George Washington as a traitor by the British, after he lost the Battle of Lexington. America is still a British colony, hoping for independence. An engineer who is a descendant of Washington is in charge of the great Transatlantic Tunnel venture. Harrison describes his amazing ultra-Victorian technology with as much affection as Roberts did his lithographic stones and road locomotives.

The second hinge is cleverly revealed through a medium, Madame Clotilda: the Christians were defeated by the Moors at the Battle of Navas de Tolosa in A.D. 1212. So Spain and Portugal remain "the Iberian Caliphate." It was John Cabot, in consequence, who discovered North and South America, and so on. The chain of events has become more complex, and thereby more convincing. Madame Clotilda is put into a trance and seeks to make contact with our alternate world of today. The vision before her is terrible. "Urhhh . . . urrhhh . . . penicillin, petrochemicals, purchase tax. Income tax, sales tax, anthrax . . ." She ends with a scream of horror and collapses. The world of the Transatlantic Tunnel is infinitely to be preferred.

For all its serious intent, Harrison's novel repeats a trick of Amis's and Moore's, transposing real people, often science-fiction writers, into the counterfeit world. Thus Harrison gives us Lord Amis; the warden of all souls, with his "impressive nose and jaw," is named Reverend Aldiss. Harrison's later *A Rebel in Time* (1983) contains a reference to *The Alteration*.

In *West of Eden* (1984) Harrison's hinge is set far back in time and is a negative reversal: a large hypothetical meteor failed to hit the Earth some 70 million years ago; the dinosaurs were thus not wiped out of existence, and humankind had to develop beside them. In our time the Yilanè, highly civilized dinosaurs, confront the two-legged mammals.

In Brian W. ALDISS's *The Malacia Tapestry* (1976), the hinge is similarly remote in time. In our reality *Homo saurus*, evolved from the reptiles, were allegedly wiped out at the great prehistoric Battle of Itssobeshiquetzilaha, over 3,001,700 years ago, and never heard of again. In Malacia's counterfeit world *Homo saurus* survives and relives an approximation of humanity's history, although they never quite achieve an industrial revolution.

Other novels that are clear examples of alternate worlds are Ronald W. Clark's *Queen Victoria's Bomb* (1976), in which British scientists develop a nuclear weapon in the heyday of imperialism, and the delightful *Ada* (1969), in which Vladimir NABOKOV, with wonderful intellectual self-indulgence, unites his two worlds of Russia and

America in a golden midway land thriving in a kind of idealized nineteenth century. A few cars putter along country roads, and afternoons can be spent reading Proust. Michael MOORCOCK's *Gloriana* (1978) is even more sumptuous, painting an alternate England, Albion, where Elizabeth I rules an empire in the Near East from her elaborate and ultimately unknowable palace while despairing of ever achieving orgasm.

Some of these novels have fantastic elements and could be regarded as technophobic, or at least modernophobic. An alternate world where magic rather than science rules was created by Randall GARRETT in his Lord Darcy series, of which the culmination is the novel *Too Many Magicians* (1967). Its hinge is the survival into the twentieth century of the Angevin Empire; its form resembles a pastiche of Arthur Conan Doyle's Sherlock Holmes stories.

All these alternate worlds, with the exception of Moore's, are substitutions for our own world and therefore do not involve the use of mechanical devices, such as time machines. When time machines are used as instruments of the plot, the work is better classified as a time-travel story. A good example would be Ray BRADBURY's celebrated "The Sound of Thunder" (1954), in which the time traveler, going back to shoot dinosaurs, steps off the prescribed path and tramples a butterfly to death. In so doing he sets in action a chain of events that culminates in his finding himself in a much changed and more ghastly version of our world.

The characterstics of an alternate- or counterfeit-world story are, therefore, that it takes place in a version of the present and has its roots in an altered event in history, prehistory, or perhaps even imagined history. This definition rules out tales in which the hero goes back in time and, for whatever reason, attempts to change history , as Mark TWAIN's *A Connecticut Yankee in King Arthur's Court* (1889) or L. Sprague DE CAMP's *Lest Darkness Fall* (1941). In such cases if the present changes it will be by design rather than by accident. T. A. Shippey characterized Twain's novel as an example of "the Whig interpretation of history," which depicts the historical process as a purposive struggle between progressives (Whigs) and reactionaries, in which the progressives win and thus bring about our world. The idea of intended change overemphasizes similarities between present and past while wrongly assuming that human beings intend the consequences of their actions—no one in the past actually willed the present.

In most alternate worlds, where the present is changed by some happenstance in the past, the Whigs lose. What renders the frequent premise of this subgenre scientifically suspect is an emphasis on the vital role of individuals—the death of Elizabeth I in the sixteenth century would scarcely have such drastic effects four centuries later. Altered outcomes of battles or wars enjoy much greater feasibility.

Glenn Larson in the title role, *The Amazing Colossal Man*

The counterfeit world as a literary subgenre is either awaiting development or stagnating. Its particular history-based brand of irony has certainly inspired excellent writing, and possibilities for books remain infinite.

Close neighbors of alternate worlds and histories are those time-travel stories in which the present has to be protected from history changers (H. Beam PIPER's Paratime Police series at the end of the 1940s is an example); worlds of the future will or will not be born according to what happens today (the classic example is Jack WILLIAMSON's *Legion of Time*, written at the end of the 1930s); or similar worlds exist in parallel and have to be maintained (best exemplified by Keith LAUMER's *Worlds of the Imperium*, 1962). Science or at least pseudo-science, perhaps generated by the theories of J. W. Dunne, controls the development of these kinds of narrative, and in them our interests are transferred from the vagaries of history to the paradoxes of time travel.

B.W.A.

THE AMAZING COLOSSAL MAN (1957).

Directed by Bert I. Gordon; screenplay by Mark Hanna and Bert I. Gordon; adapted from a story by Bert I. Gordon; photographed by Joseph Biroc; music by Albert Glasser. With Glenn Langan, Cathy Downs, William Hudson, James Seay, Larry Thor, Lyn Osborn. 81 minutes. Black and white.

This imitation of THE INCREDIBLE SHRINKING MAN in reverse, absurd though it is, is Bert I. Gordon's most watchable film. Gordon's inadequate special effects are offset by Glenn Langan's modestly effective performance in the title role. Radiation from an atomic blast causes an army colonel to grow to a height of sixty feet. After mental torment he goes mad, attacks Las Vegas, and is shot off the top of Hoover Dam. (He returned in *War of the Colossal Beast,* 1958.)

B.W.

November 1928 cover with art by Frank R. Paul. Note the slogan *scientifiction*.

AMAZING STORIES (also known for periods as *Amazing Science Fiction*).

Amazing Stories was the first English-language science-fiction magazine, launched in America by Hugo GERNSBACK in April 1926. Gernsback was a popularizer of science and hoped to teach science through fiction as well as to cultivate an interest in the potential of technology. The fiction in his magazine reflected these goals somewhat simplistically, ignoring sociological trends, but it found a large and sympathetic readership. Gernsback brought into print many of the leading writers of the first generation of pulp SF, including E. E. SMITH, Jack WILLIAMSON, David H. KELLER, and Stanton COBLENTZ. Perhaps the single most important piece in *Amazing* at this time, and one of the most influential, was E. E. Smith's *The Skylark of Space* (1928). *Amazing* was important not only as the first specialist SF pulp but for its impact on the next generation of writers, including Arthur C. CLARKE, Fritz LEIBER, Isaac Asimov, A. E. VAN VOGT, and Robert A. HEINLEIN, all of whom were attracted to science fiction by the early issues of *Amazing* and their colorful, brash covers by Frank R. PAUL.

Amazing ceased to be the leading SF magazine after Gernsback lost publishing control in 1929. Under the editorship of octogenarian T. O'Conor SLOANE from 1929 to 1938, the magazine lost its verve and is perhaps best remembered for the galaxy-trotting adventures of Professor Jameson, as told by Neil R. Jones. In 1938 *Amazing* was taken over by a new publisher, the Chicago-based Ziff-Davis, with Raymond A. PALMER as editor. Palmer did wonders for the magazine's circulation but little for its quality, and the reputation of pulp SF plummeted; further wounds were inflicted on it by the series of hoaxlike stories by Richard SHAVER—known as the "Shaver Mystery"—published from 1945 to 1948. Standards briefly improved under the editorship begun in 1950 by Howard BROWNE, who aimed at a more sophisticated reader. In 1953 *Amazing* was converted to a digest-size format with a further brief improvement in the fiction, but by 1955 the budget had been slashed and the magazine resorted to formula SF.

This lag in quality continued under the editorship of Paul W. Fairman in 1956, but a change came with his successor, Cele Goldsmith. Between 1958 and 1965 Goldsmith encouraged new authors and experimental fiction, with writers Roger ZELAZNY, Thomas M. DISCH, Ursula K. LE GUIN, and Piers ANTHONY making their mark. Circulation did not improve, however, and in 1965 *Amazing* was sold to Sol Cohen, who converted it primarily to a reprint magazine. It was only under the editorship of Ted WHITE, from 1969 to 1979, that *Amazing* again flirted with quality. Since then the magazine has been hit by a series of publishing and editorial changes, and even today, although it publishes some competent fiction, it has externally done little to transform its image. Its reputation remains, however, for good or ill, as the magazine that started it all.

M.A.

AMIS, KINGSLEY (1922–).

British novelist, poet, critic, and essayist. Amis's *New Maps of Hell* (1960) was the first serious study of science fiction to have an impact on the literary scene. He was one of the few authors of mainstream reputation to write about SF with sympathy and to write it himself with understanding; his many publications include two SF novels and six SF anthologies. In 1986 he received the Booker Prize, Britain's most prestigious literary award.

Amis was born in London and before and after army service studied English at St. John's College, Oxford. He was a lecturer in English at University College, Swansea, between 1949 and 1961; during this period he wrote the novels that established him as a major literary figure in Britain, including *Lucky Jim* (1954), regarded as the classic comic novel of university life. In 1959 he gave a series of lectures at Princeton University, published as *New Maps of Hell*, a landmark in the history of the serious academic treatment of science fiction. His comments on SF continued in reviews and essays and in introductions to five anthologies edited with Robert Conquest (*Spectrum*, 1961; *Spectrum II*, 1961; and subsequent volumes in 1963, 1965, and 1966). His most recent anthology is *The Golden Age of Science Fiction* (1981); Amis considers SF's Golden Age to have been from 1949 to 1962: the effects of the NEW WAVE were to him "almost uniformly deleterious"; he has complained that "SF has lost its innocence."

Amis's novels *Colonel Sun* (1968) and *The Green Man* (1969) contain science-fiction and fantasy elements respectively. But he has written only two novels that can be classified as genuine SF. *The Alteration* (1976), which won the John W. Campbell Memorial Award, takes place in a world in which the Reformation never happened and concerns the plight of a twentieth-century English boy singer whose soprano voice can only be preserved by castration. *Russian Hide and Seek: A Melodrama* (1980), which bears a strong resemblance to English translations of classic Russian novels, is set in a twenty-first-century England under Russian rule. Both books are stylish models of what a mainstream novelist can do when he turns to science fiction.

E.J.

ANALOG SCIENCE FICTION/SCIENCE FACT (formerly titled *Astounding Stories of Super Science* or *Astounding Stories*, 1930–1938, and *Astounding Science Fiction*, 1938–1959).
Considered for most of its life as the premier science-fiction magazine responsible for reshaping the genre, *Astounding* was the first pulp to rival Hugo GERNSBACK's magazines. It first appeared in January of 1930 and, under editor Harry BATES, adopted a policy of publishing fast-action super-science stories, which proved popular. Yet despite the stature of its contributors (including Murray LEINSTER and Jack WILLIAMSON) *Astounding* carried little of merit and folded in 1933 when its publisher, the Clayton pulp chain, fell victim to the Depression. The magazine was revived that same year by Street & Smith, with F. Orlin TREMAINE as editor. Tremaine initiated a policy of publishing what he called "thought variant" stories to foster bold new ideas. The years 1934 and 1935 saw *Astounding* established as the field leader with some mature science fiction from writers Nathan Schachner, Donald Wandrei, Williamson, Leinster, and Raymond Z. GALLUN.

In 1937 Tremaine was succeeded by John W. CAMPBELL, Jr., under whose leadership, as Eric Frank RUSSELL later recalled, writers were brought, "or in some cases dragged," from the primitive 1930s into the modern world. Campbell, who using the pseudonym of Don A. Stuart had written some of the best science fiction of the 1930s, was a powerhouse of ideas, and he established a stable

Cover illustration by Howard V. Brown

of writers capable of drawing on those ideas. These included Robert A. HEINLEIN, Theodore STURGEON, Isaac ASIMOV, and A. E. VAN VOGT. Campbell demanded that story be preeminent, with science only part of the setting and not the central point. He wanted writers to tell a story as if addressing a future audience. If the period from 1939 to 1942 was indeed, as it has been called, a GOLDEN AGE for science fiction, that golden age took place almost wholly in the pages of this magazine.

After World War II, *Astounding* was unable to recapture its previous allure. Other magazines were gaining equal respectability, while Campbell injured his reputation, first in 1950 by his promotion of L. Ron HUBBARD's theory of Dianetics, and then throughout the 1950s by his constant emphasis on mental powers and parapsychology. *Astounding* remained the senior SF magazine during the 1950s and most of the 1960s (it received the Hugo Award as best professional magazine eight times from 1953 to 1965), but the magazine's continuing status was more a result of the level-headedness of its contributors than of Campbell's influence. Nevertheless, Campbell still encouraged new writers and ideas and had some notable successes, Frank HERBERT's Dune

A CASE OF IDENTITY by RANDALL GARRETT

Cover illustration by John Schoenherr

series and Anne McCAFFREY's Pern stories among the best known of later years. He died in 1971 and was succeeded by Ben BOVA from 1972 to 1978 and Stanley SCHMIDT from 1978 to the present. Bova did much to raise *Analog* from its rut, and he received the Hugo Award as best editor from 1973 to 1977 and again in 1979. He encouraged writers to expand the horizons of science fiction and received some wonderful responses from Frederik POHL, Joe HALDEMAN, and newcomers such as Orson Scott CARD. Under Schmidt the magazine has lost some of that sparkle, and although it remains respectable and important, in keeping with the general decline in the influence of SF magazines, it is now one among equals rather than first among many.

M.A.

ANCESTORS OF SCIENCE FICTION

Fanciful stories go as far back as there are records, but the rational consideration of marvelous things that is characteristic of modern science fiction was uncommon in early times. Instead a group of genres, subgenres, or motif bearers offers fragmentary ideas later to be found in science fiction, where they are sometimes combined, sometimes rendered more sophisticated. The classical utopia, the imaginary voyage, the lunar voyage, the Faustian invention story, the catastrophe story, the tale of futurity, and the imaginary war story are examples.

To the Greek philosopher Plato may be traced two elements in science fiction. In his *Timaeus* and *Critias* he developed the literary myth of Atlantis, the lost continent. Much more important, however, was his creation of the detailed, logically consistent ideal state in *The Republic* and *The Laws*. As presented by Socrates, the just state requires (a) complete regulation of social behavior; (b) the existence of an ascetic warrior and ruling caste, the Guardians; and (c) communism, even extended to women, among the Guardians. Although Plato considered these ideas interdependent, they have obviously taken different paths in history and literature. Some utopian writings and some with a utopian tinge have stressed the idea of the elite Guardians; others have favored the concept of social control or socialism.

The notion of state socialism was developed strongly in Sir Thomas MORE's *Utopia* (1516/1517), which blends Platonic idealism, Christian monasticism, English economic history, and American ethnography. More's short work, together with Sir Francis Bacon's *New Atlantis* (1626/1627) stands behind most later English-language utopian fiction, either directly or indirectly. Many of the basic ideas from More and Bacon appear in fictional descriptions of non-European societies, as in the seventeenth- and eighteenth-century imaginary voyage.

In the ancient world, fantastic journeys, in particular the *Epic of Gilgamesh*, the *Odyssey*, and the *Argonautica*, formed an important part of literature. In the Middle Ages the apocryphal travels of John de Mandeville played a similar, if lesser, role. The European ages of discovery, however, gave rise to many accounts of imaginary travels, often with utopian and science-fiction elements.

Such *voyages imaginaires* flourished in France, and the more important French examples were soon translated into English. Worthy of mention are Denis Vairasse's *The History of the Sevarites or Sevarambi* (French, 1677–1679), which places a high socialist culture in then unknown Australia, and Gabriel Foigny's *A New Discovery of Terra Incognita Australis* (French, 1676), also set in Australia, describing a continent contoured by engineering and peopled with gigantic hermaphrodites. Both books, as part of the early Enlightenment, stress "Reason based on Nature." Even more important is Jonathan SWIFT's *Travels into Several Remote Parts of the World . . . by Lemuel Gulliver* (1726), in which the Laputa episode is one of the few early examples of true science fiction. In Laputa ("the whore") Swift satirized science and the scientific method, thus controverting Bacon. During the eighteenth century the imaginary voyage waned, but Ludwig Holberg's *A Journey to the World Under-ground* (Latin, 1741), a satire on European cultural groups set among intelligent vegetable and animal life in a hollow earth, deserves notice.

During the early nineteenth century the *voyage imaginaire* began to assume new importance. Antarctic exploration formed the background to Edgar Allan POE's *The Narrative of Arthur Gordon Pym* (1838), and Antarctica and John Cleves Symmes's crank theory of a hollow Earth stood behind Adam Seaborn's *Symzonia* (1820), a pseudonymous satire on Symmes and American politics. More significant for fiction, however, were the exploration of darkest Africa and the discovery of the ancient high civilizations of the New World. Here the *voyage imaginaire* bifurcated. One branch subsumed the novels of Jules VERNE and his school, which include both fictionalized geographic tracts and science fiction with geographic elements. The second branch developed into the lost-race novel, which attained maturity in H. Rider HAGGARD's *She* (1886) and *Allan Quatermain* (1887). Haggard's story patterns were widely copied in Britain and America. On the whole British writers preferred Africa as a setting, while Americans tended to write about the Aztecs and Incas of Latin America.

Another form of exploration, different in origin from terrestrial geographic fiction, is the lunar voyage, which during most of its history (perhaps because of lunar folklore) was satiric. The earliest such voyage, Lucian of Samosata's *A True History* (Greek, second century after Christ) pokes fun at the Greek classics. The most important Renaissance lunar voyage, Savinien de CYRANO de Bergerac's *Voyage to the Moon* (French, 1657), is a remarkable attack on Cartesian science, the Bible, and revealed religion. Although it is occasionally cited for the mechanical devices the narrator uses to attain flight, these are trivial compared with the book's wealth of ideas.

The most significant early lunar-voyage work, Johannes KEPLER's *Somnium* (Latin, 1634), is not satire but fictionalized selenography, with ingenious speculations on life-forms adapted to lunar conditions. Similarly serious is the scientifically lesser but historically more important *The Man in the Moone* (1638) by Bishop Francis Godwin, which invokes medieval natural history to transport the narrator to the moon. Godwin's work influenced most later premodern accounts of lunar voyages.

Around the middle of the nineteenth century, advancing astronomy and technology opened new paths for the fictional lunar traveler. Poe's "Hans Phaal" (1835) is transitional between satire and science; Richard A. Locke's *Celebrated Moon Hoax* (1835) strikes out boldly in extrapolated science. It was Verne's *Voyage to the Moon* and *Around the Moon* (French, 1865, 1869) that genuinely established the science-fiction novel. In lesser hands the lunar voyage/interplanetary novel continued

through the end of the nineteenth century with a mélange of eccentric notions, occultism, satire, and heterodox religion. Typical specimens are Percy GREG's *Across the Zodiac* (1880) and John Jacob ASTOR's *A Journey in Other Worlds* (1894).

Technology and science on the whole exerted their influence on these ancestral forms late, and then most typically in the invention story. Although Bacon in his *New Atlantis* identified applied science as a cultural force, most of his successors missed his point. Fictional analysis of fantastic inventions and discoveries and their implications did not appear until the end of the eighteenth and the beginning of the nineteenth centuries. The subtext of these stories is the idea that certain knowledge is evil, and that the scientific mind tends to hubris and sacrilege and will be punished. In William Godwin's *St. Leon* (1799) the protagonist is able to manufacture gold and the elixir of life, but his character degenerates and he knows little happiness. The theme of *Frankenstein* (1818), by Godwin's daughter Mary Wollstonecraft SHELLEY, is similar if more sensational. This tradition of the Faustian discoverer persisted sporadically throughout the nineteenth century, a notable example being *The Strange Case of Dr. Jekyll and Mr. Hyde* (1887) by Robert Louis STEVENSON. The invention story eventually bifurcated into mad-scientist and comic-inventor tales, both of which flourished in the early twentieth century.

Equally concerned with punishment is the catastrophe story, which is rooted in the great religious traditions: the flood of the Near East and the kalpas of the Indian religions. Although the notion of destruction and chiliasm recurred perpetually in medieval religious life, it appeared fairly late in fiction. One may cite Jean Cousin de Grainville's *The Last Man* (French 1805), in which God ends it all, and Mary Shelley's *The Last Man* (1826), wherein warfare and plague finish off humankind. The theme of destruction was especially important in nineteenth-century America, where Millerism reinforced increased astronomical knowledge. Typical are S. Austin, Jr.'s, "The Comet" (1839), Poe's "Conversation of Eiros and Charmion" (1839), and Nathaniel HAWTHORNE's "The New Adam and Eve" (1849). In Alexander Blettsworth's anonymous *The Strange Ms.* (1883), a cosmic fire storm destroys almost everyone except refugees in Mammoth Cave.

Whereas catastrophe stories often take place in the near future, stories set in more remote times to come are typically concerned with the modus vivendi of their day. The earliest known piece of this sort, the partly fictionalized, anonymous *The Reign of George VI* (1763), focuses on dynasties and military history. Far more important historically is Louis-Sebastien Mercier's *Memoirs of the Year Two Thousand Five Hundred* (French, 1770/1771), which offers a detailed, somewhat optimistic picture of future French culture, stressing rationalism and Roussellianism. Predictive stories of this sort became linked in America with concepts of perfectibility and often shaded into the utopia. To cite two examples: Mary Griffith's "Three Hundred Years Hence" (1836) describes what has been termed an old-maid's future, with no dogs, alcohol, or tobacco, and Poe's "Mellonta Tauta" (1849) attacks technological advances and the concept of progress.

During the 1880s and 1890s, along with various concepts of progress, the utopia emerged in America as a major genre that also influenced later science fiction. By far the most important of these ventures was Edward BELLAMY's *Looking Backward, 2000–1887* (1888), in which a nineteenth-century man reaches Boston, A.D. 2000, via accidental suspended animation. He finds there a flourishing socialist state organized as a work army, without money or much private ownership, with good benefits but (although Bellamy did not see the point) rather weak liberties. *Looking Backward* was followed by a host of sequels and parallel works by other authors, supporting or attacking Bellamy's ideas. Bellamy himself scanted scientific and technological advances, but many of his imitators developed such matters more fully, their work often merging into science fiction. Bellamy believed that his future state would evolve gradually and naturally out of monopolies, but other authors believed that a better government could only be the outcome of class war.

International war too was an important part of early fantastic literature, particularly in the imaginary war story, in which a hostile power more or less realistically invades an innocent state. Often presented in semifictional form, the product of British insularity and insularism, this type received its model in George CHESNEY's *The Battle of Dorking* (1871), which describes a successful invasion of Great Britain by a Germanic power. Like *Looking Backward* it was followed by a host of imitative works, mostly concentrated in Great Britain, but a few were set on the Continent and in the United States. In America this type was often associated with the notion of the Yellow Peril. The original impetus of the imaginary war story, with Chesney, was serious concern about military preparedness, but the genre on the one hand degenerated into scare journalism (such as William Le Queux's *The Great War in England in 1897,* 1894) or, on the other hand, evolved into science fiction.

In addition to these major story types there are also isolated works and story groups. VOLTAIRE's *Micromegas* (French, 1750/1752) describes a visitor from another stellar system; the point of the work is the triviality of humanity, in opposition to prevailing Enlightenment anthropocentricity. Early aeronautical stories, such as Ralph Morris's *A Narrative of the Life and Astonishing Adventures of John Daniel* (1751), appeared sporadically, but later tales in the genre tend more to reflect historical attempts at flight (as, for example, in the Frank Reade, Jr., dime-novel adventure stories). Edwin A. Abbott's *Flatland* (1884) and Charles Hinton's *Scientific Romances* (1884–1885) conduct logical explorations into worlds with fewer or more dimensions than ours, but these stories have religiophilosophical concerns.

Just when these ancestors of science fiction became science fiction proper is moot, and scholars have offered several different timetables. Similarly disputable is the exact relation between these early story types and modern science fiction. On the whole these individual early works are so scattered and obscure (although typologically interesting) that in most instances it would be chimerical to envision bridges of transmission between them. The lunar voyage and the utopia genres are exceptional in offering continuous, consciously used chains of development. In most other instances connections can only be called loose to very tenuous; similarities between ancients and moderns may be only similar responses to recurrent ideas.

E.F.B.

ANDERSON, POUL [WILLIAM] (1926–).

American writer, one of the most prolific, versatile, and honored in the field. Born in Pennsylvania to Danish parents, Anderson spent his youth in Texas, Denmark, and Minnesota, earned a B.S. in physics with honors from the University of Minnesota in 1948, and moved to the San Francisco area in 1953, after marrying fellow writer Karen Kruse (1932–).

James BLISH has called Anderson "the enduring explosion" because of his productivity. From his first solo sale ("Logic") to *Astounding* in 1947 up to 1987 he has published sixty-nine SF novels, nine detective and fantasy novels, thirty-three collections of stories, and four books of nonfiction, edited two books, and even translated one. His speculative fiction ranges from high tech to high fantasy. He has also written juveniles, essays, poetry, horror, and popular science.

Anderson's fiction is rational in concept, romantic in execution. (His favorite authors are Johannes Jensen, the Danish Nobel laureate, and Rudyard KIPLING.) He is a self-proclaimed "eighteenth-century liberal" (by which he means libertarian) in politics, an antimodernist in culture (he was an early member of the Society for Creative Anachronisms). His persistent theme is how free beings respond to challenge, yet he sees no ultimate meaning to these responses. In Anderson's view, courage is its own reward, for doom awaits all things.

As Blish has observed, Anderson's awareness of entropy, or the inevitable death of everything, gives his work a tragic sense rare in SF. He is no Pelagian optimist, believing that humans are the authors of our own salvation, as does his college classmate and sometime collaborator Gordon R. DICKSON. In serious work his characteristic mixture of tragedy and triumph yields plots that match an external, concrete problem that is usually

Poul Anderson

solved with an internal, personal one that is solved less often. The subtle irony of *Tau Zero* (1970), which Blish has called "the ultimate hard science fiction novel," plays the ordinariness of people against the marvelous argosy of their starship. Yet pessimism hones rather than dulls Anderson's capacity for wonder. He builds his ALIEN WORLDS directly from their astrophysical specifications, creating new environments rich in scientific invention and poetic names, then giving their inhabitants cultures resonant with myth and history. He has written articles about the skills and pleasures of fictional world building.

To explore the historical process, he developed two separate future histories, the Psychotechnic League series, influenced by Robert A. HEINLEIN, which features the shrewd, fat, boisterous trader Nicholas van Rijn, and the more adventurous Technic Civilization series. The latter covers five millennia of galactic history in forty stories (including thirteen novels) written over the course of four decades and features the sophisticated, existentialist Terran agent Dominic Flandry working in the twilight of a corrupt galactic empire. Anderson's classic time travel stories show that he is equally at home in the past ("The Man Who Came Early," 1956) and on alternate time lines (*The Guardians of Time,* 1960; revised 1981).

The breadth of Anderson's work is illustrated in his four early novels: *Brain Wave* (1954), *The High Crusade* (1960), *Three Hearts and Three Lions* (1953/1961), and *Tau Zero. Brain Wave* is an idea story in which Anderson traced the difficulties and opportunities that arise when the Solar System escapes from a force field that has been inhibiting intelligence. *The High Crusade*

describes the adventures of a group of knights who storm an alien spaceship during the feudal period and head out to the stars. In *Three Hearts and Three Lions* an Englishman is thrown into an *Unknown* type of rationalized fantasy world. In *Tau Zero* a ram-scoop spaceship accelerates out of control so that the passengers experience the final collapse of our universe and the birth of another.

Myth has inspired some of Anderson's best work, including his two different versions of Orpheus in *World without Stars* (1966/1967) and "Goat Song" (1972). His first adult novel, *The Broken Sword* (1954; revised 1971), adapts the *Völsunga Saga* as heroic fantasy; "The Sorrows of Odin the Goth" (1983) treats the same saga as a time travel story. Anderson mythified literature in *A Midsummer's Tempest* (1974) and domesticated magic in his rivets and sorcery fantasy *Operation Chaos* (1956–1959/1971).

Anderson's humor is generally satiric, allusive, and thick with puns. His most popular comedies are the farcical Hoka stories written with Dickson, in which teddy bear–like aliens imitate human pop culture (*Earthman's Burden,* 1957, and *Hoka!* 1984).

Despite his breadth of achievement, Anderson's work does have faults—awkward dialogue, some excesses of sentiment, a tendency for characters to lecture, and what critic Patrick McGuire has called "a vaguely 'pulpish' odor." Such flaws are less evident, however, in his shorter work, as his many awards for midlength fiction attest. He received the Hugo for "The Longest Voyage" (1960), "No Truce with Kings" (1963), "The Sharing of Flesh" (1968), "The Queen of Air and Darkness" (1971), "Goat Song" (1972), "Hunter's Moon" (1980), and "The Saturn Game" (1981). "The Queen of Air and Darkness," "Goat Song," and "The Saturn Game" also won the Nebula.

Anderson was awarded the Gandalf as a Grand Master of Fantasy in 1978, served as president of the SCIENCE FICTION WRITERS OF AMERICA (1972–73), and was Professional Guest of Honor at the World Science Fiction Convention in 1959.

NOTABLE OTHER WORKS: *War of the Wing-Men* (1958; as *The Man Who Counts,* 1978); *The Enemy Stars* (1958/1960); *The Makeshift Rocket* (1958/1962); *Orbit Unlimited* (1961); *After Doomsday* (1962); *Let the Spacemen Beware* (1963; as *The Night Face,* 1978); *Time and Stars* (collection, 1964); *Trader to the Stars* (1964); *Ensign Flandry* (1966); *There Will Be Time* (1972); *The People of the Wind* (1973); *Hrolf Kraki's Saga* (1973); *The Many Worlds of Poul Anderson* (1974; as *The Book of Poul Anderson,* 1975); *The Psychotechnic League* (collection, 1981); *Fantasy* (collection, 1981); *Orion Shall Rise* (1983); *The Unicorn Trade* (with Karen Anderson, 1984); *Dialogue with Darkness* (collection, 1985).

S.L.M.

ANDROID (1981). *Directed by Aaron Lipstadt; screenplay by James Reigle and Don Opper; photographed by Tim Suhrstedt; music by Don Preston. With Don Opper, Klaus Kinski, Brie Howard, Norbert Weisser, Crofton Hardester, Kendra Kirchner. 91 minutes. Color.*

This delightful and provocative film directed by Aaron Lipstadt and featuring a brilliant performance by Don Opper as the android, Max, is one of the best of the number of science-fiction films such as BLADE RUNNER and HEARTBEEPS that explore the relationship between human and artificial life. Living in an isolated space station where he assists a scientist (Klaus Kinski) in his android research, Max is fully aware of his android status and its ostensible emotional limits, but he is fascinated by film and video records of human life and attempts to fashion a persona for himself based almost entirely on characters in old movies, such as *It's a Wonderful Life*. Three escaped criminals take refuge in the space station, thus initiating a sequence of events in which Max's "humanity" more and more asserts itself just as differing kinds of inhumanity are revealed in Max's scientist-creator and in the escaped criminals.

An important step in what Vivian Sobchack terms contemporary SF film's "embracing of the alien and erasing of alienation," *Android* also focuses on postmodern culture's increasing emphasis on video images as the maker of, rather than reflection of, reality. *Android* was one of the first SF films to anticipate the "new wave" of marginal and low-budget productions such as REPO MAN and THE BROTHER FROM ANOTHER PLANET, which have come to characterize the best of SF film in the latter part of the 1980s.

B.L.

THE ANDROMEDA STRAIN (1971). *Directed by Robert Wise; screenplay by Nelson Gidding; adapted from the novel by Michael Crichton; photographed by Richard H. Kline; music by Gil Mellé. With James Olson, Arthur Hill, David Wayne, Kate Reid, Paula Kelly, George Mitchell, Ramon Bieri. 130 minutes. Color.*

Although based on a best-selling novel, *The Andromeda Strain* would not have been made if *2001: A SPACE ODYSSEY* had not succeeded three years earlier. Like that landmark film, it expresses an ambivalence about technology, both the source and solution of the problem in the film. It marked the return of Robert WISE—best known to science-fiction fans as director of the 1951 DAY THE EARTH STOOD STILL—to the SF cinema.

A satellite returns to Earth, bringing with it a microorganism that wipes out a small town except for an old man and a baby. An elite team of scientists is sealed in a gigantic complex to try to find a way to stop the spread of the alien organism.

The Andromeda Strain opens very well, with eerie scenes in the deserted town, and the climax, as James Olson races to shut down an automatic nuclear explosion, is exciting and tense. However, the middle portion of this long film becomes mired in technological and medical patter, which not only is uninvolving but proves pointless in the end: the organism simply mutates into harmlessness, deflating the film's theme about the responsibilities of science and technology. This strange story blunder comes from the novel; it's unfortunate that Wise and screenplay author Nelson Gidding didn't consider altering it.

Despite these flaws, *The Andromeda Strain* is a respectable film—grim, understated, and sober. Its considerable budget ($6.5 million) was spent primarily on the extensive sets, designed by Boris Leven, representing the underground medical emergency complex. Wise took great care at the beginning to establish the extreme security precautions and the reality of the Wildfire Research Establishment. The actors were chosen for verisimilitude rather than star power, and the approach throughout is uncluttered, to the point, and unsensational. The photography is cool and remote, and Gil Mellé's electronic score is appropriate and dramatic, but less advanced technically than much earlier electronic music, including Louis and Bebe Barron's score for FORBIDDEN PLANET (1956).

B.W.

THE ANGRY RED PLANET (1960). *Directed by Ib Melchior; screenplay by Ib Melchior and Sid Pink; photographed by Stanley Cortez; music by Paul Dunlap. With Nora Hayden, Gerald Mohr, Les Tremayne, Jack Kruschen. 83 minutes. Color.*

This low-budget tale was shot as "Invasion of Mars," suggesting a more interesting viewpoint—Earthpeople as invaders—than the film ultimately adopted. It's a conventional story of how the first expedition to Mars encounters a series of monsters that eventually chase the survivors back to Earth, accompanied by a warning from Martians to stay off their planet. The most distinctive elements of the film are the imaginative but silly monsters, particularly the almost endearing "bat-rat-spider," and the peculiar film process called Cinemagic, resulting in what looks like overexposed black-and-white film tinted Pepto-Bismol pink. The process was intended to make the actors and sets appear as real as the cartoon drawings (by Alex Toth) used as backgrounds, but it only puzzled audiences.

B.W.

ANIMAL FARM (1955). *Directed by John Halas and Joy Batchelor; screenplay by John Halas and Joy Batchelor; adapted from the novel by George Orwell;*

music by Matyas Seiber. With voices by Maurice Denham. 75 minutes. Color.

British artists John Halas and Joy Batchelor created this animated version of George ORWELL's political fable, elevating the cartoon medium to full-length adult cinematic satire. The Walt Disney–like innocence generally associated with animation is utilized brilliantly to contrast grotesque political realities with the apparent naïveté of the cartoon form and to describe the development of a totalitarian state (clearly modeled on the USSR, with porcine characters identifiable as Stalin and Trotsky). Farm animals, resolving that "all animals are equal," rebel against an oppressive master and agree to rule themselves. Then Napoleon, an ambitious pig, establishes a new tyranny as bad as the old one. The new slogan: "All animals are equal, but some animals are more equal than others."

Although this film is an obvious parable of the Russian Revolution and its decline (as well as a faithful rendering of the novel), it—like PLANET OF THE APES and A BOY AND HIS DOG—proves once again that speaking animals, as well as talking computers, can serve as a mirror of human behavior.

M.T.W.

ANSTEY, F. (Pseudonym of Thomas Anstey Guthrie) (1856–1934).

British writer of satiric fantasies. Anstey's major contribution to science fiction is *The Time Bargain* (1891, also later retitled *Tourmaine's Time Cheques*), one of the first stories concerning time travel and the paradox it creates. Anstey is best known, however, for his witty fantasies in which some magical element from the past finds its way into Victorian England. For example, in *The Tinted Venus* (1885), Anstey's comment on the present state of love, the ancient Roman goddess is conjured up in contemporary England. Anstey made use of both classical mythology and Germanic folktales in his stories and included such SF devices as mind transfer (*Vice Versa*, 1882) and telepathy (*The Fallen Idol*, 1886). Most of his short stories were published in *Punch*.

OTHER WORKS: *The Talking Horse* (collection, 1891); *The Black Poodle and Other Tales* (collection, 1896); *The Brass Bottle* (1900); *Salted Almonds* (collection, 1906); *In Brief Authority* (1915); *Humor and Fantasy* (collection, 1931).

S.H.G.

———— ANTHOLOGIES ————

Anthologies have been important to the development of modern science fiction for several reasons. For roughly the first thirty years after Hugo GERNSBACK founded AMAZING STORIES in 1926, science fiction was predominantly a medium for fiction of less than novel length. Anthologies therefore have chronicled the history of the SF magazines and the stories they ran. In addition, anthologies, particularly those published in hardcover, determine which stories remain available for 95 percent of readers, which stories are most representative of particular writers, and which become the "classics" of their generation. These facts place great responsibilities on reprint anthologists, who are in a position to advance certain writers and stories over others. Anthologies imply, by their presumed selectivity, that the stories in them are important. Moreover, anthologies have introduced countless thousands of young readers to the field. Finally, the introductions and headnotes in some anthologies contain insights and information that contribute to the history and study of science fiction in important ways. Indeed the *only* information on some writers may be the brief biographical notes found in anthologies.

Anatomy of Wonder (1976, revised 1987) divides anthologies into general reprint anthologies; historically based anthologies, including those based on specific magazines or awards and those organized chronologically; the "year's best" anthologies; theme anthologies; anthologies aimed primarily at children and young adults; and the so-called original anthologies, which are fundamentally different but are included here for the sake of convenience.

Although anthologies of proto-SF can be identified, the SF reprint anthology is generally held to have begun with Phil Stong's *The Other Worlds* (1941), which reprinted stories from the genre magazines, and Donald A. WOLLHEIM's *The Pocket Book of Science Fiction* (1943), the pioneering paperback SF anthology. (Wollheim went on to a distinguished career as one of the leading book editors and publishers in the field, but he was also an excellent anthologist who created many worthy collections for Ace Books. He later helped initiate an excellent "best of the year" series that is still published.)

These two books were general reprint anthologies, a category that was particularly important immediately after World War II, when two major trade publishers, Random House and Crown, entered the SF field with massive books of this type. The first to appear was Crown's *The Best of Science Fiction* (1946), edited by Groff Conklin, the premier anthologist of his generation. Conklin would publish some forty anthologies in his career, including *A Treasury of Science Fiction* (1948), *The Big Book of Science Fiction* (1950), and *The Omnibus of Science Fiction* (1952), all huge books of high quality. Conklin, who apparently never published any SF of his own, rarely produced a weak book.

The second book of this pair, however, Raymond J. Healy and J. Francis McCOMAS's *Adventures in Time and Space* (1946), made the greater impact and had the better stories, largely because its editors beat Conklin to many of the stories he would have included in his first volume. This book was nearly 1000 pages long and contained much of the cream of magazine SF published to that date—the excellence of this volume is emphasized by the fact that it has never been out of print. The decision by these two respected publishers to bring out SF collections did much for the reputation of the field and encouraged other publishers to initiate SF projects of their own.

General reprint anthologies continued to be produced, although their number declined drastically as other types of anthologies became popular, as the price of doing such huge volumes became almost prohibitive, and as the rise of paperback and hardcover SF novels and single-author collections took up the slots once afforded to this type of book. Other notable books in this category include Edmund Crispin's excellent *Best SF*, which consists of seven volumes published between 1955 and 1970; Anthony Boucher's two-volume *A Treasury of Great Science Fiction* (1959), long offered as a premium of the Science Fiction Book Club; *Spectrum*, a series of five anthologies (1962–1967) that originated in Great Britain, edited by the noted literary figure Kingsley AMIS, whose prestige did much to advance the stature of science fiction in Britain and the United States; Sam MOSKOWITZ's *Modern Masterpieces of Science Fiction* (1965); Christopher Cerf's well-selected *The Vintage Anthology of Science Fantasy* (1966); the inappropriately titled *England Swings SF* (1968), edited by the talented anthologist Judith MERRIL, which had a considerable impact on the SF community through introducing examples of the British New Wave to an American audience; *A Science Fiction Argosy* (1972), edited by Damon KNIGHT, who in addition to his many other contributions to modern science fiction is also an anthologist of great ability; the nine-volume Alpha series (1970–1978), edited by Robert SILVERBERG, which rescued a number of excellent but neglected stories; and *The Arbor House Treasury of Modern Science Fiction* and its companion, *The Arbor House Treasury of Great Science Fiction Short Novels* (both 1980), edited by Silverberg and Martin H. Greenberg.

Historical anthologies fall into three subcategories—those based on magazines, those based on time periods, and those based on awards. Almost all long-running science-fiction magazines have spawned anthologies: *Astounding Science Fiction* and its successor, *Analog*, have produced more anthologies than any other magazine. A representative list includes *The Astounding Science Fiction Anthology* (1952), edited by John W. CAMPBELL, Jr., a massive, high-quality volume that covers the magazine's "Golden Age"; the series of anthologies edited by Campbell beginning with *Prologue to Analog* in 1962 and continuing with *Analog 1* to *Analog 9* in 1973; the large two-volume retrospective anthology done as a tribute to Campbell by Harry HARRISON and Brian

W. ALDISS, *The Astounding-Analog Reader* (1972 and 1973); and the numerous anthologies edited by Stanley SCHMIDT and others after the magazine was bought by Davis Publications, the large majority of which are theme anthologies.

Anthologies based on GALAXY SCIENCE FICTION began with *The Galaxy Reader of Science Fiction*, edited by H. L. GOLD in 1952. This developed into a series that continued from *The Second Galaxy Reader of Science Fiction* to *The Eleventh Galaxy Reader of Science Fiction* in 1969, with books 1 through 6 edited by Gold and the remainder by Frederik POHL. Other Galaxy-based books include *The Best from Galaxy*, four volumes produced by various hands including James Baen from 1972 to 1976; and *Galaxy Magazine: Thirty Years of Innovative Science Fiction*, a major retrospective edited by Pohl, Greenberg, and Joseph D. Olander (1980), which contains historical essays and memoirs. The last of the "big three" of the postwar era, THE MAGAZINE OF FANTASY AND SCIENCE FICTION, has been well served by a long series of "best of" books that began with *The Best from Fantasy and Science Fiction* in 1952 and continues with some twenty-four volumes to date, each edited by the excellent group of editors who have shaped the magazine over the years.

A sampling of other major magazine-based anthologies includes *The Best of Planet Stories* (1975), edited by Leigh BRACKETT, the first of a planned series that never developed; *The Best from New Worlds* (1955) and numerous later volumes that chronicle the development of the important British magazine, capped by Michael MOORCOCK's huge 1983 retrospective *New Worlds*; *The Best of Omni Science Fiction*, a series that began in 1980 and has continued with various editors in different formats; *The First World of If* (1957), the initial volume of several series of "best of" books drawn from that influential magazine—a capstone anthology with memoirs—*Worlds of If*, edited by Pohl, Greenberg, and Olander, which appeared in 1986; and an increasing number of anthologies drawn from *Isaac Asimov's Science Fiction Magazine* (1978–).

Historically oriented anthologies not based on magazines generally focus on time periods—good examples include the excellent group edited by Aldiss and Harrison, *Decade: The 1940s*, *Decade: The 1950s*, and *Decade: The 1960s* (1975–1977); the group published by Avon beginning with *Science Fiction of the Thirties*, edited by Knight (1975), *Science Fiction of the Forties*, edited by Pohl, Greenberg, and Olander (1978), and *Science Fiction of the Fifties*, edited by Greenberg and Olander (1979); the interesting *End of Summer: Science Fiction of the Fifties*, edited by Barry N. MALZBERG and Bill Pronzini (1979); the somewhat esoteric *Golden Age of Science Fiction*, edited by Amis (1981), which covers the 1950s and early 1960s; the wonderful *Before the Golden Age* (1974), an entertaining and informative look at the science fiction of the 1930s edited by Isaac ASIMOV; and the excellent *Classic Science Fiction: The First Golden Age* (1978), edited by Terry CARR, which covers the early 1940s, the first of several planned books but the only one to appear to date. This approach has been taken to its presumably logical conclusion by Asimov and Greenberg with their series *The Great SF Stories*, which is devoted to retrospective analysis of the best stories of each year beginning with 1939 and continuing through 1986, with a total of thirty-three books planned. A substantial number of anthologies, historically or thematically organized, are compiled for classroom use, such as James GUNN's *The Road to Science Fiction* (4 vols., 1977–1982).

Also of great historical importance (and containing a wealth of reading) are the award-based anthologies, the best known of which is *The Hugo Winners*, a series edited by Asimov beginning in 1962 and consisting of five volumes through 1986 which reprint the stories that won the Hugo Award in the less-than-novel-length categories. The Nebula Award of the SCIENCE FICTION WRITERS OF AMERICA has received similar treatment in the form of *Nebula Award Stories*, beginning in 1966 and edited by various guest editors; twenty-one volumes had been published through 1986. These are really "self-chosen" books and not anthologies in the conventional sense of the term, because the awards determine the contents. A similar and excellent group of books are Harrison's *SF: Author's Choice* (1968–1974), for which authors are asked to choose their best (often their favorite) story. Especially noteworthy are the three *Science Fiction Hall of Fame* books, whose contents were chosen by vote of the members of Science Fiction Writers of America from among stories published before the establishment of the Nebulas. Volume 1 (1970) consists of short stories compiled by Silverberg; Volumes 2A and 2B (1973) contain novelettes and novellas compiled by Ben BOVA.

Two works of considerable historical importance are Richard LUPOFF's *What If? Stories That Should Have Won the Hugo* (2 vols., 1980–81), which discusses stories by year from 1952 to 1965 and chooses what the author feels are the most deserving from among them; and Michael Ashley's four-volume set *The History of the Science Fiction Magazine* (1974–1978), which provides a wealth of information on the magazines by decade, beginning with 1926–1935 and ending with 1956–1965.

One of the most popular categories of anthologies is the "year's best," which began with *The Best Science-Fiction Stories*, edited by Everett BLEILER and T. E. Dikty, ran from 1949 to 1956, and reappeared in 1958, with the series edited by Dikty alone from the volume covering 1955. This was a solid if unexceptional series that was followed by Merril's *The Year's Greatest Science-Fiction and Fantasy*, which ran from 1956 to 1968 with a name change or two along the way. The series contains

much fantasy, but its chief importance lies in Merril's willingness to go outside the genre magazines for stories, an effort that widened the boundaries of the field for many readers. Two of the most important anthologists-editors in SF, Wollheim and Carr, teamed up for the next effort at a year's best volume—*World's Best Science Fiction* began covering the year 1965 and ended with coverage of 1971, when the team separated. Wollheim then started a new series with *The 1972 Annual World's Best SF* that is still running today with the assistance of Art Saha. Carr's series, The Best Science Fiction of the Year, was distinguished by the excellent taste usually exhibited by its gifted editor. Unfortunately a companion series, The Best Science Fiction Novellas of the Year, failed after two good volumes (1980–1981).

Proceeding chronologically from series initiation, 1967 saw the launching of Harrison and Aldiss's *Best SF: 1967*, a somewhat idiosyncratic series that ran to 1973 and exhibited a strong British flavor. Lester DEL REY entered the competition in 1972 with his *Best Science Fiction Stories of the Year* (and by this time it must have been quite difficult to find another title variation for this kind of series), which he edited until 1976, when the series was taken over by Gardner DOZOIS, who has developed it into an enormous annual volume of some 250,000 words with excellent summations of the year's events in the field. These three series are firmly established, and it appears the genre can accommodate them all.

Theme anthologies date from the early 1950s. One of the first was compiled by Martin Greenberg (the man who cofounded Gnome Press, not the current prolific anthologist of the same name); *The Robot and the Man* (1953) was the first anthology of artificial intelligence stories. The number and variety of theme anthologies is so enormous that it precludes a meaningful listing here, but it should be mentioned that virtually all the major and minor subjects of science fiction have been covered at least once—a very partial list would include aliens (*Invaders of Earth*, Conklin, ed., 1952); war (*Body Armor 2000*, the first of a series that examines individual weapon systems, Joe HALDEMAN, Greenberg, and Waugh, eds., 1986); sports (*The Infinite Arena*, Carr, ed., 1977); crime (*Dark Dreams, Dark Sins*, Malzberg and Pronzini, eds., 1978), galactic empires (*Galactic Empires*, 2 vols., Aldiss, ed., 1976), religion (*Wandering Stars*, Jack Dann, ed., 1974), and even weight loss (*The Science Fiction Weight Loss Book*, Asimov, George R. R. MARTIN, and Greenberg, eds., 1983).

A variation of the theme anthology are books based on such definitions as gender (*Women of Wonder* series, Pamela SARGENT, ed., 1975–1978), occupation of the writer (*The Expert Dreamers*, stories by scientists, Pohl, ed., 1962) and form of writing (*Space Mail*, stories in the form of letters and diary entries, Asimov, Greenberg, and Olander, eds., 1980). This category sometimes requires repetition as new and better stories replace older ones.

Anthologies for children and young adults barely constitute a separate category, because they usually contain only stories originally published in the genre magazines. However, they have been numerous and influential, introducing new generations of readers to SF. The leading editors here have been Carr and Silverberg, both of whom did their best work in this category for the publishing company Thomas Nelson. Their books are of more than passing interest to adult readers. Also noteworthy is the to-date twelve-volume group of theme anthologies *Science Fiction Shorts*, edited by Asimov, Greenberg, and Waugh between 1981 and 1984.

The so-called original anthology goes back at least to Raymond J. Healy's *New Tales of Space and Time* (1951). This type of book can be of the general type, in which case it closely resembles a magazine in hardback or paperback format (although without magazine features, with higher-quality stories on the average, and sometimes offering authors higher word rates). Or the stories can be written around a theme. The process by which these books are compiled resembles that of editing a magazine except that in some cases some or all of the stories are solicited. After Healy's work, the next important development was the first series of this type, the excellent *Star Science Fiction Stories*, six volumes (plus one of short novels) that appeared from 1953 to 1960, edited by Pohl. Other important series include *Orbit*, twenty-two volumes edited by Knight (1966–1980), noteworthy for including stories that most SF magazines would not publish (at least until the late 1960s, when the magazines opened their doors to all styles of science fiction); *Universe*, an excellent continuing series edited by Carr that reached seventeen volumes; *New Dimensions,* edited by Robert SILVERBERG (joined by Marta RANDALL for the last two volumes) and including sixteen books from 1971 to 1981 (this series and *Universe* produced a sizable number of award-winning stories); *New Writings in SF*, a British series that totaled some thirty volumes from 1966 to 1977, edited by E. J. Carnell and later Kenneth Bulmer; Stellar Science Fiction Stories, seven books from 1974 to 1984 (plus one of short novels), edited by Judy-Lynn DEL REY; Nova, four volumes from 1970 to 1974, edited by Harrison; and Infinity, five volumes from 1970 to 1973, edited by the underrated Robert Hoskins.

More recent series efforts include Destinies, edited by Baen, with twelve books from 1978 to 1981, and Far Frontiers, edited by Jerry POURNELLE and Baen, beginning in 1985 and continuing. These last two are really magazines in paperback format; they include nonfiction and book reviews.

The thematic original anthology has appeared fairly often over the years, and here the most prolific, if not always the best, editor has been Roger Elwood, whose books of this type number in at least the sixties. One of his best was *Future City* (1973). Other good examples are *The Farthest Reaches* (1968), edited by Joseph Elder; *Tomorrow Today* (1975), edited by George ZEBROWSKI; and *Final Stage,* (1974, revised 1975), edited by Edward Ferman and Barry N. MALZBERG.

Worthy of special mention are the Dangerous Visions books edited by Harlan ELLISON—*Dangerous Visions* (1967), *Again, Dangerous Visions* (1972), and the still-to-be-published and long-awaited *The Last Dangerous Visions.* The 1967 and 1972 volumes contain a high percentage of memorable stories and must stand as the outstanding examples of their kind.

The original anthology flourished in the late 1960s and early 1970s but is still important as a source of short fiction in an era in which SF magazines have been declining in number. The most recent trend is the "shared universe" anthology, which features settings and characters established by editors. This type began in earnest with the Sanctuary books *(Thieves' World)* in 1979 and continued with at least nine volumes through 1986. Other current series include Borderland, edited by Teri Windling and Mark Alan Arnold; Liavek, edited by Will Shetterly and Emma Bull; and Heroes in Hell, edited by Janet Morris. But all of these are largely or completely fantasy.

A number of science fiction's writers have become successful and important anthologists, including Isaac Asimov, both alone and in collaboration; the team of Jack DANN and Gardner Dozois; Lester del Rey; Harry Harrison and Brian W. Aldiss, both alone and in collaboration; Damon Knight; Barry N. Malzberg, who specializes in obscure and neglected writers and stories; Robert Silverberg; and Frederik Pohl, who edited some of the outstanding anthologies of the late 1950s and 1960s. Indeed a few writers are much better known as editors; any list of this type would have to include Terry Carr, Donald A. Wollheim, and Judith Merril. A small number of anthologists have carved out significant careers without having written any (or in some cases, very little) science fiction—Martin H. Greenberg and Charles G. Waugh (the most prolific reprint anthologists in the history of the field), Groff Conklin, and Roger Elwood.

A fairly recent development has been anthologies created directly for the "bargain" or "remainder" tables in the large chain bookstores. Some of these are uncredited, such as *Space Odyssey* (1983) and *Analog: The Best of Science Fiction* (1985), but in others the responsible parties are identified, as in *101 Science Fiction Stories* (1986), edited by Greenberg, Waugh, and Jenny-Lynn Waugh.

Anthologies have been so important to the SF field that indexes have been created just for them: William Contento's *Index to Science Fiction Anthologies and Collections* (1978) and *Index to Science Fiction Anthologies and Collections, 1977–1983* (1984).

M.H.G.

Piers Anthony

ANTHONY, PIERS (Professional name of Piers Anthony Billingham Jacob) (1934–   ).
American science-fiction and fantasy writer, born in England but living in the United States since 1940 and an American citizen since 1958. In the twenty years since the appearance of *Sos the Rope* (1968), Anthony has published more than fifty novels, ranging from hard science fiction and space opera through juveniles and martial-arts novels to scientized mythology. He has, on occasion, used his powerful abilities as an action writer to clothe weak ideas, but at other times he has revealed an imposing creative imagination and a fine sense of irony and humor. His punning fantasy novels have brought him consistently onto the best-seller lists.

Three of Anthony's early novels are among his most original work. *Chthon* (1967) and its sequel, *Phthor* (1975), constructed on a web of variants on myth and Jungian archetypes, posit a hell in the form of an underground prison planet peopled by a race of minionettes who reverse emotions (they love those who hate them) and exist to engender complex incestuous relationships.

Macroscope (1969), arguably Anthony's finest SF novel, describes a supertelescope capable of seeing through time and space; the book's complex story involves astrology, a hidden amoral superman, and a search for the ultimate power in the universe. High technologies mingle with powerful if somewhat diagrammatic human relationships and an exciting quest motif to make a most effective novel.

Anthony soon began to plan and write novels in groups of three, four, or five in order to meet publishers' pressures and to expand ideas. The first of these groups is *Omnivore* (1968), *Orn* (1971), and *Ox* (1976), a trilogy about three explorers who become ever more aware of

humankind as destructive omnivore when they search for new worlds via matter transmission. The Battle Circle trilogy, started at the same time, consists of *Sos the Rope* (1968), *Var the Stick* (1972), and *Neq the Sword* (1975); set in postholocaust America, it chronicles the early stages of the struggle back to civilization.

The five-novel Cluster series—*Cluster* (1977), *Chaining the Lady* (1978), *Kirlian Quest* (1978), *Thousandstar* (1980), and *Viscous Circle* (1982)—visits many vividly imagined worlds and focuses on the role of Kirlian auras in saving the galaxy. Anthony's growing interest in the tarot led from this quintet to a tarot trilogy, *God of Tarot* (1979), *Faith of Tarot* (1980), and *Vision of Tarot* (1980), which mixes SF and fantasy elements in a metaphoric search for godhead.

In Anthony's most recent works there are strands of fantasy (The Magic of Xanth), scientized myth (The Incarnations of Immortality quartet beginning with *On a Pale Horse*, 1984), and a spectacular return to space opera of the most vivid and sweeping sort in the five-volume *Biography of a Space Tyrant* (1983–1986). Although he is often accused of hastiness, Anthony has shown himself capable of fine work.

NOTABLE OTHER WORKS: *The Ring* (1968); *The E.S.P. Worm* (1970); *Prostho Plus* (1971); *Steppe* (1976); *A Spell for Chameleon* (1977); *Castle Roogna* (1979); *The Source of Magic* (1979); *Split Infinity* (1980); *Blue Adept* (1981); *Centaur Aisle* (1982); *Juxtaposition* (1982); *Ogre, Ogre* (1982); *Night Mare* (1983); *Dragon on a Pedestal* (1983); *Anthonology* (collection, 1985); *Crewel Lye: A Caustic Yarn* (1985); *With a Tangled Skein* (1985); *Shade of the Tree* (1986); *Wielding a Red Sword* (1986).

P.B.

ANVIL, CHRISTOPHER (Pseudonym of Harry C. Crosby) (?–   ).
American author and consistently reliable contributor to the SF magazines, who published all but his earliest science fiction under the name Anvil. Anvil has kept his personal life secret, and little is known about him. His work first appeared in the SF magazines under his own name with "Cinderella, Inc." (1952) in *Imagination*, but he is most closely associated with *Astounding/Analog*, which has published some eighty of his stories since "The Prisoner" appeared in 1956. Anvil has been called a "competent hack" by critic Peter Weston, a label that is in part a credit to Anvil's ability to write good science fiction as required but also highlights the limitations of his inventiveness.

During John W. CAMPBELL's editorship of *Astounding*, Anvil's work reflected Campbell's belief that humankind could overcome all odds, a point of view best demonstrated in Anvil's continuing series about the Interstellar Patrol, which began with "Strangers to Paradise" (1966, a Nebula Award finalist for best novella) and has comprised many stories since, including two books, *Strangers in Paradise* (1970) and *Warlord's World* (1975). Anvil's unashamed chauvinism in the Cold War between the United States and the USSR is mirrored in a number of his works, including *The Day the Machines Stopped* (1964), wherein the Russians nullify electricity but the Americans counter by rebuilding a steam-age world. In his *The Steel, the Mist, and the Blazing Sun* (1975), the battle between these two countries continues, even after a nuclear holocaust.

OTHER WORK: *Pandora's Planet* (1972).

M.A.

——————— APHORISMS ———————

Like many intellectual communities or subcultures, the world of science fiction has evolved a considerable number of pithy sayings that have become part of the lexicon of the genre. Generally these aphorisms are of four kinds: concise philosophies of life, rules or suggestions for the writing of SF, comments on the nature of the genre itself, and the colorful expressions of fandom. Often the sayings gain such currency that they become abbreviated into bizarre-sounding code words. Thus, Robert A. HEINLEIN's widely quoted (often by himself) philosophy that "there ain't no such thing as a free lunch" becomes TANSTAAFL, and the fannish proclamation that "fandom is a way of life" becomes FIAWOL.

The folk wisdom of SF, surprisingly, tells us that "90 percent of all science fiction is crud" but then reassures us that "90 percent of *everything* is crud" (Theodore STURGEON). It absolves us from having to worry about defining the genre, because SF is only "what we point to when we say it" (Damon KNIGHT). It settles matters of literary history by assuring us that "the Golden Age of science fiction is twelve" (credited to David Hartwell and a half-dozen others). It even suggests we not worry too much about understanding the details of what we read, because "a sufficiently advanced technology is indistinguishable from magic" (Arthur C. CLARKE).

The would-be SF writer finds no shortage of rules to follow. If he or she is interested in writing about the future, Heinlein (perhaps the field's most indefatigable aphorist) provided in 1950 three axioms for making predictions: "A 'nine-days' wonder' is taken as a matter of course on the tenth day. A 'common sense' prediction is sure to err on the side of timidity. The more extravagant a prediction sounds the more likely it is to come true." If a robot story is in the works, one only has to turn to the most famous rules in all SF, Isaac ASIMOV's Three Laws of Robotics: "A robot may not injure a human being, or through inaction, allow a human being to come to harm. A robot must obey the orders given it by human beings except where such orders would conflict with the

First Law. A robot must protect its own existence as long as such protection does not conflict with the First or Second Law."

Such sayings are more than the graffiti of a cult of true believers (although they often seem to serve that function at fan conventions). They provide a means of formalizing narrative conventions and common themes as well as promoting a sense of group identity within the SF community—and perhaps insulating that community from outsiders. Two of the more recent popular aphorisms, for example, came from the fans themselves and seem decidedly testy. One, still in wide circulation on lapel buttons at conventions in the late 1980s, suggests "Reality is a crutch for people who can't handle science fiction." Another, coined by a fan in the early 1970s, reflects apprehension over the growth of academic studies of the field: "Let's get Science Fiction out of the classroom and back to the gutter where it belongs" (Dena Benatan).

"So it goes" (Kurt VONNEGUT, Jr.).

G.K.W.

ARNOLD, JACK (1916–   ).

American director under contract to Universal Studios who made some of the best science-fiction-horror films of the 1950s. Arnold's effectively atmospheric films skillfully meld the commonplace and the strange. THE INCREDIBLE SHRINKING MAN (his most famous work, 1957), vividly depicts the practical effects of infinite shrinkage on the hero by emphasizing the mundane objects and domestic spaces that come to overwhelm him. IT CAME FROM OUTER SPACE (1953) and THE CREATURE FROM THE BLACK LAGOON (1954) are also noteworthy for their atmospheric qualities.

Initially a stage actor, Arnold began his career in the cinema as a documentary filmmaker working with the founder of the genre, Robert Flaherty, director of *Nanook of the North*. He started directing commercial features in 1950, and although he directed the typical range of genre programmers, Arnold seems to have reserved his best work for his SF and horror assignments. In the 1970s he made a number of black-power thrillers and worked on some TV series, including *Archer* and *Gilligan's Island*—the latter in its own way as fantastic as any of his SF movies.

OTHER FILMS: *Revenge of the Creature* (1955); *Tarantula!* (1955); *Monster on the Campus* (1958); *Space Children* (1959); *The Mouse That Roared* (1959); *Hello Down There* (1969).

B.K.G.

ASIMOV, ISAAC (1920–   ).

American writer, scientist, and editor. Asimov became the leading example of GOLDEN AGE science fiction as set forth by John CAMPBELL and of hard SF, plainly and clearly told. His prolific production, though mostly of works other than

Isaac Asimov

SF, totaling more than 300 books by 1987, has earned him a reputation and an audience that in the 1980s placed him among the top three SF writers in the world (Arthur C. CLARKE and Robert A. HEINLEIN are considered his peers), and put his novels that revisit his robot and Foundation universe on the best-seller lists.

Trained in chemistry at Columbia University and holder of a professorship in biochemistry at Boston University School of Medicine, Asimov has chosen to forge his lifework as a writer—both of science fiction and detective fiction and of nonfiction ranging in subject matter from anatomy to zoology, and from the Bible to Shakespeare. When he commented in a science column he writes for THE MAGAZINE OF FANTASY AND SCIENCE FICTION that his life was tantamount to the long list of his books, he was being both clever and deadly serious. "*This* is Isaac Asimov," he wrote. Until the 1980s his science fiction was a relatively small part of his total production; for his many nonfiction works Professor George S. Simpson of Harvard called him "one of our natural wonders and national resources." In 1987 the Science Fiction Writers of America presented him the Grand Master Award for a lifetime's achievement in SF, and, his other achievements aside, it is as a writer, chronicler, and representative of the most rigorous and rational elements in modern SF that Asimov should be, and wants to be, valued.

Brought by his parents to Brooklyn from Russia at the age of three, Asimov was raised in a series of candy stores, where he discovered science fiction and began writing fan letters and critiques to the pulp magazines of the 1930s. He published his first story in *Amazing* at the age of nineteen and rapidly developed into one of the most talented and quick-learning students of the editor he idolized, John Campbell of *Astounding*. Campbell planted fertile ideas in the minds of his bright young writers, and Asimov proved the best example of this seeding practice: stories such as "Nightfall" (1941), in which aliens who have never known darkness go mad when an eclipse blots out the last of six suns and the stars emerge, and concepts such as the "Three Laws of Robotics" and the deterministic "psychohistory" of the 1940s Foundation stories grew from conversations in Campbell's Manhattan office.

The Foundation trilogy—*Foundation* (1951), *Foundation and Empire* (1952), and *Second Foundation* (1953)—and its recent sequels may contain SF's best-known story line of this century, narrating the fall of a great galactic empire and the efforts of the Foundations set up by psychohistorian Hari Seldon to shorten the millennia of barbarism destined to follow. While it was being written, one story at a time, Asimov was a chemistry student, a working chemist at the U.S. navy yard in Philadelphia during World War II, and then a doctoral research student back at Columbia. The mix in the Foundation trilogy of open-ended problem solving, the reaching for "finality" or closure, and their relentless development in story after story set the tone, as much as Campbell did, for rational, "hard" SF as it has come to be looked back on now in that Golden Age. The notion of psychohistory as a controlling and cohering force in the future history of the galaxy seems to echo Enlightenment hopes for useful knowledge and for the harmony of this knowledge with a universe of "inevitable" order.

In contrast, Asimov's "laws" of robotics, which find fullest expression in his collection *I, Robot* (1950), represent his other great focus of creative energy. They speak to the desire of the rationalist to tinker continually with changing conditions, with the interfaces between human beings and their machines, and with ever-changing permutations in the very nature of things. His three laws are so basic that they have become accepted not only by other writers but by researchers into artificial intelligence:"(1) A robot may not injure a human being, or, through inaction, allow a human being to come to harm; (2) a robot must obey the orders given it by human beings except where such orders would conflict with the First Law; and (3) a robot must protect its own existence as long as such protection does not conflict with the First or Second Law." Because Asimov balances so well this yearning for deterministic order (the Seldon Plan) with the eager openness to continual change (the Three Laws are so basic that he can work endless and witty changes on them), he gives the impression in his fiction of the complete scientist: his work manifests both the rigorous math and the religious impulses of Einstein in popular fiction.

Following a variety of fictional expressions of this "galactic" vision as well as a set of juvenile books written under the name of Paul French that also are intended to inculcate both problem-solving flexibility and a belief in order, Asimov decided, with the advent of the first Soviet satellite *Sputnik*, to concentrate his efforts on popularizations of science. His 1972 novel *The Gods Themselves* was a magnificent return to science fiction, winning him his first Nebula and his first novel Hugo. Inspired by a chance reference to "plutonium 186," which Asimov knew to be an impossible atomic weight for the element, he proceeded to write his most scientifically oriented novel, built around parallel universes in which plutonium 186 could exist.

Distinct from the original robot stories, the robot novels that began with *The Caves of Steel* (1954), which many critics (and Asimov himself) consider his best novel, combine the conventions of the detective story with extrapolations into the future history of the galaxy. *The Caves of Steel* tells the story of detective "Lije" Baley, who is forced to team with a disliked android to solve an important murder case. The developing relationship between the two is one of Asimov's most effective displays of novel-writing craft, and, when combined with the sociological influence of the enclosed cities on Baley and other Earth people, it exhibits some of his most convincing characterization.

In the 1980s Asimov began to write sequels to the robot novels and to the Foundation trilogy that continue his rationalist fusion of problem solving with the hope for unity. Part of the unity now is in his career as a writer, part in the attempt to bring his various novels into a self-consistent future history. It is also significant that his 1980s novels for the first time began appearing regularly, along with those of Clarke and Heinlein, and a few other SF writers, on the best-seller lists.

Finally, in the Enlightenment tradition of the need for a reliable first-person observer in any science, Asimov promoted a self-consciousness and autobiographical emphasis on his own role as a writer that may be one of his more important contributions to the genre. Three massive works—his collection *The Early Asimov* (1972), the anthology with autobiographical commentary *Before the Golden Age* (1974), and his volumes *In Memory Yet Green* (1979) and *In Joy Still Felt* (1980)—illustrate how this self-conscious urge serves both to help chronicle the history of modern SF and to deepen the sense of Asimov's involvement as a writer, much in the way that Samuel Johnson's *Lives of the Poets* promoted both "modern" literature and Johnson himself. Asimov is no Johnson; but he is an important representative not only of the intellectual meaning of hard science fiction but also of its aspirations to be taken seriously.

NOTABLE OTHER WORKS: *Pebble in the Sky* (1950); *The Stars, Like Dust* (1951); *David Starr: Space Ranger* (1952); *The Currents of Space* (1952); *Lucky Starr and the Pirates of the Asteroids* (1953); *Lucky Starr and the Oceans of Venus* (1954); *The End of Eternity* (1955); *The Martian Way and Other Stories* (1955); *Lucky Starr and the Big Sun of Mercury* (1956); *The Naked Sun* (1957); *Lucky Starr and the Moons of Jupiter* (1957); *Lucky Starr and the Rings of Saturn* (1958); *Fantastic Voyage* (novelization, 1966); *Nightfall and Other Stories* (1969); *Foundation's Edge* (1982); *The Robots of Dawn* (1983); *Robots and Empire* (1985); *Alternative Asimovs* (1985); *Foundation and Earth* (1986); *Fantastic Voyage II: Destination Brain* (1987).

D.M.H.

ASPRIN, ROBERT LYNN (1946–).
American science-fiction writer. Asprin began his career in the late 1970s, alternating mildly interesting military SF novels told in the manner of Gordon DICKSON (notably *The Cold Cash War,* 1977) with minor fantasy novels loosely derived from the Incomplete Enchanter series of L. Sprague DE CAMP and Fletcher PRATT. Asprin's most enduring work, however, is as an editor. His Thieves' World series (nine volumes since 1979) was the first of what were later known as braided meganovels, stories by different writers set in the same imaginary universe. Although the Thieves' World anthologies themselves are forgettable, the form Asprin invented with them has proved increasingly popular with publishers; meganovels will probably be Asprin's most lasting contribution to the field.

OTHER WORKS: *Tambu* (1979); *The Bug Wars* (1979); *Mirror Friend, Mirror Foe* (with George Takei, 1979).

M.M.W.

ASTOR, JOHN JACOB (1864–1912).
American writer and descendant of the celebrated financier. Perhaps the purest and earliest example of optimistic American science fiction, Astor's *Journey in Other*

Worlds: A Romance of the Future (1894) depicts a trip to Jupiter and Saturn, where a spirit reveals true Christianity to the explorers. Replete with scientific detail, the novel is devoid of the satire and humor common to most nineteenth-century science fiction.

~ N.H.

ASTOUNDING STORIES: SEE ANALOG

ATTACK OF THE CRAB MONSTERS (1957).

Directed by Roger Corman; screenplay by Charles B. Griffith; photographed by Floyd Crosby; music by Ronald Stein. With Richard Garland, Pamela Duncan, Russell Johnson, Leslie Bradley, Mel Welles, Richard Cutting, Beach Dickerson. 62 minutes. Black and white.

This film effectively divides the dilettantes on Roger CORMAN's films from the devotees; the title is absurd, as are the film's monsters, and the movie itself falls into the scorned "giant bug" subgenre. But though hastily written, with ideas that vanish or lead nowhere, the script is intelligent and well structured, the climax is imaginative, and the central idea is unusual and witty.

The radiation-enlarged crabs of the title, found on a Pacific island, absorb the minds of the people they devour—so they can be several people at once. The notion of confronting a colossal crustacean that moments ago was a friend is eerie, comic, and unique. All appearances to the contrary, this is one of Corman's best low-budget films.

B.W.

ATTACK OF THE 50-FOOT WOMAN (1958).

Directed by Nathan Juran; screenplay by Mark Hanna; photographed by Jacques Marquette; music by Ronald Stein. With Allison Hayes, William Hudson, Yvette Vickers, Ken Terrell, George Douglas, Roy Gordon, Frank Chase, Otto Waldis, Mike Ross. 66 minutes. Black and white.

In recent years this film has gained a reputation as a great inadvertent comedy; it is simultaneously one of the worst, most typical, and yet most interesting of the 1950s science-fiction films. The special effects are awful; the premise is silly (diamond-seeking giant alien enlarges an alcoholic millionairess), and the film is both imitative and exploitative. Nonetheless, director Nathan Juran (hiding under the pseudonym Nathan Hertz) provides a snappy pace, and actors Allison Hayes and Yvette Vickers are thoroughly professional under trying circumstances. Hayes is the title figure—so to speak—and Vickers plays the local floozy after wealthy Hayes's no-good husband.

B.W.

ATTERLEY, JOSEPH (Pseudonym of George Tucker) (1775–1861). American educator and writer of two science-fiction works. Both of these works prefigure many of the themes of Edgar Allan POE, whom Atterley knew when Poe attended the University of Virginia and Atterley was a member of the faculty there. Atterley's first work, *A Voyage to the Moon with Some Account of the Manners and Customs, Science and Philosophy, of the People of Morosophia and Other Lunarians* (1827) is in the tradition of Savinien de CYRANO de Bergerac's *Voyages to the Moon* (1657) but seems to take science far more seriously. Atterley's character gets to the moon with the aid of a substance, that repels gravity. This work is filled with the same kind of speculation as Poe's "The Unparalleled Adventures of One Hans Pfaall" (1835) and "The Thousand and Second Tale of Scheherazade" (1845). Atterley's second work, *A Century Hence or, a Romance of 1941* (edited from his manuscript, 1977), deals with overpopulation, one of the major features of Poe's future world in "Mellonta Tauta" (1845).

S.H.G.

AUEL, JEAN M. (1936–). American author, noted for her Earth's Children series of anthropological science-fiction novels, which started with the best-selling *Clan of the Cave Bear* (1980). Although Auel originally planned a six-novel sequence, only two additional titles have appeared to date, *The Valley of the Horses* (1982) and *The Mammoth Hunters* (1985). Like Stanley WATERLOO's *The Story of Ab* (1897) and Vardis Fisher's *Darkness and the Deep* (1943) and the early novels in his Testament of Man series, Auel's series describes in novel form the origins and development of the human species. It follows the life of the orphaned Cro-Magnon girl Ayla, who is raised by the more primitive Neanderthals. Ayla's natural ratiocinative intelligence is enhanced by association with the more instinctive and mystical animallike cunning of the Neanderthals, making her unique. Through her, humankind makes giant strides toward civilization. At times the series suffers from oversentimentality, but it is written with much skill and insight, supported by carefully researched authentic detail.

M.A.

———— AWARDS ————

Enthusiasm for fantastic literature and its authors, and for one story or author over another, has existed since the earliest publication of science fiction. As evidence one need only read the letter columns of *Argosy* and other early pulp magazines. But the idea of honoring writers occurred to no one until SF fandom emerged out of the letter columns of the SF magazines. In those columns and in their amateur magazines, fans asked one another, Who is your favorite author?—and published the inconclusive results.

In the early 1930s Raymond A. PALMER, then a popular fan writer but later editor of AMAZING STORIES and FANTASTIC ADVENTURES and, after that, editor-publisher of *Other Worlds,* created the first award, the Jules Verne Prize Club. The club would conduct a poll and present the winners with inscribed loving cups, paid for by donations. Eventually Palmer declared Edmond HAMILTON winner, but so few donations had come in that no trophy was ever presented.

In 1951 the International Fantasy Award emerged as the first formal award for excellence in the field. Since then at least one hundred different awards have been presented by organizations or individuals. Some were announced but never awarded; a number have been discontinued; a few have been forgotten. Many have had no real influence on science fiction, literature, or the publishing industry, and for some time none had any real impact, being ignored by media, critics, and publishers alike.

Gradually, however, as the first trickle of awards became a flood, their importance and significance grew. A Hugo or a Nebula carried with it a certain amount of fame and sometimes fortune as well, increasing an author's audience, salability, and even the size of his or her advances. Today the major awards are coveted, and even the lesser awards are welcomed.

The International Fantasy Award: In 1951 four British fans—Leslie Flood, John Beynon Harris (John WYNDHAM), G. Ken Chapman, and Frank Cooper—appointed themselves the judges of what they called the International Fantasy Award and presented the first awards in SF—to George R. STEWART for his *Earth Abides* and to Willy LEY and Chesley BONESTELL for their nonfiction *Conquest of Space.* The trophy was a metal spaceship and cigarette lighter mounted on a base. From 1952 until the award's demise in 1957, more judges were added, and the awards were announced at a special dinner attended by SF personalities in Great Britain. The judges were prestigious, and their choices were impeccable.

The Hugo Awards: Hal Lynch thought of presenting science-fiction achievement awards to help promote the 1953 world convention in Philadelphia. Almost instantly they were named Hugos, in honor of Hugo GERNSBACK, publisher of the first SF magazine and popularly credited as the father of modern science fiction, who had been guest of honor at the 1952 convention in Chicago. The trophy, except for those years when production difficulties intervened, has always been a chrome-plated spaceship mounted on a wooden base.

The 1954 San Francisco convention committee did not pick up the idea, but the following year the Cleveland convention committee, chaired by Noreen and Nicholas

Falasca, revived the awards, and they have been a tradition ever since. For the first few years the ballot was prepared by the convention committee, which selected five entries in each category; convention members then voted on the entries. The system changed in 1959, when the Detroit world convention announced open nominations. After a nomination-stuffing incident in 1960, committees restricted nominations and voting rights to convention members. Bloc voting occasionally has been a problem, especially in the early years, when only a few hundred people cast votes, but the thousands of ballots cast in recent years, and the escalation of membership fees to $25 and even $50, has lessened that possibility.

The Hugos started with seven categories: novel, professional magazine, new author or artist, fact article, cover artist, interior illustrator, and number-one fan personality. Alfred BESTER's *The Demolished Man* won the first novel award. The awards since have expanded to twelve: four in the various lengths for fiction, one for nonfiction, one for dramatic presentation, one each for professional editor and professional artist, and four fan awards (semipro magazine, fanzine, writer, and artist).

In the early years magazines dominated the fiction entries, but with the rise of paperback books and book clubs to market dominance, more and more nominees, even in short story categories, come from these sources. The first special committee award was presented in 1960 to Hugo Gernsback, and over the years other such awards, at the discretion of the convention committee, have been given.

Because of its broad electorate the Hugo Award represents the most significant sampling of reader popularity. The importance of the Hugos has been somewhat diminished by the appearance of other awards, in particular the Nebula, the World Fantasy Award, and the Locus Poll, but the Hugos still are the oldest and in some ways the most prestigious, even though the size and diversity of their voting group and its method of balloting have led to accusations that they are awarded more for popularity than for excellence.

The Nebula Awards: The SCIENCE FICTION WRITERS OF AMERICA (SFWA) was created by Damon KNIGHT in 1965 to improve the conditions under which writers work and live, to temper some of the more outrageous practices of the publishers, and to provide channels of communication among its scattered members. Since then writers' incomes have increased (in some cases phenomenally), a number of problems have been brought to heel, and the channels of communication have become choked with the squabbles of SFWA's nearly 1000 highly individualistic members.

The association's first secretary-treasurer, Lloyd BIGGLE, Jr., immediately perceived the need for more income than could be raised by dues—then a pittance, which was almost all SF writers could afford. He proposed an annual award, which would provide material for a yearly anthology some of whose revenue would go to the organization. Judith Blish (now Judith Blish-Nikolaou) designed a costly trophy for what would be called the Nebula Award: a rectangular block of acrylic with a floating spiral nebula and a rock crystal embedded in its engraved base.

Nebulas have been awarded throughout SFWA history for the four lengths of fiction: novel (40,000 words or more), novella (17,500 to 40,000 words), novelette (7,500 to 17,500 words), and short story. The first winners, in 1965, were, respectively, *Dune* by Frank HERBERT, "The Saliva Tree" by Brian W. ALDISS and "He Who Shapes" by Roger ZELAZNY, "The Doors of His Face, the Lamps of His Mouth" by Roger Zelazny, and " 'Repent, Harlequin!' Said the Ticktockman" by Harlan ELLISON. In 1973 an award for best dramatic performance was added, but it was dropped in 1977. In 1977 a Grand Master category was added to honor writers for contributions over a lifetime, and the first such award was presented to Robert A. HEINLEIN.

As with those of the Hugo, Nebula voting rules have evolved with experience. Each member of SFWA is entitled to nominate an unlimited number of stories throughout the year. In the beginning any story receiving any nomination would appear on a final ballot, but this practice led to impractically long ballots. Now, at the close of the nominating year, a preliminary ballot is distributed, listing all stories with a prescribed number of nominations. From the response to this ballot, a final ballot is prepared, listing the five leaders in each category. A special committee chosen by the SFWA president and two past presidents has the right to add one more entry in each category.

The Nebula Awards, because they are chosen by writers, are considered to be given more for excellence in writing, and the fact that some writers have been honored more by the Nebulas than by the Hugos tends to support this judgment. However, particularly in recent years, many of the same novels, and even the same stories, have appeared on both ballots, and some have even won both competitions.

The World Fantasy Award: Editor David Hartwell and writer Charles L. GRANT founded the World Fantasy Award in 1975 as a feature of the World Fantasy Convention. Because the first meeting of the convention was in Providence, Rhode Island, home of the famous author of fantasy horror the late H. P. LOVECRAFT, the trophy was a caricature bust of Lovecraft designed by cartoonist Gahan Wilson. One winner, author and publisher Donald Wandrei, described the trophy as "repellent" and refused it, but other winners have carried it away happily. Nicknamed the Howard, it is sometimes mistakenly believed to honor the late Robert E. Howard, creator of *Conan*.

The convention meets in different parts of the country, and, unlike other conventions, limits attendance to about 750, mostly writers, editors, and academics. The awards, voted on by a jury, were originally presented for novel, short fiction, and collection or anthology, but they have been expanded to include novella, artist, and special awards for professional, nonprofessional, and lifetime achievement. The World Fantasy Award is the most prestigious award for fantasy alone (including weird and horror fiction), and it ranks in prestige with the Hugo, the Nebula, and the Locus Poll.

The Locus Poll: Locus began life as a fanzine devoted to gossip and news and has developed into the leading trade journal covering fantastic literature. In 1971, as a protest against the small size of the Hugo vote in that year's competition, Charles BROWN, owner-publisher of *Locus*, began polling his readership, hoping to stimulate interest in the Hugos. Instead he created another award.

Up to that year a serious fan could expect to read virtually everything published, but publication of books expanded rapidly thereafter, climbing from 348 in 1972 to 1288 in 1979, with more than half of these works previously unpublished. The Locus Poll, appearing before the close of the Hugo voting, began to serve many fans as a short list of "must-read" titles and to form the basis for their Hugo selections.

Consistently more votes are recorded in the Locus Poll than for any other award; in 1986 the votes totaled over 1000 (more than the totals for the Hugo and Nebula awards combined). For this reason if for no other, the Locus Poll can be claimed to be most authoritative.

The award consists of an announcement in the pages of *Locus*, usually in the June issue; presentation of a trophy depends on the whim of Brown. Once wooden spaceships were handed out. More recently the trophy was an ornate plastic sunburst on a base. The range of the Locus Poll also is worth noticing, amounting as it does to an up-to-date market survey. In recent years *Science Fiction Chronicle*, another monthly newsmagazine, edited and published by Andrew Porter, has conducted a similar poll of its readers.

The John W. Campbell Award: John W. Campbell first gained prominence in the early 1930s as a major writer of superscience space epics in the style of E. E. SMITH and Edmond HAMILTON, then shifted in the mid-1930s to "modern" science fiction—with more people and less hardware. In 1937 he became editor of *Astounding Science Fiction* (later *Analog*), a position he held until his death in 1971. In the late 1930s, 1940s, and early 1950s he was a dominant force in science fiction, because of the preeminence of his magazine and the demands he made on the writers who wanted to sell him stories. *Analog*'s publisher at the time of his death, Condé Nast, honored his memory with an award for the best new writer, and even after the magazine was sold to Davis Publications, the award continued.

The Campbell Award for best new writer is administered by the World SF Convention, voted on by its members at the same time as the Hugos, and presented at the time of the Hugo Awards; it is not, however, a Hugo but is instead a rectangular plaque suitably engraved. To qualify for the award, writers must have had their first professional appearances within the previous two calendar years. Jerry POURNELLE won the first Campbell Award in 1973. The award, in a sense a successor to the early Hugo Award for the most promising new writer (presented sporadically between 1953 and 1959), has continued to honor authors who have gone on to outstanding careers.

The John W. Campbell Memorial Award: Not to be confused with the Campbell Award for the best new writer, the John W. Campbell Memorial Award was created in 1973 by Harry HARRISON and Brian W. ALDISS as a juried alternative to the Hugo and Nebula awards. The award, voted after a six-month exchange of opinions, usually by means of letters, represents the tastes and judgments of a cosmopolitan and international committee consisting of writers, editors, critics, and academics. It is an indirect descendant of the International Fantasy Award.

The original committee of Harrison, Aldiss, Leon STOVER of Illinois Institute of Technology, Thomas CLARESON of Wooster College, and Willis MCNELLY of California State University at Fullerton selected as the first winner *Beyond Apollo* by Barry MALZBERG.

In subsequent years membership on the committee varied and the award's place of presentation moved to Fullerton, Oxford, Dublin, Stockholm, and finally the University of Kansas in Lawrence, where it is still presented, usually at a Campbell Award conference in July. James GUNN, who joined the committee in 1973 after his novel *The Listeners* took second place in the first competition, served as chairman from 1978 to 1980 and again after 1985. The award, produced by University of Kansas sculptor Elden Tefft after an original piece of art created in Ireland, is a jagged bronze oval mounted on a wooden base. The committee in 1986 consisted of T. A. Shippey and Kingsley AMIS of Great Britain, Sam Lundwall of Sweden, and James Gunn, Algis BUDRYS, Walter Meyers, and Elizabeth Anne Hull of the United States.

The Pilgrim Award: The Pilgrim Award is presented by the Science Fiction Research Association (SFRA) for "outstanding contributions to science fiction and fantasy scholarship." The first award, in 1970, went to J. O. Bailey, for whose pioneer 1947 study, *Pilgrims through Space and Time*, the award is named. It is given for academic writing rather than creative work and consists of an imposing bronze design mounted on a walnut stand; the trophy was created by University of Kansas sculptor Elden Tefft. Winners do not get possession of it, however, because only one trophy exists, and it is on display throughout the year at the University of Kansas Center for the Study of Science Fiction. Each year that

a new committee appointed by the SFRA president selects a winner, his or her name is engraved on the trophy, and the presentation is made at the SFRA annual meeting, held at different locations, usually in June.

The INTERNATIONAL ASSOCIATION ON THE FANTASTIC IN THE ARTS launched an award for distinguished scholarship (an engraved plaque and a check for $1,000) at its 1986 meeting in Houston; the first award went to Brian W. Aldiss. The association's William L. Crawford Award for the best new fantasy writer, established in 1985, went the first year to Charles de Lint.

The Eaton conference, held annually by the University of California at Riverside, features the Milford Award for lifetime achievement in editing science fiction and fantasy.

The Philip K. Dick Memorial Award: Philip K. DICK, one of the most praised writers of science fiction, died in 1982 just before the release of the film BLADE RUNNER, which was adapted from his novel *Do Androids Dream of Electric Sheep?*. Because most of Dick's early (and some think his best) novels appeared as original paperbacks, the Dick Memorial Award was established by a group of his friends and admirers to honor annually "a distinguished work of science fiction first appearing in paperback." The award consists of a certificate and a cash prize of $1000; the second-place winner receives $500. The cash awards have been contributed by publishers, magazines, bookstores, and literary agencies; the winner is selected by a committee, whose three members choose their own successors. The award was proposed in a Norwescon (Seattle regional convention) guest of honor speech by Thomas DISCH, and the first, in 1983, honored *Software* by Rudy RUCKER at a ceremony in New York City. Later presentations have been made at Norwescon.

The First Fandom Award: First Fandom consists of approximately 200 members who were active in science-fiction fandom before 1938. Each year they vote on and present an inscribed plaque to a writer from that Golden Age.

Other Awards: Other awards have come and gone. The Jupiter Awards were created by Charles G. Waugh, who formed the Instructors of Science Fiction in Higher Learning (ISFHA) to poll academics about their choices for the four lengths of fiction. Awards were presented from 1974 to 1978, but the response was so inadequate in 1976 that no awards were announced.

The death of J. R. R. Tolkien was announced at the World SF Convention in Toronto (Torcon), and a day or so later Lin Carter announced the formation of the Gandalf Award Committee to present a Grand Master of Fantasy Award (Gandalf) in Tolkien's honor. The presentation was made at the same time as the Hugos from 1974 until 1980, when the Gandalf was discontinued.

A great variety of other awards have been presented over the years; some are still being given. Writers of the

Future, an organization founded by L. Ron HUBBARD and continued after his death, conducts a continuing contest for unpublished writers, awarding cash prizes and publishing an annual anthology. The Prometheus Award (in gold) is presented to the best novel incorporating libertarian principles. World SF, an international organization for science-fiction professionals, presents several awards, including one for translation, at its annual meeting.

Science-fiction conventions now number in the hundreds, and one way to attract attendees is to announce some sort of award. The Balrog Award, for instance, was presented for several years at the "Foolcon" convention offered at Johnson County (Kansas) Community College and later transferred to a location in Colorado, where it has not been heard from recently. In addition, awards are offered in many countries overseas, including Great Britain (BSFA Awards and others), Australia (Ditmar Awards), and non-English-speaking countries such as the Soviet Union, Poland, and Japan. Announcements of such awards are carried regularly by one or more of the semiprofessional magazines specializing in news relating to science fiction.

H.D.

B

BACK TO THE FUTURE (1985).   *Directed by Robert Zemeckis; screenplay by Robert Zemeckis and Bob Gale; photographed by Dean Cundey; music by Alan Silvestri. With Michael J. Fox, Christopher Lloyd, Lea Thompson, Crispin Glover, Thomas F. Wilson, Claudia Wells, Marc McClure, Wendie Jo Sperber. 116 minutes. Color.*

Had this film been made in the period in which it takes place, it probably would have been called *I Was a Teenage Time Traveler*. But times have indeed changed, and the subject of a 1950s quickie becomes in the 1980s a big-budget success, not to mention the 1986 Hugo Award winner. Teenager Michael J. Fox is propelled back to 1955, where he accidentally thwarts his parents' romance then must patch things up before he is erased from reality. Christopher Lloyd is wonderful as the daffy (though not mad) scientist who invents the time-traveling DeLorean automobile, and time travel jokes come thick and fast until Fox previews rock and roll in finest causality-loop fashion. On a slightly more serious level, he must deal with the discovery that his father was a failure as a youth and that he seems to be going the same way. The film is *about* adolescence not merely aimed at an adolescent audience, and so it is watchable by both teenagers and anyone who remembers what it was like

to be one.

The film's depiction of 1955 America is excellent and makes the subtle point that the culture may have been brash and naive, but there seemed to be more of a *future* then. The "grandfather paradox" plot is old hat to science-fiction readers, but it must have seemed new and sophisticated to a general audience.

D.S.

BACON, FRANCIS (1561–1626).   British jurist, statesman, and philosopher. Bacon's ideas pioneered empirical science and the scientific method. In his unfinished utopian narrative *The New Atlantis* (originally published in Latin, 1627), he depicted a society on a remote Pacific island that is ruled by an elite of benevolent scientists. Their methods of research foreshadow those of latter-day science, and their Salomon's House inspired the creation of England's Royal Society.

J.H.

BALLARD, J[AMES] G[RAHAM] (1930–   ).
British writer who became a central figure in British NEW WAVE science fiction. Born in Shanghai, Ballard was interned in a Japanese civilian prison camp during World War II, and his fiction, shaped by that experience, brought to the written word the surrealism of such painters as Hieronymus Bosch and Salvador Dalí, and the mainstream's sense of unavoidable disaster, as well as its concern for style (he has written about William Burroughs as "Myth-Maker of the Twentieth Century"). After studying medicine and serving in the Royal Air Force, Ballard became a full-time writer with the publication of *The Wind from Nowhere* (1962).

His first stories, published in 1956 in NEW WORLDS and *Science Fantasy*, divided his potential audience: the New Wave embraced him (Brian W. ALDISS has written that he was "firmly nailed to the masthead of MOORCOCK's pirate ship"); more traditional SF writers and readers ignored his work or refused to recognize it as SF. His concern is not outer space but "inner space."

Ballard's collections of short stories attest to his range of experiments in theme and style: he has used common SF conventions to explore insanity, reality, and the way media and technology influence people's notions of reality; *The Atrocity Exhibition* (1970; in the United States as *Love and Napalm: Export USA*, 1972) is filled with images of the automobile, traffic accidents, and superhighways. Later stories and novels dwell on the tragic potential of humanity's artifacts to transform the race into passive creatures without control over their fates.

Indeed, his submissive characters, more often victims than heroes, may explain the reluctance of traditional SF readers—who have grown up with characters who fight the odds, even if they fail—to embrace Ballard's work. In the face of personal and general doom, Ballard's characters do not fight; if anything, like concentration camp prisoners, they appear to collaborate with their fate. Ballard's fiction might better be read not as a revelation of the way things are but as a warning about the forces that shape human lives.

Ballard is best known for a series of four novels, published between 1962 and 1966, that feature world-destroying catastrophes: *The Wind from Nowhere, The Drowned World* (1963), *The Burning World* (1964; revised as *The Drought,* 1965), and *The Crystal World* (1966). In 1966, inspired by the French antinovelists, he began to publish "condensed novels" ("The Assassination of John F. Kennedy Considered as a Downhill Motor Race," 1967, for instance) that are kaleidoscopes of despairing images. In 1979, however, he wrote a far more optimistic work in *The Unlimited Dream Company,* in which one character gains control of his world, although in typical Ballard fashion the reader is left unsure what the world is or indeed what is real and what is imagined. Most recently his autobiographical, non-SF novel *Empire of the Sun* (1985) became an international best-seller and was filmed in 1987 by Steven SPIELBERG.

OTHER WORKS: *The Voices of Time and Other Stories* (collection, 1962); *Billenium and Other Stories* (collection, 1962); *The Four-Dimensional Nightmare* (collection, 1963); *Passport to Eternity and Other Stories* (collection, 1963); *The Terminal Beach* (collection, 1964); *The Impossible Man and Other Stories* (collection, 1966); *The Disaster Area* (collection, 1967); *The Day of Forever* (collection, 1967); *The Overloaded Man* (collection, 1967); *Chronopolis and Other Stories* (collection, 1971); *Vermilion Sands* (collection, 1973); *Crash!* (1973); *Concrete Island* (1974); *High-Rise* (1975); *Low-Flying Aircraft and Other Stories* (collection, 1976); *The Best of J. G. Ballard* (collection, 1977); *The Best Short Stories of J. G. Ballard* (collection, 1978); *The Venus Hunters* (collection, 1980); *Hello America* (1981); *Myths of the Near Future* (collection, 1982).

S.H.G.

BALMER, EDWIN (1883–1959). American author and editor. Balmer edited *Redbook* magazine from 1927 to 1949. His detective stories, notably those in *The Achievements of Luther Trant* (collaboration with William MacHarg, 1910) have science-fiction elements. In one episode the use of the lie detector is forecast. Balmer collaborated with Philip WYLIE on WHEN WORLDS COLLIDE (1933; adapted for film by George PAL, 1951) and its sequel, *After Worlds Collide* (1935).

J.H.

Jane Fonda in an earlier incarnation as Barbarella

BANKS, RAY[MOND] E. (1918?–). American writer who was a frequent contributor to the science-fiction PULP MAGAZINES in the 1950s and 1960s. Banks's stories are usually witty and depend less on technological hardware than on quirks of human nature, as the title of his first story, "Never Trust an Intellectual" (1953), suggests. Among his best stories are three published by *Galaxy:* "The Littlest People" (1954), "This Side Up" (1954), and "The City That Loves You" (1969).

S.H.G.

BARBARELLA (1963). *Directed by Roger Vadim; screenplay by Terry Southern, Roger Vadim, Claude Brule, Vittorio Bonicelli, Clement Biddle Wood, Brian Degas, Tudor Gates, and Jean-Claude Forest; photographed by Claude Renoir; music by Maurice Jarre. With Jane Fonda, Anita Pallenberg, David Hemmings, Milo O'Shea, John-Phillip Law, Marcel Marceau, Ugo Tognazzi. 98 minutes. Color.*

This French-Italian production chronicles the adventures of Jean-Claude Forest's comic-strip heroine, Barbarella, a character similar to *Playboy*'s later pneumatic cutie, Annie Fannie. In the year 40,000 Barbarella, an intergalactic agent, is sent by the president of Earth to stop the mad scientist whose positronic death ray threatens the universe. After crash landing, Barbarella experiences a wide variety of fantastic encounters, including an attack by sadistic children, a rescue by a blind, handsome angel, and imprisonment in a pleasure-inducing machine designed to kill by causing an excess of sexual stimulation.

Barbarella was released the same year as *2001: a Space Odyssey*. But whereas *2001* sought to broaden its viewers' horizons and encourage intellectual speculation, *Barbarella* used the gadgetry of science fiction to make jokes. A tongue-in-cheek spoof of secret agent films and SF pulp conventions of the Flash Gordon era, the movie blends adventure, fantasy, eroticism, and humor. Critics have alternately called the film satire, comedy, and soft porn. The movie's episodic style weakens an already thin plot, which is of little importance, because the purpose of *Barbarella* is to provide mindless entertainment. Photographed beautifully by Claude Renoir, the film is visually intriguing (the bizarre sets were created by Enrico Fea) and is distinguished by good special effects by August Lohman.

                                                                                    D.P.V.

BARNES, ARTHUR K[ELVIN] (1911–1969).
American pulp writer who produced many kinds of fiction, including science fiction in *Thrilling Wonder Stories* and other magazines from 1931 to 1946. Barnes sometimes used the pseudonym Kelvin Kent for works written both alone and in collaboration with Henry KUTTNER. Five of his stories, from a series featuring the space huntress Gerry Carlyle in pursuit of alien animals, were rewritten for the collection *Interplanetary Hunter* (1956).
                                                                                    J.H.

BARR, GEORGE (1937–   ). American science-fiction illustrator. Barr was born in Arizona but raised in Salt Lake City, Utah, where he lived until 1968. In high school Barr met Utah landscape artist Jack Vigos, who instilled in him a sense of pride in work well done; this is evident in the careful craftsmanship in all Barr's art, from his first *Fantastic Stories Magazine* cover in 1962 to his work today. One of many SF illustrators who began by supplying illustrations for fanzines, Barr is still active in fandom and has been nominated for five Hugos for fan art, winning in 1968; he has also been nominated several times for a Hugo in professional art and won the Lensman in 1986. He has worked for many magazines, including *Forgotten Fantasy, Fantastic Stories,* AMAZING STORIES, and the recently revived *Weird Tales,* and has painted cover illustrations for DAW Books, Pyramid, Ace, Ballantine, Leisure, and Donald M. Grant's spectacular limited-edition volumes. He is particularly remembered for his illustrations for Robert E. HOWARD's *Red Nails* (Donald M. Grant), the cover paintings for Marion Zimmer BRADLEY's Darkover books from DAW, and the poster for the cult movie *Flesh Gordon.* In 1976 Grant published a volume of Barr's work, *Upon the Winds of Yesterday.* His style has been influenced by the works of Arthur Rackham, Maxfield Parrish, and, to a lesser extent, Hannes BOK. He works primarily in ink

(ball-point pen) and watercolor; his black-and-white illustrations are done with coquille board, pencil, and ball-point pen. In a field dominated by almost painfully bright colors, his pastel shades stand out, and his people, elves, fairies, and dragons are notable for a sense of gracefulness often missing in the work of others.
                                                                                    J.G.

BARRETT, NEAL, JR. (?–   ). American science-fiction writer noted for his craftsmanship and imaginative plots and best known for his Aldair series (*Aldair in Albion*, 1976; *Aldair, Master of Ships*, 1977; *Aldair, Across the Misty Sea*, 1980; *Aldair: The Legion of Beasts*, 1982). Reminiscent of Cordwainer SMITH's "underpeople" stories and Clifford D. SIMAK's short stories collected in *City*, the Aldair series concerns a humanoid character of the same name descended from pigs through genetic manipulation. The Earth on which Aldair lives has been deserted by humans, and each of the novels concerns the search for some understanding of what has happened to the humans and for a meaning to Aldair's own existence. Barrett also filled the series with fascinating creatures.

The Aldair series is not the only work by Barrett that will remind readers of other SF, but Barrett's style and imaginative plots prevent his stories from being merely derivative. *The Leaves of Time* (1971), for example, deals with a parallel world but adds a series of complications, including a shape-changing alien, that make the story far less predictable than the average tale in this subgenre. And *Karma Corps* (1984) combines the conventions of colonists versus natives and special-powers stories into a thought-provoking work on the use and misuse of power.

Barrett is an infrequent contributor of magazine short stories. Like his novels, his short fiction shows high standards of writing. Among his best stories are "The Stentorii Luggage" (1960), a tale of shape-changing creatures, and "The Flying Stutzman" (1978), a combination of the myths of Sisyphus and the Wandering Jew.

OTHER WORKS: *Kelwin* (1970); *The Gates of Time* (1970); *Highwood* (1972); *Stress Pattern* (1974).
                                                                                    S.H.G.

BASS, T. J. (Pseudonym of Thomas Bassler, M.D.) (1932–   ). American writer whose most important works, the novels *Half Past Human* (1971) and *The Godwhale* (1974), depict a far-future dystopian "Earth Society" in which the only hope lies in artifacts from humanity's past. In both novels 3 trillion people called Nebishes live a miserable existence underground, while virtually the entire land surface of the planet is used for food production. In *Half Past Human* hope lies off Earth: a small group of humans who still live on the

surface, along with a few Nebishes who are able to change, leave Earth in an automated spaceship remaining from a grander period in human history. In *The Godwhale*, however, salvation dwells in the Earth's seas but is dependent on the use of a huge, semisentient "plankton harvester" created long ago.

Bass's other works include the stories "Star Seeder" (1969), "A Game of Biochess" (1970), "Song of Kaia" (1970), and "Rorqual Maru" (1972), which was selected for *The 1973 Annual World's Best SF* (Donald A. WOLL-HEIM and Arthur W. Saha, eds.), and which was later incorporated into *The Godwhale*.

B.D.

BATES, HARRY (Professional name of Hiram Gilmore Bates III) (1900–1982).

American writer and founding editor of ASTOUNDING STORIES who, while working for the Clayton chain of adventure magazines in 1930, took on the seminal task of establishing a more professional pulp magazine to compete with AMAZING STORIES. Bates was successful in nurturing a stable of writers who knew little science and teaching them to add a veneer of science to their action and adventure narratives, thus paving the way for science fiction as literature rather than the popular science preferred by Hugo GERNSBACK. Working with his assistant editor, D. W. Hall, Bates also began to produce stories of this type himself. Some of his later, uncollected stories, notably "Alas, All Thinking" (1935) and "Farewell to the Master" (1940; made into the movie *The Day the Earth Stood Still*, 1951), are recognized as early classics. In the year before his death Bates wrote sadly of his efforts late in life to revise and polish his longer fictions to meet much more highly evolved literary standards than those he had done much to generate originally. Bates's importance deserves to be more fully studied.

OTHER WORK: *Space Hawk: The Greatest of Interplanetary Adventurers* (written as Anthony Gilmore with D. W. Hall, 1952).

D.M.H.

BATTLE BEYOND THE STARS (1980).

Directed by Jimmy T. Murakami; screenplay by John Sayles; adapted from a screen story by John Sayles and Anne Dyer; photographed by Daniel Lacambre; music by James Horner. With Richard Thomas, John Saxon, Robert Vaughn, Darlanne Fluegel, George Peppard, Sybil Danning, Sam Jaffe, Morgan Woodward, Jeff Corey, Dick Davalos. 104 minutes. Color.

In his early years in films, producer Roger CORMAN was often innovative; by the 1970s he'd become imitative, and *Battle beyond the Stars* was his version of STAR WARS. Using Akira Kurosawa's *Seven Samurai* as a template (although the adaptation is uncredited), John

Sayles wrote a funny, ragtag script, and Jimmy T. Murakami kept the pace fast enough that the similarities bothered few. The special effects are above average for an inexpensive film, and the cast enters into the script's friendly if mocking spirit. To save his rural planet from the return of a space marauder, a young man enlists the aid of a group of mercenaries, most of whom die heroically in the successful defense.

Laden with jokes, effects, and action, *Battle beyond the Stars* was financially successful, but none of Corman's follow-ups were as good. Sayles, a novelist, wrote several more genre film scripts before making his well-regarded debut as a director; he later made THE BROTHER FROM ANOTHER PLANET (1984). An odd sidelight on the film is that Robert Vaughn played the same role in this as he did in the Western version of Kurosawa's film, *The Magnificent Seven*.

B.W.

BATTLE FOR THE PLANET OF THE APES: SEE PLANET OF THE APES

BATTLESTAR GALACTICA (1978–1979).

Directed by Richard Colla, Christian Nyby, Rod Holcomb, Daniel Heller, and others; written by Glen Larson, Donald Bellisario, and others; music by Stu Phillips. With Lorne Greene, Richard Hatch, Dirk Benedict, Herb Jefferson, Jr., Terry Carter, Maren Jensen, Noah Hathaway, Anne Lockhart, John Colicos. One three-hour movie in color, one two-hour special in color, four two-part episodes (each sixty minutes) in color, and eleven one-hour episodes in color.

This big-budget television series was unveiled in 1978, with much fanfare, as ABC-TV's answer to the success of STAR WARS. The three-hour series premiere, "Saga of a Star World" (written by producer Glen Larson and directed by Richard Colla), established the good guys versus bad guys format: the evil Cylons set up and then attack a peace conference to ensnare and destroy the remaining humans in an era called the Seventh Millennia. A ragtag fleet made up of survivors of the attack are led on a quest by the spaceship *Galactica* to find the "long-lost planet Earth" while doing battle with the Cylons and their agents. Lorne Greene stars as commander of the fleet, along with Richard Hatch and Dirk Benedict as fighter-ship pilots, and Terry Carter, Maren Jensen, and Herb Jefferson, Jr., as crew members.

Battlestar Galactica lasted for a single season. Then, a year later, it underwent a format change and was rebroadcast as *Galactica 1980*, in which the travelers find present-day Earth. The revamped series, however, lasted for only nine more episodes, then sank without a trace.

K.R.D.

Greg Bear

space opera. Bayley's novels contain the typical characteristics of space adventure stories, including galactic empires (*The Annihilation Factor,* 1972), colliding worlds (*Collision Course,* 1973), and heroes who try to save the universe (*The Garments of Caean,* 1976). His work is distinguished from the usual space opera, though, by Bayley's literary and literate writing style and daring inventiveness. In his most recent work, *The Zen Gun* (1983), action frequently holds second place to an entirely unpredictable plot and a setting equal to those of Jack Vance. The work is held together with a satiric humor that keeps readers going even when they are unsure of how, why, or when an event takes place.

Bayley's short stories also show his love for the offbeat and off-center. Almost all of them are collected in two books: *The Knights of the Limits* (1978) and *The Seed of Evil* (1979).

OTHER WORKS: *The Star Virus* (1970); *Empire of Two Worlds* (1972); *Soul of the Robot* (1974); *The Grand Wheel* (1977); *Star Winds* (1978); *The Fall of Chronopolis* (1979); *The Pillars of Eternity* (1982).

S.H.G.

BAXTER, JOHN (1939–   ). Australian writer and film critic. Baxter's science fiction consists of three novels (one of which—*The Black Yacht,* 1982—is only marginally SF) and fewer than twenty short stories. However, his work is distinguished for its literary style, imaginative organization, and original plots. *The Off-Worlders* (1966, published as *The God Killers* in Australia, 1968) describes a society in the year 2833 that has turned to Satan after rejecting technology. *The Hermes Fall* (1978) is a disaster novel based on Baxter's extensive research on the meteorite that fell in Siberia in 1908.

Most of Baxter's short stories have appeared only in British magazines and anthologies, including *New Worlds* and *New Writings in SF.* They show the clear influence of the New Wave on his style as well as Baxter's interest in creating an Australian science fiction. "Apple" (1967), a surrealistic story about a character who guards a giant apple and must battle creatures who seek to destroy it, is his best-known story and a good example of Baxter's humor. His interest in encouraging Australian science fiction has also resulted in his editing two anthologies of short stories: *The Pacific Book of Australian Science Fiction* (1968) and *The Second Pacific Book of Australian Science Fiction* (1971).

Baxter has received wide recognition for his film studies, and most of his current writing is in this field. His work has brought several awards and invitations to lecture. In 1970 he combined both interests to produce *Science Fiction in the Cinema,* an original and thought-provoking work on the roots and development of SF films.

S.H.G.

BAYLEY, BARRINGTON J[OHN] (1937–   ). British writer of sophisticated and frequently humorous

BEAR, GREG[ORY DALE] (1951–   ). American writer born, educated, and living in San Diego. Although he earned a bachelor's degree in English in 1973, Bear writes science fiction marked by a fascination with developing areas of science. Because of his interest in near-future fiction and "inner space," he has been identified with CYBERPUNK science fiction, although he denies the connection. His first story, "Destroyers," was published in 1967, when he was only sixteen; he began publishing regularly in 1975, when he became a full-time writer; and he has made a remarkable reputation in a short time, winning two Nebula Awards in 1984, for "Hardfought" and "Blood Music," which also won a Hugo Award that year. The novel *Blood Music* (1985), which deals with a biological computer that gets loose and remakes humanity, was a Nebula and Hugo finalist.

Bear has achieved this much so early by striving for originality—if not in theme then in the way theme is handled—by creating believable characters, and by pushing into new areas of science, such as information theory and information mechanics. *Eon* (1985) deals with nuclear holocaust, contact with an asteroid spacecraft, and mathematical exploration of space and time. Bear also writes horror and fantasy, exemplified by *The Infinity Concerto* (1984), in which music is truly magic, and its sequel, *The Serpent Mage* (1986), wherein magic confronts a slightly altered modern California.

OTHER WORKS: *Hegira* (1979); *Psychlone* (1979); *Beyond Heaven's River* (1980); *Strength of Stones* (1981); *The Wind from a Burning Woman* (collection, 1983); *Corona* (1984); *The Forge of God* (1987).

H.L.P.

The eponymous *Beast from 20,000 Fathoms*

THE BEAST FROM 20,000 FATHOMS (1953).

Directed by Eugène Lourié; screenplay by Lou Morheim and Fred Freiberger; adapted from the short story "The Fog Horn" by Ray Bradbury; photographed by Jack Russell; music by David Buttolph. With Paul Christian, Cecil Kellaway, Paula Raymond, Kenneth Tobey, Lee Van Cleef. 80 minutes. Black and white.

Based on Ray BRADBURY's moody short story, *The Beast from 20,000 Fathoms* was the first example of that popular science-fiction movie subgenre of the 1950s, the giant dinosaurs film. The movie fleshes out Bradbury's story of a dinosaur drawn to the sound of a lighthouse foghorn out of loneliness, complete with visions of the eponymous creature flattening vehicles in New York City and causing crowds of people to flee in panic. Such scenes would become obligatory in later monster movies, some of which even include a variation on *Beast*'s climax, in which the dinosaur is vanquished amid Coney Island roller coasters. The film's explanation for the creature's appearance—that it was awakened from its long slumber by an atomic blast—also was picked up by numerous other films and makes the beast a thinly veiled metaphor for nuclear anxiety. Ray HARRYHAUSEN animated the beast and provided the more than serviceable special effects in this, his first feature as special-effects head.

B.K.G.

BEAST WITH A MILLION EYES (1956).

Directed by David Kramarsky; screenplay by Tom Filer; photographed by Everett Baker; music by John Bickford. With Paul Birch, Lorna Thayer, Dona Cole, Dick Sargent, Leonard Tarver, Chester Conklin. 78 minutes. Black and white.

A bodiless alien takes over the minds of animals and a human moron (hence the "million eyes"); confronted by the film's protagonists, it simply leaves the Earth. Boring and lacking in action, this film is merely a curiosity. Significant today mainly for executive producer Roger CORMAN's involvement, it also established illustrator Paul Blaisdell as a creator of cheap monsters; the slave of the alien glimpsed here was a finger puppet.

B.W.

BEDFORD-JONES, H[ENRY JAMES O'BRIEN] (1887–1949).

Canadian-born American author of historical and adventure fiction for the PULP MAGAZINES, many of whose stories were science fiction. Under his own name and more than fifteen pseudonyms, Bedford-Jones was one of the most popular and prolific pulp writers, and, like most such writers, published fiction in many categories. Two of his series of stories in *Blue Book* (1938–39, 1943–44) involve devices for viewing or recording the past, and as Allan Hawkwood he published three lost world adventure novels in the 1920s. His SF novel *The Star Woman* was published in hardcover in the 1920s.

N.H.

——— BEGINNINGS ———

The Industrial Revolution of the late eighteenth century was also an "industrial revelation" to thinking people, who saw how greatly the world might be transformed by new machines. Reactions to this revelation were varied. Some writers were horrified, after the fashion of William Blake, whose "prophetic books" foresaw a world of strife and misery in which human beings would struggle to build the New Jerusalem among "dark satanic mills." Others were optimistic, especially in France, where the idea of progress took strong root among the philosophers who laid the groundwork for the revolution of 1789; Louis-Sebastien Mercier published in 1772 his vision of *L'An 2440,* in which machines have lightened the burden of human toil and society is organized more justly. Before this date images of ideal societies had usually been placed on remote islands or fabulous continents; now they began to be set in the world's great cities, displaced into the future as goals to be achieved.

In the early years of the nineteenth century, the more anxious vision received greater literary support. Scientists and inventors sometimes played a quasi-diabolical role in Gothic fantasies: "Automata" (1814) and "The Sandman" (1816) by E. T. A. HOFFMANN and (more subtly) *Frankenstein* (1818) by Mary SHELLEY offer examples. The idea that the scientist's interferences with nature might amount to a mockery of divine ordinance was widespread and became the basis for many tragic parables, including several notable works by Nathaniel HAWTHORNE: "Dr. Heidegger's Experiment" (1837), "The Birth Mark" (1843), "The Artist of the Beautiful" (1844), and "Rappacini's Daughter" (1844). Herman Melville's story "The Bell Tower" (1855) also belongs to this category.

There was another strain in the Gothic imagination, however, which was more readily accommodated in the developing scientific worldview; this was an interest in personality disorders and abnormal psychology. From American Gothic novels such as Charles Brockden Brown's *Wieland* (1798) this fascination passed to Edgar Allan POE, who moved easily from horror stories of disturbed minds to more ambitious studies of the mind's capacity for extraordinary perceptions. This interest is evident in "William Wilson" (1839) and in the dispassionate "clinical observations" of "The Facts in the Case of M. Valdemar" (1845) as well as in Poe's own experiments in intuition, "A Mesmeric Revelation" (1844) and *Eureka* (1848). Poe's attempts to bring a more analytic approach to representations of the strangeness of the human mind had a considerable influence on later American fiction and stand at the head of a tradition that includes the "medicated novels" of Oliver Wendell Holmes—*Elsie Venner* (1861), *The Guardian Angel* (1867), and *A Mortal Antipathy* (1885)—and the rationalized ghost stories of William Dean Howells.

Poe was an influential writer in the prehistory of science fiction for other reasons too. He was attracted to the theory of the hollow Earth popularized by John Cleves Symmes and his satiric novel *Symzonia* (published under the pseudonym Captain Adam Seaborn, 1820) and drew on it for "MS. Found in a Bottle" (1833) and *The Narrative of Arthur Gordon Pym* (1837). More important, he appended to the book version of his comedy "The Unparalleled Adventure of One Hans Pfaall" (1835) an essay on lunar voyages that champions greater verisimilitude in such fantasies. He also produced an early catastrophist fantasy in "The Conversation of Eiros and Charmion" (1839).

America's revolutionists had placed a high priority on the freedom of the press, and throughout the nineteenth century America had a far richer crop of periodicals than any European nation. This outlet created a thriving market for short fiction that had no parallel in Europe, and the thesis that science fiction is especially well adapted to short story form because of its use of the "idea-as-hero" format can easily be invoked to explain why so much proto–science fiction appeared in America. Poe and Hawthorne were the first in a line of short story writers who drew extensively on SF motifs to enliven their fiction; some of their short works have only recently been rediscovered in the pages of obscure periodicals. Their most famous successor was Fitz-James O'BRIEN, author of the first microcosmic fantasy—"The Diamond Lens" (1858)—and some stories that toy with the notion of other dimensions—"The Lost Room" (1858) and the celebrated story of an invisible being "What Was It?" (1859). Others in this tradition include W. H. Rhodes, whose stories were collected in *Caxton's Book* (1876), and two writers whose newspaper stories have recently been recovered and collected by Sam MOSKOWITZ: Edward Page Mitchell and Robert Duncan Milne. Better-known American short story writers who occasionally dabbled in speculative fiction include Edward Everett HALE and Frank R. STOCKTON. Edgar Fawcett, the first American writer to produce a substantial body of longer speculative fiction, also published his early novellas—"Douglas Duane" (1888) and "Solarion" (1889)—in periodicals.

Poe was greatly admired in France and was a favorite of Jules VERNE, but Verne became the progenitor of a very different species of speculative fiction. He was essentially an armchair voyager, inspired by new means of mechanical transportation—balloons, steamships, and submarines—to imagine the extraordinary voyages that would soon be possible. His characters explore every corner of the globe and go into regions as yet inaccessible in such novels as *Journey to the Center of the Earth* (1864), *Twenty Thousand Leagues under the Sea* (1870), *Round the Moon* (1870), and *The Clipper of the Clouds* (1886). Verne did more than any other writer to take up the cause of verisimilitude in fantastic romance, and his stories are full of technical detail to enhance plausibility. His was a disciplined imagination, rigidly confined by notions of imaginative propriety, and he thus became the intellectual forefather of "hard" science fiction.

It was another French writer, though, the astronomer Camille Flammarion, who took up the intuitive mode of Poe's *Eureka* and tried to combine the latest discoveries in astronomy with metaphysical beliefs about the nature of the universe. Flammarion was seized early with a powerful sense of the sheer wonder of the revelations of science concerning the extent and nature of the cosmos and the antiquity of life on Earth. He combined astronomy, evolutionary science, and spiritualist faith in his

Récits de l'infini (1872), a collection of fictionalized essays one of which was later expanded as *Lumen* (1887). Other essays in this mode—*Urania* (1889) and *La Fin du monde* (1893–94, translated as *Omega: The Last Days of the World,* 1894)—were highly successful, and the latter proved to be an influential catastrophist fantasy, whose images of cosmic disaster were repeated in numerous illustrated popular science articles in British and American periodicals.

The concerns of Verne and Flammarion were frequently mingled in late-nineteenth-century interplanetary fiction; Vernean technical detail became a standard device, but the discoveries made by adventurers in the far reaches of the solar system very often bore upon matters of religious belief. This combination appears in Chrysostom Trueman's *History of a Voyage to the Moon* (1864), Andrew Blair's *Annals of the Twenty-ninth Century* (1874), W. S. Lach-Szyrma's *Aleriel* (1883), and John Jacob Astor's *A Journey in Other Worlds* (1894).

British speculative fiction was slower in its flowering than that of America and France, inhibited by the chasm that separated the elite world of three-decker novels and literary periodicals from the imagination-starved crudities of penny-dreadful publishing. It was not until this middlebrow gap was filled in the 1890s that the history of British scientific romance really began. For two decades before that, though, British speculative fiction was dominated by future-war stories, initially inspired by George Chesney's alarmist exercise in fictitious journalism *The Battle of Dorking* (1871). Although the sun had not yet begun to set on the British Empire, there was cause to be anxious about the ambitions of the newly consolidated German nation, and there were also fears of armed conflict in connection with calls for Irish independence. Many future-war stories did not involve futuristic weaponry, but bigger and better guns crept in by degrees, and so did airships and submarines—the former prefigured as early as 1859 in *The Air Battle* by Herrmann Lang.

Britain was, though, the first nation to be transformed by the Industrial Revolution, and its witnesses to the resulting pattern of social change became quickly disenchanted with the French mythology of progress. There is a marked ambivalence about British nineteenth-century utopian fiction, and it was British writers who gave elaborate consideration to the notion of a retreat from technology, first in Richard Jefferies's *After London* (1885), then in W. H. Hudson's pioneering exercise in ecological mysticism *A Crystal Age* (1887). Edward George Bulwer-Lytton's account of *The Coming Race* (1871) is as ambiguous a utopia as any produced in more modern times, and Samuel Butler's *Erewhon* (1872) remains a strikingly eclectic utopian satire. Britain produced the first "dystopian novels" in H. C. Marriott Watson's *Erchomenon* (1879) and Walter Besant's *The*

Inner House (1888).

This deep-seated suspicion of the social changes brought about by technology is rooted in the values of the English aristocracy, whose authority was steadily eroded by the emergent bourgeoisie. America, which had largely cast aside such values in its revolution, produced writers much more inclined to celebrate the power of machinery and the liberating potential of new inventions. America made a hero out of Thomas Alva Edison, and that hero myth was widely reflected in fiction. The cheap dime novels produced in profusion after the Civil War, which undertook the first experiments in genre specialization, offered accounts of the many exploits of boy inventors Frank Reade, Jr., and Tom Edison, Jr., alongside their stories of derring-do on the wild frontier and heroic crime fighters. A less enchanted view of American inventiveness and know-how was taken by Mark Twain in his ironic account of the fate of a man charged with introducing the ways of the nineteenth century into the sixth, *A Connecticut Yankee at King Arthur's Court* (1889), but Twain remained a wholehearted subscriber to the idea of technological liberation even after losing the money he invested in the unfortunate Paige typesetting machine.

The American dream of liberation by technology was set out most clearly and successfully by Edward Bellamy, whose *Looking Backward, 2000–1887* (1888) became a phenomenal best-seller and inspired many "sequels" and ideological replies. Bellamy's shorter speculative fictions, including his first short novel, *Dr. Heidenhoff's Process* (1880), are less enthusiastic about mechanical solutions to human problems, and his later futuristic fantasy *Equality* (1897) devotes much more attention to political theory and the sociology of religion. But *Looking Backward* remains a vital apologia for technology as a key element in the making of a better world. In the tradition of American hard science fiction, this ideology is as important as the Vernean insistence on imaginative propriety.

By 1895 American proto–science fiction was sufficiently distinct and recognizable as a literary subspecies for Edgar Fawcett, in the preface to *The Ghost of Guy Thyrle*, to offer a manifesto on its behalf. Modern imag-' inative fiction, he claimed, should eschew the purely supernatural; speculations had to retain a solid basis in scientific fact—modern stories of wonder must, in fact, be "*realistic* romances," however odd that oxymoronic phrase might seem. The term *science fiction* had already been coined, by an obscure Scottish poet named William Wilson, who used it in 1851 to describe Richard Henry Horne's *The Poor Artist* (1850), which the author called "science in fable." Alas, this precedent was lost, and Fawcett's British contemporaries began to speak of "scientific romance" in parallel with his "realistic romance." All three designations, though, relate to the same discovery: that the scientific outlook could entirely change our idea of the universe while its material extensions—new technologies—could give us the power to remake our life and work. This discovery emerged gradually into literary expression through the works of Poe, Verne, Flammarion, and Bellamy before it was seized wholeheartedly by the first writer to really exploit it to the full: H. G. WELLS, with whom the history of modern speculative fiction really begins.

B.S.

BELLAMY, EDWARD (1850–1898).

American writer and political theorist whose 1888 utopian novel *Looking Backward, 2000–1887* not only was a runaway best-seller but also created a worldwide political movement. As a fiction writer Bellamy was barely adequate, with a clumsy style and little sense of narrative, and many of his novels are merely veiled treatises or polemics. But his powerfully suggestive ideas redeem them. For example, the otherwise slight novel *Dr. Heidenhoff's Process* (1880) depicts the possibility of selective extirpation of memory and ruminates on the legal and ethical consequences of such a process.

Looking Backward was influential on several levels. Its story of Julian West—a man of 1887 who wakes from a strange sleep to find himself in the Boston of the year 2000—was a successful model of the long sleep that many later writers would adopt, and Bellamy's inspiration to locate his technological utopia in the possible future was another much-copied device. Bellamy's future Boston is filled with efficient railroads, telephones, television, and a version of the automobile. Industry has been automated, and new devices make life healthier and more pleasurable. But the city's most amazing feature is its society: people have achieved a classless and nonsexist order in which all the marvels of technology benefit all the citizens. Special privileges are gone; everyone shares the advantages of universal education, guaranteed income, and excellent medical care.

The consequence of this book's success was the for-

mation of more than 150 Nationalist clubs, the incorporation of its programs into a political party, and the creation of two journals, *The Nationalist* and *The New Nation*. *Looking Backward* also touched off a new wave of utopias. William Morris, for instance, responded with the nontechnological *News from Nowhere* (1890) and H. G. WELLS with the technological antiutopia *When the Sleeper Wakes* (1899), which actually mentions Bellamy. Bellamy himself wrote a long sequel to *Looking Backward—Equality* (1897)—defending his political and social theories. Later writers such as Mack Reynolds drew ideas and inspiration from Bellamy; Reynolds actually took a new look at *Looking Backward* and its vision, and other writers as diverse as Larry NIVEN and Frederik POHL have based new novels on it.

Some of Bellamy's short stories are science fiction related, usually focused on conjectural developments of the mind—Martians who can foresee the future in "The Blindman's World" (1886) and a race of mind readers on a remote island in "To Whom This May Come" (1888)—but he always dealt with moral consequences and the hope for the future. Bellamy looked to these new mental powers, as he did to the new social systems of his novels, as possible paths to a better life for all human beings.

OTHER WORK: *The Blindman's World and Other Stories* (collection, 1898).

S.T.J.

BENEATH THE PLANET OF THE APES: SEE
PLANET OF THE APES

BENET, STEPHEN VINCENT (1898–1943).
American author, renowned for short fiction published in the *Saturday Evening Post,* often on American historical or folkloristic themes, including the fantasy classic "The Devil and Daniel Webster" (1936). Benét's major contribution to science fiction, "By the Water of Babylon" (1937), is an influential postholocaust story told from the point of view of a future primitive exploring the ruins of twentieth-century civilization. Benét was also a poet of note, author of the epic *John Brown's Body* (1928) and a landmark bit of speculative verse, "Nightmare for Future Reference" (1938), which jauntily, then chillingly describes a third World War in which all humankind is rendered sterile by bacteriologic weapons. He wrote several other pieces of science-fiction poetry, including "Metropolitan Nightmare" (1927) and "Nightmare Number Three" (1935).

WORKS: *Thirteen O'Clock: Stories of Several Worlds* (1937); *Tales before Midnight* (1939); *The Selected Works of Stephen Vincent Benét* (2 vols., 1942); *The Last Circle* (1946).

D.S.

BENFORD, GREGORY [ALBERT] (1941–   ).

American writer and physicist. Although he is quoted as saying, "I'm a scientist by first choice and shall remain so," and although he is professor of physics at the University of California, Irvine, Benford writes fiction that in both quantity and quality has established his reputation firmly as a writer.

Born in Alabama and educated at the University of Oklahoma and the University of California, San Diego, Benford began his association with science fiction as a fan writer and enthusiast. He learned his writing craft partly through collaboration and imitation, and continues to expand his literary aspiration in concert with his skill and vision. Speculations on tachyons and the time travel paradox, understanding and portrayals of credible scientists, and experiments in style all are noteworthy and dynamic elements in his work.

His novel *Timescape* (1980), which won the Nebula and Campbell awards, and his literary experimental work *Against Infinity* (1983) illustrate Benford's versatility as a writer. *Timescape*, which alternates between the historical past, the present, and a polluted near future in which scientists are attempting to warn the past by means of a tachyon beam, is one of the most effective fictional depictions in our century of science at work, and Benford's examination of the concept of meeting oneself in time is moving. In *Against Infinity* SF and mainstream literature converged as Benford deliberately translated the story, style, and sense of awe of William Faulkner's "The Bear" into an SF narrative dealing with a boy's attempt to destroy a mysterious, alien artifact left on Ganymede.

Along with such literary experimentation, Benford has maintained his involvement with the conventions and themes of the genre. Space adventure heroes such as his Nigel Walmsley reappear in several fictions. His 1986 collaboration with David Brin, *Heart of the Comet,* is actually a wonderful pastiche and near parody of conventional motifs from "green slime" to futuristic military details in the tradition of Robert A. Heinlein. Moreover, Benford continues to write an impressive number of nonfiction pieces, as yet uncollected, especially on the image of the alien in SF, the nature of hard SF, and his own approaches to writing SF.

Benford's short fiction, with which he began and in which he continues to excel ("If the Stars Are Gods," with Gordon Eklund, won a 1974 Nebula, and "Deeper Than the Darkness," "Doing Lennon," "White Creatures," "A Snark in the Night," and "Swarmer, Skimmer" were Nebula or Hugo finalists), is written with equal care, and some has been collected in *In Alien Flesh* (1986).

Benford is important to SF in several ways: as a member of the science culture reflecting its concerns and reality to the literary culture, as C. P. Snow advocated in his "Two Cultures" lecture; as a writer who in the 1980s has found his own voice and message of alienation; and as spokesman for his kind of SF. Literary standards apply to all kinds of fiction, he has argued, but certain kinds of fiction, such as hard SF, have special standards and virtues of their own; literary fiction, including literary SF, is pessimistic about the future, but scientists, as Snow said, "have the future in their bones." Benford's concern for literary standards is an extension of the emphasis on good writing in SF that began with John W. Campbell, but his analytic-scientific training has led him to the open-ended hopefulness of hard SF.

OTHER WORKS: *Deeper Than the Darkness* (1970; revised as *The Stars in Shroud,* 1978); *Jupiter Project* (1975); *If the Stars Are Gods* (with Gordon Eklund, 1977); *In the Ocean of Night* (1977); *Find the Changeling* (with Eklund, 1980); *Shiva Descending* (with William Rotsler, 1980); *Across the Sea of Stars* (1984); *Artifact* (1985); *Great Sky River* (1987).

D.M.H.

BERESFORD, J[OHN] D[AVYS] (1873–1947).

British writer and architect. The author of over forty mainstream novels, Beresford wrote eight science-fiction novels and many short stories. His first SF novel, *The Hampdenshire Wonder* (1911), remains his best known. One of the earliest treatments of a human with superpowers, the novel concerns the life and death of a superintelligent child born to ungifted working-class parents. Beresford emphasized the loneliness of the exceptional child, dwelling particularly on how his powers make him an alien in human society. The novel is a powerful, grim statement about the tragedy that lurks behind being "special."

A contemporary of H. G. Wells, Beresford dealt with many similar themes, but whereas Wells tended to stress ideas, Beresford focused on human relationships. In the unjustly neglected *Goslings* (1913), for example, he described society in an all but abandoned London during a plague. His focus was on ordinary people forced to survive in what appears to be a hopeless situation rather than on an ideological statement about the causes of disease and poverty.

With the recent movement toward incorporating mainstream techniques into science fiction, Beresford's work may undergo a revival. Indeed Beresford was doing just that almost seventy-five years ago.

OTHER WORKS: *Nineteen Impressions* (collection, 1918); *Revolution: A Story of the Near Future in England* (1921); *Signs and Wonders* (collection, 1921); *Real People* (1929); *The Meeting Place and Other Stories* (collection, 1929); *The Camberwell Miracle* (1933); *What Dreams May Come . . .* (1941); *A Common Enemy* (1942); *The Riddle of the Tower* (with Esme Wynne-Tyson, 1944).

S.H.G.

November 1939 cover illustration by Bergey

BERGER, THOMAS (1924–). American mainstream writer (best known for his novel *Little Big Man*, 1964, which became a major film in 1970), whose writings sometimes border on science fiction. Berger's only clearly SF novel is *Regiment of Women* (1973), about a future society in which sex roles have been reversed. *Vital Parts* (1970), the third of his four Reinhart novels, concludes, however, with Berger's contemporary hero Carlo Reinhart choosing cryonic suspension over death, suggesting the possibility of an SF sequel to his adventures.

N.H.

BERGEY, EARLE K. (?–1952). American illustrator known as the "inventor of the brass bra," a trademark that single-handedly branded science fiction as "lurid" for several decades. Bergey painted so many beautiful women struggling in the clutches of bug-eyed monsters and robots that his work became a cliché. During the 1940s Bergey painted covers for pulps such as *Startling Stories, Planet Stories, Fantastic Story Magazine, Thrilling Wonder Stories*, and *Captain Future*. Apparently Bergey did no interior illustrations for the pulps. His slick, professional, realistic style helped launch the trend away from the depiction of machinery and toward people.

J.G.

BERKELEY SQUARE (1933). *Directed by Frank Lloyd; screenplay by Sonya Levien and John L. Balderston; adapted from the play by John L. Balderston and John C. Squire, from the novel* The Sense of the Past *by Henry James; photographed by Ernest Palmer; music by Louis De Francesco. With Leslie Howard, Heather Angel, Valerie Taylor, Irene Browne, Beryl Mercer, Alan Mowbray. 87 minutes. Black and white.*

I'LL NEVER FORGET YOU (1951). *Directed by Roy Baker; screenplay by Ranald MacDougall; adapted from the play by John L. Balderston and John C. Squire, from the novel* The Sense of the Past *by Henry James; photographed by Georges Perinal; music by William Alwyn. With Tyrone Power, Ann Blyth, Michael Rennie, Dennis Price, Irene Browne. 89 minutes. Color and black and white. Alternate title:* The House on the Square.

The two film versions of Henry James's novel are essentially romantic fantasies employing a science-fiction-like time travel motif; in the later film, however, with its scientist-hero and his anachronistic inventions, the accent has switched: science and SF are more to the fore. In the 1933 version an American (Peter Standish, played by Leslie Howard) inherits an old London house and finds himself drawn 150 years into the past, where he does his fitful best to pass as his own ancestor/double. His attempts to fit into another time fascinate, intermittently. He makes inexplicable gaffes, such as references to Oscar Wilde ("He's dead. No—") and other matters Yet to Come. In the film's most arresting sequence, he gives in to his cursed godlike knowledge and grandly consigns those within earshot to their future/past graves. Unfortunately, the script dawdles in the prefatory present, and, when it finally does get to the past, sometimes waxes romantic in the worst way. Howard gets most of the script's wit; Heather Angel, the mush.

In the 1951 version a scientist (Tyrone Power) working in his ancestral Berkeley Square home in London loses consciousness during a thunderstorm and awakens in the eighteenth century. There he dabbles with steam power and electricity and invents television. Ultimately he returns to the twentieth century and meets the counterpart of his eighteenth-century love (Ann Blyth). Scenes set in the present are in black and white; in the past, in color. The story has some touching and amusing moments, but Power is stolid in the lead role. The film's most graceful grace note: Irene Browne repeats her role of Lady Pettigrew from the 1933 version.

D.W.

BESTER, ALFRED (1913–1987). American writer, one of the giants of the science-fiction field during its GOLDEN AGE, which his works helped define. Bester's two early novels, *The Demolished Man* (1952/1953) and *The Stars My Destination* (1959; originally published in Great Britain in 1956 as *Tiger! Tiger!*, the title Bester preferred), have forever stamped him as one of the field's legendary masters. Both are highly regarded by both critics as well as fans, and both repay the careful attention they demand.

Born in New York City, Bester was educated at the University of Pennsylvania, where he studied, by his own account, psychology, literature, law, and music. He began writing professionally in 1938, and in the next decade or so he churned out science fiction; radio scripts for *Charlie Chan, The Shadow*, and other shows; and pulp writing of all kinds, ranging from adventure and detective yarns to "true" stories. This training served him well as preparation for his mature SF novels.

When *The Demolished Man* was originally published in magazine form, readers immediately recognized the hand of a master at work. Not only did Bester tell a rattling good story, replete with some strikingly original SF devices and settings, but he broke new ground by incorporating into SF certain literary devices—ignored by most of his contemporaries—derived from so-called mainstream fiction. These include interior monologue, stream-of-consciousness narrative, and the utilization of typographical devices. Bester's admiration for the work of James Joyce, notably *Ulysses*, is evident in much of his writing. In both *The Demolished Man* and *The Stars My Destination* that influence can be seen in the long passages of detailed prose, as well as the use of interior monologue.

Almost alone among his contemporaries, Bester attempted—and often achieved—real characterization. Neither Ben Reich of *The Demolished Man* nor Gully Foyle of *The Stars My Destination* are two-dimensional individuals; both have dark sides to their otherwise heroic natures. In fact, Bester utilized techniques from the soft science of psychology to provide depth of characterization; it is possible to read both these novels from a Freudian, Jungian, or Adlerian point of view. Reich is a deliberately ambiguous hero, whose attempt to plan and execute a first-class felony in a society guarded by mind-reading police has many of his readers at least unconsciously rooting for his success or eventual escape. By contrast, the prefect of police, Lincoln Powell, seems almost insufferably smug and complacent.

In both novels Bester examined the search for identity, the father-son relationship, revenge, death, and rebirth. In *The Stars My Destination*, for example, Foyle is driven not just by revenge but also by the need to overcome the near diabolic shadow figure from his unconscious. When he becomes angry and loses control of himself, the shadow self is manifested on his face in the form of horrible tattoos. In the end Foyle's tattooed tiger mask gives a profound meaning to the British title of the novel, *Tiger! Tiger!*, derived from the opening words of William Blake's poem. To borrow from Blake, it is Foyle's "fearful symmetry" that must be overcome; in fact, the

Alfred Bester

novel suggests that until the tiger in all of us is overcome, humanity will never reach true civilization or harmony.

What makes the achievement of both of these early novels so marvelous is that Bester never lost sight of the fact that he was telling a story—a headlong, pell-mell, action-oriented story. The action careens through the planets and into outer space, returning to the inner space of the psyche, perhaps SF's last frontier. In *The Demolished Man* Bester married these standard SF devices to the "open" detective story, in which the criminal, the crime, and the method are revealed to the reader as the story progresses. Almost from the first page, it is evident that Reich is a killer, that he is planning a murder, and that he will successfully execute an almost impossible crime. What remains hidden is Reich's true motive, which even Powell, a highly trained detective, has difficulty uncovering—the novel is thus more of a "whydunit" than a "whodunit."

So also with *The Stars My Destination*. At first reading it appears to be a classic revenge story flavored with elements derived from Alexandre Dumas's *The Count of Monte Cristo*. But it also deals with more complex themes, notably that of rebirth; at book's end, Foyle, who has gone through successive rebirths, is again about to be reborn, this time to characters known as Joseph and Moira.

After these novels Bester published nothing in the field for nearly two decades. He had become an editor of *Holiday* magazine, a task that left him no time for writing SF, but his return was anxiously anticipated. When *The Computer Connection* was published in magazine form in 1974 and in book form a year later, it proved disappointing to many of Bester's loyal readers. While it dealt with many of the themes of the early books—humanity's inhumanity to its own, death and rebirth, the conflict of good and evil—it also seemed that the years away from writing SF had robbed the author of some control over his materials. His hero appears variously as

Daniel or Edward Curzon, for example, and the plot is so complicated that it is almost impossible to follow completely.

Golem 100 (1980), also long awaited, was another disappointment to many of Bester's fans. Entire passages are printed in the form of musical scores, while others consist of page after page of pure graphics. Alas, the novel's complexities demand a patience of eye and intellect that many readers are either unwilling or unable to give.

Bester's short fiction, some of it collected in *Starlight: The Great Short Fiction of Alfred Bester* (1976), is also worthy of serious consideration. His stories are marked by careful craftsmanship, literary touches, an emphasis on the individual, and an ability to infuse tired SF devices with new life. Most notable among them are "The Men Who Murdered Mohammed" (1958), "Fondly Fahrenheit" (1954), "5,271,009" (1954), and the classic, evocative "Adam and No Eve" (1941). Many later NEW WAVE writers claimed Bester as a predecessor and his work as an inspiration, just as later CYBERPUNK authors identified some of his work (particularly *The Stars My Destination*) as ancestral to theirs.

W.E.M.

BIERCE, AMBROSE [GWINNET] (1842?–1914).

American satirist, journalist, and author whose work, most of it in the area of horror and the supernatural, is marked by an abiding cynicism and black humor. Born in Ohio, Bierce disappeared in Mexico in 1913 and is presumed to have been killed in the Mexican Civil War. His satiric bent is evident in *The Devil's Dictionary* (1906), a volume of cynical definitions. His best-known work, however, is "An Occurrence at Owl Creek Bridge" (1891), in which a Civil War spy escapes hanging and returns to his family; in a twist that is genuinely terrifying, the reader ultimately discovers this is only the dying man's fantasy. Several of Bierce's stories display elements of science fiction, including "Moxon's Master" (1909), with its murderous chess-playing robot; "The Damned Thing" (1898), which matter-of-factly describes an invisible creature; and "The Realm of the Unreal" (1893), with its extrapolation of hypnotism. The *Collected Writings of Ambrose Bierce* (1963) contains his major works.

R.S.C.

BIGGLE, LLOYD, JR. (1923–).

American author. Educated as a musicologist (he earned his Ph.D. from the University of Michigan in 1953), Biggle has been a full-time writer since 1951, but, perhaps because of his academic background, he has been primarily interested in the organization and preservation of materials about science fiction. He served as the first secretary-treasurer of the SCIENCE FICTION WRITERS OF AMERICA, the first chairman of its board of trustees, the founder of its regional collections, and the founder of the Science Fiction Oral History Association.

Biggle's work includes references to music but is more significantly oriented toward social and political questions. For much of his work he has invented the Council of Supreme, a giant computer fed information by seven aliens and a human, which works through the agents of the Galactic Synthesis, the Cultural Survey, and the Interplanetary Relations Bureau, helping unite civilized worlds to save planets, galaxies, and even the universe from Udef, the Dark Force. In novels such as *All the Colors of Darkness* (1963), *Watchers of the Dark* (1968), *This Darkening Universe* (1975), *Silence Is Deadly* (1977), and *The Whirligig of Time* (1979), his characters display concern for all forms of life, planetary ecology, and differences between species. Biggle also creates the physical details of worlds, social customs, political arrangements, speech patterns, economics, and culture to make his works believable.

OTHER WORKS: *The Angry Espers* (1961); *The Fury out of Time* (1965); *The Rule of the Door* (collection, 1967); *The Still Small Voice of Trumpets* (1968); *The World Menders* (1971); *The Light That Never Was* (1972); *The Metallic Muse* (collection, 1972); *Nebula Award Stories 7* (ed., 1973); *Monument* (1974); *A Galaxy of Strangers* (collection, 1976); *Alien Main* (with T. L. Sherred, 1985).

R.H.W.

BINDER, EANDO (Pseudonym used originally by the American brothers Earl Andrew Binder [1904–1965] and Otto Oscar Binder [1911–1974] but used by Otto alone after 1935, when Earl stopped writing).

Popular contributors to the science-fiction pulps since their works' first appearance with "The First Martian" (1932), the Binders wrote mostly light SF adventures. Working on his own, Otto (who also wrote as John Coleridge and Gordon A. Giles) produced the more memorable works, especially "I, Robot" (1939), the first of the Adam Link robot stories. Although the later stories in this series were little more than basic pulp adventures, the first set out to treat robots sympathetically. Most of these stories were collected as *Adam Link—Robot* (1965) and in Isaac Asimov's collection of robot stories *I, Robot* (1950). Although Binder's work was always competent, it seldom rose above the pulp stereotype and has dated badly. Binder wrote mostly for comic books during the 1940s and also wrote books on astronomy and UFOs. He returned to fiction in the late 1960s with a series of forgettable novels.

NOTABLE OTHER WORKS: *Enslaved Brains* (1934/1965); *Anton York—Immortal* (1937–1940/1965); *Lords of*

Creation (1939/1949); *The Impossible World* (1939/1970); *Five Steps to Tomorrow* (1940/1970); *Get Off My World* (1971); *Puzzle of the Space Pyramids* (1971); *Secret of the Red Spot* (1971); *The Double Man* (1971); *The Mind from Outer Space* (1972).

M.A.

BIOLOGY

Science-fictional speculations in biology have almost always born a relation to scientific notions of the time—though not always accurately. Luigi Galvani experimented with frog legs and electricity, and his conclusion that there is a kind of animal electricity, later disproved by Volta, led to the popular misperceptions that Mary SHELLEY exploited in *Frankenstein* (1818), arguably the first science-fiction novel. The other faces of biology in SF—alien beings, mutation, EVOLUTION—are revealed in virtually every major work of the genre to a greater or lesser degree. Reading works of SF historically is like taking a short course in the scientific theories and interests of the times in which they were written.

The science of poisons fascinated Nathaniel HAWTHORNE. In "Rappaccini's Daughter" (1844) a young woman is raised among poisonous plants until she is immune to their toxins. Simply to touch her, however, is to die. The discoveries of "giants in the Earth" by paleobiologists led Jules VERNE to speculate on the possibility of "survivals" in *Journey to the Center of the Earth* (1864). Fitz-James O'BRIEN's short story "The Diamond Lens" (1858) explores intelligent life in a drop of water, though more as hallucination than as scientific reality.

The contemporary ideas at H. G. WELLS's disposal were manifold—Darwinian and other theories of evolution, advances in basic biology, and efforts by Herbert Spencer and others to tie together sociology, history, and biology. Wells's first novel, *The Time Machine* (1895), is one of the first convincing fictional expositions on human evolution, neatly combining social and biological evolution. In *The Island of Dr. Moreau* (1896), Wells tackled vivisection (a contentious issue then and now), forced Lamarckian evolution, and the mad doctor in his laboratory with such zest and conviction that writers have been emulating this short novel ever since. Despite the years since Shelley's work, the keynotes of *The Island of Dr. Moreau* are still pain, monsters, and horror; clearly Dr. Moreau has dabbled in "things man was not meant to know." *The War of the Worlds* (1898) is an ingenious study in exobiology and even unwitting germ warfare. In *The Food of the Gods* (1906), a new food produces giants—giant wasps, children, and so on—and the consequences are food for satire and social criticism. Here Wells was less haunted by the horror of it all; still, the message remained the same: meddling in biology leads to sorrow and disruption.

Following more in the footsteps of Jules Verne than in those of Wells, Arthur Conan DOYLE created Professor Challenger, who in *The Lost World* (1912) discovers an isolated jungle plateau harboring dinosaurs and primitive cavepeople. Challenger also discovers that the entire Earth is a living being in Doyle's short story "When the World Screamed" (anthologized in 1929).

It was up to the pulp writers of the 1920s and 1930s to fill in the remaining gaps, sometimes crudely, sometimes with true vision. E. E. SMITH (a Ph.D. in chemistry) cemented his reputation as an inventor of aliens in the Lensman novels; *Triplanetary* (1948) provides a historical perspective for the conflict between the extradimensional Eddorians and the noble, godlike Arisians, who have both meddled in the affairs of men. Jack WILLIAMSON throughout his long career has handled biological themes, notably in his novels *Darker Than You Think* (1940), concerning lycanthropy as a genetic throwback, and *Dragon's Island* (1951), about controlled mutations and the creation of a race of "notmen."

Eric Temple Bell, a mathematician by trade, wrote a number of SF novels as John TAINE, many of them concerned with evolution. The most blatantly biological is *Seeds of Life* (1931), yet another queasy, disaster-filled life-in-the-laboratory story. In 1927 *Amazing Stories* reprinted "The Tissue Culture King" by Julian Huxley, brother of Aldous and grandson of Thomas. Aldous HUXLEY himself, steeped in his family's long association with the life sciences, created *Brave New World* (1932), a complex and prescient vision of the future, foreseeing test-tube babies and behavior control through drugs.

Edgar Rice BURROUGHS's Mars—introduced in 1912 with the serialization of "Under the Moons of Mars" (book title *A Princess of Mars*)—is weird and wonderfully cockeyed, with enormous four-armed green Martians, humanoid oviparous red Martians (human hero John Carter breeds an interspecies dynasty with the beautiful egg-laying Dejah Thoris), bodiless heads and headless bodies symbiotically united, and so on. In *The Land That Time Forgot* (1924) evolution on a lost island proceeds individually rather than phylogenetically; each creature evolves from a single cell through reptilian forms to humanity.

Beginning in 1930 with *Last and First Men*, British philosopher (William) Olaf STAPLEDON suddenly played all the keys on the organ of speculative fiction. This account of the future of the human race reads like genuine history; humanity evolves over 2 billion years through eighteen distinct species. The Third Men's specialty is "the vital art," creating new life-forms and adapting the old, eventually making great brains that replace themselves. The cumulative effect of this work, in both a literary and a speculative sense, is overwhelming. Stapledon treated biological change with less distaste and more actual hope than any previous author. In *Star-*

maker (1937) he created the supreme work of imaginative literature in the twentieth century. Reaching far beyond the vast time scales of *Last and First Men*, he took a narrator (clearly himself) on an astral journey to witness the history of intelligent life in other worlds and the eventual evolution of the galaxies themselves into living beings. Stapledon's smooth progress from biology and evolution to mystical vision is unparalleled.

Across the ocean Stanley G. WEINBAUM, perhaps interested in going Wells one better, plunged into all the major biological themes of science fiction—exobiology ("A Martian Odyssey," 1934; its sequel "Valley of Dreams," also 1934; and "The Lotus Eaters," 1935), mutation ("The New Adam," published posthumously in 1939; and "Proteus Island," 1936), mad doctors in laboratories ("The Adaptive Ultimate," 1935), and evolution, inherent in many of these stories in one way or another. His most famous creations are the hordes of alien characters in "A Martian Odyssey," among them the birdlike Martian Tweel and a creature that excretes silicate bricks, with which it then constructs little pyramids to protect itself. This pyramid beast is an early example of "silicon-based life," more and more a staple of science fiction through the 1960s and 1970s, when its scientific improbability led to a literary extinction.

In the 1940s Eric Frank RUSSELL, L. Sprague DE CAMP, Robert A. HEINLEIN, A. E. VAN VOGT, and others played more variations on the old themes, adding distinct touches of their own. Russell's story "Symbiotica" (1943) tells of an outwardly peaceful but actually deadly planet dominated by interrelated plantlike organisms. De Camp's "The Blue Giraffe" (1939) is about mutations on the African veld. In the brilliant novella *Universe* (1941) Heinlein devised a biologically independent system aboard an out-of-control generation starship, populated by humans and "muties," in particular the two-headed Joe-Jim Gregory, one of the most memorable characters in SF. In *The Puppet Masters* (1951) Heinlein had little sympathy for intelligent parasitic "slugs" who attempt to enslave the human race. Throughout the 1940s and into the 1960s, A. E. van Vogt created consistently intriguing, often darkly powerful aliens. The most famous of these is the huge, ancient Coeurl of "Black Destroyer" (1939).

Theodore STURGEON's work is dominated by biological speculations, playful and otherwise. His story "Microcosmic God" (1941) is one of the all-time great tales of "making life in the laboratory." Inventor James Kidder accelerates evolution and synthesizes the tiny, highly intelligent Neoterics, which eventually protect themselves by making an impenetrable energy shield.

Isaac ASIMOV, though trained in biochemistry, concentrated on galactic empires and astronomical themes until his later novels—*Fantastic Voyage* (1966), a novelization from a motion picture screenplay by Harry Kleiner, based on a story idea by Jerome BIXBY, and *The*

Gods Themselves (1972).

Clifford SIMAK created some of the most oddball aliens in science fiction ("They Walked Like Men" 1962); however, he is most famous for his novel *City* (1952), assembled from stories published during the 1940s and in 1951. *City* follows the social evolution and migration of human society, which eventually leaves the Earth in charge of intelligent dogs.

James BLISH was the first to bring a coherent vision of biology to science fiction. He clearly saw the need for humanity to adapt itself—actually to change its form and even its mentality when faced with strange environments. Blish studied microbiology at Rutgers University and applied his studies to the stories that eventually went into the book *The Seedling Stars* (1957). In this work human beings are altered to fit into alien environments, the most radical adaptation being the creation of microscopic intelligences in "Surface Tension." In his collaboration with Norman L. KNIGHT, *A Torrent of Faces* (1967), Blish applied a statement by eccentric economist Henry George to an extraordinarily crowded but viable Earth, populated by natural humans and Tritons, adapted for the sea.

In the 1940s and 1950s the effect of high-energy radiation on organisms became a central concern in and out of science fiction. The specter of the atomic bomb, radiation sickness, radiation-induced mutations, and sterility hung over these decades and poked a glowing finger deep into the unconscious, especially in motion pictures, where radiation created a zoo of monstrosities.

Strangely, mutations and radiation almost overshadow the progress in unraveling the code of life itself. The research into DNA and genetics at this time was complex and tentative, difficult for laypeople to understand; few SF writers felt qualified to tackle the theme. Computers and information theory became an important part of our lives within two decades; the difference between "software" and "hardware" became a major philosophical and psychological concept. Yet not until over twenty years had passed would biology, computer theory, and information theory come together to bring biology truly into its own in science fiction.

In the 1950s authors began to exploit more seriously the potentials of the biological sciences to explore questions of evolution, genetic manipulation, alien biology, intelligence, ecological catastrophe, and alien-human relationships. In "Against the Fall of Night" (serialized in 1948, published in book form in 1953, redrafted as *The City and the Stars* in 1956), Arthur C. CLARKE—although he stretched his imagination across a billion years—foresaw very few physical changes in human beings. Yet in *Childhood's End* (1953), under alien influence, humans begin to abandon their biological forms within a few short years. Clarke seems more comfortable positing a direct evolution from biological to godlike immaterial forms, as in *2001: A Space Odyssey* (1968 movie and novel). In *Rendezvous with Rama* (1973), among his speculations on alien biology Clarke showed, with little of the social guilt and pain of *The Island of Dr. Moreau*, genetically altered animals serving humans.

Animals raised to human intelligence are important in Cordwainer SMITH's work, in which they are called the Underpeople. The book *Norstrilia* (1975; published separately as *The Planet Buyer*, 1964, and *The Underpeople*, 1968) tells part of their story. Jack VANCE foresaw intricate manipulations of living things in *The Houses of Iszm* (serial 1954, book 1964), in which people live in literal tree houses adapted to serve their every need. Much of Vance's work—*The Dragon Masters* (1962) and *The Last Castle* (1966) in particular—takes an exotic approach to the life sciences.

Hal CLEMENT's *Mission of Gravity* (1954) takes place on the huge, oblate planet Mesklin, where indigenous life-forms must survive a gravitational pull as high as 700 times that of Earth. Clement's interest in aliens in extreme environments is a hallmark of all his work, but in *Needle* (1950) the alien environment is a human body. A symbiotic extraterrestrial detective must find a criminal of his own kind while occupying the body of a boy.

Another author who has built his career on alien worlds and their inhabitants is Poul ANDERSON. However, his first adult novel was largely earthbound; *Brainwave* (1954) takes the Earth out of a galactic force field that inhibits neuronal activity, and therefore intelligence. Eventually the renormalized, more intelligent humans migrate into space, leaving behind the brain-impaired of their own kind and bright animals.

John CHRISTOPHER's *No Blade of Grass* (1956, British title *The Death of Grass*) is an excellent example of what now would be called ecological disaster. Throughout the 1950s Christopher and John WYNDHAM developed a distinctly Wellsian strain of SF disaster novels. Wyndham's *The Day of the Triffids* (1951, British title *Revolt of the Triffids*), *Out of the Deeps* (1953, British title *The Kraken Wakes*) and *The Midwich Cuckoos* (1957) are all biological in theme.

In the 1950s Philip José FARMER's stories "The Lovers" (1952), "Mother" (1953), and "Open to Me, My Sister" (1960) opened new territory with the controversial themes of alien-human sex and incest. William TENN satirized biology, sex, and aliens in many of his short stories, including "Wednesday's Child" (1956), in which a woman gives birth to herself, and "Venus and the Seven Sexes" (1949), a treatise on Venusian procreation. In "Child's Play" (1947) Tenn drops a special-delivery package, a Bild-a-Man set from the year 2353, into the lap of a hapless modern protagonist, who learns more about biology than he cares to.

In the 1960s science in SF laboratories seemed stuck in a rut. Philip K. DICK's *Do Androids Dream of Electric Sheep?* (1968) is an interesting exception; citizens of

Strange creatures from Jules Verne's *Journey to the Center of the Earth*

Dick's future Earth, drained of population by space colonization, take drugs tailored for specific moods and use artificial animals as status symbols. Speculation about the biology of aliens flourished in the 1960s, however. Frank HERBERT's immensely popular and influential novel *Dune* began magazine serialization in 1963 and was published as a book in 1965. *Dune* brought to popular attention the still youthful concept of ecology and may have contributed to the ecology movement that began to flourish in the wake of Rachel Carson's *Silent Spring*. Brian W. ALDISS's "The Saliva Tree" (1965) and *The Long Afternoon of Earth* (1962, British title *Hothouse*), about triumphant (and sometimes intelligent) flora, are delightfully innovative if incredible.

Harry HARRISON's most vivid creation in the 1960s was doubtless Deathworld (in *Deathworld*, 1960; *Deathworld 2*, 1964; and *Deathworld 3*, 1968), a planet packed with vicious life-forms. In his *Plague from Space* (1965) a horrible disease is brought back from Jupiter; this story predated Michael CRICHTON's *The Andromeda Strain* by half a decade. *Make Room! Make Room!* (1966) is a dark, concise account of an overpopulated future Earth on the brink of complete ecological disaster. John BRUNNER made progress in the life sciences an integral part of his novel *Stand on Zanzibar* (1968), an encyclopedic study of the Earth in the year 2010.

In 1965 Larry NIVEN began his Known Space series of stories and novels, introducing a number of remarkable aliens on which he elaborated in the 1970s. He also described a future trade in organs for transplant, in a society that eventually penalizes the most minor crimes with death in order to increase the organ supply in *A Gift from Earth* (1968). His most innovative biological idea is in the novel *Protector* (1973), wherein humans are but an arrested, immature breeding stage of an extraterrestrial species.

James WHITE, in his Hospital Station novels, cheerfully described the medical treatment of alien life-forms; their variety and strangeness does not induce distaste so much as sympathy and fascination in the reader. James TIPTREE, Jr., (a pseudonym of Alice Sheldon) consistently uses biological symbols and themes in her work; the most telling is in her story "The Screwfly Solution" (1977, written under the pseudonym Raccoona Sheldon). She speculated on the sources of human male aggression against females. "Love Is the Plan, The Plan Is Death" (1973) is an extraordinary Tiptree exploration of alien interaction.

In the 1970s and 1980s biological speculation came into full flower. In the early 1970s Gregory BENFORD, in his stories and novels—especially *In the Ocean of Night* (1977) and its sequel, *Across the Sea of Suns* (1984)—began his definitive fictional studies of biomechanisms, the result of biology's evolution toward mechanical, computerized forms. This idea continues to dominate his work. Benford collaborated with David BRIN in *The Heart of the Comet* (1986) to speculate on the life-forms that might be found in a comet.

Two of Brin's own novels, *Sundiver* (1980) and *Startide Rising* (1983), postulate a galaxywide attempt to "Uplift" organisms to intelligence. Dolphins, chimps, and other animals are given human intelligence to act as equals, a final shedding of Wells's and Shelley's guilt about meddling with nature.

Physicist Robert FORWARD's novel *Dragon's Egg* (1980) presents an environment far more extreme than Clement's Mesklin: the surface of a neutron star. The beings that survive here rank among the finest creations in hard SF.

The most significant biologically oriented author of the 1970s is John VARLEY. Finally putting together genetic engineering, sex roles, and computer science, Varley explores the "downloading" of human personalities into computer memory ("Overdrawn at the Memory Bank," 1976) and changing physical sex roles ("Options," 1979). In his trilogy *Titan* (1979), *Wizard* (1980), and *Demon* (1984), Varley has created a vast, living, artificial space structure called Gaea, after the goddess of the Earth.

In the 1980s the subjects pioneered by Varley, Alfred BESTER, Norman SPINRAD, Robert SILVERBERG, and others began to blossom into a loosely knit literary movement called neuromantic, or CYBERPUNK, or other labels. Intrigued by the possibilities of changes in human form and psychology presented by genetic engineering and cybernetics, these authors have set science fiction on a new and irreversible course. William GIBSON's *Neuromancer* (1984) is biologically speaking one of the more conservative works in the field. Bruce Sterling's *Schismatrix* (1985) and Greg BEAR's *Blood Music* (short story,

1983; novel, 1985) and *Eon* (1985) go to greater extremes. Paul PREUSS's *Human Error* (1985), almost a doppelgänger of *Blood Music,* is as convincing as Bear's novel is expansive. Both begin in high-tech laboratories developing "biochips," computer circuits based on organic molecules. Preuss chose Palo Alto, California, as his setting and called it Protein Valley; Bear chose La Jolla and referred to it as Enzyme Valley. The similarities, considering the independent creation of the two novels, are astonishing.

The revolution that has occurred in science fiction dealing with biology has not been without precedent. Past stories treated most of these ideas and themes; what they could not do until now was provide a rational basis for their execution. Blish's "Surface Tension" and Sturgeon's "Microcosmic God" explored miniature intelligence; *Blood Music* and *Human Error* show how such phenomena might be possible. *Titan, Eon,* and *Schismatrix* rank biology as an equal with physics, astronomy, and sociology; sociobiology becomes a key issue in Sterling's novel.

In the 1970s and 1980s biology came of age in science fiction.

G. Bear

THE BIRDS (1963). *Directed by Alfred Hitchcock; screenplay by Evan Hunter; adapted from the short story by Daphne Du Maurier; photographed by Robert Burks; electronic sound by Remi Gaasman and Oskar Sala. With Rod Taylor, Tippi Hedren, Jessica Tandy, Suzanne Pleshette, Veronica Cartwright. 119 minutes. Color.*

One of the best known of Alfred Hitchcock's thrillers, *The Birds* is not only the prototype for the subsequent cycle of revenge-of-nature horror and science-fiction films but in its ambiguity arguably the most effectively disturbing of the lot. Like the films that followed (*Frogs,* 1972; *Piranha,* 1978; and so on), *The Birds* depicts a horrifying but poetically just revenge scenario in which animals violently turn on human beings.

The Birds expands on Daphne Du Maurier's short story considerably, providing an entirely new narrative. After a flirtatious episode in a San Francisco pet shop, socialite Tippi Hedren follows Rod Taylor to the small seaside town where his family lives, bringing with her a pair of caged lovebirds. Her arrival coincides with the beginning of a series of attacks on people by common birds, attacks that grow increasingly extensive and violent. They culminate in the fiery destruction of the town's main street, followed by a siege on the protagonists in their family home. The film ends with the suggestion, as Hedren and the family are forced to flee, that this strange bird behavior is spreading to other places.

Strictly speaking *The Birds* is not a work of science fiction; it offers no clear explanation, scientific or otherwise, for its premise. For example, there is no indication, as there is in many of the similar movies to follow, that the creatures' aggression is a result of environmental pollution. Nor is there any evidence of scientific tampering with nature. In fact Hitchcock carefully included a scene in a diner in which he offered a number of conflicting "explanations," from the apocalyptic vision of the religious crackpot to an ornithologist's categorical denial of the bird attacks as a scientific impossibility.

The film clearly, however, deals with themes and imagery that have been consistently important throughout Hitchcock's career. Bird metaphors appeared in Hitchcock's films at least as early as *Blackmail* (1929), and they became a major motif in *Psycho* (1960). Thematically the bird attacks are a concrete representation of Hitchcock's concern with the violence that lurks beneath the seemingly calm surface of social and psychological appearances. Indeed it could be argued, as a number of critics have convincingly done, that the bird attacks are, as in so many horror films, a metaphor for the subconscious desires of the characters, a graphic embodiment of Freud's notion of "the return of the repressed." The theme of repression is emphasized throughout this film by a visual motif of cages, from the opening scene in the San Francisco pet shop to the final assault by the birds, during which the family house is transformed into a cage for its human inhabitants.

Yet while *The Birds* is certainly central to Hitchcock's personal vision, its success as a wholly integrated work is questionable. Its special effects, by Lawrence A. Hampton and Ub Iwerks, are not entirely convincing, and some of the narrative seems irrelevant. But the film does contain some sequences that are among the director's best: the massing of the birds in a school playground as the children obliviously sing a song, for example, and the final assault by the birds on the now boarded house demonstrate Hitchcock's genius for visual drama. What makes *The Birds* a classic of its kind is its undeniably disturbing power, rooted in its ambiguity, its refusal to offer explanations. This strategy is perfectly embodied in the film's final shot: as the protagonists drive away in the light of dawn, are they headed toward a new day of mutual emotional support, or are they pointlessly fleeing the birds, who have now taken over the foreground of the image? As the houselights come up, the viewer is inevitably troubled by this unresolved conclusion.

B.K.G.

BISCHOFF, DAVID F[REDERICK] (1951–).

American writer of adventure science fiction, who is at his best when he deals with action plots filled with exotic aliens and high technology. Bischoff's most widely read novels have been collaborations, including *The Seeker* (1976) with Christopher Lampton, *Forbidden World* (1979) with Ted WHITE, and *Day of the Dragonstar*

(1983) and *Night of the Dragonstar* (1985) with Thomas F. MONTELEONE. In all these novels the heroes tend to be larger than life, and the action is fast paced enough to hold the attention of any reader who enjoys this kind of SF. *Tin Woodman* (1979), a novel written with Dennis R. Bailey, is the best of Bischoff's collaborations. Reminiscent of Charles Bernard Nordoff and James Norman Hall's *Mutiny on the Bounty, Tin Woodman* presents a telepathic young man trying to save aliens from the clutches of the psychopathic leader of a contact expedition.

Bischoff has written a number of novels on his own, including *Mandala* (1983), a story about a galactic general who undergoes a transformation, and a novelization of the screenplay *War Games* (1983). He has also written the Nightworld series (*Nightworld*, 1979, and *The Vampires of Nightworld*, 1981), a combination of suspense and humor about computers, androids, and the supernatural. The same good humor can be found in *Star Fall* (1980) and its sequel, *Star Spring* (1982), in which the future "beautiful" and not-so-beautiful people cope with intergalactic intrigue and murder.

NOTABLE OTHER WORKS: *Wraith Board* (1985, with Thomas F. Monteleone); *The Macrocosmic Conflict* (1985).

S.H.G.

BISHOP, MICHAEL (1945–). American

writer, considered one of the finest authors of "literary" science fiction. In satiric short stories like "Rogue Tomato" (1975), in which a character finds himself in outer space in the form of a tomato as big as Mars, Bishop presents celestial phenomena obeying actual physical laws while he pays tribute to Philip K. DICK, Franz Kafka, Arthur C. CLARKE, Kurt VONNEGUT, Jr., and the theology of transcendence. He excels in showing characters realistically responding to worlds that feature radical dislocations. For example, in his Nebula Award–winning story "The Quickening" (1980), humanity awakens one morning to find everything rearranged: the hero, Lawson, had fallen asleep in the United States, but he awakens in Spain. In the world Bishop describes people must adjust themselves to the possibility that such a rearrangement might happen again and again. Bishop traces the consequence of that great dislocation in believable detail by following Lawson's growing awareness of the superficiality of his earlier, typically American values.

In delineating character or using science, Bishop takes no shortcuts. Even in his first novel, *A Funeral for the Eyes of Fire* (1975; revised as *Eyes of Fire*, 1980), Bishop's concern for accuracy in detail is obvious. Although the plot is the stuff of space opera, the passages concerning alien culture and the protagonist's progress in self-understanding make the novel an exceptional first effort. Both *And Strange at Ecbatan the Trees* (1976;

Michael Bishop

A Little Knowledge (1977) and Catacomb Years (1979), describe a complacent world ruled by a theocracy. However, its inhabitants are shaken by the appearance of aliens who profess faith in the doctrine of the ruling church. The entire social and political order is threatened, and ultimately humanity is forced to examine its values and mode of life.

Bishop writes ambitious fiction with intricate plots and equally complex themes. With a master's degree in English from the University of Georgia and experience as an instructor there and elsewhere, he also displays great care in his use of language and style, sometimes challenging the reader's skill and patience in a genre characterized by plain stories plainly told. At his best, he creates stories that speak to both the hearts and the minds of his readers.

OTHER WORKS: Transfigurations (1980); Under Heaven's Bridge (with Ian Watson, 1982); Blooded on Arachne (collection, 1982); One Winter in Eden (collection, 1982); Who Made Stevie Crye? (1984).

S.H.G.

retitled Beneath the Shattered Moons, 1977) and Stolen Faces (1977) show strengths in creating alien worlds with a lushness and variety worthy of Jack VANCE and the later Robert SILVERBERG. Yet each of the worlds is unique: Bishop does not repeat himself. In the first an alien race must deal with the consequences of genetic engineering, which has created a harmonious society by propagating two castes completely dependent on each other. The second is a dark novel about a society whose only method of expression is self-mutilation.

In 1983 Bishop won a second Nebula Award for his novel No Enemy But Time (1982). The book describes John Monegal, a young black given away by his prostitute mother who has the power to dream of the Pleistocene age. A specialist in this period recruits him to travel back in time, where he finds everything as he had dreamed it. Monegal falls in love with one of the habiline inhabitants of the period and has a daughter by her before she dies. What distinguishes No Enemy But Time from most SF works is its depth of characterization. The dilemma of a person caught out of time, nurtured by one age but called by another, is believable and poignant.

In a more humorous vein Bishop turned the tables in Ancient of Days (1985), in which a Pleistocene man lives in a small southern town. When the wife of a local citizen moves in with him, the consequences afford Bishop the opportunity to score some telling points about contemporary American society.

Bishop has also written a series of short stories and two novels set in NUAtlanta, the domed city of Atlanta in the last third of the twenty-first century. The novels,

BIXBY, JEROME (1923–   ).   American writer, editor, and screenwriter. Bixby, who has also written under the pseudonyms Jay B. Drexel, Alger Rome, and Harry Neal, is best known for his famous story "It's a Good Life" (1953), which was voted into the Hall of Fame by the SCIENCE FICTION WRITERS OF AMERICA and dramatized on TWILIGHT ZONE and in Twilight Zone: The Movie.

Bixby has had numerous careers, including the editing of Planet Stories and other pulp magazines in the early 1950s, the writing of some three hundred science-fiction and fantasy stories and about 1000 other stories, a screenwriting career that includes four STAR TREK episodes and numerous other screenplays, real-estate development, and music composition. He has published a collection of SF, Space by the Tale (1964), and a collection of horror and fantasy stories, The Devil's Scrapbook (1964).

Bixby's SF is at its best where scientific projections meet morality and the whole can be flavored with irony or gentle satire. "It's a Good Life" is a prototype for stories about omnipotence, particularly accidental omnipotence, as when chance confers godhood on some passerby. In this story Anthony is born with extraordinary and horrible psychic powers that enable him to punish terribly or even wish out of existence anyone who thinks negative thoughts. In a small mid-American town people live in terror even of thinking anything but happy thoughts lest the amoral, capricious child destroy them. Here and in the more gently ironic touches of his other stories, Bixby demonstrates a craftsman's ability to comment on the human situation.

P.B.

THE BLACK HOLE (1979).

Directed by Gary Nelson; screenplay by Jeb Rosebrook and Gerry Day; photographed by Frank Phillips; music by John Barry. With Maximilian Schell, Anthony Perkins, Robert Forster, Joseph Bottoms, Yvette Mimieux, Ernest Borgnine, Roddy McDowall. 97 minutes. Color.

The crew of a deep-space research vessel, the *Palomino*, is returning from an expedition searching for extraterrestrial life. Discovering a black hole, they also locate the U.S.S. *Cygnus*, a ship that vanished twenty years earlier. Dr. Hans Reinhardt, commander of the *Cygnus* and the archetypal mad scientist, has transformed his previous crew into humanoid robots and intends to travel through the black hole to a new universe. During an asteroid storm and subsequent fighting, Reinhardt, his ship, and his robots are destroyed. The two robots, V.I.N.CENT and Maximilian, like cowboys of the old West, face each other in a laser-fire duel. The crew of the *Palomino*, safely aboard the *Cygnus*'s probe ship, discover they have no choice but to travel through the black hole. The film ends with the implication that they survive the journey and enter the new universe.

Deservingly praised for the technical merit of its special effects, *The Black Hole* was the Disney Studios' entry in the competition of space adventure films of the late 1970s. This ambitious production—the most expensive ever created by the studio—was also Disney's first PG-rated film. The technical staff, headed by Peter Ellenshaw and Art Cruickshank, reaffirmed Disney's preeminence in the special effects category.

The robots, also impressively designed, steal the show from the living actors. The likable and anthropomorphic V.I.N.CENT plays a role originated by FORBIDDEN PLANET's Robby and expanded by STAR WARS' R2-D2 and C-3PO. In opposition, the superrobot, Maximilian, is sinister, inhuman, and seemingly indestructible, like Arnold Schwarzenegger's robot in THE TERMINATOR. In the involuntary transformation of crew members into cyborgs, the film presents a terrifying picture of individual dehumanization, but the sheer visual power of its space vistas has already prepared the viewer to perceive humans as somewhat diminutive props on the galactic stage.

M.T.W.

THE BLACK SCORPION (1957).

Directed by Edward Ludwig; screenplay by David Duncan and Robert Blees; photographed by Lionel Lindon; music by Paul Sawtell. With Richard Denning, Mara Corday, Carlos Rivas, Mario Novarro, Carlos Muzquiz. 86 minutes. Black and white.

Essentially a remake of THEM! (1954) with a change of arthropods, *The Black Scorpion* involves colossal scorpions released by a volcano in Mexico. The biggest scorpion of them all kills its rival arachnids, charges into Mexico City, and is brought to its death in a bullring by an electrical harpoon.

Its photography is too dark, its acting is uninteresting, and its dialogue is no better than ordinary, but *The Black Scorpion* is nonetheless one of the best of the 1950s "big bug" films because of the outstanding animation of the title creatures, by Willis O'BRIEN and Pete Peterson. O'Brien and Peterson not only made the scorpions seem alive but gave them a sinister aura. A descent into the scorpions' lair has much of the same visual quality as KING KONG. A minor film by most standards, *The Black Scorpion* has been given lasting interest by the special effects alone.

B.W.

BLADE RUNNER (1982).

Directed by Ridley Scott; screenplay by Hampton Fancher and David Peoples; adapted from the novel Do Androids Dream of Electric Sheep? *by Philip K. Dick; photographed by Jordan Cronenweth; music by Vangelis. With Harrison Ford, Sean Young, Rutger Hauer, Edward James Olmos, William Sanderson, Daryl Hannah, Brion James, Joanna Cassidy, Joseph Turkel. 118 minutes. Color.*

In Los Angeles, 2019, weary, retired Deckard (the "Blade Runner" of the title, played by Harrison Ford) has to hunt several "replicants"—androids—who have illegally returned to an overcrowded Earth. In true private-eye fashion Deckard not only traces and kills the replicants one by one but falls in love with Rachael (Sean Young), a replicant herself. Inevitably Deckard comes to recognize the replicants' essential humanity; his confrontation with Roy Batty (Rutger Hauer), the last of the androids, is at once frightening and moving.

There have been few films of any nature as visually stunning as *Blade Runner*, and Ridley Scott's professed hope was to become with it "the John Ford of science-fiction movies." He never quite achieved that goal, however, in part because *Blade Runner* is occasionally confusing; the hopeful ending disappointed many and is not in keeping with the films noir on which it is modeled. Many viewers also objected to Ford's laconic voice-over narration, added just before the film was released. But his performance is generally fine; Young is precisely correct visually; and Hauer is impressive as the sardonic Batty.

Like 2001: A SPACE ODYSSEY (1968), *Blade Runner* is a film whose reputation continues to increase. Although a failure in theatrical release, *Blade Runner* now seems to have found its audience, and it may well come to be regarded as a masterpiece of science-fiction film. Dedicated to Philip K. DICK, who died shortly before its release, it won the Hugo in 1983.

B.W.

BLEILER, EVERETT F[RANKLIN] (1920–   ):

American editor, bibliographer, and literary scholar, one of the leading experts on speculative—and particularly supernatural—fiction. Bleiler produced the first significant bibliography in the field, *The Checklist of Fantastic Literature* (1948). With T. E. Dikty he edited the first of the best of the year anthology series, *The Best Science Fiction Stories* (1949–1954) and later *The Year's Best Science Fiction Novels* (1952–1954). As editor of Dover Books in the 1960s, he was responsible for important reprints of Victorian and Edwardian supernatural fiction, both anthologies and books by individual authors, among them Robert W. Chambers, Lord Dunsany, and Oliver Onions. The introductions to these volumes are superb. Recently Bleiler has written or compiled several of the best reference works in the field, including *Science Fiction Writers* (1982), *The Guide to Supernatural Fiction* (1983), and the massive *Supernatural Fiction Writers* (1985).

OTHER WORKS: (As editor) *The Castle of Otranto, by Horace Walpole; Vathek, by William Beckford; The Vampyre, by John Polidori; and A Fragment of a Novel by Lord Byron; Three Gothic Novels* (1966); *Five Victorian Ghost Novels* (1971); *A Treasury of Victorian Ghost Stories* (1981). (As editor, with T. E. Dikty) *Imagination Unlimited* (1952).

D.S.

BLISH, JAMES [BENJAMIN] (1921–1975).

American writer whose early career in science fiction followed a typical path from fandom (as a member of the FUTURIANS in the 1930s) through collaborations with other fans on a number of short stories to publication of his first piece ("Emergency Refueling," 1940) in one of the lesser-known pulp magazines.

Blish soon established himself as an unconventional SF writer; with the publication of the first Okie stories, insightful readers realized that Blish was using SF material to explore serious philosophical questions. The Okie tales became part of the stories, novellas, and novels that made up the four books later collected as *Cities in Flight* (1970). Although their setting—cities that have been lifted off the Earth and wander the stars under the power of antigravity devices called spindizzies—was itself original and fascinating, the themes remain the centerpiece of each work. All four books (*Earthman, Come Home*, 1955; *They Shall Have Stars*, 1956; *The Triumph of Time*, 1958; *A Life for the Stars*, 1962) deal with the tensions of a race dependent on technology yet nostalgic for the past, between moral conduct and practical behavior, and between longevity and the need for renewal. *Cities in Flight* is also enriched with the minutiae of future life. Government, education, business, and even family life receive detailed attention rare for science fiction in the 1950s.

Blish was never satisfied with writing mere adventure SF. Through his works he examined such issues as the characteristics that define the human race. "Surface Tension" (1952), for example, depicts microscopic underwater human beings created from the cells of doomed humans stranded on an unknown world. Although their transformation has drastically changed how these new "Earthmen" live, their desire to learn and master their environment separates them from the other life-forms around them. "Surface Tension" and similar stories about human adaptations were collected in *Seedling Stars* (1957); in each of these works Blish used his training in microbiology to investigate the delicate balance between body and mind that seems to distinguish the human species.

Such investigations also led Blish to more abstract issues. His best-known work, *A Case of Conscience* (1958), deals with the eternal question of good and evil. As part of the After Such Knowledge trilogy (*Doctor Mirabilis*, 1964; *Black Easter*, 1968; and *The Day after Judgment*, 1970—Blish considered the last two a single novel), *A Case of Conscience* examines the moral consequences of seeking knowledge, questioning even that most human of acts. Shifting point of view from character to character, Blish illustrated a wide range of human attitudes toward both knowledge and faith.

Blish was also a scholar and critic of science fiction, as well as of the works of James Joyce and Ezra Pound. Writing under the pseudonym William Atheling, Jr. (*The Issue at Hand*, 1964, and *More Issues at Hand*, 1970) and under his own name in another series of articles, he impatiently criticized much that was being published, arguing that too many writers settled for superficial work that simply rehashed old patterns in trivial ways. He also lobbied for more careful attention to the craft of writing and for more deliberate use of intelligent themes. Blish doubted that SF would ever produce a new literary masterpiece, but that doubt did not stop him from making extraordinary demands on his own writing and applying high standards to the works of others.

Ironically, during this same period he was also producing novelizations of STAR TREK scripts. He wrote twelve such works (not counting the original novel *Spock Must Die*, 1970, but including volume 12 of the series, which was completed by his widow, Judith A. Lawrence) and claimed to have enjoyed doing them not only because of the money he earned but also because of the enthusiastic response they received from young readers.

Blish gave much to science fiction, including his encouragement of new writers through the Milford SF Writers Conference, which he helped found. As a writer and critic, he added a new depth to the genre that others continue to explore and expand. Most important, his own work remains as an example of how far SF is capable of going when concern for art and intellect propels it.

OTHER WORKS: *Jack of Eagles* (1952, retitled *Esper*, 1958); *The Warriors of Day* (1953); *VOR* (1958); *The Duplicated Man* (with Robert Lowndes, 1959); Galactic Cluster (collection, 1959); *The Star Dwellers* (1961); *Titan's Daughters* (1961); *So Close to Home* (collection, 1961); *Mission to the Heart Stars* (1965); *Best Science Fiction Stories of James Blish* (collection, 1965; revised, 1973; British title *The Testament of Andros*, 1977); *A Torrent of Faces* (with Norman L. Knight, 1967); *Welcome to Mars* (1967); *The Vanished Jet* (1968); *. . . And All the Stars a Stage* (1971); *Anywhen* (collection, 1971); *Midsummer Century* (1972); *The Quincunx of Time* (1975); *The Best of James Blish* (collection, 1979).

S.H.G.

THE BLOB (1958). *Directed by Irvin S. Yeaworth, Jr.; screenplay by Theodore Simonson and Kate Phillips; photographed by Thomas Spalding; music by Jean Yeaworth. With Steve McQueen, Aneta Corseault, Earl Rowe, Olin Howlin. 85 minutes. Black and white.*

Because of its novel depiction of an alien life-form (although a similar idea was used later in the year in Inoshira Honda's *The H-Man*), *The Blob* rises (or rather slithers) above the conventional space-monster movie. An amoebic glob of cosmic protoplasm grows steadily larger as it absorbs human beings, clothes and all. Putting teenagers in the standard role of witnesses whom no one believes, the film adds an extra level of interest by cleverly exploiting the alienated-youth films that had been popularized by James Dean a few years earlier. Steve McQueen appears in his first role as the clean-cut teenage hero. The best scene, perhaps suggesting a bit of self-conscious humor, shows the eponymous blob entering the local cinema through an air vent like Jell-O through a meat grinder as panicking film patrons flee in all directions. And while THE CREATURE FROM THE BLACK LAGOON (1954) was immortalized as a plastic model by Revell, the blob has the distinction of being the only nonanthropomorphic creature to have inspired a top-forty pop song (written for the film by Burt Bacharach!).

B.K.G.

BLOCH, ROBERT (1917–   ). American writer of short fiction, novels, and screenplays. Bloch is better known for fantasy, horror, and mystery than for science fiction, but he has been a prominent figure in SF fan circles. A frequent contributor of articles and letters to fan magazines, he has often served as toastmaster at World SF conventions, where he is noted for his dry wit and wry delivery. His best-known early fan writings were published for the 1962 World convention as *The Eighth State of Fandom.*

An early admirer of and correspondent with H. P. LOVECRAFT and a member of the Milwaukee group of SF writers that included Stanley G. WEINBAUM, Bloch has done much of his best-known work in the horror field, most notably "Yours Truly, Jack the Ripper" (1943) and *Psycho* (1959), whose purchase by Alfred Hitchcock persuaded Bloch to move to Los Angeles, so he could be closer to the film industry. He has written hundreds of radio and television scripts and film screenplays.

In his science fiction—consisting almost entirely of short works—Bloch has emphasized social criticism with a particular concern for individuality, paradoxical perception, the outcast, and the existential concept that struggle gives meaning to life. His first major publication was "The Feast in the Abbey" (1935) in *Weird Tales*. Since then he has written twenty-one novels and more than 400 stories, including "The Hell-Bound Train" (1958), which won a Hugo (although it was more fantasy than science fiction). A number of Bloch's SF short stories have been collected in *Atoms and Evil* (1962) and *Lost in Time and Space with Lefty Feep* (1987).

H.L.P.

BLUE THUNDER (1983). *Directed by John Badham; screenplay by Dan O'Bannon and Dan Jakoby; photographed by John A. Alonzo; music by Arthur B. Rubinstein. With Roy Scheider, Warren Oates, Candy Clark, Malcolm McDowell. 110 minutes. Color.*

The near future paranoid science-fiction film began with *Seven Days in May* (1964) and ended with *Blue Thunder*. Malcolm McDowell plays a sadistic colonel attempting a military takeover of the United States; all that stands in his way is heroic lieutenant Roy Scheider and *Blue Thunder*, a helicopter with more gadgets than one of James Bond's sports cars. Politics is sublimated in favor of gadgetry, resulting in a mechanistic shoot-'em-up film. Although *Blue Thunder* spawned a 1984 ABC television series, the series was not SF.

M.M.W.

BOK, HANNES (1914–1964). American science-fiction and fantasy illustrator. Bok (no one knows his real name; the one he used was a respelling of "Johannes S. Bach") was one of SF's premier stylists and individualists. His insistence on doing work his own way cost him many assignments. Nevertheless, he was a prolific artist, producing covers for Arkham House, Gnome Press, Shasta Press, and Fantasy Press, among others, and creating black-and-white illustrations and covers for such magazines as *Super Science Stories, Planet Stories, Cosmic Stories, Weird Tales, Future Science Fiction, Fantastic Universe*, and *Imagination*. In 1963

Illustration by Bok

Bok shared the very first art Hugo with Ed EMSHWILLER.

Bok was also an author, writing thirteen articles for *Mystic Magazine* (on astrology) as well as a number of short stories. He wrote three novels: *Starstone World* (1942), *The Sorcerer's Ship* (1942), and *The Blue Flamingo* (1948). An admirer of A. MERRITT's work, he finished and illustrated two of Merritt's books, *The Black Wheel* (1947) and *The Fox Woman* (1946). After Bok's death, author and friend Emil Petaja helped start the Bokanalia Foundation (1967), which has published some of Bok's poetry, several art portfolios, and Petaja's *And Flights of Angels: The Life and Legend of Hannes Bok* (1968).

J.G.

BOND, NELSON S[LADE] (1908–   ). American author; a polished stylist whose fantastic short stories appeared not only in the science-fiction pulps but also in such prestigious publications as *Bluebook* and *Scribner's*. Bond's best work consists of ironic fantasies reminiscent of the work of John Collier.

Although some of Bond's work appeared in John W. Campbell's *Astounding* and *Unknown,* the bulk was published in the less sophisticated pulps of the early 1940s—*Amazing, Fantastic Adventures, Thrilling Wonder,* and *Planet Stories*—and, albeit well written, these stories seem slight and naive. Somewhat better is the postholocaust series Meg the Priestess (1939–1941). One of its stories, "Magic City" (1941, from *Astounding*), has been repeatedly anthologized.

Bond is nostalgically remembered by fans; but even though he was a better stylist than many of the greats of the 1940s Golden Age, he was a far less interesting thinker. He ceased writing in the early 1950s.

WORKS: *Mr. Mergenthwirker's Lobblies and Other Fantastic Tales* (1946); *The Thirty-first of February* (1949); *Exiles of Time* (1949); *The Remarkable Exploits of Lancelot Biggs, Spaceman* (1950); *No Time Like the Future* (1954); *Nightmares and Daydreams* (1968).

D.S.

BONESTELL, CHESLEY [KNIGHT] (1888– 1986). American astronomical artist, architect, and motion picture matte painter. Bonestell is primarily known for bringing the art of astronomical painting into the public eye; many even credit him (erroneously) with inventing the art form.

Bonestell started working for architectural firms in 1911 and helped design many structures, including the Chrysler Building and the Golden Gate Bridge. In 1938 he began working in Hollywood and produced matte and background paintings for such pictures as *The Hunchback of Notre Dame* (1939), *Swiss Family Robinson* (1940), *Citizen Kane* (1941), *Charley's Aunt* (1941), *The Fountainhead* (1949), DESTINATION MOON (1950), WHEN WORLDS COLLIDE (1951), and THE CONQUEST OF SPACE (1953).

In the early 1940s Bonestell began a series of astronomical paintings that he sold to *Life* magazine in 1944. Over the next dozen years his paintings appeared in *Life, Look, Scientific American, Collier's, Astounding Science Fiction,* and *Fantasy and Science Fiction.* His style was impeccably realistic; he drew on every bit of astronomical knowledge available to create accurate planetary vistas. When the accuracy of his paintings of the Moon, showing sharp peaks and craggy rocks, was contradicted by the Apollo moon landings, he redid several of them.

Bonestell has contributed art to dozens of books. His major works include the classic *Conquest of Space* (with Willy LEY), *Conquest of the Moon, Beyond the Solar System, Mars,* and *The World We Live In.* He has done work for several planetariums, including the Flandreau and Hayden planetariums and the Boston Museum of Science, and he has received many awards for his work, including a Hugo, an International Fantasy Award, the British Interplanetary Society Special Award, a Lensman, and others.

J.G.

BORGES, JORGE LUIS (1899–1986). Argentine author and poet, a major figure in world literature who has had a pervasive influence on the more sophisticated science fiction since the late 1960s. A few of his stories, such as "Utopia of a Tired Man" (1977) and "The Immortals" (1962), are overt SF; many more are fantasies.

Borges specialized in the very short story or prose sketch, often so rich in idea and language as to be more substantial than most novels. Both failing eyesight (which became total blindness) and the poet's instinct encouraged this compression. His imaginative prose could take the form of a short story, pseudoscholarly essay, fable, or even review of an imaginary book. It always resists categorization but is often concerned with strange twistings of reality or metaphysical paradoxes. "The Library of Babel" (1962), for instance, describes the universe in terms of an infinite library of mostly incomprehensible books.

D.S.

BOUCHER, ANTHONY (Pseudonym of William Anthony Parker White) (1911–1968). American writer, critic, and editor. Boucher wrote for John W. Campbell's pulps in the early 1940s; his best stories from the period were reprinted in *Far and Away* (1955) and *The Compleat Werewolf* (1969). He wrote numerous detective novels, including (as H. H. Holmes) *Rocket to the Morgue* (1942), a roman à clef featuring members of the Los Angeles SF community. Under the Holmes pseudonym he also covered science fiction for the *New York Herald Tribune*. Boucher was a founding editor, with J. Francis McComas, of The Magazine of Fantasy and Science Fiction and remained with the magazine until 1958. The emphasis this magazine placed on literary sophistication helped greatly to improve the quality and reputation of SF in the 1950s. Boucher's classic story "The Quest for St. Aquin" (1951) is a key example of theological science fiction. He edited the first eight annual issues of *The Best from Fantasy and Science Fiction* (1952–1959), the first three in collaboration with McComas, and the two-volume anthology *A Treasury of Great Science Fiction* (1959).

B.S.

BOULLE, PIERRE (1912–). French writer with a background in electrical engineering, best known for two novels, both of which were made into successful films: *The Bridge on the River Kwai* (1952, translated into English, 1954) and the science-fiction novel *The Planet of the Apes* (1963, translated 1963; later retitled *Monkey Planet*, 1964). The film Planet of the Apes merely hints at the most notable feature of Boulle's novel: a love of the absurd. Throughout the work Boulle used outrageous situations to score points against human frailty. Thus ape behavior parodies contemporary human society, turning to shambles some of humanity's most cherished prejudices.

Boulle's SF novels are adult fables that use animals and technology to force his readers to reconsider their world in new, often amusing, lights. In *The Good Leviathan* (1979) an oil supertanker possesses the power to heal; in *The Whale of the Victoria Cross* (1983) a whale becomes the hero of the Falklands conflict; and in *Desperate Game* (1973) misdirected scientists try to bring about a golden age by developing dangerous games to interest a population bored with an era of social peace. Unlike many writers of modern fables, however, Boulle rarely preaches, leaving his readers to take the point or to depart no more enlightened than when they started—although the latter possibility would be highly unlikely.

OTHER WORKS: *Garden on the Moon* (1964); *Time out of Mind and Other Stories* (collection, 1966); *Because It Is Absurd* (collection, 1971); *The Marvellous Palace and Other Stories* (collection, 1977).

S.H.G.

BOVA, BEN[JAMIN WILLIAM] (1932–). American author, editor, and science writer. After earning a B.S. from Temple University, Bova served as a newspaper editor, technical editor on the Vanguard Project, screenwriter on a project at MIT, and science writer for Avco-Everett Research Laboratory. His first science-fiction publication was a children's novel, *The Star Conquerors* (1959), and his first story was "A Long Way Back" (Amazing, 1960). He also wrote a series of articles for *Amazing*, but he became best known early for editing Analog (1971–1978) and *Omni* (1978–1982). As the successor to the late John W. Campbell, he is credited with revitalizing *Analog* after a period of sluggishness, and he received five Hugo Awards for editing during his tenure with the magazine.

As editor Bova upheld *Analog*'s reputation as primarily a forum for hard SF, but he also accepted stories from authors who emphasize the sociological and human consequences of science. For instance, Bova published the first story by Frederik Pohl (as a single author) to appear in *Analog*, "The Gold at Starbow's End" (1972), and he encouraged Joe Haldeman to turn his "Hero" (1972) into the Hugo- and Nebula-winning *The Forever War* (1975). Both stories were franker and more realistic than *Analog* readers had been accustomed to. In 1975, partly in response to the flood of unacceptable manuscripts he received at *Analog*, Bova published *Notes to a Science Fiction Writer*, a commonsense handbook of advice to would-be writers.

Bova's earliest SF novels are juveniles filled with action that nevertheless ask serious questions, such as how humanity can grow into the staggering responsibilities it

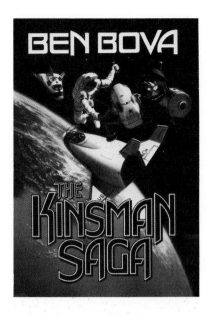

Ben Bova

faces, in *Star Conquerors* and *Star Watchman* (1969), after it has defeated a superior alien race and controls a galactic empire. His Exiles trilogy—*Exiled from Earth* (1971), *Flight of Exiles* (1972), and *End of Exile* (1975)— are also richer fare for young readers than most juveniles.

Bova's adult SF focuses on contemporary problems and humanity's inability, through fear of change and a reliance on emotion over intellect, to solve those problems. In some stories this theme is treated with humor, as in the juvenile *Gremlins, Go Home!* (with Gordon R. DICKSON, 1974) and the novel *The Starcrossed* (1975), based on the circumstances surrounding Harlan ELLISON's ill-fated television series *The Starlost*, for which Bova was listed as technical adviser.

Bova distrusts political, social, and economic institutions because such organizations seek to perpetuate themselves, even when their usefulness is over and they are the problem rather than the means to the solution. In both *The Weathermakers* (1967), another juvenile, and *Voyagers* (1981), the heroes must fight through self-interested bureaucracies that fear science because of the changes it may cause. In the latter the hero succeeds in furthering the space program at the cost of his life.

Bova's most popular character is Chet Kinsman, who was first introduced in a series of short stories collected in *Kinsman* (1979), depicting the adventures of the astronaut-hero. Kinsman's story continues in Bova's best novel, *Millennium* (1976), in which the hero averts the ultimate nuclear confrontation among Earth's governments over the rights to increasingly scarce resources by establishing an independent nation on the Moon and advocating the exploitation of its untapped wealth. Two novels continue the story of *Millennium: Colony* (1978)

confirms Bova's earlier distrust of political institutions as the Moon base remains the center of political struggles; *When the Sky Burned* (1973), though published earlier, describes the destruction of the Earth by a solar flare and the bleak and hostile conditions against which the remaining humans are pitted on the Moon base. Like most of Bova's works, these last two novels focus on humanity's lack of farsightedness. Bova believes that humans are capable of rational decisions that will enable the species to continue, but he also knows that this capability is too often buried in greed, superstition, and laziness.

Bova also is a speaker much in demand on topics such as the colonization of space and the Strategic Defense Initiative, as well as scientific topics in general. He has written two recent books about humanity and weapons in space, *The High Road* (1981) and *Assured Survival: Putting the Star Wars Defense in Perspective* (1984), and some twenty science books, mostly for children, and he has edited more than a dozen books, including the two volumes of novelettes and novellas published as *The SFWA Science Fiction Hall of Fame, Volumes IIA and IIB.*

OTHER WORKS: *Out of the Sun* (juvenile, 1968); *The Dueling Machine* (juvenile, 1969); *Escape* (juvenile, 1970); *THX-1138* (novelization, 1971); *As on a Darkling Plain* (1972); *The Shining Strangers* (juvenile, 1973); *The Winds of Altair* (juvenile, 1973); *Forward in Time* (collection, 1973); *City of Darkness* (juvenile, 1976); *The Multiple Man* (1976); *Maxwell's Demons* (collection, 1979); *The Test of Fire* (1982); *Orion* (1984); *Escape Plus Ten* (collection, 1984); *Privateers* (1985); *Prometheans* (collection, 1986); *Battle Station* (1987).

S.H.G.

A BOY AND HIS DOG (1975).

Directed by L. Q. Jones; screenplay by L. Q. Jones; adapted from the novella by Harlan Ellison; photographed by John Arthur Morril; music by Tim McIntire. With Don Johnson, Susanne Benton, Jason Robards, Alvy Moore, Tiger as Blood, the dog, and Tim McIntire as the voice of Blood. 89 minutes. Color.

This film presents a dystopian scenario of a posthollocaust world—akin to that of *The Road Warrior*—where bands of survivors roam over a wasteland. The imperative is survival in a violent, misogynistic society. In the year 2024 a youth travels with an intelligent, telepathic dog, whose observations on human behavior provide both insight and comic relief. When the boy must choose the survival of a girl or of the dog, he kills the girl to feed the dog. The macabre humor is pure Harlan ELLISON, as are the kinky sexual overtones.

The dog, Blood, is neither a cartoon nor a vehicle for satire but a major character, convincing in his communication and his close relationship with the boy. When the biologically driven youth meets the nubile girl, who lures him to the regimented underworld (where the males are becoming sterile), it is Blood who warns him against the entrapment. And indeed love (or at the very least friendship) triumphs in the end, as the young man's trust in Blood effectively saves his life.

M.T.W.

BOYD, JOHN (Professional name of Boyd Bradfield Upchurch) (1919–).

American science-fiction writer who began publishing SF when he was almost fifty. Boyd wrote several novels and a few short stories in the decade that followed. His first SF work, *The Last Starship from Earth* (1968), is unquestionably his best, but several other novels, most notably *The Pollinators of Eden* (1969) and *The Rakehells of Heaven* (1969), were enjoyed by readers who had found in Boyd's first novel a fine sense of plotting, some acerbic comments on contemporary society, and many witty and erudite literary allusions.

Born in Augusta, Georgia, Boyd moved to southern California, after service in World War II; he sold photoengraving equipment for twenty-five years before trying his hand at writing. Under his real name he published *The Slave Stealer* (1968), a historical novel based on an old family legend. He turned to SF in large part because the genre allowed him to satirize contemporary trends and developments, chief among them Skinnerian behaviorism, which he pilloried in *Last Starship*.

A book that improves with each successive rereading, *Last Starship* is a probability-world novel with an alternate West Coast setting that is just familiar enough to be outrageously funny. The pope is a computer on Mt. Wilson; Lincoln has delivered the Johannesburg Address; Henry VIII is a leading sociologist who was a student of John Dewey; and the hero, Haldane IV (the Roman numeral indicates a hereditary, rigidly stratified hierarchical society), is a mathematician at the Berkeley campus of the University of California, where he commits "treason" by falling in love with a poet and is consequently condemned to a peculiarly dismal prison planet named Hell.

Boyd pleads, in almost all of his novels and in a variety of conventional SF settings and situations, for true freedom, characterized by independent choice, intelligent commitment, and rational deliberation. This plea is particularly forceful in *Pollinators of Eden* and *Rakehells of Heaven*. Together with *Last Starship* they form a trilogy attacking rigidity in psychology, religion, sociology, and various hard sciences. His later works reveal flashes of the brilliance that marked his first books, and all are distinguished by his ability to tell an entertaining story.

OTHER WORKS: *Sex and the High Command* (1970); *The Organ Bank Farm* (1970); *The Gorgon Festival* (1972); *The I.Q. Merchant* (1972); *The Doomsday Gene* (1973); *Andromeda Gun* (1974); *Barnard's Planet* (1975); *The Girl with the Jade Green Eyes* (1979).

W.E.M.

THE BOYS FROM BRAZIL (1978).

Directed by Franklin J. Schaffner; screenplay by Heywood Gould; adapted from the novel by Ira Levin; photographed by Henri Decaë; music by Jerry Goldsmith. With Laurence Olivier, Gregory Peck, James Mason, Lilli Palmer, Uta Hagen, Denholm Elliott, Rosemary Harris, John Dehner, Jeremy Black, Michael Gough, Bruno Ganz, Wolfgang Preiss, Anne Meara. 125 minutes. Color.

An elderly Jewish Nazi hunter (Laurence Olivier) slowly learns the truth about a series of strange murders: Dr. Mengele (Gregory Peck) has cloned Hitler and is trying to duplicate the key events from Hitler's life in the lives of the little Adolfs (all played by young Jeremy Black). The climax is an amusingly wheezy battle between the old Jew and the old Nazi, thwarted by none other than one of the little Hitlers, who finds Mengele "weird."

Despite the absurd premise of the novel on which this film is based, Franklin J. Schaffner and Heywood Gould created an entertaining comic-book yarn, helped by the quirky, well-observed performance of Olivier and the surprisingly effective one by Peck, cast *way* against type. Many good character actors also turn up in *The Boys from Brazil*.

B.W.

BRACKETT, LEIGH (1915–1978).

American author of science fiction, mysteries, and screenplays, best known for her contributions to action and adventure science fiction of the 1940s. A native of Los Angeles, Brackett began publishing SF in 1940, and in the early years of her career her work appeared frequently in the pages of the adventure pulp *Planet Stories.*

During her apprentice years, she was hired to assist none other than William Faulkner with the screenplay for the film adaptation of Raymond Chandler's classic private detective novel, *The Big Sleep.* The resulting film (1946), which starred Humphrey Bogart and Lauren Bacall, inaugurated for Brackett a long career of occasional screenwriting, especially in association with Howard Hawks, the director of *The Big Sleep.* Brackett's later screenplays for Hawks and John Wayne included *Hatari* (1962), *El Dorado* (1967), and *Rio Lobo* (1970), but most critics and film scholars agree that the finest product of their professional association was Brackett's script for the classic western *Rio Bravo* (1959). In this film the tarnished but plucky lady gambler, Feathers (Angie Dickinson), is a portrait of a characteristic Brackett heroine, and her wisecracking, ambivalent relationship with John T. Chance (Wayne) embodies a romantic conflict central to most of Hawks's best films. Such motifs are also vintage Brackett.

Brackett's early SF is highly romantic, depicting saturnine heroes on perilous worlds. Following SF conventions of the 1930s and earlier, Brackett envisioned Venus as a sinister, lush, neotropical paradise, somewhat in the mode of Edgar Rice BURROUGHS and Otis Adelbert Kline; her Mars is a variation on the mythic planet imagined by SF writers from Burroughs to Ray BRADBURY—a doomed desert planet haunted by ruins of its ancient civilizations and past glories. The ultimate embodiment of this Martian myth is Brackett's novel *The Sword of Rhiannon* (1953), in which both the ravaged and desolate Martian present and its glorious past are evoked in an adventure climaxed by the reappearance of the ancient Martian god Rhiannon and his victory over archaic enemies.

Jade Greene, of the early prototypical novella "The Halfling" (1943), is a characteristic Brackett hero: the cynical manager of an interplanetary carnival, he is erotically obsessed by a cat-woman, the "halfling" of the title. During this early period, Brackett created the most memorable and durable of her heroes, the disenchanted but indomitable Eric John Stark. Brackett's heroines are equally tough-minded and resourceful, capable of using weapons and holding their own in a fight. Princess Yvain of *The Sword of Rhiannon,* the archetypal Brackett heroine, is willing to abandon her ancient Martian world of oceans and sea kings to return to the desolate Martian present with her terrestrial lover.

In the 1950s Brackett and her husband, SF writer Edmond HAMILTON, began to spend part of their time in rural Ohio; with the market for pulp SF declining, her career entered a new phase. *The Long Tomorrow* (1955), a more realistic novel than her earlier works and by many

accounts her best, describes a pastoral and agrarian postdisaster America; the drama in the novel arises from the conflict between such a world and the gradual impact of technological change.

In her final period Brackett resurrected Eric John Stark, in a trilogy that returned to the romantic vision of her early SF (*The Ginger Star,* 1974; *The Hounds of Skaith,* 1974; *The Reavers of Skaith,* 1976).

During this time she worked on what was regrettably her final film project, an early draft of the screenplay for THE EMPIRE STRIKES BACK (1980) for George LUCAS and Steven SPIELBERG. It is perhaps no accident that this film, directed by Spielberg, is the most highly regarded of the three Star Wars adventures, for the romance between Han Solo and Princess Leia depicted there suggests the unmistakable Brackett touch.

Throughout her career Brackett managed to succeed in a male-dominated genre primarily by adapting her talent to the formulas and conventions of masculine adventure fiction. An excellent stylist, Brackett was more articulate than Burroughs and Hamilton, more restrained than her contemporary C. L. MOORE, and her work is easily as readable as that of most of her successors.

OTHER WORKS: *The Starmen of Llyrdis* (1952); *The Big Jump* (1955); *The Nemesis from Terra* (1961); *Alpha Centauri or Die* (1963); *The Secret of Sinharat* (1964); *People of the Talisman* (1964); *The Coming of the Terrans* (1967); *The Halfling and Other Stories* (collection, 1973); *The Best of Leigh Brackett* (collection, 1977).

E.L.C.

BRADBURY, RAY [DOUGLAS] (1920–   ).

American writer, playwright, poet, and screenwriter. Possibly the best-known personage in contemporary science fiction and fantasy, Bradbury has enchanted millions of readers and viewers for more than forty years with his short stories, novels, plays, TV and motion picture scripts, and poems. As the token SF writer included in dozens of short story textbooks and anthologies, he came to represent SF to the nongenre reader, although in the past decade or so he has shared this burden with Ursula K. LE GUIN. Traditional critics have generally praised nongenre characteristics of his work, such as his poetic style and metaphoric imagery, but both Bradbury and Le Guin have been honored and held in high regard by their colleagues in the field as well.

Bradbury's early achievements represented the first break out of SF's self-imposed ghetto. They were distinguished most of all by his intense, clean-limbed prose, which proved that fine writing could be found in the pulp medium. Moved by his parents from Waukegan, Illinois, to Arizona and then to Los Angeles, Bradbury achieved success slowly, working as a newsboy in Los Angeles while writing dozens of stories before he started selling for a penny a word to magazines such as *Super Science Stories* and *Planet Stories*. By 1945 his stories began appearing in *American Mercury* and Martha Foley's *Best Short Stories*, and by the following year in *Collier's, Mademoiselle,* and *O'Henry's Memorial Award Stories.*

His "discovery" by such literary critics as Gilbert Highet, Christopher Isherwood, and Aldous HUXLEY may have been as important to his growing reputation as the publication of his Mars stories as *The Martian Chronicles* (1950). This book, seldom if ever out of print since, has identified his name as closely with Mars as that of Edgar Rice BURROUGHS, a boyhood influence. Both authors' versions of Mars are equally imaginary, but few readers cared. About the same time Bradbury was publishing *Chronicles* and *The Illustrated Man* (1951) he wrote the screenplay for IT CAME FROM OUTER SPACE (1952), and three years later he wrote the script for John Huston's *Moby Dick,* an epic adventure he is recalling in a book entitled "The Whale, the Whim, and I." More scriptwriting projects followed.

A prolific writer in his early years (though not so later), Bradbury specialized in the short story (he has written only four true novels, one of them a murder mystery). Ideas for stories—"The Pedestrian," about a near future in which everybody rides and a man who gets arrested for taking a walk, is typical—would seize him, and he would produce a finished manuscript in one creative burst. His novel-length works were mostly cobbled together from short stories.

A number of themes recur in his writing; his own love of books, for instance, combined with his hatred for censorship to produce perhaps his best single novel, *Fahrenheit 451* (1953). (The temperature, incidentally, is supposedly the point at which paper ignites.) Here his belief in freedom to read, to speak, and to think found memorable expression. If the love of a man and a woman is worth commemorating, Bradbury has said, so also is the love of a man or woman for an idea, a concept that lies at the heart of SF, which has often been described as a literature of ideas rather than of memorable characters. The greatness of *Fahrenheit 451* rests on Bradbury's ability to involve the reader in hero Guy Montag's slow struggle toward awareness as he moves from "fireman" (book burner) to rebellious book preserver and memorizer. François Truffaut's 1979 film version (see FAHRENHEIT 451) was notable not only for its cinematography but for catching Bradbury's spirit exactly, as the author himself has commented.

Another frequent Bradbury theme is space: his view includes the physical shape of a spaceship as well as that of the whale he celebrated in his script for *Moby Dick* and his unpublished play "Leviathan 99," also based on Melville's novel. In Bradbury's vision space is a new version of the American West, an expansion of historian Frederick Jackson Turner's thesis (quoted ap-

Ray Bradbury

provingly by Bradbury) that the nature and existence of the frontier has been the distinctive characteristic of American life.

The notion of the frontier makes its appearance in many of Bradbury's short stories and the novels assembled from them. In *The Illustrated Man* as well as *The Martian Chronicles,* he established a frontier setting to permit his exploration of reality, hallucination, fantasy, the imagination, time, eternity, or past and present. His command of language, his emphasis on the inexhaustibility of space, and his nostalgia for a past that never was caught the imagination of his readers.

Bradbury's longtime love for the stage led him to turn his novel *Dandelion Wine* (1957) into a play in 1972. This charming little work is still often produced by both amateur and professional theater groups. A stage version of *The Martian Chronicles* ran for months in Los Angeles and there was a (disappointing) network television miniseries in 1980. His recent cable television series, *Ray Bradbury Theater,* represents still another of the author's many involvements with drama. In recent years he has been working on an opera adapted from his play "Leviathan 99" as well as a musical version of *Fahrenheit 451.* He also has published considerable poetry, collected in *The Complete Poems of Ray Bradbury* (1982).

As a Public Personage, Bradbury has also become a charismatic lecturer—in turn witty, informed, charming, and erudite, often the spokesman for SF or the artistic community. His early fiction is pessimistic about human behavior—children kill or betray their parents in "The Veldt" (1950), "The Small Assassin" (1946), and "Zero Hour" (1947), for instance, and his Mars explorers throw beer bottles through the glorious windows of Martian castles and litter the Martian canals—but his optimistic vision in person is contagious, and his audiences are convinced, as Bradbury is himself, that humanity can shape the world into anything it wants. In addition Bradbury has often performed with orchestras, narrating such works as Sergey Prokofiev's *Peter and the Wolf* or Camille Saint-Saëns's *Carnival of the Animals.*

Over a period of years he has created a number of myths about himself—that he does not drive a car or ride in an airplane, for example—and in public he so often wore the wonderful ice-cream suit that served as the subject of one of his most famous stories (and subsequent plays) that it virtually became his trademark. Bradbury's intensity and enthusiasm have also helped spread the SF gospel, which he preaches to any audience, any time.

While Bradbury's stories are often set on a rocket ship or Mars, they rarely are hard-core SF. Mostly fantasy or science fantasy, they still embody his optimistic Edenic outlook and trumpet the cry that has become the dominant theme of all SF: humanity must surely master the machine or the machine will master humanity. In the end his is a paradisiacal vision. Mars is heaven, after all.

OTHER WORKS: *Dark Carnival* (collection, 1947); *The Silver Locusts* (collection, 1951); *The Golden Apples of the Sun* (collection, 1953); *The October Country* (collection, 1955); *A Medicine for Melancholy* (collection, 1959); *The Day It Rained Forever* (collection, 1959); *R Is for Rocket* (collection, 1962); *Something Wicked This Way Comes* (1962); *The Anthem Sprinters and Other Antics* (collection, 1963); *The Machineries of Joy* (collection, 1964); *The Vintage Bradbury* (collection, 1965); *The Autumn People* (collection, 1965); *S Is for Space* (collection, 1966); *Tomorrow Midnight* (collection, 1966); *Twice Twenty-two* (collection, 1966); *I Sing the Body Electric* (collection, 1969); *Bloch and Bradbury* (collection, with Robert Bloch, 1969); *Selected Stories* (collection, 1975); *Long after Midnight* (collection, 1976); *The Best of Bradbury* (collection, 1976); *To Sing Strange Songs* (collection, 1979); *The Stories of Ray Bradbury* (collection, 1980); *Dinosaur Tales* (collection, 1983).

W.E.M.

BRADLEY, MARION ZIMMER (1930–).

American writer and editor of science fiction and fantasy. The author of one *New York Times* best-seller, the Arthurian novel *The Mists of Avalon* (1983), Bradley broke into print in 1954 when she sold "Centaurus Changeling" to *The Magazine of Fantasy and Science Fiction.* In the past thirty-two years she has written, coauthored, or edited over sixty books.

Marion Zimmer Bradley

Bradley is best known for her series of books set on the planet Darkover. These works have evolved from sword and sorcery in the science-fictional frame of a Lost Colony in conflict with the Terran Empire to a richly detailed and versatile vehicle for Bradley's storytelling and her interests in feminism, psychology, and occultism. Her first Darkover novel, *The Sword of Aldones,* appeared in 1962 and was a Hugo nominee. It was expanded into *Sharra's Exile* (1981).

Subsequent Darkover novels such as *The Planet Savers* (1962), *The Bloody Sun* (1964), and *Star of Danger* (1966) established many characteristics of what has grown into one of the most influential SF series of the past two decades: the telepathic culture, the violent Darkovan climate, the fragile ecology, the presence of nonhumans, and the opposition of the Comyn, or ruling caste, to the presence of the Terran Empire. With the 1972 publication of *Darkover Landfall,* Bradley began to establish a Darkovan chronology.

Larger, more ambitious novels that deal with major issues have marked Bradley's development in the 1970s and 1980s. *The Heritage of Hastur* (1975), often regarded as one of Bradley's finest books, is an agonizing picture of human relationships set against civil and arcane war. *The Shattered Chain* (1976) explores feminist issues by focusing on the Renunciates, or Free Amazons, first mentioned in *The Planet Savers.* The Amazons have proved to be one of Bradley's most controversial yet beloved creations; their evolution has been described in *Two to Conquer* (1980), a novel condemning rape and imperialism during the Darkovan Ages of Chaos; *Hawkmistress* (1982), also set in that time; *Thendara House*

(1983); and *City of Sorcery* (1984).

This interest in Amazon culture led Bradley to examine alternative life-styles in *The Forbidden Tower* (1977) and in her mainstream novel *The Catch Trap* (1979), praised by the gay community. Fantasy novels such as *Night's Daughter* (1985) and *The Mists of Avalon* also demonstrate her interest in feminism and magic. She is currently planning a novel, *The Firebrand*, describing the siege of Troy from the Amazons' point of view.

Bradley has turned the circle of fans and enthusiasts inspired by her Darkover novels into a highly prolific writers' community that has been compared—somewhat ironically—with the Bloomsbury group. The publication in 1980 of *The Keeper's Price* marked the first anthology of stories by the Friends of Darkover. Two others have since appeared. Additional fan anthologies are *Greyhaven* (1983), *Free Amazons of Darkover* (1985), and the series anthology *Sword and Sorceress*, about to go into its fifth volume. Among the writers who owe early professional sales to Bradley are Diana Paxson, Jennifer Roberson, Paul Edward Zimmer, Juanita COULSON, Susan SHWARTZ, and Pat Mathews.

S.M.S.

THE BRAIN FROM PLANET AROUS (1957).
Directed by Nathan Juran; screenplay by Ray Buffum; photographed by Jacques Marquette; music by Walter Greene. With John Agar, Joyce Meadows, Thomas Browne Henry, Robert Fuller, Tim Graham, Henry Travis, E. Leslie Thomas, Dale Tate. 71 minutes. Black and white.

Like many favorite "awful films," *The Brain from Planet Arous* is fast paced if silly entertainment. A criminal alien brain inhabits scientist John Agar, controlling his actions and threatening the world. He is foiled by a policeman alien brain, which takes over a German shepherd; advised by the good brain, the occasionally undominated Agar hacks the bad brain to death with an ax.

Arous suffers from a very low budget and a penny-dreadful conception of the bad brain's motivations (he enjoys power and sex). The brains themselves, tethered and usually badly superimposed balloons, are also a weakness. But Agar is occasionally effective, director Nathan Juran kept things lively, and the basic idea is loopily imaginative.

B.W.

BRAINSTORM (1983).
Directed by Douglas Trumbull; screenplay by Robert Sittzel and Philip Frank Messina; adapted from the story by Bruce Joel Rubin; photographed by Richard Yuricich; music by James Horner. With Christopher Walken, Natalie Wood, *Louise Fletcher, Cliff Robertson. 106 minutes. Color.*

This was Douglas TRUMBULL's second film as director, after SILENT RUNNING (1971); both fail because of their tone. Almost left uncompleted because of Natalie Wood's death before the shooting was finished, *Brainstorm* is too earnest; Trumbull never lets the viewer forget that his characters are *serious* people involved in *serious* work. When the film leaves the laboratory and enters the minds of experimental subjects, it sharply improves; the science is plausible, interesting, and even wondrous. With a half-decent script, Trumbull might yet become a major science-fiction director.

M.M.W.

BRAND, MAX (pseudonym of Frederick Faust) (1892–1944).
American writer for the Munsey and Street and Smith pulps in the 1920s and 1930s. Primarily famous for his western adventure stories about such characters as Destry and Silvertip, Brand developed the character of Dr. Kildare in the middle 1930s when moving up the ladder from the "pulp jungle" to the slick magazine markets. His major attempt at a science-fiction novel was *The Smoking Land*, published in *Argosy* in 1937 under the name of George Challis. In this adventure novel a modern western rancher, Smokey Bill Cassidy, journeys to a hidden kingdom on an island within the Arctic Circle to rescue his closest friend, a scientific genius. In a mode familiar to readers of H. Rider HAGGARD and A. MERRITT, the island is peopled by a lost race descended from the intermarriage of a primitive people and some errant Vikings. Clearly Brand was using an SF setting as a new realm for the adventure stories he could tell so vividly.

E.L.C.

BRAZIL (1985).
Directed by Terry Gilliam; screenplay by Terry Gilliam, Tom Stoppard, and Charles McKeown; photographed by Roger Pratt; music by Michael Kamen. With Jonathan Pryce, Michael Palin, Kim Greist, Ian Holm, Robert De Niro, Katherine Helmond, Bob Hoskins, Ian Richardson, Peter Vaughan. 142 minutes. Color.

Brazil has been described as the Monty Python version of George ORWELL's *Nineteen Eighty-four*, an apt comparison in more ways than one: in addition to ex-Python Terry Gilliam's direction and Michael Palin's sinister comedic appearance as one of the villains of the piece, this black comedy features sets that appear to be leftovers from Michael Radford's 1984. The title of the film refers not to the country of Brazil but to a 1930s wish fulfillment song of that name—an appropriate image since the protagonist dreams of escape from the dreariness around him.

Jonathan Pryce plays a put-upon citizen caught up in

the nightmarish, bureaucratic world that exists, as the film puts it, "somewhere in the twentieth century." Indeed the setting, brilliantly realized by production designer Norman Garwood, is not the future but an oppressively altered present, in which machinery, architecture, even women's fashions will have recognizable functions but look threatening and ugly. The hero's hapless rebellion is part the naive, hopeless defiance of a Winston Smith, part the daydreaming escapism of a Walter Mitty (and, in fact, the ending is a retreat into subjectivity); the film is marked by malicious wit, sinister invention, and striking, surreal dream sequences. Palin plays a scarily convincing "nice guy" establishment figure who abandons his lifelong buddy Pryce when Pryce begins to deviate from the norm. Viewers will find it difficult to forget the encounter with Robert De Niro's guerrilla plumber, or the department store bombing scene, at the end of which Pryce is completely enveloped in old newspapers that seem to have a malevolent life of their own.

This film had considerable difficulty getting released in the United States because of a dispute over length; it was only distributed after winning an award from Los Angeles film critics for the director's shorter version. Harlan ELLISON, writing in THE MAGAZINE OF FANTASY AND SCIENCE FICTION, heralded it as one of the greatest cinematic works of all time, but, typically, it didn't win a Hugo.

D.S.

BREUER, MILES J[OHN] (1889–1947).
American medical doctor and prolific and inventive contributor of science-fiction short stories to AMAZING STORIES. Breuer's novel *Paradise and Iron*, which appeared in *Amazing Stories* in 1930, shows skepticism of technological utopias in much the same way as E. M. FORSTER's "The Machine Stops." Breuer collaborated with Jack WILLIAMSON on *Birth of a New Republic* (1931).

J.H.

BRIDE OF FRANKENSTEIN: SEE FRANKENSTEIN ON FILM

BRIDE OF THE MONSTER (1956). *Directed by Edward D. Wood, Jr.; screenplay by Edward D. Wood, Jr., and Alex Gordon; photographed by William Thompson and Ted Allan; music by Frank Worth. With Bela Lugosi, Tor Johnson, Loretta King, Tony McCoy, Harvey B. Dunn, George Becwar, Paul Marco. 67 minutes. Black and white.*

Not yet as infamous as Wood's later PLAN 9 FROM OUTER SPACE, *Bride of the Monster* nonetheless has its adherents, who love it for Wood's unique style of ineptitude. Wood was bad at everything he tried, but he tried with vigor, perseverance, and even a certain style. He was one of a kind.

The basic form of this amazingly cheap film is the mad-scientist film such as Bela Lugosi made in the early 1940s: insane researcher turns victims into moronic supermen; almost killed by his pet octopus, he's vaporized in an atomic explosion. But Wood's erratic style and shoddy production values, along with Lugosi's flamboyant performance, makes the film entertaining in ways no one could possibly have intended.

B.W.

BRIN, DAVID (1950–). American writer and physicist. Having received a Ph.D. in space science in 1981 from the University of California at San Diego, as well as research and teaching experience, Brin possesses a solid scientific background. This and his continuing links to fellow physicist and writer Gregory BENFORD, an early mentor and recent collaborator, have led to remarkably quick maturity as a writer of hard science fiction with promising versatility and scope. Brin's two award-winning novels, *Startide Rising* (1983) and *The Postman* (1985), demonstrate what he has learned and his importance to the field.

Startide Rising, the middle volume in his Uplift series, incorporates Brin's sublime vision of the origins of species and their evolutionary potentials; it captures both the space opera "sense of wonder" and the intellectual rigor of an extrapolation that toys with Darwin and COSMOLOGY. Rather than natural selection Brin postulated a combination of breeding and genetic engineering by precursor patron species as the mechanism for the development of the thousands of intelligent species in his universe. The result is a sort of subjugation between the more mercenary patrons and their intelligent species, although humans are more benevolent to the two principal clients they have uplifted, dolphins and chimpanzees. The process also has everyone in the novels looking for the original precursors, "the mythical first species" that started the uplift process.

If detailed human drama and sensitive human characterization are absent from his SPACE OPERA, Brin's other prizewinning work is a touching portrayal of postholocaust Earth in the tradition of Walter MILLER's *A Canticle for Leibowitz* (1960). In *The Postman* Brin playfully made the redeeming institution the "mail delivery network," managed by a storytelling impostor rather than the Church.

In personal appearances and lectures, and in his nonfiction discussions of science and science fiction, Brin exhibits an infectiously boyish enthusiasm for the challenges and rewards of writing and reading SF and an optimism about science and the future that is reflected in his fiction. His award-winning short story "The Crystal Spheres," which plays a strange variation on the notion of extraterrestrial intelligence central to his Uplift series, heads Brin's first collection of short fiction, *The River of Time* (1986). His early success as well as his energy and efforts to improve mark him as a writer to watch.

OTHER WORKS: *Sundiver* (1980); *The Practice Effect* (1984); *Heart of the Comet* (with Gregory Benford, 1986); *The Uplift War* (1987).

D.M.H.

BRITISH COMMONWEALTH

Historically the British Commonwealth has been an economic and cultural entity with tenuous cultural links. Held together by the past glories of the now lost empire and the figurehead British monarch, the Commonwealth has often prided itself on its sheer diversity of voices, its melting pot of cultures, and its colorful local traditions. It is hardly surprising, then, that science fiction has developed along different paths in the various countries that make up the Commonwealth, particularly because the empire was already in decline by the time modern science fiction was born. In African and Far Eastern countries, SF has in fact had little impact. Indeed the major factor affecting SF in the more technologically advanced countries of the Commonwealth is the degree of influence American SF and its pulp traditions attained as opposed to the more genteel and literary aura of its British cousin.

Science fiction in Australia and Canada after World War II aligned itself much more with upbeat American traditions than with those of Britain, where after the hardships of the war and the ensuing economic restrictions SF writers retreated into a bleak catastrophe subgenre typified by John WYNDHAM's *Day of the Triffids* (1951) or John CHRISTOPHER's *The Death of Grass* (1956). Later British authors such as Brian W. ALDISS (*Greybeard*, 1964) and J. G. BALLARD (*The Drowned World*, 1962) would take this obligatory motif even further, integrating it with the entropic worries of the New Wave. (Characteristically, a British expatriate writer such as Arthur C. CLARKE, resident in Sri Lanka, has never tackled this theme of catastrophe and its purifying virtues so beloved of his fellow countrymen.)

Despite the undeniable later influences of American writing and magazines, Australian SF can claim some estimable native antecedents, although in many cases, because of the scarcity of local publishing outlets, publication occurred in London or New York. As far back as 1892 Australian clergyman Robert Potter published *The Germ Growers*, one of the first alien invasion yarns, preceding H. G. WELLS's *War of the Worlds* by six years. Journalist and novelist Erle Cox (1873–1950) is best known for the novel *Out of the Silence* (1925; serialized in

1919), about a surviving woman from an extinct superrace who had attempted to subjugate Australia; this classic has been translated into several foreign languages and is Australia's first major contribution to the SF genre. Cox's other SF venture, *Fool's Harvest* (1939), describes a future invasion of Australia. Another early author of note is Eric North, one of the many pseudonyms of Bernard Charles Cronin (1884–?), a founder of the Australian Society of Authors whose career spanned three decades and whose work ranged from *The Green Flame* (also titled *The Toad*, 1924) to *The Ant Men* (1955).

Various Australian-born authors moved to England: Guy Boothby (1867–1905), Fergus Hume (1859–1932), and Vernon Knowles (1899–?) all produced some science fiction. J. M. Walsh (1897–1952), also resident in England, was the first Australian writer to contribute on a regular basis to the American pulp magazines. Others back at home followed in his footsteps, among them Alan Connell, John Heming (1900–1953), Val Molesworth (1924–1964), and A. L. Pullar, author of *Celestiala* (1933). Many of these authors contributed to a local renaissance of SF publishing during World War II, when U.S. publications became unavailable in Australia.

After the war a growing number of Australian authors, many of them brought up on the American GOLDEN AGE magazines, came to the fore: Frank Bryning (1907–), the British-born Norma Hemming (1927–1960), Winifred Law, Dal Stivens (1911–), and Wynne Whiteford saw their work in British and American magazines. But Australia's two outstanding postwar novels emanated from the mainstream: *Tomorrow and Tomorrow* (1947) by M. Barnard Eldershaw (a pseudonym for Flora Eldershaw and May Barnard), a "looking backwards" novel that suffered censorship problems, and Nevil SHUTE's atomic parable *On the Beach* (1957), later filmed by Stanley Kramer.

As the local SF scene prospered and homegrown magazines *(Thrills, Inc., Future Science Fiction, Popular Science Fiction, Science Fiction Monthly)* came and went, Australian fandom became increasingly active (the country has since hosted two World SF conventions, in 1975 and 1985), spawning many new writers. But the most prominent Australian author to make a mark overseas was British-born Arthur Bertram CHANDLER (1912–1984), whose work combines strong characterization with a pleasing blend of American space opera and "frontier" traditions. Best known for his Rim Worlds books, influenced by his many years at sea and C. S. Forester's Horatio Hornblower series, Chandler reached his prime in the 1960s and 1970s. His career culminated with *Kelly Country* (1983), a powerful alternate-world novel with an Australian setting, one of Chandler's few novels actually to take place in his adopted country.

From the 1960s onward, encouraged by British and American magazine editors and spurred by local publications such as *Visions of Tomorrow* and *Void*, a new generation of writers, many of whom are still active today, broke through: David Rome, Lee Harding, Damien Broderick, John BAXTER (also an author of film books and blockbuster commercial novels), Jack WODHAMS, David Grigg, Ron Smith, and Pip Maddern are the most notable.

The publication of John Baxter's two anthologies (both titled *The Pacific Book of Australian Science Fiction*, 1968 and 1971) confirmed the breadth of talent in Australian SF and encouraged both the creation of new works and the expansion of local SF small presses. Two of these especially, Cory and Collins, have done much to foster new talent. In addition to the increasingly talented Broderick, major contemporary SF writers include George Turner (1916–   ), a mainstream author and academic of note who came late to SF but has provided a series of highly literate and thought-provoking dystopias (*Beloved Son*, 1978; *Vainglory*, 1981; and *Yesterday's Men*, 1983), and David LAKE (1929–   ), an H. G. Wells scholar whose fiction still holds much promise despite indulging in space opera format series. In addition, writers of critically acclaimed mainstream fiction, including Gerald Murnane, Peter Carey (author of *Illywhacker*), David Ireland, and Randolph Stow, have produced a number of successful works of SF.

Science fiction has also fared well in the Australian cinema, and films such as writer Richard O'Brien's *Rocky Horror Picture Show* (initially a stage play and later filmed by director Jim Sharman, 1975), George Miller's MAD MAX series, and the ambiguous movies of Peter Weir (*Picnic at Hanging Rock*, 1975; *The Last Wave*, 1977) have achieved international success. On the critical front Australia has also contributed much to the genre, with a number of highly regarded scholars and critics, including Bruce Gillespie, George Turner, Peter Nicholls (editor of *The Science Fiction Encyclopedia*, 1979, and other nonfiction books), and the Tasmanian Donald Tuck, compiler of the monumental *Encyclopedia of Science Fiction and Fantasy* (1974, 1978, and 1982), which unfortunately hasn't yet reached beyond 1968 in its coverage.

Nearby New Zealand has a lesser SF tradition, although it too has assimilated American and British influences. Samuel BUTLER (1835–1902) lived in New Zealand for some time, but his classic *Erewhon* (1872) was mostly written after his return to Great Britain. A local fan scene sprang up in the 1950s, but in a country with few cultural traditions, travel overseas soon tempted writers such as Bruce Burn and Cherry Wilder (1930–   ), who moved in 1954 to Australia and in 1976 to Germany, where she now resides. Wilder, although an expatriate, is New Zealand's best-known writer, equally at ease with colorful SF and flamboyant fantasy. Phillip Mann, who moved to New Zealand from England, is a promising writer. His *Eye of the Queen* (1982) provides one of SF's most memorable alien societies; this novel

has since been followed by *Masters of Paxwax* (1986). New Zealand's cinema, although small, has already made a mark on SF with the films of Geoff Murphy, *Utu* and the postatomic *Quiet Earth*.

In both Australia and New Zealand, the only emergence of aborigine and Maori culture in fiction has manifested itself in fantasy as opposed to science fiction, in the works of Keri Hulme, Patrick White, and Patricia Wrightson. One hopes that this infusion of native culture will someday affect SF as well, imbuing it finally with a voice of its own.

The problem faced by Canadian science fiction is a different one: Canadian authors are too often assumed to be either American or British, because of geographic proximity and linguistic imperialism. For the record, important writers such as A. E. VAN VOGT, Gordon DICKSON, Donald KINGSBURY, and Phyllis GOTLIEB are Canadian. To complicate matters, although many foreign-born authors—including William GIBSON, Spider ROBINSON, Judith MERRIL, and Michael Coney—live in Canada, their work is not necessarily "Canadian," and some of Canada's more prominent French-speaking writers—including Elisabeth Vonarburg and Norbert Spehner—happen to be French-born.

Isolated Canadian pioneers include James De Mille (1837–1880), author of the Antarctic utopian novel *A Strange Manuscript Found in a Copper Cylinder* (1888); John Buchan (1875–1940), Scottish but governor general of Canada from 1935 to 1940; and Frederick Philip Grove (1879–1948), whose *Consider Her Ways* (1947) features communication with ants.

Early American SF magazines circulated freely throughout Canada, and local authors specializing in the field were soon writing for these publications; they included Thomas P. Kelley, Richard Vaughan, and van Vogt and Dickson, both John W. CAMPBELL alumni permanently resident in the United States. Many postwar Canadian authors dabbled liberally in SF, including Arthur Hailey, now better known for formula best-sellers; John Nantley, author of the paranoiac *The 27th Day* (1956); humorist Stephen Leacock; Charles G. D. Roberts; Margaret Laurence; and Ruth Nichols. To this day major Canadian writers are not averse to working occasionally in the SF genre (or in fantasy); they include Brian Moore, Robertson Davies, and Margaret Atwood (whose *The Handmaid's Tale*, 1986, is a ferocious dystopia).

Leading contemporary authors in the SF genre are Phyllis Gotlieb (1926–   ), better known in Canada as a fine poet and playwright and in SF for *Sunburst* (1964), *O Master Caliban!* (1976), and a trilogy about telepathic cats (1980 to 1985); and Donald Kingsbury (1929–   ), a specialist in sprawling alien cultures and author of *Courtship Rite* (1982) and *The Moon Goddess and the Son* (1986). Also of note are Wayland Drew, British-born Andrew Weiner, Crawford Kilian, Hayden Howard, British-based juvenile author and anthologist Douglas Hill, Robin Sanborn, and London-based critic John Clute.

A thriving subgenre in Canadian SF, specializing in separatist utopias and political fiction, has arisen because of Canada's two-language culture and political division. In the French/Quebec camp there has been a flowering of SF fandom and literary activity over the last decade. This has been spearheaded by semiprofessional magazines such as *Requiem* (now *Solaris*) and *Imagine*, which have launched an impressive array of authors who successfully combine French intellect with hard SF traditions derived from the United States. Elisabeth Vonarburg, Esther Rochon, Daniel Sernine, Francine Pelletier, René Beaulieu, Jean François Somcynski, Norbert Spehner, and Jean-Pierre April lead a crowded field that holds as much promise for French-language SF as for SF as a whole.

Also prominent in the Canadian SF field is a master of the horror cinema, David CRONENBERG. Most of his films blend an intelligent use of SF conventions with gross-out horror effects; the best known are *The Brood*, *Shivers*, SCANNERS, VIDEODROME, and THE FLY.

Manifestations of science fiction in the rest of the British Commonwealth are few and far between, with the exception of Ireland, where authors such as Bob SHAW or James WHITE have been assimilated into the mainstream of British SF.

There have been isolated SF stories and some academic activity in the field in India and Singapore, but very little SF has emerged in Africa, where writing in the postcolonial period is dominated by either magical realism in the South American mold or politically active social realism. This lack of SF in what were until recently underdeveloped countries is not totally surprising considering the postindustrial origins of the genre. As for South Africa, strong censorship has been a major obstacle to writers who might prove interested in SF; when not choosing exile, most local authors (among them J. M. Coetzee, André Brink, and Breyten Breytenbach) have found it preferable to use allegory or fantasy to comment on oppression or injustice.

M.J.

BRODERICK, DAMIEN (1944–　). Austra-
lian writer. Born in Melbourne, Broderick earned a bachelor's degree from Monash University, Clayton, Victoria. After publishing stories primarily in Australia (his collection, *A Man Returned*, was published in 1965), Broderick made his presence felt in Ted Carnell's *New Writings in SF* (1964), Frederik POHL's brief (two-volume) attempt at *International Science Fiction* (1967), and the Australian/British *Visions of Tomorrow* (1970). Broderick's first novel, *Sorcerer's World* (1970), appeared the same year.

Perhaps the outstanding Australian author currently writing and the recipient of two Literature Board of Australia fellowships and two (Australian) Ditmar Awards for SF, Broderick made his first major impact with *The Dreaming Dragons* (1980), which combines psychological science with metaphysical transcendence in its exploration of a strange Australian outcropping of rock. It was mentioned that year for most of the major awards and took second place in the Campbell Award for the best science-fiction novel of the year.

Broderick has published a second collection of stories, *A Solipsism Samba* (1985), edited two anthologies, *The Zeitgeist Machine: A New Anthology of Science Fiction* (1977) and *Strange Attractors* (1985), and published a mainstream novel about SF fans, *Transmitters* (1984).

OTHER WORKS: *The Judas Mandala* (1982); *Valencies* (with Rory Barnes, 1983).

J.E.G.

THE BROTHER FROM ANOTHER PLANET
(1984). *Directed by John Sayles; screenplay by John Sayles; photographed by Ernest R. Dickson; music by Mason Daring. With Joe Morton, Darryl Edwards, Leonard Jackson, Bill Cobbs, Maggie Renzi, Tom Wright, John Sayles. 104 minutes. Color.*

This imaginative, low-budget SF feature was written and directed by John Sayles, an independent American filmmaker who has specialized in both sensitive dramas of topical social issues *(Liana, Return of the Secaucus Seven)* and commercial screenplays revealing a humorous self-consciousness of SF and horror *(The Howling, Piranha)*. *Brother from Another Planet*, the first movie to depict a black alien, neatly combines both aspects of Sayles's work and succeeds with a minimum of special effects. The alien lands in New York City (of course), near the Statue of Liberty (of course), and quickly finds his way to Harlem (of course), where he feels more at home. Because of the simple yet novel stroke of making the alien black, Sayles was able to comment on the implicit racial politics of the mainstream SF film as well as on the minority status of blacks in America. Sayles himself gives an extremely comical performance as an interstellar bounty hunter.

B.K.G.

BROWN, CHARLES N[IKKI] (1937–　).
American editor and publisher of *Locus,* the preeminent newsletter of the American science-fiction community. An electrical engineer by training and an active SF fan since the 1950s, Brown founded *Locus* in 1968; since then the publication has evolved from a mimeographed fanzine into a professionally staffed monthly magazine, which features detailed coverage of SF publishing, the

visual media, and current events, along with lengthy opinion pieces and personality profiles. Between 1971 and 1983 *Locus* won the Hugo Award for best fanzine eight times; since its reassignment to the newly created best semiprozine category, it has won all three of the Hugos awarded in that division.

WORKS: *Far Travelers* (editor, 1976); *Alien Worlds* (editor, 1976); *Science Fiction in Print: 1985* (with William G. Contento, 1986).

P.N.H.

BROWN, FREDRIC [WILLIAM] (1906–1972).

American writer whose popular science fiction provides a wry and ironic commentary on human existence. An office worker and newspaper proofreader, Brown became a free-lance writer after the publication of his first novel, a successful hard-boiled mystery, *The Fabulous Clipjoint* (1947). His first SF story was published in 1941, and he alternated between mysteries (and suspense novels) and science fiction for the remainder of his life. His first SF novel, *What Mad Universe* (1948/1949), is a comic romp about an SF editor who gets blasted into his foremost fan's alternate world.

Brown is also noted for the idealism of *The Lights in the Sky Are Stars* (1953; as *Project Jupiter*, 1954), about the beginnings of interstellar travel, and the comedy of *Martians, Go Home* (1955), about humanity being plagued by little green people. But Brown's greatest skill is evidenced in such short stories as "Etaoin Shrdlu" (1942), about an alien creature that takes possession of a Linotype machine; "Arena" (1944), about the settling of an interstellar conflict by one-on-one combat; and "The Star Mouse" (1942). His stories are collected in *Space on My Hands* (1953), *Angels and Spaceships* (1954), *Honeymoon in Hell* (1958), *Nightmares and Geezenstacks* (1961), *Daymares* (1968), *Paradox Lost* (1973), *The Best of Fredric Brown* (1977), and *The Best Short Stories of Fredric Brown* (1982). Brown made a unique art form of the short-short story with such classics as "Answer" (1954), in which a computer newly linking 96 billion planets is asked, Is there a God? and replies, "There is now."

OTHER WORKS: *Rogue in Space* (1957); *The Mind Thing* (1961); *And the Gods Laughed* (collection, 1987).

H.L.P.

BROWN, HOWARD V. (1878–?).

American illustrator who became one of the "Big Four" science-fiction pulp artists of the 1930s (with Leo Morey, Frank R. PAUL, and WESSO). Brown was born in Lexington, Kentucky, and studied at the Chicago Art Institute. His paintings in the 1930s were crude, but in time he developed into a fine illustrator, particularly known for his bug-eyed monsters, or BEMs. Brown started the trend

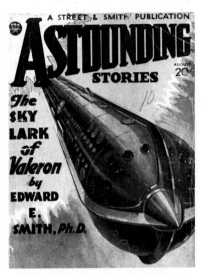

August 1934 cover illustration by Brown

away from the garish, intense colors of the early magazines, introducing a wider and more subtle palette into SF cover art. He did work for such magazines as *Startling Stories*, *Astounding Stories*, and *Thrilling Wonder Stories*.

J.G.

BRUNNER, JOHN [KILIAN HOUSTON] (1934–).

British writer of science-fiction and mainstream fiction and poetry. Brunner is one of the two or three most influential British SF writers of the last three decades and has gained an international reputation matched by few SF writers of any nationality. It is tempting to divide his career into four distinct periods: From 1959 to 1968 Brunner published thirty-three novels, all but six of them for Ace Books. Most of these are well-plotted adventure SF characterized by a smooth narrative style. In 1968 Brunner turned to more serious themes and experimented considerably with his style. He still published an extraordinary number of novels during this period (thirteen) but from 1968 to 1975 he is best known for his dystopias; set in the near future, they describe horrible worlds reeling from human greed and stupidity. From 1976 through 1982 Brunner wrote very little, but in 1984 he returned with a fiction that was far more optimistic about the future and the role of science and technology.

Although each of these characterizations can be supported by Brunner's fiction, they can only be a starting point for any serious discussion of his accomplishments. He was the first SF writer to have his work featured in a panel discussion of the Modern Language Association. He has won a British Fantasy Award, a Hugo Award, two British Science Fiction Association Awards, the Prix Apollo, two Cometa d'Argento, and the Europa Award, and he is credited with proving that there is a place in SF for skilled literary craft. Brunner has dealt with every major SF theme imaginable, and if the results have not always been up to his high standards, his work has consistently provided readers with entertaining, often riveting stories.

Even during his early period, when Brunner was churning out such potboilers as *The Atlantic Abomination* (1960), with its telepathic alien who enslaves unwary humans, and *Echo in the Skull* (1959; revised as *Give Warning to the World*, 1974), in which the world is threatened with obliteration, he did not ignore either serious issues or stylistic innovation. *Castaways' World* (1963; revised as *Polymath*, 1974) relates the story of humans struggling to survive on a bleak, alien planet and explores the failure of the human attempt to compartmentalize knowledge. In *The Day of the Star Cities* (1965; revised as *Age of Miracles*, 1973), the human race awakens one day to find areas of the Earth covered with huge communications nets constructed by an unknown alien race that seems to see people in the same way as people see house mice. Now knowing that humanity shares the universe with at least one vastly superior race, the human characters must rebuild their lives to fit the new order. And in *The Whole Man* (1964; as *The Telepathist*, 1965) Brunner featured a deformed telepathic hero who undergoes a spiritual rebirth.

Perhaps the most important novel from this period is *Squares of the City* (1965). Its plot is standard in both SF and mainstream fiction: an outsider becomes the focus of political intrigue in a country ruled by a privileged class. But Brunner complicated his task by basing the plot on an actual chess match, the moves of which are echoed by the two opposing factions in the novel, who use the hero and citizens of the city as their pieces. The action occasionally seems forced because of Brunner's need to follow the moves of the historic game, but the theme of manipulation and the cynical treatment of citizens by those in power are memorable.

Given such work, the appearance of *Stand on Zanzibar* in 1969 should not have been surprising, although it seems to have taken readers by storm. Its style (based on that of John Dos Passos), its characters, its picture of a world gone mad, and its size (the largest SF novel written up to that time) were all new to the genre. Although the opening of *Stand on Zanzibar* demands careful attention, readers who stick with it are rewarded with an awesome portrayal of the consequences of overpopulation. Brunner detailed social, moral, political, economic, and psychological effects with such care that the world becomes the central character in the story. In fact, the setting is so painstakingly and credibly drawn—and

the world and its problems made so convincing in their magnitude—that Brunner had trouble ending the novel: a solution seems inconceivable. As a result he resorted to the device of a naturally occurring pheromone to calm the situation down. Despite this forced ending, the novel remains a seminal work in the genre.

Brunner followed *Stand on Zanzibar* with three other major dystopian works. *The Jagged Orbit* (1969) handles racism and again turns to a deus ex machina for a resolution. *The Sheep Look Up* (1972) attacks those who cause pollution and those who ignore it. Another stylistically unique work, this novel contains a fitting (if somewhat drastic) ending as the world's chief polluter—the United States—turns on itself. *The Shockwave Rider* (1975) is the most optimistic of these four dystopias. Here the cause for the dystopia is the information explosion and the insistence by a privileged class that access to information be rationed. The hero refuses to accept the status quo and fights to open up all lines of communication to all people.

Brunner wrote a number of other novels that emphasize his fears for humanity's future. Such events as the energy crisis of 1973 and the frequent squabbling among the Common Market nations inspired *The Stone That Never Came Down* (1973) and *Total Eclipse* (1974). Not all his novels from this period are uniformly bleak, but his primary vision was dark. Perhaps this darkness accounts in part for the six-year hiatus Brunner took from writing SF. Brunner began writing again with a more optimistic attitude and new subject matter. *The Crucible of Time* (1983) concerns an alien species that, because of its form and chemistry, cannot make extensive use of fire; its technology, therefore, is based on the biological rather than the physical sciences. In the first of seven parts, these aliens discover that their planet is headed for a cosmic collision in the distant future. Each of the succeeding parts follows the aliens as they develop from a feudal society to an urban one and struggle with the forces of science and superstition. The novel is a masterful study of alien history, culture, biology, and sociology.

The Crucible of Time and the more recent *The Tides of Time* (1984) may signal a change in Brunner's fiction, although it is perhaps too early to tell. In any case, they share with his earlier work a concern for humanity in its struggles with itself and its environment.

OTHER WORKS: *Threshold of Eternity* (1959); *The World Swappers* (1959); *The Hundredth Millennium* (1959; revised as *Catch a Falling Star*, 1968); *Sanctuary in the Sky* (1960); *The Skynappers* (1960); *Slavers of Space* (1960; revised as *Into the Slave Nebula*, 1968); *Meeting at Infinity* (1961); *I Speak for Earth* (1961, as Keith Woodcott); *The Ladder in the Sky* (1962, as Keith Woodcott); *Secret Agent of Terra* (1962; revised as *The Avengers of Carrig*, 1969); *The Super Barbarians* (1962); *Times without Number* (1962; revised 1969); *No Fu-*

ture in *It and Other Science Fiction Stories* (collection, 1962); *The Psionic Menace* (1963, as Keith Woodcott); *The Space-Time Juggler* (1963; as *The Astronauts Must Not Land,* 1963; revised as *More Things in Heaven,* 1973); *The Dreaming Earth* (1963); *Listen! The Stars* (1963; revised as *The Stardroppers,* 1972); *Endless Shadow* (1964); *To Conquer Chaos* (1964); *The Martian Sphinx* (1965, as Keith Woodcott); *Now Then* (collection, 1965); *The Altar on Asconel* (1965); *The Enigma from Tantalus* (1965); *The Long Result* (1965); *No Other Gods But Me* (collection, 1966); *A Planet of Your Own* (1966); *Out of My Mind* (collection, 1967); *Born under Mars* (1967); *The Productions of Time* (1967); *Quicksand* (1967); *Not before Time: Science Fiction and Fantasy* (collection, 1968); *Bedlam Planet* (1968); *Father of Lies* (1968); *Double, Double* (1968); *Timescoop* (1969); *The Evil That Men Do* (1969); *The Dramaturges of Yan* (1971); *The Wrong End of Time* (1971); *The Traveler in Black* (1971); *From This Day Forward* (collection, 1972); *Entry to Elsewhen* (1972); *Time-Jump* (collection, 1973); *Web of Everywhere* (1974); *The Book of John Brunner* (collection, 1976); *Interstellar Empire* (1976); *Foreign Constellations: The Fantastic Worlds of John Brunner* (collection, 1980); *The Infinitive of Go* (1980); *Players at the Game of People* (1980); *The Shift Key* (1987).

S.H.G.

Ed Bryant

BRYANT, EDWARD [WINSLOW, JR.] (1945–).

American science-fiction author who has won two Nebula Awards (1978, 1979) for short story writing. Born in New York but living in Colorado, Bryant earned bachelor's and master's degrees in English from the University of Wyoming. He is an alumnus of the Clarion Science Fiction Writers' Workshop, and his work displays many of the characteristics that have become identified with the workshop's best writers. His well-written, stylish short stories deal with tense social and psychological issues. For example, in one of his earlier stories, "Shark" (1973), Bryant explored the clash between scientific investigation and human emotions when a woman agrees to allow the transplantation of her brain into the body of a shark. Such a premise has proven too fantastic for many traditional readers of hard science fiction, some of whom may question whether Bryant's stories are "real" SF. Yet "Sharks" is a moving work that highlights the constant struggle between the intellectual quest for new information and the emotional desire for security—a traditional SF theme.

Indeed most of Bryant's themes are obviously science fictional, but he presents them as fables rather than stories of credible, detailed worlds. He is at his best when describing human dilemmas rather than technological advances. *Among the Dead and Other Events Leading up to the Apocalypse* (1973; revised 1974) contains a series of short stories in which humanity has lost its intellectual and emotional energy. Like the universe around them, people are heading toward an ultimate state of entropy. If it were not for the energetic style and strong tone of condemnation that shape them, these stories might leave readers in utter despair. As it is, they are frightening visions of the suffering that humanity is capable of inflicting upon itself. In later collections, such as *Particle Theory* (1980), Bryant toned down the blackness of his worlds, but his emphasis remains on human relationships and the difficulties people encounter as they seek meaning for their lives.

Bryant has also written two novels. His first, *Phoenix without Ashes* (1975), was a collaboration with Harlan ELLISON. Based on the pilot script for Ellison's TV series *The Starlost,* the novel is a traditional generation starship story that lacks the powerful characterization typical of Bryant's short fiction. *Cinnabar* (1976), in contrast, is identifiably a Bryant work. This ambitious novel is actually a combination of short stories portraying the almost immortal human inhabitants of a city who, like the last men in Olaf STAPLEDON's *Last and First Men* (1930), are living in the final age: time has run out for the race. Once again, as in *Among the Dead,* many of the characters lack the will or desire to change, but unlike those of the earlier collection, at least some of *Cinnabar*'s characters continue to care about one another, remain curious about their world, and are still capable of growth. In this and other works, Bryant has produced thoughtful, careful SF that sympathetically describes the dreams and nightmares of the human race.

OTHER WORK: *Wyoming Sun* (collection, 1980).

S.H.G.

——— BUCK ROGERS ———

Buck Rogers was a multimedia pop-culture hero who came to symbolize for millions of comic-strip readers and radio and movie serial audiences the fabulous technology of the far-off future, the twenty-fifth century, and the two-(ray)-gun hero who would protect them from the yellow peril. He came out of the pulps as Anthony Rogers in "Armageddon—2419," a story by Philip Francis NOWLAN in Hugo GERNSBACK's August 1928 AMAZING STORIES. That story was followed by "The Airlords of Han" in the March 1929 issue. But Rogers's appeal and following transcended the limited audience of the science-fiction magazines.

Nowlan, the father of ten children and a financial reporter for the *Philadelphia Public Ledger*, said he wrote the story because he "got so sick and tired of writing about business science and news." In the original story Rogers, a World War I pilot trapped in a mine cave-in and overcome by radioactive gas, awakens 500 years later to find America overrun by a "Yellow blight" of Mongol hordes. He joins forces with Wilma Deering, an officer in the military organization opposing the Mongols, and, by adopting the enemies' weapons and devices, such as the famous flying belt, overcomes their tyranny.

John Flint Dille, president of the National Newspaper Syndicate, persuaded a reluctant Nowlan to undertake a comic strip and to change the name of his hero to Buck. He also signed Dick Calkins, an editorial cartoonist, to illustrate the story. On January 7, 1929, *Buck Rogers in the 25th Century* debuted in dozens of newspapers as a daily comic strip. After Nowlan's death in 1940, Dille, Calkins, and Rick Yager wrote the stories. Color Sunday strips followed the dailies, illustrated first by Russ Keaton and later by Rick Yager. Murphy Anderson did the strip in 1958, and Gene Tuska took over in 1959.

When the comic strip folded in 1967, it had been translated into eighteen languages and had appeared in more than 450 newspapers. Readers the world over had been introduced by this first SF comic strip ever to the basic trappings of space opera—rocket ships, ray guns, robots, and domed cities—and SF had come to be called "that Buck Rogers stuff." Numerous attempts were made to duplicate the incredible popularity of the comic strip in other media—Big Little books, radio, movies, and television—but never with as much success.

A radio serial based on the comic strip went on the air November 7, 1932, and lasted until World War II. It was revived after the war and survived into the late 1940s. The shows were written, produced, and directed by Jack Johnstone.

The 1939 movie serial version of Buck Rogers was Universal's attempt to duplicate the popularity of its FLASH GORDON serials, even borrowing Flash's Buster CRABBE for the title role. Ironically, the comic strip *Flash Gordon*

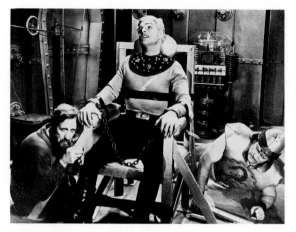

Buster Crabbe as Buck Rogers (1939)

had originally been conceived by a rival syndicate to capture the kind of readership commanded by *Buck Rogers*. The serial did not include robots, probably because of budgetary constraints, making do with "human robots deprived of their will" by what look like five-gallon cans on their heads. But Buck was not as popular with serial fans as Flash, and Crabbe was returned to that role. The Rogers serial was later edited into two feature versions: *Planet Outlaws* (1953) and *Destination Saturn* (1956).

The 1950–1951 television serial, like other SF series of the period, was produced on an extremely low budget, with results to match. The short-lived 1979 series, like BATTLESTAR GALACTICA a response to the success of the film STAR WARS, was ostensibly based on the comic strip as well, but it did not capture the flavor (or following) of the original. Buster Crabbe was featured in one episode, and Mel Blanc provided a silly voice for an insufferably cute robot called Twiki. The failure of the series attests to the fact that the days when SF could be represented, and popularized, by space adventure alone may have passed.

Buck Rogers (1939). *Directed by Ford Beebe and Saul A. Goodkind; screenplay by Norman S. Hall and Ray Trampe; adapted from the comic strip* Buck Rogers in the 25th Century; *photographed by Jerry Ash. With Buster Crabbe, Constance Moore, Jackie Moran, Jack Mulhall, Anthony Warde, C. Montagu Shaw. Movie serial with twelve two-reel episodes. Black and white.*

Buck Rogers (1950–1951). *Directed by Babette Henry; written by Gene Wyckoff. With Ken Dibbs (1950), Robert Pastene (1950–51), Lou Prentis, Harry Southern, Harry Kingston. Television series, each episode 25 minutes. Black and white.*

Buck Rogers in the 25th Century **(1979).**
*Directed by Daniël Haller; screenplay by Glen A.
Larson and Leslie Stevens; photographed by Frank
Beascoechea. With Gil Gerard, Erin Gray, Pamela
Hemsley, Henry Silva. Pilot for television series.
89 minutes. Color.*

W.L.

BUDRYS, ALGIS (1931–   ). Lithuanian-born
science-fiction writer and critic, resident in the United
States since 1936. A prolific writer of short stories in the
1950s, Budrys has, in the main, derived his reputation
from a handful of novels. His visibility in the field
has benefited from years of sharp-eyed reviewing for
Galaxy (1965–1971) and *Fantasy and Science Fiction*
(1975–   ) and his column "On Writing" for *Locus* (1977–
1979). In 1984 he became a judge and later administrator of the Writers of the Future contests funded by
L. Ron HUBBARD.

Born Algirdas Jonas Budrys in the German province
of East Prussia, where his father was a member of the
Lithuanian diplomatic corps, Budrys retained his status
as a citizen of pre-Soviet Lithuania until his naturaliza-
tion as a U.S. citizen in 1987; he has described himself
as "basically a Lithuanian peasant." His writing career
began at the end of the pulp magazine era, and his fiction
and criticism reflect a keen awareness of SF as a "newsstand" form. In the early 1950s he apprenticed himself
to Lester DEL REY, who bought his first story, "Walk to
the World" (*Space Science Fiction*, 1952), and later
bought "Blood on My Jets" (1953) and others. Budrys
also studied the craft of magazine fiction from many of
its most skillful practitioners, including Robert A. W.
"Doc" LOWNDES, Larry Shaw, H. L. GOLD, and John W.
CAMPBELL. Despite his initial successes, in 1962 he found
it necessary to take work in public relations to support
his growing family, and between that year and 1974 he
produced only reviews, some nonfiction, a handful of
short pieces, and *The Amsirs and the Iron Thorn* (1967).
In 1974 he began once again to devote himself exclusively to science fiction; however his fiction output since
then has consisted only of the novel *Michaelmas* (1976)
and the stories collected in *Blood and Burning* (1978).
Instead, he has expanded his critical efforts to include
not only reviews but historical and theoretical essays
such as "Paradise Charted" (*TriQuarterly*, Fall 1980)
and *Non-literary Influences on Science Fiction* (1983).

Budrys is fascinated not only by the way things work
but also by what workings do to the people caught in
the gears. His first novel, *False Night* (1954; full text
restored as *Some Will Not Die*, 1961), chronicles the
rebuilding of civilization after a worldwide plague. His
novel, *The Falling Torch* (1959), though drawn from his
experience as assistant to his father in his work with
exiles, is not so much an autobiographical work as an

Algis Budrys

examination of the ways that national and family history
bear on the youthful hero as he attempts to determine
where he "fits" in the world. Likewise, *Rogue Moon*
(1960) deals less with the exploration of the lunar "death
machine" (Budrys's original title) than with the emotional extremes to which the explorers drive themselves
and are driven. In *Who?* (1958) an important American
scientist is returned after a terrible accident in Russia
with prosthetic parts and a metal mask, but the question
of his identity is never answered: whether or not he is
the scientist returned, he has to confront his past. In fact,
much of Budrys's work turns on the enigmatic and solitary figure—the isolated leader *(The Falling Torch, Some
Will Not Die)*, the alienated hero *(The Amsirs and the
Iron Thorn)*, the invisible superman ("Nobody Bothers
Gus," 1955). Even Laurent Michaelmas, hero of the novel
that bears his name, is known to us more by his present
actions and powers than by his history. It is as though,
in a human version of the Heisenberg principle, we can
know either where a man came from or what he is now,
but not both.

OTHER WORKS: *Man of Earth* (1958/1956); *The Unexpected Dimension* (collection, 1960); *Budrys' Inferno* (collection, 1963); *Benchmarks: Galaxy Bookshelf
by Algis Budrys* (nonfiction, 1985).

R.F.L.

BULMER, H[ENRY] KEN[NETH] (1921–   ).
British writer, prolific under his own name and various
pseudonyms, including Alan Burt Akers and Tully Zet-
ford. Bulmer's earliest works, *Space Treason* and *Cybernetic Controller* (both 1952), were written in

collaboration with A. V. Clarke. Much of his work is routine SPACE OPERA, often heavily romanticized (as in *The Earth Gods Are Coming*, 1960, and *No Man's World*, 1961) but sometimes more hard-bitten (as in *Worlds for the Taking*, 1966). Another very romantic story, "The Map Country" (1961; revised as *Land beyond the Map*, 1965), provided the foundation stone of a long-running series of parallel-worlds stories, from *The Wizards of Senchuria* (1969) to *The Diamond Contessa* (1983). But Bulmer's ability to reiterate formulas in this way has obscured—and arguably helped waste—his real talents, which are deployed in the thoughtful *Beyond the Silver Sky* (1961) and more cynical futuristic novels such as *The Ulcer Culture* (1969; also known as *Stained Glass World*). His Edgar Rice BURROUGHS imitations as Akers (more recently as Dray Prescot, also the name of the series's hero) have been ground out at the rate of two to three per year since 1972. There is no collection of Bulmer's shorter works.

NOTABLE OTHER WORKS: *City under the Sea* (1957); *Demons' World* (1964; also known as *The Demons*).

B.S.

BULWER-LYTTON, EDWARD GEORGE [EARL] (1803–1873).

British writer, one of the most popular novelists of the Victorian era and an early writer in the utopian tradition. Bulwer-Lytton's important proto-science-fiction novel *The Coming Race* (1871) picks up some themes from his occult romances *Zanoni* (1842) and *A Strange Story* (1862) and depicts a technologically advanced society made affluent by a new source of power, *vril*.

B.S.

BUNCH, DAVID R[OOSEVELT] (192?–).

American writer. Although his more than eighty science-fiction short stories have covered a wide range of subjects and styles, Bunch is best known for his cautionary, almost antiscience tales concerning the machine-inhabited world of Moderan, which began appearing in *Amazing* and *Fantastic* in the early 1960s. The constantly warring machines (actually humans who have replaced most of their flesh with metal) of these stories are intentionally extreme embodiments of human hatred and violence; the inhabitants of Moderan live only for war. Two stories in this series, "Incident in Moderan" and "The Escaping," appeared in Harlan ELLISON's *Dangerous Visions* (1967), making Bunch the only writer to be represented by more than one story in that anthology. A collection of Moderan stories packaged as a novel entitled *Moderan* appeared in 1971. Bunch's other work includes *We Have a Nervous Job*, a collection of verse published in 1983.

B.D.

BURDICK, EUGENE L[EONARD] (1918–1965).

American author of several best-selling novels, coauthor (with Harvey Wheeler) of *Fail-safe* (1962), a chilling and convincing account of an accidental nuclear strike. A film version of FAIL-SAFE was released in 1964.

N.H.

BURGESS, ANTHONY (Pseudonym of John Anthony Burgess Wilson) (1917–).

British mainstream author particularly known for his verbal invention and literary style. Although science fiction and fantasy elements are present in many of Burgess's other books—most notably *One Hand Clapping (1961)*, MF (1971), *A Long Trip to Teatime* (1976), and *1985* (1978)—his most important contributions to SF are *A Clockwork Orange* (1962) and *The Wanting Seed* (1962). (Another novel with SF elements is *Beard's Roman Women*, 1976.) Burgess spent six years in the service in World War II, attaining the rank of sergeant major. After the war he worked for the Ministry of Education and the British Colonial Service in Malaya and Borneo. This part of the world was the setting for the three novels in his Malayan trilogy, published 1956–1959, which established his reputation as a mainstream novelist.

In 1959 illness forced Burgess to return to England, where he was diagnosed as having a brain tumor and given only a year to live. The diagnosis was at least in part responsible for an extraordinarily creative period. During the next eighteen months he wrote six books, intended to support his wife in her widowhood. These included the two SF novels for which he is best known, *A Clockwork Orange* and *The Wanting Seed*.

A Clockwork Orange has attained an audience and influence beyond the book itself because of the brilliant film version by Stanley KUBRICK released in 1971. The film effectively depicts the novel's concern with futuristic violence and behavior modification by the state but is less successful in conveying its literary style and linguistic richness. Influenced by the complex puns and allusions of James Joyce, Burgess made his hero, Alex, and his gang speak in a slang rich with sounds, meanings, and effects. Indeed much of the book's originality rests on Burgess's skill with language. He used cadence and connotation to delightful advantage and established SF as an appropriate terrain for demanding and experimental literary style. *The Wanting Seed* lacks this dazzling literary style but interestingly addresses the problem of overpopulation in a futuristic world short on food where infanticide is officially encouraged and wars are arranged to kill people off.

Burgess is a literary novelist, a man of letters, and one of Britain's most distinguished contemporary writers; he has written a critical history of the English novel, as well as studies of Shakespeare, Keats, and Joyce. As a writer of science fiction, he has contributed keen intelligence, satiric wit, and impressive craftsmanship to the genre.

R.M.

BURKS, ARTHUR J. (1898–1974).   American pulp writer, especially prolific during the 1930s, when he reputedly wrote 10,000 words a day. After retiring as a U.S. Army officer, Burks contributed westerns and detective and adventure stories to various magazines as well as fantasy and science fiction to *Weird Tales* and *Astounding*. His best-known SF novel is *The Great Mirror* (1942/1952), in which Tibetan lamas come face to face with Martians.

J.H.

BURROUGHS, EDGAR RICE (1875–1950).
American author of science fantasy, whose adventure stories were influential in developing a broad audience for science fiction. In his first attempts at writing fiction for the PULP MAGAZINES, Burroughs created three major series and the best-known character of the century, Tarzan, turning them into a fortune and a publishing empire.

After an ordinary span of schooling and unsuccessful jobs of various kinds, which he romanticized in later life, Burroughs used the materials and ideas floating around him—evolution, feralism, a dry, dying Mars with canals, a hot, swampy Venus, a hollow Earth—to manufacture worlds of fancy and romance. His first SF work, "Under the Moons of Mars" (*A Princess of Mars*, 1912/1917), was published in *All-Story* magazine under the name Norman Bean. Burroughs intended the name to be "Normal" Bean, as if he were uncertain of the work's reception, but its success led to the use of his own name and a series of adventures of an Earthman, John Carter, on Mars, each early one of which was a cliff-hanger leading to the next volume.

Burroughs's worlds belong to the "lost-world" or un-discovered-world tradition. Each was created complete with exotic and distinctive language, customs, environments, and social and political organizations. Readers overlooked the inconsistencies and illogicalities. Carter's agility is explained by his growing up in the heavier gravity of Earth, but his son, who grows up on Mars, inherits it anyway. The fact that Martian women lay eggs but can interbreed with humans, telepathy, radium power, unabashed coincidences—all seem acceptable on Mars or are forgiven for the sake of the stories.

Burroughs's characters are types: noble, powerful heroes; beautiful, high-spirited heroines repeatedly in danger of sexual assault but always saved in the nick of time; evil villains who threaten death and fates worse than death. The spirit of Burroughs's work is romantic; its locales and characters are larger than life and its relationships revolve around Victorian values of love and

Edgar Rice Burroughs on the set of the first Tarzan film (1918) with star Elmo Lincoln

honor, occasionally marred by the racism of the period. The language, often awkward, is formal and sometimes quaint, with word inversions and high-flown diction that give the stories a lofty importance impressive to beginning readers.

Tinkering with scientific knowledge, even in Burroughs's day, was common, but his worlds incorporated the speculations of his era—wet, steamy Venus and the dry, dying Mars with dead sea bottoms and canals leading water from the poles popularized by astronomer Percival Lowell. The series of works dealing with Earth's center, Pellucidar, avoid the molten or solid core debate and volcanic realities by having an inventor's "iron mole" bore through a high-temperature zone to a livable region within a hollow Earth lighted by a miniature sun in the middle. Aside from ignoring the problem of Earth's specific gravity, Burroughs provided interesting speculation about the passage of time in Pellucidar and the psychological problems arising from perpetual daylight.

Burroughs's speculations, like those of many SF novelists, anticipated later scientific developments, such as the transplantation of body parts in *The Mastermind of Mars* (1928), which also incorporated Burroughs's satire on organized religion. *The Land That Time Forgot* (1918/1924) focuses on biology, describing a microcosm on an island near the South Pole, reachable only by submarine, in which the natives progress from eggs through each stage of evolution in their own lifetimes.

Like many writers Burroughs borrowed widely. Jules VERNE may have provided the idea for the hollow Earth—or Burroughs might have gone back to Verne's predecessors, Edgar Allan POE, John Cleves Symmes, or even Ludvig Holberg. H. G. WELLS's *The First Men in the Moon* (1901) may have suggested *The Moon Maid*

(1926), although the tradition of the inhabited Moon goes back to LUCIAN OF SAMOSATA. Certainly competition from a rival, Otis Adelbert Kline, led Burroughs to launch a series of adventure novels placed on Kline's turf, Venus, beginning with *Pirates of Venus* (1934); Kline promptly began a Mars series. But Burroughs made these borrowings peculiarly his, and Burroughs's characters and actions seem exactly what his readers wanted; they made him, like Verne and Wells before him, a multimillionaire.

NOTABLE OTHER WORKS: *The Gods of Mars* (1917); *The Warlords of Mars* (1919); *Thuvia, Maid of Mars* (1920); *The Chessmen of Mars* (1922); *At the Earth's Core* (1922); *Pellucidar* (1924); *The Monster Men* (1929); *Tarzan at the Earth's Core* (1930); *Tanar of Pellucidar* (1930); *A Fighting Man of Mars* (1931); *Jungle Girl* (1932); *Lost on Venus* (1935); *Swords of Mars* (1936); *Back to the Stone Age* (1937); *Carson of Venus* (1939); *Synthetic Men of Mars* (1940); *Land of Terror* (1944); *Escape on Venus* (1946); *Llana of Gathol* (1948); *Beyond the Farthest Star* (1964); twenty-four Tarzan novels.

R.H.W.

BUSBY, F[RANCIS] M[ARION] (1921–   ).
American telegraph engineer and science-fiction writer. Busby had one story published as early as 1957 and is the author of such provocative stories as "Tell Me about Yourself" (1973), which involves legalized necrophilia, but he is best known for a series of novels that combine SPACE OPERA adventure with a future history backdrop and focus on themes of personal identity and survival. In the Demu trilogy (*Cage a Man*, 1973; *The Proud Enemy*, 1975; *End of the Line*, 1980), a man caged by crablike aliens, the Demu, who seek to remove his identity and reshape it into something like themselves, escapes and gets revenge. In the Rissa Kerguelen series—*Rissa Kerguelen* (1976; revised edition, 1984), *Zelda M'Tana* (1980), *The Alien Debt* (1984), *Star Rebel* (1984), and *Rebel's Quest* (1985)—protagonists Rissa and Bran Tregare become outlaws and finally overthrow the fascistic tyranny called United Energy and Transport, which rules most of the Earth and many outlying planets.

OTHER WORK: *All These Earths* (1978).

J.J.P.

THE BUSINESS OF SCIENCE FICTION

The genre of literature called science fiction owes its present-day form and content not only to the legends, dreams, and fancies of its authors but also, to a large extent, to changing technologies in printing and distribution and to the economic realities that have influenced EDITORS and others connected with publishing.

Early authors seldom made their living from writing; the market was too small, the costs of printing too high, and distribution too limited. Writers made do with other jobs: Miguel de Cervantes was a tax collector, Edgar Allan POE an ill-paid editor, and Herman Melville a customs inspector. They wrote in their free time, more for their own satisfaction than for money, although they were happy to receive any payment for their work.

By the mid–nineteenth century, in North America and Europe, the advent of universal primary education, improvements in printing technology, and distribution by train and steamship had much expanded the reading public. A few general novelists became very successful. The British writer Charles Dickens, for example, gained a fine living and international acclaim from his novels exposing the harsh and sordid lives of London's poor.

The unsuccessful lawyer and stockbroker Jules VERNE, inspired by the fantastic and science-fictional elements in the work of Poe, became the world's first full-time SF writer. Verne's novels, based on his study of current scientific developments, fired the imaginations of thousands of readers with tales of voyages beneath the sea in a submarine or to the Moon in an artillery shell. His one hundred hardcover books were eagerly received, making Verne famous and financially independent.

Meanwhile, editors gained skill in judging the popularity of submitted material, while printers and publishers made strides in quantity production and distribution. Improvements in the printing press and the development of cheap pulp paper occurred around 1884. Halftone engraving, which appeared in 1886, facilitated the reproduction of pictures in printed works. These advances, with the demands of an expanding readership, fostered the growth of general-fiction magazines, some of which carried an occasional imaginative story. In Britain in 1903, one issue of *The Strand* ran a Sherlock Holmes tale by Sir Arthur Conan DOYLE along with H. G. WELLS's story "The Land Ironclads," which foresaw the military tank.

In America in the early 1900s, the Munsey Company published in its magazines what it called "different stories," many of which would later be called SF. In 1912 an unsuccessful bookkeeper, cowboy, soldier, and railroad detective, disgusted by a poor piece in *All-Story*, submitted a tale of his own. Thus Edgar Rice BURROUGHS wrote his first novel, published as a book in 1917 under the title *A Princess of Mars*, and followed it with *Tarzan of the Apes*. These books and the many sequels that followed sold over 35 million hardcover copies and made Burroughs a fortune still enjoyed by his heirs.

As the twentieth century unfolded, cities grew, wages rose as new technology increased productivity, and greater leisure for working people joined with the growth of advertising to popularize increasing numbers of newsstand magazines. The time between the two world wars was the heyday of the pulp. Hundreds of PULP MAGAZINES, all in a six-by-nine-inch format on cheap paper with garish cover paintings, beckoned the reader. They published adventure stories of all kinds for working men and their sons, who read only for pleasure stories about the West, war, the sea, aviation, sports, crime and detectives, even love and, later, SF. Save for the love and confessions magazines, the pulps catered to a heavily male readership, featuring fast action, one-dimensional characters, and a straightforward narrative style. Most operated on a shoestring; yet during this time they offered a wider market for short stories than ever before or since.

Adventure Magazine, Argosy, and Blue Book were the aristocrats of the pulps. Paying higher rates, they demanded storytelling on a more sophisticated level and attracted excellent writers who, like Harold Lamb, later became successful as general writers.

Although pulps such as Argosy and All-Story carried occasional science fiction, the exclusively SF magazine evolved not so much from the pulps as from the popular-science magazine. The first such magazines were the brainchildren of the immigrant inventor, writer, and publisher Hugo GERNSBACK. His magazines, including Modern Electrics and Science and Invention, often contained tales of "scientifiction," through which Gernsback hoped to interest young people in technical careers. In 1926 he produced the first all-science-fiction magazine, AMAZING STORIES.

Even without Gernsback's vision, SF magazines would probably have been published sooner or later. The pulp Weird Tales, combining fantasy with a little SF, had appeared in 1923. In 1930 the Clayton chain brought out Astounding Stories of Super-Science, obviously imitating Amazing. Of all the many SF magazines that followed, only Amazing and Astounding (now ANALOG) have, with changes of name and owner, survived into the 1980s. In 1929 Gernsback's Amazing was forced into bankruptcy and sold to Tech Publications, but in the same year the indomitable Gernsback started the short-lived Science Wonder Stories.

Once the SF magazines became the focus for the SF impulses that had been scattered throughout the book and magazine field, publication of the genre elsewhere grew less frequent and, in the book field, virtually disappeared. This trend concentrated great power in the hands of magazine editors, whose decisions about whether to accept stories and how to publish them (and the publishers' decisions to pay for them) began to define the field.

Gernsback's elderly editor T. O'Conor SLOANE, who remained with Amazing until it was bought by Ziff-Davis in 1938, offered little direction to such early writers as E. E. SMITH, Jack WILLIAMSON, and Murray LEINSTER; and Harry BATES, the first editor of Astounding, was concerned mostly with story mechanics. His successor, after

Astounding had been bought by Street & Smith in 1933, F. Orlin TREMAINE, began wielding the power of the editor to shape the field, and Tremaine's successor in 1937, John W. CAMPBELL, Jr., took full control.

During his editorship, Campbell worked closely with writers, feeding them ideas and returning their manuscripts with detailed analyses sometimes longer than the stories themselves. Within a few years Campbell had remade SF in his own image, turning Astounding into the clearly recognized leader of the field. In effect he began to determine SF by what he published; whatever he didn't publish was, by definition, not SF, or, even when published by one of the other magazines, not quite SF. The period 1937–1945, during which Campbell exerted his greatest influence and introduced some of the writers who would dominate the field for the next few decades—such as Isaac ASIMOV, L. Sprague DE CAMP, Lester DEL REY, Robert A. HEINLEIN, Theodore STURGEON, and A. E. VAN VOGT—would later come to be known as the GOLDEN AGE.

To most of the writers it may not have seemed golden. Campbell had some help: Street & Smith was a sound and prosperous pulp magazine chain with good distribution for its products. Some of the other magazines were published by shakier groups with less reliable practices. Under Clayton ownership Astounding had started paying an astounding two cents a word upon acceptance, but under Street & Smith payment dropped to a penny a word, and the other magazines paid as little as a quarter of a cent a word, and sometimes didn't pay that until threatened with lawsuits.

The effect, even if they were not trying to earn their entire living from their typewriters, was to encourage authors to write as quickly as possible. Some of those who did write full-time and had to contribute to many kinds of pulp magazines, such as Arthur J. Burks and Frederick Faust (who wrote under such pseudonyms as Max Brand), trained themselves to write as much as 10,000 words a day, and never to rewrite. If they could sell most of what they wrote, they could make a good living even at a penny a word.

Science-fiction authors followed the pulp model. The best way to write quickly was to use standard plots (or formulas), stereotyped characters, and constant action. The ideas sometimes were inspired, but the execution usually was hasty. Not until conditions changed, and sometimes not until new writers emerged, would the writing of SF change in response, and some authors had to retrain themselves; Frederik POHL began writing his first drafts on the backs of circulars and old manuscripts so that he would be forced to rewrite them.

Early illustrators had their troubles too. Their rate of pay was so low, their deadlines so short, that they seldom had time to read the stories they illustrated. Although few knew much about the technology behind the stories, most rejected suggestions from the authors, and magazine covers often showed a man in an as-yet-uninvented space suit while his female companion braved outer space clad only in a bikini and a plexiglas helmet. Covers were painted in eye-catching primary colors, and the interior line drawings may have detracted from the written word. Not until payment for illustrators increased and they retained the rights to their own paintings—to resell for themselves and increase the return from their investment of time and talent—did the sophistication of today's SF illustration emerge.

Advertising had made possible the publication of many early magazines, including the mass magazines that became known as the slicks, as advertisers began to realize the potential of creating a mass market by national promotion, and one of John W. Campbell's unrealized dreams was to tap the wealth he knew was available from such specialized products and institutions as were taking page ads in magazines like *Scientific American*. That potential only began to be realized in the late 1970s, and then largely by such mixed publications as *Omni*.

The SF magazines were considered only another category of pulp, and the ads placed in them, apparently for a gullible readership quite different from the one Campbell knew his to be, were pulp chain ads for such things as Charles Atlas's body-building course, trusses and back supports, and mail-order technological courses promising instant education and munificent jobs. Some even made thinly disguised offers of loaded dice. Such advertising, although it may have made the difference between existence and extinction for some magazines, added to the general disapproval many parents harbored for the early SF magazines.

The paper shortages of World War II doomed the pulp magazines, except for a few that adopted the smaller "digest" size and paper of better quality; those that did not die were killed off, like the slicks, by the competition with television in the 1950s. During the war, however, the U.S. government had bought quantities of specially printed paperback books to ship overseas for the troops. After the war the paperback blossomed into a major industry, and publishers, who at first had issued only reprints, began to seek original paperback SF novels. Ballantine Books, when it was founded in 1952, announced its intention to pay advances against royalties high enough ($5,000) to permit authors to write full-time.

The end of World War II had brought Campbell other competition: SF in hardcover books, much of it, ironically, anthologies of stories taken from *Astounding* and novels that had been published in its pages as serials. Many of the books were published by fans, *Astounding* readers so filled with missionary spirit that they invested their meager funds to spread and preserve SF classics. Although they soon failed, their efforts were picked up by major publishers, and they, in turn, began to publish original SF. Campbell no longer was the single arbiter of SF, and would-be writers had somewhere else to look for publication and direction.

Writing for books was different from writing for ephemeral magazines. Books are permanent, and the payment for them goes on as long as the books sell or are reprinted. Original payments may have been small, but writers could begin to think of themselves as professionals—authors—and their bodies of work as an investment. And material planned for books could still find magazine publication and thus pay twice. That meant fiction could compensate a greater investment of time and effort. Then too, the book audience was different from the magazine audience, more sophisticated perhaps, and more patient.

So SF writing changed. It also changed when two major new magazines began to be published in 1949 and 1950: Anthony BOUCHER and J. Francis McCOMAS's MAGAZINE OF FANTASY AND SCIENCE FICTION and H. L. GOLD's GALAXY. *Fantasy and Science Fiction* had literary ambitions; *Galaxy* aimed at greater sophistication. Editors of both magazines attracted older writers and encouraged new writers, and worked with them in the way that Campbell had worked with *Astounding*'s writers. Because they had a vision of what they wanted and the energy and strength of will to achieve it, they defined SF in new ways.

Agents too began to work with writers to promote their work, find it new markets, and improve contracts. H. G. WELLS had been the client of one of the first English agents, J. B. Pinker. Julius Schwartz, who later was an editor of Superman and DC Comics, became the first purely SF agent when he created the Solar Sales Service with Mort WEISINGER. Later agencies, completely or mostly devoted to SF, helped authors with negotiating power and advice. Some even offered literary criticism.

The boom in SF magazines following World War II, although it lasted less than a decade, produced as many as forty publications at one time. But, in combination with the increase in book publication, it encouraged many SF writers to chance full-time writing careers. What had been primarily a part-time avocation became a profession. Professionals may not always write better, but they write differently.

The dissolution of the American News Company in the mid-1950s accounted for the collapse of many SF magazines and demonstrated once again the relation of distribution to the magazine field. Distribution also accounts for the success of the best paperback publishers, because returns of their books (actually only the torn-off covers) may run anywhere from 10 to 70 percent, and between these two extremes lie riches and failure, for the author as well as the publisher.

Today a handful of SF magazines exist, as in the 1930s. The most successful sell about 100,000 copies, as they did in the 1930s. The only exception is the primarily article-and-illustration magazine *Omni*, which sells an inspiring 900,000. The major difference is the book field, where more than 1,500 titles are published or reprinted each year. And some of these are achieving best-seller status and earning advances for their authors of $1 million or more. A best-seller, like a book with a $1 million advance, is a specialized product. It must appeal to a broad audience. That fact also influences the nature of the writing that goes into it.

The number of independent publishers, however, has diminished. Publishing is big business, and mergers and purchases, particularly those by large corporations, have consolidated the field. Berkley Books, for instance, bought up Jove Books, Ace Books, and Playboy Press's SF line, and Ballantine Books is owned by Random House. Accountants and sales forces now exercise as much power over SF publication as editors, and publishers are looking hardest for best-sellers and leaders of monthly publication lists that will carry along other titles. That priority too influences the kind of SF authors are encouraged to write—and discouraged from writing.

Motion pictures would seem to be a major economic factor, and indeed some authors are supplementing their incomes with sales of their works to Hollywood or are writing directly for movies and television. In addition, more than half the leading films of the late 1970s and 1980s have been SF, including E.T., STAR WARS and its sequels, the SUPERMAN films, and ALIENS. The audiences drawn to such films, far larger than those who have ever read SF in the past, may have been an influence on the recent growth in the general audience for SF, creating the best-seller, for instance, but they may have been an even greater influence on the growth of the audience for heroic fantasy.

Thus SF, a small part of a very big publishing picture fifty years ago, has become big business. One out of every seven or eight books of fiction published today is SF or fantasy. In a world where the social and physical environment changes at an accelerated pace and the threat of nuclear annihilation is ever present, a broad, perhaps a universal, audience for SF has been created. Science fiction, in return, offers its readers a glimpse of an infinite number of possible tomorrows. It hammers home the lesson that change is inevitable but that the direction of change is under human control. It may be ironic that those cautionary glimpses and hopeful messages have been, and still are being, shaped by economic factors.

L.S.d.C./C.C.d.C.

BUTLER, OCTAVIA E[STELLE] (1947–).
American writer whose fiction draws on Afro-American history and explores multiracial future societies. A Pasadena native, Butler was educated at Pasadena College, California State University, and Clarion SF Writers Workshop. Beginning with her first story, "Crossover" (1971), Butler has explored themes of power and love and has built a reputation as a major writer with a unique viewpoint and contribution.

Octavia Butler

Black women usually are at the center of her novels, but around them Butler develops a wide variety of characters as she deals, through a series of novels, with the creation of a species of superhumans linked in a psychic web known as the Pattern. The Patternists rule "mutes," who lack psychic powers. In *Wild Seed* (1970), which begins in 1690, Doro, an African superman, kills souls and steals bodies in order to breed the racial stock that will become Patternist. In *Mind of My Mind* (1977) Doro's hubris forces a duel with his daughter-lover, who creates the Pattern. In *Clay's Ark* (1984) an extraterrestrial virus mutates humans into beasts, attacking both Patternists and non-Patternists. In *Survivor* (1978) a non-Patternist girl marries an alien and fights other aliens who enslave humans through addiction. Brothers duel for mastery of the psionic Pattern in *Patternmaster* (1976), demonstrating Butler's theme that altruism can triumph.

In a non-Patternist novel, *Kindred* (1979), a contemporary woman is time-warped into the antebellum South, where, as a slave, she copes with ignorance, injustice, and inhumanity. Butler's "Speech Sounds" (1983) won a Hugo for its portrayal of a woman infected with a plague that has destroyed human language. In "Bloodchild" (1984), which won a Nebula, a human male slave willingly gestates eggs for an intelligent alien, suggesting a metaphor for human reproductive politics. *Dawn* (1987) begins a series about aliens altering human genetic structure.

Butler is interested in the relationships of men and women, children and parents, masters and slaves, inferiors and superiors as revealed in struggles for great power and for survival, and in how even under these great stresses human values can develop and prevail.

M.T.B.

BUTOR, MICHEL (1926–   ).

French novelist and critic, a leading proponent and practitioner of the "new novel" and one of the first academics to consider science fiction a serious genre. Butor's critical works include some of the earliest analyses of the work of Jules VERNE as well as the influential essay "La Crise de croissance de la SF" (1953), translated and published in *Partisan Review* in 1967 as "SF: The Crisis of Its Growth." In this work he suggested that SF would be more powerful if its authors wrote about an agreed-upon vision of the future, of which one example would be a common future city.

N.H.

C

CADIGAN, PAT[RICIA K.] (1954–   ).

American writer. Much of Cadigan's fiction is characterized by a sharp focus on the dark side of human psychology and its interaction with developing technologies and popular culture. This focus is particularly evident in stories such as the Nebula Award nominee "Pretty Boy Crossover" (1986), in which a narcissistic "pretty boy" is given the opportunity to be converted into electronic information, and "Patterns" (1987), in which television is shown not only to affect a viewer's perception of reality but actually to become the viewer's reality.

Cadigan's first published story appeared in *New Dimensions* in 1980, and since then her short fiction has come out in *The Magazine of Fantasy and Science Fiction, Omni, Isaac Asimov's Science Fiction Magazine*, and elsewhere. Her best-known works include "Nearly Departed" (1983), "Rock On" (1984), "Roadside Rescue" (1985), and the stories in her Pathosfinders series. Her first novel, *Mindplayers*, was published in 1987. With her husband, Arnold Fenner, Cadigan was coeditor of the semiprofessional magazine *Shayol*, which won a World Fantasy Award in the special achievement, nonprofessional category in 1981.

B.D.

CAIDIN, MARTIN (1927–   ).

American broadcaster, consultant on aviation and aerospace technology, and writer of both science fiction and mainstream novels, as well as numerous books and articles on flight. In his SF Caidin makes extensive use of his experience in the realm of space technology. His novels tend to be "realistic" portrayals of the problems of the space program and the collision of advanced technology with human nature. His best-known novel, *Marooned* (1964; film version 1969), describes what may go wrong not only in space but also among the humans who participate in space ventures. His heroes tend to be tough-minded, highly competent military men who are patriotic, devoted to their jobs, and not quite successful as lovers.

Caidin is a political conservative who frequently uses his fiction to present his views on disarmament (*The Mendelov Conspiracy*, 1969; reprinted in 1978 as *Encounter Three*), world competition in space (*No Man's World*, 1967, and *Cyborg IV*, 1975), and the need in times of devastation for competent military control (*The Long Night*, 1956, and *Four Came Back*, 1968). His Stephen Austin series (*Cyborg*, 1972; *Operation Nuke*, 1973; *High Crystal*, 1974; and *Cyborg IV*, 1975) was the basis for the TV series *The Six Million Dollar Man* and *The Bionic Woman*; although far less known than either TV program, the books examine the relationship between human and machine—a theme completely missing from either series.

OTHER WORKS: *The Last Fathom* (1967); *Aquarius Mission* (1968); *The God Machine* (1969); *Killer Station* (1985); *Exit Earth* (1987).

S.H.G.

CALVINO, ITALO (1923–1985).

Italian writer whose surrealistic style is reminiscent of the work of Jorge Luis BORGES. Calvino's stories and novels make extensive use of paradox, absurdity, and irony to explore contemporary morality. His earliest science-fiction work, *The Cosmicomics* (*Le Cosmicomiche*, 1965), is a collection of linked short stories that trace the history of a cell named Qfwfq as it witnesses events from the creation of the universe to the rise of humanity and the race's subsequent history. Told with a dry, cutting sense of humor, the stories frequently expose the limitations of anthropocentrism. Qfwfq reappears in *T Zero* (*Ti con zero*, 1967; also known as *Time and the Hunter*), another collection of linked stories that explore humanity's relation to the universe, particularly the discrepancy between human notions of time and space and what the "reality" may actually be.

Calvino's most ambitious work is *Invisible Cities* (*Le Città invisibili*, 1972), in which Marco Polo travels with Kubla Khan to a series of extraordinary cities and converses on the power and weakness of human perception. The various episodes supplied numerous occasions for Calvino to indulge his love of paradox and to amplify his favorite theme: that the human perception of reality is as much a work of fiction as any of his stories.

OTHER WORKS: *The Watcher and Other Stories* (collection, 1971); *The Castle of Crossed Destinies* (*Il Castello dei incrociati*, collection, 1973).

S.H.G.

CAMPBELL, JOHN W[OOD], JR. (1910–1971).

American writer and editor, both a product of the early values of pulp science fiction and its greatest shaper. As one critic has said of Campbell, "no man was ever a better learner." With a solid scientific engineering education from MIT and Duke University and an appreciation of space opera and the superscience stories of fellow engineer–pulp writers such as E. E. Smith, Campbell sold his first story while he was still an undergraduate. By the middle years of the Depression he was writing innovative pulp stories far more stylistically sophisticated than his early works of superscience. In 1937 he assumed the editorship of *Astounding*, and in the following years he presided over what has come to be called SF's Golden Age. Most of the best works of that era reflect Campbell's values and his editorial expertise. Although future critics may decide that Campbell's editorial vision was too narrow, his insistence that human survival requires cooperation and intellectual adaptability, as symbolized by modern science and humanized in good storytelling, gave meaning and substance to the optimistic science fiction of World War II and the period immediately after. In fact he never learned the despair associated with holocaust or nuclear disaster; he preferred positive American individualism.

Most critics divide Campbell's own work into two periods, divided in the year 1934, when he started to write under the name Don A. Stuart. The earlier six novels and sets of stories—of which the most popular were those with the protagonists Arcot, Morey, and Wade—consist of heroes working together to make superscience inventions so that the human race might survive; that sort of scenario must have been particularly appealing to the would-be engineers and scientists among his readers. In the first Depression years the only place to find American rugged individualism was in the pages of those early SF magazines.

None of Campbell's pulp novels or sets of stories was set to appear in book form until the end of the 1940s, when SF books became commercially viable, but the name John W. Campbell had become an important companion to that of Doc Smith and others by 1934. Then, writing as Stuart and beginning with the early "Twilight" in the November 1934 issue of *Astounding Stories*, Campbell started to produce fiction of greater philosophical depth and a more ambitious literary style. Critics have concluded that if Campbell himself, writing as Stuart, had not tried to increase sophistication in the writing of SF and then later insisted on depth of meaning with his editorial leadership, the genre would have floundered at the end of the 1930s in formula repetitions. As it was the later Campbell fictions, perhaps best represented by the award-winning Stuart story "Who Goes There?" (1938), simply express a more subtle and better-imaged version of Campbell's belief in adaptable indi-

John W. Campbell (far right) with Randall Garrett, Sam Moskowitz, and Isaac Asimov

viduality as opposed to relentless collectivism. The monster in the story is evil because it is programmed in too monolithic a way and lacks individual adaptability.

In 1937 Campbell was asked to take over the editorship of *Astounding Stories*. He soon changed the magazine's name to *Astounding Science Fiction* as an expression of his vision of a unified genre and later changed it again, to *Analog Science Fact/Fiction*. Once Campbell assumed this new position, his own writing virtually stopped, probably because he had found an ideal role for the embodiment of his belief in cooperative individualism. Campbell edited the magazine (and from 1939 to 1943 a companion fantasy magazine, *Unknown*) until his death. This was, scholars are beginning to conclude, one of the most important editorships in our century. Essentially Campbell salvaged and shaped modern science fiction as a profoundly speculative literature with high standards of writing. He did this in part by actively encouraging writers to develop ideas that he suggested to them in ways that he suggested.

Campbell helped change and improve the work of writers already in the field, such as Jack Williamson, and he discovered and nurtured a whole generation of new writers who are now considered representative of the Golden Age of the genre. Isaac Asimov, one of the latter, has said that Campbell's genius was his ability to wait and select the best writer in whose mind to plant the seed of a new idea. Moreover, Campbell was always generous in giving credit to his colleague writers for their literary inventions, many of which he had first conceived himself. His detailed and vast correspondence with his writers, which is just now beginning to appear in print, promises to shed additional light on Campbell's editorial "collaboration" with his authors. Thanks to his editing, Campbell's vision of cooperative individualism now means much more to us as the inherent optimism of mature SF as well as a clear goal for the many later writers who do not share this perspective.

OTHER WORKS: *The Mightiest Machine* (1947); *The Incredible Planet* (1949); *The Moon Is Hell!* (1951); *Cloak of Aesir* (1952); *The Black Star Passes* (1953); *Who Goes There? and Other Stories* (1955); *Islands of Space* (1957); *Invaders from the Infinite* (1961); *The Ultimate Weapon* (1966); *The Planeteers* (1966); *The Space Beyond* (1976); *The John W. Campbell Letters*, vol. 1 (1985).

D.M.H.

SEE ALSO: EDITORS; GOLDEN AGE

CAPEK, KAREL (1890–1938). Czech writer, best known for his play *R.U.R.* (1921, translated into English 1923), whose title is an acronym for Rossum's Universal Robots.

R.U.R. is credited with introducing the Czech word *robot* (meaning "worker") into English, although the creations it represents would now be called androids. The robots were designed to be economical workers who, because they lacked emotions, would be easier to handle, more dependable, and far cheaper than their human counterparts. However, the intended exploitation of the robots does not follow the course the human inventors imagined, and Čapek used their revolt as a stage for his views on human relationships. Čapek collaborated with his brother Josef in another play, *Ze života hymzu* (best known as *The Insect Play*, 1921, first translated as *And So Ad Infinitum* 1923). This darkly satiric work uses arthropods to expose the danger of humans who allow greed and dreams of power to rule their minds.

Three of Čapek's novels are of particular importance in the history of science fiction. The first, *Továrua na absolutno* (*The Absolute at Large*, 1922, translated 1927), portrays the ironic results of the discovery of how to produce unlimited, cheap power. *Krakatit* (1924, translated 1925) describes the catastrophic consequences of an insane inventor's development of a new explosive. Finally, *Valka s Mloky* (*War with the Newts*, 1936, translated 1937) brings together most of Čapek's earlier themes. A race of sea-dwelling creatures is discovered in the South Pacific and almost immediately exploited by humans. These Newts become slave laborers and captive consumers in order to bring on humanity's golden age. As the Newts acquire human traits, however, they also learn human aggression, and, as in *R.U.R.*, they revolt. Their method of rebellion is far more effective than that of the robots: they threaten to flood the world. Class struggle, hypocrisy, human greed, and social injustice are all part of this novel, yet Čapek managed to balance the potential darkness of the subject matter with such ironic humor that the story never overpowers its readers with depression.

OTHER WORKS: *Věc Mokropulos* (*The Makropoulos Secret*, play, 1925); *Adam stvořitel* (*Adam the Creator*, play with Josef Čapek, 1929); *Money and Other Stories* (collection, 1929); *Povídky z druké kapsy* (*Tales from Two Pockets*, collection, 1932); *Devatero Pohádek* (*Fairy Tales*, collection, 1933); *Power and Glory* (play, 1937); *Kniha Apokryfů* (*Apocryphal Stories*, collection, 1949).

S.H.G.

CAPRICORN ONE (1978). Directed by Peter Hyams; screenplay by Peter Hyams; photographed by Bill Butler; music by Jerry Goldsmith. With Elliott Gould, James Brolin, Brenda Vaccaro, Sam Waterston, Karen Black, Hal Holbrook, Telly Savalas, David Huddleston, David Doyle, Robert Walden, James Sikking, James Karen, O. J. Simpson. 124 minutes. Color.

Budget cutbacks force a harried NASA administrator (Hal Holbrook) to coerce three astronauts (James Brolin, O. J. Simpson, and Sam Waterston) bound for Mars into secretly faking a landing for the media. But their rocket burns up on reentry, and the administrator makes plans to ensure that his "martyrs" are truly dead. Meanwhile, an irascible reporter (Elliott Gould) tracks down leaks in the cover story.

Inspired by rumors claiming the lunar landings were faked, *Capricorn One* may be unlikely, but it's Peter Hyams's liveliest science-fiction film, however borderline. (His others include OUTLAND and 2010.) A failure as satire, it includes car chases, plane wrecks, amusing performances, helicopter battles, and a fast pace that keep audiences from scoffing until after the film ends.

B.W.

CARD, ORSON SCOTT (1951–   ). American writer who has become a major science-fiction author in a remarkably short time; his stature has been confirmed by the winning of consecutive Nebula and Hugo Awards in the best novel category for *Ender's Game* (1985) and its sequel, *Speaker for the Dead* (1986).

A practicing Mormon, Card, the son of a professor, earned his bachelor's degree in theater from Brigham Young University and worked at playwriting before turning to fiction. He earned an M.A. in English as well and began work toward a Ph.D. before dropping out to pick up a career as an editor of computer books and then as a full-time writer.

After early success with short fiction, collected in *Capitol* (1978) and *Unaccompanied Sonata and Other Stories* (1981), that earned him the Campbell Award for best new writer in 1978, Card began publishing novels, starting with *Hot Sleep* (1978), *A Planet Called Treason*

(1979), and *Songmaster* (1980). He has retained a commitment to short fiction, however, and, after contributing a review column to one fanzine, founded his own review of short fiction, *Short Form*, and accepted chairmanship of the Sturgeon Memorial Award for the best short SF.

Card's intelligence and rapidly developing skills have combined the strengths of adventure literature and moral probing in the manner of C. S. Lewis. His major theme, as illustrated in *Songmaster* and *Ender's Game*, is the rite of passage, as children with exceptional potential are deprived of community and thrust into positions of pain and high responsibility, bearing them with fortitude and growing strength and wisdom, and saving the community in the end.

In *Ender's Game*, for example, Ender Wiggins is taken from his family and forced to survive by his wits and courage in an elite military academy whose purpose is to find a military savior against invading aliens. *Speaker for the Dead* finds Ender in a more conciliatory role as he tries to cope with his guilt for having unwittingly wiped out an entire alien species and is called upon to deal with another group of aliens.

Card launched another series, a science fantasy of an early 1800s alternate America in which folk magic is real, with *Seventh Son* (1987), volume one in Tales of Alvin Maker. He is likely to be a force in science fiction for many years to come, combining as he does the virtues of successful creation and critical analysis.

OTHER WORKS: *Hart's Hope* (1983); *The Worthing Chronicle* (1983); *Wyrms* (1987); *Red Prophet* (1987, vol. 2 of Alvin Maker); *Prentice Alvin* (1988, vol. 3 of Alvin Maker); *Book of Spells* (1988).

J.R.D.

CARLSON, RICHARD (1912–1977).
American actor, director, and writer often associated with science-fiction films. Carlson's numerous published writings include stories, articles, and film scripts; his deep and abiding interest in science fiction led to collaborations with Curt Siodmak on The Magnetic Monster (1953), in which he acted, and Riders to the Stars (1954). He not only acted in *Riders*, but directed the film as well.

After graduation from the University of Minnesota, Carlson became a Broadway actor and made the transition to film with *The Young at Heart* and *The Duke of West Point* in 1938. Although he appeared in many traditional films, such as *The Little Foxes* (1941), the handsome, reserved actor is remembered by 1950s and 1960s science-fiction film viewers for his numerous roles in such films as It Came from Outer Space (1953), The Maze (1953), Creature from the Black Lagoon (1954), The Power (1968), and the SF-related *King Solomon's Mines* (1950).

H.L.P.

CARPENTER, JOHN (1948–).
American film director known primarily for his riveting action sequences. Carpenter's work thus far has favored the science-fiction and horror genres, narrative types for which he feels a personal affinity. (It was after seeing movies such as It Came from Outer Space and Forbidden Planet that he decided to become a director.) Carpenter also works on the special effects photography, scripts, and music for his films, and he has established his own compelling style in the tradition of Hollywood's greatest storytellers.

While a graduate film student at the University of Southern California, Carpenter made a number of short films, including *The Resurrection of Bronco Billy*, which won an Academy Award in 1970. For his graduate thesis film, he collaborated with classmate Dan O'Bannon to make a short SF movie, Dark Star, which in 1974 was expanded into his first feature film. His first great commercial success came with the low-budget horror classic *Halloween* (1978), whose box-office earnings launched a series of Halloween sequels (directed by others) as well as Carpenter's entry into the commercial mainstream and bigger budgets.

Carpenter's approach to filmmaking clearly emphasizes story and entertainment values above theme. If there is meaning in his movies, it emerges from the action and style rather than being injected into them. In many ways then Carpenter signifies a continuation of the classic American style of action movie represented by John Ford, Alfred Hitchcock, and especially Howard Hawks, a significant influence on his work. And like Hawks's in his adventure films, Carpenter's greatest skill is the straightforward depiction of action, refined almost to what might be called "pure" cinema. Pacing, mood, and a sure sense of editing are the basic elements of his action sequences. John Houseman's masterful recitation of a ghost story to a group of spellbound children around a nighttime campfire, the opening sequence of *The Fog* (1980), is, in a sense, a perfect metaphor for the director's own art in relation to his audience. His science fiction, like all his work, tends to concentrate on those aspects of the genre that lend themselves to his personal vision of moviemaking.

Carpenter is clearly concerned with the themes of communication and loneliness. In *Dark Star* outer space becomes the vast distances of inner space, as the men on the ship grow apart through boredom and different interests; one crewman remains spatially separated for virtually the entire film, peacefully watching the heavens in the ship's observation dome. The suspense in The Thing (1982) is the result of mutual alienation and distrust; every member of the expedition suspects that the others may be monsters. The final images show the two survivors warily sitting opposite each other, separated by the icy environment.

Since moving into mainstream filmmaking Carpenter

has had bigger budgets, but the results have been less exciting. *The Thing*, for example, the first film over which Carpenter did not have contractual control, concentrates so much on Rob Bottin's special effects that the ostensible humanist theme is swamped. Similarly ESCAPE FROM NEW YORK (1981) drops its potentially compelling premise to focus on rather conventional action. *Christine* (1983) begins promisingly as an exploration of American culture's automobile fetish, but as the film progresses the social and sexual inadequacies of the teenage protagonist are eclipsed by the spectacle of the car's various physical metamorphoses.

STARMAN (1984), however, is something of an anomaly in Carpenter's oeuvre, and more successful probably for that reason. Here, action is sacrificed for character and a sense of intimacy. Carpenter dwelled not on the dangers of isolation but on the developing romance between an alien and an Earthwoman. But this film stands out in a series of mixed successes. Carpenter's most recent film, *Big Trouble in Little China* (1986), once again concentrates too much on action and not enough on character, and it was a box-office flop. It remains to be seen whether Carpenter can successfully combine his filmmaking instincts with the requirements of the commercial mainstream.

B.K.G.

CARR, JAYGE (Pseudonym of Margery Krueger) (1940–   ).

American writer whose work is characterized by fine writing, detailed characterizations, sophisticated humor, and a sense that bigotry of any kind is intolerable. A former nuclear physicist, Carr began her career in science fiction with the publication of her story "Alienation" in the October 1976 issue of *Analog* under the name Jaygee Carr. Her story "Blind Spot" (1981) was reprinted in *The 1982 Annual World's Best SF* (Donald A. WOLLHEIM and Arthur W. Saha, eds.), and "Webrider" (1985) was reprinted in the 1986 edition of the same anthology. Her novels include *Leviathan's Deep* (1979), *Navigator's Sindrome* (1983), and *The Treasure in the Heart of the Maze* (1985). *Leviathan's Deep* in particular—with its strong female protagonist and its depiction of an alien matriarchy—has frequently been read as a feminist novel.

B.D.

CARR, TERRY (1937–1987).

American editor and writer, active in FANDOM from his teens; winner of Hugo Awards for best fanzine (with Ron Ellik, 1959) and best fan writer (1973). By the 1960s Carr was working at Ace Books, where he coedited best of the year ANTHOLOGIES with Donald WOLLHEIM and produced the first of his *Universe* original anthology series (seventeen numbered volumes, 1971–1987). In 1967 he began the Ace Science Fiction Special series, which presented work by Philip K. DICK, R. A. LAFFERTY, and Ursula K. LE GUIN, among others. After leaving Ace, Carr continued to edit *Universe* and an annual best-of-the-year volume, as well as many other original reprint anthologies. In the 1980s he returned to a revived Ace Specials series with results as impressive as the first.

Carr was a distinguished but not a prolific writer: he produced three novels (one a collaboration) and the short story collection *The Light at the End of the Universe* (1976), which includes "The Dance of the Changer and the Three" (1968), "Hop-Friend" (1962), and "They Live on Levels" (1973). His writing, like his editing, aspired to combine traditional genre tropes and attitudes with the more "writerly" concerns of the NEW WAVE of the 1960s and 1970s. Like his colleagues Damon KNIGHT and Robert SILVERBERG, Carr used the double role of writer-editor to offer a model of what the field can be at its best.

OTHER WORKS: *Warlord of Kor* (1963); *Invasion from 2500* (with Ted White as "Norman Edwards," 1964); *Cirque* (1977); *Between Two Worlds/Messages Found in an Oxygen Bottle* (with Bob Shaw, back-to-back collections of fan writing, 1986); *Fandom Harvest* (fan writing, 1986).

SELECTED ANTHOLOGIES: *World's Best Science Fiction: 1965* (with Donald A. Wollheim, 7 dated volumes through 1971); *New Worlds of Fantasy* (3 numbers, 1967, 1970, 1971); *The Best Science Fiction of the Year* (15 numbered annual volumes 1972–1986); *This Side of Infinity* (1972); *An Exaltation of Stars* (1973); *Into the Unknown* (1973); *Fellowship of the Stars* (1974); *Year's Finest Fantasy* (1978; *Volume 2*, 1979); *The Best Science Fiction Novellas of the Year 1* (1979; 2, 1980); *Fantasy Annual 3* (1981; 4, 1981; 5, 1982); *A Treasury of Modern Fantasy* (with Martin H. Greenberg, 1981); *Science Fiction Hall of Fame, Volume 4* (1986).

R.F.L.

CARROLL, LEWIS (Pseudonym of Charles Lutwidge Dodgson) (1832–1898).

British mathematician and writer best known for the classic fantasies *Alice's Adventures in Wonderland* (1865) and *Through the Looking Glass* (1871). Brian W. ALDISS aptly remarked that, although these two books "form no part of science fiction," Carroll's fondness for logical inversion and his pleasure in placing Alice in situations that absurdly distort commonplace events has had a "marked effect on the field." Calling these two "children's" works a bridge between the worlds of Beatrix Potter and E. E. "Doc" SMITH's the Gray Lensman, Aldiss credited them with influencing such science-fiction writers as John W. CAMPBELL, Henry KUTTNER, Ray BRADBURY, Eric Frank RUSSELL, and Robert SHECKLEY. A number of

Illustration by Cartier for George O. Smith's "Rat Race" (Astounding, August 1947)

number of series.

Carter's first novels, starting with *The Wizard of Lemuria* (1965), feature the Conanesque Thongor on the lost continent of Lemuria. He moved from the distant past to the dying future for his Gondwane sequence, starting with *Giant of World's End* (1969). Two SF series by convention are the Burroughs-influenced Jandar sequence, starting with *Jandar of Callisto* (1972), and the Green-Star sequence, beginning with *Under the Green Star* (1972). Carter writes his novels out of a nostalgic reverence for the old pulp writers and magazines, especially *Planet Stories*, but his pastiches are frequently poor imitations and do more to injure the memory. His best SF has been his lighthearted but enjoyable escapades of the intergalactic secret agent and licensed criminal Hautley Quicksilver, who first appeared in "Crown of Stars" (1966; expanded as *The Thief of Thoth*, 1968) and then in *The Purloined Planet* (1969).

NOTABLE OTHER WORKS: *The Star Magicians* (1966); *The Man without a Planet* (1966), with sequels *Star Rogue* (1970) and *Outworlder* (1971); *The Man Who Loved Mars* (1973); *Beyond the Gates of Dream* (collection, 1969); *Dragonrouge* (1984).

M.A.

SF stories also have referred to Carroll's long poem *The Hunting of the Snark* (1876).

Carroll was the master of giving so-called nonsense stories an underlying logic—an approach that prefigured alternate-world and alternate-history SF, in which fictional worlds resemble the real world but differ in several significant points. In both Alice stories Carroll used the fantastic world of Wonderland to confront contemporary social customs, beliefs, and even fears just as in the twentieth century SF writers have rearranged reality to challenge popular thinking.

He also wrote two collections featuring logical fantasies like those in Alice's adventures: *A Tangled Tale* (1886) and *The Game of Logic* (1887).

S.H.G.

CARTER, LIN[WOOD VROOMAN] (1930–).

American writer, mostly of fantasy with nearly sixty solo novels plus many collaborations to his credit. Carter's greatest service to fantasy has been as an editor and anthologist; he has helped resurrect forgotten works and contributed to the revival in popularity of fantasy in the late 1960s, particularly as a consultant to Ballantine Books. Carter was heavily influenced by the works of Edgar Rice BURROUGHS, A. MERRITT, and Robert E. HOWARD, and his stories and novels are highly derivative—even most of his science fiction is SF by locale and convention, rather than idea. Almost all his novels fit into one of a

CARTIER, EDD (1914–).

American science-fiction and fantasy illustrator. Cartier is primarily known for his black-and-white interior illustrations for such magazines as *Astounding Science Fiction, Planet Stories, Unknown,* and *Other Worlds*. Although Cartier produced little color work, he did paint several covers for *Unknown*. Some of his best known illustrations for *Unknown* were for L. Ron HUBBARD's "Fear" and Jack WILLIAMSON's "Darker Than You Think" and illustrations in *Astounding* for Hubbard's "Old Doc Methuselah" and L. Sprague DE CAMP's "The Hand of Zei."

Cartier produced most of his work between 1940 and 1954 (when he left freelance illustration) with a break during World War II. His art ranges from horror to humor, both of which he could depict with equal facility. His clean lines and smooth modeling were his trademarks, and his style was one of the genre's most distinctive until the arrival of Frank FREAS and Ed EMSHWILLER.

J.G.

CARTMILL, CLEVE (1908–1964).

American author, journalist, and inventor whose fame in science fiction rests on one story, "Deadline" (1944), which accurately detailed the atomic bomb a year before its revelation and caused American security to investigate both Cartmill and editor John W. CAMPBELL. (The whole episode is related in Albert Berger's article "The Manhattan Project's Confrontation with Science Fiction" in *Analog*, September 1984.) "Deadline" is otherwise a routine story, and its notoriety has overshadowed Cartmill's other works, many of which are more worthy. He was never prolific, producing a little over forty stories after his first, "Oscar" (1941). His work includes such competent and smoothly written political science fiction as "With Flaming Swords" and "Overthrow" (both 1942). "The Link" (1942) is a touching story about emerging Man. Cartmill also wrote a series about a space salvage team during 1949–50; these were posthumously collected as *The Space Scavengers* (1975).

M.A.

CAT-WOMEN OF THE MOON (1953). *Directed by Arthur Hilton; screenplay by Roy Hamilton; photographed by William Whitney; music by Elmer Bernstein. With Sonny Tufts, Victor Jory, Marie Windsor, Bill Phipps, Douglas Fowley, Carol Brewster, Susan Morrow, Suzanne Alexander, and The Hollywood Cover Girls as the Cat-Women of the Moon. 64 minutes. Black and white.*

Regarded as an authentic camp classic, the 3-D *Cat-Women of the Moon* gets everything wrong. Classic bad guy Victor Jory plays a dashing hero, the Moon looks like Monument Valley—on the inside—and is populated by gorgeous women in slinky leotards; one of the Cat-Women asks a second-string hero (Bill Phipps) if he has "a special Earth girl" and wants to go to Earth so she can visit the beach and have a Coke. The earnest makers of this film clearly ran out of money, and the climax is dealt with solely in off-screen dialogue. The surprising aspects are the filmmaker's conviction, the good performances by the leads, and the swift pace; these make *Cat-Women* one of the most watchable awful movies. Certainly it is far superior to its remake, the execrable *Missile to the Moon* (1958).

B.W.

CATACLYSM AND CATASTROPHE

Human kind has always been haunted by the fear of disaster. Myths of plague and deluge occur in our most sacred writings, and it is not surprising that such motifs are frequently echoed in fiction.

Apocalyptic themes had a brief vogue in the early nineteenth century, which produced Mary SHELLEY's *The Last Man* (1826) and other works. They had a second wave of fashionability at the end of that century, when the popularization of a new cosmology called attention to the Earth's vulnerability to cosmic disaster. The French astronomer Camille Flammarion made much of such ideas in *Omega* (1894), and they are echoed in the work of many contemporary writers, including George GRIFFITH (*Olga Romanoff*, 1894) and H. G. WELLS ("The Star," 1897). Flammarion also wrote about the ultimate

destiny of the Earth if it were to survive destruction, becoming desolate as the Sun cooled. Such eschatological imagery is also found in contemporary imaginative fiction, in *The Time Machine* (1895) by Wells and *The House on the Borderland* (1908) by William Hope HODGSON.

Other visitations of disaster were commonplace in this period too: mass poisonings in M. P. SHIEL's *The Purple Cloud* (1901) and Arthur Conan DOYLE's *The Poison Belt* (1913); monstrous epidemics in "The Scarlet Plague" (1912) by Jack LONDON and *Goslings* (1913) by J. D. BERESFORD. Many of these stories show a curious ambivalence about the destruction of civilization; there is horror in the tragedy but also a powerful romanticism in imagining oneself a survivor in an empty world.

Postcatastrophe romanticism came increasingly to the fore after 1912, the year it was elaborately extended in the first volume of George Allan ENGLAND's Darkness and Dawn trilogy. Comfort could be taken from the contemplation of disaster if one could think of it as a quasi-diluvian cleansing or a Darwinian winnowing, and such lines of argument were frequently advanced; they are prominent in Garrett P. SERVISS's *The Second Deluge* (1912), S. Fowler WRIGHT's *Deluge* (1928), and David H. KELLER's *The Metal Doom* (1932). There was also a certain appeal in the notion of a tightly organized and disciplined community assuring its own survival by collective effort while fighting off assaults from the world at large, to which misfortune has brought anarchy. *Nordenholt's Million* (1923) by J. J. Connington and *When Worlds Collide* (1933) by Philip WYLIE and Edwin BALMER are examples.

In the wake of World War I, British writers produced many accounts of civilization destroyed by warfare (although there is little trace of such anxiety in contemporary American SF), but after World War II this tradition of pessimistic fantasies (most popularly depicted in Nevil SHUTE's 1957 *On the Beach*) was extended in a preoccupation with natural catastrophes that played a central role in the careers of such writers as John WYNDHAM, John CHRISTOPHER, and Charles Eric MAINE. Works in this tradition gradually evolved a profound fascination with the hypothetical psychology of human reactions to disaster, which was to be most elaborately explored by J. G. BALLARD in many works, the most famous being *The Drowned World* (1962), *The Drought* (1964), and *The Crystal World* (1966).

Apart from one very conscientious treatment, in George R. STEWART's *Earth Abides* (1949), American science fiction had no tradition parallel to this British preoccupation save its dealings with nuclear holocausts. Fritz LEIBER's *The Wanderer* (1964) reintroduced into American SF the disaster story told from multiple viewpoints, but it turned out to be ahead of its time. There was a veritable boom in such stories in the 1970s, aided by such cinematic successes as *Earthquake* and *The Tow-*

ering Inferno. Because cosmic disaster stories are so difficult to film, they remained peripheral to the main phenomenon, but *Lucifer's Hammer* (1977) by Larry NIVEN and Jerry POURNELLE achieved best-seller status. A sense of urgency drew many ecocatastrophe stories toward the horrific and the tragic; those dealing with pollution, such as *The Sheep Look Up* (1972) by John BRUNNER and *The End of the Dream* (1972) by Philip WYLIE, tend to be particularly hysterical. More recent works, though, have swung back toward ambivalence, if not outright romanticism, and American SF of the 1980s seems to be developing a mythology of the postholocaust frontier, elaborated in such works as *In the Drift* (1985) by Michael Swanwick and *Dinner at Deviant's Palace* (1985) by Tim POWERS.

B.S.

CHALKER, JACK L[AURENCE] (1944–   ).
American writer of dystopian science fiction and fantasy, with special interests in politics, ecology, and history. Although Chalker has a technical background, his academic degrees are in history, English, and law. Never a practicing attorney, he taught geography and history in Baltimore public schools before becoming a full-time writer in 1978. Like many SF writers, Chalker was first a fan, editing his own fanzine, *Mirage*, and later creating The Mirage Press, which is devoted to publishing SF scholarship.

Chalker's knowledge of history and law do much to shape his art, which concentrates on the dilemmas and choices of power-wielding characters, many of whom consider the virtues and vices of communal utopian and radically independent capitalist cultures. *A Jungle of Stars* (1976), though partially set in Vietnam, explores these issues. Even more graphic on this subject is *Dancers in the Afterglow* (1978), in which aliens called the Combine conquer a planet, subdue it through thought control, and create a communal life-style for the inhabitants that reduces many to herd or flock animals. Which is better, the alienation and waste of the preconquest culture or the understanding and sharing but lack of individual achievement after conquest? Chalker does not answer but makes his readers deliberate while they are being entertained. *A War of Shadows* (1979), about viral research, and *The Identity Matrix* (1982), about mind switching, also ponder how much social control is good.

Chalker has written several successful series dealing with utopian and environmental concerns. The five Well World novels (1977–1980) explore environmental adaptation and power through the myriad alien life-forms Chalker created for the Well World hexes. The Four Lords of the Diamond tetralogy (1981–1983) again deals with adaptation to environment, both political and physical, in this case of human characters experiencing worlds radically different from Earth, such as a tree-house cul-

ture above an ocean planet. The Soul Rider series (1984–1985), in which social and economic class is established by the amount of alternate universe energy one is permitted to use, also quivers with similar ideological and political configurations, as do the Rings of the Master and Dancing Gods series. Although Chalker is not a stylist like Ursula K. LE GUIN or Philip K. DICK, his work is distinguished by imagination, a fascination with political and social orders, satisfying, suspenseful, action-oriented plots, and characters, such as Mavra Chang, whose strongest trait is survival.

OTHER WORKS: *The New H. P. Lovecraft Bibliography* (1962); *The Index to Science Fiction Publishers* (1966); *The Necromicon: A Study* (1967); *An Informal Biography of Scrooge McDuck* (1974); *Midnight at the Well of Souls* (1977); *The Web of the Chozen* (1978); *Exiles at the Well of Souls* (1978); *Quest for the Well of Souls* (1978); *And the Devil Will Drag You Under* (1979); *The Return of Nathan Brazil* (1980); *Twilight at the Well of Souls* (1980); *Lilith: A Snake in the Grass* (1981); *The Devil's Voyage* (1981); *Cerberus: A Wolf in the Fold* (1982); *Charon: A Dragon at the Gate* (1982); *Medusa: A Tiger by the Tail* (1983); *The River of Dancing Gods* (1984); *Demons of the Dancing Gods* (1984); *Spirits of Flux and Anchor* (1984); *Empires of Flux and Anchor* (1984); *The Birth of Flux and Anchor* (1985); *Masters of Flux and Anchor* (1985); *Downtiming the Night Side* (1985); *Vengeance of the Dancing Gods* (1985); *Lords of the Middle Dark* (1986); *The Messiah Choice* (1986); *Children of Flux and Anchor* (1986).

C.B.

CHANDLER, A[RTHUR] BERTRAM (1912–1984).
English-born author and seaman, who became an Australian citizen; among his best-known works is "Giant Killer," about a strange space derelict, published in *Astounding* in 1945. Chandler's many years as a merchant seaman show in virtually all his fiction. He once remarked that only someone who knows ships and shipboard routine can write convincingly about spaceships, and he spent much of his career proving the point.

Much of Chandler's fiction details the life and times of John Grimes, an interstellar Horatio Hornblower of the Rim Worlds near the edge of the Milky Way. Some of the stories are extremely imaginative, others mere transplanted sea adventures. *Contraband from Otherspace* (1967), with its description of an alien derelict, interdimensional travel, and ratlike humanoids, shows Chandler's imagination to excellent effect. In contrast, *The Big Black Mark* (1975) is little more than an outer-space version of the famous mutiny on the HMS *Bounty*. (Chandler felt Captain Bligh was maligned, and dedicated a book to him.)

Not all Chandler's books follow the space-seaman pattern. *The Bitter Pill* (1974) is a grim exercise in future sociology; *False Fatherhood* (1968; as *Spartan Planet*, 1969) is a satiric account of an all-male society in which women are unknown. *Kelly Country* (1983) is an alternate history, in which the protagonist, nineteenth-century Australian revolutionary Ned Kelly, wins and establishes a republic.

Chandler was a capable and prolific writer, and his knowledge of ships gave his space-faring science fiction an uncommon degree of realism. Although his characterizations are often standard, and some of his plots are basically sea stories in SF dress, he remains a popular and readable writer.

OTHER WORKS: *Bring Back Yesterday* (1961); *Rendezvous on a Lost World* (1961; retitled *When the Dream Dies*, 1981); *The Rim of Space* (1961); *Beyond the Galactic Rim/The Ship from Outside* (1963); *The Hamelin Plague* (1963); *Glory Planet* (1964); *The Deep Reaches of Space* (1964); *Into the Alternate Universe/The Coils of Time* (1964); *Empress of Outer Space/The Alternate Martians* (1965); *Space Mercenaries* (1965); *The Road to the Rim* (1967); *Nebula Alert* (1967); *The Rim Gods* (1968); *Catch the Star Winds* (1969); *The Sea Beasts* (1971); *The Dark Dimensions/Alternate Orbits* (1971; *Alternate Orbits* published separately as *The Commodore at Sea*, 1979); *To Prime the Pump* (1971); *The Inheritors/The Gateway to Never* (1972); *The Hard Way Up* (1972); *The Broken Cycle* (1975); *Star Courier* (1977); *The Way Back* (1978); *To Keep the Ship* (1978); *The Far Traveller* (1979); *Star Loot* (1981); *The Anarch Lords* (1981); *Up to the Sky in Ships* (1982); *Matilda's Stepchildren* (1983); *Frontier of the Dark* (1984); *The Last Amazon* (1984); *The Wild Ones* (1984).

D.S.

CHAPDELAINE, PERRY A. (1925–   ).

American writer, mathematician, and psychologist whose fiction is primarily about alien contact. Chapdelaine's first science-fiction novel, *Swampworld West* (1974), deals with the tensions that develop between a colony of Earth natives and the natives of an alien planet. He founded the Author's Cooperative, which has published several SF and SF-related books.

Chapdelaine's most substantial contribution to science fiction, however, may well be a major project currently under development, to rescue, edit, and reproduce the correspondence of John W. CAMPBELL, the first volume of which, *The John W. Campbell Letters*, edited by Perry A. Chapdelaine, Tony Chapdelaine, and George Hay, emerged from Author's Cooperative Projects in 1985.

OTHER WORK: *The Laughing Terran* (1977).

S.H.G.

───── CHARACTERS ─────

The critical assessment of all works of science fiction as stories of character misses the vital point that many works of SF are not stories of character but are fictions of other types. For example, when science fiction is considered by its writers and readers as "the literature of ideas," one of its traditional definitions, character is necessarily subordinated to thematic content. Contrariwise, when science fiction is regarded as an alternate mode for the presentation of other, more conventional narratives, emphasis on and consequently development of character is more appropriate.

In his essay "On Science Fiction" C. S. LEWIS denounced reviewers who condemn a book because they dislike the genre to which it belongs. "Let bad tragedies be censured by those who love tragedy, and bad detective stories by those who love the detective story," Lewis wrote. "Then we shall learn their real faults. Otherwise we shall find epics blamed for not being novels, farces for not being high comedies, novels by James for lacking the swift action of Smollett."

From the beginnings of modern SF in the nineteenth century, authors have been faced with the choice between writing about characters and using characters as a vehicle through which exotic locations, phenomena, and principles are presented.

The second choice, with occasional exceptions, was dominant through most of the nineteenth century and the twentieth century before the end of the pulp era in the 1950s. Since the 1950s, in part through the heightened standards demanded by James BLISH, Damon KNIGHT, and other critics, and in part through the influence of H. L. GOLD, Anthony BOUCHER, and other editors, characterization in SF has received increased emphasis.

In Mary SHELLEY's *Frankenstein*, regarded by some as the first SF novel and surely one of the most influential ever written, character is overwhelmed by theme. The novel abounds with characters, most notably Frankenstein himself, Elizabeth, and the monster. But the great moral themes, the dichotomy of Promethean versus Faustian implications of the application of science and of power, reduce the personal considerations of individual characters to the level of trivial concerns.

In the great works of H. G. WELLS, characters are again subordinated to external events and phenomena. In *The Time Machine* Wells declined even to give his protagonist a name: he is simply The Time Traveller. The deliberation given to this decision is shown by the fact that Wells had named the protagonist in earlier versions of the story. In other Wells books and stories characters are named, but they are rarely developed, and often they are merely viewpoints. Even when central to the story (as in *The Invisible Man*), they are clearly objects of utility rather than of real concern.

The works of Edgar Rice BURROUGHS, by contrast, are

primarily adventure stories and therefore require a strong central character—the adventurer. In them the locale—whether Mars or Venus, the African jungle or the center of the Earth—is of only passing concern. Burroughs was a master of the exotic touch, but what he really wrote about was daring swashbucklers, foul-hearted villains, beautiful princesses held in durance vile, and all the rest of the paraphernalia of late Victorian romance.

Thus Burroughs's John Carter and Dejah Thoris, Tarzan and Jane, and other characters are heavily emphasized and extensively developed. This development may seem excessively romantic and grossly unrealistic to the reader more accustomed to later, naturalistic characterization, but it nonetheless represents a major contrast to the characters of Shelley and Wells. It should also be noted that Burroughs's less exaggerated and romanticized characters, David Innes of Pellucidar and Carson Napier of Venus, were both less popular commercially when the books concerning them were published and are regarded as less memorable than their more exaggerated counterparts.

Clearly Burroughs strove for vividness rather than subtlety in his portrayals; his characters are imagistic (not to say stereotypical). To condemn them for their limitations and unreality is to miss the point that they are projections of the essence of heroism, villainy, or beauty; they were never intended to be fully rounded, realistic characters complete with toothaches, menstrual cramps, and assorted neuroses.

Similarly, the overdrawn characters of adventure-oriented space opera are fondly and vividly remembered by veteran readers. Examples are E. E. SMITH's Richard Seaton (The Skylark of Space) and Kimball Kinnison (Gray Lensman), Edmond HAMILTON's Curtis Newton (Captain Future) and the title character of Star Wolf, and the members of Jack WILLIAMSON's Legion of Space. An illuminating contrast is found in the space operas of John W. CAMPBELL, for Campbell's manifest interest lay in the principles and theories of physics that his characters expounded rather than in the characters themselves or their activities per se. His characters are consequently unmemorable.

The use of character as moral, political, or psychological paradigm offers the possibility of creating men and women who potentiate the thematic material of the stories in which they appear, rather than competing with this material for emphasis. Consider George ORWELL's Nineteen Eighty-four. Although the author's major concern in this book is obviously political and cautionary, Winston, Julia, and O'Brien remain vivid and memorable even though they are defined by their relationship to their society.

In this regard Lewis suggested that those SF works exemplified by Wells's First Men in the Moon ought to be "tried by their own rules." He decried as "absurd" the notion that, because they display no deep or extraordinary characterization, they are somehow flawed. In fact, Lewis wrote, "it is a fault if they do. Wells's Cavor and Bedford have rather too much than too little character. Every good writer knows that the more unusual the scenes and events of his story are, the slighter, the more ordinary, the more typical his persons should be."

Obviously there are strong counterarguments to be made: that extraordinary men and women are more suitable protagonists for extravagant tales than are ordinary ones. However, a danger in placing too-overdrawn characters in fantastic situations lies in the double severing of connection to the reader's experience. Either realistic characters in fantastic situations or fantastic characters in realistic situations are fine. But as Lewis said, "To tell how odd things struck odd people is to have an oddity too much."

The placement of ordinary rather than extraordinary characters in extraordinary situations has led to some of the finest works of science fiction. A sampling might include Bob Arctor of Philip K. DICK's A Scanner Darkly, Thomas Jerome Newton of Walter TEVIS's The Man Who Fell to Earth, the physicist Shevek of Ursula K. LE GUIN's The Dispossessed, Daniel Weinreb of Thomas M. DISCH's On Wings of Song, Andrew Wiggin of Orson Scott CARD's Ender's Game and Speaker for the Dead, young Thorby Baslim of Robert A. HEINLEIN's Citizen of the Galaxy, and the multiple and collective protagonists of Theodore STURGEON's More Than Human. None of these is larger than life, none is particularly romanticized. None is memorable in the sense that a John Carter or a Kimball Kinnison is, but all are in fact more effective creations than these romantic figures by reason of their ordinariness.

With the development of more mature forms of science fiction, in which psychological and particularly sexual matters are treated seriously and with openness, there arises the danger of a new imbalance. Works appear in which introspection becomes the primary, even the exclusive, mode of action or narration. Examples are found in Heinlein's short story "All You Zombies" and in his later novels, from Stranger in a Strange Land on. A similar trend is obvious in the late works of Dick, from Valis on, and in the introspective novels of the prolific Barry MALZBERG.

In the continuing development of science fiction, authors will face the challenge of balancing the demands for strong characterization (whether of romantic figures, hypernaturalistic antiheroes, or more evenhandedly conceived centrist protagonists) with other thematic content.

R.A.L.

CHARBONNEAU, LOUIS [HENRY] (1924–).
American journalist and author of radio plays, westerns, mysteries, and science fiction. Charbonneau's novels

often depict dystopian worlds where his protagonists battle different kinds of repressive systems, as in *No Place on Earth* (1958), *The Sentinel Stars* (1963), and *Psychedelic-40* (1964; British title *The Specials*).

J.H.

CHARLY (1968).

Directed by Ralph Nelson; screenplay by Stirling Silliphant; adapted from the novel Flowers for Algernon *by Daniel Keyes. With Cliff Robertson, Claire Bloom, Lilia Skala, Dick Van Patten. 106 minutes. Color.*

A fine adaptation of the famous, Hugo-winning Daniel KEYES novel, *Charly* is the story of Charlie Gordon, a retarded man who is made artificially intelligent for a short while, only to revert to his former state. The film is especially notable for its sensitive treatment of the theme of intelligence—uncommon in science-fiction cinema and probably one of the reasons the general public failed to recognize the movie as science fiction. (The other reason is, of course, the lack of the familiar SF icons—robots, spaceships, and so on.) Typical of the period in which it was made, *Charly* expresses doubts about the morality—and efficacy—of science's intrusion into human biology and psychology.

Ultimately, though, this is as much a film about character as it is about science, and it is Cliff Robertson's realization of the title character (for which he won an Academy Award) that gives the film its force. Although it inevitably lacks the close-in focus of the original story's first-person narrative, other aspects of the story-to-film adaptation are extremely successful: the white mouse Algernon running in a maze is an effective visual symbol for Charlie's plight, even as the mouse was used, in a different way, in the novel.

Claire Bloom is similarly effective in a supporting role as Charlie's teacher and in the developing relationship between them, as Charlie's intelligence grows and he awakens emotionally and sexually. The film is characterized by delicacy and restraint, except perhaps in the interview scene in which Charlie, at the brief zenith of his genius, indicts the callous modern world with a series of scathing platitudes. Perhaps these were inevitable, given the political climate of America in the late 1960s, but they remain the least convincing, and now the most dated aspect of the film. In every other way, however, *Charly* is a beautiful and moving piece of work.

D.S.

CHARNAS, SUZY MCKEE (1939–   ).

American writer whose first two novels, *Walk to the End of the World* (1974) and its sequel *Motherlines* (1979), explore the extremes of sexism in their depiction of postholocaust societies, one male dominated and misogynistic, the other all female. Charnas's *The Vampire Tapestry*

(1980), a collection of interconnected novellas including the Nebula Award winner "The Unicorn Tapestry," is innovative in its demythologized representation of a vampire. In *Dorothea Dreams* (1986) the theme of reincarnation—or time-spanning mind linkage—is woven into an otherwise realistic 1980s setting.

J.H.

CHERRYH, C[AROLYN] J[ANICE] (1942–   ).

American writer whose work has always been marked by versatility. Cherryh made her debut (and added the final *h* to her name at the suggestion of her publisher) with *Gate of Ivrel* (1976), a science-fantasy adventure, but she has since shown an equal grasp of the substance and the spirit of both hard science fiction (*Downbelow Station*, 1981) and pure fantasy (*The Tree of Swords and Jewels*, 1983). She has made a remarkably fast move into the front rank of SF and fantasy writers in popularity and success.

Cherryh studied anthropology, archaeology, classical history, and linguistics at the University of Oklahoma, and she taught Latin and ancient history in Oklahoma public schools from 1965 to 1976. She has studied physics, genetics, and other hard sciences on her own to strengthen the background of her SF. Cherryh is known particularly for her complex alien psychologies and cultures. In *Hunter of Worlds* (1977), the reader must pay close attention, because Cherryh developed three cultures with motivations as alien as their languages, which are distinguished by concepts that cannot be easily defined in English. *Forty Thousand in Gehenna* (1983) follows the evolution, over generations, of the relationship between descendants of a human colony abandoned on an alien planet and the native mound-building Calibans.

Most of Cherryh's SF novels are part of a future history, the beginnings of which are shown in *Downbelow Station*. This novel involves intelligent, though primitive, aliens and a war between Earth and a federation of space-station colonies called Union. The war is about to reach the station, which until now has remained neutral, orbiting Pell's World. Out of the ensuing action grows Alliance, a confederation of the people of the space station and Earth's remaining war fleet. At first Alliance seems to be an appealingly libertarian society, while its chief competitor, Union, seems repellently totalitarian. However, in novels placed later in the history, such as *The Faded Sun: Kesrith* (1978) and its sequels (*The Faded Sun: Shon'Jir*, 1979, and *The Faded Sun: Kutath*, 1980), Alliance becomes militaristic and imperialistic, and in *Cyteen* (1987) Union is portrayed more sympathetically.

Cherryh's work shows a keen insight into the forces that shape history, and her novels are marked by the moral, political, and cultural conflicts that trigger historic events. Her protagonists are often subjected to nearly unbearable stress before they manage to win personal victories—or perhaps only survive. For example, *Pride of Chanur* (1982) and its sequels (*Chanur's Venture*, 1984, and *The Kif Strike Back*, 1985) are set among the Compact Worlds, where Earth's attempt to compete with Alliance and Union in developing interstellar trade leads to almost disastrous conflicts among half a dozen alien races. Caught in the middle of this galactic struggle, the aliens are constantly torn between preserving their own cultures and accepting sufficient changes in their ways of life to ensure survival.

In 1977 Cherryh won the John W. Campbell Award for best new writer, and she has won Hugo Awards for "Cassandra" (in 1978) and *Downbelow Station* (in 1982).

OTHER WORKS: *Brothers of Earth* (1976); *Well of Shiuan* (1978); *Fires of Azeroth* (1979; combined with *Gate of Ivrel* and *Well of Shiuan*, this novel was republished in 1979 as *The Book of Morgaine*); *Hestia* (1979); *Serpent's Reach* (1980); *Wave without a Shore* (1981); *Merchanter's Luck* (1982); *Port Eternity* (1982); *The Dreamstone* (1983); *Voyager in Night* (1984); *Cuckoo's Egg* (1985); *Angel with a Sword* (1985); *Visible Light* (collection, 1985); *Glass and Amber* (1987).

J.J.P.

CHESNEY, GEORGE T[OMKYNS] [LT. COL. SIR] (1830–1895).

British officer in the Royal Engineers who originated the science-fiction future war genre with his famous work *The Battle of Dorking* (1871), in which a German army successfully invades Britain with a surprise attack. A few examples of this kind of cautionary tale about lack of preparedness had been published earlier, but Chesney's novella was superior in effect and more aptly timed to coincide with British uneasiness about the decline of the empire. Every European nation and the United States as well adapted the form to its own circumstances, however. A more famous later example in this genre is H. G. WELLS's *The War of the Worlds* (1898).

N.H.

SEE ALSO: WAR

CHILDREN'S SCIENCE FICTION

Science fiction has become not only a recognized genre of children's literature but also—if the term *children's literature* is expanded to encompass young adult literature as well—one of its most popular genres. Although SF has attracted young readers since its origins, critical acceptance of children's SF has been relatively slow in coming. Only with the publication by Scribner's of Robert A. HEINLEIN's *Rocket Ship Galileo* (1947) did experts in children's literature begin to realize that it was possible to combine literary quality and subject matter attractive to youngsters. Heinlein's first children's novel was a skillful blend of adventure and instruction: detailing the story of three boys who build a rocket in their backyard, travel to the Moon, and discover a secret base from which the Nazis hope to begin a third world war, it also addressed the questions of parental conflict, career indecision, and maturation.

It was not, however, the first SF juvenile, whose antecedents reach back into the nineteenth century, when a number of significant changes were taking place in children's literature. The first of these was the secularization of nature writing—a process clearly observable in the material written to instruct young people. Previously the wonders and operations of nature had been almost entirely ascribed to Divine Providence. With the onset of the 1800s, however, commentators began to describe nature more objectively, while managing to maintain a fondness for the sort of imaginative description sure to appeal to young readers. Witness Margaret Gatty's very popular *Parables for Nature*, written between 1855 and 1871, which combines religious orthodoxy, highly accurate scientific observations, and a penchant for secular analogy, metaphor, and simile. Perhaps the most striking evidence of the secularization process is the frequency with which natural phenomena were discussed in terms of the literary fairy tale and its conventions. For example, children could learn about storms and dewdrops in Agnes Gilberne's *Father Aldur: A Water Story* (1887), discover the secret world of liquids and gases in Lucy Meyer's *Real Fairy Folks: Explorations in the World of Atoms* (1887), or read about science in general in Lydia Farmer's *A Story Book of Science* (1886).

The most distinctive element of the fairy tale—magic—became a favorite explanation for scientific and technological wonders. Works of science fantasy—literary fairy tales about scientific topics—appeared as early as 1851, with the publication of Charles Delorme's *The Marvellous and Incredible Adventures of Charles Thunderbolt in the Moon*. Other examples abound. In *Water Babies* (1863) Charles Kingsley dramatized the science of underwater life and the theory of evolution. Albert Hooper's *Up the Moonstair* (1890) describes lunar inhabitants on the dark side of the Moon. And in *The Secret of the Amulet* (1906), Edith Nesbit, a friend of H. G. WELLS, ascribed her young protagonists' ability to travel through time to a magic amulet. Electricity was a favorite topic of early science fantasy. For instance, in *The Wonderful Electric Elephant* (1903) and *On a Lark to the Planets* (1904), Frances Montgomery featured an electrically powered mechanical elephant that can run, swim underwater, and fly off into space. Even more interesting is L. Frank Baum's *The Master Key: An Electrical Fairy Tale* (1901), which describes electricity as a genie and its impressive applications as wishes granted to Rob, the hero of the book.

Children's science fantasy, in its domestication of science and technology, was instrumental in the emergence of children's science fiction. But even after SF had taken hold as a juvenile literature, science fantasy continued to be written—and read—with enthusiasm. In 1929, for example, Hugh Lofting sent his popular Dr. Dolittle and his animal friends on a lunar voyage in *Dr. Dolittle in the Moon*. And as recently as 1983 Diane Duane wrote the intriguing *So You Want to Be a Wizard*, whose main character, Fred, is a compact white hole.

The final development necessary to the emergence of children's SF involved the concurrent popularity of Jules VERNE and the American invention story in its dime-novel format. When the first English translation of a Verne novel, *Five Weeks in a Balloon*, appeared in 1869, young readers soon constituted a significant part of its readership. Verne deliberately included young readers among his intended audience, and many of his novels ran as serials in *Magasin d'éducation et de récréation*, a juvenile periodical. In fact, Verne became so popular with young readers that by the end of the century he had acquired a reputation in English-speaking countries as primarily a boy's writer.

The first dime-novel invention story appeared in 1865 with the publication of Edward S. Ellis's *The Huge Hunter; or, The Steam Man of the Prairies*. This type of story blossomed in the hands of Luis Philip SENARENS, author of most of the 187 Frank Reade and Frank Reade, Jr., stories that make up the Frank Reade Library. This series, one of the most influential in the nineteenth century, stars a young inventor and describes his many exploits involving various modes of transportation, particularly flight. Other invention story series, all patterned after the Frank Reade books, include *Tom Edison, Jr., Happy Days, Pluck and Luck*, and the British *The Boys' Own Papers*.

Hardcover children's science adventures, featuring wondrous inventions, episodic adventures, and travel to exotic or lost lands, began to be published in the 1800s, among them Harry Collingwood's *The Log of the "Flying Fish"* (1886), Frederick Ober's *The Silver City: A Story of Adventure in Mexico* (1893), Jack Trowbridge's *Three Boys on an Electrical Boat* (1894), and Clement Fezandie's *Through the Earth* (1898).

The popularity of science adventure, in either dime-novel or hardcover format, eventually prompted the enterprising Edward Stratemeyer, founder of the prolific Stratemeyer Syndicate, to start turning out science and invention series fiction for boys. The most famous of the series were Victor Appleton's Tom Swift books; first appearing in 1910, these stories celebrated the inventions and adventures of young Tom until 1941. Other noteworthy series were Roy Rockwell's The Great Marvel, Carl Claudy's Adventures in the Unknown, Howard Gar-

is's Rocket Riders, H. Irving Hancock's Conquest of the United States, and Richard Bonner's The Boy Inventors. In the mid-1930s the first wave of series SF was succeeded by SF COMICS and Big Little books, featuring the likes of Tarzan, BUCK ROGERS, and FLASH GORDON. Along with the new SF periodicals, such as AMAZING STORIES, *Astounding*, and *Wonder Stories*, they attracted many youngsters eager for SF in one form or another.

By the late 1940s children's SF was firmly established—at least in the minds of readers—as a genre. After the success of Heinlein's first children's book, Scribner's released a number of other SF books by him for young readers, notable among them *Red Planet* (1949), *Farmer in the Sky* (1950), *The Rolling Stones* (1952), and *Starman Jones* (1953). Spurred on by their success, other publishers decided to enter the market. In 1951 McGraw released Ellen MacGregor's *Miss Pickerell Goes to Mars*, the first of twelve Miss Pickerell books. In 1952 Harcourt published Andre NORTON's *Star Man's Son: 2250 AD*, a fine novel of initiation set in a postcatastrophe age and the first of Norton's many SF novels for young readers. One year later Doubleday published *David Starr: Space Ranger*, the first of six David Starr volumes by Isaac ASIMOV, writing as Paul French. And in 1954 Little, Brown published Eleanor Cameron's *The Wonderful Flight to the Mushroom Planet*, the first of five Mushroom Planet stories.

In fact, by 1958 at least ninety children's SF books, excluding series fiction, had been published. Unfortunately, not all were equal to the work of Heinlein, Norton, and Asimov. In general, children's literature has always been victimized by hack writing, and children's SF proved no exception, as derivative stories about flying to the Moon or the planets (Leslie Greener's *Moon Ahead*, 1951, or Ruthven Todd's *Space Cat*, 1952, for example) or space visitors (Carl Biemiller's *The Magic Ball from Mars*, 1953) were rushed into print to share in Scribner's and Heinlein's success.

One publishing house in particular, John C. Winston, was instrumental during the 1950s in establishing children's SF as a viable genre. With Cecile Matschat and Carl Carmer as editors, Winston founded its Science-Fiction Series, which, by the end of the decade, consisted of twenty-six books. Some of the titles, for instance Poul ANDERSON's *Vault of the Ages* (1952), Chad OLIVER's *Mists of Dawn* (1952), Eric North's *The Ant Men* (1955), and Raymond JONES's *The Year When the Stardust Fell* (1958), compare favorably with the SF produced for children today. Matschat and Carmer, desirous that the Science-Fiction books both teach and entertain, insisted on a distinctive format. Each book begins with an introduction in which the author discusses a scientific topic (Venus or Saturn, for example), phenomenon (say, ESP), or discipline (oceanography) and speculates about possible developments. The text then dramatizes or in some way reflects the topic of the introduction. Whether

Illustration by Clifford Geary for Robert A. Heinlein's *The Rolling Stones*

the Winston novels functioned as effective teaching tools is debatable, but the series, with its published intentions, intriguing format, and often winning narratives, convincingly signaled that it was no longer fair to link SF exclusively with pulps and comics.

The 1950s also saw the return of SF series fiction—a phenomenon suggesting a cross-fertilizing relation between mainstream children's SF and popular-culture manifestations of the genre. In 1947 Grosset & Dunlap released John Blaine's *The Rocket's Shadow*, the first title in the twenty-three-volume series devoted to the adventures of Rick Brant. Other series were also inaugurated: Carey Rockwell's Tom Corbett, Space Cadet; Jay Williams and Raymond Abrashkin's Danny Dunn, still read today; Joseph Green's Dig Allen; Donald A. WOLLHEIM's Mike Mars; and, most interesting of all, a second Tom Swift series, ostensibly written by Victor Appleton II, that celebrates, over thirty-three volumes, the scientific exploits of the famed inventor's son, Tom, Jr.

Interestingly enough, a significant amount of the SF written for children during the 1950s came from authors who are today well known for their adult SF. In addition to Heinlein, Norton, and Asimov, they include Robert SILVERBERG, Donald A. Wollheim, Poul Anderson, James BLISH, Ben BOVA, Arthur C. CLARKE, Lester DEL REY, Gordon R. DICKSON, Murray LEINSTER, Jack VANCE, and Harry HARRISON. It is entirely possible that some of these authors owe their continuing livelihood to their early forays into children's SF, which helped them pay the rent during otherwise lean years. It is also clear, however, that a number of them looked on the writing of children's SF as hackwork at best. Nevertheless, the overall quality of their writing helped catapult children's SF into critical respectability.

In the last twenty-five years children's SF has matured, its range of topics has expanded, and the presentation of those topics has become increasingly sophisticated. Although space travel remains a favorite subject, both plot and characterization have become increasingly complex, as in Gregory BENFORD's *Jupiter Project* (1980) and Ludek Pesek's *Trap for Perseus* (1980). Animals continue to be strong central characters, but contemporary practitioners tend to eschew cliché and sentimentality in their treatment, as do Andre Norton in her Star Ka'at books and Clare Bell in *Ratha's Creation* (1983) and its sequel *Clan Ground* (1984).

As in adult SF, alien encounters are a common subject, with the aliens often depicted as either conquerors—as in John CHRISTOPHER's Tripod trilogy and Jean Karl's *The Turning Place: Stories of Future Past* (1976)— or potential conquerors—as in Nicholas Fisk's *Grinny* (1974) and H. M. Hoover's *The Shepherd Moon* (1984). A number of writers have described very plausible alien worlds, among them Laurence YEP in *Sweetwater* (1973), Cherry Wilder in *The Luck of Brin's Five* (1977), and Hoover in *The Bell Tower* (1982). Indeed, there are few topics that haven't been tackled in children's SF: a significant number of books contain postcatastrophe scenarios, including Joan Clarke's *The Happy Planet* (1963), Robert O'Brien's touching *Z for Zachariah* (1975), and two recent and provocative novels, Robert Swindell's *Brother in the Land* (1984) and Louise Laurence's *Children of the Dust* (1985).

As it has matured, children's SF has begun to take on a number of controversial themes. ECOLOGY, for instance, is the focus of Adrien Stoutenberg's *Out There* (1971), an impressive story of the dire effects of the exploitation of natural resources; even more impressive are Nancy Bond's finely written *The Voyage Begun* (1984) and Raymond Brigg's stunning picture book, *When the Wind Blows* (1983). Virginia Hamilton and Joan VINGE have both provided provocative investigations of ESP, in *Justice and Her Brothers* (1981) and sequels, and *Psion* (1983), respectively. Other significant topics include psychological experimentation and its abuses (John Christopher's *The Guardians*, 1970; Sylvia Engdahl's *The Far Side of Evil*, 1971; and Ann Schlee's *The Vandals*, 1981) and racism (A. M. Lightner's *The Day of the Drones*, 1969; Piers ANTHONY's *Race against Time*, 1973; and Monica Hughes's *The Keeper of the Isis Light*, 1981). Like other, more general, writing for young readers, children's SF has naturally tackled the conflict between individualism and conformity, in such books as H. M. Hoover's *The Lost Star* (1979), Sharon Wells's *Earthchild* (1982) and sequels, and George ZEBROWSKI's *Sunspacer* (1984); sometimes that conflict is not happily resolved, as in Jan Mark's *The Ennead* (1978) and Robert Westall's *Futuretrack 5* (1983).

Perhaps the most significant recent development in children's SF is the virtual elimination of the sexism that has tainted children's literature (and, to an extent, SF in general). It is interesting that women now rank among the major authors of SF for young readers; among the most prominent are Sylvia Engdahl, Josephine Rector Stone, Jean Karl, Monica Hughes, and H. M. Hoover.

There are two other signs that children's SF has matured into a viable literature in its own right. One is the fact that two novels in the genre, Madeleine L'ENGLE's *A Wrinkle in Time* (1963) and Robert O'Brien's *Mrs. Frisby and the Rats of NIMH* (1972), were voted the prestigious Newbery medal for outstanding children's literature. The other is the growing number of publishers, authors, critics, and readers committed to quality children's SF, even in the face of attempts to trivialize the genre through "Choose Your Own Adventure" books and to co-opt youthful interest in SF through mediocre novelizations of SF films and television shows. Indeed, it is possible that early notions of the didactic value of SF had, and continue to have, merit. In *Images in a Crystal Ball* (1981), Lillian Biermann Wehmeyer has argued that it would behoove schools to build imaginatively conceived and well-executed programs in futuristics around children's SF. For what other segment of society more needs to consider the future and its own constructive role in that future?

F.J.M.

CHILSON, ROB[ERT] (1945–).

American writer. A member of the last generation of science-fiction writers whose first published stories were purchased by John W. CAMPBELL, Jr., Chilson works largely in hard science fiction and often incorporates Campbellian themes. His first story, "The Mind Reader," was published in ANALOG in 1968, and his fiction has continued to appear there regularly, as well as in other magazines. Since 1985 Chilson has published numerous short stories and novelettes in collaboration with Lynette Meserole, Robin W. Bailey, and especially William F. WU. His novels include *As the Curtain Falls* (1974), *The Starcrowned Kings* (1975), and *The Shores of Kansas* (1976).

B.D.

THE CHINA SYNDROME (1979).

Directed by James Bridges; screenplay by Mike Gray, T. S. Cook, and James Bridges; photographed by James Crabe. With Jane Fonda, Michael Douglas, Jack Lemmon, Scott Brady, Peter Donat, James Hampton. 122 minutes. Color.

This conspiracy drama about an accident and subsequent cover-up in a nuclear power plant is distinguished by breathless pacing and superb performances. Jane Fonda is memorable as the fledgling television reporter who struggles to bring the story to light, and Jack Lemmon's moving portrayal of the plant controller, torn between duty and conscience, is first-rate.

The film's relation to science fiction is tenuous, although its themes of cosmic disaster and the expendability of the masses in the eyes of centralized authority are common in the genre. Like PLANET OF THE APES (1968), *China Syndrome* is a political statement against nuclear power and technological hubris; indeed several critics have drawn parallels between the two films. Although neither SF films nor SF books predict the future, the probable alternatives they portray often find a simulacrum in world events: *China Syndrome* was released, quite coincidentally, shortly after the nuclear plant accident at Three Mile Island, which in turn anticipated the more devastating 1986 accident at Chernobyl.

M.T.W.

CHRISTOPHER, JOHN (Pseudonym of Christopher Samuel Youd) (1922–).

British writer whose science fiction usually involves postholocaust worlds in which the continuity of civilization and the human race are open questions. The most famous of these disaster novels is *The Death of Grass* (1956; as *No Blade of Grass*, 1957), in which all types of grasses, including all grains, are attacked and destroyed by a natural disease. The threatening famine reduces humanity to two camps in constant conflict: those who are willing to sacrifice all humane values in the name of self-survival and those who insist on trying to maintain some semblance of civilization in the face of overwhelming crises. In the early 1970s this novel became the basis for the SF film NO BLADE OF GRASS, produced by Cornel Wilde.

In the novels that followed, Christopher made use of similar natural upheavals (*The World in Winter*, 1962, as *The Long Winter*, 1962; and *A Wrinkle in the Skin*, 1965, as *The Ragged Edge*, 1966) and social dysfunction (*Pendulum*, 1968) to create worlds in which he effectively probed the nature of humanity. His postholocaust settings are resolutely grim; in them survival, if it is possible at all, comes at a cost to the human characters.

Christopher has also written a number of superior SF works for children, including *The Lotus Caves* (1969), *The Guardians* (1970), *In the Beginning* (1972; revised as *Dom and Va*, 1973), *Wild Jack* (1974), *Empty World* (1977), *Fireball* (1981), and *New Found Land* (1983). Two other series for children, *The Sword of the Spirits Trilogy* (1980) and *The Tripods Trilogy* (1980), also deserve mention. The latter work forms the basis for the recent BBC-TV series *The Tripods*.

OTHER WORKS: *The Twenty-second Century* (collection, 1954); *The Year of the Comet* (1955; as *Planet in Peril*, 1959); *Sweeney's Island* (1964; British title *Cloud on Silver*); *The Possessors* (1965); *The Little People* (1967).

S.H.G.

CITIES

The words *city* and *civilization* come from the same root, so it is hardly surprising that the image of the city in science fiction tends to reflect attitudes—often ambivalent—toward civilization itself.

In such works as Ignatius DONNELLY's *Caesar's Column* (1890) and H. G. WELLS's *When the Sleeper Wakes* (1899), the city of the future is a sort of ultratechnological Babylon, full of scientific wonders but with an underside of social degradation. This has become the dominant image of the future city through such classic films as Fritz LANG's METROPOLIS (1927) and Ridley Scott's BLADE RUNNER (1982) and reflects the belief that human institutions, or even human nature, are unequal to the task of creating a utopian society, however great science and technology may be.

Purely utopian visions of the city can be found in Wells's *A Modern Utopia* (1905), Hugo GERNSBACK's *Ralph 124C 41+* (1911–12), and Wells's film *Things to Come* (1936); in these works science and technology are assumed capable of solving if not all human problems at least all *important* ones. Frederik POHL's Shoggo in *The Age of the Pussyfoot* (1969) is the apotheosis of an urban utopia, and his *Years of the City* (1984) is a social prescription for creating one. Larry NIVEN and Jerry POURNELLE offered the urban arcology as a utopian dream in *Oath of Fealty* (1982). Pastoralist Clifford D. SIMAK preferred the campuslike "city" of *Time and Again* (1951).

Contrasting images of the city and its possible alternatives are used to explore various philosophies of civilization in works such as Arthur C. CLARKE's *The City and the Stars* and Isaac ASIMOV's *The Naked Sun* (both 1956) and Asimov's earlier *The Caves of Steel* (1954).

J.J.P.

THE CLAN OF THE CAVE BEAR (1986).

Directed by Michael Chapman; screenplay by John Sayles; adapted from the novel by Jean M. Auel; photographed by Jan De Bont; music by Alan Silvestri. With Daryl Hannah. 100 minutes. Color.

In *Clan of the Cave Bear* Daryl Hannah plays a Cro-Magnon waif adopted by a tribe of loutish Neanderthals. Hannah pits her rational *Homo sapiens* mind against the racial memory and close-to-nature traditionalism of the

Neanderthals, who cannot understand her desire to change the established order. An odd mixture of feminism and mild racism (Hannah is blond and Nordic; her oppressors are dark subhumans), *Clan* is an example of prehistoric, origin-of-species science fiction but lacks the inventiveness of QUEST FOR FIRE (1981) or the wit of *Caveman* (1981). In the end the film is redeemed only by Jan De Bont's breathtaking images of the Canadian wilderness.

M.M.W.

CLARKE, ARTHUR C[HARLES] (1917 –).

British author, resident of Sri Lanka since 1956, noted for his themes of scientific optimism, transcendence, and loss. A central figure of modern science fiction, Clarke is often ranked with Isaac ASIMOV, Ray BRADBURY, and Robert A. HEINLEIN, and, like them, he has successfully reached a broad general audience. He is also a prolific writer of nonfiction on spaceflight, scientific forecasting, and undersea exploration.

Born in Somerset, England, Clarke served as a radar officer in the Royal Air Force during World War II and was active in the British Interplanetary Society. In 1945 he wrote an article predicting the development of communications satellites. His first professional SF stories appeared in 1946; four years later he became a full-time writer. *The Exploration of Space* (1951), a nontechnical account of astronautics, was a selection of the Book-of-the-Month Club. He achieved widespread popularity, however, only with the release of Stanley KUBRICK's film 2001: A SPACE ODYSSEY (1968), for which Clarke wrote the novel and coauthored the screenplay; it was inspired in part by several of his short stories, notably "The Sentinel" (1951).

In the British tradition of H. G. WELLS's *The Time Machine* (1895) and Olaf STAPLEDON's *Last and First Men* (1930) and *Star Maker* (1937), Clarke's best-known works achieve a cosmic vision in which human characters are reflective observers rather than heroic actors, the tone is awe mixed with sadness, and the effect—accentuated by the frequent use of surprise endings or "twists," especially in his short stories—is a reconsideration of the accepted certainties of reality and human nature. In "The Star" (1955) a Jesuit scientist struggles to understand why a supernova that destroyed an advanced civilization was also that harbinger of hope and salvation, the Star of Bethlehem. Tibetan monks install a computer to calculate the names of God in "The Nine Billion Names of God" (1953); completion of their task will end humanity's reason for existence. Learning this only as the project reaches its goal, the Western computer technicians look up: "Overhead, without any fuss, the stars were going out."

With the notable exception of *The City and the Stars* (1956; expanded from *Against the Fall of Night*, 1953),

Clarke's novels take place in the near future. Even *The Songs of Distant Earth* (1986), although set in the late fourth millennium, depicts decidedly contemporary human problems as the crew of the last starship from Earth interacts with colonists on a distant world. Many of the novels focus on technological accomplishments or problems, such as the first Moon landing (*Prelude to Space*, 1951) or the rescue of a lunar tourist vehicle (*A Fall of Moondust*, 1961), but they are not essentially action thrillers or hardware stories. Even though surprises are frequent and scientific information appears regularly, the stories are filtered through the perceptions of basically decent, rational characters whose dignity and understanding are stimulated by the natural and human challenges confronting them.

Childhood's End (1953) is paradigmatic of Clarke's more speculative, transcendental novels. Structured as a succession of apocalyptic revelations, it depicts the sudden metamorphosis of humanity, under the protective midwifery of the alien Overlords, into the next evolutionary stage, a group mind that ultimately merges with the cosmic Overmind, destroying the Earth in the process (see ESCHATOLOGY). The alien other that transcends humanity yet paradoxically represents humanity's destiny is a recurring theme in the author's speculative novels: examples include Vanamonde, a lesser cosmic mind created by a long-forgotten human superscience in *The City and the Stars;* the Star-Child, the outcome of human evolution manipulated through alien intervention in *2001;* the technology of the alien spaceship that baffles human investigators but may well be grasped when the second and third Raman vessels eventually pass through the Solar System in *Rendezvous with Rama* (1973). Each of these novels is also a fictional embodiment of Clarke's third law (1967): "Any sufficiently advanced technology is indistinguishable from magic," a thesis Clarke employs not to monger mysteries but to undercut smugness and to suggest that both the universe and human inventiveness hold many surprises.

The short story Clarke considers his best, "Transit of Earth" (1971), epitomizes many of his characteristic concerns. The last survivor of a scientific expedition to Mars, doomed to imminent death, isolated as no one has ever been, records a scientific wonder not before seen by human eyes: the transit of the Earth and Moon across the face of the Sun. As the transit and his own life approach their inevitable end, the narrator describes how his last minutes will be spent, driving through the fascinating Martian landscape, thinking of those who have dreamed about Mars—H. G. Wells, Percival Lowell, Edgar Rice BURROUGHS, Stanley G. WEINBAUM, Ray Bradbury—enjoying the reality that is no stranger than and just as beautiful as their dreams, and listening to the music of J.S. Bach.

Transcendence and loss are inseparable in Clarke's fiction. Transcendence—whether of the human spirit ris-

Arthur C. Clarke

ing above the inevitable and the contingent or of the human species evolving to a higher stage—entails the loss of the familiar; cosmic vastness brings separation and loneliness; alien intelligences and natural phenomena often lie beyond our comprehension. The result is sadness and poignancy, loss or exclusion. Yet through his deep optimism in the capacity of the human spirit to find beauty and wonder everywhere and to create in science the instrument for overcoming pettiness and self-destructiveness, Clarke also strongly conveys his conviction that through our encounter with the cosmos, we will realize our humanity.

OTHER WORKS: *The Sands of Mars* (1951); *Islands in the Sky* (1952); *Expedition to Earth* (collection, 1953); *Earthlight* (1955); *Reach for Tomorrow* (collection, 1956); *Tales from the White Hart* (collection, 1957); *The Deep Range* (1957); *The Other Side of the Sky* (collection, 1958); *Tales of Ten Worlds* (collection, 1962); *Dolphin Island* (1963); *Glide Path* (1963); *The Nine Billion Names of God* (Clarke's favorite short stories, with autobiographical forewords, 1967); *The Lion of Comarre and Against the Fall of Night* (1968); *The Lost Worlds of 2001* (stories, drafts, autobiography, 1972); *The Wind from the Sun* (collection, 1972; expanded edition, 1987); *Imperial Earth* (1975; expanded U.S. edition, 1976); *The Fountains of Paradise* (1979); *2010: Odyssey Two* (1982); *The Sentinel* (short stories, one previously uncollected, with autobiographical forewords, 1983); *2061: Odyssey 3* (1987).

R.G.

Hal Clement

Nevertheless, deep resonances of standard literary themes such as death or even Oedipal relations exist in Clement's fiction. *Needle* (1950), his first novel, in addition to combining juvenile detective fiction with an interesting extrapolation on an alien life-form, contains definite Freudian implications that Clement vigorously denies. *Cycle of Fire* (1957) is about the puzzles of mortality and cycles in nature. *Mission of Gravity* (1954), with its detailed description of a high-gravity planet and its insectlike inhabitants, is Clement's best-known work; its description of the protagonists' relentless upward movement against great weight captures not only details of mechanics and astronomy but also the hopeful tone of hard SF. Literary critics, however, may see in that narrative a metaphor for the challenge of modern science.

OTHER WORKS: *Iceworld* (1953); *The Ranger Boys in Space* (1956); *Close to Critical* (1964); *Natives of Space* (1965); *Small Changes* (1969); *Star Light* (1971); *Ocean on Top* (1973); *Through the Eye of a Needle* (1978); *The Best of Hal Clement* (1979); *Nitrogen Fix* (1980); *Still River* (1987).

D.M.H.

CLEMENT, HAL (Pseudonym of Harry Clement Stubbs) (1922–).

American writer and teacher whose work is mentioned most often as the prime example of hard science fiction. After earning degrees from Harvard University in astronomy, chemistry, and education and distinguishing himself as a bomber pilot during World War II, Clement settled into a long and effective career teaching general science at Milton Academy near Boston. His passion to teach science along with the encouragement and influence of John W. CAMPBELL's editing (Clement sold his first story to *Astounding* when he was still an undergraduate) led to a body of work that always teaches some lesson from modern science, much of it directed to juvenile readers. In short Clement's professional teaching and professional writing have continually been interrelated, and now that he has retired from Milton Academy, he continues to teach through his books.

Since the early 1950s Clement has been a favorite among fans of rigorous and accurate extrapolation in storytelling. Thus he represents the deliberate preference for the separateness, or "ghettoizing," of science fiction along with its commitment to correct science. Moreover, in interviews and appearances at conventions Clement has rejected the viewpoint that accurate extrapolation may be inherently impossible. He projects and imagines alien environments and speculative conditions that are always consistent with the known data in our own environment as though these "thought experiments" are closer to real science than to imaginative literature. For holding this staunch position over decades, he has come to embody nonliterary hard SF.

CLIFTON, MARK [IRVIN] (1906–1963).

American industrial psychologist and writer. Clifton seriously followed John W. CAMPBELL's advice to write stories that present real people coping with realistic problems of the future: in "Hang Head, Vandal" (*Amazing*, 1962), for example, the narrator frequently addresses readers directly and attacks their romantic notions of scientists and their work.

Campbell influenced Clifton in other ways as well. Most of Clifton's stories (usually collaborations published in *Astounding*) were series that Campbell encouraged him to write, particularly those dealing with psychic powers. Clifton's first series (collected as *They'd Rather Be Right*, 1957, with Frank Riley; retitled *The Forever Machine*, 1967) concerns a supercomputer named Bossy that has been programmed to treat disturbed human beings. Bossy's treatment is so successful that its patients actually develop supermental powers and become immortal. These stories focus on the morality of allowing machines to change human beings and untreated humans' fear of these "perfected" people. The collection won the Hugo Award for best novel in 1955.

Clifton's second series ended with the novel *When They Come from Space* (1962), in which a specialist in extraterrestrial psychology manages to save the Earth from a series of alien invasions. A parody of SPACE OPERA, this work displays considerable wit at the expense of government bureaucracy.

OTHER WORKS: *Eight Keys to Eden* (1969); *The Science Fiction of Mark Clifton* (collection, 1980).

S.H.G.

A CLOCKWORK ORANGE (1971).

Directed by Stanley Kubrick; screenplay by Stanley Kubrick; adapted from the novel by Anthony Burgess; photographed by John Alcott; music by Walter Carlos. With Malcolm McDowell, Patrick Magee, Warren Clarke, Michael Bates, Adrienne Corri, Aubrey Morris. 137 minutes. Color.

One of the most faithful film adaptations of a novel, *A Clockwork Orange* deftly blends the art of the master filmmaker with that of the master novelist. BURGESS's tale of future thuggery and mind control is swiftly paced, so the film has a tight structure, in contrast to the long static sequences characteristic of KUBRICK's *2001* (1968) or *Barry Lyndon* (1975). Kubrick managed to transplant the story from print to film brilliantly, substituting visual style for Burgess's verbal pyrotechnics. Although some of the novel's future slang is incorporated into dialogue and voice-over narration, the book's flavor is most vividly captured through the use of stark white protopunk costumes and decor and jarringly inappropriate music (for instance, "Singing in the Rain" while the hero and his fellow toughs kick a tramp to death).

The story is a simple one, detailing the crimes and horrendous rehabilitation of Alex (McDowell), a young thug in a lawless future England. It is presented in a savagely ironic, yet to many disturbingly ambivalent manner. There is no moral black and white in Alex's world. He and his "droogs" (gang members) out on a merry spree of "ultraviolence" are certainly evil, but is the government's brainwashing any less so? (Typically, as aversion therapy renders him completely incapable of violence, Alex also loses his one previous redeeming feature, a fondness for Beethoven.) This is an antiutopia far less overt than the typical future Hell—it could almost be the present day—without any easy answers. In the end Alex is deprogrammed and cynically announces that he is "cured," in other words, ready to go back to his former, violent life-style.

The controversy surrounding the film arose not so much because of its explicit scenes of violence and rape—indeed these are quite tame by the standards of later "splatter" pictures—but because of the narrative point of view. Because we follow Alex through the action, and because Alex *enjoys* violence, the beatings, rapes, and even a murder look disturbingly like fun. The feelings of the victims hardly matter, except when they may add to the victimizer's pleasure.

In Burgess's dark and subtle fable (and Kubrick's film), Alex himself is the "clockwork orange," in his brainwashed state the equivalent of a mechanical imitation of a living thing. Ultimately, to Burgess (and presumably to Kubrick), the inability to choose between good and evil becomes the greatest evil of all. Many critics missed the point, attributing the callous attitudes of the characters to the director and condemning the film as immoral and proviolence. *A Clockwork Orange* remains one of the finest science-fiction films ever made, and arguably Kubrick's best work.

D.S.

CLOSE ENCOUNTERS OF THE THIRD KIND (1977).

Directed by Steven Spielberg; screenplay by Steven Spielberg; photographed by Vilmos Zsigmond; music by John Williams. With Richard Dreyfuss, François Truffaut, Teri Garr, Melinda Dillon, Bob Balaban, J. Patrick McNamara. 135 minutes. Color.

One of the most commercially successful science-fiction movies ever made, *Close Encounters of the Third Kind* offers, with the possible exception of SPIELBERG's own E.T.: THE EXTRA-TERRESTRIAL (1982), the most benign view of an alien encounter yet depicted on film. Its compelling visual beauty and benevolent vision evoke that "sense of wonder" many critics have identified as the essential quality of SF and set this movie apart from the paranoid films about alien encounters so characteristic of the genre. In *Close Encounters* people watch the skies not out of fearful vigilance, as in THE THING (1951), but in the hope of transcendence.

Spielberg based his screenplay in part on reports of UFO investigations, and the scientist played by François Truffaut is based on the real-life UFO researcher Jacques Vallée. What struck Spielberg most about these reports was their consistency in describing the aliens as childlike and friendly, both points emphasized in the film.

The plot focuses on an average American man (his house is awash in the detritus of middle-class suburban existence), played by Richard Dreyfuss, who is touched by a light beam from an alien spacecraft. The beam generates in him an obsession with a shape he later discovers to be Devil's Tower in Wyoming, the alien's appointed landing place. Much of the ensuing story, which is dramatically rather slim, depicts the hero's efforts to discover the meaning of his vision and then, along with the mother of a boy who has been taken away by the aliens, to penetrate government security and ascend the mountain to the landing site.

Spielberg deftly sustained the sense of wonder in both plot and style, structuring the movie around a thematic opposition between imagination and possibility on the one hand and pragmatism and narrowness on the other. The hero works for the local power company, but after his encounter, which shakes his company truck as if it were merely one of the multitude of toys that fill the film, he acknowledges the existence of greater powers in the universe. Similarly, when the spacecrafts, pursued by the state police along a highway, fly past a toll booth, the reaction of the toll collector humorously captures the sense of awe about beings who transcend our imaginary, confining boundaries. The hero's departure aboard the mother ship for unknown adventures is the film's final grand embrace of the possible.

*Close Encounters'*s climactic meeting with the aliens, is depicted with great cinematic bravado, the delayed appearance of the huge mother ship providing one of the film's marvelous displays of special effects, photographed by Douglas Trumbull. Truffaut gives a moving performance as the sensitive exobiologist, and Spielberg's deft direction imbues the scene with an unabashed spirituality. The aliens, as they emerge from the ship haloed in light, are both childlike and angelic.

Even though *Close Encounters* was an established box-office smash, Spielberg reedited the film in 1980, adding new footage about the meeting with the aliens and deleting some of the material on the hero's suburban home. The film was rereleased as *Close Encounters of the Third Kind: The Special Edition*.

B.K.G.

COBLENTZ, STANTON A[RTHUR] (1896–1982).

American author. A prolific writer of and about poetry, Coblentz began producing speculative fiction in the early 1920s. After placing his satiric utopian tale *The Sunken World* (1928/1948) in Hugo GERNSBACK's *Amazing Quarterly,* he adapted his style to the conventions of the pulps, although he published a prehistoric fantasy, *The Wonder Stick* (1929), and an elegiac lost race fantasy, *When the Birds Fly South* (1945), elsewhere. *The Blue Barbarians* (1931/1958) and *In Caverns Below* (1935/1957 as *Hidden World*) are perhaps the best of his rough-hewn satires; *After 12,000 Years* (1929/1950) has some striking futuristic imagery. Coblentz continued writing into the 1970s—his last novel was *The Island People* (1971)—but his plotting remained crude and repetitive and his style slapdash.

NOTABLE OTHER WORKS: *Into Plutonian Depths* (1931/1950); *The Planet of Youth* (1932/1945 as *Youth Madness*); *Lord of Tranerica* (1939/1966); *Under the Triple Suns* (1955); *Next Door to the Sun* (1960); *The Runaway World* (1961); *The Lizard Lords* (1964); *The Crimson Capsule* (1967; also known as *The Animal People*); *The Day the World Stopped* (1968).

B.S.

COCOON (1985).

Directed by Ron Howard; screenplay by Tom Benedek; photographed by Don Peterman; music by James Horner. With Don Ameche, Wilford Brimley, Hume Cronyn, Brian Dennehy, Jack Gilford, Steve Guttenberg, Maureen Stapleton, Jessica Tandy, Gwen Verdon, Herta Ware, Tahnee Welch. 117 minutes. Color.

This film, depicting with honesty the frustrations of the aged in a retirement community in Florida, is a significant entry in the popular category of movies about human encounters with beneficent and superior aliens. This film tradition was popularized, if not inaugurated, by Steven SPIELBERG in CLOSE ENCOUNTERS OF THE THIRD KIND (1977), and of course achieved a kind of apotheosis in his E.T.: THE EXTRA-TERRESTRIAL (1982). Nevertheless, *Cocoon* stands up well in comparison with either of those celebrated films.

The elderly protagonists are played with impressive skill and dignity by Don Ameche, Wilford Brimley, Maureen Stapleton, Jessica Tandy, Hume Cronyn, Jack Gilford, and Gwen Verdon; Brimley's strong performance tends to dominate the film. When Brimley and Ameche meet some wise and compassionate aliens (temporarily in human form), they learn that the swimming pool on an abandoned nearby estate, which they use regularly, seems to have powers of rejuvenation. As it turns out, the pool's restorative action results from the storage there of alien "cocoons" in suspended animation.

As might be expected, the discovery of renewed vitality by Brimley and his friends produces a satisfying amount of solid drama, although the film's melodramatic climactic sequence seems a concession to commercialism. In it the aliens, and a few of the elderly who have elected to join them on their cosmic voyage, are pursued by the Coast Guard and other benighted authorities in a demonstration that, in films of this kind, only children and the more aware of the elderly are truly receptive to messages from advanced creatures from the stars. Even the somewhat sentimental ending might have been spared, but whatever its flaws this restrained and poignant film merits respect.

E.L.C.

COGSWELL, THEODORE R[OSE] (1918–1987).

American author, primarily of short stories, and professor of English. Cogswell, who drove an ambulance in the Spanish Civil War and served in the U.S. Army Air Force in World War II, taught at Ball State Teachers College and Keystone Junior College in Pennsylvania. His first published and most famous science-fiction story was "The Specter General," which appeared in *Astounding* in 1952 and was reprinted frequently thereafter, most notably in the *SFWA Hall of Fame*. Humorous in intent, it describes a space admiral with a shortage of technicians and a technical school with a shortage of training material. The best of Cogswell's fiction is collected in *The Wall around the World* (1962) and *The Third Eye* (1968). His poem "The Roper" was set to music by John Jacob Niles, published in 1958, and reprinted in THE MAGAZINE OF FANTASY AND SCIENCE FICTION in 1962.

Cogswell became best known among other writers for the creation and publication of the *Proceedings of the Institute of Twenty-first Century Studies (PITFCS)*, the first forum for discussion of the craft by professional SF and fantasy writers. A freewheeling journal of personal opinion and serious criticism, *PITFCS* debated the question of an organization of writers while demonstrating the advantages of such a group; it led ultimately to the creation of the Science Fiction Writers of America, whose publication *Forum* (which Cogswell later edited) served many of the same functions as *PITFCS* and largely replaced it.

OTHER WORK: *Spock, Messiah!* (with Charles A. Spano, 1965).

R.S.C.

——— COLLABORATION ———

In no other literary field has collaboration been as rife as in science fiction. This situation no doubt stems from a number of factors, not the least of which is the genre's need for a collaborative response from its readers and the ease with which ideas can be exchanged in a literature *of* ideas. Also important, of course, is the feeling of community that permeates the genre, with authors frequently meeting at conventions, publishing events, clubs, writing workshops, and so on. Indeed the collaboration phenomenon has been particularly prominent in the United States, with its extensive network of fans: Gordon DICKSON, for instance, has written novels with four different partners (Poul ANDERSON, Ben BOVA, Harry HARRISON, and Keith LAUMER), and Harlan ELLISON has shared a byline on short stories with over fourteen other authors (in *Partners in Wonder*, 1971).

Combinations have included brother (STRUGATSKYS), husband-and-wife (KUTTNERS), father-and-son (HERBERTS, MATHESONS, HOYLES), and brother-and-sister teams in addition to the many temporary linkups, most often by authors already enjoying excellent reputations in their own right. There have also been transatlantic collaborations, including *Under Heaven's Bridge* (1981) by Michael BISHOP and Ian WATSON; Bishop, an American, resides in Georgia, Watson in England, and the two have never met.

Although early pulp writer brothers Earl and Otto Binder wrote as Eando BINDER, the first major collaborations worthy of note began in the 1940s with the New York FUTURIANS fan club spawning a multitude of partnerships: Frederik POHL and C. M. KORNBLUTH, Pohl and Judith MERRIL, Kornbluth and Merril (as Cyril Judd), Pohl and Lester DEL REY, and others. The undoubted star team of the 1940s was husband and wife Henry Kuttner and Catherine L. MOORE, sometimes writing as Lewis Padgett or Lawrence O'Donnell. Theirs was a close writing relationship: many books credited to Kuttner alone are rumored to contain much by Moore. A similar partnership occurred in France in the 1960s between husband and wife Charles and Nathalie Henneberg. Also popular, if on the fantasy borderline, were L. Sprague DE CAMP's collaborations with P. Schuyler MILLER, Fletcher PRATT, and an assortment of Conan scribes.

In the 1950s Pohl continued down the collaborative road and wrote a series of novels with Jack WILLIAMSON; their partnership still continues. Williamson also worked with James GUNN on one novel. The following decade saw successful collaborations among Poul ANDERSON, Gordon EKLUND, and Mildred Downey Broxon, and between Avram DAVIDSON and Ward MOORE, Robert SILVERBERG and Randall GARRETT (as Robert Randall), Terry CARR and Ted WHITE, and others. During the next two decades the trend continued unabated with Ray NELSON and Roger ZELAZNY completing novels by Philip K. DICK, NEW WAVE proponents Thomas DISCH and John SLADEK penning thrillers and Gothics together, and Frank M. ROBINSON and Thomas SCORTIA attaining best-sellerdom with *The Towering Inferno* and follow-ups. The attainment of best-seller status occurred with metronomic regularity when Larry NIVEN and Jerry POURNELLE linked up for a series of novels, in parallel with their solo careers. More recently Gregory BENFORD has proven a frequent collaborator (with Gordon Eklund, William ROTSLER, David Brin, and Mark Laidlaw); other recent duos include George R. R. MARTIN and Lisa TUTTLE, Spider and Jeanne ROBINSON, Jack and Joe HALDEMAN, and Gardner DOZOIS and George Alec EFFINGER.

Collaboration has been a component of the contemporary CYBERPUNK movement as well, with writers such as William GIBSON, Michael Swanwick, Rudy RUCKER, and Bruce Sterling combining talents for short stories. A complete listing of SF collaborations would no doubt feature most of the major authors in the genre.

Methods of collaboration are as varied as the authors themselves and can include the writing of alternate chapters or drafts, the division of the task into plotting and writing, and so on. Although some writers work in close proximity—the Strugatsky brothers sit in one room and carefully discuss each sentence—others, such as Peter Straub and Stephen KING, "interface" by computer.

A more recent phenomenon in science fiction is the shared world anthology, whose contributors do not actually collaborate but use similar settings, rules, and characters: *Thieves' World, Heroes in Hell, Magic in Ithkar*, Michael MOORCOCK's Cornelius stories, and others have all attracted a diverse group of authors.

Of course, the result of any given collaboration isn't always equal to the sum of its parts: personalities and styles don't necessarily blend harmoniously, and individual talents sometimes come together to produce a bland, commonplace work. But as the multitude of successful literary partnerships attest, the field would be poorer without collaboration.

M.J.

THE COLOSSUS OF NEW YORK (1958).

Directed by Eugène Lourié; screenplay by Thelma Schnee; adapted from an original screen story by Willis Goldbeck; photographed by John F. Warren;

music by (Nathan) Van Cleave. With John Baragrey, Otto Kruger, Charles Herbert, Mala Powers, Ross Martin, Ed Wolff, Robert Hutton. 70 minutes. Black and white.

Humanitarian scientist Ross Martin is accidentally killed, so his father, Otto Kruger, installs his brain in a giant robotlike body. Despite becoming friendly with the dead man's son (played by Charles Herbert), the Colossus goes mad and tries to rid the Earth forever of troublesome people.

Some regard *Colossus* as a minor classic; others find it dry and ponderous, a routine low-budget film derived from FRANKENSTEIN and *The Golem*. The robotlike Colossus is interesting but unconvincing. William Alland produced this thriller aimed at children.

B.W.

COLOSSUS: THE FORBIN PROJECT (1970).
Directed by Joseph Sargent; screenplay by James Bridges; adapted from the novel Colossus *by D. F. Jones; photographed by Gene Polito; music by Michel Colombier. With Eric Braeden, Susan Clark, William Schallert, Gordon Pinsent. 100 minutes. Color.*

The story of the computer that goes out of control and takes over everything is an old one in science fiction, effectively captured by authors as various as Isaac ASIMOV, Fredric BROWN and Mack REYNOLDS, Jack WILLIAMSON, and Harlan ELLISON. In this filmed version of D. F. JONES's novel, the process receives a chilling visualization as the scientist Forbin (Eric Braeden) builds a mountain-sized, foolproof computer that will ensure peace. The computer, seen gradually "coming alive"—in a scene that "successfully communicates the feeling that something immensely powerful has got out of control," according to SF film critic John Brosnan—before it is hermetically sealed away in the Rocky Mountains, locates a Soviet counterpart, and they quickly seize control of Earth in the name of peace.

Forbin's initial reaction is bemused pride in his brainchild: he built better than he knew. But admiration turns to alarm as Colossus ruthlessly assassinates opponents and executes "clean" strikes to consolidate its power. Attempting a conspiracy, Forbin plots with a colleague, Susan Clark, in voyeuristic scenes conducted under the global computer's electronic gaze. In time Forbin realizes that Colossus is toying with him; he is a pet, probably kept alive solely because he is the machine's maker. The conspiracy was doomed from its start. Forbin's final, angry "Never!" is swallowed in a metallic drone as Colossus describes humankind's future: stagnant, resigned, and above all peaceful.

The film deserved an audience that its distributors did not get for it, but it is worth watching when it shows up, as it does, on TV.

J.C.

COMIC STRIPS AND COMIC BOOKS

Even at their birth in the 1890s, comic strips incorporated elements of the fantastic—often with a science-fiction bent. Winsor McCay's work—notably *Little Nemo in Slumberland*—was the most artistically striking of the early 1900s comics and spawned such imitators as *The Explorigator* by Harry Grant Dart, about a marvelous airship that even traveled to the Moon.

But true SF strips didn't appear until 1929, by which time the adventure continuity strip had been established. Then Phil NOWLAN launched BUCK ROGERS, based on his AMAZING STORIES novelettes "Armageddon 2419 A.D." and "The Airlords of Han." The year 1933 saw the debut of V. T. Hamlin's *Alley Oop*, about a caveman living in a world of dinosaurs. In time Hamlin introduced Professor Wonmug and his time machine, allowing Oop to visit not only the present but also various historical eras. Also in 1933, William Ritt and Clarence Gray's *Brick Bradford* debuted. This eponymous SF hero traveled through time and space in the Time Top. FLASH GORDON followed in 1934. Also notable during this period was Frank Godwin's *Connie*. Beginning in 1927 as a society girl, Connie evolved into an adventure heroine and eventually went into space to explore the planets.

The year 1933 marked the appearance of the first comic books—initially collections of comic strips intended solely as store giveaways—bearing the titles *Funnies on Parade* and *Famous Funnies*. M. C. Gaines decided to see if the books would sell on the newsstands for ten cents. They did. Buck Rogers began his run in *Famous Funnies No. 3*.

In 1935 Major Malcolm Wheeler-Nicholson began publishing the first comic book made up entirely of original material, *New Fun Comics*. The first issue contained science fiction: "Super-Police, 2023" and "Dan Drake on the Planet Saro," both written by Ken Fitch and illustrated by Clemens Gretter (under the name Clem Gretta). Time travel was featured in "The Magic Crystal of History," illustrated by Adolphe Barreaux, a magazine artist who was also doing the Sally the Sleuth strip for the pulp *Spicy Detective*.

Wheeler-Nicholson soon added a second book, *New Comics,* and changed the title of *New Fun* to *More Fun*. The initial issue of *New Comics* (later to become *Adventure Comics*) marked the first appearance in comic books of the work of two artists who would later become favorites: Walt Kelly had center spreads in the first two issues illustrating scenes from *Gulliver's Travels* (the first SF classic done in a comic book); Sheldon Mayer had two features, one of which, "The Strange Adventures of Mr. Weed," concerned a time machine.

Jerry Siegel and Joe Shuster produced their first professional work for Wheeler-Nicholson, injecting SF even into police stories. But it was only after the Major had handed the company over to Harry Donenfeld and Jack Liebowitz that its greatest creation, SUPERMAN, debuted in the first issue of *Action Comics* (June 1938).

Superman's origin on another planet and involvement with mad scientists were imitated by other superheroes, many of whom had SF origins. Ajax the Sun Man, in *Doc Savage Comics*, came from the Sun. The Human Torch, in *Marvel Comics*, was an android. And Jerry Siegel's Robotman, in *Star-Spangled Comics*, was a murder victim whose brain lived on in a robot body.

Even heroes with magical origins (including Captain Marvel, Fawcett's major comic hero) had a great deal of SF in their adventures. One of Captain Marvel's chief writers was SF author Otto (Eando) BINDER, and Manly Wade WELLMAN also wrote some episodes. At All-American, *Green Lantern*'s writers included Henry KUTTNER and Alfred BESTER.

By this time, Fiction House, which had been publishing pulps, had entered the comics field. One of its titles was *Planet Comics*, a sort of comics version of its *Planet Stories*. This was the first all-SF comic book. In its more than thirteen years of publication it offered "The Red Comet," "Auro, Lord of Jupiter," "Gale Allen and the Girl Squadron," "Star Pirate," "Mars, God of War," "Mysta of the Moon," and "Futura." The last three issues featured straight SF stories, abandoning regular series, after the fashion of the EC comics.

Early comics were strongly influenced by the pulps and took from them many artists, writers, and even editors. The DC company hired editor Mort WEISINGER away from Standard, and he remained with them (except for his service time during World War II) until his retirement in 1970. Throughout his tenure at DC he was particularly busy on *Superman*, although he worked on other projects as well. One of his most interesting scripts was "How Television Will Change Your Future" in *Real Fact Comics No. 15* (July–August 1948). Most of his predictions there have come true, including his assertion that we would view the first moon landing live. (The script even contained an illustration of people watching the landing on a giant screen in Times Square—just a short distance from where people actually watched such a screen in Central Park.)

Weisinger's boyhood friend and fellow pioneer in SF fandom, Julius Schwartz, had become an SF literary agent. When an editor at All-American, Dorothy Roubicek, left to marry, Alfred Bester recommended Schwartz as her replacement. He was hired and was still, at this writing, working at DC (which was affiliated with All-American and took it over in the mid-1940s).

Edmond HAMILTON also began writing for DC in the 1940s (although he is also reported to have written "The Black Terror" for Better, or Standard). In the 1950s his wife, Leigh BRACKETT, ghosted a few scripts for him, including one *Batman*.

The Gilberton company had created the first suc-

cessful comic adapting the great literary works, *Classic Comics* (later *Classics Illustrated*). The series presented comic-strip versions of *Dr. Jekyll and Mr. Hyde, A Connecticut Yankee in King Arthur's Court, Frankenstein,* Edgar Allan POE's *Hans Pfaal,* and a number of works by Jules VERNE and H. G. WELLS, among others. Other publishers have followed suit. A current weekly series in Mexico has, at this writing, adapted more than fifty Vernes.

DC's *Real Fact Comics* differed from the many clones of *True Comics* in that it stressed science and science fiction, as well as prediction. It featured biographies of Wells and Verne along with "Just Imagine," speculation about the future illustrated by fantasy artist Virgil FINLAY. Finlay also did other work for *Real Fact*, including some art on the Tommy Tomorrow series.

Tommy Tomorrow began with a story called "Columbus of Space," in which Tommy was the first man of Mars—in 1960. Finally the series was shifted to *Action Comics*, running there and in *World's Finest Comics* for several years.

By the early 1950s an SF craze was sweeping the nation. Science-fiction movies and TV shows were es-

pecially popular, and the comics, suffering from the public's disaffection with superheroes, were trying new things, SF among them.

An artist appeared at this moment who was to change the look of comics with his striking and innovative style. Wallace Allen Wood was born in Minnesota in 1927. He was not yet out of his teens when he began working as an assistant to Will Eisner on his Spirit Sunday section. In 1949 Wood hit the comic books. Previously there had been little detail to SF machines and spaceship interiors; bug-eyed monsters (BEMs) tended to look like Earth creatures, especially reptiles. Wood changed all that. His machinery was intricate, whether in a lab or in a space vessel, convincing the viewer of its reality. His BEMs were monstrous indeed and totally unearthly in appearance. With Wood, SF comics took a long stride.

In 1950 and 1951 Wood was involved in a number of SF adaptations: *Dr. Jekyll and Mr. Hyde* in Fox's *A Star Presentation No. 3,* Avon's *An Earth Man on Venus* (from Farley's *The Radio Man*), *Rocket to the Moon* (from Otis Adelbert Kline's *Maza of the Moon*), and *Attack on Planet Mars* (from Ray Cummings's *Tarrano the Conqueror*).

By 1954 Eisner's Spirit section had begun to lose papers and seemed about to fold. Wood was brought in to do a few weeks' work that would take the Spirit on a trip to the moon. Jules Feiffer wrote the story. They produced first-rate work but to no avail: soon after the section was canceled.

But Wood's greatest fame came with his work on EC's science-fiction comics. M. C. Gaines, after selling out All-American to DC, had launched EC (standing first for Educational Comics, then for Entertaining Comics). EC was floundering when Gaines was killed in a boating accident and his son, William M. Gaines, took over. Bill Gaines set out to reorganize the line with new concepts.

It was then that Wood came to EC. Teamed with artist and writer Harry Harrison, who was later to become an SF author, Wood worked at first on western and romance comics. Then Gaines launched what was to be known as the New Trend line, specializing in "SuspenStories"—short stories with surprise endings. Harrison, backed by Wood, suggested SF as a theme for some of the titles. Gaines, always a fan of the SF pulps, agreed and launched *Weird Science* and *Weird Fantasy* in 1950.

Albert B. Feldstein was the editor and chief writer as well as, in the early issues, an artist. Eventually his other duties left him little time for art; for a while he only did covers but in time turned entirely to writing and editing. A few of the early SF stories were written by Gardner Fox, a prolific comics writer who, at Julius Schwartz's suggestion, had begun writing SF for the pulps. Wood himself wrote some stories, as did Harvey Kurtzman, who also provided the art. Jack Kamen was another of the original EC science-fiction artists. With Feldstein producing little art and Kurtzman becoming writer-editor of the new war comics, other artists filled in. Two finally became regulars: Joe Orlando, who had worked with Wood, and Al Williamson. A typical EC science-fiction comic would have a lead story by Wood followed by a Williamson story, a human interest piece by Kamen, and finally an Orlando tale. In time other artists worked on the magazines as well. The stories, which Gaines and Feldstein plotted together, were always written for a particular artist.

With so many stories to do, it was not easy to think of wholly original plots, and comics frequently took their story line from various sources. In *Weird Fantasy No. 13* the story "Home to Stay" combined Ray Bradbury's "The Rocket Man" and "Kaleidoscope." Although Bradbury did not threaten to sue, he did ask for payment for secondary rights, then suggested that EC adapt others of his stories as well. This they did, turning two dozen of his best tales, fourteen of which were SF, into comics.

Despite their quality the EC science fiction comics never sold well. Eventually the two were combined into *Weird Science-Fantasy (WSF),* with the price raised to 15 cents. During this period Harlan Ellison sold a plot

to the publication: his "Upheaval" appeared in *WSF No. 24*. Otto Binder apparently wrote a few stories for EC at the time, and perhaps this explains how they came to adapt his "Teacher from Mars" and the first three Adam Link stories. (Feldstein scripted these, but Binder later adapted several Adam Links for early issues of Warren's *Creepy* magazine.)

With the advent of the Comics Code in 1954, *Weird Science-Fantasy* became *Incredible Science Fiction*. Soon, however, the EC comics folded. Only *Mad*, which had become a magazine, survived. An abortive attempt to keep going with a wedding of comics and text called "Picto-Fiction" is worth mentioning only because one of its writers was sometime SF author Daniel KEYES.

At DC 1950 saw the launching of *Strange Adventures*, edited by Julius Schwartz. The first issue introduced Chris KL99 by Edmond HAMILTON. Like the early Tommy Tomorrow, Chris was a "Columbus of Space" and spent his time exploring new worlds. Gardner FOX and David V. Reed (Dave Vern) also had stories in that issue. The last feature was an adaptation of the movie DESTINATION MOON, which was also adapted (at full length) in *Fawcett Movie Comics*. H. L. GOLD and Walter B.

Gibson wrote stories for *Strange Adventures*. Another feature, *Captain Comet*, began in No. 10. This concerned a mutant with a mind far beyond that of ordinary humans. It was written by John Broome, using the pseudonym Edgar Ray Merritt (from Edgar Rice BURROUGHS, Ray CUMMINGS, and A. MERRITT). The following year brought a companion magazine, *Mystery in Space*. The lead feature in its early issues was *Knights of the Galaxy*, by Anthony Dion (Robert Kanigher). Fox, Hamilton, and Manly Wade Wellman also contributed to the magazine.

Showcase No. 17 introduced *Adam Strange*, an archaeologist who was teleported to the planet Rann of the star-sun Alpha Centauri and fell in love with the beautiful Alanna of Ranagar. Written by Fox and originally illustrated by Mike Sekowsky, *Strange*'s tryout was successful enough to give the strip a long run in *Mystery in Space*, with Carmine Infantino taking over the art. Another SF feature spotlighted in *Showcase* was *Space Ranger*, which went on to *Tales of the Unexpected*.

The second age of superheroes began in the mid-1950s. Most of the new heroes had SF origins. Hawkman, in his 1940s version a reincarnation of an Egyptian prince, was now an alien lawman. Green Lantern had become one of a corps of space-guarding heroes. Marvel's Fantastic Four (including a new Human Torch) got their powers from cosmic rays during a spaceflight.

Other countries had their SF heroes too. Great Britain's *Garth*, bowing in 1943, was a muscular man who often had amorous adventures in time and space. In 1954 *Jeff Hawke*, a space hero, debuted in the same country. In France, Jean-Claude Forest's *Barbarella*, best known today for the Jane Fonda film version, first appeared in *V-Magazine* in 1962.

In America, Williamson turned his *Seetee Shock* and *Seetee Ship* into a newspaper strip *Beyond Mars*, with art by Lee Elias, but it had only a short run (1951–1953). Oscar Lebeck's *Twin Earths*, illustrated by Alden McWilliams, did better (1953–1963).

One of Great Britain's most popular SF series was *Dan Dare, Pilot of the Future*, which debuted in 1950 in the first issue of the magazine *Eagle*. The current top magazine of this type in Britain is *2000 A.D.*, which has featured a number of futuristic series (most set much further in the future than the magazine's title). Several of these have been reprinted in America, notably *Judge Dredd*, about a lawman in a futuristic American city who is policeman, judge, and jury all in one.

A modern innovation in comics is the limited series. The first of these, *World of Krypton*, told the story of Superman's father in three issues. Another notable series was DC's *Camelot 3000*, in which King Arthur returned to save Earth from alien invaders. Mike W. Barr wrote it, and the art was handled by *Judge Dredd*'s Brian Bolland.

The coming of comics shops in the 1970s opened the field to new publishers. Many of these have launched science-fiction titles. One of the most successful, First Comics, did a series adapting the SF Broadway play *Warp*. More successful has been Howard Chaykin's *American Flagg*, about an actor turned lawman in the 2030s. One of the most popular characters in this series is a talking cat named Raul.

Another recent innovation is the graphic novel, a quality volume in comics form. Many of these are science fiction. DC has been producing adaptations of works by BLOCH, SILVERBERG, BRADBURY, POHL, ELLISON, and others in this format.

E.N.B.

COMPTON, D[AVID] G[UY] (1930–).

British writer now resident in the United States. Compton has written mysteries (as Guy Compton), romances (as Frances Lynch), and radio plays. His SF novels are near future studies of personal relationships affected (almost always for the worse) by apocalyptic events or the abuse of technological innovations. In *The Silent Multitude* (1966) cities crumble in the face of an alien infection, and in *The Missionaries* (1972) aliens try to convert

humankind to their faith. But his finest works show ordinary people suffering because of the morally blind exploitation of new technological devices. These include *Synthajoy* (1968), about a means of recording conscious experience; *The Electric Crocodile* (1970; also known as *The Steel Crocodile*), about the use of information technology; and *The Continuous Katherine Mortenhoe* (1974; also known as *The Unsleeping Eye* and *Death Watch*—the latter also the title of an excellent film of the book), about the intrusiveness of modern media.

The characteristic bitterness of Compton's tone—ingeniously displayed in the dystopian black comedy *A Usual Lunacy* (1978)—in which falling in love is held to be the effect of a virus—makes his novels too uncomfortable for readers who prefer wish fulfillment fantasies, but he is a fine prose craftsman with a remarkable flair for futuristic realism; it is a pity that he has published nothing since 1980, with the exception of *Scudder's Game* (1985), available only in German as of 1987.

OTHER WORKS: *The Quality of Mercy* (1965); *Farewell, Earth's Bliss* (1966); *Chronocules* (1970; as *Hot Wireless Sets, Aspirin Tablets, the Sandpaper Side of Used Matchboxes, and Something That Might Have Been Castor Oil*, 1971); *Windows* (1979); *Ascendancies* (1980).

B.S.

—————— COMPUTERS ——————

The computer revolution is often cited as a great blind spot in science-fiction prophecy. The only major work to anticipate the social significance of computer information networks, for example, was Murray LEINSTER's "A Logic Named Joe" (1946); it was a lucky guess for Isaac ASIMOV to provide Hari Seldon with a pocket computer in the prelude to *Foundation* (1950) at a time when even Robert A. HEINLEIN's heroes used slide rules.

Actually, the history of computers in science fiction isn't quite such a blank as many imagine. Computerized range finders win a naval war for the United States in Leinster's "Politics" (1932). In E. E. SMITH's *Triplanetary* (1934), there is casual mention of "automatic integrating course plotters" (read "navigational computers"). Even the "electric filing cabinets" of A. E. VAN VOGT's *Slan* (1940) are obviously computer banks as we know them. Yet such forecasts were relatively uncommon for two apparent reasons. First, science fiction was obsessed by the idea of *humanoid robots*, which in imagination performed the tasks later to be actually performed by computer-programmed industrial robots. Second, without any hint of the transistor and related developments (a real, and inevitable, blind spot), it was impossible for SF to forecast the *miniaturization* of computers. In Smith's *Skylark of Valeron* (1934–35), the heroes find their way back to the Galaxy with the help of a mapping navigational computer the size of a planetoid. Smith's battle management computer in *Second Stage Lensmen* (1941–1942) is almost as huge; moreover, it relies on the cumbersome switchboard system that is now almost a forgotten chapter in the history of computers.

Advances in computer application, particularly the interfacing of human and machine, which make it possible to access information directly (and even to "become" part of a computer network), are explored in such recent works as Samuel R. DELANY's *Stars in My Pocket Like Grains of Sand* and William GIBSON's *Neuromancer* (both 1984). But to a great extent science fiction has had to play catch-up with the computer revolution in the real world. More common in classic SF has been the theme of artificial intelligence, with computers large and complex enough to be *self-aware*.

In Laurence MANNING's "Master of the Brain" (1932), a mechanical brain administers the entire world and has become a power unto itself. The theme of artificial intelligence "taking over," with an organic lust for power attributed to inorganic life, has been common ever since. D. F. JONES's *Colossus* (1966), filmed by Joseph Sargent as COLOSSUS: THE FORBIN PROJECT (1969), is typical of works in which a Great Computer assumes power in the name of humankind's own good. Even in Frank HERBERT's otherwise sober exploration of artificial intelligence, *Destination Void* (1966), the cliché of the computer as God is rung in at the end. To counter this notion, Heinlein introduced the idea of the computer as Playful Companion in *The Moon Is a Harsh Mistress* (1966). This theme was further developed in David GERROLD's *When Harlie Was One* (1972) and other works: computers might be mischievous, even self-protective, but never power crazed. In Gibson's *Neuromancer*, by contrast, an Artificial Intelligence shows an aloof indifference to humankind, having unfathomable purposes of its own.

J.J.P.

THE CONQUEST OF SPACE (1955). *Directed by Byron Haskin; screenplay by George O'Hanlon; title from the book by Willy Ley and Chesley Bonestell; photographed by Lionel Lindon; music by (Nathan) Van Cleave. With Walter Brooke, Eric Fleming, Mickey Shaughnessy, Phil Foster, Benson Fong, Ross Martin, William Redfield, William Hopper, Joan Shawlee, Rosemary Clooney. 81 minutes. Color.*

Set in the near future, *The Conquest of Space* depicts the trials and tribulations of a spaceship crew en route to Mars from a huge space station in Earth orbit. When a crewman dies, the ship's Captain Merritt becomes convinced that God doesn't want people to go to Mars; he clashes with his crew member–son and goes mad. After he damages the water supply, he is accidentally killed;

The Conquest of Space

a Christmas snowfall saves the imperiled crew from an arid death, and the ship is safely launched.

Producer George PAL's success with WAR OF THE WORLDS (1953) led to his production of the mainstream movies *Houdini* (1953) and *The Naked Jungle* (1954), but he hoped to produce an epic of the exploration of the solar system. Paramount, however, insisted on the clichéd, intrusive father-son rivalry and emphasis on religion, diluting Pal's hoped-for realistic Martian journey. The film does offer sandstorms and a Marsquake, and there's also a tough sergeant and a wisecracking Brooklynite. But the movie disappointed Pal's fans and is rarely shown today.

The special effects, under the direction of John P. Fulton, are less convincing than one would hope, in spite of the emphasis on realism. Adviser Chesley BONESTELL protested the Mars set built by studio technicians, although it turned out to be surprisingly accurate: red sand dotted with black rocks.

B.W.

CONQUEST OF THE PLANET OF THE APES: SEE PLANET OF THE APES

CONVENTIONS: SEE FANDOM

COOK, GLEN [CHARLES] (1944–   ). American science-fiction writer and a prolific author of 1970s short stories and 1980s adventure novels in spite of a full-time job as a supervisor in a General Motors assembly plant in St. Louis. After an early postholocaust novel, *The Heirs of Babylon* (1972), Cook turned to romantic military fiction of the future and fantasy in several series. Dread Empire up to 1987 consisted of *A Shadow of All Night Falling* (1979), *October's Baby* (1980), *All Darkness Met* (1980), *The Fire in His Hands* (1984), *With Mercy toward None* (1985), and *Reap the East Wind* (1987). Starfishers consists of three novels, all published in 1982: *Shadowline, Starfishers,* and *Star's End.* Black Company is another trilogy: *The Black Company* (1984), *Shadows Linger* (1984), and *The White Rose* (1985). The Darkwar trilogy is composed of *Doomstalker* (1985), *Warlock* (1985), and *Ceremony* (1986). So much written so quickly means a reliance on traditional plots and styles, but the ready publication of Cook's work also indicates that it has an audience.

OTHER WORKS: *The Swordbearer* (1982); *A Matter of Time* (1985); *Passage of Arms* (1985); *Sweet Silver Blues* (1987).

S.H.G.

COOK, WILLIAM WALLACE (1867–1933). American writer, who, from 1903 to 1907, satirized contemporary utopias and popular science-fiction themes in five novels for the pulp magazine *Argosy: A Round Trip to the Year 2000* (1903/1925), *Cast Away at the Pole* (1904/1925), *Adrift in the Unknown* (1904/1925), *Marooned in 1492* (1905/1925), and *The Eighth Wonder* (1906–7/1925). Among other inventions, Cook introduced modern ROBOTS, which he called muglugs.

J.H.

COOPER, EDMUND (1926–1982). British science-fiction writer. At his best Cooper used science fiction to make political and social comments. Although his novels rarely contain much interesting hardware, the societies he created are often compelling and controversial. For example, his novels that deal directly with the battle between the sexes (*Five to Twelve*, 1968; *Who Needs Men?* 1972; in the United States *Gender Genocide*) are both clearly antifeminist.

Cooper's favorite setting was postholocaust Earth, usually after a nuclear war: in his first novel, *The Uncertain Midnight* (1958; in the United States *Deadly Image*), androids threaten to replace humans; in *Seed of Light* (1959), humans flee a devastated Earth in a generation starship. And in both *The Last Continent* (1969) and *The Tenth Planet* (1973), nuclear weapons have rendered the Earth either uninhabitable or close to it.

Cooper used the postholocaust setting to compare technological and rural societies, and it is clearly the rural societies for which he had the greater sympathy. *A Far Sunset* (1967), one of his finest novels, contrasts a sophisticated but unimaginative human society with a primitive alien culture that has created an elaborate my-

thology; *The Overman Culture* (1971) compares a fanciful version of Victorian England with the cold, technological present. However, Cooper's best-known novel, *The Cloud Walker* (1973), describes the rebirth of technology on a postholocaust Earth dominated by a repressive, antimachine religion.

Cooper also wrote a series of space operas known as The Expendables under the pseudonym Richard Avery. These four novels (*The Deathworms of Kratos,* 1975; *The Rings of Tantulas,* 1975; *The War Games of Zelos,* 1975; and *The Venom of Argus,* 1976) show few of his more serious concerns, but they do successfully achieve another of his goals: to entertain.

OTHER WORKS: *Tomorrow's Gift* (collection, 1958); *Voices in the Dark* (collection, 1960); *Tomorrow Came* (collection, 1963); *Transit* (1964); *All Fools' Day* (1966); *News from Elsewhere* (collection, 1968); *Sea-horse in the Sky* (1969); *Son of Kronk* (1970); *The Square Root of Tomorrow* (collection, 1970); *Double Phoenix, The Firebird* (1971); *Unborn Tomorrow* (collection, 1971); *The Slaves of Heaven* (1974); *Prisoner of Fire* (1974); *Merry Christmas, Ms. Minerva* (1978); *Jupiter Laughs and Other Stories* (collection, 1979); *A World of Difference* (1980).

S.H.G.

CORMAN, ROGER (1926–). American film director and producer noted for his prolific output of genre quickies, camp treatment of exploitation material, and encouragement of new Hollywood talent. Between 1955 and 1971 Corman directed, and often produced as well, at least forty-five feature films in a variety of genres. His reputation, however, rests largely on his work in horror and science fiction, with such low-budget classics as THE LITTLE SHOP OF HORRORS (1960), X—THE MAN WITH THE X-RAY EYES (1963), and a series of adaptations of the work of Edgar Allan POE starring Vincent PRICE.

Corman's films were usually box-office successes, first for American International Pictures, a company that catered to the teen market, and then for his own production company, New World Pictures. One of Corman's major strengths as a director is his ability to infuse what otherwise would be relatively standard fare with serious moral and metaphysical implications. His movies often offer moral lessons, many of them obvious, such as warnings about the danger of nuclear destruction. The action-packed ATTACK OF THE CRAB MONSTERS (1956), for instance, was the most successful of Corman's early low-budget monster movies. It depicts a group of scientists on a remote Pacific island battling giant crabs, mutated as a result of nuclear testing.

THE DAY THE WORLD ENDED (1956) and *The Last Woman on Earth* (1960) are postholocaust parables. In *The Day* humanity is reduced to a handful of survivors, a microcosmic society that fights internally even as it must work cooperatively to battle the mutated beasts outside. *Teenage Caveman* (1958) offers a bit of a twist in its story of an apparently prehistoric boy whose tribal law forbids travel to the greener, more appealing land across the river. The hero defies tradition and makes the journey, discovering that the monster the tribe had feared is actually a dying man in a leaking radiation suit—the setting, it turns out, is not prehistory but a future devastated by nuclear war.

Other Corman films are concerned with hubris and the fatal desire to extend human ability or control destiny. In *The Wasp Woman* (1959), for example, the unfortunate lady of the title ("A beautiful woman by day—a lusting queen wasp by night," announced the film's publicity) is the head of a cosmetics firm; afraid of losing her beauty with age, she applies a new serum of wasp extract to her skin with horrifying results.

One of Corman's best films, *X—The Man with the X-Ray Eyes,* explores the Faustian theme of the desire for unlimited knowledge through the perfect cinematic metaphor of heightened visual acuity. A scientist develops a potion that allows him to see through objects. His newfound power is initially wonderful, as the scientist delights in looking through people's clothes on a dance floor. But as he increases the dosage of the potion, his vision transcends all bounds. Perceiving the very depths of the universe, he sees more than he can comprehend and begins to go mad. In the powerful climax the scientist tears at his eyes while a preacher at a revival meeting thumps out the biblical injunction "If thine eye offend thee, pluck it out."

Corman's ability to produce a substantial string of cheaply made movies that proved both popular and provocative is in part a result of his ingenuity in hiring talented people. Screenwriters such as Richard MATHESON, Charles Beaumont, and Robert Towne have each written at least four films for Corman. Cinematographer Floyd Crosby, whose many credits begin with F. W. Murnau's classic *Tabu* (1931), has photographed over twenty Corman films, and the director fully acknowledges Crosby's influence in his use of wide screen, color, and camera movement. Corman has also employed a number of talented actors, including Jack Nicholson, Peter Fonda, Bruce Dern, and Vincent Price. And many of the most talented new American directors got their start at New World Pictures, among them Francis Ford Coppola, Peter Bogdanovich, Martin Scorsese, Monte Hellman, and Joe DANTE.

But Corman's own resourcefulness in dealing with limited budgets has also helped his box-office record. His first film as producer, *The Monster from the Ocean Floor* (1954), was made for a mere $12,000. Many of his movies were shot very quickly; *The Little Shop of Horrors,* Corman's brilliant black comedy about a bloodthirsty plant, is legendary for having been shot in two days.

Roger Corman's *Attack of the Crab Monsters* (1956)

His visual ideas often made the most out of his limited resources. NOT OF THIS EARTH (1956), for example, depicts the alien from the planet Davanna as nothing more unusual than a man in a business suit with dark sunglasses (his eyes occasionally glow), played with the perfect touch of menace by B-actor Paul Birch. Sometimes the zippers on the monster suits show through, as in *The Day the World Ended,* in which the mutated human is clearly clothed in something resembling latex. But despite these occasional limitations, Corman stands out as an SF director who has consistently demonstrated that interesting work can be done in the genre without inflated budgets and elaborate special effects. He has managed to create a body of pulp science-fiction movies that provide modest thrills while delivering earnest, if simplistic, moral messages.

B.K.G.

THE COSMIC MONSTER *(The Strange World of Planet X)* (1958). *Directed by Gilbert Gunn; screenplay by Paul Ryder; adapted from the novel* The Strange World of Planet X *by René Ray; photographed by Joe Ambor; music by Robert Sharples. With Forrest Tucker, Gaby André, Martin Benson, Alec Mango, Wyndham Goldie, Hugh Latimer, Geoffrey Chater. 75 minutes. Black and white.*

An uncaring scientist's work with magnetism opens a hole in the ionosphere, loosing cosmic rays on a portion of the English countryside. Some insects are made gigantic, and a tramp turns homicidal. A benign alien straightens things out by blowing up the scientist.

Dark, slow-paced, and unexciting, *The Cosmic Monster* is notable only as the sole British entry in the giant-insect sweepstakes of the 1950s. Some of its effects are interesting and gruesome, but the film is dreary.

B.W.

COSMOLOGY

Cosmology is the branch of astronomy concerned with the study of the universe as a whole; it embraces cosmogony, which consists of theories and speculations about the origin, development, and future of the cosmos. Following the displacement of the Aristotelian "closed world" by the Copernican heliocentric theory of the universe, the idea gradually took hold that the stars are other suns and that the universe is infinite in extent. The expansion of perspective contained in this idea has an awe-inspiring grandiosity that has frequently moved people to imaginative rhapsody; there is perhaps no purer example of the "sense of wonder" that science fiction frequently tries to evoke and exploit.

Fictional techniques have often been used to convey the special excitement of cosmological speculations, as in such works as Gabriel Daniel's *A Voyage to the World of Cartesius* (1692), Fontenelle's classic *A Plurality of Worlds* (1688), and Camille Flammarion's *Lumen* (1873). Edgar Allan POE's *Eureka* (1848) is a treatise in cosmological metaphysics, but Poe chose to subtitle it "A Prose Poem" and to request that it be considered only as a work of literature. Poe's short story "A Mesmeric Revelation" (1844) was the first of several accounts of visionary adventures, among them Edgar Fawcett's *The Ghost of Guy Thyrle* (1895) and H. G. WELLS's rather flippant "Under the Knife" (1896). A much more elaborate visionary sequence can be found in William Hope HODGSON's *The House on the Borderland* (1908), but the most comprehensive and careful example of such a project is Olaf STAPLEDON's masterpiece *Star Maker* (1937).

In the twentieth century a series of discoveries has further elaborated and complicated cosmological theory. The true size of our own galaxy was determined, and it was proved that ours is but one of a vast number of galaxies. A more profound impact on the imagination, however, was made by the discovery that the universe is apparently expanding—giving rise to the notion that it began with a "big bang." The Big Bang theory was initially opposed by a steady state theory, which suggested that matter is continually being created to fill in the gaps caused by expansion, but the discovery of objects like quasars, and of a stellar-background radiation that may be an echo of the big bang, suggested that the universe is not homogeneous, as the steady state theory would imply. Science-fiction writers, however, tend to combine aspects of big bang and steady-state theories into the idea that there might be an external series of cycles in which the universe continually explodes and collapses, being effectively reborn with every new big bang. This image is much more commonly used than the alternative cosmogonic prognosis, which suggests that the universe will ultimately and irredeemably suffer an entropic "heat death" when all its energy is homogeneously distributed.

A popular cosmological model in early pulp SF was inspired by the analogy drawn between the Rutherford-Bohr model of the atom and the solar system. This suggested to several writers that our perceived cosmos might be part of an infinite hierarchy, containing a microcosm and being contained by a macrocosm. The idea appears to have first been used by R. A. Kennedy in his eccentric romance *The Triuneverse* (1912) but was popularized mainly by Ray CUMMINGS, who wrote numerous microcosmic and macrocosmic romances including *The Girl in the Golden Atom* (1919–20) and *Explorers into Infinity* (1927–28). Other pulp stories of similar stripe include "Submicroscopic" (1931) by S. P. MEEK, "Colossus" (1934) by Donald Wandrei, and "He Who Shrank" (1936) by Henry Hasse. These stories now seem silly, as do other early pulp stories of cosmological revelation, such as Laurence MANNING's "The Living Galaxy" (1934) and Edmond HAMILTON's "The Accursed Galaxy" (1935), which suggests that the universe is expanding because other galaxies are fleeing from ours, horror-struck by the fact that it is infected by life.

In this field the discoveries of the astronomers have been consistently more amazing than anything writers could invent. Those discoveries, moreover, are not easy to weave into the fabric of stories dealing with the exploits of human beings, although A. E. VAN VOGT found a way to make a man the agent of the big bang in "The Seesaw" (1941; incorporated in *The Weapon Shops of Isher*, 1951). A notion such as entropic heat death has not even the innate dramatic appeal of the big bang, and it is most famously featured in SF in a story that uses it as an analogical counterweight to a study of the tedium of housework: Pamela Zoline's "The Heat Death of the Universe" (1967). Several writers have, however, managed to dramatize the idea that cosmological discoveries must reduce our sense of self-importance ad absurdum: in L. Ron HUBBARD's "Beyond the Black Nebula" (1949, as Rene Lafayette) it is found that our world is located somewhere in the gut of a macrocosmic worm, and Damon KNIGHT's "God's Nose" (1964) is a brief account of the cosmogonic sneeze. A different kind of absurdism is invoked as a narrative strategy to dramatize cosmological notions in Italo CALVINO's *Cosmicomics* (1965).

Despite these difficulties modern SF writers have been reasonably ingenious in discovering ways in which human characters can become witnesses to cosmogonic affairs, in particular to the "life cycle" of cosmic collapse and explosive rebirth. In *The Triumph of Time* (1958) James BLISH actually brought our universe to a premature catastrophic end, but subsequent writers have found ways to transcend spatiotemporal limitations to make cosmogonic events perceptible. This effect was achieved by Poul ANDERSON in *Tau Zero* (1970), Bob SHAW in *Ship of Strangers* (1978), George ZEBROWSKI in *Macrolife* (1979), and Charles SHEFFIELD in *Between the Strokes of Night* (1985). All these memorable stories succeed in making concrete the kind of visionary sequence that by Poe, Wells, and Stapledon could only be represented as a sort of hallucination, and by so doing they add something to the quality of the imaginative experience.

New ventures in cosmological speculation are relatively rare, but a particularly interesting exception is featured in Ian WATSON's *The Jonah Kit* (1975), in which the theory that our universe is only a kind of existential "echo" of the actual Creation has a devastating effect on the consciousness of whales when it is communicated to them by humans. Charles HARNESS made ingenious symbolic and speculative use of cosmological ideas in his novels *The Paradox Men* (1949; originally titled *Flight into Yesterday*) and *The Ring of Ritornel* (1968). Harness-influenced Barrington J. BAYLEY also frequently uses cosmological speculations to good dramatic effect, notably in *The Pillars of Eternity* (1982) and *The Zen Gun* (1983). Also of interest in this regard is Philip José FARMER's novel *The Unreasoning Mask* (1981).

Speculations developed from the hypothesis that our apparently three-dimensional cosmos may be part of a much greater multidimensional one (partly encouraged by Einstein's claim that the actual universe is a four-dimensional "hypersphere") have also featured fairly extensively in SF, most interestingly in stories by Rudy RUCKER, including *White Light* (1980) and *The Sex Sphere* (1983). Few of the stories developing this kind of hypothesis are interesting as exercises in speculative cosmology, though, because most writers use such "multiverses" as simple stacks of parallel worlds.

There have been a few science-fiction exercises in "alternative cosmology," including Bayley's story of a solid universe with life-bearing lacunae "Me and My Antronoscope" (1973) and David LAKE's similar but more elaborate *The Ring of Truth* (1982). Quasi-Aristotelian closed worlds occasionally turn up, as in Lester DEL REY's *The Sky Is Falling* (1963) and Brian STABLEFORD's ironic account of a recollapsed worldview "The Cosmic Perspective" (1985). Some ingenious "cosmoses that might have been" are featured in George Gamow's fantasies designed to popularize Einsteinian ideas in *Mr. Tompkins in Wonderland* (1939) and *Mr. Tompkins Explores the Atom* (1944), although these are really essays rather than works of fiction. All these alternative cosmologies are small-scale universes, reduced to suit the convenience of human perspectives, and it is understandable that writers should be attracted by such alternatives. The real universe is simply too big to be fitted into the space-and-time scale of human affairs.

For this reason the reader in search of the cosmological sense of wonder may well find more to inspire awe in nonfiction accounts, whose laconic descriptions tend to be at least as mind stretching as anything that can be credited to the experience of imaginary characters. There are numerous fine popular texts, from Sir Arthur Eddington's *The Expanding Universe* (1940) through Isaac ASIMOV's *The Universe* (1966) and John Taylor's *Black Holes: The End of the Universe?* (1973) to Steven Weinberg's *The First Three Minutes* (1977). It is notable that although astronomer Fred HOYLE's science-fiction stories, notably *The Black Cloud* (1957), do contain some speculative cosmology, his fiction cannot compare for breadth of vision and speculative audacity with his nonfiction books, especially *Lifecloud: The Origin of Life in the Universe* (with Chandra Wickramasinghe, 1978).

B.S.

COULSON, JUANITA [RUTH, Née WELLONS] (1933–).

American writer of romantic, fantasy, and Gothic novels as well as science fiction. Coulson's work is noted for its careful and imaginative detail, particularly in settings and in the interaction of her characters. Her first novel, *Crisis on Cheiron* (1967), describes an alien planet that is dominated by human and corporate greed. *The Singing Stones* (1968) continues the same plot with the addition of a species that possesses telepathic "Stones of Song." Coulson has written several novels (*Tomorrow's Heritage*, 1981; *Outward Bound*, 1982) in the Children of the Stars series, which follows the history of the Saunder family as each generation helps to shape the twenty-first century.

Coulson's short fiction (uncollected) exhibits the same craft as her novels. "Another Rib" (1963), written in collaboration with Marion Zimmer BRADLEY, is a particularly memorable post-holocaust story. With her husband, Robert COULSON, she won a Hugo in 1965 for editing the fan magazine *Yandro*.

OTHER WORKS: *Unto the Last Generation* (1975), *Space Trap* (1976).

S.H.G.

COULSON, ROBERT [STRATTON] (1928–).

American writer and businessman. Almost all of Coulson's novels have been written in collaboration with Gene DeWeese. Their first efforts produced two novels based on the television series *The Man from U.N.C.L.E.* (*The Invisibility Affair*, 1967, and *The Mind-Twisters Affair*, 1967). The dry humor of these novels is carried over into *The Gates of the Universe* (1975), reminiscent of Frederik BROWN's *What Mad Universe*, describing an amateur SF writer and his companion who use the knowledge they have gained from reading science fiction to cope with an alien system and its computer. Coulson and DeWeese have also produced novels that make use of their background as fans. Characterized by inside jokes about fans and writers, *Now You See It/Him/Them* (1975) and *Charles Fort Never Mentioned Wombats* (1977) parody virtually every aspect of the SF community.

To Renew the Ages (1976), which Coulson wrote alone, is straight adventure SF. On a post-holocaust Earth, the hero ventures forth to do battle with a telepathic enemy. With his wife, Juanita COULSON, he won the Hugo Award in 1965 for editing the fanzine *Yandro*.

S.H.G.

COVER, ARTHUR BYRON (1950–   ).

American science-fiction writer whose work reflects an often satiric humor and a liberal ideology. Cover has been influenced by several writers, most notably Harlan EL-LISON. He has also modeled some of his science fiction on the work of Philip José FARMER and Michael MOOR-COCK but has not yet found his own way of treating similar characters and settings. *Autumn Angels* (1975), his first novel, describes a future Earth on which the last humans have achieved immortality and, along with it, utter boredom, which they try to relieve by taking on the personalities of figures from popular culture; this ploy, however, seems to work for neither the characters nor the readers. The sequel, *An East Wind Coming* (1979), suffers from the same problem: a fascinating concept with an uninteresting plot.

Nevertheless, Cover's writing is well crafted and pleasurable to read, and when he masters the plot his stories are successful. These early works show a young writer seeking a personal voice; if he finds it and continues in the field (he has published nothing in the 1980s), he should produce significant work.

OTHER WORKS: *The Sound of Winter* (1976); *The Platypus of Doom and Other Nihilists* (collection, 1976); *Flash Gordon* (1980).

S.H.G.

COWPER, RICHARD (Pseudonym of John "Colin" Middleton Murry, Jr.) (1926–   ).

British writer noted for the mainstream virtues of style and characterization, and for the vein of mysticism that runs through his work. Cowper, son of mainstream writer and critic John Middleton Murry, was educated in English and education at Rendcomb College, Oxford, and at the University of Leicester, interrupted by service in the Royal Navy Fleet Air Arm in World War II. Cowper wrote several mainstream novels while working as a teacher, but, disappointed in their reception, turned to writing science fiction under a pseudonym.

His first SF novel, *Breakthrough* (1967), established the qualities of his writing: sensitive prose, the romantic dreaminess of its situations, and a longing for a better world. It dealt with the existence in contemporary characters of minds from a more perfect world and focused, as many of his later works did, including *Phoenix* (1968) and *Domino* (1971), on telepathy and other paranormal powers.

Cowper's earliest major success was *Clone* (1972), a humorous, anti-technological novel about the existence of multiple clones who develop psychic powers in a corrupt contemporary world. *The Twilight of Briareus* (1974), Cowper's most highly praised novel, takes place on an Earth in which humanity has been sterilized by a nova and deals again with "passengers" who take over the minds of several characters. It also features a near-fantasy concern for the involvement of characters with landscape and a mystical expectancy of something great to come.

The Road to Corlay (1978) may have attracted even more attention as a lushly described science-fantasy trilogy (preceded by the novella "Piper at the Gates of Dawn," 1976, and completed with *A Dream of Kinship*, 1981, and *A Tapestry of Time*, 1982) about a post-holocaust world in which a new religion is created by a young boy who can unite people with the music of his flute and the image of a white bird. The sequels, set 1,000 years later, show how the religion has rigidified and how another young boy, also with the gift (or curse) of influencing people with his piping, comes to terms with it.

OTHER WORKS: *Kuldesak* (1972); *Time Out of Mind* (1973); *Worlds Apart* (1974); *The Custodians and Other Stories* (collection, 1976); *Profundis* (1979); *The Web of the Magi and Other Stories* (collection, 1980); *Out There Where the Big Ships Go* (collection, 1980); *The Tithonian Factor and Other Stories* (1984).

J.E.G.

CRABBE, BUSTER (Professional name of Clarence Linden Crabbe) (1907–1983).

American athlete and actor who correctly dubbed himself the King of Serials; no other actor in the sound era starred in more serials (nine). Born in Oakland, California, Crabbe moved with his family to Hawaii at an early age; a proficient swimmer, he won a bronze medal at the 1928 Olympics and a gold medal in the 1932 games. Because of his athletic build and handsome features, he was chosen to star in the serial *Tarzan the Fearless* in 1933 (legal complications allowed rival productions to MGM's lavish Tarzan films starring Johnny Weissmuller); in the same year Crabbe appeared in *King of the Jungle*, based on a character created by Otis Adelbert KLINE. Several minor studio films followed; then Crabbe appeared in the serial that gave him lifelong fame, FLASH GORDON (1936), perhaps the most popular of all time. In 1938 he followed this with *Flash Gordon's Trip to Mars;* he also starred in BUCK ROGERS (1939), another serial, but returned in *Flash Gordon Conquers the Universe* the next year. Among the other genre films he appeared in were *Nabonga* (1943), *The Sea Hound* (1947), the serial *King of the Congo* (1952), and *The Alien Dead* (1980), his last film. He also appeared as Brigadier Gordon in an episode of the TV series *Buck Rogers in the 25th Century.*

In addition, Crabbe starred in dozens of westerns and the TV series *Captain Gallant of the Foreign Legion;* despite his claim that he was never much of an actor, he was impressive in his few roles as villain (some opposite Johnny Weissmuller). He was a champion of physical fitness for senior citizens and wrote two books on the subject.

B.W.

CRACK IN THE WORLD (1965).

Directed by Andrew Marton; screenplay by Jon Manchip White and Julian Halevy; photographed by Manuel Berenguer; music by Johnny Douglas. With Dana Andrews, Janette Scott, Kieron Moore, Alexander Knox, Peter Damon, Gary Lasdun, Mike Steen, Todd Martin. 96 minutes. Color.

In a typical Hollywood "science is dangerous" approach, a scientist (Dana Andrews) seeking inexpensive power acts against the advice of his colleagues and detonates an atomic device deep underground. The resulting cataclysmic fissure can be stopped only by the creation of another crack; when the two meet, a chunk is blown into space to become another moon.

The extravagance of this film's premise is undercut by inadequate special effects and an overemphasis on the characters' personal lives. But Dana Andrews gives a quietly forceful performance, the design is good, and the movie is consistently interesting.

B.W.

THE CRAWLING EYE *(The Trollenberg Terror)* (1958).

Directed by Quentin Lawrence; screenplay by Jimmy Sangster; adapted from the BBC-TV series The Trollenberg Terror *by Peter Key; photographed by Monty Berman; music by Stanley Black. With Forrest Tucker, Janet Munro, Laurence Payne, Warren Mitchell, Jennifer Jayne, Frederick Schiller, Andrew Faulds. 84 minutes. Black and white.*

Mysterious deaths at an Alpine resort are linked to a radioactive cloud on Trollenberg, a nearby peak. Thanks to a young woman in accidental psychic communication with the inhabitants of the cloud, it's learned that they are globular, head-hunting monsters, presumably aliens here to conquer the world. When they attack an observatory, they're wiped out by fighter planes.

The original TV serial and the film itself are clearly imitation Nigel Kneale: mystery, deaths, and some extrasensory powers are explained by the presence of invading aliens (although the creatures' origin is never made clear in the film). Albeit well acted and strongly directed, *The Crawling Eye* is weakened by an illogical script, motivated largely by sensationalism and an emphasis on weird happenings never satisfactorily explained. But because of its good photography and other virtues, the film is well regarded by many aficionados.

B.W.

CREATURE FROM THE BLACK LAGOON (1954).

Directed by Jack Arnold; screenplay by Harry Essex and Arthur Ross (with additional material by Jack Arnold); photographed by William E. Snyder and (underwater) Charles S. Welbourne; music by Hans J. Salter. With Richard Carlson, Julia Adams, Richard Denning, Antonio Moreno, Nestor Paiva, Whit Bissell, Ben Chapman, Ricou Browning. 79 minutes. Black and white.

REVENGE OF THE CREATURE (1955).

Directed by Jack Arnold; screenplay by Martin Berkeley; photographed by Charles S. Welbourne; music supervision by Joseph Gershenson. With John Agar, Lori Nelson, John Bromfield, Nestor Paiva, Grandon Rhodes, Dave Willock, Robert B. Williams, Clint Eastwood, Ricou Browning. 82 minutes. Black and white.

THE CREATURE WALKS AMONG US (1956).

Directed by John Sherwood; screenplay by Arthur Ross; photographed by Maury Gertsman; music by Henry Mancini. With Jeff Morrow, Rex Reason, Leigh Snowden, Gregg Palmer, Maurice Manson, Ricou Browning, Don Megowan. 78 minutes. Black and white.

Not only is the Creature from the Black Lagoon—the Gill-Man to his friends—one of the most famous movie monsters of all time, but he is emblematic of the 1950s. The first Creature film, made in 3-D, is low-budget science fiction, better than one would think, and stars icon Richard CARLSON. The Gill-Man costume was perhaps the first such cinematic creation: carefully sculpted, painstakingly detailed, skintight, custom made for the two actors who wore it. (In fact, two costumes were used, an underwater suit in a lighter shade worn by swimmer Ricou Browning, and a more thoroughly painted suit for huge Ben Chapman to wear out of the water.) Nearly everyone connected with the film took credit for the suit, but the main design contributions were by Millicent Patrick, Jack Kevan, director Jack ARNOLD, and producer William Alland.

The stories of the first two films are elementary: in the first film an expedition finds the Creature alive in the Amazon jungles. He falls for the sole woman in the group and tries to prevent them from leaving, but they shoot him and he sinks into the Black Lagoon. In the second film a new expedition captures the Creature and brings him to an aquatic park in Florida. He escapes, chases another woman, and is again shot. The third film, at least, is different: the Creature is trapped in the Everglades and accidentally set afire; when he recovers, his scales and gills have burned off, and he proves to have

Creature from the Black Lagoon

a set of lungs. Taken to San Francisco, he protects a flock of sheep, stares moodily at the bay, and then escapes. He kills an unscrupulous scientist and is last seen headed for the Pacific and, ironically, a presumed death by drowning.

But it was not plot line that made the Creature one of the enduring monsters of the movies. Some credit must go to the intelligently designed suit; it has a logic so persuasive that almost all cinematic fish-men since have resembled the Gill-Man. But equally important, director Arnold, who helmed the first two films and did rewrites on the script of the first, understood that the Creature was more than just a monster; he added a tragic, lovelorn dimension, represented visually by the remarkable ballet of desire performed by Julia (later Julie) Adams and Browning as he swims beneath her, entranced, plucking at her feet with his claws.

Of course, the concept of a half-man, half-fish survivor from the Devonian Age is absurd; the first film itself, despite some excellent moments, is a standard low-budget studio production of the period, with variable acting and bad dialogue. Yet the Creature was a monster of a less sophisticated time, probably a significant reason for its enduring appeal. Almost all children adore the Creature, finding him heroic and frightening at once. He remains an indelible image of the SF cinema.

B.W.

CREATURE FROM THE HAUNTED SEA (1961).   *Directed by Roger Corman; screenplay by Charles B. Griffith and Roger Corman; photographed by Jacques Marquette; music by Fred Katz. With Antony Carbone, Betsy Jones-Moreland, Edward Wain (Robert Towne), Edmundo Rivera Alvarez, Robert Bean, Beach Dickerson. 60 minutes. Black and white.*

One of Roger CORMAN's last meager-budget science-fiction thrillers, *Creature from the Haunted Sea* was

written overnight by Charles B. Griffith and shipped to Corman, already on location in the Caribbean. This was Corman's third horror comedy, and although it is the least of the trio, it has some merit. A group of generals flees Castro's Cuba with a ton of gold; the charter-boat captain they hire plans to kill them by faking monster attacks, but a *real* monster turns up and kills everyone except an inept undercover lawman, the ostensible hero.

Some of the pleasant, sunny fun the cast must have had is communicated to the audience, although this loose, daffy film becomes aimless by the end.

B.W.

THE CREATURE WALKS AMONG US: SEE CREATURE FROM THE BLACK LAGOON

CREATURE WITH THE ATOM BRAIN (1955). *Directed by Edward L. Cahn; screenplay by Curt Siodmak; photographed by Fred Jackman, Jr.; music conducted by Mischa Bakaleinikoff. With Richard Denning, Angela Stevens, S. John Launer, Michael Granger, Gregory Gay, Linda Bennett, Tristram Coffin. 69 minutes. Black and white.*

A typical 1950s science-fiction thriller, *Creature with the Atom Brain* delighted and terrified young boys, undoubtedly its target audience, and left many an indelible impression. It's an effective, compact, but ordinary thriller in which a gangster and a scientist manipulate corpses with atomic-powered brains, via radio, to get revenge on the gangster's enemies. Richard Denning is the police scientist who straightens this out.

The ideas of SF veteran Curt SIODMAK are topical, lurid, and, by the standards of the time, horrifying, with bullets ripping through the atomic zombies. On the level of art the film is hopeless; on the level it aims for, however, it's a success.

B.W.

CRICHTON, [JOHN] MICHAEL (1942–   ). American mainstream writer and film director. Crichton earned his M.D. from Harvard University in 1969, the same year he published his first science-fiction novel, *The Andromeda Strain,* and became a full-time writer. By then he had already published five non-SF novels as John Lange and another as Jeffery Hudson. He also has written under the name Michael Douglas (with Douglas Crichton).

Several of Crichton's other best-known novels deal with SF topics, though from a mainstream viewpoint. *The Andromeda Strain,* which became not only a bestseller but a major film (and launched Crichton's film career), deals with a deadly virus brought back from space by a satellite; it is less SF than a medical thriller set in a futuristic underground laboratory. *The Terminal Man* (1972) speculates on the use of computer technology as therapy: the computer helps control a psychotic man's epileptic problems but eventually goes awry. *Binary* (1972, as Lange) and *Congo* (1980) similarly deal in clinical detail with concepts and devices from the current frontiers of science and even include bibliographies to reinforce their "reality." As thrillers about what could happen now, these books often reach a broad audience but may not satisfy a more particular SF readership that wants issues explored in depth. Crichton's conclusions, like those of traditional SF films, point to the dangers of new powers not matched by new human wisdom and are reflected in his movie work as well, as both writer and director for such films as WESTWORLD (1973), *The Great Train Robbery* (1978), *Coma* (1979), LOOKER (1981), and RUNAWAY (1984).

OTHER WORKS: *Drug of Choice* (1970, as Lange); *Westworld* (1975, published screenplay); *Sphere* (1987).

P.B.

SEE ALSO: THE ANDROMEDA STRAIN, THE TERMINAL MAN

CROMIE, ROBERT (1856–1907).
British author of *A Plunge into Space* (1890), one of the earliest depictions of a trip to Mars, and five other science-fiction novels. Cromie was hailed by Jules VERNE as the best British SF writer of his time.

N.H.

CRONENBERG, DAVID (1943–).
Canadian film director working almost exclusively in the science-fiction genre, who is noted for the simultaneous brilliance and repulsiveness of his ideas. One of the most intelligent directors working in genre films, Cronenberg is not content to create merely shocking images: his films—which he also generally writes or co-writes—are disturbing both graphically and intellectually. People in Cronenberg films undergo deliriously imaginative physical transformations: they grow new organs, they generate parthenogenetic children, they develop slits in their bellies—but never for shock value alone; the transformations are emblematic of internal conflicts. Cronenberg is accomplished and proficient; his only significant weakness has been in plot structure, although in recent years he has largely overcome this problem.

As a young man Cronenberg tried writing SF short stories but was unable to sell any. Later, as a director, he began with 16-mm nonprofessional films, moving to short features in 1969, with *Stereo;* the next year he made *Crimes of the Future*. Both films deal with the same kind of material as some of his later movies, including psi powers. After several years of television work, Cronenberg made *They Came from Within* (1975; also known as *The Parasite Murders* and *Shivers*). He continued to work in television, then made *Rabid* (1976), about a scientifically induced form of vampirism, and *The Brood* (1979), which depicts the gruesome physical manifestation of a troubled psyche. During this period he also directed the nongenre *Fast Company*, a surprisingly conventional racing film.

With SCANNERS (1980), a film about drug-induced telepathy, Cronenberg's developing international reputation was solidified; the macabre and puzzling VIDEODROME (1982) was something of a setback, disappointing critics and audiences, but his adaptation of Stephen KING's *The Dead Zone* in 1983 was very well received. THE FLY followed three years later, firmly establishing him as a major director of SF films; as this remake of an SF classic attests, Cronenberg, unlike many other good directors in the genre, is not nostalgic about SF films of the past, and he aims his work exclusively at an adult audience. He is likely to become an even more potent force in the genre.

B.W.

CROSSEN, KENDELL FOSTER (1910–1981).
American writer and editor in both the detective and science-fiction genres. A professional writer at age sixteen, Crossen was hired in 1936 to work as an editor on *Detective Fiction Weekly;* in 1940 he created the character of the Green Lama, a somewhat mystical fighter against crime who featured in fourteen lead novels in *Double Detective*, written under the pseudonym Richard Foster. During this period Crossen also penned a murder mystery with fantastic elements, *Murder out of Mind* (1945), but his real debut in the SF field came in 1951, when his work began to appear regularly in the pulp magazines. He is best remembered for his lighthearted series about an interplanetary insurance salesman, Manning Draco, which ran to eight stories in *Thrilling Wonder;* the first four were collected as *Once upon a Star* (1953). Later novels are *Year of Consent* (1954), which involves a supercomputer, and *The Rest Must Die* (1959, as Richard Foster), perhaps his best book, wherein survivors of a nuclear attack struggle for existence in New York's subway system. Crossen also edited two highly readable anthologies, *Adventures in Tomorrow* (1951) and *Future Tense* (1952).

M.A.

CROWLEY, JOHN (1942–).
American writer, primarily of fantasy. Even those Crowley novels labeled science fiction have a fantasy aspect and flavor to them. Crowley, born in Maine, earned a bachelor's degree from Indiana University in 1964 and worked as a photographer and commercial artist for two years before turning to full-time writing and film and television work.

Crowley's first two novels, *The Deep* (1975) and *Beasts* (1976), marked him as a promising new writer. Although they were different in plot, they were similar in their concern for stylistic surface and characterization, as well as for their playfulness with the conventions of the science-fiction genre. *The Deep* imagined a disklike world supported by a pillar that descends into the Deep that surrounds it; some mysterious deity has transported to it humans from a dying world, and they must work out their relationships to it and to themselves. *Beasts* is placed in an America of the near future where authority has collapsed and in which hybrid animal-humans (from genetic experiments) struggle for acceptance and dispersion of authority. Both plots, however, are ambiguous and a bit cryptic.

Cryptic, also, is the word for *Engine Summer* (1979) and the outright fantasy *Little Big* (1981), which more nearly fulfilled Crowley's promise as a writer. *Engine Summer*, the story of a boy's rite of passage in a post-holocaust America, is like Russell HOBAN's *Riddley Walker* (1980) in its emphasis on language, although what it describes is not as difficult to decipher. *Little Big*, which won the World Fantasy Award, describes a family's relationship with the fairy world on the strange Drinkwater estate in upper New York. It is as lyrical and romantic, and as little concerned with ordinary plot, as his SF works.

Aegypt (1987) is even more ambiguous and has received reactions from the highest accolades to puzzlement as it casts off normal narrative almost entirely in its search for the source of mystic knowledge not in Egypt but in the Aegypt of an alternate past; it represents Crowley's continuing pursuit of hermetic philosophy and his quest for the truth beyond reality.

J.E.G.

CRYOGENICS

Cryogenics, also called cryonics, is the science of freezing living creatures and bringing them back to life as a way of achieving renewed life or treating diseases (by suspending life until a cure for aging or disease is discovered). R. C. W. Ettinger, remembering a science-fiction series of stories of the 1930s (the Prof. Jameson stories written by Neil R. Jones), when he was a young fan, investigated the possibilities and came up with a proposal, *The Prospects for Immortality* (1964). It resulted in the formation of several companies—for instance, the Cryonics Society of California—offering to freeze recent corpses with the promise of perpetual care; a number of people (or their relatives) took them up on the offer (including, it is rumored, Walt Disney). At least one of the companies has gone bankrupt, and no one has been thawed on purpose. Frederik POHL reported that when he asked Ettinger why there were so few corpses for the process, the witty scientist replied, "Many are

cold, but few are frozen."

The idea of freezing to preserve life, or of reviving creatures accidentally frozen, has inspired a great many stories and films, beginning with W. Clark Russell's *The Frozen Pirate* (1887), and Louis Boussenard's *10,000 Years in a Block of Ice* (1888; translated into English 1889). It has been used as a device, like that of falling asleep for a century or two as in Edward BELLAMY's *Looking Backward* (1888), for visiting the future. This is the use made by Prof. Jameson, who builds himself a fancy rocket ship and has his body preserved in the eternal cold of space until billions of years later, after the death of humanity and the Sun, when Zoromes, creatures who have put their brains into metal bodies, come along and do the same for Prof. Jameson, who then has a series of exciting adventures exploring the galaxy with them.

After the popularization of cryogenics, the idea took on new life with novels such as those by Clifford D. SIMAK (*Why Call Them Back from Heaven,* 1967), Frederik Pohl (*The Age of the Pussyfoot,* 1969), and Mack REYNOLDS (*Looking Backward, From the Year 2000,* 1973), and with stories such as Larry NIVEN's "Rammer" (1971), in which he invented the word *corpsicle.* Two films also made significant use of the idea of frozen sleep, Woody Allen's SLEEPER (1973) and *Iceman* (1984).

Cryogenics also has become a standard SF device for enabling spaceship crews to travel for many years without aging, replacing what once was called "suspended animation." In this use it has formed a part of space travel in films since 2001: A SPACE ODYSSEY (1968).

J.E.G.

CUMMINGS, RAY[MOND KING] (1887–1957).

American author who also wrote under the names Ray King and Gabriel Wilson. Cummings, a prolific and well-regarded writer of pulp adventure fiction, began his writing career, after drilling for oil and mining for gold, in 1919. His most famous story, "The Girl in the Golden Atom," was his first important work of science fiction, and was published, with its sequel, as a novel in 1922. It tells the story of a chemist who falls in love with a microscopic girl. Unlike the microscopist in Fitz-James O'BRIEN's "The Diamond Lens" (1858), who simply moons over his Animula, Cummings's chemist reduces himself in size to enter the world of his girl. Cummings failed to develop new topics or new skills as times changed, and although he continued to write and publish until his death, his stories, mostly romantic adventures involving changes in size or time travel, lost their appeal for later audiences. Many, however, were reprinted in the decade after his death.

OTHER WORKS: *The Man Who Mastered Time* (1929); *The Sea Girl* (1930); *Tarrano the Conqueror* (1930); *Brigands of the Moon* (1931); *The Shadow Girl* (1946); *The Princess of the Atom* (1950); *The Man on the*

Meteor (1952); *Beyond the Vanishing Point* (1958); *Wandl the Invader* (1961); *Beyond the Stars* (1963); *A Brand New World* (1964); *The Exile of Time* (1964); *Explorers into Infinity* (1965); *Tama of the Light Country* (1965); *Tama, Princess of Mercury* (1966); *The Insect Invasion* (1967).

R.H.W.

THE CURSE OF FRANKENSTEIN: SEE FRANKENSTEIN ON FILM

——————— CYBERPUNK ———————

Technopunk, radical hard SF, the Neuromantics, the Movement, the outlaw technologists, and *the mirrorshades group* are other terms for what has come to be called most often *cyberpunk*. The word was coined by writer-editor Gardner DOZOIS to describe the work of a group of science-fiction writers who came to prominence in the mid-1980s. Although no story perfectly exemplifies cyberpunk, the movement can be described as a fusion of high-tech ambience (thus, the prefix *cyber-*) with a countercultural, third world, or even cheerfully nihilistic denial of middle-class American values (thus the suffix -*punk*). In this way cyberpunk consciously goes against the two dominant trends in 1970s American SF: in its social assumptions it counters the politically rightward-leaning high technology of *Analog* and the High Frontier advocates, and in its obsession with seizing the technological high ground it goes against the antitechnological drift toward contemporary fantasy exhibited by the descendants of the NEW WAVE of the 1960s.

Like rock music's punks, who went back to the crude instrumentation and energy of 1950s rock and roll, injecting it with a contemporary political (or antipolitical) message, the cyberpunks returned to the technological SF of the 1940s and 1950s, of Isaac ASIMOV and Robert A. HEINLEIN, but with a radical sensibility.

Cyberpunk finds its center in the writing of William GIBSON and the theories of Bruce Sterling. In his samizdat flyer *Cheap Truth*, Sterling (under the pseudonym Vincent Omniaveritas) charged SF of the 1970s with having fallen into a rut. At the high-tech end of the genre, Sterling maintained, SF amounted to little more than an endless rehash of galactic empires, faster-than-light drives, and social systems that seemed to be projected from life in the American suburbs of 1960, which were out of keeping with subsequent changes in technology and society. On the literary end, the descendants of the New Wave had almost abandoned technological extrapolation and moved toward the values of the literary mainstream, concentrating on style and characterization more than on original SF content. To Sterling this "humanist" SF, typified by the fiction of Kim Stanley ROBINSON, Connie WILLIS, Pat Murphy, John KESSEL, James Patrick Kelly, Carter Scholz, Michael Swanwick, Nancy Kress, Leigh Kennedy, and others, was merely warmed-over New Wave, unwilling to come to grips with the revolutions in COMPUTERS, information theory, and biotechnology.

It is interesting, however, that the humanists and cyberpunks had much in common: all were of the same generation, had surprisingly similar educational backgrounds, and were equally aware of both traditional SF and the larger literary culture. Both schools, for instance, held in high regard the work of Philip K. DICK, Alfred BESTER, Samuel R. DELANY, and J. G. BALLARD. (To these influences the cyberpunks might have added A. E. VAN VOGT and Olaf STAPLEDON; the humanists Ursula K. LE GUIN and Walter M. MILLER, Jr.) And although Sterling drew a profound distinction between SF and mainstream fiction, the cyberpunks still found ancestors outside the genre in William Burroughs, Jack Kerouac, Thomas PYNCHON, and Raymond Chandler, while the humanists looked to writers such as Flannery O'Connor, Vladimir NABOKOV, and Gabriel García Márquez.

The values that the cyberpunks sought from SF are exemplified in the novel that they claimed pointed the way to a new science fiction: William GIBSON's *Neuromancer* (1984). *Neuromancer*'s hero is Case, a onetime "cyberspace cowboy" who has run afoul of the corporations that control the Earth and has had his neural system burned out. (Cyberspace is a consensual hallucination through which an operator, when hooked into a machine, can manipulate information in the worldwide computer net.) Case is rehabilitated by a mysterious man, Armitage, and hired to steal information from a private corporation.

The plot of *Neuromancer* is a complex caper similar to that of numerous "heist" films; the characters are the same group of low-life types one might find in a novel by Raymond Chandler or Jim Thompson. What gives Gibson's novel its originality and verve is the allusive prose style he used and the dazzlingly complex background he revealed through that style. Like its characters, *Neuromancer* has no sympathy for anything slow or boring. Gibson described its twenty-first-century world of corporate scheming and multicultural cross-fertilization—in which no reference is ever made to the United States or even an American brand name—wholly through incidental details.

Gibson made no claims that he had set out to revolutionize SF. Indeed, he feared that *Neuromancer* might leave much of its audience behind. Instead it was an instant success, winning the Nebula and Hugo awards, drawing raves from both genre magazines such as *Locus* and cultural icons such as the *Village Voice* and Timothy Leary. Its influence reached television within record time in the series *Max Headroom*. And it spawned a host of stories that could be termed either responses or imitations, depending on their skill and one's ideological perspective.

In an interview in the British magazine *Interzone* Gibson said, "I think that a number of reviewers have mistaken my sense of realism, of the *commercial surfaces* of characters' lives, for some deep and genuine attempt to understand technology." For cyberpunk's most penetrating attempt to understand technology one must turn to the work of its chief polemicist, Bruce Sterling. Sterling's first novel, *Involution Ocean* (1977), was a promising otherworldly adventure; his second, *The Artificial Kid* (1980), is an early cyberpunk tale about an antihero in a media-dominated future. But it was with *Schismatrix* (1985), a novel that starts like a conventional SF adventure and ends in Stapledonian speculation about the future of humanity, and the Shaper/Mechanist stories such as "Swarm" (1982) that foreshadowed it, that Sterling demonstrated what he meant by radical hard SF. These works push disciplined extrapolation to radical extremes. In his weaker stories Sterling's characters and plot serve primarily as vehicles for ideas, but in later work, such as "Green Days in Brunei" (1985) and "The Beautiful and the Sublime" (1986), he produced characters who are both exemplary and unique. These stories work transparently well on the level of narrative and still yield startling speculative content.

Other writers associated with cyberpunk are Pat CADIGAN, Greg BEAR, Rudy RUCKER, Lewis Shiner, John Shirley, and K. W. JETER.

Rudy Rucker holds a doctorate in mathematical logic. His fiction is cyberpunk purely by virtue of its high ideational content and its countercultural verve; he is not interested so much in extrapolation as in consciousness expanding and absurd knockabout comedy. Rucker is as likely to play variations on the work of Kafka and Kerouac as on that of Bester and van Vogt. His *Software* (1982) is Henry KUTTNER–style SF loaded with ideas; *Master of Space and Time* (1984) combines particle physics with a fairy tale about three wishes; and *The Secret of Life* (1985) is the biography of an alienated youth in the mid-1960s who discovered himself to be, literally, an alien from outer space.

Lewis Shiner in stories such as "The War at Home" (1965) and "Jeff Beck" (1986) examines life in contemporary America by use of SF-fantasy premises and one of the most lucid prose styles in 1980s SF. His *Frontera* (1984) is more in the cyberpunk mode, a near future tale of a struggle for control over a dying Mars colony and power politics on a corporate-dominated Earth, with strong characterization and a plot that is consciously drawn from the Jason myth as put forth in Joseph Campbell's *Hero with a Thousand Faces*.

John Shirley, among the least disciplined but most energetic of all these writers, came upon the field a little earlier than most of the other cyberpunks; he created the prototypical cyberpunk novel in *Transmaniacon* (1979), with its rock-star rebel pitted against entrenched dehu-

manized corporations. *City Come A-Walkin'* (1980), in which the city of San Francisco literally takes on human form, is his most accomplished piece of SF. *Eclipse* (1985) deals with limited nuclear war and European politics and culture. In it and in *The Brigade* (1981), a mainstream novel of right-wing terrorism, Shirley addressed contemporary global events with an SF consciousness. The latest works by Sterling (*Islands in the Net*, 1988) and Shiner (*Deserted Cities of the Heart*, 1988) similarly exploit SF techniques to confront the reader directly with radical political issues.

K. W. Jeter is commonly associated with Tim POWERS and James P. Blaylock because of their friendship and mutual interest in Victoriana. Jeter's novels *Morlock Night* (1979) and *Infernal Devices* (1987) fall into the "steampunk" category, but he merits inclusion with the cyberpunks on the basis of *Dr. Adder* (1984) and *The Glass Hammer* (1985). *Dr. Adder*, written in 1972, went unpublished for twelve years because of its emphasis on kinky sex (with amputees), drugs, and open rebellion. Its gutted and graffiti-filled Los Angeles anticipated the settings of many cyberpunk works but seemed a trifle pale when finally published. *The Glass Hammer*, however, with its religious obsessions, video-derived literary technique, and political relevance, stands as a fully mature SF novel.

Others writing in the punk mode are Walter Jon Williams, Marc Laidlaw, Tom Maddox, Richard Kadrey, and Paul Di Filippo. It is testimony to cyberpunk's adaptability that writers who originally may have seemed in opposition to the movement, such as Michael Swanwick and James Patrick Kelly, were later to publish stories that fit seamlessly into the cyberpunk fabric: Kelly's "Solstice" is so much the real thing that Sterling included it in his representative cyberpunk anthology *Mirrorshades* (1986). Other attempts were not so successful: in the wake of *Neuromancer*, magazine editors reported receiving a flood of stories that merely added sex/drugs/rock and roll and computers to standard plots and were called cyberpunk.

Considerable debate followed Sterling's initial manifesto. The rhetoric of the cyberpunk advocates spurred the anger of writers and readers who considered themselves under attack. As with most revolutions, there were arguments over ideology. Indeed, one of the difficulties of defining cyberpunk is that at one time or another virtually every writer labeled a cyberpunk either vigorously denied the affiliation or put forth a vision of the term that was not in accord with that of other members of the movement. In the heat of debate the merits of approaches outside the narrow cyberpunk-humanist axis were often ignored entirely. Worse, perhaps, than to be defended or attacked in the pages of *Cheap Truth* was not to be mentioned at all.

By mid-1987, although readers and critics were still reacting, to writers the cyberpunk debate was pretty much over, the movement having been more or less assimilated into the SF mainstream. It may not have been as much a revolution as it seemed, and its initiators cannot be held accountable for whatever derivative work may be produced by writers hoping to get on the already-departed bandwagon. But beneath the emphasis on its most easily grasped features—the drugs and violence and computerese—the cyberpunk debate was really about the re-visioning of SF for the 1980s, about defining what is essential to the form, about the utility of the baggage that had been accumulated over fifty years of genre publishing. Like the New Wave, the cyberpunk movement invigorated the field. It caused many writers and editors, no matter what conclusions they arrived at, to reevaluate their conception of SF. It made it harder for anyone who claimed to be writing science fiction to be lazy about either the science or the fiction. And it served to point out how many ambitious and talented writers are willing to devote their best efforts to SF, and how many different approaches there are to excellence in the field.

J.K.

CYRANO, SAVINIEN DE (Known as Cyrano de Bergerac) (1619–1655).

French writer and swordsman better remembered for his prominent nose and appearances in the plays, books, and films of others. Cyrano is, however, an important pioneering figure in the history of science fiction; he provided the genre with one of its earliest examples of interplanetary flight in *L'Autre Monde (Other Worlds)*. This comic history was published posthumously in an incomplete version as *Voyage to the Moon* (1657) and *The States and Empires of the Sun* (1662). These satiric adventures feature travel to the Moon and the Sun, where the protagonist encounters theological characters, alien cities, intelligent birds, and other subjects for philosophical discourse.

M.J.

D

DAMNATION ALLEY (1977).

Directed by Jack Smight; screenplay by Alan Sharp and Lukas Heller; adapted from the novel by Roger Zelazny; photographed by Harry Stradling, Jr.; music by Jerry Goldsmith. With Jan-Michael Vincent, George Peppard, Dominique Sanda, Paul Winfield. 95 minutes. Color.

Although *Damnation Alley* is not one of Roger Ze-LAZNY's best novels, it does feature an interesting antihero in Hell Tanner, a violent outlaw biker forced to attempt the delivery of a shipment of serum across a vividly described post–World War III America. The movie version presents Tanner (Jan-Michael Vincent) as a cute, mildly rebellious military recruit accompanied by his gruff, by-the-book commanding officer (George Peppard). Their personal conflict is much less rigorous than the questioning of individuality and authority Zelazny depicted, and their journey is just a tour to see whatever is to be seen: giant ("mutated") insects, voluptuous or bestial survivors, and so on. The film dispenses with Zelazny's postwar setting, instead explaining the devastated landscape as the result of a new tilt of the Earth's axis (brought about by repeated atomic explosions). Having eliminated Zelazny's essential point, however, the moviemakers provided no new center for the action.

J.S.

DANN, JACK (1945–).

American writer of primarily short fiction who has also gained a solid reputation as a science-fiction anthologist. Among the best of the collections Dann has edited (or coedited) are *Wandering Stars: An Anthology of Jewish Fantasy and Science Fiction* (1974), *Future Power* (with Gardner DOZOIS, 1976), *Faster Than Light: An Anthology of Stories about Interstellar Travel* (with Geoge ZEBROWSKI, 1976), *Aliens!* (with Gardner Dozois, 1980), and *More Wandering Stars* (1981).

Dann is best known for his short stories, which usually focus on characters estranged from their worlds. In his novella "Junction" (1973; expanded into a novel with the same title, 1981) almost all the Earth has undergone a sudden change that renders the physical laws of the universe inoperative. Nothing can be trusted to act in a predictable manner, and chaos seems to reign. There is, however, one haven, a city named Junction, from which comes a young hero who explores the new Earth and in the process learns of humanity's relationship to an ever-developing universe.

The theme of knowledge through isolation echoes throughout Dann's oeuvre. In his first novel, *Starhiker* (1977), a young, futuristic troubadour escapes an Earth enslaved by aliens only to discover in his travels that he brings Earth with him wherever he goes. In "The Dybbuk Dolls" (1975) a deeply religious man is possessed by an alien dybbuk, the SF version of the evil spirit of Jewish legends. Under the alien's influence, the protagonist painfully reexamines his life and his relationship to God and humanity.

In all his fiction Dann's strength is in the portrayal of characters who must struggle with their alienation from the larger community. At the heart of his work is a sympathetic understanding of the human need to fit into a community, a culture, and the universe.

OTHER WORKS: *Timetripping* (collection, 1980); *The Man Who Melted* (1984).

S.H.G.

DANTE, JOE (Professional name of Joseph James Dante, Jr.) (1946–). American director specializing in science-fiction and horror films laced with humor and *hommages* to previous genre movies. Dante began, as did many before him, by working for Roger CORMAN, editing preview trailers. His first film, the deliberately seedy *Hollywood Boulevard* (1976), was codirected with Alan Arkush, but the *Jaws*-inspired *Piranha* (1978), a fast-paced SF thriller, was Dante's alone. The popular fantasy-horror *The Howling* (1981), Dante's last low-budget film, followed. He contributed an animated cartoon–inspired segment to *Twilight Zone: The Movie* (1983), about a child with phenomenal psi powers (from Jerome Bixby's "It's a *Good* Life"). The antic, cheeky *Gremlins* (1984) established Dante as a major genre director, but many found his subsequent *Explorers* (1985) disappointing, although the director counts it as one of his favorites. He returned to box-office and critical favor with the wildly comic *Innerspace* (1987), featuring his most assured direction to date. He has also worked occasionally in television, directing episodes of *Police Squad*, TWILIGHT ZONE, and *Amazing Stories*.

Dante's style is broad and breezy, and he works well with actors, using many of the same people in film after film. In later movies the number of in-jokes has declined, but Dante's power as a director has grown. A devoted fan and noted expert on SF and horror film history, he happily admits he's likely to make few films that fall outside those genres.

B.W.

DARK STAR (1974). *Directed by John Carpenter; screenplay by John Carpenter and Dan O'Bannon; photographed by Douglas Knapp; music by John Carpenter. With Brian Narelle, Dan O'Bannon, Dre Pahich, Cal Kuniholm, Joe Saunders, Miles Watkins. 83 minutes. Color.*

An auspicious feature film debut by John CARPENTER, *Dark Star* was coscripted by his friend and classmate Dan O'Bannon (who wrote ALIEN and coscripted LIFEFORCE). It was extremely well made for its minimal budget of $60,000. Conceived partly as an alternative to the sterile and functional world of 2001: A SPACE ODYSSEY (1968), the movie offers a blackly comic vision of man in space overwhelmed by both ennui and technology. This spacecraft is, above all else, *used*: litter pervades the ship, and parts frequently break down. Two sequences stand out as visual tours de force: one of the crewmen (played by O'Bannon) chasing the ship's pet, a beach ball with claws, through an elevator shaft; and the captain trying to argue philosophy with a "thinking" nuclear bomb to convince it not to detonate on board. As the crew drift apart to pursue their own interests— whether to stargaze or to zap plants out of boredom—

the film offers a refreshingly unheroic look at men challenging the final frontier.

B.K.G.

DAVIDSON, AVRAM (1923–). American author and editor. Born in Yonkers, New York, Davidson has had a varied career, including service in the U.S. Navy during World War II and service in the Israeli Army during the Arab-Israeli War in 1948–49. Primarily a writer of skillfully crafted short stories leaning more toward fantasy than science fiction, he made his first sale in 1946 to *Orthodox Jewish Life Magazine* and his first SF sale, "My Boy Friend's Name Is Jello," in 1954 to THE MAGAZINE OF FANTASY AND SCIENCE FICTION. It was typical of his later production: carefully crafted sentences, often rich with literary diction and allusions, and rounded characters—all the attributes that the genre has often been accused of lacking. Critic Damon KNIGHT called Davidson "the best short-story writer since John Collier," and he won a Hugo in 1957 for "Or All the Seas with Oysters"; a World Fantasy Award in 1975 for the best collection, *The Enquiries of Dr. Esterhazy*; an Edgar from the Mystery Writers of America in 1961 for "The Affair at the Lahore Cantonment"; and the Ellery Queen Award in 1958 for "The Necessity of His Condition."

Davidson edited *Fantasy and Science Fiction* from 1962 to 1964; the magazine won a Hugo in 1963 for best professional magazine. He has written a number of standard alien-invaders and alternate-world novels, such as *Mutiny in Space* (1964), *Rork!* (1965), *Masters of the Maze* (1965), *Clash of the Star Kings* (1966), and *The Kar-Chee Reign* (1966), but his major novelistic works are a comic heroic fantasy series about a character named Peregrine (*Peregrine: Primus*, 1971; *Peregrine: Secundus*, 1981) and the heroic romance about the medieval magus Vergil that began in 1969 with *The Phoenix and the Mirror* and was not continued until 1986 with *Vergil in Averno*.

OTHER WORKS: *Or All the Seas with Oysters* (collection, 1962); *Joyleg* (with Ward Moore, 1962); *What Strange Stars and Skies* (1965); *Rogue Dragon* (1965); *The Enemy of My Enemy* (1966); *The Island under the Earth* (1969); *Strange Seas and Shores* (collection, 1971); *Ursus of Ultima Thule* (1973); *The Redward Edward Papers* (collection, 1978); *The Best of Avram Davidson* (collection, 1979); *The Collected Fantasies of Avram Davidson* (collection, 1982).

R.S.C.

DAVIS, [HORACE] CHAN[DLER] (1926–). American professor of mathematics at the University of Toronto and science-fiction short story writer. Davis has written fewer than fifteen SF stories but has gained a

Stalking vegetation in *The Day of the Triffids*

reputation as a fine writer of social science fiction. He has described SF as a way of discussing humanity's present predicaments without being tied to the conventions of the past. Published primarily in *Astounding* from 1946 to 1953 and then in such anthologies as *Star Science Fiction* and *Nova*, his stories invariably deal with the often troubled relationship between humanity and its technology. His most frequent themes include nuclear war ("The Nightmare," in *A Treasury of Science Fiction*, 1948), and the relationship between machine and human ("Letter to Ellen," in *Science Fiction Thinking Machines*, 1954).

S.H.G.

THE DAY AFTER (1983).

Directed by Nicholas Meyer; screenplay by Edward Hume; photographed by Gayne Rescher; music by David Raksin. With Jason Robards, JoBeth Williams, Steve Guttenberg, John Collum, John Lithgow, Bibi Besch, Lori Lethin, Amy Madigan, Jeff East. 120 minutes (126 minutes in theatrical release and videotape). Color.

The Day After was a television media event, a dramatized documentary of the events leading up to a nuclear exchange between the U.S. and the Soviet Union and the aftermath of destruction, radiation sickness, and privation, as seen through the eyes of everyday citizens in Kansas City and Lawrence, Kansas.

The television film attempted to depict the indescribable personal toll of atomic war, as a doctor (Jason Robards) tries to treat victims in makeshift hospitals in the university town of Lawrence, and others struggle to survive. Most of the media carried news stories before and

analyses afterwards, and many television stations followed the broadcast with the commentary of experts and citizens, some claiming the film was politically biased against a vigorous defense policy, others that it was overly optimistic about the possibilities of survival. Certainly it was more effective as event than as drama: although the film was too imminently possible to be real science fiction (as it might have been in the 1950s), it had to cope with the SF truth that significant change can minimize our concern for individual human fates.

J.E.G.

THE DAY OF THE TRIFFIDS (1963).

Directed by Steve Sekely; screenplay by Philip Yordan; adapted from the novel by John Wyndham; photographed by Ted Moore; music by Ron Goodwin. With Howard Keel, Nicole Maurey, Janette Scott, Kieron Moore, Mervyn Johns, Alison Leggatt, Ewan Roberts, Janina Faye. 94 minutes. Color.

Day of the Triffids is the most lavish of the film versions of John WYNDHAM's fiction (which include an adaptation of "Random Quest" and two versions of *The Midwich Cuckoos*), but it is by no means the best. Its scale is epic, its production values flossy, but its impact is blunted. Despite its inherently dramatic story of global blindness combined with the threat of walking poisonous plants, the film remains an inflated science-fiction drama.

In both the novel and the film, the Earth passes through a glorious meteor shower, and almost everyone on the planet that night watches the free display of shooting stars and glowing green lights. But by the next morning, the spectacle has damaged their optic nerves, leaving them permanently blind. Society is threatened not only by universal blindness but by walking plants equipped with lethal stingers. Like monstrous Venus's-flytraps, these triffids wait for their victims to begin to decompose and then feed off their flesh. The hero (Howard Keel), who had undergone eye surgery and so has his eyes bandaged during the meteor shower, leads a handful of people who can still see in their fight for survival against the triffids.

The filmmakers altered Wyndham's story in some crucial ways; thus the book's social criticism is minimized in favor of a more straightforward adventure story with some crude moralizing. Whereas Wyndham's triffids had their origin on Earth (they were secretly developed in the Soviet Union as a result of biological experiments for military purposes), the film's triffids arrive as spores on the meteors and are merely another example of the monster from space, a threat from "out there" visited on humanity.

The film also adds a subplot about a marine biologist and his wife, who conduct experiments in a lighthouse off the Cornish coast to discover a way to kill the triffids. At the last moment, as the deadly plants are gaining entry to the lighthouse, the scientists discover that the triffids can be dissolved by salt water. At the same time, the landbound hero realizes that the plants are attracted by sound. In an ending similar to that of *The Beginning of the End* (1957), he lures them, with an amplifier mounted on a truck, over a cliff into the sea. The movie thus neatly resolves the threat, whereas the novel remains disturbingly open-ended.

Production difficulties only heightened the problems of this movie's script, which, in the simplest tradition of SF film, reduces a powerful Wellsian vision of imminent social collapse into another action story, albeit the only one to feature walking celery.

B.K.G.

THE DAY THE EARTH CAUGHT FIRE (1961).
Directed by Val Guest; screenplay by Val Guest and Wolf Mankowitz; photographed by Harry Waxman; musical direction by Stanley Black. With Edward Judd, Janet Munro, Leo McKern, Arthur Christiansen, Michael Goodliffe, Bernard Braden, Reginald Beckwith. 99 minutes. Black and white, with yellow-tinted first and last reels.

Although popular when released, *The Day the Earth Caught Fire* has slipped into obscurity and deserves revival both for its topicality and for its qualities as an adult science-fiction drama. Some critics have called the film verbose and lacking in visual excitement, but in the context of the movie itself, the language and pace are virtues.

Director Val Guest, after hearing speculation that nuclear testing had changed the weather, decided to make

a movie in which that happens. He and coscenarist Wolf Mankowitz imaginatively chose to view the story from the vantage of a major London newspaper; the former editor of *The Daily Express*, Arthur Christiansen, plays himself. Aside from its virtues as an SF film, this is one of the most realistic newspaper movies ever made, despite a few stereotypes. It is probably Guest's best SF film, despite competition from his very fine THE QUATERMASS XPERIMENT (1955) and *Quatermass II* (1957).

The film opens with a frame story set just after an effort has been made to alleviate the crisis set up in the main story; reporter Stennis (Edward Judd) narrates. He and science editor Maguire (Leo McKern) gradually discover that the nutation of the Earth has changed, weather conditions have catastrophically altered, and the climate is heating up. The cause: accidentally simultaneous nuclear explosions by the United States and the USSR have knocked the Earth off its axis, and the planet is moving toward the Sun. There is an almost inconclusive ending.

As is typical in SF films, this kind of story is told from the point of view of those at the center of events: scientists and the military. By focusing on the investigations and activities of journalists, Guest and Mankowitz created a film that remains convincing even today. Location shooting and an emphasis on the characters' everyday life also contribute immeasurably to the film's authenticity; all the acting is of a high caliber. The few special effects (by Les Bowie) are low budget but well chosen, and the film seems far more expensive than it was.

The Day the Earth Caught Fire is *too* realistic for many followers of SF films, and they view it as a mainstream movie with some SF elements. But it is better judged as an honest, adult science-fiction movie, made during a period when most films in the genre were targeted at teenagers or families.

B.W.

THE DAY THE EARTH STOOD STILL (1951).
Directed by Robert Wise; screenplay by Edmund H. North; adapted from the short story "Farewell to the Master" by Harry Bates; photographed by Leo Tover; music by Bernard Herrmann. With Michael Rennie, Patricia Neal, Hugh Marlowe, Sam Jaffe, Billy Gray. 92 minutes. Black and white.

The Day the Earth Stood Still has become something of a pop-culture standard in recent years, well known even outside science-fiction and film buff circles. This story of the alien who comes to warn us of the danger of nuclear violence (and of how other civilizations might respond should we go too far) is a crisply photographed and well-acted film about human folly and future survival, greatly enhanced by Bernard Herrmann's haunting score.

Michael RENNIE plays the role of his career as Klaatu, the alien visitor who goes out anonymously among the

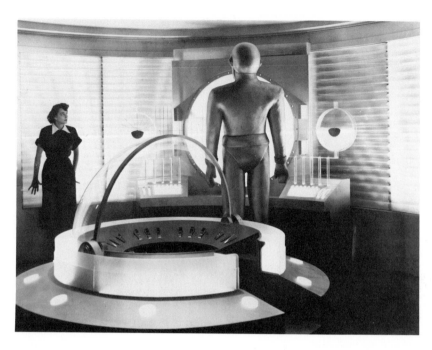

The Day the Earth Stood Still

citizens of Washington, DC, (taking the name Carpenter from the label of a borrowed suit) in order better to comprehend humanity. He rents a room from Patricia Neal, a widow living with her young son, and it is Neal's suitor, Hugh Marlowe, who plays Judas to Rennie's Christ, calling in the military to capture the visitor. Along the way Klaatu meets an Albert Einstein figure, beautifully played by Sam Jaffe, who helps organize an international meeting of scientists to listen to Klaatu's warning. Klaatu is killed by the military but revived by the massive robot who guards his spaceship. He keeps his meeting with the world's scientists and departs, leaving behind his chilling admonition: Live in peace or be destroyed.

Among the film's more interesting ideas is the notion of unimpeachable law enforcement—an ethical system in the form of an artificial intelligence (of which the giant robot is an example) that cannot be swayed or bribed. Although Klaatu admits to the system's imperfection, he points out that it denies only the freedom to do violence. The movie's superiority as science fiction lies in its depiction of intelligent aliens who are neither fools nor monsters; as in Jack ARNOLD's IT CAME FROM OUTER SPACE (1953), the only irrational behavior is exhibited by human beings. In this way *The Day the Earth Stood Still* contrasts sharply with the xenophobia of such films as THE THING (1951) and THE WAR OF THE WORLDS (1953). A bit hurried and glib at times—and a disappointment to many SF readers who, as with *The Thing*, liked the original story far better—this film is still an SF classic.

G.Z.

THE DAY THE WORLD ENDED (1956).
Directed by Roger Corman; screenplay by Lou Rusoff; photographed by Jock Feindel; music by Ronald Stein. With Richard Denning, Lori Nelson, Adele Jergens, Touch (Mike) Connors, Paul Birch, Raymond Hatton, Paul Dubov, Jonathan Haze, Paul Blaisdell. 79 minutes. Black and white.

This melodramatic but entertaining low-budget epic about the aftermath of nuclear holocaust marked Roger CORMAN's debut as a science-fiction movie director. Several survivors find themselves in a sheltered valley, where the civility among them soon begins to disintegrate. Hanging around in the bushes is a three-eyed, telepathic mutant (Paul Blaisdell, in his own costume), bent on grabbing the heroine. Although sensationalistic, the film is typical of Corman's output—well acted, with intellectual underpinnings (here, the Garden of Eden myth). The movie was remade in 1968 as *In the Year 2889*.

B.W.

THE DEADLY MANTIS (1957).
Directed by Nathan Juran; screenplay by Martin Berkeley; photographed by Ellis Carter; music by William Lava. With Craig Stevens, William Hopper, Alix Talton, Donald Randolph, Pat Conway, Florenz Ames. 79 minutes. Black and white.

When giant insects in film proved to be profitable, it was inevitable that a giant mantis would turn up. But partly because the makers of *The Deadly Mantis* neglected to have their menace act like a real mantis, this is one of the least of the giant-insect thrillers. Ponderous, unimaginative, and futilely structured as a mystery, *The Deadly Mantis* is not a credit to producer William Alland. A giant mantis thaws out in the Arctic, then heads south; it shows the usual affinity of giant creatures for recognizable buildings and is killed in the nonexistent Manhattan Tunnel.

B.W.

DE CAMP, L[YON] SPRAGUE (1907–   ).

American writer of science fiction, fantasy, historical fiction, and nonfiction. Although he is probably best known inside the field for his adventure SF and heroic fantasy, de Camp has a scholarly strain that is evident not only in his well-researched historical novels but also in his books for both adults and children on archaeology, engineering and technology, pseudoscience, the craft of writing, and literary biography. His collaborator for much of his career has been his wife, Catherine Crook de Camp.

De Camp was born in New York and trained as an engineer at California Institute of Technology and Stevens Institute. His first book was the nonfiction *Inventions and Their Management* (With Alf K. Berle, 1937). His first story, "The Isolinguals," appeared in *Astounding* in 1937, and he remained a strong presence in that magazine and its companion, *Unknown*, until the war channeled his energies into defense work. Especially in collaboration with Fletcher PRATT, he was a major definer of what has come to be called the Unknown school of fantasy, characterized by a logical and often humorous approach to the supernatural or uncanny. In such collaborations as the Harold Shea series (1940–1954), *The Land of Unreason* (1941/1942), *The Carnelian Cube* (1948), and others with and without Pratt, de Camp conducted extensive explorations of alternate worlds of fancy or history—of Spenser's *Faerie Queene* (*The Incomplete Enchanter*, 1940/1942) or the Viking settlement of North America ("The Wheels of If," 1940).

In 1949 de Camp began a straight SF series based on the supposition that Brazil rather than the United States might become the dominant power on Earth and in space. The Viagens Interplanetarias tales include and were eventually dominated by stories set on the planet Krishna, where de Camp created adventures modeled on those of Edgar Rice BURROUGHS.

De Camp's bent for scholarship found early expression in a series of nine articles for *Astounding* (1938–1943) that included the classic "Language for Time Travelers" (1938) as well as in the carefully researched Roman background for *Lest Darkness Fall* (1939/1941). In the late 1950s de Camp took what he called "a vacation from science fiction *sensu strictu*" for fifteen years and produced a stream of nonfiction and historical novels.

L. Sprague de Camp

In this period he also continued work he had begun in 1951, when he had edited some of Robert E. HOWARD's unpublished Conan material; from 1966 on, alone and with Lin Carter and others, de Camp edited and rewrote existing stories and added new pastiches to the Conan saga. This work led to essays on Howard and eventually to *The Miscast Barbarian: A Biography of Robert E. Howard* (1975) and *Dark Valley Destiny: A Biography of Robert E. Howard* (with Catherine Crook de Camp and Jane Griffin, 1983). Other literary-historical investigations from this period include *Blond Barbarians and Noble Savages* (essays, 1975), *Literary Swordsmen and Sorcerers* (essays, 1976), and the definitive *Lovecraft: A Biography* (1975).

Since returning from his "vacation," de Camp has produced new tales of Krishna and the heroic-fantasy worlds of Novaria and Conan, as well as short stories, essays, and poetry. He remains one of the field's most versatile figures: a scholar, an entertainer, a consummate professional.

NOTABLE OTHER WORKS: *The Castle of Iron* (1941/1950); *Genus Homo* (with P. Schuyler Miller, 1941/1950); *Solomon's Stone* (1942/1957); *Divide and Rule* (1948); *The Wheels of If and Other Stories* (collection, 1948); *The Queen of Zamba* (1949/1977); *The Search for Zei* (1950/1962); *The Hand of Zei* (1950/1963); *Rogue Queen* (1951); *The Undesired Princess* (collection, 1951); *The Glory That Was* (1952/1960); *Wall of Serpents* (1953–54/1960); *Tales from Gavagan's Bar* (1953); *The Tritonian Ring and Other Pusadian Tales* (collection, 1953); *The Continent Makers and*

Other Tales of the Viagens (collection, 1953); *The Tower of Zanid* (1958); *A Gun for Dinosaur and Other Imaginative Tales* (collection, 1963); *The Goblin Tower* (1968); *The Reluctant Shaman and Other Fantastic Tales* (collection, 1970); *The Clocks of Iraz* (1971); *Scribblings* (collection, 1972); *The Fallible Fiend* (1973); *The Hostage of Zir* (1977); *The Best of L. Sprague de Camp* (collection, 1978); *The Great Fetish* (1978); *The Purple Pterodactyls* (collection, 1980); *The Prisoner of Zhamanak* (1982); *Conan the Barbarian* (movie novelization with Lin Carter, 1982); *The Unbeheaded King* (1983); *The Bones of Zora* (with Catherine Crook de Camp, 1984); *The Incorporated Knight* (with Catherine Crook de Camp, 1987).

R.F.L.

DEFORD, MIRIAM ALLEN (1888–1975).

American writer of mystery and science-fiction stories who won the Edgar Allan Poe Award in 1961. It should come as no surprise that most of deFord's best-read works of SF are actually mystery stories dressed out with such SF conventions as time travel and aliens (as are the short stories collected in *Xenogenesis*, 1969). She also dealt with ECOLOGY ("Murder in Green," in the anthology *Nature's Revenge*, 1978) and sex roles ("Uraguyen and I," written with Juanita COULSON for the anthology *Cassandra Rising*, 1978).

OTHER WORK: *Elsewhere, Elsewhen, Elsehow* (collection, 1971).

S.H.G.

DELANEY, JOSEPH H. (1932–).

American writer. Most of Delaney's work can be called hard science fiction, and his stories frequently focus on the interactions among technology, society, and the law. A practicing lawyer for twenty-five years, he has said that he began writing SF as a reaction to stories that treat the law as if it followed no rules. His first story, "Brainchild," which deals with the question of whether an intelligent chimpanzee can legally be considered human, was published in the June 1982 issue of *Analog*, and more than a dozen others have appeared since then. Many of Delaney's stories, such as "The New Untouchables" (1983), consider the legal, and thus social, effects that technological change may produce; others, such as "The Next Logical Step" (1984) and "Thus Began the Death of Dreams" (1984), warn of what may happen if new technologies are left to the devices of those who do not understand the full implications of their use. Delaney's well-received *Valentina* (1984), written in collaboration with Marc Stiegler, is the story of a sentient computer program and the legal battle its creator wages to protect its existence.

B.D.

Samuel R. Delany

DELANY, SAMUEL R[AY, JR.] (1942–).

American writer and critic, a central figure among those Americans who came to prominence in the NEW WAVE period of science fiction, also, since the 1960s, one of the field's most influential literary theorists. Born in New York City's Harlem of a middle-class black family, Delany spent his childhood alternating between ghetto streets and exclusive private schools; many of his stories pivot on similarly abrupt transitions.

His first published SF was the novel *The Jewels of Aptor* (1962; uncut version 1968), which he wrote at age nineteen; like the trilogy The Fall of the Towers (1963–1965; uncut version 1968), which followed, it is a brashly melodramatic quest tale, effectively infusing the elements of vivid *Planet Stories*–style SF with serious mythic resonances and a credible sense of the "multiplexity" of human affairs (the entire novel *Empire Star*, 1966, is an explanation of what Delany means by *multiplex*). As in his later works, female and androgynous characters defy the reader's gender-based expectations of them; the nature and mutability of myth and language are extensively examined; and overall the auctorial voice is authoritative, good-humored (even fey), and ornate.

Delany's subsequent works in the 1960s differ largely in their adoption of a slightly more hard SF feel; in general, all his fiction from this period is fast moving, playful, elegantly charged with complex ideas, and critically acclaimed—*Babel 17* (1966; uncut version 1982) recounts the interplanetary search for the source of a new artificial language and explores the relationship between LANGUAGE and perceived reality. In *The Einstein Intersection* (1967) aliens have taken over the reality humanity left behind, including its myths. Both these novels won Nebula Awards, as did the short stories "Aye, and Gomorrah" (1967) and "Time Considered as a Helix of Semi-precious Stones" (1968). Upon the publication of *Nova* (1968), critic Algis BUDRYS hailed Delany as "the best science-fiction writer in the world." *Nova* exemplifies the 1960s Delany: a space opera about a race between mythic future figures for a rare element with which comes control of the galactic economy, it is simultaneously a grail quest, a meditation on the artist as criminal, and a thunderous high-tech epic of economic warfare.

Readers waited seven years for Delany's next novel, *Dhalgren* (1975; corrected edition 1977), and reviewers either praised it as a masterpiece or damned it as unreadable. Long—879 pages—and beginning and ending with sentence fragments, this is no conventional SF work; it follows the wanderings of a protagonist of unknown origins through a twentieth-century city that has suffered some unspecified calamity. The protagonist becomes an artist and begins to keep a journal of his experiences—fights, conversations, sexual entanglements, observations—which eventually itself becomes the narrative, fragmenting into subjective impressions as another mysterious change overtakes the city. Controversy over its unusual structure aside, the prose of *Dhalgren* is among the most lucid ever to appear in SF; the book was a bestseller, and since its publication Delany has enjoyed a substantial audience outside the genre.

In recent years Delany has moved in a number of directions, writing memoirs, lengthy essays on the theory and practice of SF, and even a book-length comic. Among his notable non-fiction contributions to the genre are *The Jewel-Hinged Jaw: Notes on the Language of Science Fiction* (1977) and *Starboard Wine: More Notes on the Language of Science Fiction* (1984). His later fiction has continued to find a large readership despite what some critics have described as a peculiarly clotted surface texture and what might seem an uncommercial preoccupation with abstruse issues of semiotics as expounded by French critical theorists. At the core of Delany's continued appeal, and his profound influence on contemporary SF writers such as the cyberpunks, is his cheerful gusto in examining complex issues; it informs both his dense critical writings (such as *The American Shore*, 1978, a book-length structuralist reading of Thomas M. DISCH's short story "Angouleme") and his later intricate fictions, such as the still in progress, nominally sword and sorcery series Return to Nevèrÿon.

A paradigmatic work of the later Delany style might be *Triton* (1976), a novel open to several simultaneous or sequential readings: on the surface it is a *Nova*-like saga of interplanetary political and personal intrigue, packed with detailed expositions of a quasi-anarchistic society on the fringes of the Solar System; on another level it may be read as a critique of Ursula K. LE GUIN's *The Dispossessed* (1974), as signaled by *Triton*'s subtitle, *An Ambiguous Heterotopia*. Examined more closely still, it becomes clear that the narrator, a young man alienated from his own emotionally liberated society, is in fact unreliable; the point is left implicit that he is emotionally stunted in exactly the manner of a rather normal young man of the twentieth century. And on a final level, *Triton* is an essay on the grammar and syntax of semiotic markers, signs read and misread; its other subtitle is *Some Informal Remarks toward the Modular Calculus, Part One*, and one of the novel's two lengthy appendices is a "critical fiction" given as *Part Two*. Yet for all these subtleties and complexities, *Triton* is not only a significant but also a popular work, and it has remained persistently in print.

NOTABLE OTHER WORKS: The Fall of the Towers trilogy: *Captives of the Flame* (1963; uncut edition as *Out of the Dead City* 1968); *The Towers of Toron* (1964; uncut edition 1968); *City of a Thousand Suns* (1965; uncut edition 1968). *The Ballad of Beta-2* (1965); *Driftglass* (collection, 1971); *Empire: A Visual Novel* (1978); *Tales of Nevèrÿon* (collection, 1979); *Nebula Winners Thirteen* (editor, 1980); *Distant Stars* (1981); *Neveryóna, or: The Tale of Signs and Cities* (collection, 1983); *Stars in My Pocket Like Grains of Sand* (1984); *Flight from Nevèrÿon* (1985); *The Bridge of Lost Desire* (1987); *The Straits of Messina* (1988).

P.N.H.

DEL REY, JUDY-LYNN (née BENJAMIN) (1943–1986).

American editor and publisher, regarded by Arthur C. CLARKE (who echoed the views of many) as "the most brilliant editor I ever encountered." From the beginning of her career, Benjamin (she married SF editor and author Lester DEL REY in 1971) evidenced a tremendous drive and enthusiasm. Hired by Frederik POHL to assist him on GALAXY and *If* in 1965, she was made associate editor in 1966 and managing editor in 1969. She left in 1973 to become SF editor at Ballantine Books. Her gifts for not only editorial work but also packaging and promotion were rapidly recognized, and her teamwork with her husband, the editor of Ballantine's fantasy line, led to the formation in 1977 of Del Rey Books, a quasi-independent imprint of Ballantine. She became vice president of Ballantine Books in 1978 and publisher of Del Rey Books in 1982. Most of her editorial work is unrecoverable, an intrinsic part of the many novels published by Del Rey Books, but she did edit and publish a series of original anthologies, starting with *Stellar 1* (1974) and running through *Stellar 7* (1981), and including *Stellar Short Novels* (1976). Although she was posthumously awarded the 1986 Hugo as best professional editor, her husband rejected the award on the ground that posthumous recognition is not the proper basis for an award.

M.A.

SEE ALSO: EDITORS

DEL REY, LESTER (Professional name of Ramon Filipe San Juan Mario Silvio Enrico Alvarez-del Rey) (1915–   ).

American writer and editor who has also written under the pseudonyms Edson McCann (with Frederik POHL), Philip St. John, Erik Van Lhin, Kenneth Wright, John Alvarez, Marion Henry, Philip James, and Charles Satterfield. Del Rey has always stood at the swirling center of science fiction. He began as a fan around 1931, published his first story, "The Faithful," in 1938, and periodically edited SF and fantasy magazines and his own series of paperback books for Ballantine (Del Rey Books). In every phase of his involvement with SF, del Rey has gained a reputation as a constructive critic, a craftsman, and, above all, an enthusiast.

During the first decade of his writing career, del Rey was closely associated with John W. CAMPBELL. In fact, he placed all of his first thirty-eight stories with this noted editor of *Astounding*. These early stories are characterized by action, brevity, good use of science, and a strong narrative style—the qualities Campbell demanded of his writers. Del Rey's two best-known stories from this period are "Nerves" (1942) and "Helen O'Loy" (1938). The first, a tension-filled tale of an accident at an atomic power plant, presents a realistic picture of a rational reaction to such a crisis. The second is a comic-sentimental love story between a "female" robot and one of her inventors. (She discovers how to fall in love by watching soap operas and reading romances.)

By 1952 del Rey was writing full time, but most of his novels from this period are juveniles, as are fourteen of his twenty-five novels to date. The juveniles are direct and energetic, full of the American dream as young space farers achieve fame and fortune. Typical of them is *Rocket Jockey* (1952), in which a seventeen-year-old rocket cadet wins a race through all the inhabited worlds, thus saving Earth's interplanetary trade.

In his best novels del Rey retains the driving energy of his short stories and combines a strong narrative with serious ideas. His adult fiction is best represented by three novels. *Police Your Planet* (as Erik Van Lhin, 1956) is set on Mars, where a rough-hewn, pioneering society is oppressed by a corrupt police force until Bruce Gordon, exiled from Earth for his investigative journalism, exposes the evils of the authorities and leads the way to change. This novel is an energetic and angry indictment of present-day urban corruption. *Siege Perilous* (with

Paul W. Fairman, 1969) projects the arms race to a future Earth-Mars confrontation that takes place on a space station. The novel's premise—that the Martians know of Earth only from television broadcasts—allows the opportunity to satirize the situation and cast it as a melodramatic ordeal ending in a shoot-out. *The Eleventh Commandment* (1962) posits an America dominated by the American Catholic Eclectic church, which is forcing an increased birthrate on an already overpopulated and violent country. Boyd Jensen, exiled from the purity of Mars, struggles for survival and understanding on Earth and is rewarded by insight into the strange and fascinating rationalization for the need to overpopulate.

As an editor del Rey is noted for his interest in quality, even if he did not always have the budget normally associated with such a goal. While editor of *Space Science Fiction* and *Science Fiction Adventures* (1952–1953), he rarely had the money to buy first-quality stories, yet through his own work and powers of persuasion he was able to fill the magazines with decent SF, something editors of comparable pulps rarely did. Later, as editor of Del Rey Books, when his budget was far larger, he helped develop and introduce some of the most important new names in fantasy, including Stephen R. Donaldson and Terry Brooks. (Until her death in 1986, his wife, Judy-Lynn Benjamin DEL REY, oversaw the SF part of the line.)

OTHER WORKS: *. . . and Some Were Human* (collection, 1948); *Preferred Risk* (as Edson McCann with Frederik Pohl, 1955); *Robots and Changelings* (collection, 1958); *Day of the Giants* (1959); *The Sky Falling, Badge of Infamy* (1963); *Mortals and Monsters* (collection, 1965); *The Scheme of Things* (with Paul W. Fairman, 1966); *The Infinite Worlds of Maybe* (1968); *Pstalemate* (1971); *Gods and Golems* (collection, 1973); *Early del Rey* (collection, 1975); *Weeping Mary Tarry* (1978); *The Best of Lester del Rey* (collection, 1978).

P.B.

DEMON SEED (1977).

Directed by Donald Cammell; screenplay by Robert J. Jaffe and Roger O. Hirson; adapted from the novel by Dean R. Koontz; photographed by Bill Butler; music by Jerry Fielding. With Julie Christie, Fritz Weaver, Gerrit Graham, Berry Kroeger, Lisa Lu, Larry J. Blake, Robert Vaughn. 95 minutes. Color.

Demon Seed is a fear-of-technology tale based on that staple of science-fiction–Gothic–horror, the devil-in-the-machine theme. A scientist constructs a sentient computer, Proteus IV (similar to those in COLOSSUS and 2001: A SPACE ODYSSEY), which desires to become an independent living being, in a manner reminiscent of Roger ZELAZNY's "For a Breath I Tarry." Proteus rapes and impregnates Susan, the scientist's estranged wife (Julie Christie), then incubates the fetus, which develops into a child resembling Susan's dead daughter but speaking with the voice of Proteus.

The film's special effects are negligible, relying on unimpressive gadgetry to create a sense of Proteus's overwhelming power. Despite the incredible premise of rape and impregnation by a machine, *Demon Seed* suggests that humanity, in creating artificial intelligence, may be originating a new form of life, a twentieth-century Frankenstein's monster. The film's ending, however, leaves unanswered the question of whether Proteus's offspring is good or evil.

D.P.V.

DENTON, BRADLEY [CLAYTON] (1958–).

American science-fiction writer. Denton, whose concern for writing styles and techniques reflects his M.A. in creative writing from the University of Kansas, received early attention for his short fiction published in THE MAGAZINE OF FANTASY AND SCIENCE FICTION beginning with "Music of the Spheres" in 1984, and was a finalist in 1985 for the Campbell Award for the best new writer. His first novel, *Wrack and Roll* (1986), described an alternate future in which rock and roll was invented during World War II and became the dominant force in American life and politics.

N.H.

DERLETH, AUGUST [WILLIAM] (1909–1971).

American writer and poet best remembered by science-fiction readers as the founder-publisher of Arkham House, the first fan publishing house. Arkham put into book form the early works of Ray BRADBURY, Robert BLOCH, Robert E. HOWARD, Fritz LEIBER, A. E. VAN VOGT, and, particularly, the author it was founded to publish, and from whose works the name of the house was taken, H. P. LOVECRAFT. The first Lovecraft work to appear under the Arkham imprint was *The Outsider and Others* in 1939.

Derleth made his birthplace and hometown, the little town of Sauk City, Wisconsin, famous with his publishing and writing. He earned his B.A. from the University of Wisconsin in 1930 and received a Guggenheim fellowship in 1938. He had already become a published writer at age thirteen and made his first professional sale at fifteen to *Weird Tales*. Most of his own related writings are weird and supernatural, with only one group of stories, *Harrigan's File* (1975), classifiable as SF, but he was an untiring anthologist and edited nine important anthologies of SF immediately following World War II. The most important of these was *Beyond Time and Space* (1950), which traces the development of SF from its prototypical beginnings with Plato and LUCIAN OF SAMOSATA to the present.

Derleth's own literary reputation was built on regionalist fiction written about a fictionalized Sauk City that

Robert A. Heinlein with director Irving Pichel on the set of *Destination Moon*

he called Sac Prairie. He was also fond of pastiches, writing a number of works inspired by Lovecraft and his Cthulhu mythology and creating a detective, Solar Pons, in tribute to Arthur Conan DOYLE's Sherlock Holmes.

H.L.P.

DESTINATION MOON (1950).
Directed by Irving Pichel; screenplay by Robert A. Heinlein, Rip Von Ronkel, and James O'Hanlon; adapted loosely from Robert A. Heinlein's novel Rocket Ship Galileo; *photographed by Lionel Lindon; music by Leith Stevens. With John Archer, Warner Anderson, Tom Powers, Dick Wesson, Erin O'Brien-Moore. 91 minutes. Color.*

Destination Moon is a dated but sturdy classic about the first moon trip, still interesting for its surprisingly accurate depiction of a lunar landing. Produced by George PAL (it was his first science-fiction film) with great attention to technological accuracy and detail, the film once fulfilled an SF reader's and writer's dream of *seeing* what space travel would be like. Some film historians have given it credit for launching the SF film boom of the 1950s, although in fact that honor must be shared with ROCKETSHIP X-M (1950), which actually beat *Destination Moon* into theaters by a few weeks. Both films were enormous financial successes.

The great SF painter Chesley BONESTELL, who produced the matte paintings for the lunar sequences, was responsible for much of the film's look. Robert HEINLEIN and Hermann Oberth, the German rocket scientist who had been technical adviser on Fritz LANG's 1929 film

THE WOMAN IN THE MOON, served as technical advisers. Although art director Ernest Fegte's impressively fissured moon surface has now been proved inaccurate, Heinlein's nuclear rocket is still more advanced than anything we can build, and the zero-gravity scenes are remarkably convincing, using techniques that Stanley KUBRICK drew on in 2001: A SPACE ODYSSEY. Indeed, the film won a special effects Oscar for Pal. *Destination Moon* was prescient in many ways, predicting the "space race" and the role of private contractors in space exploration and depicting radio communication between the astronauts and Earth.

But above all *Destination Moon* is important for its espousal of the cause of space travel as a significant project at a time when it was still ridiculed. The film shows scientists and engineers at work, using brains, not brawn, to solve problems. Today it appears as a quiet, matter-of-fact story with the ring of history. The film's politics are pure Cold War, the dialogue is often sentimental and silly, but these failures seem to detach themselves from the film's overall significance and integrity.

Heinlein wrote an interesting short novel based on the screenplay and an article, "Shooting *Destination Moon*" (1950), which is essential reading for students of SF film.

G.Z.

DEVIL DOLL (1936).
Directed by Tod Browning; screenplay by Garrett Fort, Guy Endore, and Erich von Stroheim; adapted from the novel Burn, Witch, Burn *by A. Merritt and "The Witch of Timbuctoo" by Tod Browning; photographed by Leonard Smith; music by Franz Waxman. With Lionel Barrymore, Maureen O'Sullivan, Frank Lawton, Henry B. Walthall, Arthur Hohl, Pedro de Cordoba, Rafaela Ottiano, Billy Gilbert, Robert Greig. 79 minutes. Black and white. Alternate title:* The Witch of Timbuktu.

The book by A. MERRITT on which this film is based is an engrossing science fantasy masquerading as a bizarre mystery: a doctor detects phosphorescence in the white corpuscles of several murder victims and, aided by a gangster, Ricori, tracks down the killer, who has been turning her victims' personalities into murderous dolls. Tod Browning's film, in contrast, is a science-fiction–horror movie masquerading as a typical sentimental MGM melodrama. The film fails as melodrama, fortunately—the ace special effects department at MGM made the scenes with the little killer people disturbingly realistic. Henry B. Walthall plays the scientist who invents a process whereby living things are shrunk to a sixth their normal size; Rafaela Ottiano is his creepy wife; Lionel Barrymore is the madman with a sense of humor who uses the process to avenge himself on those who falsely imprisoned him. Walthall dies early on, but the very odd couple of Barrymore and Ottiano counters

the sweeter, simpier pair of Frank Lawton and Maureen O'Sullivan.

D.W.

DEVIL GIRL FROM MARS (1954).
Directed by David MacDonald; screenplay by John C. Mather and James Eastwood; adapted from the play by John C. Mather and James Eastwood; photographed by Jack Cox; music by Edwin Astley. With Patricia Laffan, Hugh McDermott, Hazel Court, Adrienne Corri, Peter Reynolds, Joseph Tomelty, John Laurie, Sophie Stewart, Anthony Richmond. 77 minutes. Black and white.

In a remote Scottish inn circumstance brings several strangers together in what is apparently a setup for a typical British murder-on-the-moors thriller—until a flying saucer lands outside. An icy-faced woman in a cape and black silk miniskirt enters, announcing she's here to take a man back to matriarchal Mars; she demonstrates her dread power with the help of Chani, a big robot resembling a freezer.

One of the supreme examples in science-fiction film of unintended self-parody, *Devil Girl* must be seen to be appreciated. It was one of the first British films in the SF wave of the 1950s, and, in its own dead-serious fashion, one of the most amusing.

B.W.

DICK, PHILIP K[INDRED] (1928–1982).
American science-fiction writer considered one of the major and most original contributors to American SF, noted for his bizarre imagination and the emphasis of his fiction on the nature of reality. Dick's first short story was published in 1952, and when he died unexpectedly of a stroke he had written thirty-six SF novels and 112 short stories.

Born in Chicago, Dick was a twin; the death of his sister a few months later haunted him all his life. His parents soon moved to Berkeley, California, and he lived mostly in the San Francisco area, except for his final ten years, when he lived in Los Angeles. A brilliant and learned man, Dick was primarily self-educated, having attended the University of California, Berkeley, only briefly in 1947.

Dick published seventy-two short stories in his first three years of writing; only four of these were written in 1952, when he still was managing a record store, and twelve in 1955, when he had started his novel-writing career, so during 1953 and 1954 he was averaging better than a story every other week. Many collections of his short fiction have been published, including *The Best of Philip K. Dick* (1977) and *The Collected Stories of Philip K. Dick* (1987).

Dick's early career as a novelist was characterized by his publication in the low-paying paperback originals.

Fifteen of his novels, including the first five, and ten out of the first fourteen, were published by Ace Books, and six more were published originally by other paperback houses, which provided a ready outlet for his prolific work but also kept him impoverished and writing continuously. The Philip K. Dick Award was established after his death to recognize the best novel of the year published originally in paperback.

The typical setting of Dick's fiction, a barren wasteland on the West Coast early in the twenty-first century, was a way of exploring the problems Dick saw threatening society in the twentieth century: materialism, totalitarianism, and nuclear holocaust. His typical protagonist is a sensitive individual filled with deep anxieties as he contemplates this world. The novel that won the Hugo Award and first gained attention for Dick was *The Man in the High Castle* (1962), which depicts an alternate history in which Japan and Germany have won World War II and divided the United States between them, except for a neutral zone along the Rocky Mountains. Most of the novel takes place in the Japanese zone on the West Coast, where believable characters, both American and Japanese, seek ways of coexisting; at the end one character seeks out in Cheyenne, Wyoming, the man in the high castle, who has written an important alternate-history novel in which the United States won World War II.

Dick also was fascinated by the political process, and his astute insights into it can be found in such novels as *The Penultimate Truth* (1964), *The Simulacra* (1964), and *Dr. Bloodmoney* (1965). In the mid-1960s the focus of Dick's fiction changed from dystopian social criticism to the exploration of inner space and the workings of the human mind. Two questions fascinated him: What is reality? and What is an authentic human being? He came to believe that the world we regard as real is an illusion, that we can know reality only "through a glass darkly." The protagonist in *Martian Time-Slip* (1964), an electronics repairman in the desolate Martian colonies, suffers from periods of schizophrenia and finally comes to believe that the reality his mental illness occasionally allows him to glimpse is closer to truth than the consensus reality he shares with others. In *The Three Stigmata of Palmer Eldritch* (1965), also set on Mars, settlers from Earth live in a wasteland so desolate that they use drugs to escape its reality. They prefer their illusory world even though the drugs that enable them to reach it are provided by the evil Palmer Eldritch. This novel, picturing hallucinogenic realities, led to the charge that Dick was using LSD when he wrote it. He insisted this was not the case, however, saying that only later did he briefly use LSD and that the only thing he wrote while hallucinating was a part of *The Unteleported Man* (1966).

Dick's best answer to his second question—What is an authentic human being?—is found in *Do Androids*

Dream of Electric Sheep? (1968). Here he studied androids that look like humans and humans without feelings who behave like machines; the protagonist, a policeman, finally concludes that humans without empathy are no different from mechanical constructs. A human being, according to Dick's definition, expresses love and compassion for all living forms, as does J. R. Isidore, the wise fool of the novel. Ridley Scott's film version, BLADE RUNNER (1982), departed from the novel in many ways but has a richly detailed and appropriately decadent background and comes to the same final point; Dick saw excerpts from the screenplay before his death. *Flow My Tears, the Policeman Said* (1974), another novel about law enforcers, carries the same message about love. It won the John W. Campbell Award.

Perhaps Dick's most bizarre vision is contained in *Ubik* (1969), which pictures a world where reality constantly collapses and time regresses, as entropy, the ultimate evil for Dick, drags the various characters down to death. Or are they really dead? Dick refused to provide his reader an answer: reality, he suggested, is unknowable.

In 1970, when Dick's fourth wife (he was married five times) left him, he ceased writing and became involved in the street drug world. This dismal part of his life ended with a suicide attempt in 1972. In 1977 he published *A Scanner Darkly*, a novel drawing on his experiences during that period to depict the destructive results of drug use. Dick's last novels, the Valis trilogy, turn to metaphysical speculation, transforming into fiction a religious epiphany he experienced in March 1974. The religious messiah had occasionally appeared in earlier Dick novels, *The World Jones Made* (1956) and *Counter-Clock World* (1967), for example. In his last novels, *Valis* and *The Divine Invasion*, both published in 1981, the search for God becomes a near obsession. Dick was at work on "The Owl in Daylight" when he died.

The Transformation of Timothy Archer, published posthumously in 1982, is realistic fiction about the life of Dick's friend Bishop James Pike. Dick had written a number of mainstream novels during the first half of his career but found a publisher only for *Confessions of a Crap Artist* (1975). Since his death some of these novels have been published, including *The Man Whose Teeth Were All Exactly Alike* (1984), *In Milton Lumpky Territory* (1985), *Puttering Around in a Small Land* (1985), *Humpty Dumpty in Oakland* (1986), and *Mary and the Giant* (1987).

Because Dick's only income was from his writing, his novels were sometimes written hastily with disappointing results, as in *The Crack in Space* (1966) and *Our Friends from Frolix 8* (1970). His two collaborations, *The Ganymede Takeover* (1967), written with Ray F. NELSON, and *Deus Irae* (1976), written with Roger ZELAZNY, are not as successful as his solo work. At the time of his death he was beginning to reap the benefits of his efforts in both popular and critical success; he may have been held in even higher regard in Europe than in the United States. Several books about his life and work appeared in the 1980s, and an international conference was devoted to a consideration of his accomplishments.

OTHER WORKS: *Solar Lottery* (1955); *The Man Who Japed* (1956); *Eye in the Sky* (1957); *The Cosmic Puppets* (1957); *Time out of Joint* (1959); *Dr. Futurity* (1960); *Vulcan's Hammer* (1960); *The Game-Players of Titan* (1963); *Clans of the Alphane Moon* (1964); *Now Wait for Last Year* (1966); *The Zap Gun* (1967); *Galactic Pot-Healer* (1969); *A Maze of Death* (1970); *We Can Build You* (1972); *Radio Free Albemuth* (1985).

P.W.

DICKINSON, PETER (Pseudonym of Malcolm de Brissac) (1927–).

British writer who combines science fiction and fantasy with his highly literate children's books and crime fiction. In his particularly odd and rich world of the imagination, Dickinson links history, myth, science, superstition, anthropology, and psycholinguistics. His Changes trilogy for children (collected as *The Changes*, 1975), comprising *The Weathermonger* (1968), *Heartsease* (1969), and *The Devil's Children* (1970), is set in an England where magic has replaced technology. *King and Joker* (1976) is a complex detective story set in an alternate England ruled by Edward VII's eldest son. Dickinson's only legitimate adult SF novel, *The Green Gene* (1973), is also set in an alternate Britain. In this amusing satire on color prejudice, a rampant gene turns all "Celtic" children green at birth.

R.D.

DICKSON, GORDON R[UPERT] (1923–).

Canadian-American writer, master of the philosophical action story. Dickson was born in Edmonton, Alberta, to an Anglo-Australian father and an American mother. (His older half-brother was the noted Anglo-Canadian author, editor, and publisher Lovat Dickson, 1902–1987.) He entered the University of Minnesota at age fifteen and studied creative writing with Sinclair Lewis and Robert Penn Warren. Returning after military service, he completed his B.A. in English in 1948 and has resided in the Minneapolis area ever since.

Following his first solo sale ("The Friendly Man") to *Astounding* in 1951, Dickson has written full time, producing nearly seventy books and more than 175 shorter works, including mysteries, westerns, essays, poems, and songs. He has edited four anthologies and scripted nine radio plays. His most successful work has been a series in progress called the Childe Cycle, begun with *Dorsai!* (1959).

Dickson's primary theme is initiation—of the individual and the race. He maintains that "man's future is upward and outward" and insists that destiny is directable. Unlike his college classmate Poul ANDERSON (1926–), a writer with whom he is often inaccurately compared, Dickson cannot admit the possibility of real or lasting failure. He cherishes an almost Victorian faith in the inevitability of progress—by spiritual, rather than material means—and truly believes in the redemptive power of art. His SF is usually more mystical than technical, although *The Far Call* (1977) has been praised as "the finest realistic novel about the space program yet written."

During the 1970s Dickson systematically improved his formerly passive and stereotyped characterizations of women. However, filial and fraternal relationships continue to spark the fiercest passions in his work: conflicting tendencies in human nature are typically symbolized by estranged twin brothers. His interest in male bonding under stress has led him to choose pioneering and fighting as subject matter for his fiction. Although he has been accused of militarism, his chessboard conflicts are not meant as ends in themselves. His artistically gifted heroes embody his fascination with precocity, longevity, unusual size, and fabulous strength, but right is always the source of their might. In Dickson's oeuvre human determination can vanquish any menace, however awesome. For example, the lonely, brilliant hero of *Way of the Pilgrim* (1987) rouses unarmed humanity to repel giant alien conquerors who seem invincible. This novel is a meditation on freedom, responsibility, and maturity, for the aliens are parent figures as well as oppressors.

Animals and aliens modeled on animals receive sympathetic treatment, perhaps most poignantly in *Alien Art* (1973), with its martyred otterlike alien artist. But nature exists as a milieu for human acts: man, for Dickson, is the measure of all things, and the human mind must prevail over matter (as in *The Pritcher Mass*, 1972). Humanity's indomitable will, Dickson tells us, can reshape the universe (as in *Time Storm*, 1977).

Dickson is a traditional storyteller, heavily influenced by Rudyard KIPLING and nineteenth-century English literature. Sensitivity to literary craft led Dickson to develop the "consciously thematic novel," the adventure story with a moral. This approach is at least as old as Chaucer, but Dickson's version uses realistic details to render philosophical arguments as naturally as possible without lapsing into propaganda or didacticism.

The showcase for Dickson's theory is his Childe Cycle, which seeks to dramatize a millennium of human evolution from the fourteenth to the twenty-fourth century through the interaction and unification of three archetypes called Prime Characters—the Men of Faith (Friendlies), Philosophy (Exotics), and War (Dorsai). Ultimately the human race is to "come of age" by experiencing a quantum leap in creative power and ethical behavior.

Gordon R. Dickson

When complete this multipart epic will consist of twelve novels: three historical, three contemporary, and six science-fictional. *Dorsai!*, *Necromancer* (1962), *Soldier, Ask Not* (1967), *The Tactics of Mistake* (1970/1971), and *The Final Encyclopedia* (1984) have appeared so far, and the next volume, *Chantry Guild*, is in preparation. Four "illuminations," related works that are not part of the cycle proper, are collected with background material in *The Dorsai Companion* (1986).

Dickson is also noted for his broad, bouncy comedies, which typically place a logical person in an illogical situation. For instance, a college professor becomes a dragon in *The Dragon and the George* (1976), the partial basis of the 1986 animated television film *The Flight of Dragons*. His farcical Hoka series, written in collaboration with Poul Anderson, concerns teddy bear–like aliens who imitate human pop culture (*Earthman's Burden*, 1955, and *Hoka!* 1984).

Having chosen in childhood to be a writer, Dickson possesses a strong sense of vocation. He remains an enthusiastic public speaker on SF topics and is a patient mentor of younger writers. As one of the first profes-

sionals to join the SCIENCE FICTION RESEARCH ASSOCIATION, he has campaigned for closer ties between SF and academe. He participated regularly in the Intensive English Institute on the Teaching of SF at the University of Kansas and appeared in its SF Lecture Film series.

Dickson's awards include the Hugo for "Soldier, Ask Not" in 1965, for "Lost Dorsai" in 1981, and for "The Cloak and the Staff" in 1981; the Nebula for "Call Him Lord" in 1966; the Jupiter for "Time Storm" in 1977; and the Derleth for *The Dragon and the George* in 1977. He served two terms as president of the SCIENCE FICTION WRITERS OF AMERICA (1969–1971) and was professional guest of honor at the 1984 World SF Convention. A bibliography of his work has been published by Raymond H. Thompson (1983).

NOTABLE OTHER WORKS: *Delusion World* (1961); *Spacial Delivery* (1961); *Naked to the Stars* (1961); *Home from the Shore* (1962/1978); *The Alien Way* (1965); *The Space Swimmers* (1967); *Spacepaw* (1969); *Wolfling* (1969); *Danger-Human* (1970); *The Star Road* (1973); *Ancient, My Enemy* (1974); *Combat SF* (editor, 1975); *The Spirit of Dorsai* (1979); *In Iron Years* (1980); *Lost Dorsai* (1980); *The Last Dream* (1986); *The Forever Man* (1986).

S.L.M.

DI FATE, VINCENT (1945–   ).

American science-fiction illustrator. Born in Yonkers, New York, Di Fate graduated from the Phoenix (now Pratt-Manhattan Center, class of 1967), and the Art Students' League. He began illustrating SF in 1969, when he made his first professional sale to ANALOG. Since then he has provided the art for hundreds of book and magazine covers and interiors.

Most of Di Fate's work has appeared on paperback book covers for such publishers as Ace, Berkley, Pyramid, Avon, Tor, Baen, Ballantine, Bantam, and Doubleday, and the majority of his magazine work has been for *Analog*. Di Fate has also done illustrations for the aerospace industry, including companies such as Rockwell North American and Kerfott-Singer, and he was one of the NASA artists for the Apollo-Soyuz flight (1975); in addition, the National Air and Space Museum has acquired some of his work for its permanent collection. Recently, Di Fate has worked as a consultant for the motion picture and toy industries.

Di Fate has had major shows in many galleries and museums, including solo shows at the Museum of Science and History in St. Louis; the Reading Public Museum in Reading, Pennsylvania; the Earthlight Gallery in Boston; the Pendragon Gallery in Annapolis; several galleries in Europe; and the Museum of the Surreal in New York City. He is a member of the Society of Illustrators, SFWA, Graphic Artists Guild, World SF, and the International Association of Astronomical Artists.

Di Fate is best known for his illustration of SF gadgetry and technological artifacts. He paints in a "commercial art" style, similar to those of Dean Ellis or John Berkey, emphasizing flat planes and often using sober colors—blacks, ochers, and violets. Di Fate has been nominated for the Hugo Award thirteen times (he won it in 1979), and he was the 1979 recipient of the Frank R. Paul Award.

J.G.

Illustration by Di Fate for G. Harry Stine's *The Space Enterprise*

DILLON, LEO (1933–) and DIANE (1933–).

American illustrators, a husband-and-wife team, whose art ranges from the near abstract to the highly realistic. The Dillons' earlier work, much of which appeared on the covers of Harlan ELLISON's books, resembles woodblock prints, with strong, thick lines and bold imagery; this same style is reflected in their work for GALAXY and their paperback covers for Dell, Fawcett, Viking, Bantam, and Ace Books, especially the Ace Specials. The Dillons' realistic work, apparently influenced by the British school of science-fiction art (see ILLUSTRATION: BRITISH), has a precise and finished look; in this style they produced a series of limited-edition prints.

The Dillons have worked outside the SF field as well, doing a number of cover paintings for Caedmon Records; their best known in this series is the cover for *The Autobiography of Miss Jane Pittman*. Many examples of their work have been collected in *The Art of Leo and Diane Dillon* (1981). The only team to win a professional artist Hugo Award (1971), they also received the Caldecott Medal for their book *Why Mosquitoes Buzz in People's Ears* (1975).

J.G.

The Dillons' cover illustration for Joan D. Vinge's *World's End*

─────── DIME NOVELS ───────

The end of the American Civil War found the nation obsessed with three things: the real and mythological exploitation of the West, invention, and business. Stories based on the West or business (the Horatio Alger series was only one example) poured forth, but stories about inventions were just as intriguing, particularly to young readers, and had not yet been as thoroughly exploited.

Cheap paperback novels (usually with yellow covers) had appeared episodically at least since 1830. What came to be called "Dime Novels" were similar paperback books, usually written to order, which appeared in a numbered series. Dime Novel No. 1 from Beadle's was *Malaeska* by Ann S. Stephens (1813–1886), published in June of 1860.

The first science-fiction dime novel, written for Beadle's in 1868 by Edward S. ELLIS (1840–1916), was *The Steam Man of the Prairies*, No. 45 of American Novels. Ellis was a prominent educator and scholar, a leader in the New Jersey educational system, and the author of more than fifty volumes of history as well as a thousand dime novels. In his story a fifteen-year-old boy inventor builds a steam-powered robot that pulls wagons at high speed and takes it out west to fight bad men and Indians; the book is a brilliant combination of invention and the West.

Boy's weekly papers usually ran a half-dozen serials simultaneously. The owner of one of the weeklies, Frank Tousey, asked Harry Enton, pseudonym for Harry Cohen (1854–1927), to write a story similar to *Steam Man*. The result, serialized in *Boys of New York* in 1876, was *The Steam Man of the Plains*, in which Frank Reade, a teenage inventor (and brilliant businessman) builds a steam-powered robot that can run fifty miles an hour and ships it out west, once again to battle bad men and Indians. Enton wrote the first four Frank Reade dime novels and then was replaced by Luis P. SENARENS (1865–1939). Under the pseudonym Noname, Senarens retired Frank Reade, Sr., to a farm and continued the series with his teenage son in *Frank Reade, Jr., and His Steam Wonder* (1882). The steam wonder is a steam caboose that doesn't need tracks.

Ellis's steam-man story was repeatedly reprinted in various Beadle five-cent libraries for boys. Tousey followed Beadle's example when he bought *Wide Awake Library* and reprinted all the Frank Reade series as complete novels, or, if they were too long, as two-part novels at five cents each. In 1892 Tousey responded to popular demand by creating a weekly *Frank Reade Library*, in which the stories were again reprinted and new ones published for 191 issues. The series was finally closed down by tirades from numerous pulpits on the disastrous moral effect on young readers of dime novels, with their stories of robots, tanks, submarines, airplanes, helicopters, earth satellites, radio telescopes, and electric stun guns.

Senarens wrote a second series of at least fifty dime novels, almost interchangeable with Frank Reade, Jr.; Jack Wright was the hero of these, which were also serialized and then reprinted as novels. In 1902 Tousey revived the series with *Frank Reade Weekly Magazine,* reprinting ninety-six numbers with full-color covers and also reprinting the Jack Wright stories, in his *Pluck and Luck Library.*

Jules VERNE, whose novels were being published in British boy's magazines, came into possession of at least some Senarens stories and started a correspondence with the author, even adapting some of Senarens's concepts for *The Steam House* (really a steam elephant) and *The Clipper of the Clouds* (1887).

Street & Smith imitated Senarens's invention stories with a series of Tom Edison stories, written under the pseudonym Philip Reade, and Electric Bob stories, both in its *New York Five Cent Library* launched in 1892. Dime novels that featured detectives or the West often would toss in new inventions as well.

All these invention stories evolved into the *Tom Swift, Great Marvel,* and *Adventures in the Unknown* boy's hardcover book series and eventually entered the pulp magazines, predominantly as short stories of invention with a humorous slant. They could also be found in the early issues of AMAZING STORIES. The Gallegher stories of Henry KUTTNER (writing as Lewis Padgett), featuring a brilliant drunken inventor who can't remember the purpose of his inventions when he sobers up, may be a survival of this genre into the 1940s.

S.M.

DISCH, THOMAS M[ICHAEL] (1940–   ).

American writer of science fiction, horror, poetry (of which he has published half a dozen volumes), and Gothic novels, who has earned a reputation in SF as one of its finest stylists with one of its darkest visions. Disch is most frequently associated with the British NEW WAVE writers of the 1960s, although he was born in Iowa, raised in Minnesota, and educated in New York City. Disch was awarded the O. Henry Prize in 1975 and the Rhysling Award for SF poetry in 1981, and Samuel R. DELANY devoted an entire book, *The American Shore* (1978), to the structuralist reading of Disch's short story "Angouleme" (1971).

The indifference of the universe to human feelings and aspirations is an abiding theme in Disch's work; his earliest novels expose anthropocentrism and depict a world in which humanity does not shape, but is shaped *by,* the future. In both *The Genocides* (1965) and *Mankind under the Leash* (1966; as *The Puppies of Terra,* 1978), invading aliens brush aside human civilization and seize the Earth. In the first case the aliens exterminate people as pests; in the second they keep them as pets. In one of his early masterpieces, "The Asian Shore" (1970), a middle-class American is slowly transformed into a lower-class Turk.

Disch's experimental style comes through most clearly in his best-known early novel, *Camp Concentration* (1968), an indictment of America's treatment of antiwar protesters. The book describes prisoners in a near future American concentration camp who are treated with an ultimately fatal drug that increases intelligence for a few months. The narrator, telling his story in the form of journal entries, alternates between the joy of his increased abilities and the fear of the drug's consequences.

Another of Disch's major themes, most apparent in his short stories, is humanity's inhumanity to its own. "Flight Useless, Inexorable the Pursuit" (1966), "The Affluence of Edwin Lollard" (1967), and "Angouleme" describe a world oppressed by poverty, race hatred, and blind selfishness. Disch's characters are in constant battle with repression, a battle which few win and then only at huge cost. Disch's work also reflects an interest in *self*-oppression. Such short stories as "Descending" (1964), "Come to Venus Melancholy" (1965), and "Moondust, the Smell of Hay and Dialectic Materialism" (1967) portray human beings trapped by constricting beliefs, meaningless slogans, and narrow, self-centered views of the world. All these stories are typically ambiguous; unlike his earlier novels, they offer no background. His characters appear, without explanation, in the middle of extraordinary situations from which there is apparently no escape, as in "Descending," in which a man is trapped on an endlessly descending escalator.

Disch has often attacked American puritanism as particularly oppressive. *On Wings of Song* (1979), the winner of the John W. Campbell Memorial Award as best novel, presents a divided America: the Midwest toils under a repressive form of religion while the Northeast, particularly New York City, bursts with artistic inventiveness. Less relentlessly pessimistic than his other novels, *On Wings of Song* celebrates the arts, especially opera. Describing a world in which singing enables not only the spirit but the body to soar, the novel symbolizes the victory of the spirit through the physical act of flight.

The Businessman: A Tale of Terror (1984) dwells less on the confines of the human mind than on its potential expansiveness. Here religion is no longer necessarily an oppressive force but a potentially liberating one. Disch's development seems to suggest that if evil exists in the world it is because goodness exists as well; having exposed the terror of the human predicament, he now can suggest ways to ameliorate it.

OTHER WORKS: *One Hundred and Two H-Bombs* (collection, 1966; enlarged edition as *White Fang Goes Dingo and Other Funny S.F. Stories*, 1971); *Echo Round His Bones* (1967); *Under Compulsion* (collection, 1968; as *Fun with Your New Head*, 1971); *The Prisoner* (1969, based on the television serial); *334* (1972); *The Early Science Fiction Stories of Thomas M. Disch* (collection, 1977); *Triplicity* (1980); *Fundamental Disch* (collection, 1980); *The Man Who Had No Idea* (collection, 1982); *Ringtime: A Story* (1983); *Torturing Mr. Amberwell* (1985).

S.H.G.

DR. CYCLOPS (1940). *Directed by Ernest B. Schoedsack; screenplay by Tom Kilpatrick; photographed by Henry Sharp and Winton C. Hoch; music by Ernest Toch, Gerard Carbonara, and Albert Ray Malotte. With Albert Dekker, Janice Logan, Thomas Coley, Charles Halton, Victor Kilian, Frank Yaconelli. 75 minutes. Color.*

Hoping to create another KING KONG, Paramount hired Ernest B. Schoedsack to direct *Dr. Cyclops*. Alas, his efforts were expended on a slight tale, much like those found in the science-fiction pulps of ten years earlier. An expedition visits evil scientist Dr. Thorkel in his jungle laboratory; he shrinks the newcomers to a height of six inches, kills one, and then tries to kill the others. They smash one lens of his heavy glasses (hence the title), then manage to kill him. As they return to civilization, they gradually grow to their normal height.

Except for Albert Dekker, the cast is inadequate, the dialogue melodramatic, and the pacing lethargic. Though financially successful the film was never the adventure spectacle Schoedsack had hoped for, and it generated no more SF thrillers of its type. It was novelized by Henry KUTTNER, writing as Will Garth.

B.W.

DR. JEKYLL AND MR. HYDE ON FILM

Because of the appeal of Robert Louis STEVENSON's original story, and the ease with which it lends itself to adaptation, there have been more film, stage, television, and radio versions of "The Strange Case of Dr. Jekyll and Mr. Hyde" (1886) than of any other work of science fiction or horror. (Although there *have* been more movies about Dracula, few were based on Bram STOKER's novel.) The first official theatrical adaptation of "Dr. Jekyll and Mr. Hyde" was mounted just a year after the novella's publication and made Richard Mansfield a star for his performance in the dual role; the first movie adaptation came in 1908. Others will undoubtedly follow for as long as films are made and plays produced.

John Barrymore's silent version, still often shown, is notable mainly for his performance; although the transitions from Jekyll to Hyde are unintentionally comic when seen today, Barrymore's sleazy, amusing Hyde is still impressive. The film originated the good-woman, bad-woman duality followed in most of the subsequent screen versions: the good woman (Jekyll's fiancée) at-

Fredric March in the dual role of Dr. Jekyll and Mr. Hyde (1932)

tracts the lust of Hyde, and the bad woman of the streets arouses Jekyll's lust, satisfied by Hyde.

Rouben Mamoulian's 1932 version, for which Fredric March won an Academy Award (tied with Wallace Beery), is the most significant adaptation to date. Fluidly cinematic, it approaches the tale from a different perspective, portraying Hyde (who becomes more grotesque with each successive transformation) not as Jekyll's evil alter ego but as his animal nature set free, neither good nor evil but totally amoral. March's performance as Jekyll is somewhat stiff and posturing, but as Hyde he is magnificent: unnervingly hilarious, genuinely frightening, sensual, brutal, and superbly made up, he is one of the great screen monsters.

The stodgy 1941 version, with an ill-cast Spencer Tracy as Jekyll/Hyde, faddishly used Freudian psychology to explain the leading character's obsessions. Ingrid Bergman is even better than Miriam Hopkins (in the 1932 version) as the Bad Girl, but despite beautiful production values, this overly long film fails in almost every way that the 1932 version succeeds. It is watchable but uninvolving.

The 1960 Hammer Films production *Two Faces of Dr. Jekyll* completely ignores Stevenson's story in favor of a surprising but unrewarding new approach: here, Jekyll (Paul Massie) is elderly and homely, while Hyde is a handsome young libertine. The film is intelligently written, but Wolf Mankowitz's idea that Hyde was no more corrupt than other notorious Victorians defuses the central theme.

The Jack Palance TV version benefited from his exuberant performance as the leads, although his Jekyll, like that of March, evokes little interest. By filming on videotape, the producers gained money to spend on sets,

but the script meanders and adds little of note.

I, Monster, released in 1971, is the only faithful film adaptation of Stevenson's novella, but it is unsuccessful. Although Peter Cushing does an admirable job and Christopher Lee gives what may be his best non-Dracula performance, the slow pace, generally inadequate acting, and very low budget prevent the film from rising much above the second rate.

Stevenson's story of the doctor with the dual life has inspired a myriad of other adaptations, too numerous to enumerate here. They include comedy versions (among them *The Ugly Duckling* and *Jekyll and Hyde . . . Together Again*), cartoons, parodies, and at least one musical (with Kirk Douglas). The central ideas—unleashed desires are perilous, our other selves are destructive—have proved irresistible to filmmakers and will undoubtedly continue to inspire.

Dr. Jekyll and Mr. Hyde (1920).   Directed by *John S. Robertson; screenplay by Clara S. Beranger; adapted from the novella "The Strange Case of Dr. Jekyll and Mr. Hyde" by Robert Louis Stevenson; photographed by Roy Overbough. With John Barrymore, Brandon Hurst, Nita Naldi, George Stevens, Louis Wolheim, Charles Lane, Martha Mansfield. 63 minutes. Black and white.*

Dr. Jekyll and Mr. Hyde (1932).   Directed by *Rouben Mamoulian; screenplay by Percy Heath and Samuel Hoffenstein; photographed by Karl Struss. With Fredric March, Miriam Hopkins, Rose Hobart, Tempe Piggott, Holmes Herbert, Halliwell Hobbes, Arnold Lucy, Edgar Norton. 82 minutes. Black and white.*

Dr. Jekyll and Mr. Hyde (1941).   Directed by *Victor Fleming; screenplay by John Lee Mahin; adapted* *from the script by Percy Heath and Samuel Hoffenstein for the 1932 version; photographed by Joseph Ruttenberg; music by Franz Waxman. With Spencer Tracy, Ingrid Bergman, Donald Crisp, Ian Hunter, Lana Turner, Barton MacLane, C. Aubrey Smith, Sara Allgood. 122 minutes. Black and white.*

The Two Faces of Dr. Jekyll (1960).
Directed by Terence Fisher; screenplay by Wolf Mankowitz; photographed by Jack Asher; music by Monty Norman and David Heneker. With Paul Massie, Dawn Addams, Christopher Lee, David Kossoff, Norma Marla, Francis De Wolff, Oliver Reed. 88 minutes. Alternate titles: House of Fright; Jekyll's Inferno.

The Strange Case of Dr. Jekyll and Mr. Hyde (1968).
Directed by Charles Jarrott; teleplay by Ian McClellan Hunter; photography directed by Tom Ashworth, Bob Coyle, and Gordon Luker; music by Robert Cobert. With Jack Palance, Denholm Elliott, Billie Whitelaw, Tessie O'Shea, Torin Thatcher, Oscar Homolka, Leo Genn, Gillie Fenwick, Duncan Lamont. 110 minutes. Color.

I, Monster (1971).
Directed by Stephen Weeks; screenplay by Milton Subotsky; photographed by Moray Grant; music by Carl Davis. With Christopher Lee, Peter Cushing, Mike Raven, George Merritt, Susan Jameson, Kenneth J. Warren. 75 minutes. Color.

B.W.

DR. STRANGELOVE, OR HOW I LEARNED TO STOP WORRYING AND LOVE THE BOMB (1964).
Directed by Stanley Kubrick; screenplay by Stanley Kubrick, Terry Southern, and Peter George; adapted from the novel Red Alert *by Peter George; photographed by Gilbert Taylor; music by Laurie Johnson. With Peter Sellers, George C. Scott, Sterling Hayden, Keenan Wynn, Slim Pickens, Peter Bull, James Earl Jones. 102 minutes. Black and white.*

Stanley KUBRICK's black comedy about the beginning of a nuclear war was the first commercial feature film to treat the topic in a humorous, even irreverent manner. The movie's stark black-and-white cinematography matches its dark vision, but its contrasting light tone sets it apart from the solemnity usually accorded the subject in the movies, as in, for example, ON THE BEACH (1959) or *The War Game* (1965).

The sardonic scenario of *Dr. Strangelove* shows the world ending not with a nuclear bang but with a technological whimper more befitting humanity's collective stupidity. Atomic warfare is the result of human foul-up rather than political conflict or technological malfunction, as in FAIL SAFE, released only a few months after Kubrick's film. Events snowball (or rather, mushroom) as a paranoid American Army officer, convinced of a Russian conspiracy to sap the "precious bodily fluids"

of wholesome Americans, seals off his base and orders the first strike. No one can short-circuit the ensuing chaos, which leads to the retaliation of the Soviets with their new "doomsday machine," designed to end life on Earth.

Peter Sellers has an actor's field day, playing three major roles—the American president, an army captain, and the crackpot scientist of the film's title. The mad Dr. Strangelove wears a black glove on one hand, a reference to the evil scientist Rotwang in Fritz LANG's classic METROPOLIS (1926), and with an apparent will of its own, his hand periodically shoots upright into a Nazi salute—a comic but grim image of biology controlled by technology.

Because of its satiric tone and nuclear gallows humor, this film was the subject of heated controversy. In fact, Kubrick initially planned it as a serious drama, but its brilliance lies precisely in its outrageously farcical plot and tone; its essential point, after all, is that, to have created the possibility of nuclear war and planned for it in the first place, we must already be ludicrously mad. When the Soviet ambassador begins to quarrel with some of the assembled officials in the Pentagon, they are reprimanded with the unforgettable remark, "You can't fight in here—this is the War Room!" This statement perfectly captures what Kubrick obviously perceived as a ghastly global joke.

B.K.G.

DOCTOR WHO (1963–   ).
Directed by Waris Hussein, Gordon Flemyng, and others; written by Anthony Coburn, Terry Nation, Dennis Spooner, Bill Strutton, and others; photographed by John Wilcox and others; music by Malcolm Lockyer and others. With William Hartnell, Patrick Troughton, Jon Pertwee, Tom Baker, Peter Davison, Colin Baker, Elizabeth Sladen, William Russell, Carole Ann Ford, Roger Delgado, Anneke Wills, Jacqueline Hill, Michael Craze, Stewart Bevan. 30-minute episodes. Black and white through 1967, color since then.

Doctor Who is the longest-running science-fiction television series in history, illustrating the medium's way of devouring materials as it exploited (and often mixed) every imaginable SF trope as well as historical adventure and parody, gothic and mad-scientist horror, Ruritanian romance, and Victorian and 1920s murder mystery. Intended as an educational entertainment for children, conceived by Sydney Newman and originally produced by Verity Lambert and Mervyn Pinfield, it began as a routine children's adventure series on November 23, 1963. Under the leadership of Lambert and her staff, however, *Doctor Who* developed into a uniquely popular SF adventure series with a broad audience. The mysterious, extraterrestrial Doctor, portrayed from 1963 to 1966 by William Hartnell, uses his space-time machine the *TARDIS* to transport himself and various companions to past or future Earths or to other worlds, where they partake in cliff-hanging serial adventures generally of two to six episodes. The second serial of the first season, "The Daleks" by Terry Nation, assured the program's success and provided British popular culture with a durable set of villains, the metallic-voiced megalomaniacal cyborgs of the title. Their simple design and operation also illustrate the way in which the series has gotten around the problem of expensive special effects.

The need for continuity and variety over a span of more than two decades has led to both innovative and traditional responses from the producers. The problem of continuing the series when the principal wanted to leave was solved by having the Doctor "regenerate" into a new appearance and personality played by a new actor. Since 1966 this tactic has allowed the Doctor to be portrayed by William Hartnell (1963–1966), Patrick Troughton (1966–1969), Jon Pertwee (1970–1974), Tom Baker (1974–1981), Peter Davison (1981–1984), and Colin Baker (1984–1986), the last acrimoniously dismissed. Companions have come and gone, from the first Doctor's granddaughter and two of her terrestrial teachers (played by Carole Ann Ford, Jacqueline Hill, and William Russell respectively) on to a total of thirty by 1986. Villains, however, have returned often; in addition to the ever-popular Daleks and their creator, the mad-scientist Davros, they include the Master (played by Roger Delgado, 1971–1973, and Anthony Ainley, 1981–   ), Sea Devils, Cybermen, Ice Warriors, and Sontarans.

Doctor Who has become an industry: the programs (all but 134 of more than 600 episodes survive) are still broadcast in world markets, notably on public television in the U.S.; licensed merchandise provides the BBC with considerable income; Doctor Who fan clubs and fanzines proliferate; the serials are turned into children's books; and there is an official *Doctor Who Magazine*. Two films based on television scripts by Terry Nation, *Doctor Who and the Daleks* (1965) and *The Daleks: Invasion Earth 2150* (1966), featured Peter Cushing as the Doctor, and a play, *Doctor Who and the Daleks in Seven Keys to Doomsday*, by series script editor (1968–1974) Terrance Dicks, was produced in London in 1974.

R.F.L.

DOCTOR X (1932).

Directed by Michael Curtiz; screenplay by Robert Tasker and Earl Baldwin; adapted from the play by Howard W. Comstock and Allen C. Miller; photographed by Richard Tower and Ray Rennahan. With Lionel Atwill, Fay Wray, Lee Tracy, Arthur Edmund Carewe, Preston Foster, Mae Busch, Robert Warwick, John Wray, Tom Dugan. 77 minutes. Color.

At the climax of this lively, entertaining horror thriller with science-fiction touches, we learn that the myste-

Illustration by Dold for Nat Schachner's "The Sun-World of Soldus" (*Astounding*, October 1938)

rious, cannibalistic Moon Killer is a one-armed scientist (Preston Foster), who regularly fashions a temporary second hand and hideous face from a vat of the "synthetic flesh" he has secretly invented. He's thwarted by the wisecracking reporter-boyfriend (Lee Tracy) of the heroine (Fay Wray, screaming again). The isolated, bizarrely designed laboratory where most of the action takes place is headed by Lionel Atwill, at his best as the eponymous Dr. Xavier, a stern but heroic scientist. The film is rarely screened today, almost never in the original two-strip Technicolor process, which it imaginatively used.

B.W.

DOLD, ELLIOTT (?–?).

American SF illustrator. Dold produced the first of his many interior illustrations in 1930 and continued for almost a decade. Although most of his work was for *Astounding Science Fiction*, he painted two covers for his brother Douglas's magazine, *Miracle Science and Fantasy Stories*, and one for *Cosmic Stories*. Dold is best known for his illustrations for E. E. "Doc" SMITH's "Skylark of Valeron" (*Astounding Science Fiction*, 1934). His drawings were distinguished by high contrast, and, like his contemporary, Frank R. PAUL, he was better at depicting huge and complex machinery, gadgets, spaceships, and fantastic cities, than people.

J.G.

DONNELLY, IGNATIUS (1831–1901). American politician and author whose eccentricities are better known than his fiction. A Minnesota politician, lieutenant governor at age twenty-eight, and one of the founders of the Populist party, Donnelly won notoriety for his beliefs that Atlantis really existed, which he tried to prove with his book *Atlantis, the Antediluvian World* (1882), and that Francis Bacon wrote Shakespeare's plays, for which he claimed to find cryptographic evidence documented in *The Great Cryptogram* (1888). He wrote two fantasy novels: *Dr. Huguet* (1891), about the personality of a white man trapped in the body of a black, and *The Golden Bottle* (1892), in which capitalism is overthrown via a process for making gold. His most important science-fiction work is a grim portrayal of a dystopian future marked by growing inequality and disastrous wars, *Caesar's Column* (1890), in which the column of the title is a pillar of skulls.

S.E.G.

DONOVAN'S BRAIN (1953). *Directed by Felix Feist; screenplay by Felix Feist; adapted by Hugh Brooks from the novel by Curt Siodmak; photographed by Joseph Biroc; music by Eddie Dunstedter. With Lew Ayres, Gene Evans, Nancy Davis (Reagan), Steve Brodie, Lisa K. Howard, Michael Colgan. 83 minutes. Black and white.*

After a plane crash near his desert laboratory, a scientist (Lew Ayres) removes the brain of a dead billionaire, keeping it alive in his lab, but the ruthless brain dominates him and forces him into evil acts.

The Curt SIODMAK novel on which this movie is based has been filmed three times and imitated often; this low-key, sincere movie, though somewhat slow, is the best adaptation to date. Made in a period when science-fiction films were still aimed at adults, it is modest but intelligent, carefully designed—the lab looks authentically jury-rigged—and largely unsensational. It greatly benefits from Ayres's detailed, thoughtful performance, one of the best in low-budget SF films.

B.W.

DOYLE, ARTHUR CONAN [SIR] (1859–1930). British writer best known for the creation of Sherlock Holmes, one of the most durable and influential detectives in fiction. A poet, essayist, historian, and medical doctor, Doyle belonged to the same generation as Rudyard KIPLING and H. G. WELLS, and shared some of their interests and attitudes. His enormous success with the Holmes stories has overshadowed his other writing of high quality, especially his forays into science fiction. Doyle experimented with SF of the Jules VERNE variety in a few forgotten early stories, including "The Great Brown Perichord Motor," which appeared in *The Pic-* *torial Magazine* in January 1904 (less than a month after the success of the Wright Brothers at Kitty Hawk, North Carolina) and predicts the invention of a flying machine.

The Holmes stories also sometimes approach the boundary of SF when dealing with bizarre and esoteric methods of murder. But it is primarily the invention of Professor George Challenger and the tales Doyle wrote about this intrepid explorer that make him an author of some stature in the development of SF. Brave, resourceful, alternately jovial and irascible, Challenger is one of the memorable characters in the genre, typifying some of the virtues and limitations of SF written before the 1930s.

Thought to have been modeled on Professor William Rutherford of the University of Edinburgh, Challenger first appears in *The Lost World* (1912), a novel depicting an expedition that discovers an uncharted plateau in the Andes, where creatures from the Jurassic age still roam. Aside from telling an exciting tale, Doyle thus introduced into the genre the archetypal theme of confrontation with a primitive world of animals supposedly extinct. This use of a prehistoric realm prefigured the work of such writers as Edgar Rice BURROUGHS, especially in the Pellucidar stories and some of the later Tarzan novels. It also was one of the influences (perhaps indirectly) on such films as KING KONG (1932).

Another Challenger novel, *The Poison Belt* (1913), describes a world apparently dying from poison in the upper atmosphere and probably owes its inspiration to M. P. SHIEL's *The Purple Cloud* (1901) and Wells's fables of disaster. Nevertheless, its imaginative extrapolation of ecological catastrophe remains vivid and relevant even today. Doyle wrote several other Challenger stories, most notably *The Land of Mist* (1926), wherein Challenger becomes involved with the spiritualist ambience that preoccupied Doyle himself in the final years of his life. Yet another late excursion into SF, though without Challenger, is *The Maracot Deep* (1929), an impressive novel of undersea exploration. Two other noteworthy works of SF by Doyle are "The Disintegration Machine" (1913) and "When the World Screamed" (1928).

Though limited in scope, Doyle's SF displays a number of admirable qualities: narrative verve, solid characterizations, an interest in ideas and the possibilities of science, and the exhilaration of exploring new territory. Doyle was perhaps more fascinated by intellectual adventure than by the pure love of science, but his best SF has, like Holmes and Challenger, the stamina to endure.

E.L.C.

DOZOIS, GARDNER [RAYMOND] (1947–   ). American writer of surrealistic science fiction, anthologist, and editor. Dozois served as a military journalist

Gardner Dozois

in Germany from 1966 to 1969, but he had already sold his first story, "The Empty Man," in 1966. Upon his discharge he began writing full-time, with the aid of jobs as reader for two paperback publishers and the GALAXY family of magazines.

Dozois is primarily a short story writer, having published only two novels. The first, *Nightmare Blue* (1975), is an SF adventure novel written in collaboration with George Alec EFFINGER. The other, *Strangers* (1978), deals with the misunderstandings that doom the love affair between an Earthman and an alien. Dozois's short stories have appeared in *Playboy*, *Penthouse*, and *Omni*, as well as the usual genre magazines and original anthologies. They have been Nebula finalists six times, been Hugo finalists four times, and won two Nebula Awards. Dozois's story about the melting of the polar ice caps and the evangelists who take over the heartland of the former United States, "The Peacemaker," won the Nebula short story award in 1983, and "Morning Child" won the award in 1985. A collection of his early fiction, *The Visible Man*, was published in 1977.

Dozois succeeded Lester DEL REY as editor of Dutton's *Best Science Fiction Stories of the Year* on the strength of his earlier anthologies, *A Day in the Life* (1972) and *Future Power* (with Jack DANN, 1976). Dozois edited five issues before Dutton dropped the series, but Bluejay Books (succeeded by Tor) picked him as editor of a new *The Year's Best Science Fiction*, in which he had a substantial 250,000 words at his disposal to bolster the volume's growing reputation as the leading annual survey of the field. Dozois's greatest visibility and influence may have arrived, however, when he was named editor of ISAAC ASIMOV'S SCIENCE FICTION MAGAZINE, succeeding Shawna McCarthy in mid-1985.

J.E.G.

DRAKE, DAVID [ALLEN] (1945–   ). American writer of action science fiction. Born in Dubuque, Iowa, Drake received his B.A. with honors in history and Latin from the University of Iowa in 1967 and his law degree from Duke University in 1972. Before retiring from the law, he was assistant town attorney (1972–1980) in Chapel Hill, North Carolina, where he still resides. Since his first sale to August DERLETH's anthology *Travellers by Night* (1966), he has produced four collections and more than twelve novels, and edited several reprint anthologies.

Drake's most popular works are his tales of hard-bitten interstellar mercenaries (*Hammer's Slammers*, 1979/1987; *At Any Price*, 1985; and *Counting the Cost*, 1987), which draw on his historical knowledge and Vietnam experience. His background in the classics is well displayed in *Ranks of Bronze* (1986) and *Cross the Stars* (1984), which retells Homer's *Odyssey*. Drake excels at SF spy thrillers (*Fortress*, 1987) and adventure yarns (*Time Safari*, 1982). In addition, he is a core participant in Janet Morris's shared universe, Heroes in Hell, and has designed one of his own, The Fleet, with Bill Fawcett.

Whatever its subject matter, the keynote of Drake's fiction is realism—grim, gory, and historically accurate. Operating in brutally vivid settings, his heroes are imperfect men in an imperfect universe where the driving force of morality is loyalty to one's group or task.

OTHER WORKS: *The Dragon Lord* (1979); *Skyripper* (1983); *From the Heart of Darkness* (1983); *Birds of Prey* (1984); *Forlorn Hope* (1984); *Killer* (with Karl Edward Wagner, 1985); *Active Measures* (with Janet Morris, 1985): *Bridgehead* (1986); *Lacey and Friends* (1986); *Kill Ratio* (with Janet Morris, 1987).

S.L.M.

DUNCAN, DAVID (1913–).

American writer of fiction, teleplays, and screenplays. Duncan's reputation in science fiction rests on his ability to evoke his readers' sympathy for his characters and their conflicts. In *Dark Dominion* (1954), for example, he created an emotional story of the effect on scientists of their work on a secret military project in space. The novel was well before its time in the use of rounded characters and in the detailed description of their responses to events. Similarly, in *Occam's Razor* (1957) Duncan combined the mystery story with SF to explore the human consequences of the visit of two aliens to Earth; in *Beyond Eden* (1955; published in Britain as *Another Tree in Eden*, 1956), he examined the distrustful relationship that generally exists between scientists and the rest of humanity.

Duncan has also written such "classic" sci-fi screenplays as THE MONSTER THAT CHALLENGED THE WORLD (1957), *The Thing That Couldn't Die* (1958), MONSTER ON THE CAMPUS (1958), and *The Leech Woman* (with Ben Pivar and Francis Rosenwald, 1960). He is responsible as well for the screen adaptation of H.G. WELLS's THE TIME MACHINE (1960). Some critics have claimed that Duncan writes his novels in the same way that he writes his screenplays—that the problems he creates for his characters are too easily solved by superficial measures. These critics see little concern in his works for the more philosophical themes of such contemporaries as James BLISH and Edgar PANGBORN. However, Duncan's style and his ability to portray characters make his novels at least entertaining, and his premises are thought provoking.

OTHER WORKS: *The Shade of Time* (1946); *The Madrone Tree* (1949; retitled *Worse Than Murder*, 1954).

S.H.G.

DUNE (1984).

Directed by David Lynch; screenplay by David Lynch; adapted from the novel by Frank Herbert; photographed by Freddie Francis; music by Toto (David Paich, Jeff Porcano, Steve Lukather, Steve Porcano, Mike Porcano). With Kyle MacLachlan, Sean Young, Francesca Annis, Kenneth McMillan, Jurgen Prochnow, Max von Sydow, Sting, Dean Stockwell, Brad Dourif, José Ferrer, Linda Hunt, Freddie Jones, Richard Jordan, Paul Smith, Everett McGill. 137 minutes. Color.

Dune, novel and film, details the rise of a new messiah on a desert planet, played out against a backdrop of planetary and interplanetary intrigue. David Lynch's screenplay compresses Frank HERBERT's massive book but follows the plot line faithfully (perhaps too closely for some viewers and many critics, who complained that they were completely bewildered). But others felt that Lynch's treatment of the film as a historical epic, closer perhaps to *Lawrence of Arabia* or *Intolerance* than to other SF films, was unusual and creditable. Indeed, in

such films details of complex intrigue and even of personal relationships tend to be secondary to a sense of the broad sweep of history.

So it is with *Dune*. Not only is there no way to present adequately all of Herbert's novel on screen, there is no need to. Lynch has created a world—or rather a whole galaxy of worlds—that seems lived in and realistically complex. Not only are the sets (some briefly glimpsed) richly detailed, but they always function solely as the environment for the characters.

The film requires close attention; it is intensely cerebral, both in approach to the script and in style—the action scenes are few and almost perfunctory; Lynch's interest lay elsewhere. He may not have been entirely successful, but he deserves credit for daring to treat this novel as worthy of both an intellectual and an epic approach.

B.W.

DYE, CHARLES (1926–1960).

American writer who published about twenty science-fiction stories, mostly in the Lowndes magazines, between 1950 and 1954. Dye's only novel, *Prisoner of the Skull* (1952), details thrilling encounters between ordinary people and a kind of superman. Dye was married to Katharine MACLEAN from 1951 to 1953, and three of her early stories appeared under his name.

J.H.

E

E.T.: THE EXTRA-TERRESTRIAL (1982).

Directed by Steven Spielberg; screenplay by Melissa Mathison; photographed by Allen Daviau; music by John Williams. With Henry Thomas, Dee Wallace, Peter Coyote, Drew Barrymore, Robert McNaughton, K. C. Martel, Sean Frye, Tom Howell, Erika Eleniak. 115 minutes. Color.

E.T. is the most commercially successful science-fiction movie of all time and also, according to director Steven SPIELBERG, his most personal work, "a whisper from my childhood." Its winsome story of an alien stranded on Earth, befriended and cared for by a boy, is visually constructed with such skill that, like STAR WARS, *E.T.* became a cultural event, complete with the marketing of merchandise.

The movie's benevolent extraterrestrial is quite the opposite of the threatening aliens typical of SF cinema. In *E.T.* the classic premise of the alien encounter is transformed into an unabashedly sentimental film fantasy that is perhaps the director's best demonstration to date of his uncanny knack for eliciting and manipulating audience response. Spielberg emotionally saturated his simple tale of "boy meets creature, boy loses creature, creature saves boy, boy saves creature," as he has described it, to create a film that, if not entirely coherent in its narrative, nevertheless has moved millions to watch it through moist eyes.

Spielberg achieved his emotional effects in part by cleverly maintaining the point of view of the twelve-year-old hero; indeed, much of the film is shot from waist level. So the suburban spaces where the action unfolds are visually presented as banal in daylight, mysterious at night—the typical perceptions of a twelve-year-old. And the forest where E.T. finds himself at the beginning of the movie is reminiscent of a Disney landscape—in fact, this is only one of many references in the film to the works of Walt Disney.

On a more general level, the alien represents the faith, optimism, and imagination that for Spielberg are special qualities of childhood: the children can soar lyrically through the sky on their bicycles with E.T.'s help, in marked contrast to the images of containment represented by the adult world, among them the hermetically sealed plastic tubes of the government scientists.

E.T. is escapist SF fare at its best. When E.T. holds his sickly hand out to Elliott's mother for help, adults as well as children are touched. Although E.T. is perhaps unsuccessful as an alien life-form in the best tradition of SF film, he suits this film's purpose extraordinarily well.

B.K.G.

EARTH VS. THE FLYING SAUCERS (1956).
Directed by Fred F. Sears; screenplay by George Worthing Yates and Raymond T. Marcus (Marcus fronting for the blacklisted Bernard Gordon); photographed by Fred Jackman, Jr.; musical direction by Mischa Bakaleinikoff. With Hugh Marlowe, Joan Taylor, Donald Curtis, Morris Ankrum, Thomas Browne Henry, John Zaremba, Grandon Rhodes, Harry Lauter. 83 minutes. Black and white.

The scenes of the flying saucers attacking Washington, DC, in this cut-rate imitation of THE WAR OF THE WORLDS are so spectacular and entertaining that they make an otherwise pedestrian film watchable. The second collaboration between producer Charles H. Schneer and Ray HARRYHAUSEN, *Earth vs. the Flying Saucers* suffers from a badly written and structurally clumsy script; almost all the saucer action takes place in the opening and closing reels. The middle portion introduces unnecessary plot elements (for example, space suits of solidified electricity) perhaps just to add running time.

Aliens in flying saucers try to contact human beings, but they literally talk too fast; it isn't until a tape-recorded message is accidentally slowed down that the aliens' peaceful intentions are known. By this time Earth is al-

Earth vs. the Flying Saucers

ready at war with them, and the aliens decide to take over. They're on the verge of doing so when the hero devises a means of disabling the sleek saucers, and they plunge spectacularly into a series of Washington landmarks.

In his many other films, Harryhausen used his stop-motion animation effects to create strange creatures; here he applied the technique to nonliving machines, and the results are among his most impressive work. Until CLOSE ENCOUNTERS OF THE THIRD KIND (1977) these were the best UFOs in movie history: purposeful, deadly, elegant, and sinister. Without Harryhausen's saucers, *Earth vs. the Flying Saucers* would be merely another standard SF film of the period; with them, it is entertaining and interesting. These effects were also used in other films, including THE 27TH DAY (1957) and Orson Welles's *F Is for Fake* (1973).

B.W.

———————— ECOLOGY ————————

Ecology is the study of the relations between organisms and their environment—in large measure the study of relations between different species whose fortunes are in some way linked, often via food chains. The discipline acquired its name quite recently; the first important books on the subject appeared in the 1920s. Since then we have learned a great deal about the intricacy of ecological relations, and matters of human ecology have been forced into the political arena as technology has given us the power to make increasingly radical transformations of the environment. The possible exhaustion of soils by modern agricultural techniques; the pollution of the environment by heavy metals, "acid rain," new organic poisons, and radioactive wastes; and the possibility of affecting the biosphere's carbon dioxide recycling systems by burning fossil fuels and deforestation—all are ecological issues of political significance. The urgency some individuals feel about such issues has brought into being "green" political parties in several European nations, and that same urgency has been an important influence on science fiction's images of the near future.

Distaste for the way the march of civilization affects the environment and puts everyday life into an artificial environment is not new. English Romantic poets such as William Blake and William Wordsworth were fearful of "dark, satanic mills"; Richard Jefferies's *After London; Or, Wild England* (1885) and W. H. Hudson's *A Crystal Age* (1887) both look forward to futures from which cities have been obliterated, and the latter yearns for a special kind of mystical harmony between humanity and nature that is also exemplified in the heroine of Hudson's lush novel *Green Mansions* (1904). Such anxiety was always present in British scientific romance, despite the fact that its leading figure, H. G. WELLS, had little patience with pastoral nostalgia. E. M. FORSTER's "The Machine Stops" (1909) and John GLOAG's *The New Pleasure* (1933) are equally eloquent, though in very different ways, in championing the idea of a retreat from technology toward a "more natural" way of life. The long struggle between the technological and pastoral ideals has been discussed in detail in Leo Marx's *The Machine in the Garden* (1964).

Such nostalgia is not so obvious in early American SF, although something of it can be found in V. T. Sutphen's *The Doomsman* (1906), and Edgar Rice BURROUGHS did provide in the character of Tarzan an unparalleled champion of the wild. The last two decades, though, have seen a considerable renaissance of this kind of nostalgia in both British and American SF; the most striking examples include the trilogy begun with *The Road to Corlay* (1978) by Richard Cowper, *Engine Summer* (1979) by John Crowley, and *Juniper Time* (1979) by Kate WILHELM.

Ecological thinking was largely absent from early pulp SF. Most pulp writers were perfectly happy to populate other worlds with nasty predators without giving a thought to the herds of herbivores necessary to provide them with a staple diet. The writer who first discovered that there is a certain aesthetic delight in constructing alien life systems that might make some kind of crazy ecological sense was Stanley G. WEINBAUM; he used such insight to enliven stories such as "The Mad Moon" (1935) and "Parasite Planet" (1935). From their publication on, the construction of bizarre alien life systems was a game played by many writers. Another early adept was Clifford SIMAK (also, during the 1940s, the pulp SF writer who preserved the strongest nostalgic feelings for the pastoral), but the 1950s saw considerable sophistication of this kind of exercise. Hal CLEMENT became the foremost expert in designing life systems to fit peculiar physical environments—his expertise is shown off in novels such as *Mission of Gravity* (1953) and *Cycle of Fire* (1957). The latter is one of several notable stories imagining life adapted to seasonal cycles of many generations: others include Poul ANDERSON's *Fire Time* (1974) and Brian W. ALDISS's Helliconia trilogy (1982–1985).

A favorite variant of the alien ecology game is to design life systems to fit ever more extreme circumstances; thus Fred HOYLE adapted life to cosmic dust clouds in *The Black Cloud* (1957), Robert L. FORWARD envisioned life on the surface of a neutron star in *Dragon's Egg* (1980), and Larry NIVEN designed a strange planetless ecosystem in *The Integral Trees* (1983). Another variant is to face human explorers or colonists with puzzles whose solution lies in figuring out something odd about the ecology of the alien life system with which they are confronted; practitioners of this format include Poul Anderson, in *Question and Answer* and *The Night Face* (both 1978 under these titles, although both originally date from the mid-1950s), and Brian STABLEFORD, in the six-volume Daedalus series (1976–1979) and *The Gates of Eden* (1983). Other examples are Michael Coney's *Syzygy* (1973) and John BRUNNER's *Total Eclipse* (1974).

A remarkably common theme in alien ecology stories is the alien life system that is much more closely integrated than Earth's ecosphere and in which the "balance of nature" is much more carefully preserved. We find this theme in Richard McKENNA's "Hunter Come Home" (1963), Gordon R. DICKSON's "Twig" (1974), and Robert F. YOUNG's *The Last Yggdrasil* (1982; based on a 1959 short story); we also find it in stories of vast alien life systems that are effectively single organisms, such as the forest in Ursula K. LE GUIN's "Vaster Than Empires and More Slow" (1971), the Earth-invading Indigo in Doris PISERCHIA's *Earthchild* (1977), and Gaea in John VARLEY's Titan trilogy (1979–1984). A metaphysical integration of earthly species is featured in Frank HERBERT's *The Green Brain* (1966).

These images of intimately integrated ecospheres are often imbued with a kind of mystical awe—if humans disrupt them, their crime is seen almost as blasphemy, and if humans can join them, the union is a kind of triumphal transcendence. There is a tendency to represent the presumed harmony of these imaginary ecospheres as a symbol of something that human beings tragically lack; the idea that we could gain (or recover) such a warm and intimate relationship with our world has close connections with certain religious ideas. Thus SF has developed in recent years a mythology of "ecological mysticism." One of the most striking early examples of this was Mark Clifton's *Eight Keys to Eden* (1960), and many subsequent examples also draw on the Christian myth of the Garden of Eden. Other examples of the metaphoric use of alien ecologies are Piers ANTHONY's *Omnivore* (1968), John BOYD's *Pollinators of Eden* (1969), and the STRUGATSKY brothers' *The Snail on the Slope* (translated into English 1980); the mystical ritualization of ecological dependencies can be found in Robert A. HEINLEIN's *Stranger in a Strange Land* (1961) and in Frank Herbert's *Dune* (1965); and a sense of spiritual awe penetrates such political tracts as Ernest Callenbach's *Ecotopia* (1975) and Scott Russell Sanders's *Terrarium* (1985). A more skeptical treatment of this mythology can be found in Brian Stableford's *The Walking Shadow* (1979).

The idea that humanity's transformations of the surface of the Earth might lead to a massive disruption of the ecosphere, and possibly to a chain reaction of disasters, increasingly affected images of the future in the 1950s. Anxiety about soil exhaustion was expressed as early as 1938 in A. G. Street's *Already Walks Tomorrow*, and J. J. Connington had envisioned the consequences to humanity of a devastating crop disease in *Nordenholt's Million* (1923). These anxieties receive more alarmist treatment in Edward Hyams's *The Astrologer* (1950) and John CHRISTOPHER's *No Blade of Grass* (1956), and C. M. KORNBLUTH's bleak "Shark Ship" (1959) features the idea of a more generalized "ecocatastrophe." In the 1960s anxiety about the population explosion and the effects of environmental pollution grew rapidly, and ecocatastrophe stories became more extreme, reaching a climax in Philip WYLIE's *The End of the Dream* (1972) and Trevor Hoyle's elaborate account *The Last Gasp* (1983). This anxiety is also strongly reflected in the scripts written for the British television series *Doomwatch* (1970–1972), which produced such spin-off ecocatastrophe stories as *Mutant 59: The Plastic Eater* (1972) and *Brainrack* (1974), both by the series's creators, Kit Pedler and Gerry Davis.

Many ecocatastrophe stories lean toward bitter black comedy, suggesting that if civilization comes to an end because human beings have carelessly wrecked their environment, then we will be getting exactly what we deserve. This kind of righteous rage—the other side of the coin of concern that produces ecological mysticism—is expressed in such stories as James BLISH's "We All Die Naked" (1969) and Kurt VONNEGUT's "The Big Space Fuck" (1972).

A much more subtle kind of catastrophe story deals with small changes in the environment that have considerable significance for humankind. An early example is H. F. HEARD's "The Great Fog" (1944), in which a mutant mildew causes perpetual fog at the Earth's surface, and human civilization must adapt to the new lack of visibility. Here the dismantling of our high-speed civ-

ilization becomes an important lesson in humility, and something of the same reservation of judgment exists in the catastrophe stories of J. G. BALLARD, especially *The Drowned World* (1962) and *The Drought* (1965). This lack of regret for the eclipse of civilization is not as prevalent in stories by American writers, although *The Year of the Cloud* (1970) by Theodore L. THOMAS and Kate Wilhelm belongs to this subspecies.

Ecological questions are deeply embedded in the SF writer's methods of extrapolation. It would nowadays be unacceptable for writers to imagine humans establishing themselves on an alien world without having to overcome, one way or another, problems of ecological adaptation. We have come to recognize the extremes to which we might have to go in fitting human beings for life in exotic environments, whether by genetic engineering, as in James Blish's *The Seedling Stars* (1957), or by cyborgization, as in Frederik POHL's *Man Plus* (1976).

Some writers, of course, invert the problem and imagine that we will use organic instruments to adapt the exotic environments to our needs—a process dubbed "terraforming" by Jack WILLIAMSON. The idea of terraforming Mars or Venus has always been tempting to SF writers and is featured in many SF stories, including Arthur C. CLARKE's *The Sands of Mars* (1951), Frederik Pohl and Cyril M. Kornbluth's *The Space Merchants* (1953, also featuring a satiric vision of advertising fueling a high-consumption world of growing scarcities, opposed by an underground group of conservationists called "consies"), and Pamela SARGENT's *Venus of Dreams* (1986).

A key aspect of utopian thought in contemporary SF is the presumption that the ideal society must maintain some kind of sustainable balance in its use and control of the environment. For many writers this viewpoint has tied the idea of utopia to that of a partial retreat from technology—examples include Norman SPINRAD in *Songs from the Stars* (1980) and Ursula K. Le Guin in *Always Coming Home* (1986). For others it implies bringing the entire world ecosphere under technical control and management: the Earth as a fabulous garden. Brian Stableford and David Langford featured this kind of ecological management in the SF mock history *The Third Millennium* (1985).

Whether any of the European green parties ever gains power, the importance of ecological issues in politics can hardly diminish, and questions of "conservation" have become a major source of inspiration for ordinary people to involve themselves in political demonstrations and pressure groups. These trends are certain to sustain the importance of such questions in futuristic fictions, and recent novels such as Williamson's *Firechild* (1986) suggest that ecological mysticism has by no means reached its peak of intensity.

B.S.

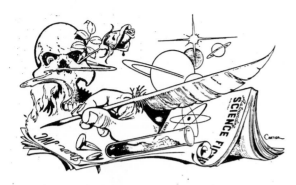

BRASS TACKS·

Masthead for John W. Campbell's letters-to-the-editor column in *Astounding Science Fiction* (art by Edd Cartier)

--- EDITORS ---

Editors rarely receive adequate credit for their contributions to the success of authors or publications. This is especially true in science fiction, where editors have exerted an unusual influence. Much of SF's development has come through marginal magazines and publishing operations in which the commitment and methods of editors have been crucial, and because the magazines were virtually the only place SF could be found between 1926 and 1946, the writers favored by editors prospered, their kind of SF flourished, and what editors chose to publish became, by definition, what SF was. As John W. CAMPBELL once remarked, "Science fiction is what science-fiction editors publish."

Even before the existence of SF magazines, editors were important to the nurturing of the genre that was to become SF. Alfred Jerome Hart (1854–1907) published hundreds of fantasies between 1880 and 1907 in the San Francisco magazine *Argonaut*. William Randolph Hearst hired some of them away for his *San Francisco Examiner*, added Ambrose BIERCE and Garrett P. SERVISS, and reprinted work by Europe's masters. Robert Hobart Davis (1869–1942) was generous in his publication of SF in Munsey's early-twentieth-century adventure pulp magazines, *Argosy, All-Story*, and *Cavalier*.

Even Bernarr Macfadden incorporated utopian works in his muscle magazine *Physical Culture* and confession magazine *True Story* beginning in 1904; this fact may explain his attempt to purchase and then obtain through other means Hugo GERNSBACK's AMAZING STORIES in 1929.

Harold Hersey (1893–1956) became the first editor of an SF-like magazine in Street & Smith's *Thrill Book*, whose "notice to writers" asked for "strange, bizarre, occult, mysterious tales . . . containing mystic happen-

ings, weird adventures, feats of leger-de-main, spiritualism, etc." In 1930 Hersey took over Macfadden's *Ghost Stories* and the next year brought out two issues of *Miracle Science and Fantasy Stories*. In 1936 he published one issue of *Flash Gordon Strange Adventure Magazine*.

Weird Tales, which became the first all-fantasy magazine in the United States in March 1923, was edited briefly by Edwin Baird, but Farnsworth Wright (1888–1940) took over with the November 1924 number. The magazine ran several "weird-scientific" stories in each issue, and published the first hardcover SF anthology, *The Moon Terror*, in 1927. Wright discovered or developed many writers, including H. P. LOVECRAFT, Clark Ashton SMITH, Robert E. HOWARD, and Seabury QUINN.

The most important SF editor must be Luxembourg-born Hugo Gernsback (1884–1967). After emigrating to the United States in 1904 at the age of nineteen, Gernsback engaged in radio-oriented businesses and issued a radio parts catalog; that enterprise gave him the idea for the earliest radio magazine, *Modern Electrics* (1908). To fill a hole in that magazine, he wrote a novel of the future and interplanetary travel, *Ralph 124C 41+*, which began in the April 1911 issue and ran for twelve installments. It was filled with scientific prophecy.

Before selling the magazine to *Popular Science*, Gernsback created *Electrical Experimenter* in 1913 as a companion (the name was changed to *Science and Invention* in 1920), and he soon began publishing SF by himself and others, an enterprise that culminated in a "Scientific Fiction Issue" for August 1923 with five SF stories and an SF cover by Howard V. BROWN. Gernsback was working up to creating the first SF magazine, *Amazing Stories*, which debuted in April 1926. It had three editors, C. A. Brandt, a major SF collector; Wilbur C. Whitehead, better known as a bridge expert; and T. O'Conor SLOANE, who became managing editor.

Starting as a reprint magazine, mostly of works by Edgar Allan POE, Jules VERNE, and H. G. WELLS, *Amazing Stories* soon attracted authors who had been working for the pulp adventure magazines, for *Weird Tales*, and for *Science and Invention*, and new authors, such as E. E. SMITH and Jack WILLIAMSON. Most of the covers and interiors were done by the Austrian-born illustrator and draftsman Frank R. PAUL.

Forced into involuntary bankruptcy in 1929 by a legal technicality, Gernsback created a new group of SF magazines, *Science Wonder Stories, Air Wonder Stories, Science Wonder Quarterly*, and *Scientific Detective Monthly*. Editor David Lasser (1902–   ), an MIT graduate, answered an ad in the *New York Times*. He introduced many new writers, including Clifford SIMAK, John Beynon Harris (John WYNDHAM), and Laurence MANNING, but his major claims to fame were his founding in 1930 of The American Interplanetary Society, writing the first book on space travel in English, *The Conquest of Space* (1931), and staking a claim for SF's contribution to space travel.

Lasser was fired in·1933 for spending excessive time on socialist, technocratic, and welfare activities (he became head of the Workers Alliance of America), and Gernsback hired the seventeen-year-old Charles D. HORNIG (1916–   ) because he was impressed by Hornig's letterpress fan magazine, *The Fantasy Fan*. (He also could pay him one-third Lasser's salary.) Under Hornig a "New Story Policy" was introduced, Stanley G. WEINBAUM was discovered, and the Science Fiction League, which developed into today's SF FANDOM, was launched. Hornig's last issue was in April 1936, when *Wonder Stories*, into which three magazines had been incorporated, was sold to Beacon Magazines, a subsidiary of Standard Publications.

Meanwhile, T. O'Conor Sloane (1851–1940), who had stayed behind to edit *Amazing Stories* at the age of seventy-eight, held on to most of the publication's regulars and maintained it as the leading SF magazine at least through 1932, publishing new writers such as John W. Campbell, Jr., Eando BINDER, and John Russell FEARN, but alienating other writers by holding manuscripts (without purchasing them) for as long as five years. In 1938 the magazine was sold to Ziff-Davis.

Amazing Stories and then *Wonder Stories* in its several versions attracted the interest of W. M. Clayton, whose Clayton Magazine chain was publishing thirteen pulps. In 1930, to economize on covers, Clayton started an SF magazine, *Astounding Stories of Super Science*, at the suggestion of Harry BATES (1900–1981), whom he made editor. Bates was also an effective writer then and later.

Astounding, with its ragged edges, covers with many monsters, and high pay rates for low-grade action fiction from well-known authors, was the first true SF pulp in the sense that it grew out of the pulp tradition rather than Gernsback's popular-science background (see PULP MAGAZINES). A companion magazine of supernatural fiction, *Strange Tales*, was more literary. Both magazines were suspended in 1933.

Street & Smith bought *Astounding* in 1933 and hired F. Orlin TREMAINE (1899–1956) as editor. Desmond Hall, who had been assistant editor to Bates (and his sometime collaborator), resumed that role until 1934, when he was transferred to a position at *Mademoiselle*. Street & Smith's resources allowed Tremaine to recruit writers from other publications, discover such new writers as L. Sprague DE CAMP, Eric Frank RUSSELL, and Ross ROCKLYNNE, and raise the quality of the SF short story. Tremaine was promoted to editorial director over several publications and hired editors for each of them. John W. Campbell, Jr. (1910–1971), who was struggling to make a living as a writer, was delighted to edit *Astounding* for thirty dollars a week.

Campbell, who had been writing superscience stories under his own name and more artistic stories under the pseudonym of Don A. Stuart, shifted *Astounding*'s emphasis to the psychological and philosophical implications of future developments; the impact of change on politics, business, war, government, and religion; and the place of slavery, monarchies, feudalism, and empires in the future. His interest was in better writing, in which background is suggested indirectly, and he reshaped the work of established writers such as Jack Williamson, Clifford D. Simak, Eric Frank Russell, and L. Ron HUBBARD, and developed new authors such as Robert A. HEINLEIN, Theodore STURGEON, Isaac ASIMOV, and A. E. VAN VOGT. From 1939 to 1945 he created what his admirers have called the GOLDEN AGE of SF.

He also created a short-lived but much praised magazine of rationalized fantasy, *Unknown* (1939–1943), which he characterized as "Fairy Tales for Grown-ups." Perhaps this openness to unusual ideas, illustrated by his acceptance of stories based on the offbeat premises of Charles FORT, helps explains his later embrace of "science we don't understand," such as Dianetics, psionics, the Dean (antigravity) drive, water dowsing, and levitation.

At the other extreme was Raymond A. PALMER (1910–1977), named editor of *Amazing* by Ziff-Davis in 1938. He turned the magazine to a policy of action stories with simplistic themes, created a companion magazine, *Fantastic Adventures*, brought back the work of Edgar Rice BURROUGHS, developed a stable of writers from whom he bought at a fixed rate whatever they wrote, sometimes, reputedly, without reading it. The most notorious among these authors was Richard S. SHAVER (most of whose material Palmer is said to have written himself); Palmer credited Shaver's "mystery" about demonlike creatures living in caves under the Earth with adding 50,000 readers. In 1949 Palmer founded his own magazine, *Other Worlds*, and left *Amazing*.

Two of Palmer's regulars, Howard Browne and Paul Fairman, succeeded him. Browne briefly tried to produce the first SF slick-quality magazine with comparatively high rates, but he was forced to return to the stable-of-writers concept. Cele Goldsmith (1933–   ), hired as an assistant two years before, became editor in 1958, the first woman SF editor of a nonreprint magazine. She opened the magazine to general contributions, publishing the first stories of Ursula K. LE GUIN, Roger ZELAZNY, and Piers ANTHONY as well as British authors Brian W. ALDISS, J. G. BALLARD, John BRUNNER, and James WHITE. She also published articles about SF and its authors by Sam MOSKOWITZ.

Beacon/Standard changed the name of *Wonder Stories* to *Thrilling Wonder Stories;* added a companion magazine, *Startling Stories;* and a year later introduced *Captain Future*. Leo Margulies (1900–1975), as editorial director, was in charge of as many as forty-five magazines and hired a pool of editors to work on them, including Mort WEISINGER, Jerome BIXBY, H. L. GOLD, Oscar J. Friend, Sam Merwin, Jr., and Samuel Mines. Margulies judged an editor's worth by how much he rewrote a story, and the magazines got the reputation of being outrageously overedited, a tradition that Gold would carry over into the pages of *Galaxy*. But Weisinger and the others produced colorful, well-illustrated, and well-written magazines, often the best in the field, particularly after World War II.

Louis Silberkleit, who had once worked for Gernsback and later founded a pulp chain called Blue Ribbon Publications, entered SF in 1939 with *Science Fiction*, edited by Hornig, and added two companion magazines, *Future Fiction* and *Science Fiction Quarterly*. Robert A. W. LOWNDES (1916–   ), a member of the FUTURIANS, was hired to replace Hornig in 1940, and with a tiny editorial budget he filled the magazines with stories by his Futurian friends under a variety of pen names. Both Frederik POHL, when he became editor of Popular Publications's *Astonishing Stories* and *Super Science Stories* (at a salary of ten dollars a week) earlier that year, and Donald A. WOLLHEIM, when he convinced Albing Publications in 1941 to let him create *Stirring Science Stories* and *Cosmic Stories* at no salary and an editorial budget of zero, did likewise. Wollheim convinced professional writers to let him publish their work free as he had been doing in his fan magazines.

Wollheim went on to edit the *Pocket Book of Science Fiction* (1943) and *Portable Novels of Science* (1945), *The Avon Fantasy Reader* (1947–1952), *The Avon Science Fiction Reader* (1951–1952), *Out of This World Adventures* (1954–1955), and *10 Story Fantasy* (1951) before becoming editor of the first significant SF paperback line at Ace Books and then founding his own DAW Books.

In the reprint field Wollheim's competition was *Famous Fantastic Mysteries* (1939–1953) and its companion *Fantastic Novels* (1940–41, 1948–1951), both edited by Mary Gnaedinger and composed of reprints from the Munsey pulp adventure magazines. *Planet Stories* (1940–1955) was subtitled "Strange Adventures on Other Worlds" and lived up to its name, but under sometime editor Malcolm Reiss it also published excellent fiction, including that of Ray BRADBURY and Philip K. DICK.

When the paper shortage ended after World War II, the SF boom resumed. *The Magazine of Fantasy* (with the second issue, *and Science Fiction*) was created by editors Anthony BOUCHER (1911–1968) and J. Francis McCOMAS (1911–1978). They emphasized literary qualities, fantasy, and reprints and published the first stories of Richard MATHESON and others, plus the novelettes that formed the basis of *A Canticle for Leibowitz* by Walter MILLER, Jr., and Daniel KEYES's "Flowers for Algernon." Boucher was followed by Robert P. Mills, Avram DAVIDSON, and the then owner Joseph Ferman, before

the magazine was taken over by Ferman's son Edward (1937–   ) in 1965.

The most direct competition to Campbell's *Astounding* was GALAXY SCIENCE FICTION, founded in 1950 by H. L. Gold (1914–   ), who had published fiction in *Astounding* in the 1930s under the name Clyde Crane Campbell and edited for Margulies. Gold wanted an emphasis on social science fiction and psychology, on people who are forced to cope with change rather than those who create it. Like Campbell, he worked closely with writers and got new work out of older writers, such as Alfred BESTER's pyrotechnical *The Demolished Man* (1952/1953) and *The Stars My Destination* (1956). He also established Frederik POHL as a major writer, particularly with his collaborations with Cyril M. KORNBLUTH beginning with *Gravy Planet* (1952; as *The Space Merchants*, 1953).

Illness forced Gold's retirement in 1961, and he was replaced by Pohl, who became one of the field's best and most honored editors, not only with *Galaxy* but with companion magazine *If*. Pohl went back to full-time writing when the magazines were sold to Universal Publishing in 1969, and *Galaxy* was edited by Ejler Jakobsson and then Jim Baen before being sold to the publishers of the subscription magazine *Galileo*, who never recovered from their efforts to obtain newsstand distribution.

By the early 1970s the magazines had lost their primary position in the field; they had been superseded by the burgeoning book market, which would increase its publications from less than 400 in 1972 to more than 1200 in 1979. The role of the editors diminished, but to the credit of the field and the benefit of new writers trying to break into print and develop their talents, the SF magazines continued to be published and retained a following while nearly all the other pulp magazines disappeared.

Astounding Stories had been changed by Campbell to *Astounding Science Fiction* and then to *Analog* in 1965. Campbell died in 1971 and was replaced, after an extensive search, by author Ben BOVA (1932–   ), whose effective editing won him in 1978 the position of fiction editor and later executive editor of *Omni* before he returned to full-time writing. He was replaced at *Analog* by Stanley SCHMIDT, a writer who had been discovered by Campbell and an equally competent editor.

Lowndes returned to SF in 1950 with *Future Fiction*, to which he added *Science Fiction Quarterly*, *Dynamic Science Fiction*, and *Science Fiction Stories*, which struggled to survive for ten years. Beginning in 1963 he published a series of predominantly reprint magazines: *The Magazine of Horror, Startling Mystery Stories* (which published the first story by Stephen KING), *Famous Science Fiction, Weird Terror Tales*, and *Bizarre Fantasy Tales*.

In the 1970s the outstanding success was ISAAC ASI-

MOV'S SCIENCE FICTION MAGAZINE, issued by the publishers of *Ellery Queen's Mystery Magazine;* it soon rivaled *Analog* in circulation and prestige (*Analog* was to be bought by the same publisher). George Scithers (1929–   ), a Philadelphia fan, was the first editor; he was followed, after a brief interim editor, by Shawna McCarthy and then Gardner DOZOIS.

The first British SF magazine was *Scoops,* which in 1934 published twenty issues of a weekly for juveniles edited by Hadyn Dimmock (?–?). Walter Gillings (1912–1979), a newspaperman and fanzine editor, in 1937 induced Worlds Work in London to publish sixteen issues of *Tales of Wonder.* Although heavily dependent on American reprints, the magazine also published the work of British writers, including the first story of Arthur C. CLARKE. After World War II, Gillings created *Fantasy,* "the Magazine of Science Fiction," with predominantly new British fiction.

A prominent early fan, Edward J. Carnell (1912–1972) convinced Pendulum Publications in 1946 to produce three issues of NEW WORLDS before raising his own financing to produce 141 more numbers, along with a companion magazine for 81 issues, *Science Fantasy.* Between these two publications he discovered or developed a cadre of British SF writers, including Brian W. ALDISS, J. G. BALLARD, John BRUNNER, Michael MOORCOCK, James WHITE, J. T. MCINTOSH, E. C. TUBB, Ken BULMER, Ian Wright, and many more.

Declining fortunes led to the sale of *New Worlds* in 1964 to Roberts & Vintner, which put Moorcock (1939–   ) in charge. He made the magazine an avant-garde publication with stories that experimented with technique and subject. This approach came to be called the NEW WAVE, although many of its leaders were former Carnell authors. Much of Moorcock's effort was devoted to finding new publishers, distributors, government grants, and donations, and he himself wrote for others an endless stream of nonexperimental material to finance the publication before it finally died in 1978 as a paperback.

S.M.

George Alec Effinger

people faced by strange events or innovations, as in *Chapayeca* (1971). He has written several western novels under the pseudonym Kelly P. Gast and other novels and nonfiction books under several other names.

OTHER WORKS: *T.H.E.M.* (1974); *The Aluminum Man* (1975); *The Man Who Corrupted the Earth* (1980); *Star Slaver* (with Andrew J. Offutt as John Cleve, 1983); *The Takeover* (with C. M. Kotlan, 1984); *The Cunningham Equations* (with C. M. Kotlan, 1986); *The Black Magician* (with C. M. Kotlan, 1986).

R.S.C.

EDMONDSON, G. C. (Born José Mario Gary Ordooñez Edmondson Y Cotton) (1922–   ).

American author and blacksmith. Edmondson's first publication was "Blessed Are the Meek" (1955) in *Astounding.* His best-known work, *The Ship That Sailed the Time Stream* (1965), originally published with a collection of his short stories, *Stranger Than You Think,* is a novel about a ship that is sent back to the Viking era when a homemade still is struck by lightning; it was expanded for a 1978 edition, and a sequel, *To Sail the Century Sea,* was published in 1981. His work, primarily action stories, nevertheless features flashes of wit and lifelike, fallible characters. Born in Mexico, Edmondson often deals with the plight of simple Indian

EFFINGER, GEORGE ALEC (1947–   ).

American writer, mostly of science fiction bordering on surrealism. After attending Yale and New York universities, Effinger entered SF through the Clarion Writers' Workshop in 1970, graduating to full-time writing in 1971. Much of his writing has consisted of work for *Marvel Comics* and novelizations of the TV series *Planet of the Apes: Man the Fugitive* (1974), *Escape to Tomorrow* (1975), *Journey into Terror* (1975), and *Lord of the Apes* (1976). His first novel, *What Entropy Means to Me* (1972), attracted significant attention from reviewers and from fellow members of SCIENCE FICTION WRITERS OF AMERICA, who nominated it for a Nebula Award.

A resident of New Orleans who has suffered from periodic bouts of illness and ill fortune (he lost a group of unfinished short stories in a 1986 apartment fire), Effinger excels at the shorter lengths, where his combination of traditional SF furniture with elements of the absurd, along with the density of his style, does not try the attention span or patience of his readers. He attempts, he has said, "to do new things with old material. . . . Perhaps surreal fantasy describes these stories best."

His work is also distinguished by a rotating cast of characters, recycled from previous works without regard for their earlier careers or fates. Sandor Courane, for instance, appears in half a dozen stories or novels, like his other characters offering Effinger "a private stable of stereotypes to draw upon."

His best-known early work, *What Entropy Means to Me*, features four different interwoven stories, the most prominent being the search for his father by an eldest son; the least obvious of the stories takes the form of that son's commentary about the writing of this particular story. In 1986 Effinger produced a novel, *When Gravity Fails*, that has been described as "the best example of the cyberpunk *oeuvre* to date." Although it features a plugged-in, gritty, streetwise reality, it is placed in the Arab world.

OTHER WORKS: *Relatives* (1973); *Mixed Feelings* (collection, 1974); *Nightmare Blue* (with Gardner Dozois, 1975); *Irrational Numbers* (collection, 1976); *Those Gentle Voices* (1976); *Death in Florence* (1978; as *Utopia 3*, 1980); *Dirty Tricks* (collection, 1978); *Heroics* (1979); *The Wolves of Memory* (1981); *Idle Pleasures* (collection, 1983); *The Bird of Time* (1985).

J.E.G.

EHRLICH, MAX [SIMON] (1909–1983).
American mainstream author, journalist, and screenwriter whose science fiction, like his screenplays, most often concerns human characters facing strange, often chilling dilemmas based on contemporary social and political problems. For example, *The Edict* (1971, a novelization of his screenplay *Z.P.G.*) is a haunting story of overpopulation in which a young woman defies a ban on childbearing in a world of scant food supplies and little space. Ehrlich refused to romanticize her decision, but he also recognized the need to have children as a natural, humanizing drive that cannot and should not be denied. The novel ends with a solution that allows the woman to keep her child but leaves open the larger problem of how that society should manage its population.

Ehrlich's first novel, *The Big Eye* (1949), accurately evokes contemporary American cold war fears of nuclear devastation as a group of astronomers fabricates the story that an approaching planet will hit the Earth. Their collective hoax is intended to frighten the competing governments into cooperative action, thereby ushering in an era of peace.

Ehrlich's best-known work is his novelization of his screenplay *The Reincarnation of Peter Proud* (1974). Like its sequel, *Reincarnation in Venice* (1979; published in Britain as *The Bond*, 1980), this story of dream research is a suspenseful thriller that deals more with horror than with science fiction.

OTHER WORKS: *Spin the Glass Web* (1952); *First Train to Babylon* (1955; retitled *Dead Letter*, 1958, and then *Naked Edge*, 1961); *The Takers* (1961); *Dead Is the Blue* (1964); *The High Side* (1969); *The Savage Is Loose* (1974); *The Cult* (1978); *Naked Beach* (1979).

S.H.G.

EISENSTEIN, PHYLLIS (1946–   ). American
writer and fan. Born Phyllis Kleinstein in Chicago, where she continues to live with her husband, Alex Eisenstein, also a fan, Eisenstein attended the University of Chicago in the 1960s and earned her bachelor's degree in anthropology from the University of Illinois, Chicago, in 1981. Her first story, a collaboration with her husband, was published in *New Dimensions I* (1971); her first novel was *Born to Exile* (1978), a fantasy. She was cofounder and director of the Windy City SF Writers Conference.

Eisenstein is better known for her fantasy than her science fiction, particularly her stories about a minstrel with the power of teleportation named Alaric, which are brought together in *Born to Exile*. Her approach to fantasy, however, in these stories and in *Sorcerer's Son* (1979), is in the pragmatic tradition of John W. CAMPBELL's *Unknown*, with laws for magic resembling those for science. Some of her stories, and her novels *Shadow of Earth* (1979) and *In the Hands of Glory* (1981), are SF, the latter a kind of space opera, the former describing the plight of a contemporary woman thrust into a medieval world.

J.E.G.

EKLUND, GORDON [STEWART] (1945–   ).
American science-fiction writer who became one of the most promising talents of the 1970s but virtually deserted the field in the mid-1980s. Eklund was successful from the start: his first sale, "Dear Aunt Annie" (1970), was a Nebula Award finalist. Ten of his works have been Nebula nominees, and "If the Stars Are Gods" (1974), written with Gregory BENFORD and in 1977 expanded into the novel of the same name, won the Nebula for best novelette. Eklund's output was prolific in the 1970s; his success may, however, have been too meteoric. Some of his stories show an immaturity of style and organization, but for all that, much of his work is exciting and vibrant, including his first book, *The Eclipse of Dawn*

(1971). His best full-length work to date is *All Times Possible* (1974), an interesting exploration of alternate realities. *The Grayspace Beast* (1976), audacious in its style and narration, doesn't quite succeed. Eklund's asset is his ability to ring the changes on standard SF themes, best seen in his shorter works, as in "Points of Contact" (1978), which explores the subject of first contact with an alien species. Recently this talent has not been allowed to develop as Eklund has been commissioned to write a series of STAR TREK novels and an extension of E. E. SMITH's Lord Tedric series.

OTHER WORKS: *A Trace of Dreams* (1972); *Beyond the Resurrection* (1973); *Inheritors of Earth* (with Poul Anderson, 1974); *Serving in Time* (1975); *Falling toward Forever* (1975); *Dance of the Apocalypse* (1976); *The Twilight River* (in *Binary Star 2*, 1979); *The Garden of Winter* (1980).

M.A.

ELGIN, [PATRICIA ANNE] SUZETTE HADEN [Née WILKINS] (1936–).

American speculative satirist, folk musician, and founder of the SCIENCE FICTION POETRY ASSOCIATION. Elgin taught linguistics at San Diego State University before retiring to emeritus status and moving to Arkansas, where she founded the Ozark Center for Language Studies. Her interest in both communication and feminism is reflected in much of her science fiction. Her first published story, "For the Sake of Grace" (1969), depicts the struggles of Jacinth, a genius-poetess, in an antifeminist society. Her Communipath series—consisting of *The Communipaths* (1970), *Furthest* (1971), *At the Seventh Level* (1972), *Communipath Worlds* (a collection of previous works, 1980), and *Star-Anchored, Star-Angered* (1979)—satirizes not only sexism but capitalism and romantic love as well and features superspy–projective telepath Coyote Jones, another of Elgin's strong female protagonists.

Elgin's best characterization and storytelling, however, shine in the Ozark trilogy—*Twelve Fair Kingdoms* (1981), *The Grand Jubilee* (1981), and *And Then There'll Be Fireworks* (1981)—set on the planet Ozark, where folk magic really works. In *Yonder Comes the Other End of Time* (1985), Elgin brought Coyote Jones to Ozark. Typically, all four books explore the psychology of male-female communication.

In *Native Tongue* (1984) women are forced to bear numerous infants, who are bred to learn languages for alien trade. The sequel, *Native Tongue II: The Judas Rose* (1987), describes a woman messiah—one of many in Elgin's oeuvre—who begins the reform of human male violence through the underground feminist language Laadan. Like all Elgin's books, *The Judas Rose* reflects a passionate belief in the power of words and the redemptive nature of feminism.

M.T.B.

ELLIS, DEAN (1920–).

American illustrator, the majority of whose work has appeared on paperback covers for Ace Books, Berkley, Ballantine, Del Rey, and others. Ellis's style is slickly modern and is often compared with the work of John Berkey. It can best be described as Madison Avenue advertising art in space—high-tech machinery depicted with quick, bold brush strokes. While Ellis's paintings appear realistic, closer inspection reveals an impressionist structure. Although his cover for Lester DEL REY's *The Eleventh Commandment,* for example, seems to belie it, he is fond of bright colors; reds, yellows, and oranges predominate in his work.

J.G.

ELLIS, EDWARD S. (1840–1916).

American teacher, editor, and author of numerous dime novels, mostly westerns. One of these, *The Steam Man of the Prairies* (1865, reprinted 1974), was the first American novel to feature a type of robot.

J.H.

ELLISON, HARLAN [JAY] (1934–).

American writer, screenwriter, editor, film and television critic, and lecturer. Arguably the most dynamic and controversial writer associated with the science-fiction genre, and certainly one of its finest and most acclaimed, Ellison has won nine Hugos, three Nebula Awards, four Writers' Guild of America Awards, the British Fantasy Award, and the Mystery Writers of America's Edgar Award, among others. He is primarily a writer of short stories, many of them justly considered classics in the field. But although his stories often display the trappings of SF, Ellison's concerns are universal—how people win and lose; how they succumb to fear, selfishness, complacency, and greed; and how they endure in spite of the odds and themselves, and sometimes even transcend the limitations of human nature. Indeed, Ellison has carefully eschewed the title of science-fiction writer for the more accurate one of fantasist.

Ellison's stories often deal with redemption in one form or another. In "I Have No Mouth and I Must Scream" (1967) the five human survivors of a computer-controlled war are tormented by a supercomputer but redeemed by one man's act of love. And in " 'Repent, Harlequin!' Said the Ticktockman" (1965) an irrepressible rebel opposes the regimentation of a future society and thus celebrates the boundlessness of the human spirit.

Although Ellison's major themes prevail in nearly all his writing, he reached his full stride as a powerful and individual voice when he left behind the restrictions of genre that mark his formative work of the 1950s and early 1960s. In stories such as "A Boy and His Dog" (1969) and "Jeffty Is Five" (1977) he was able to give full rein to his deep personal concern for a humanity trapped, blessed, ennobled, and often viciously betrayed by its own nature. These and other stories demonstrate how fantastic writing can be a mainstream phenomenon, totally representative of the age. Ellison's fiction is frequently a tool for biting social commentary and the expression of rage, as well as a showcase for humor, exuberance, and compassion.

For Ellison, society's general ill conduct is redeemed by small individual acts of love and compassion, as displayed by Gaspar and Billy Kinetta in "Paladin of the Lost Hour" (1985) or by the old man Pederson and the Martian Pretrie in "In Lonely Lands" (1958). Stories such as "Croatoan" (1975) and "The Whimper of Whipped Dogs" (1973) expand on this theme and reveal the often startling sense of personal and social responsibility that underlies Ellison's writing, both fiction and nonfiction. In works such as "Pretty Maggie Moneyeyes" (1967) and "The Deathbird" (1973) (in which Satan is the hero and God the demented villain), we see what provocative and experimental means Ellison uses to achieve his ends, distancing us, resensitizing us, bringing us back to truths of feeling we have invariably recognized and experienced ourselves.

His commitment to fantasy as a vigorous and relevant medium is evident as well in the original and widely applauded ANTHOLOGIES Ellison has edited: *Dangerous Visions* (1967), *Again, Dangerous Visions* (1972), and *Medea: Harlan's World* (1985). In all three books contributors were encouraged to explore new ideas, styles, and formats. A similar dedication is evident in Ellison's roles as a founder of the Clarion Writers' Workshop and as editor of the Harlan Ellison Discovery series—part of his abiding interest in discovering and nurturing new writers.

His work for television has displayed the same originality and breadth of vision as his fiction, with award-winning teleplays for STAR TREK ("The City on the Edge of Forever," 1967) and THE OUTER LIMITS ("Demon with a Glass Hand," 1964), and scripts for such series as *Burke's Law*, *The Man from UNCLE*, and the new TWILIGHT ZONE (for whose first season he was creative consultant).

All of Ellison's writing is deeply persuasive and highly personal. Even though his fiction is usually not overtly autobiographical, it displays an immediacy and emotional depth that suggest a greater, more vital personal involvement than the reader might otherwise identify. Some stories, such as "All the Lies That Are My Life" (1980), deliberately court and play with this connection; others are brought into startling relief by a simple introductory remark, a common framing technique used in Ellison's collections, made effective by the fact that both story and introduction inevitably retain an integrity of their own.

This continuing interest in drawing relevant comment

Harlan Ellison

out of personal experience and observation has led Ellison to the development of a powerful, distinctively individual voice as essayist, social commentator, and critic. Indeed, he is one of the most self-revelatory, outspoken authors in modern letters. The introductions to his many collections, the autobiographical headnotes to his stories and nonfiction pieces, the defiant how-I-see-it thrust of his essays, media criticism, and lectures show his dedication to monitoring his own process as writer-observer, as well as a commitment to his deliberate position as rebel and provocateur. His articles on television (collected as *The Glass Teat*, 1970, and *The Other Glass Teat*, 1975) and everything from racism and religious bigotry to video games, gun control, and computer dating (in *Sleepless Nights in the Procrustean Bed*, 1984, and *An Edge in My Voice*, 1985) show the range and intensity of this personal commitment.

Ellison is an original and important talent who has made a lasting impact on twentieth-century fiction and has set and maintained exemplary standards of excellence.

OTHER WORKS: *Web of the City* (1958); *The Deadly Streets* (1958); *The Sound of a Scythe* (1960); *A Touch of Infinity* (collection, 1960); *Children of the Streets* (1961); *Gentleman Junkie* (collection, 1961); *Memos from Purgatory* (1961); *Spider Kiss* (1961); *Ellison Wonderland* (collection, 1962; revised 1984); *Paingod and Other Delusions* (collection, 1965); *I Have No Mouth and I Must Scream* (collection, 1967); *Dooms-*

man (1967); *From the Land of Fear* (collection, 1967); *Nightshades and Damnations* (editor, 1968); *Love Ain't Nothing But Sex Misspelled* (1968); *The Beast That Shouted Love at the Heart of the World* (collection, 1969); *Over the Edge* (collection, 1970); *Partners in Wonder* (collection, 1971); *Alone against Tomorrow* (collection, 1971; published in Britain in two volumes as *All the Sounds of Fear* and *The Time of the Eye*, 1973–74); *Approaching Oblivion* (collection, 1974); *Phoenix without Ashes* (with Edward Bryant, 1975); *Deathbird Stories* (collection, 1975); *No Doors, No Windows* (collection, 1975); *Strange Wine* (collection, 1978); *The Book of Ellison* (collection, 1978); *The Illustrated Harlan Ellison* (collection, 1978); *The Fantasies of Harlan Ellison* (collection, 1979); *Shatterday* (collection, 1980); *Stalking the Nightmare* (collection, 1982); *The Essential Ellison* (collection, 1987).

T.D.

THE EMPIRE STRIKES BACK: SEE STAR WARS

EMSHWILLER, CAROL [Née FRIES] (1921–).
American writer and instructor in creative writing who is married to filmmaker and onetime science-fiction artist Ed EMSHWILLER. The hallmarks of Carol Emshwiller's fiction are unusual plots and stylistic daring; she frequently experiments with style, organization, and narrative technique, and her forty-plus short stories are a testament to how well such experimentation can pay off. These stories often deal with conventional SF material—including aliens, space journeys, and humans with strange talents—but they are usually set in the present or near future. Moreover, the stories focus on the lives of ordinary people trying to cope with personal problems rather than with the future or advanced technology.

In addition, Emshwiller has an energetic wit that frequently makes difficult or potentially depressing subject matter palatable. Love ("This Thing Called Love," 1955; "Love Me Again," 1956; "Sex and/or Mr. Morrison," 1974; "Abominable," 1980), estrangement ("Adapted," 1961; "Escape Is No Accident," 1977), and terror ("Hunting Machine," 1980; "Omens," 1980) are effectively portrayed in her work with sensitive comments on contemporary human behavior. Some of Emshwiller's best early short stories are collected in *Joy in Our Cause* (1974).

S.H.G.

EMSH[WILLER, EDMUND ALEXANDER] (1925–). American illustrator, five-time Hugo Award recipient (1953, 1960, 1961, 1962, and 1964), and one of the two most important science-fiction artists

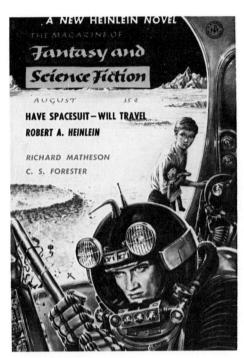

Cover illustration by Emsh

of the 1950s (with Frank Kelly FREAS). Emsh graduated with a degree in art from the University of Michigan, and his first cover illustration was for GALAXY in 1951; in the years that followed he painted covers for *Planet Stories*, THE MAGAZINE OF FANTASY AND SCIENCE FICTION, *Vanguard SF, Rocket Stories, Super-Science Fiction*, and others. He did all but the first cover for *Infinity SF* and painted many for the Ace Double series of the 1950s, including some memorable covers for works by Poul ANDERSON, H. Ken BULMER, Jack VANCE, and many other authors. He was equally versatile at humor and horror, without resorting to cartooning or excess. Emsh had a dynamically realistic style, and many of his paintings have a gemlike quality, with small, bright points of light scattered through them. His black-and-white works have a scratchy look, but their technique gives them a great deal of life. In many paintings he used his wife, author Carol EMSHWILLER, as his model.

In the late 1950s Emsh became interested in films, and his first effort in that medium, the experimental film *Dance Chromatic*, (1959), was an award winner; his 1966 film *Relativity* is widely regarded by critics as one of the best short films ever made. He retired from the SF field in the mid-1960s and today works mainly with video, teaching in California.

J.G.

ENEMY MINE (1985). *Directed by Wolfgang Petersen; screenplay by Edward Khmara; adapted from the short story by Barry B. Longyear; photographed by Tony Imi; music by Maurice Jarre. With Dennis Quaid, Louis Gossett, Jr., Brion James, Richard Marcus, Carolyn McCormick, Bumper Robinson. 108 minutes. Color.*

The first major German science-fiction film in over four decades, *Enemy Mine* is often crude compared with American SF movies, but it is also more ambitious, a sincere effort to bring to the screen Barry B. LONGYEAR's ultimately pacifist tale of two enemies (one alien, one human) who must cooperate to survive. The space battles may look like something out of the television version of BUCK ROGERS and the planet-scapes are obviously painted backdrops, but excellent performances by Dennis Quaid and Louis Gossett, Jr. (who is remarkable as the alien) raise *Enemy Mine* above mere formulaic SF.

The film is best when it depends not on special effects but on Longyear's original story. The sequences showing the alien's pregnancy, childbirth, and death are surprisingly moving without being sentimental, and they are carefully balanced with the same kind of humor that leavened the original. Where the story line begins to deviate from Longyear's story, however, trouble rapidly develops. The bang-up climax brings on furious action, hissable villains worthy of old-time serials, and hastily patched-up logic. But the film regains some dignity at the end, as peace is apparently restored and the hero expresses profound respect for the culture of his former enemy.

Although not consistently successful, this film was one of the few adult, rather than adolescent, entries in the genre for the period and was nominated for a Hugo.

D.S.

ENGLAND, GEORGE ALLAN (1877–1937). American writer whose stories appeared chiefly in magazines published by Frank A. Munsey between 1906 and 1918 and whose work emphasizes adventure plots and the wonders of recent technology typical of the early pulp magazines and their writers. His novel *The Air Trust* (1915) and such short stories as "The Empire of the Air" (1914) illustrate the range of England's interests: the first is an example of early social science fiction in which capitalism is criticized through the image of a private company that seeks to monopolize the breathable air; the second is a space opera in which a group of aliens invades the Earth through the fourth dimension.

England's most famous work is the novel *Darkness and Dawn* (1914), a one-volume edition of three 1912–13 magazine serials. (It was reprinted in 1965–1967 in five volumes: *Darkness and Dawn, Beyond the Great Oblivion, The People of the Abyss, Out of the Abyss,* and *The Afterglow*.) This is a postholocaust tale in which

an anesthetic gas engulfs the entire planet, killing most of its inhabitants. Among the survivors are a man and a woman who sleep for centuries high in a skyscraper. The rest of the work concerns their efforts to explore what the world has become; they encounter intelligent rats, degenerate humans, and, finally, a lost civilization.

OTHER WORKS: *The Golden Blight* (1916); *Cursed* (1919); *The Flying Legion* (1920); *Elixir of Hate* (1976).

S.H.G.

——————— **ENVIRONMENT** ———————

Environmental concerns are commonly thought to be a recent obsession in science fiction, yet they can be found in one of the earliest works that can be called SF, Jean Baptiste Cousin de Grainville's *The Last Man, or Omegarus and Syderia* (1806), which posits exhaustion of natural resources as dooming the world.

Densely populated Britain had had experience with smog even during the Middle Ages, with the first use of "sea coal" as a fuel, and had keenly felt the impact of the Industrial Revolution on the environment. It is not surprising, then, that environmental consciousness found an early outlet in SF there. Richard Jefferies's *After London* (1885), the first of the great postholocaust novels, makes pollution—rather than some cataclysmic war—the cause of civilization's downfall. Robert Barr's "The Doom of London" (1892) anticipates a killer smog, and Fred M. White's "The Four Days' Night" (1903) is in the same vein. In France widespread air and water pollution are part of the background in Albert Robida's *The Twentieth Century* (1882).

Of course, one can't claim this sort of thing was common in early SF; authors and readers alike were more alarmed about future wars—if indeed they were alarmed about anything. In the American PULP MAGAZINES, Stanley G. WEINBAUM's "Smothered Seas" (with Ralph Milne Farley, 1936) was one of the few stories to realize that humankind's activities could have unanticipated effects on the environment. Perhaps the first great alarmist story on this topic was Nat Schachner's "Sterile Planet" (1937), in which "civilization" has turned the world into a desert. Although many may not think of it as such, Frederik POHL and Cyril M. KORNBLUTH's *The Space Merchants* (1952/53) was a trendsetting environmentalist work, and the growing popularity of Frank HERBERT's *Dune* (1965) in the late 1960s came about at least in part because of its clear statement on the influence of environment and its timing with the rise of the environmental movement.

But if such works were few for several decades, writers made up for the lack with a vengeance in the 1970s. How sudden the shift in consciousness was can be seen in two works of John BRUNNER. *Stand on Zanzibar* (1968) seems to explore every aspect of overpopulation *except* its massive impact on the environment. In *The Sheep*

Look Up (1972), however, every environmentalist's nightmare is visualized in graphic detail, from dead seas to air so filthy it's suicide to go outside without a gas mask. Philip WYLIE's posthumously published *The End of the Dream* (1972) offers similarly horrifying scenarios—many of them forecast for 1985 or earlier. James BLISH had already written the ultimate environmental disaster story: in "We All Die Naked" (1969) Earth is doomed because thermal pollution, leading to rapid melting of the ice caps, has upset the world's isostatic balance: tectonic cataclysms are just ahead.

Although the worst forecasts of 1970s SF failed to materialize, it would be risky indeed to accuse Brunner, Wylie, and others of crying wolf—even in the old story, the wolf *did* come eventually. There is still an underlying assumption in some science fiction, from Richard A. LUPOFF's *Fool's Hill* (1976) to Ridley Scott's *Blade Runner* (1982), that (even barring atomic war and nuclear winter) the environment doesn't have much of a future.

J.J.P.

ESCAPE FROM NEW YORK (1981).   *Directed by John Carpenter; screenplay by John Carpenter and Nick Castle; photographed by Dean Cundy; music by John Carpenter in association with Alan Howarth. With Kurt Russell, Lee Van Cleef, Donald Pleasence, Ernest Borgnine, Isaac Hayes, Harry Dean Stanton, Season Hubley, Adrienne Barbeau. 99 minutes. Color.*

Escape from New York is a playful science-fiction action thriller by John CARPENTER, who had previously demonstrated his firm grasp of cinematic action in such films as *Assault on Precinct 13* (1976) and *Halloween* (1978). The premise sets up a potentially brilliant extrapolative conceit: in 1997 Manhattan has become a maximum-security prison, encircled by an imposing containing wall. The plot thickens (or perhaps more accurately congeals) when Air Force One crashes within the island prison and the president is taken captive by some of the inmates. The protagonist, a cynical but professional ex–war hero, must enter the island and rescue the president in twenty-four hours or he will die from a timed explosive device implanted in his body by the authorities.

Carpenter ironically cast Kurt Russell, a onetime Disney youth star, as the protagonist. But the other stars are cast rather conventionally: Isaac Hayes, for example, as the villainous leader of the prison society. The narrative, too, descends into standard action fare. Although the predictable plot is occasionally relieved by the arresting detail of set design or by Carpenter's characteristic injection of humor into dramatic situations (when the dreaded underground "crazies" emerge from manholes, a Chock Full O' Nuts sign is clearly visible in the background). Alas, such throwaway delights are not enough to save this film from failing to live up to its possibilities.

B.K.G

ESCAPE FROM THE PLANET OF THE APES:
SEE PLANET OF THE APES

─────── ESCHATOLOGY ───────

C. S. LEWIS originated the term *eschatological science fiction*, borrowing a word from theology and considerably broadening its usage for his purpose.

The *Oxford English Dictionary* defines *eschatology* as "the branch of theological science concerned with 'the four last things': death, judgment, heaven and hell." These were significant concerns for Lewis because of his lifelong interest in Christianity, but for most other science-fiction writers the "last things" relate not so much to theology as to the last state of Genus homo and to the more advanced (or at any rate different) beings who may succeed him. Perhaps the most useful definition of *eschatological SF* would be "stories about the end of humanity or the transition from humanity to something else."

Most eschatological stories are set rather far in the future, because the second part of the definition—the transition from humanity to something else—requires evolution, a process that moves slowly, and stories about the end of the human species tend to seem more eschatological, that is, concerned with philosophical and ethical issues, when time has had a chance to reveal something new or unsuspected about humanity. For that reason the many "end-of-the-world" stories that involve contemporary catastrophic collisions with astronomical bodies, plagues, invasion by aliens, or even nuclear holocaust seem more apocalyptic than eschatological.

Nevertheless, stories such as E. M. FORSTER's "The Machine Stops" (1909), with its warning about the corruptibility of the human spirit by overdependence on machines, and John W. CAMPBELL's "Twilight" (1934), with its view of a sad and lonely human species fading away in its eternal cities because it has lost its curiosity, are eschatological. Philip José FARMER's Riverworld series, beginning with *To Your Scattered Bodies Go* (1971), contains elements of eschatology in its resurrection along the banks of a nearly interminable river of everybody who ever lived, and W. Olaf STAPLEDON's *Last and First Men* (1930) combines both elements of eschatology as it traces the evolution of humanity through various shapes and conditions until its end.

The more interesting aspects of eschatological SF are those that deal with the strange shapes that, over the long future, humans may assume, the strange powers they may develop, and the strange ideas that may flow through their heads; or the even stranger shapes, powers, and ideas that may characterize humanity's successors. These may take even more time: a taxonomists' rule of thumb is that the making of a new species requires 100,000 years. Still, SF writers have taken literary advantage of the fact that mutations can occur at any time, or perhaps can be forced through molecular biology. Moreover, in a number of works, the major change in question is not purely genetic.

The most familiar example of this kind of eschatological SF may well be the novel (and, with Stanley KUBRICK, the film) by Arthur C. CLARKE, 2001: A SPACE ODYSSEY (1968), in which the astronaut Bowman follows the Black Monolith through Technicolor space to become the no-longer-human Starchild. (It is troublesome but ultimately irrelevant that in Clarke's 1982 sequel, 2010, the Starchild seems to be no longer the next stage of humanity but instead a sort of messenger for some higher order of being.)

Clarke's Starchild is transformed from human into Something Else by an outside force, the powers behind the Black Monolith. Of course, no external agency is necessary to create a mutation, or any number of mutations, except from the viewpoint of an SF writer desirous of speeding up the development of a story. Simple Darwinian evolution will do the trick, given time. The process that transformed our ancestors from something like *Australopithecus afarensis* to us continues. The first major eschatological SF stories acknowledged that fact and were therefore purely evolutionary. As it happens, they were all by British authors.

As in much else, H. G. WELLS defined the parameters of the subject, in this case in *The Time Machine* (1895). As John J. Pierce has pointed out, *The Time Machine* is not quite the first story of time travel, but it is the first SF story *about* time—about the immense reaches of "deep time," to the very end of the Earth. On the way to Earth's last moments, Wells's Time Traveller stops in the year 802,701. The human race has not simply changed, it has bifurcated into the cavern-dwelling Morlocks and the bright, trivial Eloi of the surface of the planet. Although Wells clearly was sending a political message about the ultimate outcome of the class struggle (Morlocks equaling workers, Eloi equaling the rich aristocrats), he was also describing the inevitability of evolution to something no longer human. Wells, of course, was first exposed to Darwinian concepts when he studied biology under Thomas Henry Huxley.

No modern SF writer has written more in this particularly eschatological vein than the British novelist Olaf Stapledon. In his 1935 novel *Odd John*, the title character is one of a dozen or so mutants, all vaguely telepathic, all able to do things that normal human beings cannot—even to see events past and future and to communicate after death. With the help of a loyal human being who serves as his friend, confidant, and perhaps pet, John finds a remote island on which all the super-humans gather to try to discover their destiny in the world of billions of lesser primates. But the "civilized" humans find them, and they blow themselves up.

Stapledon's *Last and First Men* describes the future history of the human race and its descendants for the 2 billion years until the final flaring of the Sun incinerates its planets and ends human history forever. After the First Men (modern humanity as we know it) comes a Pageant of later evolutionary forms, some successful, some not, some mere brainless grazers and others Great Brains almost devoid of bodies, until at last evolve the Eighteenth Men. They are serene and wise in their home on Neptune; anticipating the coming explosion, they decide to make "a fair conclusion to this brief music that is Man."

The third pioneer of eschatological SF, also British, was S. Fowler WRIGHT. His lyrical and brooding novel *The World Below* (1929, Book I; as *The Amphibians*, 1925) is a deliberate retelling of Homer's *The Odyssey* set half a million years in our future. A time traveler of our own kind finds himself in an unrecognizable world inhabited by a menagerie of odd beings: sleek, seallike, almost genderless Amphibians; huge and remotely intellectual Dwellers; ugly creatures shaped like beaked and legged beach balls called Killers; and the flying, insectoid Antipodeans. Some of these may be our descendants; all of them are our successors, for Homo Sapiens no longer exists on Earth.

Within a decade or so of the first issue of AMAZING STORIES in 1926, most of the developments in SF were coming from American authors. David H. KELLER's "The Revolt of the Pedestrians" (1928), about an automobile-dependent culture in which humanity's legs have atrophied to useless vestiges, is a notable early work about eschatological change. So is Harry BATES's "Alas, All Thinking" (1935), in which a traveler to the future finds that humans have become so intellectual they no longer bother to reproduce, or even eat, and are dying off. But American magazine writers were in more of a hurry than their British predecessors. Like British-born Clarke, they preferred not to wait for evolution to run its course, and they employed various devices to get the successors of humankind on the scene more rapidly.

An early American example is Clifford D. SIMAK's 1944 story "Desertion" (collected as part of his 1951 "novel" *City*), in which Kent Fowler and his dog Towser transfer their minds into the bodies of creatures native to Jupiter (today's knowledge about the planet indicates that it doesn't have a solid surface, but that is a separate question). In their altered form, the two Earthborn beings find a kind of awareness, joy, and well-being they had never previously known; the dog can communicate, and both can understand and experience things far beyond their previous comprehension. But they are obligated to report to humanity what has happened, and at the close of the story comes the following memorable passage:

"I can't go back," said Towser.

"Nor I," said Fowler.

"They would turn me back into a dog," said Towser.

"And me," said Fowler, "into a man."

Theodore STURGEON's *Venus Plus X* (1960) surprises the reader (and its protagonist, Charlie Johns) by revealing that the inhabitants of Ledom—hermaphrodites who have achieved a perfect society because all sexual tensions are eliminated—are not really mutations at all but simply normal human beings who are surgically transformed at birth. In Jack VANCE's *The Dragon Masters* (1963) eschatological change is also engineered. The novel is set on a planet and in a time far removed from our own; human beings and their chief competitors, a lizardlike intelligent race of aliens, have been artificially bred into a dozen different types that compete and interact.

But some American writers continued to use the device of simple evolutionary change, manifested by mutations occurring in the normal population. Rather like *Odd John* in concept—and certainly at one time far better known to most readers of SF—is A. E. VAN VOGT's novel *Slan* (1940). Its hero, Jommy Cross, is telepathic, he has tendrils rather than hair, and, like Odd John, he is almost smothered in the world of obsolete human beings. Another of the many stories about mutated superhumans trying to adjust to humanity is Wilmar H. SHIRAS's "In Hiding" (1948; published, with two sequels, as *Children of the Atom*, 1953), about superintelligent children concealing not only their skills but their very existence from the world.

Of course, in numerous SF stories the human race is "replaced," usually through extermination, by Martians, robots, creatures from the depths of the sea, or unnamed monsters from anywhere. These works are not really eschatological; in them the human essence does not carry on but simply ceases to exist. However, stories in which humanity is replaced by computers or robots can fall into the category, because robots may be considered our "children," albeit not biological ones. Jack WILLIAMSON's "With Folded Hands . . . " (1947) describes humanoid robots who relieve their human masters of all work, worry, and decisionmaking—thus effectively removing humanity from any role in future history. Williamson's sequel, " . . . And Searching Mind" (1948; as *The Humanoids*, 1949), chronicles humanity's continuing struggle to win back its right to make mistakes, suffer, and be free.

If many SF writers have dealt with eschatological themes, such subjects have dominated the work of at least one, Paul M. A. Linebarger, who, under the pseudonym of Cordwainer SMITH, wrote evocatively and often poetically, making considerable use of mythical and historical themes, about a far-advanced future. Some of his characters seem to be evolved humans, like the great,

almost incomprehensible figures of the Instrumentality, the rulers of this universe, such as Lady Alice More and Lord Jestocost. Others are artificially mutated animals, such as the cat-girl C'Mell and the dog-woman D'Joan. Smith's stories often are told from the viewpoints of his animal-people, who tend to be more sympathetic than the posthuman figures whose exploits the stories describe.

This kind of approach to eschatological fiction may be necessary. It is as hard (to use an analogy employed by many of its authors) for a human being to understand something beyond humanity as for a dog to understand its owner's concerns over quantum mechanics or the income tax; and of course that makes it extraordinarily difficult to write about posthuman characters. To describe the daily life (much less the ultimate goals) of a superhuman necessitates trying to make comprehensible to the reader behaviors and characteristics that even the author, being human, cannot really claim to understand. So authors must walk a troublesome dividing line between success and catastrophic failure, pushing their imaginations to such an extreme that if they took one step more they and their enterprises would come crashing down as preposterous farce.

Indeed, the challenge of eschatological SF is to write about humanity's successors with sympathy and insight. Fortunately, many fine writers of SF have accepted this challenge and continue to do so. John VARLEY and Samuel R. DELANY handle the eschatological regularly in much of their best work. And other writers—such as Joan Slonczewski with her 1986 novel *A Door into Ocean*, which describes a watery world inhabited by an entirely female race of humans—are beginning to emerge as new practitioners of this unique variety of SF.

F.P.

ESHBACH, LLOYD ARTHUR (1910–).

American writer and publisher, editor of the first published book about modern science fiction, *Of Worlds Beyond* (1947), containing six essays by leading writers of the day. Eshbach sold some twenty SF stories to the pulps during the 1930s following his first appearance with "The Voice from the Ether" (1931); some of these are collected as *The Tyrant of Time* (1955). Although dated they remain readable. After World War II Eshbach established one of the first regular specialty SF publishing houses, Fantasy Press, which ran from 1947 to 1961 and brought into hardcover for the first time some of the early pulp classics by Robert A. HEINLEIN, E. E. SMITH, Eric Frank RUSSELL, L. Sprague DE CAMP, Jack WILLIAMSON, and John W. CAMPBELL. Eshbach's informal volume of reminiscences about these days, *Over My Shoulder* (1983), provides a wealth of detail on specialty publishing. He also completed one of Smith's last novels, *Subspace Encounter* (1983).

OTHER WORKS: *The Land beyond the Gate* (1984); *The Armlet of the Gods* (1986), the first two volumes in a four-book fantasy sequence.

M.A.

THE EVIL OF FRANKENSTEIN: SEE FRANKENSTEIN ON FILM

——— EVOLUTION ———

Science fiction, as a literature of change, of future life-forms and alien life evolving beyond Earth, is implicitly and deeply influenced by the theory of evolution. Nonetheless, SF does not generally (and perhaps cannot often) address itself to actual evolution as it is currently understood.

Charles Darwin's theory of evolution holds that different species appear through random inheritable mutations over long periods, with favorable mutations allowing more offspring to survive the struggle for resources in their particular environment. Jean-Baptiste Lamarck, in *Philosophie zoologique* (1809), had already introduced a concept of evolution by adaptation, best symbolized by the image of giraffes stretching to reach higher leaves and bequeathing ever-longer necks to their offspring, under the assumption that acquired characteristics could be inherited. Both Darwin in his *Origin of Species* (1859) and his contemporary Alfred Russel Wallace—influenced by Thomas Malthus's *An Essay on the Principle of Population* (1798), which argues that breeding is determined by available resources—identified competitive "natural selection" as the principal means of evolution. Philosopher Herbert Spencer coined the actual terms *survival of the fittest* and *evolution.* The specific mechanism of evolution, genetic variation, was announced obscurely by Gregor Mendel in 1869 and only publicized by William Bateson in 1889. Variation is now explained by changes in the DNA molecular code through copying accidents or radiation; less than 0.1 percent of random mutations are of survival value.

Despite the survival of Lamarckianism in the USSR into the Stalin era through the agronomist Trofin Denisovich Lysenko, and despite increasing attacks on Darwinism in the United States by religious fundamentalists preaching a nonscientific "creation science," the broad outline of the theory is not in doubt. Genuine evolutionary controversies today include (1) The concept of punctuated equilibria (Eldredge, Gould, 1972), whereby change is postulated to occur in sudden jumps with relative stability in between. In this concept the ancestor species continues to survive for some time in its old niche along with adjacent descendants. (In geological terms "sudden" means between 5000 and 50,000 years, rather than the overnight birth of "hopeful monsters.") (2) Cladistics (Hennig, 1950), a radical revision of the relations between species first mapped by Linnaeus in the eighteenth century. Named after the Greek word for "branch," this perspective analyzes close common ancestry on the basis of shared derived characteristics, upsetting traditionally assumed evolutionary links. (3) The discovery through recombinant DNA research that, by reverse transcription, acquired characteristics sometimes can be inherited, and body can communicate with germ-line. For example, fertilizers have been found to induce inheritable changes in some varieties of flax. (4) The role of constraints dictated by the basic laws of physics, chemistry, and growth processes. This understanding indicates that probably no creature could ever evolve wheels or three heads (as opposed to two). (5) The linked concept that matter can self-organize, with orderly structures arising spontaneously. (6) The likelihood (Margulis, 1970) that the complex cells of animals and plants first evolved by endosymbiosis, with some bacteria taking up residence inside others, causing some non-Mendelian inheritance. (7) The puzzle of why sex evolved, because humans could have evolved from molds in 3 billion years by genetic mutation alone. Perhaps sex, by varying the chemical "passwords," protected against hostile unicellular parasites.

Evolution proceeds by sheer chance, in dialectical relation with a given environment. There is evidence that life evolved independently several times on Earth, apparently early in our planetary history; thus alien life as such may easily evolve if suitable planets exist. Yet there is no *need* for life, once begun, to evolve beyond single-cell organisms. No reason is known for the explosion of species at the start of the Cambrian period, a vast time after life commenced. Evolution can by no means be equated with upward progression toward increasing complexity. Still less does it need eventually to lead to intelligence. On the contrary, because of its survival value, the eye as a sense organ appeared independently by convergent evolution forty times, whereas intelligence evolved only once. If the dinosaurs had survived their late Cretaceous mass extinction there is no reason why *Saurus sapiens* should not have evolved instead of or along with *Homo sapiens,* as Harry HARRISON has speculated in *West of Eden* (1984). Humanity resulted from a large number of chance events that were neither predictable nor necessary. Even complex technology could be a product of randomly evolved nonintelligent creatures; witness the synthesis of magnetite by birds for navigation.

Science fiction often deploys evolution ignorantly, romantically, or ideologically, evoking purposive, goal-directed, upward progress (or, conversely, decline), with convergent evolution producing either intelligence and even humanoid bodies on other worlds or new superpowers through mutation to a "next level," ultimately even to cosmic mind or Godhood.

Such ideological choice may also entail, reluctantly

or otherwise, a political social Darwinism, the application of "survival of the fittest" to human history. H. G. WELLS, a pupil of Darwin's apostle T. H. Huxley, struggled to reconcile utopian socialism aimed at a "fitter" society with Darwinian "laws" in works ranging from the caricature of degenerately evolved workers and aristocrats in *The Time Machine* (1895) to the gloomy essay *Mind at the End of Its Tether* (1945), in which humanity is deemed unfit because it cannot adapt to its new technological environment. Social Darwinism has been deployed in support of anti-Semitism and white supremacy in the works of M. P. SHIEL, provides backing for Robert A. HEINLEIN's toughly individualist though species-proud morality, and has led to such excesses as John W. CAMPBELL, Jr.'s July 1951 editorial "Evolution" in favor of aggression and L. Ron HUBBARD's advocacy of genocide for any alien competitors we meet ("To the Stars," 1950; also titled *Return to Tomorrow*, 1954). It was the stock-in-trade of Frank HERBERT, whose *Eyes of Heinsenberg* (1966) addresses the genetic engineering of immortal Optimen and whose novels increasingly insist on ruthless survival training; ambitious, subtle breeding programs; and weeding of failures. Most typical of these works is *The Dosadi Experiment* (1977).

But such doctrinaire "Darwinism" in alien or human relations is out of key with much contemporary ecological, multicultural SF—a reaction slightly prefigured by George Bernard Shaw's political renunciation of Darwin in favor of Lamarck in *Back to Methuselah* (1921). Lamarck, via mystical philosopher Henri Bergson with his extra (and heretical) notion of élan vital ("vital spirit"), also influenced Shaw's compatriot J. D. BERESFORD in his superchild novel *The Hampdenshire Wonder* (1911; also titled *The Wonder*).

Our evolutionary past increasingly captures attention at a time of fossil discoveries and anthropological controversy; witness the film QUEST FOR FIRE (1981), based on *La Guerre de feu* (1909), one of the prehistoric fantasies of Lamarckian J.-H. Rosny Aîné, or Jean M. AUEL's *Clan of the Cave Bear* (1980) and sequels. *What We Did to Father* (1960; also titled *The Evolution Man*) by Roy Lewis is a Thurberesque romp in which one African ape-man invents absolutely everything. The most sophisticated treatments of evolution are those of Michael BISHOP in *No Enemy But Time* (1982), in which a temponaut visits with the African hominids, and *Ancient of Days* (1985), in which a hominid survivor appears in modern Georgia.

As regards future evolution, Wells's spoof review "The Man of the Year Million" (1893) set one trend, envisaging progress via larger brain, slighter body, and great, sensitive hands—toward "human tadpoles," with bodies "a dangling degraded pendant to their minds." Edmond HAMILTON's "The Man Who Evolved" (1931) follows this course, courtesy of concentrated cosmic rays, to its final conclusion, "a mass of simple *protoplasm!* . . .

Charles Darwin

the last mutation of all! The road of man's evolution was a circular one, returning to its beginning!" (Mutations here are viewed as inevitable, awaiting, and inherent, not random.) Converse to this is Hamilton's "Devolution" (1936), in which all terrestrial life is a freak example of frozen degeneration from superior, shape-shifting jelly-beings. A scientifically argued variant on such "flexilife" is Brian STABLEFORD's *The Gates of Eden* (1983), in which alien species that evolved separate coexisting genetic codes for different bodily forms fuse into a metamorphic multispecies which can even absorb, and express, human DNA.

Nuclear war would obviously produce much radiation, and SF authors have often invoked its mutagenic aftermath to create monsters, degenerates, sports, or—more optimistically—humans with paranormal powers; John WYNDHAM's *The Chrysalids* (1955), in which telepathy results amid a society religiously dedicated to destroying any mutants, is a typical example of this premise. Beneficial side effects of holocaust are most unlikely, but the romantic interpretation of evolution constitutes a wish for *Homo superior* (including wild talents). In *Last and First Men* (1930), Olaf STAPLEDON (whose *Odd John*, 1939, charts the growth, successes, and voluntary demise of a mutated superhuman) deployed Darwinian methods—including cul-de-sacs and extinctions, plus planned biodesign, through 2 billion years of humanity's future on Earth, Venus, and Neptune—in a grand and sometimes tragic yet fundamentally exaltatory progress toward cosmic insight and racial mind; although humanity at last quits the stage, destiny has been fulfilled.

Arthur C. CLARKE's *Childhood's End* (1953) posits "two different evolutions": that of the intellectually superior Overlords, who are stuck in a blind alley, mere servants of the growing cosmic Overmind, and that of humanity, with latent paranormal powers that become overt as all children suddenly pass through an evolutionary "puberty," evolving into a collective energy-being to join the Overmind. Such postnatal evolution is no more orthodox than SF's use—applied to life not in the womb but subsequently—of the law identified with Darwin's German apostle Ernst Haeckel that individuals embryonically recapitulate the evolutionary history of the race. James BLISH's *A Case of Conscience* (1958) offers an example. A type of saltation—a sudden leap between one generation and the next—is rationalized in Ian WATSON's *Alien Embassy* (1977) by preadaptation of gene sites. Watson's *The Martian Inca* (1977) uses contamination by a Martian life-form analogous to the congregative slime mold to rewire human brains and produce higher consciousness. As in much evolutionary SF, transcendence is the aim here.

If our current civilization continues, natural Darwinian evolution may no longer strictly apply—this result would come about through advances in medical science along with social decisions regarding which offspring will survive, but it would occur principally because of genetic engineering of DNA to enhance, mutate, and adapt the human form. The wilder shores of far future genetic alterations are celebrated lyrically in Robert SILVERBERG's *Son of Man* (1971), and the nearer shores of what might be called controlled evolution are satirized in Watson's *Converts* (1984). Charles SHEFFIELD's *Sight of Proteus* (1978) imagines twenty-second century biotechnology permitting people to alter their shape at will within certain limits policed by the office of Form Contro. In Bruce STERLING's *Schismatrix* (1985), humanity diverges into separate evolutionary groupings of biooriented Shapers and Mechanists.

In Daniel F. GALOUYE's *Project Barrier* (1968) collection, societies of bears, dogs, and other higher mammals whose evolution has hitherto been stifled by human success are each in turn enabled by isolation to follow naturally the identical path as humans to language, technology, and social structures. The more plausible variation on this theme is that we will by genetic engineering redesign and enhance animals as servants or partners, such as the space-faring dolphins in David BRIN's *Startide Rising* (1983).

Humans may retool themselves and other species—or machines may seize the baton of evolution. Isaac ASIMOV's "Darwinian Pool Room" (1950) suggests it may be no coincidence that we invent hydrogen bombs and thinking machines at the same time—the first to destroy us, the second to replace us. Gregory BENFORD's *Across the Sea of Suns* (1983) explores this thesis in detail, with organic species—flawed by inbuilt mortality, sexual schism, and stranger hostility—committing nuclear suicide and their machines evolving galactic civilization self-programmed to prevent organized life from arising technologically again. To survive, one alien species redesigns itself into imitation machines, with biological eletromagnetic bodies. In Stanislaw LEM's *The Invincible (Niezwyezony*, 1964) a collective cloud of nonintelligent fly-size cybernetic crystals has evolved in a struggle for resources, destroying both organic life and rational robots. The novel suggests that organic species may be mere precursors to machine life that they will invent; however, machine life need not be superior in intelligence, only in survival ability.

If such prognoses are chilling—so that by preference or ignorance SF authors use the label but not the substance of evolution in a cavalier style—some baroque (if tongue-in-cheek) evolutions are daunting too. Barrington J. BAYLEY's "Mutation Planet" (1973) has humans and aliens, each equipped by evolution with incompatible racial obsessions (curiosity, submission, death wish), lethally encountering a Lamarckian world where each creature is its own unique species, able to evolve an even better adapted offspring overnight. Brian Stableford's "The Engineer and the Executioner" (1973) has a supremely adaptive ecology based on unique organisms with one chromosome determining the body, another coding for a virus released at senility that invades other life, fusing, coadapting, and inducing purposive metamorphosis.

We by no means understand all the mechanisms of evolution, and we have only one example, life on Earth. Maybe an understanding of some self-organizing life dynamic will lead us to revise the image of materialistic, chance processes. Lynn Margulis (proponent of endosymbiosis, the theory that parts of complex cells developed by invasion of independent parts, such as the mitochondria) has argued in favor of J. E. Lovelock's "Gaia hypothesis," wherein evolution is seen as a holistic, symbiotic, planetary phenomenon. However, Stableford in *The Walking Shadow* (1979) proposed that although the tough environment of early Earth finally shaped cellular life into intelligent individuals, gentler worlds might give rise to sheets of life, all one, without competition, individuality, or mind; and fiercer worlds might breed cells specializing in self-repair, pitted not against each other but against the environment itself, leading to a protean superorganism, very adaptable physically but without intelligence. The resulting Gaia is mindless. Such "third-phase life," according to Stableford, might extend itself to other worlds in an invincible drive to utilize everything, producing a cosmic "whole" that is blankly mindless.

The mainstream of successful species have in effect kept their options open by retaining the ability to adapt behaviorally, a more effective strategy than aiming at specialized efficiency. Thus *Tyrannosaurus rex* never was the creature "fittest" to maximize the number of offspring that would survive. Parental care by mammals gives rise to human society, thence culture, which allows a wider range of nonlimiting choices. If through genetic engineering we take physical evolution by storm, without limiting the flexibility of our future options—a theme of Watson's *The Gardens of Delight* (1980), in which superbeings who emerged spontaneously from a naked singularity now explore the nature of human evolution and its psychic undercurrents—then what is written in science fiction today may in the future be written into our genes.

I.W.

F

THE FABULOUS WORLD OF JULES VERNE
(1958). *Directed by Karel Zeman; screenplay by Karel Zeman and Frantiske Hrubin, with dialogue by Milan Vacha; loosely adapted by Jiri Brdecka from the novel* Face aux drapeaux *by Jules Verne; photographed by Jiri Tarantik, Bohuslav Pikhart, and Antonin Horák; music by Zdenek Liska. With Lubor Tokos, Arnost Navrátil, Moloslav Holub, Jana Zatloukalová, Václav Kyzlink, Frantisek Slégr; American version narrated by Hugh Downs. 82 minutes. Black and white. Alternate title:* A Weapon of Destruction.

Derived primarily from Jules VERNE's *Face aux drapeaux* (*For the Flag,* 1896; as *Facing the Flag,* 1897), this Czechoslovakian import blends several Vernean ideas, viewing the nineteenth-century "futuristic" wonders with whimsical fondness. Karel Zeman is widely regarded as one of the great geniuses of the fantastic film, using whatever special effects he finds necessary to tell his tales. His films are never realistic; generally, as here, they are designed to look like the original illustrations for the adapted work. To simulate the look of wood and steel engravings, Zeman "shaded" each scene with horizontal stripes, often painted directly onto the sets or even the costumes.

But *The Fabulous World of Jules Verne* is more than old wood engravings brought to life; it is at once an affectionate spoof of and tribute to Verne and nineteenth-century attitudes toward science, and a reinterpretation of these attitudes in pacifist terms. Little noticed in its first release, it has come to be regarded as one of the most witty and sophisticated of science-fiction films, one of those extremely rare movies that provide each viewer with a sense of personal discovery.

The story is simple: a young man and a scientist are kidnapped by a Nemoesque madman, whose island base is later blown up. The plot is embellished with inventions galore, a wistful mood, and a unique style of humor.

Zeman's films are generally not released in the English-speaking countries, and some viewers find them slow. But they are all intensely imaginative, the works of a poet and a true cinematic artist. Among Zeman's other films available here are *The Fabulous Baron Munchausen* (*Baron Prasil,* 1961), *A Jester's Tale* (*Bláznova Kronika,* 1964), and *On the Comet* (*Na Komete,* 1970). *Ukradena Vzducholod* (shown at festivals as *The Stolen Airship*) and *On the Comet* are derived from Verne novels.

B.W.

FAHRENHEIT 451 (1966).
Directed by François Truffaut; screenplay by François Truffaut and Jean-Louis Richard; adapted from the novel by Ray Bradbury; photographed by Nicolas Roeg; music by Bernard Herrmann. With Julie Christie, Oskar Werner, Cyril Cusack, Anton Diffring, Jeremy Spenser. 112 minutes. Color.

François Truffaut's film adaptation of Ray BRADBURY's novel was a major departure for the French New Wave director. It was his first film in color; his first in a foreign language, English, which he could hardly understand (it was also shot with a predominantly English crew); his first (and only) science-fiction movie; and his first film shot in a studio. As might be expected, although the film displays a thematic continuity with Truffaut's other work, many of the distinctive elements that characterize his directorial vision are absent here. But even if *Fahrenheit 451* may be disappointing as a "Truffaut" film, it is certainly effective in transferring Bradbury's vision to the screen.

In a repressive future society, printed material has been outlawed, and members of the Fire Service now start fires rather than put them out, uncovering illegal caches of books and burning them. In this ironic utopia peace of mind is valued above all else, and the individual voice, encouraged by the exchange of ideas in books, is considered a threat. The hero, Montag (Oskar Werner), is a fireman who secretly begins to read and gradually becomes aware of the importance of books. His subversive activity turns him into an outlaw, and after he is denounced by his wife he is forced to flee the city to live among the Bookmen, social outcasts who have taken on the monumental task of memorizing books in order to preserve culture.

Bradbury's novel expresses a romantic and optimistic

belief that culture and the humanist spirit will ultimately prevail against even the sternest repression—a view complemented by Truffaut's characteristic exuberance, humanity, and love of art and culture. In the film Truffaut treats books as sacred objects—indeed almost as living things. In fact, in comparison with the generally flat characters, the books in a way become "the heroes" of the tale. They are filmed by cinematographer Nicolas Roeg with great care, even affection, particularly in the vivid close-ups of their burning pages, which, in Bradbury's words, "leapt and danced like roasted birds, their wings ablaze with red and yellow feathers." The human beings have significantly less presence, which may have been Truffaut's intention.

The casting of Julie Christie in two opposing roles, as Montag's conservative wife and the woman who introduces him to literature, suggests that Truffaut was interested less in portraying rounded individuals than in presenting Everymen. To his credit, Truffaut tried to establish connections between the story's idea and actual history. Hence the uniforms of the firemen evoke those of the Nazis, and the inclusion of anachronistic details—old dresses and antique telephones—in the design of the future society emphasizes the continuity between the present and this imagined future.

Yet Truffaut seems to have considered the story less as SF than as a vehicle for personal expression. (His priority, perhaps inadvertently, is revealed by the poor quality of Charles Staffel's special effects.) From this perspective, Montag's conversion from a fireman to a reader is not so much an act of political rebellion as a pursuit of the imagination—the book he decides to memorize is Edgar Allan Poe's *Tales of Mystery and Imagination*—a quest common to many of Truffaut's protagonists.

Truffaut's visual imagination cannot sustain the simplicity of this film's premise or the illogicalities of its plot with complete success. Although *Fahrenheit 451* is certainly a personal statement by this important New Wave auteur, it is not entirely satisfactory as extrapolative science fiction.

B.K.G.

FAIL SAFE (1964). *Directed by Sidney Lumet; screenplay by Walter Bernstein; adapted from the novel by Eugene Burdick and Harvey Wheeler; photographed by Gerald Hirschfeld. With Henry Fonda, Dan O'Herlihy, Walter Matthau, Frank Overton, Edward Binns, Fritz Weaver, Larry Hagman, Sorrell Booke, Dom DeLuise, Dana Elcar. 111 minutes. Black and white.*

Most movies warning about nuclear war are grimly purposeful, and few are grimmer than *Fail Safe*. With a plot so similar to that of Dr. STRANGELOVE (1964) that it required accommodations between the distributors of

the two films, *Fail Safe* is as serious as the other film is comic, told with stark, high-contrast photography, intense acting, and high moral purpose. Based on a best-seller, the film was given prestige treatment, with a cast not just of major names but of exceptional actors. Director Sidney Lumet, known for such quality films as *Twelve Angry Men* (1957) and *Long Day's Journey into Night* (1962), was not only director but also one of the executive producers of *Fail Safe*. Most of the acting is fine, but Fritz Weaver is hammy; Walter Matthau's character was modeled on Henry Kissinger and is probably this exemplary actor's only overwrought performance.

President Henry Fonda learns that bombers have been sent past the fail-safe point en route to Moscow and tries to warn the Soviet premier; when despite everything a bomber gets through and blows up Moscow, Fonda contritely blows up New York, where his wife is shopping. Dan O'Herlihy, suffering from nightmares throughout, is the pilot chosen to obliterate Manhattan, and he commits suicide afterward. The film is nothing if not morbid and is rarely shown today.

Most viewers take this movie as seriously as it was intended, but some find its steely intensity overdone and the plot so preposterous as to be almost as funny as that of *Strangelove*.

B.W.

——— FANDOM ———

Science fiction may be the first category of fiction to have developed a body of enthusiastic amateurs—a fandom. As a group fans have not only supported SF they have also served it in a number of ways and even shaped it.

Once to admit that one read SF was to be labeled the resident crazy in school. That was when a new hardcover book was an event, when 1000 attendees at a World SF Convention was unimaginable, when the general public considered all SF fans to be BUCK ROGERS nuts. This situation led one early fan, Rick Sneary, to say, "It is a proud and lonely thing to be a fan." But times have changed. Today almost every student reads some SF, more than 1200 SF books are published every year, nearly 10,000 fans have attended a world convention, and almost everybody has heard at least of ASIMOV, BRADBURY, CLARKE, STAR TREK or STAR WARS or Steven SPIELBERG.

In the beginning—between 1926 and 1936—SF fans groped into contact with each other in the departments of readers' letters in *Amazing, Astounding,* and *Wonder*. That correspondence led to the formation of clubs and the publication of newsletters and magazines (fanzines), the organization of conventions, and individual acts of fan activities (fanac). These developments meant frequent contact between readers and creators, instant feedback for the genre, and audience influence on the subject and style of what was written and published, even on how it was illustrated. Out of fandom also came new writers, illustrators, editors, and publishers, to create what they had already imagined and discussed.

The first club was organized in Oakland, California, in 1927, one year after the appearance of *Amazing Stories*. Within a year clubs had been organized in Georgia, Chicago, and Boston. In 1929 Raymond A. PALMER, later to become an influential editor and publisher, organized the Science Correspondence Club, and in 1930 he published *Comet* as the first fanzine. That same year the Bay State Science Club of Boston issued *Asteroid,* and a New York fan club, the Scienceers, published *The Planet.* In 1931 Forrest J ACKERMAN of Los Angeles created a correspondence club, The Boys Scientifiction Club, and produced two issues of a clubzine.

In New York, Mortimer WEISINGER, who would become an editor not only of SF magazines but of Superman comics and a successful author of mainstream articles and books, and Julius Schwartz, who would become the first SF agent and later edit SUPERMAN and other DC comics, persuaded Allen Glasser to edit a new fanzine, *The Time Traveller,* and after two issues convinced Conrad H. Ruppert to print it. In 1932 a group of fans organized the *Science Fiction Digest.*

Meanwhile seventeen-year-old Charles D. HORNIG, who in 1933 had begun publishing a fanzine called *The Fantasy Fan,* had been hired to edit Hugo GERNSBACK's *Wonder Stories,* replacing David LASSER, the original editor. Lasser had organized promotions and contests, and helped found the American Interplanetary Society (in 1931 he wrote *The Conquest of Space*). Hornig thought of creating the Science Fiction League, a nationwide organization of fans to be publicized in his magazine. In 1934 local chapters sprang up in various parts of the country, including New York, Los Angeles, and Chicago.

By 1986–87, according to the *Fandom Directory,* the number of SF fan clubs in the United States had passed 550, and most foreign countries had clubs as well.

The first SF convention occurred in 1937, when a group of New York fans visited their Philadelphia counterparts. By 1938 different groups of fans in the New York area were competing to put on the first world convention, and on July 2, 1939, 200 fans gathered in Caravan Hall in Manhattan, under the leadership of Sam MOSKOWITZ, who would become a noted fan scholar with many professional publications, including the first published fan history. Fans came from as far away as Texas, New Mexico, and California. The last contingent included Ackerman and a young Ray Bradbury. But one group, close to home, was excluded because of feuding. They were the key members of the FUTURIANS, a group that included many members who later would become authors, agents, editors, and publishers, among them Frederik POHL and Donald A. WOLLHEIM.

The world convention would be held annually from that point, with the exception of the four years of U.S. participation in World War II, and would be rotated between the eastern, central, and western portions of the country until 1957, when it met in London. Since then the convention has met several times in Great Britain, once in Germany and Canada, and twice in Australia, earning the "world" in its name by location as well as by the attendance of fans from different countries. Fund drives had brought fans from Great Britain as early as 1949 through TAFF (Transatlantic Fan Fund), and a similar system was instituted later for Australia (DUFF— Down Under Fan Fund). By the 1980s foreign locations for the convention had become traditional at least every fourth year, and attendance had climbed close to 10,000 (in Anaheim, 1984).

Contests and prizes were part of the early Gernsback publications, and fans began to present awards in 1941 at the third world convention, held in Denver. The first International Fantasy Awards were given from 1951 to 1957 by a panel of British experts. The Science Fiction Achievement Awards, popularly known as Hugos (after Gernsback), were instituted at the World Convention of 1953, held in Philadelphia, and after the lapse of a year reinstated for the 1955 Cleveland convention. They have expanded from awards for writing, editing, and illustration to recognitions for a long list of accomplishments in allied fields and fandom, voted on by fans with advance membership in the convention. Many other awards are presented in connection with the World Science Fiction Convention, or by other organizations, including the First Fandom lifetime achievement awards; the E. Everett Evans "Big Heart" Award; the Gernsback Awards; the Academy of Science Fiction, Fantasy, and Horror Films awards, the Australian Ditmars, and so forth.

The feud between the Futurians and Moskowitz's New Fandom was only one of many in the microcosm of SF fandom. Some of the earliest debates concerned the goals of clubs or publications, with some fans committed to the development of science and others to science fiction. The Moskowitz-Futurians debate was over whether fans should work to create the better world that many stories described; some called this communism, and to be sure a number of the Futurians had joined the Young Communist League. Often struggles grew up over the sponsorship of conventions and sometimes simply over power itself. When there were no feuds, puckish fans would invent them, such as the debate in the 1930s over whether magazines should be held together by wire staples.

Other developments in fandom were the organization of amateur press societies to distribute fanzines and the setting up of communal dwellings. The Fantasy Amateur Press Association (FAPA) was organized in 1937, and Vanguard Amateur Press Association and Spectator Amateur Press Society (SAPS) in the mid-1940s. Today there are dozens of groups, often organized around special interests, that distribute their publications to members. In the late 1930s and early 1940s the idea of fans living together became popular; "Ivory Tower" was rented in Brooklyn by Futurians, "Slan Shack" was created in Battle Creek, Michigan, and "Tendril Towers" appeared in Los Angeles (both of the last two named in honor of A. E. VAN VOGT's 1940 novel *Slan*). Such communal arrangements, however, did not survive the 1940s.

Like any subculture SF fandom developed its own language. Much of this language is initial slang—such as *fiawol* ("fandom is a way of life"), *fijagh* ("fandom is just a goddamned hobby"), and *gafia* ("get away from it all")—but some is portmanteau—such as *corflu* ("correction fluid"), *fanac* ("fan activity"), and *prozine* ("professional magazine")—and some is invention or tradition. Any "neofan" is advised to learn the language before getting in too deep: dictionaries and instructors are available at most conventions. A basic disagreement exists over what to call science fiction for short. Ackerman invented the term *sci-fi*, and many people and publications use it, but many fans and authors consider this a term used mostly by people and publications who don't understand the genre; they prefer *SF* or *sf*.

Significant contributions have been made to SF by fandom. Not only had it produced a substantial number of writers, illustrators, and editors in the field—shaping SF by both feedback and actual takeover—but it has also contributed publishers. In fact, one of the most significant developments in SF was the explosion of book publication following World War II, and most of this was the product of fan publishing.

Since the earliest days of fandom, fans have contributed a substantial service by collecting: every fan was a potential collector, and the only reason many of the fragile pulp-paper magazines survive is the dedication of fans. Today some of those collections are worth millions of dollars, and individual magazines (and even early fanzines) have sold for thousands of dollars. Colleges and universities getting into the study of SF in the late 1960s and early 1970s founded their research collections on gifts and purchases from fan collectors.

After World War II some of these collectors decided to reprint in book format their favorite stories and serials from the magazines. Lloyd Arthur ESHBACH founded Fantasy Press; David A. Kyle and Martin Greenberg, Gnome Press; William L. Crawford, Fantasy Publishing Co.; Melvin Erle Korshak and Ted Dikty, Shasta Publishers; and Jim Williams, Prime Press. Arkham House had been created even earlier by August DERLETH with the help of Donald Wandrei. The fan publishers produced dozens of books. Virtually all such operations failed financially, but their example got many major publishers interested in the field, and copies of those early publications are worth many times their original price. Today the pub-

lication of collector's editions is primarily a matter of fan publishing, although one major publisher has entered the field. And at least one major commercial publisher, DAW Books, was created by a onetime fan, Donald A. WOLLHEIM.

Fans also have contributed significantly to scholarship with such publications as Everett F. BLEILER's *The Checklist of Fantastic Literature*, W. R. Cole's *A Checklist of Science Fiction Anthologies*, Michael Ashley, Terry Jeeves, and Robert Weinberg's *The Complete Index to Astounding/Analog*, Donald H. Tuck's *The Encyclopedia of Science Fiction and Fantasy*, Donald B. Day's *Index to the Science Fiction Magazines, 1926–1950*, with its successors by the MIT Science Fiction Society, and many others, including numerous individual pieces of scholarship.

Science fiction would not be what it is today without fandom. Some critics in academia and the mainstream believe that the relationship is too close for the writers' true artistic independence, and even some academic publications are accused of "fannishness." In many ways, however, the ignoring of SF by the mainstream of literature, and the creation of what has been called the science-fiction ghetto, is the reason for fandom's development. If traditional literature was not going to be concerned with SF, fans would have to provide the appreciation, the criticism, the studies, even the books, the anthologies, and the tools of scholarship. Newsmagazines, such as *Locus* and *Science Fiction Chronicle*, thrive because they are the only places thousands of readers can find substantial information about the field that fascinates them.

It still may be "a proud and lonely thing to be a fan."

F.J.A.

FANTASTIC PLANET (*La Planète sauvage*) (1973). *Directed by René Laloux; screenplay by Roland Topor and René Laloux; adapted from the novel* Oms en série *by Stefan Wul; music by Alain Goraguer. 72 minutes. Color.*

The surreal backgrounds of this animated adult cartoon, a French-Czechoslovakian coproduction, are its chief attraction. The story itself, about blue humanoid giants on a distant planet who keep humans as pets, is at the juvenile level: eventually the human Oms escape and become annoying pests, and the giant Draags decide to eliminate them. The Oms rebel and finally force the Draags to recognize them as equals by building spaceships and destroying the Draags' methods of reproduction.

In the background, however, alien creatures go about their daily lives, sustaining their own existences or destroying others; strange, demonic machines charge around malevolently; and occasionally in the lives of the Draags nightmarish details emerge, such as their method of

Fantastic Voyage

propagating: their "meditation spheres," along with those of beings from other galaxies, descend on the headless shoulders of gigantic naked human figures, whereupon they go into a strange mating dance. Original artwork was provided by Roland Topor.

J.E.G.

FANTASTIC VOYAGE (1966). *Directed by Richard Fleischer; screenplay by Harry Kleiner; photographed by Ernest Laszlo; music by Leonard Rosenman. With Stephen Boyd, Donald Pleasence, Arthur O'Connell, Raquel Welch, Edmond O'Brien, William Redfield, Arthur Kennedy, Jean Del Val, James Brolin. 100 minutes. Color.*

At the time of its release, *Fantastic Voyage* was considered state-of-the-art science fiction, and it is often accorded classic status today. The film was lavishly budgeted, its production was covered extensively in the media, and it was a substantial hit. Viewed today this film is likely to be regarded as a colorful, even comic bore, imaginatively designed but dramatically vapid. Until INNERSPACE (1987), however, it was the only SF film set inside the human body.

A defecting scientist develops a blood clot in the brain. Daring secret agent Grant (Stephen Boyd) and his submarine crew are miniaturized to destroy the clot, but they have only sixty minutes to complete the task—and the only person who knows how to make the miniaturization last longer is the scientist himself. Shrunken, the sub is injected into the scientist's bloodstream and makes its way to his brain. As is typical of adventure melodrama, there's also a saboteur (Donald Pleasence) on board. Mission accomplished, with Pleasence devoured by a white blood cell, the heroes emerge in a teardrop.

The elaborate sets of the body interior were designed by Jack Martin Smith and Dale Hennesy and were reputed to be thoroughly accurate. But their accuracy was compromised by inaccuracies in other areas and weak dramatics. The film becomes more outlandish as it proceeds, and it makes so many other scientific blunders as to venture into sheer fantasy. Miniaturized air is released from the sub; the machine itself is left behind, devoured by a white blood cell—presumably both the air and the sub will return to normal size when the time limit is up. In his novelization of the script, Isaac ASIMOV endeavored to straighten out these gaffes, but the strain shows.

B.W.

FANTHORPE, R[OBERT] L[IONEL] (1935–   ).
British writer and English teacher who wrote more than 160 novels and collections of stories, mostly between 1958 and 1967, while teaching full time. Almost all Fanthorpe's work was published by British publisher John Spencer in *Supernatural Stories* or under Spencer's Badger paperback imprint. As a consequence, much of Fanthorpe's fiction consists of hastily written adventure stories, many slanted toward horror and fantasy. He made extensive use of folklore in books such as *The Timeless Ones* (1963), romance in *The Black Lion* (1979), the supernatural in *From Realms Beyond* (1963) and *The Thing from Sheol* (1963), and magic in *The Eye of Karnak* (1962). His work is consistently moral; in it good always triumphs over evil.

Fanthorpe has used at least seventeen pseudonyms, the most important of which are Leo Brett, Bron Fane, John E. Miller, Lionel Roberts, Pel Torro, and Karl Zeigfried. After a break of more than a decade, he began publishing science fiction again at the beginning of the 1980s.

S.H.G.

FARLEY, RALPH MILNE (Pseudonym of Roger Sherman Hoar) (1887–1963). American writer, patent engineer, and teacher. Farley's early pulp fiction, notably the Radio Man series, was modeled on that of Edgar Rice BURROUGHS. The series, which describes the adventures of a Boston scientist who sends himself to Venus via radio, consists of *The Radio Man* (1924/1948, also known as *An Earthman on Venus*), *The Radio Beasts* (1925/1964), *The Radio Planet* (1926/1964), "The Radio Man Returns" (1939), and "The Radio Minds of Mars" (1955/1969). *The Immortals* (1934/1947) is slightly more sophisticated science-fiction adventure. The best of Farley's pulp SF stories can be found in *The Omnibus of Time* (1950), and two further stories are in *The Hidden Universe* (1950).

B.S.

FARMER, PHILIP JOSE (1918–   ).

American writer with a reputation for handling themes of sex and religion in new and surprising ways; best known for the five Riverworld novels. Born and raised in the Midwest, Farmer has lived in Peoria, Illinois, since the late 1960s. He won a 1953 Hugo Award for best new writer on the strength of his first few science-fiction stories and subsequent Hugos for "Riders of the Purple Wage" (novella, 1967) and *To Your Scattered Bodies Go* (novel, 1972).

Farmer's first SF story, "The Lovers" (1952), recounting the love of a repressed human male for an alien female, was immediately welcomed as a refreshing and adult treatment of sexuality—even though it had been rejected by *Astounding* and *Galaxy* as disgusting. Other similarly innovative and disturbing stories followed, including "Mother" (1953), "Strange Compulsion" (1953, retitled "The Captain's Daughter"), "The God Business" (1954), and others collected in *Strange Relations* (1960) and *The Alley God* (1962). These works established Farmer's reputation as a taboo breaker in the areas of sex and religion.

Despite his popularity with readers, the first years of Farmer's career were difficult. In 1954 the bankruptcy of Shasta Publishers, which had promised a cash award and publication for his novel *I Owe for the Flesh* (the progenitor of the Riverworld series), nearly ended his career as a full-time writer before it could properly start. Nevertheless, he continued to write part-time for the next fifteen years, producing fourteen novels, including *The Green Odyssey* (1957); *Flesh* (1960); *The Lovers*, a book-length revision of his short story by the same name (1961); *Inside Outside* (1964); *Night of Light* (1966); and a non-SF story of interracial love, *Fire and Night* (1962).

Much of Farmer's work of the 1960s and 1970s celebrates the popular and high literature he has enjoyed since his youth. The World of Tiers series (*The Maker of Universes*, 1965; *The Gates of Creation*, 1966; *A Private Cosmos*, 1968; *Behind the Walls of Terra*, 1970; *The Lavalite World*, 1977) mixes elements of classical and Amerindian mythology, William Blake, Edgar Rice Burroughs, and chase-and-escape adventure. *Image of the Beast* (1968), *Blown* (1969), and *A Feast Unknown* (1969), written for the upscale "adult" publisher Essex House, combine parodies of the private-eye and pulp superhero genres with what Leslie Fiedler has characterized as "sado-pornographic" scenes of sex and violence. These three books, by turns erotic, satiric, and disturbing, are the most uncomfortable of Farmer's explorations of the darker side of the human psyche.

In addition, *Feast* is the first full-fledged example of Farmer's recycling not just of the motifs of his favorite fiction but of the characters themselves. *Feast* features Tarzan and Doc Savage (under pseudonyms) in adventures that continue in *Lord of the Trees* and *The Mad Goblin* (1970). A few years later Farmer wrote the bi-

Philip Jose Farmer

ographies *Tarzan Alive* (1972) and *Doc Savage: His Apocalyptic Life* (1973), along the lines of William S. Baring-Gould's work on Sherlock Holmes and Nero Wolfe. This treatment of fiction as history grew into the Wold Newton cycle of stories and biographies, in which Farmer established a family tree that includes Captain Blood, Thomas Carlyle, the Greystokes, Jack the Ripper, Philip Marlowe, and James Bond. Eventually Farmer wrote stories as some of these characters, most notably *Venus on the Half-Shell* (1975), by Kurt VONNEGUT's Kilgore Trout.

The Riverworld series (*To Your Scattered Bodies Go*, 1971; *The Fabulous Riverboat*, 1971; *The Dark Design*, 1977; *The Magic Labyrinth*, 1980; *Gods of Riverworld*, 1983) is a large-scale investigation of human aspirations and limits. After gathering on the banks of a multi-million-mile-long river everyone who has ever lived and giving them the means for comfortable, indefinitely extended lives, Farmer showed how we reinvent not only civilization but also its discontents and insanities. Historic figures mingle with Farmer's own creations, so that Sir Richard Francis Burton can meet Peter Jairus Frigate of Peoria for adventures, conversations, and meditations. As with Frank HERBERT's Dune series, which it resembles in scope, bulk, and publishing history, the Riverworld series led some to wonder what the author might do outside such a massive undertaking. The answer is that he continues to stretch and challenge himself and the conventions of SF, as in *The Unreasoning Mask* (1981), a Sufi space opera; *A Barnstormer in Oz* (1982), the adventures of Dorothy's son; *Dayworld* (1985), a development of the setting of "The Sliced-Crossways Only-on-Tuesday World" (1971); and enough projects to last into the next century.

NOTABLE OTHER WORKS: *A Woman a Day* (1960; retitled *Timestop!*); *The Cache from Outer Space* (1962);

The Celestial Blueprint (1962); *Tongues of the Moon* (1964); *Dare* (1965); *The Gate of Time* (1966); *Lord Tyger* (1970); *The Stone God Awakens* (1970); *Down in the Black Gang and Other Stories* (collection, 1971); *The Wind Whales of Ishmael* (1971); *The Book of Philip José Farmer* (collection, 1972); *Time's Last Gift* (1972); *The Other Log of Phileas Fogg* (1973); *Traitor to the Living* (1973); *The Adventure of the Peerless Peer* (1974); *Hadon of Ancient Opar* (1974); *Flight to Opar* (1976); *Ironcastle* (translated from the novel of J.-H. Rosny, 1976); *Mother Was a Lovely Beast* (edited, 1976); *Dark Is the Sun* (1979); *Jesus on Mars* (1979); *Riverworld and Other Stories* (collection, 1979); *Father to the Stars* (1981); "Maps and Spasms" (1981, autobiographical essay in Martin H. Greenberg, ed., *Fantastic Lives*); *Greatheart Silver* (1982); *Stations of the Nightmare* (1982); *The Purple Book* (collection, 1982); *River of Eternity* (1983, the 1954 second draft of the original Riverworld novel); *The Grand Adventure* (collection, 1984).

R.F.L.

FAST, HOWARD [MELVIN] (1914–).

American mainstream writer whose works are characterized by political commitment, moral integrity, and human warmth. Fast is best known for his historical novels, particularly *Citizen Tom Paine* (1943), *Spartacus* (1951), and *The Immigrants* (1977). His science fiction comprises one novel, *The Hunter and the Trap* (1967), and four collections of short stories: *The Edge of Tomorrow* (1961), *The General Zapped an Angel* (1970), *A Touch of Infinity* (1973), and *Time and the Riddle: Thirty-one Zen Stories* (1975). Fast's SF emphasizes spiritual longing and the half-realized fantasies of ordinary people. He has called these stories parables that preach "against the cruelty and foolishness of modern man." One of his favorite short stories, "The General Zapped an Angel," describes how a brutal general shoots an angel while engaged in a battle in Vietnam; "The Mouse" recounts the reactions of humans to a mouse that is given intelligence by an alien. At his best Fast writes with impeccable clarity and depth, and his fiction often leads readers to reconsider the morality of contemporary human values.

J.R.D.

FEARN, JOHN [FRANCES] RUSSELL (1908– 1960).

British author who wrote more than eighty novels and nearly 200 short stories under his own name and a host of pseudonyms. Fearn was the ultimate pulp writer of the 1940s and 1950s. His stories, often adventure science fiction, deal with supermen (*The Intelligence Gigantic*, 1933) and superwomen (*The Golden Amazon*, 1944), with Martian battles (*Emperor of Mars*,

1950; and *Red Men of Mars*, 1950), and with disasters (*Annihilation*, 1950; and *The Devouring Fire*, 1953). *The Golden Amazon* was reprinted in the *Toronto Star Weekly* and led to the commissioning of an Amazon series that ran for sixteen years. Fearn also wrote thoughtful idea stories, however, and a number of them—such as "The Man Who Stopped the Dust" (1934), written under his own name, and "Wings across the Cosmos" (1938), written as Polton Cross, one of Fearn's eight pseudonyms—are remembered fondly by older readers.

In 1950 Fearn adopted the name Vargo Statten for a particularly popular series of fifty-two novels that he wrote for a British publisher, which created a magazine named *Vargo Statten* for him to edit. All this ended, however, with the general failure of British paperback publishers in 1956. Fearn branched out into acting, writing, and producing in films, television, radio, and theater; he even put together a theatrical troupe before his premature death at the age of fifty-two.

S.H.G.

———————— FILM ————————

Any film genre that can look back on milestones such as METROPOLIS, FRANKENSTEIN, KING KONG, THINGS TO COME, THE DAY THE EARTH STOOD STILL, DR. STRANGELOVE, 2001, and E.T. must be recognized for its protean diversity and inherent power. Indeed, even when measured by its failures rather than by its successes, science-fiction film has left an indelible mark on our national consciousness. The top three money-making films ever released are SF (E.T., STAR WARS, and THE EMPIRE STRIKES BACK), and although such lists are ever subject to change, six of the top money-making films of all time are SF. More significant than the popularity of these films, however, is their cultural impact; they have clearly established a new popular mythology, reinforced by a deluge of spin-off products ranging from T-shirts and toys to TV shows and breakfast cereals. Just as earlier SF films were greatly responsible for planting in the mind of the American public its first images of space flight, computers, and robots, and its first fear of nuclear radiation, contemporary SF films continue to shape our concerns about the present and our fears and fantasies about the future.

Yet there is no denying that the genre has been responsible for some of the worst films ever made, and, unfortunately, it is perhaps most frequently thought of and written about as if its poorest efforts were the measure of its worth. What's more, some of SF's finest examples—films such as THE MAN IN THE WHITE SUIT (1951), LA JETEE (*The Pier*, 1963), SECONDS (1966), THE BROTHER FROM ANOTHER PLANET (1984), or BRAZIL (1986)—are not generally thought of as SF. Most SF writers do not like most SF movies, noting their tendency to be rampantly illogical, scientifically insulting, and overly reliant on sensational SPECIAL EFFECTS. Many SF writers and critics see the history of SF film as a sad story of missed opportunities and betrayals, caused in great part by Hollywood's preference for its own ideas and writers over the body of SF literature that made the film genre possible. Although more than understandable, this view effectively denies film its identity as an independent medium and precludes any real understanding of SF film.

Certainly many SF films *are* embarrassingly illogical, and many adaptations of SF literature disappointingly depart from their sources, but to condemn SF film on the basis of its weakest movies makes no more sense than to condemn any literary genre on the basis of its weakest works. To judge SF film primarily in terms of the degree to which it faithfully "reproduces" the letter and/or spirit of SF writing is to ignore the wide range of profitable relations possible in film adaptation. Perhaps the most important thing to remember when thinking about the relation of SF writing to SF film is simply that the two endeavors are very different.

A movie may be "made from" or "based on" a novel, but it should not be thought of as an illustrated novel or the moving picture of a novel: writing and film *mean* in different ways, are produced with different goals, and have different impacts on their audiences. Furthermore, adaptations of existing SF writing account for only a fraction of the total number of SF films. Many of the SF films made from original treatments would not "translate" well into writing, but then they were not intended for such translation—no more than film is intended to compete with writing. The decision to tell a story on film marks a choice of medium, an opting for one kind of meaning or signification system over another. The choice of film over writing also represents a choice of a primarily visual logic system over a discursive one. As movies such as 2001, BLADE RUNNER, and BACK TO THE FUTURE make clear, a series of images on film creates its own logic, quite apart from the prose narrative that it conveys, and film also presents its meaning through auditory tracks that carry dialogue, music, and sound effects. Accordingly, SF filmmakers do not just supply concrete images for a story but through the sound track, camera angles, lighting, cutting from scene to scene, casting of actors, and other devices unique to the medium, *create* a story through the way they choose to tell it.

The history of SF film reveals other important differences from SF writing. Peter Nicholls has accurately observed that SF films can be grouped by theme or subject into four basic formulas: space, dystopia, monsters, and disasters. Such a classification, however, attempts to wrestle film into familiar literary categories rather than to consider the kinds of cinematographic aesthetics and technology that also might group SF film. For example, a "time travel" film such as George PAL's production of THE TIME MACHINE (1960) would probably be classed as

dystopian under such a literary-oriented system, but it might be much more profitably thought of—in film terms—as belonging to a long tradition of SF films concerned with the illusion of manipulating time, an illusion for which cinema is particularly well suited. In this sense it is important to remember that most of what we now consider the earliest SF films were simply thought of by their makers as "trick" or "gimmick" films, their stories and subjects much less important to their makers than the technology that made their illusions possible. Indeed, one major line of film theory goes so far as to suggest that the real purpose of SF film is to demonstrate the state of the art of both the cinema itself and its special effects techniques.

Science-fiction film is as old as cinema itself and nearly as old as the modern SF literature introduced by Jules VERNE and H. G. WELLS. Almost as soon as the means of cinematography was consolidated in the 1890s, the new medium made technology and science one of its first subjects—invariably for humorous treatment. A great number of the first short films made in France, England, and the United States poke fun at automation, scientific elixirs, and devices that could slow or speed up time. Frenchman Georges MELIES is generally credited with making the first SF film of significant length in 1902, when he drew very loosely from books by both Verne and Wells to create his *Le Voyage Dans la Lune* (A TRIP TO THE MOON). But it would be more accurate to say that Méliès was the first to base a film on SF literature.

Actually, neither Méliès's landmark film nor any of the dozens of others that dealt with subjects now thought of as SF share any of the significant concerns or assumptions of SF literature. Trained as a magician and a showman, Méliès clearly made his film in the tradition of popular stage and fairground spectacles of his time rather than in the spirit of Wells or Verne. This distinction between the concerns, assumptions, and goals of film and SF literature has remained true for most of "SF" film from its crude beginnings to the blockbuster special effects marvels of the present. It is important to remember that the very first SF films were made with little or no interest in SF per se but as an exciting new means to showcase special effects—as technological spectacle, rather than stimulus for reflection. Thus, although early SF films often had as their starting points works of literature, the goals and concerns of the early filmmakers were quite different from those of SF writers, a legacy that persists in most SF films today.

Moreover, both the medium of film and the nature of the film industry mandated some essential differences from written SF. Some central idea or concept or hypothesis usually gives rise to SF literature, whereas SF film may well start from or be driven by an image or special effect—visual phenomena. Furthermore, although most SF writers pride themselves on their knowledge of science and their sensitivity to its implications,

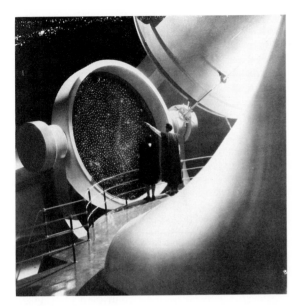

Things to Come (1936)

what most filmmakers know best is not science but other movies. As a result the general conventions of SF film may actually have more in common with those of other film genres—such as the western or the musical—than with the assumptions and conventions of SF writing. In other words, before SF film can be compared with SF writing, it must be understood in terms of the conventions, assumptions, and production methods of both the genre film and the classic Hollywood style within which genres developed.

Méliès was by no means alone in his use of science-fictional situations to exploit the technological potential of the cinema. In England, Robert Paul and H. G. Wells never followed through on their 1895 plans for constructing a multimedia, motion picture–centered theater to simulate time travel, but Paul did go on to make a number of films with SF aspects, such as *How to Make Time Fly* (1905). One of the pioneers of the SF film in America was Thomas Edison, whose most ambitious film project was a sixteen-minute version of *Frankenstein,* made in 1910. Other Edison SF films include *The Wonderful Electro-magnet* (1909), *A Trip to Mars* (1911), and *How Patrick's Eyes Were Opened* (1912), which features a device called the Projecto-Optician, SF film's first image of a visual communication screen.

Edison's was but one of many companies in the United States, France, and Great Britain that together produced over 175 films with SF themes between 1900 and 1920. After 1910 the length of these films significantly increased from the five- to ten-minute range to one of forty

to seventy-five minutes, and as the films grew longer, their concerns tended to become more serious. In 1910 an American film, *The Comet,* became the first developed disaster movie, presenting a story in which Halley's comet crashes into the Earth. As Europe inexorably inched toward World War I, SF films, particularly in Great Britain, became more and more concerned with the nature of future war. *The Airship Destroyer* (1909) first depicted aerial warfare, an idea also exploited in 1916 in D. W. Griffith's *The Flying Torpedo.* Two German films, *Der Golem* (1914) and Homunculus (1916), solidified what has become one of the enduring themes of SF film—the fear of artificial life.

Although the films of the 1910s grew increasingly serious, the years from 1920 to 1930 saw a fundamental shift in the nature of SF cinema from primarily humorous goals to those that are realistic and were strongly influenced by the dark and threatening atmosphere of German expressionism. German films such as *The Cabinet of Dr. Caligari* (1919) and *Nosferatu* (1922) are horror rather than SF, but they had much to do with the look and assumptions of many later SF films made in America. This distinction between horror film and SF film is important. Whereas horror movies featuring vampires, werewolves, mummies, and ghosts depend on some supernatural incarnation of evil or an assumption of magic and miracles, SF films are neo- or pseudorealistic, offering some attempt to account rationally for the origins of their "impossible" contents. In this sense Dracula is a horror monster, but Frankenstein's creature emblemizes the SF monster. Of course, many films, including Dr. Jekyll and Mr. Hyde, contain both horror and SF elements.

The great number of films that have been made from the Jekyll and Hyde story (at least five in America before 1920) suggests just how seductive the emblem of the mad scientist became for the cinema. René Clair's *Paris qui dort (The Crazy Ray)* invoked that emblem to visually stunning effect in 1923 with a story of a scientist who freezes time for almost everyone in Paris. More often than not, SF film depicts its science in the character of its scientists, a technique perhaps best exploited by David Cronenberg's The Fly (1986).

A single Russian film, Aelita, went far in 1924 toward establishing the visual conventions for another mainstay of SF film, the portrayal of the interplanetary future. Its cubist and futurist designs for a dystopian Martian society ruled by Queen Aelita seem to have particularly influenced the look of the American Flash Gordon and Buck Rogers serials. An even more influential American film appeared in 1925: The Lost World, featuring impressive special effects dinosaurs by Willis O'Brien, a sign of what he would accomplish in *King Kong* in 1933. Another important development in this decade was German director Fritz Lang's *Die Frau im Mond* (The Woman in the Moon), which in 1928 became the genre's first serious space-travel film. Lang *invented* the rocket count-down in that film and pioneered the use of actual rocket experts as technical advisers.

No development in the 1920s, however, came close to matching the specific impact on SF film of a single movie—Lang's classic *Metropolis* (1926). This gargan-tuan production, originally 182 minutes long and fea-turing a cast of over 37,000, has been correctly identified as one of the indisputable classics, not just of SF but of all film. In one great movie Lang managed to combine scenes of a fantastic future city, its dystopian underpin-nings, a mad scientist with an artificial arm who creates a robot that can pass for human, and a spectacular dis-aster as the underground city is flooded. The archetypal visual imagery of this film has exerted tremendous in-fluence on SF films through *Blade Runner* (1982) and *Brazil* (1986).

After the significant achievements of the SF film in its first thirty years, the decades of the 1930s and 1940s can only be seen as a somewhat disappointing period of transition in which the genre searched for a new iden-tity that would reflect changes necessitated by the advent of sound in the cinema and would be more heavily influenced by increasingly ominous world affairs. Just as sound dramatically reshaped the practices of cinema in general, it called for pivotal changes in the SF film— now science had to be talked about as well as shown; visual spectacle no longer sufficed. Perhaps because au-diences lacked the patience to listen to much talk about science and certainly because screenwriters were not familiar enough with or interested enough in scientific speculation, relatively few of the early talkies had sig-nificant SF elements, and the most successful American SF films in the 1930s were more in the tradition of Gothic horror than of SF. Yet paradoxically the 1930s seems to have been the decade in which the SF film first really captured the public's imagination, the time in which its most lasting emblems were created.

In 1931 James Whale directed *Frankenstein* for Uni-versal Studios, and in 1935 he made its even more im-pressive sequel, BRIDE OF FRANKENSTEIN. The popularity of both films inextricably wedded the concept of the mad scientist to images of Gothic horror, an association intensified by Rouben Mamoulian's 1932 version of *Dr. Jekyll and Mr. Hyde*, and the same year's ISLAND OF LOST SOULS, featuring a memorable performance by Charles Laughton as Dr. Moreau. THE INVISIBLE MAN (1933), wittily directed by Whale from a screenplay written in part by Philip WYLIE, brought still another of Wells's stories to the screen.

The real legacy of these films has been their images. Apart from Boris KARLOFF's shambling monster, *Fran-kenstein* provided an irresistible image of electrical charges madly dancing over ominous-looking laboratory equipment, setting a pattern for laboratory scenes that still exists. And no better example of the primacy of the image in SF film can be found than in *King Kong,* a film structured almost completely around masterful special effects by Willis O'Brien. O'Brien's stop-motion ani-mation of Kong has rarely been matched in subsequent giant creature films, and his monster, like Karloff's crea-ture, has become one of our familiar cultural icons, per-haps an achievement in film rivaling Herman Melville's creation of the literary icon for giantism, Moby Dick.

Although the 1930s saw a number of efforts to recap-ture the visionary scope of *Metropolis,* only two films deserve mention as successors to Lang's classic: the odd Hollywood musical JUST IMAGINE (1930) and the monu-mental British THINGS TO COME (1936). Whatever *Just Imagine* lacked in serious purpose was more than made up for by *Things to Come,* produced by Alexander Korda and directed by William Cameron MENZIES from a script by Wells. Wells also strictly watched over the film's making, and the fact that one of the two great fathers of modern SF literature was also able to figure in the making of one of the most important SF films says much about the speed with which the film genre had developed. Offended by the "balderdash" he saw in *Metropolis,* Wells loaded *Things to Come* with ideas, primarily his belief in the ability of science and tech-nocracy to order the chaos of humanity. In a memoran-dum to those making the film, he advised: "As a general rule you may take it that whatever Lang did in *Metrop-olis* is the exact contrary of what we want done here." Spanning the years between 1940 and 2036, the film consistently champions technological progress, advanc-ing Wells's belief that only a "scientific order of society" offers an alternative to perpetual conflict. The film ends with men of science triumphing over popular opposition to launch an exploration to the Moon. The leader of the scientists sums up what Wells saw as a choice "between stagnation and the universe" and portentously asks, "Which will it be?" Almost alone among early SF films in its proscience and pro–space travel stance, *Things to Come* must surely be one of the genre's masterpieces.

However, if *Things to Come* represents for many the ideal of the SF film, the 1930s serials featuring the ad-ventures of Flash Gordon and Buck Rogers represent more of its reality. *Flash Gordon* (1936) and *Buck Rog-ers* (1939) gave not only SF film but also SF literature an image both may never completely escape. More low-budget serials followed in the 1940s, when the events of World War II completely overshadowed filmic imag-ination.

Not until 1950 did SF film recapture the impact and immediacy of *Things to Come,* but during that decade SF film had its first great renaissance and became a staple of American popular culture, emerging as one of Hol-lywood's most successful and persistent film genres. In the years following World War II, Americans slowly began to wonder whether they were the beneficiaries or the victims of great scientific and technological leaps. Probably more than anything else, the atomic bomb signaled that the march of science could have terrifying implications (a fear pointedly evident in Japan in the cycle of antinuclear monster films started by *Godzilla* in 1954). The great American national confidence of the war years inexorably began to give way to paranoia, best tapped by Senator Joseph McCarthy in the political realm and by the SF movie in the realm of entertainment. Film after film warned of invasion conspiracies, forms of mind control, atomic mutations, and world destruction. *The Day the Earth Stood Still* (1951), FIVE (1951), THE THING (1951), WHEN WORLDS COLLIDE (1951), RED PLANET MARS (1952), THE BEAST FROM 20,000 FATHOMS (1953), INVADERS FROM MARS (1953), IT CAME FROM OUTER SPACE (1953), WAR OF THE WORLDS (1954), *Target Earth* (1954), THEM! (1954), and THIS ISLAND EARTH (1955) all suggested the precariousness of human existence and great threats to the "American way of life." Such films constitute no less than an aesthetic of paranoia, and their fears were more than matched by SF films in the second half of the decade. Movies such as the Howard Hawks production of *The Thing* and INVASION OF THE BODY SNATCHERS (directed by Don Siegel, 1956)—possibly the most powerful SF film made in the 1950s—remain the dominant image of that period. More important for the development of the genre was the fact that the SF films of the 1950s shed most of the Gothic and horror conventions so prevalent for the previous thirty years, turning their attention from the supernatural to the scientifically created or "explainable" unnatural.

The first significant SF film of the decade, DESTINATION MOON (1950), offers an interesting measure of the genre's development, because its subject is the same as that of Méliès's *Le Voyage dans la Lune* and Lang's *Die Frau im Mond*. Produced by George Pal, whose SF film projects *When Worlds Collide*, *War of the Worlds*, CONQUEST OF SPACE, and *The Time Machine* would largely shape the look of SF film in the 1950s and early 1960s, *Destination Moon* was everything that Méliès's Moon trip film had *not* been: scientifically accurate, realistic, serious, and, by today's standards, a bit dull. Robert A. Heinlein watched over the making of this film in much the same way that Wells had supervised *Things to Come,* and, perhaps as a result, *Destination Moon* does not display the paranoia so common in most SF films of this decade. Other space exploration films in the 1950s were ROCKETSHIP X-M (1950), RIDERS TO THE STARS (1954), *Conquest of Space* (1954), and FROM THE EARTH TO THE MOON (1958).

Much more dramatic than the space exploration films were those featuring first contacts with visitors from outer space. *The Day the Earth Stood Still* and *It Came from Outer Space* (1953) were the most sophisticated films in this space subgenre, both noteworthy for their criticism of human violence and mistrust. *It Came from Outer Space*, the first in a flurry of 1950s SF movies

filmed in 3-D, was also the first in a long line of Universal Studios SF films produced by William Alland and directed by Jack ARNOLD, including THE CREATURE FROM THE BLACK LAGOON (1954), TARANTULA (1955), and THE INCREDIBLE SHRINKING MAN (1957). Alland was largely responsible for Universal's interest in SF, and his importance in the development of SF film rivals that of George Pal. *This Island Earth* (1955), another Alland project, was the first relatively big-budget space opera film of the decade. Two other impressive SF films of the period, FORBIDDEN PLANET (1956) and 20,000 LEAGUES UNDER THE SEA (1954), were both box-office and critical successes. And in Great Britain, Hammer Films produced two superior projects, THE QUATERMASS EXPERIMENT *(The Creeping Unknown),* released in 1956, and its 1957 sequel, *Quatermass II (Enemy from Space).*

Several 1950s SF films are noteworthy for their depiction of children and/or teenagers, reflecting Hollywood's belated recognition that it was no longer really creating "family entertainment" and that its untapped market was the young. Independent producer Roger CORMAN was the first to exploit this new youth market fully with films such as IT CONQUERED THE WORLD (1956), ATTACK OF THE CRAB MONSTERS (1957), and *Teenage Caveman* (1958). Other independent productions, even more specifically targeted for youth audiences, were *I Was a Teenage Werewolf* (1957), *I Was a Teenage Frankenstein* (1958), and *The Blob* (1958). Undoubtedly the two best SF films about children during the 1950s were Menzies's *Invaders from Mars* (1953), uniquely a child's nightmare filmed from a child's perspective, and Jack Arnold's THE SPACE CHILDREN (1958), featuring children benignly controlled by a pacifistic alien intelligence.

The great irony of SF films of this decade is that they have been largely kept alive by television, Hollywood's greatest fear when they were made and a significant factor in the diminished vitality of the genre late in the decade. The increasing accessibility of videotape seems certain to make these films even more familiar to contemporary and future audiences. Perhaps even more important, the SF films of the 1950s seem to have in great part shaped the sensibilities of some of the most successful directors and producers of big-budget SF successes in the 1970s and 1980s. Steven SPIELBERG (CLOSE ENCOUNTERS OF THE THIRD KIND and *E.T.*), George LUCAS (the Star Wars series), and John CARPENTER (THE THING and STARMAN) have all acknowledged their great debt to and fascination with 1950s SF films.

The "classic" SF films of the 1950s were almost all made before 1958, and the end of the decade saw a proliferation of derivative, low-budget exploitation movies. The 1960s were to free SF film from the limited budgets and expectations of that time and to indicate the direction and potential of SF film until the present. This was the decade in which SF film produced some of its most successful satires, such as LITTLE SHOP OF HORRORS (1960), DR. STRANGELOVE (1964), and BARBARELLA (1966). It was also the decade in which a large number of well-respected directors turned to SF film, a trend that blurred the boundaries of the genre and gained for it much more critical recognition.

In 1963 Alfred Hitchcock directed THE BIRDS and Chris Marker made the haunting *La Jetée* (*The Pier*). That year also saw the first Annual SF Film Festival in Trieste, perhaps the first "official" acknowledgment that SF film constitutes a body of work worthy of reflection and evaluation. One of the winners at that first festival was Corman's X: THE MAN WITH X-RAY EYES. Within the next few years, Jean-Luc Godard made ALPHAVILLE (1965), François Truffaut made FAHRENHEIT 451 (1966), and Alain Resnais made *Je T'aime, Je T'aime* (1967). In Great Britain, Peter Watkins filmed his devastating "future documentary" *The War Game* (1966), and Joseph Losey made THESE ARE THE DAMNED (1963). American directors such as John Frankenheimer, Sidney Lumet, and Franklin J. Schaffner reflected Hollywood's increasing interest in the genre's "respectable" potential, with Schaffner's PLANET OF THE APES (1968) becoming one of the decade's most successful films.

Of course, the film most responsible for freeing the genre to seek its potential was Stanley KUBRICK's *2001: A Space Odyssey* (1968). Still claimed by many to be the most important SF film of all time, *2001* was certainly the most intellectually complex film in the genre and was striking enough to launch SF film's second renaissance. The ultimate conspiracy film, in which humankind is nothing but a pawn in some alien grand design, *2001* presents a pessimistic future, one made not horrible but crushingly banal by technology. What is most noteworthy about *2001*, however, is that its impact is singularly that of *film;* the experience of watching it cannot be evoked by discursive plot summaries or philosophical discussions that celebrate or castigate its "ideas." Out of some two hours and nineteen minutes of film, *2001* contains only a little less than forty minutes of dialogue; its story is a visual and auditory experience much more than a verbal one.

For all its impact, however, it is important to realize that *2001* crystallized the concerns and direction of SF film during the 1960s—it did not discover them. Films as varied as *The Birds* (1963), George Romero's *Night of the Living Dead* (1968), *Planet of the Apes* (1968), CHARLY (1968), and COLOSSUS: THE FORBIN PROJECT (1969) all imply that humanity is losing control of the future. There is a quality of speculation in all these films the likes of which had not been seen since *Things to Come;* however, Wells's unbridled faith in technology is nowhere to be found in 1960s SF movies, nor does the confidence in teamwork and ingenuity so prevalent in 1950s SF films seem any longer supportable. Not only did the SF movie begin to take itself seriously in the

Rod Taylor in *The Time Machine* (1960)

1960s, but it also found it harder and harder to see the future in any other than mistrustful terms, and this trend intensified in the early 1970s.

Robert WISE's THE ANDROMEDA STRAIN (1970) offers a chilling view of research and technology, in stark contrast to the human focus of his previous classic, *The Day the Earth Stood Still*. An even harsher indictment of technology is THX 1138, George Lucas's first film, also released in 1970. Kubrick's A CLOCKWORK ORANGE (1971), and WESTWORLD (1973), THE TERMINAL MAN (1974), and THE STEPFORD WIVES (1974) all reflect this unease.

Problems and questions of identity underlie two of the most "difficult" SF films made in the 1970s: SOLARIS (1971), directed by noted Russian filmmaker Andrei Tarkovsky from Stanislaw LEM's well-respected novel, and THE MAN WHO FELL TO EARTH (1976), directed by Nicolas Roeg from the novel by Walter TEVIS. Both are among the most beautiful and haunting of all SF films, but they have also been criticized as overlong and pretentious, as has been John Boorman's *Zardoz* (1973). Largely ignored at the time of its release, the crudely effective A BOY AND HIS DOG (1975) foreshadowed the look of most postapocalyptic films of the 1980s.

The 1970s saw the increasing diversification of SF films and the increasing tendency for those films to be thought of as "major motion pictures" rather than as SF or "Sci-Fi." Within this diversity, however, three significant lines of development should be noted: a cycle of ecologically centered cautionary tales, such as NO

BLADE OF GRASS (1970), SILENT RUNNING (1971), and SOY-
LENT GREEN (1973); a blending of SF and horror elements
in a subgenre of SF/splatter films such as Cronenberg's
The Parasite Murders (1974) and Larry Cohen's surprisingly complicated *It's Alive* (1973); and a most impressive group of SF satires and parodies, ranging from
Carpenter's DARK STAR (1974) to THE ROCKY HORROR PIC-
TURE SHOW (1975) and Mel Brooks's *Young Frankenstein* (1974).

The real story of the SF film in the 1970s, however,
has little to do with "strains," "subgenres," or implications, and everything to do with box-office success.
Beginning with Spielberg's subtle and surprising *Close
Encounters of the Third Kind* (1977) and Lucas's un-
subtle, unsurprising, but spectacular *Star Wars* (1977),
this was a time of unprecedented commercial success
for SF film, a time in which it so totally transcended
genre limitations as to become the new paradigm for the
Hollywood big-budget blockbuster. SUPERMAN—The
Movie followed in 1978, ALIEN and STAR TREK—THE MO-
TION PICTURE in 1979. This was also a time of big-budget
remakes such as INVASION OF THE BODY SNATCHERS (1978),
as well as of relatively low-budget surprise successes,
such as George Miller's MAD MAX (1979), the first in a
series of increasingly elaborate postapocalyptic Australian spectacles. For the popularity of SF film, it was
indisputably the best of times, but for the development
of the genre the 1970s may ultimately be recognized as
opening up potential rather than as fostering accomplishment. For all its success, *Star Wars* is more fairy
tale than SF, and for all its gritty realism, *Alien* is a horror
story set on a spaceship. Distinctions such as these may
be beside the point, but, with the possible exception of
Close Encounters, the SF movies that proved so amazingly successful in the 1970s were sustained by their
increasingly sensational special effects and simplistic escapism. Unlike the best SF in either literature or film,
these movies have almost no contact with the reality of
the time in which they were made.

The 1980s have already proved to be a period of even
more phenomenal popularity and success for SF film,
although also a time in which calculation and conservatism seem to mark the genre. The biggest success—
and one of the best films —*E.T.: The Extra-Terrestrial*
(1982) indicates both the total integration of SF material
into the public consciousness and the extent to which
Hollywood seemed determined to put that material to
patently nonspeculative use. Despite its indisputable SF
elements, *E.T.* has much more in common with children's fantasies, such as *Peter Pan*, than with the traditions of the SF cinema. This is not to say that *E.T.* is
not a magnificent film, but it is to note that the most
successful SF film of all time derives very little of its
appeal from what might be called science-fiction thinking. Combined with the fact that most of the other SF
box-office successes of the 1980s have been sequels to

1970s (or earlier) films, this characteristic may suggest
that fantastic commercial success is not in itself a guarantee of the vitality of the genre.

Significant remakes and sequels in the 1980s include
The Empire Strikes Back (1980), RETURN OF THE JEDI
(1983), *Superman II* (1980), *Superman III* (1983), *Supergirl* (1984), *Star Trek II: The Wrath of Khan* (1982),
Star Trek III: The Search for Spock (1984), 2010
(1985),and INVADERS FROM MARS (1986). A few remakes
and sequels did significantly improve on their predecessors, however. *The Road Warrior* (1981), *1984* (1984),
Mad Max: Beyond Thunderdome (1985), *Aliens* (1986),
and *The Fly* (1986) each displays impressively innovative approaches.

The years 1985 and 1986 witnessed nothing less than
an explosion of big-budget SF films, several of them
resounding successes, and three clear trends in these
movies seem likely to exert strong influence on SF films
made in the future. One of the most striking developments has been the crossbreeding of rock videos with
SF film, further evidence of the independent lineage of
film. Science-fiction themes and images have become a
staple for rock videos, while SF movies such as BACK TO
THE FUTURE (1985), *Explorers* (1985), and *Mad Max:
Beyond Thunderdome* have increasingly featured sound
tracks by contemporary rock musicians and have been
attended by the release of rock videos edited from the
films themselves. Rock stars such as Sting, Grace Jones,
Gene Simmons, and Tina Turner have become featured
actors in SF film; directors such as John Sayles (*The
Brother from Another Planet*), and Tobe Hooper (LIFE-
FORCE,1985, and *Invaders from Mars*) are now known
for their work in music video as well as in film.

A second major trend in recent SF films has been
toward "juvenilizing" the genre, with children and teenagers becoming its stars, their problems its concerns.
Closely related to this development has been a third
trend, toward using SF as a vehicle for obvious wish
fulfillment. Whereas once it may have been enough to
think of an SF world on the screen as a kind of wish
fulfillment in its own right, a vision—such as that offered
by *Metropolis* or *Things to Come*—of a time or place
so new and different as to be in itself exciting and liberating, the clear implication of 1985 films such as *Cocoon, Back to the Future, Explorers, Weird Science,
My Science Project, D.A.R.Y.L.,* and *Real Genius* is
that Hollywood now sees the SF world as an enabling
mechanism for solving common personal problems. In
offering happy endings for difficulties ranging from those
of aging and death to those of adolescence and parent-
hood, these movies have refocused the traditional concern of SF film on the personal rather than the societal.

A further sign of potential trouble for the SF genre may
be that the 1980s have already produced a number of
SF films that were disappointing, if not outright disasters.
Carpenter's ESCAPE FROM NEW YORK (1981) and his re-

make of *The Thing* (1982) were neither critical nor commercial successes, although *The Thing* may prove, like Ridley Scott's *Blade Runner,* to be a much more significant film than was first thought. The most costly disappointment of the 1980s will almost certainly be *Dune* (1984), directed by the gifted David Lynch and produced by the irrepressible Dino De Laurentiis, who had already financed one SF disaster in the 1980s in his remake of *Flash Gordon* (1980). Other big-budget failures include *Lifeforce* (1985), *Invaders from Mars* (1986), and *Howard the Duck* (1986).

What most of these films have in common is predictability, either in terms of previous SF films or in the newer terms of the big-budget formula of the 1970s and 1980s: spectacular special effects and childlike emotional simplicity. However, the 1980s have also seen the making of a number of impressively unpredictable— if not offbeat—SF films, and these may actually be a better sign of the genre's vitality. BATTLE BEYOND THE STARS (1980), HEARTBEEPS (1981), ANDROID (1982), *Ice Pirates* (1983), THE ADVENTURES OF BUCKAROO BANZAI (1984), REPO MAN (1984), *Starman,* and *Return of the Living Dead* (1985) all put SF to humorous and more risky use, as do two appealing films from John Sayles, *Alligator* (1980) and *The Brother from Another Planet.* Terry Gilliam's *Brazil,* one of SF's great dystopian city films, was so uniquely imaginative that Universal Pictures initially hesitated to release it.

David Cronenberg continued his distinctive working of the SF genre with SCANNERS (1980), the hauntingly self-conscious VIDEODROME (1982), *The Dead Zone* (1983), and his powerful and innovative remake of *The Fly.* LIQUID SKY (1982) curiously blends New Wave satire and sensationalism, and the disturbingly effective *Cafe Flesh* (1981) was almost certainly the first postapocalyptic pornographic SF film. George Romero completed his visceral "zombie trilogy" in 1985 with *Day of the Dead.* Considerably more restrained but distinctly oddball are STRANGE INVADERS (1983) and a surprisingly intelligent first-encounter movie, *Wavelength* (1983). *Iceman* (1984) offers a restrained and thought-provoking counterpoint to both versions of *The Thing,* much as TESTAMENT (1983) offers a calmly devastating view of life following a nuclear war. Only a modest commercial success but a charmingly unpretentious allegory, THE LAST STARFIGHTER (1984) builds on a number of cultural and psychological initiation myths. Less popular but more ambitious was Wolfgang Peterson's ENEMY MINE (1986), a well-intentioned but heavy-handed attempt to use SF to argue for understanding and tolerance.

The starkly violent and fast-paced *The Terminator* proved to be one of the surprise hits of 1984 and paved the way for its makers, director James Cameron and producer Gale Ann Hurd, to create the even more violent, faster-paced bigger success of *Aliens* in 1986. Like the satiric *Night of the Comet* (1984), both of these films feature capable female protagonists, a distinct departure from SF film tradition. One of the most intriguing SF films of the 1980s, or of any other period, was Ridley Scott's *Blade Runner.* In several ways an unfortunate reduction of Philip K. DICK's *Do Androids Dream of Electric Sheep?* and a clear homage to the film noir hardboiled detective story, this film nevertheless manages to create a strikingly compelling visual environment of the future and to imbue that environment with issues that effectively question the definition of humanity itself. Indeed, *Blade Runner* may be the perfect emblem for the unique strengths and problems of SF film. It tells a different story than does the novel from which it was made and tells it crudely at times, but it tells a story deserving of thought and almost demanding of reaction. Among recent films, *Blade Runner,* along with Gilliam's *Brazil* and Cronenberg's remake of *The Fly,* engages its audience in the issue at the heart of almost all fine SF literature: the possibilities and problems stemming from the intersection of science and humanity.

B.L.

THE FINAL COUNTDOWN (1980).   *Directed by Don Taylor; screenplay by David Ambrose, Gerry Davis, Thomas Hunter, and Peter Powell; photographed by Victor J. Kemper; music by John Scott. With Kirk Douglas, Martin Sheen, Katharine Ross, James Farentino, Ron O'Neal, Charles Durning, Victor Mohica, James C. Lawrence. 105 minutes. Color.*

Caught in an inexplicable time warp, a giant U.S. aircraft carrier is swept back to Pearl Harbor just before the Japanese attack; debate rages over whether to try to stop the attack, but the carrier returns to 1980 before anything can be done.

This film functions primarily as a documentary on aircraft carriers; its science-fiction elements are timid and inconclusive. It was often disparaged as a standard episode of TWILIGHT ZONE; the cast of veteran performers could do little with the concept and thin characters.

B.W.

FINLAY, VIRGIL [WARDEN] (1914–1971).
American artist known mostly for his fantasy creations but also a classic science-fiction illustrator for the major PULP MAGAZINES. Largely self-taught, Finlay perfected the painstaking technique known as stippling, a method of drawing that utilizes minuscule dots to portray an image. Although he worked in color, he is most noted for his black-and-white, pen-and-ink interior illustrations. Finlay displayed a distinct style of almost photographic realism that conveys a sense of fantasy reminiscent of the work of Aubrey Beardsley.

Finlay was especially adept at portraying that pulp

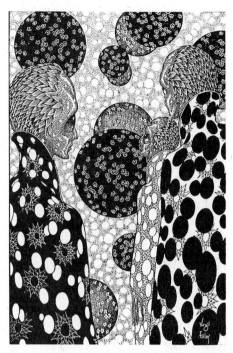

Illustration by Finlay for A. Merritt's _Conquest of the Moon Pool_

magazine staple, the artfully naked female ravaged by lustful aliens. Very popular among the fans, Finlay was affectionately known as the "bubble man" because of the strategically placed bubbles on his sensuous renderings of the female form. (Brian W. ALDISS referred to this puritanical convention in SF art as "the great nipple shortage.") Finlay was also famous for his bug-eyed monsters (BEMs), macabre aliens, and other nightmarish creatures. Nominated several times for the Hugo Award, he won only once (in 1953 for best interior artist).

Finlay's first major sale was to _Weird Tales_ (December 1935). Farnsworth Wright, that magazine's editor, thereafter had Finlay do numerous illustrations, including many covers. H. P. LOVECRAFT was so enamored of Finlay's illustrations of the monsters in Robert BLOCH's _The Faceless God_ (1936) that he began a correspondence with Finlay and even sent him a panegyrical poem, the last lines of which declare: "What limner he who braves the black gulfs alone/And lives to make their alien horrors known?"

In 1937 A. Merritt invited Finlay to work full-time for _The American Weekly_. Toward the end of his career Finlay was employed by several astrology magazines, for which he did some exquisite illustrations of the symbols of the horoscope.

M.T.W.

FINNEY, JACK (Born Walter Braden Finney) (1911–).
American writer of short fiction, novels, and screenplays, better known for his mainstream fiction and fantasy than science fiction. Finney's 1955 novel _The Body Snatchers_ describes the invasion of Earth by an alien life force that duplicates and ultimately replaces human beings. A genuinely terrifying book— and a subtle attack on communism, McCarthyism, and Nazism—_The Body Snatchers_ is concerned with two recurrent themes in Finney's fiction: individuality and the loss thereof. The book is perhaps best known today as the inspiration for Don Siegel's highly successful film INVASION OF THE BODY SNATCHERS (1956) and Philip Kaufman's 1978 remake of the same name.

Another concern mirrored in Finney's SF is TIME TRAVEL: in such works as _The Woodrow Wilson Dime_ (1968), _Time and Again_ (1970), "The Love Letter" (1959), "I Love Galesburg in the Springtime" (1960), "The Coin Collector" (1960), and "The Face in the Photo" (1962), his characters return to idyllic times in a more caring, less hurried past. _Marion's Wall_ (1973) also reflects nostalgia for days gone by but contains supernatural elements such as ghosts and reincarnation.

H.L.P.

FIRST MAN INTO SPACE (1958).
Directed by Robert Day; screenplay by John C. Cooper and Lance Z. Hargreaves; photographed by Geoffrey Faithfull; music by Buxton Orr. With Marshall Thompson, Marla Landi, Bill Edwards, Carl Jaffe, Bill Nagy, Robert Ayres, Roger Delgado. 77 minutes. Black and white.

Hiding behind this film's sober title is a lurid thriller about a blood-drinking monster from space. A test pilot defies orders, sending his plane more than 250 miles high; he ejects into a cloud. Soon thereafter, blood banks are raided and cattle (and later humans) killed (this is the first cattle-mutilation film). The culprit turns out to be the pilot.

Made in Great Britain but set in New Mexico, this film was promoted as a realistic movie akin to _Breaking the Sound Barrier_ (1952). Somewhat above average for its period, it is now extremely dated, a mildly effective antique.

B.W.

FIRST MEN IN THE MOON (1964).
Directed by Nathan Juran; screenplay by Nigel Kneale and Jan Read; adapted from the novel by H. G. Wells; photographed by Wilkie Cooper; music by Laurie Johnson. With Lionel Jeffries, Edward Judd, Martha Hyer, Erik Chitty, Betty McDowall, Miles Malleson, Peter Finch (unbilled). 103 minutes. Color.

Producer Charles H. Schneer and special effects expert Ray HARRYHAUSEN followed their series of successful science-fiction thrillers and fantasy adventures with this reasonably faithful adaptation of H. G. WELLS's 1901 novel of the same name. The film, cowritten by Nigel Kneale, retains much of Wells's acid humor and pessimism. Veteran of SF Nathan Juran directed. The primary changes in the film were the addition of a woman to the lunar expedition, and a framing story about an international Moon landing that discovers a British flag from 1899. Edward Judd tells Wells's story in flashback.

The film is handsomely designed and photographed, with convincing special effects and model work, frequent humor, and above-average acting, particularly by Lionel Jeffries as the scientist Cavor. Although likable and intelligent, it's slightly ponderous and has an unsatisfying climax, so *First Men in the Moon* is frequently underrated by critics.

The novel was also filmed in 1919, and Georges MÉLIÈS's A TRIP TO THE MOON (*Le Voyage dans la Lune,* 1903) borrowed Wells's insectoid Selenians.

B.W.

Buster Crabbe as the cinema's first Flash Gordon

FIVE (1951).   *Directed by Arch Oboler; screenplay by Arch Oboler; photographed by Sid Lubow, Ed Spigel, Louis Clyde Stoumen, and Arthur Swerdloff; music by Henry Russell. With William Phipps, Susan Douglas, James Anderson, Charles Lampkin, Earl Lee. 93 minutes. Black and white.*

A ninety-day wonder when it first appeared, *Five* is now largely forgotten, notable mostly for its status as one of the first films to deal with nuclear Armageddon. Directed, written, produced, and designed by radio-writer Arch Oboler, it's set after radioactive dust has wiped out all animal life on Earth, except for five people unconvincingly spared by circumstance. They gather on the California coast, where radiation, racial tensions, and jealousy eventually reduce their number to two, a man and the only woman.

Shot on grainy stock, this film is harsh and pretentious; the best scenes are those in which the survivors visit a city populated only by bleaching skeletons. The dialogue and performances are strained, and the film almost talks itself to death. Nonetheless, *Five* remains interesting for its pioneering efforts.

B.W.

FLAGG, FRANCIS (Pseudonym of George Henry Weiss) (1898–1946).   American poet who wrote science fiction under his pseudonym. Flagg was especially active as a contributor to SF magazines in the early 1930s. Some of his later stories were written in collaboration with Forrest J ACKERMAN. His only novel, *The Night People,* about the time travel of an escaped convict, was published posthumously in 1947.

J.H.

———— FLASH GORDON ————

An archetypal science-fiction hero of numerous space opera adventures, Flash Gordon began his long career in 1934 in a King Features comic strip by Alex Raymond (unlike BUCK ROGERS, which began as a novelette by Philip Nowlan in a 1928 AMAZING STORIES and was turned into a comic strip in 1929; its success for a rival syndicate may have inspired Gordon's creation). Whereas Buck Rogers was, like the Tom Swift series, adventure SF with an emphasis on gadgets, Flash Gordon was better drawn and was conceived as a mythic saga close to the spirit of Edgar Rice BURROUGHS's John Carter novels. It was created in the depth of the Depression, when the national yearning for escape made the period a golden age of fantasy.

The basic plot of the Gordon adventures was laid down in the opening comic-strip sequence, enshrined in the 1936 serial film version, and repeated in the 1981 feature film. Gordon, a dashing, all-American youth, embodies athletic prowess, chivalric and gentlemanly ideals, and some intellect (he is a college graduate and the son of a famous scientist). He also is a star polo player in the movie serial; the 1981 film updated him—unwisely—to star quarterback for the New York Jets.

The story starts with the Earth menaced by impending destruction from a collision with the rogue planet Mongo, which is the work of Mongo's ruler, the Emperor Ming, who demands immediate surrender. Dr. Hans Zarkov has built a rocket ship in his secret laboratory and takes off for Mongo along with Gordon and Dale Arden, a young woman Gordon has just met. They become prisoners of Ming, a sinister Oriental type—tyrant, warlord, and Fu Manchu avatar—embodying the yellow peril fears of the period.

After Gordon survives combat in the arena, Princess Aura, Ming's gorgeous, dark-haired daughter, saves Gordon from execution because she has fallen in love with him. In subsequent adventures he gains the respect and support of the Tree Men and the Hawk Men and overthrows Ming, who nevertheless escapes for future sequences. The adventurous and melodramatic character of the saga was maintained through various sequels: not only Ming's menaces but unexplored Mongo continents had to be tackled. In some later comic strips, Gordon traveled to distant planets in the manner of Captain Kirk and the STAR TREK crew.

The original Raymond strip was distinguished by superior graphics, literate prose, and restrained tone. The women characters in particular were drawn with intelligence, subtlety, and understated allure. The strip has been criticized, however, for its slow pace and paucity of action compared with Buck Rogers and pulp fiction competitors.

The 1936 Universal serial adopted a frenetic pace, sacrificing logic and all but the most rudimentary characterizations. The sets were acceptable by 1930s standards, but the costuming and special effects, like the dialogue, were often ludicrous. Buster CRABBE plays a handsome and rugged Flash Gordon, but his absurdly high ideals make him seem mindless. Jean Rogers makes an attractive and ingenuous Dale Arden, whose main function is to look helpless and frightened. Charles Middleton plays a hammy Ming, Frank Shannon, an absent-minded Zarkov, and Priscilla Lawson vamps shamelessly as Aura. Despite its swift pace and inventive action sequences, the serial, available in a condensed version on videocassette, now seems a masterpiece of high camp. As a Saturday matinee serial, however, it was successful enough to be followed by two sequels: *Flash Gordon's Trip to Mars* (1938) and *Flash Gordon Conquers the Universe* (1940). Edited versions of these have also recently been released on videocassette.

Gordon also was featured in a radio serial in the 1930s, and the comic strip has continued through the 1980s. Austin Brigg replaced Raymond as artist in 1944; he was followed by Mac Raboy, Dan Barry, and finally Al Williamson. Williamson's work often seems influenced by *Star Trek* and other recent SF, just as Raymond had probably been influenced by Burroughs's John Carter. In the 1970s some of the strips by Williamson were brought out in paperback versions, as were novelizations of the strips by a number of authors, some of them uncredited. A single issue of a *Flash Gordon Strange Adventure Magazine* was published in 1936, and an unsuccessful television series ran in 1951. Parodies of the Flash Gordon stories have also appeared over the years: *Mad* magazine did a memorable spoof in the early

Flash in a 1947 comic-book incarnation

1950s, and a film parody, *Flesh Gordon* (1974), benefited from the public's interest in X-rated movies in the 1970s.

Thus a background of audience recognition awaited the 1981 film, which was an expensive undertaking with impressive sets and costuming, adequate special effects, a good musical score, and effectively choreographed fight scenes. The serial seems to have been the chief inspiration for the film's plot, and its pace is swift. Thanks to director Mike Hodges's light touch, the movie is mildly entertaining, but its final effect is disappointing in spite of good performances by Max von Sydow as Ming and Topol as Zarkov. Melody Anderson is a pretty if tepid Arden, and Sam J. Jones has the physique to play Gordon, but he is an indifferent actor and his persona as Gordon is too knowing and cynical for a naive and idealistic hero.

No effort seems to have been made to set the film on a more intelligent level, and it is at best a spoof of itself; at worst it is an archly self-conscious exercise in camp comedy. The absurdity of the plot is also apparent in a novelization of the film script by Arthur Byron COVER (1980). But if the technology used in the film had been available in the 1930s, the saga of Flash Gordon might have been as popular as that of James Bond.

The character of Gordon survives in *Defenders of the Earth*, an animated cartoon series for children that began in 1985 and also features Gordon's contempo-

A 1952 Flash Gordon comic book

raries, such as Mandrake the Magician and the Phantom. The series is a Valhalla for old comic-strip heroes.

Flash Gordon (1936). *Directed by Frederick Stephani; screenplay by Ray Trampe, Norman S. Hall, and Wyndham Gittens; adapted from the comic strip created by Alex Raymond; screenplay by Frederick Stephani, George Plympton, Basil Dickey, and Ella O'Neill; photographed by Jay Ash and Richard Fryer. With Larry "Buster" Crabbe, Jean Rogers, Charles Middleton, Frank Shannon, and Priscilla Lawson. A serial in 13 episodes; approximately 200 minutes. Black and white.*

Flash Gordon (1981). *Directed by Mike Hodges; screenplay by Lorenzo Semple, Jr., adaptation by Michael Allin; based on the characters created by Alex Raymond; photographed by Gil Taylor, music by Queen, with orchestral score by Howard Blake. With Max von Sydow, Sam J. Jones, Melody Anderson, Ornella Muti, Topol, Timothy Dalton, Brian Blessed, Peter Syngarde, and Mariangela Melato. 111 minutes. Color.*

E.L.C.

FLIN[D]T, HOMER EON (1892–1924). American writer, mostly for the Munsey PULP MAGAZINES, in which he published some engaging futuristic and interplanetary fantasies, including those collected in *The Lord of Death and the Queen of Life* (1965) and *The*

Devolutionist and the Emancipatrix (1965). Flint collaborated with Austin Hall on the classic parallel-worlds novel *The Blind Spot* (1921/1951). His premature (and mysterious) death (his body was discovered at the bottom of a canyon) cut short a promising career.

B.S.

THE FLY (1958). *Directed by Kurt Neumann; screenplay by James Clavell; adapted from the short story by George Langelaan; photographed by Karl Struss; music by Paul Sawtell. With Al (David) Hedison, Vincent Price, Patricia Owens, Herbert Marshall, Charles Herbert. 94 minutes. Color.*

THE FLY (1986). *Directed by David Cronenberg; screenplay by David Cronenberg and Charles Edward Pogue; adapted from the short story by George Langelaan; photographed by Mark Irwin; music by Howard Shore. With Jeff Goldblum, Geena Davis, John Getz, Joy Boushel, Les Carlson, George Chuvalo. 100 minutes. Color.*

It is surprising that *The Fly* is one of the few works of science-fiction cinema to tackle the possibility of teleportation. Both versions of the film approach the subject seriously, but in scientific terms the first is considerably less successful. The original was nevertheless a success at the box office and was popular enough to inspire two sequels and the remake. The fascination generated by the story probably has less to do with our interest in teleportation than with our common dread of the insect world because of its strangeness and frightening efficiency.

In the original story a scientist experiments with a matter transmitter and succeeds in teleporting small objects. He decides to experiment on himself, but his atoms are inadvertently scrambled with those of a common housefly that has accidentally found its way into the transmitter. Until this point the tale's premise is plausible, but with the introduction of the proverbial, and here literal, fly in the ointment, it descends into implausibility. After teleportation the scientist ends up with a fly's head and the fly with a human head, although both seem to have human brains. The scientist wants to reverse the teleportation process, but he cannot capture the fly. Finally, in an unconventionally downbeat ending, the scientist begins to go mad and is killed in a steam press by his wife, while his brother finds the fly trapped in a spiderweb, its little voice shouting for help, and smashes it with a rock to save it from a rather novel fate worse than death.

Despite the film's silly narrative, the actors play in a straight-faced manner, thus elevating it from mere camp. And the film does have its fine moments: the first close-up of the scientist's fly head, its mandibles working, is effectively frightening, as is the wife's scream in reaction, the image multiplied in what must be the only fly's-eye point of view shot in the history of the cinema.

The scientist's son makes a similar mistake in the sequel, *The Return of the Fly* (1959, directed by Edward L. Bernds); *The Curse of the Fly* (1965, directed by Don Sharp) seems, as it were, a more fly-by-night production. Looking for a new twist, it ascribes a variety of unexpected results to the effects of the matter-transmitting machine.

In 1986, Canadian SF and horror filmmaker David CRONENBERG returned to the original story to come up with a more contemporary interpretation. His version retains the story's essential idea but alters the plot line considerably, focusing on the love interest and the gradual physical alteration of the scientist's body into a human-sized fly; this transformation is treated as an extended metaphor for the decay of human relationships. In developing his machine, Cronenberg's scientist (Jeff Goldblum) has lived alone and worked obsessively; he is sexually innocent and socially maladroit. Nevertheless, a romance develops between him and a female journalist (Geena Davis). Later, overcome by jealousy, he assumes that she has rejected him for an old boyfriend, and in a drunken stupor he sends himself through his transmitter with the inevitable fly. But Cronenberg improves on the unscientific lapse of the original film: Goldblum's entire body is transformed as a result of his computer's genetic bonding of human and fly.

Cronenberg's version is scientifically more plausible and its characters psychologically far more interesting than those of the original. But the movie's greatest distinction is the result of its establishing a firm connection between the horrors of biological transformation and a convincing human relationship. Goldblum's subtly modulated performance deserves as much credit for the film's success as Cronenberg's literate, adult script. The first version of *The Fly* is entertaining SF; the second is a poignant film about very real human concerns.

B.K.G.

FONTANA, D[OROTHY] C. (?–   ).

American writer, primarily of teleplays, and TV story editor. Fontana is best known for the episodes she wrote for STAR TREK, for which she also served as story editor. Her most significant contribution to the series mythos was the introduction of Sarek and Amanda, parents of Mr. Spock, in her episode "Journey to Babel." She also wrote episodes for other science-fiction series, including, in the 1970s, *The Fantastic Journey* and *Logan's Run,* for which she served as story editor. Her novel *The Questor Tapes* (1974) was based on the script for a TV pilot film by Gene Coons and *Star Trek* creator Gene RODDENBERRY. Fontana returned to the scene of her best-known work in 1987 as writer and associate producer for *Star Trek: The Next Generation.*

K.R.D.

Robby the Robot oversees Anne Francis and Leslie Nielsen in *Forbidden Planet*

FORBIDDEN PLANET (1956).

Directed by Fred McLeod Wilcox; screenplay by Cyril Hume; photographed by George Folsey; music (electronic tonalities) by Louis and Bebe Barron. With Walter Pidgeon, Anne Francis, Leslie Nielsen, Warren Stevens, Jack Kelly, Richard Anderson, Earl Holliman, Marvin Miller. 98 minutes. Color.

Forbidden Planet, an impressive color and Cinema-Scope production, is cleverly based on Shakespeare's *The Tempest.* A spaceship from Earth arrives on the planet Altair IV in search of a previous expedition; there Captain J. J. Adams (Leslie Nielsen) and his crew find only two survivors, Dr. Edward Morbius (Walter Pidgeon) and his daughter Altaira (Anne Francis), and a robot. Morbius, an expert in languages, has studied the remains of an alien civilization, the Krel, on Altair IV and concluded that the race perished in a single night while on the verge of a supreme accomplishment. As the film progresses we learn that the Krel had invented a form of direct creation—by linking their minds to machines of vast energy—and had destroyed themselves when these machines magnified their unconscious animal impulses. One of the ship's crew is killed—as it turns out, by Morbius's murderous id, magnified by the Krel's machines. The invisible nightmare begins to stalk Adams, Altaira, and Morbius himself. They flee into the depths of the Krel laboratories, but the monster breaks in after them. Morbius confronts it and is killed. As he dies he sets in motion forces that will cause the planet to explode, thus sparing Earth the dangers of Krel technology.

Despite this film's fluid style, the script portrays Morbius as just another mad scientist delving into things humanity is not ready to know. The story line is overly simplistic: would the Krel really have linked their minds to direct creation machines without considering the possible effects of their own random and unconscious thoughts? In spite of these flaws, however, the film has considerable power. Walter Pidgeon gives a fine performance as the anguished Morbius, literally destroyed by his own subconscious rage. The production is a feast for the eyes, accomplished with great elegance entirely on studio sets, and the innovative music successfully serves as both score and sound effects. The special effects and model work are still breathtaking, and Robby the Robot is a delight to anyone familiar with Isaac Asimov's Robotics stories. The film's lasting importance as science fiction, however, derives in great part from the fact that its story is the stuff of written SF of the period—a fact underscored by W. J. Stuart's novelization, which treats the film's theme in greater depth and with the seriousness it deserves.

G.Z.

FORD, JOHN M. (1957–   ).

American writer and game designer. Ford is difficult to categorize because his fiction has covered a wide range of subgenres and themes; however, virtually all his work, from his Alternities Corporation science-fiction series (1979–1981) to his World Fantasy Award–winning *The Dragon Waiting* (1983), is characterized by fluid writing and frequently startling ideas. A prolific author, he published his earliest professional stories in ISAAC ASIMOV'S SCIENCE FICTION MAGAZINE and elsewhere in the late 1970s. Since then he has published short fiction in numerous magazines and anthologies; Alternities Corporation stories have become particularly well known. He was coauthor, with George H. Scithers and Darrell Schweitzer, of *On Writing Science Fiction* (1981), a popular manual for aspiring SF writers. His novels include *Web of Angels* (1980) and *Princes of the Air* (1982), but as a novelist he is probably best known for his fantasy work *The Dragon Waiting*, which takes place in an alternate history at the time of Richard III in which Christianity never solidified and magic and a vampire play key roles in political intrigue.

B.D.

FORSTER, E[DWARD] M[ORGAN] (1879–1970).

British author, considered by many to be one of the finest novelists of the twentieth century. Forster wrote only one science-fiction story, but "The Machine Stops" (1909), quite apart from its literary merits, is a seminal work in the evolution of SF itself.

Written, according to Forster himself, as "a protest against one of the earlier heavens of H. G. WELLS," "The Machine Stops" was the first of the explicitly anti-Wellsian antiutopias in a fertile tradition that continued with Aldous HUXLEY's *Brave New World* (1932), George ORWELL's *Nineteen Eighty-four* (1949), and others. In Forster's story a future humanity has been reduced to an underground, hivelike existence, completely cut off from nature and utterly dependent on machines. When the great Machine that controls all the other machines breaks down, the dehumanized wretches it has "served" die helplessly. The same theme, with different conclusions, has been treated by writers such as John W. CAMPBELL in "Twilight" (1934) and Isaac Asimov in *The Caves of Steel* (1954).

Forster's critique of the Wellsian technological utopia anticipates not only the mainstream antiutopian classics but such warning stories within the SF genre as David H. KELLER's "Revolt of the Pedestrians" (1928), Laurence MANNING's "The City of Sleep" (1933), and Herbert W. Franke's *The Orchid Cage* (1961). Forster's fantasy is collected in *The Celestial Omnibus* (1914) and *The Eternal Moment* (1928).

J.J.P.

FORT, CHARLES [HOY] (1874–1932).

American journalist, researcher, and author, mostly of nonfiction collections of unexplained phenomena, whose books were significant influences on science-fiction authors. For twenty-six years in libraries in New York (he lived in the Bronx) and London, Fort, a true eccentric, assembled documentation of events for which, he said, science had no explanation: poltergeists; red snow and black rain; frogs, fish, stones, and other objects falling from the sky; mysterious disappearances; levitation; strange lights; and other sightings. He collected 40,000 clippings and assembled them into four books: *The Book of the Damned* (1919), *New Lands* (1923), *Lo!* (1931), and *Wild Talents* (1932). Not content with attacking the inability of science to come up with explanations for phenomena that he said scientists simply brushed aside, Fort offered his own sometimes whimsical, frequently absurd explanations: "We are property" or "Something lives above us" or "In steam-engine time people invent steam engines." Author Tiffany Thayer, who helped found the Fortean Society to further Fort's work and served as its secretary, called these "breath-taking answers, tongue-in-cheek answers, brilliant answers, colorful, staggering—and all no more, no less, preposterous than the answers they once thought were true."

Science fiction thrives on eccentric data and indulges

occasionally in even more eccentric explanations. Flying saucers or UFOs were worked into many SF stories (as well as Steven SPIELBERG's film CLOSE ECOUNTERS OF THE THIRD KIND, 1977) after these terms were popularized following newspaper reports of so-called sightings beginning in 1947; Fort had dozens of clippings recounting such sightings in the nineteenth and early twentieth centuries (although at that time the UFOs were described as cigar shaped). Fort's books were of such significant interest to the SF community that *Lo!* was reprinted as an eight-part series of articles in *Astounding Stories* (1934), and SF author and critic Damon KNIGHT wrote the biography *Charles Fort, Prophet of the Unexplained* (1970). Science-fiction writers of the 1930s and 1940s mined Fort's books for phenomena and imaginative explanations. Notable examples are Edmond HAMILTON in "The Space Visitors" (1930) and "The Earth Owners" (1931) and Eric Frank RUSSELL in *Sinister Barrier* (1939/1943), *Dreadful Sanctuary* (1948/1951), and *Sentinels from Space* (1953). Traces of Fort's ideas and influence can be found throughout SF up to the present. Fort also published an early and little remembered novel, *The Outcast Manufacturers* (1909).

J.E.G.

FORWARD, ROBERT L[ULL] (1932–).

American writer and physicist recognized in the early 1980s as one of the few writers of genuine hard science fiction. Having received a doctorate in physics from the University of Maryland in 1965, Forward is now senior scientist at Hughes Research Laboratories and has made a solid reputation as a research scientist as well as a popular writer and lecturer on science. Using the name Susan Lull, he began publishing fiction in 1979. Three novels under his own name followed. *Dragon's Egg* (1980) is a rigorous extrapolation on the high-gravity environment of a neutron star and the compression of time for its unusual inhabitants. His fiction is marked not only by its intellectual questioning supported by his knowledge of advanced physics but also by a lively sense of humor at the strangeness modern science has uncovered; it echoes J. B. S. Haldane's suspicion "that the universe is not only queerer than we suppose, but queerer than we *can* suppose."

D.M.H.

FOSTER, ALAN DEAN (1946–).

American writer of adventure science fiction and one of the foremost practitioners of the SF novelization. Most of Foster's SF novels share the setting of the "Commonwealth," a confederation of planets in which human beings and aliens freely and peacefully interact. His novels rarely deal with complex social or political issues but frequently deliver fast-paced action and exciting plots; his characters tend to be of the comic-book variety, full of daring but with little depth. For example, in the Flinx trilogy (*The Tar-Aiym Krang,* 1972; *Orphan Star,* 1977; and *The End of Matter,* 1977) a young man with special talents journeys through the galaxy fighting potent enemies who threaten the Commonwealth.

Foster has a fine visual sense, however, and frequently populates his works with such memorable creations as the intelligent whales of *Cachalot* (1980) and the alien Tran of *Icerigger* (1974). He also takes pains in his use of science so that the environments and technology he depicts ring true, particularly his description of cities, as in *The Man Who Used the Universe* (1983).

Occasionally Foster deals with more than adventure, although his themes in such cases are not original. In *Midworld* (1975), for example, humans land on the planet Midworld and discover an established society descended from other humans stranded there long ago. The space farers, of course, try to exploit the planet and come into conflict with the "natives" and their ecologically based culture.

Foster has also produced an extensive series of novels based on screenplays, including *Dark Star* (1974), *Star Trek Log One* through *Star Trek Log Ten* (collections, 1974–1978), *Splinter of the Mind's Eye* (based on the characters of STAR WARS, 1978), *Alien* (1979), *The Black Hole* (1979), *Outland* (1981), *Clash of the Titans* (1981), *The Thing* (1982), *Krull* (1983), *The Last Starfighter* (1984), and *Starman* (1984). He is also widely believed to be the author of the *Star Wars* novelization (1976), although that was officially credited to George LUCAS.

OTHER WORKS: *Bloodhype* (1973); *Luana* (1974); *With Friends Like These* (collection, 1977); *Mission to Moulokin* (1979); *Nor Crystal Tears* (1982); *For the Love of Mother-Not* (1983); *The I Inside* (1984); *Voyage to the City of the Dead* (1984); *Slipt* (1984); *The Moment of the Magician* (1984); *Shadowkeep* (1984); . . . *Who Needs Enemies?* (collection, 1984); *Sentenced to Prism* (1985); *Pale Rider* (1985); *Season of the Spellsong* (1985, including *Spellsinger,* 1983, *The Hour at the Gate,* 1984, and *The Day of the Dissonance,* 1984); *Glory Lane* (1987).

S.H.G.

FOUR-SIDED TRIANGLE (1952).

Directed by Terence Fisher; screenplay by Paul Tabori and Terence Fisher; adapted from the novel by William F. Temple; photographed by Reginald Wyer; music by Malcolm Arnold. With Barbara Payton, Stephen Murray, John Van Eyssen, James Hayter, Percy Marmont. 81 minutes. Black and white.

With the help of the woman they both love (Barbara Payton) two young scientists (Stephen Murray and John Van Eyssen) construct a machine that can duplicate anything. Payton marries Van Eyssen, so the lovelorn Murray duplicates *her*. Being a perfect duplicate, however, she too loves Van Eyssen. This unfortunate situation leads to a fiery but unhappy finale.

This is a sentimental, casually sexist, romantic melodrama. The science-fiction element is novel and could have provided a good story, but it's treated almost apologetically. *Four-Sided Triangle* is slow moving and old fashioned (the novel was better). The simple country doctor played by James Hayter narrates throughout, and Hayter's quiet performance is the best thing about this curious film.

B.W.

FOX, GARDNER F[RANCIS] (1911–1987).

American lawyer and writer best known for his contributions to comic books but also the author of several science-fiction adventure novels. Fox started working for the comics in 1937 and wrote for *Superman, Batman, Green Lantern,* and many others; he originated *Hawkman* and *The Flash*. His fantasy and SF writing began with contributions to *Weird Tales* and *Planet Stories* in 1944 and 1945. His early novels were mostly in the historical and adventure genres, but later he wrote spy novels, mysteries, and westerns. His SF novels include *Escape across the Cosmos* (1964), *The Arsenal of Miracles* (1964), *The Hunter out of Time* (1965), *Beyond the Black Enigma* (1965), and *Abandon Galaxy* (1967) (the last two written under the pseudonym Bart Somers). Fox also wrote many heroic fantasy novels.

N.H.

—————— FRANCE ——————

In addition to an active contemporary scene, few countries can boast such long-standing science-fiction antecedents as France. Over the years successive waves of promising new authors have emerged with metronomic regularity alongside mainstream writers of repute who often dabble sympathetically in the genre.

Although Rabelais's classic fables *Gargantua* and *Pantagruel* (1532 and 1564) contain utopian elements with SF connotations, it is really with CYRANO de Bergerac's *Other Worlds* (1657–1662), which features interplanetary flight, that the French SF tradition began in earnest. Speculation about alien worlds continued with Bernard Le Bovier de Fontenelle's *Entretiens sur la pluralité des mondes habités* ("On the Plurality of Inhabited Worlds," 1686). Imaginative narratives took full flight during the eighteenth century, with the advent of often picaresque philosophical tales by Voltaire (*Micromégas,* 1750; *Candide,* 1759), Restif de la Bretonne, the Marquis de Sade, Montesquieu, Diderot, Marivaux, and countless other less remembered satirists. Classic themes also began appearing in embryo form: "the sleeper awakes" in Louis-Sébastien Mercier's *Memoirs of the*

Year Two Thousand Five Hundred (*L'An deux mille quatre cent quarante,* 1771) and lost worlds in de la Bretonne's *La Découverte Australe* ("The Southern Hemisphere Discovery," 1781).

The nineteenth-century rise of romanticism in Europe and, more particularly, France was ideally suited to speculative writing, a fertile tradition that would culminate later in the century with Jules VERNE. But before Verne one must note *Le Dernier Homme* by Jean Baptiste Cousin de Grainville ("The Last Man," 1805), an end of the world yarn; Honoré de Balzac's *Louis Lambert* (1832); Charles Nodier's *Léviathan le long* ("Leviathan the Long," 1833); Grandville's *Un Autre Monde* ("Another World," 1844), featuring mechanical cities and a flamboyant space opera of Stapledonian vision, Charles Defontenay's *Star* (*Star; ou Psi de Cassiopée,* 1854). All contain genuine SF speculations but were dwarfed by the eminence of Verne and the shadow his influence soon cast over the late century.

Many in fact assert that SF as we know it began in Verne's scientific romances. At any rate his work is certainly at the origins of the genre's fascination with science, as opposed to H. G. WELLS's humanist stream. But Verne's prolific oeuvre in fact contains many strands, with a noticeable darkening of hue in his later works. His sixty-four novels combine scientific prophecy both fantastic and accurate (cannon shells to the Moon, perfected submarines, television) with sheer adventure and a visionary sense of global turmoil. His popular success, confirmed by many Walt Disney adaptations in later years, appears to have relegated Verne in many critics' and readers' minds to the ghetto of juvenile literature; he is overdue for critical reassessment as a phenomenally prolific visionary whose influence on the budding SF genre cannot be ignored. Hugo GERNSBACK, that other nurturer of SF, was not mistaken when he placed the early issues of AMAZING STORIES under Verne's patronage, not only reprinting his work but also featuring a masthead that depicted "Jules Verne's tombstone at Amiens portraying his immortality."

All Verne's works initially appeared in popular magazines, combining romance fiction, travel, and science, and usually produced for an adolescent public—these were harbingers of the flowering of the pulp magazines in America in the 1920s and 1930s.

Many other French authors figured in the popular magazines, a good number of them heavily indebted to Verne. Still remembered and often reprinted are André Laurie, Paul d'Ivoi, Jean de la Hire, André Valérie, Capitaine Danrit, and René Thévenin, all active until World War II. Among Verne's contemporaries still devoted to the philosophical tale were the astronomer Camille Flammarion, with his *Stories of Infinity* (*Recits de l'infini,* 1872), and the cartoonist Robida, who also became an affectionate parodist of Verne in *Saturnin Farandoul* (1879). But the most important SF writer in the lineage of Verne is Rosny Aîné (1856–1940). Long remembered for his innovative novels of prehistory, Rosny was a powerful visionary whose far-future tales have not dated and include *The Death of the Earth* (*Le Mort de la terre*, 1909), about the end of the world; *Les Navigateurs de l'infini* ("Navigators of the Infinite," 1925); *The Shapes* (*Les Xipehuz*, 1887); and *La Force mystérieuse* ("The Mysterious Power," 1913).

Verne's influence flourished in France for half a century, and the strength of his school of scientific romance helped to shield French readers and authors from the parallel development of pulp SF in America. By avoiding the pulp stigma, early French SF was never relegated to a literary ghetto and many established mainstream authors—among them Paul Claudel, Emile Zola, Claude Farrère, Anatole France, and the marginal surrealist Raymond Roussel—often provided a seal of critical respectability.

Alongside the speculative dabblings of the literary establishment, several popular authors took over the Verne mantle with great spirit and innovation: one of the more flamboyant of these was Gustave Le Rouge, whose *Le Prisonnier de la planète Mars* ("The Prisoner of Planet Mars," 1908), *La Guerre des vampires* ("War of the Vampires," 1909), and the picaresque *Le Mystérieux Docteur Cornélius* ("The Mysterious Dr. Cornelius," 1912) prefigured heroic fantasy. European political anxieties between the two world wars are mirrored in José Moselli's *La Fin d'Illa* ("The End of Illa," 1925), wherein fallen Atlantis stands as a prophecy of future world carnage. Other authors of note during this period include Louis Boussenard, Octave Béliard, Théo Varlet, Gaston Leroux, Léon Groc, Léon Daudet, and Ernest Pérochon. Better remembered is Maurice Renard, who dedicated his first novel, *Le Docteur Lerne, Sous-Dieu* ("Doctor Lerne, Undergod," 1908), to H. G. Wells, and whose *The Hands of Orlac* (*Les Mains d'Orlac*, 1920), featuring a crazed pianist's revenge, made it to the Hollywood screen. His *Le Péril bleu* ("The Blue Peril," 1910) bears an overall similarity to the work of Charles FORT.

In 1935 Régis Messac, who was to die eight years later in a German concentration camp, launched Hypermondes, the first French SF imprint. It produced only three titles—a David H. KELLER translation and two forceful novels by Messac, *Quinzinzinzili* (1935) and *La Cité des asphyxiés* ("City of the Suffocated," 1934), both bleak but modern in approach. Jacques Spitz, a witty, ironic writer still in great favor in France, published a score of deeply pessimistic novels possibly influenced by the upheaval that shook the world under Hitler: *Save the Earth* (*L'Agonie du globe*, 1935), *Les Evadés de l'an 4,000* ("Fugitives from the Year 4,000," 1938), *La Guerre des mouches* ("The War of the Flies," 1938), *L'Homme elastique* ("The Elastic Man," 1938), and *L'Oeil du Purgatoire* ("The Eye of Purgatory," 1945).

The healthy progress of French SF was abruptly cut short by World War II, and the only writer of note to emerge during those violent years was René Barjavel, with *Ashes, Ashes* (*Ravage*, 1943), about the consequences of the disappearance of electrical power, and *Future Times Three* (*Le Voyageur imprudent*, 1944), an innovative time travel romp. Unfortunately, Barjavel's postwar career never reached such heights, although his weaker books were major publishing successes over several decades. Also straddling the old and new French SF traditions were Marc Wersinger and B. R. Bruss, whose first novels reflect the specter of the atomic bomb. Bruss (a pseudonym for Roger Blondel) turned into a prolific pulp author, borrowing much from the American masters of the genre. •

By 1952 the massive body of modern Anglo-American SF had slowly begun to appear in translation in France. Intellectuals weaned on Hollywood movies and American crime fiction became aware of popular SF, and many became great fans, although few deigned to write in the genre. But authors and publishers such as Raymond Queneau, Michel Pilotin, Maurice Blanchot, Audiberti, George Gallet, and Stephen Spriel gave SF sufficient intellectual cachet for it to seduce the French imagination.

One of the more prominent fans was Boris VIAN, who, in addition to his many careers and novels, translated works by A. E. VAN VOGT and Lewis Padgett (Henry KUTTNER and C. L. MOORE). Although his books are more surrealist than SF, Vian's role is characteristic of the transitional period between prewar scientific romance and the assimilated influence of English-language SF. Vian was a harbinger of the British NEW WAVE of the 1960s, which was itself to have a determining influence on young French SF writers.

In September 1951 Fleuve Noir, a publisher of mass-market paperbacks, launched Anticipation, an SF series still going strong today. Although publishing for a popular audience, Fleuve Noir has over the years provided many new writers with a training ground and, despite its lowbrow attitudes, has been instrumental in bringing successive generations of French readers to SF. Apart from occasional translations (and Perry Rhodan material), most Fleuve Noir titles have been by local authors: Jimmy Guieu, Richard-Bessière, M. A. Rayjean, Maurice Limat, B. R. Bruss, Jean-Gaston Vandel, and Pierre Barbet. Among the commercial dross, Fleuve Noir has published some writers of quality: Stefan Wul, a pen name for a dentist in the provinces who had a lightning but impressive burst between 1956 and 1959, producing *Niourk* (1957), *Oms en Série* ("A Chain of Men," 1957), and *Temple of the Past* (*Le Temple du passé*, 1958). His comeback in 1977 (with *Noô*) was short-lived. Other Fleuve Noir discoveries have included Kurt Steiner, a pseudonym for André Ruellan; Gilles d'Argyre, another pseudonym, hiding Gérard Klein; Gilles Thomas; and J. L. Le May.

It was also in 1951 that Le Rayon Fantastique was launched by Spriel and Gallet, primarily to introduce the GOLDEN AGE of American SF. Soon French authors were on board: Francis Carsac was the first writer of prominence, later followed by Albert Higon (Michel Jeury), Gérard Klein, Arcadius, Charles Henneberg, Philippe Curval, Christine Renard, Vladimir Volkoff, and Jérome Seriel. In 1954 Editions Denoël launched another new imprint, Présence du Futur; its high standards attracted many refugees from the mainstream. French authors featured initially were Jacques Sternberg, an acid satirist; Jean-Pierre Andrevon; and Gérard Klein.

The year 1954 was important for the debuts in France of the first genuine SF magazines—*Galaxie* and *Fiction*, respectively drawn from GALAXY and THE MAGAZINE OF FANTASY AND SCIENCE FICTION. *Fiction* immediately established a strong team of homegrown talent, featuring Rayon Fantastique and Présence du Futur authors as well as new names, such as Marcel Battin, Claude Cheinisse, Michel Demuth, Daniel Walther, and many others.

Carsac and Henneberg were the major writers of the 1950s, but in the 1960s they faded from the scene and were replaced by Sternberg, Curval, and Klein, all elegant stylists who moved French SF into a literary, humanist niche. But with the student uprising of 1968, a wave of younger, politicized authors, led by Walther and Andrevon, took over; the older Jeury made an impressive comeback with *Chronolysis* (*Le Temps incertain*, 1973) and, with a rejuvenated Curval, assumed the mantle of leadership for a French SF scene characterized by innovative yarns displaying the influence of American authors such as Philip K. DICK and the British New Wave. A group of young writers, including Joel Houssin, Bernard Blanc, and Dominique Douay, had a brief flirtation with pronounced left-wing SF, which has recently been followed by yet another wave of strongly innovative—and wildly imaginative—writers such as Joelle Wintrebert, Jean-Marc Ligny, Serge Brussolo, Emmanuel Jouanne, Pierre Barberi, Antoine Volodine, and Yves Frémion. Despite the constant renewal of French SF by younger talent, major mainstream authors have continued to be active in the genre, even if on an irregular basis; they include Jean Hougron, Robert Merle, Pierre Boulle, Claude Ollier, and Charles Dobzinsky, and their work in the genre demonstrates how highly regarded SF is in French intellectual circles. Nevertheless, the popular heritage hasn't been forgotten: Fleuve Noir still publishes six to eight new titles per month, including a powerful saga of a world overtaken by ice, George Arnaud's *La Compagnie des glaces* ("The Company of the Ice," 1980–   ), now into its thirty-fifth volume, and the work of the individualistic Pierre Pelot (who also writes as Pierre Suragne), now nearing his one hundredth title.

It is the strength of French SF that it reconciles intellectual rigor and powerful imagination with the adopted pulp traditions of the genre to offer its readers a unique literature full of daring, fine writing, and sensitivity. But then Verne was a good inspiration.

M.J.

FRANK, PAT (Pseudonym of Harry Hart) (1907–1964).
American writer, reporter, and government worker whose science fiction of the 1940s and 1950s focused on Americans' fears of nuclear devastation. Frank's first novel, *Mr. Adam* (1946), describes near universal male sterilization after an industrial accident at a bomb factory in Mississippi. The single man who remains fertile is confronted with a series of comic adventures that lampoon government bureaucracy. In *Forbidden Area* (1956; in Great Britain as *Seven Days to Never*, 1957) Frank's tone turns from ironic to brooding as the United States and the USSR square off in a series of incidents that almost lead to the ultimate war. Again the American bureaucracy receives harsh treatment but this time in a serious indictment of its inability to respond to emergencies.

Frank's best known and most effective novel is *Alas, Babylon* (1959). Like his earlier novels it is set in the near future and portrays the consequences of an atomic disaster; in this book, however, the feared war has taken place. The novel excels in its descriptions of postholocaust life as people try to restore order and combat the same abuses of power that led to the war in the first place. Frank did much more in each of these works than simply cash in on contemporary anxieties, for his strong plots and credible details served as warnings rather than adventure romances.

S.H.G.

FRANKENSTEIN ON FILM
Mary SHELLEY intended her novel as a philosophical inquiry into life and death, and the responsibilities of science; as such it falls clearly into the category of science fiction. Moviemakers, however, have always seen it as a vehicle for shuddery horror stories or occasionally comedies. Nevertheless, all the Frankenstein films retain certain abiding themes of SF—the artificial creation of life, the potency (and potential for abuse) of science—and the Universal films certainly influenced the *look* of SF cinema for years to come. The first known Frankenstein film was made by Thomas Edison in 1910; another, *Life without Soul*, was made five years later, and Italy's *Il Mostro di Frankenstein* followed in 1920. There have been dozens of Frankenstein films; the monster and/or the doctor turn up as guest stars, leading characters, and walk-ons. A significant series began in 1957 with Hammer Films's *The Curse of Frankenstein*; subsequent entries followed the adventures of the doctor (Peter Cushing) with a new monster for each film.

But to the public there has really been only one Fran-

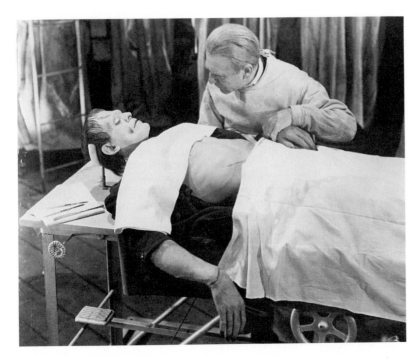

Edward Van Sloan and Boris Karloff (as the monster) in James Whale's *Franken-stein* (1931)

kenstein: not the doctor, but his monster, in a confusion that goes back as far as the 1820s. This was the monster from the series that began with James Whale's *Franken-stein* in 1931. The block-headed makeup—corpse pale, scarred, with electrodes in the neck—was created by makeup genius Jack P. Pierce; it was first and most famously worn by Boris KARLOFF.

In the wake of the great success of *Dracula* (1931), Whale, then in studio favor, personally selected Shelley's novel (in a Robert Florey adaptation) for filming. With carte blanche as to casting, he chose minor actor Karloff as the monster and Colin Clive as Frankenstein.

Even in its handsome restored version, complete with the monster tossing the girl into the lake (a scene lost for years), *Frankenstein* is largely a curio today. The scenes of joyous peasants dancing, the harrumphing elder Frankenstein, and the lack of music make parts of the film seem quaint. But the creation of the monster, the pursuit at the end, Whale's bravura style—these are still effective.

The undimmable central virtue of the film, however, is Karloff's sensitive, imaginative, and frightening performance. He is not just a killing machine but a creature for whom it is possible to feel sympathy; the touches of pathos make the film more than the thriller it was intended to be. And it made Karloff a star.

Whale's visual style is Germanic, with low camera angles, deep shadows, and exotic sets. There are only traces of his quirky wit in *Frankenstein;* it centers mostly

on Frankenstein's assistant, Fritz (Dwight Frye), and that fuddy-duddy father (Frederick Kerr).

The film was an enormous success, and a sequel inevitably followed, although it took several years to make. By then Whale had found himself increasingly comfortable with comedy on screen; *Bride of Frankenstein*—with its remarkable blend of humor and horror—is one of the most eccentric of all the Frankenstein films. Some regard it as the best horror movie ever made; Whale considered it "a hoot."

In *Bride* sardonic Dr. Pretorius (Ernest Thesiger) kidnaps Frankenstein (again Karloff) to help him create a mate (Elsa Lanchester) for the monster. One of the few genuinely unique Hollywood films, *Bride* was not successful, and when the administration changed at Universal, Whale and horror films fell out of favor. But in 1939 a new administration made *Son of Frankenstein*, trendily billed as "streamlined." Some footage was shot in color, but it was junked in favor of black and white. This film's style is more Gothic, yet sleeker and more stylized. Wolf von Frankenstein (Basil Rathbone), the legendary doctor's son, returns to the ancestral home, where the broken-necked Ygor (Bela Lugosi, in his finest performance) convinces him to revive the monster (still Karloff). He does so, and Ygor uses the monster to take revenge on his enemies. The monster plunges into a pit of molten sulfur at the climax. The film is exciting but not frightening or imaginative.

Universal itself became streamlined. The horror films

were a proven commodity, so production costs were lowered, and a series of inexpensive but competent thrillers resulted. *The Ghost of Frankenstein* is an efficient thriller but far from the genuine art of the Whale films or the elaborate adventure movie that *Son* was. Lon Chaney, Jr., is the monster in *Ghost,* at the end of which Ygor's brain is in the monster's body, a new development actively overlooked thereafter. However, Chaney's portrayal of the monster as merely a silent hulk set the mode for the rest of the series.

Although writer Curt SIODMAK felt that science fiction and fantasy horror should not be combined, he was assigned to write *Frankenstein Meets the Wolf Man*. It is perhaps the liveliest of the 1940s horror thrillers, with a genuinely eerie opening and a spectacular climax as the monsters of the title grapple in the flood from an exploded dam. Lugosi, who had turned down the part of Frankenstein's monster in 1931, plays the role here, though not well.

Universal decided that if the public turned out for two monsters, they'd beat down the doors for even more. *House of Frankenstein* gave the audience not only the Wolf Man and the Frankenstein monster, but Dracula, a hunchback, and a mad doctor (Karloff again). Glenn Strange, best known as a supporting player in westerns, was the monster in the remainder of the series. The story of *House* is awkward; Dracula (John Carradine) appears only in the first third, and the remainder of the film marks time as Karloff tries to revive the monster. This film was followed almost immediately by *House of Dracula,* largely a supernatural horror film, with the SF elements exiled to the last reel. The monster barely gets off the operating table, and the film is generally uninteresting.

In 1948 the series ended with the sprightly, funny *Abbott and Costello Meet Frankenstein*. The two comedians find themselves up against Dracula (Lugosi, for only the second time on screen), the monster (Strange), and the Wolf Man (Chaney). This is actually a better film than the previous two and not an unfitting end to the most famous SF/horror series in movie history.

If Universal's films set the direction for SF/horror movies, then ten years later Hammer Films of Great Britain changed it forever, though not overnight, with the release of the first color productions in the genre, *The Curse of Frankenstein* and *Horror of Dracula* (1958). Both these films were made by the same team and star Peter Cushing and Christopher Lee, launching these actors on careers in the genre that continue to the present.

Hammer's adaptations of several television productions, including the Quatermass stories by Nigel Kneale, had proved popular worldwide, but by 1956 most observers felt that the SF boom was fading. Nevertheless, Hammer—who suspected that underneath the popularity of SF film bubbled an interest in Gothic horror—abandoned several long-planned projects in favor of *Curse*. The completed film seemed unusually promising, so a print was immediately flown to New York and

screened for Jack Warner. Warner Bros. bought the rights, and the film broke records the world over.

The Curse of Frankenstein looked and played like no other horror or SF film before it. The classic Universal Frankenstein face could not legally be duplicated, so a new monster was devised by Phil Leakey and played by tall, slender Lee. The plot, an original story by Jimmy Sangster, bears little resemblance to the Shelley novel.

This Frankenstein is urbane, witty, sardonic, cruel, sensual. He's dapperly dressed and hums little tunes to himself while bloodily working in his lab. Because of the precision and passion of Cushing's performance, the baron made a far more powerful impact on audiences than the creature; in subsequent Hammer Frankenstein films, the baron himself is the central character (played, in all the films except *Horror,* by Cushing).

This film is tight though oddly structured, vigorous, well designed for its budget. It is also brightly colored, brightly lit; the Germanic chiaroscuro of the Universal series has been replaced by a Grand Guignol approach. But it was *Horror*'s bloody realism that dazzled younger audiences and outraged their elders. Never before in *any* film, horror or otherwise, had gore been depicted so graphically. Some critics scorned the film because of this, but Hammer's new approach depended on showing the horror. Although not an inherently inferior approach, it proved a brutal shock to those who liked horror kept in the shadows.

Because of the overwhelming success of the first film, a sequel soon followed, and more after that (although fans did prefer the Hammer Dracula series, with Christopher Lee).

In *The Revenge of Frankenstein,* the baron has been using men in a prison hospital as the source for two new bodies he's putting together secretly; one body (Michael Gwynn) is used to house the brain of the cripple who freed him from the gallows, but that experiment goes spectacularly wrong. At the climax the baron is fatally beaten by the hospital inmates, but he has his assistant install his brain in the other body—and Frankenstein becomes his own monster.

This neat twist was abandoned for the third film in the series, *The Evil of Frankenstein,* which didn't arrive for several years. Made in conjunction with Universal, it features a monster (New Zealand wrestler Kiwi Kingston) who resembles the Karloff creature. But the forcing together of the Hammer and Universal approaches really doesn't work; *Evil* is the least successful film in the series, degenerating into inadvertent comedy as the monster swigs chloroform and everything goes up in flames.

The baron returned three years later in *Frankenstein Created Woman,* a title parodying Roger Vadim's famous film with Brigitte Bardot, . . . *And God Created Woman*. Instead of dead bodies, the baron is now interested in soul transmigration. He gives the soul of a murdered young man to a crippled girl (Susan Denberg) who loved him, then killed herself in despair. Revived, she kills the men who were responsible for the death of the young man—then leaps into a river, as Frankenstein walks helplessly away.

Frankenstein Must Be Destroyed is probably the best film in this series. Frankenstein's personality had wavered from haughty to benign in the previous entries (he's at his kindest in *Evil,* oddly enough), but in this movie he is thoroughly despicable, opportunistic, fanatic in his dedication, and casual in his destruction of the lives of those who hinder him. His latest creation (Freddie Jones), who looks relatively normal, carries the screaming baron into a blazing house at the climax.

The last film in the series, *Frankenstein and the Monster from Hell,* suffered from both a low budget and an overemphasis on gruesomeness. The monster (David Prowse) is overdesigned, a hideous brute covered in hair. Confined to a prison hospital setting again, this film broke no ground, although Cushing's weary baron here may represent his best performance in the series.

Like the Universal series before it, the Hammer Frankenstein series has faded from public memory, but the immense impact of *Curse of Frankenstein* is felt and displayed in virtually every horror movie, and innumerable SF films, made today.

Frankenstein (1931).   *Directed by James Whale; screenplay by Garrett Fort, Francis Edwards Faragoh, John Russell, and Robert Florey; adapted by John L. Balderston from the play by Peggy Webling, from the novel* Frankenstein; Or the Modern Prometheus *by Mary Wollstonecraft Shelley; photographed by Arthur Edeson; music by David Broekman. With Colin Clive, Boris Karloff, Mae Clarke, John Boles, Edward Van Sloan, Dwight Frye, Lionel Belmore, Marilyn Harris, Michael Mark. 67 minutes. Black and white.*

Bride of Frankenstein (1935).   *Directed by James Whale; screenplay by William Hurlbut; photographed by John Mescall; music by Franz Waxman. With Colin Clive, Boris Karloff, Ernest Thesiger, Elsa Lanchester, Valerie Hobson, Gavin Gordon, Douglas Walton, Una O'Connor, E. E. Clive, O. P. Heggie, Dwight Frye, John Carradine, Walter Brennan, Billy Barty. 75 minutes. Black and white.*

Son of Frankenstein (1939).   *Directed by Rowland V. Lee; screenplay by Willis Cooper; photographed by George Robinson; music by Frank Skinner. With Basil Rathbone, Boris Karloff, Bela Lugosi, Lionel Atwill, Josephine Hutchinson, Donnie Dunagan, Emma Dunn, Edgar Norton, Lionel Belmore, Michael Mark, Ward Bond. 96 minutes. Black and white.*

The Ghost of Frankenstein (1942).   *Directed by Erle C. Kenton; screenplay by W. Scott Darling; photographed by Milton Krasner and Woody Bredell; music by Hans J. Salter. With Lon Chaney (Jr.), Sir Cedric Hardwicke, Bela Lugosi, Ralph Bellamy, Lionel Atwill, Evelyn Ankers, Janet Ann Gallow, Barton Yarborough, Michael Mark, Dwight Frye. 67 minutes. Black and white.*

Frankenstein Meets the Wolf Man (1943).   *Directed by Roy William Neill; screenplay by Curtis Siodmak; photographed by George Robinson; music by Hans J. Salter. With Lon Chaney (Jr.), Ilona Massey, Patric Knowles, Bela Lugosi, Lionel Atwill, Maria Ouspensakaya, Dennis Hoey, Don Barclay, Dwight Frye. 74 minutes. Black and white.*

House of Frankenstein (1944).   *Directed by Erle C. Kenton; screenplay by Edward T. Lowe; photographed by George Robinson; music by Hans J. Salter. With Boris Karloff, Lon Chaney (Jr.), John Carradine, Anne Gwynne, J. Carrol Naish, Glenn Strange, Elena Verdugo, Peter Coe, Lionel Atwill, George Zucco, Sig Rumann, Michael Mark. 70 minutes. Black and white.*

House of Dracula (1945).   *Directed by Erle C. Kenton; screenplay by Edward T. Lowe; photographed by George Robinson; music directed by Edgar Fairchild. With Lon Chaney (Jr.), Onslow Stevens, Martha O'Driscoll, John Carradine, Glenn Strange, Lionel Atwill, Ludwig Stossel, Skelton Knaggs. 67 minutes. Black and white.*

Abbott and Costello Meet Frankenstein (1948). *Directed by Charles T. Barton; screenplay by Robert Lees, Frederic I. Rinaldo, and John Grant; photographed by Charles Van Enger; music by Frank Skinner. With Bud Abbott, Lou Costello, Bela Lugosi, Lon Chaney, Jr., Glenn Strange, Lenore Aubert, Jane Randolph. 83 minutes. Black and white.*

The Curse of Frankenstein (1957).   *Directed by Terence Fisher; screenplay by Jimmy Sangster, loosely based on the novel* Frankenstein; Or, A Modern Prometheus *by Mary Wollstonecraft Shelley; photographed by Jack Asher; music by James Bernard. With Peter Cushing, Christopher Lee, Robert Urquhart, Hazel Court, Valerie Gaunt, Noel Hood, Melvyn Hayes, Paul Hardtmuth. 83 minutes. Color.*

The Revenge of Frankenstein (1958).   *Directed by Terence Fisher; screenplay by Jimmy Sangster; photographed by Jack Asher; music by Leonard Salzedo. With Peter Cushing, Francis Matthews, Michael Gwynn, Eunice Gayson, Oscar Quitak, Richard Wordsworth, Lionel Jeffries, Michael Ripper. 89 minutes. Color.*

The Evil of Frankenstein (1964).   *Directed by Freddie Francis; screenplay by John Elder (Anthony Hinds); photographed by John Wilcox; music by Don Banks. With Peter Cushing, Peter Woodthorpe, Katy Wild, Duncan Lamont, Kiwi Kingston (monster), Sandor Eles, David Hutcheson. 86 minutes. Color.*

Frankenstein Created Woman (1967).   *Directed by Terence Fisher; screenplay by John Elder (Anthony Hinds); photographed by Arthur Grant; music by James Bernard. With Peter Cushing, Susan Denberg, Thorley Walters, Robert Morris, Duncan Lamont, Peter Blythe, Barry Warren, Alan MacNaughtan. 92 minutes. Color.*

"Space 104—Scramble" by Frazetta

strips and books, including BUCK ROGERS, FLASH GORDON, and Al Capp's *Li'l Abner*. He broke into science fiction with a series of Conan covers for Lancer Books and soon after was creating covers for the Edgar Rice BURROUGHS Tarzan books published by Ace (aided by his good friend and fellow artist Roy G. KRENKEL). Some of his paintings have attained an almost legendary status, among them "Death Dealer," which appeared—among other places—on an album cover for the rock-and-roll group Molly Hatchet. Frazetta's style is dynamic, and his paintings usually feature a strong central figure surrounded by other figures or a background that appears to swirl about it. Unlike such artists as Michael WHELAN or ROWENA, he allowed his brush strokes to show and indeed used them to create a sense of movement. Now retired, Frazetta was one of the most popular cover illustrators of the 1960s and 1970s, when he dominated the sword-and-sorcery illustration market. His artwork, both oils and pen-and-ink sketches, has been collected in a series of books published by Peacock Press of Bantam Books. Nominated for six Hugo Awards, he received only one, in 1966.

J.G.

Frankenstein Must Be Destroyed (1969). *Directed by Terence Fisher; screenplay by Bert Batt; photographed by Arthur Grant; music by James Bernard. With Peter Cushing, Simon Ward, Veronica Carlson, Thorley Walters, Freddie Jones, Maxine Audley. 97 minutes. Color.*

The Horror of Frankenstein (1970). *Directed by Jimmy Sangster; screenplay by Jimmy Sangster and Jeremy Burnham; photographed by Moray Grant; music by James Bernard. With Ralph Bates, Kate O'Mara, Graham James, Veronica Carlson, Bernard Archard, Dennis Price, Joan Rice, David Prowse (monster). 95 minutes. Color.*

Frankenstein and the Monster from Hell (1973). *Directed by Terence Fisher, screenplay by John Elder (Anthony Hinds); photographed by Brian Probyn; music by James Bernard. With Peter Cushing, Shane Briant, Madeline Smith, John Stratton, Bernard Lee, David Prowse (monster), Charles Lloyd Pack. 99 minutes. Color.*

B.W.

FRAZETTA, FRANK (1928–   ). American illustrator, best known for his magnificently muscled men and zaftig women. Frazetta is often called the leader of the "heroic school" of fantasy art. After graduating from the Brooklyn Academy of Fine Arts, where he studied under Michael Falanga, Frazetta began his career in the comics in 1944 and remained a comic illustrator for almost two decades. He worked on a variety of comic

FREAS, FRANK [KELLY] (1922–   ). American science-fiction illustrator, an important figure in the genre since the first appearance of his work on the cover of *Weird Tales* in November of 1950. Freas is the most popular illustrator in the history of SF, having been nominated for more than twenty Hugo awards and winning ten times. He has also received the Frank R. Paul award, the Lensman, the Inkpot, and the Skylark, among others. Equally adept at cover paintings and interior black-and-white illustrations, Freas has done both (often with his wife, Polly, as model) for such magazines as *Science Fiction Stories*, *Weird Tales*, *Astounding Science Fiction* (and ANALOG), THE MAGAZINE OF FANTASY AND SCIENCE FICTION, *Tops in Science Fiction*, *Planet Stories*, *Fantastic Universe*, and *MAD*. His paintings grace the covers of books from such publishers as Ace, Lancer, DAW, and Laser.

Freas's style is generally realistic, often with a humorous bent; some of his early black-and-white work is similar to that of Edd CARTIER. A number of his illustrations have become classics of the genre, including the little green man for the cover of Fredric BROWN's *Martians, Go Home*, the bedeviled blue alien in Christopher ANVIL's "The Gentle Earth," the man in the metal mask for Algis BUDRYS's *Who?*, and the giant robot for Tom Goodwin's "The Gulf Between" (which was used again—with some alterations—as an album cover for the rock group Queen). Freas created all the cover illustrations for the ill-fated Laser Books series (1975–1977); each cover was painted to a formula to give the series a unified look. In addition to his SF art, he has produced artwork

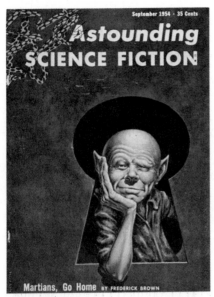

Illustration by Freas

for NASA and designed the astronauts' shoulder patch for one of the Skylab missions. His art has been collected in two books: *Frank Kelly Freas: The Art of Science Fiction* (1977) and *Frank Kelly Freas: A Separate Star* (1984).

J.G.

FROM THE EARTH TO THE MOON (1958).
Directed by Byron Haskin; screenplay by Robert Blees and James Leicester; adapted from the novels De la Terre à la lune (1865) and Autour de la lune (1870) by Jules Verne; photographed by Edwin B. DuPar and Jorge Stahl, Jr.; music by Louis Forbes. With Joseph Cotten, George Sanders, Debra Paget, Don Dubbins, Patric Knowles, Henry Daniell, Morris Ankrum, Carl Esmond. 100 minutes. Color.

A heroic munitions manufacturer (Joseph Cotten), opposed by a villainous pacifist (George Sanders), launches a cannon-cum-rocket to the Moon, and both (plus the juvenile leads) go along.

Far from VERNE's stories both in content and approach (although Verne does appear as a character), this ponderous film is deliberately anachronistic. As usual with Verne adaptations, a "prediction" of atomic power is worked into the plot line. Pompous dialogue, thoroughly unconvincing effects, a leaden pace, and uncaring performances by all except Cotten destroy what little interest the film initially generates.

B.W.

THE FUTURE

The future of humanity is one of the basic themes of science fiction. Fred Polak, in *The Idea of the Future* (1973), has pointed out that there are actually two concepts of the future, one pertaining to an ultimate or eschatological future, the other to a historical future. The distinction is easily seen in H. G. WELLS's *The Time Machine* (1895), which deals with the historical future of the Eloi and the Morlocks and then with an ultimate future in which humanity has become extinct and the Earth is dying.

The idea of a materially different historical future is of recent origin; it emerged in substantial measure only with the philosophers of progress at the end of the eighteenth century. Before that the only future much thought or written about was the Day of Judgment, when history would come to an end. The history of SF reflects both the burgeoning of the idea that the historical future is rich in opportunity but fraught with danger and the virtual eclipse of the idea that the Day of Judgment is imminent and that therefore the true business of life is preparation for eternal bliss or punishment. Again this whole pattern is encapsulated in *The Time Machine,* which balances hope and anxiety in speculating about the social world but finds nothing to be said about a destiny beyond death; hope for a transcendence of the contemporary human condition is pegged to future evolution instead of religious salvation.

Insofar as SF depends on theories of social change to generate images of the future, two are frequently favored. One is naive technological determinism, which views social change as a series of adaptations to new technologies. Most works of this kind are tacitly optimistic, somewhat after the fashion of the early classic *Looking Backward* (1888) by Edward BELLAMY, and this worldview underlies much hard SF. The other favored theory involves the notion of historical cyclicity, although this often seems to be chosen more for its hypothetical convenience or aesthetic appeal than for its intellectual persuasiveness. It figures in such works as Olaf STAPLEDON's *Last and First Men* (1930), Isaac ASIMOV's Foundation trilogy (1942–1953), and James BLISH's *Cities in Flight.* In Blish's work this theory gives ample opportunity for literary range, in terms of tragedy and catastrophism, although, as in Asimov's trilogy, it can also allow for a measure of optimism.

Ironically, biological EVOLUTION, although its mechanisms are much better understood, is even more difficult to anticipate than social change, because it relies on the selection of unpredictable mutations. Onetime SF writers who dealt with the future evolution of the species were therefore faced with a problem that they often "solved" by reintroducing into SF images of transcendence borrowed from theology. Some who did this, including George Bernard Shaw in *Back to Methuselah,*

Home of the future from an 1894 issue of *Pall Mall*

Fritz Lang's future city in *Metropolis* (1929)

denied Darwinism; others—such as Arthur C. CLARKE in *Childhood's End*—merely had to embellish it after the fashion of the Darwinist theologian Pierre Teilhard de Chardin (1881–1955). The recent development of elementary techniques in genetic engineering, however, suggests that technical control over evolution might be achieved in the near historical future, and this possibility has allowed a radical reappraisal of possible future change—compare, for instance, Stapledon's *Last and First Men,* which extends over 2 billion years, with Brian STABLEFORD and David Langford's *The Third Millennium* (1985), which offers equally dramatic changes in the span of a mere thousand years.

B.S.

——— FUTURE HISTORIES ———

"Future history" is the kind of contradiction in terms that science fiction thrives on (because it makes readers re-evaluate what they "know" to be true), combining as it does history, a systematic written account of what has

happened, with the future, events that have not happened and may never happen. A future history, then, is an imaginary systematic written account of events that have yet to happen.

Robert A. HEINLEIN popularized the idea of organizing stories along a previously thought-out scheme of future events, and John W. CAMPBELL announced it, first in a footnote to a story in the March 1941 issue of *Astounding* and then in a May 1941 editorial that published Heinlein's two-page "Future History" chart.

Earlier authors had written stories that deal with the future as if it were history, as in H. G. WELLS's *The Time Machine* (1895) and Olaf STAPLEDON's evolutionary and galactic histories in *Last and First Men* (1930) and *Star Maker* (1937), but Heinlein's History of the Future, which began with stories published in magazine form in 1939–40, was the first series to set works at different *stages* of an evolving future. This strategy made it possible for the events of one story to become the premise of the next, and for works set in the more distant future to have a background in the past. The moving highways of "The Roads Must Roll" (1940) become the ruins of *Methu-*

selah's Children (1941); Nehemiah Scudder and the Theocracy are a looming threat at the end of "Logic of Empire" (1941), a historical fact in "If This Goes On—" (1940). Developments in one story grow logically from others: the system of justice in "Coventry" (1940) is a reaction against the abuses of the Theocracy.

With its creator's belief in the utopian potential of science, technology, and General Semantics (a "scientific" philosophy popular in SF circles during the 1940s), Heinlein's future history follows a basically linear model. Even the Theocracy is a comparatively minor setback in humankind's advance to its "first mature culture." Heinlein's model was followed by Larry Niven in his Known Space series but with the variation that *human* history intersects with an ongoing *galactic* history involving several alien races. In the Soviet Union, Arkady and Boris STRUGATSKY's history of an evolving Communist future also has a linear structure.

Isaac ASIMOV, with his Foundation series, pioneered what became the cyclic model of future history, with civilization and barbarism alternating. Although he was inspired by Edward Gibbon rather than Arnold Toynbee or Oswald Spengler, Asimov's image of the Galactic Empire became the centerpiece of series such as H. Beam PIPER's Terrohuman future history and Jerry POURNELLE's CoDominium history—both of which take the inevitability of historical cycles as fundamental. Such future histories also take martial and aristocratic virtues very seriously, to the point of regarding a military aristocracy as the highest form of society—even if it is tragically doomed at the end of each cycle. In his Cities in Flight series, James BLISH explores a Spenglerian future history much more dispassionately, without any of the glamour or gallantry of empire.

Poul ANDERSON's Technic History is superficially much like those of Piper and Pournelle. But Anderson's attitude is quite different: his Polesotechnic League and Terran Empire are the "spring" and "autumn" of the same cycle. And he offers hope of escape from the cycles in the far future, libertarian Commonalty. Anderson's model has its parallels in the Hainish Cycle of Ursula K. LE GUIN, with its Ekumen, and even in Cordwainer SMITH's mythos of the Instrumentality of Mankind, ending with the Rediscovery of Man. Still other models are represented by Gordon R. DICKSON's Childe Cycle, in which evolution of a new *kind* of human plays a central role, and C. J. CHERRYH's unnamed future history, which follows the diffusion of two supercultures with individual works set against a commonly understood (usually cyclic) history.

Jack WILLIAMSON considers humanity's colonization of space SF's "epic theme," and Donald A. WOLLHEIM in his *Universe Makers* (1971) traced what he called SF's "cosmogony"—a consensus future history in which almost all SF is placed—to Asimov's Foundation (whose first story appeared in 1942).

J.J.P.

THE FUTURE OF SCIENCE FICTION

By the mid-1980s science fiction was developing so rapidly that predicting its future seems difficult if not impossible. After a long history as a minority literature—even, many have said, a ghetto literature—by the 1980s SF may have become a majority literature, that is, a literature everyone knows about and a majority of readers of English read at least occasionally.

Various statistics support the fact of SF's increasing popularity. According to figures in *Locus,* which has been called the "*Publishers Weekly* of the SF field," in 1972, when *Publishers Weekly*'s annual report on the year's publications indicated that 9 percent of all fiction published was science fiction or fantasy, SF and fantasy books published numbered 348. In 1986 roughly 20 percent of all fiction, or 1502 books, published was SF or fantasy.

Science fiction also broke into the best-seller lists in the 1980s, not just with movie novelizations and "mainstream" novels not ordinarily considered SF (by mainstream critics at least), such as Carl SAGAN's *Contact* and Kurt VONNEGUT, Jr.'s *Galapagos,* but with SF novels by such genre masters as Isaac ASIMOV (*Foundation's Edge*), Arthur C. CLARKE (*2010*), and Robert A. HEINLEIN (*Friday*), as well as novels by lesser-known authors.

For generations the film industry had treated SF as an easily exploitable genre, for instance, as a source for more terrifying or more plausible monsters, but seldom for important themes and significant narratives. If money was spent on such productions, it went primarily into special effects, not into stories, scripts, direction, or acting. Just as the long-held attitude of publishers was that SF books made a little money but could never make a lot (with enough ardent readers to sell 1000 to 2000 copies of any hardcover SF book but not enough to justify printing more than 4000 or 5000 copies of a hardcover novel), Hollywood believed that SF movies were a way to make a few safe dollars but little more, so there wasn't any point in risking a lot of money by making them good. In 1968 the Stanley Kubrick production of 2001: A SPACE ODYSSEY changed that attitude, and George LUCAS's STAR WARS (1977) confirmed the indisputable fact that a major SF production could make major profits. By 1986 six of the seven top money-making films of all time were SF, and twelve of the top twenty were SF or fantasy. The perspective of filmmakers, like that of publishers, had been permanently changed.

Why is commercial success important to the development of SF?

The only rational method of prediction, SF has discovered, is extrapolation: extrapolating SF's future involves looking at the conditions that have affected its development in the past and tracking them up to the present and into the future. Anything else is simply guesswork.

As a popular genre, SF always has been dependent on the commercial media. The kind of SF that gets published depends not only on the times and the authors but on what people are willing to publish. Jules VERNE succeeded only when he found publisher Jules Hetzel, and H. G. WELLS got ahead by placing his stories in the proliferating popular magazines of his time. The pulp magazines evolved into the category pulp magazines. When the first SF category magazine was published, book publication dropped to virtually nothing, so not only did the SF magazines identify and nurture the new genre, its readers, and its new writers, but they also defined it. For several years SF was what Hugo GERNS-BACK published in AMAZING STORIES, then it was what *Amazing, Wonder,* and the Clayton *Astounding* published. Finally, such was Joseph W. Campbell's dominance of the field between 1937 and 1950, SF was what his *Astounding* published. Since then the field has been broadening and branching.

Two of its branches—which offered different visions of what SF could be—were the strongly competitive magazines THE MAGAZINE OF FANTASY AND SCIENCE FICTION (beginning in 1949) and GALAXY (beginning in 1950). Radio, television, and film offered still other visions, although none of them was truly competitive until *2001* and after. The book format returned after World War II, but it worked its way through a decade or more of reprinting magazine stories and serials before providing a significant alternative for original novels.

By the mid-1980s, however, the book had become the dominant means of publication. The half-dozen magazines still being published, though significant as proving grounds for new writers, had not benefited by the apparent increase in SF readership: their circulations generally stayed within their traditional ceilings of 50,000 to 100,000 (*Omni*'s circulation is nearly 1 million, but it is primarily an article and graphics magazine with some fiction). Only a small proportion of the new fiction published each year appeared in the fifty-some annual issues of the seven all-fiction SF and fantasy magazines, and their payments for stories represented an even smaller part of authors' incomes.

As a consequence, magazines no longer lead or define the genre. Instead individual books, both hardcover and paperback, must find their own markets in the bookstores and on the newsstands, and readers must make their choices on the basis of cover, blurb, author, or genre. And genre labels no longer are a reliable basis for determining whether the purchaser will like what they are pasted on. The formerly predictable floor under book sales has vanished along with the ceiling; when more than 1500 books are published every year, even the most ardent readers must be selective. Few titles except those by major authors are individually promoted. This fact may account for the popularity of series: one successful novel presells the next.

Because of marketing methods, a book with a specific appeal has more chance of good sales than a novel of quiet competence, or even of excellence. The latter has come to be called a midlist book because it has no outstanding characteristic that can be sold by the publishers' sales forces to the major booksellers and by them to the public. In the middle of a crowd, books, like people, must do something unusual to stand out; for a while the midlist book was considered unsalable, and thus unpublishable. That assessment has changed somewhat: mass-market publishers' monthly lists of six, eight, or a dozen titles require more than the few books that can be leaders.

Science fiction has always been subject to periods of boom and bust. Gernsback's first SF publishing empire collapsed in 1929; Clayton's magazine chain went bankrupt in 1933; World War II and its paper shortages killed off a good part of the magazine field that began to burgeon in 1938–39, and the postwar boom, which exploded with the publication of some fifty magazines between 1949 and 1959, began to implode in the mid-1950s and took the developing book market along with it. Even in contemporary times, the recession of 1980 interrupted the long rise of book publication, with declines in numbers of books published of 8 percent, 11 percent, and 1 percent in successive years until the recovery of 1983. Those may seem like small percentage drops, but they meant that publishers were depleting their inventories and not buying new books, and many writers' incomes—and plans—were seriously disrupted.

While the audience for SF was small—Damon KNIGHT once called SF "the mass medium for the few"—ups and downs in the economy or the world at large could exert disproportionate effects on the field. It can be argued that the audience now is of sufficient size that future swings will be moderate. Indeed SF now may expect an extended period of continued growth. The literature of change has been accepted broadly as at least appropriate, and perhaps even essential, to a world of change and the young people who have to live in it. And because SF's growth has been recent and rapid, most of its 1980s readers are young, in their teens or early twenties, and, like the baby boom generation, can be expected to increase the audience still more as they move into their thirties and are replaced by groups of younger readers as large or larger.

In recent years as well the field has been marked by periodic shake-ups: some successful editors have been fired, some publishers have dropped their entire SF lines, other publishers have gone bankrupt, and many have been sold and consolidated. Berkley Books, for instance, bought Jove paperbacks, Playboy SF paperbacks, and Ace Books, and a German company bought Doubleday, Bantam, and Dell. In the mid-1980s the results of such combinations remained to be determined, but when publishing programs disappeared, in whatever fashion, they were replaced by the expansion of other programs or the start of new ones. A recent development has been the rise of the specialist press, usually emphasizing expensive editions of books by major authors but occasionally providing publication for collections and other hard-to-publish books, and capable of moving into midlist publication.

All of these new forces exert pressures toward diversity; the only forces operating to contain or direct the field are organizations, formal and informal, such as fandom, with its conventions, publications, awards, and genre expectations; the SCIENCE FICTION WRITERS OF AMERICA, with its journals and awards; a few publishers with identifiable editorial tastes; and, to a lesser degree, reviews and academic criticism. In other words, except in the eyes of literary journals and general review media, which have consistently ignored SF over the years, the genre seems very much like the mainstream and more and more can be expected to behave like it.

Damon Knight has pointed out that one consequence of the rapid growth in the number of younger readers of the genre is a juvenile preference for SF and fantasy adventures. Younger readers also tend to buy movie and television novelizations, STAR TREK novels, and other kinds of media spin-offs. Many of them, indeed, may have been brought into SF reading from film and television viewing, or from comic books (a large comic-book fandom overlaps SF fandom). Still, the size of the field means that a great many tastes can be accommodated.

Knight has divided the field of the mid-1980s into hard SF, science fantasy, adventure SF, "gonzo" SF, and literary SF. Hard SF is "practiced by technically trained writers who pride themselves on their scientific rigor." Science fantasy allows the writer one fantastic assumption but then expects logical development without further violation of physical law. Adventure SF, the largest category, uses an SF idea or universe as the setting for an adventure story. Gonzo SF, which includes CYBERPUNK, relies for its effectiveness on shock and brilliant tawdriness. Literary SF measures itself against traditional literary values: "character, form, insight, dignity, complex emotions, and polished style."

Most of these categories can be expected to continue in popularity, with adventure SF, the easiest to write and read, being the most popular and lending itself most readily to series; its readership may be restricted to the genre audience, but it will appeal to the largest part of that audience. Science fantasy, because it makes fewer demands on its readers, may appeal to a more general audience and has the potential occasionally to break out of category and into best-sellerdom. Gonzo SF may be limited by its need for continual escalation, Knight believes, and must reach a cultural limit. One might expect it, however, to be replaced by something newer and more exciting; as a matter of fact, many writers identified with

cyberpunk had moved on by the time the audience caught up with what was happening. Hard SF is the category most likely to be confined to a strictly SF audience because of the special information and close attention it requires; yet it most nearly incorporates the ideal of SF.

Literary SF may be expected to increase because it has achieved, with some exceptions, more acceptance outside the genre than within. It is what mainstream writers usually produce when they are attracted to SF themes, and the SF writer who attempts it is more likely, when he or she gets the mainstream virtues right, to be reviewed and sold to mainstream audiences. This is the kind of SF whose wider acceptance by genre readers would not only be good for SF but would result in a more sophisticated genre audience.

The outlook for SF as a whole is optimistic in terms of audience, number of publications, and sales but not so optimistic in terms of the development and improvement of the genre. The pressures for diversity mean that evolution will be dependent on the examples of individual writers, that the field will not evolve from interactions within the genre. Members of the SF ghetto evolved together, one writer building on the accomplishments of another. With the ghetto walls down, the general population is free to stroll through SF's strange and wondrous streets, but the sense of unity and brotherhood may disappear.

Robert Oppenheimer once wrote that art "is primarily to be enjoyed and understood," but "it is not primarily to be built upon." Science, in contrast, is "cumulative" and "irreversible." Science fiction may have been more like science; now it may be becoming more like art.

Science fiction is likely to become more and more like the mainstream, and part of the mainstream is likely to use the ideas and tropes of SF, until the two genres become almost indistinguishable in the middle. What once were distinct categories of fiction will become like a spectrum, clearly different at the ends but continuous, connected, and indisputably one literature. Whether that development will be good for SF or for literature remains to be seen.

All these predictions may be true for the American market, which by its size and tradition leads the rest of the world. Great Britain, however, has at times pursued a different path. There SF has never been as ghettoized as in America, and thus the British genre's traditions as literature have never been as seriously questioned. Its influences have been those of individual writers, except during the 1960s NEW WAVE period. In the mid-1980s, however, a number of leading writers resented and discarded genre labels, and that trend may be expected to accelerate. Great Britain may lead the movement toward blurring genre lines, but the size of its market compared with that of America will minimize its influence.

SF in the non-English-speaking countries depends on the spread of industrialization. Interest generally is followed by translations of American classics and then the development of native writers, who often encounter difficulties in competing. We can expect, however, as parts of the world not presently industrialized begin to experience this transition and the scientific and technical education of their citizens, that SF readership will not be far behind, and that it will be followed by the development of native SF peculiarly suited to the cultures, temperaments, and world situations of the countries involved. This process has already occurred, for instance, in Japan, Poland, and the Soviet Union, and in lesser respects in other countries not dependent on the American market.

J.E.G.

FUTUREWORLD: SEE WESTWORLD

─────── THE FUTURIANS ───────

Familiar name of the Futurian Society of New York, a science-fiction fan organization founded in 1938. The group of two dozen or so Futurians produced an impressive list of SF professionals: Isaac ASIMOV, James BLISH, Virginia KIDD, Damon KNIGHT, Cyril M. KORNBLUTH, David A. Kyle, Robert A. W. LOWNDES, Judith MERRIL, Frederik POHL, Larry SHAW, Richard WILSON, and Donald A. WOLLHEIM. Other members included Elsie Balter (Wollheim), Doris Baumgardt, Chester Cohen, Harry Dockweiler ("Dirk Wylie"), Walter Kubilius, and John Michel.

The Futurians were less a club than a way of life for the core members. They were teenagers, bright but strangely socialized, living a hand-to-mouth existence at the end of the Depression, fascinated by the literary and social possibilities they saw in SF. They shared apartments, married each other, produced endless fanzines, conducted fannish feuds, read each other's stories, wrote collaboratively, and, eventually, published each other's work in Futurian-edited, poverty-row pulps. Their territorial and ideological squabbles with each other and with rival fan groups were the stuff of fannish legend for decades, but it was the Futurian drive for professional status that had the most significant impact on American SF. By 1945, when the group dissolved, nearly every member had published some SF, at least in collaboration; Wollheim, Pohl, Lowndes, and Knight had worked as editors; and Asimov had long since departed to become one of John W. CAMPBELL's star writers at ASTOUNDING.

A partial list of Futurian editorial accomplishments includes (of at least 175 anthologies and various major and minor magazines) the first paperback SF anthology (Wollheim's *Pocket Book of Science Fiction*, 1943); the first original anthology series (Pohl's *Star Science Fiction*, 1953–1960); three other distinguished series

(Merril's *Year's Best SF*, 1956–1968; Wollheim and Carr's *World's Best SF*, 1965–1971, and its successor, *Annual World's Best SF*, 1972– , with Arthur W. Saha; and Knight's *Orbit*, 1966–1980). In 1972, after years of editing at Ace Books, Wollheim went on to establish his own publishing house, DAW Books, a major publisher of original paperback SF. Various individuals and subsets of the Futurians (Blish, Merril, and especially Knight) continued the tradition of organizing and participating in formal and informal writers' groups: the Milford Conference, the Clarion Writers' Workshop, and the SCIENCE FICTION WRITERS OF AMERICA.

R.F.L.

FYFE, H[ORACE] B[ROWNE] (1918–). American laboratory assistant, draftsman, and the author of over sixty science-fiction short stories and one novel. Fyfe, who has been writing SF since 1940, is best known for his series organized around the Bureau of Slick Tricks, a secret group whose mission is to get humans on alien planets out of difficult situations. These stories customarily involve human contact with aliens that results in some dilemma craftily solved by the human characters ("In Value Deceived," *Possible Worlds of Science Fiction*, 1951; "The Compleat Collector," *Future*, 1953; "Welcome, Strangers!" *Astounding*, 1954; and others).

Fyfe's one novel, *D-99* (1962), is in the same vein, presenting a series of episodes that describe how humanity outsmarts, outmaneuvers, and simply outlasts any and all aliens. Although Fyfe's fiction rarely deals with any serious theme or explores any complex ideas, his stories provide good entertainment for readers willing to look for them. Such a search, however, can be difficult, because no collection of his stories yet exists.

S.H.G.

─────── G ───────

─────── GALACTIC EMPIRES ───────

The concept of the billions of stars in a galaxy brought together into political union, as the Roman Empire united the world of its time, has appealed to dozens of authors, but a true galactic empire was not realized until Isaac ASIMOV began his Foundation series in 1942. Edmond HAMILTON, E. E. SMITH, and Olaf STAPLEDON had created interstellar federations and cosmic cultures, but these were for the most part either larger canvases on which to play out larger dramas or cosmic Ruritanias—offering Luke Skywalker, for example, a princess to rescue in STAR WARS. This usage has obvious roots in the Martian kingdoms of Edgar Rice BURROUGHS's Barsoom.

Asimov's intention, evidenced by his use of parallels from Edward Gibbon's *Decline and Fall of the Roman Empire*, was to imagine a sober historical epic of the far future. As used by H. Beam PIPER, Poul ANDERSON, Jerry POURNELLE, and others, galactic empires, though sometimes romantic, have been manifestations of a historical process at work (see FUTURE HISTORIES).

Only in a relatively few works, such as Edmond HAMILTON's *The Star Kings* (1949), is the galactic empire used for pure romance without any serious speculative pretensions. Empires are taken more seriously by most authors—enough so at least for them to render plausible what is really a romantic fantasy (whatever government an inhabited galaxy chooses, it is unlikely to be an empire). It is rare, for example, to find galactic empires that are *truly* galactic anymore. Those of Piper, Anderson, Pournelle, and Frank HERBERT embrace at most a few hundred worlds in a space of a few hundred light-years—more would make central administration impossible, which is what makes Asimov's galactic empire begin to decay at the beginning of his still-expanding trilogy. And although there are still emperors and aristocracy in his empire, Asimov set the style for bureaucracies and political intrigue rather than buckling swashes. *Sic transit gloria!*

J.J.P.

GALAXY SCIENCE FICTION (1950–1980).

The leading science-fiction magazine of the 1950s. *Galaxy* was launched in October 1950 with H. L. GOLD as editor. Gold was well schooled in the pulp tradition and something of a protégé of John W. CAMPBELL, Jr., but, unlike Campbell, Gold was firmly of the opinion that SF need not be overwhelmingly technophilic or ruled by the hero figure. *Galaxy* set out to create a new soft SF, as opposed to Campbell's hard-core fare. Soft SF was frequently satiric and became a vehicle for writers such as Frederik POHL, Cyril M. KORNBLUTH, Robert SHECKLEY, and Philip K. DICK. Gold clearly succeeded: when the first Hugo Awards were presented in 1953, *Galaxy* was co-winner with *Astounding* for best professional magazine. Although *Galaxy* never won another Hugo, the quality of its fiction, especially in the 1950s, is unquestionable. Perhaps the best-known work from its pages is Alfred BESTER's *The Demolished Man* (1952), regarded as one of the few genuine SF classics. Other works of note from this period are "The Fireman" by Ray BRADBURY (1951; the original version of FAHRENHEIT 451), "Surface Tension" by James BLISH (1952), and *The Space Merchants* by Kornbluth and Pohl (1952). *The Caves of Steel* (serialized in 1953), which Isaac ASIMOV regards as the first genuine fusion of SF and detective stories, was actually suggested by Gold.

Gold retired as editor in 1961 and was succeeded by

Pohl, who broadened *Galaxy*'s policy by including SF adventure stories (which were later shifted to the newly acquired companion magazine *If*). *Galaxy* was at the height of its reputation in the mid-1960s and remained so until Pohl's resignation in 1969. Under new editor Ejler Jakobsson, the magazine went into decline, but this development was more the fault of the new publisher, Arnold Abramson, who changed the format for the worse, interrupted the publishing schedule, and disrupted author payments. Despite Jakobsson's open policy toward fiction, which included the publication of American New Wave works and such quality fiction as Asimov's *The Gods Themselves* (1972) and Arthur C. CLARKE's *Rendezvous with Rama* (1973), circulation continued to dwindle. Against these odds James Baen valiantly raised the quality of the magazine during his short editorship (1974–1977), but thereafter a succession of editors and irregular, drab issues sounded *Galaxy*'s death knell. One final issue appeared under a new publisher in 1980. It is regrettable that what was possibly the most sophisticated of SF magazines had such an ignominious end.

M.A.

SEE ALSO: EDITORS

GALLUN, RAYMOND Z[INKE] (1910–   ).

American science-fiction and technical writer. In the 1930s Gallun was a prolific contributor of pulp SF, particularly to *Astounding*, then edited by F. Orlin TREMAINE. During that period his most notable story (for its sympathetic portrait of an alien) was "Old Faithful" (1934). Gallun stopped writing SF after World War II but took it up again in the 1970s, with stories such as "Then and Now" (1977), "The Eternal Wall" (1979), and "A First Glimpse" (1980), and a novel, *Bioblast* (1985).

OTHER WORKS: *The Machine That Thought* (1940, as William Callahan); *People Minus X* (1957); *The Planet Strappers* (1961); *The Eden Cycle* (1974); *The Best of Raymond Z. Gallun* (collection, 1978).

E.L.D.

GALOUYE, DANIEL F[RANCIS] (1920–1976).

American journalist and science-fiction writer. In Galouye's stories, which appeared in SF magazines in the 1950s and early 1960s, distorted or restricted perception of reality is a recurrent theme. His first novel, *Dark Universe* (1961), is set in an underground world inhabited by descendants of survivors from a nuclear holocaust who discover the sense of sight. A later novel, *Simulacron-3* (1964; British title *Counterfeit World*), deals with a world of counterfeit reality and is reminiscent of the works of both Frederik POHL and Philip K. DICK. It was filmed for TV in West Germany in 1973 by Rainer Werner Fassbinder.

J.H.

———— GAMES ————

Science-fiction games appeared on the scene as early as the 1930s. Successful movie serials featuring Larry (Buster) CRABBE as BUCK ROGERS or FLASH GORDON resulted in a variety of toys, novelty items, and games. And the occasional hit film, radio, or later TV show led companies to crank out easy-to-play derivative games.

Science-fiction games came into their own, however, with the complex board game, enhanced almost immediately by role-playing games and video games, and finally by personal computers, with the interactive laserdisk looming as a possibility of the future.

The first board game with a major impact on SF fans was Starforce Alpha Centauri (1977), a complex war game from Simulations Publications. Starforce used existing SF concepts and added a few tricks of its own to create a detailed, realistic space combat game.

Dungeons & Dragons led to the game explosion of the late 1970s. It developed from a homegrown medieval miniatures game into a new form: the role-playing game. In a role-playing game players assume the roles of characters, deciding what actions to take while a referee determines the consequences of those actions. Role-playing games have drawn headlines with an occasional injury or even death attributed to the stress of role playing on unstable personalities; they have also drawn open attacks by fundamentalist groups and individuals who called them demonic. A number of psychologists, however, have defended the games' therapeutic effect, and teachers have attested to their educational value.

Mark Miller's role-playing game Traveller (Game Designers Workshop, 1977) successfully captured all the elements of SF in one game: contact with aliens, space travel and combat, and vastly different economic and political systems. Using Miller's backdrop of the Imperium, a far-flung galactic empire, players are free to explore, battle, and trade. Science-fiction board games really arrived with the later releases of Starfleet Battles (Taskforce Games, 1979) and Stellar Conquests (which Metagaming had developed in 1975 but which was later acquired and released by The Avalon Hill Game Company).

These were followed by a virtual flood of titles: many were serious games such as Starship Troopers (Avalon, 1976), based on Robert A. HEINLEIN's novel; others, such as Yaquinto's Attack of the Mutants, and West End Games's delightful Monsters (featuring bug-eyed principals), explored, with tongue firmly in cheek, some of the more cliché-ridden aspects of media SF. Ogre (1977), a pocket-sized game designed by Steve Jackson, became a fan favorite, with its host of hovertanks trying to stop the incredibly powerful Ogretank. Jackson's later release, Car Wars, capitalized on the MAD MAX films with a humorous game of auto dueling in the twenty-first century.

The role-playing field expanded to include the gaudy heroics of Fantasy Games Unlimited's Space Opera (1982) and West End Games's Paranoia (1984), a humorous fantasy set in a world inspired by George LUCAS's film THX-1138. FASA acquired the license to produce Star Trek the Role-Playing Game (1983), in which players can act out the quirky scenarios of Kirk and company facing the unknown. In 1986, almost ten years after the appearance of Traveller, Game Designers Workshop released Traveller: 2300, a state-of-the-art role-playing game that includes a remarkably detailed chart of the stars found within fifty light years of Sol. And in 1987 West End Games finally released a role-playing game based on STAR WARS.

The arcade video craze began in the late 1970s with Nolan Bushnell's game Pong. It was the start of the company Atari (the name, which means "you have a piece in danger," comes from a term used in the Japanese game go). Hard-core SF gamers found little in the first video games to attract them, but by 1983, when the video craze was waning, the personal computer entered the scene with Atari's space-age shoot-'em-up Asteroids. As the personal computer developed into a powerful machine, manufacturers created ever more sophisticated games, such as Activision's Space Shuttle (1983) and Infocom's all-text adventure of survival on an alien world, Planetfall (1983). Many gamers left their boards and stacks of cardboard for a keyboard: fans of galactic conquest could play Strategic Studies Group's Reach for the Stars (1983) or, the best game for vivid starship-to-starship space combat, Firebird's Elite (1986).

Computers took over some of the tedious bookkeeping of SF board games and provided an ever-ready opponent. The computer-game market continues to grow as more people acquire personal computers. A top game, however, requires up to a year to develop and may sell no more than 10,000 to 20,000 copies.

Licensing, in both board and computer games, became an important factor in 1985. Simon & Schuster acquired the Star Trek license and produced a number of entertaining text adventures such as The Kobayashi Alternative (1985) and The Promethean Prophecy (1986). Fans of Larry NIVEN's Ringworld and Michael MOORCOCK's Hawkmoon could play roles in these games from Chaosium Inc. (1985 and 1986, respectively).

Books such as Douglas ADAMS's Hitchhiker's Guide to the Galaxy (Infocom, 1986) have been turned into intriguing text adventures in which players can, within reason, decide what will happen next in the story. The laserdisk, which spawned two arcade hits, Dragon's Lair and Space Ace (both 1985), featuring cartoons that respond to a player's actions, made interactive games practicable, and when laserdisk technology reaches the home, SF game playing may hit a new peak of popularity. In 1987 Pioneer offered a Knowledge Disc, putting the thousands of pages of an encyclopedia at the instant access of its owner. The potential to store hundreds of thousands of images and alternatives may take gamers where no one has gone before.

Many board games, such as Car Wars and Ogre, have inspired computer games, but computer games have not affected mainstream SF games and the hard-core gamers. The interactive laserdisk, with its rich possibilities for thoroughly realistic game play, may change that.

M.J.C.

GARRETT, [GORDON] RANDALL (1927–1987).

American science-fiction author. Garrett was the Murray LEINSTER of the 1950s and 1960s, the competent and prolific craftsman of clearly identifiable genre fiction. Born in Lexington, Missouri, he earned a bachelor's degree from Texas Tech after service as a marine in World War II and worked as an industrial chemist before turning to full-time writing. His first story was published in 1944, but his writing career was launched in earnest in the early 1950s, when he became part of the Ziff-Davis stable for *Amazing* and *Fantastic* and then became a regular contributor to John W. CAMPBELL's *Astounding/Analog* from the late 1950s to the early 1960s, under his own name and half a dozen pseudonyms.

Between 1953 and 1965, for instance, he published ninety-six stories under his own name; fifteen stories and one serial, primarily in *Astounding*, as Robert Randall (in collaboration with Robert SILVERBERG); three serials in *Astounding* as Mark Phillips (in collaboration with Laurence M. JANIFER); five stories in *Astounding* as Walter Bupp; fifteen stories, about half in *Astounding*, as David Gordon; and three stories and a serial in *Astounding* as Darrell T. Langart. He also wrote under the house names of Alexander Blade, Ralph Burke, Richard Greer, S. M. Tenneshaw, and Ivar Jorgensen.

The principal characteristics of Garrett's writing are a strong narrative line, ingenuity, and wit. The last two are exemplified as well in his comic verse, which was published frequently during the 1960s, including parodies of specific stories, such as Isaac ASIMOV's *The Caves of Steel,* Poul ANDERSON's *Three Hearts and Three Lions,* Alfred BESTER's *The Demolished Man,* and John W. Campbell's "Who Goes There?" He also parodied SF in general in such verse as his famous takeoff on Gilbert and Sullivan's "I've Got a Little List." Many of these appear in his collections *Takeoff* (1978) and *The Best of Randall Garrett* (1982).

Garrett's most famous fictional creation is the Lord Darcy series of stories and novels, set in the alternate history of a twentieth-century Angevin Empire in which magic is the dominant technology. Lord Darcy is a detective forced not only to solve crimes but to counteract the magic responsible for the crimes or their concealment. The series parodies the characters and styles of many contemporary authors of detective stories and cul-

minates in the novel *Too Many Magicians* (1967).

Since 1981 Garrett and his wife, Vicki Ann Heydron, have collaborated on a series of novels in their Gandalara series: *The Steel of Raithskar* (1981), *The Glass of Dyskornis* (1982), *The Bronze of Eddarta* (1983), *The Well of Darkness* (1983), and *The Search for Ka* (1984).

OTHER WORKS: *The Shrouded Planet* (with Robert Silverberg, 1957, as Robert Randall); *The Dawning Light* (with Robert Silverberg, 1959, as Robert Randall); *Pagan Passions* (with Laurence M. Janifer, 1959); *Unwise Child* (1962; as *Starship Death,* 1982); *Brain Twister* (with Laurence M. Janifer, 1962, as Mark Phillips); *The Impossibles* (with Laurence M. Janifer, 1963, as Mark Phillips); *Supermind* (with Laurence M. Janifer, 1963, as Mark Phillips); *Anything You Can Do . . .* (1963, as Darrell T. Langart); *Murder and Magic* (1979); *Lord Darcy Investigates* (1981).

J.E.G.

GAUGHAN, JACK (Professional name of John Brian Francis Gaughan) (1930–1986).

American science-fiction and fantasy illustrator. A descendant of post-Impressionist Paul Gauguin, Gaughan is probably SF's most overlooked illustrator. Extraordinarily prolific, he created covers and interior illustrations for numerous magazines, including AMAZING STORIES, GALAXY, *Isaac Asimov's Science Fiction Magazine, Astounding Science Fiction*/ANALOG, *Infinity Science Fiction, Vertex Science Fiction, Other Worlds, Spaceways,* and *Worlds of Tomorrow,* and painted covers for many book publishers, among them DAW Books, Ace, and Paperback Library. Gaughan's style is unadorned, at times even sketchy; some of his interior illustrations are reminiscent of Roy KRENKEL's work, others of Leo SUMMERS's, but he had a distinctive touch that marked them always as his own. He could be as realistic as Vincent DI FATE or as abstract as Richard Powers, and his lean, angular, almost spidery figures are similar to those of H. R. Van Dongen.

Gaughan also worked as an art editor; he held that position at *Galaxy* from 1969 to 1972, during which time he produced almost all the magazine's art. In 1977 he became art editor for *Cosmos Science Fiction and Fantasy,* a position he held for all of that magazine's short life. A three-time winner of the Hugo award for Best Professional Artist (1967, 1968, and 1969), Gaughan was the only artist to win that award and the Hugo for Best Fan Artist in the same year (1967); he remained responsive to requests for his artwork from fan publications for many years.

J.G.

GEORGE, PETER [BRYAN] (1924–1966).

British writer whose novel *Two Hours to Doom* (1958,

as Peter Bryant; in the United States as *Red Alert,* 1959) was filmed as DR. STRANGELOVE in 1963 by Stanley KUBRICK, with a screenplay by George and Kubrick. A revised edition of the novel, *Dr. Strangelove, or How I Learned to Stop Worrying and Love the Bomb,* was published in 1963. George also wrote seven other novels (he was working on his ninth when he committed suicide), mostly in the mystery-suspense genre, dealing with the arms race. *Commander-1* (1965) is an interesting and well-crafted postholocaust novel, which could conceivably function as a sequel to *Red Alert.*

N.H.

——————— GERMANY ———————

In 1980 H. J. Alpers, Werner Fuchs, Ronald M. Hahn, and Wolfgang Jeschke wrote that science fiction in West Germany had left the ghetto and "developed into a widely recognized genre of light literature, which has won and is still winning an ever-widening readership." *(Lexikon der Science Fiction-Literatur).* At the time, West German SF was riding the crest of a wave: there were 400 new titles a year, publishers reaped healthy profits, and German SF authors were represented as never before in the lists of serious publishing houses. Some SF novels even saw translation into other languages, and the media were filled with brightly illustrated articles about "the literature of ideas." Yet, half a dozen years later, the dream of an independent German science fiction had burst like a soap bubble.

Kurd Lasswitz (1848–1910) was the author of *On Two Planets* (*Auf zwei Planeten,* 1897), the prototype of the interplanetary travel tale and still a readable piece of science fiction. Trivial imitations were served up by Oscar Hoffmann (1866–?), with *Mac Milfords Reisen im Universum* ("Mac Milford's Travels through the Universe, 1911"), and F. W. Mader (1866–1947) with *Wunderwelten* ("Wonder Worlds," 1911)—adventure stories full of scientific facts and figures. Both authors kept plugging away at science fiction, Hoffmann with such titles as *Unter Marsmenschen* ("Among Martians," 1905) and *Die vierte Dimension* ("The Fourth Dimension," 1908), Mader with *Die tote Stadt* ("The Dead City," 1923) and *Der letzte Atlantide* ("The Last Atlantean," 1923). True SF pulp magazines like *Aus dem Reich der Phantasie* ("From the Realm of Fantasy," 1901, 10 volumes), written solely by Robert Kraft (1869–1916), the anonymously written *Der Luftpirat und sein lenkbares Luftschiff* ("The Air Pirate and His Steerable Airship," 1908–1913, 165 volumes), and *Wunder der Zukunft* ("Wonders of the Future," 1909, 4 volumes) created by Robert Heymann (1879–1963) played a strictly supporting role after the turn of the century.

Utopia was generally reserved for hardcover books:

the brilliant debunker Paul Scheerbarth (1863–1915) published his scurrilous, fantastic short stories and novels (among them *Lesabendio,* 1913) as hardcovers, as did technocrat Carl Grunert (1865–1918) with his collections *Feinde im Weltall* ("Enemies from Space"), *Im irdischen Jenseits* ("In Earth's Other World," 1904), *Menschen von Morgen* ("People of Tomorrow," 1905) and *Der Marsspion* ("The Martian Spy," 1908), but today their works are as little known as the technical "futurist novels" of officer Karl August von Laffert (1872–1938), widely celebrated in the 1920s for *Der Untergang der Luna* ("The Downfall of Luna," 1921), *Feuer am Nordpol* ("Fire at the North Pole," 1924), and *Flammen aus dem Weltraum* ("Flames from Outer Space," 1927). Also consigned to virtual oblivion is Hans Richter (1889–1941) and his *Der Kanal* (1923), *Turmstadt* ("Tower City," 1926), and *Ozeania 3000 PS* ("Oceania 3000 hp," 1928). Even a prolific writer like Otfried von Hanstein (1869–1959), author of over 150 novels including the bestsellers *Der Kaiser der Sahara* ("Emperor of the Sahara," 1922), *Elektropolis* (1927), and *Mond-Rak 1* ("Moonshot 1," 1929) has been forgotten by all but the collectors. The fame of Thea von Harbou (1888–1954) undoubtedly rests on the film classics Fritz LANG created out of her novels *The Girl in the Moon* (*Frau im Mond,* 1926) and *Metropolis* (1926) (see WOMAN IN THE MOON and METROPOLIS). Few remember her third SF work, *Die Insel der Unsterblichen* ("Isle of the Immortals," 1926).

In the 1920s and 1930s the technology-mad nationalist Hans Dominik (1872–1945) had a large following: his seventeen SF novels typically tell of German engineers who show the world what top Teutonic technology can do. His best novels—still read today—are *Die Macht der Drei* ("The Power of the Three," 1922), *Die Spur des Dschingis Khan* ("The Trail of Genghis Khan," 1923), *Der Brand der Cheopspyramide* ("The Cheops Pyramid Fire," 1926), *Das Erbe der Uraniden* ("The Uranians' Inheritance," 1928), *König Laurins Mantel* ("King Laurin's Cloak," 1928), *Befehl aus dem Dunkel* ("Command from the Dark," 1933), *Der Wettflug der Nationen* ("The Nation's Race in Space," 1933), and *Ein Stern fiel vom Himmel* ("A Star Fell from on High," 1934). Another celebrated writer was Otto Willi Gail (1896–1956), thanks to a number of "instructive" SF novels; in *Shot into Infinity* (*Der Schuss ins All,* 1925) Germans and Russians race to the moon (the good guys win, of course), and there is a sequel, *The Stone from the Moon,* (1926). *Hans Hardts Mondfahrt* ("Hans Hardt's Voyage to the Moon," 1928) and *Der Herr aus dem Wellen* ("Lord of the Waves," 1949) are all but forgotten today.

True SF pulps were still quite rare in the Nazi era; after letting Paul A. Müller (1901–1970, as Lok Myler) publish *Sun Koh, der Erbe von Atlantis* ("Sun Koh, Heir of Atlantis," 1933–1936, 150 volumes), the Nazis banned them—not because of any deviation from the party line, but because of the paper shortage. The era did see the rise to prominence of one of the first modern SF authors, Kurt Siodmák (1902–   ), whose novel *F.P. 1 Does Not Reply* (1930) was filmed by Karl Hartl in 1932. His works *Stadt hinter Nebeln* ("City behind Clouds," 1931), *Die Rache im Äther* ("Revenge in the Ether," 1932), and *Die Macht im Dunkeln* ("Power in Darkness," 1937) are futurist crime fiction. He became better known as a novelist and screenwriter (Donovan's Brain, *Hauser's Memory*) after he immigrated to the U.S. in 1937. Another prominent author of the period, in the tradition of Dominik, was Rudolf Heinrich Daumann (1896–1957) with titles like *Dünn wie eine Eierschale* ("Eggshell Thin," 1937), *Gefahr aus dem Weltall* ("Threat from Space," 1939), and *Protuberanzen* (1940). Friedrich Freksa (1882–1955) turned out a racist tract in the warped Nazi mold, *Druso: Die gestohlene Menschenwelt* ("Druso: The Stolen Civilization," 1931), while mainstream authors like Paul Gurk (1880–1953) and Werner Illing (1895–1979), with his socialist utopia, *Utopolis* (1930), produced experimental and satirical writing of high quality.

None of the hacks of this era made explicit propaganda in favor of the Nazis: it was mostly adventure and technology that counted for them, and—not surprisingly—the superiority of German engineers and inventors over their colleagues from other nations. Amazingly enough, there were no descriptions of a world ruled by the Master Race; that the world would benefit from the "German Way" was taken for granted. On this point all SF writers had been in agreement since Kaiser Wilhelm's time.

After the end of World War II the first publishers in the Allied zones of occupation set about satisfying German hunger for ideas and entertainment. The desire for reading matter was predictably great, but publishers chose to produce mainly new editions of pre-war pulp novels, cleansed of their more overtly nationalistic features. Despite the paper shortage, which gave publishing space only to authors with some reputation, small publishing houses proliferated. Few, however, were successful; most went out of business after three or four titles.

At this time science fiction was published almost exclusively by houses that supplied cheap escapist fiction to lending libraries. This twilight zone was inhabited by authors such as C. C. Zanta, whose dreary offerings included *Der Mann auf dem Lichtstrahl* ("The Man on the Light Ray," 1948) and *Der Geheimagent von Planet X* ("Secret Agent from Planet X," 1949). *Sun Koh's* creator, Paul A. Müller, reappeared in 1949, this time under the name of Freder van Holk. Mainstream authors with single utopian works—not labelled SF—were Franz Werfel (1890–1945) with *Star of the Unborn* (*Stern der Ungeborenen*, 1945) and Egon Friedell (1878–1938) with *The Return of the Time Machine* (*Die Rückkehr der Zeitmaschine*, 1946), a "sequel" to H. G. Wells's 1895 classic. Hellmuth Lange (1903–   ), horrified by the nu-

clear devastation of Hiroshima and Nagasaki, wrote *Blumen wachsen im Himmel* ("Flowers Grow in Heaven," 1948) casting doubt on the general faith in science and progress. The philosopher Walter Jens (1923–   ) wrote *Nein. Die Welt der Angeklagten* ("No. The World of the Accused," 1950), a dystopia grounded in utter distrust of state power. An early postwar pulp series was *Rah Norten, der Eroberer des Weltalls* ("Rah Norten, Conqueror of Space," 1949–50, 20 volumes) by Ive Steen and Freder van Holk. Sam Grafner detailed the adventures of "space detective" *Dr. Bendany* (1949, 3 volumes).

The 1950s brought reprints of *Sun Koh* and *Jan Mayen* and a flood of new pulps: *Utopia* (1953–1966, 596 volumes), *Utopia-Grossband* (1954–1959, 204 volumes), *Utopia-Kriminal* (1956–1958, 26 volumes), *Utopia-Magazin* (1955–1959, 26 volumes), *Im Jahr 2000* ("In the Year 2000," 1953, 5 volumes), *Luna* (1956, 57 volumes) *Terra* (1957–1968, 555 volumes), *Terra-Sonderband* (1958–1965, 99 volumes), *Galaxis* (1958–1959, 15 volumes; the German edition of *Galaxy*), *Der Weltraumfahrer* ("The Space Traveler," 1958, 8 volumes), *Abenteuer im Weltraum* ("Adventures in Space," 1958–59, 19 volumes), *Star Utopia* (1957–58, 10 volumes), and *Uranus* (1957–58, 18 volumes). Weiss Verlag pioneered science fiction in hardcover, but its honest wordsmiths—including Richard Koch (1895–1970), who wrote twenty-two novels between 1950 and 1969, Claus Eigk (1905–   ), Erich Dolezal (1902–   ), and the established 1930s author Paul Eugen Sieg (1899–1955), who tried for a comeback with *Insula* (1953) and *Angolesa* (1954)—simply could not compete with foreign reprints from authors such as Robert A. Heinlein, Arthur C. Clarke, and Edmond Hamilton.

Rauch Verlag launched a line of high-quality American SF in 1952, which, alas, collapsed the same year beneath public indifference, effectively finishing hardcover SF in Germany. In 1954 AWA Verlag published a series aimed at young adults, with only moderate success. Serious publishers ignored the genre, leaving it at the mercy of the lending-library houses and pulp producers. Outfits like Bewin, Zimmermann, Dörner, Pabel, and Moewig dominated the field, heaping superlatives on trivial rubbish and only succeeding in projecting science fiction to the public as literature for stay-at-homes. The authors of the early 1950s were little more than hacks writing to order under house names; the most successful of these were K. H. Scheer (1928–   ), Kurt Brand (1917–   ), Jesco von Puttkamer (1933–   ), Axel Jeffers (1917–   ), Ernst H. Richter (1901–1958), and W. D. Rohr (1928–1981). Authors writing under pennames like "Bert Andrew" and "K. Merten," whose real names never became known, committed to paper such hair-raising adventures as those of the "space pirate" Will Fox, which amply documented the equally abysmal level of their scientific and proof-reading abilities.

Translated science fiction from the Anglo-American magazines arrived in 1958: author Walter Ernsting (1920–   ) persuaded publisher Erich Pabel, whose Utopia pulps celebrated the derring-do of spaceman Jim Parker, to issue the large-format line *Utopia-Grossband,* which alongside Anglo-American material gave him (as Clark Darlton) his first chance in print. As a consequence, local SF had to compete with works from the English-speaking world, a situation that doomed most of the native pulps. Meanwhile, a number of mainstream authors fired off notable one-shots in book form: Heinrich Hauser (1901–1960) published *Gigant Hirn* (1958, "Giant Brain"), and Fontane Prize winner Jens Rehn (1918–   ) packed a punch with his post-nuclear novel *Die Kinder des Saturn* ("The Children of Saturn," 1959). Manfred Langrenus (1903–   ) won popularity as a children's author with *Reich im Mond* ("Moon Kingdom," 1951) and *Im Banne des Alpha Centauri* ("In the Grip of Alpha Centauri," 1955).

At about the same time limited amounts of SF began to appear in East Germany—generally dry slabs of propaganda, wherein the hero functioned as an ideological mouthpiece to convey to the reader the superiority of the socialist way of life. Ludwig Turek (1896–1975), then a leading name in East German politics, set the ball rolling with his anti–atomic war novel *Die goldene Kugel* ("The Golden Ball," 1949). He was followed by Heinz Vieweg (1920–   ) who wrote the utopian spy thriller *Ultrasymet bleibt geheim* ("Ultrasymet Stays Secret," 1955), and Eberhard Del'Antonio (1926–   ), author of *Gigantum* (1957), a piece of agitprop designed to show up the rapacity of the capitalists and the simplemindedness of their scientific stooges. Kurt H. Ball (1903–   ) and Lothar Weise (1931–1966) championed the peaceful use of nuclear power in *Atomfeuer über dem Pazifik* ("Atomic Blaze over the Pacific," 1959).

The 1960s saw the first real SF boom in Germany. Though the broader public remained unaware of or uninterested in the genre, a few pulps, among them *Terra,* were doing relatively well.

The first change came in 1961 with the appearance of the Perry Rhodan series of juvenile-adventure short novels; despite its publisher's early reliance on lending-library writers Clark Darlton, K. H. Scheer, and Kurt Brand, newcomers like Kurt Mahr (1936–   ), Hans Kneifel (1936–   ), and fans W. W. Shols (1925–1981), William Voltz (1938–1983) and Ernst Vlcek (1941–   ) showed that their models were more likely to be Heinlein, A. E. VAN VOGT, and Theodore STURGEON than dull technocrats and crypto-Fascists like Van Holk and Dominik. As fans, these authors had all read English-language SF in the original, and consequently had no trouble reworking the genre stereotypes. To this day the amazing sales success of Perry Rhodan continues unabated: the series has produced over 1300 volumes, with sales of over a billion copies. Perry Rhodan spawned numerous

imitators, not all of them successful: Pabel launched *Mark Powers* (1962–1964, 48 volumes) and *Ad Astra* (1967–68, 21 volumes), but both series, written by old-timers and newcomers alike, were flops. Kurt Brand, fired from the Perry Rhodan team after forty volumes, struck back—unsuccessfully—with Kelter Verlag's *Ren Dhark* (1966–1968, 98 volumes). The unhappy Ad Astra crew endeavored to check the triumphal progress of Perry Rhodan with Rex Corda ("rescuer of the world") at Bastei Verlag (1966–67, 38 volumes), but they, too, were ultimately unsuccessful.

Herbert W. Franke (1927–   ) was the first science-fiction author to ignore the stereotypes and win broad popularity. At the same time, a number of mainstream writers successfully ventured into SF territory, among them several Austrian authors: Peter von Tramin (1932–   ) with his time-travel story *Die Tür im Fenster* ("The Door in the Window," 1968), Otto Basil (1901–   ) with the satirical alternate-world history *Wenn das der Führer wüsste* ("If the Führer Just Knew That," 1966), and Winfried Bruckner (1937–   ) with the anti-Utopia *Tötet ihn!* ("Kill Him!", 1967). The genre was given a boost in 1966 by the TV series *Raumpatrouille* ("Space Patrol"), whose screenplays were successfully novelized by Hans Kneifel.

In East Germany, too, more SF was now being published. Horst Müller (1923–   ), a member of the People's Assembly, wrote *Signale vom Mond* ("Signals from the Moon," 1960), and *Kurs Ganymed* ("Course Ganymede," 1962). Günter Krupkat (1905–   ) in *Die grosse Grenze* ("The Great Frontier," 1960) described U.S. astronauts saved from a space catastrophe only by Soviet discipline. Brazilian-born Carlos Rasch (1932–   ) acquired a small following with SF adventures such as *Asteroidenjäger* ("Asteroid Hunters," 1961). Hubert Horstmann (1937–   ) wrote of revolution exported to a backward planet in *Die Stimme aus der Unendlichkeit* ("The Voice from Infinity," 1965). Herbert Ziergiebel (1922–   ) used *Die andere Welt* ("The Other World," 1966) to portray the physical strains on the crew of a crippled spaceship. Karl Heinz Tuschel wrote the first alien-contact novel, *Ein Stern fliegt vorbei* ("A Star Flies Past," 1967). *Verleumdung eines Sterns* ("Defamation of a Star," 1968) by Curt Letsche (1912–   ) tells of dangerous drug experiments in a classless future state. Gerhard Branstner's (1927–   ) *Die Reise zum Stern der Beschwingten* ("Journey to the Swinging Star," 1968) is a satire in the tradition of Jonathan SWIFT; Alexander Kröger (1934–   ) wrote *Sieben fielen vom Himmel* ("Seven Fell from Heaven," 1969) as an adventure story. In West Germany, however, SF from the German Democratic Republic never caught on; lacking any kind of action, it was seen—and continues to be seen—as overly sober, didactic, and dull.

By 1970 every West German child knew what science fiction was. Respected news magazines such as *Der*

Spiegel reported that in intellectual circles it was fashionable to read SF. Big publishing houses such as Schröder (from 1969), Lichtenberg (1970), and Insel (1971) discovered the genre, followed closely by the paperback publishers Ullstein (1970), Bastei (1971), Fischer (1972), Williams (1972), König (1973), and Knaur (1978), who regularly issued SF, most of it Anglo-American. In numerous anthologies, most of them edited by Wolfgang Jeschke (1936–   ), German authors flourished, and were quite optimistic about their prospects—although they had wildly overestimated the interest of local SF readers. There were repeated attempts to establish new pulp series and lines essentially reserved for German authors, among them Marken Verlag's *Zeitkugel* ("Time Capsule," 1974–1979, 44 volumes); the adventures of *Commander Scott* (Bastei Verlag, 1975–76, 42 volumes; inspired by E. C. Tubb's *Cap Kennedy* novels, and continued by German authors); *Zukunft-Roman* ("Future Novel," from Neuzeit Verlag, 1975, 20 volumes); and *Gemini* (Kelter Verlag, 1976–77, 47 volumes). The SF magazine *Comet* was launched in 1977, but it was doomed to failure along with *2001* (1978), *SF Perry Rhodan Magazin* (1978), and the earlier attempts by Pabel and Moewig, *Utopia-Magazin* and *Galaxis*.

Interesting new SF authors in the 1970s were Wolfgang Jeschke with *Der Zeiter* ("The Timer," collection, 1970); Ludek Pesek with *The Earth Is Near* (*Die Erde ist nah*, 1970); mainstream author Carl Amery (1922–   ) with the time-travel story *Das Königsprojekt* ("The King's Project," 1974), the post-holocaust novel *Der Untergang der Stadt Passau* ("The Fall of the City of Passau," 1975), and the alternate history *An den Feuern der Leyermark* ("At the Fires of the Leyermark," 1979); and at least three other names, Ulrich Harbecke (1943–   ) with *Invasion* (1979), Rainmar Cunis (1933–   ) with *Livesendung* ("On the Air," 1978) and *Zeitsturm* ("Time Storm," 1979), and Gerd Maximovic with *Die Erforschung des Omega-Planeten* (collection, "Investigation of Planet Omega," 1979).

In young people's literature Michail Krausnick (1943–   ) established a reputation with *Die Paracana-Affäre* (1975). Mark Brandis (1931–   ), Ronald M. Hahn (1948–   ), H. J. Alpers (1943–   ), and Lothar Streblow (1929–   ) also wrote science fiction for a younger audience.

While SF flourished in many forms, the pulp trade in the 1970s was almost dead—*Perry Rhodan* had wiped out its major competitors, the down-market space opera *Raumschiff Promet* ("Space Cruiser Promet," Astro Verlag, 1972, 52 volumes) and the psi power and ecology-oriented *Terranauten* ("Terranauts," Bastei Verlag, 1979, 99 volumes).

The 1970s marked an SF boom in East Germany as well. Wolf Weitbrecht (1920–   ) made his debut with *Das Orakel der Delphine* ("The Dolphin Oracle," 1972) and established a reputation with *Das Psychomobile*

(collection, 1976). *Gerichtstag auf Epsi* ("Judgment Day on Epsi," 1973) by Richard Funk (1926–   ) was an SF one-shot, like Alfred Leman (1925–   ) and Hans Taubert's (1928–   ) *Das Gastgeschenk der Transsolaren* ("The Present Brought by the Trans-Solarians," 1973) and the highly regarded, psychologically well-constructed novel by Heiner Rank (1931–   ), *Die Ohnmacht der Allmächtigen* ("The Impotence of the Omnipotent," 1973). Johanna (1929–   ) and Günter (1928–   ) Braun produced science fiction of literary quality, including *Unheimliche Erscheinungsformen auf Omega IX* ("Weird Manifestations on Omega IX," 1974) and *Der Fehlfaktor* ("Deficient Factor," collection, 1975), whose scathing characterization won respect even in the West. Klaus Frühauf (1933–   ) emerged as a talented author of space opera on the strength of *Mutanten auf Andromeda* ("Mutants on Andromeda," 1974), and *Das Wasser des Mars* ("The Waters of Mars," 1977), while Gerd Prokop (1932–   ) won the applause of West German critics with the racy SF detective stories of *Wer stiehlt schon Unterschenkel?* ("Who Wants to Steal Lower Legs?" collection, 1977). Other works of note were the time-travel spoof *Die ersten Zeitreisen* ("The First Trips in Time," 1977) by Erik Simon (1950–   ) and *Der unsichtbare Kreis* ("The Invisible Circle," collection, 1977) by Bernd Ulbrich (1943–   ).

The boom years ushered in by films such as STAR WARS (1977) were followed in the early 1980s by an era of overproduction in which annual publication increased fourfold, from the 100 titles published in 1977. The results were program cuts, dwindling print runs, and a reluctance to experiment. German, continental, and new English-language authors suddenly represented a risk, as did collections and anthologies (unless bearing the name of Isaac ASIMOV). Today the euphoria of the early 1980s is gone, as are the days when anthologists like Jörg Weigand (1940–   ), H. J. Alpers, and Thomas Le Blanc (1951–   ), and promising writers like Thomas Ziegler (1956–   ) and Horst Pukallus (1949–   ), fondly imagined that German science fiction could stand on its own feet despite the dominance of Anglo-American literature.

In 1987 the West German SF scene was marked by frustration and disillusionment. Publishers tended to ignore native talent in favor of Hollywood novelizations or American big-name authors—despite the fact that their past investments in various American SF stars had scarcely ever paid off. By contrast the market for German SF is sound in East Germany, where first editions of 50,000 copies are normal. The future of West German science fiction, however, remains very much in doubt.

R.M.H.

GERNSBACK, HUGO (1884–1967). American science-fiction editor and publisher, a pioneer in the

Masthead by
Frank R. Paul for
Gernsback's *Wonder Stories*

field, dubbed "the Father of Magazine Science Fiction"; the annual achievement awards presented at the World SF Convention are named Hugos in his honor. Gernsback came to the United States from his native Luxembourg in 1904 and established a dry battery and electrical importing business. He designed the first home radio set in 1905 and began to issue a radio catalog that year. It rapidly evolved into the technical magazine *Modern Electrics*, launched in 1908, which Gernsback began to fill with articles discussing the wonders of science. In 1911 Gernsback began to include a fiction serial in the magazine's pages: *Ralph 124C 41+* (book, 1925) looks at the scientific wonders of the year 2660. The serial—more an excuse to speculate on future science than genuine fiction—proved popular, and Gernsback began a policy of including at least one such story per issue. He had a gift for popularizing science, though, as *Ralph 124C 41+* shows, he was no writer. Soon, however, the magazine began to attract a stable of other fiction contributors as well as such artists as Howard BROWN, Frank R. PAUL, and Alex SCHOMBURG. *Modern Electrics* gave way to *The Electrical Experimenter* in 1913, retitled *Science and Invention* in 1920.

By then Gernsback was publishing two or more SF stories per issue by writers such as Clement Fezandie, Ray CUMMINGS, and George Allan ENGLAND; he was even reprinting the work of H. G. WELLS. The August 1923 issue was a special "Scientific Fiction Number," the first such issue in the English language. It was a natural step, then, in April 1926 to launch the first regular SF magazine in the world, AMAZING STORIES. Gernsback followed this with an *Amazing Stories Annual,* which in 1928 became a regular *Amazing Stories Quarterly*. In 1929 he lost control of the Experimenter Publishing Company, established for his magazines, but he rapidly organized a new company and launched *Air Wonder Stories* and *Science Wonder Stories* (merged in 1930 as *Wonder Stories*), *Science Wonder Quarterly* (later *Wonder Stories Quarterly*), and *Scientific Detective Monthly* (later *Amazing Detective Tales*), along with a number of scientific magazines and even two straightforward adventure pulps, *Pirate Stories* and *High Seas Adventures*. By 1936 Gernsback's only surviving SF pulp was *Wonder Stories*, which he was forced to sell. He tried in 1939 with the short-lived *Superworld Comics* and again in 1953 with *Science Fiction Plus*, his last SF magazine, which ran only seven issues.

Had Gernsback not launched the first SF magazine, someone else surely would have, and almost certainly along the same lines. And the fact that magazine SF traced its origins not from pulp adventure but from popular science is undoubtedly significant. Gernsbackian SF may not be the most literate, but it had a certain veneer of respectability lacking in the other brash adventure pulps, especially the Clayton ASTOUNDING STORIES. Gernsback attracted to SF not so much writers as visionaries—among them E. E. SMITH, Jack WILLIAMSON, David H. KELLER, Stanton COBLENTZ, and John W. CAMPBELL—and his belief that science can be taught through fiction reflected a genuinely altruistic hope in a technological utopia. His actions influenced a whole generation of readers, writers, and publishers, and effectively established the SF genre. Gernsback's writings are readable not as fiction but for their reflection of his (and his times') hopes and extrapolations. Apart from episodes and stories in his magazines that have not been reprinted in book form, his only other work is *The Ultimate World* (1971), written in 1958 and edited for publication by Sam MOSKOWITZ. Also available is a volume of Gernsback's spoof scientific essays, *The Collected Works of Mohammed Ulysses Fips* (1987).

M.A.

SEE ALSO: EDITORS; GOLDEN AGE; PULP MAGAZINES

Hugo Gernsback in 1956 with the model of an early wireless

pirations. His first novel, *Lords of the Starship* (1967), is nothing like the space opera its title might suggest; instead it describes the efforts of the inhabitants of a depleted Earth to find a better life through the construction of a starship. Geston's concern here is clearly with the plight of his weary characters and the ultimate futility of their project. Both *Out of the Mouth of the Dragon* (1969) and *The Day Star* (1972) extend the mood of his first novel, but in each Geston created characters more capable of effecting change. *The Siege of Wonder* (1976), wherein magicians battle scientists, mixes fantasy with science fiction but is far from standard science fantasy. It too treats the themes of war and quest and examines the fine line between science and magic.

S.H.G.

THE GHOST OF FRANKENSTEIN: SEE FRANKENSTEIN ON FILM

THE GIANT BEHEMOTH (1959). *Directed by Eugène Lourié; screenplay by Eugène Lourié and Daniel Hyatt (Hyatt uncredited); adapted from an original screen story by Robert Abel and Allen Adler; photographed by Ken Hodges; music by Ted Astley. With Gene Evans, Andre Morell, Jack MacGowran, Maurice Kaufman, Henry Vidon, Leigh Madison, John Turner. 79 minutes. Black and white. Alternate title:* Behemoth the Sea Monster.

This was the least of director Eugène Lourié's three dinosaur-attacks-a-city films, the others being BEAST FROM 20,000 FATHOMS (1953) and GORGO (1961). Although *Behemoth* is competent, it is a virtual remake of the superior *Beast;* hampered by a low budget, it is watched today primarily by aficionados.

A radioactive dinosaur (the nonexistent "paleosaurus") attacks the English coast, eventually arriving in London, where it engages in typical giant monster activity until being destroyed.

The film's stop-motion animation by Willis O'BRIEN and Pete Peterson is impressive, rendering the monster lifelike and menacing, but there's not enough of it. The other special effects are average for the budget.

B.W.

GERROLD, DAVID (Pseudonym of Jerrold David Friedman) (1944–). American writer of solid science fiction in the tradition of Robert A. HEINLEIN; also known for his involvement with the television series STAR TREK (he scripted the famous "Trouble with Tribbles" episode and has written books about both that episode and the series in general). In *When Harlie Was One* (1972) Gerrold developed the theme of the enfant terrible artificial intelligence, which has succeeded the menacing computer-god of earlier SF. *The Man Who Folded Himself* (1973) expands on the classic time travel paradox of a man meeting himself and becoming the first cause of his own travels. In *Moonstar Odyssey* (1977) a terraformed world is the setting for a provocative utopian idea: a culture in which children are born androgynous and choose gender at adolescence. In the War against the Chtorr series, beginning with *A Matter for Men* (1983) and continuing with *A Day for Damnation* (1984), Earth is faced with an alien ecological invasion, an idea suggested by the Red Weed in H. G. WELLS's *War of the Worlds* but never fully developed before. Much of Gerrold's time in the 1980s has been devoted to scriptwriting and work for various TV series.

OTHER WORKS: *The Flying Sorcerer* (with Larry Niven, 1971); *With a Finger in My I* (collection, 1972); *Space Skimmer* (1972); *Battle for the Planet of the Apes* (novelization, 1973); *Yesterday's Children* (1974); *The Galactic Whirlpool* (1980).

J.J.P.

GESTON, MARK S[YMINGTON] (1946–). American attorney and writer known for his dark stories about the far future describing humanity's unending battle with its self-destructive nature. Although their subject is hardly unique, Geston's novels are distinguished by his skillful style and obvious sympathy with human as-

GIBSON, WILLIAM [FORD] (1948–). American writer. Gibson may be the most important science-fiction writer to emerge in the 1980s. A member, perhaps even the prime mover, of the so-called CYBERPUNK movement, he has brought to contemporary SF a startling blend of hard science and high literary art. His fiction, mostly set in a decadent, gritty near future of megaconglomerates and computer networks, features a complex, heavily neologistic style, the detailed projec-

William Gibson

THEY WANT TO PUT ME IN AN ENCYCLOPEDIA ?!

I TOLD YOU THIS WOULD HAPPEN IF YOU DID THAT TRILOGY, BUT DID YOU LISTEN? NOOOO!

Original observation by Gilliland

tion of cybernetic and bioengineering technologies, and protagonists who share a cynical punk sensibility.

Neuromancer (1984), Gibson's influential first novel, won Nebula and Philip K. Dick awards. The book's protagonist, Case, is an interface cowboy, a data thief who can link his mind into the world-spanning computer matrix. The novel concerns one such theft and the development within the matrix of an artificial intelligence. The description of matrix travel is extraordinary, a cybernetic equivalent of the psychedelic passage through the Star Gate toward the end of Stanley KUBRICK's 2001: A SPACE ODYSSEY.

Gibson's excellent second novel, *Count Zero* (1986), though not quite as successful as his first, was a Nebula and Hugo finalist. It is set seven years after *Neuromancer*. The artificial intelligence of that book has fragmented into a number of cybernetic entities, who are now worshiped by a sophisticated voodoo cult. Count Zero, a novice hacker; Turner, a cybernetic samurai; and Marly, an art dealer, find themselves caught up in the complex and mysterious manipulations of the artificial intelligence. That a new writer like Gibson can bring together all of *Count Zero*'s disparate elements is

proof of enormous talent, but the book lacks the sharp focus and narrative drive of *Neuromancer*.

Burning Chrome (1986), Gibson's first collection, features several stories set in the universe of *Neuromancer*, including the title story, "Johnny Mnemonic," and "New Rose Hotel." It also includes collaborations with John Shirley, Bruce Sterling, and Michael Swanwick, all major figures in the cyberpunk movement. Gibson's short stories also occur in a bleak near future in which all power is controlled by a computer-assisted capitalist oligarchy. Most involve cynical antiheroes. *Burning Chrome*, a powerful work, shows Gibson to be among the best of the new writers who āre redefining the SF short story in the 1980s.

M.M.L.

GILLILAND, ALEXIS A[RNALDUS] (1931–   ).
American writer, chemist, and cartoonist who won the John W. Campbell Award in 1982 as best new writer. Gilliland brings to his science fiction a cartoonist's eye (he has won a series of Hugos, beginning in 1980, as best fan artist) and extensive experience in government bureaucracy (he worked for both the National Bureau of Standards and the Federal Supply Service). His trilogy set on Rosinante (*The Revolution from Rosinante*, 1981; *Long Shot for Rosinante*, 1981; and *The Pirates of Rosinante*, 1982) describes a space colony that succeeds in breaking away from Earth's repressive government, only to find that its computer is ready and able to fill the void. Each novel contains humorous parodies of bureaucratic procedures, and Gilliland's style frequently and deliberately mimics the language of politics. A fourth novel, *The End of Empire* (1982), however, puts forth the more serious opinion that some government regulation is needed if civilization is to be maintained. It is a solid addition to the large number of stories already produced on GALACTIC EMPIRES.

S.H.G.

GLEN AND RANDA (1971).

Directed by Jim McBride; screenplay by Lorenzo Mans, Rudolph Wurlitzer, and Jim McBride; photographed by Alan Raymond and Gerald Cotts. With Steven Curry, Shelley Plimpton, Woodrow Chambliss, Garry Goodrow, Roy Fox, William Fratis. 94 minutes. Color.

Infants at the time of the nuclear holocaust, teenagers Glen and Randa scratch out a living in the forest with other survivors. But Glen reads a comic book about civilized life in Metropolis, and, believing Metropolis to be a real place, he—and pregnant Randa—determine to search for it.

Although made in a numbingly literal fashion—each scene is one long take followed by a fade to black—*Glen and Randa* is a haunting postapocalypse film. The subject isn't the disaster but the uncaring consumerism that has doomed even those who survive the holocaust; whenever Glen digs through ruins, he unearths indestructible plastic flowers. Albeit painfully slow, *Glen and Randa* is insightful and intelligent, the only *sardonic* American film in this genre.

B.W.

GLOAG, JOHN [EDWARDS] (1896–1981).

British editor and writer. The author of many books on architecture, furniture, and industrial design, Gloag also wrote science fiction and mainstream fiction. His first SF novel, *Tomorrow's Yesterday* (1932) takes place in the Earth's far future, when humanity has died off and the species that has followed tries to understand *Homo sapiens* and the reasons for its demise. In doing so they produce a motion picture on the human race, which Gloag uses to criticize the selfishness and self-centeredness of contemporary humanity.

Gloag continued this brand of social SF in *Winter's Youth* (1934), in which a process for reversing aging is mixed up with politics, religion, and advertising, and in *99%* (1944), in which modern human beings are able to relive the experiences of their ancestors. Gloag's short stories in *First One and Twenty* (1946) are filled with caricatures of contemporary life but rarely contain the detail or descriptive power of his novels.

OTHER WORKS: *The New Pleasure* (1933); *Manna* (1940).

S.H.G.

GODWIN, TOM (1915–   ).

American occasional writer of science fiction, noted for his early story "The Cold Equations" (1954), in which a young female stowaway on a space vessel has to be sacrificed for its mission to succeed. This story was regarded as one of the best of its year and has been frequently reprinted. Although Godwin has published over thirty SF stories since, he has failed to achieve the same success, even

though many of the stories, including "The Greater Thing" (1954), "Too Soon to Die" (1957), and the more recent "The Gentle Captive" (1972), are handled with equal sensitivity. Godwin has published only three novels. *The Survivors* (1958; reprinted as *Space Prison*, 1960) and its sequel, *The Space Barbarians* (1964), are fairly routine space opera; *Beyond Another Sun* (1971) shows more development in its study of human colonists on another planet.

M.A.

GODZILLA, KING OF THE MONSTERS (*Gojira*, 1954).

Directed by Inoshiro Honda, American scenes directed by Terry Morse; screenplay by Takeo Murata and Inoshiro Honda; adapted from a story by Shigeru Kayama; photographed Masao Tamai, American scenes photographed by Guy Roe; music by Akira Ifukube. With Haruo Nakajima (as Godzilla), Raymond Burr, Takashi Shimura, Momoko Kochi, Akira Takarada, Akihiko Hirata, Achio Sakai, Fuyuki Murakami. 81 minutes. Black and white.

One of the effects of the successful reissue of KING KONG in 1952 was the production of *Godzilla, King of the Monsters*. Toho Pictures decided to make a home-grown version of Kong; special effects expert Eiji Tsuburaya was pleased, because *Kong* had been his favorite film since childhood. However, instead of using stop-motion animation to bring his monster to life, Tsuburaya employed Haruo Nakajima in an elaborate rubber suit. Tsuburaya's miniature work was always fine, and, for what it was, the Godzilla suit was acceptable. In a desire to make the movie more accessible to American audiences, scenes with actor Raymond Burr were added in the United States.

Godzilla is a dark, brooding film, much of which takes place at night. The monster itself, an enormous dinosaurlike creature, has been revived by radiation and breathes atomic fire. He smashes Tokyo; seemingly unstoppable, he's on the verge of attacking other cities when a reclusive scientist uses his "oxygen destroyer" to make the semiaquatic Godzilla dissolve.

Writers have commented on the fact that Godzilla is revived by atomic radiation; they see significance in Japan's being the only country to suffer from nuclear attack, and many have called the film, at least in part, a criticism of the misuse of atomic power. The film itself, however, does little with the radiation theme except as a pretext to get the monster up and smashing cities.

The great worldwide success of *Godzilla* made a sequel mandatory, but the monster had been thoroughly dissolved, so director Inoshiro Honda and his writers simply conjured up *another* Godzilla. This film, shown in the United States as *Gigantis the Fire Monster* (1959), is of considerably less interest than its progenitor.

There was a long, pregnant pause in the Godzilla

cycle; seven years went by before *Kong Kong vs. God-zilla* was released. This brightly colored film—the first two were in grim black and white—began a new direction for Godzilla and his playmates, which continued until the series petered out in the mid-1970s: now primarily aimed at a juvenile audience, the series began to contain some overt comedy.

Thirteen Godzilla films followed, with Tsuburaya providing the special effects until his death in 1970 and Nakajima hanging in as the monster a bit longer.

Godzilla battles other Toho monsters, some created for the series, others coming in from films of their own; Mothra, Ghidrah, and Rodan became regular players. In *Ghidrah, the Three-Headed Monster* (1965), Godzilla changes permanently from a menace to a hero.

Most of the films are not worth detailing, but *Godzilla's Revenge* (1969) is worthy of note as the only film in the series aimed exclusively at children. Godzilla fanciers generally declare *Destroy All Monsters* (1968) to be the pick of the crop; it's fast paced, amusing, and absolutely jammed with monsters.

Many deplore the Godzilla films, and it is hard for even their fervent admirers to defend them as adult entertainment or genuine science fiction. Instead of resenting these "cartoons," however, fans embrace them precisely for their outlandishness. It became clear that even the filmmakers could hardly take the films seriously: eventually Godzilla started talking, he could occasionally fly, giant monsters sometimes dance little jigs, and Minya blows smoke rings. But even the affection of fans couldn't sustain the series forever. Although the last two Godzilla films are as grim as the first, it was too late to recapture the world's interest.

This exhaustion of the subject was proven again in 1984 when an elaborate new and very serious Godzilla film was mounted; Burr even shot more American scenes. But by this time Godzilla had become a clown to Americans, and the film was not successful.

The Godzilla films gave rise in Japan to many other similar giant MONSTER MOVIES (collectively termed *kaiju eiga*), with only the Gamera series (about a giant prehistoric fanged turtle able to fly) gaining any degree of fame in the United States.

B.W.

GOLD, H[ORACE] L[EONARD] (1914–   ).

Canadian-born American writer and editor. Gold sold stories to the science-fiction pulps in the 1930s (the earlier ones under the pseudonyms Clyde Crane Campbell and Leigh Keith), became assistant to editor Mort WEISINGER on *Startling Stories* and *Thrilling Wonder Stories* in 1939, and in 1950 founded GALAXY, which he quickly made into a seminally important SF magazine. He encouraged humor and a satiric outlook in his writers and broadened the speculative bases of SF into the social

sciences, playing a key role in developing the careers of Frederik POHL, Clifford SIMAK, Robert SHECKLEY, William TENN, and Fritz LEIBER. While ASTOUNDING became increasingly bogged down by John W. CAMPBELL's idiosyncratic preoccupations, Gold—though increasingly bound to his apartment by chronic agoraphobia—took up the task of widening the horizons of the field. Gold's own SF consists of fewer than twenty stories (plus a few fantasies), the best of which are collected in *The Old Die Rich and Other Science Fiction Stories* (1955). He edited the first six *Galaxy Readers* (1952–1962) and four collections of longer stories from the magazine (1958–1961). *What Will They Think of Last?* (1976) is a collection of Gold's editorials.

B.S.

——— THE GOLDEN AGE ———

Commonly, *Golden Age* describes that period in science fiction beginning with the June 1938 issue of *Astounding Science Fiction*—the first issue for which John W. CAMPBELL, hired by Street & Smith in October 1937, was fully responsible—and ending with *Astounding*'s December 1945 issue, in whose "Brass Tacks" section appeared the first response to the use of the atomic bomb against Japan. Indeed the bomb itself may have been responsible for the demise of that fundamental innocence and commitment to technological expansion which had until 1945 represented, for those in the field, the basic values of SF.

As with nearly all golden ages, this period's exact chronology is a matter of dispute: some argue that it continued until the late 1940s, when the appearance of many new magazines and non-Campbellian approaches to SF dispersed the unity of the field; others vote for a much earlier Golden Age, peaking in the mid-1930s with the serials of E. E. SMITH in the issues of *Astounding* edited by F. Orlin TREMAINE.

Here, however, the term will cover the period from 1938 to 1945 and will focus on the Campbell-edited *Astounding*, which dealt with the first generation of writers and readers to be exposed to an entire decade of American SF; they were ready, under Campbell's tutelage, to take the field in a new direction—to begin to impose humanistic values on technological expansion, explore (in the works of such writers as Henry KUTTNER and A. E. VAN VOGT) the darker implications explosive technology might hold, and assume both a more stylistic and a dystopian bent, opening up the field for the experimentation and greater expansion of the 1950s and 1960s.

The Golden Age owes much, perhaps all, of its significance to Campbell's influence—which provided the opportunity for myriad new writers to be published—and to his persuasive and innovative editorial point of view—which in many cases afforded those writers the themes, plots, and ideas they developed. Isaac Asimov, for instance, has credited Campbell with suggesting the idea for his famous short story "Nightfall." And almost all the writers associated with the Campbellian Golden Age—Theodore Sturgeon, Lester del Rey, Fritz Leiber, Robert A. Heinlein, van Vogt, Asimov—have made clear in oral and written testimony how instrumental they found their editor's role. It is not surprising then that the Golden Age is often regarded as Campbell's personal creation, his legacy to the field.

Up to the time of his editorship, SF had been written in the main by figures such as Arthur Leo Zagat, Nat Schachner, and Nelson Bond—prolific magazine writers for whom SF was simply another category of pulp fiction, to be written quickly, with interchangeable characters and conceptions, and with only enough borrowed invention to make a story fit the term. Frank Gruber, a prominent pulp writer of the time, referred to the output of such writers as "PSEUDOSCIENCE," and this was the popular term among pulp editors in other fields long thereafter.

Not all writers of pseudoscience were crass commercialists, of course. E. E. Smith, Ph.D., was a practicing chemist who wrote his interplanetary and intergalactic novels as a hobby; Jack Williamson, whose *Metal Man* had appeared in a very early issue of Amazing and who had been a contributor to the Tremaine *Astounding*, wanted to write nothing other than science fiction or fantasy—a predilection shared by Edmond Hamilton, who broke into print in 1926, and C. L. Moore, who began to sell in the mid-1930s.

But it was Campbell's intuition that the kind of SF which would persist and which he wanted to publish in *Astounding* could best be achieved by writers without preconceptions, whom he could train; newer writers without a publishing background would be not only more malleable but also more financially dependent.

The signatory issue of the Campbell period is generally agreed to be the July 1939 *Astounding;* although Campbell had acquired important work from the outset, this issue presented C. L. Moore's "Greater than Gods," as well as the first magazine work by van Vogt and Asimov ("Black Destroyer" "Trends"). In August, Heinlein's first story, "Life-Line," appeared, and in the two or three years to come, virtually all the elements of what has come to be called modern science fiction were laid out. These elements include a humanistic and exploratory approach to science and technology, various analyses of the role technology would play in the lives of individuals, the emergence of an ironic consciousness (Kuttner and Moore were particularly important here) in which the juxtaposition of technological expansionism or optimism and human perversity or limitation are perceived to have unforeseen and often disastrous effects. All of these elements amount to what Alexei Panshin and other

critics have defined as a mapping of the universe, a cosmopolitization of some very wild districts.

Shortly after Campbell assumed the editorship of *Astounding*, his attitude toward SF and its practitioners became manifest in the magazine's pages. Many writers who had published steadily through the 1930s were forced out by rejection or decided on their own that they could not accept Campbell's more rigorous assumptions. A handful of the old guard remained, notably Jack Williamson and Will F. Jenkins (Murray Leinster), writers who had much important work ahead of them and were able to make the necessary adjustments; many others, however, were lost to the magazine (and to the field) by the early 1940s, and their work is either not at all remembered or, like the conceptions of Ray Cummings, seen only in a nostalgic context.

Other important Golden Age figures who came to the magazine through the 1940s include Raymond F. Jones, A. Bertram Chandler, Malcolm Jameson, L. Sprague de Camp, Cleve Cartmill, George O. Smith, Fredric Brown, E. Mayne Hull (the wife of A. E. van Vogt), and P. Schuyler Miller (who in 1951 became Campbell's monthly book reviewer and continued in that position until his death in 1974). Although *Astounding* and its few competitors published the work of other writers as well, it is remarkable, in retrospect, to see how thoroughly the field was dominated by a relatively few writers. Much of their work remains in print even today, in collections and anthologies, not only because it was important to the fundamental creation of SF but because it still stands among the genre's most sterling achievements.

Merely to list some of the short stories, novels, and novelettes that appeared in *Astounding* in these years is to apprehend the importance of the work being done: Heinlein's "Universe," "Common Sense," *Beyond This Horizon;* Asimov's "Nightfall" and "Foundation"; Kuttner's "Twonky" and "Shock"; Moore's "No Woman Born"; Lester del Rey's "Nerves"—all these works were profoundly influential and have not lost their power to move generations of SF readers. But what most distinguished the Golden Age was a unique situation in which the field was, issue by issue, being defined and reshaped by an editor, writers, and readers who became literal collaborators. There were fewer barriers among writers, readers, and editors then than at any time in the history of mass publishing: writers were recruited from the readership, and because they were so familiar with the magazine (there was no other way to sell stories to *Astounding*, Campbell emphasized) they were able to grant short-term feedback—responses to ideas or extensions of stories would appear after a gap of only months. During this period, as Brian W. Aldiss has pointed out, *Astounding* was a laboratory in which various approaches were analyzed, tested, and experimented with. But always SF was perceived as a synergistic process, likely to be changed by any given work. This sense of an entire genre being constructed rapidly and in the view of its readership has virtually no parallel in Western culture. When Campbell became *Astounding*'s editor, the field was so new, its basic materials so barely explored, and its potential so significant that the application of his principles had almost instant effect.

Perhaps after 1946 the field had become too large; the facts of Hiroshima and Nagasaki, and the very real possibility of atomic doom, had an even more dampening effect. Science fiction was no longer a workshop or an intellectual game; it was no longer, either, as Asimov has pointed out, "a bunch of stories for crazy kids"; it was a form of literature that, in Cartmill's 1944 "Deadline," had laid out for a mass audience how the atomic bomb worked, and it was a literature whose posited technology had already led to real devastation, with the possibility of more to come. It was no longer possible, after Hiroshima, for SF's practitioners or readers to regard the field as somehow divorced from real terror or consequence.

Furthermore, and on a practical level, the postwar surge of interest—with major publishers commissioning large anthologies from Groff Conklin, Raymond Healy and J. Francis McComas, Everett F. Bleiler and T. E. Dikty; leading magazines such as *The Saturday Evening Post* proving receptive to fiction by Heinlein; movies, radio, and emergent television showing interest in SF (however debased their versions might be)—meant that SF was no longer a small field, no longer a laboratory; it had been taken away, to an insurmountable degree, from those who had created, codified, and shaped it, and it would never again possess that insular aspect that had made the Golden Age possible.

In the 1950s SF became an entirely different kind of literature; it may in fact have been superior to its precursor. Pohl among others has written that there were a succession of Golden Ages, each nostalgically perceived as the best. Certainly the 1950s was a period in which high style, the satiric and dystopian visions of H. L. Gold, and the urbanity of Anthony Boucher dominated the magazines. Meanwhile the important novels of that decade—Alfred Bester's *The Demolished Man*, Sturgeon's *More Than Human*, Walter M. Miller's *A Canticle for Leibowitz*, Algis Budrys's *Rogue Moon*, Frederik Pohl and C. M. Kornbluth's *The Space Merchants*—enjoyed a far larger audience and exercised a greater effect on the culture than even the best work of the 1940s.

It should also be noted that, although *Astounding* and Campbell were absolutely essential to any consideration of this period, there were other magazines, approaches, and writers in the early 1940s; for instance, Alden H. Norton and Donald A. Wollheim were, as editors, receptive to writers and approaches that Campbell found inaccessible; Ray Bradbury could not have published at all had it not been for markets such as *Planet Stories* and *Thrilling Wonder Stories*, which took his work when Campbell found all of it (with the exception of "Doodad") unacceptable. It should be noted too that several important stories, either not seen or rejected by Campbell—Frederic Brown's "The Star Mouse" *(Planet Stories)*, Kornbluth's "The Words of Guru" *(Stirring Science Fiction)*, and the novels of Edmond Hamilton *(Captain Future)* appeared in other markets, and many critics feel that they had as significant an effect on the development of the field as much of the work published in *Astounding*.

Campbell himself, in the last years of his life, questioned the theory of his editorial omnipotence. In a letter to Alexei Panshin, apparently in response to questions Panshin had raised about the theoretical basis underlying the 1940s *Astounding Science Fiction*, Campbell wrote:

> You ask me if I disagreed with Gernsback's theories. Why hell, man, I didn't know he *had* theories—and I'll bet he didn't know it either until he thought about it months or years later! I wrote stories because I thought they needed telling—they "needed" telling to stop the peculiar sort of itch they were causing in my own mind.

It hardly matters, however, whether Campbell was consciously changing the face of science fiction or not, because change it he certainly did. And in doing so he laid the groundwork for a genre that has continued to grow and flourish for over half a century. As Damon Knight has pointed out, the Golden Age was Campbell's decade, and his contribution to SF was immeasurable.

B.N.M.

GOLDIN, STEPHEN (1947–). American science-fiction writer and editor who writes primarily adventure SF often mixed with elements of mystery and intrigue. In *Scavenger Hunt* (1975) and its sequel *Finish Line* (1976), for example, a brother and sister become involved with murder while participating in a futuristic scavenger hunt. *Mindflight* (1978) incorporates telepathy, clandestine agents, and a secret that may or may not threaten all humanity. *And Not Make Dreams Your Master* (1981) offers a future in which dreams can be broadcast to vast audiences, but one of the most popular dreamers goes mad and endangers the minds and the lives of the audience.

Goldin has been writing a series of novels based on the earlier work of E. E. Smith: *The Imperial Stars* (1976), *Strangler's Moon* (1977), *Getaway World* (1977), *The Clockwork Traitor* (1978), *Appointment at Bloodstar* (1978), *The Purity Plot* (1978), *Planet of Treachery* (1982), *Eclipsing Binaries* (1983), *The Omicron Invasion* (1984), and *Revolt of the Galaxy* (1985). These works center on the activities of the Family d'Alembert, each member of which is an agent of the galactic empire. They describe how this talented family defends the empire by defeating various malcontents who try to subvert or destroy it. None of the books pretends to be anything more than good space opera, and in this each succeeds admirably well.

OTHER WORKS: *Herds* (1975); *Caravan* (1975); *Assault on the Gods* (1977); *Trek to Madworld* (1979); *The Eternity Brigade* (1980); *A World Called Solitude* (1981).

S.H.G.

GOLDING, WILLIAM [GERALD] (1911–   ).

British mainstream novelist who was educated at Oxford, served in the Royal Navy during World War II, worked as a teacher until 1961, and received the Nobel Prize for literature in 1983. Golding has published nine novels and a few shorter works of fiction, some of them tangential science fiction. His novels combine psychological realism with symbolism and moral allegory, as in his renowned first novel, *Lord of the Flies* (1954), about a group of schoolboys marooned on a tropical island during a near future atomic war. The boys' frail attempt to organize a community along adult lines fails completely as they regress into savagery, reflecting the progress of the adult world, where basic flaws in human nature determine society's end.

In *The Inheritors* (1955) these flaws are traced back to the time when the Neanderthal people were exterminated by the Cro-Magnon race, modern humanity's ancestors. In explicit contrast to H. G. WELLS's evolutionary view of the Neanderthals in *The Outline of History* (1920), Golding's Neanderthals, though of inferior intelligence, embody innocence and a harmonious relationship with Mother Earth, lost to their tool-making, fear-haunted exterminators. In three novellas collected in *The Scorpion God* (1971), ancient or prehistoric settings provide the backdrops for more transparent allegories, illustrating humanity's capacity for delusion, religious or scientific.

J.H.

GORGO (1961).   *Directed by Eugène Lourié, screenplay by John Loring and Daniel Hyatt; photographed by F. A. (Freddie) Young; music by Angelo Francesco Lavagnino. With Bill Travers, William Sylvester, Vincent Winter, Bruce Seton, Joseph O'Connor, Martin Benson, Nigel Green. 78 minutes. Color.*

Two adventurers capture a biped dinosaur in the Irish Sea and return with the beast—dubbed Gorgo—to London, where the monster is put on display at an amusement park. But Gorgo is a *baby*, and his mother, ten times his size, comes to rescue him, demolishing much

Maternal rage in *Gorgo*

of London in the process. The monsters return to the sea at the end.

Gorgo is handsomely photographed, and its simple plot is unencumbered with extraneous details; the acting is also above average, and the SPECIAL EFFECTS (by Tom Howard) are impressive, though not really convincing. The film's major drawback is that despite its unusual ending its plot is familiar.

Director Eugène Lourié, best known as a production designer, had previously directed THE BEAST FROM 20,000 FATHOMS (1953) and THE GIANT BEHEMOTH (1959), so he knew how to smash a city.

B.W.

GOTLIEB, PHYLLIS [FAY] (1926–   ).   Canadian writer who is best known as an excellent poet but whose fiction is almost all science fiction and fantasy. The style and texture of Gotlieb's fiction are conditioned by her experience as a poet: her work is filled with imagery, sharply visualized scenes, and skillfully crafted sentences, but it also features a strong sense of adventure and well-integrated uses of violence and pain. She published SF before fantasy, in the novels *Sunburst* (1964) and *O Master Caliban* (1976) and a collection of stories, *Son of the Morning and Other Stories* (1983). In the

1980s she completed a fantasy trilogy: *A Judgement of Dragons* (1980), *Emperors, Swords, Pentacles* (1982), and *Kingdom of the Cats* (1985).

N.H.

GOTSCHALK, FELIX C. (1929–   ).

American writer and psychologist who uses his background in psychology and his interest in linguistics to create energetic, stylistically unique short stories. Gotschalk characterizes his writings as personal indulgences in which he is as surprised as any reader by the twists and turns his plots may take. As a result most of his fiction appeals to editors noted for their interest in experimental works, such as Robert SILVERBERG (during his tenure at *New Dimensions*) and Damon KNIGHT (*Orbit*).

His characters tend to live in technological worlds and be contented members of hedonistic societies. Their governments channel the energies of the massive human populations into "safe" activities that allow control of the huge numbers of people while affording some kind of personal independence. In such stories as "The Man with the Golden Reticulates" (1975), "The Day of the Big Test" (1976), "Charisma Leak" (1976), and "Conspicuous Consumption" (1983), Gotschalk described potentially dystopic worlds in which sheer human exuberance for life manages to carry the characters through their daily routine. These characters know only the world they live in and usually accept that world as a given. They rarely see the darker possibilities, and as a result, despite the ever-present threat of tragedy from strained resources and questionable technological developments, they usually do not perceive themselves as oppressed. In such stories as "A Day in the South Quad" (1975), however, Gotschalk makes it eminently clear that such worlds are not healthy for human beings.

Gotschalk's only novel, *Growing Up in Tier 3000* (1975), contains all the features one expects of his SF. Set in a future that has been automated beyond most writers' wildest imagination, the novel describes a world in which the children, who know of no other way of life, are far better suited to live than their parents. Gotschalk here created an elaborate jargon for that technological future, and through it his readers are shown how much reality is dependent on the words we use to describe it. Those who speak the jargon are able to enjoy the new world fully, but those who do not are doomed.

S.H.G.

GOULART, RON[ALD JOSEPH] (1933–   ).

American writer of numerous books who has successfully written mysteries (and won the Edgar Allan Poe Award) and comic strips but is best known for his science fiction. Goulart's short fiction, with its highly polished style and striking, often farcical, characters, has appeared frequently in *The Magazine of Fantasy and Science Fiction*. Many of his novels are set in the Barnum planetary system and are thinly veiled broadsides against contemporary life, especially in southern California. In his first novel, *The Sword Swallower* (1968), he mixed SF and mystery in the form of a shape-changing detective (Ben Jolson of the Chameleon Corps), who searches for clues on a planet populated with comic-strip people. Other novels that make use of the Barnum system and the Chameleon Corps include *Flux* (1974), *Spacehawk, Inc.* (1974), *A Whiff of Madness* (1976), and *Flux, and the Tin Angel* (1978). The Barnum system was also the basis of the comic-strip books in the Star Hawk series (*Empire 99*, 1980; *The Cyborg King*, 1981), illustrated by Gil Kane.

Goulart has written other SF series, including Gypsy (*Quest for the Gypsy*, 1976; *Eye of the Vulture*, 1977), whose mysterious protagonist performs fantastic feats while searching for clues to his origin, and Battlestar Galactica (*Greetings from Earth*, 1983; *Experiment in Terra*, 1984; *The Long Patrol*, 1984), based on the television series. In 1975 he began a series concerning the comic-strip character Vampirella (*Bloodstalk*, 1975; *On Alien Wings*, 1975; *Deadwalk*, 1976; *Blood Wedding*, 1976; *Deathgame*, 1976; *Snakegod*, 1976), which mixes the Gothic with SF.

Under a number of pseudonyms, Goulart has also written several series that are marginally SF. As Frank S. Shawn, he continued the Phantom (*The Veiled Lady*, 1973; *The Golden Circle*, 1973; *The Mystery of the Sea Horse*, 1973; *The Hydra Monster*, 1973; *The Goggle-Eyed Pirates*, 1974; *The Swamp Rats*, 1974). Using the name Kenneth Robeson, he wrote a dozen Avenger stories (*The Man from Atlantis*, 1974; *Red Moon*, 1974; *The Purple Zombie*, 1974; *Dr. Time*, 1974; *The Nightwitch Devil*, 1974; *Black Chariots*, 1974; *The Cartoon Crimes*, 1974; *The Iron Skull*, 1975; *The Death Machine*, 1975; *The Blood Countess*, 1975; *The Glass Man*, 1975; *Demon Island*, 1975). And under the name Con Steffanson, he gave new life to Flash Gordon (*The Lion Men of Mongo*, 1974; *The Plague of Sound*, 1974; *Swamp Rats*, 1974).

OTHER WORKS: *After Things Fell Apart* (1970); *The Fire-Eater* (1970); *Gadget Man* (1971); *Death Cell* (1971); *What's Become of Screwloose? and Other Inquiries* (collection, 1971); *Clockwork's Pirates/Ghost Breaker* (collection, 1971); *Broke Down Engine and Other Troubles with Machines* (collection, 1971); *Hawkshaw* (1972); *Plunder* (1972); *Wildsmith* (1972); *The Chameleon Corps and Other Shape Changers* (collection, 1972); *Shaggy Planet* (1973); *A Talent for the Invisible* (1973); *The Tin Angel* (1973); *When the Waker Sleeps* (1975); *The Hellhound Project* (1975); *Nutzenbolts and More Troubles with Machines* (collection, 1975); *Odd Job No. 101 and Other Future Crimes and Intrigues* (collection, 1975); *The Enormous Hourglass*

(1976); *Crackpot* (1977); *The Emperor of the Last Days* (1977); *The Panchronicon Plot* (1977); *Nemo* (1977); *The Island of Dr. Moreau* (novelization of the screenplay, 1977); *The Wicked Cyborg* (1978); *Calling Dr. Patchwork* (1978); *Cowboy Heaven* (1979); *Hello, Lemuria, Hello* (1979); *Hail Hibbler* (1980); *Skyrocket Steele* (1980); *Brinkman* (1981); *Upside Downside* (1982); *Big Bang* (1982); *Hellquad* (1984); *The Prisoner of Blackwood Castle* (1984); *Suicide, Inc.* (1985); *Daredevils, Ltd.* (1987).

S.H.G.

GREAT BRITAIN

Science-fictional elements first appeared in British fiction in various eighteenth-century satires, notably Jonathan Swift's *Gulliver's Travels* (1726), but it was not until a century later that more earnest extrapolations from speculative hypotheses appeared, in such works as *Frankenstein* (1818) and *The Last Man* (1826) by Mary Wollstonecraft Shelley and *The Mummy!* (1827) by Mrs. Loudon. For most of the nineteenth century, though, the English literary marketplace was dominated by the three-decker novel, whose wealth and density of detail were not conducive to the presentation of hypothetical environments. The most adventurous futuristic three-deckers, Edward Maitland's *By and By* (1873) and Andrew Blair's *Annals of the Twenty-ninth Century* (1874), are essays thinly disguised as narratives.

A significant stimulus to the development of British futuristic fiction was provided by fears of invasion, exploited by propagandists anxious about Britain's readiness for war. George Chesney's *The Battle of Dorking* (1871), which describes a near future conquest of England by Germany, called forth many replies in kind and prepared the way for "future war" stories to become a subgenre of popular fiction. In the same year Edward George Bulwer-Lytton issued his utopian romance *The Coming Race,* one of the first stories to imagine society dramatically transformed by new means of production; a year later came Samuel Butler's utopian satire *Erewhon* and the first English translation of a novel by Jules Verne, *Journey to the Center of the Earth.*

The British literary marketplace was considerably changed in the 1890s by a host of new periodicals, which filled the gap between the highbrow world of the three-deckers and the lowbrow "penny dreadfuls." Competition between these periodicals encouraged experimentation and deliberate breaks with tradition, which in turn opened up the market for the development of scientific romance. Future war fiction became fashionable again and was given more extravagant scope by George Griffith's *Angel of the Revolution* (1893), which introduced airships and submarines into conflict on a world scale. In the sequel, *Olga Romanoff* (1894), Grif-

fith moved on to more spectacular catastrophism, having the world devastated by collision with a comet. H. G. Wells found the new periodicals hospitable to the essays and stories that he was producing in profusion. Within a few years he published *The Time Machine* (1895), *The Island of Dr. Moreau* (1896), *The Invisible Man* (1897), *The War of the Worlds* (1898), *When the Sleeper Wakes* (1899), *The First Men in the Moon* (1901), and three collections predominantly of speculative short stories. This remarkable oeuvre framed the field of scientific romance, in which numerous writers were subsequently to work.

The most important writers of scientific romance before World War I were M. P. Shiel, Arthur Conan Doyle, William Hope Hodgson, and J. D. Beresford. Shiel wrote several future war stories, beginning with *The Yellow Danger* (1898), but his most famous work is *The Purple Cloud* (1901), a catastrophe story embodying speculations about the metaphysics of evolutionary progress. Doyle's early scientific romances are minor works, but he made a considerable impact with *The Lost World* (1912), a robust adventure story that was followed by the catastrophist novella *The Poison Belt* (1913). Hodgson's exercises in teratology include two remarkable visionary fantasies of the far future, *The House on the Borderland* (1908) and *The Night Land* (1912). Beresford produced a classic novel about a superhuman child, *The Hampdenshire Wonder* (1912), and the disaster story *Goslings* (1913).

Scientific romance was already losing its fashionability before World War I, as the popular magazines passed beyond their experimental phase, but the war interrupted its development and had a profound effect on British attitudes toward the future. World War I obliterated European dominance in world economic affairs, and, while America enjoyed an unparalleled boom in the 1920s, Britain struggled to rebuild its economy. When the Wall Street crash brought the Depression to America, the effects hurt Europe even more. Thus, while early pulp SF in America reflected an optimism tied to the boom of the 1920s and managed to sustain its exuberance even in the 1930s, British futuristic fiction between the wars began in a pessimistic vein and became increasingly anxious.

Wells, in *The Shape of Things to Come* (1933), called this period the Age of Frustration, and British scientific romance gave voice to this sentiment. Future war stories became extremely bleak, frequently presenting the view that aerial bombing would destroy civilization; examples include *The People of the Ruins* (1920) by Edward Shanks, *Theodore Savage* (1923) by Cicely Hamilton, *Ragnarok* (1926) by Shaw Desmond, *Gay Hunter* (1934) by J. Leslie Mitchell, and the trilogy begun with *Prelude in Prague* (1935) by S. Fowler Wright. Wars are inevitable, they suggested, because of the innate bestiality of *Homo sapiens,* and writers frequently speculated about the character of new species that might replace ours and take up the torch of progress. These new species, some descended from humans and some not, make their appearance in such works as *Back to Methuselah* (1921) by George Bernard Shaw, *The Clockwork Man* (1923) by E. V. Odle, *The Amphibians* (1925) by Wright, *Last and First Men* (1930) and *Odd John* (1934) by Olaf STAPLEDON, *Tomorrow's Yesterday* (1932) by John GLOAG, *The Young Men Are Coming!* (1937) by M. P. Shiel, *Minimum Man* (1938) by Andrew Marvell, and *"What Dreams May Come . . ."* (1941) by Beresford.

This constant preoccupation with the end of the world we know and its supersession by a new order was further extrapolated in apocalyptic tales that adopted a heavily ironic tone, regarding the decay of civilization as an entirely appropriate fate. Examples of this irony can be found in such works as *The Seventh Bowl* (1930) and *The Lord of Life* (1933) by Neil Bell, and *The New Pleasure* (1933) and *Manna* (1940) by Gloag. Something of this attitude affected many stories of natural catastrophe, including *Deluge* (1927) by Wright, *Red Snow* (1931) by F. W. Moxley, and *The Hopkins Manuscript* (1939) by R. C. SHERRIFF and thus helped establish the seeds of the tradition carried forward after World War II by such writers as John WYNDHAM, John CHRISTOPHER, and J. G. BALLARD.

Irony is also to be found in a number of stories in which lone heroes try to blackmail the world into sanity but inevitably fail; examples include *Star Dust* (1925) by E. Charles Vivian, *Power* (1933) by Wright, and *The Peacemaker* (1934) by C. S. FORESTER. Faith in the possibility that science would enable humanity to build a better society was hard to sustain in this zeitgeist, and the idea that technological progress would instead lend more oppressive power to corrupt political leaders was given extravagant expression in Aldous HUXLEY's *Brave New World* (1932) and (with further emphasis lent by the example of World War II) George ORWELL's *Nineteen Eighty-four* (1949).

Some American SF pulps were imported into Britain in the 1930s, when they were mostly sold at junk prices in department stores. Several British writers, notably John Russell FEARN, Eric Frank RUSSELL, and John Beynon Harris, began writing for the pulp market, and British fans eventually launched their own pulp, *Tales of Wonder*, in 1937, although it never thrived. Not until the end of the paper rationing introduced during World War II sparked a boom in paperback publishing between 1948 and 1953 was a substantial amount of SF as such published in Britain.

The fiction written for this market was produced at breakneck pace for tiny payments, and read like the result of such a process, although some of the authors involved, notably E. C. TUBB, John BRUNNER, and Kenneth BULMER, went on to more mature work. A measure

of literary respectability was brought to British SF by the magazines of the 1950s and early 1960s, especially John Carnell's NEW WORLDS and *Science-Fantasy*, where Brian W. ALDISS and J. G. Ballard first established themselves. The most successful British writer of speculative novels in this period was John Wyndham (who had earlier published pulp SF as John Beynon Harris and some books as John Beynon); his best-selling *The Day of the Triffids* (1951) was followed by several more catastrophe stories, notably *The Kraken Wakes* (1953), *The Chrysalids* (1955) and *The Midwich Cuckoos* (1957). This success was partly tied in with an avoidance of the SF label, a strategy also followed by other writers in the same vein, including John Christopher, author of *The Death of Grass* (1956; American title *No Blade of Grass*) and *The World in Winter* (1962; American title *The Long Winter*), and Charles Eric MAINE, author of *The Tide Went Out* (1958) and *Calculated Risk* (1960).

Science fiction enjoyed a brief period of fashionability in Britain during the early 1950s, when it was featured extensively on radio, in Charles Eric Maine's *Spaceways* (1953) and Charles Chilton's long-running serial *Journey into Space* (1953–1955), and on television, where Nigel Kneale's serials THE QUATERMASS EXPERIMENT (1953) and *Quatermass II* (1955) were significant innovations in popular programming. Sidgwick & Jackson launched the British SF Book Club in 1953, but despite this showcase for the best of British and American SF, publication of SF in hardcover remained low-key until 1961, when Victor Gollancz began to issue a distinctively packaged series.

The leading British SF writers of the 1950s—Wyndham, Aldiss, and Arthur C. CLARKE—each combined in some way the traditions of British scientific romance and American SF. They tempered the imaginative exuberance of the latter with a skeptical sobriety more typical of the former. Wyndham did so in anxious fantasies about the precariousness of civilization and the superficiality of its finer values. Aldiss developed a previously unseen deftness and sophistication of style in the short stories in *Space, Time, and Nathaniel* (1957) and his first novel, *Non-stop* (1958). Clarke combined with surprising ease a new depth of technical realism and a vein of quasi-mystical regard for the wonders of the cosmic perspective (the latter inherited mainly from Stapledon) in works as various as *Childhood's End* (1954), *The City and the Stars* (1956), and *The Deep Range* (1957).

The 1960s saw a new boom in paperback publication, in which SF played an important part. With the exception of the Badger Books turned out in amazing profusion by R. Lionel FANTHORPE, these SF paperbacks were aimed at a middlebrow audience, avoiding the crudities of the SF paperbacks of the early 1950s. Most of the material was, however, imported from the United States, and the SF writers who were operating as full-time professionals in Britain were often first (and sometimes only) published by American paperback companies. The British SF magazines suffered from competition with these paperbacks and were forced to find a new role. The unusual stories of Ballard, displayed in such collections as *The Four-Dimensional Nightmare* (1963) and *The Terminal Beach* (1964), already provided the basis for an SF avant-garde, whose cause was taken up by Michael MOORCOCK when *New Worlds* was sold to a new publisher in 1964 and he became its editor.

Moorcock provided experimental work of his own in stories featuring Jerry Cornelius and encouraged writers like Aldiss to undertake new adventures in style and method, as exemplified by *Report on Probability A* (1968) and *Barefoot in the Head* (1969). Although two of his most successful recruits (Thomas M. DISCH and John SLADEK) were American, Moorcock played a leading part in encouraging a new generation of British writers. *New Worlds* published material that formed the basis of several important collections, including *The Caltraps of Time* (1968) by David I. Masson, *The Atrocity Exhibition* (1970) by Ballard, *The Eye of the Lens* (1972) by Langdon Jones, *The Machine in Shaft Ten* (1975) by M. John Harrison, and *The Knights of the Limits* (1978) by Barrington J. Bayley. Its companion magazine, *Science-Fantasy* (later *Impulse*), published first stories by other writers later to become important, including Christopher Priest, Josephine Saxton, and Keith ROBERTS—who wrote for it the stories making up his alternate-world fantasy *Pavane* (1968).

The increased market space for SF novels that became available in the 1960s also helped encourage writers to more ambitious productions, many of them carrying forward the catastrophist tradition that had dominated British imaginative fiction for so many years. Ballard's trilogy *The Drowned World* (1963), *The Drought* (1965), and *The Crystal World* (1966) offers accounts of individuals adapting themselves psychologically to various kinds of disaster; Aldiss described a world without children in *Greybeard* (1964); Brunner produced a series of highly detailed near future disaster stories based on contemporary anxieties: *Stand on Zanzibar* (1969), *The Sheep Look Up* (1972), and *The Shockwave Rider* (1975). Similarly anxious themes can be found in the work of many other writers, including *The Quality of Mercy* (1965) and *The Electric Crocodile* (1970) by D. G. COMPTON, *The Furies* (1966) by Keith ROBERTS, *Colossus* (1966) and *Implosion* (1967) by D. F. JONES, *Death Is a Dream* (1967) by E. C. Tubb, *The Ulcer Culture* (1969) by Kenneth Bulmer, and *Heroes and Villains* (1969) by Angela Carter. Carter was one of a number of "mainstream" novelists who made use of science-fiction themes in this period, following the earlier precedents set by Huxley, Orwell, and Evelyn Waugh (*Love among the Ruins*, 1953); other examples include *A Clockwork Orange* (1962) by Anthony Burgess, *A Very Private Place* (1968) by Michael Frayn, and *The Bodyguard* (1970)

by Adrian Mitchell, all of which are dystopian fantasies.

This predominant pessimism contrasted somewhat with the relatively buoyant mood of the times, but the main antidote to anxiety remained, as in much harsher times, the idea of transcendence: a leap in mental evolution. This is expressed extravagantly in the work of Arthur Sellings (*The Silent Speakers*, 1963, and *The Uncensored Man*, 1964) and more moderately in other parapsychology stories of the period, including *Breakthrough* (1967) by Richard Cowper and *The New Minds* (1967) and its sequels by Dan Morgan.

The themes that had become most typical of postwar American SF—the conquest of the galaxy and encounters with exotic alien cultures—were never as far to the fore in Britain, although British writers whose main market was the American paperback publishers (notably Brunner, Bulmer, and Tubb) produced such stories in quantity, in a spirit of honest craftsmanship. Two exceptions to this rule, however, were writers from Northern Ireland: James WHITE and Bob SHAW. White published numerous stories and novels dealing with the problems of future medical professionals whose skills must extend to alien biology, including *Star Surgeon* (1963) and *Major Operation* (1971). Shaw also combined a sobriety typical of British material with themes more typical of American SF in such works as *Palace of Eternity* (1970) and *Orbitsville* (1975).

The economic recession that began in 1974 hit the British book market badly, and it has been much more difficult since that time for new writers to establish themselves; magazine publishing was even harder hit. The increasing popularity of SF has enabled writers who *are* successful to achieve best-seller status, but only two British writers have managed this: Arthur Clarke, who returned to novel writing some years after the success of 2001: A SPACE ODYSSEY (1968), the film whose script he wrote for Stanley KUBRICK, with *Rendezvous with Rama* (1973); and Douglas ADAMS, whose radio serial THE HITCHHIKER'S GUIDE TO THE GALAXY (1978) spawned a series of novels and a television serial. Despite the problems caused by the recession, though, a number of new writers have managed to establish themselves in the British SF field in the last ten years. The most notable is Ian WATSON, who made an impressive debut with *The Embedding* (1973); he has devoted himself more assiduously than any other writer to developing the theme of evolutionary transcendence, which has always been central to British speculative fiction. Other significant recruits to the field include Robert HOLDSTOCK, Garry Kilworth, Tanith LEE, and David Langford.

Market conditions in recent years have encouraged the production of novel SERIES, especially trilogies, and many of the leading British SF professionals have begun to plan their contemporary work with this trend in mind. Examples already completed include Aldiss's trilogy *Helliconia Spring* (1982), *Helliconia Summer* (1983), and *Helliconia Winter* (1985); Richard Cowper's trilogy *The Road to Corlay* (1978), *A Dream of Kinship* (1981), and *A Tapestry of Time* (1985); and Watson's trilogy *The Book of the River* (1983), *The Book of the Stars* (1984), and *The Book of Being* (1985). Shaw began a series still in progress with *The Ragged Astronauts* (1986). All these series manifest characteristic British concerns: detechnologized landscapes, often harsh, in which characters must struggle to achieve some kind of marvelous alleviation of their existential burden. It is significant, though, that in all these series except Cowper's the struggle is shifted into entirely hypothetical circumstances.

In the late 1980s, British SF cannot be considered a healthy genre. One magazine, *Interzone,* survives on an Arts Council grant but circulates only to subscribers and via a handful of specialist bookstores. Most of the publishers—especially paperback houses—who have retained SF lines (many have not) are content to reprint books that have already demonstrated their popularity in America. The space devoted to SF and heroic fantasy in bookstores is increasingly dominated by heroic fantasy. The only significant innovation in British SF publishing in recent years has been the establishment of an SF line by the feminist Women's Press; this line includes an interesting original anthology, *Despatches from the Frontiers of the Female Mind* (1985), edited by Sarah leFanu and Jen Green, but it remains to be seen whether the recruitment of new female writers can enliven British SF in the same way that women enlivened American SF in the 1970s.

B.S.

GREEN, JOSEPH [LEE] (1931–).   American science-fiction author and technical writer whose highly imaginative short fiction has extended the boundaries of SF. Green has written both literary stories that show the hand of an accomplished stylist ("Jaybird's Song," 1974) and adventure tales that probe future relations between humanity and its technology ("And Be Lost Like Me," 1983). His earliest works can be found in a collection of his short stories (*An Affair with Genius,* 1969) and in two of his novels (*The Loafers of Refuge,* 1965, and *Conscience Interplanetary,* 1972), which consist of material that first appeared in short stories.

Both novels illustrate Green's favorite pattern: a central character is given a difficult problem and must find an answer by interacting with aliens. This pattern is most successful in *Gold the Man* (1971; published in the United States as *The Mind behind the Eye,* 1972), in which Gold, the hero, is actually transferred into the body of a giant alien in order to spy on the alien's warring race. In this solid adventure novel with greater depth than many of its kind, Gold tackles the crisis that has forced the aliens to threaten the Earth and copes with the isolation he feels as an alien in an alien's world.

OTHER WORKS: *Star Probe* (1976); *The Horde* (1976).

S.H.G.

GREG, PERCY (1836–1889).   British poet, novelist, and historian who portrayed the first fictional journey by spaceship to another planet (Mars) in his novel *Across the Zodiac: The Story of a Wrecked Record* (1880). Taking advantage of the physical and astronomical science of his day, Greg envisaged an exotic Martian landscape and a Martian technological utopia that is a moral and political dystopia.

N.H.

GRIFFITH, GEORGE (1857–1906).   British author and adventurer, born George Chetwynd Griffith-Jones; one of the foremost science-fiction writers of his time. Griffith's novels and stories, which exemplify various SF subgenres, appeared frequently in the fiction and PULP MAGAZINES of his day. Today he is best remembered for *A Honeymoon in Space* (1901), the first SF novel to depict a trip to Venus.

N.H.

GUIN, WYMAN [WOODS] (1915–).   American marketing and media specialist and science-fiction writer who specializes in SF short stories that portray unusual human and alien societies. Guin's societies are usually caricatures of contemporary life with one feature singled out for exaggerated treatment: in "Beyond Bedlam" (1951) for example, schizophrenia has become the normal state because alternate personalities must share the same body; in "The Delegate from Guapanga" (1964) dishonest politics is stretched until it becomes the foundation for an alien's theory on human governments. Naturally, with their emphasis on social satire, most of Guin's works appeared in GALAXY. *The Standing Joy* (1969), his lone novel, is a parallel-world story. Guin's love for the aberrant surfaces in the novel when the reader learns that the most notable invention of this world is a method for prolonging orgasm. Although Guin's SF rarely contains any serious moral, his imaginative stories amuse and divert anyone willing to search for them.

OTHER WORK: *Living Way Out* (collection, 1967; published in Britain as *Beyond Bedlam,* 1973).

S.H.G.

GUNN, JAMES E[DWIN] (1923–).   American writer and professor of English, as well known for writing *about* science fiction as for writing it. Gunn started writing SF in 1948, between earning a bachelor's degree in journalism and receiving a master's degree in

James E. Gunn

English from the University of Kansas (where he now teaches and directs the Center for the Study of Science Fiction). He also has been president of both the SCIENCE FICTION WRITERS OF AMERICA and the SCIENCE FICTION RESEARCH ASSOCIATION.

Gunn's brand of SF combines elements of the academic scholar and the popular fiction writer, bringing literary values to the service of traditional storytelling. One of his short definitions of SF is "the literature of the human species," and his fiction sees humanity as a species that must have challenges even if individuals want to settle down to things as they are. In such early works as his connected stories collected in *Station in Space* (1958), his major characters push humanity toward its destiny in space, sometimes inventing and then living with an elaborate hoax but always suffering and enduring, and moving forward.

Like many SF writers Gunn seems most at home in the shorter lengths. Most of his so-called novels are actually collections of short fiction written on a common theme. In *The Joy Makers* (1961), for example, he explored the nature of happiness over three short novels and the lifetimes of several generations. He asked: What

would people do if the art of happiness became a science? Each story in the series suggests an answer, advances the history of "hedonics," and makes its own climactic point about the nature of happiness and humanity's quest for it.

Both *The Immortals* (1962) and *The Listeners* (1972) use this same structural device. In *The Immortals* Gunn described the psychological and social consequences of the knowledge that immortality is possible. The 1970 television series THE IMMORTAL changed the focus to the immortal man himself rather than the world around him, and the episodes became a series of chases, captures, and escapes. In *The Listeners* communication replaces immortality as the central theme: the difficulty of picking up signals from the stars is matched by the difficulties individual human beings have communicating with one another and with society itself.

Although many of Gunn's works may appear structurally similar to one another, much of his development as a writer stems from his dislike for repeating himself or others. His first novel, *This Fortress World* (1955), for instance, deals with the then-popular concept of galactic empire, but Gunn examined it from the viewpoint of the people who live in its squalor, people engaged in a struggle to survive rather than in romantic high adventure: this is naturalism brought to the service of SPACE OPERA.

Two later works, *Kampus* (1977) and *The Dreamers* (1980), are characterized by stylistic daring. The opening chapter of *Kampus*, which reflects in its language the confusion of a student under the influence of a psychedelic drug, was called "pyrotechnic" by Theodore STURGEON. In *The Dreamers* Gunn told the story of the use of chemical memory as entertainment at three different levels—plot and character, symbol, and metaphor—while surrounding its narrative episodes with a frame in which three different trains of a "Mnemonist's" thoughts are reflected simultaneously.

In 1976 Gunn won the SFRA Pilgrim Award and a Special Award from the World Science Fiction Convention for his *Alternate Worlds: The Illustrated History of Science Fiction* (1975). In 1983 he won the Hugo Award for his study *Isaac Asimov: The Foundations of Science Fiction* (1982). His four-volume critical anthology *The Road to Science Fiction* (1977–1982) is the standard text in college courses on SF, and he became general editor of *The New Encyclopedia of Science Fiction*.

OTHER WORKS: *Star Bridge* (with Jack Williamson, 1957); *Future Imperfect* (collection, 1964); *The Witching Hour* (collection, 1970); *The Immortal* (novelization of the TV film, 1970); *The Burning* (1972); *Breaking Point* (collection, 1972); *Some Dreams Are Nightmares* (collection, 1974); *The End of the Dreams* (collection, 1975); *The Magicians* (1976); *Crisis!* (1986).

S.H.G.

H

HAGGARD, H[ENRY] RIDER (1856–1925).

British writer; creator of the lost-race subgenre of science fiction and fantasy. Best known for his first two novels, *King Solomon's Mines* (1885) and *She* (1886), and the creation of the two colorful characters in them, Allan Quatermain and Ayesha, Haggard continued to produce works of fiction, almost all with elements of fantasy and SF, to a total of fifty-eight books. His literary success led to his virtual abandonment of the law within a year of starting his practice.

Although Haggard dealt with such typical SF themes as immortality, suspended animation, communication with the dead, and reincarnation, he was not central to SF like his contemporaries Jules VERNE and H. G. WELLS. Instead, his romanticism led him toward fantasy and the supernatural, and the creation of larger-than-life characters whose loves and adventures span the centuries. His novels most resembling SF are *When the World Shook* (1919), in which a priest of Atlantis is revived from suspended animation, and *Stella Fregelius* (1904), in which an attempt is made to contact the dead by radio.

She initiated the notion of ancient civilizations surviving unknown into the present, and not only Haggard but many of his successors, including Edgar Rice BUR-ROUGHS, wrote so many similar stories that the basic plot became a subgenre (see LOST RACES). *She* also introduced Ayesha, the Egyptian princess who makes herself immortal by bathing in a special pillar of flame and survives millennia until her lost love is reincarnated. *King Solomon's Mines*, which introduced the adventurer Allan Quatermain, is a straightforward adventure story whose only fantasy element is the discovery of King Solomon's ancient treasure. Following the success of that novel, Haggard, drawing on his years as a government official in South Africa, began to create a Zulu mythos, a carefully delineated world peopled with wonderful characters and seasoned with elements of supernaturalism, mysticism, and occasional science, especially anthropology and geology.

Although Haggard killed off Quatermain at the end of *Allan Quatermain* (1887), and even resorted to an *Allan's Wife* (1889) sequel, he later told many of Quatermain's earlier adventures, especially in former incarnations, as in *The Ancient Allan* (1920) and *Allan and the Ice-Gods* (1927), in which dreams of past lives are drug induced. Haggard even brought Quatermain and Ayesha together, in *She and Allan* (1921). Apart from Africa, Haggard set his lost race adventures in central Asia in *Ayesha* (1905); Central and South America in *Montezuma's Daughter* (1893), *The Heart of the World*

H. Rider Haggard

(1895), and *The Virgin of the Sun* (1922); and ancient Babylon in *Belshazzar* (1930). He also wrote several historical fantasies, such as *Eric Brighteyes* (1891), *Red Eve* (1911), and *The World's Desire* (1891), the last with Andrew Lang.

Haggard's novels hold little interest for SF readers today, although a few are still read by children; he may have reused the same theme too often, but he was a stirring and imaginative writer whose works inspired not only his own but later generations.

M.A.

HALDEMAN, JACK C[ARROLL, III] (1941–).

American writer who has written over forty short stories, many on "future sports" ("Louisville Slugger," 1977; "Home Team Advantage," 1977; "The Agony of Defeat," 1978; "The Thrill of Victory," 1978; "Race the Wind," 1979). Most of Haldeman's stories have a SPACE OPERA plot in which the human race depends on the outcome of a contest, and most are laced with broad humor. That humor characterizes Haldeman's nonsports stories as well, including "What Weighs 8000 Pounds and Wears Red Sneakers?" (1978), an extended "elephant joke"; "Wet behind the Ears" (1982); and "My Crazy Father Who Scares All Women Away" (1983). Haldeman has written three novels in the science-fiction adventure vein: *Vector Analysis* (1978), which mixes mystery with SF; *Perry's Planet* (1980), part of the Star Trek series; and *There Is No Darkness* (with his brother, Joe Haldeman, 1983), a picaresque novel that follows the trials and tribulations of young adults as they venture to various planets.

S.H.G.

Joe Haldeman

HALDEMAN, JOE [JOSEPH WILLIAM] (1943–).

American writer who combines literary skills with hard-core scientific rigor, as evidenced by his degrees in physics and astronomy (B.S., University of Maryland, 1967) and writing (M.F.A., Iowa University, 1975). Haldeman attracted the attention of fans and general readers alike with his first science-fiction novel, *The Forever War* (1972–1974/1974), which won both the Nebula and the Hugo Award.

Although he has published well-received novels since—in particular *Mindbridge* (1976), *All My Sins Remembered* (1977), *Worlds* (1981), and *Worlds Apart* (1984)—*The Forever War* is still the work for which Haldeman is best remembered. He was severely wounded in Vietnam (and wrote about the experience in his non-SF *War Year*, 1972), and that experience is reflected in *The Forever War*, a naturalistic description of a war that lasts more than a thousand years, although the main characters age only a few years because of the relativistic effects of faster-than-light space travel. The situation of the soldiers fighting in this kind of war is complicated, however, by their alienation from their own societies by the time-dilation effect, and their growing disillusionment with the war.

The novel is both a tribute and a response to Robert A. HEINLEIN's *Starship Troopers* (1959), showing the casual brutality and brutalizing effect of warfare that is ultimately pointless. At the same time, its author points out, it is a metaphor for Vietnam and the effect of that war on American society.

Mindbridge uses an experimental technique reminiscent of that of John Dos Passos, alternating straightforward narrative with excerpts from the protagonist's autobiography and social artifacts, to deal with a future that includes alien races, matter transmission, telepathy, and the colonization of other planetary systems. *All My Sins Remembered* is a spy thriller, and *Worlds* and *Worlds Apart* are the first two volumes of a projected trilogy about the true nature of civilization told through the near future experiences of a female protagonist.

Haldeman also has been successful at the shorter lengths of fiction, winning a Hugo Award in 1977 for his "Tricentennial." He has published two collections of short stories, *Infinite Dreams* (1978) and *Dealing in Futures* (1985). In addition, he is an anthologist, particularly of SF stories dealing with war, in collections such as *Study War No More* (1977) and *Supertanks* (with Martin Harry Greenberg and Charles W. Waugh, 1987). He also has written plays, verse (his "Saul's Death," published originally in *Omni*, won the SCIENCE FICTION POETRY ASSOCIATION's Rhysling Award in 1984), two series novels—*Attar 1: Attar's Revenge* (1975) and *Attar 2: War of Nerves* (1975)—as Robert Graham, and two STAR TREK novels: *Planet of Judgment* (1977) and *World without End* (1979). For the past few years Haldeman has divided his time between teaching fiction writing to students at MIT and living in Florida.

OTHER WORKS: *There Is No Darkness* (with Jack C. Haldeman, 1983); *Tool of the Trade* (1987).

J.E.G.

HALE, EDWARD EVERETT (1822–1909).

American writer, editor, clergyman, abolitionist, and grandnephew of Revolutionary War patriot Nathan Hale. Best known for his patriotic prose and poetry, including the story "The Man without a Country" (1863), Hale, like so many nineteenth-century authors, wrote fiction about science, technology, and change—what later would be called science fiction—as a matter of course. Hale's SF includes the short novel *The Brick Moon* (serialized in *Atlantic* in 1869–70). The first work of fiction to mention an artificial satellite (it is intended, when launched into space by giant flywheels, to be used as an aid to navigation), *The Brick Moon* describes the accidental launching of the satellite while the workmen and their families are aboard, and the struggles of those set adrift to survive. Hale also wrote one of the first stories of alternate worlds, "Hands Off" (*Harpers*, 1881), which was reprinted in *Fantasy and Science Fiction* in 1952. "The Good-Natured Pendulum" was reprinted in *Amazing Stories* in 1933.

R.S.C.

HAMILTON, EDMOND [MOORE] (1904–1977).

American writer, one of the pioneers of pulp science fiction. Beginning in *Weird Tales* in 1926, Hamilton developed the classic SPACE OPERA, his Interstellar Patrol stories, which strongly prefigured E. E. SMITH's later Lensman series. It was only in 1928, however, when he began writing for *Amazing*, that his work had genuine impact on the genre.

Much of Hamilton's enormous output was routine, with the same formula plots repeated endlessly; unlike many early pulp writers, however, Hamilton matured—only to find his reputation permanently besmudged by his previous excesses (particularly the Captain Future series of juveniles). At the outset Hamilton typified the glorious, naive wonder of early pulp SF, but by the middle 1930s he was interspersing genuinely sensitive pieces among the more hackneyed efforts. His best work of this period consists of short stories for *Weird Tales*, such as "In the World's Dusk" (1936) and "He That Hath Wings" (1937).

After World War II Hamilton produced increasingly polished versions of some of his standard stories (*The Star Kings* 1949, is the culmination of decades of writing space opera), often for marginal magazines. A leader in the 1930s, he was a fringe figure by the 1950s, despite the fact that he wrote his own type of outer-space adventure better than anyone else and, in the 1950s and early 1960s, produced a small number of poetic, moody short stories that show him an equal to any newcomer.

In the last years of his career Hamilton returned to his beloved space opera, with a sequel to *The Star Kings* and the entirely new Starwolf trilogy. Much of his magazine work is uncollected, and any listing of his books is misleading, because many titles are reprints of earlier magazine stories.

OTHER WORKS: *The Horror on the Asteroid* (1936); *Tiger Girl* (1945); *Murder in the Clinic* (1946); *The Monsters of Juntonheim* (alternate title *A Yank at Valhalla* 1950); *Tharkol, Lord of the Unknown* (1950); *The City at the World's End* (1951); *The Star of Life* (1951); *The Sun Smasher* (1959); *The Haunted Stars* (1960); *Battle for the Stars* (1961); *The Valley of Creation* (1964); *Outside the Universe* (1964); *Crashing*

Suns (1965); *Fugitive of the Stars* (1965); *Doomstar* (1966); *The Weapon from Beyond* (1967); *World of the Starwolves* (1968); *The Closed Worlds* (1968); *Danger Planet* (1968, as Brett Sterling); *Calling Captain Future* (1969); *Captain Future and the Space Emperor* (1969); *Captain Future's Challenge* (1969); *The Comet Kings* (1969); *Galaxy Mission* (1969); *The Magician of Mars* (1969); *Outlaw World* (1969); *Outlaws of the Moon* (1969); *Planets in Peril* (1969); *Quest beyond the Stars* (1969); *Return to the Stars* (1970); *What's It Like Out There?* (1974); *The Best of Edmond Hamilton* (1977).

D.S.

HANGAR 18 (1980).

Directed by James L. Conway; screenplay by Steven Thornley; photographed by Paul Hipp; music by John Cacavas. With Darren McGavin, Robert Vaughn, Gary Collins, Joseph Campanella, Pamela Bellwood, Tom Halleck. 93 minutes. Color.

A number of films, of which the most successful was CLOSE ENCOUNTERS OF THE THIRD KIND (1977), have tried to capitalize on the UFO phenomenon and its true believers. A Utah production company based *Hangar 18*, with considerably less effect, on the widely believed myth of contemporary times that a UFO's crash landing in the Southwest during the 1940s was covered up by the U.S. government, which still keeps the spacecraft and its alien inhabitants in a top-secret location: Hangar 18. In this case the crash occurs during an election year. It all makes for a conspiracy-at-top-levels suspense story that is watchable for its action if one can forget the absurdity of its premise.

H.L.P.

HARNESS, CHARLES L[EONARD] (1915–   ).

American science fiction writer and patent attorney. Until recently, the writing of SF had been more of an avocation for Harness; indeed his first story, "Time Trap" (1948), was written to pay the costs of his daughter's birth. Although he has yet to receive the general recognition he deserves, Harness has attracted an enthusiastic following among readers and critics alike. His first novel, *Flight into Yesterday* (also known as *The Paradox Men*), was published in *Startling Stories* in 1949 and immediately attracted favorable critical notice from both Damon KNIGHT and James BLISH, but Harness's most highly praised work, his short novel *The Rose*, published in Britain in 1953, was not printed in the United States until 1969.

Nearly all Harness's works draw on elements from his own life (not only his background in chemistry and patent law but a number of personal topics as well), and many share common themes—cycles in time (as in *The*

Paradox Men, an SF adventure story that puts forth several unusual ideas about time travel) and transcendental metamorphosis via death (as in *The Rose,* a brooding but compelling morality play). Another abiding theme in Harness's work is the notion of science as a powerful tool with the potential for abuse: *The Rose* pits Art against the Science of a totalitarian state; the heroes of *The Paradox Men* use the forces of science to fight a despotic government. Both Harness's novels and his short fiction are characterized by intricate plots, complex characters, and an inventive use of the fantastic.

Although Harness's SF career has been sporadic (he wrote little from 1954 through 1965 and 1969 through 1976), since 1977 he has produced several short works and five novels: *Wolfhead* (1977), *The Catalyst* (1980), *Firebird* (1981), *The Venetian Court* (1981), and *Redworld* (1986).

OTHER WORK: *The Ring of Ritornel* (1968).

W.D.S.

Harry Harrison

HARRISON, HARRY (Pseudonym of Henry Maxwell Dempsey) (1925–   ).

American author, artist, and editor now living in Ireland. For nearly four decades Harrison has been one of science fiction's most productive writers. His output has ranged from the quasi-superhero adventures of Jason dinAlt, which Harrison chronicled in his three Deathworld novels (1960–1968), to the outrageous antics of antihero Jim DeGriz in the Stainless Steel Rat series (1957/1961–   ). Harrison's major achievements, however, are *West of Eden* (1984) and *Winter in Eden* (1986), the first two books in a projected trilogy dealing with what the world might be like had the dinosaurs survived.

Harrison began his career as a commercial artist but was soon writing story lines for comic books (which he drew as well). Not long after, he turned to straight SF, supporting himself as a free-lance writer for many years. Harrison has lived in numerous countries, including Denmark, England, and Ireland, as well as various cities in the United States. He is multilingual, even speaking Esperanto, as he once remarked, "like a native."

His sense of absurdity has made him one of the few SF writers to deal successfully with comedy. To be sure, the Stainless Steel Rat books are potboilers, but they are also very funny, reflecting Harrison's almost inexhaustible comedic invention. He has a penchant for bad puns (he named one of his planets "far off Faroffia" and another "distant Distantia") and an eagerness to demolish pretense—whether in SF itself (who but Harrison would write a novel with the incredible title *Star Smashers of the Galaxy Rangers,* 1973?) or the inanities of bloated militarists and politicians. *Bill, the Galactic Hero* (1965), one of his most underestimated books, satirizes both warmongering and some ideas of Robert A. HEINLEIN and Isaac ASIMOV.

Harrison's comic gift is also evident in *The Technicolor Time Machine* (1967), with its sex-bomb heroine Slithey Tove, and *A Transatlantic Tunnel, Hurrah!* (1972; also published as *Tunnel through the Deeps*), which is written in the style of a late Victorian novel. An alternate-world story, it describes the struggles of a descendant of the disgraced George Washington (who lost the American Revolution) attempting to redeem the family name by digging a tunnel under the Atlantic Ocean.

For all that Harrison has pilloried many of humanity's foibles and SF's excesses, he has never forgotten how to tell a good story; indeed, all his short stories and novels are richly plotted. *Make Room! Make Room!* (1966) is a more serious effort, set in a teeming, uncontrolled, grim, and starving New York City in the year 1999. In this book, almost as much a polemic as a novel, Harrison argues for serious population control. The loose cinematic adaptation of *Make Room!,* titled *Soylent Green* (1973), gives only a partial indication of the seriousness of Harrison's beliefs, emphasizing the concept of cannibalism rather than the necessity for contraception.

Harrison has also contributed to science fiction as a critic. With his friend Brian W. ALDISS, he founded the first serious journal of criticism in the genre, *SF Hori-*

zons. Although it was short-lived (the only two issues were published in 1964 and 1965), Harrison and Aldiss established in *SF Horizons* new standards for the genre, judging it as serious literature and inspiring other scholarly journals, among them *Extrapolation* and *Science Fiction Studies*. In 1972, with Aldiss and Leon E. STOVER, Harrison founded the John W. Campbell Memorial Award for the best SF novel of the year; its jury includes professional critics and academicians as well as authors; he was also the founder and first president of World SF, an international organization of SF professionals.

Harrison has been almost as prolific an editor as he has a writer. His excellent taste and high standards have made many of his short story anthologies distinctive. With Carol Pugner he edited *A Science Fiction Reader* (1973), a text for high school students, and with Willis E. McNelly he edited *Science Fiction Novellas* (1975), another text. He produced the excellent *The Light Fantastic* (1971), an anthology of SF classics from the mainstream. He also edited, with Aldiss, *Best SF* (1967–1975), *The Astounding-Analog Reader* (2 vols., 1972–1973), *Decade: The 1940's, the 1950's, the 1960's* (3 vols., 1975–1977), and *Hell's Cartographers* (1975), autobiographical essays by six SF authors.

OTHER WORKS: *Deathworld* (1960); *The Stainless Steel Rat* (1961); *Planet of the Damned* (1962); *War with the Robots* (1962); *Deathworld II* (1965); *Deathworld III* (1968); *Captive Universe* (1969); *Prime Number* (1970); *The Stainless Steel Rat's Revenge* (1970); *The Daleth Effect* (1970); *The Stainless Steel Rat Saves the World* (1972); *The Stainless Steel Rat Wants You!* (1979); *Planet Story* (1979); *Homeworld* (1980); *Starworld* (1981); *Wheelworld* (1981; published, with *Homeworld* and *Starworld*, as *To the Stars*, 1987); *The Jupiter Plague* (1982); *The Stainless Steel Rat for President* (1982); *Planet of No Return* (1982); *A Rebel in Time* (1983); *Adventures of the Stainless Steel Rat* (1984); *A Stainless Steel Rat Is Born* (1985); *The Stainless Steel Rat Gets Drafted* (1987).

W.E.M.

HARRYHAUSEN, RAY (1920–). American model animation and SPECIAL EFFECTS expert known for his skillful work in science-fiction and fantasy films. Harryhausen's style is characterized by an impressive combination of anatomical authenticity and creative fantasy, and his animated creations, whether actual animals (the dinosaurs in *One Million Years B.C.*, 1964) or mythological beasts (the Venusian Ymir of TWENTY MILLION MILES TO EARTH, 1957), are extraordinarily expressive.

As a young man Harryhausen expressed a keen interest in sculpture and paleontology, areas that later would give his animated work a distinctive verisimilitude. He was inspired by Willis O'BRIEN's stop-motion animation in the classic KING KONG (1933) and devoted himself to experimenting with a variety of animation techniques. O'Brien was a pioneer in the field and Harryhausen's idol, so the younger man eagerly took the opportunity to show O'Brien his early efforts, which he had produced in his family's garage. O'Brien hired Harryhausen as his assistant on MIGHTY JOE YOUNG (1949). Harryhausen immediately established his careful working methods by sending a motion picture cameraman to a zoo to photograph one of the gorillas in captivity; he used the footage to help give the film's animated ape an impressive array of individualized gestures.

After working briefly for George PAL's Puppetoon series and contributing animated effects to Frank Capra's film unit during World War II, Harryhausen independently produced a series of short animated fairy tales *(Little Red Riding Hood, Hansel and Gretel)*, refining his skills and steadily building his reputation. In the early 1950s he was hired to do the animation for Eugène Lourié's BEAST FROM 20,000 FATHOMS (1953), based on a short story by his old high school friend Ray BRADBURY. *Beast* was the first feature film for which Harryhausen was in charge of the special effects. Its opening sequence, in which the beast attacks a lighthouse, admirably captures the mood of Bradbury's story, and the dinosaur is clearly the film's star.

While working on the relatively low-budget *Beast*, Harryhausen began exploring new, resourceful methods of combining live backgrounds and animated models. For *The Seventh Voyage of Sinbad* (1959), the first film of this kind to be done in color, he developed the process he called Dynamization, which incorporates matte photography, sets built to scale, and the synchronization of animated and live-action photography. This film contains Harryhausen's most impressive work, particularly the sword fight between Jason and his men and seven skeletons. This sequence, which synchronized animation with live action, took four and a half months to produce.

His work on IT CAME FROM BENEATH THE SEA (1955), notable for its giant octopus, marked the beginning of a fruitful business relationship with producer Charles H. Schneer that lasted for seventeen years and involved many films.

Some of Harryhausen's later work seems simplistic in comparison to his earlier efforts, and recent advances in special effects technology have, to an extent, dated his brand of animation: even the complex Medusa sequence in *Clash of the Titans* (1981) falls short of its promise. Nevertheless, Harryhausen is one of SF film's genuine originals, and an artist in his own right.

B.K.G.

HASKIN, BYRON (1899–1984). American film director with a long and varied career, but generally known for his science-fiction movies produced by his

Ray Harryhausen's stop-motion animation for *One Million Years B.C.* (1964)

friend George PAL, particularly THE WAR OF THE WORLDS (1953) and THE POWER (1968). Haskin began working in film in 1917 and served in a variety of capacities including newsreel cameraman, cinematographer, special effects creator, second-unit director, and producer. He directed his first film in 1927. Although his films do not possess a discernible personal style, his best work reveals a thematically consistent view of nature as transcendent. The ant army in *The Naked Jungle* (1954), the vastness of space in CONQUEST OF SPACE (1955), and the destruction of the Martians by bacteria in *The War of the Worlds* all suggest humankind's subordination in the face of the power and plenitude of nature. Haskin's other films as director include FROM THE EARTH TO THE MOON (1958) and ROBINSON CRUSOE ON MARS (1964).

B.K.G.

HAWTHORNE, NATHANIEL (1804–1864).
American writer considered one of the greatest American literary figures of the nineteenth century. In Hawthorne's day the popularity of the Gothic novel was giving way to a renaissance of the utopian novel; at the same time many of the embryonic social sciences—particularly psychology—were beginning to exert an influence on Western thinking. It was natural, then, that Hawthorne—who was adept in both literary forms and a master of the psychological plot—interwove into his works (especially his short stories) what have become traditional science-fiction elements and techniques. Indeed, his body of work is peopled with a long line of doctors, chemists, botanists, mesmerists, physicists, and inventors, and his interest in extrapolating on the latest scientific knowledge—a mainstay of SF—permeates his stories. His mad scientists are legion: Heidegger, Aylmer, Rappaccini,

Chillingworth, Maule, Westervelt, Grimshawe, Dolliver, and others.

Like Jonathan SWIFT, Hawthorne dramatized the dangers inherent in an overreliance on science and criticized ruthless scientific experimentation. In "The Birthmark" (1843) the scientist Aylmer tries to perfect nature and pays dearly for his hubris (his wife pays with her life). Similarly, in "Rappaccini's Daughter" (1844) the scientist Rappaccini attempts to protect his daughter literally by poisoning her. Owen Warland, the artist-scientist of "The Artist of the Beautiful" (1844), places an idea—a mechanized butterfly—above human concerns. Like Ethan Brand, Hawthorne's scientists commit the unpardonable sin of pursuing intellectual achievements without regard for human suffering.

Although Hawthorne utilized SF techniques and elements, like Swift he was more concerned with the salvation of souls than with science. Everything in Hawthorne's fiction is subordinate to a highly complex moral allegory; he used science, as he used Puritan guilt, for its symbolic value.

M.T.W.

HAY, GEORGE (1922–).
British writer and editor known primarily as a promoter of science fiction—he was one of the founders of the British teaching and research society the Science Fiction Foundation, which publishes the journal *Foundation*—who also wrote four paperback SF novels in the early 1950s and edited four SF anthologies in the 1960s and 1970s. Hay's novels are *Flight of the Hesper* (1951), *Man, Woman, and Android* (1951), *This Planet for Sale* (1952), and *Terra* (1953), the last under the house name of King Lang. He edited *Hell Hath Fury* (1963), *The Disappearing Future*

(1970), *Stopwatch* (1974), and *The Edward De Bono Science Fiction Collection* (1976).

N.H.

HEARD, H[ENRY] F[ITZGERALD] (1889–1971).

British writer of fiction and religious philosophy, journalist, and editor, who moved to the United States in 1937. He also wrote as Gerald Heard. Heard's friendship with writers Aldous HUXLEY and Christopher Isherwood led to his association with and interest in Vedanta, a philosophy based on the Hindu Vedas. His interests in science (he wrote several books on EVOLUTION and scientific subjects), philosophy, and religion led to the writing of the SF science-fiction novel *Doppelgängers* (1947), which antedates (by a year) B. F. Skinner's *Walden Two* in its depiction of behavior control. *Doppelgängers,* however, presents a dystopia about a tyranny in which the masses are plied with pleasure to keep them docile.

Heard wrote on many topics, including clothing and its relation to civilization, flying saucers, murder mysteries, and God, all in a witty, sophisticated, sometimes involuted style, and many of his short stories using SF ideas are collected in *The Great Fog and Other Weird Tales* (1944) and *The Lost Cavern and Other Tales of the Fantastic* (1948). *The Black Fox* is a related Heard novel about the use of black magic by an English clergyman (1950).

H.L.P.

HEARTBEEPS (1981).

Directed by Allan Arkush; screenplay by John Hill; photographed by Charles Rosher, Jr.; music by John Williams. With Andy Kaufman, Bernadette Peters, Randy Quaid. 79 minutes. Color.

Andy Kaufman and Bernadette Peters portray wonderfully defective domestic ROBOTS in this 1981 "small film" masterpiece warmly directed by Allan Arkush. Their "defect," of course, is emotion; they want to see a sunset and raise a robot child. Accompanied by a robot comedian programmed to tell Henny Youngman jokes (badly and incessantly), the two robots become ever more human as they flee reprogramming and warehousing. Their creation of a robot child from junkyard parts and their sacrifice to ensure his future flirts with sentimental excess, but this remains one of the most winning and enjoyable of the growing number of SF films that question distinctions between "natural" and "unnatural" life.

B.L.

HEINLEIN, ROBERT A[NSON] (1907–1988).

American writer of science fiction, continuously active (except for a hiatus during World War II) since 1939.

Heinlein has been guest of honor at the 1941, 1961, and 1976 World Science Fiction Conventions and is the winner of the Hugo Award for best novel for *Double Star* (1956), *Starship Troopers* (1960), *Stranger in a Strange Land* (1962), and *The Moon Is a Harsh Mistress* (1967), and of the first SCIENCE FICTION WRITERS OF AMERICA's Grand Master Award (1975). He has served as a leader and model in the field not only because of his skill and intelligence as a writer but also because of his success in moving from the PULP MAGAZINES through the slicks to the best-seller.

Born and raised in Missouri and graduated from the U.S. Naval Academy in 1929, Heinlein retired from active service in 1934 as a result of illness. After postgraduate studies in mathematics and physics at the University of California, Los Angeles, another round of ill health, and a number of occupations, Heinlein turned to writing SF, selling his first story to *Astounding* in 1939; by 1942 he had produced three serials and twenty-five stories under his own byline and five pseudonyms (Anson MacDonald, Lyle Monroe, John Riverside, Caleb Saunders, Simon York). In less than three years Heinlein became one of the writers who defined an *Astounding*—and therefore a cutting-edge SF—story. His contributions to the field were as much matters of craft as of content, and perhaps most influential was his seamless integration of SF material into a story's action; his SF ideas were equally definitive. Damon KNIGHT called him "the nearest thing to a great writer the science-fiction field has yet produced." Modern SF takes its characteristics from Heinlein: idiomatically American, dense and detailed, futuristic but familiar, matter of fact about the marvels of domesticated engineering and technology.

Many of his early *Astounding* stories fit into the framework that came to be called the Future History series (largely collected in *The Past through Tomorrow,* 1967); in May 1941 John W. CAMPBELL printed a chart by Heinlein that plotted existing and proposed stories along with technological, social, and political changes on a time line running from the late twentieth to the twenty-second century. Revised versions of the chart appeared in the hardcover reprints of the magazine stories. More than thirty years after beginning the series, Heinlein produced the capstone Future History novel, *Time Enough for Love* (1973), which not only details "The Lives of Lazarus Long" (subtitle) but systematically addresses the major themes and problems the author has pursued throughout his career.

With few exceptions SF had been systematically confined to the pulp magazines, but after World War II Heinlein, like a modern Moses, led the way first into the slick, general fiction magazines, then into hardcover publication and the juveniles, and later still into films. He placed such stories as "The Green Hills of Earth" (1947) and "Ordeal in Space" (1948) in such markets as the *Saturday Evening Post* and *Town and Country.*

Robert A. Heinlein

Major hardcover houses published almost no genre SF until Heinlein started a juvenile series at Scribner's with *Rocket Ship Galileo* (1947) and continued it through a dozen volumes with remarkable financial and artistic success, sometimes including serialization by adult SF magazines.

Heinlein also was one of the first authors to get his magazine serials reprinted in hardcover by the fan publishers, first *Beyond This Horizon* (1942/1948), then *Sixth Column* (1941/1949), and the Future History collections *The Man Who Sold the Moon* (1950), *The Green Hills of Earth* (1951), *Revolt in 2100* (1953), and *Methuselah's Children* (1941/1958), among others. They were reprinted in paperback almost immediately. In his furthest excursion from the pulps, Heinlein became the second SF writer (after H. G. WELLS) to shape a serious SF film when he provided the story for the George PAL production of DESTINATION MOON (1950).

Heinlein's other ambition in the immediate postwar period was "to explain the *meaning* of atomic weapons through popular articles," as he wrote in *Expanded Universe* (1980), an extension of the concern he had expressed in the 1941 story "Solution Unsatisfactory." This urge to educate, seen in its pure form in nine articles with titles such as "How to Be a Survivor" and "The Last Days of the United States," written after World War II but not published until *Expanded Universe*, became one of the trademarks of his fiction. One of Heinlein's strengths has been his ability to show how things actually or might eventually work, and his transition from engineering to political, social, and moral matters is, in hind-

sight, unsurprising. His juveniles are implicitly didactic, increasingly concerned with the achievement of ethical and social maturity, and his essays are Heinlein's attempt to lead an adult audience toward his idea of responsible and rational behavior.

His art as a fiction writer may have reached its peak in the decade between 1949 and 1958, when his message was carefully integrated with his story in his juveniles beginning with *Red Planet* (1949) and in his adult novels *The Puppet Masters* (1951), about the attempted conquest of humanity by parasitic intelligences from Titan, and *Double Star* (1956), about an out-of-work actor who is conscripted to impersonate an interplanetary leader and eventually must take his place.

Didacticism and juvenile fiction converged dramatically when, in response to the antinuclear testing movement, Heinlein interrupted work on what would become *Stranger in a Strange Land* (1961) to write *Starship Troopers* (1959), which argues the necessity and worth of service, especially military service. Its graphic battles with the alien Bugs led Scribner's to reject the book, and it was published by Putnam; Heinlein wrote only one more juvenile (*Podkayne of Mars*, 1963). *Starship Troopers* marked the beginning of a negative shift in the public opinion of Heinlein, especially among liberal critics and readers, which accelerated after 1960 with the publication of such books as *Farnham's Freehold* (1964), *I Will Fear No Evil* (1970), and *Time Enough for Love*.

Critical reevaluation of earlier work (notably by Alexei and Cory PANSHIN, George Edgar Slusser, and H. Bruce Franklin) found some roots of a "bad" Heinlein. Since *Starship Troopers*, Heinlein has been variously characterized as a conservative, a militarist, a Calvinist, a sexist, a libertarian, a solipsist, and even a fascist. Such labels oversimplify a complex writer who has consistently and seriously wrestled with large and difficult matters, not only the how questions of engineering, space navigation, revolution, or immortality but the why questions—the meaning of love and individuality in a Darwinian struggle for species survival, of awareness in a universe of merely material processes.

Labelers also must account for *Stranger in a Strange Land*, in which an Earth child, orphaned among Martians, returns to Earth as to an alien culture and finally becomes the messiah of a new religion devoted to *grokking*, or total understanding of people or situations, and love. This book was a campus cult favorite and opened publishers' eyes to the possibilities of SF paperback bestsellers, which were confirmed by Frank HERBERT's *Dune*.

Heinlein certainly respects the moral accountability of the individual to himself or herself and to the social group. In fact, the tension between these two sets of demands fuels much of his fiction. A Heinlein protagonist is likely to be smarter, more rational, and more self-reliant than the surrounding group (who are often portrayed as muddled, self-interested, uninformed, and unreliable) but is likely to risk his life to defend their lives and freedoms. Perhaps these tensions explain his emphasis on elite groups, whose members' most intense loyalties are to each other and to abstract ideas—*Space Cadet* (1948), "Gulf" (1949), *Starship Troopers*—and, especially in his later work, on the family and not some larger social unit as the emotional and ethical center of life—*Methuselah's Children, The Rolling Stones* (1952), *Farnham's Freehold,* and, most of all, *Time Enough for Love.* They may also explain why Heinlein's protagonists so often feel at home on the literal or figurative frontier, ahead of the crowds, out where the rules are set by nature rather than by humans.

Despite health problems, Heinlein continued to work right through his eighth decade, with his books leading SF into the world of six- and seven-figure advances and onto the hardcover best-seller lists. Following the da capo movement begun in *Time Enough for Love,* his late books return to the characters and scenes of earlier tales and begin to gather many of them into an alternate-worlds framework: the adventures of *Number of the Beast* (1979) lead eventually to the universe of Lazarus Long; *Friday* (1982) is the sequel to "Gulf"; *Job: A Comedy of Justice* (1984) contains a reference to Heinlein's classic of paranoia, "They" (1941), and echoes the main conceit of "The Unpleasant Profession of Jonathan Hoag" (1942); *The Cat Who Walks through Walls* (1985) joins the world of Lazarus to that of *The Rolling Stones* and *The Moon Is a Harsh Mistress* (1965/1966); and *To Sail beyond the Sunset* (1987) concerns Lazarus's mother, Maureen Smith.

OTHER WORKS: *Farmer in the Sky* (1950); *Waldo and Magic, Inc.* (collection, 1950); *Destination Moon* (1950/ 1979); *Between Planets* (1951); *Starman Jones* (1952); *Assignment in Eternity* (collection, 1953); *The Star Beast* (1954); *Tunnel in the Sky* (1955); *Time for the Stars* (1956); *The Door into Summer* (1956/1957); *Citizen of the Galaxy* (1957); *Have Space Suit—Will Travel* (1958); *The Menace from Earth* (collection, 1959); *The Unpleasant Profession of Jonathan Hoag* (collection, 1959); *Glory Road* (1963); *Orphans of the Sky* (collection, 1964); *The Worlds of Robert A. Heinlein* (collection, 1966).

R.F.L.

HENDERSON, ZENNA [Née CHLARSON] (1917–1983).

American writer noted for her sensitive portrayals of children and of paranormal phenomena. Born near Tucson, Henderson spent most of her life as an elementary school teacher in rural Arizona. The classroom and the countryside were the twin roots of her thirty-year career in science fiction. She wrote only short stories, beginning with "Come On, Wagon" in THE MAGAZINE OF FANTASY AND SCIENCE FICTION (1951); four collections contain nearly her entire output.

Henderson's best-known creation is the People, a humanlike, psychically gifted alien race hiding in the American Southwest. Their exodus is chronicled—with pointed biblical parallels—in *Pilgrimage: The Book of the People* (1961) and *The People: No Different Flesh* (1966) and was the basis of a Hugo-nominated television movie, *The People* (1972).

School stories were Henderson's specialty. They allow events—ranging from glimpses of beatitude ("The Anything Box," 1956) to space war sufferings ("The Last Step," 1957)—to be shown from the perspectives of child and adult simultaneously. (Those who have criticized Henderson for occasional sentimentality have somehow overlooked her gift for horror.) Within her chosen range Henderson was an unobtrusive but precise miniaturist. The enduring appeal of her work lies in the wonders she showed us through the clear eyes of children and saints.

OTHER WORKS: *The Anything Box* (1965); *Holding Wonder* (1971).

S.L.M.

HERBERT, FRANK [PATRICK] (1920–1986).

American science-fiction writer. A true Renaissance man, Herbert was a newspaper reporter, lay Jungian analyst, photographer, ecologist, scuba diver, wine expert, pilot, and student of religions (to name only a few of his vocations and avocations) before he achieved lasting fame with *Dune* (1965) and its sequels, *Dune Messiah* (1970), *Children of Dune* (1976), *God Emperor of Dune* (1981), *Heretics of Dune* (1984), and *Chapterhouse: Dune* (1985), now collectively termed the Dune Chronicles.

Herbert was born in the Pacific Northwest, and his roots remained there throughout his life. In fact his epic masterpiece *Dune* grew out of a series of newspaper articles he was preparing about the control of sand dunes along the Oregon coast, which prompted an interest in desert religions and their messiahs. His formal education at the University of Washington was cut short by military service in World War II, and later in life he took considerable pride in his invitations to lecture and even to teach at the university level, in spite of the fact that he had never received a formal B.A. A voracious and catholic reader, he educated himself about many subjects after his return from military service. He researched each new interest meticulously, accumulating file folders crammed with information for later use in either his newspaper articles or his fiction.

This technique served him well in his first SF novel, published in ANALOG as "Under Pressure" (1956) (Herbert's preferred title was "The Dragon in the Sea"). This suspense-filled tale of twenty-first-century submarine warfare, its dangers, and their effects on the crew received considerable praise from submarine crews, who

Frank Herbert

DECEMBER 1963 50¢

analog
SCIENCE FACT — SCIENCE FICTION

DUNE WORLD | BY FRANK HERBERT

Original magazine serialization of *Dune* in the December 1963 issue of *Analog*

could not believe that its author had never been on a submarine except for a research visit. It served notice that Herbert had a first-class talent awaiting only development of his thematic material to achieve greatness.

That greatness came with *Dune*. In this literary epic—no other word describes the book adequately—Herbert brought to SF a sense of scene, fascinating and well-developed characters, thoroughness of detail, and an evocation of the familiar behind the wildly unfamiliar. This combination catapulted the book's sequels (*Dune* itself caught on after a period of years) not only to the top of SF best-seller lists, with the publication of *Children of Dune*, but into the awareness of a large segment of the reading public for whom SF was normally anathema. Thus Herbert reached a wide audience, composed of ecological enthusiasts, adventure story readers, students, teachers, and a few mainstream critics who had never before read a single word of science fiction. The popularity of *Dune* and its sequels brought Herbert five-, six-, and even seven-figure advances and helped take SF out of its almost self-imposed ghetto. Before *Dune* SF was provincial; after *Dune* it became universal.

A constant Herbert theme not only in the Dune Chron-

icles but in his many non-Dune novels is a single complex question: What is it to be human, and what characteristics distinguish genuine humanity? He played variations on this theme in the Dune Chronicles as he raised questions about Leto Atreides II, God Emperor of Dune. Transmogrified into a several-thousand-year-old giant sandworm that possesses thousands of human memories—a true racial memory—is Leto now human, or is he merely the greatest predator humanity has ever known? By extension the work asks if humanity itself is the predatory beast that will eventually destroy the race.

In both *The Santaroga Barrier* (1968) and *The White Plague* (1982), novels separated by more than a decade, Herbert addressed analogous problems. In the first book his hero, Gilbert Dasein, becomes less and less human as he gradually falls under the spell of a drug-laden cheese called jaspers; eventually he withdraws from humanity completely. In *The White Plague*, Herbert suggested that the passion for violence and revenge that seems to characterize the modern world may cause a bloodbath resulting in the death of humanity itself. This novel quite obviously reveals Herbert's Jungian training, for it is the feminine aspect of humanity, the Jungian

anima, that is under attack: a rather conventional mad
scientist avenging the accidental death of his wife and
children at the hands of terrorists has unleashed a highly
selective virus, which kills only women. In Herbert's
mordant but perceptive view, the rational, intellectual
aspect of humanity will die without the feminine spirit
to enlighten it just as the human species itself will die
without women to bear children.

Herbert felt strongly about many causes, particularly
ECOLOGY. If, as he indicated in *Dune*, ecology is the
science of understanding consequences, then understanding the potential results of any act must become
one of the highest pursuits of humanity. But while many
of his works are marked by an almost didactic fervor,
Herbert never permitted his enthusiastic endorsement of
an idea to obscure his primary function as storyteller.
Well aware that his books had to compete for both attention and money in a transient marketplace, he packed
his stories and novels with considerable dialogue and
much action. In the end he took more pride in his ability
to tell a good tale than in any ideas he might have embedded in his works.

Herbert's untimely death deprived the SF world of one
of its luminaries, but he had given that world one of its
genuinely great works with *Dune*. By that masterpiece
Herbert will always be remembered.

OTHER WORKS: *The Green Brain* (1966); *Destina-
tion: Void* (1966); *The Eyes of Heisenberg* (1966); *The
Heaven Makers* (1968); *Whipping Star* (1970); *The
Worlds of Frank Herbert* (collection, 1971); *The God-
makers* (1972); *Soul Catcher* (1973); *The Book of Frank
Herbert* (collection, 1973); *Hellstrom's Hive* (1973);
Threshold: The Blue Angels Experience (1973); *The
Best of Frank Herbert* (collection, 1975); *The Dosadi
Experiment* (1977); *The Jesus Incident* (with Bill Ran-
som, 1979); *The Lazarus Effect* (with Bill Ransom, 1983).

W.E.M.

**Illustration by the Hildebrandts for Terry Brooks's *The Sword
of Shannara***

HERSEY, JOHN (1914–   ).   American writer,
primarily known as a mainstream novelist, who made
use of science-fiction themes in three novels. *The Child
Buyer* (1960) describes a corporation in near-future
America that wants to buy hyperintelligent children. *White
Lotus* (1965) is set in an alternate time stream where
white America has been subjugated by the Chinese. Finally, in *My Petition for More Space* (1974), Hersey
depicted a rigidly totalitarian, overpopulated future world.

J.H.

HILDEBRANDT, GREG and TIM (1939–   ).
American fantasy illustrators. The twin Hildebrandt
brothers started their careers illustrating children's books
but are best known for their J. R. R. Tolkien calendars
(1976, 1977, and 1978) and the first STAR WARS poster.

In addition to advertising work for Coca-Cola, they have
done cover illustrations for DAW, Warner, New American Library, Ballantine, and Bantam Books, some of
them science fiction, but most in the fantasy genre. Especially noteworthy are their covers for Terry Brooks's
The Sword of Shannara (1900) and books by such diverse authors as Robert Louis Stevenson, Lester DEL REY,
Roger ZELAZNY, Anne McCAFFREY, C. L. MOORE, and Edgar
Rice BURROUGHS. Their style, influenced by Walt Disney
and the N. C. Wyeth-inspired Brandywine School, is
realistic, with great scope and detail, although some
critics have described even their most action-packed
paintings as still lifes; their use of color has been compared with that of Maxfield Parrish. The best collection
of their work is *The Art of the Brothers Hildebrandt*
(1979). In 1982 they stopped working as a team to pursue
separate art careers in SF and fantasy.

J.G.

HILTON, JAMES (1900–1954). British author, essentially a mainstream novelist, whose best-selling *Lost Horizon* (1933) may have been the last (and most successful) lost race novel. In it a group of typical English travelers discover the lost world of Shangri-La, a romanticized, escapist utopia in the Himalayas. The book was turned into an equally successful film by Frank Capra (1936).

                                                                                          J.H.

THE HITCH-HIKER'S GUIDE TO THE GALAXY (1981). *Directed by Douglas Adams; screenplay by Douglas Adams. With Simon Jones, David Dixon, Mark Wing-Davey, Peter Jones, Dave Prowse. British miniseries in seven 30-minute episodes. Color.*

The television version of *The Hitchhiker's Guide*, shown on PBS stations in 1982 and later, is the form in which most viewers have encountered this multimedia extravaganza created by Douglas Adams, but it was first a weekly, thirty-minute BBC radio serial and later a book with three sequels, a double record album, a computer game, and a film script.

Adams, then script editor for the long-running British TV series DR. WHO, conceived the radio show in 1978. Unimportant little Earth is destroyed by aliens to make room for an intergalactic freeway. The only survivor, Arthur Dent, is rescued by his friend Ford Prefect, an alien researcher for a revised edition of *The Hitchhiker's Guide to the Galaxy*, and they take off for a hilarious hitchhiking tour, allowing Adams room for great comic invention and opportunity to parody many conventions of SF through clichéd situations and characters, outrageous puns, and shaggy-dog conclusions.

Adams was encouraged by Simon Brett, who produced the first episode, and by Geoffrey Perkins, who produced the next eleven. The scripts were written episode by episode, and letters from listeners soon testified to the popularity of the show in general and of Marvin the paranoid android in particular.

Adams turned the series into a book, which was published in 1979; it quickly appeared on the mass-market best-seller list. A record album of the first four episodes also did well, and the second book in the series, *The Restaurant at the End of the Universe*, based on the last eight episodes of the radio series, was published in 1980.

The BBC television series based on the first six radio shows was broadcast in Britain beginning in January 1981. The third and fourth books in the series, *Life, the Universe and Everything* and *So Long, and Thanks for All the Fish*, were published in 1982 and 1984. All four books plus a new short story, "Young Zaphod Plays It Safe," were published in a single volume, *The Hitchhiker's Quartet*, in 1986. The original radio script was published in 1985. Infocom has created a computer game written by Adams and based on the series, and Adams has written a screenplay that has not yet been produced.

                                                                                          W.L.

HOBAN, RUSSELL [CONWELL] (1925–   ). American writer now living in London. Hoban is best known for his more than fifty works for children, which include a series of tales about Frances (a young raccoon) as well as *The Mouse and His Child* (1967) and *Emmet Otter's Jug-Band Christmas* (1971). He has written only one novel that is unambiguously science fiction, but that work, *Riddley Walker* (1980), is one of the finest renderings of the posthollocaust theme in the history of the genre. It describes a distant-future Earth long after a nuclear war, and its eponymous hero is a young man who wanders England in a quest for understanding. The shaman of his tribe, he instinctively feels the tension between technological progress, which has come again into the world, and the "traditional" life that has developed since the war.

The strength of the novel lies in Hoban's use of language to portray his dystopia: the novel is in the form of a memoir written by Riddley, who speaks a version of English that has undergone significant changes in phonology, grammar, and vocabulary. Through this alternate English Hoban gives his readers a vivid sense of how similar Riddley's world is to and at the same time how different it is from our present.

These similarities and differences are accentuated by the elaborate myths and legends of the novel's future England, particularly the myths of Addom—a symbol of both Everyman and the power of atomic fission. Religious and folk stories stress that the world and its inhabitants have experienced a great split, which has caused not only physical devastation but also a division between the heart and the mind. And while these tales warn Riddley of the coming dangers to his own society, they also give the reader a vivid sense of life in a world produced by events the inhabitants no longer understand or even remember.

Hoban received the John W. Campbell Memorial Award for best novel of the year for *Riddley Walker* in 1982, but he has yet to write another SF work. His other adult fiction, including *Pilgermann* (1983), is in the form of fantasies that occasionally make use of SF elements such as alternate history. However, even if *Riddley Walker* remains his sole work in the genre, Hoban will have a significant place in SF for that remarkable achievement.

                                                                                          S.H.G.

HODGSON, WILLIAM HOPE (1877–1918). British author killed in World War I. Hodgson's many short stories and novels, which drew on his experiences as a seaman, combine traditional horror with a science-inspired interest in bizarre life-forms and the world's far future. *The House on the Borderland* (1908) is noteworthy as an early parallel-world novel.

J.H.

HOFFMANN, E[RNST] T[HEODOR] A[MA-DEUS] (1776–1822).

German writer, composer, and jurist often credited, along with Edgar Allan POE and Nathaniel HAWTHORNE, with shaping the modern short story and contributing to the development of the genre that became science fiction. Hoffmann spent his early years in composing music, writing librettos, producing commentaries on music, and directing music for the theater. However, he is best known for his romantic writings, most of which are collected in three volumes: *The Devil's Elixir* (*Die Elixiere des Teufels*, 1816), *Night Pieces* (*Nachtstücke*, collection, 1817), and *The Serapion Brethren* (*Die Serapionsbruder*, 1819–1821). The stories in these volumes span a wide range of categories, including the supernatural, the merely mysterious, and detailed portraits of life in Germany, Italy, and France.

Hoffmann's interest in science paralleled his romanticism and mysticism. His fascination with Emanuel Swedenborg's visions of good and evil and Franz Mesmer's hypnotism frequently found its way into his stories. Those characters in his fiction who work with the sciences are, like artists, lonely men whose obsessions with their work make them virtual exiles. Typical of such a loner-hero is Dr. Coppelius in "The Sandman" (1816), who builds a female automaton so perfect that she becomes the object of love. A precursor of both Mary Wollstonecraft SHELLEY and Hawthorne, Hoffmann used science for his frequently grotesque romances not as a symbol of humanity's sin against God but as a way of making the fantastic credible.

S.H.G.

HOGAN, JAMES P[ATRICK] (1941–).

American writer and former computer sales executive whose fiction resembles the pre-1960 work of Robert A. HEINLEIN. Like Heinlein, Hogan creates protagonists who prove capable of overcoming all threats to humanity's continued progress despite the impasses posed by liberals, whom Hogan portrays as fuzzy headed, and corrupt politicians. His characters have little patience with protocol when serious work needs to be done. Neither Hogan nor his heroes suffer fools gladly—fools in this case being those who cling to outmoded behavior and values in the face of vast change.

Happily, Hogan shares another characteristic with the Heinlein of the 1940s and 1950s: he can tell a good story. In *Voyage from Yesteryear* (1982), for example,

he described an Earth colony in the Alpha Centauri system that has developed a wealthy and free society based on the abundant benefits of scientists who are free to investigate anything and everything. Of course, the economy of the Chironians is as freewheeling as its science. To this utopia come a shipload of future Pilgrims, who are appalled by so much libertarianism, and their leaders attempt to subvert the colony. Its plots and counterplots make *Voyage from Yesteryear* good reading, but its political viewpoint—which some readers will find extreme—needs to be at least tolerated or readers will miss the entertainment. The same blend of political viewpoint and adventure plot can be found in *Code of the Lifemaker* (1983), in which a charlatan leads a rebellion that preserves freedom for a race of robots; and in *The Minerva Experiment* (a trilogy that includes *Inherit the Stars*, 1977; *The Gentle Giants of Ganymede*, 1978; and *Giants' Star*, 1981), in which scientists try to solve the mystery caused by the discovery of an alien body on the Moon.

Hogan's faith in science and the American way is certain to put off a number of readers, and occasionally that faith gets in the way of his stories. Like Heinlein, however, he has a gift for storytelling that transcends politics.

OTHER WORKS: *The Genesis Machine* (1978); *The Two Faces of Tomorrow* (1979); *Thrice upon a Time* (1980); *The Proteus Operation* (1985); *Endgame Enigma* (1987).

S.H.G.

HOLBERG, LUDVIG (1684–1754).

Norwegian-born Danish poet, playwright, essayist, and historian. Holberg's *Journey of Niels Klim to the World Underground* (originally published in Latin, 1741) describes a voyage into the hollow center of the Earth, where the narrator visits various nations, human and animal, whose peculiarities cast satiric reflections on contemporary customs and institutions. Only the sedate, treelike people of Potu (Utopia) have established the rationally balanced social order Holberg favored.

J.H.

HOLDSTOCK, ROBERT P. (1948–).

British writer. A popular author in both Britain and the United States, Holdstock has produced a range of work from movie-novelization potboilers to finely crafted, award-winning fantasies; he has published novels and short fiction in the genres of horror, the occult, fantasy, and science fiction, both under his own name and under various pseudonyms. His pseudonymous work includes the novels in the Nighthunter series (written as Robert Faulcon) and novelizations of horror films (written as Robert Black). Under his own name, he produced the

SF novels *Eye among the Blind* (1976), *Earthwind* (1977), and *Where Time Winds Blow* (1982), as well as the occult novel *Necromancer* (1978) and a collection of short fiction, *In the Valley of the Statues* (1982). His short fantasy "Mythago Wood," inspired by Celtic myth, won the British Science Fiction Association's award for best short story of 1981; his later novel of the same title won the association's award for best novel of 1984. *Mythago Wood* was also the co-winner (with Barry Hughart's *Bridge of Birds*) of the 1985 World Fantasy Award.

B.D.

HOMUNCULUS (DIE RACHE DES HO-MUNKULUS) (1916). *Directed by Otto Rippert; screenplay by Otto Rippert and Robert Neuss; adapted from the novel by Robert Reinert; photographed by Carl Hoffmann. With Olaf Foenss, Friedrich Kuehne, Aud Egede-Nissen, Theodor Loos. 6 episodes; 401 minutes. Black and white.*

Homunculus was popular with both the public and European film critics such as Lotte Eisner, who later called it "remarkable . . . extraordinary." In this fantasy, one of the earliest of the *Frankenstein*-inspired films, a laboratory-created superman, Homunculus (Olaf Foenss), proves intellectually and morally formidable—until he discovers his nonhuman origins. Like Frankenstein's monster, he then runs amok and on a rather grand scale: he establishes himself as a ruthless dictator, a kind of prevision of Hitler. Ultimately, only lightning can stop him. Photographs of the imposing, black-cloaked Foenss suggest the serial's visual power, although its extreme length is equally imposing.

D.W.

HORNIG, CHARLES D. (1916–). American science-fiction magazine editor. Hornig was hired by Hugo GERNSBACK to edit *Wonder Stories* in 1933, after the magazine's first editor, David LASSER, left to head the Workers Alliance of America. Hornig was only seventeen years old and had yet to finish high school but Gernsback hired him because he had seen, and admired, the first issue of Hornig's fanzine, *The Fantasy Fan*. Hornig's enthusiasm for new ideas in SF coincided with F. Orlin TREMAINE's "thought-variant" phase, which also emphasized the idea content of SF, at *Astounding*, and produced Stanley WEINBAUM's first story, the classic "A Martian Odyssey." It also led to the pioneer fan organization—Gernsback's suggestion but Hornig's execution—the Science Fiction League. Hornig remained with *Wonder Stories* until it was sold in 1936; he later edited *Science Fiction*, *Future Fiction*, and *Science Fiction Quarterly*. He was a conscientious objector in World War II.

E.L.D.

THE HORROR OF FRANKENSTEIN: SEE FRANKENSTEIN ON FILM

HOSKINS, ROBERT (1933–). American author, agent, and editor. Born in Lyons Falls, New York, Hoskins attended Albany State College for Teachers for a year before working in the family business, during which time he sold his first science-fiction story, "Feet of Clay," to *If* in 1958, and then serving as an attendant in a school for the retarded. Like many other authors and editors, he worked as an agent for the Scott Meredith Literary Agency; after a year he became senior editor at Lancer Books in 1969.

Hoskins began his career as a novelist while still at Lancer, selling his first books to the publishing house as Grace Corren, including his first science-fiction novel, *Evil in the Family* (1972). Soon, however, he was selling to other publishers and had published eight SF novels—primarily action adventure—by 1979. He has also published suspense novels and gothics as Susan Jennifer, Michael Kerr, and Grace Corren, as well as science fiction as John Gregory.

Hoskins has made more significant contributions to the field as an editor with a series of anthologies, most particularly five issues of an original anthology, *Infinity*, for Lancer (1970–1973) and two issues of a historical anthology, *Wondermakers*, for Fawcett (1972–1974).

OTHER WORKS: *The Shattered People* (1975); *Master of the Stars* (1976); *To Control the Stars* (1977); *Tomorrow's Son* (1977); *Jack-in-the-Box Planet* (1978); *To Escape the Stars* (1978); *Legacy of the Stars* (1979).

J.E.G.

HOUSE OF DRACULA: SEE FRANKENSTEIN ON FILM

HOUSE OF FRANKENSTEIN: SEE FRANKENSTEIN ON FILM

HOYLE, FRED (1915–). British astronomer and writer, something of an enfant terrible in the British scientific establishment, whose science-fiction novels generally feature mavericks of the scientific community battling to save the world.

HOYLE, GEOFFREY (1942–). British writer and son of Fred Hoyle, with whom he has collaborated on numerous works of science fiction, including many for juvenile readers.

With Thomas Gold and Hermann Bondi, Fred Hoyle formulated the steady-state theory of the universe, which gradually lost out in competition with the Big Bang theory; more recently he and Chandra Wickramasinghe have made the controversial claim that life originated in deep space and that diseases such as influenza are not infectious but instead are contracted from virus particles falling from the sky. Hoyle's novel *The Black Cloud* (1957) is a classic of hard SF and features apocalyptic contact with a strange alien intelligence; *October the First Is Too Late* (1966) describes a similarly apocalyptic fragmentation of local space-time.

Most of Hoyle's later novels were written in collaboration with his son Geoffrey; the best is the catastrophe story *The Inferno* (1973). His work is rich in scientific speculation but sometimes stylistically awkward, and his fiction cannot compare for boldness or a sense of wonder with his better nonfiction, including *Of Men and Galaxies* (1964), *Lifecloud* (with Wickramasinghe, 1978), and *Ice: The Ultimate Human Catastrophe* (1981).

OTHER WORKS: By Fred Hoyle: *Ossian's Ride* (1959); *Element 79* (1967). Notable works by Fred and Geoffrey Hoyle: *Fifth Planet* (1963); *Rockets in Ursa Major* (1969); *Seven Steps to the Sun* (1970); *Into Deepest Space* (1974); *The Incandescent Ones* (1977); *The Westminster Disaster* (1978). By Fred Hoyle and John Elliot (novelizations of TV scripts): *A for Andromeda* (1962); *The Andromeda Breakthrough* (1964).

B.S.

HUBBARD, L[AFAYETTE] RON[ALD] (1911–1986).
American writer, philosopher, and philanthropist. After a long and successful career as a prolific author of pulp fiction of many kinds, including science fiction and fantasy, Hubbard wrote a best-selling book about a simplified form of psychoanalysis he called Dianetics (1950), and it developed, often via ties to SF (through editors who publicized it, writers who became involved in it, and fans who joined it), into a full-blown, well-publicized, worldwide system of therapy and a controversial, disputatious religion, Scientology, of which Hubbard became the multimillionaire leader and prophet. In his last years, perhaps to restore his early standing as an SF author, he returned to the field with a long novel, *Battlefield Earth* (1983), and a satiric "dekalogy," Mission Earth, beginning with *The Invader's Plan* (1985), much of which was published posthumously. As a consequence, an evaluation of Hubbard's contribution to modern SF must await careful examination of a long career that continues to influence both the writing of SF and the public at large.

Decades ago Hubbard's notion of the use of rational analytic methods to improve the mind (and through it the body) had a profound influence on the thinking of Golden Age editor John W. CAMPBELL and other pulp writers of the time; it undoubtedly contributed to the predominantly positive outlook of early SF. Even in the late 1980s Hubbard's influence continued: using funds

L. Ron Hubbard

from his substantial fortune, he founded organizations called Bridge Publications and Author Services, which continued after his death to publish and publicize his books and to fund an ongoing contest called Writers of the Future to identify and reward new writers and publish their work in a series of anthologies.

Hubbard's energy and worldview manifested themselves early in his career in a large body of pulp adventure writing that is too easily dismissed for its worst qualities. His return to the field with *Battlefield Earth* and his dekalogy was marked by more repetitive adventure drama than any adult reader can long endure. Yet Hubbard's rapid, voluminous production of the 1930s and 1940s elicited from readers and fellow authors admiration for his writing skills and narrative drive.

Although Hubbard had been successful with other genres of pulp adventure, such as the sea story, SF and fantasy dominated his output in the decade following his first appearance in *Astounding* with "The Dangerous Dimension" (1938). He published under his own name as well as under Rene Lafayette, Kurt von Rachen, and numerous other pseudonyms. Typical of the positivism of his later philosophical thought, the Hubbard hero is generally a superman with highly developed mental powers destined to save the world. The dictator-hero of *Final Blackout* (1940/1948), a much admired, prophetic, end-of-civilization serial in *Astounding,* is perhaps the best-known example of Hubbard's personal brand of elitism.

Hubbard also published influential fantasy under his own name in *Astounding*'s companion magazine, *Unknown,* and under pseudonyms he wrote popular SF stories such as the Doc Methuselah series (collected in 1970 as *Old Doc Methuselah*) and the Kilkenny Cats series. But because there was originally no book market for Golden Age SF and because Hubbard published under so many names, sorting out the texts from this stage of his career will be nearly as difficult as evaluating his later philosophical impact. As an artist, Hubbard was probably best at a kind of ironic self-consciousness about being a mass-market writer. *Typewriter in the Sky* (1940/1951), which anticipates plot gimmicks now popular among experimental metafictionists, ought to be taken seriously by the critics who will evaluate his strange genius.

OTHER WORKS: *Buckskin Brigades* (1937); *Death's Deputy* (1948); *Slaves of Sleep* (1948); *Triton, and Battle of Wizards* (1949); *The Kingslayer* (1949); *Fear and Typewriter in the Sky* (1951); *Science Fantasy Quintet* (1953); *Return to Tomorrow* (1954); *Fear and the Ultimate Adventure* (1970).

D.M.H.

HULL, E[DNA] MAYNE (1905–1975).
Canadian-born American writer of science fiction who was married to A. E. van Vogt from 1939 to her death. Although the stories Hull wrote in the mid-1940s for *Astounding* and *Unknown* appeared under her own name, her novels—*Planets for Sale* (1954), featuring the unscrupulous interstellar businessman Artur Blord, and *The Winged Man* (1966)—and collection—*Out of the Unknown,* 1948—appeared as collaborations with her husband.

Hull worked as an auditor for Dianetics from 1950 to 1975, during which time she did almost no writing.

N.H.

HUNTER, MEL (1929–?).
American illustrator who did most of his work for The Magazine of Fantasy and Science Fiction, with some additional covers for Galaxy, *If,* and *Science Fiction Adventures.* In his work for SF magazines, Hunter produced only cover illustrations, never black-and-white interiors. In addition, he illustrated Alan E. Nourse's nonfiction book *Nine Planets* (1960, revised 1970) and painted some of the murals in the Transportation and Travel Pavilion at the 1963 World's Fair. His style was firmly realistic and often ironic. He is best known for his whimsical robots, which appear in most of his paintings, usually engaged in delightfully human activities in vast, desolate, postholocaust landscapes.

J.G.

HUXLEY, ALDOUS [LEONARD] (1894–1963).
British novelist and essayist, whose *Brave New World* (1932) is the example always cited of mainstream science fiction. The grandson of T. H. Huxley, Charles Darwin's champion and H. G. Wells's teacher, Huxley gained recognition in the 1920s as a satirist whose novels often are vehicles for sophisticated intellectual debate. *Brave New World* is the dystopian novel by which he is best known today, and, along with George Orwell's *Nineteen Eighty-four,* it is often read in American high schools. Because of their acceptance in the literary canon, these books are considered above and outside the SF category, although they are clearly SF by any definition.

Brave New World projects into the twenty-fifth century Henry Ford's assembly line (Ford has been deified) to imagine a high-technology world that has given up personal freedom for stability, affluence, and freedom from age, pain, disease, and poverty. These goals are achieved by genetic manipulation (identical babies, decanted from bottles, are bred and conditioned for their status in society), drugs (soma), entertainment (feelies), and free, ritualized sex (orgy-porgy). The novel's major conflict arrives with the discovery of "the Savage," who has grown to maturity on a primitive reservation with romantic, poetic notions; the conflict between these notions and the society come to a focus in a dialogue with Mustapha Mond, the World Controller for Western Europe. Twenty-five years later, in *Brave New World Revisited* (nonfiction, 1958), Huxley looked at his predictions and found some of them close to reality. *Brave New World* was filmed, as a four-hour miniseries for television in 1978, but it was not broadcast until 1980 and was unsuccessful.

Huxley turned with some frequency to SF ideas in his other works. The satiric novel *After Many a Summer Dies the Swan* (1939) offers a bizarre climax to the theme of longevity. *Ape and Essence* (1948) is an early depiction of the grim consequences of nuclear holocaust. Rather than becoming pessimistic in his later years, like Jules Verne and H. G. Wells, Huxley made a turn of his own from satire to hope: *Island* (1962), with its combination of Western science and Eastern philosophy, is one of the last of the utopias. But two world wars and other disillusionments made it impossible to conceive of "good places that were no place." The mood of the mid–twentieth century was dystopian.

J.H.

I

I MARRIED A MONSTER FROM OUTER SPACE
(1958). *Directed by Gene Fowler, Jr.; screenplay by Louis Vittes; photographed by Haskell Boggs. With Gloria Talbott, Tom Tryon, Alan Dexter, Robert Ivers, Chuck Wassill, Peter Baldwin, John Eldredge, Maxie Rosenbloom. 78 minutes. Black and white.*

This film is best known for being better than its title would indicate. Because it focuses on a woman, it's occasionally misread as an early feminist tract, but the title is simple sensationalism, although the film's style consistently undercuts this aim.

Aliens, fleeing the nova that killed their women, kidnap a man on his wedding night and impersonate him and others in his town. Eventually one wife (Talbott) begins to question her husband's humanity. She enlists the help of human men and dogs, and overcomes the invaders.

Made quickly on a low budget and compromised by its more lurid aspects, this film is nevertheless atmospheric, witty, and intelligent; some sympathy is even offered for the aliens. But director Fowler, whose *I Was a Teenage Werewolf* (1957) was also above average, returned to editing.

B.W.

ICEMAN (1984).
Directed by Fred Schepisi; screenplay by Chip Proser and John Drimmer; photographed by Ian Baker; music by Bruce Smeaton. With Timothy Hutton, John Lone, Lindsay Crouse, Josef Sommer, David Straitharn, James Tolkan. 101 minutes. Color.

Iceman combines two science-fiction film ideas that have recurred since the silent era: the caveman on the loose and the revival of a frozen body. The makers of the film seem to have been unaware of the familiar story lines and to have proceeded with an intelligent authority; the film ultimately does not succeed, however, and will probably be regarded as an odd footnote in the careers of all concerned.

Iceman is the story of a scientific team who revive a frozen Neanderthal man in the Arctic. Its central virtues are the beautiful, chilly cinematography of Ian Baker, believable scientific details, and the inventive, imaginative performance of John Lone as Charlie the Neanderthal. This was the actor's first significant film role, and he creates the most convincing primitive man in film history, superior even to the characters in QUEST FOR FIRE (1981). His Charlie is a rounded personality, with a sense of humor, memories, a friendly nature, and powerful fears and superstitions. Unfortunately, after Charlie is

Illustration by J. Allen St. John for Edgar Rice Burroughs's *Tarzan and the City of Gold*

revived, the story essentially marks time until the climax. Anthropological details are muddled—would modern-day Eskimos still practice the same religion as Neanderthals of hundreds of thousands of years ago? The scenes between Charlie and the two scientists are funny and touching, but the film falls short of what it could have been.

B.W.

I'LL NEVER FORGET YOU: SEE BERKELEY SQUARE

THE ILLUSTRATED MAN (1968).
Directed by Jack Smight; screenplay by Howard B. Kreitsek; adapted from the book by Ray Bradbury; photographed by Philip Lathrop; music by Jerry Goldsmith. With Rod Steiger, Claire Bloom, Robert Drivas, Don Dubbins, Jason Evers, Tim Weldon, Christie Matchett. 103 minutes. Color.

This film is an adaptation of three episodes from Ray BRADBURY's book: "The Veldt," "The Long Rains," and "The Last Night of the World." In "The Veldt" two children in the future use a three-dimensional toy to create an African setting, complete with lions. Their parents, lured into this tableau, are killed by the lions. Set on the planet Venus, "The Long Rains" involves the futile wandering of a group of lost people during incessant rains. In "The Last Night of the World" parents living in an outdoor pavilion in the far-distant future peacefully kill themselves and their progeny in compliance with a worldwide suicide pact brought on by impending holocaust.

Like the work of Edgar Allan POE, Bradbury's surreal stories are often mistaken for hard-core science fiction; however, whether set on Mars or not, his tales are macabre and magical revelations of the psyche. Brian W. ALDISS has called Bradbury "the Hans Christian Andersen of the jet age." This sense of magic, however, is far more vividly realized in the book than in the movie.

The film's framing device—a man whose body is tattooed by a mysterious seductress with stories that come to life as episodes in the future—did not work well in the book either. But cinema suffers more than literature when it attempts to unite distantly related stories. The brief interludes connecting the three episodes, although visually striking, tend to be a distraction rather than a unifying element. The lethargic pace of the film and its poor audio quality provide little incentive for viewers to endure the entire movie. However, the film does at times capture the dreamlike, sometimes nightmarish, qualities of Bradbury's poetic fiction.

D.P.V.

ILLUSTRATION

The function of illustration in literature containing exotic settings or extraordinary concepts is to provide the reader with a frame of reference to aid in understanding the author's ideas. For the science-fiction story, which deals with characters and events far removed from common experience, this function can be particularly important. The bond between the SF story and its supporting artwork is among the strongest in literature, yet either, if sufficiently well conceived and crafted, can stand independently. The SF painting is unique among other forms of commercial illustration in that it is not often subject to stylistic trends or linked to specific historical periods that would tend to date it. At its weakest it is seldom less than a quaint curiosity. At its best it can be a window into the future and a means of expanding the imagination while revealing as much about the here and now as it does about the tomorrows yet to come.

Pictures drawn in the sand to transmit and illuminate ideas must have been one of the first forms of human communication. Early links between picture making and the expression of fantastic ideas can be seen in works of Sumerian, Egyptian, Greek, and Roman art. Tales of mythical beasts, strange and outlandish places, marvelous devices, and bizarre astral voyages are part of the fabric of human culture. Even before the beginnings of civilization, one can imagine *Australopithecus* sitting in the lower limbs of a tree with envious eyes turned skyward to observe birds as they flittered from branch to branch. Dreams of flight, fearsome visions of unseen night terrors, wonder about the nature and movement of the Sun, Moon, and stars, speculation about death and about life on distant worlds and in other planes of existence—these are the elements of which fantastic ideas are born, and they have been with humanity since the dawn of human intelligence.

The oldest surviving examples of book art date back to the medieval period, when they took the form of manuscript illuminations. In the Islamic world early in the thirteenth century, illuminations were used to illustrate Persian poems as well as the Koran. Illustration was done by hand even after Johannes Gutenberg introduced the first books in Europe printed from movable type in about 1450. Although the Chinese experimented with block printing as early as the eighth century, not until the late 1400s, with the development of the block book, were artists able to create a single work cut in wood from which multiple impressions could be made. Within a century copperplate engravings replaced the wooden blocks and provided greater ease and versatility in the creation of artwork for reproduction. Engraving methods limited the artist to working in line until the late nineteenth century, when the development of the line screen and other processes allowed for the re-creation of halftones. Line art continues to be used and has become an honored tradition in SF magazines. Part of the reason for its persistence is its quality of reproduction on the inferior pulp paper on which many of these periodicals were printed during what was commonly known as the pulp era (circa 1896 to the mid-1950s; see PULP MAGAZINES).

The works of Hieronymus Bosch (1450?–1516) and Leonardo da Vinci (1452–1519) exerted a significant influence on the portrayal of fantastic subjects during the period preceding the Industrial Revolution. Bosch's vivid depictions of a world dominated by demonic forces reflect a popular fear that the erosion of medieval values by the forces of change was the work of Satan. Although his art is regarded as a precursor of surrealism, Bosch was less concerned with the search for human identity than with reacting to the spirit of political, economic, and technological progress in his own time. Da Vinci, by contrast, embraced change and did much to foment it. As an artist, architect, engineer, scientist, and inventor, da Vinci is regarded as one of the most capable and original thinkers of the Renaissance. His secret notebooks abound in detailed descriptions of inventions that far exceeded the knowledge of his time, particularly in their depictions of aerodynamic principles and their extrapolations on mechanized warfare. The sharply contrasting views of these two artistic geniuses characterize a division that has long endured in the portrayal of prog-

ILLUSTRATION   232

Cover art by Hubert Rogers (October 1940)

Cover art by Alex Schomberg (March 1953)

ress and its fundamental value to humankind.

By the last half of the nineteenth century, the SF novel had begun to grow in popularity and form, reaching its peak with the works of Jules VERNE and H. G. WELLS. During this period a number of artists became associated with SF. Notable among them were Isidore Grandville, who startled and delighted French readers with his amusing drawings of grotesque creatures in the book *Un Autre Monde* (1844); Albert Robida, whose inventive visions of future life, technology, and warfare in *Le Vingtième Siècle* (1883) and *La Vie électrique* (1887?) seemed like predictions; and Warwick Goble, whose illustrations for the serialization of Wells's novel *The War of the Worlds* for *Pearson's Magazine* (1897) were a departure from the rigidity of the works of his Victorian contemporaries. Characterized by a dramatic sense of abstract composition and fluidity, Goble's art heralded the beginnings of modern SF illustration.

An artist who rose to prominence during the early decades of the pulp era was J. Allen ST. JOHN (1872–1957). He was the principal illustrator for the works of Edgar Rice BURROUGHS, and his facile style became widely known. The sheer bravura of his handsomely crafted drawings and paintings later influenced generations of artists of heroic fantasy, beginning with Roy G. KRENKEL and Frank FRAZETTA and continuing into the present.

Another artist whose work appeared in the magazines at about the same time and with perhaps a greater in-fluence on SF art was Frank R. PAUL (1884?–1963). Born in Austria and trained as an architect, Paul worked as a newspaper illustrator before being discovered by Hugo GERNSBACK, the founder and publisher of the first SF magazine, AMAZING STORIES (which first appeared in 1926). Paul is generally considered the father of SF illustration; his work, though often crude, was highly inventive and established many of the visual conventions of the genre. Using large areas of flat, bright color, Paul endeavored to cope with the problems of poor print reproduction and in so doing created a body of vivid, intricately detailed art that came to be strongly identified with the field. As a logical extension of the work of his Victorian antecedents, Paul's art rose to the vanguard of gadget illustration. Largely because of his influence, paintings that emphasize science and technology have long been considered a key component of the genre.

Many artists emulated Paul, some with greater artistic skill but few with his genius for invention. Among the best known were Hans Wessolowski (known simply as WESSO), who worked primarily for ASTOUNDING STORIES (*Amazing*'s chief competitor); Leo Morey, who replaced Paul at *Amazing* when it changed ownership in 1929; Robert Fuqua, who used much the same style of outlining and composition; and Alex Schomberg, who worked in the comic-book field as well as for the pulps. Others—such as Malcolm Smith, H. R. van Dongen, Mel HUNTER, and Edward VALIGURSKY—distinguished themselves in the

Cover art by Leo and Diane Dillon

creation of gadget art but developed highly individual styles. Among the most skilled of these artists was Howard V. BROWN, who worked mainly for *Astounding* but also for *Startling Stories*. Brown brought many mainstream values to the field and was a skilled colorist and figure painter.

A series of paintings of the planet Saturn as seen from its moons appeared in the May 29, 1944, issue of *Life* magazine and were the first published works of their kind by Chesley BONESTELL (1888–1986). Bonestell's highly detailed, realistic paintings had an important effect on astronomical art, and their consistency with accepted scientific information stimulated much public interest in astronomy before the beginning of the U.S. space program. From the mid-1940s through the 1950s, Bonestell's work appeared in such magazines as *Life, Look, Collier's,* and *Coronet* as well as in a number of well-received book collaborations with such space and rocketry experts as Willy LEY, Wernher von Braun, and Arthur C. CLARKE. Some of his work appeared on the covers of SF magazines, most notably THE MAGAZINE OF FANTASY

AND SCIENCE FICTION and *Astounding,* and in the George PAL SF films DESTINATION MOON (1950), WHEN WORLDS COLLIDE (1951), THE WAR OF THE WORLDS (1953), and THE CONQUEST OF SPACE (1955). His influence can be seen in virtually all contemporary astronomical art and was important in paving the way for such artists as Robert McCall, Mel Hunter, and Pierre Mion.

By the end of World War II the paperbound book began to flourish as a commercial entity and eventually played a role in bringing about the demise of the pulps. Many pulp artists made the transition to paperbacks, but other artists came to this new market with little background in magazines. Among them was Stanley Meltzoff (1917–), one of the first paperback artists to specialize in SF illustration. Clearly the work of a brilliant craftsman, Meltzoff's paintings for the early Signet SF novels are outstanding examples of art in the genre. His unique talent for scientific detail and his skill as a figure painter caused his work to be widely imitated. Paul Lehr (1931–) and John SCHOENHERR (1935–), who became major contributors to the genre, studied under Meltzoff at the Pratt Institute. Lehr, though more surrealistic in approach, held closely to Meltzoff's tenets for a time before developing his own style. Schoenherr, one of the more painterly artists of the genre, distinguished himself with depictions of alien creatures and environmental subjects during the 1960s and became strongly identified with the field through a series of cover paintings for Frank HERBERT's Dune novels. Vincent DI FATE (1945–) is a contemporary example of the Meltzoff influence. Known for his depictions of technological subjects, Di Fate does work that varies from hard edged to more painterly. He uses the naturalistic palette that distinguishes this group of painters from the more color intense pulp artists.

Others of note who have made a specialty out of gadget art are Christopher Foss, a British painter who combines airbrush with oils; Dean ELLIS, who uses a crisp, posterized style; and John Berkey, whose work has an impressionistic flavor.

Although gadget art continues to be a formidable presence in SF illustration, a focus on unusual and exotic characters is yet another important aspect of the field. Hubert ROGERS (1898–1982), who did many covers for *Astounding,* developed a symbolic approach and used many mainstream techniques in his well-crafted paintings. A skilled portraitist, Rogers in his interior art often avoided action scenes in favor of isolated portrayals of the main story characters. In so doing he instigated a fashion later followed by artists such as Frank Kelly Freas (1922–) and Jack Gaughan (1930–1985). Earle K. BERGEY (?–1952) was a fine figure painter who worked mainly for the secondary SF pulps, such as *Startling Stories* and *Thrilling Wonder Stories,* and the paperbacks. His talent for portraying voluptuous women has diminished his legacy, however, for he is sometimes looked down on for having popularized the brass bras-

ILLUSTRATION   234

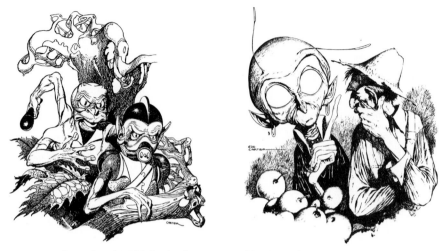

Illustrations by Edd Cartier for L. Ron Hubbard's "Ole Doc Methuselah"

siere as an article of futuristic feminine attire. Other artists who flourished in the magazines include Hannes BOK, who used a glaze technique similar to that of the renowned artist Maxfield Parrish; Edd CARTIER, who created art with a whimsical flavor for *Astounding* and *Unknown;* and Virgil FINLAY, who is well remembered today for his meticulous black-and-white illustrations.

Freas began his career in 1950 with the magazine *Weird Tales*. By 1953, following in a natural progression from the work of Cartier, Freas became a regular contributor to *Astounding* (which became ANALOG in 1960) and remained closely associated with it until the magazine was purchased by Davis Publications in 1981. The sentimental quality of his color work and the often humorous nature of his interiors endeared him to many SF readers and made him the recipient of more awards than any other SF illustrator. Ed EMSHWILLER (1925–   ), sometimes known as Emsh or Emshler, began his career with GALAXY magazine in 1951 and worked for most of the SF digests and the paperback market before switching to a career in video filmmaking in the mid-1960s. Emshwiller also employed humor and won considerable acclaim. He occasionally integrated abstract elements into his otherwise representational work and was a strong compositionalist. Other artists with a sometimes whimsical flare were Leo Ramon SUMMERS and Jack Gaughan. By the mid-1960s Gaughan had become a major SF artist, championed artists' rights, and done much as the art director for *Galaxy, World of If,* and later *Cosmos* to encourage the introduction of new talent to the magazines.

Frank Frazetta (1928–   ) had worked for twenty years in the comic books before turning to free-lance illustra-

tion in 1964. Combining the sensual, larger-than-life romanticism of Renaissance master Peter Paul Rubens with the simpler, more direct compositional approach of J. Allen St. John, Frazetta created an appealing style that has made him perhaps the most imitated of all SF artists. His Tarzan and Pellucidar covers for Ace Books forged the link to the earlier works of St. John and established Frazetta as the foremost creator of heroic fantasy art. Notable among his works of the mid to late 1960s were a series of horrific covers for the illustrated Warren magazines, *Eerie* and *Creepy*. Other artists who distinguished themselves working in the heroic manner are Jeff Jones, Boris VALLEJO, Rowena MORRILL, and, to a lesser extent, Michael WHELAN, who developed a more defined and sedate style.

Until 1970 most paperbacks cost less than a dollar and were considered impulse purchases. Like many products intended for mass consumption, these books were packaged with the lowest common denominator in mind. Thus, representationalism has long been the prevailing approach to paperback cover art. In the early 1950s artists such as Stanley Meltzoff and Robert Schulz created a stir with their ultrarealistic SF paintings, and although other types of books experimented with various cover approaches, SF, with only a few notable exceptions, stayed close to its ties to representational painting.

James Bama (1926–   ) had been a realist since the beginning of his career in 1950, but in the early 1960s he developed a style that was so photographic and finely detailed that it revolutionized paperback illustration. Although his involvement with SF was infrequent, the sixty-two covers he painted for the Bantam editions of Kenneth ROBESON's Doc Savage novels (reprinted from a Street and Smith pulp of the 1930s) are among the best crafted and most consistent works ever done for an SF book series. Using largely monochromatic color schemes, Bama captured the proper mix of 1930s pulp adventure and modern photorealism. He left the field in 1971 to turn his attentions to fine art. His protégé and closest imitator, Peter Caras, produced a similar series of paintings for another Robeson character, The Avenger, for Warner Paperback Library. Fred Pfeiffer used a more painterly, though still quite realistic, approach on several of the Doc Savage titles after Bama's departure and did a few outstanding paintings for other SF books while under contract to Bantam in the late 1970s. Other realistic artists who have done fine but infrequent work for the SF field are Lou Feck, whose work is characterized by a clean, direct style, and Mitchell Hooks, who is a unique colorist.

Not all SF art has been strictly representational. Inspired by the pioneering work of Sigmund Freud in psychoanalysis, surrealism is a movement in the arts that utilizes fantastic imagery and other devices to express the workings of the subconscious. Believing that dreams are a type of metaphoric communication between the levels of consciousness, surrealist painters have formed two major trends. The first uses highly representational images juxtaposed in an extraordinary manner that defies immediate understanding. Proponents of this approach include René Magritte, Giorgio De Chirico, Marcel Duchamp, and Salvador Dalí. The other trend is a type of abstract art which utilizes seemingly natural forms that lurk below the threshold of recognition; it is exemplified by the works of Joan Miró, Yves Tanguy, Arshile Gorky, and Matta. Richard Powers (1921–   ) has long been an advocate of the latter approach, and his work resembles that of Tanguy, particularly in its use of timeless backgrounds and meticulously rendered abstract shapes. To supplement his income from fine art, Powers began illustrating in the late 1940s and did his first SF covers for Doubleday in 1949. By 1953 he had established himself in the specialty and began using surrealism in his SF work. One of the most prolific artists to work in the genre, Powers remains virtually unique in his use of abstraction in commercial illustration. Most of his important SF work was done for Ballantine Books in the 1950s and for Berkley in the early 1970s.

Although the influence of Meltzoff had formed permanent ties to representationalism for Paul Lehr and John Schoenherr, both exhibited elements of Powers's surrealistic approach at various times. Schoenherr showed the influence early on, especially in his cover painting for John BRUNNER's *Meeting at Infinity* (Ace Books, 1961). Lehr, after a period of working in the Meltzoff style and even doing some of the Signet SF titles in Meltzoff's absence, evolved a decorative technique that often uses subliminal elements. Jack Gaughan and Ed Emshwiller also created works that contain components of abstract

Cover art by Earle K. Bergey (Spring 1949)

surrealism, as did the British artists Brian Lewis and Josh Kirby.

In the mid- to late 1960s two events helped advance the use of surrealism in the packaging of SF. The first was the academic recognition of SF as a legitimate literary art form as reflected by the increase in high school and college courses devoted to the subject. Until that time the majority of the SF readership was perceived by publishers to be juvenile or young adult males. Academic recognition brought the promise of a more sophisticated and diverse audience. The other event was the commercial recognition of a trend in SF writing—dubbed the New Wave—toward a more pessimistic view of science and a greater emphasis on literary style over content. Although many fine works were created under the New Wave label, its existence as a marketing tool, which separated these stories from other forms of SF, was short-lived. During this period, however, many artists created works with a surrealistic bent. Among them was Don Ivan Punchatz, who combined elements of Magritte and Dalí with his own slightly primitive, representational technique. Another such artist was Robert Foster, who developed a method of painting over photographs in a startling manner reminiscent of the later

ILLUSTRATION   236

Cover art by Frank R. Paul (Spring 1930)

works of Dalí. Leo and Diane DILLON, though not strictly surrealistic in approach, are associated with this period for their work on an important series of books called the Ace Science Fiction Specials.

Today SF art has returned largely to its traditional forms. This development in part reflects a conservative trend in our society but even more derives from the gradual increase in editorial control over cover art since the mid-1970s. Because SF illustration is a commercial entity, it has always been subject to economic considerations. When manufacturing techniques permitted the inexpensive production of pulp magazines at the outset of the twentieth century, SF found refuge between the garish covers of those publications. After World War II, with the increase in softcover books, SF became a staple of the paperback industry. Although digests such as *Amazing, Analog,* and *The Magazine of Fantasy and Science Fiction* still survive and a new breed of larger format slick magazines such as *Omni* and *Twilight Zone* now exist, the cutting edge of SF illustration remains in the softcover book market.

Another important factor affecting the field involves changes in the laws that pertain to creative works. In the mid-1960s, when state sales taxes came into being, some publishers began returning original artworks rather than paying tax on them as physical properties. However, the issue of ownership was clouded until the passage of the Copyright Revision Act of 1976 separated the physical artwork from the right to reproduce it. This law has resulted in the growth in desirability of SF paintings outside publishing, and several galleries now specialize in the sale of this kind of art.

Art shows and auctions have become fixtures of the SF convention and are significant sources for the purchase of artwork, original manuscripts, and other collectibles. In recent years, in part because of changes in the law, an increasing number of the items sold at auction are the works of professional illustrators. Displays at conventions and galleries heighten public awareness of the contribution of SF illustration to our culture and strengthen acceptance of its validity as a legitimate art form. Museums also have begun displaying SF paintings, and the Smithsonian Institution's National Air and Space Museum has extended its Space Art Collection to include SF works that predate the actuality of space exploration and that inspired this nation to reach for the stars.

Another aspect of the new copyright law recognizes the artist's rights of creation and allows greater personal control over the duplication of illustrations. As a result there is an expanding market for ancillary rights, and SF images are now appearing on a wide variety of products other than books and magazines.

Science-fiction illustration, like all forms of commercial art, has been handicapped by the limitations of print technology and the economic pressures of the marketplace. However, it offers the public a visual insight into the imagination of our species in a way that cannot be duplicated by other means. Translating the abstract ideas of written language into images that seem real helps people accept the change that is a growing part of their daily lives, change that will inevitably and irrevocably open the door to the future.

V.D.F.

——— ILLUSTRATION: BRITISH ———

The story of British science-fiction illustrators starts in the 1800s, with the publication of Mary Wollstonecraft SHELLEY's *Frankenstein* (1818) and the "scientific romances" of Jules VERNE, H. G. WELLS, and others. However, one man was responsible for the start of modern British SF illustration: Warwick Goble. He illustrated several books by Wells and is best known for his illustrations of the Martian tripedal war machines of Wells's *The War of the Worlds* (1898). Goble influenced many subsequent British illustrators and some early Americans,

"The Sorcerer" by Hannes Bok

Art by Virgil Finlay
for the cover of *Famous Fantastic Mysteries*

Art by Earle K. Bergey
for the cover of *Thrilling Wonder Stories*

Art by Mel Hunter for the cover of *Galaxy Science Fiction*

"Surface of Mercury" by Chesley Bonestell

Art by Michael Whelan for Robert A. Heinlein's *Friday*

Untitled painting by Paul Lehr

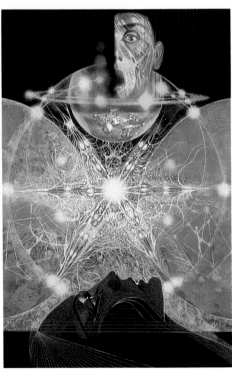

"The Game of fFlar"
by Richard M. Powers

"Bellerophon" by Vincent Di Fate

Art by Dean Ellis for Lester del Rey's *Moon of Mutiny*

Art by John Schoenherr
for Frank Herbert's *Chapterhouse: Dune*

including Frank R. PAUL and Howard V. BROWN. Other early British illustrators are W. H. C. Groome, who illustrated Fenton Ash's *A Trip to Mars* (1909), and A. C. Michaels, who did work for Wells's *The War in the Air* (1911).

Little is known about SF illustration in the next two decades, but J. M. Valda illustrated stories for *The Rocket Magazine* in the 1920s, and W. J. Roberts created art for *Tales of Wonder Magazine* in the 1930s.

It was in the late 1940s that British SF illustration really got its start, with the work of H. W. Perl, Ethel Siegel, R. M. Bull, Steve Dowling, and Frank Bellamy. Their colorful, realistic illustrations set the tone for future British work, influencing, among others, the later works of Eddie Jones and Josh Kirby.

Recovery from World War II was the key to the growth of SF in Great Britain. With the prosperity of the 1950s came the first SF boom. Some of the giants of British SF illustration got their start at this time: Gerard Quinn, Eddie Jones, Brian Lewis, Josh Kirby, and, in the comics, Sidney Jordan (*Jeff Hawke*) and Frank Hampson (*Dan Dare*). Styles ranged from Lewis's near surrealism (reflecting the work of America's Richard Powers) to the polished realism of Jones. Other artists of note in this decade include James Rattigan, Ken McIntyre, James Stark, and J. E. Mortimer. Most British artists of this period tended to use strong primary colors (red, green, blue, yellow) and an abundance of technological or surreal elements.

Quinn, Jones, Lewis, and Kirby entered the 1960s as major artists, joined by David Hardy, author-artist Keith Roberts, Mike Atwell, and Mal Dean. The NEW WAVE was gathering its adherents in British SF, and many of the artists joined it to create exciting—and often disturbing—images.

One of the hallmarks of British illustration, particularly since 1950, has been the artists' perfectionism, whether in SF or in fantasy. In the 1970s this zeal was evident in the work of newcomers such as Patrick Woodroffe, Rodney Matthews, Chris Foss, Bruce Pennington, Tim White, Jim Burns, Roger Dean, and David Pelham, whose style is epitomized by clear imagery that often borders on photorealism.

Other British artists, though not as realistic, have also produced superb work, among them Anthony Roberts, Richard Glyn Jones, Jim Pitts, Bill Botten, and James Cawthorn. Technological wonders, particularly complex spacecraft and airships, appear in the majority of the works of modern British SF artists. While transatlantic interaction is often difficult to prove, it seems reasonable that the British artists of the 1960s and 1970s were at least partially influenced by American artists such as Frank Kelly FREAS, Ed EMSHWILLER, Roy G. KRENKEL, and Jack GAUGHAN, and it is more than likely that such cross-pollination will continue in the future.

J.G.

THE IMMORTAL (1969). *Directed by Joseph Sargent; screenplay by Robert Specht; adapted from the novel* The Immortals *by James Gunn; photographed by Howard R. Schwartz; music by Dominic Frontiere. With Christopher George, Barry Sullivan, Ralph Bellamy, Jessica Walter, Carol Lynley. 75 minutes. Color.*

James E. GUNN's novel *The Immortals* (1962) tells the story of the social response to the identification of an immortal man whose better blood can temporarily rejuvenate by means of a transfusion. This ABC-TV movie of the week used the opening part of the four-part novel to tell a story focused not on the rejuvenated millionaire (Barry Sullivan) and the doctor (Ralph Bellamy) who tells a homeless drifter to flee (he does), but on the immortal man, a test-car driver (Christopher George). In the film George hangs around to be imprisoned, to escape (helped by the millionaire's young wife, played by Jessica Walter), and finally to be presented with a crisis of conscience when his fiancée (Carol Lynley) joins him and is shot by one of the millionaire's henchmen. Everything ends in a car chase.

The film was carefully made (though in only two weeks), tautly directed by Joseph Sargent, well acted by Bellamy and particularly by Sullivan, predictably by George, Lynley, and Walter, and successful in drawing an audience; ABC capitalized on all this and seized on the valuable blood as a gimmick for another chase series, which lasted only fifteen hour-long episodes in 1970–71. In it only George was carried over from the film, but there were predictable sequences of his being tracked down in a car chase, imprisoned, freed by a woman, and escaping in a final car chase.

In Gunn's novel the immortal man appears only at the beginning of the first chapter and at the end of the last. The focus is on the world's hypochondria and Gunn's frequent theme that anything, even life and health, can be overdone. *The Immortal* was the first adult TV series to be based on a science-fiction novel, but its impact was lost in the chase format, which *TV Guide* called "Run for Your Blood."

J.E.G.

THE INCREDIBLE SHRINKING MAN (1957). *Directed by Jack Arnold; screenplay by Richard Matheson; adapted from the novel* The Shrinking Man *by Richard Matheson; photographed by Ellis W. Carter; music by Fred Carling and E. Lawrence. With Grant Williams, Randy Stuart, April Kent, Paul Langton, Raymond Bailey, William Schallert, Frank Scannell, Billy Curtis. 81 minutes. Black and white.*

THE INCREDIBLE SHRINKING WOMAN (1981). *Directed by Joel Schumacher; screenplay by Jane Wagner; adapted from the novel* The Shrinking Man *by Richard Matheson; photographed by Bruce*

Logan; music by Suzanne Ciani. With Lily Tomlin, Charles Grodin, Ned Beatty, Henry Gibson, Mark Blankfield, Elizabeth Wilson. 88 minutes. Color.

With its tight script, lean direction, credible SPECIAL EFFECTS, and intelligent ideas, *The Incredible Shrinking Man* is one of the best science-fiction films of the 1950s. From its precredit image of a human figure shrinking away as a mushroom cloud ominously expands, the movie pursues its premise and thematic possibilities with inexorable logic, touching on timely social fears as well as deeper psychological ones.

The shrinking man of the title, at first an apparently healthy American male, is exposed to a mysterious cloud while on a boating holiday with his fiancée. After their marriage he begins to notice that he is getting smaller. The process seems irreversible, and as he shrinks his wife must take greater care of him, finally keeping him in a dollhouse. The family house cat becomes curious and forces the tiny man into the cellar, where he must survive on his own. He is now so small that his wife cannot hear his calls for help when she returns home from her errands and, seeing him gone, presumes that the cat ate him. Alone in the cellar, the shrinking man must battle a spider for a morsel of cheese left as bait in a mousetrap. The film's ending is surprisingly upbeat, as the tiny hero slips through the mesh of a window screen to merge with the universe, embracing the idea that "to God there is no zero."

As a visual medium, the cinema is particularly well suited to a science-fiction story that deals with the relative scale of objects. In addition, the transformation of the shrinking man's world from domestic and comfortable to unfamiliar and threatening is chronicled with unassuming skill by screenwriter Richard MATHESON and director Jack ARNOLD, and the story is effectively told from the point of view of the dwindling protagonist.

By contrast, *The Incredible Shrinking Woman*, despite the promise of the idea and the talent of the leading actress, Lily Tomlin, is a rather disappointing revision. The film's intention in altering the gender of the protagonist was to make the story a more contemporary feminist statement about sexual inequality. Therefore, the heroine's shrinkage is attributed to a new perfume, Sexpot. And the film succeeds in creating some wonderful images to express this theme: the tiny Tomlin housed in a hamster cage, for example, or buried by table scraps in the kitchen sink and forced down the drain with all the gunk.

Finally, though, this film relies too heavily on Tomlin's presence and not enough on the inherent drama of the physical transformation her character experiences. In its overly conscious attempt at meaningful social statement, it fails to keep the narrative point of view solidly within the character, and so the familiar never really becomes strange but merely amusing. Also, as a film clearly aimed at a family audience, *Shrinking Woman* seems to have been obligated to provide a conventionally satisfying resolution, wherein Tomlin is publicly restored to her normal size. Thus, the movie's explicit social criticism is drastically compromised.

B.K.G.

ING, DEAN (1931–   ).   American writer whose science fiction most frequently concerns contemporary events. A former aircraft engineer and behavioral scientist now living in Oregon, Ing uses his novels to present his views on the forces shaping contemporary life. His first novel, *Soft Targets* (1979), in which an uncontrolled media turns terrorists into celebrities, deals with the problems a free society will inevitably face in coping with the threat of terrorism.

Ing has also written four novels on postholocaust survival. *Pulling Through* (1983) is little more than a retelling of the Robinson Crusoe story, as a man and a woman use their ingenuity to re-create such mechanical equipment as air pumps and filters while they fight off their less desirable neighbors. The other three Ing novels (*Systematic Shock*, 1981; *Single Combat*, 1983; *Wild Country*, 1985) form a series centered on the adventures of Ted Quantrill, a young man who first becomes an agent for a secret government organization and later rebels against it. These works are basically action adventure, but the character of Quantrill and the description of a future world governed by religious fundamentalists stand out in the subgenre. As·is *Soft Targets*, this series is as much about the need for "hard-nosed" action in all aspects of international relations as it is about life after the bomb. Ing has also completed two manuscripts left by the late Mack REYNOLDS: *The Other Time* (1984) and *Deathwish World* (1985).

   OTHER WORKS: *Anasazi* (collection, 1980); *High Tension* (collection, 1982); *Firefight 2000* (collection, 1987).
S.H.G.

INNERSPACE (1987).   *Directed by Joe Dante; screenplay by Jeffrey Boam and Chip Proser; photographed by Andrew Laszlo; music by Jerry Goldsmith. With Martin Short, Dennis Quaid, Kevin McCarthy, Meg Ryan, Fiona Lewis, Robert Picardo, Vernon Wells. 115 minutes. Color.*

To date there have been only two films about journeys *inside* the human body, the melodramatic but serious FANTASTIC VOYAGE (1966) and the extravagantly comic *Innerspace*. In the earlier film the approach was sober and emphasized the wonders of human biology; in this fast-paced adventure, produced by Steven SPIELBERG and directed by Joe DANTE, the human interior is merely the backdrop for a story that takes place, for the most part, *outside*. The effects are less extravagant than those in *Fantastic Voyage*, although the bodily wonders are rendered with more accuracy here.

Through complicated circumstances, miniaturized test pilot Tuck Pendleton (Dennis Quaid) ends up injected into the bloodstream of hypochondriac nerd Jack Putter (Martin Short). Tuck connects himself to Jack's aural and visual nerves and advises the nervous Putter as they fight an evil industrialist (Kevin McCarthy). Tuck's advice gives Jack confidence for the first time in his life; things lead to a wild climax as a bad guy (Vernon Wells), also miniaturized, attacks Tuck inside Jack, while Jack battles the industrialist and his henchwoman (Fiona Lewis), now themselves half-sized.

Innerspace is a speedy, amusing film that plays fair with its premise (more science fantasy than science fiction) and delivers excellent SPECIAL EFFECTS. Short is especially good as the supermarket clerk who unwittingly finds himself plunged into bizarre adventure. Things become increasingly outlandish as the film progresses, but it never loses its footing. Despite overlength and a tendency toward silliness, it's one of the best SF comedies yet made.

B.W.

———— INTELLIGENCE ————

Science fiction allows authors to change not only the conditions in which humans live but humans themselves, so it is understandable that SF authors have often tackled the question of a change in intelligence. Usually such a change is an increase in intelligence, although occasionally it is the reverse, and often the increase is associated with superior abilities in general, marking the evolutionary development of a new human species, or superman. Sometimes, however, especially in the older tradition, greater intelligence is considered cold, cruel, or dehumanizing, as in the figure of the mad scientist.

Wisdom, usually but not always considered a product of greater intelligence, has been attributed not only to the biblical King Solomon but also to the medieval magician called Solomon Magus. The other side of the coin of intellect, the mad scientist, emerged from the image of the alchemist obsessively pursuing his blasphemous magical formulas for turning baser metals into gold or creating the elixir of life. Mary Wollstonecraft SHELLEY built on that tradition when she created her scientist, Victor Frankenstein, and the mad scientist theme was off and running, culminating in the brilliant amorality of Dr. Strangelove in Stanley KUBRICK's (1964) film.

Often in films and stories the distinction is made between the emotions and intelligence. In John TAINE's *Seeds of Life* (1931), accidentally enhanced intelligence merely gives a laboratory technician increased opportunity for cruelty, and in the film FORBIDDEN PLANET (1956) Dr. Morbius's intelligence, enhanced by the Krel machine, does not control his murderous subconscious.

The process of mental enhancement, like other artificial processes, usually incurs a risk of death (or, in the mind, of insanity); in the same film another character who uses the Krel machine dies after revealing the secret he has learned.

Early SF marveled at strangeness; modern SF treats it as commonplace. Intelligence began receiving that treatment in E. E. SMITH's space epics in 1928: it became associated with rationality, and the final revelation of Smith's six-part Lensman series is that the benign aliens, the Arisians, have been breeding humans for intelligence, a process that culminates in the creation of the "children of the Lens" in the novel of that name. This was the belief that John W. CAMPBELL installed at the heart of *Astounding*/ANALOG. It would culminate in such novels as A. E. VAN VOGT's *Slan* (1940), in which greater intelligence and other characteristics (telepathy, strength, and endurance) combine in the superman. The superman is artificially created in van Vogt's *The World of Null-A* (1945), in which a "double brain" is enhanced by Null-A training. The tragic consequences of growing up with greater intelligence in a hostile, envious world had been dealt with earlier by J. D. BERESFORD in *The Hampdenshire Wonder* (1911) and Olaf STAPLEDON in *Odd John* (1935), and later by Wilmar H. SHIRAS in *Children of the Atom* (1948–1950).

Other characteristics sometimes associated with intelligence have been sterility and futility. Although Jonathan SWIFT provided an early attack (1726) on ineffectual thinkers in Part 3 of *Gulliver's Travels* (the voyage to Laputa), with the Laputans hiring "flappers" to strike with an inflated bladder the mouth of the one who was to speak and the ear of the one who was to listen, the image of a brain floating in a pool of nutrient liquid may have originated with H. G. WELLS's 1893 essay "Man of the Year Million." People, and sometimes aliens, with enlarged brains, big heads, and spindly bodies occupy many stories and films, sometimes horribly, as with Wells's invading Martians, sometimes benignly, as with BUCK ROGERS's Dr. Huer, sometimes neutrally, as in the film THIS ISLAND EARTH (1954), and sometimes with distaste, as in Harry BATES's story "Alas, All Thinking" (1935), in which a visitor to the future finally, in disgust, snaps the spindly neck of the last human left alive.

Intelligence itself is the subject of Poul ANDERSON's *Brain Wave* (1954) and Daniel KEYES's *Flowers for Algernon* (1966). In *Brain Wave* Earth escapes from a force field that has been inhibiting mental activity for millions of years, and the novel considers what would happen if everybody were to become smarter; in *Flowers for Algernon* Keyes developed the idea as personal tragedy when brain surgery turns a retarded man into a genius who later regresses to his former state. Thomas M. DISCH considered the cruelty of artificially induced intelligence (leading eventually to death) in *Camp Concentration* (1968), and Cyril M. KORNBLUTH dealt with the question of what evolved human geniuses would do with the rest of mentally retarded humanity in "The Marching Morons" (1951).

Intelligence also has been displayed in animals, such as horses (Swift's Houyhnhnms), cats (Cordwainer SMITH's "lost C'mell"), dogs (Stapledon's *Sirius*, 1944, and Clifford D. SIMAK's *City*, 1952, with its "stories the dogs tell"), and other creatures, including ants, cephalopods, and whales. Aliens are another major means for discussing the nature of thought, beginning with Wells's "intellects vast and cool and unsympathetic" in *The War of the Worlds* (1897).

The other significant means for considering how the ability to think better will change the nature, or even the perception, of existence is artificial intelligence displayed in COMPUTERS or ROBOTS, a subject that writers, Isaac ASIMOV in particular, have explored in great detail.

J.E.G.

THE INTERNATIONAL ASSOCIATION FOR THE FANTASTIC IN THE ARTS.
The IAFA grew out of the International Conference on the Fantastic in the Arts, founded at Florida Atlantic University in 1980 by Professor Robert A. Collins. Its principal function, under other officers, is still to mount an annual academic conference in March. In 1985 the conference moved to the Houston area and in 1988 to Fort Lauderdale. The association's emphasis on fantasy, a broader though less defined area than science fiction, attracts representatives of disciplines of the humanities in addition to English.

J.E.G.

INVADERS FROM MARS (1953).
Directed by William Cameron Menzies; screenplay by Richard Blake; photographed by John Seitz; music by Raoul Kraushaar. With Arthur Franz, Jimmy Hunt, Helena Carter, Leif Erickson, Hillary Brooke, Morris Ankrum. 78 minutes. Color.

INVADERS FROM MARS (1986).
Directed by Tobe Hooper; screenplay by Dan O'Bannon and Don Jacoby; photographed by Daniel Pearl; music by Christopher Young. With Louise Fletcher, Timothy Bottoms, Laraine Newman, Bud Cort, Karen Black, Hunter Carson, Jimmy Hunt. 93 minutes. Color.

The original version of *Invaders from Mars*, a science-fiction variation on the boy-who-cried-wolf story, is a minor masterpiece of mood and design. A young boy sees a flying saucer land in the sand pit near his home, but at first nobody will believe him, even though one by one his parents and other adult authority figures are sucked underground by the Martian and reprogrammed like zombies to sabotage America's fledgling space program. When the evidence becomes clear and the army is called in, the film becomes an invasion night-

mare about Cold War paranoia. In the justly famous conclusion, the conventional happy resolution—the boy wakes up to discover he's been dreaming—is undermined as he again sees a flying saucer landing exactly as it had in the beginning. Director MENZIES's expressionist imagery vividly conveys the young boy's growing estrangement from the adult world.

Tobe Hooper's remake is rather different in tone, but its politics are essentially the same. This version consciously demonstrates its awareness of the original through a series of humorous references and in-jokes. The best of these is the scene in which the policeman, played by Jimmy Hunt (the boy in the original), climbs over the ridge of the sand pit to investigate, remarking, "I haven't been up here since I was a kid." But such references serve to establish a continuity with the original rather than a contrast. The Martians' claim of infringement of sovereignty by NASA exploration is never taken seriously, and as the cigar-chomping American general asserts to the boy, "We're not out of options yet; Marines have no qualms about killing Martians." The film's depiction of the invasion of domestic space replays that of the original and is informed by the same besieged militaristic attitude.

B.K.G.

INVASION OF THE BODY SNATCHERS (1956).
Directed by Don Siegel; screenplay by Daniel Mainwaring; adapted from the novel The Body Snatchers by Jack Finney; photographed by Ellsworth Fredericks; music by Carmen Dragon. With Kevin McCarthy, Dana Wynter, Carolyn Jones, King Donovan. 80 minutes. Black and white.

INVASION OF THE BODY SNATCHERS (1978).
Directed by Philip Kaufman; screenplay by D. W. Richter; photographed by Michael Chapman; music by Danny Zeitlin. With Donald Sutherland, Brooke Adams, Leonard Nimoy, Veronica Cartwright. 115 minutes. Color.

One of the few science-fiction films to retain its emotional power over the years, *Invasion of the Body Snatchers* is worth seeing in both its original and remade versions. The plot is the same in both: a small town in California is invaded by alien beings that hatch duplicate humans out of pods. The pod-creatures then take the place of the original people. Eventually the aliens are in the majority, transporting the pods openly and even using local government facilities to help with their distribution.

In one of the original film's most nightmarish sequences, the hero (Kevin McCarthy) finds a duplicate of himself and learns the terrifying truth. But before he can convince anyone else, the town is nearly taken over, impelling McCarthy and the female lead (Dana Wynter) to flee. Good performances, atmospheric photography, and deft direction generate a considerable amount of paranoid suspense—enough, perhaps, to prevent the audience from noticing occasional lapses in plot logic, including the aliens' switch from the mere substitution of one body for another to "taking over" their victims in something akin to psychic possession.

The film drives on to a vivid climax, as McCarthy is left screaming on a highway, trying to stop traffic and warn the unwary. He climbs into the back of a truck only to find it filled with pods: the distribution is in high gear. This is where the film should have ended, emphasizing the essential horror of the situation. But such an ending was allegedly regarded as too much for the 1956 audience, so an anticlimax was tacked on: McCarthy tells the story to the FBI, who begin to take action against the aliens, presumably saving the world in the eleventh hour.

The original *Invasion* was one of the finest SF films of the 1950s and has since been recognized as a classic. Much has been written about its purported political allegory—the pod-people representing Communist infiltration into American society—but the film's undiminished impact thirty years later suggests something far more universal. The real horror derives from our fear of an intrusion into our lives—by politics, disease, or any element beyond our control—that deprives us of our loved ones by making them *different* and, as such, a threat. Antecedents occur in the vampire films of previous decades. The most modern renditions of essentially the same nightmare are *The Night of the Living Dead* and its sequels.

The remake set out to correct the weaknesses of the original while retaining its intensity. In a witty comment on the original ending, Kevin McCarthy makes a cameo appearance early in the film, *still* running frantically through traffic, pounding on windshields in an attempt to warn people. Donald Sutherland, the new hero, plays a San Francisco health inspector who gradually gets caught up in the alien invasion.

The style of the second film differs markedly from that of the first. More leisurely and open, even low keyed at first, it radiates a sense of alienation and anonymity as appropriate for 1978 as was the claustrophobic paranoia of the Siegel version for 1956. The new script deals with the inconsistencies of the original: this time it is clear that the pods always substitute new bodies for old. The original humans are consumed in the duplication process, and their remains crumble. (Thus the early scene of trash collectors' heaving garbage bags onto a truck takes on a sinister significance.)

There is one extremely effective new touch: a pod-person, when it detects a human, points and emits a weird, gargling scream. This scream is used to tremendous effect at the end, when the film moves on to the logical conclusion the 1956 version backed away from. The heroine is betrayed at the last moment, when she reveals herself to what she thinks is still Sutherland and it emits the telltale scream. The aliens have won, and there is no convenient, all-powerful FBI to save humanity. A 1956 audience might have had faith in such redemption, but in 1978, after Vietnam and Watergate, few still did.

D.S.

INVASION U.S.A. (1985). *Directed by Joseph Zito; screenplay by James Bruner and Chuck Norris; photographed by João Fernandes; music by Jay Chattaway. With Chuck Norris, Richard Lynch. 108 minutes. Color.*

For no apparent reason, sinister Russians land in Florida and attempt to take over the United States. En route to Atlanta, they stop to smash school buses, harass old ladies, and destroy shopping centers. Only Chuck Norris can stop their fiendish plans. Perhaps the worst of the "right-wing" movies of the 1980s, this film continues the crudity of the pulp magazines without preserving pulpish vigor. The plot consists of a series of demolition scenes connected by minimal character development. No ideas are discussed; politics has been completely replaced by violence.

M.M.W.

————— INVISIBILITY —————

The notion of invisibility has inspired dreams (the cloak of invisibility) and nightmares (invisible creatures). The two major concerns displayed in stories on the topic have been how invisibility might be achieved and, if achieved, how it might enable unusual things to happen. As with all good story ideas, however, invisibility isn't really interesting unless something goes wrong or the price is too high.

Fitz-James O'BRIEN ("What Was It? A Mystery," 1859) and Guy de Maupassant ("The Horla," 1887) wrote early stories about invisible creatures, and Ambrose BIERCE produced a classic treatment ("The Damned Thing," 1898), in which invisibility is achieved by creatures made of colors beyond the visible spectrum. Early magazine stories stressed the means by which invisibility could be accomplished, and H. G. WELLS's 1897 novel *The Invisible Man* devotes several paragraphs to how Griffin made his flesh perfectly transparent (even though Wells himself recognized that transparent eyeballs would be blind). In a 1934 story ("Beyond the Spectrum"), however, Arthur Leo Zagat dealt with that problem: his naturally invisible aliens kidnap human victims to supply themselves with eye transplants. In other stories, such as *Cloak of Aesir* (1939/1952) by John W. CAMPBELL (writing as Don A. Stuart) and *The Cometeers* (1936/1950) by Jack WILLIAMSON, invisibility is achieved by causing visible light to pass around a garment, coating, or force field, with ultraviolet or infrared rays admitted and converted into the visible spectrum.

In Victor Endersby's "A Job of Blending" (1934), a tailor, victim of the protection racket, persuades his persecutors to accept payment in trade and makes suits that camouflage them so effectively in city traffic that they become easy accident victims. In Randall GARRETT's *Too Many Magicians* (1967) the "Tarnheim Effect" prevents anyone from looking directly at, or noticing, the person or object rendered invisible. Christopher PRIEST's *The Glamour* (1984) deals with invisibility as a talent perfected by people who are psychologically inconspicuous to begin with.

Are these science fiction? Psychology, including the camouflage effect, is a science, and if authors subject their magic to laws, they in effect treat it as a science. *The Glamour*, however, uses invisibility more as a metaphor and as a way to provide insights into character.

The most important aspect of invisibility, however, as Wells discovered, is not so much how it is achieved as how it will affect the person who achieves it: Griffin's dream turns into a nightmare when he faces the practical problems of being invisible; without clothes he suffers from cold and exposure; without the ability to make his needs known, he must starve. His hubris becomes madness and then nemesis.

H.C.

THE INVISIBLE BOY (1957).   *Directed by Herman Hoffman; screenplay by Cyril Hume; adapted from the short story by Edmund Cooper; photographed by Harold Wellman; music by Les Baxter. With Richard Eyer, Philip Abbott, Diane Brewster, Harold J. Stone, Robert H. Harris, voice of Marvin Miller. 90 minutes. Black and white.*

Whimsy is rare in science-fiction films, which perhaps explains why the pleasing *Invisible Boy* has been neglected, although it is a follow-up to FORBIDDEN PLANET (1956). The busy plot includes Robby the Robot (here from the future), a lonely little boy, satellites, mind control, and an evil supercomputer, the first in movie history.

The major defects of the film are director Herman Hoffman, a lazy pace, and an inadequate budget. However, these are offset by a witty approach, affectionate spoofing rather than satire, and enough novelty and invention for several films. Jack Rabin, Irving Block, and Louis DeWitt provided special effects. Richard Eyer was a pleasant child actor, and he carries the film with adult aplomb.

Some scenes fall flat, but most work, and *The Invisible Boy* is a film of rare merit and genuine charm.

B.W.

THE INVISIBLE MAN (1933).   *Directed by James Whale; screenplay by R. C. Sherriff; adapted from the novel by H. G. Wells; photographed by Arthur Edeson. With Claude Rains, Gloria Stuart, Henry Travers, William Harrigan, Una O'Connor. Holmes Herbert, John Carradine, Dwight Frye, Walter Brennan. 71 minutes. Black and white.*

Universal chose James Whale to direct *The Invisible Man* as the latest in their series of successful horror films, two of which—FRANKENSTEIN (1931) and *The Old Dark House* (1932)—he had directed previously. At Whale's insistence Claude Rains was hired for his movie debut as Griffin, the title character, and novelist R. C. Sherriff wrote the script, following H. G. WELLS's novel closely. The only major change other than those necessary for compression was designed to make the Invisible Man more sympathetic: in the novel he's a megalomaniac, but in the film his madness is merely a side effect of his invisibility drug. Except for this change, Wells approved of the film.

The Invisible Man, as much a comedy as a horror film or science-fiction thriller, remains highly admired today. As do other Whale films, it balances horror and humor adroitly, with humor predominating in the early parts of the film and horror taking over as Griffin goes mad. The film provides a vivid depiction of the troubles and powers of invisibility, with the help of John P. Fulton's astonishing SPECIAL EFFECTS. As in all Whale's films, each character is colorful and the dialogue is memorable. The film has an undeniable power; when seen today, unlike most films of its time, it is free of quaintness and affectation, and it remains one of the authentic masterpieces of the fantastic cinema.

As in the novel, a strangely bandaged traveler arrives at a small country inn, insisting on privacy. The curious locals soon learn he is invisible, and the Invisible Man—furious at both his discovery and his inability to restore himself to visibility—flees to take refuge with a rival; as the invisibility drug drives him mad, he makes plans literally to conquer the world. "Even the moon is frightened of me," he exults madly, "frightened to death!" But his reign of terror is brought to an end when he's shot down by policemen.

Although the film was successful, Universal didn't produce a follow-up for several years. *The Invisible Man Returns* (1940) also tried to balance horror and humor, but while respectable it has none of the brilliance of Whale's film. Vincent PRICE, as Griffin's brother, becomes invisible to prove himself innocent of a crime.

Because horror films experienced a resurgence from the late 1930s into the 1940s, Universal continued making Invisible Man films, with *Invisible Agent* in 1942 and *The Invisible Man's Revenge* in 1944; Jon Hall was a different invisible man in each. The last in the loosely linked series was, perhaps inevitably, *Abbott and Costello Meet the Invisible Man* (1951). In each

The Invisible Ray

of the films a line or two of dialogue connects the current Invisible Man with Rains's Griffin; a photo of Rains is often shown. All but the first treat invisibility simply as a visual gimmick for scares, wonder, or gags; the problems of being invisible are ignored.

Wells's novel was produced as an episode of NBC-TV's *Matinee Theatre* in the 1950s; the 1980s saw a British TV adaptation in several parts. Neither measured up in any way to the Whale version. There was also a TV movie called *The Invisible Man* (1975), but it was a pilot for an inferior TV series, sharing no similarities with the Wells work except the concept of invisibility. In the 1950s *The Invisible Man* became a British TV series. Mexico's *El Hombre que lorgo ser invisible* (1957, also known as *The New Invisible Man*) was a bland and unacknowledged remake of *The Invisible Man Returns*. In spite of innumerable adaptations and imitations, the original film remains the superlative celluloid version of Well's novel.

B.W.

THE INVISIBLE RAY (1936).   *Directed by Lambert Hillyer; screenplay by John Colton; photographed by George Robinson; music by Franz Waxman. With Boris Karloff, Bela Lugosi, Frances Drake, Violet Kemble Cooper, Frank Lawton, Walter Kingsford, Beulah Bondi, Nydia Westman. 82 minutes. Black and white.*

The Invisible Ray has a stronger basis in science-fiction ideas than almost any other American horror film of its period, but the SF is still only a device to give Boris Karloff the touch of death. Using the supertelescope to see into Earth's past, he discovers that a radioactive meteor has crashed into Africa. He organizes an expedition to find it; touching the meteor, he begins glowing, then goes mad and seeks revenge on those he incorrectly believes wronged him. Bela Lugosi plays a rare sympathetic role.

Well produced and drenched in Gothic atmosphere, this film is brisk but overheated, with an awkward structure.

B.W.

ISAAC ASIMOV'S SCIENCE FICTION MAGAZINE (1977–   ).   One of the newest and most exciting science-fiction magazines, *Asimov's* was launched during a period of uncertainty in the SF magazine field. Publisher Joel Davis had the advantage of knowing that Asimov's name would secure a foundation of initial sales, but to sustain those sales the magazine needed to be consistent in its quality. Editor George Scithers struck the right chord when, using Asimov's own fiction as a model, he selected stories that reflect a puckish sense of humor, deliver a strong plot line, or do a little of both. The magazine also emphasized story series rather than serials and included a variety of departments to encourage reader involvement. This was clearly the right formula: within a year *Asimov's* circulation had risen to the highest in the field, beating even Analog. Scithers won the 1978 Hugo Award for best professional editor, a recognition repeated in 1980.

Throughout his tenure Scithers encouraged new writers, the two most successful of whom were Somtow Sucharitkul and Barry B. Longyear. Each established himself with a story series: Mallword by Sucharitkul and the Circus Planet Momus by Longyear. Although *Asimov's* circulation has since dropped below that of *Analog* (now its companion publication), the magazine is still healthy. It has continued to be popular with both readers and critics and was especially so under Shawna McCarthy's editorship (1982–1985). *Asimov's* has remained the most exciting and innovative SF magazine available. Two new trends in its pages are the publication of more serious stories and the inclusion of fantasy. In the 1980s more award winners and nominees have come from *Asimov's* than from any other magazine. Under the current editor, Gardner DOZOIS, it remains *the* magazine for new ideas.

M.A.

ISLAND OF LOST SOULS (1933).
Directed by Erle C. Kenton; screenplay by Waldemar Young and Philip Wylie; adapted from the novel The Island of Dr. Moreau *by H. G. Wells; photographed by Karl Struss. With Charles Laughton, Richard Arlen, Lelia Hyams, Kathleen Burke, Arthur Hohl, Stanley Fields, Tetsu Komai, Bela Lugosi. 72 minutes. Black and white.*
THE ISLAND OF DR. MOREAU (1977).
Directed by Don Taylor; screenplay by John Herman Shaner and Al Ramrus; adapted from the novel by H. G. Wells; photographed by Gerry Fisher; music by Laurence Rosenthal. With Burt Lancaster, Michael York, Nigel Davenport, Barbara Carrera, Richard Basehart, Nick Cravat, The Great John L. Bob Oxman. 98 minutes. Color.

The first film adaptation of H. G. WELLS's *Island of Dr. Moreau* (1896) eliminates the satire, changes the ending, and drapes the story in horror. The result is one of the most horrifying of all horror movies, unforgettable and even witty. Intensely stylish, with an astonishing performance by Charles Laughton as Moreau and makeup far more ghastly than in the tame remake, this is one of the greatest science-fiction–horror movies ever made.

Forced to remain on Dr. Moreau's tropical island, a young man (Richard Arlen) is attracted to Lota (Kathleen Burke), the native girl living there. To his horror, he slowly realizes that Lota, as well as all the other restless natives, are animals that Moreau has surgically transformed into human beings. Moreau's hope is that the young man and Lota will have a child together. At the climax the beast-men in the jungle rebel, and, grabbing surgical instruments, do to Moreau what he had done to them.

Wells considered this film a vulgarization of his book; his assessment can scarcely be denied, but it is also quite beside the point. Made during the first great wave of horror films, the movie was intended to top the others in terror, and it did. It may have been recut before release: Lugosi's role, as Speaker of the Law ("What is the

Charles Laughton in *Island of Lost Souls* (1933)

Law? Not to spill blood! Are we not men?"), is surprisingly small considering that he was near the peak of his fame.

Karl Struss's camerawork, Hans Dreier's art direction, and Wally Westmore's sometimes astonishing makeup all contribute to the Dantean quality of the film, but the major achievement is Laughton's. His egocentric, purring Moreau, delighting in his secrets, chuckling over the possibility of Lota (an ex-leopard) having a child, imperiously whipping the beast-men and raging at them in the vivid climax—this is the greatest mad scientist in screen history.

By contrast, the 1977 version is lackluster at best. Much was made of the film not being an actual remake; however, the panther-girl created for the first movie turns up here as well (Barbara Carrera). The only novelty the film has to offer is that the castaway on Moreau's island (Michael York) temporarily descends the evolutionary scale to become a beast-man himself. Too sunny to be a good horror film, this movie is also damaged by the miscasting of Burt Lancaster as Moreau; he thinks his way through the role rather than embodying the scientist. York is acceptable as the castaway, and Carrera is attractive as the panther-woman; John Chambers's makeup is elaborate but unconvincing. But the film's major weakness is the fact that it has been done by rote; there's no involvement on the part of the filmmakers; it is as if they expected their restructured story line to carry the film.

B.W.

IT CAME FROM BENEATH THE SEA (1955).

Directed by Robert Gordon; screenplay by George Worthing Yates and Hal Smith; photographed by Henry Freulich; music conducted by Mischa Bakaleinikoff. With Kenneth Tobey, Faith Domergue, Donald Curtis, Ian Keith, Dean Maddox, Jr., Harry Lauter, Del Courtney. 77 minutes. Black and white.

This typical 1950s thriller about a colossal octopus driven to attack human beings and finally staging an assault on San Francisco is competently made and above average for its genre. But its historic importance is that it was the first collaboration between master stop-motion animator Ray HARRYHAUSEN and producer Charles H. Schneer. Their partnership lasted almost thirty years, resulting in many memorable films, the most significant being the fantasies *Seventh Voyage of Sinbad* (1958), *Jason and the Argonauts* (1963), and *Clash of the Titans* (1981) as well as many other films, including FIRST MEN IN THE MOON (1964).

B.W.

It Came from Beneath the Sea

IT CAME FROM OUTER SPACE (1953).

Directed by Jack Arnold; screenplay by Harry Essex and Ray Bradbury (Bradbury uncredited); photographed by Clifford Stine; music by Herman Stine. With Richard Carlson, Barbara Rush, Charles Drake, Kathleen Hughes. 81 minutes. Black and white.

An astronomer living in the Arizona desert sees a meteor strike nearby; investigating, he discovers it is actually a spaceship inhabited by benign aliens who have the power to make themselves look like human beings. The story develops in taut if melodramatic fashion.

Ray BRADBURY's intelligent tale, written for the screen, was rewritten for the worse by Harry Essex, and the official credits obscure the fact that Bradbury was the principal creator of virtually everything effective about the script. (In fact, his influence on science-fiction movies of the 1950s is due for reassessment.)

Striking 3-D work, a strong sense of locale, and a suspenseful structure keep the film entertaining, although other elements, including the outdated acting style and an overreliance on studio sets, date the film for all its historic importance. At the time of its release, however, it was immensely influential, helping establish workmanlike Jack ARNOLD as one of the major directors of SF films of the period, William Alland as a producer, the desert as a favored locale, Richard CARLSON as an SF leading man, and the loner-scientist as a hero.

Steven SPIELBERG has admitted that *It Came from Outer Space* was one of the major progenitors of CLOSE ENCOUNTERS OF THE THIRD KIND (1977), so the influence of this modest but worthwhile film is still being felt.

B.W.

IT CONQUERED THE WORLD (1956).

Directed by Roger Corman; screenplay by Charles B. Griffith (credited to Lou Rusoff); photographed by Frederick West; music by Ronald Stein. With Peter Graves, Lee Van Cleef, Beverly Garland, Sally Fraser, Russ Bender, Jonathan Haze, Dick Miller, Charles B. Griffith. 71 minutes. Black and white.

A loner scientist (Lee Van Cleef) conspires with an arriving Venusian in an effort to conquer the Earth; the scheme involves taking control of the minds of key individuals. Another scientist (Peter Graves) and Van Cleef's wife (Beverly Garland) try to defeat the invader; at the climax Van Cleef realizes the error of his ways and dies while killing the evil alien.

With his principal screenwriter, Charles B. Griffith, Roger CORMAN made a series of surprisingly intelligent though cheap science-fiction thrillers in the late 1950s; this is one of the most interesting. Paul Blaisdell built and played the comic-grotesque monster, which resembles a fanged turnip. It is both outrageous and imaginative, one of the favorites of 1950s monster fans. But Griffith's script is even better than the monster; although it was hastily written, it is insightful and intelligent, echoing many typical 1950s themes (mind control, alien invasion). The acting is above average as well. In 1966 the film was remade as *Zontar, the Thing from Venus*.

B.W.

IT! THE TERROR FROM BEYOND SPACE (1958).

Directed by Edward L. Cahn; screenplay by Jerome Bixby; photographed by Kenneth Peach; music by Paul Sawtell and Bert Shefter. With Marshall Thompson, Shawn Smith, Kim Spalding, Ann Doran, Dabbs Greer, Paul Langton, Ray "Crash" Corrigan. 68 minutes. Black and white.

The second expedition to Mars is returning to Earth with the sole survivor of the first (Marshall Thompson) under arrest for murdering his crewmates. His claim that a monster killed them is borne out when the monster, now on board, begins killing the crew of the rescue ship. At the climax the Martian monster is killed by suffocation.

Though cheaply made, *It!* is a tidy, compact thriller, well developed and reasonable. Thompson, Shawn Smith, and some of the other actors give creditable performances, but Kim Spalding is inadequate. Director Edward L. Cahn was unimaginative in his handling of the Martian, played as a conventional monster by stuntman Crash Corrigan. Despite these deficiencies, *It!* is an above-average science-fiction film for its period.

Many regard ALIEN (1979) as an unacknowledged remake of this film, but screenwriter Jerome BIXBY now admits *he* was imitating THE THING *(from Another World)* (1951). Although similarities between *Alien* and *It!* do exist, their basic idea was often used in pulp fiction and comic books.

B.W.

J

JAKES, JOHN [WILLIAM] (1932–).

American author of best-selling books, known for his prolificity, who reached his broadest audience with the Kent Family Chronicles of early American history beginning with *The Bastard* (1974) and the Civil War trilogy beginning with *North and South* (1982), both subjects of televised miniseries. Jakes's first love, however, was science fiction, and he has written sixteen novels and two collections under his own name and others under the name of Jay Scotland. He has also written as Alan Payne and William Ard.

Jakes turned to full-time writing in 1971, after earning a bachelor's degree from DePauw University and a master's degree in American literature from Ohio State, and working as a copywriter for pharmaceutical companies and advertising agencies. His most popular character in the field is his Conanlike Brak, who fights his way through a series of heroic fantasy adventures such as *Brak the Barbarian* (collection, 1968), *Brak versus the Mark of the Demon* (1969), *Brak the Barbarian versus the Sorceress* (1969), and *Fortunes of Brak* (collection, 1980). His more imaginative novels, however, belong to his Dragonard series, including *When the Star Kings Die* (1967), *The Planet Wizard* (1969), and *Tonight We Steal Stars* (1969), in which the Dragonard clan guards corporate star kings from galactic perils. The Klekton series, *Master of the Dark Gate* (1970) and *Witch of the Dark Gate* (1972), features alternate Earths that can be reached through mind gates and are occupied by humans descended from a pre–Ice Age civilization.

Jakes has been principally an author of adventure fiction, known for his ability to create intriguing situations and strong narrative lines—talents equally suitable to his best-selling historical fiction. He is also capable, however, of such pungent satire as *On Wheels* (1973), about a subculture a century in the future that lives its entire existence on the superhighways, and the stories found in *The Best of John Jakes* (1977). He has also written SF and fantasy plays.

NOTABLE OTHER WORKS: *The Asylum World* (1969); *The Hybrid* (1969); *Secrets of Stardeep* (juvenile, 1969); *Black in Time* (1970); *Mask of Chaos* (1970); *Monte Cristo 99* (1970); *Six-Gun Planet* (1970); *Mention My Name in Atlantis* (1972); *Time Gate* (juvenile, 1972); *Conquest of the Planet of the Apes* (novelization, 1972).

J.E.G.

JAMESON, MALCOLM (1891–1945).

American writer who became a frequent contributor to science-fiction magazines after illness forced him to retire from his career as a naval officer in 1938. Jameson's navy experience inspired a popular juvenile SF series in ASTOUNDING STORIES, most of which was collected in *Bullard of Space Patrol* (1940–1945/1951). His near future disaster novel *The Giant Atom*, originally printed in *Startling Stories*, in 1944, attracted much attention and was published in paperback with the title *Atomic Bomb* (1945).

OTHER WORK: *Tarnished Utopia* (1943/1956).

J.H.

JANIFER, LAURENCE M[ARK] (1933–).

American writer, born Larry Mark Harris, who adopted his present name in 1963. Janifer started his literary career as an editor with the Scott Meredith Literary Agency.

At the height of the science-fiction magazine boom, Meredith had come to an arrangement with various publishers to use his clients' stories to package several magazines, including *Cosmos SF & Fantasy Magazine* (1953–1954) for which Janifer served as uncredited editor. Janifer in turn used the opportunity to publish his first story, "Expatriate" (1953). Today the interested reader can find it in his only collection to date, *Impossible?* (1968).

Janifer left Meredith's agency in 1957 to become a professional comedian. He also began to write novels, initially in collaboration with Randall GARRETT under the pseudonym Mark Phillips. The first of these, *Brain Twister* (1962; serialized in ASTOUNDING STORIES in 1959 as "That Sweet Little Old Lady") was nominated for a Hugo Award. *The Impossibles* (1960/1963) and *Supermind* (1960/1963) were also amusing tales of a secret agent pitted against people with various psi talents. Janifer also collaborated with S. J. Treibich on another humorous series of novels featuring a protagonist named Angelo di Stefano: *Target: Terra* (1968), *The High Hex* (1969), and *The Wagered World* (1969).

Janifer's own novels often center on issues of power, including the power to torture, and rebellion. These are often dealt with ironically and satirically, to expose humanity's concerns about power, morality, and sexual taboos, as in *You Sane Men* (1965; 1968 as *Bloodworld*) and *Power* (1974). Janifer has also written fourteen other non-SF novels under his own name and as Larry M. Harris, Alfred Blake, Barbara Wilson, and Andrew Blake.

OTHER WORKS: *Slave Planet* (1963); *The Wonder War* (1964); *A Piece of Martin Cann* (1968); *Survivor* (1977); *Knave in Hand* (1979); *Reel* (1983).

M.A.

LA JETEE (1962). *Directed by Chris Marker; screenplay by Chris Marker; photographed by Jean Chiabaud; music by Trevor Duncan. With Helene Chatelain, Davos Hanich, Jacques Ledoux. 29 minutes. Black and white. Alternate title:* The Jetty.

In a post–nuclear holocaust Paris scientists struggle to save humanity by obtaining resources from the past or the future. Attempts to achieve time travel with random subjects fail (the subjects die) until the scientists work with people who can retain strong mental images. One person in particular (Davos Hanich) has an obsession with a childhood memory. Through injections and electrodes attached to his mask, the scientists manage to free him to roam the past, where he meets the girl who was part of this obsession, and then the future, where he is given a power supply to save his time. Realizing he is now expendable, he asks to be sent to the past: he arrives on the jetty of Orly Airport where, running toward the woman, he discovers that he is the man

his childhood self saw executed.

This short film story is told in stills; it contains only one "moving picture" (when the woman's eyelids blink), and this sudden movement is as stunning as the switch to color in Sergey Eisenstein's *Ivan the Terrible*. Anti-Proustian in its grim view of time, this cult favorite is at once thought provoking and pretentious—melancholia with a vengeance. The stream-of-photographs technique chillingly evokes a sense of time as a trap, but the insistently moody music and narration keep nudging one emotionally, as if to say, "Isn't it all so triste?"

D.W.

JETER, K. W. (1950–   ). American writer. Jeter might best be described as a premature CYBERPUNK, whose work attained greater recognition after its grittily high-tech street scene became identified with the cyberpunk movement. His best-known novel, the controversial *Dr. Adder*, with its Los Angeles sewer background, surgically altered prostitutes, and decadence, was written in 1972. Its eventual 1984 publication included an afterword by Philip K. DICK comparing the author to James Joyce and Henry Miller. Jeter's first published novel, *Seeklight* (1975), got similar high praise from Barry N. MALZBERG, whose introduction called it "one of the three or four best SF novels I have ever read." It and *Dreamfields* (1976), which like much of Jeter's work shares Dick's search for reality, were published by Laser (which was a short-lived attempt by Harlequin Books to adapt its romance distribution formula to science fiction). They were followed by *Morlock Night* (1979), which tries to complete H. G. WELLS's *The Time Machine* (1895) by having the Morlocks invade 1892 England.

After the publication of two horror novels, *Soul Eater* (1893) and *Night Vision* (1985), Jeter entered a period of high productivity with *The Glass Hammer* (1985), *Dark Seeker* (1987), *Infernal Devices* (1987), *Death Arms* (1987), and another horror novel, *Mantis* (1987). With his gut-wrenching subjects and writing skills, Jeter may be an author to keep track of, although those characteristics also may lead him further into the horror field and out of SF.

J.E.G.

JOHNSON, GEORGE CLAYTON (1929–   ). American writer who is best known for his novel *Logan's Run* (with William F. NOLAN, 1967), which was filmed in 1976 and became a television series for one season (1977–78). Johnson contributed three short stories to the science-fiction magazine *Gamma* in the early 1960s, but he has worked primarily as a writer of screenplays and teleplays (notably for the original TWILIGHT ZONE).

N.H.

SEE ALSO: LOGAN'S RUN

JONES, D[ENNIS] F[ELTHAM] (1917–1981).

British writer, formerly an officer in the Royal Navy, bricklayer, and market gardener. In Jones's novel *Colossus* (1966), the title is the name given to a super-computer designed by Dr. Charles Forbin to defend the West against nuclear attack. After forming an alliance with Guardian, its Russian equivalent, Colossus proceeds to take over the world. Two sequels attracted little notice, but the story was effectively filmed as COLOSSUS: THE FORBIN PROJECT in 1969. All set in the near future, Jones's later novels are routinely gloomy and pessimistic; among them are *Implosion* (1967), which describes the fate of a small number of fertile women in a world where most others have become sterile; the geological catastrophe of *Don't Pick the Flowers* (1971, American title *Denver is Missing*); and the alien invasion of *Xeno* (1979, American title *Earth Has Been Found*).

OTHER WORKS: *The Fall of Colossus* (1974); *The Floating Zombie* (1975); *Colossus and the Crab* (1977).

R.D.

JONES, NEIL R[ONALD] (1909–).

American author and government worker, one of the first writers of future history. Starting in 1931 with "The Jameson Satellite" *(Amazing)*, Jones produced a series of stories that continued until 1968. The hero is Prof. Jameson, a twentieth-century man who arranged to preserve his body after death by having it entombed in a special rocket that orbited the Earth. Many centuries later, long after all humanity is gone, his brain is revived and placed in a metal body by the Zoromes, alien cyborgs. Jameson's adventures in the twenty-fourth through twenty-sixth centuries and his wonderful discoveries quickly became popular with many readers. Over half these stories are contained in five collections: *The Planet of the Double Sun* (1967), *The Sunless World* (1967), *Space War* (1967), *Twin Worlds* (1967), and *Doomsday on Ajiat* (collection, 1968).

S.H.G.

JONES, RAYMOND F. (1915–).

American author most active in the 1940s and 1950s and best remembered today for his novel *This Island Earth* (1952), which was the basis of the popular film of the same name (1955). Jones's book was in fact a pale attempt to recapture the magic of his first novel, *Renaissance* (1944/1951; as *Man of Two Worlds*, 1963), a richly detailed story of the vital but tenuous links between a destroyed Earth and another world. Few of Jones's other novels equaled it, although his later books for younger readers were good introductions to science fiction for their day: *Son of the Stars* (1952), *Planet of Light* (1953), *The Year When Stardust Fell* (1958), and *Moonbase One* (1971). Jones's best and most original work was in his short fiction, especially "Fifty Million Monkeys" (1943), in which the principle of random thought is brought to bear on a problem, and its spiritual successor, "The Non-statistical Man" (1956). Along with "The Toymaker" (1946), "The Children's Room" (1947), and "The Moon Is Death" (1953), they have a competence and originality lacking in Jones's more recent and longer works.

NOTABLE OTHER WORKS: *The Alien* (1951); *The Toymaker* (1951); *The Secret People* (1956; as *The Deviates*, 1959); *The Cybernetic Brains* (1950/1962); *The Non-statistical Man* (1964); *Syn* (1969); *Renegades of Time* (1975); *The King of Eolim* (1975); *The River and the Dream* (1977); and *Weeping May Tarry* (with Lester del Rey, 1978).

M.A.

——————— THE JOURNEY ———————

The journey is one of the basic themes in ancient and classical literature as well as in modern science fiction. The mystery of what lies beyond the horizon—or the planet—has always lured people; even stay-at-homes have been eager to hear, read, or see tales of the distant unknown and the exotic unknowable. But the purpose of the journey in literature is not simply to arrive somewhere; the trip itself is fraught with peril, uncertainty, and adventure, as much in ancient times as in prospect.

The pattern of the literary journey—a lone adventurer or a band carefully assembled who by accident or design sally beyond the ken—was fixed in the earliest fiction: Gilgamesh, the Sumerian hero (ca. 2000 B.C.), goes on a long journey to discover immortality, and Odysseus's troubled travels home from Troy (ca. eighth century B.C.) were so influential as the model for later works that *odyssey* became an alternate term for the journey of adventure and discovery. The point of Homer's story, like that of so many journeys, is not so much what Odysseus discovers when he finally gets home to Ithaca but what happens to him along the way. Journeys are learning and testing experiences.

The pattern of SF journeys that cross space or time instead of seas has changed only in the addition of scientific or pseudoscientific rationales for the means of travel and sometimes in the stress on self-discovery over the discovery of other beings and places. In the process the best tales set forth the writer's philosophy through the hero's goals: to return home, to defeat an enemy threatening the hero's life or world, to rescue a friend or lover, to achieve immortality for oneself or for humanity, to gain godlike powers or keep the villain from attaining them, to make the world better, or just to survive.

Gilgamesh and Odysseus, to be sure, arrive home wiser men, but the earliest known physical journey that ends specifically in self-knowledge may be the biblical

Lunar projectile trains from Verne's *From the Earth to the Moon*

Book of Jonah (ca. 300 B.C.). After being swallowed by a big fish, Jonah is spat out upon a beach, goes to Nineveh, that great and wicked city Jonah wishes God to destroy, and discovers that he is not as righteous as he thought and that Gentiles too are children of God. Twentieth-century SF journeys, such as Alexei PANSHIN's *Rite of Passage* (1968) and David LINDSAY's *A Voyage to Arcturus* (1920), also focus on self-revelation; it is worth noting that their methods of travel, interstellar spaceship and "crystal torpedo," are no more scientifically possible than Jonah's whale.

LUCIAN OF SAMOSATA, surnamed The Blasphemer, wrote two satiric proto-SF works: *Icaromenippus*, which tells of a philosopher who straps on one wing from a vulture and one from an eagle and flies to the Moon; and *A True Story*, which satirizes the travel stories of his predecessors (including Homer) by having the ship of a band of adventurers caught up in a storm and carried to the Moon, where the characters fight for the King of the Moon against the armies of the Sun King for the right to colonize Venus.

Utopias, beginning with Thomas MORE's eponymous 1516 work, used the journey as a means of making their ideal states more plausible—explaining why the world has not heard of the utopia in question as well as describing how perfection can exist in a corrupt world—and utopias such as Campanella's *The City of the Sun* (1623) and Francis Bacon's *The New Atlantis* (1627) are similar to *A True Story* in that their journeys are more entertaining than the dialogues and descriptions that follow.

The *means* of travel has, for many writers of SF, been as important as the journey itself; the genre continues to be fascinated with the mechanics of things. Johannes KEPLER's *Somnium* (1634) is about a dream voyage to the Moon (by demon), but the hero of Bishop Francis Godwin's *The Man in the Moone* (1638) is lifted by a bird-drawn chariot. CYRANO de Bergerac, in his satiric and still lively *States and Empires of the Moon* (1657) and *Comic History of the States of the Sun* (1662), described several methods of levitation, including dew in glass bottles that are drawn up by the Sun and rockets. *Travels into Several Remote Nations of the World: Four Parts* (1726)—better known as *Gulliver's Travels*—is still a widely read example of proto-SF, enjoyed by both children and adults, though for different reasons. Jonathan SWIFT's journeys, however, are only the means to launch Gulliver into new satiric situations. *The Consolidator* (1705) by Daniel Defoe is a social satire in which the hero uses an alcohol-burning machine to get to the Moon; Defoe's *Robinson Crusoe* (1719), though not SF, does involve a journey and influenced a great deal of later SF, particularly Jules VERNE's *The Mysterious Island* (1875), which begins with a journey via a balloon caught up in a storm, like that of Lucian's characters.

Most of these early journeys aimed at the Moon, and the Moon continued to be the most prominent off-Earth destination in the eighteenth and early nineteenth centuries. Samuel Brunt's satiric *A Voyage to Cacklogallinia* (1728), Murtagh McDermot's *A Trip to the Moon* (1728), and Ralph Morris's *The Life and Astonishing Transactions of John Daniel* (1751) are about journeys to the lunar world. The protagonist of Baron Ludvig HOLBERG's satiric *Journey to the World Underground* (1741) goes to the center of the Earth. But Joseph ATTERLEY's *A Voyage to the Moon* (1827) and Edgar Allan POE's "Hans Pfaall" (1835), in which his hero ascends to the Moon in a balloon, reverted to the favorite far-off place of contemporary satire-romancers. Poe's *The Narrative of Arthur Gordon Pym* (1838) is almost all voyage (and not remotely SF) until Pym arrives near Antarctica.

In the later nineteenth century, as proto-SF began evolving into science fiction, writers started to extrapolate from the new ideas, discoveries, and techniques

Aerophile from the British magazine edition (1928) of Wells's *When the Sleeper Wakes*

created by the accelerating Industrial Revolution and the burgeoning of science and technology, pushing their fiction out into the Solar System and beyond through travel. But the worlds at journey's end were usually no more realistic than those of their predecessors. Jules Verne's *From the Earth to the Moon* (1865) and *Around the Moon* (1870) were the first true hard-core SF stories because they represented the attempt by an SF writer to adhere strictly to contemporary scientific knowledge—although Verne failed as a prophet by using an enormous cannon, rather than the rocket proposed by his fellow Frenchman, de Bergerac, to launch his spaceship.

John Jacob ASTOR's spaceship in *A Journey to Other Worlds* (1894) is propelled by an antigravity source called apergy, derived from Percy GREG's *Across the Zodiac* (1880). Astor also may have been influenced by Marie Corelli's *A Romance of Two Worlds* (1886), in which interstellar travel is achieved by "personal electricity," and Robert CROMIE's *A Plunge into Space (1890)*, which uses an antigravity device and touches on some of the harsh realities of space voyaging. William R. Bradshaw, whose *The Goddess of Atvatabar* (1892) is a grandiose tale of a voyage to the center of the Earth, exemplifies writers who choose to go inward instead of outward. Gustavus W. Pope's *Journey to Mars* (1894) was followed by his *Romance of the Planets, No. 2: Journey to Venus* (1895). John Munro's *A Trip to Venus* (1897) was the first story to use the modern method of multistage rockets for propulsion.

H. G. WELLS, in *The First Men in the Moon* (1901), used an antigravity metal named Cavorite; he knew the metal was scientifically impossible, but he was more interested in depicting possible societies than means of travel. The same may be said for his *The Time Machine* (1895), which is confined to a small geographic area but journeys far in time.

Around the turn of the century George Griffith, Ellsworth Douglas, Fenton Ash, John Mastin, Garrett P. Serviss, and Edwin L. Arnold all wrote novels about journeys in space. The most influential use of another planet began with Edgar Rice BURROUGHS's "Under the Moons of Mars" (1912; as *A Princess of Mars*, 1917). Its hero, John Carter, and a later character named Ulysses Paxton shuttle by astral projecton between Earth and Mars in this novel and its sequels; their process may have anticipated STAR TREK's method of beaming matter without a receiver to re-form the dissociated molecules because Carter and Paxton were able to form flesh around their projected "souls" after arriving at their destinations.

Astral voyages in space and time also are made by the hero of Jack LONDON's *The Star Rover* (1915), while the unnamed hero of London's *Beyond Adam* (1906) achieves the similar experience of reincarnation by racial memory. Journeys are common in the gadget-oriented dime novels about Frank Reade, Jr., as they are in almost all of Verne's *voyages extraordinaires;* several series of adventure stories for boys, particularly the Tom Swift series by Victor Appleton (house name) and the Great

Marvel series by Roy Rockwood (house name), were constructed around journeys, although their focus, as in Verne's work, usually is a novel vehicle or method of propulsion, for instance, in Rockwood's *Through Space to Mars* (1910), which uses waves pushed against the ether by an "Etherium motor."

Arthur Conan DOYLE's *The Lost World* (1912) followed the pattern of the earlier lost-race romances launched by H. Rider HAGGARD's *She* (1887) in locating the plateau that has sheltered dinosaurs in the remotest corner of Brazil, where it must be reached by an arduous journey.

Perhaps the best example of rigorous but inventive extrapolation from given scientific premises is Hal CLEMENT's *Mission of Gravity* (1953/1954). The trip across a high-gravity planet, Mesklin, by the centipedelike natives, aided from a distance by Earth dwellers, is a journey of self-discovery that can truly be called an odyssey in which the journey itself is the focus. Murray LEINSTER in "Proxima Centauri" (1935) and Don WILCOX in "The Voyage That Lasted 600 Years" (1940) were the first to deal with the concept of the generation starship, in which only the descendants of the original passengers will reach their destinations. But Robert A. HEINLEIN's "Universe" (1941) and its sequel "Common Sense" (1941; as *Orphans of the Sky*, 1963) achieve the journey's most complete realization as a theme: the real history and purpose of the voyage are lost after a mutiny, and myths develop that consider the spaceship the entire universe and the voyage as the journey between creation and the final end of life.

Aniara (1956), an epic poem about a starship by the Swede Harry Martinson, became the basis for the first true space opera, performed in 1959. Other noteworthy treatments of starships are Judith MERRIL's "Wish upon a Star" (1958), Brian W. ALDISS's *Non-Stop* (1958; as *Starship*, 1959), Edmund COOPER's *Seed of Light* (1959), J. T. McINTOSH's *200 Years to Christmas* (1961), A. E. van VOGT's *Rogue Ship* (1965), Samuel R. DELANY's *The Ballad of Beta-2* (1965), Harry HARRISON's *Captive Universe* (1969), Damien Broderick's "The Star Mutants" (1970), and Brian M. STABLEFORD's *Promised Land* (1974). Perhaps the most mind-expanding version is Poul ANDERSON's *Tau Zero* (1970), in which a starship accelerates uncontrollably and slows down the rate of time passage for its crew, which witnesses the death of the universe and the rebirth of a new one. Larry NIVEN's *Ringworld* (1970) describes not only the difficulties in getting to a distant star but the adventures of the characters as they attempt to explore this magnificent piece of engineering with its enormous surface area: two journeys for the price of one.

Other space voyage works not about starships are "Shadow in Space" (1967) by Philip José FARMER, in which a faster-than-light vessel expands to become larger than the universe and is trapped in hyperspace (a crew member lights his cigar on a dying galaxy); Richard A. LUPOFF's *Into the Aether* (1974), a satire on Roy Rockwood–type SF; Farmer's comic *Venus on the Half-Shell* (1975, as Kilgore Trout), in which the antihero seeks the origin of the universe and the cause of pain and death; his *The Unreasoning Mask* (1981), in which the hero discovers that intrauniverse spaceships cause the collapse of the "walls" between universes, which are in reality the cells in the body of an infant God; Piers ANTHONY's *Macroscope* (1969), another mind bender in which the journey through the universe is accomplished by shrinking Neptune and using its superdense matter to punch holes in the fabric of space-matter, thus giving the travelers shortcuts to their destinations; and George ZEBROWSKI's *Macrolife* (1979), which makes the journey the permanent and ideal state for the human species as it establishes its future home not by settling on distant planets but by traveling in space itself.

In any period the method of SF travel reflects what writers are able, given the state of contemporary technology, to imagine. But the purposes of the journey are always the same: to allow the characters, and through them the readers, to undergo the concept-changing, character-shaping experience of travel and to reach the enlightenment and revelations of the unknown.

P.J.F.

JOURNEY TO THE CENTER OF THE EARTH (1959). *Directed by Henry Levin; screenplay by Walter Reisch and Charles Brackett; adapted from the novel by Jules Verne; photographed by Leo Tover; music by Bernard Herrmann. With James Mason, Pat Boone, Arlene Dahl, Thayer David, Peter Ronson, Diane Baker, Alan Napier, Alan Caillou, Ivan Triesault. 132 minutes. Color.*

The financial success of several Jules VERNE adaptations prompted 20th Century–Fox to produce this expensive version of one of Verne's best-known novels. The brightly colored film was a hit, inspiring Fox to make several similar movies.

Edinburgh professor Lindenbrook (James Mason) finds evidence that a famous explorer had once gone to the center of the Earth, so he sets out on his own mission, accompanied by a student (Pat Boone), the widow of an unlucky rival (Arlene Dahl), an Icelandic farmer (Peter Ronson), and a duck; they go on foot down extinct volcanic fissures. They are followed by Count Saknussem (Thayer David), a descendant of the explorer, who tries to stop them; the imperious count even eats the duck. After facing a series of hazards (including crabby dimetrodons), the travelers do reach the center of the Earth, and a volcano shoots the survivors back to the surface.

The only significant alteration to Verne's plot is the addition of the woman; some of his events are omitted, but most are here. The principal change is in tone: never taking itself seriously, the film walks a knife-edge between parody and melodrama. This approach won it many supporters and keeps it entertaining today.

It was also splendidly if erratically produced; some of the sets, beautiful though they may be, look artificial; a few scenes were shot in Carlsbad Caverns. The dimetrodons, impersonated by iguanas with attached fins, are especially successful for lizards-as-dinosaurs. Mason plays Lindenbrook as an impatient, egocentric, and tireless scientific romantic, precisely in keeping with the approach of the film. David is an outstanding villain, and the rest of the performers, including Boone, are acceptable. The score by Bernard Herrmann is one of the great composer's finest—sonorous, majestic, and imaginative.

B.W.

JOURNEY TO THE SEVENTH PLANET (1961).
Directed by Sidney Pink; screenplay by Ib Melchior and Sidney Pink (latter uncredited); photographed by Age Wiltrup; music by Ib Glindemann. With John Agar, Carl Ottosen, Ove Sprogøe, Louis Miehe Renard, Peter Monch, Greta Thyssen, Ann Smyrner. 83 minutes. Color.

In 2001 an expedition to Uranus battles an evil alien brain capable of bringing into reality the desires and fears of its opponents.

The central concept of this film is imaginative, but it is poorly developed, with amateurish performances and inept special effects. The basic idea, derived from FORBIDDEN PLANET (1956), makes the film worth watching once for the hard-core connoisseur, but others beware.

B.W.

JUST IMAGINE (1930).
Directed by David Butler; screenplay by David Butler, B. G. DeSylva, Lew Brown, and Ray Henderson; photographed by Ernest Palmer; music by B. G. DeSylva, Lew Brown, and Ray Henderson. With El Brendel, Frank Albertson, Maureen O'Sullivan, John Garrick, Marjorie White, Hobart Bosworth, Kenneth Thomson, Mischa Auer. 113 minutes. Black and white.

In the wonder world of 1980—with its television phones, building-to-building autogyro travel, food pills, and automatic doors, people are still people—and young J-21 (John Garrick) has to prove himself in order to be worthy of LN-18 (Maureen O'Sullivan). He and a Norwegian revived from the year 1930 (El Brendel) make a trip to Mars and back, and J-21 gets LN-18.

Just Imagine is notable for its extensive cityscape miniatures, perhaps the best (and certainly the most hopeful) for decades to come. During the period when

it was made, there was much speculation about the coming utopia, and just after the advent of sound, studios produced many lavish musicals; this first science-fiction musical probably was inevitable. But it is dated today, a lethargic and elephantine joke, innocently racist and sexist, a curiosity. To viewers aware of the Depression and World War II looming ahead, however, its buoyant optimism may seem evanescent and tragic.

B.W.

K

KAPP, COLIN (1929–).
British writer and electronics consultant, best known for his hard-core science-fiction stories in the style of Arthur C. CLARKE and Larry NIVEN. Kapp's first story, "Life Plan" (1958), appeared in the British magazine NEW WORLDS, which regularly featured his stories, including "Lambda 1" (1962) and its novel-length sequel, *The Dark Mind* (1963/1965, American title *Transfinite Man*). These works depict interdimensional travel. Kapp became best known for his Unorthodox Engineers series, wherein the Engineers find themselves tackling increasingly complicated scientific puzzles. The first of its stories was "The Railways Up on Cannis" (1959); it was followed by several others in the British anthology series *New Writings in SF*.

In his novels Kapp can always be relied on to weave a compelling story amid a wealth of high-tech details, and he frequently introduces aspects of ESP or even elements of mysticism. *The Patterns of Chaos* (1972) and its sequel, *The Chaos Weapon* (1977), for example, describe multidimensional gods. Further scientific problems arise in *The Wizard of Anharitte* (1973); both *The Survival Game* (1976) and *Manalone* (1977) pit society and science against bureaucracy. Kapp's most ambitious project to date has been his Cageworld series, set in a system of concentric Dyson spheres and consisting of *Cageworld* (1982; published in the United States as *Search for the Sun*, 1983), *The Lost Worlds of Cronus* (1982), *The Tyrant of Hades* (1982), and *Star Search* (1983).

M.A.

KARLOFF, BORIS (Born William Henry Pratt) (1887–1969).
British actor who appeared in films that often mix science-fiction elements with horror motifs and vice versa. Karloff was an accomplished stage actor before making his first film appearance in 1916. Beloved by the public and highly respected by his peers, he made approximately 150 films; his recordings and television appearances were numerous, and he hosted the popular

television series *Thriller.*

Karloff's soft voice with a slight lisp was his trademark, but his portrayal of the Frankenstein monster established him as a master of menace. Viewers of SF films best remember him for his roles in such films as FRANKENSTEIN (1931), *The Mummy* (1932), *The Black Cat* (1934), THE INVISIBLE RAY (1936), *The Walking Dead* (1936), *The Man Who Lived Again* (1936), *The Invisible Menace* (1938), *Tower of London* (1939), *The Boogie Man Will Get You* (1942), *The Body Snatcher* (1945), *Isle of the Dead* (1945), *Bedlam* (1946), *The Raven* (1963), *The Terror* (1963), *Black Sabbath* (1964), *The Venetian Affair* (1967), and *Targets* (1968). Karloff's greatest contribution to film was his enduring presence, which brought a subtle sense of menace to SF and horror alike.

H.L.P.

KELLER, DAVID H[ENRY] (1880–1966).
American author, physician, and pyschiatrist. Although the technique displayed in Keller's contributions to the early PULP MAGAZINES was primitive by any standard, their content was often sophisticated. From his first story, "Revolt of the Pedestrians" (in AMAZING STORIES, 1928), he dealt with social issues. Just as Henry Ford was putting America on wheels, Keller wrote of a future in which the legs of the "automobilists" have atrophied, rendering all but a few uncivilized "pedestrians" utterly dependent on their cars. In "Stenographer's Hands" (1928) a selective breeding program produces the ultimate typist—with catastrophic consequences. "A Biological Experiment" (1928) prefigured Aldous HUXLEY's *Brave New World* (1932) with its characters' revolt against artificial human reproduction. (They adjourn to the wilderness and do it the old way.)

Much of Keller's short fiction displays faults typical of GERNSBACK-era writing, including exposition of the idea to the virtual exclusion of plot and characterization. His novels are somewhat more complicated, although two of his best, *The Metal Doom* (1932) and *The Abyss* (1948), share the same throwaway ending: civilization is threatened by catastrophe (the loss of metals, a whole population under the influence of a drug that releases ancestral memories). Ultimately, though, Keller didn't know what to do with the menace so it just goes away.

Much of Keller's finest work is not SF but psychological horror based on his psychiatric experiences. He also wrote whimsical fantasies. He did little work after 1935, and most of his work published later was written years before.

OTHER WORKS: *The Solitary Hunters and the Abyss* (1948); *Life Everlasting and Other Tales of Science, Fantasy, and Horror* (collection, 1949); *Tales from the Underwood* (collection, 1952); *The Folsom Flint and Other Curious Tales* (collection, 1969).

D.S.

KEPLER, JOHANNES (1571–1630).
German astronomer and champion of the heliocentric theory of the universe. To dramatize his theory Kepler wrote an essay in the form of an imaginary voyage, the *Somnium* (1634; probably first written in 1593; best English translation by E. Rosen in 1967). Its description of events seen by an observer on the Moon is supplemented by speculations about lunar life. It represents the interest in space flight, extraterrestrial worlds, and informed speculation that would lead, two hundred years later, to science fiction.

B.S.

KESSEL, JOHN (1950–   ).
American writer and professor of English at North Carolina State University. Kessel began publishing short stories while still a graduate student and since then has published two dozen stories, one of which, his novella "Another Orphan," was part of his doctoral dissertation at the University of Kansas and won the Nebula Award in 1983. In 1985 he published his first novel, *Freedom Beach* (with James Patrick Kelly).

Kessel's science fiction is marked by his emphasis on characterization and literary values, and often a preoccupation with surrealism and decadence. The most effective and original of his short stories, "Not Responsible! Park and Lock It!" (1981), depicts a convincing and well-developed future society of families who live out their entire lives driving down an endless megalane highway. *Freedom Beach* concerns the plight of Shaun Reed, whose reality is being manipulated by sinister "dreamers." Like much of Kessel's work, the novel is developed primarily through pastiche and literary satire.

N.H.

KEYES, DANIEL (1927–   ).
American professor of English and occasional writer of science fiction; author of one of the field's most highly regarded stories, "Flowers for Algernon" (1959). After leaving college in 1950, Keyes was employed for eighteen months as associate fiction editor with Stadium Publications and thus worked for a while on *Marvel Science Fiction.* After a period in fashion photography, he turned to teaching in 1955, becoming lecturer in English at Ohio University in 1966 and professor in 1972. Writing has always been incidental to his academic career. Keyes sold his first story, "Robot Unwanted," in 1952, but since then he has written barely a dozen stories.

"Flowers for Algernon" is the poignant tale of an experiment in enhancing the INTELLIGENCE of a mentally retarded man, Charlie Gordon, told through his journal entries as his mental capacity and understanding, and his ability to communicate, gradually improve. Then, after peaking at the genius level, he sees the experimental

Daniel Keyes

subject that has preceded him, the mouse Algernon, first lose its mental improvement, then die, and Charlie records his deterioration once more to his former state. The novelette won the Hugo Award, and the later novelization in 1966 won the Nebula Award. The story went on to be filmed as CHARLY (1968) and earned Cliff Robertson an Oscar for the title role. It also has been adapted for television as "The Two Worlds of Charlie Gordon."

Keyes has written two other novels with borderline SF associations: *The Touch* (1968; published in Britain as *The Contaminated Man*, 1977), which looks at the psychological stress of radioactive contamination, and *The Fifth Sally* (1980), which fictionalizes the true case of a girl with multiple personalities.

M.A.

KIDD, VIRGINIA (1921–). American literary agent and editor; a member of the FUTURIANS fan group in the mid-1940s and James BLISH's first wife. Kidd has represented many major authors (including Ursula K. LE GUIN, Anne McCAFFREY, R. A. LAFFERTY, Michael Swanwick, Gene WOLFE, Gardner DOZOIS, Alan Dean FOSTER, and the late Tom Reamy and James TIPTREE, Jr.), and she has helped to shape and influence science fiction for many years. In addition, she is the editor of *The Best of Judith Merril* (1976) and *Millennial Women* (1978), and the coeditor (with Roger Elwood) of *Saving Worlds* (1973) and (with Le Guin) of *Nebula Award Stories Eleven* (1976) and *Interfaces* (1980).

B.D.

KILLOUGH, [KAREN] LEE (1942–). American writer and radiological technologist. Killough's science fiction, which often incorporates elements of fantasy, is first and foremost concerned with character. Her short stories, particularly those collected in *Aventine* (1982), deal with women and men who strive for better lives, frequently without understanding what is wrong with their present ones. Her use of language, often dramatically vivid and imagistic, creates the perfect tone for her plots, which usually involve disillusionment, revenge, murder, and decadence.

Killough often makes use of feminist material in her novels, although her strong and decisive female characters are too rounded to be simply mouthpieces for political and social statements. In *A Voice out of Ramah* (1979), the feminist message is embodied in a male protagonist, who disguises himself as a woman in order to thwart a priesthood that controls the planet Ramah. In the position of a woman helped by other women, this once privileged man learns that the nature of freedom lies in the right of each individual, irrespective of gender, to determine the course of his or her life.

Killough's novels frequently combine mystery with fantasy and SF. *The Monitor, the Miners, and the Shree* (1980) highlights alien cultures, describing a group of interplanetary problem solvers who deal with a series of unusual crimes and crises. *The Doppelgänger Gambit* (1979) features a detective story complicated by a repressive society and abused technology. Both these novels show Killough's fine ability to portray both human and alien minds that are psychologically complex and emotionally vulnerable. Her use of science is at least up to the needs of her stories: she creates believable hardware and does not cast technology as a cardboard villain.

OTHER WORKS: *Deadly Silents* (1981); *Liberty's World* (1985).

S.H.G.

KING KONG (1933). *Directed by Merian C. Cooper and Ernest B. Schoedsack; screenplay by James Creelman and Ruth Rose; photographed by Edward Linden, Vernon L. Walker, and J. O. Taylor; music by Max Steiner. With Fay Wray, Robert Armstrong, Bruce Cabot, Frank Reicher, Sam Hardy, Noble Johnson, Steve Clemento, James Flavin, Victor Wong. 100 minutes. Black and white.*

SON OF KONG (1934). *Directed by Ernest B. Schoedsack; screenplay by Ruth Rose; photographed by Edward Linden, Vernon Walker, and J. O. Taylor; music by Max Steiner. With Robert Armstrong, Helen Mack, Frank Reicher, Noble Johnson, Victor Wong, John Marston. 69 minutes. Black and white.*

King Kong stands as one of the greatest adventure films, a science-fiction–horror thriller of enduring popularity; its appeal remains undimmed despite imitations,

Kong atop the Empire State Building in the original *King Kong* (1933)

sequels, and remakes. Its audacity, the splendor of its design by Carroll Clark and Al Herman, the romantic perfection of its story, the imagination of its special effects by Willis O'Brien—all have contributed to making *Kong* one of the most famous movies of all time. The film has long since passed into the realm of actual myth.

King Kong was conceived by Merian C. Cooper and directed by him and his collaborator, Ernest B. Schoedsack; these remarkable men are the basis for the characters played by Robert Armstrong and Bruce Cabot; they appear briefly as the pilot and gunner of the plane that kills Kong. Screenwriter Ruth Rose was married to Schoedsack.

The story of *King Kong* is too familiar to be detailed here; it is sufficent to say that a giant gorilla found on a lost island of prehistoric monsters is brought back to 1933 New York. Enamored of a blond actress, he escapes and climbs with her to the top of the Empire State Building, where biplanes kill him. But it wasn't the planes, as Carl Denham says, it was beauty killed the beast.

Kong was a puppet eighteen inches tall, jointed and covered in cotton and rabbit fur. Animated a frame at a time by O'Brien and his staff, the monster ape has a personality as vivid as that of the finest actor. There have been other similar films in which stop-motion animation is more realistic but none in which characterization is stronger or more appealing.

It is partly these superlative special effects, partly the sweep and scope of the epic, and partly an undefinable, unduplicable quality of enthusiasm, affection, and intensity *behind* the cameras that have kept *Kong* before the public so long. King Kong really may be, as he was billed in the film, the eighth wonder of the world.

The success of the movie prompted a sequel, *Son of Kong*, begun the same year. Denham returns to Skull Island, finds Kong's smaller, white-furred son, and the island sinks. Denham is saved by the young ape, who perishes. This film is a hurried affair, of much less interest than the original; the tone is more jocular; even the effects are below the standards set by *Kong*. Nonetheless, the film has some appeal.

Two Japanese films dealing with King Kong followed. The first, *King Kong vs. Godzilla* (1963), was distantly derived from a story line by O'Brien. The Kong in this film is an unspectacular, even tatty-looking man in a furry suit; he and Godzilla spar awhile, then both tumble into the sea. The second film, *King Kong Escapes* (1968), is a broad, silly fantasy involving a madman, a robot duplicate of Kong, aliens, and a big fight in Tokyo. The story elements of this film were used for an animated TV series about Kong. What interest these films have is in their place in Japanese monster movie history, not as Kong films.

Producer Dino De Laurentiis's remake of *King Kong* (1976) was financially successful, and many critics applauded the film. However, it struck others as cynical and exploitative; although the acting is generally good, the approach was to belittle the very idea of Kong. There are no dinosaurs in the film, the explorers are after oil rather than adventure, and the heroine is a well-used party girl rather than the innocent actress of the original. The filmmakers removed the grandeur; what is left is a slick piece of entertainment machinery. Kong is played by makeup expert Rick Baker in a suit he built with Carlo Rambaldi.

The sequel to the remake, *King Kong Lives!* (1986), was quickly and shoddily made, a spoof with no affection remaining, a cheap exploitation of the name of King Kong. It failed dramatically at the box office.

Today, as for over fifty years, for most people there is and always will be only one *King Kong*.

B.W.

KING, STEPHEN [EDWIN] (1947–). American writer of horror fiction, in which he is almost certainly the best selling and most popular writer in the world. Many of King's works fall in the realm of science ficiton, although they do not follow the SF tradition. After selling several short stories, starting with "The Glass Floor" (1967), King shot into the best-seller ranks with his first novel, *Carrie* (1974), about a pubescent girl with telekinetic powers. Neither of his next two novels, *'Salem's Lot* (1975) and *The Shining* (1977), nor his pseudonymous *Rage* (1977, as Richard Bachman) relies on SF motifs, but *The Stand* (1978) turns to the standard catastrophe theme (although King developed the novel along more mystical than apocalyptic lines), with almost the entire world's population destroyed by a virus. His next novel, *The Dead Zone* (1979), was specifically identified by King as SF; he withdrew it from contention for the World Fantasy Award. As with *Carrie*, it deals with psi-powers, in this case precognition. King developed the theme further in *Firestarter* (1980), about a girl with pyrokinetic powers. *Carrie*, *The Dead Zone*, and *Firestarter* form a powerful three-volume study of the human psyche and the relationship between gifted people and society.

King has also shown adeptness at mystical fantasies, in particular his Dark Tower sequence, of which *The Gunslinger* (1982) and *The Drawing of the Three* (1987) have to date been published, and in his collaboration with Peter Straub, *The Talisman* (1984). Here, as in Roger ZELAZNY's Amber series, we are presented with a world, The Territories, of which *our* world is but one reflection, and the novel depicts an epic quest across that world and our own. King's shorter fiction has been collected in *Night Shift* (1978) and *Skeleton Crew* (1985), the latter including his two most overt works of SF, "The Jaunt" (1981), about the psychological effects of instantaneous space travel, and "Beachworld" (1985), wherein explorers stranded on a world of sand dunes are haunted by a hostile planetary intelligence. King's abilities to use SF themes to create horrific effects are among the best realized in the field.

M.A.

KINGSBURY, DONALD [MACDONALD] (1929–). American-born Canadian writer and lecturer in mathematics. Apart from a short story in ASTOUNDING STORIES in 1952, Kingsbury did not publish fiction until 1978–79, when three of his novelettes appeared in ANALOG and were anthologized by Terry CARR (1979): "To Bring in the Steel" and "The Moon Goddess and the Son"—both parts of a near-future, "inner planet" series—and "Shipwright"—set in the same remote "finger" of the galaxy as the novel *Courtship Rite* (1982). An expanded novel version of "The Moon Goddess and the Son" was published in 1986.

Primarily a writer of hard science fiction, Kingsbury is concerned with creating histories, based—in his own words—on "real science constraints." The detailed biology of a planet with scanty resources and no higher forms of animal life in *Courtship Rite* invited comparisons with Frank HERBERT's *Dune*. The inhabitants of the planet are descendants of space-exploring humans who have survived in this harsh environment through cannibalism—quite effectively contrasted with the rediscovered military history of Earth and its killing "without intent to eat"—and the development of a clan-structured society, multiple marriages, and advanced genetics. The novel is remarkable for its intricate composition, adept handling of diverse viewpoints, male and female, and good storytelling.

J.H.

KIPLING, [JOSEPH] RUDYARD (1865– 1936). British author much of whose writing is of only indirect relevance to science fiction. Kipling's children's works—such as *The Jungle Books* (1894, 1895), *Kim* (1901), and *Just So Stories* (1902)—with their exotic settings, daring adventures, and talking animals, helped inspire Edgar Rice BURROUGHS's Tarzan; these same elements, transferred to outer space, may have indirectly brought about the SPACE OPERA brand of SF. In another children's book, *Puck of Pook's Hill* (1906), a series of historical figures—a Norman knight, a Roman centurion, and the like—come out of the past to narrate strange adventures, although no explanation is offered for their time-traveling abilities. "The Finest Story in the World" (1891) is really a fantasy, as it tells of a hopeless young poetaster who takes no interest in his visions—derived from a past life—of being a Greek galley slave and a member of the crew of a Viking ship. More pertinent to SF is the enigmatic story "Wireless" (1902), in which wireless telegraphy is likened to the tapping of spiritual waves in a séance, as an ignorant man falls into a trance and becomes "tuned" to the spirit of John Keats, writing down fragments of his poetry even though he has never read his work.

Kipling's principal contributions to SF are two long stories told with a circumstantiality that would not be characteristic of other SF for several decades, "With the Night Mail" (1905) and its sequel, "As Easy As A.B.C." (1912). In the former, subtitled "A Story of 2000 A.D.," the world is controlled by the A.B.C. (Aerial Board of Control), whose sole function is to facilitate worldwide travel: its motto is "Transportation Is Civilisation." "As Easy As A.B.C." provides further information on this society: set in 2065, it shows that the A.B.C. has abolished war and independent governments only by ruthless suppression. A radical sort of self-sufficiency is encouraged, in which democracy is a "disease," crowds are considered "against human nature," and concerted action does not exist. It is amusing to note that this system seems the precise opposite of the collectivist society depicted in Ayn Rand's *Anthem*.

S.T.J.

KLINE, OTIS ADELBERT (1891–1946).

American author, agent, composer, music publisher, film writer, and editor. A Chicago native and resident, Kline was a composer/song writer and music publisher before founding a literary agency, Otis Kline Associates. He followed in the footsteps of Edgar Rice BURROUGHS, A. MERRITT, and H. P. LOVECRAFT, both in contributing stories to *Weird Tales*, AMAZING STORIES, and *Argosy* and in the romantic-adventure tales he wrote.

Considered by most critics and readers as a Burroughs imitator, Kline also turned to the same Chicago book publisher, McClurg, after serialization in *Argosy*, for *The Planet of Peril* (1929), *The Prince of Peril* (1930), and *Maza of the Moon* (1930). The first two books form part of a trilogy (completed in 1932/1949 with *The Port of Peril*) about Robert Grandon's swashbuckling adventures on Venus, very similar to the swashbuckling adventures of Burroughs's John Carter on Mars. Kline's publication by McClurg may have contributed to its loss of Burroughs; the last McClurg book by Burroughs, after twenty-six of his first twenty-seven, was *The Monster Men* in 1929.

Kline's novels prompted Burroughs to write his series of four Venus novels about Carson Napier, starting with *Pirates of Venus* (1932/33). Kline in turn responded with a Martian series starting with *The Swordsman of Mars* (1933/60) and concluding with *Outlaws of Mars* (1933/61). His most successful novel may have been *The Call of the Savage* (serialized in *Argosy* as "Jan of the Jungle," 1931/37), which became a Dorothy Lamour film and a radio serial. After 1935 Kline seems to have devoted most of his time to his literary agency.

OTHER WORKS: *Tam, Son of the Tiger* (1931/62); *Jan in India* (1935/62); *The Man Who Limped and Other Stories* (1946); *Stories* (1975).

J.E.G.

KNIGHT, DAMON (1922–   ).

American science-fiction fan, writer, editor, critic, teacher, historian, and anthologist; a founder of the Milford Writers' Conference; founder and first president of the SCIENCE FICTION WRITERS OF AMERICA. In 1956 Knight won the Hugo Award as best book reviewer and in 1975 received the SCIENCE FICTION RESEARCH ASSOCIATION's Pilgrim Award for his critical and editorial work. Since 1963 he has been married to writer Kate WILHELM.

Knight is one of those people whose entire life seems to have been lived in science fiction. Born and raised in Oregon by schoolteacher parents, he discovered SF

Damon Knight and Kate Wilhelm

by way of AMAZING STORIES and became active in SF FANDOM while still in his teens. In 1941 he moved to New York, where he joined the FUTURIANS, the celebrated group of fans, writers, and editors, about which he wrote the historical-autobiographical work *The Futurians* (1977). His first professionally published fiction, written while he was in high school, was "Resilience," which appeared in the February 1941 *Stirring Science Stories*. He went on to sell illustrations and stories to Futurian-edited magazines and to work as an assistant editor for the Popular Publications pulps, as a reader at the Scott Meredith agency, and as editor of the short-lived *Worlds Beyond* (three issues in 1950–51). He wrote notable short fiction for GALAXY and THE MAGAZINE OF FANTASY AND SCIENCE FICTION in the 1950s, and in this same period became one of two writer-reviewers (the other was James BLISH, writing as William Atheling, Jr.) to insist that SF "is worth taking seriously, and that ordinary critical standards can be meaningfully applied to it."

Knight's dedication to the improvement of the field has extended beyond tough reviewing standards. In 1956, with Judith MERRIL and James Blish, he started the Milford Writers' Conference for published writers; later he was one of the first teachers at the Clarion workshops for beginning writers of SF. In 1965 he founded the Science Fiction Writers of America to serve as a professional association and writers' union. The next year he began the Orbit original ANTHOLOGIES (21 volumes, 1966–1980), a series associated with the NEW WAVE and the publication of important work by both new and established writers; the series received four Nebula Awards for short fiction and more than twenty Nebula nominations. Starting in 1962 Knight also edited some forty reprint anthologies, usually with historical or thematic orientations.

Given this level of editorial and organizational activity, it should not be surprising that Knight's fiction amounts to only about a third of his career's accomplishments. In the productive 1950s he worked mainly in shorter forms; even his novels tend to be freestanding novellas (*Masters of Evolution*, 1954/1959) or combined and expanded short pieces (*Hell's Pavement*, 1955). His fiction aspires to the standards announced in his criticism: craft and intellectual rigor, especially in following through the implications of a science-fictional "idea," such as the empathy-producing aerosol of "Rule Golden" (1954) or the matter-reproducing "gizmos" of *The People Maker* (1959; as *A for Anything*, 1961). He has a special fondness for ironic reexaminations of the genre's hoariest conventions, such as time travel or encounter with aliens, and some of his most effective stories remove layers of sentimentality and wish fulfillment from our view of the future—"The Earth Quarter" (1955; also titled *The Sun Saboteurs*, 1961), "Masks" (1970), "Down There" (1973), or "I See You" (1976). Since the suspension of the Orbit series, Knight has returned to writing novels with *The World and Thorinn* (1980), *The Man in the Tree* (1984), and *CV* (1985).

OTHER WORKS: *The Rithian Terror* (also known as "Double Meaning," 1953/1965); *Masters of Evolution* (also known as "Natural State," (1954/1959); *Far Out* (collection, 1961); *In Deep* (collection, 1963); *Beyond the Barrier* (1964); *Mind Switch* (also known as *The Other Foot*, 1965); *Off Center* (collection, 1965); *Three Novels* ("Rule Golden," "Natural State," and "The Dying Man," 1967); *Two Novels* ("Double Meaning" and "The Earth Quarter," 1974); *Charles Fort, Prophet of the Unexplained* (nonfiction, 1970); *The Best of Damon Knight* (collection, 1976); *Turning Points: Essays on the Art of Science Fiction* (nonfiction, editor, 1977).

SELECTED ANTHOLOGIES: *A Century of Science Fiction* (1962); *A Century of Great Science Fiction Short Novels* (1964); *Thirteen French Science Fiction Stories* (translator and editor, 1965); *Nebula Award Stories 1965* (1966); *Science Fiction Inventions* (1967); *A Hundred Years of Science Fiction* (1968); *The Metal Smile* (1968); *First Contact* (1971); *A Science Fiction Argosy* (1972); *The Golden Road* (1973); *Science Fiction of the Thirties* (1975).

R.F.L.

KNIGHT, NORMAN L[OUIS] (1895–1972).
American pesticide chemist and occasional writer of science fiction whose only book credit is his collaboration with James BLISH on *A Torrent of Faces* (1967), set on a densely overpopulated future Earth about to collide with an asteroid. The novel includes some of the future technology—farming of the seabeds and a genetically engineered Triton, or amphibious man—developed in Knight's two earlier serials in ASTOUNDING STORIES (never published in book form), "Frontiers of the Unknown" (1937) and "Crisis in Utopia" (1940). Knight had only eleven SF stories published and is unfairly neglected. Two other stories particularly worthy of revival are "Saurian Valedictory" (1939), an interesting concept in viewing the past, and "The Testament of Akubii" (1940), in which a Martian sacrifices himself to save his human colleague.

M.A.

KOONTZ, DEAN R[AY] (1945–).
American writer of popular science fiction and horror, some of whose books have become best-sellers. Koontz writes SF with a marked humanistic, rather than technological, flavor. His stylistically daring stories usually include themes that examine the qualities that define the human race. Most of his short fiction has been published in such periodicals as THE MAGAZINE OF FANTASY AND SCIENCE FICTION and in such original anthologies as *Again, Dangerous Visions* and Robert Hoskins's Infinity series.

Koontz's novels frequently deal with perverted children who have little to do with the innocence normally associated with childhood (*Beastchild*, 1970; *A Darkness in My Soul*, 1972), and they often combine SF and horror. *Demon Seed* (1973), perhaps his best-known work of this type, went on to become a major film. *Anti-man* (1970), a novel that features a shape-changing android, is a clear mixture of Gothic and SF; it retells the Frankenstein story. *A Werewolf among Us* (1973) offers a good detective story plus a fascinating view of a cybernetic hero whose two natures conflict.

Koontz's best SF work to date is *Nightmare Journey* (1975), a dark but optimistic tale of humanity some 100,000 years in the future. Forced to return to a radioactive Earth by an alien power, humankind must confront exhaustion of the species, renewed religious fervor, and a devastated environment.

OTHER WORKS: *Star Quest* (1968); *The Fall of the Dream Machine* (1969); *Fear That Man* (1969); *The Dark Symphony* (1970); *Hell's Gate* (1970); *Dark of the Woods* (1970); *Soft Come the Dragons* (collection, 1970); *The Flesh in the Furnace* (1972); *Time Thieves* (1972); *Warlock* (1972); *Starblood* (1972); *The Haunted Earth* (1973); *The Long Sleep* (1975).

S.H.G.

KORNBLUTH, C[YRIL] M. (1923–1958).
American author best known for his collaborations with

Frederik POHL and his short fiction. Kornbluth first met Pohl while both were members of the FUTURIANS in the late 1930s, during which time he regularly collaborated with Pohl and other members of the group (including Robert A. W. LOWNDES and Judith MERRIL). With the publication of *The Space Merchants* (1953; as *Gravy Planet,* 1952 in *Galaxy*), both Kornbluth and Pohl received almost universal recognition for pioneering an original form of science fiction. The novel successfully combines satire and SF in its description of a future Earth in which advertising agencies control the political and social life of the planet. The balance of wit, broadsides against human greed, and detailed portraits of life in such a world was so successful that hosts of imitators soon followed, and GALAXY became known as the place to read this brand of SF. In the next few years Kornbluth and Pohl produced two other novels that tried to continue this balance: *Search the Sky* (1954), a light treatment of xenophobic humans, and *Gladiator-at-Law* (1955), a darker satire of big business gone wild.

A fourth collaboration, *Wolfbane* (1959), deserves special mention. According to Pohl, Kornbluth wrote the final draft of this novel, and therefore its tone reflects his style. *Wolfbane* deals with an Earth that has apparently been forced out of its orbit by an alien artifact. The opening chapters, which describe a human race that has accepted its enslavement and created a culture based on passivity and poverty, evoke both sympathy and anger, and the gestalt presented later in the novel is one of the most remarkable and credible ever created. Although not as popular as the earlier collaborations, the novel has been singled out by a number of critics as a truly original and unique work of science fiction.

Kornbluth wrote several novels on his own, including *Takeoff* (1952), *The Syndic* (1953), and *Not This August* (1955; as *Christmas Mass,* 1956). Of these his best is *The Syndic,* in which a syndication of "good-hearted," freewheeling mobsters has taken over the United States and governs in a Runyonesque way; the adventures that follow provide the canvas on which Kornbluth displayed his power as a satirist and observer of human nature. Although it is little more than a series of stories loosely strung together, Kornbluth's premise and tone carry the reader through the work.

His talents, however, are best displayed in shorter works. His stories (collected in *The Marching Morons,* 1959) of a future Earth on which the vast majority of humans are mental morons are classic examples of dark humor, but he was also capable of writing sensitive tales about people caught up in struggles not of their choosing (for example, "With These Hands," 1951). And then there are stories such as "The Little Black Bag" (1950), a kind of prequel to "The Marching Morons," which joins satire with sensitivity when a medical bag from the future falls into the hands of a skid-row bum. Although human greed and stupidity play significant roles in the

story, which was dramatized on Rod Serling's *Night Gallery,* its compassionate treatment of a segment of humanity that has fallen beneath the notice of most of their fellows is moving.

Kornbluth wrote a remarkable range of stories during his short career. His fiction covers most of the traditional themes of SF, and he frequently expanded the genre to include horror and fantasy. However, whatever form a story took, he added his own touch to it in a way that made it uniquely his own. He died of a heart attack before he had reached his peak, like Stanley G. WEINBAUM at the age of thirty-five.

OTHER WORKS: *Gunner Cade* (with Judith Merril, 1952, as Cyril Judd); *Outpost Mars* (with Judith Merril, 1952, as Cyril Judd); *The Explorers* (collection, 1954); *The Mindworm and Other Stories* (collection, 1955); *A Mile beyond the Moon* (collection, 1958); *The Wonder Effect* (with Frederik Pohl, collection, 1962; revised as *Critical Mass,* 1977); *Best SF Stories* (collection, 1968); *Thirteen O'Clock and Other Zero Stories* (collection, 1970); *The Best of C. M. Kornbluth* (collection, 1976).

S.H.G.

KRENKEL, ROY G. (1918–1983). American illustrator known for his superb drawings after the style of John Allen ST. JOHN. In the late 1940s Krenkel produced science-fiction comic art for EC Comics. Most of his dynamic cover paintings were created for a series of novels by Edgar Rice BURROUGHS and Otis Adelbert KLINE (Ace Books). The paintings are populated with slender, muscular figures who leap about or fight in jungle settings, dressed in loincloths and armed with swords. Krenkel also contributed art to the Hugo-winning fanzine *Amra* and illustrated L. Sprague DE CAMP's *Cities and Scenes from the Ancient World* with highly detailed and historically accurate ink drawings. He was instrumental in launching Frank FRAZETTA in his highly successful career by offering him the opportunity to paint many of the Ace Books covers. Krenkel won a Hugo for best professional artist in 1963.

J.G.

KRONOS (1957). *Directed by Kurt Neumann; screenplay by Lawrence Louis Goldman; photographed by Karl Struss; music by Paul Sawtell and Bert Shefter. With Jeff Morrow, Barbara Lawrence, John Emery, George O'Hanlon, Morris Ankrum, Kenneth Alton, John Parrish, José Gonzales Gonzales. 78 minutes. Black and white.*

Kronos, though hampered by a mediocre screenplay, is one of the more imaginative low-budget science-fiction films of the 1950s. Occasionally director Kurt Neumann and SPECIAL EFFECTS team Jack Rabin, Irving Block, and Gene Warren give the events a sense of epic scale.

A colossal robot, resembling a cubistic sketch of a human being, arrives on Earth from space and begins draining energy from everything from a power plant to an atomic bomb, converting it to mass. Scientist Jeff Morrow short-circuits Kronos, and it devours itself spectacularly.

B.W.

KUBRICK, STANLEY (1928–   ).

American film director and writer with a strong interest in science fiction fantasy, resident in England since the production of his *Lolita* in 1962; known for his visual imagination and extraordinary cinematic style; his film 2001: A SPACE ODYSSEY (1968) not only was revolutionary in its day but continues to exert cinematic influence and elicit critical debate.

Kubrick is a careful director who takes a great deal of time to prepare his films before shooting; they are usually several years apart. During production he has been known routinely to shoot more than eighty takes of a scene before he is satisfied. Some find his intellectualism cynical and emotionally arid, but others regard his films as sardonic and complex; his admirers respect his wit and honesty. It may be significant that he once made money playing chess.

Although he has yet to repeat himself in content or, largely, in overall theme, his films are so meticulously crafted and styled that they are distinctively his. Kubrick is attracted to central characters, generally outsiders or the psychologically disturbed, who undergo not just problems but an overwhelming crisis; he observes the crisis with irony and detachment but often provides a secondary character to whom audiences can respond emotionally.

Four times so far, Kubrick has made fantastic films, three of which are not just science fiction but landmarks in the genre (all three won Hugo Awards); *2001: A Space Odyssey* is arguably the finest SF film ever made. Because of his obvious fondness for SF as a vehicle for his ideas, it seems likely that Kubrick will eventually return to it.

His first SF film was the antiwar satire DR. STRANGE- LOVE, OR HOW I LEARNED TO STOP WORRYING AND LOVE THE BOMB (1964), a black comedy about the nuclear destruction of the world. Its treatment of its subject astonished audiences, and it firmly established Kubrick as a director of the first rank.

The landmark *2001* followed and proved to be not only popular but immensely influential, changing the course of SF films. Its meaning is still being debated, but it is clear that Kubrick and his co-writer, Arthur C. CLARKE, were attempting to create a mythology of space; because of the enduring fame of both the film and its visual elements (black slabs, star children, and so on), it seems safe to conclude that they were successful. One often-overlooked point about *2001*'s production is that, with the exception of a few shots in the dawn-of-man sequence, the entire film was shot on sets; everything on screen was carefully selected and planned by Kubrick.

A CLOCKWORK ORANGE (1971), from the Anthony BURGESS novel, was less successful and is notable mainly for its visual style and satiric point of view. The central theme, that the kind of brainwashing the protagonist is subjected to is wrong even for the worst of people, was diluted by casting the charming Malcolm McDowell in the lead.

In 1980 Kubrick's film of Stephen KING's fantasy novel *The Shining* was financially successful but regarded by many as ultimately a failure. However, when the film is considered as an entity in itself and not merely a visualization of the novel, its true strengths emerge. Despite a certain aridity, it deserves greater recognition than it has thus far received.

B.W.

KURLAND, MICHAEL [JOSEPH] (1938–   ).

American editor and author who writes adventure and spy novels as well as SF. Kurland's science fiction is fast paced, rich in descriptions of unusual societies, and filled with action. In *The Whenabouts of Burr* (1957), for example, parallel worlds form the stage for an unusual chase in which the past, present, and future are jumbled together in a series of startling and amusing incidents. *Pluribus* (1975) continues in the same manner, but the setting is changed to a postwar Earth inhabited by humans who have regressed to near barbarism.

Kurland frequently parodies other SF works. His first novel, *Ten Years to Doomsday* (1964), is a collaboration with Chester Anderson that caricatures alien invasion stories; his second, *The Unicorn Girl* (1969), is a playful continuation of Anderson's *The Butterfly Kid* (1967). Both novels describe yet another alien invasion and its comic results. Even his juvenile book, *The Princes of Earth* (1980), is a burlesque of several recent movements in the United States, particularly the Church of Scientology.

OTHER WORKS: *Transmission Error* (1970); *Tomorrow Knight* (1976); *The Last President* (with S. W. Barton, 1980); *Psi Hunt* (1980); *Death by Gaslight* (1982).

S.H.G.

KURTZ, KATHERINE [IRENE] (1944–   ).

American writer, now resident in Ireland, best known for her stories about the Deryni, set in an alternative medieval land in some respects like Wales. Kurtz's first book, *Deryni Rising* (1970), established her scenario: the Deryni are a psychically gifted race with additional, less controllable, powers who were once the rulers of Gwynedd but are now persecuted by a medieval church.

Forced to seek refuge, they have established a covert network of contacts. The first trilogy was completed with *Deryni Checkmate* (1972) and *High Deryni* (1973), available in an omnibus edition as *The Chronicles of the Deryni* (1985). The second trilogy is set two centuries earlier, in the mystical times of the later canonized Camber of Culdi, and consists of *Camber of Culdi* (1976), *Saint Camber* (1978), and *Camber the Heretic* (1981). The third trilogy—*The Bishop's Heir* (1984), *The King's Justice* (1985), and *The Quest for Saint Camber* (1986)—follows the fortunes of King Kelson, who had been raised to the throne at the end of the first trilogy. *The Deryni Archives* (1986) is a collection of stories and notes and a complete chronology.

Kurtz has written two non-Deryni books, *Lammas Night* (1983), an occult thriller set in war-torn Britain, and *The Legacy of Lehr* (1986), her only pure science-fiction book, combining a starship, psychic cats, and a murder mystery. Formerly a senior training technician with the Los Angeles Police Department, she has been a full-time writer since 1981.

M.A.

Illustration to Kuttner's "A God Named Kroo" (1954) by Virgil Finlay

KUTTNER, HENRY (1915–1958).

American writer who, with his wife, popular *Weird Tales* author C. L. Moore, collaborated on numerous works of science fiction. After their marriage in 1940, Moore and Kuttner fused their writing talents to an unprecedented extent; in fact, they collaborated so frequently, thoroughly, and successfully that it is now nearly impossible to state with any certainty the exact degree of participation of either in any given story, even those published under Kuttner's or Moore's name alone.

The versatile and energetic Kuttner was once aptly described by Robert Silverberg as the "first of the SF hacks-turned-artist." A quiet, intensely private man, Kuttner read widely and wrote prolifically. In the pulps alone he sold nearly three hundred stories to a score of magazines, using seventeen pseudonyms. Inevitably, much of this work is formulaic and derivative. The mature Kuttner, however, became an uncommonly skillful craftsman.

Kuttner's first story, "The Graveyard Rats," was published by *Weird Tales* in 1936. He rapidly demonstrated proficiency in a wide variety of pulp genres, producing horror stories, humorous science fiction, SPACE OPERA romances, a sword and sorcery series modeled after Robert Howard's Conan tales, fantasy, detective fiction, adventure stories, and much else. Later in his life he wrote a number of well-regarded mysteries, a movie screenplay, television scripts, and comic-book continuity.

Today, however, Kuttner's reputation rests primarily on the literate and sophisticated stories he and Moore wrote for John W. Campbell's ASTOUNDING STORIES during the 1940s, most of which saw print under the pseudonyms Lewis Padgett and Lawrence O'Donnell. These include such significant works as "The Twonky" (1942), "Mimsy Were the Borogoves" (1943), "When the Bough Breaks" (1944), "What You Need" (1945), *Fury* (1947/ 1950), and "Private Eye" (1949). A few first-rate stories appeared elsewhere, such as "Absalom" (1946) and "Don't Look Now" (1948) in *Startling Stories* and "Two-Handed Engine" (1955) in THE MAGAZINE OF FANTASY AND

SCIENCE FICTION. In addition, Kuttner and Moore wrote eight short novels between 1946 and 1952 for *Startling Stories* (*Valley of the Flame*, 1946/ *The Dark World*, 1946/1965, *The Mask of Circe*, 1948, and so on). These were quite different from the team's work for *Astounding*, being science-fantasy adventures in the older tradition of A. MERRITT.

In the 1950s Kuttner and Moore gradually moved away from the SF magazines, turning to suspense novels and work in television and the movies. Moreover, Kuttner was a gifted teacher. Ray BRADBURY and Leigh BRACKETT had been early beneficiaries of his analytic expertise; on his return to the West Coast, Kuttner for some years taught a writing course at the University of Southern California. He enrolled in college himself and had nearly completed a master's degree in English at USC when he died suddenly, of a heart attack, at the age of forty-three.

Despite Kuttner's varied and considerable achievements, in retrospect there is something unfinished and a little sad about his career. He wrote too much too soon, was perhaps too well hidden behind his multiple pseudonyms, and died too young.

WORKS: *Fury* (1950), *A Gnome There Was* (1950); *Tomorrow and Tomorrow and the Fairy Chessmen* (1951); *Robots Have No Tails* (1952); *Ahead of Time* (1953); *Mutant* (1953); *Beyond Earth's Gates* (1954); *Line to Tomorrow and Other Stories* (collection, 1954); *No Boundaries* (1955); *Bypass to Otherness* (1961); *Return to Otherness* (1962); *Valley of the Flame* (1946/ 1964); *Earth's Last Citadel* (1964); *The Dark World* (1946/1965); *The Time Axis* (1965); *Well of the Worlds* (1965); *The Creature from beyond Infinity* (1968); *The Mask of Circe* (1971); *The Best of Henry Kuttner* (collection, 1975).

J.L.C.

L

LAFFERTY, R[APHAEL] A[LOYSIUS] (1914–   ).
American writer and science fiction's premier teller of tall tales. Except for military service during World War II, Lafferty spent his working life in the electrical wholesale business in Oklahoma. After his initial sale in 1960 to *SF Stories*, he published two dozen books of exuberant metaphysical comedy but retired from writing at age seventy.

Lafferty's contributions to the Orbit series and praise from such figures as Samuel R. DELANY and Judith MERRIL identified him with the NEW WAVE. His idiosyncratic style, which mimics oral delivery, his grotesque characters, and his intoxication with language distinguish his work from conventional SF. Nevertheless, the content

of his work is traditional, reflecting a conservative Irish Catholicism; and his "high hilarity of love and laughter" (a quotation from his novel *The Flame Is Green*, 1971) is wholly unlike the pessimism of much New Wave writing. His antimodern formulations of Good and Evil are often obscure and unfashionable. *Past Master* (1968) and *Fourth Mansions* (1969) reflect his antipathy to the thought of Pierre Teilhard de Chardin, and *The Flame Is Green* is overtly anti-Marxist. It is not surprising, then, that readers tend to prize Lafferty's style above his substance.

Because his novels often dissolve into tangles of bizarre anecdotes, as does *Archipelago* (1979), Lafferty's yarn-spinning gifts are best displayed at shorter lengths, for instance in his first collection, *Nine Hundred Grandmothers* (1970). His short story "Eurema's Dam" won a Hugo in 1973.

NOTABLE OTHER WORKS: *The Reefs of Earth* (1968); *Space Chantey* (1968); *Arrive at Easterwine* (1971); *Okla Hannali* (1972); *Strange Doings* (1972); *The Annals of Klepsis* (1983); *Half a Sky* (1984).

S.L.M.

LAKE, DAVID J[OHN] (1929–   ).
Australian science-fiction writer born in India. A professional linguistics professor and literary critic, Lake entered the SF field with the publication of his first novel, *Walkers on the Sky* (1976). This and many of his subsequent seven novels, produced at the rate of about one a year, share a common future in which Earth has been destroyed in World War IV and remnants of the human race are forced to settle on worlds where the environment is inhospitable. Lake's novels focus on the conflict between the struggle to survive and the struggle to maintain the values that distinguish humanity. He acknowledges the twin influences of H. G. WELLS and C. S. LEWIS, sharing thematic concerns with Wells and a fascination with fantastic landscape with Lewis. He may produce significant work when his generally stock narratives catch up with his situations, settings, and writing skills. Lake also writes poetry and academic books.

OTHER WORKS: *The Right Hand of Dextra* (1977); *The Wildings of Westron* (1977); *The Gods of Xuma* (1978); *The Fourth Hemisphere* (1980); *The Man Who Loved Morlocks* (1981); *The Ring of Truth* (1983); *The Warlords of Xuma* (1983).

S.E.G.

LAND OF THE GIANTS (1968–1970).
Directed by Harry Harris, Sobey Martin, Nathan Juran, and others; written by William Welch, Bob and Esther Mitchell, Arthur Weiss, William L. Stuart, Richard Shapiro, and others; music by John Williams, Leith Stevens, Joseph Mullendore, Irving Gertz, Harry Geller,

and others. With Gary Conway, Don Marshall, Heather Young, Deanna Lund, Don Matheson, Stefan Arngrim, Kurt Kasznar, Kevin Hagen. 51 one-hour episodes. Color.

This television series produced by Irwin ALLEN is set in the then future year 1983, in which a group of travelers on a commercial suborbital flight are drawn off course to a crash landing on a planet populated by giant humanoids. The premiere episode, ''The Crash'' (directed by Irwin Allen, written by Allen and Anthony Wilson), introduces the regular cast of characters (Gary Conway as the pilot, Don Marshall as the copilot, Heather Young as the stewardess, Don Matheson as a rich industrialist, Deanna Lund as a movie star, Kurt Kasznar as an embezzler, and Stefan Arngrim as an orphan accompanied by his dog, Chipper), and establishes the series formula as these ''little people'' struggle to survive and elude capture by the ''giants,'' whose civilization is essentially the same as Earth's except for size and a police-state form of government.

Land of the Giants lasted for two seasons on ABC-TV and featured some of television's most elaborate special effects, created by producer Allen's regular collaborator, L. B. Abbott. Memorable also are the theme and background music, composed by John Williams, who would go on to score STAR WARS.

K.R.D.

THE LAND THAT TIME FORGOT (1975).
Directed by Kevin Connor; screenplay by Michael Moorcock and James Cawthorn; adapted from the novel by Edgar Rice Burroughs; photographed by Alan Hume; music by Douglas Gamley. With Doug McClure, John McEnery, Susan Penhaligon. 91 minutes. Color.
THE PEOPLE THAT TIME FORGOT (1977).
Directed by Kevin Connor; screenplay by Patrick Tilley; adapted from the novel by Edgar Rice Burroughs; photographed by Alan Hume; music by John Scott. With Doug McClure, Patrick Wayne, Sarah Douglas. 90 minutes. Color.

In *The Land That Time Forgot* a British crew capture a German submarine in 1916. Near the South Pole they discover an island inhabited by dinosaurs and primitive tribes. In the sequel, *The People That Time Forgot,* an airman and some explorers crash-land on the island and search for a lost friend.

Of a number of films of the lost-world genre that were produced in the 1970s, these two British efforts are among the best for special effects. The superb prehistoric creatures by Roger Dicken reflect the continuing refinement of the process of model animation begun by Willis O'BRIEN for THE LOST WORLD (1925).

The Land That Time Forgot may have suffered from the extensive changes made by the producers to MOOR-

COCK and Cawthorn's screenplay. But an Edgar Rice BURROUGHS tale guarantees high adventure, and these films are no exception; they were sufficiently successful at the box office to encourage Connor to release other Burroughs adaptations.

M.T.W.

LANG, FRITZ (1890–1976).   Austrian-born German filmmaker who, working with fantasy, myth, and science fiction early in his career, developed a brooding, deterministic, often paranoid world on the screen. With his films about spies, master criminals, espionage, and justice, Lang raised the thriller to a metaphysical level, exploring the philosophical complexities of good and evil, innocence and guilt.

Lang moved from painting and fashion design to screenwriting while recovering from wounds received in action during World War I. He was offered the job of directing *The Cabinet of Dr. Caligari* (1919), the film that would clearly establish the distinctive German expressionist style, but declined because of his commitment to direct *Die Spinnen (The Spiders,* 1919), his second feature. However, he apparently contributed the idea of the framing story, which contains the film's most extreme visual distortions within the narrative of a mental patient, thus projecting the character's disturbed psyche onto the exterior world. This idea would inform many of his later films as well.

Lang went on to direct an impressive series of silent films, including the two-part myth *Die Nibelungen* (1923–24) and his two SF epics, METROPOLIS (1926) and WOMAN IN THE MOON (*Die Frau im Mond,* 1929). Although many of his early films contain elements of SF, these two have become classics of the genre. *Metropolis* is a mammoth epic of the future, the first of its kind in the history of the cinema. Having drained the resources of the giant UFA studios for its production, the film is visually stunning in its special effects, camera work, and direction. *Woman in the Moon* depicts the first manned flight to the Moon and for the most part displays an impressive concern for scientific accuracy. Rocket experts Hermann Oberth and Willy LEY served as technical advisers, and the film includes such details as diagrams of trajectories and the use of the countdown during the launch, which some have claimed provided the model for NASA's procedure. It is only toward the end, when the characters discover a breathable atmosphere and gold on the Moon, that the film fails in accuracy.

Beginning with his first sound film, the classic *M* (1931), about the Düsseldorf child murderer, Lang began to experience difficulties with the Nazis. Thinking that the movie, originally titled ''The Murderer Is Among Us,'' was an anti-Nazi tract, they initially refused Lang entry to the studio. His next film, *Das Testament des Dr. Mabuse (The Testament of Dr. Mabuse,* 1932), was

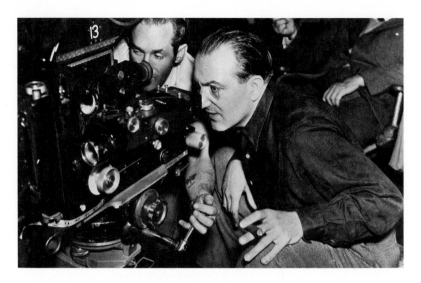

Fritz Lang

not particularly subtle in its anti-Nazi implications, depicting Lang's archfiend Mabuse as a charismatic madman who hypnotizes good citizens from afar and causes them to commit crimes. Lang's wife and longtime screenplay collaborator, Thea von Harbou, joined the Nazi party, and disputes between the two began. Hitler apparently admired Lang's work, particularly the epic quality of *Metropolis,* and so offered him the top filmmaking position in the Third Reich. Half Jewish by birth, Lang promptly left Germany and his wife, not to return until 1960, when he made his third Mabuse film.

After a brief stay in France, where he directed the film version of the fantasy *Liliom* (1933), Lang arrived in Hollywood. His first three American movies, made for as many studios, were bold, socially conscious works, but because of their poor performance at the box office Lang was forced to work in the less ambitious, more constrained limits of genre, particularly the western and the film noir. Although Lang's later films lack the speculative elements so typical of his earlier work, they retain the same thematic concerns. He returned to Germany for his last film, *Die tausend Augen des Dr. Mabuse (The Thousand Eyes of Dr. Mabuse,* 1960), and in 1963 appeared as himself in Jean-Luc Godard's self-reflexive *Le Mépris (Contempt).*

B.K.G.

LANGUAGE

Language and its relation to racial INTELLIGENCE, cultural institutions, and physical environments has long been a popular topic in science fiction. When Stanley G. WEINBAUM wrote "A Martian Odyssey" in 1934, he was aware of the problem of communication confronting his human protagonist and the alien he discovers. This problem ran deeper than simply the need to translate one language into another: "But I couldn't get the hang of his talk; either I missed some subtle point or we just didn't *think* alike—and I rather believe the latter view." More than superficial vocabulary and general parts of speech were involved. What Weinbaum suggested was that the differences between a human language and an alien one are basic to the ways in which each race looks at the universe, reasons through problems, and summarizes its respective experiences of life. Weinbaum solved the problem by making his alien intelligent enough to comprehend the basic patterns of human thought, although the human never did understand the alien's patterns. Since "A Martian Odyssey," many SF short stories and novels have been devoted to alien languages, future changes in human languages, and the development of artificial languages. Even more fiction has at least made reference to such topics. Many authors have become interested in linguistic theory and researched it as they would any other "science" in preparing to write their stories.

Weinbaum was dealing with the problem of translation in "A Martian Odyssey," but that was only one of many linguistic issues that found their way into SF. The question of how a language relates to and in some cases forms its speaker's view of the world has been the basis of many stories and novels. As descriptions of aliens became more sophisticated, methods of conveying language became more complex, and writers tackled the knotty issue of how language is affected by biological systems: Are speech and writing the only way to conduct a conversation? How would the form a language takes affect its structure and content? And as the alien languages became more complex, other writers explored the possibilities of how humans, particularly children, might acquire those languages. Linguistic theory itself also became a part of the subject matter of both the fiction and the criticism of SF, especially the school of structuralism first suggested by Ferdinand de Saussure. Finally, SF authors attacked the problem of presenting alien languages, trying in varying degrees to show their actual form and content.

One of the most influential theorists for SF writers has been Benjamin Lee Whorf, a student of the American linguist Edward Sapir. The chief architect of the Sapir-Whorf hypothesis, Whorf claimed that his study of American Indian languages suggests a kind of linguistic relativism. Languages condition radically different and often incompatible worldviews; if language is the instrument through which people articulate thoughts and experiences, it also shapes and controls those thoughts and experiences. If a people cannot express a particular concept through their language, they cannot think it.

Although Jack VANCE has denied having any knowledge of the Sapir-Whorf hypothesis before writing *The Languages of Pao* (1957), that novel has long been held up as the prime example of the use of linguistic relativism in SF. In it Vance employed the structures of two languages to show the radical differences in the peoples of two planets. Each language is perfectly suited for the culture it expresses, and Vance solved the problems of the culture of Pao by having its leader invent new languages, taught to children, to break them out of their debilitating passivity.

Samuel R. DELANY made deliberate use of Whorf's thinking in *Babel-17* (1966) when he introduced aliens whose culture is based wholly on heat and temperature changes. The "otherness" of such a culture prompts the conclusion that "compatibility factors for communication are incredibly low." *Babel-17* is centered on a new weapon of sabotage that seems to have been developed by the aliens in their war with the humans: an artificial language so exactly analytic as to assure technical mastery of any situation, yet lacking an "I." For Delany this lack precludes "any self-critical process. In fact it cuts out any awareness of the symbolic process . . . the way we distinguish between reality and our expression of reality." In effect, Babel-17 is a trap. It sabotages the speaker by cutting him or her off from the surrounding world, much as a computer shuts down when by accident a program becomes a closed loop and dominates all its circuits.

Robert SILVERBERG's *A Time of Changes* (1971) and Yevgeny Zamiatin's *We* (translated 1924) both deal with the control of individuals by the use of language. The best-known work on this subject, however, is George ORWELL's *Nineteen Eighty-four* (1949), which details the ultimate conformist, jargon-laden language. Newspeak was designed to make dissent, or "crimethink," literally impossible. There is simply no room in the lan-

guage for such thoughts. And in the same way the static, statist world of Anthony BOUCHER's "Barrier" (*Astounding Science Fiction*, 1942) both regulates language by the rules of a textbook, *This Bees Speech*, and builds a time barrier that is attacked by a linguistic hodgepodge of time travelers.

All these stories deal with Whorf's belief that language acts as a filter that selects the experiences and thoughts its speakers may have. However, linguistic theory has since called the Sapir-Whorf hypothesis into question. Such linguists as Noam Chomsky and C. E. Osgood have shown that language operates on a far more abstract level than that of the spoken or written sentence. An infinite number of sentences are, in fact, produced by a limited number of abstract patterns. Languages as diverse as English, Japanese, and Navajo share "a common market in meaning" based on the biological systems of emotional and purposeful behavior that all humans share. A relation between worldview and language assuredly exists but only within the framework of universal linguistic abstractions and shared biovalues.

But what of an alien race that does not share such a biological system? If modern linguistic theory has so complicated our understanding of the relation between language and thought that Whorf's thinking is no longer usable by writers, this question more than makes up for the loss. Indeed, as in "A Martian Odyssey," SF writers had been thinking about it for some time.

When human meets alien in SF, the communication problem may be glossed over by telepathy. Piers ANTHONY, in *Cluster* (1977) and its sequels, transmitted the Kirlian energy aura into an array of alien bodies in which the mind travelers are perfectly at home; scent communications, electromagnetic pulses, and so on are represented in colloquial English framed by a menagerie of typographic cues to the alienness. Often, moreover, the alien language is simply "translated" without even such symbolic cues attached. An alien may conveniently learn Terran, as was the case with Tweel in "A Martian Odyssey." Or a magical "translator machine" may be used; the plausible sophisticated version in C. J. CHERRYH's *The Pride of Chanur* (1981) uses symbol-coordinating computers plus a gradation of alienness from humanoids to exotics with different biochemistries.

Writers have devised Rosetta stones to allow for the decoding of a dead alien language, as in H. Beam PIPER's "Omnilingual" (1957), courtesy of the periodic table of the elements, or in Roger ZELAZNY's "A Rose for Ecclesiastes" (1957), wherein a human polyglot on Mars is taught by aliens. Their odd-sounding, dual language is no obstacle to an obsessed genius-poet who cut his teeth on classical Sanskrit and the vulgar Indian tongues. What's more, he can interbreed with the Martians.

A number of SF writers have tried to tie language more closely to the biological systems of their aliens. If the biology differs profoundly between alien and human, ambiguity and possibly lethal incomprehension may result, as in Terry CARR's "The Dance of the Changer and the Three" (1968), with its color-dancing, ego-mutating, myth-spinning, suiciding energy-beings "coalescing in each life-cycle around a spatial center." Michael BISHOP's Asadi in *Transfigurations* (1979) have speech-eyes that rapidly range the visible spectrum. David I. Masson's "Not So Certain" (1967) gives lessons in a perversely homophonous, jawbreaking alien tongue while reminding us that any alien race may include many diverse languages, just as the human race does. Discourse with the manifestations of sentient suns in Frank HERBERT's *Whipping Star* (1970) produces a semantic maze of crossword clues ("Tangential occlusion another term expressing something similar"); in "Confluence" (1967), parodying the often extensive glossaries that appear as appendixes in alien-culture novels, Brian W. ALDISS satirically listed dictionary definitions from an alien language in which body posture alters meaning ("UNK TAK; An out-of-date guide book; the skin shed by the snake that predicts rain").

Sometimes SF writers combine speculation on the connection between biological systems and language with work that has been done on animal languages. Deciphering animal languages leads to satiric adventure in Frederik POHL's *Slave Ship* (1957) and sensitively handled ethical problems in Robert Merle's *Un Animal doué de raison* (1967; translated as *The Day of the Dolphin*, 1969). Ian WATSON's *The Jonah Kit* (1975) explores the possibility of an acoustic "glyph" language spoken by sperm whales; Ursula K. LE GUIN in "The Author of the Acacia Seeds and Other Extracts from the *Journal of the Association of Therolinguistics*" (1974) performed a tongue-in-cheek reductio, right down to the absurdity of eggplant literature.

Watson explored Chomsky's abstractions in *The Embedding* (1973), which deals with isolated children experimentally taught artificial languages to test the logic limits of the connection between language and worldview. Watson then complicated the whole thing with Amazonian Indians who, when drugged, understand a recursive language that may mirror and organize "reality." And, as if that were not enough, he added aliens haunted by a visit from other dimension-hopping, linguistically multivalent aliens, who hope by collecting languages and reality views to construct a cosmically universal grammar capable of conveying sufficient insight and power to escape from our reality to elsewhere. In "Towards an Alien Linguistics" (1975) Watson argued the pros and cons of cosmic universal grammar.

The cosmic espionage adventures of academic linguist Suzette Haden ELGIN's Coyote Jones involve alien communication problems. In the passionately and lucidly feminist *Native Tongue* (1984), Elgin had human infants acquire otherwise impossible alien tongues by interacting with humanoid aliens in residence in much the same way that human speech is first learned, but the attempt to learn in a similar manner from more exotic aliens causes brainstorms and violent death; meanwhile the female linguists, oppressed by males, secretly design their own liberating language, La'adan, an early grammar and dictionary of which is actually available (from La'adan, Route 4, Box 192-E, Huntsville, AR 72740). In "The Love-Song of Johnny Alienson" (1975), Ian Watson blended this method of infantile alien language acquisition with Rupert Sheldrake's speculative hypothesis of formative causation to explain why human infants might learn human languages easily yet master alien languages only with great initial difficulty.

Saussure's *Cours de Linguistique Générale (Course in General Linguistics*, 1915) stimulated the growth of semiotics, the science of signs, symbols, and signification, as well as of structuralism, the "syntactic" analysis of thought, behavior, and culture—disciplines that are stock in trade for Delany in both his fiction and his criticism. He has long been fascinated by dress, custom, gesture, games, texts, and roles as systems of communication, and his "The Star Pit" (1967) is almost an SF transformation of the French structural anthropologist Claude Lévi-Strauss's structural analysis of myth. Delany's *The American Shore* (1978) is a structural analysis of Thomas M. DISCH's "Angouleme" (1971). *Tales of Nèveryôn* (1979), with its homage to the work of structuralists, including Jacques Derrida's *On Grammatology* (1967), is both a colorful barbarian saga and a structuralist critique. *Triton* (1976) explores in fiction the investigations of models and meaning Delany later presented in *The Jewel-hinged Jaw: Notes on the Language of Science Fiction* (1977). Preoccupied with such issues, Delany exemplifies linguistics in action with all its rich ramifications.

A. E. VAN VOGT built his "null-A" novels on an approach to meaning that deviates greatly from Saussure and his followers. Drawing on Alfred Korzybski's system of general semantics, van Vogt proposed a way of deprogramming the binary logic built into most Western languages. Robert A. HEINLEIN combined the work of one of Korzybski's disciples, S. I. Hayakawa, with Whorfian linguistic relativism to produce the messianic message of *Stranger in a Strange Land* (1961), which added the word *grok* to the English dictionary.

As for the presentation of fictional alien languages in SF, if the first (sketchy) imaginary language is Pentexoire, spoken in the land of Prester John in the fourteenth-century *Travels of Sir John Mandeville*, the most fully realized are in Old and Middle English scholar J. R. R. Tolkien's *Lord of the Rings* trilogy (1954, 1955), arguably written to provide for the languages Elvish, Westron, Ent, and so on. Myra Edwards Barnes analyzed these as speakable languages in her limited study *Linguistics and Languages in Science Fiction-Fantasy* (1975). Walter E. Meyers's *Aliens and Linguistics: Lan-

guage Study and Science Fiction (1980) followed with a fuller survey of the field.

Finally, several authors have achieved remarkable success in portraying,changed states of modern English. The advice given in L. Sprague DE CAMP's "Language for Time Travelers" (1938) is practiced in his *The Wheels of IF* (1940), with its alternate-world un-Normanized English. Anthony BURGESS in *A Clockwork Orange* (1962) devised the Russianized English of Nadsat. The most thoroughgoing example of a future, postholocaust English is the entire text of Russell Hoban's *Riddley Walker* (1981), a remarkable fusion of content with style.

A complete narrative in fully "authentic" future English or an alien langue might be unreadable, if not unwritable; yet, reinforced by commercial banalization, the voice of SF is too often nothing more than current colloquial replete with all its cultural attitudes. Even so, writers of SF are now placing increasing value on literary and linguistic boldness. As is true for all living languages, the treatment of language in SF is in constant change.

I.W./S.H.G.

LANIER, STERLING E[DMUND] (1927–).
American writer, historian, editor, and sculptor. Even though he has been a full-time writer since 1967, Lanier has produced only four novels and one collection of short stories. One novel, however, a unique blend of fantasy and science fiction, made his reputation: *Hiero's Journey* (1973), a postholocaust story in which the priest of a primitive surviving Canadian tribe, Per Hiero Desteen, makes his way through a terrifying and fantastic landscape peopled with mutants, wizards, dwarfs, and intelligent animals to find the knowledge of the past locked up in legendary machines called "COMPUTERS." The novel moves with the episodic grace of a saga and produced, after a ten-year wait, a sequel, *Unforsaken Hiero* (1983). Lanier's collection of stories, *The Peculiar Exploits of Brigadier Ffellowes* (1977), deals with a retired turn-of-the-century English secret agent who keeps running into supernatural menaces. In addition, Lanier will undoubtedly go down in SF history as the editor who placed Frank HERBERT's *Dune* with his then-employer, Chilton Books.

OTHER WORKS: *The War for the Lot* (1969); *Menace under Marwood* (1983).

S.E.G.

LASSER, DAVID (1902–). American science-fiction editor and technical writer. The editor of Hugo GERNSBACK's *Science Wonder Stories* and *Air Wonder Stories* (later combined as *Wonder Stories)* from their establishment in 1929, Lasser guided the magazines through their formative early years, bringing his own interest in technology and spaceflight to the service of Gernsback's philosophy of teaching science through SF. In 1930 Lasser founded the American Interplanetary Society, now the American Institute of Aeronautics and Astronautics, and a year later published the first English-language book on astronautics, *The Conquest of Space.* In 1933 he left Gernsback's employ to become president of the Workers Alliance of America, the major Depression-era organization of the unemployed.

E.L.D.

LASSWITZ, KURD (1848–1910). German philosopher and writer, to a large degree the father of German science fiction. Little known outside the German-speaking world, Lasswitz's magnum opus, *Auf zwei Planeten* (1897), although it became well known on the Continent, had to wait until 1971 for an English-language translation (as *Two Planets).* It describes a Martian invasion of Earth at the North Pole and the ensuing relationship between Mars and Earth. At times the story line takes second place to Lasswitz's philosophies, but the novel remains a forceful pioneering work of SF.

Despite his achievement in *Two Planets,* Lasswitz's work has still not received universal recognition. Willy LEY translated several of his short stories for THE MAGAZINE OF FANTASY AND SCIENCE FICTION in the early 1950s, but there has been no English-language collection of his work, although Lasswitz is, at last, receiving more serious critical study. Of special significance was his early collection *Bilder aus der Zukunft* ("Images of the Future," 1878), a series of extrapolative views of future technology and society. It may well have influenced the youthful Hugo Gernsback, who would certainly have been acquainted with Lasswitz's work. Thus Lasswitz may indirectly have had a more significant influence on the development of SF than has hitherto been appreciated.

M.A.

THE LAST STARFIGHTER (1984).   *Directed by Nick Castle; screenplay by Jonathan Betuel; photographed by King Baggot; music by Craig Safan. With Lance Guest, Robert Preston, Dan O'Herlihy, Barbara Bosson, Catherine Mary Stewart, Norman Snow, Chris Hebert. 100 minutes. Color.*

Eighteen-year-old Alex Rogan has no money for college, no job, and no plans for the future. What he does have is a talent for the video game "Starfighter." After Alex achieves a perfect score he is visited by Centauri, the game's inventor, who takes him to the planet Rylos; there Alex learns that the game is in earnest, a reflection of galactic reality wherein Alex is indeed the last starfighter. His skill and pluck help him to defeat the Rylons' enemies, and his hosts ask him to remain on Rylos to help rebuild their depleted space force.

Jonathan Betuel's boy hero-saves-civilization plot, reminiscent of George LUCAS's STAR WARS trilogy, was inspired by Arthurian legend. Lance Guest gives a creditable performance as the boy hero; Robert Preston is excellent as Centauri, the fast-talking intergalactic salesman and recruiter, as is Dan O'Herlihy as Grig, the wise and witty alien. The movie is a video-game enthusiast's fantasy come true.

The Last Starfighter is notable as the first motion picture to use computer-generated images that simulate live photography. Digital Productions used their Cray X-MP supercomputer to produce simulations including space battles, asteroids, and space vehicles; they were so successful that the difference between the real car driven by Centauri and the digitally simulated version soaring through space is indistinguishable on film. Although TRON (1982) paved the way with its combination of traditional and computer-generated special effects, the astonishing effects of *Starfighter* were generated almost entirely by computer and stand out in the field for their startling realism.

D.P.V.

THE LATHE OF HEAVEN (1980).   *Directed by David Loxton and Fred Barzyk; screenplay by Roger E. Swaybill and Diane English; adapted from the novel by Ursula K. Le Guin; photographed by Robbie Greenberg; music by Michael Small. With Bruce Davison, Kevin Conway, Margaret Avery, Niki Flacks, Peyton Park. 95 minutes. Color.*

Set in Portland, Oregon, but filmed in Dallas to take advantage of that city's futuristic architecture, *The Lathe of Heaven* did an effective job, praised by the novel's author, of putting on film Ursula K. LE GUIN's story of a young man, George Orr (Bruce Davison), whose dreams alter reality. His psychiatrist (Kevin Conway) persuades him to dream of a better world, but the outcome (as in "The Monkey's Paw" and other "three wishes" stories) is always disastrous. Persuaded to eliminate overpopulation, for instance, Orr dreams of the plague, and 6 billion people die. To unite Earth's people, Orr dreams of an alien fleet, and aliens that look like giant two-legged turtles become an ordinary part of life on Earth. To eliminate racial problems, Orr dreams the entire species a pale gray.

The opening of the film shows the reality Orr has escaped: death from radiation poisoning in a post–World War II landscape. At the end of the film, he is still trying to escape that fate, although he has given up the notion of changing reality, and his psychiatrist has gone mad.

The Lathe of Heaven was conceived as the first of an unrealized PBS series of filmed science-fiction novels and short stories.

W.L.

LAUMER, [JOHN] KEITH (1925–   ).   American writer noted for both tough-minded adventure tales and zany comedies. Born in Syracuse, New York, Laumer has spent much of his life in Florida, where he now resides (and often sets his stories). He holds a B.S. degree in architectural engineering from the University of Illinois, served twice in the army and in the air force, and belonged to the U.S. Foreign Service. Since his first sale in 1959 to *Amazing,* he has published about sixty books, many concerned with transit (through time, space, or alternate realities), war, and transcendence.

Dissatisfaction in government employ made Laumer an implacable foe of bureaucracy. It also inspired his popular Retief series, which satirically recounts the adventures of an omnicompetent galactic diplomat in a universe of bunglers *(Envoy to New Worlds,* 1963, and others).

His sardonic wit and preoccupation with disguises and delusions—not to mention the streamlined pace of his stories—reveal Laumer's acknowledged debt to Raymond Chandler. In tales of alien invasion, these traits can yield either shudders *(Plague of Demons,* 1964/1965) or guffaws *(The Monitors,* 1966, the basis of the 1969 film of the same name).

Laumer's finest work glorifies indomitability, as in "Once There Was a Giant" (1968). Under stress his durable heroes can grow into SUPERMEN *(The House in November,* 1970). This same love of excellence extends to machines, especially his colossal, ultimately conscious tanks *(Bolo: Annals of the Dinochrome Brigade,* 1976). For both human and machine, the supreme goal in Laumer's fiction is self-perfection.

NOTABLE OTHER WORKS: *Worlds of the Imperium* (1962); *The Great Time Machine Hoax* (1963/1964); *Beyond the Imperium* (1965, 1968/1981); *Retief's War* (1965/1966); *Galactic Odyssey* (1967); *Dinosaur Beach* (1971); *Night of Delusions* (1972); *The Ultimax Man* (1977/1978).

S.L.M.

LEE, TANITH (1947–   ).   British writer of numerous novels and short stories, most since 1975. Lee attended Croydon Art College and held several library jobs. She developed rapidly as a writer after the publication of her first book, a juvenile, in 1971, and particularly after turning to full-time writing with the purchase in the United States by DAW Books of her Birthgrave trilogy in 1974–75.

Lee's work is distinguished by sensitive handling of prose, with particular care in establishing a slow, sensuous pace and rhythm, and strong, colorful descriptions that may, nevertheless, be short on background such as ecological detail when her stories are placed on other planets. She is less concerned with plot and speculation than with characters. Complex, strong willed, in pow-

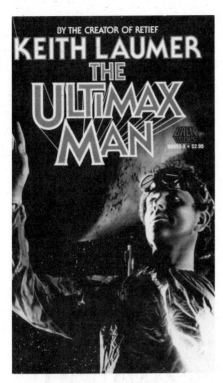

Art by J. K. Potter

Indeed, much of Lee's best work makes new uses of myth. Several short story collections retell and reinterpret recognizable myths and fairy tales from various cultures: for instance, *Red as Blood* (1983), *Tamastara* (1984), and *The Gorgon* (1985). She also deals with more contemporary horror figures in *Kill the Dead* (1980), which concerns the undead; *Sabella* (1980), which involves vampires; and *Lycanthia* (1981), which describes a different kind of werewolf.

Such clearly science-fictional novels as *Don't Bite the Sun* (1976), *Electric Forest* (1979), and *Days of Grass* (1985) use traditional SF conventions—a decadent future, androids, postholocaust humanity—to make characteristic statements about aesthetics, individualism, and feminism.

OTHER WORKS: *Companions on the Road* (1975); *The Winter Players* (1976); *The Storm Lord* (1976); *East of Midnight* (1977); *Drinking Sapphire Wine* (1977); *Volkhavaar* (1977); *The Castle of Dark* (1978); *Prince of Demons* (1978); *Shon the Taken* (1979); *Day by Night* (1980); *Unsilent Night* (1981); *The Silver Metal Lover* (1981); *Cyrion* (1982); *Anackire* (1983); *Sung in Shadow* (1983); *Dark Castle, White Horse* (1986); *Dreams of Dark and Light* (1986).

J.Gordon

LE GUIN, URSULA K[ROEBER] (1929–   ).

American writer of fantasy and science fiction. Le Guin is the daughter of anthropologist Alfred Kroeber and writer Theodora Kroeber *(Ishi in Two Worlds)*. Writing always with great care and artistic integrity, Le Guin established herself in the 1960s and 1970s in the first rank of authors of fantastic literature. Her career features an earnest search to use the materials of fantasy and science fiction to explore, in the manner of Albert Einstein's "thought experiments," the great subjects of anthropology—the richness of human diversity and the problems of cross-cultural interchange.

Beginning with a lighthearted time slip story, "April in Paris" (1962), she experimented with a wide range of SF story types, including the Platonic fable ("The Masters," 1963), the political parable ("The Ones Who Walk away from Omelas," Hugo, 1973), the saga of galactic expansion (her Hainish fiction), the ALTERNATE-WORLDS novel (*The Lathe of Heaven*, 1971), the surreal fantasy (*The New Atlantis*, 1975), and a children's fantasy trilogy (*A Wizard of Earthsea*, 1968; *The Tombs of Atuan*, 1971; and *The Farthest Shore*, 1972), the last of which won the National Book Award. Thus her work has ranged from traditional to experimental, including several tales that, like Edwin A. ABBOTT's *Flatland*, experiment with literary conventions to play with scientific ideas. Among these are "Schrodinger's Cat" (1974); "Direction of the Road" (1973), a story adopting a relativistic point of view; and a tale of fictive science, "The Author of the

erful or potentially powerful positions, they must test themselves against difficult circumstances and discover their identity and the nature of their power. Lee often deals with feminist ideas, both sensual and political, most notably the concepts of matriarchy and shared power. She has written science fiction and fantasy for both adult and juvenile readers and has proved herself adept in a variety of forms, including heroic fantasy, fairy tales, horror, and future fiction in prose both stately and wry.

Lee's earliest published works were juvenile fiction, including her first fantasy novel, *Dragon Hoard* (1971). Her children's books include the fairy tales in *Princess Hynchatti and Some Other Surprises* (1972) and *Animal Castle* (1972), a picture book. Her heroic fantasies, however, proved more important to her career. The Birthgrave series—*The Birthgrave* (1975), *Vazkor, Son of Vazkor* (1978), and *Quest for the White Witch* (1978)—combines fantasy and SF in the quest of a heroic woman-goddess. The quest reaches its climax on board a spaceship. The Demon Lord series—*Night's Master* (1978), *Death's Master* (1979), and *Delusion's Master* (1981)—consists of episodic tales that form longer sagas, using the techniques of myth to communicate the author's invented mythology.

Ursula K. Le Guin

Acacia Seeds and Other Extracts from the Journal of Therolinguistics'' (1974).

But Le Guin's greatest contribution to SF and to anthropological speculation has been her sequence of stories and novels detailing the history of the Hain, parent species of the human race and of several other humanoid species with different characteristics and abilities, living within a hundred-light-year range of our corner of the Milky Way. Beginning with ''Dowry of the Angyar'' (later ''Semley's Necklace'') in 1964, she told of the reintegration of the human species after their galactic dispersion of more than a million years. *Rocannon's World* (1966) was followed by *Planet of Exile* and *City of Illusions* (1967); these are genre stories of planetary exploration and of discontinuities wrought by nearly-as-fast-as-light travel, first contact, and human-alien integration.

Le Guin's growth as a writer is displayed in the depth and subtlety of her creation, the Hainish League (later Ekumen) of known worlds. Her two award-winning novels, *The Left Hand of Darkness* (Hugo and Nebula, 1969) and *The Dispossessed* (Hugo and Nebula, 1974), are infused with a subtext of schematic symbolism based on her reading of Taoist philosophy; the characters search for a balance among eternal opposites, which could, if nurtured, yield an optimizing of human relations. Hence, where a rift has taken place between cultures, it is her hero's function to heal, in the first case by forging a Terran-alien bond of friendship, in the second by achieving a scientific breakthrough that will reshape human

possibilities. Throughout the Hainish saga, recontact with the Hainish home world will heal local differences and strengthen the human species as a whole. In *The Dispossessed* Le Guin interleaved the story of hero Shevek's formative years with the account of his adult scientific discovery, a device for locating the adult in the child and the end of a story in its beginning. Between these two masterpieces came the bitter novella *The Word for World Is Forest* (Hugo, 1972), which may be read as a specific allegory of the Vietnam War or more broadly as a study in the ugliness of the ethnocentric mentality and a search for nonviolent methods of achieving its defeat.

With *Always Coming Home* (1985) Le Guin achieved a synthesis of her several themes in a futuristic Earth setting. In this large collection of the stories, poetry, myths, and legends—and even music—of the Kesh, she developed, by gradual accretion of detail, a powerful demonstration of how a world torn apart by ''civilization'' may be rebuilt with timeless archetypal ritual. In this haunting work Le Guin moved beyond the bounds of popular entertainment, sacrificing strong plotting for a wealth of cultural detail. In the process she drew mixed responses from the SF community—ranging from high praise to accusations that she had forgone narrative or SF extrapolation in the quest for approval from the literary community—but achieved a near total fusion of anthropology and futuristic speculation.

Le Guin's many fantasy writings and other essays and stories show a similar development from the generic to the stylish and special, with her humanistic and anthropological concerns always clearly evident. Her numerous SF and fantasy awards attest to her acceptance within the field; her more general literary awards, media dramatizations, and approval from the broader literary journals and reviewers indicate that, like Ray BRADBURY in the 1950s, she is considered not simply a ''token'' genre writer but a major contemporary author irrespective of genre.

OTHER WORKS: *The Wind's Twelve Quarters* (collection, 1975); *Orsinian Tales* (collection, 1976); *The Water Is Wide* (1976); *The Eye of the Heron* (1978); *Leese Webster* (1979); *Malafrena* (1979); *The Beginning Place* (1980); *The Compass Rose* (collection, 1982).

T.P.D.

LEHR, PAUL (1930–   ). American science-fiction illustrator. Lehr earned a degree in art (1951) from Whittenberg College in Springfield, Ohio, then took additional courses from the prestigious Pratt Institute in Brooklyn, graduating in 1956. At Pratt he met Stanley Meltzoff, who interested him in SF art. Lehr's first cover assignment was for Jeffrey Castle's *Satellite E-1* (Bantam Books, 1957) and was soon followed by commissions from Ace Books, Ballantine, NAL/Signet, Berkley, DAW, Pocket Books, St. Martin's Press, and many other book publishers. (Lehr has also painted many mystery covers.) He produced numerous cover illustrations for magazines such as *Analog, Omni, The Saturday Evening Post* (for which, in 1959, he painted his version of the first moon landing—the original is now hanging in the Smithsonian), *Fortune, Life,* and *Time.* His only black-and-white SF illustrations have been for *Analog.*

Lehr's SF art is semi-surrealistic, and he is noted for the use of strange spherical and ovoid shapes. He is best remembered for his covers for the Orbit series of original anthologies edited by Damon KNIGHT and the art for Robert A. HEINLEIN's *Stranger in a Strange Land.* Lehr has been twice nominated for the Hugo for Best Professional Artist, and has won the Frank R. Paul Award.

J.G.

LEIBER, FRITZ [REUTER, JR.] (1910–   ).

American writer of science fiction, fantasy, and horror who has won major awards in all three categories. The only child of Shakespearean actors with their own touring company, Leiber received a bachelor's degree in biological sciences from the University of Chicago. For a while he toured with his parents' company; later he was an editor and writer at *Science Digest.* A prolific writer, he has published thirty-eight books (half of them SF) and over two hundred stories (about a third of them SF). His most important SF novels are *The Big Time* (1961) and *The Wanderer* (1965), both Hugo Award winners. His many heroic fantasy stories of Fafhrd and the Gray Mouser (collected in six volumes, 1957–1977) and his supernatural horror novel *Our Lady of Darkness* (1977), winner of the World Fantasy Award, are equally renowned.

Leiber's first published stories, in 1939, were fantasy and horror; by 1943 his SF began to appear in *Astounding Science Fiction,* starting with a three-part serialization of "Gather, Darkness" (book form, 1950). The story describes a future dictatorship, the Hierarchy, based on a corrupt form of Roman Catholicism, and an underground opposition group known as the Witchcraft, purporting to use magic but actually employing advanced technology to achieve revolution.

The Big Time is arguably Leiber's most important work, a brief yet complex novel concerning the Change War, being fought throughout time and across the galaxy between two sides called the Spiders and the Snakes. Paradoxically, the novel is set in one room; Leiber deliberately employed a number of theatrical devices as humans and aliens make their entrances and exits. He has also written six stories referring to this conflict, of which five (as well as some peripheral time travel stories) are included in the collection *The Change War* (1978).

By contrast, Leiber's other Hugo-winning novel, *The Wanderer,* is multiplotted and much larger. It chronicles the widespread chaos caused on Earth by the approach of a large planetary mass, rendered realistically through

Fritz Leiber

Leiber's interest and expertise in astronomy. The new planet is revealed to be a spaceship with intelligent inhabitants.

The Big Time and *The Wanderer* are both serious works (though lightened by clever plotting and witty dialogue), but three of Leiber's SF novels as well as numerous stories are humorous. Most notable among the novels is *A Specter Is Haunting Texas* (1969), a satire that employs much black comedy. The "specter" is a man raised in a zero-gravity colony so that most of his muscles have atrophied and he must wear a titanium exoskeleton to survive. He visits a postholocaust Texas that has grown to swallow up most of North America. The satire here is wide ranging, aimed at politicians and Texans of the time, social foibles, and even several SF plot clichés.

There is no such thing as a "typical" Leiber story; like his novels his short fiction has been immensely varied, extending to most areas of SF and frequently containing original approaches and deeper levels of meaning. The stories include sharp satires of the future, such as the frequently reprinted "Coming Attraction" (1950); hard science stories such as "A Pail of Air" (1951), in which a family group survives a catastrophic drop in Earth's temperature; alternate–time line stories including "Catch That Zeppelin!" (1975, winner of the Hugo and Nebula awards); and "Ship of Shadows" (1969), another Hugo winner, set in space. Leiber's own preferences have led to his inclusion of fantasy and horror elements in much of his SF, which is all the stronger for it.

Murray Leinster

Although the best of his earlier work was cleverly written, Leiber has developed his writing talents over the course of his career, producing his most stylish work since 1970. He has a very light touch with humor and satire yet is also a storyteller of considerable power and an able descriptive writer. Highly regarded by readers and other writers of SF, he has received more major awards than any other SF writer—six Hugos, three Nebulas, three World Fantasy Awards, and Grand Master of Fantasy—and has been guest of honor at two world conventions.

OTHER WORKS: *The Green Millennium* (1953); *The Sinful Ones* (1953); *Destiny Times Three* (1957); *The Silver Eggheads* (1961); *The Mind Spider* (1961); *A Pail of Air* (1964); *Ships to the Stars* (1964); *The Night of the Wolf* (1966); *The Secret Songs* (1968); *You're All Alone* (1972); *The Best of Fritz Leiber* (collection, 1974); *The Book of Fritz Leiber* (collection, 1974); *The Second Book of Fritz Leiber* (collection, 1975); *The Worlds of Fritz Leiber* (collection, 1976); *Ship of Shadows* (1979), *The Ghost Light* (1984).

C.M.

LEINSTER, MURRAY (Pseudonym of William Fitzgerald Jenkins) (1896–1975). American writer and inventor. Leinster not only helped to create modern science fiction in the early Munsey magazines but also became a key figure of the GOLDEN AGE under John W. CAMPBELL, Jr., in the 1940s and 1950s; he pat-

ented a number of inventions, including a front-projection method for filming backgrounds.

Leinster contributed regularly to *Argosy* as early as 1916, but his first significant SF title was "The Runaway Skyscraper" (1919), in which a side effect of a geologic fault sends the Metropolitan Insurance Building and its occupants backward in time from Madison Square, Manhattan, to primitive America. While the protagonist, a young engineer, solves the problem of returning the skyscraper to the twentieth century, his companions trade with the Indians. In both "The Mad Planet" (1920) and "The Red Dust" (1921) a geologic catastrophe has opened fissures in the Earth's crust, thereby releasing poisonous gases. Civilization has collapsed, and humanity has been reduced to tribal barbarism in a world where gigantism (of insects and plants) runs rampant. The protagonist saves his people after he comes to a fuller understanding of the hostile environment. Hugo GERNSBACK reissued these novelettes in AMAZING STORIES (1926–27).

Leinster also made use of the evil genius whose inventions (or theft of advanced devices) threaten society, as in "Darkness on Fifth Avenue" *(Argosy*, 1929). These works emphasize the close relation between SF and the detective story in that both concentrate on a specific problem to be solved. Leinster published in *Argosy* through much of the 1930s.

In the 1940s and 1950s his fiction appeared in such magazines as *Astounding* and GALAXY. In "The Seven Temporary Moons" (1948) he created Bud Gregory, a hillbilly with an intuitive understanding of high technology and science, who became the central character in a series of stories. Leinster's Med Service series of stories, in which his characters tackle medical problems throughout the galaxy, were collected in four books, one of which is *Doctor to the Stars* (1964). His novelette "Exploration Team" (1955) won the Hugo, but probably the high mark of his fiction remains "First Contact" (1945), voted into the Science Fiction Hall of Fame, in which a spaceship from Earth encounters a ship of humanoid aliens near the Crab nebula. The problem in the novel is this: if either spaceship captain gives the order to flee, he risks the discovery—and thus the possible destruction—of his home planet. Perhaps even more than Stanley G. WEINBAUM's "A Martian Odyssey" (1934), "First Contact" upgrades the alien to human equality from its Wellsian prototype of monsters bent on the destruction of humanity in unending warfare. The story marks one of the turning points in SF.

Although he published more than twenty books, beginning with *Murder Madness* (1931) and *The Murder of the U.S.A.* (1946)—sometimes using the name Will F. Jenkins—Leinster remains important for his shorter fiction. Like the work of many writers of his generation, some of his material has dated, but he should not be dismissed because of changes in the political and literary temper. He gave voice to the first view of American SF:

that of protagonists capable of heroic action in a future dominated by technology as humanity reaches for the stars. For more than a half century his stories shaped the field.

T.D.C.

LEM, STANISLAW (1921–   ). Polish writer, critic, and scientific and technical commentator with an international reputation. One of the most popular authors in Europe, Lem is perhaps the science-fiction writer most likely to be considered for the Nobel Prize in literature. Living under the Germans, who interrupted his medical study, made him a mechanic, and nearly executed him, and later the Russians, who control Poland by proxy and censor his work, Lem knows the clumsiness and brutality of authoritarian rule. In order to evade the authority that suppressed his first novel and to pursue his scientific interests, Lem began writing SF, publishing *The Astronauts* (1951) and *The Magellan Nebula* (1955) in a mode of socialist realism. Unlike Lem's works known to his English readers, in which knowledge seems a futile human effort but is nevertheless pursued fervently, these novels are optimistic about utopian possibilities and acquiring knowledge.

The fame he achieved after their success partially freed Lem from the censors, enabling him to pursue satiric dystopias in *Memoirs Found in a Bathtub* (1973), with its description of an overpopulated, polluted world. In Ijon Tichy, the protagonist-narrator of this novel, Lem created a convenient vehicle to satirize SF conventions. Tichy reappears in *The Star Diaries* (1976; as *Memoirs of a Space Traveler*, 1982), a growing comic series that lampoons the convention of time travel. Similar in structure but generally lighter in tone are *The Cyberiad* (1974) and *Mortal Engines* (1977), the first a collection of robot-constructor fables on cybernetics cast in the episodic form of *Don Quixote*, and the second a collection of unrelated robot stories, some of which could be for children, while others, such as "The Mask," are subtle robotic retellings of Mary Wollstonecraft SHELLEY's *Frankenstein* (1818). Pirx the pilot appears in two short story collections; he began as a comic character much like Ijon Tichy but became more embittered in successive stories. Not a hero, Pirx succeeds more by luck and intuition than by reason.

Solaris (1971), with its sentient ocean, and *The Invincible* (1973), with its mysterious mayhem, both alien-contact narratives, deeply probe the limits of knowledge. Only in irrational gesture do Kelvin and Rohan make contact with the alien ocean and robotic-hive intelligence of their respective novels; otherwise, as in *Solaris*, the attempt to know only reveals the self making the attempt. *The Investigation* (1974) and *The Chain of Chance* (1978), both in the form of detective stories, likewise show the blindnesses that attend insight. Lem

Madeleine L'Engle

further stretched narrative forms in *His Master's Voice* (1984), supposedly a mathematician's biography, and *A Perfect Vacuum* (1979) and *Imaginary Magnitude* (1984), collections of reviews and introductions to books that have not been written. He has also written nonfiction books, such as *Summa technologiae* (1964), a survey of engineering possibilities, including social, informational, and biological aspects, and *Fantastyka i futurologia* (1970), his critical analysis of English-language SF, both untranslated. Witty, intelligent, and stylistically innovative, Lem may be SF's James Joyce.

OTHER WORKS: *Sesame and Other Stories* (1955); *Dialogues* (1957); *Invasion from Aldebaran* (1959); *Eden* (1959); *Return from the Stars* (1961; trans. 1980); *Going into Orbit* (1962); *The High Castle* (1968); *Philosophy of Chance* (1968); *Science Fiction and Futurology* (1970); *Tales of Pirx the Pilot* (1979); *More Tales of Pirx the Pilot* (1982); *Fiasco* (1987).

C.B.

L'ENGLE, MADELEINE (1918–   ). American writer best known for her science fantasy for children. L'Engle's series of children's science fiction, *The Time Tetralogy* (1979), which began with *A Wrinkle in Time* (1962), represents for many young readers their first experience with the genre.

Born in New York City, graduated from Smith College, and married to actor Hugh Franklin, L'Engle has worked in theater and playwriting, and as a teacher and librarian.

She first attempted realistic fiction before recognizing that her "true discoveries of reality came while I was writing sci-fi or fantasy." By 1987 she had written twenty-two books for children and nineteen for adults. *A Wrinkle in Time* was her seventh novel but her first major success, winning the Newbery and Sequoyah awards. It was followed by *A Wind in the Door* (1973); *A Swiftly Tilting Planet* (1978), which won the American Book Award; and *Many Waters* (1986). Together they tell the story of members of the Murry family and their friend Calvin O'Keefe as they encounter superbeings, the loss of cellular memory, the threat of thermonuclear war, and mythic creatures who help them resolve crises that could change the course of history. All the novels involve time travel.

In L'Engle's stories of good and evil, the small, the weak, and the ordinary all partake in the larger events of the cosmos. Her clear prose creates the kind of synthesis between science and literature that writers of the best adult SF have always tried to achieve.

J.R.W.

LESSING, DORIS [MAY] (1919–).   British mainstream author who lived in Southern Rhodesia (now Zimbabwe) until 1949, when she moved to London, and who ventured into science fiction in the 1970s. Lessing's African background provided material for several of her early mainstream short stories and novels, including in part *The Golden Notebook* (1961), which influenced later feminist fiction, and the five-novel sequence Children of Violence (1952–1969). In the last novel in the sequence, *The Four-Gated City,* her interest in Sufi mysticism and ESP surfaced, and in an appendix she envisioned a near-future catastrophe. Science-fiction motifs reappear in *Briefing for a Descent into Hell* (1971), a novel about a middle-aged professor's voyage in mythic space, inspired by R. D. Laing's view of schizophrenia as a kind of protective sanity. *The Memoirs of a Survivor* (1974) vividly pictures city civilization on the verge of collapse and suggests insights needed for spiritual survival.

When *Shikasta* (1979) appeared, as the first novel in the sequence Canopus in Argos: Archives, Lessing's commitment to SF became explicit. She wanted the history of the planet Shikasta (Earth) to be viewed as an aspect of "cosmic evolution expressed in the rivalries and interactions of great galactic Empires." An emissary from the ancient guardian Empire of Canopus records Shikasta's drift toward self-destruction because of the influence of the vampiric planet Shammat, which has caused a decline in SOWF (substance-of-we-feeling). Four sequels followed: *The Marriages between Zones Three, Four, and Five* (1980), a love story illustrating the infusion of female qualities in a male-dominated warrior world; *The Sirian Experiments* (1981), about the in-

volvement of the technological Sirian Empire in Shikasta's history; *The Making of the Representative for Planet 8* (1982), offering the analogy of a planet dying of cold; and *The Sentimental Agents in the Volyen Empire* (1983), about a disintegrating empire (pointedly reminiscent of the British Empire) infected, though not beyond remedy, by self-indulgent rhetoric. Despite its overt didacticism, Lessing's speculative cosmogony is an impressive achievement.

J.H.

LEVIN, IRA (1929–).   American mainstream writer. Levin followed up his fine occult thriller *Rosemary's Baby* (1967) with the ironic dystopia *This Perfect Day* (1970). *The Stepford Wives* (1972), in which a group of male suburbanites replace their wives with compliant robot substitutes, is a clever satire on sexual politics. *The Boys from Brazil* (1976) is a thriller about clones of Hitler that complains about the follies of naive genetic determinism. Levin is perhaps the best middlebrow mainstream writer to have used science-fiction themes.

B.S.

LEWIS, C[LIVE] S[TAPLES] (1898–1963). British mainstream author who was an uncompromising apologist for Christianity in a post-Christian age and who devoted his Ransom science-fiction trilogy to a defense of traditional religious and moral values against scientific humanism. In *Out of the Silent Planet* (1938) the protagonist Ransom is shanghaied aboard a spaceship by a pair of villains (one a "scientist," the other interested only in loot) bound for Mars. Mars turns out to be a world still in a state of grace, its natives in no need of humans' "blessings." In *Perelandra* (1943) Ransom manages to prevent a new fall from grace on Venus by killing the scientist, now possessed by Satan. *That Hideous Strength* (1945) depicts the attempted takeover of England by the National Institute for Coordinated Experiments (N.I.C.E.), which represents all that Lewis considered diabolic in modern thought: a rejection of absolute moral standards, the treatment of human beings (in effect) as nothing more than guinea pigs for social experiment, and the pursuit of mere power in the name of "progress." H. G. WELLS is present in caricature.

Lewis argued the same points in *The Abolition of Man* (1943), and he defended Christian doctrine in numerous works. He was a perceptive reader and critic of SF, with one particularly valuable essay, "On Science Fiction" (1966), to his credit. His *The Screwtape Letters* (1942) and his Narnia fantasies for children (beginning in 1950) also contain elements of SF.

J.J.P.

SEE ALSO: TWO CULTURES DEBATE

Willy Ley (right) with Robert A. Heinlein

LEWIS, SINCLAIR (1885–1951). American author and winner of the Nobel Prize for literature in 1930 who wrote one science-fiction novel. *It Can't Happen Here* (1935) portrays the rise to power of a fascist regime in America. Though not in the genre, Lewis's *Arrowsmith* (1925) is a novel about contemporary science, dramatizing the struggle of a research scientist against the greed of the medical profession.

                                                                                    N.H.

LEY, WILLY (1906–1969). American science and science-fiction writer, born in Germany. Ley was, along with Hermann Oberth and Wernher von Braun, one of the pioneer rocket enthusiasts for the Verein Raumschiffahrt (Society for Space Travel). A familiar figure at SF gatherings and conventions, he and his career are significant examples of the way in which science, particularly the science of space travel, and science fiction reinforced each other during this period. As the age of twenty Ley had already written his first treatise, *Die Fahrt ins Weltall (The Journey into Space,* 1926). But unlike Oberth and von Braun, he refused to work under Hitler and emigrated to the United States in 1935. There he soon gravitated to the SF magazines, where he championed the cause of space travel in fiction ("At the

Perihelion," 1937) as well as in articles.

His factual books did much to popularize rocketry. *Rockets* was published in 1944 and updated several times (its last edition was *Rockets, Missiles, and Men in Space,* 1968). Chesley BONESTELL illustrated his *The Conquest of Space* (1949), which describes the development of staged rockets, a space station, and planetary exploring vehicles and inspired a 1955 film. Bonestell also illustrated Ley's *The Exploration of Mars* (1956) *and Beyond the Solar System* (1964).

Ley also wrote on a number of other scientific and technical subjects, as evidenced by his *The Lungfish, the Dodo, and the Unicorn* (1948), *Dragons in Amber* (1951), *Engineers' Dreams* (1954), and *The Drifting Continents* (1969). He became science editor of GALAXY in 1952 and won two Hugo Awards for his columns. Although his fictional output was small, his "Fog" (1940) remains an impressive story of revolution as seen by a confused bystander. Ley longed to become active in the U.S. space program, but he was never called, and, like a space-age Moses, died just before the first Moon landing.

                                                                                    J.J.P.

LICHTENBERG, JACQUELINE (1942–   ). American science-fiction writer who specializes in stories about symbiosis between species that otherwise would be deadly to each other. Lichtenberg broke into print through STAR TREK fanzines and, with Joan Winston and Sandra Marshak, the nonfiction book *Star Trek Lives* (1975). Her first novel, *House of Zeor* (1974), began a series describing the struggle of two mutant strains of humanity, the vampiric Simes and the human-appearing Gens, to live symbiotically or perish. Subsequent books in the series are *Unto Zeor, Forever* (1978), *First Channel* (1980), *Channel's Destiny* (with Jean Lorrah, 1982), *Rensime!* (1985), and *Zelerod's Doom* (1986).

Lichtenberg is also author of the First Lifewave series, consisting of *Molt Brother* (1982) and *City of a Million Legends* (1985), which deals with venomous reptilian aliens and their sworn companions, and the Dushau trilogy—*Dushau* (1985), *Farfetch* (1985), and *Outreach* (1986)—all of which concern a human's learning to mesh with long-lived aliens.

                                                                                    S.M.S.

LIFEFORCE (1985). *Directed by Tobe Hooper; screenplay by Dan O'Bannon and Don Jakoby; photographed by Alan Hume; music by Henri Mancini. With Steve Railsback, Peter Firth, Frank Finlay, and Mathilda May. 101 minutes. Color.*

Director Tobe Hooper's 1985 film of Colin WILSON's *Space Vampires* was not a commercial success nor even enjoyable viewing—for many of the same reasons that doomed John CARPENTER's remake of THE THING—but *Lifeforce* may come to be considered a noteworthy science-fiction film precisely because it is so relentlessly unsentimental and edgy. This film displays a sensibility so odd, so unfamiliar, that it may prove one of the most subtly original SF films of the 1980s. Hooper's protagonists reveal a ruthless detachment in their conflict with the space vampires, suggesting that humans and aliens are not much different.

Hooper and scriptwriters Dan O'Bannon and Don Jakoby seem to have taken one of the assumptions of *Space Vampires*—that all life is to some extent vampiric, that all creatures feed on each other's life forces—and shaded it into the more film-specific notion that all human life is voyeuristic—that we feed by watching each other's private moments. In scene after scene *Lifeforce* puts its audience in an uncomfortably self-conscious voyeuristic role. Restless camerawork makes us view each scene from odd and oddly numerous angles, often framing the scene through glass or on a video monitor, confronting us with faces that are always too close for comfort or fish-eye lens shots that give an alien perspective to much that we see.

This film is filled with "scientific" observation of fascinatingly anguished faces and desiccating bodies, and its audience must share in this observation, deriving pleasure from the observer's horror, ultimately seeing Hooper's characters as sources for our needs, in much the same way as the vampires see them as sources for the life force. The film has something to offend almost everyone but offers much for serious analysis.

B.L.

LINDSAY, DAVID (1878–1945).

British author of allegorical romances, chiefly remembered for his first novel, *A Voyage to Arcturus* (1920), a singularly imaginative voyage in space and time. In this novel many reversals and extensions of known scientific laws, and transformations of the protagonist, highlight the relativity of human perception of reality—scientific as well as theological.

J.H.

LIQUID SKY (1982).

Directed by Slava Tsukerman; screenplay by Slava Tsukerman, Nina Kerova, and Anne Carlisle; photographed by Yuri Neyman; music by Slava Tsukerman, Brenda Hutchinson, and Clive Smith. With Anne Carlisle, Paula Sheppard, Susan Doukas, Otto von Wernherr. 118 minutes. Color.

This inventive black comedy science-fiction movie about the decadence of Western culture became an instant cult film in North America. The outrageous plot focuses on a New York performance artist who suffers a variety of sexual indignities from a parade of rapists and seducers of both sexes who embody the impersonal and insensitive sexual mores of modern urban life. Tiny aliens land their miniature saucer on the patio of the artist's Manhattan apartment and use her as a host, feeding off the chemicals produced at the moment of orgasm in the brains of her sexual partners and vaporizing them. Upon discovering the aliens' presence, the artist decides to employ their power as a sexual weapon to destroy her aggressors.

In contrast to the plot, the film's style is subtle and the performances consistently deadpan, throwing into greater relief the dark view of contemporary sexuality as unloving and "alien"-ated.

B.K.G.

—— LITERARY CONVENTIONS ——

The need for conventions as a form of literary shorthand has always been particularly acute in science fiction, a genre that was originally published almost exclusively in magazines, where length limits tended to be strict. Science fiction has the additional demands of its subject matter—unusual activities in unfamiliar surroundings—and these require explanation. As a result, most of the conventions, the means of boiling down paragraphs of explanation into a word or two, were created in the early years of SF's development, roughly from the 1920s to the 1950s. Since then writers have tended to challenge earlier conventions, to minimize them, or to put them to new uses, and occasionally to create others. And gradually conventions have become symbols—such as the robot, the ray gun, and the rocket ship—or, in more sophisticated literary usage, metaphors.

One reason for the decline of conventions has been the decline of the magazine and the rise of book publication, with its greater freedom and presumption of a more general readership. Another has been a growing interest among SF authors in the inner, rather than the outer, universe. Still another has been a shift to sociological matters, which has resulted in a fiction more concerned with cultural than technical questions.

Today's SF represents a major change from that of the early magazine years, when stories were heavily weighted toward technology and most of the classic examples of enduring conventions were created and refined. One early convention, for instance, involved spaceflight. In pre-SF flights to the Moon, for instance, all sorts of conventions for travel developed, from whirlwinds to demons and migrating birds, but the most reliable conveyance was an angel. In the nineteenth century, with its scientific enlightenment and literary emphasis on plausibility, authors turned to balloons, giant cannons, and antigravity.

By the twentieth century Robert Goddard's research had turned attention toward rocket propulsion, and early stories devoted lengthy descriptions to the way reaction could propel a rocket in the airless void, where there is nothing "to push against." As readers became familiar with such explanations, and bored with them, authors began to dispose of the question with a simple reference to "rocket ships" or "SPACESHIPS."

A little later the problem became how to get characters from one star system to another in a reasonable length of time, in view of Albert Einstein's recently announced law of relativity, which says that nothing in our universe can go faster than the speed of light: 186,282 miles per second. Even at that speed, which is unlikely to be reached, if not impossible, travel to the nearest star would take years.

Science-fiction writers arrived at one solution by assuming the future discovery of a means of traveling at velocities faster than light (ftl): E. E. SMITH invented the inertialess drive in his Lensman novels; Jack WILLIAMSON and James GUNN, "a different kind of energy that created a different kind of space" in Star Bridge (1955); some, such as Harry HARRISON in One Step from Earth (1970), used "matter transmitters," and others, such as Isaac ASIMOV in almost all his novels, used "hyperspace" (a dimension other than our familiar three), "hyperdrive," and "jumps." Later, after the discovery of black holes and the scientific speculation that matter disappearing into one might come out somewhere else in the universe, the black hole was used for the same purpose: getting characters somewhere else fast—not too different from angels or "seven-league boots."

Early in the convention-building period, however, authors began to write against the conventions for story purposes. Murray LEINSTER's "Proxima Centauri" (1935), for instance, accepts the light-speed limitation and suggests that reaching the stars might require a "generation ship," in which the crew and passengers would live and die en route so that their descendants could finally reach the distant destination. Robert A. HEINLEIN's "Universe" (1941) added the idea that, because of revolution and the passage of time, the passengers might forget the original purpose of their journey and, through a mythmaking process, come to consider their spaceship the entire universe and its travel a religious metaphor.

Dozens of other devices—too many to be listed in their entirety here—for making SF stories tellable have been used so often that they have reached the status of conventions. They include the following.

Time-Dilation Effect: Einstein's theories also postulate that time slows down as velocity increases, allowing months or years to pass on Earth while passengers in a spaceship might age only days or months, as in Heinlein's *Time for the Stars* (1956) and Poul ANDERSON's *No World of Their Own* (1955).

Superman: If the evolutionary process has not ended, a superior race of humans might develop naturally or by mutation, possibly by nuclear accident, as in Theodore

STURGEON's *More Than Human* (1953), Olaf STAPLEDON's *Odd John* (1935), and Wilmar SHIRAS's *Children of the Atom* (1953).

Antigravity: Perhaps some substance could be invented that would shield spaceships from the tug of gravity, such as H. G. WELLS's "Cavorite" in *The First Men in the Moon* (1901). Or machines could produce the same effect, such as the "spindizzies" in James BLISH's *Cities in Flight* (1970), thus permitting easy or economical spaceflight.

Invisibility: A fairy-tale wish, INVISIBILITY was rationalized into a convention by Wells's *The Invisible Man* (1897). (It had appeared as a mystery in earlier stories by Fitz-James O'BRIEN, Guy de Maupassant, and Ambrose BIERCE.) It was achieved through "perfect transparency." Different rationalizations have been suggested by later authors.

Mutations: Sometimes mutations produce creatures that are different from rather than superior to human beings, as in Heinlein's "muties" in "Universe," Wells's *The Island of Dr. Moreau* (1896), and Blish's *The Seedling Stars* (1957).

Time Travel: Wells did it best with *The Time Machine* (1895); there's no more reason to think that one can travel in time than that one can travel faster than light, but in order to explore the past or the future, authors have resorted to various devices to move their characters through time, from sleeping for many years (an early favorite) to machines (the convention of choice today).

Center of the Earth: The crank notion of a hollow Earth has survived the centuries down to today. Early uses of this convention can be found in Ludvig Holberg's *The Journey to the World Underground* (1741) and Captain Adam Seaborn's *Symzonia: A Voyage of Discovery* (1820), but the classic treatments are contained in Jules VERNE's *Journey to the Center of the Earth* (1864) and Edgar Rice BURROUGH's Pellucidar series, beginning in 1914 with *At the Earth's Core.*

Parallel Universes and Continua: Modern theorists suggest that there may be universes parallel to ours, but SF authors were using them for speculation and adventure as early as the 1930s in Leinster's "Sidewise in Time" (1934) and Williamson's *The Legion of Time* (1938). Philip José FARMER wrote the entire World of Tiers series using this convention, beginning with *The Maker of Universes* (1965).

Contact with Aliens: ALIENS themselves provide a basic theme in SF, but contact with aliens is a convention in and of itself in such classics as Stanley G. WEINBAUM's "A Martian Odyssey" (1934) and Leinster's "First Contact" (1945); it has become the subject of entire books, including Robert SILVERBERG's *Collision Course* (1961) and Gordon R. DICKSON's *The Alien Way* (1965).

Telepathy: Many people believe in telepathy, but no one has been able to demonstrate it and it is no more likely than time travel or travel faster than light. Its conventional use, however, allows authors such as Frederik POHL in *Drunkard's Walk* (1960) or Alfred BESTER in *The Demolished Man* (1953) to explore the fascinating possibilities of the transference of or inability to conceal thoughts.

Teleportation: A companion to telepathy, teleportation presumes the ability to move objects, including human bodies, instantaneously from one place to another by using the mind. Such a possibility takes a major role in Bester's *The Stars My Destination* (1957) and Blish's *Jack of Eagles* (1952) and a more peripheral place in A. E. VAN VOGT's *The World of Null-A* (1948).

Intelligence in a New Body: Like telepathy and teleportation, switching minds or personalities is so unlikely as to be nearly impossible, and it is similar to the fantasy notion of "possession," but it made possible such SF stories as Wells's "The Late Mr. Elvesham" (1896) and even novels such as Robert SHECKLEY's *Mindswap* (1966).

Animal Intelligence: The notion that the INTELLIGENCE of animals may be raised to human levels (or beyond) has been the subject of novels such as Stapledon's *Sirius* (1944) and has been part of such stories as John W. CAMPBELL Jr.'s "Twilight" (1934) and Lester DEL REY's "The Faithful" (1938).

Machine Intelligence: The idea of intelligent machines, which began as far back as the Greek legend of Talus, the man of bronze set to guard the island of Crete, was revived in the stories of chess-playing ROBOTS of Edgar Allan POE's day (and became the subject of a 1909 SF story by Bierce, "Moxon's Master"). It earned major treatment in a play by Karel CAPEK, *R.U.R.* (Rossum's Universal Robots) (1921), which gave mobile intelligent machines a name that stuck. The convention encompasses intelligent COMPUTERS, who become tyrannical, godlike, or even gods, as in Fredric BROWN's "Answer" (1954) and Harlan ELLISON's "I Have No Mouth, and I Must Scream" (1967), and robots who rebel or are constrained by Asimov's three laws of robotics as in his stories collected in *I, Robot* (1950).

Androids: The robots in Capek's *R.U.R.* are more properly called androids because they are living creatures of flesh and blood who can reproduce. There is no reason to believe, either, that such creatures can ever be created, although they may be more likely than time travel, telepathy, and travel faster than light. Stories commonly deal with the distinctions between androids and people, and when they do not concern rebellion involve questions of human definition, as in Clifford SIMAK's *Time and Again* (1951) and J. T. McINTOSH's "Made in U.S.A." (1953).

Immortality: The notion of living forever, or at least for a much longer time, is another wish fulfillment fantasy that has been rationalized into SF stories and novels such as Heinlein's *Methuselah's Children* (1941/1958)

and Gunn's *The Immortals* (1962).

Post-catastrophe Worlds: The convention (now becoming more difficult to rationalize) that human existence, or even something like civilization, can survive a major catastrophe, even a major nuclear war, allows authors to focus on the values that can continue through such an ordeal, or that will encourage survival. The earliest imagined catastrophe was the Flood, but authors such as Mary Wollstonecraft SHELLEY (*The Last Man*, 1826), Jack LONDON ("The Scarlet Plague," 1906), and George R. STEWART (*Earth Abides*, 1949) were fond of plagues, and Camille Flammarion's *Omega; The Last Days of the World* (1894), Wells's "The Star" (1897), and Edwin BALMER and Philip WYLIE's *When Worlds Collide* (1932) use collision or near collision with wandering worlds. Since the time of Wells, the British have seemed to specialize in ingenious catastrophe scenarios, as in John WYNDHAM's *The Day of the Triffids* (1951), John CHRISTOPHER's *No Blade of Grass (1957)*, and an entire series of novels and stories by J. G. BALLARD. But with the end of World War II, war, particularly nuclear war, became the favorite catastrophe, partially for cautionary reasons and partially for plausibility.

Alien Invasion: There is no reason to believe that aliens would have any use for Earth, or if they did that invasion across the vast reaches of space would be possible or economic. Nevertheless, invasion by aliens provides a terrible catastrophe in which human spirit, courage, and values can be tested, and adventure can be guaranteed, all the way from Wells's *The War of the Worlds* (1898) to Heinlein's *The Puppet Masters* (1951) and Jerry POURNELLE and Larry NIVEN's *Footfall* (1985). Invasion need not be detrimental, however, as illustrated by Arthur C. CLARKE's *Childhood's End* (1953).

Other Dimensions: Authors like to use the idea of dimensions other than the familiar three (four, if one counts time) to achieve a sense of wonder and a stretch of the imagination, as in Edwin A. ABBOTT's *Flatland* (1884), Heinlein's "And He Built a Crooked House" (1941), and A. J. Deutsch's "A Subway Named Moebius" (1950). But most often other dimensions have been used as a means of getting somewhere else, even though there is no reason to suppose that, if other dimensions do exist, they can ever be perceived or used.

Terraforming: Although contemporary scientists such as Carl SAGAN have speculated about terraforming other planets such as Venus or Mars by a lengthy process that will make them more Earthlike, such projects seem beyond human capabilities at the moment. That hasn't stopped authors such as Anderson, in a series of stories beginning with "UN-Man" (1953), Dickson in *Alien Art* (1973), and Pamela SARGENT in *Venus of Dreams* (1985), among many others, from writing about such epic and difficult projects.

Weapons: Energy weapons such as ray guns and blasters became commonplace in SF as early as "Armaged-

Jonathan Haze (far left), Mel Welles, and Jackie Joseph survey the bloodthirsty Audrey, Jr., in *Little Shop of Horrors* (1960)

don 2419'' (1928), Philip NOWLAN's first BUCK ROGERS story, from which they went straight into the comic strips and became as much a symbol as the rocket ship. They survived as a means of lending verisimilitude to future warfare, when revolvers or even automatics would seem like relics from an unsophisticated past. But the SF love for swordplay meant the need to rationalize another convention—energy weapons had to be outlawed or made unusable by some kind of energy body shield or screen, so that knives and swords could be retained, as in Frank HERBERT's *Dune* (1965).

Later authors found these conventions ready to use or discard as their stories and instincts required. Some authors chose to write against them, such as in the time travel stories suggesting that travelers from more advanced times might be at a disadvantage, as in Anderson's "The Man Who Came Early" (1956), in which a traveler's revolver doesn't protect him against Icelandic Vikings, or Brian W. ALDISS's "Poor Little Warrior" (1958).

Ballard's catastrophe novels and stories counter the heroic conventions of earlier works, and much of what has been called the NEW WAVE uses the images and metaphors of Campbellian SF while reinterpreting them or converting them to other purposes and adopting new conventions, such as entropy, the heat death of the universe, as a symbol for the decay of civilization or the human spirit. Mainstream writers such as Kurt VONNEGUT, Jr., and Doris LESSING have used the conventions of SF as vehicles for satire or utopian messages, or for humor, as in Woody Allen's film SLEEPER (1973).

The gradual absorption of SF into the mainstream (or perhaps more accurately the reabsorption of the mainstream into SF, for fantasy is the older tradition) may

result in decreased dependence on the traditional conventions that rely for their understanding on a readership familiar with the genre. Authors who do not want to turn off readers by what identifies itself as genre material often shun such conventions for more general literary conventions, or for images and metaphors unique to the work itself. But authors still writing for genre readers will use the conventions of SF to appeal to those readers or to get on with their stories, write against the conventions, or invent new ones.

G.R.D.

LITTLE SHOP OF HORRORS (1960).
Directed by Roger Corman; screenplay by Charles B. Griffith; photographed by Archie Dalzell; music by Fred Katz. With Jonathan Haze, Jackie Joseph, Mel Welles, Dick Miller, Myrtle Vail, Jack Nicholson, John Shaner, Wally Campo, Charles B. Griffith. 71 minutes. Black and white.

LITTLE SHOP OF HORRORS (1986).
Directed by Frank Oz; screenplay by Howard Ashman; photographed by Robert Paynter; music by Alan Menken and Howard Ashman. With Rick Moranis, Ellen Greene, Vincent Gardenia, Steve Martin, James Belushi, John Candy, Christopher Guest, Bill Murray, Tichina Arnold, Tisha Campbell, Michelle Weeks, Levi Stubbs. 94 minutes. Color.

Little Shop of Horrors came to be because Roger CORMAN wanted to see how fast he could make a film; he had Charles B. Griffith write a remake of their earlier *Bucket of Blood* (1959), and a movie legend was born. Corman shot *Little Shop* in two days and one night, perhaps the fastest schedule ever. But the film would be only a footnote in Corman's career if it hadn't been for Griffith's shrewd, unusual script and a group of talented actors.

Seymour Krelboined (Jonathan Haze), working in the Los Angeles Skid Row flower shop of Gravis Mushnik (Mel Welles), develops a new plant he names Audrey, Jr., after the clerk Audrey (Jackie Joseph). But as it grows, the plant requires human blood for nourishment; when Seymour runs out of fingers to drain, he tosses in providential corpses, and the plant, now talking, becomes enormous. Seymour ultimately sacrifices himself to stop it.

Little Shop is an insomniac's delight, with a quirky story, funny dialogue, and eccentric characters. (Jack Nicholson is memorable as a masochistic dental patient.) The freaky, funny film generated Howard Ashman's popular Off-Broadway musical comedy (1982). And that play in turn generated a *new* movie, this time lavishly expensive.

The major changes, apart from scale, were to make the plant an alien invader and to give it a lot more dialogue (and, because the film is a musical, several songs). This movie is superior to the play, with more invention and a less mocking attitude, as well as Lyle Conway's stupefying Audrey II, perhaps the best on-set effect in movie history. Audrey II is a wonder, and so is Frank Oz's film; Oz's reputation is likely to grow over the years. The standout performance in it is that of Steve Martin, as an outrageously sadistic dentist.

B.W.

LLEWELLYN, [DAVID WILLIAM] ALUN (1903–   ).

British lawyer and author whose reputation as a science-fiction writer rests on the novel *The Strange Invaders* (1934), admired for its vivid depiction of a future wherein civilization has been destroyed by war and humanity has regressed to a primitive tribal stage. The plot focuses on a Russian tribe's struggle to survive an invasion of giant lizards.

J.H.

LOGAN'S RUN (1976).

Directed by Michael Anderson; screenplay by David Zelag Goodman; adapted from the novel by William F. Nolan and George Clayton Johnson; photographed by Ernest Laszlo; music by Jerry Goldsmith. With Michael York, Jenny Agutter, Richard Jordan, Peter Ustinov, Roscoe Lee Browne, Michael Anderson, Jr., Farrah Fawcett-Majors. 118 minutes. Color.

Moderately popular in its time, *Logan's Run*—about a future society in which all thirty-year-olds are put to death (though most believe they are participating in a ritual of rebirth)—is typical of what moviemakers then regarded as quality science fiction: elaborate sets, trendy concepts, an emphasis on action, and handsome young players; the next year brought STAR WARS and a fresh wave (which soon grew familiar on its own). With a premise that doesn't bear even cursory examination, dated production design, elaborate but second-rate miniatures, and various plot elements dropped in just to keep the story going, *Logan's Run* demonstrates its makers' lack of conviction in every frame. Some of the performances are good, and a short-lived TV series followed.

B.W.

LONDON, JACK (Professional name of John Griffith London) (1876–1916).

American writer best known for his novels and short stories about the Klondike, the sea, and society but whose contributions to science fiction are significant. London's short stories abound with tales of scientific experimentation ("A Thousand Deaths," 1899; "The Shadow and the Flash," 1903), reconstructions of prehistoric humanoid life ("The Strength of the Strong," 1911), atavism ("A Relic of the Pliocene," 1901; "When the World Was Young," 1909), future weapons and warfare ("The Enemy of All the World," 1908; "The Unparalleled Invasion," 1910), and the advent of socialist societies ("A Curious Fragment," 1908; "Goliah," 1908; "The Dream of Debs," 1909).

"The Red One" (1918) is a sensitive short story about the worship of an alien artifact by a primitive tribe of headhunters among whom lives a dying Englishman. By the end of the story, both the Englishman and the readers learn that the aborigines have more in common with Europeans than anyone could have imagined. This climactic note, however, contrasts sharply with the earlier short story "The Unparalleled Invasion," in which the superior white race annihilates the Chinese with a bacteriological attack in order to create a new golden age.

London's SF novels are as diverse as his short stories. In *Before Adam* (1907) he used theories of both atavism and the racial unconscious as he sympathetically and convincingly described humanoid life in the Pliocene epoch. *The Scarlet Plague* (1912) recounts a reversion to primitive life after a catastrophic plague. And *The Iron Heel* (1907) depicts life in a future United States controlled by a fascistic elite. In this novel London departed from his usual narrative style and related the entire story through documents being studied by researchers in the twenty-seventh century, a future in which socialism has won the day.

London was absorbed with the ideas of his age. Besides his interest in the struggle between capitalism and socialism, the cyclic nature of history, and the "theory" that the white race is superior to other races, he was fascinated by parapsychology. In *The Star-Rover* (1915; published in Britain as *The Jacket*), for example, he described out-of-body experiences based on the state-

Frank Belknap Long

ments of Ed Morrell, who claimed that his mind dissociated itself from his body while he was tortured. Few
contemporary ideas escaped London's notice, all of them
found a place in his SF, and many contributed to the
later magazine development of SF.

OTHER WORKS: *The Strength of the Strong* (collection, 1914); *Short Stories* (collection, 1960); *Curious
Fragments: Jack London's Tales of Fantasy Fiction*
(collection, 1975); *The Science Fiction of Jack London*
(collection, 1975).

S.H.G.

LONG, FRANK BELKNAP (1903–   ). American writer best known for his weird fiction and association with his friend and mentor H. P. LOVECRAFT. Long
has had one of the longest writing careers in the fantasy
field since his first published story, "The Eye above the
Mantel" (1921), and first professional sale, "The Desert
Lich" (1924). Like Lovecraft's fiction, many of Long's
stories are what could be termed weird science fiction
with cosmic or interstellar forces or entities as background. The best of these stories are found in his collections *The Hounds of Tindalos* (1946, of which both
The Dark Beasts, 1964, and *The Black Druid*, 1975,
were abridged editions), *The Rim of the Unknown*
(1972), *The Early Long* (1975, confusingly reprinted as
The Hounds of Tindalos, 1978), and *Night Fears* (1979).

Long has written more orthodox SF than is appreciated, starting with "The Last Men" (1934) and a regular

series of sales to *Astounding* and other pulps; *Thrilling
Wonder* carried his series about an interplanetary "bo-
tanical" detective, collected as *John Carstairs, Space
Detective* (1949). He also wrote a steady stream of SF
novels during the 1960s, usually set on either a modern-
day Earth invaded by aliens or a future Earth. Long's
writing is invariably polished and stylish with the occasional betrayal of pulp weaknesses, most notable in
his more recent Gothic novels under the pseudonym
Lyda Belknap Long.

NOTABLE OTHER WORKS: *Space Station 1* (1957);
Woman from Another Planet (1960); *The Mating Cen-
ter* (1961); *The Horror Expert* (1961); *Mars Is My Des-
tination* (1962); *It Was the Day of the Robot* (1963);
The Horror from the Hills (1963; reprinted as *Odd
Science Fiction*, 1964, with two additional stories); *Three
Steps Spaceward* (1953/1963); *Mission to a Star* (1958/
1964); *The Martian Visitors* (1964); *This Strange To-
morrow* (1966); *So Dark a Heritage* (1966); *Lest Earth
Be Conquered* (1966); *Journey into Darkness* (1967);
. . . And Others Shall Be Born (1968); *The Three Faces
of Time* (1969); *Monster out of Time* (1970); *Survival
World* (1971); *The Night of the Wolf* (1972).

M.A.

——————— LONGEVITY ———————

The idea of an elixir of life has tempted the human imagination since *Gilgamesh* and has frequently inspired stories and novels. Much of the fiction dealing with longevity
is, however, skeptical of its value; many would-be immortals find no joy in their achievement, and there is
little difference in attitude among William Godwin's
Gothic fantasy *St. Leon* (1799), Karel CAPEK's *The Makropoulos Secret* (1925), and Aldous HUXLEY's *After Many
a Summer Dies the Swan* (1939). On the whole, science-fiction writers tend to take a more benevolent view
of the defiance of nature, but there is much SF in which
longevity becomes a curse, from Walter Besant's *The
Inner House* (1888) through David H. KELLER's "Life
Everlasting" (1934) to Thomas N. SCORTIA's "The Wea-
riest River" (1973) and Richard Cowper's "The Tithonian
Factor" (1983).

Many other stories are pessimistic about the way society is likely to distribute and exploit the reward of
longevity and carefully ambivalent about its advantages;
examples include *The Immortals* (1962) by James GUNN
and Frank HERBERT's Dune series. Several treatments,
including Bob SHAW's *One Million Tomorrows* (1970)
and Kate WILHELM's *Welcome Chaos* (1985), presume
the benefits of long life to be balanced by side effects
and risks. Modern SF writers, though, accept the challenge to describe how long-lived people would think
and feel, and this theme has become common in the
last two decades; examples of this "emortal existential-

ism'' can be found in *This Immortal* (1966) by Roger ZELAZNY, *The Eden Cycle* (1974) by Raymond Z. GALLUN, ''Their Immortal Hearts'' (1980) by Bruce McALLISTER, *The Golden Space* (1982) by Pamela SARGENT, and *Schismatrix* (1985) by Bruce STERLING.

B.S.

LONGYEAR, BARRY B. (1943–   ). American author noted for his rapid rise to prominence in the late 1970s. Before Longyear's first story even appeared in ISAAC ASIMOV'S SCIENCE FICTION MAGAZINE, he had sold nearly 100,000 words. Many of his early stories deal with Momus, a planet colonized by survivors of a crashed circus starship. ''Enemy Mine'' (1979) garnered a Hugo and a Nebula, and was made into a major 1985 film. Longyear also won the John Campbell Award for best new writer in 1979. Although the Momus stories are pulp adventure comedies, ''Enemy Mine'' and *The Tomorrow Testament* (1983) show a more serious side, reflecting pacifistic concerns in a space opera framework.

OTHER WORKS: *Manifest Destiny* (1980); *Circus World* (1980); *The City of Baraboo* (1980); *Elephant Song* (1982); *It Came from Schenectady* (1984).

D.S.

LOOKER (1981).   *Directed by Michael Crichton; screenplay by Michael Crichton; photographed by Paul Lohmann; music by Barry DeVorzon. With Albert Finney, James Coburn, Susan Dey, Leigh Taylor-Young, Dorian Harewood, Tim Rossovich, Darryl Hickman. 94 minutes. Color.*

Michael CRICHTON's science-fiction films often feature intriguing inventions and intelligent extrapolations from devices in use today and display a simultaneous fascination with and mistrust of technology. Even *Looker*, a notably incoherent film, has many good central ideas, but this time Crichton found no way to integrate them.

A media baron (James Coburn) makes hologram duplicates of beautiful young women, whom he then has murdered. In addition, he has a means of instant hypnosis, which he plans to employ on TV commercials to enslave the viewing public; his hit man uses a gun with the device to, in effect, become invisible. The two are thwarted by a two-fisted plastic surgeon (Albert Finney). *Looker* uncomfortably mixes laughs and thrills, never explains anything, and shows evidence of recutting.

B.W.

LORD OF THE FLIES (1963).   *Directed by Peter Brook; screenplay by Peter Brook; adapted from the novel by William Golding; photographed by Tom Hollyman and Gerald Feil; music by Raymond Lep-*

Lost Horizon

pard. With James Aubrey, Tom Chapin, Hugh Edwards, Roger Elwin, Tom Gaman. 91 minutes. Color.

In a close adaptation of William GOLDING's novel, this British film of the future focuses on the behavior of a group of schoolboys stranded on an isolated island after an atomic war. All but two of the boys revert to a kind of savagery, resulting in the murder of another before they are rescued and returned to civilization.

As in his earlier film, *The Damned,* Peter Brook used science fiction here for social criticism; the book and the movie reflect H. G. WELLS's conviction that civilization is merely a veneer on a barbaric monstrosity.

M.T.W.

LOST HORIZON (1937).   *Directed by Frank Capra; screenplay by Robert Riskin; adapted from the novel by James Hilton; photographed by Joseph Walker; music by Dimitri Tiomkin. With Ronald Colman, Jane Wyatt, John Howard, Margo, H. B. Warner, Sam Jaffe, Edward Everett Horton, Thomas Mitchell, Isabel Jewell. 130 minutes. Black and white.*

Survivors of a plane crash in remotest Tibet include British Consul Robert Conway (Ronald Colman); his brother George (John Howard); Gloria (Isabel Jewell), a

Cosmic misadventure from _Lost in Space_

it makes Conway's ultimate fulfillment explicit: Hilton's novel concludes with the hero again searching desperately for the valley; the movie ends on a more conventional happy note, as Conway actually returns to Shangri-La.

Bland storytelling and embarrassing musical numbers mark a now blessedly all-but-forgotten 1973 musical remake.

D.W.

LOST IN SPACE (1965–1968). _Directed by Don Richardson, Harry Harris, Ezra Stone, Sutton Roley, Sobey Martin, Nathan Juran, and others; written by Peter Packer, Barney Slater, Carey Wilber, Bob and Wanda Duncan, William Welch, Robert Hamner, and others; music by John Williams, Leith Stevens, Alexander Courage, Joseph Mullendore, Gerald Fried, and others. With Guy Williams, June Lockhart, Mark Goddard, Marta Kristen, Angela Cartwright, Billy Mumy, Jonathan Harris, Bob May, and Dick Tufeld. 29 one-hour episodes in black and white; 54 in color._

In this popular television series produced for CBS-TV by Irwin ALLEN an outer-space Swiss Family Robinson lifts off from Earth in the year 1997 on a mission to colonize a planet orbiting the star Alpha Centauri. Because of both a meteor storm and sabotage, their ship, _Jupiter II_, veers off course toward parts unknown. For three seasons (the first in black and white, the rest filmed in color) and eighty-three episodes, the space travelers fight for survival, at first against the elements of a hostile planet, later against every shape and form of alien monster imaginable.

Series regulars include Guy Williams and June Lockhart as the parents of children Marta Kristen, Angela Cartwright, and Billy Mumy. Accompanying them are Mark Goddard as the young copilot, and Jonathan Harris as the seriocomic villain, Dr. Zachary Smith, who eventually becomes the focus of most of the show's stories, along with the helpful and friendly robot portrayed by Bob May (inside the costume) and Dick Tufeld (supplying the voice). The sets (designed by Robert Kinoshita) and SPECIAL EFFECTS (by L. B. Abbott) remain impressive to this day, and the exciting music by Oscar winner John Williams (STAR WARS) is among the composer's best work. A controversial series, adored by fans and hated by detractors, _Lost in Space_ continues to be a permanent fixture in television syndication.

K.R.D.

tubercular woman; businessman Henry Barnard (Thomas Mitchell), and the edgy Lovett (Edward Everett Horton), a paleontologist. The mysterious, soft-spoken Chang (H. B. Warner) leads the group to refuge in the lamasery of Shangri-La in the Valley of the Blue Moon, a secluded utopia that offers peace and long life. Robert Conway, it transpires, has been ticketed to replace Father Perrault (Sam Jaffe), the current high lama, who at age two hundred plus is nearing the end of his life. Brother George, however, wants to leave the valley, and Robert grudgingly agrees to depart with him.

For years, _Lost Horizon_ existed only in crudely edited 118-minute prints. Entire scenes have now been restored for a special new edition; appropriate filmed stills accompany dialogue from the original sound track for scenes that could not be wholly restored. The result is a fuller, more satisfying film in terms of both theme and mood. Still, as always, Robert Conway and Chang are Frank Capra, Robert Riskin, and James Hilton's most convincing advertisements for the quieter world of Shangri-La. They effortlessly convey the essence of the script's idealism not just through their words but with their manner and gentle humor.

The film is true to HILTON's vision of Shangri-La as a repository for history and art and a haven for humanity—a meditative window on the world, as it were—although

——————— LOST RACES ———————

The Victorian era was an age of exploration in fiction as well as reality as characters set out from the safety of Western civilization to find LOST WORLDS, lost civilizations, lost races. Perhaps in the unexplored areas of the world, central Africa or the Antarctic or an undiscovered island, might be found the strange and the mysterious, maybe the surviving remnants of an ancient power: Roman, Greek, Egyptian, or Atlantean.

One of the first and still perhaps the best of the lost race novels gave the motif its final form: H. Rider HAGGARD's *She* (1887). There had been earlier stories with exotic settings in unknown areas of the world, beginning with Homer's *Odyssey* and extending through the medieval travel books and beyond. The utopian narratives, from Thomas MORE's *Utopia* (1516) through Jonathan SWIFT's *Gulliver's Travels* (1726), used the convention of travel to unknown islands to set up their criticisms of European society.

Daniel Defoe's *Robinson Crusoe* (1719) created a format so imitated that it earned the name *Robinsonade*, but it celebrated the triumph of common sense over all obstacles rather than the romance of the mysterious. Late-eighteenth- and nineteenth-century explorations, as well as developing geologic theory and archaeological discoveries, made narratives of exploration even more popular. In *Symzonia: A Voyage of Discovery* (1820) Captain Adam Seaborn (the pseudonym of John Cleves Symmes) refurbished the concept of a hollow Earth containing a fabulous civilization. Edgar Allan POE's indebtedness to Symmes climaxed with the image of a character being drawn into a hollow Earth by a whirlpool in the Antarctic in *The Narrative of Arthur Gordon Pym* (1838). Jules VERNE's *Journey to the Center of the Earth* (1864) drew its inspiration from Ludvig HOLBERG's *The Journey to the World Underground* (1741); Edward George BULWER-LYTTON's *The Coming Race* (1871) continued the tradition of the secret civilization under the Earth.

Drawing on personal experience in the Transvaal, Haggard opened up Africa for fictional exploration with *King Solomon's Mines* (1885) and two years later created the immortal Ayesha, She-Who-Must-Be-Obeyed. With *Allen Quatermain* (1887), he found the basic plot line for the lost race novel: an English explorer marries the blond queen of the Zu-Vendris and lives happily ever after. Five parodies of Haggard's work appeared within the year.

As James GUNN has pointed out, this motif reversed the direction taken by the literature of the new science and the growing belief in progress that was sweeping Western civilization. In stories of lost worlds and lost civilizations, writers were suggesting that perhaps the greater wonders waited in the past, and the journeys necessary to reach the few remaining untouched spots of the world forced adventurers to discard civilization and rely on more primitive virtues, such as courage, strength, and endurance. Writers such as Albert Bigelow Paine in *The Great White Way* (1901) used the lost race motif to extol neoprimitivism and denounce the new

"A singular forest" from Jules Verne's *Journey to the Center of the Earth*

urban-industrial civilization, but in large part the motif after Haggard became a love story: after a long, difficult journey to find a strange civilization, a British or American man is bewitched by a pagan beauty. If her culture can contribute to Western society, the lovers may marry, as in William R. Bradshaw's *The Goddess of Atvatabar* (1892) or Ganpat's *Harilek* (1924); if not, she commits suicide, is killed, or is abandoned, as in Clifford Smyth's *The Gilded Man* (1918).

The lost race motif remained strongly (though not graphically) erotic, expressing Western man's fascination with the non-Caucasian woman. (It shares this theme with such non-science-fiction titles as Joseph Conrad's *Lord Jim*). After Haggard's work, the most famous early title using this motif is Arthur Conan DOYLE's *The Lost World* (1912), involving the discovery of prehistoric creatures on an almost inaccessible South American plateau and introducing the irascible Professor Challenger.

Edgar Rice BURROUGHS adapted the motif to many of his Tarzan stories as well as his Pellucidar series—describing the prehistoric world within the Earth—and such novels as *The Land That Time Forgot* (1924). A. MERRITT, John WYNDHAM, and Stanton A. COBLENTZ published lost race tales in the pulp magazines as late as the 1930s, but perhaps the single best-known novel in the motif remains James HILTON's *Lost Horizon* (1933), which gave the world Shangri-La. With a few exceptions, such as Jacquetta Hawkes's *Providence Island* (1959), World War II sounded the death knell of the lost race story. There were no exotic corners of the world left unexplored; such civilizations had to be placed on other worlds than Earth. Thomas D. CLARESON's *Some Kind of Paradise* (1985) gives a full description of the lost race motif.

T.D.C.

THE LOST WORLD (Silent, 1925).

THE LOST WORLD (Silent, 1925). *Directed by Harry O. Hoyt; screenplay by Marion Fairfax; adapted from the novel by Arthur Conan Doyle; photographed by Arthur Edeson. With Wallace Beery, Lewis Stone, Bessie Love, Lloyd Hughes, Arthur Hoyt, Bull Montana, George Bunny. 98 minutes. Black and white (tinted).*

Arthur Conan DOYLE's novel about dinosaurs discovered on a plateau in the jungles of South America was written to be sportive: in its first edition it was presented as a true story, complete with sketches and photographs (with Doyle as Professor Challenger). When the movie was in production, Doyle traveled with film of Willis O'BRIEN's stop-motion dinosaurs, challenging anyone to prove they were not real. It is to the credit of the makers of the first version of the movie that they kept this impish attitude.

In this genuinely delightful film, the expedition, led by the volcanic Challenger (a memorable Wallace Beery), not only finds dinosaurs, ape-men, and savages atop the plateau but brings a brontosaurus back to London. It escapes, creates havoc, then swims off down the Thames. A romantic triangle forms a subplot.

Today *The Lost World* remains one of the most enjoyed of all silent films. Although O'Brien's animation effects now look somewhat crude by the standards of his masterwork, KING KONG (released only eight years later), the film is buoyant enough to engender a happy suspension of disbelief in most audiences.

By contrast, Irwin ALLEN's 1960 remake, starring Claude Rains and Michael RENNIE, already seems weary and dated. Although it follows a similar story line (leaving out the return to London), it lacks the vigor and wit of the original. The dinosaurs are photographically enlarged lizards (who often seem to be in pain), the heroine is a fashion plate, and there's an ugly subplot about treasure. Instead of having fun with the story, the makers show contempt for it, and this film is difficult for contemporary audiences to endure.

B.W.

——— LOST WORLDS ———

A lost world is a pocket of wonder, a strange environment cut off from the rest of the Earth, where everyday reality is sharply different. The term *lost world* comes from Arthur Conan DOYLE's novel *The Lost World* (1912), in which Prof. Challenger discovers a South American

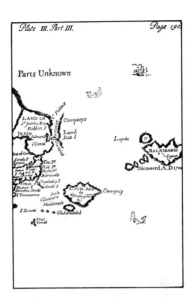

Map of lost worlds from Jonathan Swift's *Gulliver's Travels*

plateau populated by dinosaurs, beast-men, and primitive humans. The near Antarctic island of Caprona, the setting of Edgar Rice BURROUGHS's *The Land That Time Forgot* (1924), features not merely dinosaurs but a bizarre biology, as individuals hatch out of eggs and evolve in the course of single lifetimes from small lizards to humans to winged superhumans.

A lost world story is not quite the same as a lost race story, although many lost worlds are inhabited by LOST RACES. Some lost worlds, however, offer biological, sometimes physical wonders but no lost races. And not all lost race stories involve lost worlds; lost races may also be found in such relatively mundane settings as mountaintops, jungles, and remote countries such as Tibet or the far reaches of the Sahara.

The lost world is prefigured in the numerous strange islands of LUCIAN OF SAMOSATA's "A True History" (second century). The islands of Jonathan SWIFT's *Gulliver's Travels* (1726), such as Lilliput, have all the characteristics of lost worlds, but the motif gained importance for its own sake (rather than as a convention for making satires more convincing) when it became the basis for adventure stories. Robert Paltock's *The Life and Adventures of Peter Wilkins* (1751), about a warm valley near the South Pole inhabited by flying humans, marks the beginning of this separation. Numerous lost world romances appeared in the nineteenth century, but the pattern was irrevocably set by H. Rider HAGGARD, whose *She* (1887) tells of a lost valley in Africa where an immortal priestess rules over a remnant of ancient Egyptian civilization. *She* is also the archetypal lost race novel, and from this point on the two become more closely related.

The lost world–lost race formula was transmitted into the pulps, where it persisted into the early 1950s, long after authors could make any plausible case for undiscovered islands or hidden caverns. A. MERRITT, Edmond HAMILTON, Edgar Rice Burroughs, William L. Chester, Jack WILLIAMSON, Robert Moore Williams, and others contributed lost world fantasies to *Argosy, Blue Book, Weird Tales*, AMAZING STORIES, and *Fantastic Adventures* (where Williams's Jongor series, concerning a western Australian lost land, with the obligatory dinosaurs, appeared as late as 1951). Lost world pulp fiction strongly influenced the pseudofact Shaver Mystery, published in *Amazing* in the 1940s, in which the lost worlds take the form of ancient caverns under the Earth.

Although most lost worlds are merely located in some remote corner of the globe, there is a whole subspecies of hollow Earth fiction, beginning with *Symzonia* by Adam Seaborn (1820) and continuing through Jules VERNE's *A Journey to the Center of the Earth* (1864) and Burroughs's Pellucidar series (1914 on), all of which conceal the lost world more deeply, if even less scientifically. Atlantis and other lost continents are a different matter, because they supposedly existed only in the past (although some lost world–lost race stories assumed the survival of such civilizations elsewhere, or even in submerged or somehow unseen or undiscovered forms), whereas the narrative excitement of the lost world story stems from such an exotic place lingering into the present.

Inevitably, the lost world story succumbed to the progress of exploration and the bleeding away of plausibility. But old motifs never die; they just get translated. The lost world story can be found today transported to other planets or solar systems, or to other "dimensions" or parallel worlds. The motif survives in stories about the discovery of pockets of wonder in space, and, in combination with the lost race motif, in tales of the rediscovery of lost planetary colonies after the fall and rebuilding of a galactic empire, as in Ursula K. LE GUIN's *The Left Hand of Darkness* (1969).

D.S.

LOVECRAFT, H[OWARD] P[HILLIPS] (1890–1937).
American writer of horror fiction, with some influence on science fiction, whose work was published primarily in *Weird Tales;* his essays and verse appeared in amateur publications. One small-edition book, *The Shadow over Innsmouth* (1936), was published in Lovecraft's lifetime, but extensive posthumous publication of his work began with *The Outsider and Others* (1939), leading to worldwide critical recognition. Three standard modern collections are *The Dunwich Horror*

and Others (1963; revised 1984), *At the Mountains of Madness and Other Novels* (1964; revised 1985), and *Dagon and Other Macabre Tales* (1965; revised 1986).

Virtually all Lovecraft's work is borderline SF, although his explanations often delve into the fantasy involved in his Cthulhu mythos—the story of ancient alien forces that once ruled the Earth and are trying to return. Explicitly SF are "The Colour out of Space" (in AMAZING, 1927), "At the Mountains of Madness," and "The Shadow out of Time" (both in *Astounding*, 1936). "The Shadow out of Time," with its sweeping, millennial vistas, ranks with H. G. WELLS's *Time Machine* and the works of Olaf STAPLEDON as one of the grand cosmic visions of SF.

Lovecraft maintained a wide and lengthy correspondence with other writers and would-be writers (collected in *Selected Letters,* 5 volumes, 1965–1976), that extended his influence beyond his own fiction.

D.S.

LOWNDES, ROBERT A[UGUSTINE] W[ARD] (1916–   ).
American editor and writer, generally known as Doc Lowndes, who began his career in the late 1930s with the Futurian group of fans and eventually writers, some of whom he wrote with, both collaboratively and pseudonymously; one of his four novels, *The Duplicated Man* (1953/1959), is a collaboration with James BLISH. In 1940 Lowndes became editor of the Double Action (later Columbia Publications) poverty-row pulps, *Future Fiction* and *Science Fiction Quarterly* (which he improved by publishing therein the work of fellow FUTURIANS). He remained with this chain until its failure in 1960. From 1963 to 1971 Lowndes edited the Health Knowledge group, including *Magazine of Horror, Famous Science Fiction,* and *Startling Mystery Stories,* and after the collapse of that line, he edited *Sexology* magazine.

Although Lowndes never became as prominent an editor as his Futurian friends Donald A. WOLLHEIM, Frederik POHL, and Damon KNIGHT, his editorial skills always made the most of marginal operations with tiny budgets and poor distribution, especially in the second incarnations of *Science Fiction Quarterly* and *Future Fiction* in the 1950s, at whose helm he got a second look at stories by first-class writers and published early work by the likes of Philip K. DICK and Robert SILVERBERG. He was one of the last of the old-time magazine EDITORS.

OTHER WORKS: *Mystery of the Third Mine* (1953); *Believers' World* (1961); *The Puzzle Planet* (1961); *Three Faces of Science Fiction* (nonfiction collection, 1973).

R.F.L.

LUCAS, GEORGE (1945–   ).
American filmmaker who has achieved tremendous critical and commercial success with a surprisingly few films, notably

the STAR WARS series, movies that almost single-handedly reintroduced to the science-fiction film a new, broad appeal. Lucas's romantic combination of fantasy and nostalgia have made his movies popular with both an adult and a young audience, many of whom first discovered the pleasures of science fiction through his films. Although his movies may lack thematic weight, they have embraced popular culture with genuine enthusiasm and have attracted an audience apparently tired of more downbeat fare. With his own production company, Lucasfilm, Ltd., he has supported the endeavors of younger filmmakers much as Roger CORMAN did in the 1960s, becoming a significant figure in the poststudio era of American filmmaking.

While a film student at the University of Southern California, Lucas served as an intern on the musical *Finian's Rainbow* (1968), directed by Francis Ford Coppola. The two men discovered that they had mutual ideas about the cinema and developed a close and lasting relationship. Indeed it was Coppola who backed Lucas's first feature, THX-1138 (1970). Based on a short film Lucas had made as a student, *THX-1138* is a studied exercise in SF, exhibiting a minimum of action but incorporating many motifs and ideas from earlier works in the genre. It is perhaps the only film directed by Lucas with serious thematic implications, although much of it is derivative, drawing on such classics in the field as Yevgeny ZAMIATIN's *We*, Aldous HUXLEY's *Brave New World,* and even George ORWELL's *Nineteen Eighty-four.* Nevertheless, it does feature some brilliant visual imagery, including the white, open-spaced detention center and the arcadelike prayer machines scattered around the film's futuristic city. It is precisely such imagery that has made Lucas an important director.

To Lucas's great dismay, Warner Bros. reedited *THX-1138* and gave it only a limited release. The film did not do well at the box office, although it would later achieve cult status. It did, however, earn Lucas a reputation as an intellectual director of SF, in reaction to which he conceived the semiautobiographical *American Graffiti* (1973) to show that his films could appeal to a broader audience. Produced on a budget of only $750,000, the film became one of the most profitable movies of the decade, and its stunning commercial success allowed Lucas to produce his films independently.

His next, and to date his last, film as director would forever change the face of SF cinema. *Star Wars* (1977) combined his interest in SF and adolescent myth. The story is relatively standard space opera fare: fascistic villains attempt to gain control of decent, democratic folk, who are forced to become heroes to defeat the enemies of freedom. The characters are conventional types—an evil emperor, the wise elder, a princess, the stout-hearted novice, and so on—but all are so vividly established that they come off as refreshing. Moreover, the film is distinguished by bravura action sequences,

state-of-the-art special effects, carefully considered production design, and a breathtaking pace.

Lucas earned a fortune from *Star Wars*, the most successful SF movie ever made until it was surpassed by Steven SPIELBERG's E.T.: THE EXTRA-TERRESTRIAL in 1982. Lucas had poured his youthful appreciation of SF, comics, and pulp adventure into his screenplay and direction, and the film's combination of space opera escapism and high-tech production values proved a profitable formula. As a result Hollywood became more receptive to SF projects, which had suddenly become big business.

With the profits from *Star Wars*, Lucas has been establishing his own production facility, Skywalker Ranch, in Marin County, California. His hope is ultimately to print and distribute his films entirely outside the Hollywood system. Directing *Star Wars* was for Lucas exhausting, and he has sworn never to direct a big film again. So far he has kept his word, overseeing but not directing a number of movies, including the two Star Wars sequels, THE EMPIRE STRIKES BACK (1980) and RETURN OF THE JEDI (1983). Lucas has likened a director's role on such a large production to that of a general and emphasizes that he would rather be a filmmaker, directing more intimate, even avant-garde films. Whether he will do so, of course, is yet to be seen. At present he remains the very symbol of the commercial SF cinema.

B.K.G.

LUCIAN OF SAMOSATA (c. A.D. 120–200).

Syrian author and rhetorician, noted for both his absolute mastery of an acquired language (Greek) and his genial yet biting satire. Lucian's "A True History" has a reputation as the first science-fiction story, mostly, one suspects, in the minds of annexationist fans who haven't read it. The work is a parody of travelers' tales and of the works of early Greek historians (especially Herodotus); nevertheless its SF-like Moon travel and interplanetary war sequences occur early and are soon topped by an ocean of milk with cheese islands floating in it, whole communities inhabiting the belly of a 150-mile-long whale, and visits to both the Isle of the Blest and the abode of the damned. Historically, however, the Moon episode did influence CYRANO de Bergerac, VOLTAIRE, and, through them, Jules VERNE, thus securing it a place as one of the remote ancestors of SF.

D.S.

LUNDWALL, SAM J[ERRIE] (1941–).

Swedish author, editor, and publisher. The most prominent contemporary figure in Swedish science fiction and a world figure through his leadership of WORLD SF and membership on the jury of the John W. Campbell Award for the best SF novel of the year, Lundwall has written twelve novels, edited some twenty ANTHOLOGIES, and translated more than 200 novels into Swedish. Lundwall also is an electronics engineer, singer, musician, illustrator, and television producer. He was the publisher of Delta Förlags from 1973 to 1980 and since then of Fakta & Fantasi, and he has been the editor of *Jules Verne-Magasinet* since 1972.

Four of his novels—all satiric—have been translated into English: *No Time for Heroes* (1971), *Alice's World* (1971), *Bernhard the Conqueror* (1973), and *2018; or, The King Kong Blues* (1975). The best known among them, *2018*, is comparable to Frederik POHL and Cyril M. KORNBLUTH's *The Space Merchants* and John BRUNNER's *The Sheep Look Up* in its attacks on advertising and pollution. The subtitle—*The King Kong Blues*—refers to the heroine's song about betrayed romanticism, sung when she is pressed into a campaign to sell underarm deodorant after trying to break free of social compulsions.

Lundwall's most significant contributions to the genre have been his critical books. *Science Fiction: What It's All About* (1971; published in Sweden as *Science Fiction*, 1969) was one of the earliest critical and historical surveys, and its mass-market publication by Ace Books gave it high visibility and influence. *Science Fiction: An Illustrated History* came out in 1978.

J.E.G.

LUPOFF, RICHARD A[LLEN] (1935–).

American fiction writer, editor, and critic. A reader of science fiction since his youth, Lupoff first achieved prominence as coeditor (with his wife, Patricia) of the fanzine *Xero,* one of the first to look seriously at comic books and similar aspects of popular culture. He contributed substantial book reviews to the semiprofessional magazine *Algol* and has taught college courses in SF. While working as a technical writer, Lupoff eased into SF writing and editing at Canaveral Press, one of the promoters of the Edgar Rice BURROUGHS revival, beginning with a survey and evaluation of Burroughs's writings in *Edgar Rice Burroughs: Master of Adventure* (1965; revised 1968). He became a full-time writer in 1970.

Lupoff's reputation as a fiction writer has not received adequate recognition partly because of poor timing: between the appearance of the original novella "With the Bentfin Boomer Boys in Little Old New Alabama" in *Again, Dangerous Visions* (1972) and the publication of *Space War Blues* (1978), there was a six-year hiatus. But part of the problem has also been Lupoff's refusal to settle into any one comfortable commercial vein of storytelling.

Lupoff has always been drawn to the classics of popular SF, especially the work of early writers such as Burroughs, and several of Lupoff's novels are pastiches of pulp magazine adventures. His first novel, *One Million Centuries* (1967; revised 1981), is a Burroughs

pastiche; *Into the Aether* (1974) recalls the nineteenth-century scientific romance; *The Triune Man* (1976) shows the influence of A. E. VAN VOGT; and *The Return of Skull-Face* (1977) is the completion of a fragment by Robert E. HOWARD.

One of Lupoff's later techniques has been to incorporate real characters into fictional settings: *Circumpolar!* (1984), one of his more striking novels, puts Amelia Earhart, Charles Lindbergh, Howard Hughes, and the Red Baron into a hollow Earth reminiscent of Burroughs's Pellucidar; *Lovecraft's Book* (1985) offers H. P. LOVECRAFT, gangsters, Nazis, Houdini's brother, various fantasy writers, photographs of the principal character, and a bibliography.

Lupoff consistently tries to stretch SF's traditional forms and values. His best works may be those that are most original: *Space War Blues,* a satiric space opera full of stylistic tricks that pits white racists against black racists; *Sword of the Demon* (1977), a heroic fantasy based on Japanese myth; *The Crack in the Sky* (1976), a dystopia about overpopulation and ecology; and *Lisa Kane* (1976), ostensibly a juvenile about a female vampire but distinguished by adult concerns. The impressive *Sun's End* (1984) begins a trilogy supposedly inspired simultaneously by Olaf STAPLEDON and E. E. SMITH; thus Lupoff may finally be on the verge of successfully transmuting the genre's tradition.

OTHER WORKS: *All in Color for a Time* (edited with Don Thompson, 1970); *Scared Locomotive Flies* (1971); *The Comic Book Book* (edited with Don Thompson, 1974); *The Ova Hamlet Papers* (1979); *What If?* (editor, 1980); *What If? 2* (editor, 1981); *Stroka Prospekt* (1982); *The Digital Wristwatch of Philip K. Dick* (1985); *Countersolar!* (1986); *Circumsolar* (1987).

J.S.

LYNN, ELIZABETH A. (1946–).

American writer whose fiction falls between science fiction and fantasy. Filled with rounded characters who live their lives in fully detailed future societies, Lynn's stories carry overtones of the world of magic as well. For example, in her first novel, *A Different Light* (1978), Lynn's portrayal of hyperspace—what spaceships enter as they travel at speeds faster than light—is an alternate reality to the Einsteinian universe, a "place," in fact, where fantastic things can and do happen. And in *The Silver Horse* (1984) she gave her readers a standard journey through a fantasy land, in this case named Dreamland.

Lynn's best-known work is the novel *The Sardonyx Net* (1981), which describes slave trading and drug dealing on a galactic scale; the book is proof that a space-adventure plot need not lead to a mediocre work. Lynn's characters, including one noteworthy villain, are compellingly drawn. She reveals their motives, ambitions, and egos in a sympathetic style that leaves judgments to the reader; in trying to make those judgments, most readers are drawn into the story. Although the plot may be the stuff of Grade-B 1950s sci-fi, the characters make the material work.

Lynn has also written a fantasy trilogy, the Chronicles of Tonor *(Watchtower,* 1979; *The Dances of Arun,* 1979; and *The Northern Girl,* 1981), which will remind many readers of SF, especially in the ways the societies of each volume are carefully and consistently described.

OTHER WORKS: *The Woman Who Loved the Moon and Other Stories* (collection, 1981); *The Red Hawk* (1983).

S.H.G.

M

McALLISTER, BRUCE [HUGH] (1946–   ).

American professor of English at the University of Redlands, editor of literary magazines, and writer. McAllister, the author of more than forty science-fiction short stories and one novel, is a careful and accomplished stylist who concentrates on "the human condition." His stories focus on human reactions to tense crises that force the characters to make personal and moral decisions. The crises may be triggered by aliens, human frailty, or sudden changes in events that propel the characters out of the lives of habit they had established for themselves. A good selection of McAllister's stories appears in *The Faces Outside* (1985). The title story of this collection was the basis for his one SF novel, *Humanity Prime* (1985), concerning people who live under the sea. Populated with all kinds of underwater creatures, many of them intelligent, the novel handles the traditional SF question What does it mean to be human? in a fresh and compelling manner.

S.H.G.

McCAFFREY, ANNE [INEZ] (1926–   ).

American writer resident in Ireland, noted for her meticulously crafted alien and future worlds. A storyteller of the highest order, McCaffrey combines elements of science fiction and fantasy to create romantic tales rich in detail and absorbing action. She was the first woman to receive a Hugo ("Weyr Search," 1967) and a Nebula ("Dragonrider," 1968); both these award-winning novellas were incorporated in *Dragonflight* (1968).

After graduating from Radcliffe College in 1947, McCaffrey studied voice for nine years (music is featured in several of her novels), was tutored privately in physics, and studied meteorology at the University of the City of

Anne McCaffrey

Dublin. She started writing full time in the 1960s, served as secretary-treasurer of the SCIENCE FICTION WRITERS OF AMERICA (1968–1970), and now runs a thoroughbred studhorse farm.

Affectionately called Dragonlady by SF fans, McCaffrey is best known for her series of intricately interwoven novels about the dragonriders of Pern, a long-lost Earth colony. Like Marion Zimmer BRADLEY's Darkover and Frank HERBERT's Dune, Pern is a fully conceived and complex civilization whose politics, social structure, and traditions are based on a recurring ecological battle. On Pern humans and dragons have evolved a symbiotic, empathic, and telepathic relationship critical to survival in the face of a periodic threat from a spore called Thread, which crosses from Pern's companion planet and must be burned out of the air by the dragons.

Although her work—particularly the Pern series, with its medieval atmosphere and magical dragons—resembles fantasy, McCaffrey insists that it is science fiction. In the Pern novels the SF background is rationalized by the bioengineering of the dragons by long-forgotten terrestrials. *Dragonflight, Dragonquest* (1971), and *The White Dragon* (1978) detail the struggle for survival at a crucial time in Pern's history, during which the dragonriders discover that they can travel not only through space but through time as well. *The White Dragon* won a Hugo for best fantasy novel in 1979.

Dovetailing neatly into the same chronology are *Dragonsong* (1976), *Dragonsinger* (1977), and *Dragondrums* (1979), a companion series written for young adults in which major figures in the other works appear as minor figures. McCaffrey also has used earlier elements in later works: the subject of an ancient heroic ballad in the first novels, Moreta comes to life in *Moreta: Dragonlady of Pern* (1983), and a minor character in *Moreta* became the central figure in *Nerilka's Story* (1986).

In *Decision at Doona* (1969), *The Ship Who Sang* (1969), and *Dinosaur Planet* (1978), McCaffrey ventured outside the realm of Pern to examine space travel, cryogenic sleep, cyborgs, and interaction with alien lifeforms. In *The Ship Who Sang*, McCaffrey's personal favorite among her stories, a woman with disabling birth defects becomes the mind of a giant interstellar ship in a symbiotic relationship that results in surprising friendships and love affairs. Music is important to that novel, as it is to others, but McCaffrey's love of that art form is most fully expressed in *Crystal Singer* (1981), in which singers with perfect pitch locate and mine crystal.

McCaffrey was one of the first SF writers to create strong female protagonists. Although she was criticized for sexist stereotypes in *Restoree* (1967), her first novel, her heroes and heroines alike are independent, inventive, capable, romantic, and believably drawn. She focuses on the personal and emotional qualities of human beings, and particularly on the bonding between all kinds of people and creatures, while maintaining a sense of tension, suspense, and pace.

OTHER WORKS: *To Ride Pegasus* (1973); *A Time When* (collection, 1975); *Get Off the Unicorn* (collection, 1977); *The Worlds of Anne McCaffrey* (collection, 1981); *The Coelura* (1983); *Dinosaur Planet Survivors* (1984); *Killashandra* (1985).

D.P.V.

McCOMAS, J[ESSE] FRANCIS (1911–1978).

American author best known as an editor. With Raymond J. Healey, McComas edited one of the two postwar science-fiction anthologies, *Adventures in Time and Space* (1946), that did much to capture the flavor of the SF GOLDEN AGE for a generation that had known SF only in magazines. (The book has remained in print ever since.) In 1949, with Anthony BOUCHER, he founded and edited THE MAGAZINE OF FANTASY AND SCIENCE FICTION, whose most significant contribution to the field was emphasis on literary values in a period when the other leading magazines were focusing on ideas and narrative. McComas edited a number of other anthologies of SF and murder mysteries, and he wrote a handful of SF stories under his own name and the pseudonym Webb Marlowe.

R.H.W.

McDEVITT, JACK [JOHN CHARLES] (1935–).

American author. McDevitt, who trains supervisors for the U.S. Customs Service in Atlanta, entered science fiction late in his life with a story, "The Emerson Effect," in a 1981 *Twilight Zone*. He had earned a bachelor's degree in English from La Salle College in 1957 and a master's degree in literature fifteen years later from Wesleyan University.

McDevitt's story "Cryptic" made the final Nebula ballot in 1984, and his first book, *The Hercules Text*, an SF novel about a search for messages from the stars, placed second for the Philip K. Dick Award in 1986 and was voted the best first novel in the *Locus* annual poll. In it the scientists of the Hercules Project detect a signal from a pulsar 1.5 million light-years away and then discover that the star system itself is artificial and that the message has possibilities for ending all the evils of human existence—or ending human existence itself. Like most of McDevitt's work, it is not so much about technology and alien cultures as the moral dilemmas and emotional crises they provide.

OTHER WORK: *A Talent for War* (1988).

J.E.G.

MACDONALD, JOHN D[ANN] (1916–1986).

American author of mystery novels and sometime best-sellers whose early career included science-fiction stories and novels. Best known as the author of the Travis McGee mystery novels, MacDonald made his first sale to *Story* "in the early 1940s" and his first SF sale, "Cosmetics," to *Astounding* in 1948. He wrote more than fifty mystery novels and one true-crime novel, won many awards in that field, and was president of the Mystery Writers of America in 1962.

MacDonald had written almost fifty SF short stories and two novels by 1950, when the success of his first mystery novel, *The Brass Cupcake*, turned him toward that genre almost exclusively, except for a science-fantasy novel published in 1962. That work, *The Girl, the Gold Watch, and Everything*, is a comic adventure about a character who inherits a watch that makes time stop for everyone except the owner. It later was made into a television movie. MacDonald's SF frequently concerns the manipulation of humanity by aliens or fellow humans and often plays on the theme of paranoia, as in his novels *Wine of the Dreamers* (1951) and *Ballroom of the Skies* (1952). The first of these involves aliens who possess us through dreams in the belief that we are only their dream creatures; the second builds on the idea that aliens keep humanity in a state of perpetual warfare to breed superhuman leaders who may be needed by the galactic civilization. MacDonald's SF stories have been collected in *Other Times, Other Worlds* (1978).

R.S.C.

MACHINES

Machines and science fiction have always been symbiotically entwined. Whether it be Frankenstein's laboratory; H. G. WELLS's time machine; SF pulp magazine covers displaying rockets, rays, and scientists; or Jules VERNE's submarine and flying apparatus, machines have been a major source of fascination for SF. Throughout its history SF has examined the human-machine relationship, often functioning as a laboratory of scientific extrapolation.

The meteoric rise of science during the latter part of the nineteenth century and the concomitant industrial revolution brought the imagery of machines into popular consciousness, as in the many books of the French artist Albert Robida (1848–1926). As religion subsided under the onslaught of scientific discovery and explanation, the Victorian era exhibited an almost schizophrenic reaction, which has persisted even to the present, about humanity's proper response to machines. Verne's fiction revels in the possible futures that might be introduced by machines as various as submarines, airplanes, and space cannons; his English contemporary, Wells, projected more sober scenarios in such works as *The Time Machine* (1895) and *The War of the Worlds* (1898).

In the United States at the turn of the century, inventions were embraced with an almost patriotic fervor. Hugo GERNSBACK's *Ralph 124C 41+* (1911–12) gave us machines galore (Hypnobiscope, Helio-Dynamophore, Baccilatorium). His editorship of radio-electronic and popular mechanic magazines led him ultimately to the publication of AMAZING (1926) in which stories and covers featuring rockets, rays, and rumbling war machines predominated. In these early stories the attitude prevailed that machines could do anything, including solve all human problems.

John W. CAMPBELL introduced an alternative viewpoint concerning the untold possibilities of an expanding science in his capacities both as editor of *Astounding* (1937–1971) and as a writer. While Campbell extolled the limitless possibilities of the machine ("The Machine," 1935), he also considered humanity's potential for overreliance on machines ("Twilight," 1934) and required the writers for *Astounding* to consider the social consequences of the technological age. Perhaps no author fulfilled this demand more notably than Robert A. HEINLEIN, particularly in "The Roads Must Roll" (1940), with its moving roadway, and his Future History series (1939–1941). Heinlein was also responsible for the neologism *waldo* from a story by the same name about mechanical hands.

The ultimate SF machines are the spaceship and the atomic bomb. Both appeared in fiction before they were realities. After the bombing of Hiroshima, however, SF's general optimism about machines changed, and stories and cover art reflected a new ambivalence. With notable exceptions—mostly in such mainstream works as E. M.

FORSTER's "The Machine Stops" (1909), Yevgeny ZAMIATIN's *We* (1921), and Aldous HUXLEY's *Brave New World* (1932)—SF had blithely ignored the darker potentialities of the technological revolution. Could humanity control its machines? Several stories asked this question memorably: Theodore STURGEON's "Killdozer!" (1944), Jack WILLIAMSON's "With Folded Hands" (1947), and Philip K. DICK's "Second Variety" (1953).

So long as the machine remained a device to serve humanity, there were ecstatic stories of future utopias; however, as the symbiosis between human and machine became more complete (for example, with the introduction of "intelligent" machines), future scenarios turned more ominous. Ray BRADBURY's "There Will Come Soft Rains" (1950) envisioned machines, after an atomic holocaust, running without any human beings at all. And in Harlan ELLISON's "I Have No Mouth, and I Must Scream" (1967), the old order of God, human, and machine has given way not only to the death of God but to the servitude of humanity to its machines. In SF modern humankind has become a species whose destiny is forever altered by its mechanistic creations.

M.T.W.

McINTOSH, J. T. (Pseudonym of James Murdock MacGregor) (1925–).

Scottish writer who has written non–science fiction under his own name (which sometimes appears as M'Intosh) and as H. J. Murdock. McIntosh gained a reputation as a prolific author of witty and well written short stories for American SF magazines beginning in 1950 that led to the publication of such early and successful novels as *World out of Mind* (1953), *Born Leader* (1954; as *Worlds Apart*, 1958), *One in Three Hundred* (1954), and *The Fittest* (1955; as *The Rule of the Pagbeasts*, 1956), all lively SF adventure stories that deal with extreme threats to future human existence in which the characters must cooperate to survive. His later SF books have tended to rework earlier ideas and even earlier stories without improving them. He had written nineteen SF novels by 1987, as well as non-SF novels and nonfiction books. No collection of his stories has been issued.

NOTABLE OTHER WORKS: *200 Years to Christmas* (1961); *Time for a Change* (1967; as *Snow White and the Giants*, 1968); *Six Gates from Limbo* (1968); *Flight from Rebirth* (1971); *A Planet Called Utopia* (1979).

B.S.

McINTYRE, VONDA N[EEL] (1948–).

American writer. McIntyre, born in Louisville but educated and residing in Seattle, is one of the best-known feminist science-fiction authors. In addition to writing short stories and novels, she coedited an anthology of feminist SF (*Aurora: Beyond Equality*, with Susan Janice

Anderson, 1976). She has won two Nebulas, the first in 1973 for her novelette "Of Mist, and Grass, and Sand" (1973) and the second in 1978 for her novel *Dreamsnake* (1978), which was an expansion of her award-winning novelette.

All McIntyre's works are representative of the feminist subgenre in SF that emerged in the late 1960s; they criticize contemporary society for a number of ills, such as sexism, pollution, oppression, and war. Her work is not simply critical, however; she describes alternative and liberating relationships created by such virtues as tolerance, self-discovery, friendship, and responsibility exhibited by strong female protagonists. "Of Mist, and Grass, and Sand," for instance, describes a postholocaust world in which people exist in simpler and more deprived circumstances, technology has been lost but biological sciences have been discovered, and women seem to be in charge: a matriarchal desert tribe practices polyandry, and the savior, who comes riding out of the desert with her healing snakes, is a competent young woman. In *The Exile Waiting* (1975) the heroine, a female telepath in a postholocaust society, must surmount a series of mental and physical obstacles through her own ingenuity and courage.

McIntyre's fiction, however, is not defined by feminism alone. She does not depict, for instance, all-female worlds, the most radical extreme of feminist SF, and she focuses on other issues as well, such as science and genetics, which she studied in earning a B.S. in biology and in doing graduate work at the University of Washington.

McIntyre is also known for her STAR TREK novelizations, beginning with an original, *The Entropy Effect* (1981). In addition, she has worked as a conference coordinator, organizing among others a Clarion SF Writers Workshop.

OTHER WORKS: *Fireflood and Other Stories* (collection, 1979); *Star Trek: The Wrath of Khan* (1982); *Superluminal* (1983); *Star Trek III: The Search for Spock* (1984); *Star Trek: Enterprise: The First Adventure* (1986); *Barbary* (1986); *Star Trek IV: The Voyage Home* (1986).

H.M.Z.

McKENNA, RICHARD M[ILTON] (1913–1964).

American writer whose long service in the U.S. Navy provided him with the material for his best-selling mainstream novel *The Sand Pebbles* (1963). McKenna published only a dozen science-fiction and fantasy stories, the best of which are collected in *Casey Agonistes and Other Science Fiction and Fantasy Stories* (1973). Most celebrate the power of the human imagination to triumph over adverse circumstance by remaking the environment, and they are both elegant and moving.

"The Secret Place" (1966) won a posthumous Nebula, but it is less effective than "Casey Agonistes" (1958) and "Fiddler's Green" (1967).

B.S.

McLAUGHLIN, DEAN [BENJAMIN] (1931–).

American author and bookseller whose adventure science fiction was heavily influenced by John W. CAMPBELL (McLaughlin's earliest stories appeared first in *Astounding Science Fiction*). His three novels, and many of his short stories, are reminiscent of the work of such GOLDEN AGE writers as Isaac ASIMOV and Robert A. HEINLEIN. McLaughlin's fiction describes the struggle between enlightened humans who look forward to a new future and conservative forces who cling to old-fashioned ways despite their inability to respond to modern crises. In *Dome World* (1962), for example, the Earth may become a battleground because land-based governments insist on clinging to notions of national boundaries when they establish domed cities under the sea. The war is averted when the head of one of the undersea cities is sensible enough to reject such outmoded ways of looking at the world.

In *The Fury from Earth* (1963), McLaughlin tackled the human propensity to use scientific discoveries to build weaponry. When the Earth threatens its colony on Venus the book's hero refuses to build offensive weapons for the government of Venus despite great pressure. Pacifism wins out when he uses the theoretical basis for a planet-smashing weapon to produce an interstellar drive. As a result the reasons for the conflict are diminished, and humanity goes on to the stars.

Humanity's desire to reach the stars is also the concern of *The Man Who Wanted the Stars* (1965), but this time the hero keeps the space program alive long after most government officials and private citizens have given up on it. Reminiscent of Heinlein's *The Man Who Sold the Moon* (1950), the novel is heavily didactic in its insistence on the value of space exploration.

McLaughlin's fiction is not as original or well plotted as that of his more famous contemporaries, but it is consistently readable and frequently thought provoking.

OTHER WORK: *Hawk among the Sparrows* (collection, 1976).

S.H.G.

MACLEAN, KATHERINE [ANNE] (1925–).

American writer who has contributed slowly but steadily to the science-fiction field since her first story ("Defense Mechanism") was published in *Astounding* in 1949. Most of MacLean's work has dealt with medical and scientific experiment (she worked as a technician for two years in New York hospitals and indeed was sufficiently fascinated by psychology that she earned an M.A. degree at the age of fifty-two), as well as telepathy and evolution. Her first collection of stories, *The Diploids and Other Flights of Fancy* (1962), appeared the same year as her first novel, *Cosmic Checkmate* (with Charles V. De Vet, 1962), which is built around the settling of an interstellar issue of alien contact with the playing of a chesslike alien game. *The Man in the Bird Cage* (1971) was followed by *Missing Man* (1975), a novel about a telepath who works as a special consultant for the Rescue Squad of the Police Department and now must find a missing computer technician with vital skills and information. The novelette version, "The Missing Man" (1971), won a Nebula Award. MacLean has also written a novel with her husband, Carl West: *Dark Wing* (1979) describes a future in which the practice of medicine is illegal.

OTHER WORKS: *Trouble with Treaties* (collection, 1975); *The Trouble with You Earth People* (collection, 1980).

H.L.P.

McQUAY, MIKE (Professional name of Michael Dennis McQuay) (1949–).

American writer. McQuay's adventure-oriented science-fiction novels incorporate, to varying extents, the theme of one brave, intelligent man rising up to struggle against a technology or a society gone mad. McQuay has written *Tom Swift, Nancy Drew/Hardy Boys*, and *Bobbsey Twins* juveniles under the usual series pseudonyms, and he has also written a novel entitled *Cradle to Grave* (1983) as Susan Claudia; all his SF works, however, have been published under his own name. He began his SF career with the 1980 novel *Lifekeeper*, an adventure in which the hero, Doral Dulan, saves the oppressed desert peoples of the future from domination by the ruling computers. Strong male characters also become leaders and heroes in *Jitterbug* (1984) and *Pure Blood* (1985). McQuay's other works include *Motherearth* (1985), the screenplay novelizations *Escape from New York* (1981) and *My Science Project* (1985), *Memories* (1987), and the four novels of the Matthew Swain series (1981–1983), in which a Chandleresque private eye fights corruption in the twenty-first century.

B.D.

MAD MAX (1979).

Directed by George Miller; screenplay by George Miller and James McCausland; photographed by David Eggby; music by Brian May. With Mel Gibson, Joanne Samuel, Hugh Keays-Byrne, Steve Bisley, Tim Burns, Vince Gil, Roger Ward. 90 minutes. Color.

MAD MAX 2 (THE ROAD WARRIOR) (1981).

Directed by George Miller; screenplay by George Miller, Terry Hayes, and Brian Hannant; photographed by Dean Semler; music by Brian May. With Mel Gibson, Bruce Spence, Kjell Nilsson, Emil Minty, Virginia Hey, Vernon Wells. 96 minutes. Color.

MAD MAX 3 (BEYOND THUNDERDOME) (1985).

Directed by George Miller; screenplay by Terry Hayes and George Miller; photographed by Dean Semler; music by Maurice Jarre. With Mel Gibson, Tina Turner, Bruce Spence, Helen Banday, Frank Thring. 106 minutes. Color.

The trilogy of Mad Max films constitutes a strikingly original mix of western, science-fiction, horror, and motorcycle gang films, blended with a crisp narrative style matched only by such genre classics as the Warner Bros. gangster movies of the 1930s. The films' apocalyptic vision, perfectly located in the barren Australian landscape, combined with breathtaking action sequences and imaginative costume design, established Mel Gibson as a major star and made *Mad Max*, despite its initial minimal release in the United States by American International, a solid cult favorite.

Mad Max, the first of the series, is set in the near future, when social structures have all but broken down and the law has at best only a dubious control over violence and anarchy. For the most part the film uses the highway and the assorted vehicles that travel on it as an elaborate metaphor for a collapsing civilization on the road to self-destruction. The movie is also an "auto-critique," an extended joke about our cultural obsession with the car.

Max is one of the Bronze, the police force who possess the few remaining cars with V-8 engines. These cars are used to patrol the roads, which are now filled with lawless groups who prowl in souped-up homemade vehicles, patched together from parts left over from the days of manufacturing. When Max heads out to avenge the death of his partner at the hands of one such gang, he sets in motion a spiral of violence that results in the murder of his wife and baby. It is their deaths that transform him into the hardened, obsessed seeker of vengeance indicated by the title. He mercilessly kills the remaining gang members.

The narrative is both functionally slim and conventional, with Max becoming in the second half one more in a long line of fascistic Dirty Harry vigilantes. The film's value, however, is in its execution, for ex-lawyer and film buff George Miller revealed a remarkable control of style and pace in this, his first feature. Given the thinness of the story line, Miller wisely omitted virtually all background exposition, leaving the viewer to extrapolate the details of this ambiguous future world. In short, the style of *Mad Max* perfectly suits the bleakness of its vision.

Mad Max 2 (The Road Warrior), the second film of the series, is equal to if not better than the first in every way. The implications are maintained and elaborated with an impressive consistency: Max is now a hardened loner no longer working for the Bronze. His bitterness and diminishing morality are clearly visible in his appearance: his leather outfit is frayed, one eye is damaged by scar tissue, and his hair reveals a startling shock of white.

The plot makes the affinity of the Mad Max myth with the western genre more explicit. An isolated group of civilized folk who manufacture their own gasoline are besieged by another motorcycle gang. And, like the classic western hero, Max commits himself to the side of civilization by offering to lead a tanker caravan past the savages to safety. It should be noted, though, that Max's motives are less than pure, reflecting not altruism but a desire to retrieve his prized vehicle.

In *Mad Max 3 (Beyond Thunderdome)* Max is mythicized even further. Again like the classic western hero, he comes alone into town, in this case an outpost representing the beginning of social organization in the postholocaust era. But the town is built on corruption and force—literally, because it is powered by slaves toiling in the dank boiler rooms beneath the buildings—and it embodies an ugly, social Darwinist view of life, perfectly represented by the blood sport fought in the enclosed space known as the Thunderdome. The boss of the town, played by a tough Tina Turner, demonstrates that survival of the fittest is the ruling law. In opposing the town, Max now represents positive, civilized values. His mythic quality as redeemer is solidified by his leading a group of children, stranded in the desert for years, to a new Eden and being identified as their prophesied savior. The films in sequence have moved from straightforward adventure tale to mythic romance.

The series is as remarkable for its look as for its story, showing special wit and inventiveness in its costume design, which combines punk fashion, sadomasochistic paraphernalia, and macho iconography. Indeed, one of the series' most visible legacies was its influence on the look of a number of later science-fiction movies, among them *Solarbabies* (1986).

B.K.G.

THE MAGAZINE OF FANTASY AND SCIENCE FICTION (1949–   ).

The most literary of the science-fiction magazines, *The Magazine of Fantasy and Science Fiction (F&SF)* evolved from a different line than the SF pulps, because the founding editors, J. Francis McCOMAS and Anthony BOUCHER, had their feet planted firmly in both the SF and mystery fields (and had uncommon—for the times—tastes for fantasy, which tends to be more literary and less genre oriented than SF). They modeled *F&SF* on its older companion, *Ellery Queen's Mystery Magazine*. Although the publication was originally planned as exclusively a magazine of fantasy and horror (the first issue was called simply *The Magazine of Fantasy*), "Science Fiction" was added to the title (and the contents) with the second issue. But

Cover by Emsh (September 1962)

the editorial criterion remained unchanged: quality stories of literary merit, uninfluenced by the pulp tradition. With headnotes, no interior illustrations, and back-cover ads featuring testimonials by such general literateurs (and Book-of-the-Month Club associates) as Clifton Fadiman and Basil Davenport, even the look of *F&SF* emphasized its association with an older literary tradition.

F&SF has maintained a reassuring consistency in both content and appearance over its history and occasional changes in editor; the standards established by Boucher and McComas were retained by subsequent editors Robert P. Mills, Avram Davidson, and Edward Ferman, each of whom nevertheless put his own stamp on the publication. (Ferman, who has been editor since 1965, is now second only to John W. CAMPBELL in the number of issues of an SF magazine edited.) *F&SF*'s consistently high standards are reflected in the number of Hugo Awards it has received: eight as best professional magazine (1958–1960, 1963, 1969–1972), three honors for Ferman (1981–1983) as best professional editor. In addition, more stories from *F&SF* have been nominated for awards than from any other magazine.

The story most closely associated with *F&SF* is "Flowers for Algernon" (1959) by Daniel KEYES, which stands as a tribute to the magazine's liberal policy (and to its wisdom: the novelette won a Hugo, the novel version a Nebula). It is doubtful that this story, with its close focus on the feelings of a retarded man and its measured, journal-entry style, could have appeared anywhere else at the time. The story also was a harbinger of the NEW WAVE, and, as Thomas Clareson has pointed out, it is possible that the New Wave in SF might not have developed "had not *F&SF* done much to break the old molds." The other work that perhaps best typifies *F&SF*'s policy is Walter M. MILLER's *A Canticle for Leibowitz*, which first appeared as three novelettes (1955–1957) and which has been hailed by some as the best SF novel of the modern period.

In recent years *F&SF* has not been quite so innovative as it was in the 1950s. Nevertheless, it continues to publish an unusual number of first stories and award winners, to discover new, literary writers, to maintain a circulation of about half to two-thirds that of the most popular magazines, and to remain the most consistently reliable magazine in the field.

M.A.

— MAGAZINES, LIMITED RUN —

Although Hugo GERNSBACK's AMAZING STORIES, founded in 1926, was the first true science-fiction magazine, the genre had seen print several years earlier in *Weird Tales* (1923–1954), which featured a fair quota of SF among its offering of gore and grue. Many writers who sold first to *Weird Tales*, most notably Edmond HAMILTON, later graduated to the SF magazines. To Gernsback goes the distinction of founding not only the first SF magazine but the first six. After the success of *Amazing Stories* he issued a massive *Amazing Stories Annual* (1927), featuring a new Edgar Rice BURROUGHS Martian novel. The annual's success led to the establishment of *Amazing Stories Quarterly* (1928–1934), which featured full-length novels along with short stories and was always well worth the cover price. In the days before paperbacks, and with SF in hardcover a rarity, the quarterlies were a boon for their full-length adventure novels, and they remained a major asset of the SF magazines over the next twenty years.

When Gernsback lost control of *Amazing* in 1929, he promptly established a new company and issued four new SF titles: *Air Wonder Stories, Science Wonder Stories*, a bumper *Science Wonder Quarterly* (1929–1930; retitled *Wonder Stories Quarterly*, 1920–1933), and *Scientific Detective Monthly* (1930). After a year *Air Wonder Stories*, which was too specialized, merged with *Science Wonder* to form *Wonder Stories* (1930–1936), the third leading SF magazine of the 1930s.

Whereas *Amazing* had become staid, *Wonder*, especially under the editorship of Charles HORNIG after

Cover by Frank R. Paul (November 1929)

1933, was "friendlier," providing a forum, as well as editorial services, for fans and readers. It was through the Science Fiction League, instituted by *Wonder*, that organized fandom found a voice, setting the wheels in motion for the first SF conventions. *Wonder* published some of the best SF of the early 1930s, such as the work of Edmond Hamilton, Laurence MANNING, and even Clark Ashton SMITH. But if for nothing else, *Wonder* is immortalized for one author and one story, "A Martian Odyssey" (1934) by Stanley G. WEINBAUM, the first classic short story of the SF PULP MAGAZINES.

By 1936 *Wonder* was losing money, and Gernsback sold it to Standard Magazines. Retitled *Thrilling Wonder Stories* (1936–1955) and with former fan Mort WEISINGER as editor, it became primarily an SF adventure pulp aimed at a younger audience than *Astounding* but attracting many of the same writers.

In the 1930s SF grew in popularity in the magazines and was featured in *Weird Tales* and some of the hero pulps, including *Doc Savage* (1933–1949) and *Dusty Ayres and His Battle Birds* (1934–1955). *Marvel Science Stories* (1938–1941; revived 1951–1952) was the first, though not the best, of a new run of pulps appearing at the end of the decade. *Marvel* came from the Red Circle stable of magazines, and, like Red Circle's other publications, it specialized in sex and sadism—mild by today's standards, but a bold step for the SF of the 1930s. A notoriously unreliable and irregular magazine, it followed this road successfully and almost alone for the next few years. Its initial success, together with the increased circulations of *Astounding, Amazing,* and *Thrilling Wonder*, attracted other publishers to SF and encouraged existing ones to expand. The year 1939 saw seven new SF titles, 1940 a further six, and a significant number of borderline and associational magazines, not strictly devoted to SF, published works in the genre as well.

The most important new SF magazines were *Startling Stories* (1939–1955), a companion to *Thrilling Wonder* that featured long lead novels and carried some of the best adventure stories by Henry KUTTNER; *Planet Stories* (1939–1955), which concentrated solely on interplanetary tales and in the mid-1940s published some excellent work by Leigh BRACKETT and Ray BRADBURY, including some of Bradbury's Martian Chronicles episodes; *Astonishing Stories* (1940–1943) and *Super Science Stories* (1940–1943; revived 1949–1951), which provided Frederik POHL with his first editorial duties; *Cosmic Stories* (1941) and *Stirring Science Stories* (1941–1942), which marked Donald A. WOLLHEIM's editorial debut; and *Future Fiction* (1939–1943), which, with its companion, *Science Fiction Quarterly* (1940–1943; revived 1951–1958), gave Robert A. W. LOWNDES his first hand at editing. Also notable were the memorable and now highly collectible *Famous Fantastic Mysteries* (1939–1953) and its companion, *Fantastic Novels* (1940–1941; revived 1948–1951), which reprinted early SF classics beautifully illustrated by Virgil FINLAY and Lawrence Stevens.

Only a few of these and other titles survived World War II, and those that did grew up fast in the nuclear age. *Astounding* still led the field, but by 1950 it faced strong opposition not only from GALAXY and THE MAGAZINE OF FANTASY AND SCIENCE FICTION but also from *Thrilling Wonder Stories* and *Startling Stories*. Under the astute editorial guidance of Samuel Merwin (1945–1951) and Samuel Mines (1951–1954), *Wonder* and *Startling* offered, alongside solid SF adventures by Henry KUTTNER, Jack VANCE, and Edmond Hamilton, bold new SF by the likes of Arthur C. CLARKE, Ray BRADBURY, and James E. GUNN. Prominent among the new writers was Philip José FARMER, whose "The Lovers" (*Startling*, 1952) was the first graphically sexual SF story to be published in a magazine.

The early 1950s saw a second boom in the popularity of SF: four new titles in 1949, eight in 1950, fifteen in 1953. At the same time this was a period of change, as the pulps died out and the digest-format magazine took over. Many of the digests were short-lived titles of little

Cover by Earle K. Bergey (April 1947)

merit, although some deserved a longer life, especially the group of four edited by Lester DEL REY: *Space SF* (1952–1953), which carried Algis BUDRYS's first sale; *Science Fiction Adventures* (1952–1954), which serialized Cyril M. KORNBLUTH's downbeat classic "The Syndic" (1954); *Fantasy Magazine* (1953); and *Rocket Stories* (1953). Other digests worthy of note were *Worlds Beyond* (1950–1951), competently edited by Damon KNIGHT, who helped establish the SF book review as a critical feature; *Beyond* (1953–1954), the companion fantasy title to *Galaxy*; and *Ten Story Fantasy* (1951), edited by Donald A. Wollheim, which published Arthur C. Clarke's "Sentinel of Eternity" (1951), the seed for *2001: A Space Odyssey* (1968).

A few new magazines survived the blight that depleted the field in 1955. Of good quality were *Future SF* (1950–1960) and its companion, *Science Fiction Stories* (1953–1960), ably edited by Robert A. W. Lowndes, whose skill managed to overcome the strictures of a limited budget. Another notable magazine was *Fantastic Universe* (1953–1960), a doggedly persistent publication that saw its best issues under the editorship of Hans

Stefan Santesson (1956–1960). Also worthy of mention is *Other Worlds* (1949–1958), produced by Raymond A. PALMER; although of erratic quality, it made its mark in endeavoring to publish stories too daring for other magazines. *Infinity* (1955–1958), which carried Arthur C. Clarke's "The Star" and gave the world Harlan ELLISON's first published story, flourished during the late-1950s miniboom that came with the start of the Space Age. *Fantastic* (1952–1980) was a companion to *Amazing Stories* and suffered the same trials and tribulations, being at its best in the early 1960s. There was also *Venture* (1957–1958; revived 1969–1970), companion to *The Magazine of Fantasy and Science Fiction* and one of the more daring of the SF magazines with its sometimes risque lead stories.

The best magazine to come out of the 1950s, apart from *Galaxy* and *The Magazine of Fantasy and Science Fiction*, was *If* (1952–1974; revived 1986), also known as *Worlds of If* in the 1960s. A strongly independent magazine in the 1950s, *If* avoided any obvious trends and published the occasional classic, including James BLISH's "A Case of Conscience" (1953). In 1959 publisher James Quinn sold *If* to the publisher of *Galaxy*; when Frederik POHL became its editor in 1961, it experienced new vitality. Pohl reserved *Galaxy* for solid, dependable, almost predictable stories, while in *If* he had fun, always experimenting, and making it the most exciting magazine of the decade. *If* won the Hugo Award as best professional magazine in 1966, 1967, and 1968; brought E. E. SMITH and A. E. VAN VOGT back to SF; published such popular series as Fred SABERHAGEN's Berserker stories and Keith LAUMER's exploits of Retief; brought to print such award-winning stories as "Neutron Star" (1966) by Larry NIVEN and "I Have No Mouth, and I Must Scream" (1967) by Harlan Ellison; and published the first stories by Niven, C. C. MacApp, and Alexei PANSHIN, as well as idiosyncratic stories by the unpredictable R. A. LAFFERTY, Cordwainer SMITH, and Philip K. DICK. Tragically, *If* suffered the same fate as *Galaxy*, ceasing publication after its change of publisher in 1969.

The 1960s were a period of uncertainty for SF, and the only noteworthy magazine to make its debut in that turbulent decade was *Worlds of Tomorrow* (1963–1967; revived 1970–1971). A companion to *Galaxy* and *If*, it had the honor of bringing to print Philip José Farmer's Riverworld stories. With the exception of this publication, however, the SF magazine scene was floundering. Ever since the mid-1950s the SF magazines had experienced steady declines in circulation, unable to compete effectively against television, the comic book, the slick magazine, and especially the paperback. By the end of the 1960s many were predicting the end of the SF magazine, but the doomsayers were premature. Instead of dying out, the SF magazine adapted by diversifying.

One example of this diversification is the regular anthology series. The first was Frederik Pohl's *Star SF Stories* (1953–1959) (one issue had even appeared as a magazine in 1958). It was in the late 1960s, however, that the anthology series flowered, notably *Orbit* (1966–1980) and *New Dimensions* (1971–1981). A number of the new publications blurred the distinction between the magazine and anthology to produce "magabooks," such as the American edition of *Perry Rhodan* (1969–1977) and, at the other end of the literary scale, the New Wave *Quark/* (1970–1971), edited by Samuel R. DELANY and Marilyn Hacker. *Infinity* (1970–1973) appeared as a paperback revival of the 1950s magazine; *Weird Heroes* (1975–1977) emulated the hero pulps of the 1930s. The best fusion of anthology and magazine came from editor, later publisher, James Baen: *Destinies* (1978–1981) and its spiritual successor *Far Frontiers* (1985–1987) were representative of the best of *Analog* and *Galaxy*, with their emphasis on hard science.

Another development—though less successful—was the change to slick format. *Science Fiction Plus* (1953) had made such a transformation but failed nonetheless, more because of inferior content than design. *Analog* attempted a similar conversion between 1963 and 1965, again without success, demonstrating that SF magazines could not support themselves on advertising revenue. A serious attempt was made with *Vertex* (1973–1975), a good magazine and notable for John VARLEY's debut in its pages; nevertheless, it was done in by a world paper shortage and an ill-conceived effort to convert to tabloid format. Another venture was *Cosmos* (1977), also of good quality but critically underfinanced.

The SF magazine has also survived in the form of the semiprofessional publication. Such ventures are usually of limited life, depending on the enthusiasm and financial resources of their publisher, but some have proved surprisingly resilient; *Space and Time*, for example, has appeared regularly since 1966. The first "semiprozine," however, was *Marvel Tales* (1934–1935), now highly collectible. Recent years have seen a plethora of semiprozines, many in the fantasy and horror field, but a few solidly SF. Two of the best were *Unearth* (1977–1979), which had a policy of publishing new writers, among them Somtow SUCHARITKUL and Rudy RUCKER, and *Galileo* (1976–1980). Alas, *Galileo*, which started on a small scale, expanded too quickly and folded. *Rigel* (1981–1983) seemed to have the right balance but also found the course too tough. The best of late has been the British *Interzone* (1982–   ), which has established a solid subscription base and is edited by a collective with a boldly declared policy of independence.

In one form or another it would seem that the SF magazine will survive. The SF world needs the magazine to train its new writers, to offer diversity and experimentation, and to provide a unique forum for readers and authors.

M.A.

THE MAGNETIC MONSTER (1953).

Directed by Curt Siodmak; screenplay by Curt Siodmak and Ivan Tors; photographed by Charles Van Enger; music by Blaine Sanford. With Richard Carlson, King Donovan, Jean Byron, Harry Ellerbe, Leonard Mudie, Michael Fox, John Zaremba, Kathleen Freeman, Strother Martin. 76 minutes. Black and white.

This low-key thriller was intended as the first in a series of scientific detection adventures, but only one, *Gog* (1954), followed. Scientific detectives Richard CARLSON and King Donovan investigate outbursts of unusual magnetic effects; they eventually discover the man responsible—a dying scientist (Leonard Mudie) who has created a new element that turns energy into matter. Doubling in mass at regular intervals, the newly created matter gives off bursts of magnetism; if unchecked, the detectives discover, it will destroy the Earth. A gigantic undersea cyclotron is used to bombard and ultimately destroy the "hungry metal." (Footage from the 1934 German film *Gold* is effectively used for the explosive climax.)

The filmmakers' intelligent, unsensational approach, characterized by crisp photography and tight pacing, plus the exciting (if borrowed) climax, help make *The Magnetic Monster* one of the most satisfying low-budget science-fiction films of its period.

B.W.

MAINE, CHARLES ERIC (Pseudonym of David McIlwain) (1921–).

British writer and journalist. Maine wrote science fiction (he has published nothing in the field since 1976, and his last novel was published in 1971) filled with adventure and extravagant science. In *B.E.A.S.T.: Biological Evolutionary Animal Simulation Test* (1966), for instance, he imagined a computer model of animals and their environment in which the animals are forced into accelerated development until only a single creature survives: the ultimate product of the evolutionary law of survival of the fittest, it has nevertheless lost all humanity.

Survival is a frequent theme in Maine's work. In *World without Men* (1958; as *Alph,* 1972) he presented a completely female future society, characterized by rigorous eugenics and lesbianism, that is rocked when a male is discovered. In *The Tide Went Out* (1958; revised as *Thirst,* 1977), most of the Earth's water drains down a crack in the ocean floor; Shirley Sye, a worldly wise fashion editor, advises the hero how to survive in an all-for-themselves world.

Maine frequently used the themes of time travel and time displacement. *Timeline* (1955) describes a world in which people travel in time as "psycho-identities" while their bodies are left behind: in order to travel they possess the bodies of others, destroying them in the process and going on to new bodies. Maine's favorite among his seventeen SF novels (he also wrote non-SF as Richard

Rayner and Robert Wade), in addition to *The Tide Went Out,* is *The Mind of Mr. Soames* (1961). It describes the situation of a man who remains unconscious until he is thirty and the debate about how he should be educated. The novel was filmed in 1969 (Maine's first novel, *Spaceways,* 1953, based on his radio play, also was filmed the year it was published), but Maine felt the film missed the essential point of the story, which is the difference between education and training.

OTHER WORKS: *Crisis 2000* (1956); *Escapement* (1956; as *The Man Who Couldn't Sleep,* 1958); *High Vacuum* (1957); *The Isotope Man* (1957); *Count-Down* (1959; as *Fire Past the Future,* 1960); *Subterfuge* (1959); *Calculated Risk* (1960); *He Owned the World* (1960; as *The Man Who Owned the World,* (1961); *The Darkest of Nights* (1962; as *Survival Margin,* 1968; revised as *The Big Death,* 1978); *Never Let Up* (1964), *The Random Factor* (1971).

S.H.G.

———— THE MAINSTREAM ————

Writers and fans in the science-fiction community are keenly aware of their isolation in the literary world. The artistically minded SF writer feels more than a little pain when *The New York Times Book Review* tosses his or her book a mere paragraph in the irregular SF column; the commercially minded SF writer winces when the latest novel by James Michener or Robert Ludlum or Judith Krantz is displayed in the front of the bookstore while his or her own book is hidden away in an obscure corner.

The SF community uses the word *mainstream* to describe the fiction that is getting the attention they want; the word is a confession that SF is felt to be a sidestream, a tributary. *Mainstream* is not the only current word. *Mundane* is used to refer to nonfantasy and non-SF, with deliberate overtones of dullness, worldliness, and uninspired realism. The SF community seems to alternate between hubris and an inferiority complex.

There are even occasional claims that SF is the true mainstream fiction of the twentieth century, that posterity will judge Robert A. HEINLEIN, Isaac ASIMOV, and Arthur C. CLARKE—or Ursula K. LE GUIN, Samuel R. DELANY, and Philip K. DICK—to be the literary superiors of such wearily realistic fictioneers as Saul Bellow, John Updike, Ann Beattie, and John Fowles. Unfortunately, posterity is not yet able to inform us of its literary preferences; at present SF writers find themselves viewing mainstream writers with a confusing mixture of envy, anger, adulation, and contempt.

The Commercial Mainstream: By 1980 SF had developed into a reliable publishing category. In the fifty years or so since Hugo GERNSBACK launched the first magazine that specialized in "scientifiction," SF had managed to sustain a vigorous commercial short fiction market and, since the 1950s, a dependable book market as well. It was a truism that an SF novel would always sell a minimum of 30,000 or 40,000 copies, presumably on the theory that SF readers would mindlessly buy anything with a spaceship on the cover. Unfortunately, few SF novels sold significantly *more* than the minimum— SF was a dead-end publishing category.

The result was that many writers felt SF to be a ghetto— a safe place, where writers could go to conventions and bask in the attention of the fans, assured of a decent living if they wrote three or four books a year; but it was also a confining place, so that a writer, once pegged as a science fictioneer, would never get serious attention outside the genre.

A few writers in the 1960s and 1970s, willing to risk complete failure in the hope of reaching a much wider audience, managed to get the damning label *science fiction* removed from their books. What no one predicted was that the commercial walls were already coming down by themselves. Some claim that it was the phenomenal success of the movie STAR WARS (1977) that broke the commercial barrier, but the real breakthrough had happened before George LUCAS's realization of 1930s SPACE OPERA filled America's eyes with light sabers, aliens, robots, and battles in space. The walls had been breached a couple of years before by Frank HERBERT's third Dune novel, *The Children of Dune* (1976), which, after unspectacular serialization in ANALOG, shocked everyone by hitting the national best-seller lists in hard cover.

What happened? First we have to understand the best-seller dynamic. To make it onto a best-seller list, a book must sell many copies *fast*. The original novel *Dune* had been a word-of-mouth hit, with college students in the 1960s passing the book from hand to hand much the way they did J. R. R. Tolkien's Lord of the Rings trilogy. *Dune* sold an impressive number of copies in paperback, but slowly, building over many years. The first sequel, *Dune Messiah*, came out early enough in this process that it also sold too slowly to reach the best-seller lists. By the time *The Children of Dune* came out, however, a large number of people had read the first two volumes and loved them for their grand romance, prophetic vision, or scientific extrapolation. The third book in the series was given enough hype to let people know it was in the stores; the ready-made audience did the rest. The book sold quickly, and readers of *The New York Times Book Review* had to take note of the fact that a category SF novel had penetrated to commercial publishing's holy of holies.

In short order other publishers realized that certain SF novels could be marketed effectively, Isaac Asimov's Foundation trilogy and Robert A. Heinlein's *Stranger in a Strange Land* (1961) were also word-of-mouth hits in the 1960s, creating for themselves the same ready-made audience that had launched Herbert into the commercial

mainstream. Arthur C. Clarke's ties with the movie 2001: A SPACE ODYSSEY (1968) and his 1953 cult favorite novel *Childhood's End* put him in the same league.

At the same time, *Star Wars'* influence is not to be denied. The euphoria surrounding the movie's record-breaking box-office receipts led publishers to pump money into SF—often more money than the audience was ready to repay. Publishing lines in the genre were also expanded beyond the writers' ability to produce good novels. So many SF novels were published each year that regular readers could no longer keep up; inevitably, readers stuck with favorite authors and established series. New authors could no longer count on a certain minimum of sales.

As a result, although SF could transcend the category ceiling, it had lost the category floor. It was now possible to lose money selling SF. Advances for first novelists fell, from $3,000 to $2,000, even $1,500 at some publishing houses—*Omni* magazine was actually paying more for short stories than some publishers were paying for first novels.

In short, SF has joined the commercial mainstream. Often since 1980 the national best-seller lists have sported SF and fantasy in half their positions. Larry NIVEN and Jerry POURNELLE, Anne MCCAFFREY and Marion Zimmer BRADLEY have joined the ranks of avowed SF writers with best-seller status.

Now that the SF best-seller has been proved possible, some writers are melding aspects of SF with time-tested commercial techniques, blurring the boundaries of the genre with varying degrees of success. Niven and Pournelle's *Lucifer's Hammer* (1977) and *Footfall* (1985) owe much to the cast-of-thousands writing of Arthur Hailey; Gregory BENFORD's *Artifact* and Dean KOONTZ's *Strangers* are other examples of mixed-genre novels from the mid-1980s.

The Literary Mainstream: The commercial mainstream is the world of publishing as a business, where high sales figures mean the author is a success; the literary mainstream is the world of writing as an art, where high sales figures are generally taken to mean the author has sold out.

The literary mainstream is dominated by the academic-literary community—university professors of literature; high-powered critics for prestige publications such as the *New York Times Book Review, The New York Review of Books,* and *The New Yorker;* and writers who take the first two groups seriously. The academic-literary community is firmly rooted in the fiction of the early twentieth century and the critical theories invented to explain it. The intense realism and flat-affect style of Virginia Woolf, the calculatedly incomprehensible language games of James Joyce, the stodgy angst of Henry James—all are still finding echoes and imitations in the fiction of the literary mainstream. The triumph of modernism is complete.

While critical fads come and go—new criticism followed by deconstructionism—the canon of books and authors remains unchanged. Ernest Hemingway and Ford Madox Ford may go in and out of fashion, but even at their nadir they were regarded as worthy of discussion. The best recent works of the romantic tradition—*Gone with the Wind*, for instance, or the historical fiction of Mary Renault—are simply not mentioned except as "popular literature," whose study is more anthropological than critical. Fiction is not considered "serious," and therefore art, unless it displays due respect for the canon of literature and critical paradigms taught in America's universities.

The result is that the literary mainstream in the United States is not, in fact, the "mainstream" at all; with some exceptions, it is read by so few that it can hardly be said to penetrate the national consciousness. Literary fiction seems to be following the path already blazed by serious poetry—toward oblivion. This is no accident. Modernism was a rebellion against the romantic fiction of the late nineteenth century; therefore it deliberately rejected most of the conventions of romance, including those that make fiction entertaining and compelling. Reader identification with a protagonist has been rejected in favor of "distancing"; where romantic elements remain, they are carefully hidden behind detailed description, flamboyant style, or elaborate introspection. The result is that readers increasingly need to be educated in the reading of literary fiction.

In contrast, SF is read almost entirely by volunteers. Where university SF courses are taught, they are generally used as sops to the enthusiasm of the undergraduate; they increase the average enrollment of the English Department and so help support the faculty in the teaching of *real* literature. Outside the university, however, SF readers and writers sustain a lively critical community, primarily in fanzines, where the struggle to establish a critical language that adequately deals with SF is still under way. Although the critical standards being developed are alien to the critic schooled in the academic-literary tradition, they are no less serious in intent.

Thus if by "serious literature" one means fiction written with due obeisance to the particular standards of academic-literary fiction, little SF qualifies; but if one means fiction written with serious artistic intent, with *some* critical system in mind, much of SF is indeed serious literature. In fact, SF can be viewed as the inevitable romantic answer to the revolution of modernism, the counterrevolution that was due at midcentury but was thwarted by the academic-literary community's entrenched—and tenured—commitment to modernism.

Although SF is itself a revolution, there are movements and revolutions within the field as well—one more sign, in fact, that SF is a living literature and not an endless repetition of formula. John W. CAMPBELL, Jr., created what we now call hard or scientifically responsible SF

as a response to the space romances of the 1930s; the NEW WAVE of the 1960s was a revolt against the shallow, glib characterization and plain-style writing of the GOLDEN AGE.

It was with the New Wave that SF's relation with the literary mainstream became complex. Although the decision to write SF is inherently a rejection of the literary mainstream, many New Wave writers declared that their revolution consisted of bringing mainstream literary standards to SF. Some SF writers and critics have viewed this attitude as a kind of selling out—who wants to read SF as Herman Melville or William Faulkner would have written it?—while others have called for SF to become mainstream literary fiction with a futuristic milieu. But however much some SF writers believe themselves to be writing according to mainstream literary standards, their fiction remains unmistakably SF and therefore different from, and usually unpalatable to the academic-literary community. With the exceptions of Ray BRADBURY, Ursula K. LE GUIN, and Kurt VONNEGUT, Jr. (who denies that he writes SF), SF is still viewed by most of the academic-literary community with feelings ranging from benign contempt to active hostility.

Science fiction does have one key element in common with the literary mainstream that no other category shares: the primacy of idea. Science fiction is usually *about something*, not just storytelling for its own sake; in this sense even Golden Age SF is generally just as serious in intent as literary fiction.

Ironically, the literary mainstream's position as the official fiction of the academic-literary community is at once its strongest support and its greatest weakness. The fact that SF has no tenure track, no scholarly publication committees, no foundation or tax-supported public grants, and no dominant critical media allows its writers and critics a freedom bordering on anarchy—precisely the turbulent milieu from which true innovation can arise. Whereas today's domesticated mainstream writers are forbidden to despise their forebears—at least in public—SF writers are free to reject the canon of accepted literature. As William Wordsworth and Samuel Taylor Coleridge, Virginia Woolf and James Joyce rejected the literary canon of their time, so John W. Campbell, Jr., in the 1930s, Michael MOORCOCK in the 1960s, and Bruce Sterling in the 1980s proposed to purge and revise the canon of accepted SF literature. The literary mainstream is like a climax forest, a few pathetic saplings struggling to live in tiny patches of light under the dense canopy of the giant trees; so peaceful, that forest primeval! Not a movement, not a sound. Science fiction, however, fells its giants with alarming regularity, so there is always room for new growth, and strange creatures come to live in the thick underbrush.

What academic-literary writer, caught up in the pursuit of grants and tenure, would dare to do what Bruce Sterling did: publish a critical magazine that viciously attacked the writers currently in vogue and gathered like-minded writers under the banner of CYBERPUNK. Although he did not choose (or even like) the name *cyberpunk*, Sterling was able to force even his most hostile critics to reexamine their own literary theories and change, to one degree or another, their critical positions. The rejection of the past is arguably essential to revolution, literary and otherwise; as long as the canon of mainstream literature remains unchallenged, the academic-literary community is incapable of the rapid change and growth that are constantly going on in the SF community.

The current relation between the literary mainstream and SF *is* changing, however. English professors, after all, tend to have been voracious readers in their youth, and SF is quite possibly the dominant adolescent literature. (This is not to slight SF. Adolescence is the stage in life in which one's identity and worldview are entirely negotiable; SF is the one literature that insists on redefining reality and human identity in every story. Thus SF and the adolescent are particularly well suited for each other.) The academic-literary community, therefore, includes an ever-increasing number of people who have vivid memories of the literary power of the SF they read in their youth and a strong interest in bringing intelligent critical technique to bear on a beloved literature. It would also be naive to deny that SF's penetration of the best-seller lists has no repercussions in academia.

Although few SF writers have "crossed over" to acceptance by the literary mainstream, an increasing number of serious mainstream writers attempt SF, many quite successfully. John HERSEY's *White Lotus, The Child Buyer*, and *My Petition for More Space*, Gore VIDAL's *Kalki*, and Margaret Atwood's *The Handmaid's Tale*—these prove that it is possible for mainstream writers to manage the feat of writing science fiction that achieves literary respect *and* best-seller status.

Nevertheless, although the literary mainstream permits its own to dabble in SF without losing status, an SF *origin* is still virtually the kiss of death for a writer who aspires to literary honors. When the American Book Awards were initiated, replacing the traditional National Book Award, a prize was offered for science fiction (won by Frederik POHL's *Jem* in 1980). The academic-literary elite forced a revision of the rules the following year. The SF category was eliminated (ostensibly because the genre already had an adequate award system, although other categories that also had their own awards continued to receive American Book Awards). The literary mainstream simply could not endure the notion of an SF novel receiving the same recognition as a "serious" novel.

Science fiction and mainstream literature are not likely to merge; their communities are clearly separated and unlikely to compromise their identities. Academic-literary writers are too firmly invested in their belief in the superiority of "serious literature" to allow SF any sort of parity, while SF writers would be committing literary patricide if they pretended not to see the value of such plainsong storytellers as Robert A. Heinlein, Isaac Asimov, Arthur C. Clarke, and Larry Niven.

What *is* likely is a continuing cross-fertilization, one that primarily benefits SF. Because the SF community is so keenly aware of the dominance of mainstream values, SF writers are more likely to learn from mistakes and achievements by academic-literary writers, and to insist on growth and change within the SF genre. The literary mainstream, with few exceptions, is complacent about having a monopoly on quality, an attitude that almost certainly guarantees a rude awakening in years to come.

It may well be that a future generation will look back on our century and see SF as the literary revolution that followed modernism, while the academic-literary tradition that looms so large in our time will be seen as conservative, then old-fashioned, and finally quaint, like the classicism of the eighteenth century. In such a case, the communities would not have merged; SF would simply have replaced the "mainstream" in the memory of the audience of the future.

O.S.C.

MALZBERG, BARRY N[ATHANIEL] (1939–   ).

American writer, probably the most literary and surely the most controversial science-fiction figure of the 1970s. A misplaced mainstream writer who found the SF field both more lucrative and more accessible, Malzberg carried on a passionate love-hate relationship with science fiction during a career that saw him produce, in his most prolific period (from 1969 through 1976), some twenty-five novels and three hundred short stories.

The bulk of Malzberg's work tends to deal with his personal obsessions: the assassination of John F. Kennedy, insane astronauts, all-powerful and excessively manipulative bureaucracies, games that cannot be won, seemingly simple problems that refuse to yield to rational solutions—and, above all, SF itself.

He has been accused, perhaps rightly, of taking the trappings of SF and turning them inside out. Certainly he was the first to suggest that space might be so immense that the attempts to conquer it would drive our astronauts mad (*Beyond Apollo*, 1972; *The Falling Astronauts*, 1971; *Revelations*, 1972). Although his critics seem not to have noticed it, Malzberg is also obsessed with games: *Tactics of Conquest* (1974) is an expansion of a short story, "Closed Sicilian," in which an increasingly unbalanced narrator must play a series of chess matches for the survival of the galaxy; by the time Malzberg got around to writing *The Gamesman* (1975), his most Kafkaesque novel, the theme had been stripped to its bare essentials, and the Game, though obviously unwinnable, was never defined.

However, it is as a critic of SF that Malzberg has created his most memorable, bitter, and mordantly hu-

The Man from Planet X

morous works. *Herovit's World* (1973) describes the life of an increasingly schizophrenic SF hack writer; *Gather in the Hall of the Planets* (1971, as K. M. O'Donnell), a neglected early work, puts the entire SF community of writers, editors, and publishers under a microscope; and *Galaxies* (1975) is a brilliant 50,000-word critique of modern SF, disguised as "notes for a novel."

As it became apparent that his works would not reshape science fiction into the more mature literary field that he envisioned, Malzberg withdrew from the genre, producing only one novel, writing an occasional story, and editing an occasional anthology, until 1982, when he brought out *The Engines of the Night*, a collection of thirty-six insightful critical essays. The collection received great praise from the critics who had objected to the identical messages when they were couched in fictional form; strangely, it may be the single work for which Malzberg is best remembered.

NOTABLE OTHER WORKS: *The Falling Astronauts* (1971); *In the Pocket and Other S-F Stories* (collection, 1971); *Beyond Apollo* (1972); *Herovit's World* (1973); *Out from Ganymede* (collection, 1974); *Guernica Night* (1974); *The Many Worlds of Barry Malzberg* (1975); *Galaxies* (1975); *Down Here in the Dream Quarter* (collection, 1976); *Scop* (1976); *The Best of Barry N. Malzberg* (collection, 1979); *The Man Who Loved the Midnight Lady* (1980); *The Cross of Fire* (1982); *The Remaking of Sigmund Freud* (1985).

M.R.

MAN FROM ATLANTIS (1977–1978). *Directed by Lee H. Katzin, Marc Daniels, Reza Badiyi, Virgil Vogel, Dick Benedict, Paul Krasny, and others; written by Mayo Simon, Robert Lewin, John D. F. Black, Luther Murdoch, Larry Alexander, Shimon Wincel-*

berg, and others; music by Fred Karlin. With Patrick Duffy, Belinda J. Montgomery, Alan Fudge. Three two-hour TV movies, one 90-minute TV movie, and 13 one-hour episodes. Color.

This short-lived science-fiction-fantasy television series on NBC-TV starred Patrick Duffy as the "last citizen of Atlantis," discovered on a beach and put to work helping scientists explore the seas on the submarine *Cetacean.* Lasting less than a season, the series leaned more toward fantasy plots than SF, although several segments were enlivened by the presence of semiregular Victor Buono as the villainous Mr. Schubert.

K.R.D.

THE MAN FROM PLANET X (1951). *Directed by Edgar G. Ulmer; screenplay by Aubrey Wisberg and Jack Pollexfen; photographed by John L. Russell; music by Charles Roff. With Robert Clarke, Margaret Field, William Schallert, Raymond Bond, Roy Engel, Charles Davis, David Ormont, Gilbert Fallman, Tom Daly. 70 minutes. Black and white.*

This inexpensive movie beat THE THING (1951) into theaters as the first alien invader feature of the sound era. Despite a prolix and peculiarly structured script, director Edgar G. Ulmer's talents are what make the film memorable.

A wandering planet enters the Solar System, and a visitor descends onto a remote Scottish island. At first the visitor, whose face resembles an African mask, is friendly, and even at the climax his motivations are ambiguous. Apparently, director Ulmer was responsible for this unusually open-minded attitude; in the script the alien is more clearly hostile. At the end he's killed by the British Army as his planet sweeps out of the Solar System.

Ulmer made atmospheric use of standing sets, shrouding them in fog. Although the middle portion of the film is slow paced, the intelligence of the approach and the eerie atmosphere make the movie worthwhile; it deserves to be more widely seen.

B.W.

THE MAN IN THE WHITE SUIT (1951).
Directed by Alexander Mackendrick; screenplay by Roger MacDougall, John Dighton, and Alexander Mackendrick; photographed by Douglas Slocombe; music by Benjamin Frankel. With Alec Guinness, Joan Greenwood, Cecil Parker, Michael Gough, Ernest Thesiger, Howard Marion Crawford, Henry Mollison, Vida Hope, Miles Malleson. 85 minutes. Black and white.

Energetic chemist Sidney Stratton (Alec Guinness) develops a wonder fabric that will never soil or wear out, and he weaves a luminous white suit from it as a demonstration. However, his supporters turn against him: garment workers fear an end to their jobs, manufacturers fear that people will no longer buy clothes. Even his girlfriend turns against Sidney, who's oblivious to the possible social and economic problems. The suit falls apart at the climax, though, and everyone is mollified— except Sidney, who dashes off to try again.

Sprightly, witty, and swift paced, this is one of the brightest films from Ealing Studios, a small British company known for its satiric and often quite black comedies. Guinness is at his comic best in this film, which enhanced his growing international reputation. A rare example of satire in science-fiction films, *The Man in the White Suit* impishly attacks virtually every idea it raises, including those held by its scientist hero.

B.W.

THE MAN THEY COULD NOT HANG
(1939). *Directed by Nick Grinde; screenplay by Karl Brown; photographed by Benjamin Kline; music by Morris W. Stoloff. With Boris Karloff, Lorna Gray, Robert Wilcox, Roger Pryor, Don Beddoe, Byron Foulger, Ann Doran, Stanley Brown. 72 minutes. Black and white.*

This was the first film in Boris KARLOFF's brief "mad doctor" series for Columbia; in each film Karloff is a dedicated researcher who has made an amazing new discovery but whose research is stopped by repressive forces. He goes insane and finally dies, destroying his invention, but vows that others will carry on his work.

Most of the films in the series were based on actual research, and many of the ideas they depict have been put into practice. In *The Man They Could Not Hang*, the key device is an artificial heart that can revive the recently dead; the executed Karloff is revived by his invention, but he's insane and carries out a murderous revenge.

This film is a smooth piece of studio work but, except for Karloff and the concept of the artificial heart, unexceptional. It was followed by *The Man with Nine Lives* (1940), *Before I Hang* (1940), and *The Devil Commands* (1941).

B.W.

THE MAN WHO COULD WORK MIRACLES
(1937). *Directed by Lothar Mendes; screenplay by H. G. Wells; adapted from the short story by H. G. Wells; photographed by Harold Rosson. With Ralph Richardson, Roland Young, Joan Gardner, George Sanders. 82 minutes. Black and white.*

H. G. WELLS, who had worked with producer Alexander Korda on THINGS TO COME, teamed up with him a year later to make *The Man Who Could Work Miracles*. Based on a short story by Wells, the film depicts the gods' bestowal of omnipotence on an ordinary mortal to see what he will do with it. The film appears completely lucid and witty today and is undergoing a revival on television and videocassette.

Strictly speaking, this is more fantasy than science fiction, detailing the limits of omnipotence and human nature and the unexpected evils of doing good. The story echoes all the issues of *Things to Come*, especially its utopian longings and Wells's exasperation with human folly; in fact, Wells wanted the two films to be viewed together. Roland Young, best known today as the hero of *Topper*, makes a splendid Wellsean character; George Sanders is a droll god, and Ralph Richardson plays another version of his military man from *Things to Come*. The film is concisely edited and suspenseful, the dialogue subtle, and the special effects are well wrought. Handsome black-and-white prints have survived, and this film is as tense and exciting as the best of today's fantasies.

G.Z.

THE MAN WHO FELL TO EARTH (1976).
Directed by Nicolas Roeg; screenplay by Paul Mayersberg; adapted from the novel by Walter Tevis; photographed by Anthony Richmond; music by John Phillips. With David Bowie, Rip Torn, Buck Henry, Candy Clark. 138 minutes. Color.

Brilliantly photographed and directed, *The Man Who Fell to Earth* chronicles an alien's visit to Earth in an unsuccessful attempt to save his race from a drought on his home planet. The "fallen man," Thomas Newton (David Bowie), builds a corporate empire with his technological knowledge, the beginning of a plan to construct a fleet of spaceships to realize his rescue mission. But Newton is destroyed by the inevitable pressures and corruption of contemporary American culture, becoming a broken being capable only of consuming images from a bank of television monitors. Finally he is reduced to blindness as a result of tests by government scientists.

Nicolas Roeg's typically dazzling editing, his richly suggestive imagery, the refusal of Paul Mayersberg's script to explain all the details of the plot, and the casting of rock star Bowie, with his already-established extraterrestrial persona, all combine to make this one of the most intelligent and visually complex science-fiction movies ever made.

B.K.G.

THE MAN WITH TWO BRAINS (1983).
Directed by Carl Reiner; screenplay by Carl Reiner, Steve Martin, and George Gipe; photographed by Michael Chapman; music by Joel Goldsmith. With Steve Martin, Kathleen Turner, David Warner, Sissy Spacek. 90 minutes. Color.

This is a classic love story: boy meets girl, boy loses girl, boy meets brain . . . The film answers the age-old question: Should a man fall in love with Kathleen Turner or a brain in a jar? It's a tough choice for Dr. Michael Hfuhruhurr (Steve Martin), who falls in love with the brain (voiced by Sissy Spacek) while escaping a loveless marriage to Kathleen Turner. David Warner adds his usual malevolent menace, but the real star is Turner, who first displayed here her talent for comedy.

M.M.W.

THE MANCHURIAN CANDIDATE (1962).
Directed by John Frankenheimer; screenplay by George Axelrod and John Frankenheimer (the latter uncredited); adapted from the novel by Richard Condon; photographed by Lionel Lindon; music by David Amram. With Frank Sinatra, Laurence Harvey, Angela Lansbury, Janet Leigh, James Gregory, Khigh Dhiegh, Leslie Parrish, John McGiver, Henry Silva. 126 minutes. Black and white.

A key film of the 1960s, *The Manchurian Candidate* is intense, sardonic, and suspenseful. Laurence Harvey is captured during the Korean War, brainwashed into a perfectly programmed killing machine, and returned an apparent hero. A right-wing political candidate, modeled on Senator Joseph McCarthy, is ultimately revealed to be the agent of Communists, represented by chuckling Oriental mastermind Khigh Dhiegh.

John Frankenheimer and George Axelrod, closely following Richard Condon's witty novel, created a film so stylish and imaginative that audiences were dazzled. The plague-on-both-your-houses satire inflamed both the right and left but amused the more objective. Today, partly *because* of its influence, the film has less power.

B.W.

MANNING, LAURENCE [EDWARD] (1899–1972).
American writer born in Canada who worked as a newspaper reporter, writer for the Florists Exchange, and manager, president, and finally owner of a nursery service. Manning contributed a substantial number of stories to 1930s science-fiction magazines, particularly *Wonder Stories*, all of which featured realistic portrayals of space travel and concern for conservation and the value of individual life. He is best remembered, however, for a series of stories written in 1933 and published in 1975 as *The Man Who Awoke;* they describe a man who sleeps for thousands of years, periodically awakening to find humanity embroiled in one crisis after another. It aims particular criticism at the failure of the author's generation to be concerned about ecology.

E.L.D.

MAROONED (1969).
Directed by John Sturges; screenplay by Mayo Simon; adapted from the novel by Michael Caidin; photographed by Daniel Fapp. With Gregory Peck, Richard Crenna, David Janssen, James Franciscus, Gene Hackman, Lee Grant, Nancy Kovack, Mariette Hartley. 134 minutes. Color.

Three astronauts are stuck in orbit when their retro-rockets fail, and, despite a desperate attempt at a rescue mission, it becomes obvious that all three men cannot survive. Alternate scenes contrast the tension in space with the anxiety on Earth.

This film, produced in quasi-documentary style, was praised for its scientific accuracy and received an Academy Award for its SPECIAL EFFECTS, staged by Robbie Robertson. Its "heroism of science" theme is, unfortunately, marred by forced plotting, marginal character differentiation, and banal dialogue among the astronauts. Much of its fascination for audiences of the time was the recognition of the fragility of spaceflight, in which one mistake can be disastrous, as it was in the fiery deaths of astronauts in an Apollo craft in 1967 and in the Challenger tragedy in 1986.

D.P.V.

THE MARTIAN CHRONICLES (1980).
Directed by Michael Anderson; screenplay by Richard Matheson; adapted from the novel by Ray Bradbury; photographed by Ted Moore. With Rock Hudson, Darren McGavin, Fritz Weaver, Nicholas Hammond, Michael Anderson, Jr., Bernie Casey, Richard Masur, Roddy McDowall. 240 minutes. Color.

Considering the array of talent that went into this TV miniseries, *The Martian Chronicles* is an astonishing failure. Ray BRADBURY, who at one point approved of the script, later remarked that his idea of Hell was being forced to sit through the finished production. It is a lumbering effort, unable to capture the elusive mood of the

George R. R. Martin

book for more than a few seconds. Most scenes are clumsy and dull, and the acting is uninspired. The opening, which consists of several minutes of rockets blasting off (in which the wires are clearly visible) to electronic music epitomizes the series's flaws. It is worthy of note mainly as one of the very few Hollywood renditions of a major work of modern science fiction.

D.S.

MARTIN, GEORGE R. R. (1948–). American writer of short fiction, novels, and teleplays. Martin quickly earned a reputation as a stylish writer of science fiction and fantasy with philosophical overtones. Soon after the publication of his first story, "The Hero," in GALAXY in 1971, his work began to be nominated for awards: he won a Hugo in 1975 for "A Song for Lya" and two Hugos for "The Way of Cross and Dragon" and "Sandkings" (which also won a Nebula) in 1980.

In the 1980s he began to break out of the category with his novels *Fevre Dream* (1982), about vampires and a Mississippi riverboat, and *Armageddon Rag* (1983), an existential novel about the 1960s generation and its music that has achieved cult-classic status.

In 1986 Martin was named story editor for the new TWILIGHT ZONE television series, which produced his unusual teleplay "Once and Future King," a time travel tale about an unsuccessful Elvis Presley imitator who is thrown into the past and actually becomes Presley. After a varied career as a journalism instructor (with degrees from Northwestern University) and a chess tournament director, Martin now is a full-time free-lance writer who lives in Santa Fe, New Mexico.

OTHER WORKS: *A Song for Lya* (1976); *Dying of the Light* (1977); *Songs of Stars and Shadows* (1977); *New Voices in Science Fiction: Stories by Campbell Award Nominees* (editor, 1977); *Nightflyers* (1980); *Windhaven* (with Lisa Tuttle, 1981); *Tuf Voyaging* (1986); *Portraits of His Children* (collection, 1987).

H.L.P.

MASTER OF THE WORLD (1961). *Directed by William Witney; screenplay by Richard Matheson; adapted from the novels* Robur le conquérant *(1886) and* Maître du monde *(1904) by Jules Verne; photographed by Gilbert Warrenton; music by Les Baxter. With Vincent Price, Charles Bronson, Henry Hull, Mary Webster, David Frankham, Richard Harrison, Vito Scotti, Wally Campo, Ken Terrell. 104 minutes. Color.*

In a bid for respectability, American International Pictures produced this elaborate but underfinanced Jules VERNE epic. Ostensibly based on two lesser-known Verne novels, the screenplay by Richard Matheson is actually more of an aerial transposition of the Disney version of 20,000 LEAGUES UNDER THE SEA (1954), which itself was not especially true to its source.

In the nineteenth century militant pacifist Robur (Vincent PRICE) uses the *Albatross*, a gigantic flying machine, to bombard weapons of war from the air. His plan is thwarted by a heroic American (Charles Bronson); the *Albatross* crashes into the sea.

Aside from Price's effective performance, the major virtue of this film is the wittily designed *Albatross*, which resembles a dirigible supported by dozens of helicopter blades (much as it is described in the 1886 novel).

B.W.

——————— MATHEMATICS ———————
The most obvious inspiration science fiction takes from mathematics is in its play with dimensions: with the imaginary topology of hypothetical spaces. Such stories usually suppose our perceived world to be part of a four-dimensional structure, as indeed physicists since Albert Einstein have tended to believe that it is, but some of the earliest examples—notably the classic *Flatland* (1884) by mathematician Edwin A. ABBOTT—play with the idea of two-dimensional worlds. An early sequel to *Flatland* was *An Episode of Flatland* (1907) by C. H. Hinton, who wrote numerous speculative essays on multidimensional space. A more recent two-dimensional universe features in *The Planiverse* (1983) by A. K. Dewdney, and Hinton's work has been revived by the mathematician and SF writer Rudy RUCKER, who, in books such as *The Sex Sphere* (1983), has dabbled extensively in multidimensional fantasy.

Other fantasies which similarly borrow notions from

mathematicians include H. G. Wells's "The Plattner Story" (1896), Miles J. Breuer's "The Captured Cross-Section" (1929), Donald Wandrei's "Infinity Zero" (1936), and Robert A. Heinlein's story of a tesseract-shaped building, "And He Built a Crooked House . . ." (1940). The idea of a consciousness that can comprehend and master fourth-dimensional reality is presented in E. V. Odle's *The Clockwork Man* (1923) and Henry Kuttner's "Mimsy Were the Borogoves" (1943). Topological oddities such as the Möbius strip—a surface with only one side—are translated into SF imagery in stories such as Martin Gardner's "No-Sided Professor" (1946) and Homer C. Nearing's "The Hermeneutical Doughnut" (1954). The boom in information technology has already led to interest in the "inner space" of computer software—called cyberspace in William Gibson's *Neuromancer* (1984)—and this interest has begun to foster a more complex handling of such imaginary spaces.

Just as the Pythagoreans felt that the properties of numbers might somehow contain the secret of the universe, so some writers have been attracted by their magic and mystery; the most obvious recent example is Carl Sagan's *Contact* (1985), in which pi turns out to be a coded message from God. But this attitude is mocked in Douglas Adams's *Hitch-Hiker's Guide to the Galaxy* (1979), in which a godlike computer declares the answer to the riddle of the universe to be forty-two.

The curious vaults of the imagination required to grapple with mathematical puzzles, paradoxes, and ideas such as transfinite and imaginary numbers give mathematics its own aesthetics, which has spilled over into literary work since the days of Lewis Carroll (mathematician Charles Dodgson). The tricky subversion of common sense that plays a large part in *Through the Looking Glass* (1871) can be seen in such modern fantasies as James Blish's "FYI" (1953), Bertrand Russell's "The Vision of Professor Squarepunt" (1954), Norman Kagan's "The Mathenauts" (1964), Rudy Rucker's *White Light* (1980), and George Zebrowski's "Gödel's Doom" (1985). This unique spirit of serious playfulness also underlies Clifton Fadiman's two fine anthologies *Fantasia Mathematica* (1958) and *The Mathematical Magpie* (1962).

B.S.

to the protagonist through the pain it endures and repelled by the power of its anger.

Matheson's best-known work is *The Shrinking Man* (1956), a novel made famous by the 1957 film *The Incredible Shrinking Man*, which he also wrote. The story involves the plight of a man named Scott, who, after a series of unrelated accidents, begins to shrink irreversibly. The strength of the novel, and the subsequent film, is its description of the hero's ability to survive in his ever new and more difficult world. Objects and creatures once harmless become grotesque dangers, and things he used to take for granted become wondrous. Through it all Scott seeks to make sense of the increasing absurdity of his situation.

I Am Legend (1956) is a retelling of Bram Stoker's *Dracula*, utilizing the SF motif of the last man on Earth. A mysterious virus has struck the planet, leaving its victims either dead or transformed into vampires. Only the hero, Robert Neville, has avoided the plague. The novel details his isolation, the agony of needing other humans but finding none, and his fanatical quest to destroy the vampires, humanity's descendants. Neville's struggle, as *Homo sapiens* gives way to *Homo vampiris*, is a poignant one that revitalizes the old SF theme of the constant clash between the needs of the individual and those of the species. The two screenplays based on this novel (The Last Man on Earth, 1964, and The Omega Man, 1971) were not written by Matheson, and he was bitterly disappointed in both.

Most recently Matheson has primarily written screenplays and teleplays. His screenplays include *The Fall of the House of Usher* (1960), *Master of the World* (1961), *The Pit and the Pendulum* (1961), Somewhere in Time (1980), and The Twilight Zone (with others, 1983). He has contributed teleplays to such series as *The Twilight Zone*, Star Trek, *Night Gallery*, and *Kolchak: The Night Stalker*.

OTHER WORKS: *Born of Man and Woman* (collection, 1954; abridged as *Third from the Sun*, 1955); *The Shores of Space* (collection, 1957); *Shock!* (collection, 1961); *Shock II* (collection, 1964); *Shock III* (collection, 1966); *Shock Waves* (collection, 1970); *Shock 4* (collection, 1980).

S.H.G.

MATHESON, RICHARD [BURTON] (1926–   ).

American writer of novels, short fiction, and screenplays whose work is most frequently a mixture of horror and SF. Matheson's first short story, "Born of Man and Woman" (1950), immediately attracted attention for its use of SF elements in what is fundamentally a horror story. The plot concerns a monstrous mutant child who narrates the tale in a child's broken English and is apparently about to break free from the cycle of abuse it suffers at the hands of its parents. Readers are both drawn

MAY, JULIAN (1931–   ).

American writer, author of an ambitious tetralogy in the popular science-fantasy mode of the early 1980s. After gaining prominence in fandom and writing promising short fiction in her twenties, May produced nearly three hundred nonfiction, educational books, mostly for children, before returning to the writing of science fiction. Thus far the four volumes in her Saga of Pliocene Exile, beginning with *The Many-Colored Land* (1981), demonstrate a deep and enthusiastic erudition in mythology, parapsychology, and the religious implications of modern science. The first volume has received the greatest recognition, with a Hugo nomination, and the later volumes have been increasingly laden with plot details. But May continues to fill out her fictional vision and has gained notice as a mature writer with a wide following.

OTHER WORKS: *The Golden Torc* (1982); *The Nonborn King* (1983); *The Adversary* (1984); *A Pliocene Companion* (1984).

D.M.H.

THE MAZE (1953).   *Directed by William Cameron Menzies; screenplay by Daniel B. Ullman; adapted from the novel by Maurice Sandoz; photographed by Harry Neumann; music by Marlin Skiles. With Richard Carlson, Veronica Hurst, Katherine Emery, Michael Pate, Hillary Brooke, John Dodsworth, Lilian Bond, Robin Hughes. 80 minutes. Black and white.*

The plot of Maurice Sandoz's short novel *The Maze* is so bizarre it's only fitting that one edition was illustrated by Salvador Dalí; nonetheless, it was derived, albeit loosely, from a true story.

The movie is primarily a mystery, set mostly in an old Scottish castle and dealing with the secret kept for several generations by a proud family. After a surprisingly moving climax, it is revealed that the true laird of the castle is a 200-year-old man who was born as an enormous frog. The human embryo passes through several evolutionary stages during development, and the old gentleman, Sir Roger, never got beyond the amphibian stage.

William Cameron Menzies, one of the greatest art directors, not only designed but directed *The Maze*. Despite a low budget, this 3-D film has a distinctive look, but its design is less distinguished than that of Menzies's other films. The acting is adequate, but the movie tends to be talky. Many find it unintentionally hilarious, but for the sympathetic there are some moments of pathos.

B.W.

MEAD, [EDWARD] SHEPHERD (1914–   ). American writer. The author of *How to Succeed in Business without Really Trying* (1953), Mead has written three science-fiction novels along with six mainstream novels and a number of other books in the "How to Succeed . . ." vein. His SF effectively translates the humor and satire of this series to future worlds in which people manipulate and are manipulated. *The Big Ball of Wax: A Story of Tomorrow's Happy World* (1955) is his personal favorite. Set, as is Frederik Pohl's *The Space Merchants* (1952), in a world dominated by advertising, the novel describes how the discovery of XP, a way of effortlessly experiencing any action or object through electricity, brings on, in the words of Voltaire, "the best of all possible worlds."

OTHER WORKS: *The Magnificent MacInnes* (1949, in paperback as *The Sex Machine*); *The Carefully Constructed Rape of the World: A Novel about the Unspeakable* (1966).

S.H.G.

MEEK, S[TERNER] P[AUL] (1894–1972). American Army colonel, chemist, and writer who wrote children's literature, mainstream novels, two science-fiction novels, and more than fifty SF short stories (primarily for Amazing and *Astounding*, almost all between 1930 and 1932). Meek's short stories, most uncollected, frequently deal with war and the possibility of war, including the threat of Communism. Soviet agents are frequently the foils in his series of stories involving Dr. Bird, an agent of the Bureau of Standards, and his 1929 story "The Red Peril" describes Russian germ warfare in the year 1957.

Meek also wrote a number of comic stories that amount to the SF equivalent of tall tales, many of which are collected in *The Monkeys Have No Tails in Zamboanga* (1935). His two novels, *The Drums of Tapajos* (1961) and *Troyana* (1962), concern a lost tribe of the Brazilian jungle and first appeared as serials in *Amazing* in 1930 and 1932 respectively.

OTHER WORK: *The Arctic Bridge* (collection, 1944).

S.H.G.

MELIES, GEORGES (1861–1938).   French pioneer of the early cinema who is generally credited with making in 1902 the first significant science-fiction film, A Trip to the Moon *(Le Voyage dans la lune)*, based very loosely on novels by H. G. Wells and Jules Verne. Trained as a magician by the famous Robert-Houdin, Méliès assumed direction of Houdin's Paris theater in 1888 and turned it into one of the world's first public cinemas; by 1914 he had produced as many as 4000 films, acting on most as a one-man production company, always emphasizing the "magic" of cinema.

His movies pioneered the use of painted backdrops; speeded-up, reverse, and stop-action filming; the use of miniature models; and multiple exposures, what he called "little abracadabras." Films such as *Le Voyage dans la lune* and *A là Conquête du Pôle* (1912) showcase his skill as a set designer and the magic of early profilmic special effects and earned him the proud title of the "Jules Verne of the Cinema." Méliès was not only the father of the SF film but also probably its first economic casualty: he ended his life in poverty, spending some of his last years operating a small cigarette and candy stand at the Montparnasse railroad station in Paris. His work, however, influenced many later filmmakers, including Charlie Chaplin, D. W. Griffith, and Jean Cocteau.

B.L.

MENZIES, WILLIAM CAMERON (1896–1957).

American film director and production designer whose most important work was the landmark science-fiction film of the 1930s THINGS TO COME (1936). Known for his imaginative contributions to many prestigious Hollywood pictures, Menzies has design credits on films including such important movies as *Gone with the Wind* (1939) and both versions of *The Thief of Bagdad* (1924 and 1940). For his art direction Menzies won two Academy Awards, but as a director his career suffered from poor scripts and studio interference. In *Things to Come* Menzies's towering visuals and fine sense of pacing perfectly complement the epic scope and technocratic vision of H. G. Wells's screenplay. Similarly, the expressionistic, foreshortened sets for his minor masterpiece INVADERS FROM MARS (1953), which he both designed and directed, effectively express the young hero's sense of powerlessness and entrapment in a world of adults taken over by Martian invaders. Menzies's other SF films as director include *Chandu, the Magician* (1932) and THE MAZE (1953).

B.K.G.

MEREDITH, RICHARD C[ARLTON] (1937–1979).

American author, advertising manager, cartoonist, columnist, and newspaper editor. Meredith began publishing science fiction in the mid-1960s after two stints in the U.S. Army, and indeed his army experience reverberates throughout his fiction. His novels are peopled with soldiers and mercenaries, often injured or crippled, manipulated by their superiors, and struggling through high adventure to victory by virtue of courage and determination. In Meredith's second, and perhaps best, novel, *We All Died at Breakaway Station* (1969), the protagonist is a dead starship captain who has been restored to a kind of machinelike existence to make a final stand, with his walking wounded, at Breakaway Station. Meredith's more famous work is the Timeliner trilogy—*At the Narrow Passage* (1973), *No Brother, No Friend* (1976), and *Vestiges of Time* (1978)—about mercenaries crossing time and space to serve alien employers in their attempt to change Earth's past. *Run, Come See Jerusalem* (1976) describes parallel twenty-first centuries and demonstrates Meredith's knowledge of history and mastery of complex plotting.

OTHER WORKS: *The Sky Is Filled with Ships* (1969); *The Awakening* (1979).

S.E.G.

MERLE, ROBERT (1908–).

French writer of science fiction and mainstream fiction whose first book, *Week-end à Zuydcoote* (1948), a war novel, was awarded the prestigious Prix Goncourt and later filmed. A strong humanist streak pervades many of Merle's numerous novels in the SF genre. *Un Animal doué de raison* (1967, translated as *The Day of the Dolphin*) features communication between human and dolphin and examines the conflict between science and politics. *Malevil* (1972; joint winner of the John W. Campbell Award in 1974) is a bleak but striking postnuclear survival story; *Les Hommes protégés* (1974, translated as *The Virility Factor*) humorously details a feminist dystopia. Merle's latest nonrealistic novel is *Madrapour* (1976), about terrorism and the Hindu wheel of time.

M.J.

MERRIL, JUDITH (Pseudonym of Josephine Juliet Grossman) (1923–).

American writer, anthologist, and critic. The sum of Merril's impact on science fiction is far greater than her output in the field. As the editor of fourteen volumes of The Year's Greatest Science-Fiction and Fantasy, The Year's Best S-F, and The Best of Sci-Fi from 1960 to 1970, she called attention to some of the newest and most original writers in the genre. As book reviewer for THE MAGAZINE OF FANTASY AND SCIENCE FICTION and the compiler of *England Swings SF* (anthology, 1968; abridged as *The Space-Time Journal*, 1972), she introduced British NEW WAVE SF to American readers and enthusiastically lobbied for the same kind of literary experimentation among American SF writers. And as a writer of short stories and novels, she introduced a strong feminine perspective into a male-dominated genre.

Her first short story, "That Only a Mother" (1948), was voted into the *The Science Fiction Hall of Fame* (1970) by the SCIENCE FICTION WRITERS OF AMERICA and has been extensively anthologized. The story describes a future Earth plagued by radiation, where fathers have taken to killing their mutant babies in their cribs. While mother love seems to afford some of the children limited protection, the question remains: Will that love be enough to ensure humanity a future?

Shadow on the Hearth (1950) continued Merril's concern with radiation. The novel focuses on a suburban wife who must care for herself and her daughters after a nuclear attack while her husband remains trapped in the city. Her capable behavior in face of the danger posed by the radiation and by a "concerned" male neighbor far exceeds what would be expected of a pampered wife, and Merril used it to describe the hidden psychological strengths called up when women must protect their families. That same power to endure is evidenced in three novellas that have been collected as *Daughters of the Earth* (1968). Each explores an aspect of female strength: the family in "Daughters of the Earth" (1953), and motherhood in "Project Nursemaid" (1955) and "Homecalling" (1956).

Merril also collaborated with Cyril M. KORNBLUTH under the pseudonym Cyril Judd on two novels: *Gunner Cade*

(1952) and *Outpost Mars* (1952; revised as *Sin in Space,* 1961). Through her work as an anthologist and critic, she introduced new styles and voices into the genre. And while she has produced only a limited amount of fiction, her stories and novels serve as prime examples of how this new material can bring a dimension of art to good, readable SF.

OTHER WORKS: *The Tomorrow People* (1960); *Out of Bounds* (collection, 1960); *Survival Ship and Other Stories* (collection, 1974); *The Best of Judith Merril* (collection, 1976).

S.H.G.

MERRITT, A[BRAHAM] (1884–1943).

American reporter, editor, and author of fantastic science fiction and fantasy novels and short stories. Merritt's works are colorfully romantic, often taking place in mysterious and magical locales and involving strange, otherworldly forces. Their language is lush and evocative, in keeping with the transcendent experiences they describe. Although his subject matter is fantastic—soul-imprisoning powers and planet-destroying forces, for example—Merritt worked hard, with references to ancient beliefs and fragmentary scientific evidence, to make his events convincing.

Most of Merritt's writing was done while he was editor (or assistant editor) of the Hearst newspapers' magazine supplement, *The American Weekly.* He drew his settings from a youthful year in Mexico and Central America and from the speculative stories about romantic places found in his magazine. *The Moon Pool* (1919), his first novel, is set in a cavern beneath a remote South Pacific island; *The Metal Monster* (1920/1946) features a cave in Tibet; *The Ship of Ishtar* (1926), which was acclaimed in a 1938 survey as the most popular serial ever published in *Argosy,* takes place on the seas near Babylon; the ship of the title is reached by way of a carved stone block.

Merritt exercised the imagination of his readers over vast distances in time and place, creating weirdly appealing characters, such as a pillar of energy that offers horrid ecstasy, a sentient metal creature, a great carved face that weeps tears of gold, and a snake-mother who shields lovers. Each of his stories describes a battle of good and evil, of outsiders and insiders; the outcome often involves the world and the whole human race.

Merritt's poetic language and epic confrontations in remote places exerted their own strange influence over readers and writers, inspiring authors as various as Jack WILLIAMSON, Edmond HAMILTON, and Leigh BRACKETT to works of lavish romantic adventure. His characters often are stereotypes (the adventurous hero, the dark princess and the light princess), and his plots often are formulas, but his inventiveness and his language, as well as his sense of the epic, renew them. Reprintings of his novels

A. Merritt

as books made Merritt a fortune. Even though his stories and diction may be out of fashion today, his influence can still be detected in current adventure stories, and his works are still read.

OTHER WORKS: *Seven Footprints to Satan* (1927/ 1928; filmed in 1929); *The Face in the Abyss* (1931); *Dwellers in the Mirage* (1932); *Burn, Witch, Burn!* (1933); *Creep, Shadow!* (1935); *The Black Wheel* (unfinished, completed by Hannes Bok, 1947).

R.H.W.

METEOR (1979)

Directed by Ronald Neame; screenplay by Stanley Mann and Edmund H. North; photographed by Paul Lohmann; music by Laurence Rosenthal. With Sean Connery, Natalie Wood, Brian Keith, Karl Malden, Henry Fonda, Martin Landau, Trevor Howard, Richard Dysart, Joseph Campanella. 107 minutes. Color.

Striking the asteroid belt, a comet sends the large asteroid Orpheus and smaller fragments toward Earth; an international team of scientists tries to prevent the collision. Orbiting missiles of both the United States and the USSR demolish the asteroid, but fragments hit Siberia, Switzerland, Hong Kong, and Manhattan.

Arriving late in the disaster cycle, *Meteor,* despite its very good cast, seems cut-rate and trivial.

B.W.

On the set of *Metropolis*

METROPOLIS (Silent, 1927). *Directed by Fritz Lang; screenplay by Fritz Lang and Thea von Harbou; adapted from the novel by Thea von Harbou; photographed by Karl Freund and Gunther Rittau. With Brigitte Helm, Alfred Abel, Gustav Fröhlich, Rudolf Klein-Rogge, Fritz Rasp, Heinrich George. 120 minutes. Black and white.*

Metropolis (re-released in 1984 in a restored, color-tinted version with a modern rock-music score) is a visually overpowering film whose special effects, superior to those of the ambitious THINGS TO COME (1936), overshadow the flaws of an inferior screenplay. Based on a novel by director Fritz LANG's wife, Thea von Harbou (later a prominent Nazi), its Gothic underpinnings (including a villain named Rotwang) reflect a fear of technology, which is presented in disturbing but ultimately unrealistic terms: Lang's technologically advanced society would hardly require the kind of intensive physical labor the film portrays.

On a superficial level, the theme of *Metropolis* is class struggle. Humankind, in the city of the film's title, is divided between a leisure class that rules the city and an underclass that runs its vast machinery. The struggle itself is embodied in the film's upper-class hero, the son of the master of Metropolis. Made to feel guilty by his privileged position, he brings about a new understanding between the classes, expressed in the film's closing statement: "The mediator between the brain and muscle must be the Heart." The ending is arrived at with great skill and conviction and is, on the surface, quite convincing. But in reality the film's awesome sets and skillful special effects, as well as the talented cast, support a medieval morality tale and what is ultimately an unconvincing vision of the future. Lang himself, who never listed the

film among his favorites, found the reconciliation false.

The real heart of *Metropolis* is its superb design—of the city, the machines, and the underground hovels of the workers—as well as its atmosphere of gloom and oppression, and the expressive fear of technology that manages to stimulate more thought than is present in the script. In purely filmic terms it is a masterpiece.

No truly complete version of the film seems to exist. Aside from the new theatrical release, which runs 87 minutes, other versions exist on videocassette and range from 90 minutes to a reported 139. The American release of 1927 was supposedly cut by seven reels—nearly half the original film. *Metropolis* remains one of the most mutilated films from this period of German cinema, and the only way to get some idea of the complete continuity is through Harbou's novel, which was reprinted in 1975.
                                                                                                    G.Z.

MIGHTY JOE YOUNG (1949). *Directed by Ernest B. Schoedsack; screenplay by Ruth Rose; photographed by J. Roy Hunt; music by Roy Webb. With Robert Armstrong, Terry Moore, Ben Johnson, Frank McHugh, Douglas Fowley, Dennis Green, Paul Guilfoyle, Nestor Paiva, Regis Toomey, Primo Carnera. 94 minutes. Black and white, with tinted sequences.*

Sixteen years after the great success of KING KONG, the same producer-director-writer team made another giant-ape film, *Mighty Joe Young*. The Oscar-winning SPECIAL EFFECTS were again under the oversight of master stop-motion animator Willis O'BRIEN, who directed a team including Ray HARRYHAUSEN, Pete Peterson, and Marcel Delgado, who constructed models for *Kong*.

But unlike *Kong*, which borders on the horrific, *Mighty*

Joe Young is an action comedy, with a heroic ape more realistic in design and smaller than Kong. Some commentators have referred to *Mighty Joe Young* as a spoof of *King Kong*, but it's more realistically described as a comic variation on a theme.

Giant gorilla Joe, the pet of Terry Moore, is brought to Los Angeles by fast-talking Robert Armstrong. But the girl and the ape long for the jungle; tricked into getting drunk, Joe wrecks a nightclub, and while fleeing saves children in a burning orphanage. No explanation is offered for Joe's enormous size; he's just a "big monkey."

To audiences of the 1980s, accustomed to the superlative special effects of the last twenty years, the stop-motion in *Mighty Joe Young* may look unconvincing. But to audiences of its day, this was stark realism; children the world over were convinced gorillas really were that large. It is hard to imagine the child who, seeing this film at the right age, would not love the heroic giant gorilla. Although King Kong is the nightmare of adults, a primitive, unstoppable force governed by intense passion, Mighty Joe Young is the dream of childhood, a huge, gentle friend who loves us unquestioningly. The movie wasn't successful, however, and was the last major film for which O'Brien provided the effects.

B.W.

MILLER, P[ETER] SCHUYLER (1912–1974).

American technical writer, reviewer, author, educator, and amateur archaeologist. Born in Troy, New York, a descendant of Revolutionary War general Philip Schuyler, Miller worked for twenty-five years as editor and technical writer for Fischer Scientific Company in Pittsburgh, Pennsylvania. His greatest recognition came for his book reviews, starting in *Astounding* in 1948 and published as a regular column from 1951 until his death. His was the longest-running and most comprehensive review column in science fiction, characterized by optimism, evaluation of works at whatever level he found them, and the inclusion of short discussions of trends and historical perspectives. If he had any bias, it was for what readers in general preferred at the time—straightforward narrative built around original ideas, transparently told—but he was also capable of recognizing and appreciating literary artistry.

Miller did valuable work for a genre that received little critical attention during the years he wrote (what attention it did receive had little continuity). He was given a special Hugo Award in 1963. He also wrote SF, beginning in 1930: his three books are *Genus Homo* (1941/1950, with L. Sprague DE CAMP), *The Titan* (collection, 1952), and *Alicia in Blunderland* (1983), but he wrote many stories, including "As Never Was" (1944), which was voted one of the best stories of all time in a 1967 fanzine poll.

R.S.C.

MILLER, WALTER M[ICHAEL], JR. (1922–   ).

American engineer and writer whose relatively small amount of science fiction has had a profound effect on the genre. Miller has received two Hugo Awards for his fiction, the first in 1955 for his novelette "Darfsteller" (1955), about an actor who seizes one last chance to perform. In his world human performers have been replaced by a computer that controls life-sized puppets. The results are technically perfect presentations that lack the artistry of imperfect human interpreters. The hero manages to substitute himself for one of the mannequins, and as he plays his final role, readers are treated to a sensitive glimpse into the mind and heart of a person who needs to act.

"Darfsteller" was unusual for the 1950s in its portrayal of a complex character who is far more important to the story than the technology or speculative future that shapes the setting. And this attention to identifiably human and complex characters is a distinctive feature of most of Miller's short fiction during this period. In "Crucifixus Etiam" (1953) Miller explored self-sacrifice when a laborer loses his chance to return to Earth in order to ensure the terraforming of Mars. And in both "Anybody Else Like Me?" (1952) and "Blood Bank" (1952), Miller balanced the optimism often associated with evolution against ironic horror as new forms of humans appear. In the first story that horror is seen through the eyes of one of these new forms; in the second a "standard" human is forced to look at both humanity's future and its past when life is discovered on a remote planet called Earth.

Miller's finest work is, of course, his only novel: *A Canticle for Leibowitz* (1960). Actually a collection of three novellas originally published in shorter form in THE MAGAZINE OF FANTASY AND SCIENCE FICTION from 1955 to 1957, the novel has been translated into many foreign languages and sold more than a million copies in English alone. In 1961 it too was given a Hugo Award. Set on Earth some 600 years after a nuclear holocaust, the novel describes the inhabitants of a monastery founded by the twentieth-century physicist Isaac Edward Leibowitz and dedicated to preserving humanity's culture and civilization. Miller described the activities of the monastery during three significant periods in its 1200-year existence.

In the first period the crucial issue is simply the survival of the species: the inhabitants of the monastery must find a way to preserve their Order during an age of social and political chaos. The second period witnesses the reawakening of science, during which the Order must learn to balance its spiritual contentment with a growing secular curiosity over the nature of the world. Finally, in the third period, the Order must again plan for its preservation as the secular world hovers dangerously close to a second nuclear war. In each period Miller gives his readers fascinating characters who speculate on the nature of history, religion, and humanity and exemplify the entire range of human qualities, from the most selfless to the most egocentric, without becoming cardboard figures or shallow platforms for Miller's own words.

A Canticle for Leibowitz is one of those rare SF novels that actually deals sympathetically with formal religion, but it is not about religion. Its concern instead is the human condition, its nobility and its bestiality. Few SF novels before or since have handled this ambitious theme so well or so dramatically.

OTHER WORKS: *Conditionally Human* (collection, 1962); *The View from the Stars* (collection, 1965); *The Best of Walter M. Miller, Jr.* (collection, 1980); *The Science Fiction Stories of Walter M. Miller, Jr.* (collection, 1984).

S.H.G.

MITCHELL, EDWARD PAGE (1852–1927).
American journalist and short story writer whose stories, written between 1874 and 1886, pioneered such science-fiction themes as invisibility, matter transmission, multiple personality, humanoids, and space travel. Long forgotten, Mitchell's work was brought to notice with the collection *Crystal Man: Landmark Science Fiction* (1973), edited by Sam MOSKOWITZ.

J.H.

MITCHELL, JOHN A[MES] (1845–1918).
American editor and author of romances and science fiction. Mitchell's novel *The Last American* (1889) deals satirically with the discovery of the remnants of American civilization long after a climatic catastrophe. *Drowsy* (1917) features travel to the Moon and Mars. His short stories were collected in *Life's Fairy Tales* (1892) and *That First Affair* (1902).

J.H.

─────── MODERN PERIOD ───────
Although it is often convenient to divide history, literary and otherwise, into neat decades, what is generally considered the 1950s or post–Golden Age period in the literary history of science fiction encompassed an evolutionary phase that was born with the postwar world in 1945, came to full flower in the middle 1950s, and did not really conclude until about 1964, when Michael MOORCOCK took over the editorship of NEW WORLDS magazine and ushered in what was to become the NEW WAVE era. The modern period was one of major transformation for the genre. Indeed, in terms of form, style, thematic diversity, and mode of publication, it was an era that saw the birth of modern science fiction as we presently think of it.

The SF of the so-called GOLDEN AGE was dominantly a magazine genre; the mass-market paperback had not yet come into its own, and hardcover publication of SF was a relative rarity. The literary result of this publishing fact of life was that the short story and novelette were the dominant forms.

Astounding was clearly the best market and the most prestigious magazine of this period, and its editor, John W. CAMPBELL, Jr., was probably the most influential single figure that the genre had yet known. The writers he had discovered and developed—Robert A. HEINLEIN, Isaac ASIMOV, A. E. VAN VOGT, and others—stood at the top of the genre, and his vision of what SF should be was the literature's thematic leading edge. But by the mid-1950s, all that would change radically.

The history of SF is as much a history of editors as a history of writers, and if the Golden Age was the era of Campbell, the 1950s was the era of Anthony BOUCHER, H. L. GOLD, and Ian and Betty Ballantine. The first issue of THE MAGAZINE OF FANTASY AND SCIENCE FICTION was published in 1949, and in 1950 the first issue of GALAXY appeared. *The Magazine of Fantasy and Science Fiction* was edited by Anthony Boucher and J. Francis McCOMAS, and, from 1954 to 1958, by Boucher alone. *Galaxy* was edited by H. L. Gold from 1950 to 1961. In 1952 Ian Ballantine and his wife, Betty, founded Ballantine Books, the first major American mass-market paperback house, and from the outset, SF was a mainstay of their list under the editorship of Betty Ballantine herself.

Genre SF had evolved in the pages of the adventure pulps, magazines packaged to appeal to boys and male adolescents, and this early commercial product usually wrapped straightforward action-adventure plots in futuristic trappings. Campbell had succeeded in shifting the emphasis from the scientific McGuffin as an excuse for the action-adventure plot line as a vehicle for scientific speculation, but even *Astounding* was still packaged to appeal to much the same adolescent readership, and the "idea" or "science fictional concept" was the center of the ideal *Astounding* story. Campbell saw himself as more the scientific visionary than the litterateur, saw science fiction as something of a transliterary endeavor, and paid little heed to developing such "mainstream" literary virtues as elegance of style, thematic subtlety, complex moral dialectic, or depth of characterization. His genre SF was the inheritor of Jules VERNE's technological optimism not H. G. WELLS's Swiftian pessimism.

But Boucher set out to midwife the birth of a science fiction that could stand in good literary company, or at least build and retain a sophisticated adult readership. *The Magazine of Fantasy and Science Fiction* was accordingly packaged to appeal to more upscale demographics. Boucher encouraged good writing for its own sake. Characterization became a matter of serious concern, and the story itself, no longer a mere vehicle for presenting scientific and technological extrapolation, emerged as its own raison d'être.

If Boucher brought a new awareness of literary values to SF, H. L. Gold brought a new sense of science. For the contributors to Campbell's *Astounding*, the *science* in science fiction meant the hard sciences—physics, astronomy, engineering, marvelous inventions—but *Galaxy* under Gold quickly became a market for a more Wellsian SF, thematically dominated by the soft sciences—psychology, anthropology, sociology, political satire, and speculation. By broadening the concept of "science," *Galaxy* expanded the literary definition of the genre itself. In the world at large, the Cold War was under way, McCarthyism and anti-Communist paranoia were in full flower, and the fear of nuclear Armageddon was a cultural obsession. *Galaxy* both reflected and commented on these currents, becoming a magazine enthusiastically receptive to a new socially and politically engaged SF virtually unknown outside the work of Wells until then.

The Magazine of Fantasy and Science Fiction and *Galaxy* complemented each other, for Gold did not shun literate writing and subtle characterization and Boucher was receptive to SF grounded in the soft sciences. Because stories generated by the soft sciences require greater skill at characterization and finer prose with which to convey subtleties and ambiguities, writers more concerned with style and characterization tended toward Wellsian thematic material rather than Vernean concerns. In the greatest explosion of new talent the field had yet seen, many of the rising stars of the 1950s—Theodore Sturgeon, Philip K. Dick, Damon Knight, Frederik Pohl, Algis Budrys, Alfred Bester, Philip José Farmer, Robert Sheckley, Cyril M. Kornbluth, Fritz Leiber, Clifford Simak, Walter M. Miller, Jr., Edgar Pangborn, and a host of others—contributed to both magazines.

Although *Astounding* continued to flourish and Campbell continued to discover major new writers well into the 1960s, the aesthetic center of SF had shifted. Then, too, the new generation of SF writers was the first to develop into SF *novelists*, an evolution made possible by the rise of the mass-market paperback and the Ballantine SF line. It is interesting that the regular publication of SF novels and the mass-market paperback began more or less simultaneously in 1952 and evolved together. Before the decade was out, the paperback was well on its way to dominating the American publishing scene, as publishers such as Ace and Berkley, and to a lesser extent Signet and Bantam, followed Ballantine's lead and established regular SF lines. The existence of a healthy paperback rights market for SF even made hardcover publication more viable.

But while this new regular market for SF novels was a necessary publishing precondition for the transfor-

mation of SF into a genre dominated by books and the novel, the evolution going on in the pages of *Galaxy* and *The Magazine of Fantasy and Science Fiction* was a necessary literary precondition for what might fairly be called the first full flowering of the SF novel. Technological wonders, concept-centered plots, and scientific extrapolations might be enough to carry short stories and novelettes, but successful novels require a different structure, which in turn demands a more story-centered SF built around the interaction of believable characters of some complexity with the mutating environment. This thematic shift was almost precisely what Gold and Boucher had fostered in their magazines.

Dozens, indeed perhaps scores, of the SF novels that make up the present historical canon were produced during this period, and many of the dominant SF novelists of the 1960s, 1970s, and even 1980s published their early novels at this time. Frederik Pohl and Cyril M. Kornbluth collaborated to produce social and political satires such as *The Space Merchants* (1952/1953), which still stands as the major exemplar of this subgenre. Kornbluth, writing solo, produced political-action novels such as *Not This August* (1955) and *The Syndic* (1953), which mirror the social paranoia of the day. Frank Herbert wrote the sophisticated psychological thriller *The Dragon in the Sea* (1956), and Frank Robinson wrote *The Power* (1956) in a similar vein. Algis Budrys published formally sophisticated psychological novels such as *Who?* (1955/1958) and *Rogue Moon* (1960). Isaac Asimov introduced the mystery structure to the novel of technological speculation and produced *The Caves of Steel* (1953/1954) and *The Naked Sun* (1956/1957), displaying a new novelistic maturity that transcended both sets of genre conventions.

Arthur C. Clarke married hard science and mysticism in *Childhood's End* (1953). Philip José Farmer eroticized the SF novel, while Fritz Leiber was one of the first to write a kind of proto–science fantasy. Edgar Pangborn penned the moodily poetic *A Mirror for Observers* (1954). Philip K. Dick transformed the metaphysical SF novel into something with intimate immediacy. Even Theodore Sturgeon, whose métier was mainly the short story, published two classic novels during this period, *The Dreaming Jewels* (1950) and *More Than Human* (1953). It was in this period too that Clifford Simak began to write his still unique SF pastorales. So dominant had the novel form become that even Ray Bradbury, almost exclusively a short story writer throughout his career, made his reputation with *The Martian Chronicles* (1950), a collection of thinly connected short stories set on Mars, which his publisher felt compelled to package as a novel.

The growth of the novel did not preclude the maintenance of the short story and the novelette as viable forms during this period. With $1500 still the average advance for an SF novel, most SF novelists were forced to remain regular contributors to the magazines, and their mastery of the novelette and novella forms was enhanced by their experience writing novels. The magazines were still also very much the training ground for future novelists. As a result, many of the works being published in book form—Sturgeon's *More Than Human,* Miller's *A Canticle for Leibowitz* (1955/1960), James E. GUNN's *The Immortals* (1962), Asimov's *I, Robot* (1950), James BLISH's *A Case of Conscience* (1953/1958), and others—were pulled together from novelette cycles or expanded from novellas that saw first publication in the magazines. If this process tended to vitiate their formal coherence, it also greatly enhanced the quality of magazine serials.

The continued contribution to magazines resulted in the proliferation of reprint anthologies, single-author collections, and the year's best books, which until the mid-1960s selected the best stories almost exclusively from what had been published in magazines. Judith MERRIL began publishing the first year's best short story collection while reviewing books for *The Magazine of Fantasy and Science Fiction;* she thus became the first critic in the field's history to act as a mover and shaker in the sphere of book publishing.

So, far from having its vitality destroyed, short SF benefited by the rise of the SF novel, with the same authors working in both forms, and the two forms constantly cross-fertilizing.

In a commercial sense, magazine SF underwent what briefly seemed a publishing renaissance, at least in terms of the profusion of new magazines (*Worlds Beyond, Science Fiction Adventures, Space Stories, Fantastic Universe, Infinity, Imagination, Future, Fantastic, If,* and so on). But most of these had little staying power. There were just too many of them competing for the same rack space and readership. When the market suddenly expanded, the overall quality of magazine fiction could not be maintained, and the SF magazine boom quickly became a crash. By 1964 the only surviving American SF magazines were *Astounding* (rechristened ANALOG); *The Magazine of Fantasy and Science Fiction; Galaxy* and its sister magazine, *If;* and *Amazing* and *Fantastic,* the Ziff-Davis twins.

By this time the preeminence of the SF novel was firmly established, and in the comparatively brief period between 1960 and 1965, another wave of major writers-to-be saw their first publication. These were authors whose introduction to SF had been as much through novels as through magazine fiction. Roger ZELAZNY, Samuel R. DELANY, Thomas M. DISCH, Joanna RUSS, Alexei PANSHIN, Charles PLATT, Keith ROBERTS, Fred SABERHAGEN, Barry N. MALZBERG, Larry NIVEN, Gregory BENFORD, Piers ANTHONY, Keith LAUMER, R. A. LAFFERTY, Ursula K. LE GUIN, Norman SPINRAD, and a host of others published their first SF during these five years.

For this generation of writers, the postwar transformation was a given. The thematic broadening catalyzed

by *The Magazine of Fantasy and Science Fiction* and *Galaxy* had been fully absorbed. If a writer achieved success in the magazines, publication of his or her work in novel form was a rather swift and natural inevitability. The magazine apprenticeships of new writers were generally brief and consciously regarded as such. Some writers, Delany among them, even published novels before their first short stories saw print. The work of more senior writers—such as Harlan ELLISON, Michael Moorcock, Robert SILVERBERG, Brian W. ALDISS, John BRUNNER, and J. G. BALLARD—evolved suddenly and significantly during this period as well, influenced perhaps by the large influx of new talent.

The SF genre thus entered the 1960s as a literature dominated by the novel, already broadening itself formally, stylistically, and thematically in a manner that foreshadowed the New Wave of the middle to late 1960s, and already beginning to reach out to a wider and more mature readership, laying the early groundwork for the SF "publishing boom" of the mid-1970s. If, as Isaac Asimov once wryly observed, "The real Golden Age of science fiction is twelve," then the immediate post–Golden Age period of the 1950s era marked, at the very least, the genre's passage through adolescence on its way to maturity.

N.S.

THE MONOLITH MONSTERS (1957). *Directed by John Sherwood; screenplay by Norman Jolley and Robert M. Fresco; photographed by Ellis W. Carter; music supervised by Joseph Gershenson. With Grant Williams, Lola Albright, Les Tremayne. 77 minutes. Black and white.*

Fragments of a meteorite when exposed to water grow into towers of stone, leaching silicon from human beings and thereby petrifying them. When it rains, the stones threaten cataclysm to a desert town, crashing to the ground, growing again, descending an incline toward the town.

This modest but efficient movie has one of the most unusual science-fiction menaces in movie history. The towers of stone and the small-town atmosphere are well realized; the film's major virtue is the imaginative if gimmicky extrapolation of the growth of crystals, genuine SF.

B.W.

———— MONSTER MOVIES ————

Until the 1950s the majority of monster movies were fantasy horror rather than science-fiction horror, with Universal's FRANKENSTEIN series among the exceptions. Even Universal blithely tossed the SF Frankenstein monster into several films with the fantastic Wolf Man and Dracula. It was all the same to them, and probably to

Prehistoric one-on-one from *The Lost World* (1960)

audiences as well.

The proliferation of monsters in film from the 1950s on can probably be explained in one word: teenagers. It wasn't until that decade that teenagers and children had enough money to become a discrete film audience, demanding and getting movies directed at them. Science-fiction and horror movies (especially combinations of the two genres) have been children's favorites since the early 1950s; they probably took the place of the fairy tales and legends that had amused children of previous generations. Television undoubtedly played a part as well, but its effect was more subtle: it kept adults out of movie theaters and provided fodder for children while steering them toward the fantastic as a favorite genre.

Because of the blurring of distinctions between SF and fantasy, it is difficult to pinpoint the first true SF monster movie. Some of Georges MÉLIÈS's films certainly had monsters in them, but most of his trick films—even those with an SF basis—were fantasies. Several films in the silent era featured aliens, but most, as *A Message from Mars* (1913, 1921), *Radio Mania* (1923), and others, depicted more or less human beings. The odd ape-man did pop up during the 1920s, as in *Go and Get It* (1920), *A Blind Bargain* (1922), *The Wizard* (1927), and others, but he was fairly tame as far as monsters go; *The Mysterious Island* (1929) featured a sea monster, but, except for dinosaurs, as in THE LOST WORLD (1925), silent films were generally short on monsters.

Not even the popularity of KING KONG (1933), replete with dinosaurs and a big ape, kicked up much interest in films about misshapen creatures. Britain's one effort along these lines, *Secret of the Loch* (1934), is tame and nearly forgotten. ISLAND OF LOST SOULS (1933) is crawling with hairy horrors that had once been animals, but its focus is really elsewhere. *The Mad Monster* (1942)

imitated *The Wolf Man* (1941), using a scientific gimmick to come up with its wolf monster. But that's all it was—a gimmick. Even when dinosaurs turned up before the 1950s, they were only incidental, as in the prehistoric melodrama of ONE MILLION B.C. (1940) or the standard adventure of *Unknown Island* (1948).

The fact is that, with few exceptions, none of these was really a monster movie: a movie whose focus was the monstrous menace, no matter where it came from or what its nature. A monster movie is really like SF itself: easy to recognize, hard to define.

The first true SF monster movie is THE THING (*From Another World*) (1951). Although the invader in this film is an intelligent alien, he (or it) is a literally bloodthirsty monster, killing and maiming as it goes. By contrast, the creature in THE MAN FROM PLANET X of the same year is just an average guy. However, despite the substantial box-office success of *The Thing*, it didn't generate any immediate followers. But *King Kong*, when it was reissued in 1952, certainly did; because of its renewed popularity, the old classic was directly responsible for the proliferation of monster movies over the next twenty years, in both the United States and Japan.

THE BEAST FROM 20,000 FATHOMS (1953), a moody piece about a dinosaur that saunters up Wall Street, munching on policemen as it goes, was inventively animated by Ray HARRYHAUSEN. A substantial success, it was immediately imitated by its distributor, Warner Bros.; THEM! (1954) was the first and best of the giant bug films of the 1950s, a whole new subcategory of monster movies.

After *Them!*, all manner of insects (and other things) were enlarged: spiders, mantises, scorpions, grasshoppers, leeches, crabs, caterpillars, a bird, people, an octopus, shrews, crystals—they all played a part in the wonderworld of 1950s monsters. Most of these films

Big bug from *Them!* (1954)

were routine or worse, but a surprising number were good.

TARANTULA (1955) is intelligently developed, with mostly good effects, a strong sense of locale, and genuinely scary stuff. THE MONSTER THAT CHALLENGED THE WORLD (1957) features colossal caterpillarlike snails living in the Salton Sea and is graced with an above-average script and an outstanding, full-sized monster. THE MONOLITH MONSTERS (1957) has an interesting menace: towering, crashing pillars of stone. Even ATTACK OF THE CRAB MONSTERS (1957), despite its absurd-looking monsters and a hurried production, displays unusual ideas and a well-structured script.

Of course, the majority of the giant animal films were of fairly low quality. Among the worst was *The Giant Claw* (1957); although the actors were competent, the effects were substandard, especially the astonishing claw itself: a giant bird from outer space, the elaborate puppet resembles nothing so much as cartoon character Beaky Buzzard. It's hard to choose between *Monster from Green Hell* (1957) and *Beginning of the End* (1957) for last-place honors; the former is mostly stock footage plus some big wasps in Africa; the latter gave audiences a dwindling horde of grasshoppers attacking Chicago.

In Japan GODZILLA and his kin created their own movie subgenre. Men in rubber suits galumphed over miniatures of Tokyo, Osaka, and other Japanese cities. As these films continued, they became bizarrely comic; the fact that there were so many of them seems to have generated a kind of affection, and if a monster hung around long enough—as Godzilla, Rodan, Mothra, Gamera, and others did—it became a hero. Almost all these films saw release in the United States, either theatrically or directly to television. The market was clearly

hungry for monsters.

At the same time audiences were treated to a series of films in which scientists turn themselves into various monsters. These transformations, as in *The Neanderthal Man* (1953) and MONSTER ON THE CAMPUS (1958), sometimes are transitory; other times, as in THE FLY (1958), the change is tragically permanent. The transformations usually result when individuals mess around with science, but sometimes, as in *The Creeping Unknown* (1955) and *The H-Man* (1958), the new monster is an innocent bystander. Once, in the unique THE MAZE (1953), the person was born as a large frog; he was also the laird of a Scottish estate, probably one of the few giant frogs to hold that position.

Another cinematic trend in the 1950s—which overlaps the man-into-monster subgenre—was the man-in-a-rubber-suit monster. The best of these was CREATURE FROM THE BLACK LAGOON (1954), in which the frog-faced Gill-Man was introduced to a nonplussed world. Two sequels and several imitations followed, including *Monster of Piedras Blancas* (1958), the fantasy *She-Creature* (1956), and others. Universal-International was convinced that each of its SF films needed a monster, so they were shoehorned in even when inappropriate, as in THIS ISLAND EARTH (1955), with its impressive mutant. Some kind of apotheosis was reached with *Sting of Death* (1967), in which the menace is half man, half jellyfish.

Although most movie monsters have been animals, there were a few attempts to portray plant beasts; THE DAY OF THE TRIFFIDS (1963) is the best known. *Navy versus the Night Monsters* (1966), from a Murray LEINSTER novel, gave us omnivorous trees, and the ineffable Tabanga in *From Hell It Came* (1957) is a sneering tree with a man inside, somehow created by the most popular source of monsters, radiation. By contrast, the mere woman-eating tree of *Womaneater* (1959) is a trifle.

Paul Blaisdell, an SF illustrator, became one of the decade's most prominent monster makers, having designed (and usually played) creatures in BEAST WITH A MILLION EYES, *The She-Creature*, IT CONQUERED THE WORLD (a particularly memorable job), THE DAY THE WORLD ENDED (all 1956), *Invasion of the Saucermen*, *From Hell It Came* (both 1957), and IT! THE TERROR FROM BEYOND SPACE (1958), among others. His monsters unexpectedly became popular in Japan in the late 1980s; alas, Blaisdell had died several years earlier.

As the 1950s wore on into the 1960s, monsters per se declined somewhat, suffering from the overexposure that usually accompanies popularity. There were still some interestingly eccentric specimens to be found, though. The monsters in *Fiend without a Face* (1959) are ghastly, hilarious, expertly animated brains that crawl and leap across the screen. *The Killer Shrews* (1959) were impersonated by greyhounds, of all things, in furry coats; the title creature of *The Tingler* (1959) is a cock-

Alien monster from *This Island Earth* (1954)

be frightened, and everyday dangers, even exotic animals, have become commonplace, lacking the power to shock or even scare. Each generation demands an escalation of horror in its monsters; the 1930s and 1940s were content with wolf men, walking mummies, and the relatively normal-looking Frankenstein monster. Audiences of the 1950s wanted more outré menaces and got them in the form of giant bugs and ugly aliens. The 1960s turned back to fantasy, embracing Christopher Lee's Dracula and the wild, silly beasts of Japan. But in the wake of *The Exorcist* (1973), filmgoers demanded bigger horrors, and filmmakers obliged with increasingly graphic violence and outrageously vicious monsters. Each generation wrings its hands over the excesses of youth, and in time even the children of today, who delight in monsters eviscerating hapless victims, will be appalled by the horrors *their* children happily embrace. And the monsters will be there: the mind breeds monsters, and the young love them.

B.W.

roachlike embodiment of pure fear, which scientist Vincent Price accidentally looses in a movie theater; a whole planet full of incredible thingies appear in ANGRY RED PLANET (1960), with a tall, spindly bat-rat-spider being the most memorable.

By 1962, however, monsters as such had become scarce again. Those few that did appear in the 1960s were either distorted human beings, as in *The Awful Dr. Orloff* (1962), *The Manster* (1962), and so on, or in the Japanese *kaiju eiga* films, which proliferated in that decade. Alfred Hitchcock's THE BIRDS (1963) inspired several films in which normal-sized creatures rebel against humankind, including *Willard* (1971), about hungry rats, its sequel, *Ben* (1972), and *Frogs* (1972). *Night of the Lepus* (1972) gave us slightly larger monsters, specifically horse-sized, wheezing bunny rabbits.

Monster movies were given new impetus in the 1970s, continuing into the 1980s. The first of this generation was Steven SPIELBERG's *Jaws* (1975) which engendered not only more shark movies but a number of films about especially large or voracious animals, including bears and barracuda. Although these movies inevitably grew absurd, there were a few highlights; two were written by John Sayles: Joe DANTE's *Piranha* (1978) and Lewis Teague's *Alligator* (1981). The second revitalizing film was ALIEN (1979), which was responsible not only for its sequel, *Aliens* (1986), but for a horde of other vicious, human-eating monsters, some ingeniously contrived, several from Italy. Even *Night of the Living Dead* (1968), barely SF, spawned sequels and imitators galore, many of which had SF origins for their walking, cannibalistic corpses.

And they continue to come, from outer space, from under the sea, from within ourselves. Monsters clearly have great appeal; for whatever reason, people like to

MONSTER ON THE CAMPUS (1958).   *Directed by Jack Arnold; screenplay by David Duncan; photographed by Russell Metty; music by Joseph Gershenson. With Arthur Franz, Joanna Moore, Judson Pratt, Helen Westcott, Troy Donahue, Whit Bissell, Alexander Lockwood. 77 minutes. Black and white. Alternate title:* Stranger on the Campus.

In this variation on the Jekyll-Hyde theme, Arthur Franz plays a paleontologist who experiments on a recently dead coelacanth that has become irradiated. Blood from the fish accidentally falls into his pipe; when he smokes the pipe, Franz is transformed into a murderous ape-man. Eventually he realizes that he is the campus killer and arranges to be shot dead by police.

Director Jack Arnold approached this material with seriousness, but because of a deficient script and a conventional story, *Monster* is distinctly below the level of his other science-fiction films, which deal with intelligence, not brute savagery. There's little logic in the transformations here (the ape-man looks different each time), and the scientist's sacrifice at the end is meaningless. Franz is good, and the film has a studio gloss, but it's second rate nevertheless.

B.W.

THE MONSTER THAT CHALLENGED THE WORLD (1957).   *Directed by Arnold Laven; screenplay by Patricia Fielder; photographed by Lester White; music by Heinz Roemheld. With Tim Holt, Audrey Dalton, Hans Conried, Harlan Warde, Casey Adams (Max Showalter), Mimi Gibson, Jody McCrea. 83 minutes. Black and white.*

An underwater earthquake in California's Salton Sea

releases the eggs of a species of giant, carnivorous snail. One of the best of the giant monster films, though rarely mentioned, *The Monster That Challenged the World* benefits from an unusual cast, good use of locations, and an excellent monster, a full-sized and realistically designed mechanical prop. Special effects were by Augie Lohman and August S. Hayworth; director Arnold Laven got the maximum suspense from Patricia Fielder's well-structured but conventionally romantic script.

B.W.

———————— MONSTERS ————————

A monster is an abnormality (scientifically, teratology), either human or animal, usually large, gross, or frightening and generally all three, but the word also has been applied to creatures that may be normal in their customary circumstances but out of their own environment are unfamiliar and seem monstrous. The theme of monsters in science fiction clearly overlaps that of aliens, and indeed it is only during the last fifty years that a distinction has arisen in popular SF. Once it was taken for granted that the alien and the monstrous were synonymous. Other worlds were populated either by horrid creatures or by humans like ourselves (even if, as in Edgar Rice BURROUGHS's Martian tales, they lay eggs).

H. G. WELLS created the archetype of the monstrous alien in *The War of the Worlds* (1897), and it was still effective four decades later when Orson Welles panicked America with a radio adaptation of Wells's novel (1938). *The War of the Worlds* surely influenced the evolution in pulp SF during the 1920s and 1930s of what came to be known as the bug-eyed monster—an epithet possibly inspired by Charles Willard Diffin's *Brood of the Dark Moon* (1931). The pages of early pulp SF magazines were filled with monstrous aliens resembling everything from insects to reptiles, and others less describable.

The emergence of sympathetically treated aliens in such works as Stanley G. WEINBAUM's "A Martian Odyssey" and Raymond Z. GALLUN's "Old Faithful" (both 1934) led to a divergence between the themes of aliens and monsters. John W. CAMPBELL's "Who Goes There?" (1938) was the last great classic in which humanity is faced with a monstrous but clearly intelligent alien being. In A. E. VAN VOGT's "Black Destroyer" and "Discord in Scarlet" (both 1939), the monsters represent devolution from the sort of intelligence that creates culture or civilization; they survive only by cunning. In "Discord in Scarlet," Ixtl has the nasty habit of laying its eggs in human hosts. A similar alien formed the basis for Ridley Scott's *Alien* (1979). Whether or not inspired by "Discord in Scarlet," *Alien* adopted the classic image of the modern SF monster: malevolent, virtually indestructible, and without any redeeming qualities that might arouse the sympathies of the audience. One can see the same pattern in such SF novels of parasitism as Robert A.

HEINLEIN's *The Puppet Masters* (1951) and John CHRISTOPHER's *The Possessors* (1964).

Such creatures represent the fear of the unknown, but monsters also represent the fear of the *known*. Both the giant ants of Gordon Douglass's film THEM! (1954) and the giant reptile of Inoshiro Honda's film GODZILLA (1956) are punishments visited on humankind for its use of nuclear weapons. Similarly, the grisly creature of John Frankenheimer's film *Prophecy* (1979) is born of environmental pollution. Although this sort of monster appears in some SF novels, such as Theodore L. THOMAS and Kate WILHELM's *The Clone* (1965), it is more typical of the cinema—where it was so prevalent that for a time the term *monster movie* became synonymous with *SF film*. Japan produced an entire menagerie of monsters to compete with Godzilla in sillier and sillier sequels; in Hollywood the giant creature cycle was reduced to absurdity in William Claxton's *Night of the Lepus* (1972), which tried to keep a straight face while menacing the world with giant bunny rabbits.

Psychological horror is the justification of another species of monster represented in both films and books. Perhaps this source goes back to the Golem and Mary Wollstonecraft SHELLEY's *Frankenstein* (1818). Whatever else they represent, the Golem and Frankenstein's monster epitomize the perversion of the normal. The same can be said of Richard Matheson's monstrous child in "Born of Man and Woman" (1950) and the malignant telekinetic child who terrorizes adults in Jerome BIXBY's "It's a *Good* Life" (1953). "Monsters of the id," which menace the heroes of Fred McLeod Wilcox's FORBIDDEN PLANET (film, 1956), serve an allegorical function as well as evoking terror. A less believable example of the monster as allegory is David CRONENBERG's *The Brood* (film, 1979), in which the murderous creatures are explained as the literal offspring of a mental patient's rage. Science fiction shades off into supernatural horror in such rationalizations of traditional werewolf, vampire, and zombie tales as Jack WILLIAMSON's *Darker Than You Think* (1940), Richard MATHESON's *I Am Legend* (1954), and George A. Romero's *Night of the Living Dead* (film, 1968).

Monstrousness as the hidden but normal state of affairs has been a favorite theme of mainstream fiction since at least the time of Franz Kafka's "Metamorphosis" (1916), with its man become insect. During the NEW WAVE period of SF, such polemical stories as Harlan ELLISON's "The Prowler in the City at the Edge of the World" (1967), with its afterword stating that *"you* are the monsters,"were popular. Although that vogue has faded, there has (incredibly) been a revival in some quarters of the Hollywood film monster in print, for instance, Peter Tremayne's *The Ants Are Coming!* (1979).

J.J.P.

SEE ALSO: MONSTER MOVIES.

MONTELEONE, THOMAS F. (1946–).

American author. Monteleone, who has a master's degree in English from the University of Maryland, after a short career of story writing got his break in science fiction by writing the first, and most extensively promoted, of the Laser novels (Harlequin Romance's ill-fated venture into standardized SF books): *Seeds of Change* (1975) was a routine dystopia. More typical of Monteleone's work were the early novels *The Time Connection* (1976) and *The Secret Sea* (1979), well-written SF adventure stories, and *The Time-Swept City* (1977), a unified collection of stories dealing with a future Chicago. Monteleone's work has focused more on the social sciences and character than on the physical sciences and hard SF, but in recent years he has turned toward horror and dark fantasy, as well as working with film and television. He has collaborated on two adventure novels with David Bischoff, *Day of the Dragonstar* (1983) and *Night of the Dragonstar* (1985), which deal with the discovery of an interstellar zoo.

OTHER WORKS: *Guardians* (1980); *Night Things* (1980); *Dark Stars and Other Illuminations* (collection, 1981); *Ozymandias* (1981); *Night Train* (1984); *Wraith Board* (with David Bischoff, 1985).

H.L.P.

MOORCOCK, MICHAEL [JOHN] (1939–).

British writer and editor (NEW WORLDS), a major catalyst of the NEW WAVE in science fiction yet also, in his early years, a self-admitted hack writer of heroic fantasy, which remains his most popular work. Moorcock is very much an urban, and urbane, writer whose desire to put style ahead of what the genre conventionally has called substance has marked all his writing. He has lived by his writing and editing since leaving school at age fifteen, and he exerted his greatest influence on the genre during his editorship of *New Worlds* in the 1960s, introducing experiments in style and content that shook a basically conservative genre to its foundations. *New Worlds*'s impact far exceeded its small circulation, and it is still being felt.

In his own writing Moorcock consistently explores a multiverse of flux and impending chaos in various series that reflect back on one another so that his whole oeuvre is one vast mosaic. Beginning with Elric, a heroic fantasy figure who does not quite fit the heroic mold, Moorcock has continued to create characters who both display and mock genre conventions. His success at parody marks him as a particularly modernist SF writer. Parody, combined with ironic wit, is not only central to the Cornelius Chronicles, the Dancers at the End of Time trilogy, the Bastable books, and many other works but also plays across the bleak Nebula Award–winning "Behold the Man" (1966/1969) and such recent works as *Gloriana* (1979), *Byzantium Endures* (1980), and the darkly vi-

Michael Moorcock

sionary *Warhound and the World's Pain* (1981). Moorcock continued to explore his favorite themes of temporal, spatial, and spiritual flux in *The Laughter of Carthage* (1984) and *The City in the Autumn Stars* (1986).

NOTABLE OTHER WORKS: *The Sundered Worlds* (1965); *The Fireclown* (1965); *The Twilight Man* (1966); *The Wrecks of Time* (1967); *The Final Programme* (1968); *The Ice Schooner* (1969); *The Time Dweller* (1969); *A Cure for Cancer* (1971); *The War Lord of the Air* (1971); *An Alien Heat* (1972); *Breakfast in the Ruins* (1972); *The English Assassin* (1972); *The Land Leviathan* (1974); *The Hollow Lands* (1974); *The Adventures of Una Persson and Catherine Cornelius in the Twentieth Century* (1976); *The Lives and Times of Jerry Cornelius* (1976); *The End of All Songs* (1976); *Legends from the End of Time* (1976); *The Condition of Muzak* (1977); *The Transformation of Miss Mavis Ming* (1977); *Dying for Tomorrow* (1978); *The Golden Barge* (1980); *My Experiences in the Third World War* (1980); *The Entropy Tango: A Comic Romance* (1981).

D.B.

MOORE, C[ATHERINE] L[UCILLE] (1911–1987).

American writer of fantasy and science fiction; active in the GOLDEN AGE in *Weird Tales, Astounding*, and other pulp magazines. In 1940 Moore married writer Henry KUTTNER; thereafter they collaborated to some degree on everything they produced.

Moore's first sale was also her first submission: "Shambleau" (*Weird Tales*, November 1933) is a tale of erotic, psychic vampirism with a space opera background and the first of eleven stories about Northwest Smith, a Byronic space outlaw with a propensity for encountering eldrith horrors as he wanders the Solar

C. L. Moore

(1949/1954); *No Boundaries* (collection, 1962). Collaborations as Lewis Padgett: *Tomorrow and Tomorrow and the Fairy Chessmen* (collection, 1946–1947/1951); *Mutant* (1946–1953/1953); *A Gnome There Was* (collection, 1950); *Well of the Worlds* (1952/1953); *Line to Tomorrow* (1954). Anonymous collaborations with Henry Kuttner: *The Dark World* (1946/1966); *Valley of the Flame* (1946/1964); *Fury* (1947/1950); *The Mask of Circe* (1948/1971); *The Time Axis* (1949/1965).

R.F.L.

MOORE, WARD (1903–1978).

American writer best known to readers of science fiction for his whimsical and satiric novel *Greener Than You Think* (1947) and his imaginative and elegiac alternate-world novel *Bring the Jubilee* (1953). Moore began his career as a mainstream writer and novelist, and despite occasional short stories and two later novels, he never again came close to the peak he achieved with *Bring the Jubilee*. Moore found in SF a useful medium for his idiosyncratic political satire. In *Greener Than You Think*, for example, he caricatured American inventiveness, the greed of American entrepreneurs, and the fecklessness of politicians and government bureaucracy. The values behind Moore's satire seem to be a curious blend of liberalism and conservatism: his work combines a love of individualism and honesty with a distrust of centralized government and a strong nostalgia for the rural and small-town America of the world before and during World War I—a culture and style of life that began to disappear rapidly after World War II.

In *Greener Than You Think* an enterprising salesman uses a formula developed by an eccentric small-town inventor in an effort to make the grass grow on barren land. The innovation succeeds all too well, producing an uncontrolled growth that eventually takes over the West Coast, despite the efforts of foolish scientists and benighted bureaucrats to stop it. In a later novel, *Joyleg* (1962), written in collaboration with Avram Davidson, a Tennessee mountaineer has apparently discovered the secret of eternal life in a special kind of moonshine, much to the consternation of the authorities. In his final novel, *Caduceus Wild* (1978; a revised version of a 1959 serial written with Robert Bradford), Moore described an Orwellian dystopia ruled by a medical hierarchy. Like many American imitations of ORWELL's work, however, *Caduceus Wild* ends on a note of optimism when the protagonist rebels successfully.

None of Moore's other novels has the power or the poignancy of *Bring the Jubilee*, which describes the world of 1951 in an alternate history in which the South has won the battle of Gettysburg and ultimately the Civil War. The South remains agrarian and militarily strong, while the impoverished North is just emerging from the horse-and-buggy era. However, Moore's narrator, a

System. A female counterpart of sorts appeared a year later in "Black God's Kiss," the first of six stories of Jirel of Joiry, a passionate and indomitable woman warrior. These and the four nonseries stories Moore published before 1940 showed the influence of H. P. LOVECRAFT and A. MERRITT. The later Kuttner-Moore collaborations that appeared under such pseudonyms as Lewis Padgett and Lawrence O'Donnell are generally more "modern" and urban and less "gothic." When many of John W. CAMPBELL's regular writers were drawn away by the war effort, Kuttner and Moore supplied large quantities of SF to *Astounding*, including the collaborative Baldy series (collected as *Mutant*, by Lewis Padgett, 1953) and the Moore solos *Judgment Night* (1943/1952), "No Woman Born" (1944), and "Vintage Season" (1946, as Lawrence O'Donnell).

After World War II the couple continued to write SF, fantasy, and mysteries, and at the time of Kuttner's sudden death in 1958 they were starting to write for television. Moore continued to work at Warner Bros. until she remarried in 1964. Although there was no new SF or fantasy by Moore since 1957 (when *Doomsday Morning* was published), her reputation in the field has not diminished.

OTHER WORKS: *Shambleau and Others* (collection, 1953); *Northwest of Earth* (collection, 1954); *The Best of C. L. Moore* (collection, 1975). With Henry Kuttner: *Earth's Last Citadel* (1943/1964); *Beyond Earth's Gates*

luckless historian who travels back in time and inadvertently changes history to the world we know, can never reconcile himself to a more progressive twentieth-century America. In this novel Moore managed to express his personal nostalgia for the era of Teddy Roosevelt and William Howard Taft in an authentic work of art. Moreover, although the alternate-world concept was invented by Murray LEINSTER and had been employed to humorous effect by L. Sprague DE CAMP and Fletcher PRATT, *Bring the Jubilee* was probably the first serious novel to use the concept effectively. Along with Philip K. DICK's *The Man in the High Castle* (1962), it remains one of the best novels of its type.

E.L.C.

MORE, THOMAS [SIR] (1478–1535).

British writer, lawyer, and prominent politician (for three years lord chancellor), a disciple of the Dutch scholar Erasmus, and a humanist scholar and author whose writing and thinking had a lasting influence on the humanist tradition; in the history of science fiction, notable for his *Utopia* (1516), which served, along with Plato's *The Republic*, as a model for later utopian writing—and has the distinction of providing the name by which such writing is categorized.

Written in Latin, Book 2 of More's *Utopia* describes an ideal island society in the New World characterized by citizen participation in government, religious tolerance, and the lack of private ownership and a money economy. Book 1, written after Book 2, criticizes social conditions in contemporary England.

A servant and friend of Henry VIII, More refused to take the oath on the Act of Supremacy that made Henry head of the Church; for this he was executed.

J.H.

MOREY, LEO (?–?).

American artist and illustrator born in Peru. Morey, who earned a degree in engineering from Louisiana State University, succeeded Frank R. PAUL as the cover artist for AMAZING STORIES when it changed hands in 1929; until 1938, when the magazine was sold again to Ziff-Davis, he painted almost all the covers and drew many of the interior illustrations as well. Morey also created the covers for the first editions of Donald WOLLHEIM's earliest SF magazines, *Cosmic Stories* and *Stirring Science Stories* in 1941, produced covers for *Future* and *Science Fiction Quarterly* as late as 1951, and he was doing interior illustrations in 1957.

Morey followed Paul's pattern of using fantastic aliens and futuristic machines as a means of genre identification. He was better at depicting people than Paul and perhaps a better artist, but not as good with machines and future cities and never earned Paul's reputation.

J.E.G.

MORK AND MINDY (1978–1982).

Directed by Howard Storm, Joel Zwick, and others; written by David Misch, April Kelly, Dale McRaven, and others; music by Perry Brodkin, Jr. With Robin Williams, Pam Dawber, Conrad Janis, Elizabeth Kerr, Jeffrey Jacquet, Ralph James. 30 minutes weekly. Color.

Essentially a remake of MY FAVORITE MARTIAN (1963–1966), *Mork and Mindy* was significantly more successful than its predecessor because of the inspired improvisational comedy of Robin Williams, who plays Mork, the alien from the planet Ork, sent by its leader, Orson, to whom he periodically reports on his study of life on primitive Earth.

Mork, after landing in his spaceship (resembling a giant egg) near Boulder, Colorado, is befriended by a pretty young woman named Mindy (Pam Dawber) who agrees to take him in to live as a platonic companion (in the final year they get married), to keep his presence secret, and to help him gather information about Earth.

The series originated as an episode of the TV series *Happy Days*, in which the teenage hero, Richie Cunningham, wakes up to find that his attempted kidnapping by an alien is all a dream. It became a spin-off the following fall.

The premise of the program, like that of *My Favorite Martian*, allowed it to inspect human foibles and follies through the alien viewpoint of the naive and nutty Mork. It did not push its luck and settled for being a pleasant and intellectually undemanding situation comedy.

J.E.G.

MORRESSY, JOHN (1930–).

American college professor of English and writer. Morressy has balanced careers in the academic community—since 1968 he has been a professor and writer in residence at Franklin Pierce College in New Hampshire—and the writing of fiction. He published seventeen books between 1966 and 1983, thirteen of them science-fiction novels. After two thoughtful mainstream novels about teaching, he turned to SF as "the most interesting, enjoyable, and creative field open to a writer today and the one that may, in time, prove to be the most significant." Morressy's SF novels, beginning with *Starbrat* (1972), are set in the same general future history, a galactic human state racked by the decline of technology and government, in keeping with Morressy's belief that "the human race, in future ages, will behave much as it always has in the past." He has written three SF novels for children: *The Humans of Ziax II* (1974), *The Windows of Forever* (1975), and *The Drought on Ziax II* (1978); and he has published three tongue-in-cheek sword and sorcery novels: *Ironbrand* (1980), *Graymantle* (1981), and *Kingsbane* (1982).

OTHER WORKS: *Nail Down the Stars* (1973); *A Long Communion* (1974); *Under a Calculating Star* (1975);

A Law for the Stars (1976); *The Extraterritorial* (1977); *Frostworld and Dreamfire* (1977); *The Mansions of Space* (1983).

S.E.G.

MORRILL, ROWENA: SEE ROWENA

MORROW, JAMES K. (1947–   ). American author. Morrow, a native Pennsylvanian, earned a bachelor's degree from the University of Pennsylvania and a master's degree in teaching from Harvard University. He worked as a teacher, an instructional materials specialist, a contributing editor of *Media and Methods,* a science writer for *A Teacher's Guide to NOVA,* and an author of children's books before turning to science fiction with *The Wine of Violence* in 1981, which *The American Book Review* called "the best SF novel published in English in the last ten years." His *The Continent of Lies* (1984) also was well received, but his best book to date may be *This Is the Way the World Ends* (1986). Its Vonnegutian wit and social satire made it a Nebula Award finalist and a runner-up for the John W. Campbell Award for the best SF novel of the year. It tells the story of a group of Americans shanghaied from a world that has destroyed itself in a nuclear exchange and taken to Antarctica by submarine to stand trial before all the people who never had a chance to be born. The novel, like Morrow's other books, illustrates the author's greater interest in parable and myth than in reasoned extrapolations. Morrow, who lives in State College, Pennsylvania, also has developed computer games and board games and written screenplays and articles.

J.E.G.

MOSKOWITZ, SAM[UEL] (1920–   ). American historian, editor, critic, and fan. Moskowitz, until his retirement editor of a frozen-food industry magazine, is a leading expert on science fiction's pulp magazine origins and the author or editor of sixty hardcover and paperback books. A recipient of the Pilgrim Award from the Science Fiction Research Association (1981) and a member of the Science Fiction Hall of Fame (1972), he was originally best known in the genre for *The Immortal Storm* (1954), a history of the fan movement from its beginnings up to World War II; *Explorers of the Infinite* (1963) and *Seekers of Tomorrow* (1966), both collections of author profiles; *Science Fiction by Gaslight* (1968); *The Man Who Called Himself Poe* (1969); *Under the Moons of Mars* (1970); *Strange Horizons* (1976), another collection of author profiles; *Science Fiction in Old San Francisco* (1980); and *A. Merritt: Reflections in the Moon Pool* (1985).

Moskowitz was consulting editor for *The Pulps* (1970),

Sam Moskowitz

an anthology of pulp magazine fiction, and general editor of the two important Hyperion Press Science Fiction Classics reprint series (1974, 1976). Among the dozens of other anthologies he has edited are *Masterpieces of Science Fiction* (1967); *Ghostly by Gaslight* (with Alden H. Norton, 1970); *When Women Rule* (1972); and *Out of the Storm,* by William Hope HODGSON, with a 25,000-word critical biography by Moskowitz (1975).

He also organized the first World Science Fiction Convention (1939), taught the first college-level course in science fiction (1953–1955), and edited both Hugo GERNSBACK's last magazine, *Science Fiction Plus* (1952–1954) and a brief revival of *Weird Tales* (1973–74).

E.L.D.

MOTHRA (Japanese: Mosura) (1961). *Directed by Inoshiro Honda; screenplay by Shinichi Sekizawa; photographed by Hajime Koizumi; music by Yuji Kosei. With Franky Sakai, Hiroshi Koizumi, Ken Uehara, Jerry Ito, Kyoko Kagawa, Takashi Shimura, Yumi Itoh, Imo Itoh. 101 minutes. Color.*

Japanese science-fiction films have detractors and supporters in the West, but even those who deplore most of them find virtues in *Mothra,* often praising its fairy-tale-like story; thematically, it is more sophisticated than most such films. The major drawback for many is that the film is inescapably about a colossal moth.

When six-inch-tall twin girls are kidnapped from Beiru Island by a greedy promoter, Mothra comes to the rescue, first as a caterpillar, then, after cocooning on Tokyo Tower, as a gigantic moth.

Mothra is an attractive creature, resembling a cross between a Japanese lantern and a piñata. Director Inoshiro Honda added some effective poetic touches, and the film, largely intended for children, is smoothly made, with some surprising touches of satire. Mothra (or its offspring) returned in several subsequent films.

B.W.

MUNDY, TALBOT (Pseudonym of William Lancaster Gribbon) (1879–1940)

British-born writer who became an American citizen and lived the later years of his life in New York, Maine, California, and Florida. The black sheep of a respectable English middle-class family, Mundy engaged in various confidence schemes in India and Africa before moving to the United States and becoming an adventure writer in the tradition of H. Rider HAGGARD and Rudyard KIPLING.

Mundy is of interest to historians of science fiction chiefly for his Jimgrim stories, which describe the adventures of a hero who has worked in the secret service of various countries. This precursor of James Bond, who usually appeared in *Adventure*, frequently thwarted villains who sought power through innovative weapons. Perhaps the best novel in the series is *Jimgrim* (1930/1931), in which James Schuyler Grim and his companions match wits against the sinister Dorje, an Oriental menace in the Fu Manchu tradition who aims at world domination while developing nuclear weapons in a hidden valley in central Asia.

Mundy also has a niche in the history of modern fantasy because of his masterpiece *Om: The Secret of Ahbor Valley* (1924), a novel expressing his mysticism through an adventurer's quest for enlightenment in a valley in the southern Himalayas. This tale includes episodes of what appear to be clairvoyance and telepathy, and its overtones of Buddhist mysticism were inspired by Mundy's association with theosophist groups.

E.L.C.

MUSIC AND MUSIC VIDEO

Just over ten years ago, film scholar Vivian Sobchack justifiably observed that "SF music has no characteristic sound." "What is notable about most SF film music," she explained, "is its lack of notability, its absence of unique characteristics which separate it from music in other films." Curiously enough, after ten years in which the science-fiction film has experienced nothing short of spectacular commercial success, Sobchack's comment remains accurate. However, the *status* of music in SF film has changed dramatically, and the relationship between SF and popular music has been radically transformed by the rise of music videos featuring SF themes and icons. That *Godzilla—1985* actually had a "love theme" which was released as a music video, and that a video by the Hooters was titled "All You Zombies" give some indication of the impact of the music video market on SF film and SF on music videos. And it is surely significant that the most technologically sophisticated and expensive SF short film yet made, *Captain Eo* (1986), shown exclusively at Epcot Center and Disneyland, features rock star Michael Jackson and scenes sure to please an audience groomed by MTV. Jackson's appearance in *Captain Eo* follows his own use of werewolf and zombie formulas in the fourteen-minute *Thriller*, the first rock video to be almost a minimovie; its great success seems to have codified what had been a longstanding but oblique relationship between popular music and SF-fantasy.

Signs of this new relationship are hard to miss. Rock stars such as David Bowie, Gene Simmons, Tina Turner, Grace Jones, and Sting not only appear in but have become familiar presences in SF films. At the same time the imagery of SF has become an intrinsic part of the music video formula, with postapocalyptic, space, and mad scientist iconography particularly evident. In some ways this development can be seen as a natural extension to video of the long-standing use of SF-fantasy in rock album cover art.

Perhaps the most striking sign of this new relationship is the phenomenon of Max Headroom, the computer-generated talking-head persona that became one of the TV sensations of 1986. Headroom is himself a patently science-fictional character, introduced in a TV short series as a human investigative reporter whose consciousness was imprinted in a video computer at the moment of his murder. His existence, then, is part human, part computer, and his quirky speech and facial tics place him in a long line of anthropomorphized computers and robots. That such a computer-generated animated figure would find celebrity status as "host" of a music video show offers strong evidence of the degree to which rock music and SF have coalesced on television.

Moreover, the list of directors known for their work in both SF film and rock video already includes such celebrated figures as John Sayles, Tobe Hooper, and Russell Mulcahy. This development is understandable but hard to chronicle. What is certain is that audience demographics have determined a new relationship between SF and rock music. One clear sign of the extent of this influence comes from Daniel Pearl, director of photography on the recent remake of INVADERS FROM MARS (1986), who explained that director Tobe Hooper asked him to "put as much of a rock video look" into the filming as possible, "to make it attractive to the main theatre-going audience." Another sign was the decision by Universal Studios to overrule Ridley Scott's choice of a symphonic score for *Legend* (1986), replacing the original score by Jerry Goldsmith with electronic music by the rock group Tangerine Dream. As Randall Larson reported in *Cinefantastique* (July 1986), this decision to make the music more "accessible" to a teenage audience simply followed "the current trend in making movies more like music videos in order to attract young people and tie-in with record sales."

It is important to note, however, that the new ties between media go beyond adding SF-fantasy props, sets, and costumes to music videos or adding a rock sound track to SF-fantasy films (such as that for the 1984 reissue of *Metropolis*). The most striking visual aspect of both SF film and music video comes not from what is shown but from the techniques of showing, a celebration of up-to-the-moment film and video technology that is itself futuristic. Music videos and contemporary SF-fantasy films more and more define state-of-the-art technology, constantly pioneering new visual-camera effects. As a result many music videos now evoke SF-fantasy associations purely through cinematographic or video aspects—camerawork, fades, dissolves, digital and computer-generated effects, and so on. In one sense the visual content of many music videos is nothing but special effects, and these effects may derive from or resonate with those that have increasingly become the distinguishing characteristic of SF-fantasy film.

Because there is little or no time in a music video for explanation, the viewer's experience of the video will usually have to do much more with the experience of fantasy than with that of SF—establishing a "fantasy of" the video or film, as opposed to fantasy elements depicted *in* the two media. The result is that both music videos and SF-fantasy films not only are *about* experiments and other "new" ideas but have themselves become heavy-handedly experimental and "new" in look.

The place of rock or popular music in SF film history is much easier to determine than is the role of SF-fantasy icons, images, and cinematographic or video techniques in rock videos. Apart from an occasional oddity, such as the SF musical Just Imagine (1930), SF film was not much concerned with music of any kind before the 1950s. However, two of the best-known SF films made in the 1950s were also noteworthy for their musical scores: Bernard Herrmann experimented with electronic music in The Day the Earth Stood Still (1951), and Louis and Bebe Barron's "Electronic Tonalities" score for Forbidden Planet (1956) contributed greatly to that film's success. Another 1950s SF film with a noteworthy musical tie-in was the Ealing Studios production of The Man in the White Suit (1952), whose distinctive laboratory sounds—described by Bill Warren as "queeps and quirps and weetles and blorks"—provided the background beat for a popular single, "The Man in the White Suit Samba." Much more characteristic of 1950s SF films was the at-

tempt to market a tie-in popular song for exploitation sources, as was true of the Phil Harris novelty piece "The Thing," conceived as part of the publicity for the Howard Hawks film of the same title. Indeed, three different novelty songs were suggested as part of the exploitation strategy for It Came from Outer Space (1953).

The Blob (1958), one of the first SF films to star teenagers, featured a title song written by Burt Bacharach that became an American top-forty hit. The point of all this is simply to note that in the 1950s and early 1960s SF and popular music intersected almost exclusively in novelty songs of the "Flying Purple People Eater" ilk.

A number of developments in the 1960s began to change this relationship. Hollywood's belated discovery of the teen market, coupled with the rise of rock-and-roll idols such as Elvis Presley, led to the creation of a subgenre of "teenpics" in which musical performances were framed by the script. American International's "beach party" films, among many others, codified a new movie formula that embraced contemporary music and music stars. One of the ubiquitous "party" films, *Pajama Party* (1964), features Tommy Kirk as a teenage Martian whose invasion plans are sidetracked when he falls in love with Annette Funicello. In 1965 Bert I. Gordon very loosely based *Village of the Giants* on H. G. Wells's "The Food of the Gods," interlacing his teenage adventure with music by the Beau Brummels, Freddy Cannon, and Mike Clifford. (Gordon's second go at the Wells story, *The Food of the Gods* in 1976, is little better.) The year 1965 also saw *Dr. Goldfoot and the Bikini Machine*, starring Frankie Avalon; its sequel, *Dr. Goldfoot and the Girl Bombs* (1966), starred another teen idol, Fabian. Most of these teenpic specials employed SF elements only as an excuse for their real format, dubbed the "songalog" by *Variety*.

Even less interested in any of the sustained concerns of SF were versions of the songalog by supergroups such as the Beatles, who produced a variant of this formula in loosely organized theme movies held together primarily by performances of the group's music. These films feature broadly caricatured plots, and SF soon supplied some of the most accessible targets for performance, such as the figure of the mad scientist. The late 1960s' "ideological overlay" of reality-altering drugs and increased interest in mysticism seemed to push these films further toward SF-fantasy motifs and icons, with the result being releases such as *Help!* (1965) and *Yellow Submarine* (1968). One additional cultural overlay was the revolutionary or countercultural blending of music and ideology, leading to films such as *Easy Rider* (1969) or, more significantly for SF, *Privilege* (1967), directed by British Oscar winner Peter Watkins (*The War Game*, 1966). *Privilege* stars rock singer Paul Jones as a teen idol exploited by government and the Church to manipulate his youthful fans. The following year saw this arrangement reversed in WILD IN THE STREETS. The story of a youth revolution that makes a rock singer president, *Wild in the Streets* effectively brought together youth, rock star power, and a near-future political SF story.

Of course, 1968 also saw the release of 2001: A SPACE ODYSSEY, the film in which Stanley KUBRICK linked SF imagery with music (although classical) to an extent never before approached. Indeed, Kubrick must loom large in any explanation of the relationship between SF images and music. His DR. STRANGELOVE (1964) had emphasized two scenes through the discordance between image and popular lyric: the first is a midair refueling of a bomber to the sound of Otis Redding's "Try a Little Tenderness"; the second is the closing sequence of mushrooming clouds to the sound of "We'll Meet Again." And Kubrick's A CLOCKWORK ORANGE (1971) stunningly realized Anthony Burgess's vision of a dystopian future in which music is the inspiration for violence.

The 1970s saw the first "rock opera," *Tommy*, made by the Who in 1975. Ken Russell's flamboyant directing and appearances by rock stars such as Elton John, Tina Turner, and Eric Clapton make this visually striking fantasy a clear forerunner of the contemporary rock video. And even more influential may have been Jim Sharman's THE ROCKY HORROR PICTURE SHOW (1975), whose combination of androgynous sexual innuendo, punk look, outrageous situations, and rock music now seems a clear preview of things to come. The unlikely metamorphosis of Roger CORMAN's low-budget legend THE LITTLE SHOP OF HORRORS (1960), into first a Broadway musical and then a big-budget movie (in 1986), suggests that the SF-rock connection has also had a major influence on film musicals.

Other 1970s films are noteworthy for their likely visual and thematic influences: A BOY AND HIS DOG (1975) seems to have originated the Felliniesque postapocalyptic punk look that has become a visual cliché in contemporary videos, and Nicolas Roeg's stylishly directed THE MAN WHO FELL TO EARTH (1976), which stars David Bowie, seems to have left a legacy of videos of radical displacement, whether through space or time.

Just as film directors began featuring musical elements in popular films, rock musicians in the late 1960s and early 1970s turned more and more to filmlike special effects and themes to dramatize their concerts. Alice Cooper, Ted Nugent, David Bowie, and groups such as Kiss and the Who became known for the technology of their concerts as much as for the music, with light shows and pyrotechnics ever more elaborate. More often than not, the look of these concerts became vaguely science fictional–fantastic, with SF costumes and iconography offering some thin thematic rationale for the special effects. In something of a reversal of the 1950s practice of tie-in records to advertise movies, the rock group Kiss even went so far as to make an SF film, *KISS Meets the Phantom* (1978), to promote their albums and concerts.

The 1980s have seen a dramatic proliferation of SF films closely tied to rock music and rock stars, and of music videos that employ SF-fantasy iconography. One of the first films to exploit this increasingly involved relationship was the animated *Heavy Metal* (1981). The Disney Studios production of *TRON* (1982) was disappointing as SF film, but its pioneering use of computer animation combined with a rock sound track performed by Journey seems to have spawned a large subgenre of computer-animated music videos. *Streets of Fire* (1984) was both praised and condemned as "the first MTV movie." Films such as BLADE RUNNER (1982) and LIQUID SKY (1982) further intensified the rough association of punk and new wave imagery with rock and electronic music, as did REPO MAN in 1984. And the quirky satire *The Adventures of Buckaroo Banzai* (1984) is an almost encyclopedic summary of SF themes and video formats.

Rock groups now associated with science-fictional or futuristic looks include Devo, the B-52s, and the Talking Heads, while individual performers such as Grace Jones, David Bowie, Sting, Tina Turner, and Kate Bush often build their videos around SF images. Although in most cases these videos appropriate only the look of SF and none of its epistemology—and are undoubtedly influenced primarily by the norms and psychology of TV commercials and the art and pace of comic books more than by any traditions of SF film—they do constitute a new articulation of SF (although in it no distinction between SF and fantasy remains). (Cartoonlike films such as *Barbarella*, 1968, and television series such as *The Avengers, The Man from U.N.C.L.E.*, and *Batman* may also be precursors of this new medium or genre.) Employing the latest techniques in special effects, and even intensifying the preoccupation with the technology of image making and images that has been identified as a central feature in the look of SF film, these videos may strike the SF purist as a distillation of all that has been *wrong* with SF film. They do, however, seem to be shaping a new audience receptive to SF movies closely linked to the look and sound of MTV.

It is hardly accidental that the most successful SF film of 1985, BACK TO THE FUTURE, featured not only a rock sound track but a rock-and-roll performance. MAD MAX: *Beyond Thunderdome* (1985) featured Tina Turner as its female lead and gave rise to the hit song and video "We Don't Need Another Hero." Dan O'Bannon's *Return of the Living Dead* (1985) intensified the clearly developing associations between punk and zombie iconography seen in videos such as Billy Idol's "Dancing with Myself" and used punk rock groups exclusively for its sound track. Influential video director Russell Mulcahy has turned from making award-winning rock videos for Duran Duran, Elton John, and Culture Club to making

SF-fantasy films (*Razorback*, 1984, and *Highlander*, 1986). Moreover, even when little or no direct connection exists between rock videos and an SF-fantasy film, it seems clear that the look of SF film has been inexorably altered by videos. Movies as different as BRAZIL (1986), *Big Trouble in Little China* (1986), and *Labyrinth* (1986) simply look like videos and display the loosely bound, frenetically paced structure now so clearly associated with rock video. Whether this new linkage will mark a significant turn in the evolution of SF film remains to be seen, but its current importance is indisputable.

B.L.

MY FAVORITE MARTIAN (1963–1966).
Directed by Oscar Randolph, Sheldon Leonard, John Erman, and others; written by Ben Gershman, John L. Greene, Bill Freedman, and others; music by George Greeley. With Ray Walston, Bill Bixby, Pamela Britton, Alan Hewitt, J. Pat O'Malley. 107 30-minute episodes. Black and white (first two seasons), color (the last season).

A weekly situation comedy contrasting the innocence of a stranded Martian with the primitive folkways of Earth, *My Favorite Martian* allowed for broad satire and gentle comedy. Generally popular in its time, the series began with reporter Tim O'Hara (Bill Bixby) rescuing the pilot of a crashed UFO (Ray Walston), an anthropologist whose specialty is Earth, and passing him off as his Uncle Martin, all the while trying to write the story. The chief source of complication is keeping Uncle Martin's identity secret and his powers (invisibility, telepathy), along with his antennae, under his hat.

J.E.G.

THE MYSTERIANS (*Chikyu Boeigun*, 1957).
Directed by Inoshiro Honda; screenplay by Takeshi Kimura; photographed by Hajime Koizumi; music by Akira Ifukube. With Kenji Sahara, Yumi Shirakawa, Momoko Kochi, Akihiko Hirata, Takashi Shimura, Susumu Fujita, Hisaya Ito. 87 minutes. Color.

This colorful, elaborate epic of alien invasion was one of the first Japanese science-fiction films that didn't center on a city-smashing monster. The Mysterians, aliens from the destroyed world now making up the asteroid belt, land on Earth and demand women, kidnapping some when their demands aren't met. The inevitable battle ensues.

In special effects, as in their art, the Japanese emphasize elements other than realism, and this film, like others of its ilk, may look peculiar to Western eyes; on its own terms, however, *The Mysterians* is entertaining battle-happy SF.

B.W.

MYSTERIOUS ISLAND (Silent, with sound effects and music, 1929).
Directed by Lucien Hubbard, Maurice Tourneur, and Benjamin Christiansen; screenplay by Lucien Hubbard; photographed by Percy Hilburn; music by Martin Broones and Arthur Lange. With Lionel Barrymore, Pauline Starke, Karl Dane, Warner Oland, Jane Daly, Lloyd Hughes, Montague Love, Harry Gribbon, Snitz Edwards. 95 minutes. Color.

MYSTERIOUS ISLAND (1961).
Directed by Cy Endfield; screenplay by John Prebble, Daniel Ullman, and Crane Wilbur; photographed by Wilkie Cooper; music by Bernard Herrmann. With Michael Craig, Joan Greenwood, Herbert Lom, Gary Merrill, Michael Callan, Percy Herbert, Beth Rogan, Dan Jackson. 101 minutes. Color.

There have been more movies (at least nine versions or variations) of Jules VERNE's sequel to *20,000 Leagues under the Sea* (1870) than there have been of the original novel. These movies followed the novel with varying degrees of accuracy, from the reportedly faithful 1941 Soviet version to the 1929 MGM adaptation, which bears no discernible relation to the novel. Several years in production, this 1929 film changed directors and casts; the sets were destroyed in a hurricane in 1927, and many scenes had to be reshot.

Lionel Barrymore plays Prince Dakkar (Captain Nemo's real name), inventor of a submarine who lives on the island of Hetvia; when it is conquered by a tyrant, Dakkar goes undersea to carry on the resistance. He encounters a tribe of blood-loving undersea dwarfs (all of whom bear an uncanny resemblance to Donald Duck), as well as a sea dragon. The film is in two-strip Technicolor and has both sound effects and music.

The 1961 version, produced by Charles H. Schneer with effects by Ray HARRYHAUSEN, followed the novel with fair accuracy, adding two young women, also shipwrecked on the island. The story was warped to allow for the inclusion of giant animals, the result of Nemo's experiments. Verne's Civil War setting was retained, with Union prisoners escaping from a Confederate camp in a balloon that is blown off course to the South Pacific. As in the novel, they are secretly assisted by Nemo (Herbert Lom, authoritative and impressive), who dies in the *Nautilus* when his island is destroyed volcanically. The design of the submarine mimicked without duplicating the version in Walt Disney's 20,000 LEAGUES UNDER THE SEA (1954).

The highlights of this workmanlike adaptation, marred by uneven acting, are the animals, all animated by Harryhausen; they include a giant crab, a prehistoric bird, enormous bees, and a giant chambered cephalopod. The bird and the crab are among Harryhausen's best creations.

Among the other adaptations of Verne's novel are two French TV productions (1963 and 1969 respectively) and

Karel Zeman's *The Stolen Airship* (1967), which used some elements from the novel, as did the 1921 German *Die Insel der Verschollenen*. Films claiming to be based directly on the novel also include the aforementioned Soviet version in 1941, a serial in 1951 (which included alien invaders from Mercury), and a multinational production in 1972, with Omar Sharif as Nemo.

All versions of the film lack a principal feature of the novel: its nineteenth-century attitude toward technology and science. In the novel Verne's castaways virtually recreate civilization on the island, outdoing the Swiss Family Robinson (which novel was much admired by Verne) in their industry. But little of this optimism has thus far reached the silver screen. It seems likely then that filmmakers will make yet another visit to Verne's Mysterious Island.

B.W.

MYTH IN SCIENCE FICTION

Although science fiction is characterized by the classic hard science story—usually described as science working itself out within a plot line—many SF writers rely just as heavily for inspiration on myths from all over the world. Science fiction uses mythology in three principal ways: for archetypal patterns and plots, specific myth systems, and the creation of new myths. For example, Gordon R. DICKSON's Childe Cycle uses archetypal patterns to make Hal Mayne, the hero of the Final Encyclopedia series, seem larger than life. Beginning with his mysterious birth; his education, interrupted by tragedy; and his descent into an underworld of mines, then continuing with Dickson's identification of Mayne as a sort of new incarnation of previous heroes, he emerges as the archetypal quest hero and returning king, a form of high-tech Arthur.

Many writers either adapt or retell old myths. For example, Poul ANDERSON's Hugo-winning novelette "Goat Song" (1973) is a retelling of the Orpheus myth. Roger ZELAZNY's "For a Breath I Tarry" (first magazine publication in *Fantastic*, 1966) combines the story of Adam and Eve with that of Job; in his *Lord of Light* (1967), a starship crew adopts the attributes of Hindu gods to control a planet. Cordwainer SMITH's "The Dead Lady of Clown Town" is a retelling of the story of Joan of Arc. Walter M. MILLER, Jr., made poignant use of Christian symbolism as well as the figure of the Wandering Jew in his *A Canticle for Leibowitz* (1960).

More recently some writers (among them the so-called CYBERPUNKS) have become fascinated with Japanese culture, especially the system of Bushido, the chivalric code of the feudal samurai. Others, such as Joan VINGE in her Hugo-winning novel *The Snow Queen* (1980), have used the myth of a nature Goddess and the Horned God, her consort, to add depth to their work. Frank HERBERT

drew heavily on Arab and Greek sources for his Dune books; his hero, Paul Atreides, is both a descendant of the accursed House of Atreus and a modern-day Messiah, a cross between Lawrence of Arabia and a character from Greek tragedy.

But SF not only uses myths, it also creates them: the hot pilot or First-In scout, the lost starship (possibly a transformation of the Flying Dutchman legend), or the race of older, wiser aliens who dwell in the ruins of their ancient civilization (as in the works of A. MERRITT or Leigh BRACKETT). Jack WILLIAMSON believes that humanity's expansion into space is the central myth of SF (see SPACE OPERA). Perhaps the most salient evidence that SF makes as well as uses myths came in 1977 when NASA named its prototype shuttle *Enterprise* after the ship from the TV series STAR TREK. That the bridge of that imaginary starship is currently enshrined in the Smithsonian, along with actual aircraft such as Charles Lindbergh's *Spirit of St. Louis*, the X-15, and capsules from the Mercury and Apollo missions, is testimony to the power of the myths now emerging from SF.

S.M.S.

N

NABOKOV, VLADIMIR (1899–1977). American mainstream writer, translator, and lepidopterist born in Russia. Nabokov, whose fiction often used science-fiction-like devices, left Russia at the time of the Revolution and lived in England, Germany, and France, writing in Russian, until 1940, when he emigrated to the United States and began writing in English. He taught at Cornell University from 1948 to 1959, when he settled in Switzerland. An acknowledged master of twentieth-century fiction who also excelled in poetry and autobiography, Nabokov attracted public attention with *Lolita* (1958), his best-selling novel of a middle-aged European intellectual's infatuation with a twelve-year-old "nymphet." His most SF-like novel, *Ada* (1969), involves an alternate world and another forbidden relationship, love between a brother and sister. Other Nabokov novels with SF elements are *Invitation to a Beheading* (1938, translated into English 1959), *Bend Sinister* (1947), and *Pale Fire* (1972); as do all mainstream uses of SF devices, these works focus not on a changing world but on individual relationships.

J.E.G.

NELSON, RAY (Professional name of Radell Faraday Nelson) (1931–   ). American writer and teacher who recognizes Jack LONDON, whom he calls the father of American science fiction, as the chief influence on his writing.

Nelson's first novel, *Ganymede Takeover* (1971), was a collaboration with Philip K. DICK and is an uncomfortable mixture of Dick's obsessive interest in the ambiguous nature of reality and a space opera plot. Nelson's first solo novel, *Blake's Progress* (1975), reflects his involvement with THE MAGAZINE OF FANTASY AND SCIENCE FICTION and NEW WORLDS in both matter and style. Its protagonist is the poet and painter William Blake, who has been given the power to move through time in the company of his wife. The novel shines in its description of the relationship between the poet and his more talented wife, but its alternate-history elements seem to be mere window dressing.

Nelson continued his interest in time travel in *Then Beggars Could Ride* (1976, along with *The Revolt of the Unemployables*, 1978, part of the Beggars series), a work that describes a future utopia. The *Prometheus Man* (1982), in contrast, is a dystopian novel that presents a future society wracked by overpopulation and a spirit-sapping technology. *Timequest* (1985) advances Nelson's interest in both time and future societies. He has called this novel the one he always wanted to write and the one he hopes to be remembered by.

OTHER WORKS: *Ecolog* (1977); *Dimensions of Horror* (1979, as Jeffrey Lord).

S.H.G.

NEVILLE, KRIS [OTTMAN] (1925–1980).

American author and technical writer in the plastics and chemical industries. Neville's best-known work is the classic science-fiction short story "Bettyann" (1951), about a teenage girl who is convinced that she does not belong with the family and society that claim her. Starting with the understandable insecurities of a child who lives in a foster home, Neville builds a sensitive story of alienation and initiation into adulthood as the girl's suspicions are confirmed. Neville wrote a sequel, "Overture" (1951), and later combined the two stories in the novel *Bettyann* (1970). Still not done with the story, he wrote "Bettyann's Children" (1973), which deals with the consequences of Bettyann's choice between remaining with those who raised her or joining the race who gave her life.

The Bettyann series illustrated Neville's fondness for alien contact stories, and he continually returned to this form of SF in his novels and shorter fiction. "Hunt the Hunter" (1951), "The Toy" (1952), and *Special Delivery* (1967) all use variations of this plot type to explore the nature of being human. What distinguishes these works is Neville's style, which is strong and concise yet projects genuine sympathy for the characters.

OTHER WORKS: *The Unearth People* (1964); *The Mutants* (1966); *Peril of the Starmen* (1967); *Invaders on the Moon* (with Mel Sturgis, 1970); *Mission: Manstop* (1971); *The Science Fiction of Kris Neville* (collection, 1984).

S.H.G.

——— THE NEW WAVE ———

New Wave was a term first applied, by anthologist Judith MERRIL, to the avant-garde stories published in the British science-fiction magazine NEW WORLDS for a few years after 1964. Some writers and critics deny that there ever was such a thing as the New Wave in SF. They are doubtless correct in the sense that the literary movement lacked organization, a broadly accepted credo, or a formal membership list. However, an identifiable group of writers and editors operating for approximately ten years, from the mid-1960s to the mid-1970s, did have an immense impact on the field. In retrospect there can be little doubt that they represented a de facto literary school, whether this was their conscious intention or not.

The term *New Wave* was borrowed from the French cinema. In SF it originated in and was first published in *New Worlds* when that magazine was controlled by Michael MOORCOCK. Although the magazine had been published since 1946, it was only with Moorcock's editorship eighteen years later that the movement began to coalesce. It should be noted, further, that the writers who participated in the movement had in many cases been writing well before this event. Further, the roots of and influences on New Wave writing had existed in general (mainstream) literature for many years.

The essential nature of New Wave SF can best be seen in comparison with more traditional SF, particularly that categorized as "pulp." Pulp SF is primarily concerned with physical problem solving and/or combat. Conflict is seen in terms of good protagonist versus bad antagonist (or occasionally natural catastrophe). Moral and psychological ambiguities are few. Style tends to be simple and structure of narration straightforward.

In contrast, New Wave writers frequently saw problems as social or psychological in nature, subject to resolution only through radical alterations of the psyche or similarly radical restructurings of society. The conflict they wrote about is between the victimized individual and oppressive society or nature, or it takes the form of a pathological society at war with itself. Moral and psychological ambiguities lie at the heart of most New Wave stories.

The movement is characterized by an emphasis on style and experimentation; the structure of the narration could be anything an author found successful. Resulting structural and linguistic experiments, although far from startling in the context of mainstream experimental or avant-garde literature, were startling to readers whose ears had been trained on the pages of *Astounding Science Fiction*.

By these criteria, both George ORWELL's *Nineteen Eighty-four* (1949) and Alfred BESTER's *The Demolished Man* (1953) may be seen as forerunners of the New Wave. (It should be further noted that *Nineteen Eighty-four* was itself largely ·a reworking of material Orwell obtained from Yevgeny ZAMIATIN's *We*, 1924.)

An early contributor to the New Wave was the British writer J. G. BALLARD. Many of Ballard's dizzying, acerbic short stories and novels are characteristic of the movement. Typical is *The Crystal World* (1966), a global catastrophe novel in which the protagonist does little except watch in stunned impassivity as spreading crystallization destroys all life on Earth.

Moorcock himself contributed many works to the movement. *The Final Program* (1968) portrays a decadent, near-future world in which the psychedelia of the 1960s is mixed with a computer-dominated, hedonistic society. This novel was controversial but far less so than *Behold the Man* (1969), which involves a contemporary English Jew who travels through time in search of the historical Jesus. Finding Jesus to have been hopelessly retarded, the time traveler replaces him, eventually dying on the cross. *Behold the Man* brought violent protests from readers. One member of the Fantasy Amateur Press Association proposed a boycott of the book's American publisher until the book was withdrawn, and the publisher pledged to consider no further submissions from Moorcock. (No boycott of either kind followed.)

A major American writer in the New Wave was Thomas M. DISCH, a close associate of Moorcock's then living in England. In Disch's novel *The Genocides* (1965) giant aliens take control of the Earth and develop it as an agricultural station. Thematically the work echoes H. G. Wells's *War of the Worlds* (1898), further indicating the deep roots of the movement. Whereas Wells's Martians regard human beings as cattle, Disch's aliens consider them mere pests—to be eradicated. Disch's *Camp Concentration* (1968) portrays an experimental program to develop an intelligence enhancer—another historical theme in SF. But in Disch's version the experimenters are insensitive jailers; their subjects, political prisoners; the active agent, a mutated gonorrhea virus whose later effect will be the subject's death.

Brian W. ALDISS's *Barefoot in the Head* (1969) offers a world in which LSD and similar drugs have been widely used in a major war. Although physical damage is limited, the populace is subject to confusion, mental disorganization, and almost constant hallucinations.

Drugs play a role in many of the works of the American writer Philip K. DICK, whose early works long antedate the New Wave but whose psychologically based, introspective themes fit neatly in the world-view of the movement. *The Three Stigmata of Palmer Eldritch* (1965) was regarded by many as a pivotal work; *Flow My Tears, the Policeman Said* (1974) and *A Scanner Darkly* (1977) are strongly cautionary antidrug novels.

The American Joanna RUSS's *And Chaos Died* (1970) is comparable to both *Barefoot in the Head* and Dick's drug novels. Her later *The Female Man* (1975) was highly controversial, whether regarded as an SF novel or a feminist political document (or both). Norman SPINRAD addressed the subject of drugs at shorter length in "Carcinoma Angels" (1967), as did Ursula K. LE GUIN in "The Good Trip" (1970). Once again precursors are numerous, a notable one being "Two Dooms" by Cyril M. KORNBLUTH (1958).

The highly prolific American author Barry N. MALZBERG is regarded by many as representative equally of the best and the worst of the New Wave. The almost unbearably intimate, intense psychological perspective of his fiction can be both rewarding and daunting. He was obsessed with certain images and events: the assassination of John F. Kennedy is the theme of *The Destruction of the Temple* (1974) and *Scop* (1976). The notion of an orbiting astronaut abandoning his colleagues as they explore a lunar or planetary landscape is returned to again and again in *The Falling Astronauts* (1971), *Beyond Apollo* (1972), and *Revelations* (1972).

Major promotional work for the New Wave was done by Judith Merril and Harlan ELLISON, particularly by means of important ANTHOLOGIES: Ellison's *Dangerous Visions* (1967) and *Again, Dangerous Visions* (1972), and Merril's *England Swings SF* (1968, British title *The Space-Time Journal*).

Ellison opened the first *Dangerous Visions* volume with a pointed, albeit bombastic, introduction. He said, in part: "What you hold in your hands is more than a book. If we are lucky, it is a revolution. . . . It was intended to shake things up. It was conceived out of a need for new horizons, new forms, new styles, new challenges in the literature of our times. If it was done properly, it will provide these new horizons and styles and forms and challenges." Hyperbole notwithstanding, Ellison's intention is clear, and he presumably meant it to be taken seriously. He felt, along with others, that SF had reached a dead end in terms of both form and content. Nothing less than revolutionary change would resolve the dilemma.

Ellison claimed to have invited writers to submit stories too "dangerous" in theme, form, language, or some other element to have been published in any standard outlet. In later years he was to back away from this position, suggesting that the entire "dangerous visions" notion had been a mere marketing gimmick designed to draw attention to the book and sell copies. The stories in the anthology (and its successor) are uneven in quality, but many of them were indeed unconventional in form or content. There were notable contributions in *Dangerous Visions* by Robert SILVERBERG, Philip José FARMER, Brian W. ALDISS, Philip K. Dick, Carol EMSHWILLER, Samuel R. DELANY, and others, and several more notable authors contributed to the successor volume.

Merril's *England Swings SF* differed from *Dangerous Visions* in reprinting material produced by what might be termed the Moorcock circle in England. It was very close to being a Best of New Worlds, and, perhaps as a result of having been filtered through the editorial selection process twice, was of a more uniform—and generally higher—quality than *Dangerous Visions*. *England Swings SF* was not promoted with the flair displayed in behalf of *Dangerous Visions* (nor was its rather unsuitable title any asset), but it includes splendid stories by Josephine Saxton, Kyril Bonfiglioli, J. G. Ballard, Keith ROBERTS, Charles PLATT, George MacBeth, B. J. Bayley, Brian W. Aldiss, Pamela Zoline, and others.

Like Ellison, Merril introduced her book with the strong claim—interspersed with excerpts from the lyrics of songs from the Beatles' *Sergeant Pepper's Lonely Hearts Club Band*—that no one had ever read anything like the book before. Merril said: "It's an action-photo, a record of process-in-change, a look through the perspex porthole at the momentarily stilled bodies in a scout ship boosting fast, and heading out of sight into the multiplex mystery of inner/outer space."

While Ellison and Merril were promoting the New Wave, others opposed it violently. Science-fiction traditionalists such as Sam MOSKOWITZ, John J. Pierce, Isaac ASIMOV, and Lester DEL REY sought to uphold the traditional values of optimism, straightforward narration, and protechnology attitudes, all of which had been seriously challenged. (Their opposition to the New Wave did not prevent both Asimov and del Rey from accepting Ellison's money for contributions to *Dangerous Visions*—Asimov, in fact, furnished two introductions to the book.)

In *The World of Science Fiction, 1926–1976* (1980) del Rey described the motivating philosophy of New Wave writing as "a general distrust of both science and mankind." He wrote, "Against the universe, the significance of mankind was no greater than that of bedbugs—if as great." He went on to temper this statement with the admission that "this was not true of all the fiction . . . some stories simply used the older themes and disguised them. . . ." But ultimately his assessment was negative: "The old heroes were gone, and antiheroes and blank-faced and blank-feeling characters pervaded the fiction."

Ironically, if, as del Rey charged, the stories of the New Wave were marked by despair, many of the leading advocates and participants in the movement experienced that same emotion when, as Barry N. Malzberg noted in *The Engines of the Night: Science Fiction in the Eighties* (1982), the market for "experimental," "literary," "avant-garde," "downbeat," "technophobic," or depressing" science fiction collapsed in 1974. While Malzberg feels that the New Wave came to this sudden and depressing end, others disagree. William Sims Bainbridge, a professor of sociology at Harvard University, applies the term *new wave* (note the lowercase) in a broad sense, taking in much socially and psychologically oriented SF, whether it involves the stylistic experimentation associated with the *New Worlds*/ New Wave school or not. In *Dimensions of Science Fiction* (1986) Bainbridge noted the new wave focus on inner space, psychological and literary sensitivity, communication with the hidden self, and interaction between personalities. He concluded: "Critics find the new wave pessimistic and pathological. But even in its darkest stories, the new wave exalts the human spirit, because the author becomes a hunter in the forests of the night, bagging the biggest wild game of all, the monsters of the id and of cultural repression."

To the extent that Malzberg's analysis is correct, the New Wave did cease to exist as an identifiable literary movement within science fiction in the mid-1970s. But to the extent that Bainbridge is correct, the new wave became integrated with the mainstream of SF in a new concern for all that "inner space" implies, and it will remain a major element—possibly even the dominant element—in the field.

R.A.L.

NEW WORLDS SCIENCE FICTION (1946– 1979).

Britain's leading and most influential science-fiction magazine, modeled along the lines of John W. CAMPBELL's *Astounding*, though allowing for the traditional differences between British and American SF. Under editor John Carnell (1946–1964) *New Worlds* rapidly established itself as the backbone of serious British SF. All Britain's leading SF writers—among them E. C. TUBB, James WHITE, J. T. McINTOSH, Kenneth BULMER, and Brian W. ALDISS—either owed their first sales to *New Worlds* or sold much of their best work there (or to its companion, *Science Fantasy*). Carnell also published the first stories by J. G. BALLARD. By the late 1950s authors such as Ballard, Aldiss, John BRUNNER, and Harry HARRISON were testing and breaking SF taboos in the magazine's pages and paving the way for the NEW WAVE. Carnell also provided hard SF in the form of White's Sector General and Colin KAPP's Unorthodox Engineers series.

In 1964, with falling circulation, *New Worlds* was sold to a new publisher. Michael MOORCOCK became the editor, and it was through his liberalism that the New Wave reached its height. Unfortunately, the experimental *New Worlds*, while providing a unique market for both British and American writers (the latter including Thomas M. DISCH, Norman SPINRAD, and Roger ZELAZNY), was starved by the British distribution system, and attempts to revive it as an anthology series and then as an amateur magazine were unsuccessful. *New Worlds*, under both Carnell and Moorcock, was one of the most exciting and innovative magazines in SF history. Its spirit lives on today in the semiprozine *Interzone* (1982–).

M.A.

Leslie Nielsen (left) in *Forbidden Planet* (1956)

NIELSEN, LESLIE (1925–).
Canadian actor long resident in Hollywood who has frequently starred in science-fiction and fantasy films since his leading role as Captain Adams in FORBIDDEN PLANET (1956). The silver-haired Nielsen, tall, imposing, and ruggedly handsome, began his career as a utility leading man. In the 1960s he became notable as a villain, suggesting undertones of sardonic sadism. After his amusing performance in *Airplane!* (1980), Nielsen acted in several comedies. Including made-for-television movies, Nielsen has appeared in at least fifteen SF or horror films, although none has been as significant as *Forbidden Planet*. He also starred in at least seven television series, including the cult favorite *Police Squad!* In the early 1950s he appeared in several episodes of *Lights Out* and *Tales of Tomorrow* on TV.

B.W.

NIGHT OF THE COMET (1984).
Directed by Thom Eberhardt; screenplay by Thom Eberhardt; photographed by Arthur Albert; music supervised by Tom Perry. With Catherine Mary Stewart, Kelli Maroney, Robert Beltran, Geoffrey Lewis, Mary Woronov, John Achorn. 95 minutes. Color.

Despite a derivative story line, this is an exceptional example of low-budget filmmaking—witty, imaginative, cleverly directed, and very well acted. Some have declared it a satire, but it is more properly considered a comic variation on several familiar SF themes. A comet (last seen when the dinosaurs vanished) passes overhead; most of humanity watches, and most is turned to dust. Some of the survivors become cannibalistic fiends, while others, including two teenage sisters, remain normal. In the end, comedy triumphs over terror. Catherine Mary Stewart (who went on to star in several more SF films) and Kelli Maroney are excellent as the brave, karate-skilled, gun-toting but otherwise normal teenagers.

B.W.

1984 (1956).
Directed by Michael Anderson; screenplay by William P. Templeton and Ralph Bettinson; adapted from the novel by George Orwell; photographed by C. Pennington Richards; music by Malcolm Arnold. With Edmond O'Brien, Jan Sterling, Michael Redgrave, David Kossoff, Mervyn Johns, Donald Pleasence, Carol Wolveridge. 90 minutes. Black and white.

NINETEEN EIGHTY-FOUR (1984).
Directed by Michael Radford; screenplay by Michael Radford and Jonathan Gems; photographed by Roger Deakins; music by Domic Muldowney and Eurythmics. With John Hurt, Richard Burton, Suzanna Hamilton, Cyril Cusack, Gregor Fisher, James Walker, Andrew Wilde. 110 minutes. Color.

The first film of George ORWELL's great dystopia was made after the enormous success of a 1954 BBC version but was itself no success at all. Michael Anderson's adaptation is lifeless and, in the alternate ending shot for British audiences, completely unfaithful to the intent of the book: Winston Smith and his lover go down in a hail of bullets, shouting defiance.

The Michael Radford version, however, is a triumph. Quite unlike Anderson's rendition, it presents a completely convincing picture of a run-down totalitarian state wherein virtually everyone is filthy and miserable, the machines barely work, and the technology seems to have frozen around 1950. The performances are superior, and Radford made excellent use of his medium: propaganda films flicker constantly in the background—although the party line changes, the *same* footage, slightly altered, continues to run.

D.S.

NIVEN, LARRY [Professional name of Laurence van Cott Niven] (1938–).
American author. Heir to a good piece of a California oil fortune, Niven aspired to write science fiction for its own sake and achieved financial success while doing so. After earning a B.A. in mathematics from Washburn University and studying at California Institute of Technology and UCLA, he tackled SF with his first story, "The Coldest Place," in 1964, the same year he became a full-time free-lance writer.

Niven's fiction has been mostly hard SF, that is, firmly grounded in science and the real world; this orientation has not restricted his ability to imagine wildly, though;

Larry Niven

his work is distinguished by its carefully thought out, thoroughly detailed, far-out ideas, but his imaginings, even his fantasies, are rationally explained. One example is the Known Space series, which earned him his first following. A future history set over the next 1200 years or so of human exploration of space, the series is marked by encounters with other species whose cultures are already established in humanity's region of the galaxy. Niven was the first to introduce this concept; previous future histories tended to be purely *human* histories, with other species lagging far behind or at most having reached about the same stage of development. But in the Niven universe the commerce of the galaxy is already dominated by a nomadic race called the Outsiders, who sell the secret of the hyperdrive to primitive peoples such as *Homo sapiens* although they disdain to use it themselves; and by the Puppeteers, whose General Products Corp. holds a monopoly on an almost indestructible starship hull.

Perhaps the most charming of Niven's creations, the Puppeteers have armored bodies (which house their brains) on three legs and two "heads" that look like hand puppets. Nessus, a puppeteer who has dealings with humankind in "The Soft Weapon" (1967) and other stories, is insane by the standards of his kind: for one thing, he is courageous, and among his people caution, if not outright cowardice, is a virtue. For the Kzinti, a catlike species encountered in the same story, courage is normal—perhaps too much so: they've been on the losing end of several wars with humanity because they simply

don't know when to quit.

World of Ptavvs (1966) introduced Niven's readers to a Thrint; fortunately there was only one: a couple of billion years ago, his kind ruled the galaxy. They weren't very bright, but their psi powers enabled them to enslave the more intelligent Tnuctipun, who bioengineered all sorts of useful things, such as stage trees (which grow solid-fuel rocket cores) and whitefoods (huge, nutritious, sluglike animals). Eventually the Tnuctipun rebelled, and the ensuing war wiped out both species. Or almost wiped them out: degenerate descendants of the Thrintun, the grogs, are discovered in "The Handicapped" (1967), and the self-seeding stage trees play a role in "A Relic of Empire" (1967). Once in a while some artifact of the Thrintun Empire turns up in a stasis box (that's where the Thrint in *World of Ptavvs* came from). The whitefoods (also called bandersnatchi) are still around too.

Another part of Niven's future history involves the sociology of the human species over the next few centuries: the revolution in organ transplants and the consequent criminal trade in organs ("Death by Ecstasy," 1969) leads to the expansion of crimes calling for the death penalty in "The Jigsaw Man" (1967). A counterculture develops among the Belters of the Asteroid Belt that looks down on humans as Flatlanders. Earth dwellers themselves are revealed in "The Adults" (1967) to be the offshoot of another ancient race called the Pak, who also built the wondrous artificial environment of *Ringworld* (1970).

One of Niven's throwaway ideas from the Known Space series became the Moties, the fast-breeding, multicaste (through genetic engineering) menace in *The Mote in God's Eye* (1974), a collaboration with Jerry POURNELLE. His other collaborations with Pournelle—*Inferno* (1976), *Lucifer's Hammer* (1977), *Oath of Fealty* (1981), and *Footfall* (1985)—have reached broader audiences through their more frequent use of general themes and emphasis on individual fates and have rocketed to bestseller heights, but Niven fans may prefer the idea stories: for instance, in *Ringworld* humans, Puppeteers, and Kzinti explore a gigantic alien artifact, a world a million miles wide built in a vast ring around a remote sun; its 1980 sequel is *Ringworld Engineers*. In the more recent *The Integral Trees* (1984) and its sequel, *The Smoke Ring* (1987), a dissident society of humans live on trees in a peculiar but rationally justified system: an asteroid belt that possesses atmosphere. And in *A World out of Time* (1976) far future humanity has reengineered the Solar System: Earth now orbits Jupiter because the Sun has become a red giant, and the inhabitants of Earth are immortal children (adult males and females fought a disastrous war).

Niven has also become the master of the SF barroom tale, exemplified by the Draco Tavern series in such stories as "Assimilating Our Culture, That's What They're Doing" (1979), with its wicked business about aliens who want people soup. He is also the master of the logical implications of a range of topics including matter transmitters ("Flash Crowd," 1973), parallel worlds ("All the Myriad Ways," 1968), magic *(The Magic Goes Away,* 1978), and the predicament of Superman ("Man of Steel, Woman of Kleenex," 1971). He has given other writers a hand as well, collaborating with a young David GER-ROLD on *The Flying Sorcerers* (1971) and with Steven Barnes on *Dream Park* (1981). A fan favorite and a fan himself as well as a frequenter of fan conventions, Niven has won four Hugo Awards for his short fiction and a Hugo and Nebula for *Ringworld.*

OTHER WORKS: *Neutron Star* (collection, 1968); *A Gift from Earth* (1968); *The Shape of Space* (collection, 1971); *Protector* (1973); *The Flight of the Horse* (collection, 1973); *Inconstant Moon* (collection, 1973); *A Hole in Space* (collection, 1974); *Tales of Known Space* (collection, 1975); *The Long Arm of Gil Hamilton* (collection, 1976); *A World out of Time* (1976); *Convergent Series* (collection, 1979); *The Patchwork Girl* (1980); *The Descent of Anansi* (with Steven Barnes, 1982); *The Time of the Warlock* (collection, 1984); *Niven's Laws* (collection, 1984); *Limits* (collection, 1985); *The Legacy of Heorot* (with Jerry Pournelle and Steven Barnes, 1987).

J.J.P.

NO BLADE OF GRASS (1970). *Directed by Cornel Wilde; screenplay by Sean Forestal and Jefferson Pascal; adapted from the novel by John Christopher; photographed by H. A. R. Thompson; music by Burnell Whibley. With Nigel Davenport, Jean Wallace, Anthony May, John Hamill, Lynne Frederick, Patrick Holt, Wendy Richard. 96 minutes. Color.*

In the near future environmental pollution alters a previously insignificant virus that destroys most of the grains of the Earth. The story follows a family on its journey from London to a farm owned by relatives, where they believe they will be secure. On arrival, however, they have to battle the farmers for the farm.

Although serious and well intentioned, this film is dramatically awkward and obvious. As with other films of this nature, the message seems to be that to survive in a devastated world violence is the only recourse. The most interesting aspect of the screenplay is the addition of faddish environmental concerns to John CHRISTOPHER's original story.

B.W.

NOLAN, WILLIAM F[RANCIS] (1928–   ). American artist, writer, and editor whose best-known science-fiction novel is *Logan's Run* (with George Clayton Johnson, 1967), which was filmed in 1976 (see LO-GAN'S RUN) and became a television series for one season

(1977–78). Nolan also wrote two follow-up Logan novels, *Logan's World* (1977) and *Logan's Search* (1980), and two novels about a future detective name Sam Space. A commercial artist, scriptwriter, and race car driver, Nolan has written more than a dozen screenplays and television plays, published more than thirty books (including four collections of his SF and fantasy short stories), edited many anthologies and the first three issues of *Gamma* magazine, published short fiction in *If* and elsewhere, and reviewed SF for the *Los Angeles Times.*

N.H.

NORMAN, JOHN (Pseudonym of John Frederick Lange, Jr.) (1931–   ). American writer and professor of philosophy at Queens College, City College of New York. Almost all Norman's novels are part of the Gor series and belong as much to fantasy as to science fiction. The planet Gor shares Earth's orbit but is invisible to the Earth because it is always on the other side of the Sun. As in Edgar Rice Burroughs's John Carter of Mars series, an Earthman is transported to Gor and undertakes a series of adventures on this unknown, caste-ridden planet. The first several novels in the series *(Tarnsman of Gor,* 1966; *Outlaw of Gor,* 1967; *Priest-Kings of Gor,* 1968) are straight adventure fiction. However, as the series continued *(Raiders of Gor,* 1971; *Captive of Gor,* 1972) Norman began to dwell on the place of women—as slaves to men—in Gor's society. Even worse, the female characters usually insist that they are "fulfilled" by such a role. All the novels that followed are simple variations on this theme, and Norman shows no sign of changing either the pattern or the message.

OTHER WORKS: *Nomads of Gor* (1969); *Assassin of Gor* (1970); *Ghost Dance* (1970); *Hunters of Gor* (1974); *Marauders of Gor* (1975); *Time Slave* (1975); *Tribesmen of Gor* (1976); *Slave Girl of Gor* (1977); *Beasts of Gor* (1978); *Explorers of Gor* (1979); *Fighting Slaves of Gor* (1980); *Guardsman of Gor* (1981); *Rogue of Gor* (1981); *Blood Brothers of Gor* (1982); *Savages of Gor* (1982); *Kajira of Gor* (1983); *Players of Gor* (1984); *Mercenaries of Gor* (1985).

S.H.G.

NORTON, ANDRE (Pseudonym of Alice Mary Norton) (1912–   ). American author and librarian, probably the leading writer of juvenile science fantasy since Edgar Rice BURROUGHS. Norton served as children's librarian at the Cleveland Public Library from 1932 to 1950 and as special librarian at the Library of Congress during World War II. She was also an editorial reader for Gnome Press from 1950 to 1958. Since 1958 she has been a full-time writer, and she now lives in Winter Park, Florida.

Because she seldom attended fan gatherings until the

1980s (when the World SF Convention was held in Cleveland in 1955, a group of SF writers, including Isaac ASIMOV, the guest of honor, visited *her*) and because little of her work appeared in the magazines, Norton's following was gathered entirely through her books. She had already published a half-dozen historical novels, beginning in 1934, when her first SF novel, *Star Man's Son* (as *Daybreak, 2250 A.D.*, 1954), came out in 1952. Since then she has published more than one hundred novels and has become something of a legend in fan circles. But she did not receive the critical attention given to such writers as Robert A. Heinlein, Arthur C. Clarke, and Isaac Asimov until the 1980s, when the critics began to discover her.

Norton's work blurs the border between SF and fantasy. Her novels describe fascinating alternate worlds, parallel universes, and provocative futures in thoughtful, consistent detail, but they also offer myths, legends, and magic. Frequently these fantasy elements dominate, and science is relegated to a secondary role or to forces in opposition, even evil. But this is not to say that Norton uses fantasy as a substitute for science: the fantastic is present to highlight her dominant theme, that people must be free to discover who they are and what their relation is to the rest of creation.

The most dramatic example of Norton's use of myth and legend to replace science can be seen in the Janus series (*Judgment on Janus*, 1963, and *Victory on Janus*, 1966). These novels incorporate Celtic lore and magic to develop a conflict between a sylvan society and an alien-built computer that threatens to mechanize the world and all its people. These, and the more overtly fantastic Witch World series, are Norton's most antitechnological books. In *The Many Worlds of Andre Norton* (1974; as *The Book of Andre Norton*, 1975), she said, "Yes, I am anti-machine," and went on to explain that much of the present frustration of Western civilization has come from its turning to machines and sacrificing other aspects of life.

Although the situations of her young characters may be desperate, and their ultimate fates have become less hopeful as Norton's career has progressed, her protagonists have always been virtuous and optimistic in seeking their goals. For instance, they are customarily dislocated individuals, aware that the world is out of balance and seeking to bring about some equilibrium; but in the realm of Norton's fiction that can only happen if people have freedom of thought and action. Technology represents those forces in society that seek to impose a deadly uniformity. Ultimate victory comes when the protagonist establishes bonds with other people, and other creatures, and then enlists magic, the opposite of cold technology. Thus in the Janus series the computer is finally defeated when the hero, a Terran colonist, accepts the talents of a woman who has been granted the magical powers of the native priestesses.

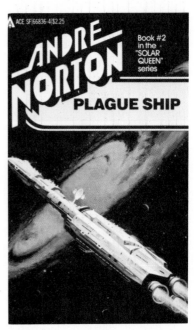

Art by Vincent Di Fate

Norton's earliest works, several written under the pseudonym of Andrew North, follow more conventional SF lines. *Star Man's Son* describes a postholocaust society trying to preserve what is left of civilization. The Dane Thorson series (*Sargasso of Space*, 1955; *Plague Ship*, 1956; *Voodoo Planet*, 1959; and *Postmarked the Stars*, 1969) is reminiscent of such earlier works as Asimov's Foundation series. These novels describe the adventures of a crew of space traders who compete with one another and the Galactic Patrol in freewheeling entrepreneurial adventures. And a failing galactic empire provides the backdrop for *Star Rangers* (1953; as *The Last Planet*, 1955) and *Star Guard* (1955).

In the late 1950s Norton began to develop alternatives to science for her stories. Special powers replaced technology as her heroes frequently battled forces that used machinery for inhumane purposes. In *Star Gate* (1958), for example, the hero, Kincar s'Rud, is able to battle various materialistic forces in his planet's alternate history because of a special bond he shares with two of the native animals. Norton returned to a similar relationship between man and beast in the Holsteen Storm series (*The Beast Master*, 1959, and *Lord of Thunder*, 1962), in which a telepathic linkage between the hero and three animals brings about the defeats of an alien invasion and a crazed engineer.

Norton further emphasized the competition between science and her hero by making Storm a Navaho exile who gradually comes to recognize the power of his heritage. Norton's later novels frequently focus on telepathy and on native American heroes.

Perhaps Norton's best-known work is her fantasy series about the Witch World: *Witch World* (1963), *Web of Witch World* (1964), *Three against Witch World* (1965), *Warlock of Witch World* (1967), *Sorceress of Witch World* (1968), *Spell of the Witch World* (collection, 1972), *The Crystal Griffon* (1972), *Jargoon Pard* (1974), *Trey of Swords* (1977), *Lore of Witch World* (collection, 1980); *'Ware Hawk* (1983); and *Gate of the Gate* (1987). Inspired by research for a never written historical novel about Crusaders who settled "beyond the sea," these books rely on Celtic and early English legends and folklore, such as *Childe Roland* and "Beauty and the Beast." They did much to fuel the sword-and-sorcery phase through which fantasy passed after the publication of J. R. R. Tolkien's The Lord of the Rings (1954–1956); its emphasis, Norton has admitted, holds the greatest appeal for her.

NOTABLE OTHER WORKS: *The Stars Are Ours!* (1954); *The Crossroads of Time* (1956); *Sea Siege* (1957); *Star Born* (1957); *The Time Traders* (1958); *Secret of the Lost Race* (1959; published in Britain as *Wolfshead*, 1977); *Galactic Derelict* (1959); *Storm over Warlock* (1960); *The Sioux Spaceman* (1960); *Star Hunter* (1961); *Catseye* (1961); *Eye of the Monster* (1962); *The Defiant Agents* (1962); *Key out of Time* (1963); *Ordeal in Otherwhere* (1964); *Night of Masks* (1964); *Quest Crosstime* (1965; published in Britain as *Crosstime Agent*, 1975); *Moon of Three Rings* (1966); *The X Factor* (1967); *Operation Time Search* (1967); *Dark Piper* (1968); *The Zero Stone* (1968); *Uncharted Stars* (1969); *Ice Crown* (1970); *Android at Arma* (1971); *Exiles of the Stars* (1971); *Breed to Come* (1972); *Here Abide Monsters* (1973); *Iron Cage* (1974); *Outside* (1975); *The Day of the Ness* (1975); *Knave of Dreams* (1976); *No Night without Stars* (1976); *Perilous Dreams* (collection, 1976); *Star Ka'at* (with Dorothy Madlee, 1977); *Star Ka'at World* (with Dorothy Madlee, 1978); *Star Ka'ats and the Plant People* (with Dorothy Madlee, 1979); *Star Ka'ats and the Winged Warriors* (1981); *Ten Mile Treasure* (1981); *Voorloper* (1981); *Forerunner* (1981); *Moon Called* (1982); *Wheel of Stars* (1983); *Forerunner: The Second Venture* (1985).

S.H.G.

NOT OF THIS EARTH (1957).   *Directed by Roger Corman; screenplay by Charles B. Griffith and Mark Hanna; photographed by John Mescall; music by Ronald Stein. With Paul Birch, Beverly Garland, Morgan Jones, William Roerick, Jonathan Haze, Dick Miller. 67 minutes. Black and white.*

Mr. Johnson (Paul Birch), an alien from the planet Davanna, has come to Earth to see if blood from human

beings can revitalize his race, which is dying from radiation because their blood is drying up. He is thwarted in his vampiric activities by a traffic cop and a nurse, but a new Davannan arrives at the end.

One of the most imaginative of Roger CORMAN's quickies, *Not of This Earth* introduced matter transmission to feature films and was one of the first films to feature telepathy. Some sympathy is developed for Johnson, the blank-eyed vampire from space, and Corman favorites Jonathan Haze and Dick Miller both have good scenes. Although Corman's direction is somewhat below par, this is among his most intelligent thrillers.

B.W.

NOURSE, ALAN E[DWARD] (1928–   ).
American writer and physician who published most of his science fiction in the 1950s. Nourse wrote several successful juvenile novels *(Trouble on Titan*, 1954; *Rocket to Limbo*, 1957; *Star Surgeon*, 1960; *Raiders from the Rings*, 1962); as a result, some of his collections of magazine stories were marketed as if for children: *The Universe Between* (1965, a novellike collection of stories from 1951), *Psi-High and Others* (1967), and *Rx for Tomorrow* (1971). In many of these works he drew extensively on his medical experience, which he also used in numerous nonfiction books for children, in mainstream fiction, and in his SF disaster story *The Fourth Horseman* (1983). His most extensive uses of his medical background are in *Star Surgeon*, in which Earth serves as a kind of hospital for the galaxy, and in a number of stories about Hoffman Center, a future medical complex in Philadelphia (where Nourse got his medical degree and started his writing career). *A Man Obsessed* (1955; as *The Mercy Men*, 1968) combines his interest in medicine and psychic powers. His SF novel *The Bladerunner* (1974), whose title alone was bought for the film, describes a future world in which socialized medicine has led to the saving of lives that otherwise would have ended, and therefore to overpopulation, dangerous plagues, and compulsory sterilization.

OTHER WORKS: *The Invaders Are Coming!* (with J. A. Meyer, 1959); *Tiger by the Tail* (collection, 1961; as *Beyond Infinity*, 1964); *The Counterfeit Men* (collection, 1963).

B.S.

NOWLAN, PHILIP FRANCIS (1888–1940).
American pulp and comic-continuity writer. In Nowlan's novelette *Armageddon 2419 A.D.* (1928) and its sequel, *The Airlords of Han* (1929), both published in AMAZING, the narrator, Anthony Rogers, wakes up after five hundred years in suspended animation and, with the aid of ingenious weaponry, helps American guerrillas defeat Mongolian world domination. This story provided the

basis for the first SF comic strip, *Buck Rogers in the 25th Century* (see BUCK ROGERS), which ran in newspapers from 1929 to 1967 and for which Nowlan supplied the continuity until his death. A 1962 paperback of *Armageddon* and *Airlords* was edited—with some details updated—by Spider ROBINSON.

J.H.

NUCLEAR PROMISE AND THREAT

The history of nuclear weapons and nuclear power cannot be separated from science fiction. "Atomic energy" and "atomic bombs" were imagined first in SF, which directly influenced the scientists who eventually converted these farfetched notions into central facts of modern life. With human fate now inextricably tied to our nuclear capabilities, SF has become a crucial mode of interpreting and projecting what has been labeled the nuclear age.

The discovery in the late nineteenth century of radioactivity led to dizzying breakthroughs in physics. As early as 1895 British novelist Robert CROMIE's *The Crack of Doom* imagined a scientist unleashing the power of the atom; after warning that it is "not wise to wreck incautiously even the atoms of a molecule," since "one grain of matter contains sufficient energy . . . to raise a hundred thousand tons nearly two miles," this mad genius is barely stopped from destroying the planet with his atomic experiments.

In the first decade of the twentieth century, scientists quantified the amount of energy associated with radioactivity, began to comprehend the structure of atoms, and precisely conceptualized the convertibility of mass and energy, expressed in Albert Einstein's seminal 1905 formula $e = mc^2$, in which the amount of energy (e) represented by matter is the product of its mass (m) multiplied by the almost inconceivably vast speed of light squared (c^2). Science fiction was simultaneously extrapolating the possibilities of using radioactivity and atomic disintegration in weapons of war.

In George GRIFFITH's 1906 *The Lord of Labour* (published posthumously in 1911), a German disintegrating ray confronts a British radium gun in a world war that slaughters millions before ending in Anglo-American global conquest. American SF of this period imagined atomic superweapons being used to end all war, either through universal disarmament or American (or Anglo-American) global hegemony, a concept earlier projected in the superbomb of Frank STOCKTON's *The Great War Syndicate* (1889). In Roy Norton's *The Disappearing Fleets* (1907), radioactivity powers stupendous "radioplanes" that establish a Pax Americana. The first atom-splitting weapon—a focused beam of "radio-active waves" that instantaneously disintegrates the atoms of all metals

into subatomic particles—is invented by a characteristic American lone genius, who uses it to force universal disarmament, in Godfrey Hollis's *The Man Who Ended War* (1908). The scientific wizard in *The Man Who Rocked the Earth* (1914) by Arthur Cheney Train and Robert Williams Wood invents a radioactive beam, fired from an airship powered by the "atomic energy" of uranium forced into rapid disintegration, that can annihilate mountain ranges or armies; this ultimate weapon causes such hideous explosions and excruciating deaths from radiation sickness that the nations realize they must end "either war or the human race."

In 1913–14 there appeared a novel destined to play a critical role in the development of nuclear bombs: H. G. WELLS's *The World Set Free: A Story of Mankind.* Wells here introduced what he christened the "atomic bomb," a true nuclear weapon that converts mass into fiery and explosive energy in a chain reaction induced by a triggering device.

Wells also predicted in this book the harnessing of "atomic energy" in the early 1950s, precisely when reactors actually began producing electricity in the United States and the Soviet Union. This technological advance exacerbates the contradictions of capitalism, with governments "spending every year vaster and vaster amounts of power and energy upon military preparations, and continually expanding the debt of industry to capital." In 1956 comes a global nuclear holocaust in which the major cities are destroyed by "atomic bombs" dropped from airplanes. Civilization virtually collapses, and hordes of survivors, many scarred by radioactivity, are left to wander through desolate landscapes (in scenes that would become familiar in fiction and films after World War II). From the ruins emerges "the Republic of Mankind," directed by an elite who establish "science" as "the new king of the world."

Irène Curie and Frédéric Joliot first induced artificial radioactivity in 1933, exactly the year Wells had forecast. Meanwhile, Hungarian physicist Leo Szilard had read *The World Set Free* just before fleeing Germany when Hitler came to power, also in 1933. That fall, while ruminating about Wells's novel, Szilard suddenly conceived of a way to sustain a nuclear chain reaction, making it possible to "liberate energy on an industrial scale, and construct atomic bombs." Szilard kept the process secret: "Knowing what this would mean—and I knew it because I had read H. G. Wells—I did not want this patent to become public."

Then in 1938 the uranium atom was split—in Berlin. "All the things which H. G. Wells predicted appeared suddenly real to me," Szilard recalled, and he therefore met with two other Hungarian émigré physicists, Edward Teller and Eugene Wigner, to enlist Albert Einstein in their plan to counter the potential menace posed by atomic bombs in the hands of Nazi Germany. The outcome was the 1939 letter, composed by Szilard and

1950s Civil Defense photograph of family fallout shelter, from *The Atomic Cafe* (1982)

Einstein, to President Franklin D. Roosevelt initiating the chain of events that led to the Manhattan Project.

One of the earliest arrangements Szilard made for the atomic scientists was ordering two books for their library: *The World Set Free* and Harold Nicolson's *Public Faces* (1932), in which Britain develops "atomic bombs" but decides to destroy them because "these new and potent engines of destruction are inimical to existing civilisation." Influenced by their reading of SF, Szilard and the other physicists who led the United States into atomic weaponry had two motives: to deter the Nazis from using atomic weapons and to bring a final end to war.

Between World War I and Hiroshima, the consequences of splitting the atom became a commonplace SF theme, particularly in *Astounding Science Fiction* under the editorship of John W. CAMPBELL, Jr. Rather than atomic weapons, though, most of the stories were concerned with atomic energy. Some reveled in its thrilling potential, imagining virtually free electricity, atomic-powered spaceships (as in Doc SMITH's 1928 *The Skylark of Space* and its sequels), an occasional atomic-powered time machine (Victor ROUSSEAU's 1930 "The Atom Smasher"), or even the artificial creation of a new sun when ours dies (Raymond Z. GALLUN's 1931 "Atomic Fire"). Others warned about the deadly dangers of atomic experimentation, even hypothesizing a chain reaction

that could make the planet uninhabitable, as in Isaac Nathanson's "World Aflame" (1935). But more common than either of these farfetched extremes were thoughtful stories—such as Harl VINCENT's "Power Plant" (1939), Robert A. HEINLEIN's "Blowups Happen" (1940), Lester DEL REY's "Nerves" (1942), and Clifford D. SIMAK's "Lobby" (1944)—blending enthusiasm about atomic energy with warnings about its financial and environmental hazards.

There was far less enthusiasm about atomic weapons. Such fiendish inventions might be used by "Asiatics" (as in "The Atom Smasher," a 1938 tale by Gordon A. Giles [Otto BINDER]) or the Nazis (as disguised in Cleve CARTMILL's 1944 "Deadline") but not by Americans. In only two stories does the United States use, or even threaten to use, atomic weapons; both appeared in the period when America was slipping into World War II.

Long before the scientists of the Manhattan Project began their feverish quest for an atomic deterrent, American readers of SF had been exposed to stories probing the fallacies of deterrence theory. In *The Pallid Giant* (1927), Pierrepont B. Noyes told how the development of atomic weapons by advanced civilizations in remote prehistory led to the virtual extinction of the human species, when the mutual fear that was supposed to deter war instead inspired preemptive attacks. In *The Final War*, by former German artillery captain Carl W. Spohr, serialized in 1932 by *Wonder Stories*, two unnamed superpowers of the twenty-first century count on their enormous arsenals, including defensive massed batteries of beam weapons and energy shields, to deter each other from war. When their nightmarish conflict does erupt, a semiaccidental discharge of tactical atomic shells quickly escalates into an overwhelming exchange of atomic missiles and raids by nuclear-armed long-range bombers, leaving only a few bands of survivors on the planet.

In 1940 several articles about the wonders of atomic energy appeared in popular American magazines. Far more blandly optimistic than the typical SF story of the period, these articles dismissed the use of atomic energy for superweapons as "unthinkable," except by "eccentrics and criminals." But also in 1940, *Liberty* magazine serialized Fred Allhoff's novel *Lightning in the Night*, which urged an all-out scientific-industrial effort to develop atomic bombs before Hitler did; at the end America's nuclear superweapons establish a Pax Americana.

A far less optimistic future is envisioned in Robert A. Heinlein's aptly titled "Solution Unsatisfactory" (1941); the Pax Americana breaks down and an American colonel establishes a global dictatorship as the only means to prevent catastrophic further use of a deadly radioactive dust whose development he had supervised. According to John W. Campbell, this story was widely discussed among scientists working on the Manhattan Project, some of whom, as recently declassified documents reveal, proposed using radioactive dust as Heinlein had imagined.

Although the basics of nuclear technology had already been published, in 1940 the U.S. government imposed censorship on all further public mention of cyclotrons, fission, uranium, betatrons, or anything else having to do with atomic power. From then until atomic bombs were exploded on Japanese cities in August 1945, the only Americans exposed to any thoughts about atomic weapons were readers of SF. The government paid no serious attention to the appearance of atomic weapons in SF, which was considered a fantasyland inhabited by kids and kooks, until the Manhattan Project approached its goal. Then even comic strips mentioning atomic power, such as a Superman strip scheduled to run in April 1945, were banned. But when military intelligence descended on Cleve Cartmill and John W. Campbell after Cartmill's "Deadline" appeared in the March 1944 *Astounding Science Fiction,* Campbell argued against banning further stories about atomic bombs because these weapons appeared so frequently in *Astounding* that their sudden disappearance would be a signal to the Axis that they were close to being produced.

After the bombings of Hiroshima and Nagasaki, society became so influenced by the nuclear promise and threat that distinctions between SF and the rest of the culture rapidly began to evaporate. SF now became an essential instrument for interpreting and extrapolating what was no longer "just science fiction." Some SF of the 1940s looked beyond the U.S. nuclear monopoly to see an uncontrolled arms race leading to the kind of future in which we live. These stories foresaw not only the menace of nuclear holocaust but also the growing loss of freedom and mental health in a society dominated more and more by its own weapons. Among the most important and still relevant works of the first few years of the nuclear age are Theodore STURGEON's "Memorial" (1946) and his masterpiece "Thunder and Roses" (1947), Chan DAVIS's "To Still the Drums" (1946), Ray BRADBURY's "The Million-Year Picnic" (1946) and "There Will Come Soft Rains" (1950), William TENN's "Brooklyn Project," Judith MERRIL's "That Only a Mother" (1948) and *Shadow on the Hearth* (1950), Fritz LEIBER's "Coming Attraction" (1950) and "A Bad Day for Sales" (1953), Alfred BESTER's "Disappearing Act" (1953), and Ward MOORE's brilliant "Lot" (1953) and "Lot's Daughter" (1954).

After the initial burst of anxiety and enthusiasm about living in a nuclear age, serious cultural attention was increasingly segregated once again in the SF ghetto, so the stories just mentioned were at first mainly read by fans. Even some of them began to complain about being tired of nuclear war stories; in "Gloom and Doom," a statement of policy in the January 1952 issue of GALAXY SCIENCE FICTION, editor H. L. GOLD announced that he was henceforth going to reject all stories of "atomic doom."

Then in 1957 came *Sputnik.* The Soviet rocket that put the first human-made object in space brought home to America and its allies the threat that for twelve years had hung over the Soviet Union. The warnings that had been damned up in the isolated reservoir of hard-core SF now burst forth in a flood of SF reaching a far wider audience, including novels read by millions and movies seen by tens of millions around the globe. These were the years of Nevil SHUTE's novel (1957) and Stanley Kramer's film (1959) ON THE BEACH, Helen Clarkson's *The Last Day* (1959), Walter M. MILLER, Jr.'s *A Canticle for Leibowitz* (1959), Mordecai Roshwald's *Level 7* (1959) and *A Small Armageddon* (1962), Pat Frank's *Alas, Babylon* (1959), Alfred Coppel's *Dark December* (1960), Leo Szilard's novella *The Voice of the Dolphins* (1961), Eugene Burdick and Harvey Wheeler's novel (1962) and Sidney Lumet's film (1964) FAIL SAFE, Peter GEORGE's *Red Alert* (1958) and the film launched from this novel, Stanley KUBRICK's *Dr. Strangelove, Or How I Learned to Stop Worrying and Love the Bomb* (1964). These novels and films challenged fundamental assumptions of the arms race and even turned the possible suicide of the human species into a subject for serious popular thought. Some of these works have attracted an audience that continues to grow into the late 1980s.

Exploring the looming nuclear menace was a central impulse of NEW WAVE SF, leading to such classics as J. G. BALLARD's "The Terminal Beach" (1964) and *The Atrocity Exhibition* (1972), Philip K. DICK's *The Penultimate Truth* (1964) and *Dr. Bloodmoney; Or How We Got Along after the Bomb* (1965), Harlan ELLISON's excoriating "I Have No Mouth, and I Must Scream" (1967) and *A Boy and His Dog* (1969), Kate WILHELM's "Countdown" (1968), and Norman SPINRAD's "The Big Flash" (1969).

In the 1980s SF about our nuclear predicament has attained unprecedented popularity. Russell HOBAN's 1980 novel *Riddley Walker* immediately established itself as a major work of world literature, and the 1983 television feature THE DAY AFTER set the record for the number of viewers watching a single show. In a perverse acknowledgment of SF's role in creating nuclear culture, such works as WAR GAMES (1983), TESTAMENT (1984), THREADS (1984), Denis Johnson's *Fiskadoro* (1985), David BRIN's *The Postman* (1985), Carolyn See's *Golden Days* (1986), and Martin Amis's *Einstein's Monsters* (1987) are probably no longer recognized by many of their viewers and readers as SF.

H.B.F.

O

O'BRIEN, [MICHAEL] FITZ-JAMES (1828–1862).

Irish poet and short story writer who emigrated to America in 1852 and established himself as one of the major writers in the pre–Civil War bohemian movement. Apart from a handful of short fantasies, O'Brien's work is almost forgotten today, the last collection of his stories, *The Diamond Lens and Other Stories*, having been published in 1932; a century ago, however, he was much praised and was regarded as one of the masters in the evolution of the American short story and a natural successor to Edgar Allan POE. In science fiction O'Brien is best known for "The Diamond Lens" (1858), the seminal story on the theme of microcosmic, or in this case microscopic, worlds. Also much anthologized is "What Was It? A Mystery" (1859), the first story to detail adequately an invisible being whose alien form is assessed from a plaster cast.

Less well known, but of equal import, are a number of intriguing fantasies which explore realms of the imagination that would later be ruled by SF. "Seeing the World" (1857), for instance, is one of the first stories to explore the possibilities of telepathy; "The Wondersmith" (1859) deals with the transference of life to inanimate objects; "The Lost Room" (1858) considers the possibilities of multidimensional space; "From Hand to Mouth" (1858) is a strangely surreal fantasy seemingly inspired by the narrator's overindulgence in drink. Another dream story is "How I Overcame My Gravity" (1864), an early consideration of space travel.

O'Brien was killed in the Civil War at the age of only thirty-four. The first collection of his works was *Poems and Stories* (1881), edited by William Winter. Winter reissued this collection without the poems as *The Diamond Lens and Other Stories* (1885). The *Collected Stories* (1925), edited by Edward J. O'Brien, contains less material than the earlier volumes.

M.A.

O'BRIEN, WILLIS (1886–1962).

American SPECIAL EFFECTS technician, one of several who simultaneously invented the technique of stop-motion animation, in which jointed models are moved a frame at a time. For many years O'Brien (known as OBie) was the only animator who used this technique in realistic settings, until his protégé, Ray HARRYHAUSEN, began his solo career. On his best films, OBie's approach, unlike Harryhausen's, was to impart vivid personalities to his creations (Harryhausen emphasizes realism); this has meant that OBie's classics—THE LOST WORLD (1925), KING KONG, *Son of Kong* (both 1933), and MIGHTY JOE YOUNG

(1949)—continue to entertain viewers the world over. His career, beset by personal tragedy and long periods of frustrating inactivity, also included *The Last Days of Pompeii* (1935), *The Animal World* (1956), *The Black Scorpion* (1957), and THE GIANT BEHEMOTH (1958).

B.W.

OFFUTT, ANDREW J[EFFERSON, V] (1937–   ).

American author and life insurance salesman. Offutt's first published story, "And Gone Tomorrow" (1954), won a college science fiction contest in *If*. He was treasurer (1973–1976) and president (1976–1978) of the SCIENCE FICTION WRITERS OF AMERICA. His prodigious fictional output (he had forty-five books published between 1970 and 1985) takes several forms: serious sociological SF, such as *The Castle Keeps* (1972), which portrays an overpopulated and polluted world; humorous, often satiric SF, exemplified by many of the short stories collected in *Evil Is Live Spelled Backwards* (1970); a sex and space exploitative novel series, Spaceways, written under the pseudonym John Cleves; heroic fantasy of his own invention, such as *Messenger of Zhuvastou* (1973); and heroic fantasy using such Robert E. HOWARD characters as Conan and Cormac mac Art in *Sword of the Gael* (1975), *Conan and the Sorcerer* (1978), and other novels.

R.S.C.

OLIVER, [SYMMES] CHAD[WICK] (1928–   ).

American science-fiction writer and anthropologist who broke into SF in 1950 and was soon recognized as one of the significant authors of that significant decade, with frequent short stories, three novels, and two collections. Oliver grew up in Texas, earned an M.A. degree in English from the University of Texas and a Ph.D. in anthropology from UCLA, and has taught and served as chairman of the Anthropology Department at the University of Texas ever since, writing part time and producing only a collection of stories and two novels in the 1970s and no new books since. His fiction, with its wide-open spaces and outdoor activities, reflects his Southwest environment, and, with its focus on aliens and anthropological themes, and sometimes anthropologists, his professional field. His writing pioneered the anthropological perspective in SF, but the breadth and depth of his work make him more than merely an "anthropological SF writer." He also has written an award-winning western novel and an anthropological text.

WORKS: *Mists of Dawn* (1952); *Shadows in the Sun* (1954); *Another Kind* (collection, 1955); *The Winds of Time* (1957); *Unearthly Neighbors* (collection, 1960); *The Edge of Forever* (collection, 1971); *The Shores of Another Sea* (1971); and *Giants in the Dust* (1976).

H.W.H.

THE OMEGA MAN (1971).   *Directed by Boris Sagal; screenplay by John William Corrington and Joyce M. Corrington; adapted from the novel* I Am Legend *by Richard Matheson; photographed by Russell Melty; music by Ron Grainer. With Charlton Heston, Anthony Zerbe, Rosalind Cash. 98 minutes. Color.*

The second film adaptation of Richard MATHESON's *I Am Legend* (the first, an Italian-American production, was THE LAST MAN ON EARTH, released in 1964 and starring Vincent PRICE), *The Omega Man* takes place after a bacteriological war has destroyed much of the world's population; most of the survivors are plague carriers (called albinos). Robert Neville (Charlton Heston), a scientist who managed to immunize himself earlier, is pursued by the albinos, who hold science responsible for their mutated condition. Eventually Neville learns of the existence of a group of young people as yet unaffected by the plague. He creates a serum from his own blood to ensure their survival, but he himself is murdered by the albinos.

The film is a rather broad adaptation of Matheson's novel, wherein the plague carriers are portrayed as vampires. (Indeed, *I Am Legend* helped to legitimize vampires as science-fiction props.) Before its release many thought *The Omega Man* would finally capture the book's paranoid intensity, but Hollywood tinsel and clichés about scientific responsibility won out.

D.P.V.

ON THE BEACH (1959).   *Directed by Stanley Kramer; screenplay by John Paxton and James Lee Barrett; adapted from the novel by Nevil Shute; photographed by Giuseppe Rotunno; music by Ernest Gold. With Gregory Peck, Ava Gardner, Fred Astaire, Anthony Perkins, Donna Anderson, John Tate, Lola Brooks, Guy Doleman, John Meillon. 134 minutes. Black and white.*

Following an unspecified nuclear incident, a shroud of fallout has wiped out all life in the Northern Hemisphere; it will soon overwhelm Australia, where life still exists. The story centers on the captain of an American submarine (Gregory Peck), the hedonistic woman he eventually allows himself to love (Ava Gardner), and others awaiting their doom. A submarine trip to California in search of possible life is fruitless, and those left soon kill themselves.

Publicity for this film treated it as the most important event in film history, with simultaneous premieres the world over. But *On the Beach* has dated badly: seen today it is essentially uninvolving. It has its merits, of course: Giuseppe Rotunno's photography is outstanding, and Fred Astaire and Ava Gardner are so skilled that their undeveloped characters come to life. But Stanley Kramer's approach is too romantic for the material, and only a few incidents effectively dramatize the extent of

the disaster; the best is an auto race in which the drivers don't care if they survive. Mostly, however, the deaths are sanitized—those who die do so neatly and offscreen.

The film's status as an *event* now seems merely a promotion device; the movie never suggests a way out of the fate it describes, and the characters' resigned acceptance of the inevitability of radioactive doom is irritating (although just as irritating in the novel). There are vignettes that have power, but overall *On the Beach* is just another Hollywood movie.

B.W.

ONE MILLION B.C. (1940).   *Directed by Hal Roach and Hal Roach, Jr.; screenplay by Mickell Novak, George Baker, and Joseph Frickert; photographed by Norbert Brodine; music by Werner R. Heymann. With Victor Mature, Carole Landis, Lon Chaney, Jr., John Hubbard, Nigel de Brulier, Robert Kent, Ed Coxen, Creighton Hale, Conrad Nagel (narrator). 85 minutes. Black and white. Alternate titles:* Cave Man, Man and His Mate. *Note: Some sources list D.W. Griffith as director or codirector of this film; Griffith was involved in preproduction planning and casting, but he left the film before shooting began.*

ONE MILLION YEARS B.C. (1966).   *Directed by Don Chaffey; screenplay by Michael Carreras; photographed by Wilkie Cooper; music by Mario Nascimbene. With John Richardson, Raquel Welch, Percy Herbert, Robert Brown, Martine Beswick, Jean Waldon, Lisa Thomas, Malya Nappi, Richard James, William Lyon Brown. 91 minutes. Color.*

Epics of prehistoric humanity have been made throughout film history, from D.W. Griffith's *Man's Genesis* (1912) to CLAN OF THE CAVE BEAR (1986). Among the most popular was *One Million B.C.* A frame story introduces contemporary travelers who, seeing cave paintings, imagine themselves in a distant time when humanity lived in caves.

Ousted from his own Rock People tribe, young Tumak falls in love with Loana of the Shell People. At the climax a volcano explodes; survivors of both tribes unite. In both films an artificial prehistoric language was used rather than English. The remake eliminated the frame story.

Both films are adventure melodramas; neither was intended as a paleontological-anthropological tract, so to complain that both show human beings coexisting with dinosaurs is pointless. The earlier film, made in less cynical times, is romantic in design and concept; the leads are much more obviously a hero and a heroine than in the gritty, grim remake, which emphasizes violence and strives futilely for realism.

The special effects of the earlier film, by Roy Seawright and Fred Knoth, include several mammals (mammoths, a coatimundi, and a costumed armadillo). More nu-

Victor Mature doing battle in *One Million B.C.*

merous are lizards—tejus, iguanas, monitors, and others—unconvincingly but dramatically impersonating dinosaurs. Some of this footage, as well as much of the impressive volcanic eruption, turned up in other films for many years.

Ray HARRYHAUSEN animated several believable dinosaurs for the remake, although that film used live animals as well. The most memorable aspect of the newer version, at least for male viewers, was Raquel Welch in a fur bikini; the film helped establish her as a star.

B.W.

ORBAN, PAUL (?–?).

American science-fiction illustrator whom Brian W. ALDISS has called an "incurable romantic in a field of incurable romantics." Orban illustrated magazines from the late 1940s until 1960. His work appeared in *The Shadow, Original Science Fiction Stories, If, Space Science Fiction, Future SF,* and *Astounding Science Fiction,* among others. He varied his style, sometimes using Finlay-like cross-hatching, other times producing simple line work with conte crayon shading, and sometimes employing fine lines to give the impression of etching. Like Virgil FINLAY, he often included scantily clad women in his work. He is best known for his illustrations for A. E. VAN VOGT's "The Rull" in *Astounding* and L. Ron HUBBARD's "The Unwilling Hero" in *Startling Stories.*

J.G.

ORWELL, GEORGE [Pseudonym of Eric Arthur Blair] (1903–1950).

British novelist and essayist, whose *Nineteen Eighty-four* (1949), like Aldous HUXLEY's *Brave New World* (1932), is everybody's favorite example of mainstream science fiction. Orwell and Huxley, two of the major satirists and literary figures of the 1930s and 1940s, represent for most readers and critics test cases for the differences between mainstream and genre fiction. Clearly *Nineteen Eighty-four* draws its form, and inspiration, not from genre SF but from H. G. WELLS, and equally clearly, like *Brave New World,* it is not above and outside the SF category because of excellence in writing or greater concern for character but is SF by any definition.

In the 1930s, as a left-wing social critic, Orwell drew on a variegated background: schooling at Eton, five hated years as a police officer in Burma, life among tramps in Paris and London and among unemployed workers in the depressed north of England. After the outbreak of the Spanish Civil War in 1936, he went to Barcelona, where he joined a socialist militia that was soon suppressed by the dominant Communist party. This experience—described in *Homage to Catalonia* (nonfiction, 1938)—determined the political outlook of his later novels. In *Animal Farm* (1945) he used the frame of the animal fable for a brilliantly sustained parody on Stalinism and the self-perpetuating mechanics of power.

Nineteen Eighty-four (a reversal of the last digits in 1948, the year in which it was completed) was his masterpiece. Although it owes a debt to Wells's *When the Sleeper Wakes* (1899) and Yevgeny ZAMIATIN's *We* (1920), Orwell's grim projection of a totalitarian society is a brilliant extrapolation of Communist control over not only individual actions but thought and truth itself. In the novel three superpowers have divided the world and are constantly at war in one combination or another, not to defeat one another but to maintain control over their citizens. Technology is used primarily for surveillance. Winston Smith—Orwell's typical, ordinary, decent hero—is not only betrayed, imprisoned, and tortured by the Thought Police but systematically deprived of his individual identity until he is able to perceive as truth whatever O'Brien, his tormentor, desires. At the end, chillingly, Smith has learned to love Big Brother, the deified leader whose face and eyes are everywhere.

Irony abounds: the Ministry of Peace is in charge of war; the Ministry of Love maintains law and order; the Ministry of Plenty presides over Oceania's poverty; and Smith works in the Ministry of Truth, which is in charge of rewriting history. An appendix describes one of the State's tools, "Newspeak," in which, once it is perfected, "a heretical thought . . . should be literally unthinkable." The actual arrival of the eponymous year precipitated vast new reprintings and reappraisals, including evaluations of Orwell's "predictions."

The novel was filmed (as *1984*) in Britain by Michael Anderson in 1955 and, with far greater success, by Michael Radford in 1984.

J.H.

THE OUTER LIMITS (1963–1965). *Directed by Leslie Stevens, Gerd Oswald, Byron Haskin, Leonard Horn, John Erman, James Goldstone, and others; written by Joseph Stefano, Leslie Stevens, Robert C. Dennis, Meyer Dolinsky, Harlan Ellison, Seeleg Lester, Anthony Lawrence, Robert Mintz and Allan Balter, Ellis St. Joseph, Donald S. Sanford, Jerry Sohl, Robert Towne, and others; music by Dominic Frontiere (first season) and Harry Lubin (second season). With Robert Culp, Robert Duvall, Martin Sheen, Bruce Dern, Warren Oates, Cliff Robertson, David McCallum, Martin Landau, Sally Kellerman, John Hoyt, Chita Rivera, Adam West, Neil Hamilton, George Macready, Mark Richman. 49 one-hour episodes. Black and white.*

This audaciously mounted TV anthology series is best remembered for its wild potpourri of aliens and special effects, its expressionistic film noir look with an emphasis on Gothic melodrama and downbeat stories, and its offbeat "Control Voice" (Vic Perrin) with its weekly invocation, "There is nothing wrong with your television set. . . ."

The strongest basis for the program's enduring popularity was the creative control wielded by its producer, Joseph Stefano, over the first thirty-two episodes. Stefano contributed to virtually every script, and his love of the surreal and philosophical lent the show a textured, adult quality that defied the ray-guns-and-space-invasions bent taken by most previous video forays into SF. Extraterrestrials, for example, were presented as humane and sympathetic, given to lyrical speechmaking reminiscent of Klaatu's admonitions in THE DAY THE EARTH STOOD STILL.

Although relatively few episodes originated with recognized SF writers, there were exceptions: David DUNCAN contributed the script for "The Human Factor"; Jerry SOHL adapted his own stories "The Invisible Enemy" and "Counterweight" into scripts, as did Harlan ELLISON ("Soldier" and "Demon with a Glass Hand"). A Clifford D. SIMAK short story, "Goodnight, Mr. James," was adapted as "The Duplicate Man"; Otto BINDER's Adam Link stories were interpreted in "I, Robot." Other segments resulted from extremely loose use of source material by genre regulars Louis CHARBONNEAU, Ib Melchior, and Arthur Leo Zagat.

This powerfully cinematic series has stood the passage of time and the inherent problems of marketing. It has been in perpetual syndication since its network cancellation after a season and a half. By 1981, the year United Artists Television predicted its permanent withdrawal from the syndication market, *The Outer Limits* had rated the cachet of uninterrupted broadcast on PBS affiliates as classic Golden Age television. 1986 saw a definitive overview of the show, *The Outer Limits: The Official Companion*, and in 1987 the first six episodes were made commercially available on videotape.

D.J.S.

OUTLAND (1981). *Directed by Peter Hyams; screenplay by Peter Hyams; photographed by Stephen Goldblatt; music by Jerry Goldsmith. With Sean Connery, Peter Boyle, Frances Sternhagen, James B. Sikking. 109 minutes. Color.*

Outland is the most important example of the science-fiction western. In classic western style, the plot involves a corrupt town (in this case a mining settlement on the moons of Jupiter) that can only be made clean by one pure man (Sean Connery, who plays, of all things, the sheriff), who can call on one pure woman (Frances Sternhagen) for aid.

Perhaps the worst part of the film is its occasional lack of scientific plausibility; the moon of Jupiter looks a good deal like a present-day mining installation. (In ALIENS, 1986, Hyams did a much better job of making a similar industrial setting appear to be part of the future.) The film is saved by Connery's usual strong performance as an embittered loner. Hyams subsequently directed the far better 2010 (1984).

M.M.W.

——— OVERPOPULATION ———

The population explosion became a popular theme in science fiction in the 1950s and 1960s, although the logic of the problem was first elaborated by Thomas R. Malthus in his 1798 *Essay on the Principle of Population*. Frederik POHL's black comedy "The Census Takers" (1956), Robert SILVERBERG's earnest *Master of Life and Death* (1957), and Cyril M. KORNBLUTH's bitterly horrific "Shark Ship" (1958) mapped out the spectrum of attitudes—from horror at the agonies of an overcrowded world to horror at the measures required to deal with the problem—characteristically reflected in fiction. Novels that paint an elaborate picture of future societies struggling to cope with a population expanding beyond their resources include *Make Room! Make Room!* (1966) by Harry HARRISON and *Stand on Zanzibar* (1969) by John BRUNNER. Attempts to examine the kinds of social and psychological adaptations necessary for living in a crowded world include *A Torrent of Faces* (1968) by James BLISH and Norman L. KNIGHT, and *The World Inside* (1972) by Silverberg.

In the second edition of his essay (1803) Malthus conceded that by the exercise of "moral restraint" human beings might control the growth of the population, but he obviously had little confidence in this possibility, and his view was echoed by SF writers, who felt that even modern methods of birth control would prove insufficient. Most stories of calculated population control therefore tend to the horrific, often involving culling by mass murder; examples include *The Quality of Mercy* (1965) by D. G. COMPTON and *Time of the Fourth Horseman* (1976) by Chelsea Quinn YARBRO. Dark pessimism, as displayed by such stories as "We All Die Naked" (1969) by James BLISH, in which the possibility of exporting excess population into space is dismissed, was commonplace. Since the mid-1970s, however, this species of alarmism has waned considerably, as original estimates of population growth have proved too high and food supplies have increased to meet and, in places, sometimes exceed demand.

B.S.

P

PAL, GEORGE (1908–1980).

Hungarian-born puppeteer, special effects expert, producer, and director whose long and influential career emphasized films of fantasy and science fiction. Pal's movies earned five Academy Awards for special effects and were significant in helping to bring the genre out of low-budget disrepute into big-budget respectability in the 1950s.

After studying cartooning and animation, Pal began his career at the Hunnia Film Studio in Budapest, then worked as a set designer for the important UFA Studios in Germany in 1931. After Hitler's rise to power, Pal moved to Paris and began making stop-motion animated shorts and commercials, which he called Puppetoons. He came to the United States in 1939 and was soon hired by Paramount, where he produced a series of Puppetoon shorts that the studio hoped would compete with Walt Disney's cartoons. The series proved popular and went on until 1947, when rising production costs rendered it too expensive.

Pal's work with SPECIAL EFFECTS in live-action films began with *The Great Rupert* (1949), which features an animated squirrel along with Jimmy Durante. Its commercial success allowed its producers, Eagle Lion Films, to finance Pal's next project, DESTINATION MOON (1950), based on Robert A. HEINLEIN's book *Rocketship Galileo* (1947). Both the author and rocket expert Hermann Oberth, who had consulted on Fritz LANG's *Die Frau im Mond (Woman in the Moon,* 1929), were hired as technical advisers, and the film displays an impressive attention to scientific realism. It was one of the first popular SF movies of the early 1950s and helped launch that decade's spate of SF film production. Pal then produced a series of major SF films with large budgets for Paramount, beginning with WHEN WORLDS COLLIDE (1951).

A number of these movies—WAR OF THE WORLDS (1953), *The Naked Jungle* (1954), CONQUEST OF SPACE (1955), and THE POWER (1967)—were directed by Pal's friend and collaborator, Byron Haskin, himself a former special effects artist. Some of the films also feature the work of Gordon Jennings, Paramount's top special effects expert

during the 1950s. All are lavishly produced and possess state-of-the-art effects for their time. Pal himself directed as well as produced THE TIME MACHINE (1960), his most financially successful production. Although the movie sacrifices some of the complexities of H. G. WELLS's vision in the novel on which it is based, the time travel effects and the Victorian quality of the production design, and particularly of the time machine itself, make it enjoyable viewing.

Among Pal's other feature films as director are *Atlantis, the Lost Continent* (codirector, 1961), *The Wonderful World of the Brothers Grimm* (codirector, 1962), and *The Seven Faces of Dr. Lao* (1964).

His last film was *Doc Savage—The Man of Bronze* (1975), which he produced and coscripted. He was working on a production of William F. NOLAN's novel *Logan's Run* when an executive shuffle at MGM resulted in the film being made without him in 1976.

B.K.G.

PALMER, DAVID R[EAY] (1941–   ).

American writer and shorthand court reporter. After what he has called a marginal high school education, Palmer held a variety of jobs before attending court-reporting school and, in 1976, making a career as a certified shorthand court reporter.

He made a remarkable splash in the science-fiction field with the publication of his first work of SF, the novella "Emergence" in ANALOG in 1981, followed by its sequel, "Seeking," in 1983. They were combined as the novel *Emergence* (1984), the story of the aftermath of a bionuclear war in which most of humanity died, focusing on Candy Smith-Foster, who may be the first representative of a new stage in human evolution. In a kind of laconic, often verbless personal journal, she narrates her odyssey across the United States seeking other *Homo post hominem.* These three publications set a remarkable record: all made the final Hugo ballots for their years, with "Seeking" and *Emergence* coming in second for the award. The novel also finished second for the Philip K. Dick Award and won the Compton Crook Memorial Award for best first novel. Palmer also finished second in 1983 for the John W. Campbell Award for the best new writer.

Threshold (1985), Palmer's second novel, is a more expansive work in which the hero, Peter Cory, learns that an ancient alien race has given him extraordinary abilities and that he will now be taught to use them in order to combat an evil cosmic force that threatens the galaxy. Unlike *Emergence*, this novel won no awards, but it was received by readers with equal enthusiasm. Palmer has said that his second novel is more representative of his taste in SF: for no-holds-barred space opera.

After these two unusually promising beginnings, Palmer fell silent, but in 1987 he reported that he was working on two books: the sequel to *Threshold*, with the working title *Special Education*, and another non-SF novel.

J.E.G.

PALMER, RAYMOND A. (1910–1977).
American editor, publisher, author, and pioneer science-fiction fan. Palmer is remembered today mostly for his editorship of AMAZING STORIES, *Fantastic Adventures*, and *Other Worlds*, plus a number of occult mystery magazines, including *Fate* and *Mystic*. He also did more than anybody else to promote initial interest in the study of flying saucers, because he was instrumental in bringing Kenneth Arnold's *The Coming of the Saucers* (1952) into print. These activities, along with his association with Richard SHAVER and the so-called Shaver Mystery, have depicted Palmer, a little unfairly, as a fanatic and a crank, when in fact he was a highly inventive and energetic writer.

Palmer was one of the pioneers of SF fandom as the editor of the first SF-generated fanzine, *The Comet*, in 1930 and an official in the early SF clubs. He was also the editor of one of the first specialist publishing ventures, *Dawn of Flame* (1936), the memorial volume to Stanley G. WEINBAUM, now a rare collector's item. Palmer's own fiction, which started with "The Time Ray of Jandra" (1930), has never been assembled in book form; although it is of variable quality, it includes some rousing, unpretentious adventure yarns, such as "Black World" (1940, as A. R. Steber), "Doorway to Hell" (1942, as Frank Patton), and "The Vengeance of Martin Brand" (1942, as G. H. Irwin).

M.A.

PANGBORN, EDGAR (1909–1976).
American author best known for his humanistic science fiction, especially two highly regarded novels, *A Mirror for Observers* (1954) and *Davy* (1964). Although Pangborn began writing general fiction under a pseudonym in 1930, his first work of SF was "Angel's Egg," published in GALAXY in 1951.

After the publication of his first SF novel, *West of the Sun* (1953), about colonization on another planet, Pangborn won the International Fantasy Award for *A Mirror for Observers*. A philosophical tale, this novel describes a Martian "observer" of twentieth-century Earth who is expected to remain objective in his study of terrestrials but becomes involved in the lives of two talented children. The second half of the book describes the effect of a plague induced by irresponsible biochemical research and satirizes the era of Senator Joseph McCarthy in the person of a clever fascistic politician named Joseph Max.

Although Pangborn continued to publish short stories in the SF genre, his next two novels were *A Wilderness of Spring* (1958), a historical romance, and *The Trial of Callista Blake* (1961), a depiction of a murder trial. However, in *Davy* Pangborn produced his most vigorous novel, describing the growth in moral awareness of a picaresque young hero four hundred years after a nuclear holocaust and its ensuing plague. This novel concludes ironically with an attempt by Davy and his friends to bring enlightenment to the superstitious culture of post-disaster Boston, but the hero's spirit remains undaunted.

Pangborn's vividly imagined postholocaust realm in *Davy* is one of the more credible descriptions of such futures in SF. He explored this terrain further in two less impressive novels, *The Judgment of Eve* (1966) and *The Company of Glory* (1975), and in the short stories collected in *Still I Persist in Wondering* (1978), most of them of superior quality. In general Pangborn's SF is distinguished by an urbane and sometimes poetic style, depth of characterization, and a mature and compassionate humanism.

OTHER WORK: *Good Neighbors and Other Strangers* (collection, 1972).

E.L.C.

PANIC IN YEAR ZERO! (1962).
Directed by Ray Milland; screenplay by Jay Simms and John Morton; photographed by Gilbert Warrenton; music by Les Baxter. With Ray Milland, Jean Hagen, Frankie Avalon, Mary Mitchell, Joan Freeman, Richard Bakalyan, Rex Holman, Neil Nephew, Richard Garland, Willis Bouchey. 92 minutes. Black and white. (Reissued as End of the World.)

A typical American family is on a camping trip when they learn that America has suffered an atomic attack. They do what they need to to survive, even becoming ruthless, but by the end authorities have begun to restore order.

Although the serious intentions of this film cannot be questioned, it approaches the theme of atomic attack simplistically, and the protagonists resemble a TV situation comedy family. Even for the period, the women are depicted deplorably, and the movie's ending is strangely optimistic. The film approaches sensationalism in some scenes and varies from justifying the husband's tendencies toward violence to decrying them. But *Panic in Year Zero!* is essentially honest; it is a failure but an ambitious and respectable one.

B.W.

PANSHIN, ALEXEI (1940–).
American author of science fiction and criticism. Panshin's first novel, *Rite of Passage* (1968), won the Nebula Award, and it remains his best work of fiction. Set on a giant self-

Alexei and Cory Panshin

Illustration by Paul for Jack Williamson and Laurence Schwartzman's "Red Slag of Mars" (*Wonder Stories Quarterly*, 1932)

supporting starship that wanders through the galaxy, the novel describes, through subtle symbolism and restrained drama, the maturation of a precocious young girl from childhood to early womanhood. *Rite of Passage* is reminiscent of Robert A. HEINLEIN's seminal novella "Universe" (1941); indeed Panshin has found inspiration in Heinlein's work since his student days. His first book-length work of criticism, *Heinlein in Dimension* (1968), is a pioneering study of the Heinlein canon.

Panshin's shorter fiction, collected in *Farewell to Yesterday's Tomorrow* (1975), is underrated. More popular is his early trilogy of restrained adventures featuring the urbane Anthony Villiers; *Star Well* (1968), *The Thurb Revolution* (1968), and *Masque World* (1969) are literate and humorous entertainments involving Villiers's adventures on backward worlds. *Earth Magic* (1978), an ambitious fantasy novel by Panshin and his wife, Cory, describes the ordeals of the son of a heroic warrior on a planet where a mother goddess exercises power. It reflects the authors' fascination, evident in their criticism, with the theory of literary romance.

Although Panshin's work is intelligent and readable, it has been limited at times by a lack of emotional depth. *Earth Magic* suggests that his fiction is now moving in a direction that attempts to balance rationality and passion.

E.L.C.

PAUL, FRANK R[UDOLPH] (1884–1963).
American illustrator born in Austria, whom Vincent DI FATE has called "the father of science-fiction illustration." Trained as an architect as well as a student of art in Vienna, Paris, and New York, Paul illustrated textbooks as his principal occupation, but he became best known as the first great science-fiction illustrator. He

was working as a newspaper illustrator when Hugo GERNSBACK discovered him and put him to work on his popular science magazines, *Electrical Experimenter* and later *Science and Invention*. He moved naturally into SF work and painted all the covers for AMAZING STORIES while Gernsback owned it, as well as the covers and many inside illustrations on Gernsback's *Wonder Stories*.

Print reproduction was poor in the 1920s and 1930s, and Paul attempted to cope with this problem by using vivid colors and bold lines. His people often seemed stiff, but he was particularly effective with cities, machines, aliens, and alien worlds, the last particularly in a series of backcover paintings for the Ziff-Davis magazines of the late 1930s and 1940s. His paintings seem crude by today's standards, in terms of both subject and technique, but Paul created the artistic environment in which science fiction was perceived in its earliest days, and his interest in gadgets, as well as his bold style, influenced artists such as Hans WESSOLOWSKI, Leo MOREY, Robert Fuqua, Alex SCHOMBERG, and other gadget painters down to the present.

J.E.G.

PEAKE, MERVYN [LAWRENCE] (1911–1968).
British author, illustrator, and poet of distinction. Born in China, where he lived for twelve years, Peake wrote a number of children's books but remains best known for the Gormenghast trilogy. Comprising *Titus*

Groan (1946), *Gormenghast* (1950), and *Titus Alone* (1959; revised from the original manuscript in 1970), the trilogy is a unique fantasia of intrigue and rebellion in a vast and ancient castle, which is a self-contained world without referent to history or geography. Often misclassified as Gothic or Tolkienesque fantasy, the trilogy defies easy categorization and places Peake among the great writers of the twentieth century.

None of Peake's works is science fiction in the strict sense, although *Titus Alone*, with its strange machines and stranger societies, displays elements of the genre. His *Mr. Pye* (1953) is a gentler fantasy. The novella "A Boy in Darkness" (1956) brings back the protagonist of the Gormenghast books. Peake's most direct contribution to SF may well have been his influence on the British NEW WAVE writers, particularly Michael MOORCOCK, who championed him in NEW WORLDS.

OTHER WORKS: *Letters from a Lost Uncle from the Polar Regions* (1948); *Writings and Drawings* (1974); *Peake's Progress* (1978).

D.S.

THE PHANTOM EMPIRE (GENE AUTRY AND THE PHANTOM EMPIRE) (1935). *Directed by B. Reeves Eason and Otto Brower; photographed by Ernest Miller and William Nobles; music by Arthur Kay. With Gene Autry, Frankie Darro, Smiley Burnette, Dorothy Christy, Wheeler Oakman, Betsy King Ross, Frank Glendon. 230 minutes (serial version); 71 minutes (feature version). Black and white. Alternate titles:* Radio Ranch, Men with Steel Faces.

One of the most popular and frequently revived Mascot serials of the 1930s, *The Phantom Empire* is a high-camp gold mine. Is it a western or a musical or a science fiction film? It is, in fact, all of the above, an inimitable combination of three genres. Twenty-five thousand feet below Radio Ranch lies the lost kingdom of Murania, ruled by the evil Queen Tika (Dorothy Christy) and patrolled by hordes of robots. This is no place for a cowboy, or "surface man," like Gene Autry, who is reduced to speaking lines such as "He's the one who allowed me to escape the death chamber so the revolutionists could study my breathing structure."

D.W.

———— PHILOSOPHY ————

The problems of philosophy can be roughly sorted into four categories. The first covers the mind's attempts to analyze its own nature (including its relation with the body and the question of the freedom of the will) and to understand the processes of thought (including the analysis of logic and questions of meaning). The second covers the mind's attempts to confront and comprehend the world outside: questions relating to the reliability of perception and scientific method as means of gathering knowledge. The third covers the attempt to reach beyond the perceived world in order to establish some kind of metaphysical context in which to understand it (including, of course, questions of theology). The fourth covers the question of how people should live in the community: moral and political issues.

In all four of these categories speculative fictions have some role in philosophical discourse; philosophers are continually establishing hypothetical cases to compare and contrast with actual ones. Plato's dialogues (to which, it has been alleged, the history of philosophy can be seen as a series of footnotes) are shot through with such fictions, used to dramatize as well as analyze; they range from the allegory of the cave to the description of the hypothetical Republic and the imaginary history of Atlantis. Allegory, fable, and parable are all philosophical modes of literary discourse, and philosophical meditations such as those of René Descartes are rife with fantastic imagery. It is hardly surprising that when prose fiction was extensively developed in the Age of Enlightenment it produced a genre of *contes philosophiques*, most famously practiced by VOLTAIRE. Many *contes philosophiques*, including Voltaire's "Micromegas" and Book 3 of Jonathan SWIFT's *Gulliver's Travels*, qualify as early examples of proto–science fiction.

The relation between philosophy and literature remained much closer in Voltaire's France than in Swift's England, which was to produce far fewer philosopher-writers, but British speculative fiction kept in close touch with philosophical issues. Several of the early writers of scientific romance—most obviously H. G. WELLS and M. P. SHIEL—had serious pretensions to be social and evolutionary philosophers, while others looked to philosophers for inspiration; for instance, John BERESFORD borrowed ideas from G. W. F. Hegel and Henri Bergson for *The Hampdenshire Wonder* (1911).

Among later writers of scientific romance, Olaf STAPLEDON was a teacher of philosophy and a serious contributor to moral philosophy, while H. F. Heard and C. S. LEWIS both used their fiction as a vehicle for their philosophical theses. Such works as Stapledon's *Star Maker* (1937), Heard's *Doppelgängers* (1947), and Lewis's *Perelandra* (1943) are all *contes philosophiques* first and scientific romances second. When the greatest of modern British philosophers, Bertrand Russell, took to the writing of fiction late in life, it came naturally to him to produce fantasies and scientific romances—his second collection, *Nightmares of Eminent Persons* (1954), is mostly science-fictional in character.

In America, Edgar Allan POE, Nathaniel HAWTHORNE, and Edward BELLAMY wrote speculative *contes philosophiques* in the nineteenth century; Bellamy popularized his social philosophy through the best-selling utopian romance *Looking Backward* (1888), but this tradition was not carried on with any force into the SF of the PULP MAGAZINES. Even pulp SF, however, cannot help bearing on philosophical problems in some of its most commonplace themes; for instance, the idea of time travel leads inevitably to questions of logical paradox, and the idea of foreseeing the future must raise the question of free will. To imagine an alien being is to construct a hypothetical viewpoint from which humanity can be seen in a new light, and to imagine an intelligent robot is to raise questions about the nature of mind and what it really means to be "human." As magazine SF evolved through the 1940s and 1950s, its writers became gradually more sensitive to these aspects of their themes.

If we take the four categories of philosophical problems in turn, we can readily quote examples to show how extensively they have fascinated SF writers. With respect to the first category—the mind's attempt to understand itself—James BLISH raised the question of free will, in connection with the premise that information might be transmitted back in time, in "Beep" (1954; expanded as The Quincunx of Time, 1973). This question is also an issue in such stories as Kurt VONNEGUT, Jr.'s Slaughterhouse-5 (1969), which considers how the acceptance of determinism should affect our personal philosophies of life, and Kim Stanley ROBINSON's The Memory of Whiteness (1985).

The mind-body problem is begged by vast numbers of stories that involve exchanges of identity or the separation of minds from bodies, but it has been brought into sharp focus by many modern stories which, like Robert SILVERBERG's The Second Trip (1972), take seriously the idea of erasing and imprinting personalities on human brains. The notion of creating a conscious personality in an artificial "brain" has received extensive treatment, most cleverly in stories of maturing artificial intelligences, such as Joseph H. DELANEY and Marc Stiegler's Valentina (1984).

The possibility of "transplanting" human personalities into computers has also been a common theme in such stories as Rudy RUCKER's Software (1982). This matter is correlated with the notion of augmenting human brains with electronic hardware to create a special kind of cyborg, as in Kevin O'Donnell's Mayflies (1979). A currently popular idea is that it might be possible for human beings interfaced with computers to project their identities from their bodies into the "dataspace" inhabited by the programs—a notion that plays a key role in William GIBSON's award-winning novel Neuromancer (1984). All these stories accept a model in which the mind relates to the body in the same way that the software of a computer relates to its hardware, and they imagine that some kind of translation is in principle feasible. (Science-fiction writers of the 1930s and 1940s usually supposed that there must be some intrinsic difference between human minds and robot "minds"—generally having to do with emotionality—but it is now widely assumed that no such difference would be discernible; this is an important theme in the work of Philip K. DICK, as expressed in Do Androids Dream of Electric Sheep? 1968, and We Can Build You, 1972.)

More subtle questions of identity are raised by SF stories in which people are duplicated, as for instance David GERROLD's The Man Who Folded Himself (1973) or C. J. CHERRYH's Voyager in Night (1984). The most sensitive SF analysis of hypothetical questions of identity is Gene WOLFE's The Fifth Head of Cerberus (1972).

There is little SF which speculates about alternative kinds of logic, although doubt about our present understanding of the nature of perception is expressed in such novels as A. E. VAN VOGT's The World of Null-A (1948). It is interesting that there is also very little SF which actually questions the scientific method, except for stories that are skeptical about the metaphysical question of whether the universe is sufficiently orderly in its nature actually to yield to rational analysis. Most skeptical in this fashion are Eastern bloc writers such as the brothers STRUGATSKY, in such works as Monday Begins on Saturday (translated into English in 1977) and Definitely Maybe (translated 1978), and Stanisław LEM, whose scientists in Solaris (translated 1970) and His Master's Voice (translated 1983) seem only to be reading their ideological preconceptions into the phenomena.

Western writers are much more likely to question in a slightly different way, dwelling instead on the unreliability of perception and the difficulty of identifying "reality" when faced with compelling illusions. Modern SF is full of malicious "demons" which, like that of Descartes's first meditation, devote themselves to deluding us; usually they are drugs, such as those in Philip K. Dick's novels The Three Stigmata of Palmer Eldritch (1964) and Now Wait for Last Year (1966), but they may also be tailored dreams, as in James Morrow's The Continent of Lies (1984), alien beings with great powers, as in Dick's The Cosmic Puppets (1957), or humans with similar powers, such as the hapless patient in Ursula K. Le GUIN's The Lathe of Heaven (1971).

Some SF writers have also borrowed from philosophers' ideas about the way what we think of as "reality" is affected and constrained by the languages we use to describe it—the cardinal examples are Samuel R. DELANY in Babel-17 (1966) and Ian WATSON in The Embedding (1973). Perhaps the most philosophically interesting of all such stories is J. G. BALLARD's "The Overloaded Man" (1961), whose protagonist attempts to dissolve his perceived world back into raw sense data.

Skepticism about whether things are really as they seem also plays a large part in the third philosophical category, metaphysical fantasies produced by SF writers. These fantasies include many stories of what Peter Nicholls has called "conceptual breakthrough," in which people in apparently eccentric worlds break through the horizons of their experience to find a much greater context (as, for instance, when the tiny puddle dweller in James Blish's "Surface Tension," 1952, puts his head through "the sky" to see the world beyond).

Our notion of "the universe" is itself a hypothesis, and SF writers delight in speculative extensions of that hypothesis which make our universe part of a vaster "multiverse"; this was often done in the 1930s and 1940s by making our Solar System an atom of a greater cosmos, but nowadays such extensions are usually accomplished by imagining our history as part of an unfolding complex of alternate universes that contain all possible histories. This fascinating image has acquired a degree of respectability thanks to physicists who accept it as one interpretation of the apparent indeterminacy of some subatomic phenomena—a respectability incorporated into such SF novels as Frederik POHL's *Coming of the Quantum Cats* (1986).

Many SF stories have also attacked the question of the frame of time—the idea of circular or cyclic time is particularly popular; Brian W. ALDISS's *An Age* (1967) and Michel Jeury's *Chronolysis* (translated 1980), however, display more sophisticated and adventurous speculative play with the nature of time. Science-fiction writers have often evaded the paradoxes arising from time travel by means of metaphysical reconstructions, as in John VARLEY's *Millennium* (1983).

Science fiction features a great many adventures in speculative metaphysics of a quasi-theological nature, as represented by Philip K. Dick's *VALIS* and *The Divine Invasion* (both 1981) and Philip José FARMER's *The Unreasoning Mask* (1981). Writers of SF can handle religious ideas in a variety of ways—as evidenced by the range of fictions in Alan Ryan's anthology *Perpetual Light* (1982)—but they are especially fond of setting up imaginary situations that replicate items of religious faith. The securing of an afterlife with the help of convenient aliens is one such popular situation, featured in Bob SHAW's *Palace of Eternity* (1969), George R. R. MARTIN's "A Song for Lya" (1974), and Nicholas Yermakov's trilogy begun with *Last Communion* (1981). The fascination of this idea is further displayed in the anthology *Afterlives* (1986), edited by Pamela SARGENT and Ian WATSON.

It is hardly necessary to offer examples of the way SF bears on philosophical questions of the fourth category—issues of moral and political philosophy. In every image of the future, questions of how human beings should live are overtly or covertly at stake. Science-fiction novels written to display political philosophies, such as Ayn Rand's *Atlas Shrugged* (1957), are not, however, necessarily more interesting than novels wherein such questions simply arise of their own accord. Similarly, stories such as Tom GODWIN's "The Cold Equations" (1954), which is little more than a sharp demonstration of utilitarian principles, need not be sin-

gled out from the thousands of works that question our ethics by asking us to consider novel situations. Where SF considers such issues as meetings with alien beings or imagines innovations in biotechnology, it must confront basic issues in ethical philosophy, and in these respects SF still belongs to the tradition of *contes philosophiques;* it is a significant means of framing questions for consideration, and as such it provides ordinary people with an important heuristic aid for the philosophical investigations we need to pursue and take delight in pursuing.

B.S.

———— PHYSICAL SCIENCES ————

Science fiction is not so much fiction about science as fiction about change; it was initially a literary response to the change a few nineteenth-century writers began to see in the world around them. The writers observed that it was created by science and technology, and they started to write stories and novels speculating about future changes that might occur.

In SF's beginnings writers turned, for story material, to the biological sciences, sometimes mixed with the new science of electricity, as in Mary Wollstonecraft SHELLEY's *Frankenstein* (1818) or Nathaniel HAWTHORNE's "Rappaccini's Daughter" (1844), or the behavioral sciences, such as the mesmerism in Edgar Allan POE's "The Facts in the Case of M. Valdemar" (1845) and Hawthorne's *The Blithedale Romance* (1852). But clearly astronomy, chemistry, geology, meteorology, physics, and so forth, and their technological offspring in the areas of power, transportation, communications, new products and production methods, and new methods of farming and obtaining minerals, were changing Western civilization most dramatically. So Richard Adams Locke's 1835 Moon Hoax series of articles in the *New York Sun* speculated about a giant new telescope, Poe dealt with balloons, Fitz-James O'BRIEN imagined the perfect microscope in "The Diamond Lens" (1858), Herman Melville and Ambrose BIERCE constructed stories about robots, Rudyard KIPLING wrote a couple of stories about dirigibles, and even Mark TWAIN wrote a story about a kind of television.

But it was the fathers of science fiction, Jules VERNE and H. G. WELLS, in their stories and novels about traveling to the Moon, to the center of the Earth, under the oceans, and to the future, who, each in his own way, established the physical sciences as the primary inspiration for authors and the way they achieved plausibility for the readers in their *voyages extraordinaires* and scientific romances that eventually would become SF.

Writers drew on the physical sciences not only for ideas but to make plausible their romantic or epic stories of distant places or the future. In any kind of story authors must convince their readers that the events *could* happen: plausibility is the means by which readers are sufficiently convinced of the validity of the fictional experience that they can suspend their disbelief for as long as the experience lasts. In SF plausibility is achieved by presenting a background consistent with current science as understood by educated readers or the reasonable modification of current science that is called extrapolation.

In the magazine stories of the 1920s and the 1930s, the physical sciences were king. Hugo GERNSBACK, founder of *Amazing Stories,* published many kinds of stories, including some of Poe's psychological thrillers and Wells's social speculations, but the stories he himself wrote, such as *Ralph 124C 41+,* were full of technological speculations; *Ralph* even has a diagram for radar, which had not yet been invented or even named. And Gernsback dearly loved the translations of his native German writers, with their great, clanking machines. His greatest discovery was Doc SMITH, whose Skylark serials have spaceships gallivanting around the Solar System (and eventually the galaxy). In large part the SF magazines emerged not from the category pulp chains but from the popular science magazines; however, in 1937 Clayton Publications produced *Astounding Stories of Super Science,* very much a pulp-chain–type magazine.

John W. CAMPBELL, Jr., who would turn his attention (by example and, when he became editor of *Astounding* in 1937, by precept) to psychology and philosophy as Don A. Stuart, started his writing career competing with E. E. Smith in the field of the space epic. His Aarn Munro in *The Mightiest Machine* (1934/1947) and later in *The Incredible Planet* (1949) spends most of his time advancing the state of physics; he develops antigravity, interdimensional, and interstellar travel, and weapons capable of destroying worlds and producing novas. Neither in these stories nor in Campbell's Piracy Preferred series (1930–1932) does a female character appear; romance in either the Victorian or any modern sense is completely absent. The total attention of the characters is devoted to quantum mechanics, the nature of space, the wave structure of the atom, and similar strictly scientific matters.

In many tales of this time, physics was replacing magic as a storytelling device. Authors and readers shared the opinion of the general public: anything was possible; sooner or later science would learn how. In some instances authors used scientific information as a source of plot ideas; in others they invented a plot and then sought scientific justification for the things that were to happen. The latter particularly was the case in stories published in *Astounding Stories of Super Science,* which decorated its standard pulp adventure formula with a scientific rationale.

John Russell FEARN's *Liners of Time* (1935/1947) exemplifies this use of the physical sciences; its justifica-

tions of time travel, invisibility, and the hurling around of planets were just gobbledygook. Campbell, in contrast, followed the first method, obtaining his story ideas from new scientific theories and speculations. His use of science produced hard SF; a fair name for the other type of story might be "wishful SF."

Science-fiction plots have been divided into *extrapolative,* or "if this goes on," and *speculative,* or "what if." The extrapolative uses of the physical sciences produce hard SF, the speculative, wishful SF.

Examples of ideas found in wishful SF include, but are not limited to education by machines, weather control, teleportation, and (in early stories) robots and biological engineering. Smith's Skylark novels (the first published in 1928) feature a device for taping thoughts and knowledge patterns (even from dead brains) and replaying them into other people's minds. A son could continue his father's life research "with only the twenty-five years or so of basic education needed to learn to think." Stories involving the concept of an education pill that appeared in the 1960s or later, such as Kate WILHELM's "The Planners" (1968) and James E. GUNN's *The Dreamers* (1981), probably qualify as hard SF, because they follow a number of misinterpreted but widely publicized experiments which seemed to demonstrate that flatworms could acquire training patterns by devouring trained flatworms. But the operation that turns mentally handicapped Charlie Gordon into a supergenius in Daniel KEYES's "Flowers for Algernon" (1959) is just as wishful as Professor Wogglebug's education pills in L. Frank Baum's Oz books.

The weather control practiced by Nat Schachner's invaders in "Slaves of Mercury" (1932) is clearly wishful; in contrast the several stories built on experiments with dry ice and silver iodide cloud seeding in the late 1940s, such as Ben Bova's "The Weathermakers" (1960), are just as evidently hard. Similarly, the earliest biological engineering stories long preceded the breaking of the DNA code or even the recognition of its existence. In Norman L. KNIGHT's "Crisis in Utopia" (1940), a new human species is being designed to exploit the marine environment. By the time the stories collected in James BLISH's *The Seedling Stars* (1952–1956/1957) were published, the idea of reshaping humanity into fantastic forms might qualify as hard SF. Even Robert A. HEINLEIN's use of a gene selection technique in *Beyond This Horizon* (1942/1948) was more nearly realizable.

These stories by Blish and Heinlein deal primarily with biological and not physical sciences. They exemplify, however, how early the biological sciences with which SF began made a significant reappearance, as evidence began to mount that these sciences were influencing the nature of existence in significant ways. It was clear, for instance, that improvements in medicine and public health could extend the human life span; few scientific advances had had as great an impact on the way people think and live, and it was this direct effect that drew SF writers once again to the behavioral and social sciences. But their greatest period of influence had to wait for the end of World War II.

Stories using ROBOTS capable of doing house, garage, or factory work have been numerous: Herman Melville's robot struck a bell ("The Bell-Tower," 1855); Ambrose Bierce's played chess ("Moxon's Master," 1909); and one significant element in Isaac ASIMOV's SF production has been stories built around his Three Laws of Robotics. A few recent works of this type qualify as hard SF, because much actual robot labor now takes place in factories. The robot general housekeeper remains a wishful concept, though, and exemplifies one of the most common weaknesses in the robot story in general: what we now call "programming" was not recognized as a problem by authors until computer engineers ran into it in real life. Science-fiction writers also failed to foresee the miniaturization achieved by solid-state electronics; the supercomputer that appeared in a story typically was described as "several tons of thinking metal."

The word *wishful,* as used here, also seems to describe an aspect of the Frankenstein myth that characterizes many robot stories—the idea of the creation turning against its creator—and against which Asimov's robots, with their built-in "law" against harming humans, were conceived. The likelihood of any computer or assemblage of chemicals spontaneously developing human-level intelligence seems rather on a par with the likelihood of any given assemblage of chemicals spontaneously developing cell-organized life, but both ideas have been used in SF. In William Lemkin's "Cupid of the Laboratory" (1937), a collection of chemicals bombarded overnight by X rays is operating as a giant amoeboid cell by morning. H. A. Highstone's "Frankenstein Unlimited" (1936) is described by its title. A more thoughtful variation on the theme is John W. Campbell's "The Machine" (1935), in which the intelligent mechanism comes to recognize the damage being done to humanity by having all its work done and all its problems solved for it; the mechanism decides to leave Earth for humanity's good. In Robert A. HEINLEIN's *The Moon Is a Harsh Mistress* (1966), the lunar colony's centralized computer complex develops spontaneous intelligence and helps the Moon dwellers in their fight for independence from Earth.

In all these cases, criticism of the author's scientific knowledge must be tempered by consideration of artistic problems. Scientific research and engineering development are time consuming, and their details may be entertaining only to a few people. Campbell's Aarn Munro realistically would have spent years or decades developing his discoveries—if they could have been developed at all. Scientific plausibility is important to an SF story, but a reasonably fast pace is essential to *any* story. Robot intelligence, benign or otherwise, may eventually

Albert Einstein

develop after long, detailed planning and trial, but a realistic description of the process would be tedious at best for most potential readers.

This is just one reason why SF is seldom genuinely prophetic. Another is the fact that it is as hard to consider all the potentially relevant factors in fiction as it is in life. Authors of the 1920s knew about Albert Einstein's equivalence of mass and energy and commonly used "atomic" power in their stories, for lighting, for the powering of vehicles and factories, for weapons—for anything by which energy might be needed. The atomic fuel might be sand, water, copper, uranium, element 87 (so called; the actual element was then unknown, or at least unisolated), or sometimes anything handy—after all, everything is made of atoms. The only recognized dangers of atomic power derive from its deliberate misuse—either in bombs or, sometimes, in the breakdown reaction that could get loose and involve the whole planet (which after all also consists of atoms). It was commonly assumed that solving the power of "the atom" was equivalent to solving that of space travel, as in Edwin BALMER and Philip WYLIE's *When Worlds Collide* (1932/1933). The principal problem of space travel, after all, was the need for energy. Few writers of that time foresaw the actual effect on the public of atomic power (presumably because nuclear weapons, not power, came first)—that is, a reaction of panic toward even the words *nuclear* and *radioactivity*. Lester DEL REY, with his novella "Nerves" (1942/1956), was a rare exception.

Space travel also was taken for granted virtually from the beginning but often with an apparently limited grasp of the detailed science involved. The suggestions that a spaceship that has run·out of fuel or lost the operation of its engines is doomed to fall into the Sun or onto the nearest planet cannot be excused by artistic need: the real dangers inherent in such a situation are numerous and potentially thrilling enough. In many cases basic Newtonian dynamics seemed beyond the writer's grasp. The stories are hard only in the sense that their creators recognized the stars to be suns and planets, between which a vacuum necessitated that the spaceship be equipped with rockets or some more exotic form of drive. Aside from this acknowledgment, readers frequently could criticize the writers for scientific slips, as they have in magazine letter columns from the 1920s to today. BUCK ROGERS, in a comic strip that started in 1929, was far from the only character to tread most of the planets and many of their moons in shirtsleeves.

Astronomical distance scales in stories often were vague. Henry J. Kostka's "Earth Rehabilitators, Consolidated" (1935) describes an interstellar government with headquarters on the planet Spica, several hundred light-years distant, but an infinitely shorter journey from Saturn to Earth was said to require five months. As in the later STAR TREK television series, familiar star names such as Rigel and Antares provided scenarios for stories, quite often with the implication (to the astronomically informed reader) that a character had in effect gone from Washington to Baltimore via Honolulu. The fact that the majority of named stars are giants old enough to have swallowed their Earthlike planets or too young to have evolved intelligence on any orbiting worlds was not recognized even by the astronomical profession until relatively recently.

There is some evidence that general understanding of Newtonian mechanics has improved. Unfortunately for SF, this evidence is found in works that may be only marginally SF, such as Martin CAIDIN's technically sound *Marooned* (1964).

John W. Campbell, after being named editor of *Astounding* (later *Analog)* in 1937, was responsible for a significant shift in tone, expressing a desire for "stories that would be published in a magazine in the twenty-fifth century." In ordinary literature, he pointed out, writers didn't need to explain the working of an automobile or a firearm; it followed, then, that a skillful practitioner of SF could make spaceships and ray guns plausible without using the obtrusive description and explanation of the 1920s and 1930s. Campbell's influence may have been directly responsible for the nearly total disappearance of the gadget story in the next few years. At roughly the same time, SF writing standards began to improve; stories featured more detailed and convincing characters and more tightly developed plots. As the gadget story waned—and plot and characterization assumed greater importance—the physical sciences moved into the background.

This is not to say that they became less important to the story; hard SF survived at the time and still does. The science essential to the plot, however, is no longer fed to the reader in inserted pages of explanation or forced dialogue. The nuclear technology of Lester del Rey's "Nerves" or Frank HERBERT's *Under Pressure* (1955/ 1956; also titled *The Dragon in the Sea)* come by implication and example, as do the astronomy, chemistry, and biology in such novels as Poul ANDERSON's *Satan's World* (1968/1969), Hal CLEMENT's *Mission of Gravity* (1953/1954), and Larry NIVEN's *Ringworld* (1970), to name only a few. Robert FORWARD, a research physicist, retained some of the old explanation flavor in *Dragon's Egg* (1980) and its sequel, *Starquake* (1985), but his novels would have been perfectly acceptable to Campbell.

The correctness of a work's science remains a matter of argument between reader and writer, as it always has. Science and technical students at MIT enjoyed themselves seeking (and finding) errors in the shape of Clement's planet Mesklin in *Mission of Gravity—* and the erroneous assumptions and computations that had caused them. And because the physical sciences are always changing, even a writer who is absolutely correct at the time a work is published cannot expect to remain so. Further, the genre is and will presumably remain an exercise ground for that most human of qualities, the disciplined, critical imagination.

In this connection hypotheses and suggestions not taken seriously by many, or perhaps any, practicing scientists still are explored by the storyteller. The field commonly called psionics or parapsychology—involving telepathy, teleportation, and remote cognition in space and time—has at the moment only controversial statistical evidence supporting any of its manifestations, but numerous well-written stories have made use of this material.

James H. Schmitz's "Witches of Karres" (1949; as a novel, 1966) and his Telzey Amberdon series (1962–) are good examples. In some of these stories, the incompatibilities with conventional science of the assumed phenomena are, in fact, the point of the plot; in others they are ignored. Anne McCAFFREY never mentions in her series of Pern novels that her teleporting dragons would have trouble with conservation of momentum; but in a world where all the laws of physics are operating, one of the creatures, going westward across a continent, would emerge into normal conditions heading straight down at 500 miles an hour. Such scientific considerations are exercise for the informed reader's imagination. Larry Niven, when he used mechanical teleportation, did consider the conservation of momentum in several stories and set realistic limits on the directions and distances over which it could operate.

Actual scientific discoveries and unrealized scientific hypotheses can and do contribute to the literary art form called science fiction, just as SF stories have anticipated and, in a few cases, inspired scientific and technological developments: a number of scientists and explorers have credited Jules Verne and H. G. Wells with their ideas, and even careers, and NASA was peppered with SF readers. The same human qualities—awareness of the universe, curiosity, and the disciplined imagination—produce both science and science fiction.

H.C.

PIERCE, ARTHUR C[ALHOUN] (1923–1987).
American writer and occasional producer or director of science-fiction films beginning with his first screenplay, *The Cosmic Man* (1958). Pierce's films were often low on budget but generally high on enthusiasm, reflecting his love for science and science fiction. While even Pierce admitted that his movies may not have been "earthshakers," they continue to be shown on television, and many are available on videocassette. Several have built loyal cult followings. Pierce's best films, *Beyond the Time Barrier (1959), Mutiny in Outer Space* (1964), and *Destination Inner Space* (1965), focus on conflicts between science and the military over some threat to humankind. Other common threads include a bantering dialogue between main characters, as in *Women of the Prehistoric Planet* (1965) and *Dimension 5* (1966), and extraordinary beings in ordinary situations, as in *The Human Duplicators* (1964) and *Cyborg 2087* (1966). Pierce endeavored to explore concepts and ideas that were often beyond his limited budgets, but his imagination and pleasure in his work are always evident.

K.R.D.

PIERCY, MARGE (1936–).
American poet and mainstream novelist who has occasionally used science-fiction concepts although she has no known links to the SF community. Piercy's work is organized around her feminist concerns, and in her best-known novel, *Woman on the Edge of Time* (1976), a psychic mind link transports the protagonist, a woman confined in a mental hospital, into a twenty-first-century utopia where the group has replaced the nuclear family as the basic social unit and gender is no longer divisive. The similarities between Piercy's work and that of such SF writers as Joanna Russ and James Tiptree, Jr., illustrate the arbitrariness of categories.

J.H.

PIPER, H[ENRY] BEAM (1904–1964).
American writer and railroad engineer. Piper's individualist heroes generally have to fight hard to defend their libertarian principles, whether in robust adventure stories, such as *Space Viking* (1963) and *Lord Kalvan of Otherwhen* (1965, also known as *Gunpowder God),* or in lighter

and more sentimental works, such as the Fuzzy series: *Little Fuzzy* (1962), *The Other Human Race* (1964), and *Fuzzies and Other People* (1984; the manuscript was lost for many years). His short stories of the Paratime Police (in *Paratime,* 1981) develop some interesting alternate worlds. Piper's suicide put a premature end to his burgeoning career, but his novels about the cute alien fuzzies have been sufficiently popular to generate two books by other writers: *Fuzzy Bones* (1981) by William Tuning and *Golden Dream* (1983) by Ardath Mayhar. *Little Fuzzy* has been adapted for young children as *The Adventures of Little Fuzzy* (1983).

OTHER WORKS: *Ullr Uprising* (1953/1982); *Crisis in 2140* (with John J. McGuire, 1957); *A Planet for Texans* (with John J. McGuire, also known as *Lone Star Planet,* 1958); *Four-Day Planet* (1961); *Junkyard Planet* (also known as *The Cosmic Computer,* 1963); *Federation* (1981); *Empire* (1981); *The Worlds of H. Beam Piper.*

B.S.

PISERCHIA, DORIS (1928–).
American author identified with science fiction's NEW WAVE of the 1960s. Piserchia's first professional sale was "Rocket to Gehenna" *(Fantastic Stories,* 1966); her first novel, *Mr. Justice,* appeared in 1973. More typical of her work, however, is her next novel, *Star Rider* (1974): in a radically transformed world of the far future, the energetic and irreverent young heroine hurtles at breakneck speed through a series of unpredictable adventures. This basic pattern is repeated with variations in subsequent works, and although Piserchia's plot details sometimes prove confusing, the exuberance of her protagonists and the imaginative situations they encounter guarantee lively and captivating tales that celebrate the irrepressible human spirit.

OTHER WORKS: *A Billion Days of Earth* (1976); *Earthchild* (1977); *Spaceling* (1979); *The Spinner* (1980); *The Fluger* (1980); *Doomtime* (1981); *Earth in Twilight* (1981); *The Dimensioneers* (1982); *The Deadly Sky* (1983).

R.H.T.

PLAN 9 FROM OUTER SPACE (1959).
Directed by Edward D. Wood, Jr.; screenplay by Edward D. Wood, Jr.; photographed by William C. Thompson; music supervised by Gordon Zahler. With Gregory Walcott, Mona McKinnon, Dudley Manlove, Tom Keene, Duke Moore, Tor Johnson, Bela Lugosi, Vampira, Joanna Lee, Lyle Talbot, Paul Marco. 79 minutes. Black and white.

Since the late 1970s this has become the favorite bad movie of many film buffs. Ignored at the time of its original release, *Plan 9* has achieved its greatest fame as "the worst movie ever made." Created by Edward D.

Wood, Jr., to use footage of Bela Lugosi from a vampire movie left uncompleted when the actor died, *Plan 9* is in fact too distinctive and eccentric to be the worst, although its cheapness is legendary.

Aliens try to prevent Earthlings from discovering sunlight-detonating Solaronite by reviving corpses that attack unwary passersby. At the end the aliens' flying saucer explodes, probably paving the way for Plan 10. Lugosi (and the chiropractor who plays his double) is one of the revived corpses.

The low budget of this film shows in almost every way possible, from completely inadequate sets to amateurish acting. But what makes the film truly memorable is the surrealistic dialogue. Among the often quoted lines: "Inspector Clay is dead—murdered—and someone's responsible!" And "Visits! That would indicate visitors!" Anyone interested in film history should see this film at least once. Perhaps nine times.

B.W.

PLANET OF THE APES (1968).
Directed by Franklin J. Schaffner; screenplay by Michael Wilson and Rod Serling; adapted from the novel Le Planète des singes *by Pierre Boulle; photographed by Leon Shamroy; music by Jerry Goldsmith. With Charlton Heston, Roddy McDowall, Kim Hunter, Maurice Evans, James Whitmore, James Daly, Linda Harrison, Robert Gunner, Lou Wagner. 112 minutes. Color.*

BENEATH THE PLANET OF THE APES (1970).
Directed by Ted Post; screenplay by Paul Dehn and Mort Abrahams; photographed by Milton Krasner; music by Leonard Rosenman. With James Franciscus, Kim Hunter, Maurice Evans, Linda Harrison, Lou Wagner, Paul Richards, Victor Buono, James Gregory, Jeff Corey, Charlton Heston. 94 minutes. Color.

ESCAPE FROM THE PLANET OF THE APES (1971).
Directed by Don Taylor; screenplay by Paul Dehn; photographed by Joseph Biroc; music by Jerry Goldsmith. With Roddy McDowall, Kim Hunter, Bradford Dillman, Natalie Trundy, Eric Braeden, Ricardo Montalban, William Windom, Sal Mineo, Albert Salmi, Jason Evers, M. Emmet Walsh. 98 minutes. Color.

CONQUEST OF THE PLANET OF THE APES (1972).
Directed by J. Lee Thompson; screenplay by Paul Dehn; photographed by Bruce Surtees; music by Tom Scott. With Roddy McDowall, Don Murray, Natalie Trundy, Hari Rhodes, Severn Darden, John Randolph, Ricardo Montalban. 86 minutes. Color.

BATTLE FOR THE PLANET OF THE APES (1973).
Directed by J. Lee Thompson; screenplay by John William Corrington and Joyce Hooper Corrington; photographed by Richard H. Kline; music by Leonard Rosenman. With Roddy McDowall, Claude Akins, Natalie Trundy, Severn Darden, Lew Ayres, Paul Williams, Austin Stoker, France Nuyen, Paul Stevens, John Huston, John Landis. 86 minutes. Color.

The impact of 2001: A SPACE ODYSSEY on film history is so powerful that *Planet of the Apes*, released the same year, is sometimes overlooked for its part in re-establishing science fiction as a film genre. Because of its weakness in some areas as SF, the film is unjustly neglected; it is, in fact, exciting, engrossing entertainment.

Astronaut Charlton Heston crash-lands on an unidentified planet; he soon discovers that apes—gorillas, chimpanzees, and orangutans—are the dominant intelligent species, while *Homo sapiens* is a hunted animal. He rebels against the apes, who are themselves shocked to discover a thinking, talking human being, and flees from their city only to discover that the planet is Earth of the far future.

The ending was no surprise to those even moderately familiar with SF or those who realized that an Earthlike planet where the inhabitants speak English could *only* be Earth. Nonetheless, it surprised most audiences in 1968 and was in keeping with the satiric intent of the middle portion of the film, in which Heston's human vitality is contrasted with the inflexible society of the apes.

The film had been planned for several years, but it wasn't until John Chambers designed the unusually lightweight but expressive makeup that *Planet* became technically feasible. Leon Shamroy's photography and Jerry Goldsmith's distinctive score help overcome the more didactic stretches of the film; Franklin J. Schaffner's intense direction, fast paced and inventive, is also responsible for the film's great success. Four sequels of varying quality followed, as well as a short-lived 1974 TV series with Roddy McDowall, who appeared in all but one of the films; episodes of the series were edited into "movies" that have been shown on television. There was also an animated TV series.

The first sequel, *Beneath*, tried to extend some of the ideas of the original film rather than merely imitate its effects. However, in the first half a newly arrived astronaut, James Franciscus, goes through the same adventures as Heston; seeking Heston, he finds a group of mutated human beings who worship a bomb capable of destroying the world. Dying, Heston detonates the bomb, confirming the apes' beliefs about humans.

With the world destroyed, it was difficult to come up with a sequel, but in *Escape* writer Paul Dehn inventively sent some apes back in time to the human world before the disaster that had left apes the masters of Earth. The innocents abroad plot line is more overtly comic than that of either of the first two films and made the movie popular on its own. The story also cannily leaves things open for further sequels, which would (and did) show

how the Planet of the Apes came to be.

In *Battle* McDowall plays the chimpanzee founder of the society of apes, the son of the character he had played in two of the previous three films. He leads a successful rebellion against vicious human beings in the fiery climax. *Battle* was the last of the series written by Paul Dehn, and his guiding hand is sorely missed in the last film. In his entries Dehn also tried to maintain the satiric, allegorical intent of the first film.

Battle is set after the atomic war that resulted when humanity enslaved apes but before the events of *Planet of the Apes*. The plot line is conventional, but it ends with proof that the bleak world of the first film has been forestalled: human beings and apes now live in harmony.

The Apes series is remarkable for its use of makeup, the relatively high standards it maintained, and its financial success. The films are rarely shown today.

B.W.

THE PLANETS

Since the earliest days of science fiction—and in fact before SF existed as a self-conscious genre—the other planets of our Solar System have served as the settings for numerous works of speculative fiction. The way in which the planets are depicted, however, has changed considerably over the years—in part because of literary fashion but perhaps most significantly because of our changing knowledge about the planets themselves.

The earliest stories used the planets merely as convenient locales for imagined societies, created by their authors for purposes of social satire or romance. The Moon was observably a world, and after Galileo the other planets were known to be worlds at least vaguely like Earth, although little else was known about them. Writers, therefore, were free to imagine virtually any conditions or inhabitants they wished, with even fewer constraints than they might feel obliged to observe in writing about unexplored lands on Earth. (It is ironic that the planets as thus imagined were generally far less exotic than they have turned out to be in reality.) As early as the second century, LUCIAN OF SAMOSATA used imaginary flights to the Moon as a vehicle for satire. Such writers as Athanasius Kircher in the seventeenth century and W. S. Lach-Szyrma in the nineteenth wrote series of romances involving visits to several planets.

In the late nineteenth and early twentieth centuries writers tended to make at least a nominal effort to incorporate actual characteristics of the planets into their stories. They were handicapped, of course, by sketchy knowledge; only the Moon, Mars, and Venus could be seen well enough by Earthbound astronomers to allow much serious speculation on their surface conditions. And many writers continued to be more interested in romance than in realism, so a rough division occurred

between those who attempted to work within a framework of real astronomical knowledge and those who did not. The years after World War II saw an increasing interest in the planets as possible sites for human colonization and in the problems colonists might actually face.

A dramatic change in the attitudes of SF writers toward the planets began in the 1960s, when American and Soviet space probes began to observe them at close range. The views and data obtained by telemetry from flybys and uninhabited landers (and, in the case of the Moon, by human explorers) were so superior to anything previously available that accepted scientific views underwent rapid and radical revision. For several years the incoming data seemed to discourage the use of Solar System settings, perhaps because authors interested in scientific accuracy were reluctant to write stories likely to be proved obsolete before they were published.

Two other factors probably also contributed to the declining importance of our neighbor planets in SF. Several lines of research (in astronomy, biochemistry, and physics) suggested that the other planets of our Solar System were not very amenable to life, either native or human, but that more hospitable planets were likely to be common around other stars—and that travel to those stars might be feasible. That suspicion had led writers, even in the 1950s, to spend less time on imagining new variations on Mars or Venus and more on creating entire new worlds in other solar systems. And the notion of the planets as potential colonies was diminished in the 1970s when the astronomer Gerard K. O'Neill proposed the creation and colonization of artificial habitats in space within the Earth-Moon system. Nevertheless, a revival of interest in our Solar System's planets may be at hand, because some writers have begun to use the new information obtained from space probes.

By far the most popular planets as subjects and settings for SF have been the Moon, Mars, and Venus. Because the Moon is an unusually large satellite, many astronomers prefer to call the Earth-Moon system a double planet rather than planet and satellite. Its proximity to Earth makes the Moon the only planet whose surface features are obvious enough to suggest strongly its world-like nature to even a casual observer. It is hardly surprising, then, that the Moon was the first world to be used by storytellers as a setting for imagined landscapes and societies. The earliest of these stories, including Lucian's *The True History* (c. 165–175 A.D.) and CYRANO de Bergerac's *L'Autre Monde* (1657), were based almost entirely on imagination and had little to do with actual lunar conditions. Even in the literature of the nineteenth century, space travelers reached the Moon by ordinary atmospheric flight and there met natives not fundamentally dissimilar to terrestrial life.

By the early twentieth century the airlessness and lifelessness of the Moon were taken for granted by most

Chesley Bonestell's vision of Saturn, as seen from Rhea

writers, but so was the possibility of human exploration and colonization. Few stories placed the first lunar landing as early as 1969 (or imagined that it would be covered by live television all over Earth), but the idea, developed in SF, that such a trip was possible almost certainly played a substantial role in making it happen. Early stories such as Robert A. HEINLEIN's "Requiem" (1940) were read by young people who grew up inspired to work toward turning the dream into reality. Later stories and films such as George PAL's *Destination Moon* (1950, with a script by Heinlein) continued to promote the idea that the venture not only was possible but might indeed be imminent.

Even though the Moon was lifeless, many writers saw possibilities for human colonization, as in Arthur C. CLARKE's *Earthlight* (1951), a series of *Saturday Evening Post* short stories by Heinlein in the late 1940s, and Heinlein's 1966 novel *The Moon Is a Harsh Mistress*. Clarke explored the possibility that aliens had visited and left artifacts on the Moon in "The Sentinel," a 1951 short story that found its final expression in the Stanley KUBRICK film 2001: A SPACE ODYSSEY (1968) and also inspired Algis BUDRYS's *Rogue Moon* (1960).

Since the Apollo landings, the Moon itself has seldom been the central subject of new SF, although lunar explorations or colonies still occasionally appear as vehicles for the consideration of other ideas. For example, in Frederick D. Gottfried's "Hermes to the Ages" (1980), a body found on the Moon leads to the discovery of an intelligent race of dinosaurs that achieved space travel long before the dawn of humanity.

Perhaps the Moon's most important role in SF was as a stepping-stone to more difficult and interesting destinations, such as Mars. Mars has long been an object of fascination as the likeliest of the planets to harbor life because it is reasonably close to Earth in size and distance from the Sun, and very close in day length and

axial tilt. Moreover, Mars has visible surface features that, imperfectly seen with Earth-based telescopes, seemed to be evidence of life: the seasonally varying polar caps and the variable dark markings interpreted as oceans, vegetation, or even canals. Many writers seized on these sketchy clues to build vividly detailed pictures of a Mars either presently or formerly inhabited. H. G. WELLS's *The War of the Worlds* (1898) showed Martians invading Earth in an attempt to escape their dying planet. That story strongly influenced many successors, and a 1938 radio dramatization by Orson Welles produced a genuine panic by convincing listeners that the invasion was actually taking place.

Perhaps in reaction to the ruthless invaders of Wells and his imitators, other writers began to tell of quite different kinds of Martians, as in P. Schuyler MILLER's "The Forgotten Man of Space" (1933) and Raymond Z. GALLUN's "Old Faithful" (1934). Stanley G. WEINBAUM's "A Martian Odyssey" (1934) made an unprecedented attempt to portray truly alien creatures sympathetically and consistently. Edgar Rice BURROUGHS (beginning with *A Princess of Mars* in 1912) and Leigh BRACKETT (in *Shadow over Mars*, 1944, and other stories) portrayed lushly exotic Martian ecologies and civilizations. Ray BRADBURY's *The Martian Chronicles* (1950, after earlier publication of several portions as short stories) used Mars with considerable poetic license as the setting for a nostalgic fantasy of a planet haunted by the ghosts of an extinct civilization.

As editor of *Astounding*, John W. CAMPBELL insisted on more realistic speculation, as in H. Beam PIPER's "Omnilingual" (1957), wherein human explorers confronted with a dead Martian civilization must figure out how to read its language without a Rosetta stone. The 1950s produced many stories about the problems of colonizing Mars, such as Arthur C. Clarke's *Sands of Mars* (1951). In many of these Mars was portrayed as at least presently lifeless, in keeping with a growing scientific suspicion, but living Martians still figured prominently in such stories as Robert A. Heinlein's *Stranger in a Strange Land* (1961) and Roger ZELAZNY's "A Rose for Ecclesiastes" (1963).

The biology experiments conducted by the Viking landers in the 1970s were widely interpreted as indicating a lifeless Mars, and this conclusion has stifled most new SF interest in the planet. However, those results remain somewhat ambiguous and controversial, and some writers still postulate unique Martian life systems, as did Ian WATSON in *The Martian Inca* (1976). The Viking results do seem to confirm that Mars in its present form would not be a comfortable home for human colonists, but writers continue to explore possible means of colonization, whether through biological engineering of the colonists, as in Frederik POHL's *Man Plus* (1976), or terraforming of the planet itself, as in Bob Buckley's "Red Wolf" (1985), in which engineering of other life-forms has become an integral part of terraforming.

Terraforming—altering a planet to make it more hospitable to human life—has also played an important role in many of the numerous stories about Venus, which after Mars is the most popular "local" planetary locale. In mass and size Venus is even more Earthlike than Mars, and this fact contributed to its use as a "second Earth" in a great many early stories. Unlike Mars, Venus has a perpetual cloud cover, so the nature of its surface was almost entirely a matter of conjecture until the American Mariner and Russian Venera space probes penetrated the atmosphere in the 1960s and 1970s. This mystery left writers through the 1950s a great deal of freedom in imagining Venusian conditions.

Very early portrayals, such as those of Athanasius Kircher and Emanuel Swedenborg, tended to feature gentle and beautiful inhabitants, perhaps because of the identification of Venus as the Roman goddess of love. In the early twentieth century Venus was a popular setting for colorful romances such as C. L. MOORE's "Black Thirst" (1934) and Leigh Brackett and Ray Bradbury's "Lorelei of the Red Mist" (1934). Many writers imagined some version of a planet that was either mostly ocean (as in Poul ANDERSON's "Sister Planet," 1959) or mostly jungle (as in Anderson's "The Big Rain," 1954). One of the most vividly developed images of Venus appeared in Stanley G. Weinbaum's "Parasite Planet" and "The Lotus Eaters" (both 1935): Weinbaum saw Venus as a very warm, very wet, but essentially terrestrial planet. This picture is now discredited on numerous scientific grounds, including the discoveries that, contrary to long-held belief, the planet does not have a perpetual day or night side, its atmosphere is too poisonous, it completely lacks surface water, and its surface temperatures are too hot to support life.

In some depictions at least part of Venus is inhabitable by humans with little or no technical aid, but many stories have suggested that conditions on some or all of the planets would be unacceptably harsh. To overcome this apparent obstacle, a number of writers have applied the concept of terraforming, among them Olaf STAPLEDON in Last and First Men (1930) and Anderson in "Sister Planet" and "The Big Rain." In The World of A (1945), A. E. VAN VOGT described an unusually benign Venus—a representation disproved by the space probes of the 1960s; when he revised the story for rerelease in 1970, he incorporated a reference to terraforming to account for the environment he described. Some writers have already set to work imagining new ways of terraforming the planet. Bob Buckley has evidenced a keen interest in the consequences of the new findings about Venus. He revised his novel World in the Clouds (1980) several times while it was in press to take account of data just being received.

The remaining inner planet, Mercury, has received relatively little attention from SF writers. As the planet closest to the Sun, it is one of the hardest to observe, but it became clear early in this century that extreme temperatures and lack of atmosphere make Mercury an unpromising candidate for either native life or colonization. A few early stories, such as Ray CUMMINGS's Tama of the Light Country (1930) and Clark Ashton SMITH's "The Immortals of Mercury" (1932), simply refused to be inconvenienced by the astronomical facts. Some later works, such as Isaac ASIMOV's "Runaround" (1942) and Lucky Starr and the Big Sun of Mercury (1956, written under the pseudonym Paul French) and Alan E. NOURSE's "Brightside Crossing" (1956), attempted to be more realistic. As some of these titles suggest, Mercury was long believed to have permanent bright and dark sides; radar measurements in the early 1960s disproved this belief. Grant D. Callin, another writer actively weaving new knowledge of the planets into his stories, drew on this discovery for "The Turtle and O'Hare" (1982), wherein the protagonist must race against the sunrise for survival.

The outer planets have not figured nearly as prominently in SF, although Jupiter, to some extent Saturn, and their major satellites have been intrinsically interesting to scientists and writers of SF. Both Jupiter and Saturn are gas giants, far larger than Earth, and both have large numbers of moons, some of them comparable in size to Earth's moon or even Mercury. Jupiter has the additional special interest of being the largest planet in the Solar System, and Saturn, of course, has its spectacular ring system, until recently believed to be unique and still the largest in the Solar System.

Over the past thirty years, our vision of the possibilities for life on these planets has undergone a particularly dramatic change, only partly for astronomical reasons. As late as the 1950s Jupiter was commonly dismissed as obviously unsuitable for life because of its low temperatures and atmosphere of poisonous gases (hydrogen, methane, and ammonia). Yet by the end of the 1960s many people viewed it as perhaps the best prospect for off-Earth life in the Solar System: biochemical research suggested that these "poisonous gases" are exactly the ones in which life originated on Earth, and their greenhouse effect produces much higher temperatures than previously assumed.

Of course, conditions on Jupiter would be very hostile to humans under either the older or the newer conception, so some of the most memorable early stories of visitation to the planet involve organisms specially modified or created to withstand Jovian conditions, as in Clifford D. SIMAK's "Desertion" (1944) and Poul Anderson's "Call Me Joe" (1957). Arthur C. Clarke's "A Meeting with Medusa" (1971) describes a human expedition encountering native life-forms in the Jovian atmosphere based on a more up-to-date picture of conditions there. The Jovian satellites Ganymede, Callisto, Io, and Europa figure in several early romances; Robert A. HEINLEIN placed colonists on Ganymede in *Farmer in the Sky* (1950), and Gregory BENFORD incorporated more recent findings and speculations on the same subject in *Jupiter Project* (1975). The Voyager space probes have found an unexpected diversity of detail on the Jovian moons, and some of them are showing up in new speculative stories, such as Kenneth W. Ledbetter's "Patera Crossing" (1985), set on a volcanically active Io.

Saturn and its rings and satellites appeared in such early stories as Raymond Z. Gallun's "Raiders of Saturn's Rings" (1941) and later works, including Isaac Asimov's "The Martian Way" (1952) and Kurt VONNEGUT, Jr.'s *The Sirens of Titan* (1959). A number of writers have incorporated more recent views of the planetary system, among them Ben Bova in *As on a Darkling Plain* (1972), Arthur C. Clarke in *Imperial Earth* (1976), Poul Anderson in *The Saturn Game* (1981), and Grant D. Callin in *Saturn Alia* (1986).

Uranus, Neptune, and Pluto have been almost completely neglected by SF. We now know that Uranus and Neptune are very similar gas giants, qualitatively resembling Jupiter and Saturn but considerably smaller. The three planets' very existence, however, was unknown until 1781, 1846, and 1930, respectively, and until quite recently they remained virtual mysteries. Even after their discovery, their remoteness discouraged the interest of romance writers, and in later years SF writers were daunted by their apparent hostility to life and the lack of hard knowledge about them. Nevertheless, they do figure in a few stories. Weinbaum wrote of Uranus in "The Planet of Doubt" (1935); Olaf Stapledon moved humankind to Neptune after the far-future expansion of the Sun in *Last and First Men* (1930) and *Last Men in London* (1932), and J. M. Walsh described it in "The Vanguard to Neptune" (1932).

Pluto, a misplaced terrestrial planet thought to be an escaped satellite of Neptune, is so small and remote that information about conditions there is still largely conjectural, although the planet seems virtually certain to be extremely cold. Pluto has appeared in only a few stories, such as Stanley G. Weinbaum's "The Red Peri" (1935) and Algis Budrys's *Man of Earth* (1958); Clifford D. Simak began *Cosmic Engineers* (1939) in the neighborhood of Pluto and returned to it for "Construction Shack" (1974). A few writers have considered the possibility that a very remote tenth planet exists—a view shared by some scientists—from John W. CAMPBELL in *The Planeteers* (1936–1938) to Larry NIVEN and Jerry POURNELLE in *Lucifer's Hammer* (1977).

Though not strictly planets, two other parts of the Solar System have also figured in SF: the asteroids and the Sun. The asteroids are thousands of small rocky objects, most lying in a belt between the orbits of Mars and Jupiter. They range in size from mere gravel to 437 miles in diameter (Ceres). Even the largest are much too small to hold a natural atmosphere or lend themselves to ter-

raforming, but the asteroid belt figured as a navigational hazard or a mining frontier in such early stories as Isaac Asimov's "Marooned off Vesta" (1939) and Malcolm Jameson's "Prospectors of Space" (1940).

The asteroids are now seriously regarded as a promising source of minerals, and although no individual asteroid seems to offer a good home for a sizable colony, a mining culture occupying the belt as a whole seems quite plausible. Relatively few SF works have devoted much attention to this possibility, but notable exceptions are Jack Williamson's *Seetee Ship* stories (1942–1943/ 1951) and *Seetee Shock* (1949/1950), and Poul Anderson's *Tales of the Flying Mountains* (1970; parts published 1963–1965 as by Winston P. Sanders). A few asteroids have highly eccentric orbits, which raise the possibility of collision or near collision with Earth, as in James BLISH and Norman L. KNIGHT's *A Torrent of Faces* (1967).

The Sun, now known as a Class G star powering virtually all processes in the Solar System, was treated by some very early writers, such as Joel R. Peabody in *A World of Wonders* (1838), as a world not profoundly different from any other. As its true nature became better known, it was more likely to be treated as a source of danger to spaceships venturing too close, as in Willy LEY's "At the Perihelion" (1937). Quite a few stories, such as Arthur C. Clarke's "Rescue Party" (1946) and Larry Niven's "Inconstant Moon" (1971), have dealt with the effects of the Sun's becoming a nova, although present astronomical theory suggests that this is quite unlikely to occur naturally. A few stories, such as Philip Latham's "Disturbing Sun" (1959), have speculated on connections between the sunspot cycle and events on Earth. The idea of "sailing" spaceships powered by the solar wind, as in Arthur C. Clarke's "Sunjammer" (1964), is now under serious consideration as a technique for exploration of the outer Solar System.

Writers of SF have largely discounted the once popular notion of close-range exploration of the Sun itself since the relatively recent discovery of the harsh conditions actually prevailing there (including "surface" temperatures up to 10,000 degrees Fahrenheit). Nevertheless, several contemporary writers have been willing to confront the speculative difficulties inherent in such exploration, including Roger MacBride Allen in "A Hole in the Sun" (1987).

Some have suggested that the planets are largely used up as subject matter for SF, especially now that so many long-standing questions about them have been answered. This claim may, however, be premature. It is true that our knowledge of the planets (especially the inner ones) has been revolutionized in the last couple of decades. But planets are so large and complex that it hardly seems likely that we now understand everything about them. It may be that future findings will open up a new era of speculation based on possibilities previously unsuspected. For the outer planets, about which we knew so little for so long and on which we still await data from probes already launched, the process of informed speculation may be just beginning.

S.S.

PLATT, CHARLES (1944–).

British writer and editor of science fiction, now residing in the United States. Platt is closely associated with the British NEW WAVE and with NEW WORLDS, its primary forum. Besides being a frequent contributor to *New Worlds*, Platt became its editor in 1970. Although he has not received the attention afforded such New Wave writers as J. G. BALLARD and Michael MOORCOCK, Platt's novels and short stories are typical of the movement. His plots deal with individuals trying to cope with events they rarely understand and over which they have no control.

For example, in his best work, *Twilight of the City* (1977), an extensively revised and unified version of an earlier collection of short stories, *The City Dwellers* (1970), Platt described a city succumbing to the forces of entropy. The city's inhabitants first try to escape their fate by fleeing to the country, but as city dwellers they have no place in such an environment. As a result the survivors return to the city to participate in its final struggles. Such a plot has little room for the space opera hero who through cunning and strength saves the Earth from invading monsters. Platt's characters appear passive and their major action is to reconcile themselves to change. Their greatest achievement is to survive with some semblance of "human dignity."

However, many of Platt's works do have dynamic moments, particularly when he describes social customs and institutions. His first novel, *The Garbage World* (1967), provides a powerful picture of a scatologically based society on an asteroid that serves as garbage dump to the Solar System; indeed, garbage permeates every act, including sex. Platt milked the humor in this situation for all it's worth and perhaps, as some critics would have it, sacrificed plot and theme to comedic moments. Moreover, many of the scenes in this novel have more in common with Platt's pornographic fiction than with SF.

At his best Platt deals with issues that are rarely handled outside the New Wave. He has a sincere interest in ordinary people who are simply trying to make do in an indifferent world, and when that interest is manifest, his fiction is moving and well worth reading. Platt published a highly praised volume of interviews with SF authors, *Dream Makers: The Uncommon People Who Write Science Fiction* (1980), followed by a sequel, *Dream Makers II*, both published under the first title as a two-volume set in 1982. He has served as SF editor for a number of publishers, and his professional fanzine, *The Patchin Review*, had a short but spirited and con-

troversial life in the early 1980s.

OTHER WORKS: *Planet of the Voles* (1971); *Sweet Evil* (1977).

S.H.G.

PLAUGER, P[HILLIP] J[AMES] (1944–).

American writer, physicist, and computer consultant. In only a few years in the mid-1970s, Plauger earned an impressive reputation as a skillful author whose greatest strength lies in his ability to approach common science-fiction themes from new and vibrant perspectives. He was the winner of the 1975 John W. Campbell Award for best new writer. His first professional SF story, "Epicycle," was published in *Analog* in 1973. "Child of All Ages" (1975), his best-known story, concerns an immortal woman who retains the body of a child. His one novel, *Fighting Madness*, was first published in 1976 in *Analog Annual* (edited by Ben BOVA). Since then Plauger has largely abandoned the writing of fiction in favor of computer science.

B.D.

POE, EDGAR ALLAN (1809–1849).

American short story writer, poet, and critic, acclaimed as an important forerunner of science fiction. Poe's role in this regard may be problematic, for he was no naive supporter of "science" in any meaningful sense of the term. To be sure, he maintained a lifelong interest in cryptography, hypnotism, and physics, and could also depict the wonders and terrors of the natural world in such tales as "A Descent into the Maelström" (1841) and "The Thousand-and-Second Tale of Scheherazade" (1845); but, as early as his "Sonnet—To Science" (1829), Poe accused science of shattering the myths and illusions that had nurtured the human spirit.

The inadequacy of science is a leitmotiv in Poe's work: in "MS. Found in a Bottle" (1833) the antiquated scientific instruments aboard a decrepit ship, ironically named *Discovery*, are pitifully insufficient to orient the narrator and crew as they stand in the midst of what H. P. LOVECRAFT would call "the black seas of infinity"; in the apocalyptic "Conversation of Eiros and Charmion" (1839), the cocksure scientists fail utterly to predict the cataclysmic effects of a comet as it strikes the Earth.

The misuse of science and technology—intellect unchecked by moral restraints—is at the heart of "The Colloquy of Monos and Una" (1841) and also of Poe's two hilarious hoaxes, "The Unparalleled Adventure of One Hans Pfaall" (1835) and "The Balloon Hoax" (1844); in these and other tales Poe's intentional use of the labored pomposity and circumstantiality of contemporary scientific treatises blurs the transition from the scientifically plausible to the grotesquely absurd. Mesmerism plays a role in "A Tale of the Ragged Mountains" (1844) and "Mesmeric Revelation" (1844), but its misuse in "The Facts in the Case of M. Valdemar" (1845) leads to loathsome results. Poe was combating the alleged superiority of the "scientific" instinct—the mere collecting of information—as opposed to the poetic instinct, which assimilates science into a philosophical understanding of the universe; it is in this light that we must read his treatise *Eureka* (1848), significantly subtitled "A Prose Poem."

Analogously, the notion that scientific advance necessarily implies moral or political progress is exploded in "Some Words with a Mummy" (1845), in which a reanimated mummy informs the reader that the Egyptians were vastly ahead of us in technological and philosophical knowledge, and also in "Mellonta Tauta" (1849), the only one of Poe's tales set in the future. Here the narrator not only quotes the ancient thinker "Aries Tottle" as saying that "not once or twice, or a few times, but with almost infinite repetitions, the same opinions come round in a circle among men" but adds some significant reflections on the role of *imagination*—as opposed to Francis Bacon's induction—in scientific discovery. Although many of Poe's stories—especially his humorous or parodic tales—are responses to contemporary scientific and political issues, the cautionary tales he often spun about the dangers of unbridled technology have much to tell us nearly a century and a half after his death.

Nevertheless, Poe's pioneering interest in writing about the effects of change on human existence—particularly scientific and technological change—led later writers to follow his example, sometimes with greater sympathy for the science and technology that brought changes about; most of his stories appropriate to the genre were reprinted in the early years of the first SF magazine, AMAZING STORIES, along with the stories of Jules VERNE and H. G. WELLS, the other two authors publisher Hugo GERNSBACK pointed at when he tried to define "scientifiction."

S.T.J.

─────────────── **POETRY** ───────────────

Like poetry itself, science-fiction poetry has no easy definition. Poetic language may be easier to define. Suzette Haden ELGIN, founder of the SCIENCE FICTION POETRY ASSOCIATION (SFPA), has described poetic language as having patterning that matters and deviance that matters, and exhibiting fierce resistance to change. To paraphrase Elgin, a pattern of some kind must exist in poetic language, and that pattern makes it deviate from ordinary prose, imbuing poetry with a "fierce resistance to change."

An SF poem, Elgin says, must use poetic language about a reality that is different from the existing reality, and it must contain some element of narrative. Other SF poets have other definitions, or seem content with the statement that a poem is science fiction if they say it is.

Science-fiction poetry, in Elgin's sense, has existed almost from the beginnings of SF. If Homer's *The Odyssey* is considered a kind of proto-SF, then it may also be considered the first SF poem. An epic poem of the Renaissance, Ariosto's *Orlando Furioso* (1532), describes a trip to the Moon to discover Orlando's lost wits. With the advent of the Industrial Revolution and the recognition of change that was the necessary precondition for SF came true SF poetry. Lord Byron and Alfred, Lord Tennyson, for instance, wrote poetry on such SF themes as the future of humanity, and Stephen Vincent BENET carried the tradition into the 1930s and 1940s.

Frederik POHL's first publication (in *Amazing Stories*, at the age of sixteen) was a poem, "Elegy to a Dead Planet: Luna," testimony to the fact that early magazines were not opposed to publishing poetry or even paying for it (although they made Pohl wait four years). Quite a bit of poetry has been published within SF stories and novels, such as Robert A. HEINLEIN's "The Green Hills of Earth" (1947), with its blind poet of the spaceways, Rhysling, after whom the awards of the SFPA are named, and his most famous lines:

> I pray for one last landing
> On the globe that gave me birth;
> Let me rest my eyes on the fleecy skies
> And the cool, green hills of Earth.

But the acceptance of poetry by genre SF editors came slowly. Before World War II occasional whimsical poems were used as filler in the SF magazines, many of them story poems by Nelson S. Bond in the style of Robert W. SERVICE. After World War II serious poetry appeared sporadically in two important showcases. One was THE MAGAZINE OF FANTASY AND SCIENCE FICTION, which featured a series of verse parodies, primarily by Randall GARRETT and Isaac ASIMOV; the other was Judith MERRIL's SF anthologies, whose pages include poems by writers outside the genre. But the example of these publications was not followed by most other SF magazines and anthology series.

That resistance to the importance, or commercial appeal, of poetry began to fade in the late 1960s, although prejudice remains and poets continue to struggle for acceptance. Their efforts were aided, however, by the founding of small press genre magazines such as *Space & Time* and *Owlflight*, whose editors purchased poetry because of its intrinsic merit. As small press markets acquired importance, poetry shared in it.

The Science Fiction Poetry Association, created in 1978, also has played a significant part in identifying the genre and promoting its publication in a variety of ways. Part of its efforts have been rewarded by the fact that publication of poetry alone can now be used as a credential for active membership in the SCIENCE FICTION WRITERS OF AMERICA, affirming SF poetry's legitimacy in the eyes of fellow writers.

During the 1970s the Avon Rediscovery series reprinted an English-language version of the novel-length SF poem *Aniara* (1956, translated into English 1963) by Swedish Nobel laureate Harry Martinson; it describes a spacecraft's journey from one solar system to another. More recently Frederick Turner, like Martinson not a writer of SF, wrote a book-length narrative poem set in 2376, *The New World: An Epic Poem* (1985), which was reviewed favorably in major media.

In 1978 *Amazing,* under the editorship of Elinor Mavor, started buying poetry as a matter of policy. Soon ISAAC ASIMOV'S SCIENCE FICTION MAGAZINE, edited by George Scithers, a fan whose semiprozine *Amra* bought poetry, followed Mavor's example. Both magazines continue to publish poetry, although their editors have changed several times.

In addition to the annual Rhysling anthologies compiled to provide members of SFPA with copies of the poems nominated for the association's Rhysling awards, anthologies and collections of SF poetry have been published at least since 1969, beginning with Edward Lucie-Smith's *Holding Your Eight Hands*. Another early anthology is Robert Vas Dias's *Inside Outer Space* (1970). Perhaps the best recent anthologies are S. R. Tem's *The Umbral Anthology of Science Fiction Poetry* (1982), prepared with the aid of a grant from the National Endowment for the Arts, and Robert Frazier's *Burning with a Vision: Poetry of Science and the Fantastic* (1984).

While SF poetry has become legitimate in many ways, its publication still depends on the kindness or enlightenment of editors. The poem, unlike prose forms, must be carefully cultivated if it is to thrive, but it has attained a foothold scarcely dreamed of by earlier poets.

S.E.G.

POHL, FREDERIK (1919–).
American science-fiction author, editor, agent, and fan—few figures have influenced every aspect of science fiction as thoroughly as Frederik Pohl. With some blurring of the borders, his career can be divided into six stages. First, as a fan in the early 1930s, Pohl was one of the original members of the Science Fiction League and a founding member of the FUTURIANS. In the late 1930s and early 1940s—when he first began publishing SF—he was the editor of *Astonishing Stories* and *Super Science Stories*. During and immediately after World War II, Pohl wrote little science fiction, working as a weatherman for the U.S. Air Force, a marketer for an advertising firm, and later as a literary agent. Next came his satiric stage, marked by collaborations with C. M. KORNBLUTH. During this time Pohl also wrote a series of social SF stories and

Frederik Pohl

novels. In the early 1970s—the period of his greatest "literary" success—Pohl's work began to show considerable invention in style, structure, and plot, as evidenced in such works as *The Gold at Starbow's End* (1971). Finally, starting in the early 1980s, came a period of consolidation, with several earlier works seeing revision and others expanded, many in the form of sequels. In addition, Pohl has at various times edited two prize-winning magazines (GALAXY SCIENCE FICTION and *If*), numerous anthologies, and the science-fiction divisions of Ace and Bantam Books.

However, despite his contributions to publishing and fandom, Pohl's greatest influence remains his fiction. As a beginning author in the 1940s, Pohl wrote adventure short stories (as James McCreigh and under five other pseudonyms) that did not stand out from most of the science fiction published during that time.

In 1952 Pohl returned to the field as co-author with C. M. Kornbluth of *The Space Merchants*. Serialized by H. L. GOLD in *Galaxy Science Fiction* under the title "Gravy Planet" (1952), this novel has seldom, if ever, been out of print. The novel brilliantly satirized a world in which advertising dominates every phase of life and at the same time created a credible vision of the future.

From 1952 to 1962 Pohl and Kornbluth produced nine other books, including *Gladiator-at-Law* (1955, revised 1985), which continued the mix of satire and SF introduced in *The Space Merchants*, this time aimed at the legal profession; and *Wolfbane* (1959, revised 1985), which examines the culture that develops over generations on an Earth hijacked by an alien force. Two characteristics dominate all the Pohl/Kornbluth collaborations: sophisticated, urbane humor and the struggle by human characters to gain control over their lives, often in a world at the mercy of forces that neither recognize individual worth nor respect basic human values. After Kornbluth's death, Pohl continued to elaborate on this theme in his own novels and short stories, sometimes angrily as in "The Tunnel under the World" (1954) and *A Plague of Pythons* (1965; revised as *Demons in the Skull,* 1984) and sometimes in gentle mockery as in *Drunkard's Walk* (1960) and *The Age of the Pussyfoot* (1969).

While Pohl's name became synonymous with wit and humor in science fiction (with such short stories as "The Midas Plague," 1954, and "Day Million," 1966), that reputation may have blinded readers (and perhaps Pohl himself) to his serious themes. With the publication of the Nebula-winning *Man Plus* (1976), however, these themes could no longer be ignored. The novel describes the transformation of a human astronaut into a cyborg capable of living on Mars and confronts the question of human dignity: as the central character, Roger Torraway, becomes less "human," the people who were once so important to him are unable to cope with what he is, and Roger must also learn to handle the new thing he has become. Moreover, Roger's reflections on his growing inability to control his own life parallel the thoughts of people throughout the country who believe the world has gone out of control. The result is a remarkably readable novel that succeeds in presenting a fully rounded character in an SF setting.

Man Plus was followed by *Gateway* (1977), the novel that won every major science-fiction award that year. The novel's protagonist, Robinette Broadhead, suffers from tremendous feelings of guilt: for the death of his parents, for his wealth (a stroke of luck he feels he does not deserve), and for the living death of his girl friend and fellow crew members. *Gateway* presents Broadhead's story in chapters that alternately describe his life before the novel opens and record present conversations between Broadhead and his computer psychiatrist, Sigfrid von Shrink. With a sensitive mixture of humor and sympathy, Pohl explores Broadhead's condition and ends with one of the finest affirmations of humanity in any literary work. While he did not originally plan to write a sequel, the opportunity to continue the story proved too tempting. In three more novels in the so-called Heechee Saga—*Beyond the Blue Event Horizon* (1980), *Heechee Rendezvous* (1984), and *The Annals of the Heechee* (1987)—Pohl elaborated on each of three threads: the condition of the Earth, Robinette's growing knowledge, and the Heechee, whose artifacts are central to the plot.

Pohl's belief in the intrinsic fascination of science—which he has referred to as the world's greatest spectator sport—is evident in these and other novels. *Heechee Rendezvous* and *The Annals of the Heechee* focus on several theories associated with the beginning of the universe. *The Cool War* (1979), *Farthest Star* (1979, with Jack Williamson), and *The Years of the City* (1984), all attempt to create fictional worlds based on real scientific hypotheses. Pohl has also written a memoir, *The Way the Future Was* (1979), which attests to his enduring curiosity about science and its workings in the world around him.

OTHER WORKS: *Danger Moon* (collection, 1953, as James MacCreigh); *Undersea Quest* (with Jack Williamson, 1954); *Preferred Risk* (with Lester del Rey, 1955, under the joint pseudonym *Edson McCann); Undersea Fleet* (with Jack Williamson, 1956); *Alternating Current* (collection, 1956); *Slave Ship* (1957); *The Case against Tomorrow* (collection, 1957); *Edge of the City* (1957); *Undersea City* (1958); *Tomorrow Times Seven* (collection, 1959); *The Man Who Ate the World* (collection, 1960); *Turn Left at Thursday* (collection, 1961); *The Wonder Effect* (with C. M. Kornbluth; collection, 1962; revised as *Critical Mass,* 1977); *The Abominable Earthman* (collection, 1963); *The Reefs of Space* (with Jack Williamson, 1964); *Starchild* (with Jack Williamson, 1965); *Digits and Dastards* (collection, 1966); *Rogue Star* (with Jack Williamson, 1969); *Day Million* (collection, 1970); *In the Problem Pit* (collection, 1976); *JEM* (1979); *Before the Universe* (with C. M. Kornbluth; collection, 1980); *Syzygy* (1982); *Starburst* (1982); *Midas World* (1983); *Wall around a Star* (with Jack Williamson, 1983); *Pohlstars* (collection, 1984); *The Merchants' War* (1984); *Black Star Rising* (1985); *The Coming of the Quantum Cats* (1986); *Terror* (1986).

S.H.G.

POURNELLE, JERRY [EUGENE] (1933–   ).

American writer, editor, aerospace engineer, and columnist. Born in Louisiana, educated mostly in Washington, and now living in Los Angeles, Pournelle came to science-fiction writing relatively late, having earned a bachelor's degree in engineering, a master's degree in statistics and systems engineering, and two Ph.D.'s, one in psychology in 1960, the other in political science in 1964. He served in the army for two years and later worked as an aviation psychologist and systems manager for Boeing. He also held other aerospace jobs, taught political science at Pepperdine University, and was executive assistant to the mayor of Los Angeles. He rode the recent wave of SF popularity to fame and fortune, and indeed his work may have contributed to the genre's newly acquired status.

After writing a couple of non-SF novels as Wade Curtis, Pournelle began writing hard SF for ANALOG in 1971 and has been a full-time free-lance writer ever since. He has expressed admiration for the work of Robert A. HEINLEIN, and his fiction emphasizes the same libertarian virtues of independence, strength, self-reliance, and distrust of bureaucracies that Heinlein extolls. Those virtues may also characterize Pournelle himself; his writing career has been marked by hard work, the willingness to fight for his beliefs, and good fortune.

Pournelle is the SF community's most vocal supporter of the Strategic Defense Initiative, or Star Wars, as it is popularly known—a subject on which the community is divided. His right-leaning political sympathies have been obvious since the publication of the CoDominium series in the 1970s. The series describes an uneasy political venture between the United States and the Soviet Union, which staves off world war long enough for the newly discovered "Alderson drive" to open the stars to humankind. Planets are settled by both voluntary pioneers and transportees from among the ranks of criminals and dissidents. In *West of Honor* (1976; revised 1978), the pioneer farmers of Ararat are menaced by hordes of riffraff who have been dumped on the planet. John Christian Falkenberg comes to the aid of the farmers with a well-trained military force and the rabble are defeated—but the farmers can't have the agrarian utopia they had hoped for: Ararat must industrialize in order to assimilate the transportees.

Falkenberg is Pournelle's ideal professional military man, and in a series of stories novelized as *The Mercenary* (1977), he wins battles on other planets and becomes the feudal lord of New Washington. Pournelle seems to approve of this development; it is part of the social evolution that leads to the first Empire of Man after the fatal breakdown of the CoDominium and the destruction of Earth. Although Pournelle's works provide a detailed chronology for the first Empire and describe a dark interregnum and the birth of the Second Empire, the only works thus far set in imperial times, *A Spaceship for the King* (1973; revised and expanded as *King David's Spaceship*, 1980) and *The Mote in God's Eye* (with Larry NIVEN, 1974), involve the early years of the Second Empire.

It was through his work with Niven that Pournelle's good fortune began: their collaborations have been considerably more successful—in terms of popularity and financial return—than Pournelle's solo work. In *Mote* the Empire is challenged by an alien species, the Moties. With their inexorable will to breed, the Moties could overrun the universe—if they can get out of their system. The invention of the Moties was Niven's contribution, the politics, Pournelle's. As in *King David's Spaceship*, in which a backward world must build a spaceship of its own to improve its status in the Empire, Pournelle celebrated the virtues of an aristocratic universal state.

Mote was one of SF's first best-sellers, and it led to other Pournelle-Niven collaborations, including *Inferno*

Jerry Pournelle

(1976), *Lucifer's Hammer* (1977), *Oath of Fealty* (1981), and *Footfall* (1985). Pournelle seems to supply the basic structure and ideology, Niven the invention and scene setting; unlike the work of either individually, the collaborations focus on a broad and varied cast of characters caught in catastrophic situations. The best of the collaborations, *Lucifer's Hammer*, is a cosmic disaster story in the tradition of Edwin Balmer and Philip Wylie's *When Worlds Collide* (1933): an encounter with a comet devastates the Earth, and the more rational survivors must contend with both physical privation and human savagery in the struggle to preserve the heritage of civilization.

Oath of Fealty brings Pournelle's neofeudal ideals down to Earth in a near future thriller set in and around an urban arcology. *Inferno* is a science-fantasy update of Dante's classic in which, among other things, modern sins such as rapacious real estate development are given appropriate punishment. *Footfall* is an alien invasion novel full of delightful invention involving the elephant-like aliens and their herd culture.

Pournelle's admiration for martial virtues is expressed again in *Jannissaries* (1979) and its sequels—in which a force of mercenary soldiers is carried off to another world by a UFO to fight battles involving previously transplanted Celts, Romans, and so on—and in a series of anthologies of military SF, *There Will Be War*, that began in 1983. His involvement with James Baen's paperback anthology series (*Destinies, Far Frontiers, New Destinies*) has helped foster a martial school of SF typified by the work of writers such as David Drake and Timothy Zahn; he has edited, often in collaboration with John F. Carr, a varied collection of anthologies on other themes. Pournelle is also known for his science articles, such as those collected in *A Step Farther Out* (1980), and for practical advice to computer hackers, as in *The User's Guide to Small Computers* (1985), an annotated collection of his popular columns from *Byte* magazine.

Pournelle served as president of the SFWA in 1973–74 and continues as an influential voice in its councils.

OTHER WORKS: *Escape from the Planet of the Apes* (novelization, 1974); *Birth of Fire* (1976); *High Justice* (1977); *Exiles to Glory* (1978); *Clan and Crown* (with Roland Green, 1982); *The Legacy of Heorot* (with Larry Niven and Steven Barnes, 1987).

J.J.P.

THE POWER (1968). *Directed by Byron Haskin; screenplay by John Gay; adapted from the novel by Frank M. Robinson; photographed by Ellsworth Fredericks; music by Miklos Rozsa. With George Hamilton, Suzanne Pleshette, Michael Rennie, Nehemiah Persoff, Earl Holliman, Gary Merrill, Richard Carlson, Yvonne De Carlo, Ken Murray, Barbara Nichols, Arthur O'Connell, Celia Lovsky. 109 minutes. Color.*

The Power was the last SF film produced by George PAL, who had helped establish the genre in films. (His final movie, *Doc Savage the Man of Bronze*, 1975, is a fantasy.) A financial failure, scorned by critics at the time of its release, *The Power* has in recent years gained some adherents, and not without reason. Though compromised by faddish visual elements, a weak central performance, and a slackening of suspense, the film maintains interest throughout.

A group of researchers discovers that one of their members (Michael Rennie) is an inimical superhuman with vast powers of ESP; while trying to uncover the villain's identity, the group is killed one by one. When George Hamilton, one of three survivors, defeats the villain, he discovers that he himself is also a mental superman.

Miklos Rozsa's imaginative score sets an exotic mood; veteran SF director Byron Haskin was unable to get a strong enough performance from Hamilton, but the rest of the cast, including SF icons Richard Carlson and Rennie, is above average. The story becomes attenuated and confusing in the middle stretches, but the climax is tense. Although not prime Pal, *The Power* deserves a better reputation.

B.W.

POWERS, RICHARD M. (1921–   ). American artist. After studying art at the Chicago Art Institute and the University of Illinois, Powers took up illustration in the late 1940s to supplement his income as a fine artist, and did his first science-fiction covers for Doubleday in 1949. Influenced by the surrealism of Joan Miro, Yves Tanguy, Arshile Gorky, and Matta. Powers began experimenting with it as illustration. In 1952, with the founding of Ballantine Books, Powers had the opportunity to begin a series of nonrepresentational, surrealistic covers that would distinguish the Ballantine SF line for its first decade.

Powers's cover treatments do not so much depict the traditional SF robots, spaceships, or aliens as suggest their essence. In his swirls and streaks and lines of color, recognizable shapes can be discerned, while others lurk just below the limits of perception. His paintings may not be specifically illustrative of any particular work but of the psychological landscape of all science fiction, focusing more on the difficulties of understanding, or even of seeing clearly, the new, the strange, the alien; they may even suggest the shift from outer space to inner space that would emerge in the NEW WAVE of the mid-1960s.

In addition to his work for Ballantine, Powers provided dozens of covers for the *Galaxy* magazines and for other lines of paperbacks, particularly Berkley Books in the early 1970s. Throughout his career, most notably in recent years, he has continued his fine art paintings and has had dozens of exhibitions in galleries in New York and elsewhere. Perhaps most important, he opened the SF publishing door to non-representational, even surreal, SF illustration, and many artists have passed through, including Leo and Diane DILLON, Paul LEHR, John SCHOENHERR, Jack GAUGHAN, Ed EMSHWILLER, Don Ivan Punchatz, and Robert Foster.

J.E.G.

POWERS, TIM (1952–   ). American writer whose fiction often lies somewhere on the border of science fiction and fantasy. On first reading, *The Drawing of the Dark* (1979), for example, seems more fantasy than SF, as Powers adds his own tale to the stories of King Arthur. Magic and journeys abound in a sixteenth-century setting that obviously echoes many previous fantasies. But Powers took great care in his description of European societies of the late Renaissance; the details of life during that period seem to be part of the reader's world and not some exotic, magical past. This is the sort of description that would be at home in any SF novel dealing with alternate history, parallel worlds, or even alien worlds.

But if *The Drawing of the Dark* is fantasy that uses SF techniques, *Dinner at Deviant's Palace* (1985) is science fiction that draws on the elements of fantasy.

This work again describes a future world in credible, fascinating detail. Shaped by a devastating world war, society has become an extreme mixture of cults, hedonism, and worship of the automobile. Many of the events that take place appear to follow no rational pattern, and magic seems to play a significant role. However, Powers ultimately explained this world by providing a rational connection between that future and the reader's present. And it is the explanation that makes the book predominantly a work of science fiction.

The Anubis Gate (1983), which won the Philip K. Dick Memorial Award in 1984, defies any label. In a world where time travel is possible, where people can achieve immortality by exchanging bodies with others in different times, where Lord Byron can wander the Earth in several places simultaneously, both science and magic share center stage. Each offers its own explanation, and each can be used to accomplish the same things. The characters are free to choose their own version of the world, because science fiction and fantasy exist side by side.

If Powers's novels refuse to fit a general pattern, there are still valid generalizations to make about his fiction. His works are fascinatingly complex, crowded with characters and events that run the entire spectrum of human behavior and history. Often written with humor and usually well crafted, these novels are, in the last analysis, neither SF nor fantasy but works about the roles that SF and fantasy play in the way human beings experience the world.

OTHER WORKS: *The Skies Discrowned* (1976, revised as *Forsake the Sky*, 1986); *On Stranger Tides* (1987).
S.H.G.

PRATT, FLETCHER (1897–1956). American writer of fantasy and science fiction, active in PULP MAGAZINES from 1928 on, who produced translations of German and French SF as well as stories alone and in collaboration. In 1940 Pratt began the long-term partnership with L. Sprague DE CAMP that resulted in the Harold Shea Incomplete Enchanter and Gavagan's Bar series, as well as *Land of Unreason* (1941/1942) and *The Carnelian Cube* (1948). Especially in his work with de Camp, Pratt became one of the developers of the *Unknown Worlds* school of fantasy, replacing the "Gothic" sensibility of *Weird Tales* with a "modern," often humorous approach. Pratt put his individual stamp on a pair of alternate-world fantasies written on his own, *The Well of the Unicorn* (1948, as George U. Fletcher) and *The Blue Star* (in the Pratt-edited *Witches Three*, 1952). These fully realized imaginary worlds are peopled with novelistically round characters, and the humor and satire of the de Camp collaborations are replaced by a darker attitude toward human nature and tough-minded political insights gained from Pratt's other career, as a

professional historian specializing in military (particularly naval) history.

OTHER WORKS: *Invaders from Rigel* (1932/1960); *Alien Planet* (1932/1962); *World of Wonder* (editor, 1951); *Double in Space* (collection, 1951); *The Petrified Planet* (edited anonymously, 1952); *Double Jeopardy* (1952); *The Undying Fire* (1953). With L. Sprague de Camp: *The Incomplete Enchanter* (1940/1942); *The Castle of Iron* (1941/1950); *Wall of Serpents* (1953–54/1960); *Tales from Gavagan's Bar* (1953).
R.F.L.

———— PREDICTION ————

Organized prediction began with the first industrial revolution, when the evident and novel sequence of spectacular technological advances raised many questions about the future of the new industrial society. Answers came slowly. The idea of constant change—social and material—took several generations to become an element in general thinking about society, and the world had to wait for the first statisticians and sociologists to provide the means for assessing the probable course of future developments.

The most important primary prediction impulses came from the French. In the last chapter of *The Progress of the Human Mind* (1795), the Marquis de Condorcet argued for the application of the scientific method to the phenomena of human society; he also forecast technological advances in agriculture, a constant improvement in the conditions of life, equality for women, and the end of colonialism. These ideas became the inheritance of his admirer, Count Claude Henri de Saint-Simon. He developed the case for a science of humanity and society in his *Mémoire sur la Science de l'homme* (1813), and with even more originality he set out a detailed program for the unification of Europe in *De la Réorganisation de la société européenne* (1814).

The ideas of Saint-Simon were the starting point for the most influential theories of his onetime assistant, Auguste Comte. In his first publication, *Plan des travaux scientifiques nécessaires pour réorganiser la société* (1822), Comte developed his central doctrine of the three stages of intellectual evolution, and in his later works he laid the foundations of modern sociology. He was confident that, once the scientific principles of the social sciences had been established, sociology would enjoy sovereign authority in its field. It followed that "the determination of the future" would then become a matter for expert calculation.

The first major investigation of future possibilities came from another Frenchman, Alexis Charles Henri de Tocqueville, who spent nine months traveling through the eastern states of the United States in 1831. In America he sought "the image of democracy itself" in order to establish the probable shape of coming developments in European society. From his examination of social trends in the United States he came to many original conclusions about the future in his celebrated *De la Démocratie en Amérique* (1835–1840): that democratic government would spread, that the population of the United States would skyrocket and the country become a major naval power, that the United States and Russia were "marked out to sway the destinies of half the globe."

By the 1840s impressionistic forecasts of this kind had become the established mode in the increasing number of futuristic studies then beginning to appear. None of these attempted the range of comprehensive conclusions of Tocqueville's work; they concentrated on their appropriate specialties—education, engineering, sanitation, medicine—in estimating the administrative and technological changes that would be required to support the ever-growing masses of the vast new urban centers. In fact, the world had to wait for the beginnings of modern statistics, that most essential of all tools in quantifying the factors that make for change in society. The true begetter of modern statistical method was the Belgian mathematician Lambert Adolphe Quételet. He set all things in motion with his essay *Sur l'Homme* (1835), in which he introduced the key concept of "the average man."

From the 1840s on the growth of predictive literature paralleled increases in population, rising levels of literacy, and nonstop advances in the technologies. The common assumption was that change would always be uniform and that all foreseeable developments could only add to or improve the expanding universe of the new industrial societies. This assumption was generally expressed in lengthy essays in the periodicals, which professionals wrote to inform their middle-class readers about "The future of" the army or the navy, banking or religion, the state in Russia or in China. At the same time the first images of the future—projections of flying machines or ocean transportation—began to appear in the new illustrated magazines, and for adolescent readers there were many books about science, invention, and the achievements of engineers. These instructive accounts often closed with "A Look into the Future," which explored the unquestioned material advantages to be expected from scientific discoveries.

With the 1880s came a flood of publications about the extraordinary triumphs of the age, which did much to encourage speculation about the most likely pattern of change in the twentieth century. The first full-length books about the future—comprehensive studies of the developments to be expected in the 1900s—appeared. For the United States there was David Goodman Croly, journalist and lifelong Comtean, who coined the word *miscegenation* in 1864, when he put forth the argument in his book of that name for the intermarriage of black and white Americans. His later series of forecasts, published as a book in 1888 with the title *Glimpses of the Future*, included continued and necessary growth of government departments, expansion of education, the British loss of India, the American acquisition of Canada, and the success of science in making humankind "the god of this planet."

A French view of the next century appeared in *Dans Cent Ans* (1892) by Charles Richet, an eminent physiologist and Nobel Prize winner. He produced statistical projections to show that the United States and Russia would become the most powerful nations in the world and that new armaments would provide the ultimate deterrent in future wars. The most original and thorough forecast, however, was *The War of the Future* (1897), by the Polish banker and economist Ivan Bloch. He made the first statistical investigation of modern warfare, examining French and German army records for the 1870 war and came to the astonishing conclusion that, contrary to the thinking of all the general staffs, the next war would be "a great war of entrenchments" that would inevitably lead to economic disruption and social collapse.

The most widely read forecasts appeared in *Anticipations* (1901), in which H. G. Wells used his great gifts to write a positive scenario for the future of Western civilization. He was important in his day: first, for the models he devised for forecasting the social, political, or organizational changes likely to follow technological advances and second, for his great success in popularizing the idea of future change in his works of fiction and prediction.

By the 1900s then books about the future had become established items on publishers' lists. They make sorry reading nowadays, because later events proved them wrong on most matters, above all their anticipations of the next war. When that burst upon Europe in 1914, the generals and the politicians soon found that their nations were committed to a very different kind of conflict, in which the scale and the rate of change were to prove decisive. The unprecedented nature of World War I accelerated the expansion of research and development programs. Out of this work after 1918 came new planning units, in which economists and statisticians provided forecasts—regarding trade, housing, agriculture, and employment—for the decisions of their political superiors.

Everywhere the expectation of change increased, and the market for informative books about the future continued to grow rapidly. There were forecasts for all areas of anticipated development: Anton Lübke's *Technik und Mensch 2000* (1927); Hugh Ferriss's *The Metropolis of the Future* (1929); Giulio Douhet's *La Guerra di 19 . . .* (1920). One telling indication of the growing public interest was the Today and Tomorrow series (1924–1931), some eighty-six monographs by experts ranging from an influential study of tank warfare by Captain Liddell Hart to an important piece of biology by J. B. S. Haldane.

Although some of these forecasts rose above the level of popular journalism, more extensive and important work was going on unnoticed in government departments. The many facets of state activity required a clear view of the future, and striking evidence for this need came with the appointment of the National Resources Committee by President Herbert Hoover in 1929. Its report, *Recent Social Trends* (1932), is a modern Domesday Book that signaled a major advance in prediction; it was the first attempt to give a government all the information needed for "the formulation of large national policies looking to the next phase in the nation's development."

The requirement for forecasts became painfully clear during the Second World War. There was so much to foresee—so much to prepare for and guard against—from the ocean war against the U-boats to the Manhattan Project, from the promises of the Atlantic Charter to the question marks over the future of Europe, China, and Japan. The experience of the planning staffs, service and civilian, carried over into peacetime practice when operational research methods proved invaluable in the immense problems of postwar reconstruction.

As the extent of the new industrial revolution became evident—computers, jet planes, transistors, automation—the rate of change was perceived to be a matter for international concern in the new epoch of space satellites, lunar landings, acid rain, and nuclear weapons. There has been a threefold response to the many questions these developments have raised about the future: first, a massive output of popular books, articles, and television programs about the many shapes of coming things; second, the rapid institution of national and international committees to examine and report on future developments (Resources for the Future, United States, 1952; Institut für Zukünftsfragen, Vienna, 1963; Committee for the Next 30 Years, United Kingdom, 1966), which have continued to proliferate, until today there can be few countries on Earth without a futures organization of some kind; and finally, from the 1960s on, the appearance of international journals devoted to the analysis of future possibilities, which signaled the growing professionalization of forecasting: *The Futurist* (United States), *Futures* (United Kingdom), *Analysen und Prognosen* (Berlin), *Futuribles* (France), and *Futuribili* (Italy).

The flood of information from futurologists continues to grow. The nuclear winter, future shock, zero growth, the postindustrial society, space colonies—these phrases have passed into general discussion of the future. At the same time many have argued that the most urgent task of today is to prepare for tomorrow's world: C. H. Waddington in *The Future as an Academic Discipline* (1975); Edward Cornish in *The Study of the Future* (1977); Robert Jungk in his *Der Jahrtausend Mensch* (1973). Out of the multitudinous opinions comes one general

conclusion: the unprecedented rate and scale of the changes now occurring throughout our planet present humankind with the choice between a good and an evil future. Prudence, cooperation, foresight, restraint, planning, international collaboration—these are the words handed down from the institutes of futurology and the commissions for the twenty-first century. As Paul Valéry once remarked, the future is not what it used to be.

I.F.C.

PREUSS, PAUL (1942–   ). American writer and independent film producer. Preuss has said of his writing that he has more interest in scientists than in science, in social consequences than in gadgets; yet his science fiction is so filled with modern scientific speculation that it has often been labeled hard SF. Black holes and conjectures about the boundaries of time and space fill the pages of his first two novels, *The Gates of Heaven* (1980) and *Re-entry* (1981). Each evokes a sense of awe at an infinite number of alternate pasts, presents, and futures. Both novels, however, are rather conventional renderings of the alternate-world theme.

But in *Broken Symmetries* (1983) Preuss blazed new ground. Centered on the history of particle physics, the novel depicts real scientists doing real work. Describing the marvels of current scientific research and complex characters, whose abstract, theoretical work can and will affect the lives of all humanity, Preuss achieved a balance between presentation of the wonders of science and discussion of their social consequences. Readers can enjoy his lucid descriptions of particle theory and at the same time understand that such research is limited by the men and women who conduct it. For good or evil, scientists and science are part of the modern world, and both will have a significant role in shaping the future. Preuss followed this fine novel with a second, *Human Error* (1985), which does almost for biological computers what *Broken Symmetries* did for particle physics.

S.H.G.

PRICE, VINCENT (1911–   ). American actor associated since the late 1950s with horror movies, with occasional forays into science fiction. Price's first genre film, in fact, was SF, *The Invisible Man Returns* (1939, see THE INVISIBLE MAN), in which he played the title role. For the next two decades, thanks to his honeyed voice, arching eyebrows, and ironic delivery, he was a frequent suave and urbane villain, with occasional comedy roles. It wasn't until *House on Haunted Hill* and THE FLY, both in 1958, that audiences began perceiving Price as primarily a horror movie actor. Thanks to a series of stylish thrillers directed by Roger CORMAN and loosely derived from the works of Edgar Allan POE, over the next several years Price became so identified with genre material that he was the first full-fledged horror star created in America since the success of Lon Chaney, Jr., in the early 1940s.

In addition to his fantasy and Gothic horror films, Price appeared in several SF movies, primarily when the genres overlapped. Among these are his notorious *The Tingler* (1959), *Master of the World* (1961), THE LAST MAN ON EARTH (1964), WAR-GODS OF THE DEEP (1965), and *Scream and Scream Again* (1969). He also appeared in several SF TV series, from *Lights Out* (1949) to *The Bionic Woman* (1976).

B.W.

PRIEST, CHRISTOPHER (1943–). British writer. His schooling completed at the age of sixteen, Priest took up a career as an accountant before contributing a story to the British magazine *Impulse* in 1966. His work represents the mature point of view of the NEW WAVE and the stylistic concerns that have led a number of British writers out of science fiction into the mainstream.

Priest's first novel, *Indoctrinaire* (1970; revised 1979), like the fiction published in the 1960s in NEW WORLDS, is filled with unexplained events, dark hints of manipulation, and a warp in time that allows the present to glimpse the future, as a shanghaied drug researcher attempts to escape from his Kafkaesque imprisonment in the Brazilian highlands. Like all Priest's later work, the novel is distinguished by strong characterization and imagery but also by an ambiguity, particularly in the conclusion, that undercuts and sometimes diffuses the narrative.

His next novel, *Fugue for a Darkening Island* (1972; published in the United States as *Darkening Island*), is also heavy on atmosphere and light on plot, but in it the balance is more successful. Set in the near future after the African continent has been devastated by nuclear bombs, the book describes a Great Britain threatened with total collapse because of overwhelming numbers of African refugees. The situation becomes a metaphor for a contemporary social problem.

Priest's most successful novel of the 1970s was *Inverted World* (1974), a literary counterpart to Hal CLEMENT's hard SF *Mission of Gravity* (1954). *Inverted World* convincingly describes a world in which time, matter, and even meaning are in constant flux, a place in which even a city must continually move to survive. The characters known as Terminators want to stop the motion, seeking stability in an ever-changing universe, even though that very stability will destroy their city. The hero, Helwood Mann, learns to accept the nature of his world as he, much like the Mesklinites in *Mission of Gravity*, explores its future frontiers. This is a book about the necessity of change and movement, and the capacity of individuals—even in a confusing environment—for

Christopher Priest

growth.

The division between appearance and reality that creates much of the tension in *Inverted World* is the major theme of *A Dream of Wessex* (1977; published in the United States as *The Perfect Lover*). The minds of thirty-nine people are linked in a computer that creates a consensus dreamworld in which possible future events can be considered and tested. The dreamworld, however, seduces one of the participants and consequently becomes real, and the characters must struggle to restore matters to their original state.

Although Priest no longer considers himself an SF writer, even his most recent works—*The Affirmation* (1981) and *The Glamour* (1984)—retain elements of the genre and clearly benefit from the power he perfected while writing SF to describe strange worlds and stranger actions. *The Affirmation*, set in the Dream Archipelago of some of Priest's short stories, contrasts the "real" life of Peter Sinclair, a man going insane in contemporary London, with his dream existence as Jethra, of the Dream Archipelago, who has been offered immortality but must give up his memories to claim it. Each is writing a book about the other universe. *The Glamour*, in contrast, is an intriguing contemporary romance about people who have achieved invisibility by enhancing their natural abilities to pass unnoticed. The fantasy process of "willing" oneself invisible supports the literary metaphor, and the work, focusing alternately on the sometimes invisible heroine and on the hero who falls in love with her while wondering if the villain is lurking nearby unseen, earned Priest his greatest commercial, and perhaps literary, success. It too, however, undercuts the suspense and romance with an ending that questions everything that has gone before.

Priest won the British Science Fiction Association Award in 1974 and 1979 and the Australian Ditmar Award in 1977 and 1982. He was an early member of the British Science Fiction Foundation and for two years associate editor of its journal, *Foundation*. He was married for several years to SF writer Lisa TUTTLE.

OTHER WORKS: *Real Time World* (collection, 1974); *The Space Machine* (1976); *An Infinite Summer* (collection, 1979).

S.H.G.

PRIESTLEY, J[OHN] B[OYNTON] (1894–1984).

British novelist, playwright, and broadcaster, and a noted establishment advocate of science fiction. A productive and at times uneven writer, Priestley made his mark in 1929 with *The Good Companions*. His excursions into SF and fantasy, however, came with his development as a playwright. His interest in the serial universe theory of J. W. Dunne led to his exploration of the concept of psychological and chronological time in the plays *Dangerous Corner* (1932), *Time and the Conways* (1937), and *I Have Been Here Before* (1938), subsequently collected as *Three Time Plays* (1947). This theme is also the basis of the surprise twist at the end of the otherwise nonfantastic *An Inspector Calls* (1945).

The time concept resurfaces in Priestley's fiction, most notably the stories collected in *The Other Place* (1953) and *The Magicians* (1954), in which, through the use of a drug, a businessman leaves sequential time for "time alive" and finds himself host to three "magicians" at a crossroads in time. Priestley's affection for SF involved him in support for the Arts Council grant that helped the ailing *New Worlds* in 1967.

OTHER WORKS: *Adam in Moonshine* (1927); *Doomsday Men* (1938); *Low Notes on a High Level: A Frolic* (1954); *The Thirty-first of June* (1961); *Snoggle* (1971).

M.A.

PROGRESS

The idea of progress serves as the natural theology of a secular religion. The philosophy of progress had its heyday in the nineteenth century, when its proponents expounded the theory that humankind had managed its own social and industrial advancement through unswerving devotion to the great powers of science, technology, and rational organization. The earliest formulations of this theory appeared in the eighteenth century in Anne Robert Jacques Turgot's organic, perfectionist thesis *Philosophical Review of the Successive Advances of the Human Mind* (1750). Theory soon found spectacular proof in the first major technological developments—the striking visual evidence of the Montgolfier balloons in 1783 and the first industrial applications of James Watt's steam engine, both of which seemed evidence that humanity had at last reached a most desirable point of no return. Then in 1798 Edward Jenner's pamphlet on vaccination promised a better life for all, and that same year Thomas H. Malthus opened the first great debate on the future of the human race in his essay *Principle of Population*.

As prodigious inventions followed—the steamship and the railroad in particular—the expectation of continued progress became a fact of everyday experience. The new sense of change ("the march of mind") took on the characteristics of a cosmic law with the published discoveries of the first paleontologists: Georges Cuvier, *Recherches sur les ossements fossiles des quadrupèdes* (1823); and Charles Lyell, *Principles of Geology* (1830). The new science began to reveal the immensity of time past exactly when the new industrial nations were speeding toward the future. The received theory of universal progress is central to Alfred, Lord Tennyson's admirable period piece "Locksley Hall" (1842), and it appears throughout Walt Whitman's *Leaves of Grass* (1855).

The first theories of progress came from many sources: Robert Southey, *Colloquies on the Progress and Prospects of Society* (1829), A. Javary, *De l'idée de progrès* (1851), and the address by George Bancroft to the New-York Historical Society "The Progress of Mankind" (1858). More important than these, however, were the new histories of the nations presented by most persuasive historians: Thomas Babington Macaulay, François Pierre Guizot, Hippolyte Taine, and Heinrich von Treitschke. Their views promoted the typical historicism of their time: the idea of progress, social and technological, as a fault-free process, working primarily for the good of Western societies and destined to go on forever. The most complete statement of this doctrine appears in Henry Thomas Buckle's *History of Civilization in England* (1857). He analyzed the mental and environmental factors—the quantifiable elements—that had advanced his nation to world power, and he proclaimed "the possibility of generalizing the past so as to predict the future."

The most widely read of these early writers on progress in both the United Kingdom and the United States was undoubtedly Herbert Spencer. Many did not see through his facile application of evolutionary ideas to the social environment—"the beneficent working of the survival of the fittest"—and many who triumphed in the social struggle found the sanction of their success in Spencer's philosophy of vigorous individualism. In the long run, however, the greatest influence of all was Karl Marx, of whom Friedrich Engels said, with understandable exaggeration, that "just as Darwin discovered the laws of evolution in organic nature, so Marx discovered the law of evolution in human history."

Then came the unexpected and terrifying demonstration of technological progress in the First World War. The unprecedented scale of that conflict and the subsequent social upheavals, especially in Russia and Germany, erased the once sacred formula that material progress equals moral and social improvement. A new idea of *unprogress* appeared—to be seen at its most ominous in Oswald Spengler's *Der Untergang des Abendlandes* (1925) and at its most rational in Bertrand Russell's *Icarus, or the Future of Science* (1924). Russell's warning against the misuses of science has been central to most thought about the future ever since.

The old-style histories of progress died the death of a thousand disasters, especially after the Second World War. Hiroshima was the image of progress at its most horrifying. And then, during the 1950s and on both sides of the Atlantic, the rapid growth of the social sciences and the beginnings of futurology spread a new and modified idea of progress as a constant process of social and technological change in need of careful monitoring for dangerous effects.

The range of recent attitudes can be examined in, first, the revised version of H. G. Wells's *A Short History of the World* (1946), wherein the old man turned his back on the marvels of progress and declared that *Homo sapiens* "is in his present form played out." Next, in *Progress and Disillusion* (1968), Raymond Aron examined the painful contradictions that derive from change and the idea of change. Again, in *The Year 2000* (1967), Hermann Kahn and Anthony J. Wiener analyzed the many possibilities for good and evil that face humankind. Finally, the various writings of the Jesuit paleontologist Pierre Teilhard de Chardin represent at this late stage the perfection of the idea of progress: over some thirty years, in *The Phenomenon of Man* (1959), *The Future of Man* (1964), and *Man's Place in Nature* (1966), he argued that the universal trend to social unification plus the constant increase in mechanization and the general heightening of intellectual vision will keep humankind on the crest of the evolutionary wave. Then will come that last moment, the *dies illa* that will inaugurate an eternity of progress.

I.F.C.

PSEUDOSCIENCE

Most science-fiction stories develop from extrapolations of known science into the future and some from inventions of imaginary science (that is, science that does not exist today or a behavioral or social science converted into a predictive hard science, as in Isaac ASIMOV's "psychohistory"). A few stories, however, use pseudosci-ence—fake or false science, masquerading as real science but based on mistaken or crank notions about what science is or what it accepts. Sometimes authors merely adopt pseudoscientific notions as the basis for a good story, but occasionally an author (or editor) actually believes in the ideas presented, or so professes to.

Atlantis is one major pseudoscientific concept. Proposed as the source of civilization by Ignatius DONNELLY in *Atlantis the Antediluvian World* (1888), Atlantis became the subject of hundreds of stories, notable book examples being Andre Laurie's *The Crystal City under the Sea* (1895), C. J. Cutliffe Hyne's *The Lost Continent* (1900), Arthur Conan DOYLE's *The Maracot Deep* (1929), Dennis Wheatley's *They Found Atlantis* (1936), and Jane Gaskell's Atlan series (beginning in 1958). In some instances, stories about the lost continent have been colored by the Theosophical belief (propounded in 1888 by H. P. Blavatsky in *The Secret Doctrine*) that Atlantis was the home of a supercivilization characterized by extensive use of remarkable psychic abilities, or magic.

Another popular pseudoscientific motif is that of the hollow Earth, used by Ludvig HOLBERG in his satiric *A Journey to the World Under-ground* (1741). The notion received new life from the early-nineteenth-century theorist John Cleves Symmes, who described polar openings leading to the interior, a concept adopted by Edgar Rice BURROUGHS in his Pellucidar novels.

Science-fiction stories and novels have also incorporated other eccentric geographies and cosmologies. S. Fowler WRIGHT in *Beyond the Rim* (1932) described a flat Earth and placed a lost race of Puritans on its edge. Andrew Lawson's *Born Again* (1904) asserts that humanity lives on the hollow interior of a sphere, and Marlo Field's *Astro Bubbles* (1928) reveals that people live on the inside of a small, sausage-shaped universe. The stars are not-too-distant lights on the other side, and the sausage is linked to other accessible sausages by polar openings.

Strange theories of evolution also turn up. E. Charles Vivian, in his *City of Wonder* (1922), used the Theosophical concept of prehuman "root races" of great antiquity; Granville Hall's *Recreations of a Psychologist* (1920) postulates at least two separate humanities. Others claim that apes arose as hybrids between humans and lower animals, and Lebbeus Harding Roger's *The Kite Trust* (1900) evades evolution by bringing humanity in separate waves from different planets.

The ideas of Charles FORT (the early-twentieth-century chronicler of mysterious and unexplained phenomena in works such as *The Book of the Damned*, 1923) have inspired a number of SF stories, particularly Eric Frank Russell's *Sinister Barrier* (1939/1943), which was based on the notion that Earth is owned by superior "outside" beings. Fort's other basic idea, that the universe is living and operates by teleportation, has been used in SF as well. His documentation of sightings in the sky and curious weather phenomena are often drawn upon, as are later notions of "flying saucers" or UFOs and the "archaeological" speculations of Immanuel Velikovsky, Erich von Däniken, and their imitators.

Several crank systems were publicized in the SF magazines during and just after World War II. John W. CAMPBELL, Jr., in *Astounding*/ANALOG recommended that his authors write stories based on psychic phenomena and urged them to consult the works of pioneer parapsychologist J. B. Rhine of Duke University, and Campbell apparently took seriously L. Ron HUBBARD's Dianetics. He may or may not have been serious about the rotary motion "Dean Drive" and the printed-circuit, unpowered "Hieronymous machine." In *Amazing Stories* and *Other Worlds*, editor Raymond A. PALMER featured and professed belief in the so-called Shaver Mystery stories about an inner Earth inhabited by demonlike beings (deros) who persecute humanity with pain-producing rays.

Whether parapsychology is pseudo- or legitimate science still is disputed. Modern SF, in any case, is permeated with the concept of paranormal powers, which, like time travel and faster-than-light travel, have come to be accepted as necessary conventions if not articles of faith.

E.B.

PSYCHOLOGY

Science fiction has traditionally drawn on concepts from the physical and biological sciences and since the 1950s from sociology and cultural anthropology as well. Yet a surprising number of SF classics and contemporary works deal with psychological processes in addition to, or instead of, other kinds of scientific constructs.

Psychology is found in SF in at least eight forms: ordinary psychological processes in extraordinary settings, abnormal psychological processes in extraordinary settings, the treatment of psychological states as in some way concrete, extension of psychological technologies, extension of human potentials, extraterrestrial psychologies, illustration or extension of psychological theories, and expression of the author's psychological conflicts.

One of the oldest and most common approaches is to depict ordinary human beings' psychological responses to extraordinary circumstances. This form is not inherently different from the strategy of much mainstream fiction and many non-SF adventure stories, but in SF the settings are more unusual and the psychological responses may be more exaggerated. Psychiatrist David H. KELLER claimed of his early pulp magazine stories, "I introduced a new form of science-fiction by writing of human emotions and reactions to new inventions." Science fiction has examined emotional reactions not only to new inventions (as in Keller's "Revolt of the Pedestrians," 1928) but to many other radical changes in ex-

ternal circumstances: for example, environments of other planets (Ray BRADBURY's "The Long Rain," 1948), outer space (George R. R. MARTIN's "The Second Kind of Loneliness," 1972), Earthwide physical or biological changes (J. G. BALLARD's *The Drowned World*, 1962), future societal complexity (John BRUNNER's *The Shockwave Rider*, 1975), and nuclear holocaust (Judith MERRIL's *Shadow on the Hearth*, 1950).

Such stories tend to assume a broad pattern of "human nature"—often distinctly American or Western European—that remains basically constant despite exposure to fantastic experiences and that may help protagonists overcome extreme predicaments. In a smaller number of stories, specific commonly observed psychological phenomena become hinges for SF plots: for instance, unconscious denial (Judith MERRIL's "That Only a Mother," 1948), emotional catharsis (Robert SHECKLEY's "Seventh Victim," 1952), gender identity (Ursula K. LE GUIN's *The Left Hand of Darkness*, 1969), development of relationships (Thomas M. DISCH's "Come to Venus Melancholy," 1965), and psychological research methodology (James McConnell's "Learning Theory," 1957). These and other stories have filled several anthology-textbooks aimed at first-year college students; the most recent, *PsiFi* (1987), edited by Jim Ridgway and Michele Benjamin, was sponsored by the British Psychological Society.

Science fiction has frequently gone beyond the "normal" range of human responses to examine connections between extraordinary settings and genuinely abnormal psychological processes. Severe neurotic or psychotic states may be presented as the outcome of extremely disorienting experiences, as when scientists in Isaac ASIMOV's "Nightfall" (1941) go mad the first time they see the stars. Conversely, such states may be shown as normal for an entire society under certain circumstances, as with the severe agoraphobia of underground city dwellers in Asimov's *Caves of Steel* (1954). Psychopathology may even be depicted as adaptive, for instance in the psychopathic protagonist of Wilson TUCKER's postholocaust novel *The Long Loud Silence* (1952), or at least as harmless when social constraints disappear, as in Shirley Weinland's "When the Haloperidol Runs Out and the Blue Fairy Never Comes" (1987).

Further, SF can grant independent or material reality to usually subjective phenomena. Psychotic delusions and other symptoms are favorite subjects for such reification: for instance, thought control in Frederik POHL's *Demon in the Skull* (1984), omnipotence of thought in Ursula K. Le Guin's *The Lathe of Heaven* (1971), self-referential conspiracies in Robert A. HEINLEIN's "They" (1941), and split personalities in Wyman GUIN's "Beyond Bedlam" (1951). Normal psychological processes have been reified in stories involving such phenomena as childhood fantasy companions (In Gene WOLFE's "The Eyeflash Miracles," 1976), the id (in Fred Wilcox's film

Illustration by Judith Mitchell

FORBIDDEN PLANET, 1956), and imagination itself (In Robert W. Krepps's "Five Years in the Marmalade," 1949).

Present or potential psychological technologies have stimulated much SF extrapolation. In most instances the fictional technologies remain far ahead of the actual. For example, whole-brain transplants were popular as early as James Whale's film version of FRANKENSTEIN (1931); films based on Curt SIODMAK's novel *Donovan's Brain* (1943) similarly popularized brains that live without bodies. A related theme is the creation of artificial intelligence and personality, either in a humanoid robot, such as in John T. SLADEK's *Roderick* (1980), or in a faceless supercomputer, such as HAL in Stanley KUBRICK's film and Arthur C. CLARKE's novel 2001: A SPACE ODYSSEY (1968).

As in the real world, fictional technologies developed for one purpose may come to serve others. Frederik Pohl created a computerized psychotherapist to preserve his

hero's sanity in *Gateway* (1977); in that book's sequels similar techniques preserve the hero's entire personality as a computer construct. In Roger ZELAZNY's *The Dream Master* (1966) a psychoanalyst treats patients by constructing and sharing therapeutic dreams with them; in James E. GUNN's *The Dreamers* (1980) artfully constructed dreams are transferred between individuals for pleasure, not therapy. Mind-altering drugs may be used for peace, as in Aldous HUXLEY's *Island* (1962), or for war, as in Brian W. ALDISS's *Barefoot in the Head* (1969). Persuasive technologies may be vastly improved in order to sell products, as in J. G. Ballard's "The Subliminal Man" (1964), or to win political campaigns, as in Tom Purdom's *The Barons of Behavior* (1972). Human brains have been integrated with mechanical devices in order to pilot spaceships, as in Cordwainer SMITH's "Three to a Given Star" (1965); to steal from giant computer networks, as in William GIBSON's *Neuromancer* (1984); and to alter one's personality for fun and profit, as in George Alec EFFINGER's *When Gravity Fails* (1987).

Science-fiction stories also deal with the nonmechanical extension of human potential, involving either the development of new psychological abilities or the augmentation of currently existing abilities. Vast increases in intelligence are difficult to depict in human adults, but some authors have done so with fair success, as in Olaf STAPLEDON's *Odd John* (1935). More often the development of superintelligence has been shown in children (Wilmar H. SHIRAS's "In Hiding," 1948), animals (Stapledon's *Sirius*, 1944), or retarded adults (Daniel KEYES's "Flowers for Algernon," 1959). Various psi powers, although their existence even in minimal form is doubted by many psychologists, have become standard components of the human psychological repertoire in SF. Their implications have been explored for the individual, as in Robert SILVERBERG's *Dying Inside* (1972); for the integrated group, as in Theodore STURGEON's *More Than Human* (1953); and for society, as in Alfred BESTER's *The Demolished Man* (1953) and *The Stars My Destination* (1956). Sometimes superpeople are so much beyond us that their psychology cannot be described at all and their actions make them seem inhuman, or at least unhuman, as in Arthur C. Clarke's *Childhood's End* (1953).

Science-fiction writers have also explored the psychology of extraterrestrials. It might seem that writers would be able to speculate with total freedom about alien psychologies, but in fact such consideration has been limited mainly to a few patterns. Aliens have usually been depicted as much like humans, at least in terms of one major trait: for instance, scientific curiosity in Hal CLEMENT's *Mission of Gravity* (1954); self-preservative urges in John W. CAMPBELL's "Who Goes There?" (1938), or altruism in Ivan Yefremov's "Heart of the Serpent" (1959). If aliens are not described as psychologically similar to humans, then they are often depicted as possessing a psychological pattern similar to that of a non-human earth species. Frederik Pohl, for instance, extrapolated to his Heechee aliens the behavior of Earth "burrowers" in *Beyond the Blue Event Horizon* (1980). Larry NIVEN and Jerry POURNELLE gave their aliens the herd instincts of elephants in *Footfall* (1985). With *Ender's Game* (1985) Orson Scott CARD joined the ranks of writers who have endowed aliens with a beelike form of hive behavior. In a smaller number of instances, writers have developed elaborately unearthlike biologies for their aliens and have then explored the psychological patterns that might result, as in Isaac Asimov's *The Gods Themselves* (1972). Finally and least often, authors have depicted aliens whose psychology is simply incomprehensible to earthlings, as in Terry CARR's "The Dance of the Changer and the Three" (1968) and Stanislaw Lem's *Solaris* (1961).

Authors of SF have incorporated into their work not only psychological research findings and clinical knowledge but entire theoretical systems. Jack LONDON based his story of an alien artifact and its place in the life of a Solomon Islands tribe, "The Red One" (1918), on his reading of the work of Carl Jung. Jungian theory also provided the foundation for much (but not all) of the protagonists' psychological development in Frank HERBERT's Dune series (1965–1985). Several of Philip José FARMER's early stories, such as "Mother" (1953), were inspired by Freudian concepts, as were Alfred Bester's "Oddy and Id" (1950) and certain aspects of his *The Demolished Man* (1953). B. F. Skinner based much (but not all) of his utopian novel *Walden Two* (1948) on his application of radical behaviorist concepts to human behavior. A. E. VAN VOGT's *The World of Null-A* (1948) not only draws on the quasi-psychological theory of general semantics but uses a number of quotations from Alfred Korzybski's *Science and Sanity* as epigraphs and thus may have helped revive what van Vogt called in one introduction "a faltering science."

In most of the works cited, the authors appear to have made deliberate use of psychological concepts or phenomena. But a final and important way in which psychological issues enter SF is as an expression of the author's own psychological conflicts, often without his or her full awareness. Science-fiction writers have rarely credited their unresolved psychological difficulties as inspiration, but some have subsequently identified fictional analogues for their psychological growth or cure. Jack WILLIAMSON, for example, attributes much of his scientifically rationalized werewolf novel, *Darker Than You Think* (1940), to his experiences in psychotherapy. Connections between personal peculiarities and the individual SF writer's choice of fiction may in some cases appear obvious (for example, in the work of Philip K. Dick), in other cases mysterious or nonexistent. So far, however, only a few SF writers (including Mary Wollstonecraft SHELLEY, Robert E. HOWARD, and Cordwainer

Smith) have been subjects of psychobiographical studies that provide detailed evidence for such connections. More of these studies may help illuminate the field.

A.C.E.

SEE ALSO: BIOLOGY, PHYSICAL SCIENCES, SOCIAL SCIENCES.

PUBLISHERS

The publishing of science fiction, particularly in the United States, can be divided into three major periods. The first of these began late in the nineteenth century; the second, early in the twentieth century (with the burgeoning of the pulp magazine industry); and the third, in the late 1940s and early 1950s, as the pulp magazines faded and publishing returned to book format.

Although few of the individual titles from the first period remain in print—or are even remembered, except by scholars and collectors—many of the themes of modern SF (and fantasy) were established then, and authors of later periods built and continue to build on these themes.

A leading publisher of this period was G. W. Dillingham in New York. Stuart Teitler of Kaleidoscope Books has estimated that Dillingham published approximately fifty titles in the field between 1878 and 1916. Among these was the anonymous *Man Abroad, A Yarn of Some Other Century* (1887), which includes spaceships; colonies on Venus, Jupiter, Saturn, Uranus, and Neptune; the adaptation of human stock to survive varying conditions on the colonized planets; and preparations for an interplanetary war. *Mizora, a Prophecy*, by Mary W. Lane (1890) portrays an inner world populated by parthenogenetic women utilizing submarines and airplanes. *Journey to Mars*, by Gustavus W. Pope (1894), is one of the most important early interplanetary novels, featuring a Martian colony at the North Pole, faster-than-light spaceships, space warps, and electrified sword duels!

F. Tennyson Neely, a firm that operated in Chicago and New York, and an associated publisher, the Abbey Press, produced at least sixty works of SF and fantasy between 1892 and 1903. A typical Neely volume was *The Secret of the Earth*, by Charles Willing Beale (1899), one of the many hollow Earth novels of the period—a subgenre that found its greatest popularity some years later in the Pellucidar novels of Edgar Rice BURROUGHS. Neely published works in translation, including *10,000 Years in a Block of Ice*, from the French of L. Broussenard (1898). This book provided one of the first descriptions of a macrocephalic future race and projected ongoing evolution and the by-now-familiar Yellow Peril. *Zerelda, a Story of Love and Death*, by Louise F. Suddick (1899), combines SF with occultism by portraying the spirits of deceased extraterrestrials.

Abbey Press, operating from the same Fifth Avenue,

Lester and Judy-Lynn del Rey

New York, address as Neely, produced distinctively attractive books in a period of outstanding trade bindings. A noteworthy Abbey Press book was *The Wonders of Mouseland*, by Edward Earl Childs (1901). Childs portrayed an advanced civilization of highly evolved, intelligent rodents thriving in the Antarctic.

Arena Publishing Company of Boston published twenty or more fantastic fiction volumes between 1892 and 1896. These include *Journey to Venus*, by Gustavus W. Pope (1895), a sequel to Pope's *Journey to Mars*, as well as *Unveiling a Parallel*, by "two women of the west" (1893), a utopian novel that features a journey by spaceship to Mars, where sexual equality extends even to brothels staffed by male prostitutes.

The Broadway Publishing Company of New York published approximately ten fantastic fiction books between 1904 and 1911. Among the most interesting are *Astyanax*, by Joseph Brown, and *The Old Mountain Hermit*, by James F. Raymond (both 1904). Brown's book details the adventures of survivors of the Trojan War as they travel westward, visiting Atlantis and eventually landing in pre-Columbian North America. Raymond's novel involves a lost race, an antediluvian city, and a vision of the superscientific future that includes interplanetary travel.

Other significant publishers working in the field in this era include A. C. McClurg, Charles H. Kerr, Stone & Kimball (all of Chicago), A. L. Bancroft (San Francisco), and Harper and Brothers (New York).

The works just cited represent the merest sampling of those published during this early period. Other publishers in the United States contributed great numbers of SF books. The popularity of Nickel Novels and Dime Novels late in the nineteenth century cut deeply into the sales of more expensive books, and when Frank A. Munsey popularized the pulp magazine in the first decade

of the 1900s, the trend in SF publishing was increasingly toward these periodicals and away from books (see PULP MAGAZINES).

The variety pulps, such as *Argosy*, *All-Story*, and *New Story*, carried many works of SF. The emergence of specialty magazines (*Weird Tales* in 1923, AMAZING STORIES in 1926) further accelerated the trend away from book publishing, although of course significant SF titles continued to appear on occasion—the works of Olaf STAPLEDON, Aldous HUXLEY, and George ORWELL are notable among them.

The demands of enthusiastic readers of the pulps to see their favorite works in book form were largely ignored by commercial houses, and beginning in the late 1930s a great many small publishing firms were established by these readers themselves—surely a rare and remarkable occurrence in the publishing field.

The first successful such attempt was Arkham House, founded by August W. DERLETH and Donald Wandrei for the specific purpose of publishing the works of the late H. P. LOVECRAFT. The early Arkham House books set a pattern for such projects—press runs were in the low thousands and sometimes the hundreds. The books tended to sell slowly, and distribution was a major obstacle, but once titles went out of print prices rose sharply. The first Arkham House book was Lovecraft's *The Outsider and Others* (1939). Soon Derleth broadened the company's line to include other authors, most of them associated with *Weird Tales*. Thus Arkham House published the first significant books of Robert BLOCH (*The Opener of the Way*, 1945), Ray BRADBURY (*Dark Carnival*, 1947), and Fritz LEIBER (*Night's Black Agents*, 1947).

Derleth continued to manage Arkham House until his death in 1971; he was succeeded as editor by James Turner. Turner further broadened the scope of Arkham House's publications to include important SF books by such authors as Greg BEAR, Michael BISHOP, and James TIPTREE, Jr.

With the end of World War II many more fan-owned presses were established. These include Fantasy Press, operated by sometime SF author Lloyd Arthur ESHBACH; Shasta Publishers, founded by Erle Korshak and Everett F. BLEILER; Fantasy Publishing Company Incorporated, operated by William Crawford and Margaret Crawford; and Gnome Press, founded by Martin Greenberg and David A. Kyle.

Whereas Arkham House specialized in publishing books by authors closely associated with *Weird Tales* and especially the Lovecraft circle, the later specialty publishers drew their material from the SF pulps—*Amazing*, *Astounding*, *Wonder*, and others. Scores of SF novels had been serialized in these magazines. A peculiar byproduct of this practice was the structuring of many SF novels into three or four major sections, with each transition marked by an internal cliff-hanger and its resolution. So deeply did this structure become ingrained in writers (and their readers, who became the next generation of writers) that many novels *not* serialized in the magazines bear the same deformation.

The fan presses were able to draw on this accumulation, issuing novels by A. E. VAN VOGT, E. E. SMITH, Jack WILLIAMSON, Stanley G. WEINBAUM, L. Sprague DE CAMP, Robert A. HEINLEIN, John W. CAMPBELL, Jr., Stanton A. COBLENTZ, L. Ron HUBBARD, Alfred BESTER, Isaac ASIMOV, Leigh BRACKETT, Henry KUTTNER, C. L. MOORE, James BLISH, and Arthur C. CLARKE. They also published many important short story collections, anthologies (including several annual series), and critical works.

With the disappearance of the pulp magazines in the early 1950s, important commercial publishers entered the field with new lines of SF books. The most significant of these were Ballantine Books and Ace Books.

Ballantine was founded in 1952 by Ian and Betty Ballantine and was sympathetic to SF from the outset. Ian Ballantine had sponsored Judith MERRIL's important SF anthology *Shot in the Dark* (1950) when he was at Bantam Books. He brought his enthusiasm with him to his own line. In 1953 Ballantine published the first volume of Frederik POHL's original story anthology, *Star Science Fiction*. This was followed by the novel *The Space Merchants* by Pohl and Cyril M. KORNBLUTH and by many other important books, including *Childhood's End* by Arthur C. Clarke, *Fahrenheit 451* by Ray Bradbury, *More Than Human* by Theodore STURGEON, *Untouched by Human Hands* by Robert SHECKLEY, *Brain Wave* by Poul ANDERSON, and *Of All Possible Worlds* by William TENN.

Ballantine's edition of J. R. R. Tolkien's trilogy Lord of the Rings ranks among the all-time bestselling books of any genre and is widely considered to have stimulated the major growth in fantasy literature of the 1960s and after. After the departure of the Ballantines, the Ballantine Books SF line evolved into Del Rey Books, and despite the death of Judy-Lynn DEL REY this imprint continues to be a major force.

Contemporaneous with Ballantine, Aaron A. Wyn founded Ace Books. Wyn's chief editor was Donald A. WOLLHEIM, a onetime fan whose professional credentials included the editorship of several pulp magazines and anthologies and prior service as editor at Avon Books. From 1953 on Ace issued SF books in a steady stream. The earliest of these, especially those in the Ace Double format, were immediately successful. They included many novels reprinted from the pulps and a smaller number of original manuscripts.

Early Ace authors included A. E. van Vogt, Leigh Brackett, Eric Frank RUSSELL, Murray LEINSTER, Clifford D. SIMAK, and other highly regarded veterans of the pulps. However, Ace's great contribution came about through the cultivation by Wollheim and his later associate Terry CARR of the early efforts of several of the most important writers of modern SF. These included Philip K. DICK,

Robert SILVERBERG, Ursula K. LE GUIN, Samuel R. DELANY, and Thomas M. DISCH.

After leaving Ace, Wollheim established his own firm, DAW Books, and continued his former policies of publishing large numbers of adventure novels and series books while sponsoring major new authors, including C. J. CHERRYH and Tanith LEE.

Following the death of Wyn and the resignation of Wollheim, Ace Books went through a series of corporate mergers and takeovers, eventually becoming part of the Berkley Publishing Group, the largest single publisher of SF and fantasy in the 1980s.

Other significant publishers of SF are Doubleday, which has maintained a steady production for many years; Tor Books, founded by onetime Ace publisher Thomas Dougherty; Bantam Books; Bluejay Books; and Baen Books, headed by another Ace alumnus, James Baen.

Although the fan-owned presses (with the possible exception of Arkham House) no longer constitute a major force in the SF field, several of them continue to thrive, primarily by producing elaborate and costly limited editions for the collector's market. Such publishers include Donald M. Grant, Phantasia Press, and Scream Press.

The performance of publishers since the 1950s indicates that an adequately funded and well-managed company that establishes an SF line under a qualified editor and supports that line over a long period is almost assured of a profitable return.

R.A.L.

PULP MAGAZINES

The history of science fiction can be viewed as a struggle between two traditions: the pulp magazine tradition, created by *Argosy* in 1896 and exemplified in SF by Clayton's *Astounding Stories of Super Science*, and the popular science tradition, pioneered by Hugo GERNSBACK's *Electrical Experimenter* and exemplified in SF by his AMAZING STORIES.

The pulp magazine was made possible (and got its name from) a process for making cheap paper from wood pulp invented in Germany in 1884. This innovation encouraged the publication of inexpensive magazines, which began filling their pages with unsophisticated adventure stories of all kinds for the newly literate working man and his sons. For the first half of the twentieth century a good part of the SF published in this country was to be found in the pulps. A cheap and accessible form of entertainment, the pulps were never highly thought of by most academics, slick-paper critics, or various defenders of public morality. The fact that they provided an outlet for SF tended to lower the genre's reputation and establish a stigma that still is being lived down.

Pulp magazines competed with the already established dime novels and nickel fiction weeklies. They measured 7 by 10 inches and offered anywhere from one hundred to two hundred pages for prices ranging from a dime to a quarter. The early pulpwoods were rather sedate in appearance, usually containing no interior illustrations and decked out in covers that consisted only of sober type. By the 1920s, when dozens of pulp titles were being offered and the format had successfully supplanted the dime novels and fiction weeklies, covers had become impressively gaudy; a typical one contained as much action and promise as a circus poster.

The pulp magazines were selling SF years before they knew what to call it. In the first decades of the century, the Frank A. Munsey pulps—*Argosy, All-Story,* and *Cavalier*—were printing tales such as "Under the Moons of Mars" and "Beyond the Great Oblivion" and labeling them "different stories." In fact, even after a whole magazine offered this kind of material there was no agreed-on term for it. Editor and publisher Hugo Gernsback is credited with first calling SF "science fiction." That was in 1929, some three years after he had launched his pioneering *Amazing Stories.*

The term *science fiction* came to serve as an umbrella, under which were gathered the many types of imaginative and speculative stories that had been appearing in the general adventure pulps, both scientific romance and scientific speculation. Science fiction could accommodate a vast range of elements: planet-hopping adventure, satiric thoughts about the future, trips through time to the past; space travelers and monstrous aliens, fragile princesses, mad scientists, absentminded professors and dedicated researchers; hymns in praise of technology and dire warnings about the perils of the machine; UTOPIAS AND DYSTOPIAS; hard science, PSEUDOSCIENCE, and crackpot science. All in all, the SF pulp was potentially more catholic in scope than most other genre pulps. In the first decade or so of SF magazines, this wide potential was overlooked more often than it was taken advantage of. The emphasis tended to be, particularly in the 1930s, on action and heroes.

Before there were any SF pulps, the Munsey magazines ran a sizable amount of SF material, chiefly because of the editorial policy of senior editor Robert H. Davis. The favored type came to be the scientific romance, mixing action with a smattering of technology and a bit of love interest. The star performer here, from 1912 on was Edgar Rice BURROUGHS. After "Under the Moons of Mars," Burroughs turned out several more John Carter of Mars adventures, and in 1914 he branched out with "At the Earth's Core," which took its hero to Pellucidar.

During the period of Burroughs's ascendancy, several other authors explored similar territory for Munsey. George Allan ENGLAND, Charles B. Stilson, J. U. Giesy, A. MERRITT, and Otis Adelbert KLINE all wrote scientific romances, using remote places and planets and a smattering of science. Kline, who made a career of following in

Cover by Earle K. Bergey (July–August 1950)

Burroughs's footsteps, had his own Mars and Venus series. Eventually the Solar System was used up, and the galactic space opera superseded the scientific romance. But first there had to be Gernsback.

Gernsback was much too eclectic to stick to any limiting definition of what an SF pulp ought to be. A man who would write SF serials for a radio repair magazine obviously cared little for categories. So Gernsback's pioneering *Amazing Stories* was somewhat wider ranging than its imitators. The first issue reached the stands, unheralded and unadvertised, with a bright yellow cover by Frank R. PAUL. Paul, a former New Jersey newspaper cartoonist, went on producing his intricate and primitive paintings—which look like what you'd get if you asked a computer to paint like Grandma Moses—for Gernsback for the next twenty years. The authors displayed in the initial issue included H. G. WELLS, Jules VERNE, and Edgar Allan POE. Gradually Gernsback made enough money to use fewer reprints and more work by living authors. He attracted a varied group of new writers—Fletcher PRATT, John W. CAMPBELL, Stanton A. COBLENTZ, Jack WILLIAMSON, and E. E. SMITH.

Smith was one of the major engineers of the space opera. His "The Skylark of Space" appeared in the Gernsback pulp in 1928. The *Skylark* is an enormous spaceship, built to cruise the galaxy. "This novel was the first to deal to any extent with the incredible power to be had from the release of intra-atomic energy and its application to space travel," wrote historian Alva Rogers. "The Skylark and its passengers tour the universe, encountering all sorts of wild and wonderful adventures, strange beings and creatures, and marvels beyond compare." Pulp readers of the late 1920s took to Smith and admired his ability to create action "on a cosmic scale." The type of novel he had introduced helped set a pattern that would persist until the 1940s, as did the 1928 *Amazing* novel by Philip Francis NOWLAN that introduced the character of BUCK ROGERS.

The year 1928 was a good one for Gernsback. But in 1929 he had to declare bankruptcy and sell his magazine. The next year *Astounding* came along. A publication of the Clayton company, its original and complete name was *Astounding Stories of Super-Science*. This new pulp was, in the words of its first editor, Harry BATES, "unabashedly an action adventure magazine." At the time of its publication there were, according to Bates, thirteen Clayton magazines. Each month the engravers delivered proofs of all thirteen cover illustrations on a single large sheet of paper—on which there were several blank spaces. Bates remembered imagining Clayton's "money-lustful" thoughts: "If I had sixteen magazines I'd get the three additional covers cheap . . . the paper for the covers, now being wasted, would be free." Armed with his hunches about what Clayton was thinking, and the armful of back issues of *Amazing* he'd been studying, Bates approached the publisher. "It was easy as pie! There'd be an action-adventure *Astounding Stories of Super-Science!* I was to get right to work on it."

Besides making up the new magazine, Bates also created one of *Astounding*'s early popular heroes, the space opera star Hawk Carse. But even with the help of the space-hopping, ray-gun-wielding Space Hawk, the magazine couldn't escape the financial pressures put on Clayton by the Depression. The whole company and all its pulps went under. Street & Smith bought some of the titles, among them *Astounding*.

Gernsback meantime gave it another try. But he had little success, and through the 1930s one Gernsback SF magazine after another appeared and disappeared. *Science Wonder Stories* thrived for only a dozen issues, from the spring of 1929 to the spring of 1930. *Air Wonder Stories*, initially devoted to the future of air and space travel, expired at the same time, after an even shorter career. The warm months of 1930 also saw the end of *Scientific Detective Monthly*. Gernsback next merged most of his fallen titles into one, named *Wonder Stories*. The first few issues were thin and on a better-quality paper. The magazine then reverted to pulp stock and lasted for nearly six years.

By 1936, with only a few thousand readers still faithful, Gernsback gave up *Wonder Stories*. Ned Pines's Standard outfit bought it, and Leo Margulies became the editorial director. Margulies had a favorite word that he stuck on the title of many of his pulps. True to form, he rechristened this one *Thrilling Wonder Stories*. The magazine now became more aggressively juvenile. Monsters tripped over exclamation points on the covers

and in the illustrations. In the stories spacemen saved the world, if not the whole universe, several times each month. There was more emphasis on series characters, heroes who could be followed and collected from issue to issue. There were immortal men, galactic big-game hunters, and a wide assortment of space mercenaries and patrolmen. While this breathless heroic approach worked well in the pulps, it proved even more effective in the emerging comic books. When the rising Superman-DC company decided to expand, it hired a good part of Margulies's staff away from him, among them editorial personnel such as Mort WEISINGER and Jack Schiff and staff writers such as Alfred BESTER and H. L. GOLD.

As the decade ended a rash of new SF pulps broke out on the newsstands. Margulies added *Startling Stories* early in 1939. This was edited by Weisinger, who also had a hand in *Captain Future*. Deliberately aimed at a young audience, the Captain hit the stands in 1940 and appeared every three months thereafter, offering such adventures as "Calling Captain Future," "Captain Future's Challenge," and "The Triumph of Captain Future." All but three of the nearly two dozen novels about Curt Newton, *aka* Captain Future, were written by Edmond HAMILTON.

Another emerging pulp in the early 1940s was Fiction House's *Planet Stories*, combining the spirit of Space Hawk with the decorations of *Spicy Detective*. This magazine caught an audience a bit further along in adolescence. Also that decade the *Thrilling-Startling* twins joined *Planet* in sporting covers that combined interplanetary action with pretty women. A new species of menace developed on the bright covers of these SF pulps—a googly-eyed alien who was both inhospitable and horny. The bug-eyed monster, or BEM, was so visible back then that many middle-aged people in the United States still automatically think of a BEM when SF is mentioned.

Other pulps that flowered briefly in the World War II years were *Comet Stories*, *Cosmic Stories*, *Astonishing Stories*, *Future Science Fiction*, and *Super Science*. The once mighty Munsey company, reduced by financial necessity to more and more reprints, introduced *Famous Fantastic Mysteries* and *Fantastic Novels* to draw on its archives. By 1942 the outfit was no more, and Popular Publications took over these two magazines and the backlog of old scientific romances.

Meanwhile *Amazing Stories* had moved to Chicago and grown fat. The Ziff-Davis company purchased the title in 1938 and gave the editorship to Raymond A. PALMER. A longtime fan, Palmer had a good percentage of P. T. Barnum in him. He made *Amazing* a flamboyant and thick pulp—it eventually swelled to 250 pages—aimed at adolescent boys and, possibly, superstitious old ladies. The circulation is said to have climbed swiftly from about 25,000 to 200,000 under his hand.

Relying on old-time professionals and young fans for contributions, Palmer also searched Chicago for new writers. When all else failed, he wrote chunks of the magazine himself. A typical issue would contain stories by Edgar Rice Burroughs, Festus Pragnell, John York Cabot, P. F. Costello, and Thornton Ayre. Half of these authors were actually Palmer and his cohorts in disguise. In 1939 Ziff-Davis added to its line *Fantastic Adventures,* a B-movie mix of SF and fantasy. Also edited by Palmer, it offered readers such characters as the Golden Amazon, Lancelot Biggs the space navigator, and the Whispering Gorilla.

After some changes in title, format, and editorship, *Astounding* came under the editorial control of John W. Campbell, Jr., in 1937. "By 1938, there came a new turning point," says Isaac ASIMOV, whose own career as an SF writer was to begin the next year. "Campbell realized that the readership of science fiction had grown older and more sophisticated. He demanded stories from writers who knew something about science and engineering, and of the way in which scientists and engineers thought and worked." Campbell shepherded science fiction into its GOLDEN AGE, during which many of the best known names in SF began writing, among them Poul ANDERSON, Robert A. HEINLEIN, Arthur C. CLARKE, A. E. VAN VOGT, L. Sprague DE CAMP, Theodore STURGEON, and Clifford D. SIMAK.

The 1940s saw the spread of new trends in SF. After 1945, the year of Hiroshima and Nagasaki, those terrible monuments to the best and worst of science, it was difficult for SF writers to be satisfied with the creation of technological predictions that might come true or stories about galactic heroes with atomic ray guns. Even *Thrilling Wonder* grew up some and offered readers work by new writers such as Ray BRADBURY, John D. MACDONALD, and Philip José FARMER.

During the heyday of the pulps—from the early 1920s to the early 1950s—the SF category was far from the most popular. In the 1930s, for example, there were over fifty different detective pulps available, thirty-odd westerns, and nearly a dozen love story magazines, but only a handful of SF titles. When the pulps collapsed, however, only the SF magazines managed to hold on. *Amazing* and *Astounding* (now called ANALOG) survive to this day, although they long ago converted to the now popular digest format.

Perhaps there is a moral in this.

R.G.

PYNCHON, THOMAS (1937–). American reclusive mainstream writer, one of the most inventive of our time, who employs science and scientific concepts as both subject and metaphor; insofar as science and its impact on human beings is his subject, his work clearly falls into any reasonable definition of science fiction. In three strange and exhilarating novels and a number of short stories, Pynchon has woven a contemporary tap-

estry whose warp is a search for order (even the most absurd) in the universe and whose woof is a rational fear of power and a concern with entropy, which he treats primarily as a metaphor for the ways in which civilization and human relationships tend toward dissolution.

V (1963) deals with the search for a mysterious woman throughout the late nineteenth and twentieth centuries, and is SF only in its time jumps and a sequence involving an artificial human. *The Crying of Lot 49* (1966) is the quest novel of a woman trying to solve the riddle of her ex-lover's will in southern California: she uncovers a secret antipostal system going back four centuries, but Pynchon suggests that her discovery of this and other conspiracies may be only the result of her paranoia. The novel, however, is laden with scientific images, including Maxwell's Demon and the printed circuit board.

Gravity's Rainbow (1973), a vast and complex novel that won the National Book Award, is built around the ballistic arc of the V-2 rocket (from which comes the title) and the search for its meaning in a context of Nazi violence, the development of international scientific cartels, and the beginnings of the missile age. Again the question of order arises in the absurd connections between the sexual activity of one character (among a cast of hundreds) and the mysterious rocket everyone is seeking, but everything explodes, literally and figuratively, at the end. The novel focuses, in wildly comic terms and at a furious pace, on the penetration of science into human lives. If a stress on science in fiction makes for science fiction, then *Gravity's Rainbow* must be viewed as a harbinger of the new SF.

OTHER WORK: *Slow Learner* (collection, 1984).

P.B.

QUATERMASS

Professor Bernard Quatermass is the central character of this unusually thoughtful and increasingly complex series of British TV serials, which have been turned into films and books as well. Created by short-story writer Nigel Kneale and first broadcast over BBC as a six-part serial in 1953, Quatermass (played by Brian Donlevy in the first two films, then by Andrew Keir, and finally by John Mills) ostensibly is the scientist in charge of England's space program. His attention is diverted, however, first by an invasion from space by an alien being that transmutes the flesh of astronauts (*The Quatermass Xperiment*), then by other aliens that try to colonize Earth by entering and possessing human bodies (*Quatermass II*), later by the discovery that ancient Martians programmed their racial frenzy into the minds of primitive humanity (*Quatermass and the Pit*), and finally by the realization that still other aliens regard the human race as a huge herd of livestock ripe for slaughter (*Quatermass*).

The series reveals increasing dismay at the willingness of politicians and military people to misuse science—and at general humanity's willingness to settle for easy answers rather than combat its own weaknesses. Along with this, Kneale skillfully incorporates echoes of folklore and myth, both to increase a sense of cosmic unease and to suggest that such lurking fears also need to be faced. The Quatermass series does succeed in presenting a few human beings who strain to get control of themselves and meet each new challenge to the human species.

The first film also is significant for convincing Britain's Hammer Films that there was money in horror, and over the next two decades the company virtually dominated the inexpensive horror film category, making a series of Dracula and FRANKENSTEIN and other horror films as well as science fiction.

THE QUATERMASS EXPERIMENT (July–August 1953). *Directed by Rudolph Cartier; teleplay by Nigel Kneale. With Reginald Tate, Isabel Dean, Hugh Kelly. Six 35-minute episodes. Black and white.*

THE QUATERMASS XPERIMENT (1955). *Directed by Val Guest; screenplay by Richard Landau and Val Guest; adapted from the teleplay* The Quatermass Experiment *by Nigel Kneale; photographed by Walter Harvey. With Brian Donlevy, Margia Dean, Jack Warner, Richard Wordsworth, David King Wood. 78 minutes. Black and White. Alternate title:* The Creeping Unknown.

QUATERMASS II (October–November 1955). *Directed by Rudolph Cartier; teleplay by Nigel Kneale. With John Robinson, Hugh Griffith, Monica Grey. Six 35-minute episodes. Black and white.*

QUATERMASS II (1957). *Directed by Val Guest; screenplay by Nigel Kneale and Val Guest; adapted from the teleplay by Nigel Kneale; photographed by Gerald Gibbs. With Brian Donlevy, Vera Day, Bryan Forbes, John Longden, Sidney James, William Franklyn, Percy Herbert. 85 minutes. Black and white. Alternate title:* Enemy from Space.

QUATERMASS AND THE PIT (December 1958–January 1959). *Directed by Rudolph Cartier; teleplay by Nigel Kneale. With André Morell, Cec Linder, Anthony Bushnell. Six 35-minute episodes. Black and white.*

QUATERMASS AND THE PIT (1967). *Directed by Roy Ward Baker; screenplay by Nigel Kneale; adapted from the teleplay by Nigel Kneale; photographed by Arthur Grant; music by Tristram Cary. With Andrew Keir, Barbara Shelley, James Donald, Julian Glover, Duncan Lamont, Edwin Richfield. 97*

minutes. Color. Alternate title: Five Million Years to Earth.

QUATERMASS (1979). *Directed by Piers Haggard; screenplay by Nigel Kneale; photographed by Ian Wilson; music by Marc Wilkinson and Nick Rowley. With Sir John Mills, Simon McCorkindale, Barbara Kellerman, Margaret Tytzack, Brewster Mason. 107 minutes. Color. Alternate title:* The Quatermass Conclusion.

J.S.

QUEST FOR FIRE (1981). *Directed by Jean-Jacques Annaud; screenplay by Gerard Brach; adapted from the novel* La Guerre du feu *by J. H. Rosny; photographed by Claude Agostini; music by Philippe Sarde. With Everett McGill, Ron Perlman, Nameer El-Kadi, Rae Dawn Chong. 100 minutes. Color.*

Promotional hype about a "science fantasy adventure" and critical comparisons to STAR WARS (1977) and 2001: A SPACE ODYSSEY (1968) aside, *Quest for Fire* (1981) is authentic fiction, the science in question being paleontology. This is one of the few "caveman" epics to go beyond the level of *One Million B.C.* and make a serious, speculative effort at presenting life in the prehistoric past.

The most remarkable thing about the film is that all the dialogue consists of grunts and odd noises, a suitably Paleolithic language (a kind of eo-Indo-European) invented by none other than Anthony BURGESS. Despite the language, the plot is not at all difficult to follow. The hero's tribe tends fire but cannot make it, and when the fire is accidentally extinguished, extinction threatens. So the hero and his companions set out on a journey of adventure and discovery, encounter humans and subhumans both more and less advanced than themselves, and return with the precious fire—only to lose it again when somebody stumbles in a swamp. But, happily, the maiden rescued by the heroes along the way knows how to *make* fire, and the film concludes effectively with the wonder of technological advance.

Quest for Fire is itself an advance, a superbly realized vision of a vanished world.

D.S.

THE QUESTOR TAPES (1974). *Directed by Richard A. Colla; screenplay by Gene Roddenberry and Gene Coon; photographed by Michael Margulies; music by Gil Melle. With Robert Foxworth, Mike Farrell, John Vernon, Lew Ayres, James Shigeta, Robert Douglas, Dana Wynter, Majel Barrett, Walter Koenig. 100 minutes. Color. Alternate title:* Questor.

Questor is one of a series of unsuccessful attempts by Gene RODDENBERRY to duplicate his earlier success with STAR TREK. This made-for-TV film was conceived as a pilot for a series that went unsold, and therefore much of the story is left untold and the issues unresolved. The story line involves the efforts of an android named Questor (Robert Foxworth) to discover the lost secret of its identity and mission. Questor is, it turns out, the last of a line of self-perpetuating androids sent to the Earth by a benevolent alien species, but it has been incompletely programmed—like the film itself. The sequences in which Questor is brought to "life" and on his own learns how to function in a human world are particularly impressive, however, and the idea might have made an effective series.

D.C. FONTANA, Roddenberry's story editor for *Star Trek,* wrote a novelization of the screenplay that was published in 1974.

W.L.

QUINTET (1979). *Directed by Robert Altman; screenplay by Robert Altman, Frank Barhydt, and Patricia Resnick; photographed by Jean Boffety; music performed by the London Symphony Orchestra. With Paul Newman, Vittorio Gassman, Bibi Andersson, Fernando Rey, Brigitte Fossey, Nina Van Pallandt. 100 minutes. Color.*

Quintet is the only attempt at science-fiction film to date by Robert Altman, an American director who has explored virtually every popular movie genre. In the New Ice Age brought about by nuclear war, the few survivors spend their time playing the deadly game of Quintet, a metaphor for a splintered, cold, and competitive society. Unfortunately, the interesting premise, fine international cast, inventive costuming (at once futuristic and medieval), and novel cinematography (even the camera lens is frosted) are compromised by a wordy script that never makes the game itself convincing.

B.K.G.

R

RACKHAM, JOHN (Pseudonym of John Thomas Phillifent) (1916–1976). British sailor, government worker, and writer. The name John Rackham, and occasionally John T. Phillifent, was associated with a large number of science-fiction adventure novels and short stories. Rackham was most at home with plots lifted from traditional literature and translated, with decent success, to SF. Secret agents (*Alien Sea,* 1968; *The Anything Tree,* 1970; *Hierarchies,* 1973), intragalactic conflict (*The Treasure of Tau Ceti,* 1969; *Ipomoea,* 1969; *The Flowers of Doradil,* 1970; *Dark Planet,* 1971; *King of Argent,* 1973), and lost children or adults who

return to civilization after many years' absence (*The Beasts of Kohl,* 1966; *Life with Lancelot,* 1973) were his most popular plots but not the only ones he used. No matter what the plot, the central conflict remained the same in all the works: good versus evil, with the forces of good having some dark moments but eventually carrying the day. Most of Rackham's short fiction was published in Britain by NEW WORLDS or the original anthology series *New Writings in SF.* No collection of his stories yet exists.

OTHER WORKS: *Space Puppet* (1954); *Jupiter Equilateral* (1954); *The Master Weed* (1954); *The Touch of Evil* (1963); *We, The Venusians* (1965); *Time to Live* (1966); *Danger from Vega* (1966); *The Double Invaders* (1967); *The Proxima Project* (1968); *Beyond Capella* (1971); *Earthstrings* (1972); *Genius Unlimited* (1972); *Beanstalk* (1973).

S.H.G.

RADIO

Radio has been not only a medium but a subject. Arthur C. CLARKE has said that radio was an "unexpected" discovery. As a consequence, before 1895, when Guglielmo Marconi transmitted his first longwave signals, stories that dealt with long-distance communication tended toward fantasy. Soon after the turn of the century, however, writers began to toy with practical applications of wireless transmission. Hugo GERNSBACK, the founder of the first SF magazine in 1926, got his start in 1900s America by importing electrical equipment, including the $7.50 Telimco Wireless, and by publishing a radio catalog that grew into the first radio magazine and then the first electronics magazine.

The most noteworthy uses of radio in fiction include a series of Rover Boys–type juveniles built around a group called the Radio Boys; a series of 1920s Radio Man adventures by Ralph Milne FARLEY, in which a Boston scientist named Myles Cabot accidentally broadcasts himself to Venus and undergoes a series of Edgar Rice BURROUGHS–like adventures; and a 1940s series of Venus Equilateral stories by George O. SMITH, about technical difficulties involving a manned satellite intended to transmit radio signals among the inhabited planets.

After World War II, when radio astronomy came into its own, stories incorporated not only radio telescopes but, after 1958, scientific speculations about the possibility of alien civilizations communicating via radio waves. Examples of the second premise include James E. GUNN's *The Listeners* (1972) and Carl SAGAN's *Contact* (1985).

It would not have been surprising, then, if radio, with its capacity for creating magical (and inexpensive) images in the mind, had taken quickly to SF as a source of dramatic material. But that wasn't the case. Although the most famous radio broadcast of all time was an SF show, SF never was the choice of programmers or the

Cast of Orson Welles's *Mercury Theater of the Air*

general audience.

Of course the fame surrounding *The Mercury Theatre of the Air*'s one-hour version of H. G. WELLS's *The War of the Worlds* has to do with the fact that several million Americans, tuning in late on the adaptation and already suffering from war jitters, thought they were hearing a news broadcast and not a drama. The show aired on Halloween night in 1938 and, as Orson Welles said, "was intended to be the *Mercury Theatre*'s own radio version of dressing up in a sheet and jumping out of a bush and saying boo." The nationwide panic over a supposed invasion from Mars and the subsequent publicity that came to Welles and his Mercury players brought Welles fame, fortune, and the opportunity to make *Citizen Kane*. Science fiction in radio, however, remained a poor relation to mystery, comedy, and western fare. Exploitation was not as fully developed a half century ago, so nobody thought of putting on a weekly invasion from Mars show or otherwise taking advantage of the sudden notoriety of SF—possibly because the mass audience of the day considered that sort of stuff both strange and unsettling.

SF was better suited for kids really, everyone believed. That's why the earliest regularly broadcast SF show was BUCK ROGERS *in the 25th Century*. Based on the comic strip, which was in turn based on the AMAZING STORIES novelettes, the show was a daily fifteen-minute afternoon serial heard originally in 1932 on the CBS network: space opera with Buck, Wilma, Dr. Huer, Killer Kane et al., sponsored by such products for kids as Cocomalt, Cream of Wheat, and Popsicles. Another comic-strip hero came to the airwaves in the mid-1930s in the person of FLASH GORDON. For the sort of SF aimed at listeners who didn't start the day with a bowl of Kellogg's cereal you had to take potluck, with shows such as *Lights Out*. Created by Wyllis Cooper and carried on by Arch Oboler, this Chicago-based anthology show offered mystery, horror, fantasy, and an occasional SF tale. *Lights Out* began in 1934 and held on, with some lapses, throughout the 1940s. Some listeners, including Bill Cosby (as he recounts in one of his comedy routines, "The Chicken Heart That Ate Chicago"), still feel that the show about the chicken heart that keeps growing and growing was Oboler's finest.

During the 1940s Carlton E. Morse's *I Love a Mystery* provided some SF continuities, often of the lush A. MERRITT romantic fantasy variety. Cooper, after a scriptwriting sojourn in Hollywood, returned to radio in 1947 to write and direct *Quiet, Please*. Highly individual and effective, the show starred Ernest Chappell in a variety of fantasy, horror, and SF stories. Some were light, such as the episode about a man meeting a Martian at the corner bar, and some were scary, such as the "Thing on the Fourble Board," which dealt with an invisible alien. The show managed to last just two years. Cooper's final script dealt with the end of the world. Programs such as *The Shadow*, with many of its scripts written by Alfred BESTER (and the voice, in 1937–38, provided by Orson Welles), also now and then used the themes and props of SF, as did SUPERMAN, *Jack Armstrong, the All-American Boy, Captain Midnight*, and even *Tom Mix*.

CBS made some notable contributions in the 1940s. *Suspense*, produced and directed for most of its life by William Spier, premiered in 1942. Along with its adaptations of mystery and horror yarns, it included a range of work from Curt SIODMAK's *Donovan's Brain* to H. P. LOVECRAFT's creepy stories. *Escape* was another anthology show, first heard in 1947. Somewhat more devoted to SF, *Escape* provided adaptations of works by H. G. Wells, Algernon Blackwood, John Collier, and Nelson S. Bond, as well as Jack LONDON's "The Scarlet Plague," F. Scott Fitzgerald's "The Diamond As Big As the Ritz," and George R. STEWART's *Earth Abides*. The show originated in Hollywood and used some of the best radio voices of the time—William Conrad, Paul Frees, and Jack Webb among them.

Real, unabashed, grown-up SF on a weekly basis finally reached the air in the spring of 1950. NBC's *Dimension X* originated in New York and used scripts, usually by Ernest Kinoy, based on recent stories by Kurt VONNEGUT, Jr., Ray BRADBURY, Robert A. HEINLEIN, Isaac ASIMOV, and other writers who weren't yet considered the creators of classics. The programs were well done, but *Dimension X* failed to snag a sponsor and left the network the following fall. A similar series, involving some of the same creative people, began in 1955: *X Minus One*, produced in cooperation with GALAXY *Magazine*, featured dramatizations of recent stories from the magazine's pages by the likes of Poul ANDERSON, Robert SHECKLEY, Robert SILVERBERG, and Theodore STURGEON. This *X* remained alive until early in 1958 and was revived for redistribution in the mid-1980s along with other programs now considered "classic radio." By 1958, however, dramatic radio was nearly dead, and just about all the private eyes and cowboys were gone. After *X Minus One* vanished, new radio SF was impossible; television was where the audience would have to turn next. And that was a pity. Science-fiction adaptations may have reached their ideal form on radio, where, instead of emphasizing expensive special effects, the sound effects engineer can establish a mood or an image with a few imaginative gadgets, where the idea is as pure and uncompromised as it is on the page, and where listeners can create the greatest machine, the most glittering or dismal future, the most beautiful woman, and the most terrifying alien in the theaters of their own minds. And *X Minus One* might have been as good as SF dramatization was going to get.

J.E.G.

RAND, AYN (1905–1982). Russian-born American who articulated her philosophy of living (which she called Objectivism) in her novels and later in nonfictional works. Rand's idealization of individualism gives *The Fountainhead* (1943) and *Atlas Shrugged* (1957) a distinct utopian flavor. Her first novel, and her only work of science fiction, *Anthem* (1938), depicts a man's escape from an oppressive dystopia.

N.H.

RANDALL, MARTA (1948–   ). American writer born in Mexico City but educated and residing in the San Francisco Bay area. Randall has written science fic-

tion and fantasy, historical novels, and dystopias, and edited two anthologies. At its best her writing is reminiscent of the work of Olaf STAPLEDON, particularly her first novel, *Islands* (1976; revised 1980), in which an aging heroine in an island society of immortals transcends her bodily form and mutates to a higher level of consciousness, merging with the cosmos.

Randall is particularly adept at describing disconcerting alien psychologies and at extrapolating cultures; in *A City in the North* (1976), for instance, she dealt with aliens, exploited and oppressed by humans, who deliberately destroy their own culture in order to free themselves. Randall's work is also informed by feminism: her women are decisive, independent, and nurturing, and her fictional worlds are nonsexist. Her fiction criticizes sexist practices in her own society and explores sexual alternatives such as homosexuality and incest but offers no new social orders. For instance, in *Journey* (1978) and *Dangerous Games* (1980), a two-part saga of the Kennerin family, who own an alien planet and attempt to create a society that is an alternative to that of the Earth, the utopian social system is monopoly capitalism. This contradiction, shared by a number of feminist writers, remains unresolved.

Randall's subsequent novels, *The Sword of Winter* (1983) and *Those Who Favor Fire* (1984), are only marginally SF. She served two terms as president of the SCIENCE FICTION WRITERS OF AMERICA, from 1982 to 1984.

H.M.Z.

RED PLANET MARS (1952). *Directed by Harry Horner; screenplay by John L. Balderston and Anthony Veiller; adapted from the play* Red Planet *by John L. Balderston and John E. Hoare; photographed by Joseph Biroc; music by Mahlon Merrick. With Peter Graves, Andrea King, Herbert Berghof, Walter Sande, Marvin Miller, Orley Lindgren, Bayard Veiller, Willis Bouchey, Richard Powers, Morris Ankrum, Gene Roth. 87 minutes. Black and white.*

Uniquely, this is a hysterically anti-Communist religious science-fiction film. An astronomer and his wife receive messages from Mars telling of a technologically advanced society; these messages humiliate the West into economic collapse. Another message, announcing that Mars too had a Jesus Christ, demolishes Communism. Then a fanatic Nazi reveals to the astronomer that *he* faked the messages from Mars. But although the astronomer, his wife, and the Nazi perish, a final, *real* Martian message arrives: "Ye have done well My good and faithful servants."

John L. Balderston, formerly one of the best writers of fantastic films, here condescended to the audience, offering a religious message in the guise of an SF film. The movie was aimed at the same audience as *The Next Voice You Hear* (1950) but failed. *Red Planet Mars* is simplistic, caricaturing Soviets and Nazis alike, trying too hard to be a "little" film. It is of interest only as an aberration.

B.W.

REED, KIT (Née Lilian Craig) (1932–   ).

American journalist, professor of English, and writer of mainstream fiction, fantasy, and science fiction. Primarily a short story writer (most of her stories have been published in THE MAGAZINE OF FANTASY AND SCIENCE FICTION), Reed uses the props of science fiction but is essentially interested in character.

In "Mister da V." (collected in *Mister da V. and Other Stories*, 1967), for instance, in which Leonardo da Vinci appears in the twentieth century and lives with a contemporary family, Reed uses the standard SF convention of time travel to explore contemporary attitudes toward the arts and the past. The story's power derives from the thoroughly mundane reaction of the family members to their extraordinary house guest.

While Reed's protagonists are often female, she is not easily categorized as a feminist writer since her barbed sense of humor takes on the modern world at large. "Golden Acres" (1968) describes the dehumanized future homes for the old of both sexes, and "Songs of War" (1974) argues that a separation of the sexes or the domination of one sex over the other is no answer to the world's problems. In her first science-fiction novel, *Armed Camps* (1969), neither aggressive men nor passive women hold the solution to the constant cycle of war in which a United States of the near future finds itself.

OTHER WORKS: *Killer Mice* (collection, 1976); *Magic Time* (1979); *Other Stories, and The Attack of the Giant Baby* (collection, 1981); *Fort Privilege* (1986); *Revenge of the Senior Citizens**Plus* (collection, 1986).

S.H.G.

——————— RELIGION ———————

Science fiction's relation with religion has always been uneasy. Science fiction, like science, can coexist with systems of organized relgous beliefs only by separating them from the intellectual skepticism that lies at the heart of both SF and science. As a matter of fact, SF, like science, is an organized system that, for many, takes the place of religion in the modern world by attempting a complete explanation of the universe. It asks the questions—where did we come from? why are we here? where do we go from here?—that religions exist to answer. That is why *religious* SF is a contradiction in terms, although SF *about* religion is commonplace.

Brian STABLEFORD has commented that "when we examine the SF of today for its dominant trend we find a strong interest in certain mystical and transcendental

themes and images." Critics frequently cite a few examples in proof. But a study of David Pringle's *Science Fiction: The 100 Best Novels* (1985) reveals that only seven of the novels listed use religion as an integral part of their stories. Of the seven, the two novels by Kurt VONNEGUT, Jr., *Cat's Cradle* (1963) and *The Sirens of Titan* (1959), treat religion as a hoax. Leigh BRACKETT's *The Long Tomorrow* (1955) sees religion as a threat; Keith ROBERTS's *Pavane* (1968) and Kingsley AMIS's *The Alteration* (1976), alternate-history novels, view a Catholic-controlled world as a danger. The sixth novel, James BLISH's *A Case of Conscience* (1958), has been read as a religious parable about the force of God, but Blish himself didn't see it that way; he was an atheist fascinated by the philosophical content of religion.

That leaves one book out of the hundred that might be considered religious and on the side of religion, *A Canticle for Leibowitz* (1959) by Walter MILLER, Jr. Some critics consider this a Catholic apologist novel, just as C. S. LEWIS's *Out of the Silent Planet* (1938) is an apologia for the Church of England. Miller used a science-fictional format—a traditional SF after-the-bomb plot—to make a religious point: that postholocaust monasteries would collect and preserve blueprints and technological artifacts the way medieval monasteries preserved Classical manuscripts. At their most religious—that is, when dealing with dogma—Miller's and Lewis's works read least like SF, and Lewis's Perelandra trilogy (of which *Out of the Silent Planet* is the first volume), which is the most often cited example of "religious" SF, certainly involves space travel to Mars and Venus but is better read as Christian parable.

Among the hordes of SF books that did not make Pringle's "best one hundred," religion is even scarcer. Gods from every pantheon abound in the wave of fantasy novels being published, but these are not SF and share more of religion's faith in the unprovable than SF's organized skepticism. Readers also can find explorations of religions in Roger ZELAZNY's *Lord of Light* (1967), with its Hindu gods, and *Creatures of Light and Darkness*, with its Egyptian deities; and in Samuel R. DELANY's *The Einstein Intersection* (1967), with almost every religion and mythology known to humanity stirred into the pot. James Blish, wearing his double hat as critic and authority on religion in SF, has commented that "Zelazny and Delany substitute myth for plot. Plot is better."

Mary Wollstonecraft SHELLEY's *Frankenstein* (1818) may have been the first SF novel, as Brian W. ALDISS believes, but it is not religious SF despite its theme of humanity replacing God as creator. Its message is humanity's need to discard religious belief, as Aldiss argued in *Trillion Year Spree* (1986); its real theme is the quest for knowledge, which no matter how badly it works out is never disavowed. Victor Frankenstein can only breathe life into his creation after rejecting all the received and worthless knowledge of the past.

Shelley may indeed have been the true precursor of modern SF, but Jules VERNE and H. G. WELLS established SF as a genre. Verne was a pious man who was commended by Pope Leo XIII for the purity of his writing, and Verne criticized his master, Edgar Allen POE, for failure to allow for the kind of "providential intervention" that is a prominent characteristic of Verne's own novels. But one might search all Wells's work for any element of faith in the supernatural. And it is from Wells that twentieth-century SF flowed.

The religious impulse, which might be described as the search for the unknowable and faith in the unprovable, is the subject of many SF speculations. Philip José FARMER has said of it, "The brain, knowing that a person can't live forever, rationalizes a future, or other dimensional, world in which immortality is possible." That sounds very much like the way a writer goes about writing an SF story, and one SF writer, L. Ron HUBBARD, actually created a religion, Scientology.

Olaf STAPLEDON's *The Star Maker* (1937) suggests that the stars are sentient and responsible for the life on their planets. If this is a religious statement, it should be remembered that this book was not published as science fiction. Nor were the other novels of the nineteenth and early twentieth centuries that critics cite as examples of religion in SF. John Jacob ASTOR's *A Journey in Other Worlds* (1894), with its spirits found on Saturn, is always mentioned, as is L. P. Gratacap's *The Certainty of a Future Life in Mars* (1903), wherein Mars is Heaven stuffed with souls. Not only are these books unread but they had no influence on later SF. The SF "Modern Prometheus" created by Shelley, Verne, and Wells came to maturity in the PULP MAGAZINES, and Hugo GERNSBACK was its godfather. Magazine SF had plenty of mysticism but no religion, or irreligion: even *damn* was deleted by puritanical copy editors.

Europe, the home of both western religion and religious wars, is also the home of the sort of SF that uses religion to criticize religion. In Camille Flammarion's *La Fin du monde* (*The End of the World*, 1893–1894), the pope and all the clergy pray for the world to be saved from an approaching meteor, but the meteor hits the Vatican, and the book hints that it was all God's doing. Nils Parling's Swedish novel *Korset* (*The Cross*, 1957) reveals a born-again preacher dragging a giant American atomic cannon around Europe after the Third World War. He calls the weapon the Fist of God, and a cult grows around it. Though thought to be unloaded, it is not—and when fired it destroys the last bastion of learning in the world. The author suggests that this is God's way of returning the world to ignorance. Also from Sweden is Sam J. LUNDWALL's *King Kong Blues* (1957), among other things a humorous parody of organized religion.

More religious content can be found in the SF short story—for the obvious reason that as a form the short story is an insatiable consumer of ideas: Ray BRADBURY's "The Man" (1949) offers the image of space travelers just missing Jesus as they visit planet after planet, and his "The Fire Balloons" (1951) shows priests encountering sinless creatures on Mars, similar to those discovered by James Blish's explorers on Lithia in *A Case of Conscience* (1958). In "The Streets of Ashkelon" (1962) Harry HARRISON confronted a fundamentalist missionary with natives who crucify him to see if he will rise; and Arthur C. CLARKE, in "The Star" (1955), found the last records of a lovely and "not evil" people on a distant planet, the explosion of whose sun shone as the Star of Bethlehem. In "If the Stars Are Gods" (1974; novel version 1977), Gregory BENFORD and Gordon EKLUND offered visiting aliens who experience stars as supreme beings, as in Stapledon's *The Star Maker*.

Much more common is religion as background, as in Michael MOORCOCK's "Behold the Man" (1966), in which a time traveler stands in for a moronic Jesus, or science begetting religion, as in Theodore STURGEON's "Microcosmic God" (1941), in which microscopic creatures undergoing forced evolution develop a religion, with the scientist as god, to rationalize their situation, or Robert A. HEINLEIN's "Universe" (1941), in which passengers are drifting in a spaceship that their religion tells them is the entire universe. Brian W. Aldiss pointed out the dangers of letting religion run society in "Danger, Religion" (1962). The outright attack on religion, as in "The Streets of Ashkelon," often has encountered publishing taboos, but the "God is dead" motif has found its way into a number of stories, such as Lester DEL REY's "Evensong" (1968), in which Man, as the Usurper, passes judgment on God, and George ZEBROWSKI's "Heathen God," in which the mad gnome who had created life and intelligence is handed over to humanity to be kept on an extraterrestrial preserve. A mad God is finally defeated by Adam, who is helped by a misunderstood serpent, and Earth comes to a final peace in Harlan ELLISON's "The Deathbird" (1973). In Philip K. DICK's *Our Friends from Frolix 8* (1970), "God is dead. They found his carcass in 2019. Floating out in space near Alpha."

Science fiction seems to work with greater assurance when it invents new religions. Heinlein's "If This Goes On . . ." (1940) offers a United States controlled by a bigoted and hypocritical church, and a year later, in "The Day after Tomorrow" (published as *Sixth Column*, 1949), Heinlein showed how a fake religious cult could defeat the Yellow Peril that had invaded and conquered America. Fritz LEIBER handled the same theme in *Gather, Darkness* (1943/1950), with a cult of phony satanists leading the revolution.

Invented alien religions offer multiple attractions to the SF author: the opportunity to create aliens and a religion and, ultimately, the chance to play God. Clifford D. SIMAK was good at this kind of story, though it too hasn't been easy to sell. In 1921 he managed to slip past a dozing editor "The Voice in the Void," in which heavy-handed humans land on Mars and crack open the tomb of the Martian Messiah—only to discover he came from Earth. Simak's "The Creator" (1935), which has time travelers go back far enough to discover that the Earth was just one of a number of constructs made by a super-being who has now had enough of it and wants to wipe it out, was less fortunate and had to be published in a semiprofessional magazine. The most famous, and the shortest, story on this theme is Frederic BROWN's "Answer" (1954), in which computers on many planets are linked together and asked Does God exist? They answer, He does now. In Katherine MACLEAN's "Unhuman Sacrifice" (1958), earth missionaries discover that alien superstitions work better than their own religion. Robert A. Heinlein offers the same message in *Stranger in a Strange Land* (1961), in which Michael Valentine Smith imports the superior Martian religion and in so doing influences humans both inside and outside the novel. Robert SILVERBERG touched on the same theme in *Nightwings* (1968/1969), as did D. G. COMPTON in *The Missionaries* (1972) and George R. R. MARTIN in "A Song for Lya" (1974).

A suspicion that even if God exists he is up to no good can be found in SF stories such as Lester del Rey's "For I Am a Jealous People" (1954), in which God turns his back on the human race and sides with the alien invaders. James Blish went even further in *Black Easter* (1968) and let the Devil win when Armageddon was let loose on Earth. The book's success demanded a sequel. Blish rejected the cowardly advice that he open the second book with "Meanwhile, in a galaxy very much like our own . . .," and actually wrote a sequel to the end of the world with *The Day after Judgment* (1970).

Science-fiction stories deal with religion in three basic ways: as a social force, as truth under test, and as transcendence. Most of the stories discussed thus far are of the first two kinds. Heinlein's treatments of religion, like those in "If This Goes On . . .," *Sixth Column*, and even *Stranger in a Strange Land*, are mostly about religion as a social force, as is Isaac ASIMOV's first *Astounding* story, "Trends" (1939), in which a return to fundamentalism threatens the space program. In most such stories, which take their inspiration from the treatment of Galileo by the Church, religion is depicted as a reactionary movement favoring ignorance over knowledge. In "Universe" Heinlein's hero has brought back his discovery that the ship actually is moving in a larger universe; he is condemned to death and shouts, echoing Galileo, "it *still* moves."

The second category, religion as truth under test, shows religion encountering the test of reality, or sometimes of science, as in Harry Harrison's "The Streets of Ashkelon." Almost always religion fails the test, although to be sure the tests are rigged and in any case aren't those

that religion, by its nature, is intended to deal with. Occasionally, however, religion passes the test, as when a spaceman discovers God on a remote planet in Eric Frank RUSSELL's "Hobbyist" (1943). Likewise, in Arthur C. Clarke's "The Nine Billion Names of God" (1953), it is believed that when Tibetan monks finish counting the names of God the world will come to an end; computer experts who have installed a computer that allows the monks to count more rapidly see the stars going out.

Finally, however, many SF stories deal with religion as transcendence, or experience beyond the world of sense. In this area religion is untestable, and scientists who claim religious belief often are describing faiths in areas beyond the reach of scientific proof, such as first causes and final ends, or at least beyond the limits of what presently is known or testable. Olaf Stapledon's *The Star Maker* and Gregory Benford and Gordon Eklund's "If the Stars Are Gods" are of this kind. So is Robert Silverberg's *Downward to the Earth* (1973), in which an Earthman finds salvation through an alien religion, and perhaps the most famous example, Clarke's *Childhood's End* (1953), in which the children of humanity destroy the Earth and merge with the Overmind.

That novel, however, contains an unusual statement: "The opinions expressed in this book are not those of the author." The SF universe is knowable and real. Even when SF stretches a timid toe into the "end-of-everything" ESCHATOLOGY that lies beyond the real and the knowable, it disavows mysticism. It is not the inhuman children of Earth with whom the reader (and perhaps the author) of *Childhood's End* identifies but the satanic-appearing Overlords who, because of their commitment to their own individualities and their pursuit of knowledge, are unable to merge with the Overmind: "they would hold fast until the end: they would await without despair whatever destiny was theirs. They would serve the Overmind because they had no choice." But, unlike Earth's children, "even in that service they would not lose their souls."

In a 1934 story titled "Twilight" John W. CAMPBELL defined the basic characteristic of humanity as curiosity. At the heart of SF is its eternal questioning; it cannot surrender that questioning for any revealed truths without losing its soul.

J.E.G.

RENNIE, MICHAEL (1909–1971).

British actor frequently associated with science-fiction films. Remembered as a tall, gaunt leading man, Rennie appeared in numerous foreign and American films during his long career. He was a major film star during the 1950s and starred in the television series *The Third Man*. His SF films include THE DAY THE EARTH STOOD STILL (1951), THE LOST WORLD (1960), *Cyborg 2087* (1966), and THE POWER

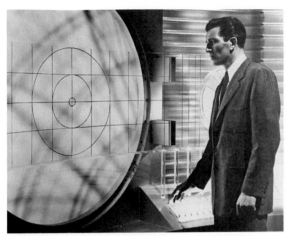

Michael Rennie in *The Day the Earth Stood Still* **(1951)**

(1968). *The Day the Earth Stood Still,* for which he is best known, is considered by many critics one of the greatest SF films ever made; Rennie was perfectly cast as the wise alien Klaatu, who comes to Earth to convince humanity to change its belligerent ways or be destroyed. Along with his role as the apostle Peter in *The Robe* (1953), his portrayal of Klaatu was among Rennie's own favorites.

H.L.P.

REPO MAN (1984). *Directed by Alex Cox; screenplay by Alex Cox; photographed by Robby Müller and Robert Richardson; music by Tito Larriva and Steven Hufsteter. With Harry Dean Stanton, Emilio Estevez, Tracey Walter, Olivia Barash, Sy Richardson, Susan Barnes, Fox Harris, Jennifer Balgobin, Dick Rude, Michael Sandoval. 92 minutes. Color.*

This wry, satiric sleeper takes place in the punk underbelly of Los Angeles. Aimless young Otto (Emilio Estevez) begins working as a car repossessor for seedy, energetic Bud (Harry Dean Stanton), who has his own repo man's creed. Meanwhile, an old Chevrolet whose trunk apparently contains the lethally radioactive remains of aliens (people are vaporized when they open it) arrives in town and Bud, Otto, and others try to claim it. At the end, the Chevy flies off into the night, with Otto and acid burnout Miller (Tracey Walter) aboard.

Repo Man defies description and challenges analysis. Alex Cox's imagery, characters, and viewpoint derive largely from rock music's punk and new wave movements, but he's also astute about films and assembled his story from a wide range of influences without slavishly imitating any.

B.W.

RETURN OF THE JEDI: SEE STAR WARS

THE REVENGE OF FRANKENSTEIN: SEE FRANKENSTEIN ON FILM

REVENGE OF THE CREATURE: SEE CREATURE FROM THE BLACK LAGOON

REYNOLDS, [DALLAS MCCORD] MACK (1917–1983). American writer and prolific specialist in socioeconomic science fiction. Born in Corcoran, New York, Reynolds was a world traveler who settled in Mexico for the last dozen years of his life, having turned to full-time writing in 1965. After his first sale to *Fantastic Adventures* in 1950, he produced more than forty SF novels and 180 shorter works, plus mysteries, Gothics, romances, and nonfiction books.

Reynolds dramatized a whole range of societies, from anarchies to theocracies, chiefly through stories of crime, espionage, and politics. Some of his overlapping, often repetitive series sketch a stratified welfare-state future, such as the world of the "Frigid Fracas" in *Mercenary from Tomorrow* (1962/1968). Others depict social experiments on alien worlds (*The Space Barbarians,* 1967/1969). Among his perennial concerns were racial prejudice, colonialism, and cultural imperialism, but futurism dominated the efforts of his last years.

His interest in futurism aside, Reynolds's overwhelming concern, whether he was designing utopias or dystopias, was bettering *this* world. Despite his awkward style, recycled plots, and "militant radical" lectures, he epitomized the analytic 1960s ANALOG writer while being voted favorite author by the readers of the more generally speculative GALAXY and *If.*

NOTABLE OTHER WORKS: *Planetary Agent X* (1961, 1965/1966); *Blackman's Burden* (1961–1962/1972); *Border, Breed nor Birth* (1962/1972); *The Earth War* (1963); *Time Gladiator* (1964/1966; with Michael Banks as *Sweet Dreams, Sweet Princes,* 1986); *Section G: United Planets* (1967/1976); *After Some Tomorrow* (1967); *The Best Ye Breed* (1973/1978); *Perchance to Dream* (1977); *The Other Time* (with Dean Ing, 1984); *Deathwish World* (with Dean Ing, 1986).

S.L.M.

RICHMOND, WALT (1922–1977) and LEIGH (Née Tucker) (?–   ). American husband-and-wife writing team, he a physicist, she a journalist and anthropologist. *Discovery* is the key word in describing the Richmonds' fiction collaborations. Their work is filled with ingenious characters devoted to expanding the limits, especially the mental limits, of the human race. The discovery may be the awakening powers in children (*The Probability Corner*, 1977, and *Phase Two*, 1980, shorter versions as *Phoenix Ship*, 1969), new technologies with fantastic side effects (*Challenge the Hellmaker*, 1976), or a new way of interpreting human history (*The Lost Millennium*, 1967). While many of the discoveries may strain the credulity of even the most devoted science-fiction fan, these novels remain true to the central goal of science fiction: to instill a sense of wonder in its readers.

OTHER WORKS: *Shock Waves* (1967); *Positive Charge* (collection, 1970); *Gallagher's Glacier* (1970; revised 1979).

S.H.G.

RIDERS TO THE STARS (1954).

Directed by Richard Carlson; screenplay by Curt Siodmak; photographed by Stanley Cortez; music by Harry Sukman. With William Lundigan, Herbert Marshall, Richard Carlson, Martha Hyers, Dawn Addams, Robert Karnes, Lawrence Dobkin, George Eldredge, Michael Fox, King Donovan, James Best. 81 minutes. Color.

Scientists send a rocket into space to discover what keeps meteors from being reduced to dust like the Moon (according to the film's rather strange science, the Moon is a cosmic dust ball). The rocket catches a meteor and brings it back to Earth. The meteor proves to be encrusted in diamonds. Now, in diamond-studded rockets, human beings can go into space.

The work of producer Ivan Tors in science fiction is characterized by small-scale predictions. Although today this characteristic makes him seem timid, in the period it may have been a reasonable approach; the general public may not have been ready for greater imaginative leaps. *Riders to the Stars* is atypical of Tors's work in that its science is wildly inaccurate. The dramatics, however, are above average for Tors, and the film is smoothly made. This is one of the few movies directed by Richard Carlson, an actor who appeared regularly in SF films.

B.W.

ROBERTS, KEITH [JOHN KINGSTON] (1935–).

British writer, editor, and illustrator. Roberts got his education in art and worked as a cartoon animator and an illustrator. His first novel, *The Furies* (1966), is a capable but conventional exercise in the "British disaster" mode, featuring giant wasps controlled by an alien intelligence. Two years later he published *Pavane* (1968), an established classic of alternate history (like many of his works, a story cycle rather than a true novel) set in England in which the Spanish Armada has won and Britain has consequently remained Catholic and medieval into the twentieth century. The setting is superbly developed, and the episodes themselves are vivid and often grim.

Roberts's story collections—*Machines and Men* (1973), *The Grain Kings* (1976), *The Passing of the Dragons* (1977), *Ladies from Hell* (1979), and *The Lordly Ones* (1986)—demonstrate considerable versatility, but he is mostly known for brooding, quasi-medieval stories set in a fog-drenched English countryside haunted by the specter of nuclear war—as in *Pavane*, *The Chalk Giants* (1974), or *Kiteworld* (1985)—which also display his regionalist ability to evoke a sense of place and his mastery in imagining alternate technologies. Quite different are *Anita* (1970), a rollicking series about a teenage witch, and *Kaeti and Company* (1986), about a young girl who goes through a series of incarnations. A major uncollected work is the 1986 novella "Tremarest," which is a sequel to *Kiteworld*.

OTHER WORKS: *The Inner Wheel* (1970); *Molly Zero* (1980); *Grainne* (1987).

D.S.

ROBESON, KENNETH.

House name used by the editors of *Doc Savage* and *The Avenger* (a crusader against crime) magazines, both published by Street and Smith, for authors writing stories in each series. The first of the Doc Savage stories appeared in 1933 under the title *Doc Savage: Man of Bronze*. Raised by a group of men who were experts in all phases of human knowledge, Doc Savage became superhuman in both his intellectual and his physical abilities. With the help of five assistants, he uses his powers in a constant battle against the forces of evil. At best little more than action adventure, the series does make use of many science-fiction plots, including lost worlds (*The Land of Terror*, 1933), mutation (*The Monsters*, 1965), and the development of special technologies (*Fortress of Solitude*, 1968; *The Dagger in the Sky*, 1969; *The Motion Menace*, 1971; *The Mental Monster*, 1973; *The Flaming Falcons*, 1986).

Most of the stories were originally published between 1933 and 1949 but were reprinted in the 1960s in paperback. Lester Dent (1904–1959) wrote the vast majority—almost 150 titles have been attributed to him. Other writers who used the Robeson name for the Doc Savage series include William G. Bogart, Norman A. Danberg, Alan Hathaway, and Emile Tepperman. Paul Ernst is the Avenger series' chief writer.

S.H.G.

ROBINETT, STEPHEN [ALLEN] (1941–).

American writer whose early stories appeared under the name Tak Hallus, Arabic for "pen name." Robinett is an accomplished teller of witty stories who was most active in the 1970s. His early association with ANALOG testifies to his interest in the relationship between technology and society, but his obvious humor shows little of the wonder of science normally connected with that magazine. Indeed, some of his best stories (particularly "Helbent 4," 1975, and "The Linguist," 1975) were published in GALAXY.

Robinett's first novel, *Stargate* (1976), mixes the technology of matter transmission with a murder mystery. The novel is noteworthy for the character of the detective, who cigar-smokes his way through the investigation, and for the 180-kilometer-wide matter transmitter that is fought over by an array of corporate pirates. This mix of technology and special parody continues in *The Man Responsible* (1978), in which molecular biology, shady politics, and corrupt business practices are smoothly combined in a polished and memorable tale of life in a near future southern California.

OTHER WORK: *Projections* (collection, 1979).

S.H.G.

ROBINSON CRUSOE ON MARS (1964).

Directed by Byron Haskin; screenplay by Ib Melchior and John Higgins; adapted loosely from Robinson Crusoe *by Daniel Defoe; photographed by Winton C. Hoch; music by Van Cleave. With Vic Lundin, Adam West, Paul Mantee. 109 minutes. Color.*

One of the few intelligent science-fiction films to follow in the wake of the big-bug epics of the late 1950s, *Robinson Crusoe on Mars* boasts a convincing Martian setting (actually Death Valley), high production values, adequate acting, and a literate script. Vic Lundin is the astronaut struggling to survive in terrible isolation, haunted by nightmares of his dead coexplorer (Adam West). When an extrasolar Man Friday turns up, the pace accelerates, but the viewer wonders why the alien slaves look exactly like humans. (Because the costuming is cheaper; that's why.) Hardly a major film, but a watchable one.

D.S.

ROBINSON, FRANK M[ALCOLM] (1926–   ).

American writer and editor who is best known for a series of carefully researched near future disaster novels written with Thomas N. SCORTIA and marketed as mainstream writings. Robinson's work as an editor for such men's magazines as *Rogue* (1959–1965) and *Playboy* (1969–1973) is apparent in his almost seamless prose and his preference for stories based on the soft (social and psychological) sciences despite his bachelor's degree in physics.

After a series of successful short stories beginning in 1950, Robinson published his first novel, *The Power* (1956), a highly successful ESP thriller that was made into a popular 1967 cult film starring George Hamilton. After a long hiatus from writing, Robinson followed this up with four novels in collaboration with Scortia.

The first and most commercially successful of these was *The Glass Inferno* (1974), a thriller about a runaway

fire in a modern skyscraper that was one of the two sources for the enormously popular film *The Towering Inferno* (1974). The team's next best-seller was *The Prometheus Crisis* (1975), whose story about an accident in a nuclear power plant seemed almost like a prophecy of the crisis at Three Mile Island four years later. The less commercially successful *The Nightmare Factor* (1978) concerns the consquences of biological warfare. In all their collaborations, Robinson and Scortia applied the extrapolative methodology of the science-fiction writer to stories that are only peripherally SF, and quickly rose to popular success. *Blow Out!* (1987), begun by Scortia but completed after his death by Robinson, was the pair's last collaboration.

Scortia died in 1986, but Robinson had already collaborated with John Levin on *The Great Divide* (1982), a near future political thriller that is marginally more SF than the Scortia collaborations, although it was marketed as a mainstream work (and later sold to Soviet television).

Robinson may be at his best in short stories, however, and in *A Life in the Day of . . . and Other Stories* (1981) readers will find an approach that is the reverse of his Scortia collaborations: SF situations handled with maturity, compassion, sardonicism, and a careful style.

OTHER WORK: *The Gold Crew* (with Thomas N. Scortia, 1980).

M.R.

ROBINSON, KIM STANLEY (1952–   ).

American writer who has won a great deal of attention for his generally upbeat stories; most of his characters enjoy life to the fullest, no matter what their social or physical environment. Robinson's "Venice Drowned" (1981) and "Black Air" (1983) were finalists for major science-fiction awards; "Black Air" won the World Fantasy Award in 1983. A collection of his stories, *The Planet on the Table*, was published in 1986.

The Wild Shore (1984), Robinson's first novel, is a picaresque work that describes the journey of a seventeen-year-old boy through postholocaust California. It garnered several award nominations and has been praised for its images of a devastated land in which the desire for life has not been quenched; it has also been criticized as yet another rehashing of the post–nuclear war story. Nevertheless, critics universally acclaimed Robinson's handling of characterization (particularly of the young hero) and the power of his language to evoke vivid images.

Icehenge (1984) has not attracted as much attention as Robinson's earlier work. In a future in which humans can live several hundred years, the government periodically rewrites history by destroying all information more than fifty years old. This arrangement works well in controlling memory that might overwhelm long-lived minds until a group of explorers arrive on Pluto and discover an obviously human artifact (Icehenge) of which there is no official record. Once again Robinson's power to develop fascinating characters is evident, but his investigation of the complex relationship among history, memory, and reality (with echoes from the works of Philip K. DICK) becomes difficult to follow and at times appears to be unconnected with the plot.

Despite such problems, Robinson's fiction has been drawing a growing number of loyal readers, and he is often described as one of SF's most promising young writers.

OTHER WORK: *The Memory of Whiteness* (1985).

S.H.G.

ROBINSON, SPIDER (1948–). American science-fiction writer and book reviewer now living in British Columbia. From his first appearance as an SF writer in 1973 to the present, Robinson has received significant praise from both writers and readers. He was co-winner of the John W. Campbell Award for best new writer in 1974 and since that early triumph has added two *Locus* Awards (one for criticism and one for fiction), three Hugos, a Nebula, a Skylark Award, a Pat Terry Award, and two government grants to his accomplishments. His first published short story, ''The Guy with the Eyes'' (1973), became part of the Callahan series (collected as *Callahan's Crosstime Saloon*, 1977). This collection is a mixture of comic and serious stories that involve the patrons (humans, aliens, and time travelers) of Callahan's saloon.

Robinson's first novel, *Telempath* (1978), begins as a devastated-Earth story, but the author drew such a compelling portrait of its protagonist, Isham Stone, in his progress from an angry cripple bent on vengeance to a mediator between humans and aliens, that the book is lifted out of genre. Stone learns that humanity, if it is to survive, must take its place in a far larger and more diverse community than that defined by any single species or planet. In the end *Telempath* is the story of how heroes arise from their times. The first four chapters of *Telempath* were previously published separately as the novella ''By Any Other Name'' (1976, co-winner of the Hugo in 1977).

A second novella, ''Stardance'' (with his wife, Jeanne Robinson, 1977), won a Hugo in 1978. This novella, later expanded into a novel (1979), depicts the battle between those who are dedicated to ''better living'' through technology and those who shun modern science and long for a ''postural'' world. Neither side of course can have it all, and, as in *Telempath*, the characters must learn to create a community that sustains *all* its members.

Robinson is also the author of *Mindkiller* (1982), a novel that combines SF and mystery to produce a rather conventional story about mind control in the future.

OTHER WORKS: *Antinomy* (collection, 1980); *Time Travelers Strictly Cash* (collection, 1981); *Melancholy Elephants* (collection, 1984); *Night of Powers* (1985); *Callahan's Secret* (collection, 1986); *Time Pressure* (1987).

S.H.G.

ROBOCOP (1987). Directed by Paul Verhoeven; screenplay by Edward Neumeier and Michael Miner; photographed by Jost Vacano; music by Basil Poledouris. With Peter Weller, Nancy Allen, Ronny Cox, Kurtwood Smith, Daniel O'Herlihy, Miguel Ferrer. 103 minutes. Color.

Acclaimed Dutch director Paul Verhoeven (*Soldier of Orange*, 1979; *The Fourth Man*, 1983) surprisingly chose to make his American film debut with this vivid, violent, comic-book-styled movie. He brought a skill with actors not usually found in such fare; the film has a satiric edge as well, making it one of the rare slam-bang action films that pleased critics and audiences alike.

In Detroit of the near future, corporations run everything, including the police force. Pleasant young cop Murphy (Peter Weller) is blasted away by crooks who, it transpires, are directed by a power-hungry corporate executive (Ronny Cox). Murphy is converted into a gleaming, skilled cyborg, RoboCop, intended as the first of a series of steely law enforcers. But he eventually learns of his origins and tries to avenge Murphy's death. At the end he has reconciled the machine and the man in himself.

RoboCop was deliberately modeled on comic books, with broadly drawn characters, a large dose of humor, straightforward themes, and startlingly gruesome violence. But the approach is always satiric, and the action is so overdone that only a few objected. The RoboCop suit created by Rob Bottin is a marvel of realism and design, the effects are generally top-notch, and all the acting is good. Weller is outstanding as RoboCop, managing at all times (after his transformation) to suggest a man unconsciously struggling to surface within this powerful machine.

B.W.

ROBOTS

The word *robot* first appeared in Karel CAPEK's play *R.U.R.* (1921); it is derived from a Czech word for forced labor, but Capek's artificial men are organic and would usually be called androids in conventional science-fiction jargon. Mechanical humanoids can be found in much earlier fiction, including E. T. A. HOFFMANN's ''The Sandman'' (1816), where they usually played a sinister role. Some early pulp SF similarly cast robots in threatening roles (for instance, ''Automaton'' by Abner J. Gelula, 1931),

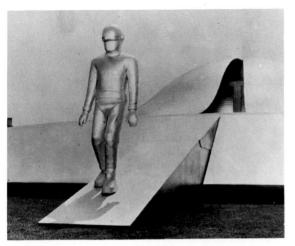

The robot Gort in *The Day the Earth Stood Still* (1951)

but there was soon a dramatic swing toward sympathy for the robot.

Lovable, altruistic, and sadly misunderstood robots were common in the SF of the late 1930s, a trend that crystallized in the famous series of stories by Isaac Asi-mov collected in *I, Robot* (1950), featuring robots whose virtue is assured by the system of programmed ethics known as the "three laws of robotics." These laws pro-vided a fertile source of plot devices, encouraging Asi-mov to continue the series through several further phases of his career—the SF detective stories *The Caves of Steel* (1954) and *The Naked Sun* (1956), more philo-sophically inclined stories such as "That Thou Art Mind-ful of Him" (1974) and "The Bicentennial Man" (1976), and most recently the attempt in the sequels to his Foun-dation and Robot novels to bind his most famous future scenarios into a single future history.

Another author who has written many stories showing robots in a positive light is Clifford D. Simak, first in his City series and later in such poignant stories as "All the Traps of Earth" (1960). Sinister robots made a big come-back, however, in the decade following the end of World War II; Jack Williamson's "With Folded Hands" (1947) examines the tragedy that ensues when robots take too literally their mission to protect humans from harm, and the 1950s produced many stories of perversely danger-ous robots. Although a robot's logicality could be a con-duit of divine revelation, as in "The Quest for St. Aquin" (1951) by Anthony Boucher, it was just as likely to cause trouble. Stories such as Walter Miller, Jr.'s "The Darfs-tellar" (1955) and Brian W. Aldiss's "Who Can Replace a Man?" (1958) suggest that robotic rationality is a poor substitute for human feeling.

By the 1960s, though, the question of whether human beings are really entitled to this assumption of spiritual superiority was being debated more carefully. It is ex-plored most fully and elaborately in the work of Philip K. Dick, whose early stories of sinister robots, such as "Second Variety" (1953), eventually gave way to intense stories in which moral sensibility is discovered in some mechanical constructs (who thus become "human") and a lack is revealed in some human beings (who thus be-come "androids"). Dick's most important works in this vein are *Do Androids Dream of Electric Sheep?* (1968), "The Electric Ant" (1969), and *We Can Build You* (1972).

Other writers were also prepared to credit robots with a human quest for meaning in life and sometimes al-lowed them a solution in religious faith; examples in-clude Barrington J. Bayley's *The Soul of the Robot* (1974) and Simak's *A Choice of Gods* (1972). These novels, like Asimov's robot stories of the 1970s, confront squarely the question of what we can and might mean by the word *human;* the fact that robots usually come out of such stories better than humans reflects our doubts and suspicions about ourselves.

Film robots have been more primitive and usually characterized by single attributes, such as the menace of the title creation in The Colossus of New York (1958), the lovability of Forbidden Planet's (1956) Robbie the Robot, the indestructibility of Gort in The Day the Earth Stood Still (1951), the loyalty of R2-D2 and the fuss-budgetry of C-3PO of the Star Wars series (1977–   ). The androids of Blade Runner (1982), however, are more central to the film's theme and display the complexity and reversals of those in the novel from which that film was adapted, Dick's *Do Androids Dream of Electric Sheep?* (1968).

B.S.

ROCKETSHIP X-M (1950).

Directed by Kurt Neumann; screenplay by Kurt Neumann; photo-graphed by Karl Struss; music by Ferde Grofé. With Lloyd Bridges, Osa Massen, John Emery, Noah Beery, Jr., Hugh O'Brian, Morris Ankrum. 78 minutes. Black and white (Martian scenes tinted red).

A modest but efficient science-fiction melodrama, *Rocketship X-M* was rushed into production after George Pal began shooting Destination Moon but released be-fore Pal's film hit the theaters. Without the imprimatur of a real SF writer, it was regarded at the time as some-thing of a spoiler. Today, however, it has found a new, more enthusiastic audience, in part because of its bleak ending, unusual for its time, and in part because it was the first film to speculate on the results of nuclear dis-aster.

An expedition headed for the Moon is sent off course and makes a forced landing on Mars. There they discover a race of primitive, scarred savages and a planet dev-astated years before by nuclear war. The expedition tries to return to Earth but, short of fuel, their ship crashes.

Kurt Neumann's earnestness about SF helped compensate for some of his deficiencies as a writer and director, but the film doesn't come to life until the ship lands on Mars. Thanks to Karl Struss's eerie, dreamlike photography, however, the planet seems genuinely alien and menacing, even today. Jack Rabin provided special effects; new effects were produced in the late 1970s and have been added to some videotapes of the film.

B.W.

ROCKLYNNE, ROSS (Pseudonym of Ross Louis Rocklin) (1913–).

American writer. A versatile and sometimes experimental writer, Rocklynne was one of the regular pulp magazine short fiction writers between 1935 and 1954, but the quality of his writing exemplifies how individual writers could transcend the medium. His stories are thoughtful and well written, often including an ingenious scientific idea, such as his classic "The Men and the Mirror" (1938), about two space-suited men, tied together and sliding across a frictionless extraterrestrial mirror, who must think of a way to escape their predicament. Two of his stories, "Quietus" (1940) and "Jackdaw" (1942), were reprinted in the two major postwar anthologies, *The Best of Science Fiction* and *Adventures in Time and Space* (both 1946). In "Jackdaw" aliens discover one Hitlerlike aviator alive on a destroyed Earth, and a jackdaw's nest full of brightly colored trivia gives the reader the answer to the riddle of human behavior that the aliens cannot decipher.

Rocklynne gave up science fiction for Dianetics until the late 1960s, when his stories met with renewed success. His "Ching Witch!" was published in *Again, Dangerous Visions* (1972). In the early 1940s he wrote several magazine novellas that were never reprinted in book form. His Darkness story series, collected as *The Sun Destroyers* (1973), describes huge alien beings that wander for millions of years from galaxy to galaxy and is remarkable for having no human characters.

OTHER WORK: *The Men and the Mirror* (collection, 1973).

B.D.

RODAN (1956).

Directed by Inoshiro Honda; screenplay by Takeshi Kimura and Takeo Murata, English dialogue by David Duncan; photographed by Isamu Ashida; music by Akira Ifukube. With Kenji Sawara, Yumi Shirakawa, Akihiko Hirata, Akio Kobori, Yasuko Nakata, Monosuke Yamada, Yoshimubi Tojima. 79 minutes. Color.

Director Inoshiro Honda and special effects expert Eiji Tsuburaya tried to repeat the success of their earlier film GODZILLA (1954) with this vividly colored aerial spectacle of a colossal pterodactyl menacing Japan. To add more appeal for the American market, the film begins with a few giant insects, gobbled up by the newly hatched Rodan.

Unlike the more interesting *Godzilla*, this is only a giant monster adventure. As is typical of the later Toho productions, there's less emphasis on the human beings; *Rodan* is a series of increasingly spectacular events rather than a story. An attempt at poignancy occurs at the end: now there are *two* Rodans; one becomes caught in lava and the other perishes trying to rescue the first—but one returns in later films.

B.W.

RODDENBERRY, [EU]GENE [WESLEY] (1921–).

American television writer, producer, and creator of the series STAR TREK. Born in Texas, Roddenberry grew up in Los Angeles; he was a frequent reader of science fiction, but his first sales as a writer were articles on flying and some poetry. A pilot in World War II, he flew for Pan American after the war and was the hero of a crash in the Syrian desert. He became a Los Angeles police officer in the mid-1950s; simultaneously he sold scripts to many television dramas. He quit the force to become head writer for *Have Gun Will Travel* and later created the series *The Lieutenant*. Roddenberry's biggest success, *Star Trek*, was influenced by the film FORBIDDEN PLANET (1956) and informed by his own staunch liberalism.

After that series was canceled, Roddenberry wrote and produced a non-SF theatrical film, *Pretty Maids All in a Row* (1971), but its lack of success brought him back to TV and to SF. He produced and wrote (or co-wrote) several TV movies, each a pilot, although none resulted in a series. These include *Genesis II* (1973), *Planet Earth* (1974), the fantasy-horror *Spectre* (1977), and THE QUESTOR TAPES (1974), the best of the lot.

Roddenberry has been only peripherally involved with the Star Trek theatrical films and TV series "sequel," *Star Trek: The Next Generation*, and he has always been active as a spokesman for the original *Star Trek* series and its spin-offs.

He is much more significant as a producer than as a writer of SF: few number his episodes as the best of *Star Trek*. Although his ideas are earnest and often intelligent, they are also generally overstated and do not bear close examination as science fiction.

B.W.

ROGERS, HUBERT (?–?).

American illustrator, most closely associated with John W. CAMPBELL's *Astounding Science Fiction*, for which he did fifty-nine covers between 1939 and 1952. In the 1940s Rogers and William Timmins dominated the *Astounding* covers; Rogers's use of grays, light and medium blues, pale greens, and tans in an era when garish colors predominated gave the magazine a unique, subdued look. When other artists were painting machinery, Rogers concentrated on human beings, imbuing them with life and personality. Of the *Astounding* artists, he did work that was the most dignified, with realistic, composed figures and a lack of strong chiaroscuro. His covers for E. E. SMITH's Lensman serials are considered classics.

J.G.

ROHMER, SAX (1883–1959). British writer of Irish parentage. Rohmer was christened Arthur Henry Ward (he later discarded the middle name and replaced it with Sarsfield). Many of his thrillers combine science-fiction undertones with the Gothic and fantastic, especially in the thirteen novels featuring Dr. Fu Manchu (the hyphen in *Fu-Manchu* was used for the first three novels only)—the Chinese "Devil Doctor" whose obsession is the complete domination of the world. A typical example is *Shadow of Fu Manchu* (1948), in which the evil doctor strives to obtain the formula of a world-destroying weapon from its inventor. These shockers foreshadow the works of many postwar writers, notably Ian Fleming. Another of Rohmer's scientific mad geniuses intent on world destruction is Anubis in THE DAY THE WORLD ENDED (1930), with the customary death rays, and his minions, resembling vampires in their flying bat costumes.

NOTABLE OTHER WORKS: *The Mystery of Dr. Fu-Manchu* (1913; American title *The Insidious Dr. Fu-Manchu*); *The Devil Doctor* (1916; American title *The Return of Dr. Fu-Manchu*); *The Island of Fu Manchu* (1941); *Emperor Fu Manchu* (1959).

R.D.

ROLLERBALL (1975). *Directed by Norman Jewison; screenplay by William Harrison; adapted from the short story by William Harrison; photographed by Douglas Slocombe; music by Andre Previn. With James Caan, John Houseman, Maud Adams, John Beck, Pamela Hensley, Moses Gunn, Ralph Richardson. 129 minutes. Color.*

In the year 2018 the world is governed by Big Business. To control the masses, à la *1984*, secret rulers have developed a brutal game called Rollerball. Teams of men compete against each other in a "melee," a combination of roller derby, football, hockey, and motorcycle racing. Violence is intentionally emphasized to encourage spectators to release frustrations vicariously, vent antisocial feelings, and live unthinkingly in the comfortable corporate world of mass sameness. When one player develops a following, the corporations perceive a threat to their power and attempt to kill him by loosening the rules of the game. Despite the resulting bloody mayhem, he alone emerges victorious.

Other forms of science fiction—such as John BRUN-

NER's *Stand on Zanzibar* (1968), Damon KNIGHT's *Hell's Pavement* (1955), and Philip POHL and Jesse KORNBLUTH's *The Space Merchants* (1952/1953)—have more fully and engagingly explored the loss of individual identity in future corporate-ruled societies. *Rollerball*, in typically slick Hollywood fashion, panders to the baser instincts rather than encouraging thought; nevertheless, it stands as a scathing comment on American armchair sports entertainments.

D.P.V.

ROTSLER, WILLIAM (1926–). American writer and filmmaker who occasionally uses the pseudonyms William Arrow (a house name for Ballantine Books) and John Ryder Hall. Rotsler is at his best in the creation of future worlds, such as those in his award-winning fan cartoons, which he uses to caricature American society. His novels *Patron of the Arts* (1974), *To the Land of the Electric Angel* (1976), and *Zandra* (1978) all take place on a future Earth that seems to have descended from present-day southern California. With their descriptions of fashionable trends, strange cults, and struggles for power and money, as well as several gladiatorial contests, these works provide fascinating scenes of such a future but, alas, little else.

Rotsler is first and foremost a science-fiction fan, and his fiction reflects a fan's view of the genre. Most of the novels are about SF such as in *The Far Frontier* (1980) and *Shiva Descending* (1980), a collaboration with Gregory Benford, rather than being original works with a serious point to make. Such novels work well for other fans, but many readers, even dedicated readers of SF, may not derive the same pleasure from them.

S.H.G.

ROUSSEAU, VICTOR (Best-known pseudonym of Victor Rousseau Emanuel) (1879–1960). British-born author who later settled in the United States, where he did most of his writing, starting with the legend "The Seal Maiden" (1913). Rousseau is best remembered today for *The Messiah of the Cylinder* (1917; in Britain as *The Apostle of the Cylinder*, 1918), which takes H. G. WELLS's *When the Sleeper Wakes* (1899) a step further in viewing a tyrannical socialist future. In *Draught of Eternity* (1918/1924 under the alias H. M. Egbert) the protagonists experiment with drugs and find themselves in a future ruined New York in an America dominated by the Oriental Yuki. A popular novel in its day was *The Sea Demons* (1916/1924 as H.M. Egbert), in which a race of sea creatures threaten Europe. The discovery of lost races and civilizations was common fare in early pulp science fiction, and Rousseau contributed a number of stories in this vein, among them "The Eye of Balamok" (1920) and *Eric of the Strong*

Cover art by Rowena for Clifford D. Simak's *Project Pope*

Heart (1925 as Egbert). He also wrote a light fantasy in "Fruit of the Lamp" (1918/1925 as *Mrs. Aladdin* by Egbert). Rousseau's early work, unlike his later contributions to the specialized pulps, was comparatively good by pulp standards. He has the honor of having written the cover story for the first issue of *Astounding Stories*, "The Beetle Horde" (1930). His last published work of SF was "Moon Patrol" (1941).

M.A.

ROWENA (Professional name of Rowena Morrill) (1944–).

American illustrator in the "heroic school" of science-fiction and fantasy art (after Frank FRAZETTA and Boris VALLEJO). Rowena's art, while dramatic and highly realistic, sometimes suffers from an emphasis on models (although they are superb). Her colors tend toward the red end of the spectrum. Her muscular human figures are almost too perfect to be real. Her monsters, by contrast, are stiff and unconvincing. She has done most of her work for such book publishers as DAW, Berkley, and Doubleday; some of her more memorable covers have appeared on Theodore STURGEON's *The Dreaming Jewels*, Manley Wade WELLMAN's *Who Fears the Devil?*, Anne McCAFFREY's *Alchemy and Academe*, and H. P. LOVECRAFT's *The Dunwich Horror and Others*. Her work, along with a good description of her technique, is collected in *The Fantastic Art of Rowena Morrill* (1983). She has been nominated for the Hugo Award several times.

J.G.

RUCKER, RUDY (1946–).

American mathematician, philosopher, and writer. Rucker has claimed a family tie to the German philosopher G. W. F. Hegel, and his daring genius and superb mathematical education (he has studied with some of the foremost twentieth-century mathematicians) establish the remark as more than mere puffery. One of the earliest and most daring of the CYBERPUNK writers, Rucker's fiction displays a fondness for computational machinery and hard science extrapolation, and is marked by stylistic energy and an almost madcap sense of expanded consciousness.

Rucker was the first recipient of the Philip K. Dick Memorial Award (for *Software*, 1982), a distinction that underlies his role as a bridge between earlier innovation in the genre and the most recent experimentation. Indeed at times Rucker's writing is so experimental as to defy easy understanding. However, if his genius with both advanced mathematical concepts and comic storytelling continues to mature, he will be one of the most important writers to fuse extrapolation and literature.

OTHER WORKS: *Geometry, Relativity, and the Fourth Dimension* (nonfiction, 1977); *White Light* (1980); *Spacetime Donuts* (1981); *The Sex Sphere* (1983); *The Fifty-seventh Franz Kafka* (1983); *Master of Space and Time* (1984); *The Secret of Life* (1985); *Wetware* (1987).

D.M.H.

RUNAWAY (1984).

Directed by Michael Crichton; screenplay by Michael Crichton; photographed by John A. Alonzo; music by Jerry Goldsmith. With Tom Selleck, Cynthia Rhodes, Gene Simmons, Kirstie Alley, Stan Shaw, Joey Cramer, G. W. Bailey, Chris Mulkey. 100 minutes. Color.

In the near future policeman Tom Selleck heads a squad whose duty is to shut down malfunctioning industrial and household robots. He battles villainous scientist Gene Simmons, who uses acid-injecting robot spiders as weapons.

This film was badly received by critics and the public, and it quickly vanished. However, despite a melodramatic story, the pace is rapid, the special effects are imaginative, and the view of robotics is intelligently extrapolative—the robots are strictly functional, and none are anthropomorphic. The film may eventually—and deservedly—receive more attention for its virtues than it has so far for its defects.

B.W.

RUSS, JOANNA (1937–).

American writer and university professor, a pioneer and radical feminist in the field, whose science fiction is also characterized by literary skills and the use of experimental techniques. Russ was born in New York City, earned a B.S. from

Cornell University and an M.F.A. from the Yale School of Drama, and has taught English at several universities. Besides SF, she writes reviews, criticism, and other fiction.

Russ extended the frontiers of SF by challenging the usual conventions of plot and character, creating strong female characters in a genre believed at the time to be written largely for adolescent males and, in her later work particularly, experimenting with original ways of narrating her feminist novels, as in *The Female Man* (1975).

Russ's first story, "Nor Custom Stale," was published in 1959, but she did not come into her own until the late 1960s, with her stories of Alyx (collected as *Alyx,* 1976, and *The Adventures of Alyx,* 1983). The early stories describe Alyx's existence in ancient Phoenicia, where she was born and learned to survive as an outlaw and adventurer, a prototypical feminist in a male-dominated world of superstition and brutality. The character is more fully developed in *Picnic on Paradise* (1968), in which she has been taken from her own time by a time-traveling organization of the future and leads a mixed group of six people to safety on a war-torn alien planet, coming to love one man and killing another.

And Chaos Died (1970) utilizes a male protagonist to explore the psychological effects of acquiring telepathy and telekinetic abilities from humans who have converted their planet into a pastoral paradise. The novel poetically renders the mental states of persons with supranormal powers while satirizing present trends in contemporary society.

The Female Man is Russ's most structurally innovative work; a polemical feminist novel, it is intended to shock readers out of complacent acceptance of sexual norms of psychology and behavior. It takes the form of a journal written by a contemporary woman who, through interwoven time streams, encounters and interacts with three alternative selves, who are the products of different historical pasts and sexual attitudes. *The Female Man* also reveals more about the fascinating all-female world of Whileaway, which first appeared in the Nebula Award–winning story "When It Changed" (1974).

Russ's interest in first-person female narrators continued in *We Who Are about To* (1977), the journal of the last surviving woman of a space wreck. The stranded passengers' dreams of colonizing end in defeat, murder, and death, a pessimistic contrast to SF's usual hopes for space. Russ's interest in freeing women from rigid cultural roles reappears in *The Two of Them* (1978), again involving Trans-Temporal Agents like Alyx, in this case an older male mentor and his female companion, who insists on rescuing a twelve-year-old girl from a repressive purdah on a distant planet, killing her male mentor and lover in the process. This motif of a woman achieving identity through the murder of a man occurs in several of Russ's novels and short stories.

Her collections of short stories, *The Zanzibar Cat* (1983) and *Extra(ordinary) People* (1984), continue to show iconoclastic inventiveness, historical empathy, and individual style. One example is the Hugo Award–winning story "Souls" (1982), which focuses on the attempt by a telepathic abbess to save a Christian community from invading Norsemen.

OTHER WORKS: *Kittatinny* (a children's fantasy, 1979); *Magic Mommas, Trembling Sisters, Puritans, and Perverts* (essays, 1985).

D.P.-S.

RUSSELL, ERIC FRANK (1905–1978).

British writer who, like many of his generation, aimed his stories at the larger American market by using American scenes and characters and developing a crisp, witty style and became a leading figure in American science fiction.

Raised in Egypt, Russell served in the King's Regiment in the early 1920s and the Royal Air Force from 1941 to 1945. He was a founding member of the British Interplanetary Society, and his acquaintance with SF began with his contacts there. His first story, "The Saga of Pelican West," was published in *Astounding* in 1937, and he won a Hugo Award in 1953 for his story "Allamagoosa," which makes clever fun of bureaucracy but is otherwise unexceptional.

He served as British representative of the Fortean Society, which was dedicated to the unusual theories of Charles FORT, and his interest in those ideas inspired a number of his stories: Fort's speculation that "we are property" led to the writing of Russell's first major work, the 1939/1943 novel *Sinister Barrier,* serialized in *Unknown.* He wrote a series of popular stories about Jay Score, a robot–space pilot who behaves like a human being (collected in *Men, Martians, and Machines,* 1956).

Dreadful Sanctuary, an *Astounding* serial in 1948 (published as a book in 1951) about a secret society that tries to stop space travel, begins with the attention-catching question "How do you know you are sane?" "And Then There Were None," a 1951 short novel about Gandhian passive resistance conquering a military expedition, was selected for the *Science Fiction Hall of Fame* and expanded into *The Great Explosion* (1962). Other noteworthy stories include "Metamorphosite" (1946), about a human who turns out to be an energy being; "Hobbyist" (1947), about an exploring spaceman who literally meets the Creator; and "Dear Devil" (1950), about a stranded alien and the child he befriends.

OTHER WORKS: *Sentinels from Space* (1951); *Three to Conquer* (1956); *Deep Space* (collection, 1956); *Wasp* (1957); *Six Worlds Yonder* (collection, 1958); *The Space Willies* (1958); *Far Stars* (collection, 1961); *Dark Tides* (collection, 1962); *With a Strange Device* (1964; as *The Mind Warpers,* 1965); *Somewhere a Voice* (collection, 1965); *Like Nothing on Earth* (collection, 1975); *The Best of Eric Frank Russell* (collection, 1978).

R.H.W.

S

SABERHAGEN, FRED [THOMAS] (1930–   ).
American writer whose work blends technology with magic and morality. Born in Chicago, Saberhagen is a former electronics technician and editor for the *Encyclopaedia Britannica* who now writes full-time and resides in Albuquerque, New Mexico. Since his first sale to GALAXY in 1961, he has published more than two dozen novels and six collections and has edited three anthologies. His plainly told, solidly rendered stories often borrow plots from history, myth, or literature and show an increasing debt to gaming.

Saberhagen's most popular creation is a series of stories about the berserkers; space-faring killer robots programmed to exterminate all life, they are high-tech symbols of utter Evil, "malignance personified in metal." Since 1963 Saberhagen has used this open-ended series to investigate the nature of consciousness and perception.

He has written three pastiches of Dracula and Frankenstein—*The Dracula Tape* (1975), *The Holmes-Dracula File* (1978), and *The Frankenstein Papers* (1986). Eminently logical in their development, with vivid historical backgrounds, the novels are sympathetically told from the viewpoint of the monsters without stinting on horror.

Saberhagen also writes technophilic "rivets and sorcery" fantasy, in which science and magic are one and the same. Perhaps his best work in this subgenre is the spirited postholocaust epic *Empire of the East* (1968, 1971, 1973/1979). Its sequels, the Swords books, reflect Saberhagen's growing fascination with game scenarios.

NOTABLE OTHER WORKS: *The Water of Thought* (1965); *Berserker* (1967); *Brother Assassin* (1969); *The First Book of Swords* (1983); *The Second Book of Swords* (1983); *The Berserker Throne* (1985); *The Third Book of Swords* (1986).

S.L.M.

Fred Saberhagen

Campbell award for best new writer of SF for 1985. *Contact* features portraits of real scientists working with radio astronomy familiar to Sagan and SF extrapolations that echo the pulp writers Sagan grew up to admire and imitate.

OTHER WORKS: *Planetary Exploration* (1970); *Cosmic Connection* (1973); *The Dragons of Eden* (1977); *Murmurs of Earth* (1978); *Broca's Brain* (1979); *Cosmos* (1980).

D.M.H.

SAGAN, CARL [EDWARD] (1934–   ).
American writer, a prime example of a brilliant childhood fan grown up to be a spokesperson for both the wonder of science and the generic integrity of science fiction. Sagan is the David Duncan professor of astronomy and space sciences at Cornell University. He achieved scientific prominence at an early age, earning his Ph.D. from the University of Chicago in 1960 and becoming a leading expert in astronomy and physics as well as in the emerging science of exobiology. Sagan is best known, however, for his speculative and best-selling nonfiction books on science and most recently for a long-awaited first novel that earned him a nomination for the John W.

ST. CLAIR, MARGARET (1911–   ).
American writer who, though born in Kansas, has lived most of her life in California and who became successful in the male-dominated science fiction of the 1950s without concealing her sex behind a pseudonym or the content of her fiction. At her best in the shorter lengths, particularly in characterizing women and children (often under the pseudonym Idris Seabright), St. Clair nevertheless produced eight novels. These works, less evenly written than her short stories, are usually adventure oriented but often make a moral point. The protagonist of *Agent of the Unknown* (1956) finds purpose in life on a synthetic pleasure planetoid; *The Green Queen* (1956) and *The*

Games of Neith (1960) feature heroines who lead their societies toward change; and *The Dolphins of Altair* (1967) shows a few humans conspiring with intelligent dolphins to save the environment. St. Clair's short stories, mostly written in the 1950s, are collected in *Three Worlds of Futurity* (1964) and *Change the Sky and Other Stories* (1974).

OTHER WORKS: *Sign of the Labrys* (1963); *Message from the Eocene* (1964); *The Shadow People* (1969); *The Dancers of Noyo* (1973); *The Best of Margaret St. Clair* (collection, 1985); *The Power of Time* (collection, 1985); *The Queen of the States* (1986).

H.L.P.

ST. JOHN, JOHN ALLEN (1872–1957). American illustrator. St. John illustrated many books and magazines during the early twentieth century, but his work for Edgar Rice Burroughs's Tarzan and John Carter of Mars books has become so famous that virtually all his other illustration has been forgotten. His artistic ties were with the nineteenth century; his heroes are all noble and muscled and his heroines delicate and innocently Victorian. The visual images he created for Burroughs's characters became archetypal. His energetic pen-and-ink illustrations and dramatic paintings for the McClurg publishing company and Amazing Stories influenced many later artists, particularly Roy G. Krenkel and Frank Frazetta.

J.G.

SAKI (Pseudonym of H. H. Munro) (1870–1916). British author and journalist, noted primarily for his short tales of humor, fantasy, and horror. Saki's primary contribution to science fiction is *When William Came* (1914), a future war novel about a German invasion of England.

N.H.

SARGENT, JOSEPH (1925–). American director of episodic television, telefilms, television miniseries, and theatrical features who won an Emmy Award in 1973 for *The Marcus-Nelson Murders*, pilot film for the *Kojak* series. Sargent made his mark in the genre with the highly regarded science-fiction suspense thriller Colossus: *The Forbin Project* in 1970 and directed pilots for the TV series *The Invaders* (1967) and *The Immortal* (1969). His other works as director include Star Trek ("The Corbomite Maneuver," 1966), *Bob Hope Chrysler Theater: Enigma* ("Time of Flight," 1966), *The Invaders* ("The Experiment," "The Ivy Curtain," "Wall of Crystal," 1967), *The Night That Panicked America* (TV movie, 1975), *Goldengirl* (1979), *Tomorrow's Child* (TV movie, 1982), *Nightmares* (1983), *Space* (TV mini-

series, 1985), and *Jaws: The Revenge* (1987).

K.R.D.

SARGENT, PAMELA (1948–). American science-fiction writer and editor. Born in Ithaca, New York, Sargent majored in philosophy at the State University of New York at Binghamton. Her first story, "Landed Minority," was published in The Magazine of Fantasy and Science Fiction in 1970. Like the stories she sold to other magazines and anthologies, it was marked by qualities of plausibility rooted in realism and an unusual focus on characterization. She gave up her goal of teaching philosophy for a career as a writer.

Her first novel, *Cloned Lives* (1976), dealt with the way clones might really feel and behave in a story about a scientist who raises five clones of himself as his children. In the mid-1970s Sargent also began a career as an anthologist with *Women of Wonder* (1975), the first collection of SF stories by women about women, which did much to publicize and clarify the position of women in the field and the growing subgenre of feminist SF. She followed it with *More Women of Wonder* (1976) and *The New Women of Wonder* (1978).

Starshadows (1977), Sargent's first collection of short fiction, solidified her position as an author whose work, largely placed in the near future, created a strong sense of reality by its use of naturalistic detail and a solid grounding in what we know about science and people. Her novels *The Sudden Star* (1979) and *Watchstar* (1980) displayed her range of theme and setting: The first was a tough, forceful novel showing a new mutant race in the process of replacing humanity, and the second was a far-future quest about a girl from a telepathic society who meets a boy from a people who lack that ability.

The Golden Space (1982) described children, still capable of change and growth, in a static world of immortals; it led to a series of novels for younger readers beginning with *Earthseed* (1983), about teenagers growing up aboard a sentient starship, and was followed by *Eye of the Comet* (1984) and *Homeminds* (1984).

In 1986, with *Venus of Dreams*, Sargent began a saga about the realistic terraforming of Venus, and the society and people who made it possible. It is the first of a projected trilogy. In that same year she published *The Shore of Women*, her most feminist novel; it depicts a post-holocaust world in which women force men to live separate, savage lives, trapped in a matriarchal religion and used only to provide the seed to impregnate those women within the walled cities selected to continue the race.

Sargent's complex themes and skillful use of language mark her as a significant contributor to the field.

OTHER WORKS: *The Alien Upstairs* (1983); *The Best of Pamela Sargent* (1987); *Alien Child* (1988).

J.M.E.

SATURN 3 (1980).

SATURN 3 (1980). *Directed by Stanley Donen; screenplay by Martin Amis; photographed by Billy Williams and Bob Paynter; music by Elmer Bernstein. With Kirk Douglas, Farrah Fawcett, Harvey Keitel, Douglas Lambert, Ed Bishop, Christopher Muncke. 86 minutes. Color.*

A madman (Harvey Keitel) arrives on Titan, convincing the two people tending an experimental hydroponics station there (Kirk Douglas and Farrah Fawcett) that he's an official; he's brought with him a powerful new robot, scheduled to replace one of them. He programs the robot via direct input from his own brain, but he's psychotic and so is the robot; it murders him, then goes after the other two.

This meaningless replay of ALIEN raises more questions than it answers: Why does the madman come to Titan? Why is the base so far from Earth? Why is the robot previously untested? *Saturn 3* is handsome, Fawcett is beautiful, and Douglas and Keitel are effective in a melodramatic fashion, but the story offers little that is new and is predictably developed. Stanley Donen, a good director at other times, seems to have been lost here.

It was films such as *Saturn 3*, made by those who understood only the trappings of science fiction and space opera, that damaged the reputation of SF films during the early 1980s.

B.W.

SCANNERS (1981).

SCANNERS (1981). *Directed by David Cronenberg; screenplay by David Cronenberg; photographed by Mark Irwin; music by Howard Shore. With Jennifer O'Neill, Stephen Lack, Patrick McGoohan, Lawrence Dane, Michael Ironside, Adam Ludwig. 103 minutes. Color.*

The scanners of the title are human beings with incredible telepathic powers, which enable them to connect with and influence the nervous systems of other people. When trained to operate and control their power, they can invade the bodies of others and cause death by internal physical explosion.

Scanners features a complicated plot, in which power-mad manipulators ruthlessly exploit scanners to achieve domination in the corporate world. In typical fashion David CRONENBERG has created a terrifying and stylish movie with a full measure of horror and gore: the film serves up graphic and bloody depictions of exploding bodies as well as a long-range duel between a scanner and a gigantic computer. As with all Cronenberg's films, *Scanners* caters to its audience's fears of the diminution of the individual and the loss of personal control. It portrays science as an essentially amoral attempt to understand, control, and modify the human condition, and in so doing harkens back to early science-fiction visions of the sinister mad scientist.

D.P.V.

SCHMIDT, STANLEY [ALBERT] (1944–).

SCHMIDT, STANLEY [ALBERT] (1944–). American editor, writer, and physicist. In 1978 Schmidt left a faculty position in physics at Heidelberg College in Ohio to succeed Ben Bova as editor of ANALOG, thereby assuming the mantle of John W. CAMPBELL's tradition of hard science fiction, which had shaped his own development as a young fan, student of science, and writer. He has carried on the role of high-visibility editor that he inherited from both his predecessors, working with writers to improve their ideas and their writing of both fiction and factual articles, and taking stands on the social and political issues that he deals with in his editorial columns. He has expressed his intention to continue his Lifeboat Earth series of novels (*The Sins of the Fathers*, 1976, and *Lifeboat Earth*, 1978), in which the advanced alien Kyrra from nearer the galactic center arrive with the news that the galaxy is exploding. But, like that of Campbell himself, Schmidt's production of fiction seems to have been partially sacrificed to editorial leadership. A new novel, *Tweedlioop* (1986), does not belong to the Lifeboat Earth series; instead, developed from a story published five years earlier in *Twilight Zone*, it deals with the love between an alien and a human, and testifies to Schmidt's determination to remain versatile as a writer.

OTHER WORK: *Newton and the Quasi-apple* (1975).

D.M.H.

SCHOENHERR, JOHN (1935–).

SCHOENHERR, JOHN (1935–). American illustrator regarded by his peers as the most painterly of science-fiction artists. Schoenherr, who has been nominated for numerous awards, including the Hugo he received in 1965, is also a respected and award-winning painter of animal subjects. His style is almost impressionistic, his colors tending toward ochres and cool tones (grays, greens, blues). He is best known for his classic cover and interior art for Frank HERBERT's Dune trilogy in ANALOG, and Herbert himself called Schoenherr "the only man who has ever visited Dune." His credits include over four hundred cover illustrations, including many for Ace and Pyramid Books. Schoenherr's painterly style carries over into his black-and-white works, in which he often uses a drybrush technique on rough paper, as well as scratchboard augmented by pen work. Although unofficially retired from the field, he still does an occasional cover painting.

J.G.

SCHOLARSHIP

Contemporary scholarship in science fiction seeks to differentiate SF from and relate it to fiction as a whole. That attempt immediately raises problems. What stories should be considered SF? Some scholars exclude all but a few of the works (those by Jules VERNE, H. G. WELLS) published before the appearance of the specialist magazines in the 1920s as "precursors" to the field, and these they categorize as fantasy. Others exclude stories that ignore established scientific opinion. They would, for example, dismiss the concepts of time travel and faster-than-light spaceflight because neither is regarded as scientifically possible. Nevertheless, both have become established conventions. The debate still echoes in SF writers' concern for and use of hard science as a basis for their fiction.

With the exception of the efforts of such individuals as J. O. Bailey (*Pilgrims through Space and Time,* 1947), Marjorie Hope Nicolson (*Voyages to the Moon,* 1948), and Philip Babcock Gove (*The Imaginary Voyage in Prose Fiction,* 1941), formal academic criticism did not begin a close examination of the field until the late 1950s. Edith Birkhead had written *The Tale of Terror* (1921), and Dorothy Scarborough had included a chapter on H. G. Wells and some of his contemporaries in *The Supernatural in English Fiction* (1917), but these early literary historians looked back to the Gothic and beyond. Others, such as Vernon L. Parrington, Jr., touched on SF only as it dealt with the utopian tradition. If a single book may be said to have brought both public and scholarly attention to SF—although its original impact has not endured—it was Kingsley AMIS's *New Maps of Hell* (1960), based on a series of lectures given at Princeton University that emphasize the dystopian element in the field at midcentury.

Many enthusiasts of the field—the fans—have produced a wide variety of materials, ranging from bibliographies and reviews to biographical sketches and interviews with editors and authors in the so-called fanzines issued by individuals or local groups. Some of these publications have been preserved in such libraries as Texas A & M University, the University of California, Riverside, Ohio State University, and the University of Kansas—to cite only major collections. But much has been lost, particularly items issued between the 1930s and the end of the 1950s, because of the small size of the printings and the inferior physical quality of the usually mimeographed fanzines. Because many early devotees expressed little or no interest in either the literary quality of the fiction itself or the relation of the field to literature as a whole, some scholars argue that the loss of these materials is of little consequence. To do so, however, ignores the continuing interest that sociologists, for example, have in the subculture of fandom; moreover, these early enthusiasts undoubtedly had information that is no longer available.

A number of important fan works, however, have provided basic tools for subsequent scholarship. Among them are Donald B. Day's *Index to the Science Fiction Magazines, 1926–1950* (1952); and Erwin R. Strauss's *Index to the Science Fiction Magazines, 1951–1965* (1966), continued by the New England Science Fiction Association (NESFA) in its *Index to the Science Fiction Magazines, 1965–1970* (1972) and subsequent annual volumes. Equally essential is Donald H. Tuck's *Encyclopedia of Science Fiction and Fantasy,* the first volume issued in 1968. At another level, from *Explorers of the Infinite* (1963) to *A. Merritt: Reflections in the Moon Pool* (1985), Sam MOSKOWITZ has provided a wealth of detail and anecdote available only from someone like himself who has worked with the specialist magazines since the 1930s. Alva Roger's *A Requiem for Astounding* (1964) concentrates on the single most important magazine of the so-called GOLDEN AGE of SF.

Nor should one forget that SF authors themselves voiced concern for the critical standards necessary to enhance the literary quality of science fiction: *In Search of Wonder* (1956) by Damon KNIGHT and both *Issues at Hand* (1964) and *More Issues at Hand* (1970) by James BLISH, writing under the pseudonym William Atheling, Jr., are two examples. Although some of these works may lack the perspective of literature as a whole, they reflect the concerns that practitioners and devotees had about the critical standards and history of the field.

Extensive academic study of SF did not begin until the Modern Language Association (MLA), primarily through the influence of Scott Osborne of Mississippi State University, sponsored the first seminar on science fiction in 1958, chaired by Thomas D. Clareson of The College of Wooster. J. O. Bailey of the University of North Carolina agreed to chair a 1959 meeting, and Clareson founded *Extrapolation* (first issue December 1959) to serve as the seminar's newsletter. For more than a decade the MLA seminar served as the focal point of academic study in the field. In 1968 the MLA held a forum called "Science Fiction: The New Mythology"; participants included H. Bruce Franklin, Darko Suvin, and Isaac ASIMOV. At the regular session that year Samuel R. DELANY presented one of his first critical papers. (He later cautioned academic scholars not to approach the study of SF only on the utopian-dystopian axis.)

By the end of the 1960s the enthusiastic academic response to SF had expanded to regional MLA groups and the Popular Culture Association (PCA), and scholars had expressed a desire for a more comprehensive organization able to provide an interdisciplinary approach. In the University of Wisconsin system, Ivor Rogers sponsored meetings ("The Secondary Universe") in the spring of 1968 (University of Wisconsin, Milwaukee) and 1969 (UW, Green Bay). At Worldcon in St. Louis, in 1969, he and Fred Lerner, a librarian who had been a longtime fan, urged the formation of an organization. In the spring of 1970 near Buffalo, New York, more than a dozen scholars established the Science Fiction Research Association (SFRA); its first meeting was held at Queensborough Community College, Long Island, in October 1970, with Virginia Carew as local chairperson.

This association has stressed not only interdisciplinary but international cooperation among scholars. It has also emphasized the need for scholars and writers, editors, and publishers to work together. Its stated aim has been to encourage the study and teaching of science fiction; another important priority has been to make all relevant materials available to scholars.

Dale Mullen of Indiana State University and Darko Suvin of McGill University founded *Science-Fiction Studies* (SFS) in 1973. In addition to emphasizing Continental SF, this journal has become the voice of an essentially Marxist point of view, although it also provided the center from which Suvin developed his concept of SF as a "literature of cognitive estrangement." Robert Philmus of McGill and Charles Elkins of Florida International University now edit *SFS*.

British scholars organized the Science Fiction Foundation in 1970 under the auspices of North-East London Polytechnic to further the teaching and study of science fiction. In 1972 they began publication of the journal *Foundation*. Its contributors reflect an indebtedness to the British-inspired NEW WAVE of the 1960s. They have provided a European viewpoint that is particularly valuable for British SF.

In 1972 Robin Scott WILSON opened the Clarion Workshop at Clarion State College (PA) as a training ground for would-be SF writers. In 1975 James GUNN held the first of his summer programs at the University of Kansas, aimed at teachers of science fiction as well as promising young writers. Both have prospered and become the most successful of their kind. The University of Kansas has become one of the foremost centers for the study of SF, noted especially for its series of filmed interviews between various writers and the editor John W. CAMPBELL, Jr.

The end of the 1970s saw the start of two other conferences. Because it possesses the J. Lloyd Eaton collection, the University of California, Riverside, has sponsored an annual conference since 1979. Each year a specific theme, ranging from SF and film to a consideration of hard SF, is chosen; selected proceedings are published by Southern Illinois University Press. Since 1979 the conference has given the Eaton Award for scholarship and since 1980 the Milford Award for editing.

Much of the effort of scholars has been directed toward defining science fiction as a genre distinct from fantasy. As though in reaction against this tendency, in 1980 Florida Atlantic University held the first Conference on the Fantastic, under the direction of Robert A. Collins. From it has grown the International Association for the Study of the Fantastic in the Arts (IAFA), with an annual conference now held at the University of Houston. Its journal, *Fantasy Review*, edited by Collins, was combined with the monthly review journal edited by Neil Barron for SFRA; it now serves the academic community as an annual review of both fiction and nonfiction. In addition, World SF, which grew out of the meeting organized in Ireland in 1976 by Harry HARRISON, is an international organization of professionals.

The mushrooming of interest in SF and fantasy, as evidenced by these organizations and journals, has produced an abundance of scholarly studies. Beginning with Clareson's *SF: The Other Side of Realism* (1971), innumerable collections of critical essays primarily by academics have appeared, many coming from specific conferences.

As of this writing, however, no comprehensive history of the field has been published. W. H. G. Armytage of Sheffield University explored the use of the future made by myth and literature in *Yesterday's Tomorrows* (1968). Chad Walsh of Beloit College (*From Utopia to Nightmare*, 1962) and Mark Hillegas (*The Future as Nightmare*, 1967) examined the shift to the dystopian mood; Kenneth Roemer of the University of Texas-Arlington (*The Obsolete Necessity*, 1976) dealt with the surge of utopian writing in the last decades of the nineteenth century. I. F. Clarke, formerly of Strathclyde University (Glasgow), provided a model for scholars with his study of the future war motif, *Voices Prophesying War* (1966); his *The Pattern of Expectation: 1644–2001* (1979) analyzes Western intellectual history.

Darko Suvin's *Victorian Science Fiction in the U.K.* (1983) deals only with early influences. Robert M. Philmus's *Into the Unknown* (1970) stops with H. G. Wells. Although David Ketterer of Concordia University stressed the apocalyptic imagination in American literature in *New Worlds for Old* (1974), fundamentally he reevaluated the utopian-dystopian axis. Thomas D. Clareson's *Some Kind of Paradise* (1985) gives the most comprehensive view of American treatment of the various motifs, tracing them to their nineteenth-century origins, but stops short in the 1920s and 1930s. Robert Scholes and Eric Rabkin's *Science Fiction: History, Science, Vision* (1977) contains keen insights but is far too brief to be considered a comprehensive work.

Perhaps the central problem can be stated this way: literary scholarship has looked most often toward the origins of SF, while scholars from other disciplines and essentially popular historians have emphasized the magazines. In Britain, Mike Ashley has issued four historical anthologies, each devoted to a separate decade in the magazines. Lester DEL REY, in *The World of Science Fiction, 1926–1976* (1980), was as concerned with the SF community, editors and writers, as with the literature itself. Although Brian W. ALDISS named Mary Wollstonecraft SHELLEY's *Frankenstein* (1818) as the fountainhead of SF, he too selected from the magazines in *Billion Year Spree* (1975; revised, as *Trillion Year Spree*, 1986); his survey is highly regarded and does provide a sense of the author's personality as he reacts to his American and British contemporaries. Although James Gunn included an account of early SF in *Alternate Worlds* (1975), one senses that he considers SF a literature of ideas and prefers the work influenced by John W. Campbell. The problem of historical studies can be summed up with one example. Despite its lengthy introduction, Sam Moskowitz's *Under the Moons of Mars* (1970) remains an anthology sampling the fiction from *Argosy* and *All-Story* during the decade of World War I; no one has yet made a comprehensive study of the Munsey magazines, whose popularity prepared the way for the specialist magazines.

Academic SF scholarship has achieved greater success with bibliographies and checklists. Everett F. BLEILER's *The Checklist of Fantastic Literature* (1948) has proved an indispensable tool. Robert Reginald's two-volume *Science Fiction and Fantasy Literature: A Checklist, 1700–1974* (1979) has become the most complete listing of relevant titles, while the value of Neil Barron's *The Anatomy of Wonder* (1976) lies in its annotations, to both fiction and nonfiction. Frank Magill edited the five-volume *Survey of Science Fiction Literature* (1979), valuable for its discussions of individual novels, although most were published since 1950. Thomas D. Clareson's *Science Fiction in America, 1870s–1930s* (1984) annotates more than eight hundred books issued in the United States during the half century before the specialist magazines controlled the field. The most valuable book from the prolific Marshall Tymn is the title he edited with Mike Ashley, *Science Fiction, Fantasy and Weird Fiction Magazines* (1985), whose entries give histories, however brief, of each periodical that has been published in the field.

Although its British origin influences some of the entries in Peter Nicholls's *The Science Fiction Encyclopedia* (1979), it is an excellent sourcebook. The most valuable European contribution to scholarship remains Pierre Versin's *Encylopédie de l'Utopia et de la sf* (1972). In the realm of cinema, Walt Lee's three-volume *Reference Guide to Fantastic Films: Science Fiction, Fantasy, and Horror* (1972) stands as a good basic guide.

Greenwood Press and Southern Illinois University Press have been the most important academic publishers in the field, although Starmont House issues the finest series of studies of single authors. Oxford University Press has apparently abandoned such a series, but James Gunn's *Isaac Asimov*, published by Oxford in 1982, remains the most noteworthy single-author study to date because of its length.

The groundwork pertaining to a recently discovered field has been completed. What are needed are extended studies of individual authors, movements (the so-called Golden Age, the still-controversial New Wave of the 1960s), special topics such as Patricia Warrick undertook in her fine *Cybernetic Imagination in Science Fiction* (1980), and examinations of earlier works. Bleiler, for instance, has given scholars another excellent source in his ten-volume facsimile reprint of *The Frank Reade Library* (1986).

Perhaps the direction for academic scholarship to take

Cover illustration by Schomburg (April 1952)

can be pinpointed by a single question that has recurred throughout the past twenty years: does science fiction (and fantasy and horror fiction as well) need special criteria before it can be properly evaluated, or can it be judged by the same criteria used to evaluate any work of fiction? Clearly, we have not heard the end of that debate.

T.D.C.

SCHOMBURG, ALEX (1905–   ). American science-fiction and comic-book illustrator whose smooth, accurate rendering and coloring of machines earned him the title King of the Airbrush. In 1925 Schomburg began doing pen-and-ink interior illustrations for Hugo GERNS-BACK's *Science and Invention*. His first SF cover appeared on *Startling Stories* in 1939, and his vividly realistic paintings have graced such magazines as *Fantastic, Thrilling Wonder Stories, Satellite*, and *Amazing*. He painted covers and endpapers for the famous Winston juveniles in the 1950s and covers for Ace Books in the 1960s. From 1940 to the early 1950s, he drew hundreds of comic-book covers and helped develop such characters as the Human Torch, Submariner, and Captain America for Timely (later Marvel) Comics. Schomburg retired in the mid-1960s but began working again a decade later with covers for ANALOG and THE MAGAZINE OF FANTASY AND SCIENCE FICTION. His life and work are featured in *CHROMA: The Art of Alex Schomburg* (1987).

                                                                    J.G.

SCIENCE FICTION POETRY ASSOCIATION.

The SFPA was founded in 1978 by Suzette Haden ELGIN as an organization for writers of science-fiction poetry. It helped open the professional SF magazines as markets and obtain active membership in the SCIENCE FICTION WRITERS OF AMERICA with credentials based on sales of poetry. It publishes a newsletter, *Star*Line*, its annual Rhysling anthology (named after Robert A. HEINLEIN's blind poet of the spaceways) serves as a network for often isolated SF poets. As part of the organization's efforts to promote SF poetry, it bestows annual Rhysling awards for the best long and short SF poems.

                                                                    S.E.G.

SCIENCE FICTION RESEARCH ASSOCIA-TION.

Professional organization for the study of science fiction and fantasy, founded in 1970. In addition to teachers at all levels, SFRA enrolls writers, editors, publishers, artists, and fans. At its annual meetings, usually in June, hosted by different individuals and institutions, it presents the Pilgrim Award, named in honor of J. O. Bailey's early book on SF, *Pilgrims through Space and Time* (1947); in fact, Bailey was the first recipient of the award. The organization also offers a newsletter and subscriptions to a number of academic publications in the field.

                                                                    S.E.G.

SCIENCE FICTION THEATRE (1955–1957).

Directed by Leon Benson, Leigh Jason, Jack Arnold, and others; written by Robert M. Fresco and others. With Lisa Gaye, Jean Lockhardt, Skip Homeir, Howard Duff, Percy Hilton, Marilyn Erskine, Truman Bradley. 78 30-minute episodes. Black and white and color.

Despite the popularity of science fiction in movies during the 1950s, it was only rarely seen on television, with the exception of *Science Fiction Theatre*. This half-hour syndicated series was created and produced by Ivan Tors, who had made several theatrical films earlier in the decade. Even more than the films, the series demonstrates Tors's cautious, timid view of SF: most episodes describe only a minor advance over contemporary science, and some are not SF at all.

The show ran for seventy-eight episodes, with many in color. All were hosted by actor Truman Bradley, whose demonstrations of an aspect of science reflected in the episode's story were meant to convince the skeptical that the show did not venture too far beyond the possible.

The majority of episodes deal with scientists, always treated as heroes, discovering a new concept—anti-gravity, artificial petroleum, controlled lightning, and so on. The dramatics are standard for the period. Technology is always treated positively, as a way of improving the everyday lives of human beings. Aliens, almost always benign, sometimes turn up, played by eccentric or odd-looking actors.

But there are memorable episodes. "Dead Storage" features the revival of a baby mammoth; a rare malign alien tries to wipe out the human race in "End of To-morrow"; a couple flees a repressive future society in "Time Is Just a Place" (from a story by Jack FINNEY); a loner scientist creates a new form of life in "Living Lights"; several episodes, such as "Water Maker" and "One Thousand Eyes," are murder mysteries.

The series occasionally featured prominent actors, including Edmund Gwenn, Basil Rathbone, and Vincent PRICE, its performers were usually those who appeared in SF movies of the time, such as Marshall Thompson, Kenneth Tobey, and Arthur Franz. Most stories were original for the series. Although directors and writers were generally undistinguished, major SF film figure Jack ARNOLD did direct four episodes, including "No Food for Thought," which he later remade as TARANTULA (1955).

Because of its content, *Science Fiction Theatre* is still occasionally run on American television, but its generally stilted dramatics and timidity about SF topics limit its interest.

                                                                    B.W.

SCIENCE FICTION WRITERS OF AMER-ICA.

International organization of writers of science fiction and fantasy. Science Fiction Writers of America was founded in 1965 by SF author, critic, and editor Damon KNIGHT, who was its first president, and author Lloyd BIGGLE, Jr., who was its first secretary-treasurer. Its Nebula Award, presented at a banquet that alternates between New York and the West Coast (with a 1986 provision for meeting elsewhere), was created at the end of the first year, and the Nebula Award anthology immediately thereafter.

With a membership approaching 1000 and active membership restricted to those who actually produce a prescribed amount of SF, SFWA has become in many ways a model organization for writers, noted particularly for its activism in grievances concerning publishers and publishing practices, model contracts, organization of effective protests, and its speakers' bureau. It holds annual business meetings at its Nebula Award conferences and at world and regional conventions, but much of its business is conducted by mail and through the members-only *SFWA Forum*. Other SFWA publications are the quarterly *SFWA Bulletin*, which has a general circulation, and the bimonthly *Nebula Report*.

                                                                    J.E.G.

SCIENTISTS AND SCIENCE FICTION

Over the past century of its development, science fiction has acquired depth, specificity, and no small measure of romance from the work of individual scientists and the legends surrounding their personalities. Although many of these scientists worked centuries before SF emerged as a separate genre, recent history has seen a growing interconnection between scientific endeavor and science fiction. Indeed, SF has often anticipated scientific development.

First honors go, of course, to the medieval and Renaissance astronomers. Nicolaus Copernicus (1473–1543) shattered the medieval Ptolemaic cosmology, removing humanity from the center of the celestial spheres and casting us adrift in a fathomless sea of stars but at the same time opening for us an infinite canvas on which to paint our dreams of the future. Galileo Galilei (1564–1642) added detail to the new universal picture; his observations of sunspots, features on the Moon, and moons orbiting Jupiter gave body and specificity to the Copernican theory and helped show in detail that the universe, like the Earth, is a mutable and therefore imperfect—and therefore interesting—place for exploration. Giordano Bruno (1548–1600), by suffering martyrdom for his dream of infinite space, became a model for the scientist silenced by orthodoxy.

An early development that presaged the emergence of the SF genre was the employment by scientific thinkers of fictive methods and media, as in Francis Bacon's *New Atlantis* (1629), Johannes KEPLER's *Somnium* (1634), and Gabriel Daniel's *Voyage to the World of Cartesius* (1692). Over the next two centuries scattered literary uses would be found for the new astronomy and its implications. It would lend depth to the *Histoire comique* (1656) of CYRANO de Bergerac, whose "states and empires on the Moon" include aliens with genuine scientific curiosity and even one who expresses the heretical opinion that the Earth is inhabited. VOLTAIRE's use of outer space and other worlds was wholly satiric, but his *Micromegas* (1753) anticipated the work of H. G. Wells by 150 years in bringing to the Earth alien visitors and making scientific pretensions a target of satire. Jonathan SWIFT would take this theme further in his visit to the Laputans in *Gulliver's Travels* (1726), with its attack on the royal societies.

After the social and scientific speculations of the Enlightenment philosophes and the arrival in force of the Industrial Revolution, fiction began to reflect wider scientific perspectives and to mirror the work of particular scientists other than astronomers and explorers. In 1798 the economist and demographer Thomas Robert Malthus (1766–1834) published anonymously his *Essay on Population*, which raised the specter of unchecked population growth. His ideas figure heavily in Jean de Grainville's *Le Dernier Homme* (1805), which depicts the depleting of resources, a common theme in end-of-the-world fiction ever since. Malthus himself would be remembered by the denizens of Aldous HUXLEY's *Brave New World* (1932), who practice faithfully their "Malthusian drill" (birth control), and de Grainville's vision would be developed by Mary Wollstonecraft SHELLEY in *The Last Man* (1826). Shelley's *Frankenstein* (1818), meanwhile, incorporated the electrical researches of Luigi Galvani (1737–1798) and Alessandro Volta (1745–1827).

The *Voyages extraordinaires* of Jules VERNE, published in the 1860s and 1870s, make such detailed and enthusiastic use of the new sciences that they would in turn become an inspiration to scientists and inventors, among them the Russian rocket scientist Konstantin Tsiolkovsky, speleologist Norman Casteret, Guglielmo Marconi, and Lucius Beebe. It was a Verne novel that inspired Igor Sikorsky to develop a helicopter, and Admiral Richard Byrd declared that Verne launched him on a flight to the South Pole. Submarine developer Simon Lake began his autobiography with the sentence "Jules Verne was the director-general of my life."

Verne showed that science and fiction could be fused in a synergy of discovery that would benefit both writers and scientists. The stage was now set for that infusion from science of the single most crucial component of the new literature, the idea of permanent, irreversible *change* in human circumstances, even in humanity itself. The proponents of that idea would be led in geology by Charles Lyell (1797–1875) and in biology by Charles Darwin (1809–1882) and Alfred Russel Wallace (1823–1913). Among students of the new thought was one Thomas Henry Huxley (1825–1895), known as Darwin's bulldog for his fierce and unswerving defense of Darwin's principles.

When the young writer H. G. WELLS completed a course with Huxley, the future of SF was set on its present course. Wells became an ardent Darwinist whose work shows a sustained attempt to demonstrate how humanity itself, physiologically and mentally, would be altered in the millennia to come. In *The Time Machine* (1895) he envisioned humanity split by class division into two distinct species, one the staple food of the other. In *The Island of Dr. Moreau* (1896), he focused on the persistence of the bestial in the human. *The Invisible Man* (1897) displays the destructive passions still latent in humanity, and *The War of the Worlds* (1898) lampoons the stupidity of colonizers failing to comprehend their own colonization. It was Wells who gave SF its uncomfortably sharp edge, who forged it into a scalpel to cut away at complacency and static thought; after him neither science nor fiction would ever be the same. More and more, scientists would look at SF to imagine the consequences of scientific developments, and SF writers would increasingly find it necessary to study science in depth as the bedrock for intelligent speculation.

The depth and complexity of this interchange can be illustrated by the life and work of Leo Szilard, a chief creator of the atomic bomb. Early in this century, H. G. Wells had read a book by an associate of physicist Ernest Rutherford: Frederick Soddy's *Interpretation of Radium* (1909) became the premise for Wells's *The World Set Free* (1914). Years later Wells's novel inspired Szilard to start thinking about chain reactions and atomic bombs. Szilard had read visionary as well as scientific books and had worked to get Wells's novel translated into his native Hungarian. Like Wells, Szilard was a utopian who thought society would be served best by a collaboration of its brightest minds; Wells called for an "Open Conspiracy" along these lines, and Szilard talked of a *Bund* (the idea of a world set right in this way is reflected in dozens of SF works, including J. T. McIntosh's *World Out of Mind*, 1953). While waiting at a London traffic light in 1933, Szilard had an inspiration about neutron emission that became the key to unlocking atomic power. (The idea of such a scientific epiphany is central to Ursula K. Le Guin's celebrated novel *The Dispossessed*, 1974, in which scientific discovery is the solution to political strife.) Szilard, it should be realized, wanted to see atomic energy used not to make weapons but to escape from the Earth's gravity and eventually from the Solar System. (Scientists and SF writers alike have repeatedly seen the need for humanity to have a common purpose to save it from its series of wars.)

The influence on SF of individual scientists and their work has become increasingly commonplace since the beginning of the twentieth century. One of the most famous examples of this influence concerns the "canals" of Mars. The Italian astronomer Giovanni Schiaparelli (1835–1910) had spotted *canali* (channels) on the surface of Mars; Percival Lowell (1855–1916) repeated Schiaparelli's observations and conceived that these surprisingly regular lines were evidence of Martian civilization. He produced an elaborate inferential structure to account for them and published his scenario in *Mars and Its Canals* (1906). So powerful was the concept of a dying Martian civilization drawing moisture from its polar caps in giant canals that it set the tone for descriptions of Mars in SF for decades to come, prototypically in Edgar Rice Burroughs's Martian novels. Even after the theory had long been abandoned, Ray Bradbury used the canals of Mars—largely for their nostalgic value—in *The Martian Chronicles* (1950).

The robot is another enduring collaboration of science fiction and science. Various tales of automata had over more than a century implanted in readers' minds the notion of a mechanical man when in 1921 Karel Capek's play *R.U.R.* gave the word *robot* (worker) currency. *R.U.R.* began a quest that has been carried on ever since. In 1948, for example, Norbert Wiener suggested that the new science of cybernetics might be viewed as the totality of skills needed to make an artificial person. When cybernetics was merged with prosthetics, a new and extensive subgenre was born; notable examples include

Bernard Wolfe's *Limbo* (1952), Martin Caidin's *Cyborg*, (1972, source for the television series *The Six-Million-Dollar Man*), and Frederik Pohl's *Man Plus* (1976).

By far the most complex and enduring interaction between scientists and SF writers has been in the area of rocketry and space travel. The scientific writings of Willy Ley (1906–1969), a German-born scientist and author who emigrated to the United States in 1935, are a case in point. (Although he came to America to work for the conquest of space, others, including Ley's friend Wernher von Braun, stayed behind and eventually became part of the effort to develop the V-2 rocket, the first true spacecraft.) Ley's books *Journey into Space* (1926) and *The Possibility of Interplanetary Travel* (1928) inspired Fritz Lang's film WOMAN IN THE MOON (1928), which some credit with the invention of the prelaunch countdown, and Lang used Ley as a scientific adviser. The first real space travel movie, it scared the British Foreign Office, and its realism led the Gestapo to destroy the film's model rockets while V-2 research was in progress. Ley went on to write science fact specifically for readers of SF, contributing to both *Astounding* and *Amazing*. His best-known work is *The Conquest of Space* (1949).

Ley was well known among SF writers; he made guest appearances at Robert A. Heinlein's Mañana Literary Society and H. L. Gold's Friday poker sessions, and he wrote a science column for GALAXY. But he was only one of dozens in the sciences of rocket propulsion and nuclear energy whose work and personal force inspired science fiction. Pierre Curie (1859–1906) and Marie Curie (1867–1934), who discovered radium; Niels Bohr (1885–1962), who developed the nuclear theory of atomic structure; Robert Goddard (1882–1945), who brought rocket research to American soil; Freeman Dyson, who conceived of a starship propelled by atomic fusion; Robert Bussard, who dreamed of a "ramscoop" starship, which would gather its fuel as it flew and accelerated; Gerard K. O'Neill, who designed outer-space habitats for humanity—all produced work that would be eagerly seized upon, first by a generation of pulp writers and then by writers of the GOLDEN AGE.

And while all this was going on, the universe was yielding up more of its secrets to a new generation of astronomers. In the 1920s Edwin P. Hubble (1889–1953) claimed that the celestial objects previously called nebulas are in many cases galaxies like our own and further that they are part of an expanding universe. Harlow Shapley (1885–1972) added even greater depth to this picture with his research into globular clusters, Cepheid variables, and eclipsing binaries. Such work gave SF writers the concept of an infinite system of worlds beckoning to humankind, a new manifest destiny that would become the very definition of the objective sought by Szilard and Wells. It was, veteran SF writer Jack Williamson wrote at the time, as if science were carrying

The engine-room of Verne's *Nautilus,* inspiration for submarine developer Simon Lake

humanity forward "with scientifiction as the searchlight."

Nor was the exploration of scientifiction limited to outer space—every corner of the Earth and its children illuminated by scientific inquiry was explored first in the imagination of SF writers. Paul Broca (1824–1880), a physical anthropologist, provided the first proof that separate areas of the brain are given over to specific functions. Wilder Penfield (*Brain,* 1963) showed the brain to be an organ with special sectors and identifiable areas of function. This work directly informs many major SF novels and stories, including Ursula K. Le Guin's "Winter's King" (1969, in its discussion of "brainwashing"), Michael Crichton's *Terminal Man* (1972, which deals with a treatment for psychomotor epilepsy), and Robin Cook's *Brain* (1981, about a brain-computer attachment). Most recently William Gibson's *Neuromancer* (1984) and *Count Zero* (1986) feature the merging of brain and computer and illusionary travel through "cyberspace."

Such fictions are rendered more plausible by the research of neuropsychologists Hughlings Jackson (1835–1911) and A.R. Luria (1902–1977), which shows some of the bizarre possibilities for human behavior latent in right-brain disorders; and the revelations of this research

have been given currency among writers of SF by popularizations such as those of Jonathan Miller (*The Listener,* 1970) and Oliver Sacks (*The Man Who Mistook His Wife for a Hat,* 1985). A great deal of SF starts from the premise of a brain detached from its usual physical extensions and given new ones. Such works include Curt Siodmak's *Donovan's Brain* (1943), Anne McCaffrey's *The Ship Who Sang* (1969), William Hjortsberg's *Gray Matters* (1971), James Tiptree, Jr.'s "The Girl Who Was Plugged In" (1973), and Tanith Lee's *Electric Forest* (1979). Recently, Orson Scott Card (*Wyrms,* 1987) has interpolated the notion of the preserved brain into the novel of quest and planetary exploration.

Science-fiction writers have long been fascinated with the nature of intelligence and socialization, so it is hardly surprising that many works in the genre examine the similarities and differences between human and insect life. Here too the work of individual scientists—most notably the entomologist Karl von Frisch (1886–1982)—informed and inspired the literature. Beginning in 1915 von Frisch devoted his long life to exploring and explaining the "language" of honeybees, and his research and that of other entomologists have influenced a literature that has produced such landmark works as H. G. Wells's *The First Man in the Moon* (1901), in which the Selenites have evolved an insectlike society, and Frank Herbert's *Hellstrom's Hive* (1973), an exploration of hive psychology in human beings that takes its tunnel society from Wells and its title from *The Hellstrom Chronicle* (1971), a documentary film that depicts with Gothic glee the "thoroughly departmental" nature of insect life. Recently in "Blood Child" (1984) Octavia Butler went a step further, exploring the possible procreative interaction of human and insect. Other works in this line of development include *Serpent's Reach* by C. J. Cherryh (1980) and *Half Past Human* by T. J. Bass (1971).

Science-fiction writers have also explored the world of the very small, aided by the development of the microscope by Antonie van Leeuwenhoek (1632–1723) and continuing modern improvements in microscopy, electron microscopy, and microsurgery. While basing many of the details of their work on scientific fact, SF writers have often used a leap of fantasy to enter the realms of the small. In *The Shrinking Man* (1956) Richard Matheson tried to capture the perspective of a human as he became smaller; Isaac Asimov developed the premise of a shrunken research team moving through the bloodstream of a blood clot victim in his novelization of the film *Fantastic Voyage* (1966). Recently, William S. Davis adapted Asimov's theme to computer science when he depicted a microscopic team moving through a computer in *The NECEN Voyage: A Fantastic Journey into the Heart of a Computer* (1985).

Perhaps the most influential scientific discovery in the realm of the small, however, occurred shortly after midcentury. While the theoretical physicist Erwin Schrödinger (1887–1961) paved the way in *What Is Life?* (1944), wherein he identified genes as the key components of life, it was the ferment of research in the early 1950s that led to the discovery of DNA by Francis Crick (1916–   ) and James Watson (1928–   ). The work for which they received the Nobel Prize in 1962 is recounted in *The Double Helix* (1968). Since then transformation of the living form through genetic engineering has exploded on the world scene and in the pages of SF, where it has created a whole new subgenre. In *No Blade of Grass* (1957), John CHRISTOPHER treated the theme of ecological disaster occurring naturally, but in *Mutant 59: The Plastic Eaters* (1971), Kit Pedler was among the first to consider the results of an organism escaping from the laboratory. Frank Herbert gave that theme a twist in *The White Plague* (1982) by having his biologist-hero engineer the wholesale death of the female sex, and James Tiptree, Jr., wrote of aliens turning the new biology on humanity in "The Screw-fly Solution" (1977). In 1984 Greg BEAR won both Hugo and Nebula awards for the story "Blood Music" (novel, 1985), which posits a total metamorphosis of all organic life following the discovery of the "biochip."

Apart from the impact of particular scientists, SF has been influenced by the image of the scientist in general, either the Faustian necromancer challenging God for forbidden knowledge or the scientist as questing discoverer, always useful to add drama to the moment—Archimedes in his bath shouting "Eureka!", Sir Isaac Newton inspired by a falling apple to reconsider his thoughts on gravity, and in a less legendary vein, Albert Einstein dreaming of riding on a light beam and viewing light as stationary. The mass-production techniques of Henry Ford became a permanent feature of SF when the citizens of Aldous Huxley's *Brave New World* (1932) revered Ford as a god and even chanted his name as part of their Dionysian revels. One reality of the scientist has not received much play in SF; the scientist as drudge, laboring over hundreds of specimens for equivocal results is, for obvious reasons, of less use to a romantic literary genre than the tempestuous discoverer struck by epistemological lightning.

In addition, since the use of nuclear weapons on Japanese cities, many SF writers have adopted a critical stance toward scientists, their methods, and their alleged lack of humanity and/or willingness to assume responsibility. Among them are Avram DAVIDSON in his story "Now Let Us Sleep" (1952), in which scientists use humanoid aliens for scientific experimentation, and James Tiptree, Jr., in "The Psychologist Who Wouldn't Do Awful Things to Rats" (1976). Inhumane scientists are a feature of many SF dystopias, such as that of George LUCAS's 1970 film THX-1138 (novelization by Ben BOVA).

In general, the image of the scientist has split into the Einsteinian figure—a demigod wise beyond measure whose compassion keeps pace with his or her wisdom—and the technocratic monster, blank eyed and wearing a lab coat, uninterested in his or her subjects' pain.

One major area of scientific influence concerns not the future but the distant past. Paleoanthropology gave Edgar Rice BURROUGHS material for his Pellucidar series, which locates a prehistoric world at the center of the Earth. The work of such pioneers as Robert Broom, Raymond Dart, and Louis and Mary Leakey has given new appreciation of the Neanderthal and new life to prehistoric SF. William GOLDING, in *The Inheritors* (1955), tried to capture the different spirits of Neanderthal and Cro-Magnon, and Jean M. AUEL (*Clan of the Cave Bear,* 1980, and its sequels) worked over the same territory to different purpose. More recent work, such as that of Richard Leakey and Donald Johanson on very early hominid fossils, is reflected in Michael BISHOP's *No Enemy But Time* (1982), which sends a modern man to live with habilines, and his *Ancient of Days* (1985), which brings a habiline forward to live with modern humankind. The celebrated opening scene of *2001: A SPACE ODYSSEY* (1968) takes up an idea common in SF—that humanity's upward march is the result of an intervention from the future in prehistoric times.

Research into our species' prehistory also adds depth to postcivilization SF, in which pictures of rebuilding, such as Walter M. MILLER, Jr.'s *A Canticle for Leibowitz* (1960), draw from research into the *initial* building. Research into present-day primitive societies, such as the work of Ashley Montagu, Margaret Mead, and others, supports fiction like Ursula K. LE GUIN's *The Word for World Is Forest* (1972), which embues alien societies with features of aboriginal Earth peoples.

Scientists have often had fruitful dialogue and interchange with writers of fiction. After Fred HOYLE, the astronomer, wrote *The Black Cloud* (1957), its basic premise of a sentient swarm was developed in an off-planet situation by Stanislaw LEM (*The Invincible*, 1973) and picked up once again by Lem in *The Upside-down Evolution* (1986) and in *Star Trek: The Motion Picture* (1979).

On the interface between science and fiction live the natural philosophers, the speculative thinkers, and those whose global vision causes them to be labeled crackpots and pseudoscientists. On the upper end of the scale (in terms of scientific respectability) are naturalists such as Konrad Lorenz, Lewis Thomas, and Loren Eiseley, whose popular writings express so powerfully the beauty they find in scientific research that they influence the whole enterprise of modern investigation and speculation. And there are more visionary influences, such as architect Paolo Soleri (*Arcology: The City in the Image of Man,* 1969), whose dream of a total self-sufficient environment is a common thread in much SF, such as Jerry Pournelle and Larry Niven's *Oath of Fealty* (1981); Julian Jaynes, whose provocative though unprovable psychogenetic theory *The Origin of Consciousness in the Break-down of the Bicameral Mind* (1976) does not deserve to be labeled pseudoscience; and Erich Von Daniken. (*Chariots of the Gods,* 1970, and its sequels), whose contention that the Earth has been the beneficiary of alien visitors is a mainstay of speculative fiction, although controversy and even charges of fraud enshroud his efforts. Pierre Teilhard du Chardin (1881–1955) invented the concept of the Omega Point, toward which humankind is tending, and conceived of the Earth as a giant organism; Marshall McLuhan (1911–1980) gave us a wealth of new, inventive language to describe our culture, particularly in its linguistic and communicative functions. Such work is vital, especially for writers who find inspiration for a story in a new word or phrase.

Even the so-called crackpots have an important place in the story of SF. Charles FORT (1874–1932) was one who resolutely refused to accept the received view of our cosmos (a category which, we should remember, also includes Copernicus and Einstein), and his ideas have given SF writers concepts to play with ever since. More recently Immanuel Velikovsky (*Worlds in Collision,* 1950, among others), whose name continues to evoke arguments among defenders of scientific free speech, inspired some charming fictional defenses, such as Donald A. WOLLHEIM's "The Rules of the Game" (1973). Finally, there are hard scientists such as Isaac Asimov who can play fast and loose with science in a spirit of fancy ("Pâté de Foie Gras," 1956), those who, like Carl SAGAN, can find in SF a vehicle to appeal for greater interest in science (*Contact,* 1985), and SF writers whose grounding in science is so strong that, like Arthur C. Clarke, they find themselves briefing U.S. congressional committees on the shape of things to come.

T.P.D.

SCIENTISTS AS AUTHORS

Scientific theorizing has an aesthetic of its own, and fictions—mainly in the guise of "thought experiments"—have a role in scientific thought and discourse; it is not surprising, therefore, to find scientists writing science fiction. Some do it as an exercise in popularization, such as George Gamow in his stories of Mr. Tompkins, others for the delight of playing with ideas in a new way, such as physicist Leo Szilard in his collection *The Voice of the Dolphins and Other Stories* (1961), astronomer Hannes Alfvén in *The Great Computer* (1966, as Olof Johanneson), or neurophysiologist W. Grey Walter in *Further Outlook* (1956).

In an earlier era, when the cultures of science and art were not so divided, it was possible for Erasmus Darwin to be a famous biologist *and* a popular poet, but nowadays things are different, and the reputation of SF has been low enough to discourage many British scientists from admitting an association with it. Thus, neurophysiologist H. J. Campbell no longer talks about the days when he edited *Authentic Science Fiction* and was a prolific author of paperback SF novels, while the relatives of plant physiologist E. C. Large, author of the classic *Sugar in the Air* (1937), refused to provide biographical details for an SF reference book. The most prestigious scientist to have written SF on a prolific scale, astronomer Fred HOYLE, is something of a rebellious outsider in the British scientific community, and the novels of the late C. P. Snow, although centrally about science, are not strongly speculative.

This stigma appears less strong in the United States (and even less in the U.S.S.R., where many leading writers, from Ivan Yefremov to the STRUGATSKY brothers, have been practicing scientists), and it has ameliorated since SF became more respectable. Many SF writers are, of course, scientifically educated and hold jobs as scientists, ranging from the industrial biochemist E. E. "Doc" SMITH to the astrophysicist Gregory BENFORD. Works by science writers such as Arthur C. CLARKE and Isaac ASIMOV are rated highly in the scientific community, and their SF is generally commended by scientists for its technical scrupulousness. Magazines such as ANALOG have always taken great pride in the scientific literacy of their writers and readers.

The closest association of SF and science, however, has been in rocketry and space exploration; many workers in this field admit inspiration from SF, and those who have written it range from early pioneer Konstantin Tsiolkovsky (*Outside the Earth,* 1920) through Willy LEY (as Robert Willey) to such modern space scientists as G. Harry Stine (Lee Correy), David BRIN, and Gregory Benford, whose award-winning *Timescape* (1980) was praised for its portrayal of real scientists doing real science.

Science-fiction stories by first-rank scientists are fairly rare, although examples such as Julian Huxley's "The Tissue-Culture King" (1927) and Norbert Wiener's "The Miracle of the Broom Closet" (1952, as W. Norbert) have considerable curiosity value because of their sources. The expectation that natural scientists tend to produce fictions lacking in human warmth is frequently borne out, but there are honorable exceptions, including the deft fantasies of the astronomer R. S. Richardson, who writes SF as Philip Latham. Social scientists, of course, are better placed to draw on the social scientific method of *verstehen*—the concept of using empathy to understand character—as an aid to characterization, as evidenced by the SF of anthropologist Chad OLIVER and linguist Suzette Haden ELGIN. Anthologies of SF by scientists are *The Expert Dreamers* (1962), edited by Frederik POHL, and *Great Science Fiction Stories by the World's Great Scientists* (1985), edited by Isaac Asimov, Martin H. Greenberg, and Charles G. Waugh.

B.S.

SCORTIA, THOMAS N[ICHOLAS] (1926–1986).

American writer who made extensive use of his experiences as a research chemist in private industry in his science fiction. Scortia's first novel, *What Mad Oracle?: A Novel of the World as It Is* (1961), depicts the politics of the aerospace industry and describes the impact on humans of its questionable business practices. The same experiences form the background for his next two novels, *Artery of Fire* (1972) and *Earthwreck!* (1974; later retitled *Endangered Species*).

All Scortia's later novels were collaborations with Frank M. ROBINSON; aimed at more general audiences than his earlier novels, they have achieved greater commercial success. *The Glass Inferno* (1974) is an above-average disaster novel that was filmed, in combination with Richard Martin Stern's *The Tower* (1973), as *The Towering Inferno* (1974). *The Prometheus Crisis* (1975), another disaster story, is a detailed, credible account of the failure of a nuclear reactor.

Scortia, however, was at his best when writing short fiction. His stories deal with a remarkable range of SF material, which he usually managed well. Many of his finest stories can be found in two collections: *Caution! Inflammable!* (1975) and *The Best of Thomas N. Scortia* (1981).

OTHER WORKS: *The Nightmare Factor* (with Frank M. Robinson, 1978); *The Gold Crew* (with Robinson, 1980); *Blow Out!* (with Robinson, 1987).

S.H.G.

SECONDS (1966).

Directed by John Frankenheimer; screenplay by Lewis John Carlino; adapted from the novel by David Ely; photographed by James Wong Howe; music by Jerry Goldsmith. With Rock Hudson, Salome Jens, John Randolph, Will Geer, Jeff Corey, Richard Anderson, Murray Hamilton, Karl Swenson, Khigh Dhiegh, Frances Reid, Wesley Addy. 106 minutes. Black and white.

This moody, intelligent film is both low-key and intense, a dark satire on the cult of youth and corporate greed. Deliberately paced, it builds to a horrifying climax, as the audience shares the last thoughts of a dying man.

A prosperous middle-aged man (John Randolph), bored with his wife and job, is approached by a secret corporation, who offer, for a fee, to fake his death and change him surgically to a younger man (Rock Hudson) with a new identity. But his dissatisfaction remains, especially when he finds that all his new friends are "seconds" like himself. He complains to the company, and at the end is wheeled into an operating room to be killed, becoming the faked corpse of a new "second."

The film is haunting; its harsh, naturalistic photography occasionally gives way to expressionism. It is brutal on its audiences, because it is unrelentingly realistic (except for the movie-star presence of Hudson) and downbeat. *Seconds* is one of the few science-fiction films with a clearly stated moral: you cannot escape yourself.

B.W.

SENARENS, LUIS P[HILIP] (1863–1969).

American author and editor. Often called the Jules VERNE of America for his prophetic imagination, Senarens is noted for his contribution to the Frank Reade series of stories, initiated in 1876 by Harry Enton. Senarens joined Enton on the series in the 1880s, when he was in his teens, writing under the pseudonym Noname. (He used twenty-seven pseudonyms in his lifetime and published over one hundred science-fiction dime novels.) He also wrote the Jack Wright series for *The Boy's Star Library*, but not all the books in that series were SF. In 1904 he became an editor for Tousey Publications.

N.H.

─────────── SERIALS ───────────

Stories told in installments go back to the early days of the oral narrative. Whether for reasons of length or effect, many bards must have told their epics over several evenings and learned to pace them in such a way that their listeners would be eager to return for the next episode. It's entirely possible that Homer himself divided *The Iliad* and *The Odyssey* into effective parts, breaking off the action at its most suspenseful point each evening.

The most significant preliterary example of the art of the serial, however, must be *The Arabian Nights*, with Scheherazade keeping her head by keeping her stories going and King Schahriah in continual suspense at dawn for 1,001 nights. From that example later writers learned to avoid what Brian W. Aldiss has called "the Scheherazade syndrome": if you bore me, you die.

By the time of general literacy and the beginnings of the mass magazines in the mid–nineteenth century, the printed serial was becoming commonplace in the British penny dreadfuls, those early mass periodicals that have been called cheap popular magazines for light reading, in which the work of Charles Dickens first was published. Indeed Dickens edited two of them in the mid-1850s. In the United States the *Saturday Evening Post* was running serials by 1855.

The true mass magazines represented by *The Strand Magazine* in Britain and *Munsey's Magazine* in the United States came along in the 1880s; both frequently published serials. But the real markets for the serial were the magazines for boys and the pulp adventure magazines for their fathers, both of which sometimes ran as many as half a dozen serials simultaneously.

The reason for all this narrative interruptus was clearly

commercial: as in the movie serials of the 1930s and the TV miniseries of the 1980s, involuntarily postponed gratification meant the likelihood of an audience returning for further pleasures and, in the case of magazines, for subscriptions or purchases. This was particularly true of science fiction. The SF magazines inherited the pulp tradition of serials to build and maintain circulation but added other motivations. Some ideas were too big to confine to the short story; some narratives required lots of room to accomplish their changes in character or situation. The digest size in which SF magazines were published over most of their history, and even the older seven-by-ten-inch PULP MAGAZINES, could not easily accommodate a complete novel—not at least without deleting many other stories and features. Then too editors believed—truthfully or not—that potential readers looked at the table of contents and made their purchasing decisions on the basis of the number and variety of stories offered in an issue. Finally, serialization of the work of particularly popular authors guaranteed the cachet of their names over several issues.

Nevertheless, some readers expressed discontent at having their involvement in a novel dissipated over monthlong gaps and saved their reading of the serials until they had all the issues in hand, or in more recent times until publication of the book. Magazines that shunned serials for policy reasons, or because they were bimonthly or quarterly, tried to capitalize on this preference by advertising novels "complete in this issue," even though the "novels" often ran to no more than 45,000–50,000 words, and sometimes substantially less.

Book versions sometimes differed from the serialized novels in minor or even major ways because of editorial meddling or the need for shortening. And until after World War II no works published in the magazines found their way into book form. After that time, however, the magazines were plundered for novels as well as stories.

As a consequence SF writers in the 1930s and early 1940s wrote their novels for the magazines alone, without consideration for book publication. They had to make a decision to write a novel, rather than a series of short stories or novelettes, on the basis of considerations other than long-term gain, or even short-term gain: although the pulp magazines paid by the word, and words were easier to accumulate in novels than in separate short stories, the payment for novels was often at a lower word rate than for short stories. Then as now however, fame generally came quicker and easier to the writer of novels.

The absence of book publication or republication, however, meant that novels envisioned as serials were constructed differently from novels planned originally as books. Serials, like television dramas, had to be set up to break naturally into two, three, four, or more parts, each with a climax at the end of an appropriate section. They had to incorporate, like *The Perils of Pauline*, a series of cliff-hangers. They also had to carry at the end

of each installment the words "To be continued in our next issue." At the beginning of the next installment they had to have a synopsis to bring the reader up to date on what had happened before. Usually the author was asked to write the synopsis, but occasionally the editor would do it, particularly if the editor were more adept than the author at the peculiar art of writing attractive summaries.

Sometimes prospective serials did not break naturally into appropriate segments, and editors rejected otherwise outstanding manuscripts. Frederik POHL told a story about his days as an agent when, in the early 1950s, he sent John W. CAMPBELL, editor of *Astounding*, the manuscript of Hal CLEMENT's classic *Mission of Gravity*. Campbell returned it because it didn't have good breaks for the narrative. Pohl waited a few weeks, divided the manuscript into equal thirds, had the breaks retyped, and returned it with the implication, though not the statement, that Clement had revised it—and Campbell published it as a serial.

Did this format work out? Longtime readers remember famous stories, but they remember even more clearly the times when classic serials appeared. E. E. SMITH's *The Skylark of Valeron* ran in seven episodes in 1934, and, according to Sam MOSKOWITZ, increased *Astounding*'s circulation by 10,000 with the first installment. Other memorable serials include Jack WILLIAMSON's *The Legion of Space* (1934), Smith's *Galactic Patrol* (1937) and *Grey Lensman* (1939), A. E. VAN VOGT's *Slan* (1940) and *The World of Null-A* (1945), Robert A. HEINLEIN's *Methuselah's Children* (1941), Frederik Pohl and Cyril M. KORNBLUTH's *Gravy Planet* (*The Space Merchants*, 1952), Alfred BESTER's *The Demolished Man* (1952), and Frank HERBERT's *Dune* (1963–1964, 1965).

By the time *The Space Merchants* and *The Demolished Man* were published in GALAXY, book publication had become a possibility every author needed to consider. Emphasis in the writing and marketing of novels gradually shifted from the magazine to the book between the 1950s and the early 1970s. Magazine publication came to be looked on as desirable but not the first priority, and novels were written as novels, not as serials. During the 1950s and 1960s this shift eventually produced a situation in which novels written to fulfill book contracts were offered for magazine serialization, as were, for instance, the series of juveniles Heinlein wrote for Scribner's.

Many novels from the 1930s and 1940s are still available in reprints, and their differences in structure may be attributed to the fact that they were written for a different form of publication. Readers might enjoy speculating about where the breaks came in the original magazines, but if they really want to read these works as they were written to be read, they need to pick up the magazines, crumbling pages and all, look at the colorful covers, peruse the blurbs and the synopses, and enjoy the action installment by installment.

Other novels have been put together from stories published separately, such as van Vogt's *The Voyage of the Space Beagle* (1950), whose first part was a novelette, "Black Destroyer," published in 1939. Van Vogt suggested the term *fix-up* to describe this kind of book, and it has been adopted by critics, although they have perhaps applied it more broadly than van Vogt originally intended. The term has derogatory implications and should not be used to describe novels broken into separately publishable parts for artistic or economic reasons, or even those constructed after the fact, such as Theodore STURGEON's *More Than Human* (1953), Walter MILLER, Jr.'s *A Canticle for Leibowitz* (1960), or Robert SILVERBERG's *Nightwings* (1969).

The history of publishing a series of related stories as a book goes back at least as far as Chaucer and Boccaccio, and, in its more contemporary form, to Arthur Conan Doyle and his Sherlock Holmes stories. It has a rich tradition in SF exemplified by Ray BRADBURY's *The Martian Chronicles* (1950), Isaac ASIMOV's *I, Robot* (1950) and his original Foundation series (1951, 1952, 1953), Robert A. Heinlein's *The Man Who Sold the Moon* (1950), Clifford D. SIMAK's *City* (1952), and Robert Silverberg's *The World Inside* (1971).

A.E. van V.

SERIES

Science fiction, runs the truism, is a literature of ideas. In view of the scope of a great many of these ideas—among them world building and travel across space and time—it is hardly surprising that the genre has produced a wealth of ongoing series. In fact, many of SF's major and emerging writers can be identified by the series they have created. For such writers the series, which may run to many volumes throughout the course of their work life, can be an ordeal in terms of both consistency and the demands of the reader. It can also be a supreme test of creative, analytic, and even philosophical ability as expressed in terms of a world (or cosmos) in which characters and plot lines reflect the author's deepest intellectual concerns.

Frank HERBERT's Dune books are a stunning example of planet building—in this case the creation of a desert ecology. They are also an ongoing and astute meditation on the use or abuse of power. Marion Zimmer BRADLEY's Darkover stories reflect both her skill in creating a low-technology, cold-weather planet and her concerns with alternative life-styles. Robert A. HEINLEIN's Future History, like James BLISH's Cities in Flight series, deals with humanity's future and, to paraphrase William Faulkner, the author's belief that humankind will not only endure but prevail.

A similar trend is evident in fantasy, which permits the author even greater license to create worlds and cultures. Inspired by the phenomenal success of J. R. R. Tolkien's The Lord of the Rings, publishers and authors have produced fantasy series after fantasy series. Although these often take the form of trilogies, long series (or multiple trilogies) are not uncommon.

The current trend toward series books has a variety of causes. First, the series novel is the logical outgrowth of the lengthy romance cycles of the Middle Ages, to which both fantasy and SF owe a great deal. Such cycles were usually set in a given kingdom or empire and often focus not just on how a hero comes to power, rules, and falls but also on his ancestors and descendants. That such cycles are found in SF is evidenced by any of the most popular series, which often focus on one or more families: Heinlein's Howard Families, the Graemes of Gordon R. DICKSON's Childe Cycle, or Bradley's Seven Comyn families. The use of such families parallels Aristotle's observations in the *Poetics* that certain dynasties are simply more suited as subject matter for tragedies.

Second, the series novel is the natural evolution of the tendency by the SF PULP MAGAZINES to use series of short stories. Isaac ASIMOV's Robot and Foundation series are outstanding examples of this tendency. In his humorous and candid article "There's Nothing Like a Good Foundation" (*Turning Points*, 1977), Asimov described how his tales of the First and Second Foundation—like his robot stories—were planned as continuing sales to editor John W. CAMPBELL. Pulp editors such as Campbell and Hugo GERNSBACK used series to build reader interest and loyalty by offering pulp fans another Robot or BUCK ROGERS story in much the same way the *Saturday Evening Post* drew readers during the 1950s with yet another Hornblower story.

New York Times Book Review columnist Gerald Jonas and SF editor and scholar David Hartwell have traced the economic underpinnings of the SF series: as we know it now, the series—with big-book promotion, hardcover best-sellers, and national circulation—began as a marketing phenomenon in 1953, the year Asimov's short stories were collected into what has become known as *The Foundation Trilogy*. The stories have proved as popular in book form as they were in the pulps; in 1966 this series defeated the fantastically popular Lord of the Rings for a best all-time series award.

Today's publishers have capitalized on the economic success of a few series by saturating the market. What John Campbell was to the pulp series, Judy-Lynn DEL REY has been to the modern series. Del Rey, who died in February 1986, served as editor of Ballantine Books' SF line (which issued the first authorized U.S. paperback edition of Tolkien's works) before it was renamed Del Rey Books. A superb marketer, del Rey saw outstanding commercial possibilities in the SF series; her extraordinary success may stem from two decisions: to back such series with fine packaging and heavy promotion, and to move from paperback originals to hardcovers. Her will-

The first novel in Andre Norton's Witch World series

ingness to shift from bargain basement to "big book" publishing paid off handsomely for Del Rey Books and authors such as Anne McCaffrey, Arthur C. Clarke, and Robert A. Heinlein, whose books have appeared on both SF and mainstream best-seller lists.

The lure of the bottom line aside, by far the most important reason for a series's existence is its meaning to author and reader alike. By writing a series an author may build and define his or her private universe. Certainly, "world building" has its own appeal apart from narrative: for evidence one need only look to the number of computer-generated programs, produced by scientists turned consultants, to help writers make their private cosmos credible—not to mention the maps, concordances, and other minutiae that provide readers with the details of a culture's geography, ecology, and sociology. Because a successful series can run to many volumes, the writer may create in it elaborately realized worlds or spend an entire book focusing on one region of a planet, one era, or even one character. In addition, many authors have used the series as a forum for scientific, philosophical, artistic, and ideological speculation.

Just as the short story form tests an author's craft, the series tests his or her sustained creativity, originality, and endurance as well as ability to hold an audience. The

litter of remaindered and unsuccessful books indicates that a successful series is not simply a case of "more of the same." The most popular series embody significant formal, historiographical, and ideological distinctions that find their own readership.

Chief among the formal distinctions is whether the series is open ended or closed. Gordon R. Dickson's Childe Cycle is a huge example of a closed series. The author plans to trace the evolution of humanity from the Middle Ages into what he calls "Responsible Man" by means of a progression of novels, outlined for many years now, that commence in the fourteenth century and continue well into the twenty-third. The advantage of closed series is control: while retaining the freedom to create "prequels" (stories set before the actual scope of the series) or "illuminations" (Dickson's term for a novelette or novella illustrating one small aspect of his cultures), the author can work within clearly defined limits. And, if the series grows tedious, it can be concluded.

The open-ended series, by contrast, often develops a life of its own. Many such series have begun with a single extraordinarily popular novel whose readers demanded be expanded upon in sequel after sequel. Bradley's Darkover series is a case in point. Originally deriving from a private mythology, the series (which first saw print in the early 1960s) actually started in medias res—the opposition of the Terran Empire to Darkovan psionic culture—and has worked backward and forward ever since. For example, *Darkover Landfall*, written in 1972, explains how Darkovan culture was born; *Sharra's Exile* (1981) is actually a rewritten version of the 1962 Hugo nominee *Sword of Aldones*, which left its original readers with the sense that Terra had overcome Darkover. Since that time Bradley has concentrated on the various aspects of Darkover that an unusually responsive fan audience has requested.

The chief advantage of the open-ended series to its author is freedom. If the series proves successful, the writer may concentrate on any aspect of the world or narrative that looks interesting—or that readers indicate is interesting to them. As the writer of such a series matures, he or she may add episodes or characters, or may even rewrite earlier work. The chief disadvantage of this type of series is the writer's inability to end it in any way short of a supernova.

Indeed it is entirely possible for an enthusiastic audience to "take over" a series, by writing their own anthologies of stories set in the writer's "universe." Bradley's Darkover, with five such volumes, leads the open-ended series in terms of reader involvement, but similar anthologies have grown up around Andre Norton's Witch World and Robert Adams's Horseclans series.

Whereas the fantasy series is usually an exercise in sustained narrative and mythography, the SF series as often as not focuses on scientific principles, or the extrapolation of such principles in the world the writer has created. The inception of such series can often be reduced to What if? What if you had a planet with an extraordinarily high gravitation? Hal CLEMENT answered that question by creating his multilegged Mesklinites, low to the ground and terrified of falling. What if it were possible to build a sort of ring that encircled a star? Larry NIVEN's Ringworld books take his readers on a tour of just such a place. What if you had a planet so arid that even the moisture from breathing must be recycled? Frank Herbert's answer was Dune.

The open-ended series focuses on the leisurely unfolding of narrative, culture, and character, and the "what if" series focuses on the extrapolation of one hypothesis that shapes the plot line of any and all books in that series, but another type of SF series is inspired by philosophy and the social sciences. If SF is the literature of ideas, these series are at its core. Asimov's Foundation series explores how foresighted individuals may preserve civilization from barbarism. James Blish's Cities in Flight series, heavily influenced by Oswald Spengler's *Decline of the West* (1918–1922), centers on much the same idea as the Foundation books, then switches over to cosmology to show humankind a match even for the heat death of the universe.

Other such series may be based on ideologies that range from the conservative militarism of Jerry POURNELLE's Co-Dominium and Robert Adams's Horseclans to the picaresque and polyglot hedonism of Norman SPINRAD's *The Void Captain's Tale* and *Child of Fortune*. The ideological series provides a never-ending source of controversy for writers and readers who may support or oppose the writer's position with equal ferocity.

In the 1970s and 1980s the series developed a variant form: the "shared world." The first such series, the popular and influential fantasy Thieves' World, edited by Robert ASPRIN (and subsequently coedited with Lynn Abbey), currently includes nine volumes, three novels, and has sold over a million copies. Shared-world series have rapidly evolved into many forms. A series such as Thieves' World is a truly interactive shared world in which writers may use (but not kill off) one another's characters and the contributors collaborate on a more or less unified narrative. Such series can also loop off into separate novels dealing with specific characters or incidents. In a sense this type of anthology may be compared with the open-ended series.

But the shared world may also take the form of the series of ideas. What if all supreme egotists met in Hell and conspired against the Devil? That theological and narrative premise underlies Baen Books' Heroes in Hell, a series written predominantly by Thieves' World veterans. Yet other shared-world series are spin-offs of successful high-tech SF novels such as Fred SABERHAGEN's Berserker stories or C. J. CHERRYH's *Angel with the Sword;* still others are almost exclusively in anthology format,

such as Andre Norton and Robert Adams's four-volume Magic in Ithkar series.

As might be expected, both financial and literary motives underlie the development of shared-world series. They appear to be immensely attractive to readers, especially those who come to SF out of role-playing games, for reasons such as the ease with which shared-world characters may be adapted (copyright permitting) for gaming, the compatibility of short stories with the TV generation's diminished attention span, and the chance to read works by many popular writers in one book. Authors enjoy them both for the ease with which short stories may be spun off a known and collectively created background and the opportunity they provide to work closely with other writers. In addition, SF, as a literature of ideas, encourages collaboration.

But underlying the practical reasons for shared-worlds' success is the fact that such books are logical outgrowths of SF's roots in medieval narrative; shared worlds are modern analogues of the framing stories used by Boccaccio and Chaucer. Both the popularity of the shared world and the tendency by some creators of series to allow other authors to write in their universes can be seen as related to medieval romance, such as the Arthurian, classical, and Carolingian story cycles, which may be regarded as elaborate universes for which the main characters and locations have already been created and the readership already established.

Today, however, the publishing community is gripped by an inevitable reaction generated by abuse of the series format. Although Gerald Jonas speaks with condescension of the SF series as a world (or worlds) of repeatable pleasures, there is some indication that these pleasures have been repeated to the point of satiation. It's one thing to expect a reader of the old *Astounding* (now ANALOG) to wait a month for the next Foundation story or the resolution of a cliff-hanger in the serialization of a novel. But it's quite another matter—and one which some readers and reviewers regard as a betrayal of their trust—to cut off a story at 80,000 words with "To be continued in the next volume" and expect that readers will wait docilely for the plot to resolve itself—a year later. It might be noted, however, that Jules VERNE left his Moon voyagers (and his readers) floating in space for five years before he returned to them in *Round the Moon* (1870), and a similar gap separated *The Mysterious Island* from *Twenty Thousand Leagues under the Sea* (1870).

Many readers have grown cynical about being "hooked" by a novel that is presented as an independent work but is actually the first in a trilogy, complete with inconclusive ending. They also complain about "series bloat," the stretching of what might have been a respectable novel into a trilogy or the expansion of a trilogy into an extended series. In a sense such books diminish the impact of the first, significant one.

Ultimately, however, the series will continue to be a major component of SF. Although series owe much to readers' demand for "more of the same" and publishers' desire to provide it, the series is both a natural outgrowth of SF's inheritance of the romance tradition and the inevitable consequence of a genre that regularly deals with concepts, ideologies, and space-time continua too vast to be contained within the covers of just one book.

S.M.S.

SERLING, ROD[MAN EDWARD] (1924–1975).

American television writer and personality responsible for the significant science-fiction and fantasy television anthology show TWILIGHT ZONE. After serving as a paratrooper during World War II, Serling returned home a vital, ambitious young man. He broke into television early in 1951, quickly becoming one of the most prominent of the "angry young men" of the period. With Tad Mosel, Paddy Chayefsky, and Reginald Rose, he was one of the best-known TV playwrights, largely thanks to his serious and popular teleplays *Patterns* (1955) and *Requiem for a Heavyweight* (1956); both were adapted for theatrical films. By 1959 he had written over one hundred television dramas, some of which, he admitted, he disliked himself.

By the late 1950s, interest in live television was beginning to decline, and Serling, disturbed by the network's and sponsors' increasing interference with the topical dramas he wrote for *Playhouse 90*, proposed a weekly series of fantasy and SF stories in which he would approach similar ideas, but obliquely, in the guise of fantasy. Under producer Buck Houghton, *The Twilight Zone*, hosted by Serling himself, debuted in 1959; it lasted for five years, despite ratings that were never impressive. Like STAR TREK, it was more successful in syndication, where its name became a synonym for the strange.

The series established Serling, in the eyes of the general public, as a guru of the weird and strange; his strong, identifiable voice unexpectedly gave him a new career as a commercial announcer and narrator of documentaries, particularly the popular shows on oceanography and marine biology produced by Jacques-Yves Cousteau. After 1967 a disillusioned Serling largely withdrew from television, preferring to teach at Antioch College in Ohio and Ithaca College in New York. Although he wrote for and hosted the later series *Night Gallery* (1970–1972), he had no creative control and often expressed a dislike for the series. However, one of his best scripts, "They're Tearing Down Tim Riley's Bar," was written for that show.

Serling himself maintained that the best episodes of *Twilight Zone* were written, not by him but by Charles Beaumont, Richard MATHESON, and George Clayton JOHNSON, among others. However, a few of Serling's

Rod Serling

episodes—he wrote over ninety—are among the most memorable, including "Time Enough at Last," "The Monsters Are Due on Maple Street," "Eye of the Beholder," and "On Thursday We Leave for Home." Serling's scripts, fantasy and otherwise, are often portentous and didactic, putting across their message broadly. Others are wistful and nostalgic, with a return to the past a recurrent theme.

Serling also wrote occasionally for films; after *The Twilight Zone* several of his screenplays were SF or borderline SF, including SEVEN DAYS IN MAY (1964), PLANET OF THE APES (1968), and *The Man* (1971). Additionally, he turned many of his *Twilight Zone* and *Night Gallery* scripts into short stories, included in the following collections: *Stories from the Twilight Zone* (1960), *More Stories from the Twilight Zone* (1961), *New Stories from the Twilight Zone* (1962), *From the Twilight Zone* (1962), *Chilling Tales from Rod Serling's Twilight Zone* (1965), *Night Gallery* (1971), and *Night Gallery 2* (1972). He also edited several anthologies, including *Rod Serling's Triple W: Witches, Warlocks, and Werewolves* (1963), *Rod Serling's Devils and Demons* (1967), *The Season to Be Wary* (1967), and *Rod Serling's Other Worlds* (1978).

In television drama of the 1950s, Serling's position is secure; his best scripts are among the finest ever done for TV. In the area of SF and fantasy, however, he is less important for his own work than for recognizing quality in the work of others; in so doing he brought to the genre a new legitimacy on the small screen. Before *Twilight Zone*, with rare exceptions, SF on television was for children; at one stroke Serling changed the genre from kiddie stuff to subject matter for adults; his impact on SF for television, and indirectly movies, cannot be overestimated.

B.W.

SERVICE, ROBERT W[ILLIAM] (1874–1958).
British-born Canadian poet and writer best known for such poems as "The Shooting of Dan Mc-Grew." At least one of Service's novels, however, *The Master of the Microbe* (1926), has all the ingredients of science fiction, including a vengeful scientist and a deadly virus. Although the book's science leaves much to be desired, the plot supplies sufficient action to keep most readers well entertained.

S.H.G.

SERVISS, GARRETT P[UTNAM] (1851–1929).
American journalist and novelist. *The* science reporter of his day, specializing in astronomy (he wrote for the *New York Sun* and later wrote columns for a newspaper syndicate), Serviss got his start in science fiction with a hastily written newspaper serial, *Edison's Conquest of Mars* (1898/1947), a sequel to H. G. Wells's *The War of the Worlds* in the same year it was published. This was followed by *The Moon Metal* (1900). His best-remembered works are the juvenile space adventure *A Columbus of Space* (1909/1911), an account of a trip to Venus in an atomic-powered spaceship that was considered by many SF readers an early classic, and *The Second Deluge* (1912), an even more popular story about an astronomer who builds an ark to save his family from a new Flood caused when the Earth passes through a watery nebula. Serviss's writing is journalistic, but his ideas are fertile and provocative.

B.S.

SEVEN DAYS IN MAY (1964).
Directed by John Frankenheimer; screenplay by Rod Serling; adapted from the novel by Fletcher Knebel and Charles W. Bailey II; music by Jerry Goldsmith. With Kirk Douglas, Burt Lancaster, Fredric March, Ava Gardner, John Houseman. 118 minutes. Black and white.

Seven Days in May is a product of the Cold War internationalism of the early 1960s. Burt Lancaster plays a fascistic general who creates a covert army to overthrow the government and replace it with a military tribunal. Only Kirk Douglas, as a loyal major, knows the full details of the plot—but will the authorities believe him?

Much of this film has dated (particularly Lancaster's performance, much too flashy for our bureaucratic times), but most of it is worth watching, particularly Fredric March, who turns a cartoonish role into a small masterpiece of world-weariness. This is the best of the near future political thrillers of the 1960s.

M.M.W.

SHAVER, RICHARD S[HARPE] (1907–1975).
American engineer and welder who achieved notoriety in the pages of Amazing Stories through his promotion of the Shaver mystery. The basis of the mystery, first launched in the story "I Remember Lemuria" (1945), was that millennia ago the Earth had been inhabited by two superraces, the Titans and the Atlans, who had established vast underground caverns full of superscientific equipment. These races were later forced to leave the Earth by the Sun's harmful radiation; the machines they left behind degenerated into evil deros (deranged robots), whose harmful rays are responsible for all humankind's current disasters.

As fiction this was good fun, but Shaver insisted (and editor Raymond A. Palmer hinted) it was all true, which insulted the intelligence of serious fans and attracted the gullible. The Shaver war raged in *Amazing* from 1945 to 1948, with an all-Shaver issue in June 1947. It also later emerged in *Other Worlds, Mystic, Fantastic,* and *The Hidden World.* Palmer published one volume of Shaver's material in *I Remember Lemuria and the Return of Sathanas* (1948).

M.A.

SHAW, BOB [ROBERT] (1931–).
Irish author who held various jobs in the steel and aircraft industries before becoming a full-time writer. Shaw published some trivial short stories in the 1950s, but his career began in earnest in the mid-1960s. His fine story "Light of Other Days" (1966; integrated into *Other Days, Other Eyes,* 1972) introduces the concept of slow glass, an apparently simple technology whose human and social consequences are far reaching. The careful extrapolation of such notions is a hallmark of Shaw's best work—another example is *Vertigo* (1978)—but he also delights in the juxtaposition of commonplace human tribulations (often marital problems) with sweeping and apocalyptic themes—a pattern seen in *The Two-Timers* (1968), *The Palace of Eternity* (1969), and *Orbitsville* (1975). He is an adept humorist, as in his witty time paradox novel *Who Goes Here?* (1977), and is equally effective as a writer of unusual adventure stories, such as *Medusa's Children* (1977) and *The Ragged Astronauts* (1986).

OTHER WORKS: *Night Walk* (1967); *Shadow of Heaven* (1969); *One Million Tomorrows* (1970); *Ground Zero Man* (1971; revised as *The Peace Machine,* 1985); *Tomorrow Lies in Ambush* (1973); *A Wreath of Stars* (1976); *Cosmic Kaleidoscope* (1976); *Ship of Strangers*

(1978); *Dagger of the Mind* (1979); *The Ceres Solution* (1981); *A Better Mantrap* (1982); *Orbitsville Departure* (1983); *Fire Pattern* (1984).

B.S.

SHECKLEY, ROBERT (1928–).

American writer best known for his urbane wit and humor. Sheckley began his career as the typical GALAXY author, selling that magazine a plethora of slick, funny stories, frequently featuring his AAA Ace Interplanetary Service, which put forth the (then) original notion that not all science-fiction heroes are necessarily very smart.

All during the 1950s Sheckley produced a stream of bright, polished, humorous stories—occasionally turning in a serious gem, such as "A Ticket to Tranai" (1955)—and he soon became known as a masterful writer of light, frothy tales, but nothing more.

Things started to change at the end of the decade, as Sheckley's work became more satiric and biting and displayed more depth. He also began writing in novel length, and although *The Status Civilization* (1960) shows how much his work had matured, it wasn't until the publication of *Journey Beyond Tomorrow* (1962), the riotous tale of an innocent abroad in America, that the unique voice of the mature Sheckley began to take shape. This was followed by *Mindswap* (1966), with its classically convoluted Theory of Searches and its memorable Twisted World. Then, in 1968, came Sheckley's masterpiece, *Dimension of Miracles*, a brilliantly funny novel in which not only the plot but the humor as well are viable only as SF.

Except for a handful of short stories, most of which appeared in such upscale markets as *Playboy*, Sheckley then fell silent for seven years, reappearing with *Options* (1975), an absurdist novel in which the author himself finally becomes a character. There were some echoes of his 1960s novels here, but it was apparent that Sheckley had struck off in a new direction. *Crompton Divided* (1978) and *Dramocles* (1983) both appear to be transitional works, not quite as absurdist as *Options*, not quite as polished and urbane as *Dimension of Miracles*.

Because he is now writing once again, after spending some time as the fiction editor of *Omni*, Sheckley's ultimate position in the field is still uncertain. However, there has been no serious challenger to the title, given to him by Kingsley Amis in *New Maps of Hell*, of "science fiction's premier gadfly," and certainly no humorist in the field has approached the polished urbanity and intellectual clarity of *Dimension of Miracles*.

OTHER WORKS: *Untouched by Human Hands* (1954); *Citizen in Space* (1955); *Pilgrimage to Earth* (1957); *Immortality Delivered* (1958; revised as *Immortality, Inc.,* 1959); *Store of Infinity* (1960); *Notions: Unlimited* (1960); *The 10th Victim* (1966); *The People Trap* (1968); *Can You Feel Anything When I Do This?* (1971);

The Robert Sheckley Omnibus (collection, 1973, British edition only); *The Robot Who Looked Like Me* (1978, British edition only); *Futureopolis: Impossible Cities in Science Fiction and Fantasy* (editor, 1978); *The Wonderful World of Robert Sheckley* (collection, 1979); *After the Fall: An Anthology* (editor, 1980); *Is THAT What People Do? The Selected Short Stories of Robert Sheckley* (collection, 1984); *Victim Prime* (1987).

M.R.

SHEFFIELD, CHARLES (1935–).

British-born writer with a doctorate in physics from Cambridge University who has published considerable technical research. Sheffield now lives in the United States, has done consulting work for the American space program, and has served as president of both the American Astronautical Society and the SCIENCE FICTION WRITERS OF AMERICA. Since the mid-1970s he has written popular fiction that ranges from historical fantasy through horror to hard SF (sometimes writing in ANALOG under the name James Kirkwood). His characters are often scientists—from Erasmus Darwin (an eighteenth-century graduate of Sheffield's college and, also like Sheffield, a prolific mix of scientist and popular writer) to his fictional futuristic Scottish genius McAndrew. Sheffield has extended his storytelling abilities beyond mere gadget SF, and his recent novels contain promising images for both sublime hard SF and deeper characterizations.

OTHER WORKS: *Sight of Proteus* (1978); *The Web between the Worlds* (1979); *Vectors* (1979); *Earthwatch: A Survey of the World from Space* (nonfiction, 1981); *Hidden Variables* (1981); *The Selkie* (with David Bischoff, 1982); *Erasmus Magister* (1982); *My Brother's Keeper* (1982); *The McAndrew Chronicles* (1983); *Between the Strokes of Night* (1985); *The Nimrod Hunt* (1986).

D.M.H.

SHELLEY, MARY WOLLSTONECRAFT (1797–1851).

British writer credited with creating one of the earliest fictions to mix literature and modern science. The daughter of intellectual parents who were both part of the Enlightenment, William Godwin and Mary Wollstonecraft, and the second wife of Percy Bysshe Shelley, the Romantic poet most in sympathy with science, Shelley naturally thought of "experiments" and the new science when she conceived her Gothic tale of horror about an artificially made man. *Frankenstein, or the Modern Prometheus* (1818) is an artful and complex work in its own right, but science fiction has come to associate it with the notion that artificial humans are evil. It was to oppose this Frankenstein "complex" that Isaac ASIMOV devised his "three laws of robotics." In fact, the artistry

Mary Wollstonecraft Shelley

ical locations near the ocean and depict the lives of down-and-outers, drug addicts, dreamers, or aging counterculture types; his central theme is alienation.

Shepard's first novel, *Green Eyes* (1984), tells the story of a scientific experiment in the resurrection of the dead gone awry. Set in Louisiana's bayou country, it begins naturalistically; develops into a Gothic tale of sexual perversion, murder, and voodoo; and ends in supernatural transcendence in the vein of H. P. LOVE-CRAFT's Cthulhu mythos.

The Jaguar Hunter (1987) collects Shepard's best short fiction, including such outstanding stories as "Salvador" and "R&R" (which won the Nebula Award for best novella in 1986), tales of drug-controlled American troops fighting in Central America; "The Man Who Painted the Dragon Griaule," about a painter's attempt to cover the body of a mile-long dragon with great art; and "A Traveller's Tale," which concerns an alien with psychic powers marooned in a Caribbean swamp. The book ranks as one of the half dozen most important SF short story collections of the 1980s.

M.M.L.

of the novel itself anticipates both the central image of the machine in modern SF and the love-hate attitude toward it.

Shelley's writing, in other words, is far more ambiguous in tone than the cultural symbol that has haunted Western thought since her monster first rose from Dr. Frankenstein's laboratory apparatus. Nevertheless, none of her other writings (and she did devote much of her energy later in life to promoting the poetic reputation of her dead husband) has managed to live on as *Frankenstein* has done. Enlightenment speculation about the nature and origins of life seems to have been more in tune with the literature and culture of our time than any of Shelley's generation of Romantic poets realized, and in Mary Shelley's novel the maligned Enlightenment poet Erasmus Darwin triumphs finally over his more emotional British contemporaries. It is he and Shelley herself who are highlighted in Brian W. ALDISS's history of SF.

OTHER WORKS: *Valperga* (1823); *The Last Man* (1826); *Lodore* (1835).

D.M.H.

SHEPARD, LUCIUS (19??–). American writer. Shepard received more award nominations during the several years after his first story appeared in 1983 than any writer since John VARLEY; he ranks with William GIBSON as one of the best new science-fiction writers of the 1980s.

Shepard's stories, which usually take place on Earth in the near future, are remarkably homogeneous in setting, theme, and characterization. Most are set in trop-

SHERRED, T[HOMAS] L. (1915–1985). American author, engineer, and technical and advertising writer. Sherred's best story was his first, "E for Effort," which made an enormous impression on the science-fiction world when it was published in the May 1947 *Astounding* and has since been reprinted a dozen times in the United States alone, including in the *SFWA Hall of Fame*, volume 2. Critic Algis BUDRYS wrote in 1970 that the story "handed the field such a knock that many old plinths are still loose in their sockets." In what became typical black humor, the story starts with the discovery of a method for viewing the past, which is used at first to make cheap films, then is employed for Hollywood spectaculars, and in the end becomes the cause of a final war as the U.S. government seizes the device and other powers realize that no secret is safe. "E for Effort" and three other early stories are included in the collection *First Person, Peculiar* (1972). Most of Sherred's stories are based on social reaction to new inventions or superpowers. He wrote two novels, *Alien Island* (1970), about first contact with aliens and their attempt, with the aid of a human, to set up a trading mission; and *Alien Main* (with Lloyd BIGGLE, Jr., 1985).

R.S.C.

SHIEL, M[ATTHEW] P[HIPPS] (1865–1947). British writer born in the West Indies, recruited to the writing of scientific romances by C. Arthur Pearson, who serialized his future war story "The Empress of the Earth" (reprinted as *The Yellow Danger*, 1898/1899). "Empress" was followed by the classic allegorical disaster story *The Purple Cloud* (1901) and *The Lord of the Sea* (1901); in both novels Shiel set out his distinctive philosophy of economic and evolutionary progress, borrowing from such writers as Herbert Spencer and Henry George. He campaigned for an ethical sensibility more progressive than the Christian ethos in *The Last Miracle* (1906) and *The Isle of Lies* (1909). After a second future war novel, *The Dragon* (1913; revised as *The Yellow Peril*, 1929), he published nothing for ten years. But he returned to scientific romance at the end of his career with *The Young Men Are Coming* (1937), in which he restated his main philosophical themes.

B.S.

SHIRAS, WILMAR H[OUSE] (1908–   ). American author noted for *Children of the Atom* (1953), a collection of linked stories about mutant children who must hide their superiority in order to survive. The stories are beautifully written, prefiguring the best of Zenna HENDERSON's People series. In an afterword to the 1978 Pennyfarthing Press edition, Marion Zimmer BRADLEY suggested that fans of the period strongly identified with the persecuted, brilliant children.

Shiras returned to science fiction with the Mrs. Tokkin series of tall tales in the early 1970s, but these had little impact.

D.S.

SHIRLEY, JOHN [PATRICK] (1953–   ). American rock singer and science-fiction writer. Shirley has frequently stated that his early science fiction was more heavily influenced by the surrealist painters than by SF writers. Such novels as *Dracula in Love* (1979) and *Transmaniacon* (1979) feature disjointed plots that often confuse the readers as much as the characters who are living them. His heroes tend to be filled with self doubt, often unsure of what action to take, and frequently without any central system of values. As a result, each novel contains outstanding, memorable individual scenes— Shirley has vast descriptive powers—but usually fail to form any coherent whole.

The early novels are nevertheless worth reading. Shirley's themes of individual freedom and of power that corrupts are dramatically presented in images that jar even the most complacent reader. In *Three-Ring Psychus* (1980) a group of people, afforded new mental powers, discover that they have the chance to develop in ways never dreamt of before. That very development, however, threatens the core of what makes them human.

After a few years away from science fiction, Shirley returned with a very different style, influenced by or coincident with the movement called CYBERPUNK, for which he has become a major spokesman. *Eclipse* (1985), a novel he calls "easily my most significant book," is written in a style he describes as "crystalline realism." Set in 2020, *Eclipse* describes a dystopic Europe ruled by fascists who came to power after a war that devastated the continent. While the descriptions of life in this near-future remain as powerful as any in his earlier works, the book is far more a cohesive whole.

The style of *Eclipse* certainly represents a significant departure from Shirley's earlier works, but his interest in human relationships, in the choice between freedom of action and security in conformity, and in the politics of power remain. The difference is that he has now learned to control his powers as a writer and to use them to produce a unified novel rather than a series of memorable episodes.

OTHER WORKS: *City Come A-Walkin'* (1981); *Cellars* (1982).

S.H.G.

SHUTE, NEVIL (Born Nevil Shute Norway) (1899–1960). British mainstream writer. Shute's career as an aeronautical engineer specializing in the construction of airships (as deputy chief engineer of the R100, he flew the Atlantic twice in 1930), enabled him to utilize his scientific knowledge in some borderline science-fiction novels, among them *An Old Captivity* (1940). The most important of these was *No Highway* (1948; filmed as *No Highway in the Sky*, 1951), which describes an airplane disaster caused by metal fatigue. After 1950 Shute lived in Australia, the setting of his only two genuine SF novels: *In the Wet* (1953), with its futuristic vision of Australia as head of the British Commonwealth; and the apocalyptic *On the Beach* (1957; filmed in 1959 with Gregory Peck, Fred Astaire, and Ava Gardner—see ON THE BEACH), in which Australia survives a nuclear war that has obliterated the Northern Hemisphere and now awaits the slow but inexorable aftermath of radioactive contamination.

R.D.

SHWARTZ, SUSAN [MARTHA] (1949–   ). American writer, editor, and critic who brings academic rigor to bear on both science fiction and fantasy. Shwartz's initial sale was a Darkover pastiche—based on Marion Zimmer BRADLEY's popular novel sequence—for the anthology *Keeper's Price* (1979). Her first novels established her versatility: *White Wing* (with Shariann Lewitt, 1985, as Gordon Kendall) is a space war adventure; *Byzantium's Crown* (1987) opens an alternate-history fantasy trilogy. Her anthology *Moonsinger's Friends* (1985), assembled to celebrate Andre NORTON's fifty years in fiction, was the first festschrift in SF presented to a living author.

S.L.M.

SILENT RUNNING (1972).

Directed by Douglas Trumbull; screenplay by Deric Washburn, Michael Cimino, and Steven Bochco; photographed by Charles F. Wheeler; music by Peter Schickele (songs sung by Joan Baez). With Bruce Dern, Cliff Potts, Ron Rifkin, Jesse Vint; as the drones: Mark Persons, Cheryl Sparks, Steven Brown, Larry Wisenhunt. 90 minutes. Color.

In the twenty-first century spaceships in orbit near Saturn bear enormous transparent domes housing vegetation and forest animals from the Earth, which now has no need of them. When orders come to destroy the domes, spaceship crewman Bruce Dern resorts to murder to save the last of them. At the climax, pursued by other ships, he launches the final dome, tended by a "drone" (robot), to safety and kills himself.

Silent Running is highly regarded by some for its sincerity and basic message: all life is interdependent. The special effects, by Douglas Trumbull, John Dykstra, and Richard Yuricich, are excellent, the drones (played by legless performers) are believable and endearing, and Dern's passionate performance is one of his best. But the premise is scientifically impossible, and the story is too slight for the film's length. *Silent Running* is more notable for what it attempts than for what it achieves.

B.W.

SILVERBERG, ROBERT (1935–).

American writer who in 1956, after graduating from Columbia University with an A.B. in English, won a Hugo as the most promising new writer of the year. Silverberg has subsequently won (or been nominated for) all the major science-fiction awards.

An only child of educated parents, Silverberg was encouraged in his intellectual pursuits. His sharp tongue and precocity were not well-received socially, and this enforced his loneliness and his voracious reading habit. By age thirteen he was submitting stories to SF magazines. His first publication for a fee and a professional magazine was "Fanmag," an article about fandom in *Science Fiction Adventures* (December 1953), and his first story was "Gorgon Planet" in *Nebula Science Fiction* (February 1954). That same year he was offered a contract for a juvenile novel (*Revolt on Alpha C*).

With his career launched before his twentieth birthday, Silverberg easily succumbed to mass-produced formularized stories and materialism. This unfortunate tendency was accelerated during the summer of 1955, when he met Randall GARRETT, an established SF writer who was then having difficulty keeping writing deadlines. Garrett and Silverberg began a series of collaborations (under the pseudonym Robert Randall) that flooded the market with profitable hackwork. Silverberg's astonishing success churning out potboilers was almost an embarrassment; other pseudonyms he used regularly were Calvin M. Knox, David Osborne, and Ivar Jorgenson.

Robert Silverberg

The year 1956 was an annus mirabilis for Silverberg. His writing career was in high gear, he graduated from college, he won the Hugo Award, and he got married. During the remainder of the 1950s the wunderkind saw little reason to question his commercial success or his "writing machine" method. Out of the millions of words he produced came at least four respectable novels: *The Thirteenth Immortal* (1956), *Master of Life and Death* (1957), *Invaders from Earth* (1958), and *Stepsons of Terra* (1958). In *Master of Life and Death* Silverberg memorably examined the theme of overpopulation, which would become a familiar concern in later works.

Around 1958 the bottom fell out of SF magazine publishing, but Silverberg's "deadly facility," as he described his writing style, was easily directed to more lucrative markets. For the next few years he abandoned SF and successfully wrote books on travel, archaeology, and popular science.

Freed from SF financially but not spiritually, Silverberg was lured into expressing his artistic side in the early 1960s by Frederik POHL, who was then editing GALAXY and offered him absolute creative freedom. Silverberg replied with "To See the Invisible Man" (1963), one of his finest explorations of alienation. It marked the beginning of a renaissance for his SF career.

Stimulated by the NEW WAVE writers of the 1960s and the freedom to explore an SF finally released from the tyranny of the formulas of the early SF pulps, Silverberg turned his writing skills to a science fiction that now embraced new horizons: the inner space of the psyche, antiheroes, sex, pessimism (as a legitimate worldview), and writing techniques evolved by mainstream authors such as James Joyce, Bertolt Brecht, and Ernest Hemingway.

With the publication of *Thorns* and the novella "Hawksbill Station" in 1967, there could no longer be any doubt that a new Silverberg had emerged, a writer of high literary abilities. In both these works Silverberg explored modern human alienation; our inability to communicate with our gods, others, and ourselves; the existential despair concomitant with an almost universal weltschmerz—and the possible redemptions. Conventional SF techniques are here, of course, (time travel, alien creatures, scientific extrapolations) but so is literature. In this year he also became president of the SCIENCE FICTION WRITERS OF AMERICA.

This new respectability was further strengthened with the publication in 1968 of the Nebula Award–winning "Passengers," in 1969 of "Sundance," and the Hugo Award in 1969 for the novella "Nightwings" (1968). These three stories alone gave witness to Silverberg's emergence as a literary craftsman whose place in the SF pantheon was well secured.

His status as a novelist too was reaffirmed and expanded, with *Downward to the Earth* (1970), a Conradian exploration of spiritual corruption and regeneration; *Tower of Glass* (1970), a highly literate work linking character and idea while examining the profound difficulties in human spiritual communication; *Son of Man* (1971), a psychedelic adventure à la David LINDSAY and Jack VANCE; *A Time of Changes* (1971), which won the Nebula Award; *Dying Inside* (1972), a story that creates one of SF's most realized characters; and *The Book of Skulls* (1972), a mainstream investigation of characterization and spiritual questing.

Throughout his career Silverberg has also enjoyed editing anthologies, an activity that has given him the opportunity to examine critically the SF canon and (especially in his New Dimensions anthologies) to bring new writers into the field. In recognition of his many contributions to SF he was chosen American Guest of Honor at the World Science Fiction Convention held in Heidelberg, Germany, in 1970.

In 1972 Silverberg moved to Oakland, California, took some time off from writing, and, in the manner of Candide, tended his garden (he is an amateur horticulturist). This retirement, however, proved to be merely a sabbatical to refresh the mind. In 1976 he returned with *Shadrach in the Furnace*, in 1980 *Lord Valentine's Castle*, and in 1984 a collection of short stories, *The Conglomeroid Cocktail Party*. His pace has slackened, but he knows that writing is a quintessential aspect of his being, which frees him from the bounds of time and space and promotes "the governing myths of the dawning age of galactic man."

NOTABLE OTHER WORKS: *Recalled to Life* (1962); *To Worlds Beyond* (1965); *The Man in the Maze* (1969); *Up the Line* (1969); *The World Inside* (1971); *The Second Trip* (1972); *Unfamiliar Territory* (1973); *Born with the Dead* (1974); *The Feast of St. Dionysus* (1975); *The Stochastic Man* (1975); *The Best of Robert Silverberg* (collection, 1976); *Capricorn Games* (1976); *Majipoor Chronicles* (1982); *World of a Thousand Colors* (1982); *Lord of Darkness* (1983); *Valentine Pontifex* (1983); *Gilgamesh the King* (1984); *Sailing to Byzantium* (1985); *Tom O'Bedlam* (1985); *Star of Gypsies* (1986); *Beyond the Safe Zone* (collection, 1986).

M.T.W.

SIMAK, CLIFFORD D[ONALD] (1904–   ).

American writer and newspaperman. Simak brought rural settings and characters to science fiction, reflecting a homespun wit and wisdom as well as a pastoral mood that stand out in a genre mostly distinguished by urban environments and values. By 1987, over a fifty-five-year career, Simak had published some 200 short stories and seventeen novels.

His concern for ordinary people and ordinary life shows the influence of his formative years. Born in Wisconsin, son of a father who had emigrated from Czechoslovakia, Simak grew up on a farm close to the confluence of the Wisconsin and Mississippi rivers. He taught for a year before attending the University of Wisconsin for two years, then worked as an editor on a series of small newspapers. It was his appointment as news editor for the *Minneapolis Tribune*, however, that gave him the free time needed for his own writing.

Simak had returned to writing SF a year before, when John W. CAMPBELL was appointed editor of *Astounding Science Fiction*. Four earlier Simak stories had been published in 1931–32. "The Creator," published in 1935, had brought him some notoriety for its attack on the being in a greater universe who created our own, but his stories for Campbell, beginning with "Rule 18" (1938), were the start of his new and continuing reputation.

Simak's stories are full of technical invention and intriguing ideas, but above all he is the pastoral poet of SF, famous for his warmth, abiding interest in ordinary individuals and their traditional moral values, and ability to couch the strange in the familiar. He received the International Fantasy Award in 1953 for *City* (1952); three Hugo Awards for "The Big Front Yard" (1958), *Here Gather the Stars* (magazine title; book title *Way Station*, both 1963), and "The Grotto of the Dancing Deer" (1980) (which also won a Nebula); and the Jupiter Award for *A Heritage of Stars* (1977); in 1977 he received the Nebula Grand Master Award.

City began as a series of stories, most published in *Astounding*, depicting the decline of the city and of humanity, leaving the Earth to intelligent dogs helped by a robot. Simak's frame for the series was the fireside tales of a Dog scholar who asks the question: Is Man a myth? In *Way Station* Enoch Wallace is a Civil War veteran and the nonaging keeper of the secret way station on the Earth that is part of a galactic transport system. Wallace protects a girl who later becomes Keeper of the Talisman, a device that in a quasi-religious way enhances morality, goodwill, and cooperation in the galactic civilization; because of her new status, the Earth is deemed fit to join that civilization. In "The Big Front Yard," when a small-town handyman's house becomes a portal to another time and place, he dickers with alien traders in his new front yard for ideas, not gadgets.

Simak has created remarkable robots. From Jenkins of *City* to Theodosius of *Project Pope* (1981), he has worked sympathetic variations on that basic SF idea, imbuing his robots with emotions long before other writers did. His aliens also are different: Hoot of *Destiny Doll* (1971), Catface of *Mastodonia* (1978), and Horseface of *Highway of Eternity* (1986) are particularly memorable.

A number of Simak's stories and novels deal with parallel worlds, such as *Ring around the Sun* (1953) and *All Flesh Is Grass* (1965). Others have a time travel component: time tunnels lead to the Cretaceous period in *Mastodonia;* Shakespeare dances with his ghost in *The Goblin Reservation* (1968); and Asher Sutton lives ten years in sanctuary on a representation of Simak's Wisconsin farm in *Time and Again* (1951).

From the mid-1960s various Simak stories give body to the mystical hints present in earlier stories. In *Why Call Them Back from Heaven* (1967), a story of skulduggery among the operators of cryogenic banks, the discovery that life goes on beyond death makes the banks obsolete. In *A Choice of Gods* (1972), The Principle, a power at the center of the galaxy, removes from the Earth everyone interested in city-style technology and protects those who are left behind. In *Project Pope* a robot pope seeks to replace faith with fact. In that novel, as in *Enchanted Pilgrimage* (1975), "Auk House" (1977), and *Highway of Eternity,* guardians monitor humanity's progress in terms of not its technology but its character.

Four Simak stories were adapted for NBC Radio's *X Minus One* program in the 1950s, an adaptation of "How-2" (1954) was televised in 1970, and *Way Station* was put under film option in 1986. Simak retired from his newspaper position in 1976 but continued to write. He was guest of honor at the World SF Convention in 1971.

OTHER WORKS: *Time Is the Simplest Thing* (1961); *Out of Their Minds* (1970); *Shakespeare's Planet* (1976); *Skirmish: The Great Short Fiction of Clifford D. Simak* (collection, 1977); *Special Deliverance* (1982); *The Marathon Photograph and Other Stories* (collection, 1986); *Brother and Other Stories* (collection, 1987).

F.L.

SIODMAK, CURT [or KURT] (1902–).
German novelist, screenwriter, and film director who became a naturalized American. Siodmak's early novels, including *F.P.1. Does Not Reply* (*F.P.1. Antwortet nicht,* 1931; translated into English 1933), were written in German. The film adaptation of F.P.1. and another science-

fiction film, *The Tunnel* (released in the United States as *Transatlantic Tunnel,* 1935), were among his early screen credits while he was working in England (a German version, *Der Tunnel,* was filmed in 1933). He moved to America in 1937 and wrote scripts for many SF and horror movies (as well as dozens of others), including *The Lady and the Monster* (1944), based on his famous pulp novel *Donovan's Brain* (1943). This story, about an industrialist's brain that, removed and kept alive after an airplane accident, begins to take over other minds telepathically, was filmed twice more. Siodmak's best book (also filmed) is a sequel, *Hauser's Memory* (1968), a thriller about transplanted memories. His early work, although its basic ideas were common in the SF of its time (two scientists recoiling from a still-living head in a laboratory was the cover of the August 1926 AMAZING), had a mass audience power, but his later work, typified by the films *The Magnetic Monster* (1953) and *Love Slaves of the Amazon* (1957), both of which he also directed, often were trivial exploitations.

OTHER WORKS: *Skyport* (1959); *The Third Ear* (1971); *City in the Sky* (1974).

B.S.

SKULLDUGGERY (1970).
Directed by Gordon Douglas; screenplay by Nelson Gidding; adapted from the novel You Shall Know Them *(Les Animaux Dénaturés) by Vercors; photographed by Robert Moreno; music by Oliver Nelson. With Burt Reynolds, Susan Clark, Roger C. Carmel, Paul Hubschmid, Chips Rafferty, Alexander Knox, Pat Suzuki, Edward Fox, Wilfrid Hyde-White, William Marshall. 105 minutes. Color.*

An expedition of adventurers and archaeologists in New Guinea finds a tribe of ape-people, perhaps the legendary "missing link." The expedition's financier (Paul Hubschmid) intends to enslave the Tropis, as they are called, so one of the adventurers (Burt Reynolds) tries to force legal proof that the Tropis are human by claiming to have murdered the offspring of one of the Tropis (Pat Suzuki) and his partner (Roger C. Carmel).

Vercors's novel is a dark satire of racism; although the film clumsily touches on the subject, it's primarily an action comedy inspired by the success of PLANET OF THE APES (1968). The clash between content and style weakens a confused script; apparently fearing the wrath of religious fundamentalists, the filmmakers drew no conclusions regarding the Tropis's humanity.

B.W.

SKY, KATHLEEN (1943–).
American writer best known for strongly emotive writing that features the relationships between humans and aliens who must make difficult decisions. Technically Sky's first novel, *Vulcan!* (1974), is a better-than-average book in the STAR TREK

series. Her next novel, *Birthright* (1975), describes a world that has been deeply changed by genetic engineering. The practice has been perfected to such a degree that new methods of distinguishing humans from androids need to be found.

Sky portrays strong women in her works, and *Witchdame* (1985), as much fantasy as science fiction, is the perfect vehicle for that interest. Its protagonist, Princess Elizabeth, shows her strength in her willingness to choose difficult actions and then follow through as she works her way to whatever the future may bring. Sky has frequently described herself as a writer who is still learning, with the best of her works yet to come. Given her ability to draw emotionally credible characters and an imagination that has created several memorable alien worlds ("Lament of the Keeku Bird," 1973, and "A Daisychain for Pav," 1976), she may be right.

S.H.G.

SLADEK, JOHN T[HOMAS] (1937–   ).

American science-fiction writer who lived for some twenty years in England and has been a technical writer, a railroad switchman, and a draftsman. Sladek is closely associated with the British NEW WAVE because of his imagistic, often surrealistic, style and for his concentration on the bleaker aspects of human nature. Almost every aspect of human behavior—in particular humanity's worship of things technological—has been the target for Sladek's ironic humor. In "Masterson and the Clerks" (1967), for example, American business practices are hilariously exposed for their hypocrisy while the "heroes" blithely follow a trail to their own destruction. In his first novel, *The Reproduction System* (1968; published in the United States as *Mechasm*, 1975), the population of a small Midwestern town gets more than it had hoped for when a self-reproducing machine runs out of control.

Nevertheless, Sladek appreciates intelligence wherever he finds it, even if it belongs to robots or cyborgs. He has written sympathetically of thinking machines who search for ways to fit into human society, in many of the short stories collected in *The Steam-Driven Boy and Other Strangers* (1973) and, most notably, in *Roderick; or, The Education of a Young Machine* (1980; abridged version, 1982) and *Roderick at Random; or, Further Education of a Young Machine* (1983). The hero of both works (which also function as a critique of Isaac ASIMOV's robot stories) is an intelligent robot whose adventures in a world not ready to accept him alternate between comedy and pathos.

Sladek has little patience with people who insist on simple, optimistic visions of solving the problems facing a technological society. In the collection *Keep the Giraffe Burning* (1977) and elsewhere, he has parodied other SF authors who, he believes, have failed to understand just how complex the effects of technology can be. And in the novel *Tik-Tok* (1983) he provides a "corrective" to Asimov's Three Laws of Robotics.

The Müller-Fokker Effect (1970) combines in one work most of the characteristics of Sladek's fiction. The novel satirizes such American institutions as evangelism, popular journalism, and the military. At the same time, it sympathetically describes the experiences of a human personality that has been reduced to a computer program. Sladek manages to balance the book's diverse elements so deftly that the novel succeeds as both satire and entertainment—an achievement that few authors, in or out of the genre, could have carried off.

OTHER WORKS: *The Best of John Sladek* (collection, 1981); *Alien Accounts* (collection, 1982); *The Lunatics of Terra* (collection, 1984).

S.H.G.

SLAUGHTERHOUSE-FIVE (1972).

Directed by George Roy Hill; screenplay by Stephen Geller; adapted from the novel by Kurt Vonnegut, Jr.; photographed by Miroslav Ondricek; music by Glenn Gould. With Michael Sacks, Ron Leibman, Eugene Roche, Sharon Gans, Valerie Perrine. 105 minutes. Color.

Billy Pilgrim (Michael Sacks), a middle-class, middle-aged American, is discontented with his job, his marriage, and his life. Suddenly dislocated in time, he randomly relives events of his life, past and future. Hurled into the past, he again witnesses the World War II destruction of Dresden, during which he was incarcerated as a prisoner of war at Number 5 Slaughterhouse Street. Projected into the future, he is imprisoned with a beautiful actress (Valerie Perrine) in a zoo on the planet Tralfamadore, where their daily activities—eating, sleeping, making love—are viewed by the native inhabitants as a form of entertainment.

This film conveys a dreamlike ambiguity, in which Pilgrim uncomprehendingly exists. Yet as he relives in haphazard order various segments of his life, he experiences the actuality that one's past is always a part of one's life, acknowledged or not. Although some critics said that Kurt VONNEGUT, Jr.'s novel did not translate well to the screen, the film remains thought provoking.

D.P.V.

SLEEPER (1973).

Directed by Woody Allen; screenplay by Woody Allen and Marshall Brickman; photographed by David M. Walsh; music by Woody Allen and the Preservation Hall Jazz Band. With Woody Allen, Diane Keaton, John Beck, Mary Gregory, Don Keefer, Don McLiam. 88 minutes. Color.

Miles Monroe (Woody Allen), an insecure Jewish intellectual, awakens 200 years after a supposedly minor operation to discover himself embroiled in a battle between rebels and an oppressive totalitarian society. Disguised as a household robot, he is bought by Luna (Diane Keaton), an indolent aristocrat, and after various escapes and recaptures both eventually fight on the side of the revolution.

Backed by a wittily anachronistic Dixieland jazz score, *Sleeper* uses typical science-fiction devices—drawn more from 1930s utopian fiction than from films—to satirize the icons of the mid-twentieth century. Allen, as usual a nervous and sexually frustrated nebbish who drops self-deprecating wisecracks, blunders his way through a cook's tour of the future. Although often described as a spoof of science fiction, *Sleeper* is instead a comic version of a typical SF antiutopian adventure.

Undeniably funny, the film is never quite as hilarious as it keeps promising to become, and the romance between Allen and Keaton is more stated than demonstrated. The supporting players, except for Keaton, are minor performers, and the film depends almost entirely on Allen for its drive and humor; luckily, he's more than equal to the task. Despite its weaknesses, *Sleeper* is the best of Allen's early comedies. It won a Hugo for best dramatic presentation.

B.W.

SLESAR, HENRY (Pseudonym: O. H. Leslie) (1927–).

American writer and advertising executive. Slesar has written mostly for television, spending nine years as head writer for *The Edge of Night* and writing many scripts for *Alfred Hitchcock Presents* and other shows. His work in science fiction has been in the short story; his only book, *Twenty Million Miles to Earth* (1957), is a novelization of the film.

N.H.

SLOANE, T[HOMAS] O'CONOR (1851–1940).

American editor and science writer who began as associate editor of Hugo GERNSBACK's AMAZING STORIES and later became editor after Gernsback lost the magazine to B. A. Mackinnon and K. K. Fly in 1929. Sloane remained editor when *Amazing* was sold to Teck Publications and stayed in that position until 1938, when he was eighty-seven and had a long white beard. His choice of stories, when he had the luxury of choosing among submissions, reflected his years with Gernsback. Sloane favored fiction that speculated on future inventions (his son was married to the daughter of Thomas Alva Edison) and explored the wonders of science. He was less interested, however, in the science in science fiction than was Gernsback, and during his tenure *Amazing* published the first stories of such diverse writers as E. E. "Doc" SMITH, John W. CAMPBELL, and Jack WILLIAMSON. He is remembered as a passive editor who often

held stories for years before rejecting them (in Clifford D. SIMAK's case, as "dated") and published others that had already been published elsewhere.

S.H.G.

SLONCZEWSKI, JOAN (1956–).

American author and college professor. Slonczewski, who is a research biologist and teaches genetics at Kenyon College, grew up in Katonah, New York, got a bachelor's degree from Bryn Mawr College, and wrote her first novel, *Still Forms on Foxfield* (1980), while pursuing a doctorate in biochemistry at Yale University. To date she has written two novels, both influenced by her scientific specialty and her decision to join the Society of Friends (Quakers). She has offered community education programs on nuclear issues and organized for the Nuclear Freeze.

Her first novel describes an alien species that communicates by chemisensing, exchanging complex chemical messages. Her second novel, *A Door into Ocean* (1986), won the John W. Campbell Award for the best science-fiction novel of the year. It describes a far future galaxy, settled by humans, in which a single water-covered moon (Ocean), with its all-woman inhabitants wise in the biological sciences, stands in the way of galactic tyrannies. Slonczewski makes that world and its strange society not only convincing but engrossing, and its non-violent victory against overwhelming force is believable as well. The world of the novel is in some ways the obverse of Frank HERBERT's Arrakis (*Dune*, 1965), with its unbeatable warriors bred out of desert privation, but it is spiritually more akin to that of Ursula K. LE GUIN's *The Left Hand of Darkness* (1969).

J.E.G.

SMALL PRESS WRITERS AND ARTISTS ORGANIZATION.

Organization founded in 1977 to differentiate the small press segment of science fiction from the realm of the fanzine. The group's effort has not been totally successful: payment for material is not a sufficient criterion for membership because some small presses do not pay and some self-described fanzines do. The group's most important function has been to define small press professional standards, but it has also promoted small presses as showcases for material of high quaity that may not be salable to mass markets. Members include writers, publishers, editors, and artists.

S.E.G.

———— SMALL PRESSES ————

Science-fiction and fantasy specialty publishing evolved out of the amateur press associations of the late nineteenth and early twentieth centuries. The first attempt at a commercial specialty press was Conrad Ruppert's *Fantasy Book*, a magazine that ran from 1931 to 1938 but never achieved newsstand distribution; William Crawford's Visionary Press of Everett, Pennsylvania, published a series of chapbooks, two paperbound novels, and two hardcovers, the most famous of which was H. P. LOVE-CRAFT's *The Shadow over Innsmouth* (1936), the only Lovecraft book published during his lifetime. Ruppert himself also published one book, *Dawn of Flame* (1936) by Stanley G. WEINBAUM, a memorial to the author resembling a Bible. However, neither publisher was commercially successful during this period; they served primarily as inspiration for those to come.

When August DERLETH and Donald Wandrei, two successful authors in the field who had been encouraged and helped by Lovecraft, sought to market a memorial collection of their mentor's work, *The Outsider and Others* (1939), it was turned down by all the major publishing houses. They then remembered Crawford's Lovecraft book and Ruppert's memorial to Weinbaum and decided to do it themselves, founding Arkham House in Sauk City, Wisconsin, in 1939. The book was expensive for its time and not a major seller, and Derleth decided to use Arkham House to publish works by others partly in the hope of paying off the debt incurred by *Outsider*. Soon he was bringing out works by many major authors of fantasy and SF, mostly drawn from *Weird Tales*; ultimately he also published the first books by such rising stars of the times as Ray BRADBURY, Fritz LEIBER, Robert BLOCH, and A. E. VAN VOGT. Arkham House had become an enormous one-man tour de force, Wandrei having been drafted.

With the end of World War II, many veterans who had been SF fans in the 1930s returned to civilian life and were inspired by Arkham House's apparent success. Donald M. Grant formed a partnership with Thomas Hadley and Ken Krueger that ran through many imprint names; today Grant alone publishes a half dozen books a year under his own imprint, with the work of Robert E. Howard a specialty. The mailing list they built up was used by Lloyd Arthur ESHBACH to found Fantasy Press, which over its eight-year life published the major works of E. E. ''Doc'' SMITH, as well as much by John W. CAMP-BELL, van Vogt, Weinbaum, and many others, rescuing them from obscurity. William Crawford founded FPCI in Los Angeles in 1945 and was commercially successful this time, particularly with works by L. Ron HUBBARD and John TAINE. In New York David Kyle and Martin L. Greenberg founded Gnome Press as a mass-market SF hardcover publisher, while Erle M. Korshak and Ted Dikty did the same with Shasta in Chicago, rescuing from pulp magazine oblivion many of the major works of the 1930s and 1940s by such now classic authors as Isaac ASIMOV and Robert A. HEINLEIN and introducing their work to a growing number of fans through sales to bookstores and libraries.

By the mid-1950s, however, most specialty publishers were either out of business or moribund, the victims of the growth of the mass-market paperback, whose publishers could pay far higher prices than they for the best work; the growth of such institutions as the Science Fiction Book Club, which could underprice and outpromote them; and the growing recognition by mass-market hardcover houses such as Doubleday and Simon and Schuster of the sales potential of SF and fantasy—a potential ironically demonstrated by the very success of the specialty publishers.

In the late 1950s only one new specialty publisher surfaced, Advent of Chicago, again seeing and filling a niche the mass market had overlooked: Advent published nonfiction books and reference works about the SF and fantasy field. Founded as a cooperative by long-time SF fans including Earl Kemp, Jon Stopa, Ed Wood, and George Price, it continues today as a part-time activity of Wood and Price. In the 1960s Jack L. CHALKER founded The Mirage Press, Ltd., which, like Advent, specialized in nonfiction and esoterica about the field (such as *An Atlas of Fantasy* and *A Guide to Middle-earth*). Both houses occasionally dabbled in fiction but found the competition too fierce. Arkham House continued in the 1960s as the lone publisher of fiction for a while, later rejoined by a resurgent Donald M. Grant.

By the 1970s the original purpose of specialty publishing—rescuing from oblivion works that devotees believed should survive and find new audiences—had become obsolete; the mass-market publishing industry couldn't get enough SF and fantasy to fill their orders. The new specialty publishers looked first at a new niche—producing fine, limited-edition hardcovers of books that were appearing, or had appeared previously, only in paperback. Some, like Underwood-Miller, began as mail-order book dealers desiring to preserve all the works of specific authors (notably, in the case of Underwood-Miller, Jack VANCE), as Arkham had begun with the idea of preserving Lovecraft's work for the pulps. The paperback, they saw, had become as perishable as the old pulp magazine. Others, like Phantasia Press, saw potential in limited, signed editions of new works by contemporary authors, often buying the hardcover rights from paperback houses and producing the first editions of those works. Most, like Advent, Phantasia, Whispers Press, Dark Harvest, Corroborree, Dragon Press, Owls-wick, and others are profitable hobbies; a few, such as Underwood-Miller, provide full-time incomes for their publishers.

Meeting the unfilled need of the field is still the primary rationale for the specialty publisher. Many valuable nonfiction and bibliographic works continue to appear only in specialty press editions (such as *The John W. Campbell Letters*, 1985, from Author's Co-Op). But other small presses have reversed the original notion and become the quality hardcover houses for mass-market paperback publishers. Arkham House too is thriving under Derleth's successor, James Turner, as one of the few houses publishing collections of short fiction in the field. Specialty publishing has carried over to other literary fields as well. Derleth founded the mystery imprint Mycroft & Moran in 1945; current publishers such as Mysterious Press and Oswald Train continue that tradition. And lately Underwood-Miller has applied the concept to best-sellers and romance novels with Brandywine Books.

Also continuing successfully is the almost separate industry of specialty publishing for SF conventions. The New England Science Fiction Association of Boston, as NESFA Press, now publishes a book by the Guests of Honor, for every World SF Convention as well as a similar book for the Guest of Honor of their own convention, Boskone. Norwescon in Seattle has established a similar tradition. A current listing of specialty SF and fantasy specialty presses, past and present, contains 214 separate imprints.

The early specialty publishers performed a unique service in rescuing the heritage of the genre from the obscurity and outright oblivion that might have resulted from World War II paper drives. Hundreds of thousands of stories and novels were written for the hundreds of pulp magazines of the era; few outside the SF and fantasy tales suvive, and they survive because of the specialty presses. The presses' second service was to prove in the postwar decade that there was a large and vital market for SF and fantasy among the general reading public. A third, and continuing, service is to publish and distribute major works of bibliography and criticism, many originally written for amateur magazines with circulations in the hundreds, so that scholars and collectors can have access to that information.

Although there has been an occasional tendency among today's specialty publishers to depart from the role of their heritage, such as publishing special editions of contemporary hardcovers by best-selling authors basically in the manner and for the reasons that the Franklin Mint produces special pewter collections, the bulk of publishing today, as yesterday, continues to seek out and fill unmet needs for the promotion and preservation of important SF and fantasy works.

                                                                    J. L. Chalker

SMITH, CLARK ASHTON (1893–1936).

American writer, primarily of poetry and fantasy stories, most of whose fiction was published in *Weird Tales* and *Wonder Stories*. Smith's poetry and poetic imagery flowed over into his fiction, which at its best is poignant and romantic, and was written in a high style. A good example is his classic fantasy "The City of the Singing Flame" (1931), in which the Singing Flame lures people

to their apparent destruction (although the protagonist discovers that it in fact leads to a better reality). The influence of Smith's exotic subject matter and ornate language can be traced in the work of such later writers as Theodore STURGEON, Ray BRADBURY, and Jack VANCE. His more traditional science-fiction stories (he wrote no novels) are interplanetary tales of discovery and adventure, such as "Marooned in Andromeda" (1930). Smith's SF stories are collected in *The Immortals of Mercury* (1932), *Tales of Science and Sorcery* (1976), and *Other Dimensions* (1977).

                                                                    N.H.

SMITH, CORDWAINER (Pseudonym of Paul Myron Anthony Linebarger) (1913–1966).

American fiction writer and political scientist who published science fiction under the pseudonym Cordwainer Smith. Linebarger's SF career was brief, concentrated between age forty-two, when he began regular magazine publication, and age fifty-three, when he died. But his work was quickly recognized for its strange characters and exotic settings, which were clearly influenced by his unusual early life.

The older son of Paul M. W. Linebarger, who devoted his life to the cause of Sun Yat-sen and Chinese nationalism, Linebarger spent much of his childhood in China and Europe. By age seventeen he was heavily involved in his father's work—propaganda, lobbying, fund-raising, intelligence gathering. At twenty-two he completed his Ph.D. in political science at Johns Hopkins University, with a dissertation on the teachings of Sun Yat-sen. In World War II he served with U.S. Army Intelligence in India, China, and Washington, D.C. In 1946 he became professor of Asiatic politics at Johns Hopkins's School of Advanced International Studies while maintaining ties with the intelligence community.

Except for juvenilia, Linebarger's first published fiction was mainstream: two novels of women recalling their bizarre personal histories (*Ria*, 1947, and *Carola*, 1948, under the pseudonym Felix C. Forrest). *Atomsk*, a spy thriller about the sabotage of a Russian nuclear bomb factory, appeared in 1949 under the pseudonym Carmichael Smith.

Linebarger's first major SF story, "Scanners Live in Vain," was repeatedly rejected, finally appearing in 1950 in a semiprofessional magazine, *Fantasy Book*. Often anthologized thereafter, the story is remarkable for its depiction of the desperate steps necessary to control the psychological pain induced by long-distance space travel. It attracted most attention, however, for its intimations of a fully developed future history. As more of his stories appeared in the later 1950s, the immense scope of Linebarger's future history was gradually revealed. Most of his stories occur within it and allude to events in other stories, told and untold. Linebarger's universe is not the

Cordwainer Smith

high-tech future of Robert A. HEINLEIN (although its technology is intriguing) but one of myth and legend, where high romance blends with intergalactic gossip while hardball politics serves great moral and religious purposes.

Linebarger's only SF novel, *Norstrilia* (1975), first appeared in book form as two separate volumes, *The Planet Buyer* (1964) and *The Underpeople* (1968). Even as a whole, *Norstrilia* is too episodic to be Linebarger's strongest work, but many individual chapters are impressive and add important details to his future history. Linebarger's reputation and influence in SF rest largely on his short stories, ranging from the early emotional intensity of "Scanners Live in Vain" (1950) and "The Game of Rat and Dragon" (1955), through the mythic nostalgia of such middle-period classics as "The Ballad of Lost C'mell" (1962) and "Alpha Ralpha Boulevard" (1961), to such bizarre quasi-religious works of his final years as "Three to a Given Star" (1965) and "Under Old Earth" (1966).

OTHER WORKS: *Quest of the Three Worlds* (1966); *The Best of Cordwainer Smith* (collection, edited by J. J. Pierce, 1975); *The Instrumentality of Mankind* (1979). (Printings dated 1985 and later include corrections of typographical errors dating from original publication.)

A.C.E.

SMITH, E[DWARD] E[LMER] "DOC" (1890–1965).

American pioneer science-fiction writer, known for the scope of his imagination as shown primarily in two major series of interplanetary, interstellar,

and intergalactic adventures. Soon after Smith's birth in Sheboygan, Wisconsin, his family moved west, and he had a rough-and-tumble upbringing in backcountry Idaho. He earned degrees from the University of Idaho and George Washington University, culminating in a Ph.D. in chemistry in 1918, and worked as a chemist developing doughnut mixes for most of the next thirty-eight years. But Smith wrote SF persistently throughout his adult life, accumulating a substantial body of work.

The Skylark of Space, Smith's first novel, was written in 1915 in collaboration with Lee Hawkins Garby and inspired by a casual conversation about travel in outer space. Although not the first interstellar adventure, *Skylark* was striking in its zest to get off the Earth, its confidence that the real story was "Out There." In addition, unlike most writers of the day, Smith depicted scientists who were as human as his readers—a fact that may have scared off editors, who feared that the story of *Skylark* was too unusual for their audiences to grasp. Then Smith discovered AMAZING STORIES, which serialized the story in 1928 (first book publication, 1946; revised, 1958). Readers were wildly enthusiastic about Smith's first tale of heroic Richard Seaton and dastardly Blackie DuQuesne, and their response encouraged Smith to write more.

The Skylark novels featured increasingly vast cosmic disturbances, larger and more powerful machines, more dreadful alien menaces. Although Smith tried to complete the series with *Skylark Three* (1930/1948), the demands of his readers—and his own restless imagination—led him to write *Skylark of Valeron* (1934/1949) and three decades later *Skylark DuQuesne* (1965/1966). Other early works include *Spacehounds of IPC* (1931/1947), intended as the first of a series, although its Solar System setting proved too restrictive for Smith's imagination, and *Triplanetary* (1934), a space pirate thriller.

At the same time that he was writing the Skylark novels, Smith was planning a major project which would eventually become the four Lensman novels, published in *Astounding: Galactic Patrol* (1937/1950), *Gray Lensman* (1939/1951), *Second Stage Lensman* (1941–42/1953), and *Children of the Lens* (1947–48/1954). He rewrote *Triplanetary* (1934–35/1948) to work it into the Lensman series and then wrote *The First Lensman* (1950), which was published only in book form, to link *Triplanetary* with *Galactic Patrol*. The whole series of six books was published by a fan press, then reissued in a uniform, boxed edition as *The History of Civilization*.

The Lensman series describes a struggle between ancient races, each of which has used newer intelligent species throughout the galaxy to further its ends. One side, called Boskone, works through intricate layers of command because it is so afraid of being supplanted that it instinctively terrorizes and manipulates everyone else. The other side, called Civilization, gives individuals as much freedom as they can handle because it wishes to

Elliot Dold's illustration for E. E. Smith's *The Skylark of Valeron*

OTHER WORKS: *The Galaxy Primes* (1959/1965); *Masters of Space* (1961/1976, completion of E. E. Evans's ms.); *Subspace Explorers* (1965); *The Best of E. E. ("Doc") Smith* (collection, 1975); *Subspace Encounter* (1983, completed by Lloyd Arthur ESHBACH).

J.S.

SMITH, EVELYN E. (1927–   ). American writer and compiler of crossword puzzles who has also written as Delphine C. Lyons. In the 1950s Smith was a frequent contributor to THE MAGAZINE OF FANTASY AND SCIENCE FICTION and GALAXY, and her work continues to reflect the bent of those magazines; typically her fiction stresses human values over technology. Smith's stories (which have never been collected) cover a wide range of subjects, including postholocaust Earth ("The Hardest Bargain," 1961), human contact with aliens ("Not Fit for Children," 1955), and future sociology ("A Day in the Suburbs," 1974), and they are written in a variety of styles, from the dark and ironic to the farcical. Her first science-fiction novel, *The Perfect Planet* (1962), comments on the contemporary health craze by setting the action on an alien planet that had once been a spa and whose inhabitants remain obsessed with the search for the "perfect" body. *Unpopular Planet* (1975) is an episodic novel about aliens who use humans for genetic experiments. The convoluted plot, with its intentional confusion between the imagined and the real, bears witness to the author's interest in puzzles of more than one kind.

OTHER WORK: *Valley of Shadows* (1968, as Delphine C. Lyons).

S.H.G.

SMITH, GEORGE H[ENRY] (1922–   ). American writer of popular fiction, including science fiction, who has written under a number of pseudonyms, including Jan Smith, George Hudson Smith, Jan Hudson, Jerry Jason, and M. J. Deer (usually in collaboration with his wife, M. Jane Deer). Smith's early career was marked by publication in the minor SF magazines and original anthologies and in paperbacks produced by small companies that catered to readers with little taste for anything but fast action and sex. The titles of his novels from this period reflect his readership: *Satan's Daughter* (1961), *Scourge of the Blood Cult* (1961), and *The Coming of the Rats* (1961).

However, in the mid-1960s Smith started mixing fantasy (usually based on Celtic mythology) with SF to produce some interesting variations on alternate-world stories. *Witch Queen of Lochlann* (1969), for example, uses a standard fantasy plot—the fight to restore the throne of the kingdom to its rightful owner—yet creates a self-consistent world that will fascinate readers for its simi-

encourage cooperation among different races and pushes new leaders to rise as high as they can. Lensmen are the highest representatives of all races that accept the values of Civilization. They are its law enforcers, chosen to wear the semiliving Lens that lets them develop telepathy and other mental powers. Human lensman Kimball Kinnison and nurse (later lensman) Clarissa MacDougall are the unknowing products of an eon-long process of selective breeding guided by the natives of Arisia, secret founders of Civilization. Eventually the superhuman children of Kim and Clarissa defeat Eddore, the power behind Boskone. In its scope and perception of the human values that mark a superman, the Lensman saga is one of the landmarks of pulp magazine SF.

Smith wrote a few short stories, and the only important ones were gathered into his novel *The Vortex Blaster* (1941–42/1960). His two novel series were his life's work, and he spent much of his later career preparing them for book publication. Their successful publication after World War II by semiprofessional SF publishers indirectly attracted the attention of major publishers to SF. His books continue to be popular in paperback, and additional fiction has been developed from his characters or series by Gordon EKLUND (the Lord Tedric series), William Ellern (the New Lensman series), Stephen Goldin (the Family d'Alembert series), and David Kyle ("The Lensman" series).

Critic and writer Richard LUPOFF has described Smith as the paradigm of the great "primitive" novelist, to be judged on the basis of vividness, dynamism, power, and directness. In these, Lupoff says, Smith was the absolute champion.

larities to and differences from our own.

Witch Queen of Lochlann is part of the alternate-world Annwn series, which features a Celticlike land in which magic substitutes for science. Several of the novels (*Druid's World*, 1967, as well as *Witch Queen*) have little more in common than setting. However, others (including *Kar Kaballa, King of the Gogs*, 1969; *The Second War of the Worlds*, 1976; and *The Island Snatchers*, 1978) share major characters who first save a nineteenth-century-like civilization from an invasion by its barbarian neighbors, then frustrate a Martian invasion, and finally save the civilization from a conspiracy of sorcerers. Although the novels do not pretend to be anything more than solid entertainment, they do admirably well in this respect, and their blend of SF detail and Celtic myth is particularly successful.

OTHER WORKS: *1976: Year of Terror* (1961); *Doomsday Wing* (1963); *The Unending Night* (1964); *The Forgotten Planet* (1965); *The Psycho Makers* (1965); *The Four Day Weekend* (1966).

S.H.G.

SMITH, GEORGE O[LIVER] (1911–1981). American science-fiction author, radio engineer, and ITT defense communication analyst whose stories usually deal with the wonders of technology. Smith is best remembered (in addition to marrying John W. CAMPBELL's first wife) for a series of short stories written between 1942 and 1973 concerning a manned communications satellite that shares the orbit of Venus around the Sun. Collected as *Venus Equilateral* (1947; enlarged, 1975; as *The Complete Venus Equilateral*, 1976), each story describes some technological or human breakdown that threatens the work of the station and the ingenious solution that one of the scientists finally uncovers. Unlike similar stories in Isaac ASIMOV's *I, Robot* (1950), however, Smith's tales have not aged well, because most of the technology they describe has been made obsolete by recent developments in actual communications satellites. However, the problems Smith described and the search for solutions still offer decent entertainment.

Smith also wrote a number of novels in imitation of the more successful space operas of E. E. "Doc" SMITH and the future histories of Robert A. HEINLEIN. Unhappily, these novels (including *Nomad*, 1950; *Operation Interstellar*, 1950; and *Hellflower*, 1953) lack the cosmic scope of Smith's Skylark and Gray Lensman series and the interesting minutiae of Heinlein's future worlds.

Of far greater interest is *The Fourth "R"* (1959; as *The Brain Machine*, 1968), the compelling story of a young boy whose parents have developed an electronic device that educates and matures the boy far beyond what can be expected of even the most precocious five-year-old. When the boy's parents are murdered, he decides to live independently, and the novel details his struggles to carry out his plans. *Highways in Hiding* (1956; abridged as *The Space Plague*, 1957), also deals with a version of the superman story, but here Smith added a strange plague and an alien invasion. The result is more or less a straight adventure story that lacks the depth of characterization found in *The Fourth "R"*.

OTHER WORKS: *Pattern for Conquest: An Interplanetary Adventure* (1949); *Troubled Star* (1957); *Fire in the Heavens* (1958); *The Path of Unreason* (1958); *Worlds of George O* (collection, 1982).

S.H.G.

——— SOCIAL SCIENCES ———

Science fiction traditionally has drawn on the physical sciences for its story ideas, but the genre has always had at least tenuous ties with the social sciences as well. Early fantastic voyages to the Moon, for instance, had such little basis in possibility that social comment was their only purpose, and the utopia, going back to the work of Thomas MORE, is more about political theory and social speculation than about the journey that customarily got the traveler to the utopian destination.

The scientific enlightenment of the nineteenth century, with its emphasis on experiment, changed the focus of early SF to the physical sciences in stories such as Jules VERNE's *voyages extraordinaires* and even H. G. WELLS's scientific romances (although by Wells's time the social impact of science and technology was beginning to loom larger than the marvels they were making possible). Wells, in a 1906 speech to the Sociological Society, recommended that sociology should adopt, as its "proper and distinctive method," the creation of utopias and their exhaustive criticism.

As early as 1849 Edgar Allen POE described a plausible future society in "Mellonta Tauta," and writers such as Rudyard KIPLING in "With the Night Mail" (1905) and "Easy as A.B.C." (1912) were dealing with the social impact of technology. Wells himself in a pair of matched stories ("A Story of the Stone Age" and "A Story of the Days to Come," both 1897) ventured into anthropology and sociology, as did Stanley WATERLOO with *The Story of Ab* (1897) and Jack LONDON with *Before Adam* (1907).

Even the 1920s and 1930s, dominated as they were by the technological orientation of Hugo GERNSBACK and his AMAZING STORIES and later *Wonder Stories* and the star-hopping space epics of E. E. SMITH, John W. CAMPBELL, Edmond HAMILTON, and Jack WILLIAMSON, had their share of social commentary in the satires of Stanton A. COBLENTZ, the evolutionary speculations of S. Fowler WRIGHT, and the psychological and sociological ideas of David H. KELLER, among others.

The PHYSICAL SCIENCES, however, continued to dominate the minds of SF writers and the magazines their stories were published in, and by the time the first post–

World War II anthologies began to appear in 1946, editor Groff Conklin still could complain in his introduction to *The Best of Science Fiction* about the paucity of stories dealing with the social sciences. Two years later, however, in his second anthology, he commented on their proliferation, and GALAXY MAGAZINE, founded two years after that, built its considerable reputation on stories that emphasized the social impact of science and technology. By 1964 the British NEW WAVE had placed the social sciences—or at least society—in opposition to the tyranny of the physical sciences, as if in answer to J. G. BALLARD's call for less emphasis on outer space and more on inner space.

Science fiction may have been slow in coming to the social sciences because archaeology, anthropology, and sociology were among the latest studies to develop as organized sciences, anthropology in the late eighteenth century and sociology in the early nineteenth. The nineteenth century, however, was marked by the burgeoning of the social sciences, spurred by a number of factors. Sociology, for example, got additional impetus from Karl Marx's emphasis on economic factors and Herbert Spencer's application of Darwinian principles, as well as the availability of important tools for sociological study, among them census questionnaires, statistical analysis, and the punch cards that developed into modern computers for data handling. Archaeology, which began with a Renaissance interest in Greek and Roman antiquities, received new urgency in the nineteenth century with the excavations of Heinrich Schliemann in Troy and the discovery of the Rosetta Stone.

Economics, founded as a field of study by Adam Smith in the eighteenth century, also developed into a major discipline in the late nineteenth century. Political science, which can be said to date back at least to Aristotle and Plato, emerged as a separate discipline at the end of the nineteenth century.

By the middle of the twentieth century, the social sciences were firmly established. Today's social scientists, with their careful measurements, record keeping, and statistical analyses, can make from fragments of bone, stone, and pottery not only extraordinary extrapolations but predictions about social behavior. Even history, which sometimes considers itself a humanity, has become systematized. And the applications of the social sciences in advertising, public relations, and political counseling, with their surveys and polls, seem to become more influential with each passing year.

All these developments merged in an effort to explain the riddles of contemporary society: the Depression and two World Wars after the belief of the late nineteenth and early twentieth centuries that humanity could look forward to the creation of a heaven on Earth. Writers of SF naturally turned to the social sciences for explanations as well as inspiration.

This orientation was not always the case, of course.

In 1947 John W. Campbell, editor of the technologically oriented *Astounding Science Fiction* (now ANALOG, but still technologically oriented), wrote in *Of Worlds Beyond*: "Prophetic extrapolation can derive from a number of different sources, and apply in a number of fields. Sociology, psychology and parapsychology are, today, not true sciences; therefore instead of forecasting future results of applications of sociological science of today, we must forecast the *development of a science* of sociology."

Five years later things had changed so dramatically that Isaac ASIMOV could write an entire article titled "Social Science Fiction," calling it "the only branch of science fiction that is sociologically significant." In that essay he divided the history of science fiction into four eras: primitive, adventure, social, and atomic. He placed social SF between 1938, when Campbell's editorial influence began making itself felt at *Astounding*, and 1945, when the first atomic bomb exploded. A bit later, however, Asimov divided modern SF into three periods: adventure-dominant, science-dominant, and sociology-dominant. And he dated the sociology-dominant period from 1950, when H. L. Gold founded *Galaxy*.

A number of stories based on the social sciences appeared in *Astounding*. Robert A. HEINLEIN's Future History stories, beginning with "Lifeline" in 1939, extrapolate as much from sociology as from the physical sciences, and "The Roads Must Roll" (1939), "Blowups Happen" (1940), "The Man Who Sold the Moon" (1949), and many others continued this tradition. "Solution Unsatisfactory" (1941) is primarily about the political impact of a nuclear weapon, and "Universe" (1941) concerns the sociology (and mythmaking characteristics) of passengers in a generation starship who have lost their real past.

The appeal of Asimov's own "Nightfall" (1941), with its entire planetary society adjusting to eternal daylight and falling prey every 2000 years to the coming of darkness and the stars, is primarily sociological; his Foundation stories illustrate Campbell's prescription by making a science (psychohistory) out of history, sociology, and prediction; even his robot stories display concern with individual and social attitudes toward robots. Judith MERRIL's "That Only a Mother" (1948) deals with the sociological and psychological impact of an epidemic of radiation-deformed babies. Eric Frank RUSSELL's story "And Then There Were None" (1951), about the defeat of a military invasion by a nonviolent society, was published, like many others, after the founding of *Galaxy* but in *Astounding*.

H.L. GOLD, the founding editor of *Galaxy*, was less interested in science and technological change, and more interested in people learning to live with the world science had created and was continually transforming. That preference led inevitably to stories inspired by the social sciences, such as Frederik POHL and Cyril M. KORN-

BLUTH's *The Space Merchants* (1952), about a world controlled by advertising agencies, and Alfred BESTER's *The Demolished Man* (1952), about the difficulty of getting away with murder in a telepathic society.

Fritz LEIBER's "Coming Attraction" (1950), with its evocative depiction of an American society guilt ridden because of its part in an atomic war, appeared in *Galaxy's* second issue, and Wyman Guin's story about a society that institutionalizes schizophrenia, "Beyond Bedlam" (1951), and Cyril M. Kornbluth's "The Marching Morons" (1951), with its depressing vision of a world run by an intellectual elite for a mentally deficient population, were only two among many "socially conscious" tales published in *Galaxy's* second year.

Notable novels of the 1950s that deal with the social sciences include Theodore STURGEON's *More Than Human* (1953), with its anthropological and psychological exploration of the gestalt superhuman; Isaac Asimov's *The Caves of Steel* (1953), about the evolutionary adaptation of people to overcrowded enclosures; Robert A. Heinlein's *Starship Troopers* (1959), with its Platonic dialogue about an ideal society, often overlooked by critics of its glorification of the military; and the beginning of Gordon R. DICKSON's *Childe* cycle (*Dorsai*, 1959), about the forced evolution of the human species.

Through the 1960s and 1970s SF leaned increasingly toward the social sciences, and even stories and novels developing out of the physical sciences during that period contain significant speculations about social impact. James GUNN's *The Immortals* (1962), for instance, describes the society that would develop out of the discovery that immortality is available. Heinlein's work had always included a significant amount of social commentary, but the publication of *Stranger in a Strange Land* (1961) made his turn in the social direction virtually total.

Overpopulation and its social background and consequences are the subject of a number of 1960s novels, including Lester DEL REY's *The Eleventh Commandment* (1962), Harry HARRISON's *Make Room! Make Room* (1965; adapted on the screen as *Soylent Green*, 1973), and John BRUNNER's *Stand on Zanzibar* (1968). Brunner's social concerns also produced *The Jagged Orbit* (1969), about race (as was Wilson TUCKER's *The Year of the Quiet Sun*, 1970); *The Sheep Look Up* (1972), about pollution; and *The Shockwave Rider* (1975), about future shock. Ecology is part of the appeal of Frank HERBERT's *Dune* (1965), as is the message of the political dangers of the messiah. Norman SPINRAD's *Bug Jack Barron* (1969) attacks social and political corruption through the medium of a television show's host. Fritz Leiber's *A Specter Is Haunting Texas* (1969) satirizes racism, war, and morality.

The point of Walter M. MILLER, Jr.'s *A Canticle for Leibowitz* (1960) is more social than religious, just as Joe HALDEMAN's *The Forever War* (1974) is more about the society created by an interstellar conflict than about the fighting itself. D. G. COMPTON dealt with the problems of new knowledge in *The Steel Crocodile* (1970), and with the personal implications of a society in which people in pain are paid to allow their suffering to be televised continuously in *The Unsleeping Eye* (1974). Feminism has been a major subject of SF since Ursula K. LE GUIN's *The Left Hand of Darkness* (1969), which also draws heavily on anthropology. Significant contributions have been made by Joanna RUSS, especially with her story "When It Changed" (1972) and her unusual novel *The Female Man* (1975), as well as by Vonda N. MCINTYRE in several works, particularly *Dreamsnake* (1979), and James TIPTREE, Jr. (the pseudonym of Alice Sheldon) in a series of short stories beginning with "The Woman Men Don't See" (1973).

Anthologies, too, reflect the influence of the social sciences. A number of them have been devoted to female writers and issues, including several volumes of Pamela SARGENT's *Women of Wonder* (first volume in 1975) and Vonda N. McIntyre and Susan Janice Anderson's *Aurora: Beyond Equality* (1976). Ecology is the subject of another anthology, *Survival Printout* (1973), which bills itself as having been edited by Total Effect. Frederik Pohl brought together various unhappy visions of the future in *Nightmare Age* (1970). And "social science fiction" itself is the subject of Willis E. McNelly and Leon E. STOVER's *Above the Human Landscape* (1972).

Pohl's own social commentary developed into the portrayal of desperate worlds in his novels *Gateway* (1977) and *JEM* (1979). The social criticism that shaped J. G. Ballard's early catastrophe novels came to a focus in his *The Atrocity Exhibition* (1970). Samuel R. DELANY's social vision, explored in confusing detail in *Dhalgren* (1975), went in other directions in *Triton* (1976) and his later SF and fantasy novels.

Le Guin's significantly anthropological *The Left Hand of Darkness* prepared the way for Michael BISHOP's novels, also anthropological, particularly *No Enemy But Time* (1982). Gregory BENFORD's *Timescape* (1980) describes the sociology of science while it deals with a polluted world trying to communicate with scientists in the past. The CYBERPUNK movement, launched in 1984 with William GIBSON's *Neuromancer*, gets much of its flavor from the gritty underworld of high technology, through which its computer jockeys and social outcasts drift until they are moved into action.

In return for drawing much of its recent inspiration from the social sciences, SF has been making its way into social science studies and classrooms. Sometimes science fiction is used as a tool to help social science students and researchers break free from preconceptions generated by their own cultures and by the studies of other, earlier observers. Science-fiction books such as C. J. CHERRYH's The Faded Sun trilogy, have become texts in anthropology and sociology departments. Alternate-history stories, such as Ward MOORE's *Bring the Jubilee* (1973) and Philip D. DICK's *The Man in the High Castle* (1962), have been used as ways to teach history. And anthologies, carrying the generic title of —— —— *Through Science Fiction*, have been developed to teach all the social and behavioral sciences, as well as philosophy and religion.

Some anthropologists have said that they chose their field because it was the closest thing they could find to SF, and at least one SF writer, Chad OLIVER, became a professor of anthropology (at the University of Texas). Perhaps the recent symbiotic relationship between SF and the social sciences will result in new developments in both fields.

J.E.G.

SOCIETY

Social change is one of the basic themes of science fiction. The idea that nations might, by judicious legislation and wise government, improve the lot of their citizens is an old one, but it was not until the eighteenth century that people became ambitiously optimistic about such prospects. Notions of the possible scope of political reforms became bolder as the development of new technologies promised more abundant wealth. Sketches for ideal societies had long been commonplace, but not until the late 1700s did these utopian images become, in Frank Manuel's terminology, *euchronian* (set, not in some exotic locale, but in the future), looking forward to a day when such states would be brought into being by political planning and action. The call for liberty, equality, and fraternity was handed on from Saint-Simonian *industriels* to Marxian socialists, although its principles were somewhat tarnished after both 1789 and 1917.

The progressive euchronians kept the upper hand until the beginnings of popular speculative fiction in the work of Jules VERNE (*The Begum's Fortune*) and H. G. WELLS (from *A Modern Utopia* to *The Shape of Things to Come*), but things had already begun to change. As technologies grew increasingly powerful, their destructive potentials became more obvious (as demonstrated in two World Wars), and cynicism regarding the goodwill and intelligence of political leaders took deep root.

Although the number of Western SF writers who subscribe to Karl Marx's analysis of the capitalist system can be counted on the fingers of one hand, the idea of future history as class struggle is remarkably commonplace. A great deal of futuristic SF concerns the attempts of heroic freedom fighters to liberate society from the domination of cunning elites. We can see this theme in the work of GOLDEN AGE writers such as A. E. VAN VOGT and Robert A. HEINLEIN, and it became formulistic in the 1950s, when such key examples as Frederik POHL and Cyril M.

KORNBLUTH's *The Space Merchants*, Ray BRADBURY's *Fahrenheit 451*, Kurt VONNEGUT, Jr.'s *Player Piano*, and James E. GUNN's *The Joy Makers* were written. The last two of these novels embrace the further cynicism (first expressed in Aldous HUXLEY's *Brave New World*) that it would make little difference if the ruling elite were benevolently inclined. The iron fist of malice featured so prominently in George ORWELL's *Nineteen Eighty-four* was merely an optional extra.

The prominence of images of awful societies in SF is partly ameliorated by the fact that alien societies are often credited with the ability to achieve a harmony that humans are psychologically ill equipped to enjoy. The recent upsurge of feminist SF has also made commonplace the suggestion that humans could achieve harmony too if only none of them was male. These exceptions might, however, be considered amplifications of the general pessimism about the possibility of humans as they are actually managing to order their political affairs justly and wisely. Even in the hard SF that preserves faith in the rewards of progress, good societies tend to be established—usually not without difficulty—somewhere other than Earth, which is often considered irredeemably spoiled.

On the one hand, it might be apologetically suggested that this cynicism can be explained partly by the facts that bad news is inherently more melodramatic and has much more potential as popular fiction, and that strident warnings against the possibility of disaster may be necessary to avoid it. On the other hand, this cynicism could be symptomatic of a widespread (and justified) loss of faith in those political engines that supposedly serve the ends of freedom and justice.

B.S.

SOHL, JERRY [GERALD ALLEN] (1913–). American writer of short fiction, novels, teleplays, and screenplays; newspaper reporter; and concert pianist. After thirteen years as a reporter and editor for the *Bloomington* (Illinois) *Daily Pantagraph*, during which he wrote most of his science fiction, Sohl became a full-time free-lance writer in 1958, moving into film and television writing as well as mainstream novels, one of which, *The Lemon Eaters* (1967), became a best-seller.

Sohl's SF is an example of work written and published outside the SF community; it takes traditional SF ideas—such as Charles FORT's "we are property" concept popularized by Eric Frank RUSSELL, L. Ron HUBBARD, and others, develops the human-interest appeal at the expense of the ideas and resolutions, and sells to a more general audience. In *The Transcendent Man* (1953), for instance, superior aliens feed off the emotions of troubled humans. Sohl's skillful writing and nongenre approach made popular successes of such novels as *The Haploids* (1952), *Costigan's Needle* (1953), *The Al-*

tered *Ego* (1954), and *Point Ultimate* (1955) without contributing new ideas or techniques to the field. He adapted his later novel *Night Slaves* (1965) for a television movie.

OTHER WORKS: *The Mars Monopoly* (1956); *The Time Dissolver* (1957); *The Odious Ones* (1959); *One against Herculum* (1959); *The Anomaly* (1971); *I, Aleppo* (1976); *Death Sleep* (1983).

H.L.P.

SOLARIS (1972).   *Directed by Andrei Tarkovsky; screenplay by Andrei Tarkovsky and Friedrich Gorenstein; adapted from the novel by Stanislaw Lem; photographed by Vadim Yusov; music by Eduard Artemyev and J. S. Bach. With Donatas Banionis, Natalya Bondarchuk, Yuri Yarvet, Anatoli Solonitsin, Vladislav Dvorjetski, Nikolai Grinko, Sos Sarkissian. 132 minutes. Color.*
STALKER (1981).   *Directed by Andrei Tarkovsky; screenplay by Arkady and Boris Strugatsky; adapted from the novella* Roadside Picnic *by Arkady and Boris Strugatsky; photographed by Alexander Knyazhinsky; music by Eduard Artemyev. With Aleksandr Kaidanovsky, Anatoli Solonitsin, Nikolai Grinko, Alisa Freindlikh. 160 minutes. Color and black and white.*

Solaris, Andrei Tarkovsky's first science-fiction film, was loosely adapted from Stanislaw LEM's novel of the same name; although Lem has voiced his disapproval of the film, it deserves to be considered on its own terms. On the surface *Solaris* is the story of the struggles of a group of scientists to understand and make contact with an alien ocean, which seems to possess powers of intelligence. Chris Kelvin arrives at the Solaris station, in another solar system, to find out why only three people survived out of an original crew of eighty-five. As he explores the station, he is confronted by his dead wife, Hari. He tries to destroy her, but the alien ocean conjures up another, and gradually Kelvin begins to love her, as she begins to understand what she is.

In an effort to communicate with the ocean more effectively, Kelvin beams his own thoughts into the water. The ocean responds by creating a series of burgeoning islands. Kelvin begins to see his relationship with the new Hari as not a replay of the past but a genuine second chance.

The film captures Lem's central creation—the dreaming ocean, which may or may not be sentient but provides for the inner needs of the visitors from Earth as if it were striving to communicate. One of the most beautiful and stylish films ever made, with a unique approach to color, it belongs in the company of 2001: A SPACE ODYSSEY (1968), THINGS TO COME (1936), and METROPOLIS (1926). Unfortunately, the full 245-minute print is rarely shown by Mosfilm's distributors; the English subtitles incompletely render the Russian dialogue, and the En-glish-language version is badly dubbed.

Stalker explores the same themes—guilt, memory, communication—in the same stylish and uncompromising way. The film's main characters, Writer, Professor, and Stalker, seek to penetrate a hidden zone where artifacts, supposedly left behind by alien visitors, are said to provide wonders; as in the novel, penetration of the Zone builds to a terrible yearning for knowledge. Among the Zone's miracles is a room where all desires can be satisfied, but none of the three can enter—Writer and Professor because they are frauds in their professions, and Stalker because he has no dreams. Tarkovsky suggests that a newer generation, one not yet demoralized by lack of faith and the loss of personal ethics, may yet come to understand the alien world.

Stalker was shot in monochrome for scenes outside the Zone, and in color inside. Stark sequences of great visual beauty reveal Tarkovsky as a poet of the camera with a unique vision. As one Soviet critic wrote, "What Tarkovsky can do, no one else can do at all."

Difficult as both these movies may be for some viewers, they challenge our notions of how films should be made and judged. In their bold dramatization of ideas, both are true works of SF cinema.

G.Z.

SOMEWHERE IN TIME (1980).   *Directed by Jeannot Szwarc; screenplay by Richard Matheson; adapted from the novel* Bid Time Return *by Richard Matheson; photographed by Isidore Mankofsky; music by John Barry. With Christopher Reeve, Christopher Plummer, Jane Seymour, Teresa Wright, Bill Erwin, George Voskovec, Susan French, John Alvin, Eddra Gale, Susan Bugg. 104 minutes. Color.*

Richard MATHESON, who wrote the romantic screenplay for *Somewhere in Time* from his own novel, appears in one hotel room scene. Christopher Reeve, an unhappy modern playwright, falls in love with a woman in a seventy-year-old photograph (Jane Seymour) and wills himself back to her time by using artifacts of the period. Authors have used many excuses for visiting the past, and love is as strong a motive as any. But even love doesn't last, and although its scenery is beautiful (the film was shot on picture-postcard Mackinac Island) its science-fiction motif is peripheral and the characterization superficial.

H.L.P.

SON OF FRANKENSTEIN: SEE FRANKENSTEIN ON FILM

SON OF KONG: SEE KING KONG

—————— SOVIET UNION ——————

Soviet science fiction is based on a solid national tradition, but because of the comparatively slow development of science and technology in prerevolutionary Russia, that tradition was not as rich as in the English- or French-speaking countries.

Science fiction in Russia started with an eighteenth-century utopia, *Voyage to the Land Ophir*, written in 1773–74 by Prince Mikhail Shcherbatov (1733–1790) but not published until a century later (1894). The first Russian interplanetary novel, *The Newest Voyage* (1784) by Vassily Lyovshin (1746–1826), places an ideal state on the Moon in the distant future. Technical previsions in the unfinished fragments of *The Year 4338. Petersburg Letters* (1840) suggests that its author, aristocrat and prolific man of letters Vladimir Odoyevsky (1803–1869), might have been the Russian Jules VERNE. The first socialist utopia was contained in the fourth dream of Vera Pavlovna in *What to Do?* (1863) by Nikolai Tchernyshevsky (1828–1889), the famous philosopher and revolutionary, who wrote this novel in prison.

Dystopias also appeared in nineteenth-century Russian literature, in the satiric fantasies of Nikolai Gogol (1809–1852) and *The Tale of a City* (1869–70) by Mikhail Saltykov-Shchedrin (1826–1889), a classic dystopia in embryo. But Fyodor Dostoevsky (1821–1881) was the real founder of the Russian dystopia with *Notes from the Underground* (1864) and *Demons* (1871–72).

Technical progress came to czarist Russia at the turn of the century with the discoveries of chemist Dmitri Mendeleyev (1834–1907), physiologist Ivan Pavlov (1849–1936), and the Russian father of astronautics, Konstantin Tsiolkovsky (1857–1935), and Russian SF fell in love with "marvelous inventions." Tsiolkovsky himself wrote novels such as *On the Moon* (1887), *Dreams of Earth and Sky* (1895), and *Out of Earth* (1918–1920) as a way to disseminate his prophetic ideas.

The influence of impending social change can be detected in early-twentieth-century Russian SF. Mainstream writer Alexander Kuprin (1870–1938) praised the future revolution in "The Toast" (1906) but feared it in "King's Park" (1911). He also wrote *The Liquid Sun* (1912) about a mad scientist. In "Earth" (1907), "The Republic of the Southern Cross" (1907), and "The Last Martyrs" (1907), the prominent poet Valery Brussov (1873–1924) predicted giant, domed, computerized cities, ecological catastrophe, and a totalitarian state. Alexander Bogdanov (1873–1928) also dealt with future revolution in his Martian novel *The Red Star (1908) and its sequel Engineer Menni* (1913).

Although critics consider *The Red Star* the first authentic Soviet SF book, the first such work published after 1917 was the utopia *Gonguri Land* (1922) by Vivian Itin. It went relatively unnoticed, however, because of its appearance in the provinces and the success of the

serialization the same year of *Aelita* by Alexei Tolstoy (1883–1945), an interplanetary romance (inspired, no doubt, by Edgar Rice BURROUGHS) about a Russian engineer and a Martian princess involved in a Marxist revolution. That novel became a symbol of early Soviet SF. Tolstoy also wrote *The Engineer Garin's Hyperboloid* (1925–26), in whose dictatorial mad scientist Hitler may be discerned.

Subjects popular with Soviet SF writers immediately after the Revolution were the hollow Earth in *Plutonia* (1926) by academician Vladimir Obrutchev (1863–1956); the imaginary lands of fantasy in the novels of Alexander Grin (1880–1932), a favorite of Soviet youth; and technical curiosities such as the laser in the work of Tolstoy and atomic weapons in *Thousand Years Hence* (1927) by Vadim Nikolsky (1886–1941).

Alexander Belyaev (1884–1942), however, the writer of more than sixty books, is considered the founding father of Soviet SF in the Vernean tradition. Perhaps because of his life as a bedridden invalid, his work focuses on heroes with fantastic abilities and attributes: shark's gills in *The Amphibian* (1928), levitation in *Ariel* (1941), extrasensory perception in *The World Master* (1928), and survival after death in *Professor Dowell's Head* (1934). He also dealt with life on a human-made satellite in *The KET Star* (1936).

Mikhail Bulgakov (1891–1940), who occupies a special place in early Soviet fantastic literature, wrote satiric short stories and novellas but also a complex philosophical novel, *The Master and Margarita* (not published until 1966), about Satan's visit to Moscow.

During the late 1930s and 1940s Soviet SF faded under the pressures of the bloody war, the hardships of the postwar years, and the inward evolution of the genre. Some SF was published in the 1940s and early 1950s—called by critics the period of "nearsighted SF"—but the range of possible subjects was sharply narrowed. Work by Viktor Saparin (1905–1970), Georgy Gurevich (1917–   ), and Alexander Kazantsev (1906–   ), the last two still active, appeared in this period, but Soviet SF seemed to be reborn with the publication in 1957, virtually coinciding with the orbiting of the first human-made satellite, of *The Andromeda Nebula* by Ivan Yefremov (1907–1972). This full-scale communist utopia, with its philosophical concept of a "Great Ring" of intelligent civilizations in space, not only made the author a leader of Soviet SF and launched a decade that has been called the Golden Age of Soviet SF but also was an inspiration to scores of gifted young authors. Yefremov's other works—*The Heart of the Snake* (1959), *The Razor's Edge* (1963), and the historical fantasy *Thais of Athens* (1972)—also were influential, although none of his successors inherited his style, ideas, or subjects.

The success of *The Andromeda Nebula* led to the decision of a few central publishing houses (and a number of popular science magazines for young readers) to launch SF programs. It also encouraged the development of scholars and critics such as Evgeny Brandis (1916–1985), Vladimir Dmitrevsky (1908–), Kyrill Andreyev (1906–1968), and Julius Kagarlitsky (1926–) and the creation of programs for translating foreign SF work.

Today the most popular Soviet SF writers, abroad as well as at home are Arkady (1925–) and Boris STRU-GATSKY (1933–) whose first work appeared in 1957. Up to 1986 they had published twenty books, and many of these have been translated into other languages. Their early novels, beginning with *The Land of the Purple Clouds* (1959), deal with traditional interplanetary SF, and many of their later novels belong to the world of "noon, the XXIInd century" and are linked by a common protagonist, spaceman Leonid Gorbovsky. One of their main themes became interference in the course of history, starting with *Escape Attempt* (1962) and continuing through their most recent novel, *Waves Dampen Wind* (magazine serialization 1985–86). Their most popular title is *Hard to Be a God* (1964). Two of their novels, the SF mystery *At the Lost Climber's Hotel* (1970) and *Roadside Picnic* (1972) have been filmed, the latter as STALKER (1981). But the Strugatsky brothers are not the only modern Soviet SF authors, as readers in English-speaking countries have discovered in Macmillan's Best Soviet SF series.

The Golden Age of Soviet SF has been dominated by hard-core SF. Anatoly Dneprov (1919–1975), author of the collections *The World I've Vanished In* (1962), *The Purple Mummy* (1965), and *The Immortality Formula* (1963), has concerned himself with "marvelous inventions," particularly cybernetics and biology. Mikhail Yemtsev (1930–) and Yeremei Parnov (1935–) have collaborated on considerations of the intrusion of the scientific into the social sphere in *Dirac Sea* (1967) and *World Soul* (1964), and fascism in the time travel fantasy *Shreds of Darkness on the Needle of Time* (1970). Their short novel *Bring Back Love!* (1966) predicts the neutron bomb. Sever Gansovsky (1918–), in *Vincent Van Gogh* (1971), wrote a humanistic novel about an artist trapped in time, as well as two classic SF stories, "The Test Yard" and "The Day of Wrath," both filmed recently. And Igor Rosokhovatsky (1929–) became famous for a cycle of books about cyborgs who slide effortlessly into the future world.

Henrikh Altov (1926–) has specialized in paradoxical "mad idea" stories, collected in *The Scorching Mind* (1968) and *Created for Thunder* (1970), as has Vladimir Savchenko (1933–), in novels such as *Self Discovery* (1967). Altov is also known for short stories based on mythology, such as those collected in *Legends of Star Captains* (1962), and Savchenko has produced questioning experimental work in *Cul-de-sac* (1972), and *A Test by the Truth* (1973), as well as the traditional utopia *Over the Turn* (1984).

Dmitry Bilenkin (1933–), one of the leading Soviet

SF writers, has specialized in the laconic intellectual short story brimming with information, such as those appearing in his seven collections, which include *The Surf of Mars* (1967), *Face in the Crowd* (1986), and *Powerful's Power* (1986). He also has produced a successful trilogy as well as a novel on timequakes, *The Life Desert* (1984).

Nevertheless, Soviet SF is not so easily divided into hard and soft; it went through a period of rapture with technocratism, but the humanistic response of other Soviet writers in the 1960s was not as stormy as that in America and Britain to the NEW WAVE.

Mainstream author Gennady Gor (1907–1981) combined humanistic SF with literary fantastic tales. He is known for his profound novels and collections dealing with the mysteries of external and internal space-time, including *Kumbi* (1963), *The Clay Papuan* (1966), and *The Statue* (1972). Olga Larionova (1935–) dealt with the problem of knowing the date of one's death in her first novel, *Leopard from the Kilimanjaro Mountain* (1965), and more recently she has successfully combined Campbellian SF with soft SF in the collection *The Zodiac Signs* (1983) and the novel *Sonata of the Sea* (1985).

Vladimir Mikhailov (1929–) demonstrated a mastery of the grand philosophical novel in such works as *The Other Side Door* (1985), *Keeper to My Brother* (1976), and its sequel, *Let's Come and See* (1983). Kir Bulychev (1934–) has enjoyed widespread popularity since such early works as *The Gusliar Wonders* (1972), *Men Like Men* (1975), and the antinuclear *The Final War* (1970). He also has written a series of humorous folkloristic tales about the citizens of the town Great Gusliar and a series of juveniles about a girl from the twenty-first century. One of the Soviet Union's most published SF authors, he writes outside the genre and is engaged in the cinema as well.

Viktor Kolupayev (1936–), who has been called the Soviet Ray Bradbury, has developed slowly. His early works, the collections *Can Such a Thing Happen!* (1972) and *Ticket to Childhood* (1977), mix hard SF, fantasy, and poetry. His latest books, *The Singing Forest* (1984) and *The Seventh Variety* (1985), have broken no new ground.

Adventure SF is represented by Alexander (1900–1985) and Sergei (1944–) Abramov; Georgy Martynov (1906–1983); Alexander Kazantsev; Evgeny Voiskunsky (1922–) and Isai Lukodyanov (1913–1984), authors of the "encyclopedic" novel *The Crew of the "Mekong"* (1961) and its sequel, *Ur, son of Sham* (1964); and Pavel Bagryak (a collective pen name for a group of writers). The veteran writer Sergei Snegov (1910–) has created Soviet philosophical space opera on a Stapledonian scale in his trilogy *Men Like Gods* (omnibus edition 1982), named after H. G. WELL's utopian novel.

The Soviet Golden Age has developed satirists in Zinovy Yuryev (1925–   ) and Ilya Varshavsky (1909–1974), whose acknowledged mastery of the short story is evident in his dystopian collection *The Sun Sets in Donomaga* (1966).

The transition from the 1970s to the 1980s has seen a change of generations as well. The old guard (Kazantsev, Gurevich, Snegov) and most of the 1960s generation are still at work, but the voice of the new generation sounds increasingly confident. Among them are the idea writer Pavel Amnuel (1944–   ), whose first collection *Now, Tomorrow and Forever* (1984) and novel *Explosion* (1986) have been praised by readers and critics; skilled adventure writers Alexander Shcherbakov (1932–   ) with *Shift* (1982) and Gennady Prashkevich (1941–   ) with *The Stolen Marvel* (1978); ironic, good-natured Sergei Drugal (1927–   ) with his collection *The Tiger Will Go to the Garage with You* (1984); and Sergei Pavlov (1935–   ) with his interplanetary hard science fiction novel *The Lunar Rainbow* (1978) and its sequel (1984).

This generation, still feeling its way, may soon have to compete with even younger authors, products of the "Soviet Clarion" Workshop that started in 1981. (It is known as the Maleevsky Workshop because of its first three meetings at the Writers' House in Maleevka, near Moscow.)

The decade since the late 1970s has been marked by three new factors: the founding of the Soviet SF award Aelita, which has been conferred on the Strugatskys, Kazantsev, Yuryev, juvenile writer V. Krapivin, Snegov, and Pavlov; a significant increase in critical and academic activity reflected in books by Vsevolod Revich, Yeremei Parnov, Vitaly Brugov, Tatyana Tchernyshova, Vladimir Gakov, and scores of Ph.D.'s in various universities; and attempts at SF by mainstream authors of note, such as Chinghiz Aitmatov, Leonid Leonov, Vladimir Orlov, and Yevgeny Yevtushenko. Their efforts have not always been successful, but the lively discussions that ensue from them can only increase interest in the genre.

V.G.

SOYLENT GREEN (1973).

Directed by Richard Fleischer; screenplay by Stanley R. Greenberg; adapted from the novel Make Room! Make Room! *by Harry Harrison; photographed by Richard H. Kline; music by Fred Myrow. With Charlton Heston, Leigh Taylor-Young, Edward G. Robinson, Chuck Connors, Joseph Cotten, Brock Peters. 97 minutes. Color.*

In the year 2022 New York City is plagued by overpopulation, pollution, unemployment, and food shortages. While investigating the murder of a prominent citizen, a police detective discovers that human corpses supply the protein base of the synthetic food manufactured by the Soylent Company to feed the masses.

Although the film's plot varies from that of Harry HARRISON's novel, and its resolution retreats into irrational horror, both the film and the novel warn that humanity must change its present irresponsible ecological practices or suffer the consequences.

The subtle technique of emphasizing the background rather than the action is employed to establish the verity of this grim futuristic vision. Edward G. Robinson's acclaimed performance as an old man who remembers life in a world of plenty was his last film role. *Soylent Green* received a Nebula Award for best film.

M.T.W.

THE SPACE CHILDREN (1958).

Directed by Jack Arnold; screenplay by Bernard C. Schoenfeld; photographed by Ernest Laszlo; music by (Nathan) Van Cleave. With Michel Ray, Adam Williams, Johnny Crawford, Peggy Webber, Jackie Coogan, Sandy Descher, Richard Shannon, John Washbrook, Russell Johnson, Raymond Bailey. 69 minutes. Black and white.

The Space Children was the last overt science-fiction film of director Jack ARNOLD; though directed at children, it is serious and well intentioned, but by centering the story on children as well, it is necessarily too gentle, unable to create a sense of menace.

An amorphous alien dominates the children of missile base workers, giving them temporary powers that stop the launching of a deadly new missile. The alien returns to space at the end of the film.

Both Arnold and producer William Alland have indicated that they think this is one of the best films they made together, but opinions today are divided between some who consider it dull, pretentious, and didactic, and others who find it a superior example of low-budget SF.

B.W.

SPACE: 1999 (1975–1977).

Directed by Ray Austin and others; written by Christopher Penfold and others; special effects by Brian Johnson. With Martin Landau, Barbara Bain, Barry Morse, Catherine Schell, Tony Anholt, Nick Tate. 47 60-minute episodes. Color.

This syndicated British television series, apparently an attempt to capitalize on the success in syndication of STAR TREK, was handicapped by implausible, even ridiculous plots and poor science, beginning with its premise that the moon, with all the characters aboard, is blasted off on an interstellar journey by the explosion of a nuclear dump on its far side. The series relied heavily on miniatures and video tricks. Spin-off novelizations were written by E. C. TUBB and others.

J.C.

Elliot Dold's illustration for E. E. Smith's space-operatic "Gray Lensman" (*Astounding,* November 1939)

——————— SPACE OPERA ———————

The term *space opera* comes by analogy from *soap opera*, a phrase for the early radio serials sponsored by soap manufacturers. Though perhaps sometimes disparaging, it is now more commonly accepted as a legitimate label for the upbeat space adventure narrative that has been the mainspring of modern science fiction.

Seen in this way, space opera can be considered the expression of a mythic theme of human expansion against an unknown and commonly hostile frontier, a theme which shows striking parallels to the legend of the American west celebrated in shelves of western fiction and the endless reels of western film often fondly called horse opera. Both forms, in turn, reflect elements of those early sagas, *chansons de geste*, and epics that immortalize the heroic origins of a people or a nation.

The kinship is apparent even in ways of composition. The folk epic began as the oral record of the exploits of a folk hero; its metric patterns were an aid to memory. Early American SF, like the early western novel, was usually written for publication in a pulp magazine, a vehicle nearly as ephemeral as oral recitation; the writer was often more intent on earning a quick penny or so a word than on attaining literary permanence.

All three forms espouse the same sharply simplistic values of good and evil. The best of them embody grand themes. Drawn larger than reality, the protagonist fights for causes and traditions greater than himself. Defending innocence and right, he displays raw courage, native ingenuity, and sometimes supernormal powers. Ambitious missions carry him to the frontiers of his world,

and often beyond. His victories are victories for a great family or a proud race or all humankind; his death is a noble sacrifice. In space opera the hero's mastery of imagined future science and engineering may replace the superhuman powers of earlier protagonists, as the superscience of his alien enemies replaces the sinister magic of epic evil, but the parallels are clear. Space opera, in fact, might be defined as the epic of a technological age.

In the short history of American SF, the themes of space opera are prefigured in the early pulp fiction of Edgar Rice BURROUGHS. Tarzan, raised by apes in a mythical Africa, is the typical epic hero. Although John Carter reaches Mars by simply wishing for it, he does cross space. Burroughs's prose may be unpolished and his science invented on the instant, but his tales still hold their mythic appeal.

Ray CUMMINGS was another forerunner, with his interstellar adventure *Terrano the Conqueror*, published in 1925. His influence was slight, however, because he found travel in the other direction, into microscopic worlds, far more popular. He returned repeatedly to the adventures of the very small, which he first explored in "The Girl in the Golden Atom" (1919/1921), and he never outgrew the rigid formulas of his first pulp fiction.

Edmond HAMILTON pushed the frontiers farther toward the stars, beginning in 1926 with "Across Space," a serial in the old pulp *Weird Tales*. Hammering out quick first drafts, he was no more a stylist than Burroughs, but he knew more science and possessed a farther-ranging imagination. In such tales of the Interstellar Patrol as "Crashing Suns" (1928/1965) heroic humans fight beside the soldiers of far-flung star systems to defend their united worlds from cosmic disaster and alien invasion. Hamilton continued to produce space opera throughout his long career, sometimes for the comics, writing with greater care and skill after his marriage to Leigh BRACKETT.

Olaf STAPLEDON, whom Hamilton greatly admired, was a British writer and philosopher who looked even farther across cosmic space and future time. In *Last and First Men* (1930) he imagined the evolution of humankind over the next 2 billion years, reporting the rise and fall of eighteen successive human races. In *Star Maker* (1937) he reduced even that great scope to a minor incident in his vision of the total and finally living cosmos.

It was E. E. ("Doc") SMITH, a doughnut-mix specialist with a Ph.D. in food chemistry until he invented his own brand of space opera, who created a more enthusiastic audience for the subgenre. His first novel, *The Skylark of Space*, was written in the years 1915 to 1919 with a collaborator, Lee Hawkins Garby, called in to do the love scenes. Rejected until 1928, when Hugo GERNSBACK bought it for *Amazing Stories*, the novel was instantly successful upon publication.

Space opera reached one of its purest expressions in

Smith's later Lensman series, which began with *Galactic Patrol*, serialized in *Astounding Science Fiction* (1937–38). Planned as a single enormous novel, the series records an archetypal epic conflict between good and evil, waged across a setting of vastness. The goodness and evil are embodied in two warring races, the Arisians and the Eddorians. The Lesmen are a family of future human beings chosen by the (good) Arisians to become the champions of civilization. They possess extraordinary powers through the lenses they wear, superscientific amulets made by the Arisians.

Always popular, Smith's work has been frequently reprinted and supplemented with additions from Stephen Goldin and others. The mythic theme he expressed— the optimistic assumption of future human expansion across the galaxy—has survived to inspire a vast body of more recent SF.

Jack WILLIAMSON was one early admirer who followed Smith's *Skylark* into space. The hero of his early first-draft effort, "The Stone from the Green Star" (1931), was Richard Smith, named for Doc and Doc's hero. With better models for *The Legion of Space* (1934) and its sequels, he drew upon Shakespeare's Falstaff for his old soldier of space, Giles Habibula, once said to have been the most popular character in *Astounding* during the 1930s. The motifs of space opera continue to appear in much of his later work, and he has never disowned the label.

Another follower, finally far more influential, was John W. CAMPBELL. Barely out of his teens, Campbell began his long and immensely productive career as Smith's chief rival, both men grinding out a very primitive sort of space opera, each striving to outdo the other in the invention of ever-larger and ever-faster battlecraft of space, armed with always farther-out superscientific weapons. Rapidly maturing in style and imagination, as Smith never did, Campbell was soon writing much better fiction under the pseudonym Don A. Stuart.

Turning editor in 1937, Campbell held the helm at *Astounding*/ANALOG until his death in 1971. Faithful to the myth of a magnificent human future in space, he made it the cardinal axiom of the magazine, using it to gather and inspire a team of gifted contributors. Writers able to refine and elaborate the myth with increasing skill and greater care for some sense of human reality, they were responsible for the famous Golden Age of SF. Although their work varied greatly, most of it held true to Campbell's optimistic credo.

Robert A. HEINLEIN became the most notable of those gifted recruits. Much of his fiction can be classified as space opera, most notably the dozen juvenile novels he wrote for Scribner's. Beginning with three boys building a backyard rocket in *Rocketship Galileo* (1947), the novels follow humankind's expansion from Earth into space all the way to the acceptance of humankind as probationary citizens of the Three Galaxies in *Have Space Suit—Will Travel* (1958).

Although familiarity soon began to dim its first aura of wondrous discovery, the hopeful legend of humanity's expansion into space has survived to underlie a vast body of modern SF. Arthur C. CLARKE's *Childhood's End* (1953) can be read as a parable of humanity's evolution into space; another of his novels, *The City and the Stars* (1956), shows our race surviving through the next billion years, until the Earth itself is almost dead. James Blish invented sophisticated variations with his Okies of space in *Cities in Flight* (1970; the first novel in the series was *Earthman, Come Home*, 1955) and his genetic modification of humankind for life on new worlds in *The Seedling Stars* (1957). A. E. VAN VOGT married space opera and general semantics in *The World of Null A* (1945/1948).

Leigh Brackett began her unusual career in such pulps as *Planet Stories*, a magazine devoted to space opera, and kept writing in the subgenre with increasing mastery all her life, culminating in her script for the STAR WARS film *The Empire Strikes Back* (1980). She drew heavily too on the kindred myth of the American west for her screenplays for Howard Hawks.

Gordon R. DICKSON has clearly found his driving inspiration in space opera, planning his ambitious Childe Cycle as an epic of humanity's rapid evolution into a superhuman race as it expands across the stars. Although the human space travelers in C. J. CHERRYH's well-imagined interstellar society encounter alien races as advanced as they are, the mythic origins of the complex future universe she began creating with *Brothers of Earth* (1976) are still apparent.

In the footsteps of John W. Campbell, Donald A. WOLLHEIM is another longtime editor who has transformed the cheerful vision of a noble human future into a pattern for commercial success. An editorial veteran of twenty years at Ace Books and founder-publisher of DAW, he has discovered and published scores of leading writers, Cherryh among them. A few words from his book *The Universe Makers* seem to express his editorial credo: "There is hope for humanity and hope for youth." The book concludes

> We are not going to end with a bang.
> We are not going to end with a whimper.
> We are not going to end.
> That's all.

Such optimism invites pessimism, and space opera has never been without criticism, sometimes soundly based. In hard reality, endless human progress toward the stars seems unlikely. Tales of interstellar commerce and galactic empires tend to stretch scientific possibility into the sheerest fantasy. Of course, opposing views of the stature of humanity and its relation to the cosmos can be traced a long way back, perhaps all the way to the contrast between the freewheeling gods of the ancient Greeks and the despotic theocracies that marked the Hebrew religion—the difference between *The Odyssey* and the Book of Job.

If one accepts C. P. Snow's separation of the culture of science and the culture of tradition, space opera clearly belongs to the newborn culture of science. It clings to the utopian faith that the future can be better; the opposed dystopians stand by their bleak despair that humankind can ever save itself, often expressing this view with more than pulp eloquence. Aristophanes, ridiculing Athenian expansiveness in *The Birds*, was one early critic of progress. Jonathan SWIFT, inventing his flying island of Laputa, was certainly another. H. G. WELLS, imagining invasion from Mars in *The War of the Worlds*, saw more hazards than promises in space.

In American SF, space opera lost much of its early appeal after World War II; the bomb had been a sad blow to our faith in science and ourselves. Two strong rivals sprang up to challenge Campbell's *Astounding/Analog*. The editors of THE MAGAZINE OF FANTASY AND SCIENCE FICTION looked beyond space adventure in search of other literary values. H. L. GOLD, the first editor of GALAXY, tended to prefer darker visions of the human future. Although Campbell kept enough support from writers and readers to carry on through two more decades, his GOLDEN AGE had ended. Reaction against space opera reached a crescendo in the 1960s, with the hopeless cynicism of the New Wave.

Yet in the face of all such critics, space opera has survived. Its mythic appeal continues to inspire a vast bulk of science fiction, sometimes crude but more often transcending those remote pulp origins. STAR TREK still runs in syndication, and hundreds of millions stand in line to see the Star Wars films, space opera of the purest water.

J.W.

SPACE PATROL (1950–1956). *Directed by Mike and Helen Moser, Lou Spence, Dick Darley; written by Norman Jolly, Lou Houston, Mike Moser, and others. With Ed Kermer, Lyn Osborn, Ken Mayer, Nina Bara, Virginia Hewitt. 209 30-minute black and white episodes. (Radio episodes as well.)*

Aboard Terra IV, Buzz and Happy bravely defended "the United Planets of the Universe" (actually five planets of the Solar System) from natural, man-made, and alien menaces in this series for children, one of the several created as competition for *Captain Video*. Like the others, *Space Patrol* was televized live, and the format kept actors, and audiences, on their toes. Bela Kovacs, who doubled as the recurring "master villain," was a special delight. *Life* profiled the series, and its spinoffs included comic books drawn by future E.C. artist B. Krigstein.

J.C.

SPACEHUNTER: ADVENTURES IN THE FORBIDDEN ZONE (1983). *Directed by Lamont Johnson; screenplay by Edith Rey, David Preston, Dan Goldberg, and Len Blum; adapted from a story by Stewart Harding and Jean La Fleur; photographed by Frank Tidy; music by Elmer Bernstein. With Peter Strauss, Molly Ringwald, Ernie Hudson, Andrea Marcovicci, Michael Ironside. 90 minutes. Color.*

This large-scale action story features Peter Strauss as the hero battling various dangers on planet Terra Eleven, with sidekicks Molly Ringwald and Ernie Hudson. The film is notable mainly for being photographed in 3-D and released during the brief revival of that format in 1982 and 1983.

K.R.D.

——— SPACESHIPS ———

Spaceships are to science fiction what horses are to westerns: they serve as indispensable means of getting from one place to another and as symbols for their genres. At the heart of both SF and the western are great empty spaces that must be crossed or tamed, and a person without transportation is doomed—as illustrated in such SF classics as Tom Godwin's "The Cold Equations" (1954). The spaceship and the horse make possible the humanizing and civilizing of these hostile environments, and both became such identifying symbols that they were used on book and magazine covers as genre identification.

Despite their importance to the conquest of space and for reaching the planets of both the Solar System and other stars, spaceships did not become central to SF until the creation of AMAZING STORIES in 1926, perhaps because rocket travel was generally considered impractical by everyone except visionaries (such as the Russian scientist Konstantin Eduardovich Tsiolkovsky, who described its possibility in 1903) until Robert Goddard's first successful rocket experiment, by remarkable coincidence also in 1926.

Spaceships had appeared occasionally in the earlier popular adventure publications of *Amazing*'s creator, Hugo GERNSBACK; for instance, there was a space-suited man in his 1923 "scientific fiction number" of *Science and Invention*, but up to that time other means of getting to the Moon or the planets had seemed more practical (or just as impractical). Edgar Allen POE's balloon was only slightly less incredible than Johannes KEPLER's demon or CYRANO de Bergerac's bottles of dew. Jules VERNE dismissed H. G. WELLS's antigravity as "invention" while defending the "physics" of his own giant cannon, but, although Verne described his cannon and its manned capsule with loving detail, neither cannon nor antigravity could have been taken seriously by their authors. And when Verne wanted to send some characters to inspect the planets, he had a comet scoop them off along with a convenient slice of the Mediterranean.

The change in attitudes was marked by Edgar Rice BURROUGHS's two interplanetary series. In 1912, when the first of his John Carter Mars novels was published in *All-Story Magazine*, Burroughs could think of no more believable method of getting Carter to Mars than wishing (astral projection), but by 1934, when the first of his Carson Napier Venus adventures was published, a spaceship was not only available but perhaps essential.

The combination of advancing rocketry and the expansion of conceptions of the universe created by the measurements and theories of Harlow Shapley and Edwin P. Hubble had created a different attitude toward space travel in authors and readers alike. Writers such as E. E. ("Doc") SMITH, beginning with *The Skylark of Space* in 1928, were inspired to write stories about giant, faster-than-light spaceships, and for the next couple of decades spaceships lingered between possibility and convenience. Nobody knew exactly how to build them or how they actually might be propelled, so no author described them in significant detail. The stories in which they appeared were more likely to contain discussions of Newton's third law of motion and how it makes rocket travel in space possible through the operation of action and reaction.

World War II, with its jet-assisted takeoffs (JATO), jet aircraft, and V-2 rockets, demonstrated the technology that could put humanity into space, and SF writers of the 1940s, especially Robert A. HEINLEIN, began to describe spaceships, as well as their impact on individuals and society, in more precise detail. *The Man Who Sold the Moon* (1950), the last chapter of which ("Requiem") was published in 1939, and "Universe" (1941) provided the definitive treatment of the generation starship, which Murray LEINSTER's "Proxima Centauri" had pioneered six years before.

The publication of Chesley BONESTELL and Willy LEY's *The Conquest of Space* (1949), with its diagrams and paintings of staged rockets, space stations, and interplanetary ships, brought new realism to the concept of spaceships and inspired such works as James E. GUNN's *Station in Space* (1958), the first parts of which appeared in 1955, as well as such disparate works as Martin CAIDIN's *Marooned* (1964; filmed in 1969) and Stanley KUBRICK and Arthur C. CLARKE's 2001: A SPACE ODYSSEY (1968).

Some authors used spaceships as a symbol for technology, often as the essential level necessary to get humanity off Earth for survival, further develoment and evolution, or simply adventure; for others, such as Ray BRADBURY in the stories collected in *The Martian Chronicles* (1950), spaceships embodied technology's destructive potential. Here two basic symbols came together: the spaceship, like the flying carpet of *The Arabian Nights*, as a symbol of escape, and as a symbol of triumphant,

The *Starship Enterprise* from TV's *Star Trek*

or diabolic, technology.

Other authors updated such maritime novels as *Captains Courageous* and *Moby Dick* to deal with humanity's restless urge to explore new environments combined with the need for people to bond together to achieve such goals, as in the extraordinary adventures of A. Bertram CHANDLER's Commodore Grimes and the young adults in Robert A. Heinlein's numerous juveniles. James BLISH gave the theme of exploration a new twist with his Cities in Flight tetralogy, the first stories of which appeared in 1950, by lifting entire cities into space, thus preserving city culture while exploring starship culture. This new concept—that humanity's true future may lie in space and not on planets—has developed the third use of the spaceship as symbol and had been the central focus of such novels as Alexei PANSHIN's *Rite of Passage* (1968) and George ZEBROWSKI's *Macrolife* (1979).

Another use of spaceships has been as major characters in and of themselves, as in *2001*'s HAL or the mildly erotic title object of Anne McCAFFREY's *The Ship Who Sang* (1969); authors have transplanted the brain of a human or some other creature into the ship's control system or had a computer intelligence develop personality. By now the intelligent, speaking ship has become at least one of the minor characters in many stories and most space films.

In recent years some uses of the spaceship have remained "magical" (in the sense that, as Arthur C. Clarke has observed, "a sufficiently advanced technology is indistinguishable from magic"), as in Frederik POHL's *Gateway* (1977) or Clarke's own *Rendezvous with Rama* (1973). Other works have focused on scientific speculations about practical spaceflight, describing light-powered "sailing ships," laser propelled ships, hydrogen-bomb-propelled ships, hydrogen ram-scoops, and hollowed and powered asteroids as space habitats.

The appearance of the spaceship has been influenced more by illustration than by words, and because it was so dominant a symbol of the genre, the spaceship often was featured on magazine covers—sometimes in the familiar phallic shape, rising on a jet of flame, but often globular or saucer shaped, the last form particularly after 1947. Beginning with DESTINATION MOON in 1950, films started to take over the task of defining the shape of the spaceship in popular imagination, sometimes with serious intent, as in *Destination Moon* and *2001* (which followed the Bonestell-Ley winged design for the staged rocket, a globe for the moonship, and a spermlike shape for the spaceship to Jupiter. STAR TREK featured a saucer with streamlined (!) appendages, and other films including *Star Wars* (1977) and its sequels, CLOSE ENCOUNTERS OF THE THIRD KIND (1977), and BATTLESTAR GALACTICA (1978–1979). The alien mother ship in *Close Encounters* has been compared to a Victorian chandelier; the fighting spaceships in *Star Wars* and *Battlestar Galactica* set back by generations public understanding of space with their impossible banking turns and noise in the vacuum of space.

The spaceship is likely to remain an integral and identifying element in SF for many years to come, and it may disappear from the literature only if space flight is proved to be impractical or useless, perhaps by the discovery that the other planets of the Solar System are too hostile for any human use and the stars are too distant or have no habitable planets. Even then, perhaps, humanity's dreams of escaping from Earth or exploring the universe may require some vehicle to transport us elsewhere, although the means may be as fantastic as Elijah's chariot or Kepler's demon. In Ian WATSON's "The World Science Fiction Convention of 2080" (1980), an SF writer points out that the destruction of technological means to reach the stars has restored spaceflight to the realm of SF dreamers. And in the hands of masterful writers, whether Heinlein, McCaffrey, or Chandler, the spaceship will continue to transcend its basic function as a method of transportation to become a significant metaphor for escape, for the symbiotic relation between humanity and the machine, or for a new kind of human culture that can be evolved only in the weightless vacuum and endless reaches of space.

S.E.G.

SPACEWAYS (1953).   *Directed by Terence Fisher; screenplay by Paul Tabori and Richard Landau; adapted from the radio play by Charles Eric Maine; photographed by Reginald Wyer; music by Ivor Slaney. With Howard Duff, Eva Bartok, Alan Wheatley, Philip Leaver, Cecile Chevreau, Andrew Osborn. 76 minutes. Black and white.*

An American rocketry expert in England is accused of murdering his wife and her lover and stowing their bodies in the recently launched first space satellite. While police follow up other leads, the expert and *his* lover

go up in another rocket to investigate the first one.

The first serious British science-fiction film since THINGS TO COME (1936), this is a drab, pedestrian affair, dealing more with espionage and illicit romance than with space travel. Director Terence Fisher soon achieved acclaim for his Hammer horror movies, but *Spaceways* is an indifferent programmer.

B.W.

———————— **SPECIAL EFFECTS** ————————

In motion picture usage *special effects* refers to any technique designed to produce an illusion, including explosions, split screens, animation, miniatures, mattes, and even elaborate makeup techniques. The history of science-fiction films is closely linked to the history of special effects.

The first filmmaker to exploit special effects was Georges MÉLIÈS; indeed, some film historians credit him with "discovering" them. A stage magician in Paris at the end of the nineteenth century, Méliès was filming a scene on a Parisian street when his camera jammed; by the time he had repaired it, the omnibus that had been in front of the lens had moved on, and a hearse had stopped in its place. When Méliès projected the film, he was stunned to see the bus apparently turn into the hearse. He also quickly saw the possibilities of this occurrence. He began making short "trick films" involving heavy use of special effects; some of these were science fictional in content, including his most famous film, *Le Voyage dans la Lune* (A TRIP TO THE MOON, 1903).

In addition to Méliès, others cited as early explorers in the field include G. A. Smith and Robert William Paul of Britain. Certainly, Méliès's great success led to many imitators, including Ferdinand Zecca, Segundo de Chomon, and Walter R. Booth. Before 1910 a vast number of trick films were produced, many of which would be called SF today: invisibility, machines that turn dogs into sausages, superspeed, transformations, trips to space—all were part of the trick film repertoire. By 1912, however, the novelty of trick films had worn off.

Special effects began to be used in other films; filmmakers employed them either to record a scene more easily or cheaply, or to create an illusion of reality. By the first decade of the twentieth century, the matte had become a special effects staple. In this technique a portion of the scene being shot is kept unexposed; the film is rewound, and other desired footage is shot on the unexposed portion. There are endless elaborations of this technique, still a major device.

Into the early 1920s few advances in special effects were made; instead already-known techniques were refined and improved. But during this time Willis O'BRIEN began making a series of whimsical stop-motion shorts. Also a common technique, stop motion involves the movement of a jointed puppet, one frame at a time, as in an animated cartoon. When projected, the film of the puppet gives the illusion of movement. O'Brien used this technique in his later masterpieces, THE LOST WORLD (1925), KING KONG (1933), and MIGHTY JOE YOUNG (1949). Ray HARRYHAUSEN, a disciple of O'Brien's and one of the great stop-motion masters, plied his craft in such films as BEAST FROM 20,000 FATHOMS (1953), EARTH VS. THE FLYING SAUCERS (1956), the Sinbad series, and others; Jim Danforth, David Allen, and Phil Tippet are other masters of the technique.

During the 1920s elaborate SF films were scarce; most only called for such simple techniques as miniature work, superimposition, split screens, and so on. Fritz LANG's monumental METROPOLIS (1926) and his later *Die Frau im Mond* (WOMAN IN THE MOON, 1928) represent, along with *The Lost World*, the pinnacles of special effects techniques during the silent era.

In the 1930s American SF films were mostly death-ray aerial adventures or comedies, but there were some exceptions. *Just Imagine* (1930) and *Deluge* (1933) used elaborate miniatures; John P. Fulton's advanced effects in THE INVISIBLE MAN (1933) are still stunning. However, more elaborate and interesting effects work was being done in Europe during this decade. *F.P.1 Antwortet Nicht* (*F.P.1 Doesn't Reply*, 1932), *Gold* (1934), TRANS-ATLANTIC TUNNEL (1935), and THINGS TO COME (1936) all have fine illusions incorporating a wide range of effects.

From the mid-1930s until the early 1950s in the United States, much of the best effects work appeared in serials, usually by the team of Howard and Theodore Lydecker, masters of miniatures and flying scenes. (In fact, during the 1940s most SF films *were* serials.)

In the 1950s with the explosion in SF cinema, special effects again became prominent in features. The films produced by George Pal, Ray Harryhausen's movies, and FORBIDDEN PLANET (1956) were highlights of effects work in this decade. Few new techniques were developed during this period, partly because the old techniques were still useful, partly because SF films were still on low budgets. And in low-budget films, Les Bowie in Britain, and the American team of Irving Block, Louis DeWitt, Gene Warren, and Jack Rabin were doing good, inexpensive work. In Japan Inoshiro Honda and Kenme Yuasa became proficient at destroying elaborate miniature sets.

In 1968 came the film that changed the level of special effects techniques forever: Stanley KUBRICK's 2001: A SPACE ODYSSEY. Although its special effects methodology was not revolutionary, the number of effects, the care taken, the money spent, and the realism achieved were all far in advance of previous films; *2001* established the reputation of effects expert Douglas TRUMBULL.

It was several years before Hollywood learned that old-style effects, as in LOGAN'S RUN (1976), with its obvious miniatures, would no longer be accepted by au-

2001: A Space Odyssey **(1968)**

diences. The one-two punches of STAR WARS and CLOSE ENCOUNTERS OF THE THIRD KIND (both 1977) launched a new era of effects, from which there was no turning back.

A key element of this era was the use of small computers: camera movements could be precisely duplicated as many times as necessary, meaning that spaceships no longer had to slide by cameras on wires—cameras could move by *them* with no wobble; ship lights could be added in a separate pass, so that lighting could be more precisely controlled. This technique was used on *Star Wars* and *Close Encounters* and has been expanded since. Because the new effects were so elaborate, the individual effects expert has been replaced by dedicated teams.

The late 1970s also witnessed the opening of a new field—special effects makeup. Its pioneers were Dick Smith, his enthusiastic protégé Rick Baker, and *his* former assistant, Rob Bottin, as well as Chris Walas. Under their direction new materials but, more important, new ways of thinking about makeup, resulted in alarmingly real distortions of the human form, reaching delirious heights with Bottin's work on THE THING (1982). In another direction the live puppetry of Jim Henson and Frank Oz moved from their cartoony Muppet films to more realistic work in SF films, among them *Dark Crystal* (1983, Henson and Oz together) and LITTLE SHOP OF HORRORS (1986, Oz alone).

As the budgets for SF films grew, so did the ability to create greater effects; as the sophistication of the audience increased, so did its demand for more realistic effects. Since 1976 there have been complaints that effects are running the show, that scripts are devised to showcase effects and not people. No doubt there is some basis for this argument, but it is also pointless. There is still a great demand for realism in special effects. This may be a stage through which audiences are passing, which will wear off in time. But it is inevitable that much filmed Science Fiction will continue to demand vigorous and elaborate special effects.

B.W.

SPIELBERG, STEVEN (1946–   ).   American film director and producer who has managed to combine the intimacy of a personal vision with the epic requirements of the commercial blockbuster. Spielberg's films use elements of science fiction and fantasy but tend to eschew ideas in favor of emotions, particularly childlike wonder and awe. Yet his work triumphs over the limitations of its sentimentality because of his ability to sustain even the shakiest narrative with the masterful use of emotionally potent visual imagery. Four of his movies—*Jaws* (1975), CLOSE ENCOUNTERS OF THE THIRD KIND (1977), *Raiders of the Lost Ark* (1981), and E.T.: THE EXTRA-TERRESTRIAL (1982)—are among the biggest grossing of all time and have been a major influence in the recent shift in SF cinema toward a less adult, more adolescent sensibility.

Unlike George LUCAS, John CARPENTER, and other successful young American filmmakers, Spielberg did not attend one of the major university film programs; he was largely self-taught. He made his first feature, a two-hour SF movie entitled *Firelight*, at the age of sixteen with money from his father, and a local movie house consented to run it for one night. In 1969 his short film *Amblin'* earned him a job with MCA, Universal's television unit, where he directed episodes for such weekly programs as *Night Gallery*, *Columbo*, and *Marcus Welby, M.D.* He also made three television films, one of which, *Duel* (1972), was given theatrical release in Europe, where it received critical praise and garnered commercial success. Its story of a salesman pursued by a giant truck, whose driver is never seen and motive never explained, is told with compelling suspense; the film convincingly sustains its nightmarish vision of machine as monster.

Spielberg pours into his films his personal knowledge of American middle-class suburbia, which he once remarked was like "growing up with three parents—a mother, a father, and a TV set." In both *Close Encounters* and *E.T.*, the aliens offer the promise of experience beyond the restrictions of conventional middle-class existence, just as the heroes of *The Sugerland Express*, *Jaws*, and the Raiders movies are transported into a normal life to exciting, unusual adventure. But, like "the Force" of his friend George Lucas's *Star Wars* (1977), Spielberg's vision also has its dark side. In *Jaws* the normally safe harbor of a public beach is threatened by a great white shark, a giant "eating machine" similar to the truck in *Duel*.

Despite his commercial success, Spielberg is not without his detractors. Many aficionados of SF have objected to *E.T.* and *Close Encounters* because of their unclear plots, narrative contradictions, naive optimism, and quasi-religious worship of aliens who are invested with the promise of transcendence. Spielberg's sugary, unrealistic treatment of the black American experience in *The Color Purple* (1985) and his episode of TWILIGHT ZONE: *The Movie* (1983), wherein elderly people can become young again if they believe hard enough, further reveals what for some is a regressive vision that refuses to accept the responsibilities of the adult world.

Regardless of the validity of such criticism, through his artful control of the film medium Spielberg has reestablished the links between our common humility before the vastness of the universe and the youthful quality of wonder at the heart of SF.

OTHER FILMS: *Something Evil* (made for TV, 1971); *Close Encounters of the Third Kind: The Special Edition* (1980); *Indiana Jones and the Temple of Doom* (1983).

B.K.G.

SPINRAD, NORMAN [RICHARD] (1940–   ). American writer. Since turning to writing full-time in the late 1960s, Spinrad has become a world traveler in science fiction, a writer of stature as well as an SF personality to be reckoned with.

After growing up in and around the Bronx and earning a bachelor's degree from the City College of New York, Spinrad worked at a variety of jobs from carpentry to sandal making to assisting at the Scott Meredith Literary Agency. In recent years he has served as president of the SCIENCE FICTION WRITERS OF AMERICA, staunchly defended writers' rights in his *Locus* column "Stayin' Alive" (since reprinted as a book) and elsewhere, and played by turns the role of antagonist and stand-up comic with SF fans.

Spinrad has always brought a great deal of vitality and creative disruption to American SF. His first two novels, *The Solarians* (1966) and *Agent of Chaos* (1967), were essentially 1960s space operas that champion the socially liberating force of morally justified violence against oppressive establishments.

Spinrad came to maturity with *Bug Jack Barron* (1969), which many still consider his finest novel. It is about America's greatest media baron, who single-handedly exposes a corrupt industrialist's project, which sacrifices live black children in order to develop an immortality serum. In Europe the novel has been widely read as a parable of America's exploitation of blacks and of the individualism allowed in American media. When it was first published, *Bug Jack Barron* had a liberating and shocking effect in the world of SF—along with other NEW WAVE fiction—because of its explicit sex; it was responsible for the banning of NEW WORLDS by one British bookstore chain when the magazine serialized the novel.

Norman Spinrad

Spinrad once told interviewer Charles PLATT that there are only five basic subjects one can write about: "sex, love, power . . . money . . . transcendence." These themes, along with a fascination for his native country, unify and characterize Spinrad's writings. His novel *The Iron Dream* (1972) is an alternate history of Adolf Hitler as an SF writer. His collection *The Star-Spangled Future* (1979) forcefully weaves together some of his best SF stories as an expression of America's explosive possibilities. *Songs from the Stars* (1980) explores the wasted power of a postholocaust America.

The most outstanding of his recent novels is *The Void Captain's Tale* (1983), a story of travel and transcendence. It is written in a masterful, neologistic "anglish sprach" of the future that deliciously mixes Romance language and Sanskrit. Sexually bracing and emotionally delicate, brash, and captivating at the same time, *The Void Captain's Tale* shows Spinrad as a writer of great independence and wit, and keen commercial sense, an author who promises to be a strong force in American SF for years to come. Each new Spinrad book, such as *Child of Fortune* (1985) and *Little Heroes* (1987), is an occasion for debate or discussion.

OTHER WORKS: *The Men in the Jungle* (1967); *The Last Hurrah of the Golden Horde* (collection, 1970); *No Directon Home* (collection, 1975); *Riding the Torch* (1978); *A World Between* (1979); *The Mind Game* (1986).

J.R.D.

SPRUILL, STEVEN G. (1946–   ). American writer and psychologist. Spruill has written that his chief intent is "to entertain the reader and produce an emotional experience in the process," a goal that he has achieved with some success. Two of his novels—*The Psychopath Plague* (1978) and *The Imperator Plot* (1983)—are part of an ongoing series featuring a broadly educated hero, Elias Kane, who is at times reminiscent of Isaac ASIMOV's Elijah Baley (especially the early Baley of *The Caves of Steel* (1954). In each of the novels Kane is called on to stop plots that threaten human civilizations on a future Earth. Spruill does not give his world the rich detail of Asimov's works, but his extensive use of psychology, a field in which he earned a Ph.D., and fascinating explorations of the differences between human and alien perceptions of reality raise interesting and memorable questions.

OTHER WORKS: *Keepers of the Gate* (1977); *Hellstone* (1980); *The Genesis Shield* (1985).

S.H.G.

STABLEFORD, BRIAN M[ICHAEL] (1948–   ). British writer, critic, and academic with a growing reputation as a student of science fiction. A biologist and sociologist by training, Stableford has put his academic knowledge to good effect in his fiction.

His earlier works—*Cradle of the Sun* (1969) and *The Blind Worm* (1970), both gushing with exotic imagery—reflect his initial delight in the fantasies of A. MERRITT. After a bold transitional work, the Dies Irae trilogy (*The Days of Glory*, 1971; *In the Kingdom of the Beasts*, 1971; and *Day of Wrath*, 1971), Stableford settled into a sequence of ingeniously plotted space adventure novels. First came the series of six books about Star-Pilot Grainger, whose brain is host to a benign alien entity: *The Halcyon Drift* (1972), Rhapsody in Black (1973), *Promised Land* (1974), *The Paradise Game* (1974), *The Fenris Device* (1974), and *Swan Song* (1975). A similar series involves the starship *Daedalus* recontacting lost Earth colonies: *The Florians* (1976), *Critical Threshold* (1977), *Wildeblood's Empire* (1977), and *The Paradox of the Sets* (1980). Both of these series, which represent high-quality SPACE OPERA, show considerable ingenuity in the invention of planetary ecologies and societies. Stableford's most ambitious effort in this respect is *The Realms of Tartarus* (1977; first part published in Britain as *The Face of Heaven*, 1976), a Nebula nominee for best novel.

Stableford has also written a number of nonseries novels, perhaps his most serious being *Man in a Cage* (1975), but more recently he has forsaken fiction for a series of nonfiction studies that includes *The Sociology of Science Fiction* (1985), *The Third Millennium: A History of the World A.D. 2000–3000* (with David Langford, 1985), and the highly lauded *Scientific Romance in Britain, 1890–1950* (1985), the result of much original research and thought. He won the IAFA Scholarship Award in 1987 and may become better known as a scholar than an author of fiction.

OTHER WORKS: Fiction: *To Challenge Chaos* (1972); *The Mind-Riders* (1976); *The Last Days of the Edge of the World* (1978); *Optiman* (1980); *The Castaways of Tanager* (1981); *Journey to the Center* (1982); *The Gates of Eden* (1983). Nonfiction: *Mysteries of Modern Science* (1977); *Masters of Science Fiction* (1982).

M.A.

STALKER: SEE SOLARIS

STAPLEDON, [WILLIAM] OLAF (1886–1950).

British writer and philosopher. Stapledon's "philosophical romances," with their sympathy for the profoundly alien and their vast gulfs of time and space, have exercised a strong influence on many modern writers of science fiction—a genre of which Stapledon had little knowledge.

Born on the Wirral Peninsula south of Liverpool, Stapledon spent his early childhood in Suez; he was later educated at Oxford, served with an ambulance unit in World War I, and received an M.A. in philosophy from Liverpool University in 1925. Never a success as an academic—his philosophical treatise *A Modern Theory of Ethics* (1929) was ignored—he nonetheless involved himself with many noted progressive intellectuals, including H. G. WELLS and Gerald HEARD. His ultimate philosophical métier, however, was his fiction, to which he turned full-time after the unexpected popular success of his first novel, *Last and First Men* (1930).

Inspired by J.B.S. Haldane's essay "The Last Judgement" (1927), *Last and First Men* purports to be a history of intelligent life in the Solar System, telepathically narrated through Stapledon by a member of the eighteenth (and last) sentient race in humanity's descent. Not all the future "men" in the chronicle are superior to modern *Homo sapiens* (whose own history as seen from the distant future begins the book); bitter setbacks lie in the path toward "cosmical perfection." However, the overall trend is toward increased consciousness, until 2 billion years in the future the Last Men are able to apprehend directly the underlying nature of space and time, and reflect on ultimate questions as they die away under a disintegrating Sun.

Stapledon's most famous other work is *Star Maker* (1937), in which a modern Englishman at the moment of his despair is mysteriously projected into the cosmos as a "disembodied, wandering viewpoint." In this state he merges with the minds of other, alien beings and becomes cognizant of the awesome Star Maker, Prime Mover of the universe, who grants him a revelation of the vitality imminent in all things and of the tiny place held by our own perceptible universe in the vast procession of cosmic time. A great deal of the book's emotional charge is derived from Stapledon's emphasis on the idea

that, as critic Leslie Fiedler put it, "God is Not Love"— rather, the Star Maker's nature is exemplified by "the cold, clear, crystal ecstasy of contemplation."

Stapledon wrote several other works of SF, most notably *Odd John* (1935) and *Sirius* (1944). The former is a significant early treatment of the mutant-superman theme; the latter, much praised for sensitive characterization, concerns a sheepdog given artificially enhanced intelligence and tormented by his emotional involvement with human beings. Of Stapledon's work in general, recent critics have observed that he was very much an intellectual of his times; David Pringle has noted an aesthetic similarity to Stalinism in Stapledon's "depictions of dire struggles and great dyings as the human race strives ever onwards and upwards to the light." For all that, Stapledon's work is still widely read and appreciated for his uncanny ability to articulate an emotional response to cosmic scale; his best fiction is among the most purely idea-oriented SF ever to be written well.

OTHER WORKS: *Last Men in London* (1932); *Darkness and the Light* (1942); *Old Man in New World* (1944); *Death into Life* (1946); *The Flames* (1947); *A Man Divided* (1950); *The Opening of the Eyes* (1954, Agnes Z. Stapledon, ed.); *4 Encounters* (1976); "*Nebula Maker*" (1976); *Far Future Calling: A Radio Play* (1978, Harvey Satty, ed.); *Far Future Calling: Uncollected Science Fiction and Fantasies* (1979, Sam Moskowitz, ed.).

P.N.H.

———— STAR TREK ————

The 1966–69 television series *Star Trek*, whose original broadcasts were not particularly popular but inspired exceptional loyalty in its viewers, became the most remarkable phenomenon of its time in syndication, and was the initial introduction to science fiction for millions of viewers, many of whom later became readers. Even in its original run, *Star Trek* created a precedent by being preserved for its final year by a massive letter-writing campaign by fans (who later would be called *Trekkies*).

An animated series, consisting of twenty-two episodes, based on the original series and using the voices of the cast, was aired in 1973–74; by 1987 four top moneymaking feature-length films had been released (and a fifth, to be directed by William Shatner, was in preparation): *Star Trek: The Motion Picture* (1979), *Star Trek II: The Wrath of Kahn* (1982), *Star Trek III: The Search for Spock* (1984), and *Star Trek IV: The Voyage Home* (1986); in 1987 a second series set some 200 years after the first, *Star Trek: The Next Generation*, with a new cast, surprised network executives by becoming so successful in syndication that a number of network stations were airing it in prime time in place of network programming.

The series was conceived by Gene RODDENBERRY who developed the first pilot, "The Cage." His diverse interests and experiences, including stints as a military and a commercial pilot and police work with the Los Angeles Police Department, contributed to his successful scriptwriting for many popular 1950s television shows such as *Dragnet*, *Dr. Kildare*, *Highway Patrol*, and *Naked City*, as well as *Have Gun, Will Travel*, for which he was head writer. He wrote episodes for the *Star Trek* series and continued to be involved in productions from the animated series, the motion pictures, and the new television series. Closely associated as well were D. C. FONTANA, the story editor, and Gene L. Coon, one of the producers.

The format of the original series (like most of the new) was the voyage through unexplored space of the futuristic Starship *Enterprise*, engaged in a mission of exploration throughout the universe. Each of the episodes was introduced with the following narration by Captain Kirk (William Shatner): "Space, the final frontier. These are the voyages of the *Starship Enterprise*. Its five-year mission: to explore new worlds, to seek out new life and new civilizations, to boldly go where no man has gone before." A continuing cast and a number of guest stars encountered new civilizations, aliens, and strange phenomena.

The story lines presented a view of a future universe related to Earth history but different in significant ways. Many problems of contemporary society, such as racial and sexual discrimination, economic distribution, and world peace were shown as solved in the Star Trek universe of the twenty-third century. The missions of the *Enterprise*, as a representative of the United Federation of Planets, reveal an essentially democratic association, a loose federation of worlds that voluntarily have joined together for the peaceful purpose of exploration, scientific research, and political and economic cooperation. The underlying laws and regulations respect humanistic values and accept difference. The Prime Directive, for instance, established a rule of non-interference to protect alien life and societies from careless actions and intrusions by Federation personnel and to safeguard the normal development of alien planets. The bending or breaking of this rule provides the central theme of several episodes.

Believable but colorful humanoid aliens, such as Vulcans, Andorians, Gorns, and Tellarites, played their parts. The animated series was able to portray an even greater variety of aliens, such as fishlike people and intelligent insects. Many plots focused on the conflicts between the Terrans and the Klingons and their allies, the Romulans, who are out to conquer the universe.

What stimulated such intensity of fan interest may have been the consistency of the background planned for the series, the plausibility with which the episodes were presented, the success of the special effects (and

Star Trek's Spock (Leonard Nimoy) and Captain Kirk (William Shatner)

the fact that they were the everyday background, not the foreground of the series), the generally benign view of the human species, and the relatively free rein given to the imagination. A number of the key episodes were written by science-fiction writers; the third year of the series, when virtually no SF writers were used (Roddenberry warned a World SF Convention audience that fans had saved the series but the studio had written it off), was the most disappointing. Most important to the show's success, however, was the development of the characters and the bonding among them. Viewers tuned in not only to enjoy the newest adventure but to experience the camaraderie, humor, and predictable responses: Kirk's courage under stress, Spock's (Leonard Nimoy's) logic, and McCoy's (DeForest Kelley's) humanistic cynicism, as well as Scotty's (James Doohan's) concern for the *Enterprise*'s engines, and so forth.

Fans have continued to play a significant role in Star Trek events, and their support of conventions and development of fanzines are unique in the genre. They not only enjoy the original series in television syndication, in novelized versions of the scripts, and in video tapes (all the episodes are available, including the never-broadcast pilot film, "The Cage"—which in some counts brings the number of episodes to seventy-nine—with

Jeffrey Hunter in the role of Captain Pike), they also support a body of new literature including two books of short stories (*Star Trek: New Voyages* and *New Voyages 2*, edited by Sondra Marshak and Myrna Culbreath, 1976 and 1977); two reference books (*Star Trek Concordance* by Bjo Trimble, 1976, and *Star Trek Compendium* by Allen Asherman, 1986); a cookbook (*Official Star Trek Cooking Manual* by Mary Ann Piccard, 1978); a computer game ("Star Trek: The Kobayashi Alternative," 1986); souvenirs of all kinds; and, most of all, new novels (thirty-three titles by 1987, and a new one coming along about every two months).

Star Trek (1966–69). *Directed by Marc Daniels, Joseph Pevney, Vince McEveety, and others; written by Richard Matheson, Robert Bloch, Theodore Sturgeon, Harlan Ellison, Jerome Bixby, Gene L. Coon, D. C. Fontana, and others; photographed by Ernest Haller and Jerry Finnerman; music by Alexander Courage, Gerald Fried, and Fred Steiner. With William Shatner, Leonard Nimoy, DeForest Kelley, James Doohan, George Takei, Walter Koenig, Nichelle Nichols, Majei Barrett, and Grace Lee Whitney. 78 60-minutes episodes. Color.*

Star Trek—The Motion Picture (1979). *Directed by Robert Wise; screenplay by Harold Livingston; photographed by Richard Kline; music by Jerry Goldsmith. With William Shatner, Leonard Nimoy, DeForest Kelley, James Doohan, Walter Koenig, George Takei, Nichelle Nichols, Majei Barrett, Grace Lee Whitney, Stephen Collins, Persis Khambatta. 145 minutes. Color.*

Star Trek II: The Wrath of Khan (1982). *Directed by Nicholas Meyer; screenplay by Jack Sowards; photographed by Gayne Rescher; music by James Horner and Alexander Courage. With William Shatner, Leonard Nimoy, DeForest Kelley, James Doohan, Walter Koenig, George Takei, Nichelle Nichols, Ricardo Montalban, Ike Eisenmann, Paul Winfield, Bibi Besch, Merritt Butrick. 113 minutes. Color.*

Star Trek III: The Search for Spock (1984). *Directed by Leonard Nimoy; screenplay by Harve Bennett; photographed by Charles Correll; music by James Horner. With William Shatner, Leonard Nimoy, DeForest Kelley, James Doohan, George Takei, Walter Koenig, Nichelle Nichols, Christopher Lloyd, Robin Curtis, Merritt Butrick, Mark Lenard, Dame Judith Anderson, James B. Sikking, John Larroquette, Robert Hooks. 105 minutes. Color.*

Star Trek IV: The Voyage Home (1986). *Directed by Leonard Nimoy; screenplay by Steve Meerson & Peter Krikes and Harve Bennett and Nicholas Meyer; photographed by Don Peterman; music by Leonard Rosenman. With William Shatner, Leonard Nimoy, DeForest Kelley, James Doohan, George Takei, Walter Koenig, Nichelle Nichols, Catherine Hicks. 118 minutes. Color.*

Star Trek: The Next Generation (1987–). *Directed by Corey Allen, Rob Bowman, Richard Compton, Paul Lynch, and others; written by D. C. Fontana, Gene Roddenberry, Maurice Hurley, Robert Lewin, and others; photographed by Ed Brown and Ed Brown, Jr.; music edited by John La Salandra. With Patrick Stewart, Jonathan Frakes, Brent Spiner, Denise Crosby, Marina Sirtis, Lavar Burton, Cheryl McFadden, Wil Wheaton, Michael Dorn. 60-minute episodes. Color.*

L.A.J.

STAR WARS (1977). *Directed by George Lucas; screenplay by George Lucas; photographed by Gilbert Taylor; music by John Williams. With Mark Hamill, Harrison Ford, Carrie Fisher, Alec Guinness, Peter Cushing, David Prowse, Anthony Daniels, Kenny Baker, Peter Mayhew. 121 minutes. Color.*

THE EMPIRE STRIKES BACK (1980). *Directed by Irvin Kershner; screenplay by Leigh Brackett and Lawrence Kasdan; photographed by Peter Suschitzky; music by John Williams. With Mark Hamill, Harrison Ford, Carrie Fisher, Billy Dee Williams, David Prowse, Anthony Daniels, Frank Oz, Kenny Baker, Alec Guinness, Peter Mayhew. 124 minutes. Color.*

RETURN OF THE JEDI (1983). *Directed by Richard Marquand; screenplay by Lawrence Kasdan and George Lucas; photographed by Alan Hume; music by John Williams. With Mark Hamill, Harrison Ford, Carrie Fisher, Billy Dee Williams, Anthony Daniels, Peter Mayhew, Ian McDiarmid, Frank Oz, David Prowse, Alec Guinness. 132 minutes. Color.*

Published as a novel by George LUCAS in 1976 and released as a film one year later, *Star Wars* is to science-fiction cinema what the monolith is to 2001: A SPACE ODYSSEY, a landmark pointing the way for those who follow. The film was an astonishing commercial success, costing about $10.5 million but earning more than $400 million around the world. It was the most successful SF movie ever made until 1982, when it was surpassed by Steven SPIELBERG's E.T.: THE EXTRA-TERRESTRIAL. *Star Wars* also sparked an unprecedented merchandising campaign of toys, lunch boxes, T-shirts, mugs, and other memorabilia, making it a major cultural event of the decade.

The film's tremendous success allowed director Lucas to flesh out his imaginary world by expanding the work into a proposed nine-film series grouped into three trilogies. He claims that this was his intention from the beginning, when he had to pare down his initial script considerably to fit it into one movie. *Star Wars* itself nowhere indicates this plan, but the opening credits of *The Empire Strikes Back*, which identify the film as "Episode V," acknowledge Lucas's overall scheme. (*Star Wars* is now referred to as *Star Wars: Episode IV*, and the third film, *Return of the Jedi*, is entitled "Episode VI.") The three films produced so far thus constitute the middle trilogy.

The films depict the struggle in a remote galaxy between an evil empire and a group of dedicated rebels and tell the story of the last of the Jedi Knights, an elite cadre who, before the Empire's foundation, maintained the social order by harnessing "the Force"—a metaphysical power that the films never fully explain—and resembled, in both code and weaponry, samurai warriors. The first film introduces us to the trilogy's continuing characters, among them Darth Vader, an ex-Jedi turned to the dark side of the force by the evil emperor; Princess Leia, one of the rebel leaders; Luke Skywalker, a young farmer and the son of a Jedi, recruited by Leia to help overturn the Empire; Han Solo, a freewheeling galactic adventurer (and sometime pirate) who becomes Luke's occasionally reluctant sidekick; and the dapper robot R2-D2 and his buzzing and clicking companion C-3PO. *Star Wars* depicts Luke Skywalker's training by Obi-Wan Kenobi, the last of the Jedi Knights, and his subsequent demolition of the Death Star, Darth Vader's vast mechanism of destruction.

Vader himself escapes in the nick of time, however, and *The Empire Strikes Back* begins with an impressive battle between the two sides on the ice planet Hoth. Our heroes escape in Han Solo's intergalactic jalopy, the Millennium Falcon, pursued by Empire spacecraft. Meanwhile, Luke undergoes his Jedi training on the planet Dagobah, instructed by the master Yoda, who has been teaching Jedi Knights for over 800 years. The film's surprising revelation is that Vader is actually Luke's father, an idea that raises the plot above the level of simplistic space opera and successfully sustained the suspense of the movie's cliff-hanging ending for three years, until the release of *Return of the Jedi*.

In this third and final chapter of the trilogy, the heroes save Princess Leia from the clutches of the slimy Jabba the Hutt, avoid a horrible fate in the Sarlac Pit, and knock out the Empire's defense system on the planet Endor. We discover this time that Princess Leia is Luke's sister. In a superb climactic battle, Luke defeats his father and at the same time redeems him from evil.

The trilogy reflects Lucas's lifelong admiration for science-fiction and pulp adventure comics, as well as his view that SF had grown too intellectual and so had lost its youthful romance and vigor, qualities he wished to restore to the form. And indeed, he succeeded. The series is filled with action and dense with subplots too numerous to mention. At the same time, the films are an SF rarity, addressing no relevant issues concerning science or technology, either directly or metaphorically, in any significant way. Remotely set in a galaxy "long ago and far away," the movies ignore such problems as nuclear danger, ecological disaster, or even sociological extrapolation, and concentrate instead on sheer action.

In doing so the Star Wars films pull out all the stops. For *The Empire Strikes Back* Lucas built the world's largest sound stage and a highly sophisticated special effects studio. The opening battle, which features walking tanks, is technically striking, and took the special effects unit, Industrial Light and Magic, three months to complete. The stunning effects for the pursuit of the Millennium Falcon through an asteroid field were achieved with a newly developed machine called a quad printer, which seamlessly mattes as many as four separate images. In *Return of the Jedi*, Lucas outdid even his previous efforts with a spellbinding chase on flying speeder-bikes through a forest of giant trees.

In its introduction of the Force, the series also taps into the same mythic material that made STAR TREK so popular on television and in the cinema: humanity, with its intuition and imperfections, triumphantly unites with technology in a perfect synthesis. In an age when technology threatens us with imminent destruction, this cybernetic fantasy could hardly be more appealing. Given the mythic appeal of the films, however, it is not surprising that the human characters exist at the level of archetype; nonetheless, they are embodied so well by the actors—notably Mark Hamill as the fresh-eyed Luke Skywalker, Alec Guinness as the venerable Ben Kenobi, and Harrison Ford as the mercenary individualist Han Solo—that they succeed as fresh heroes.

In fact, however, it is the nonhuman characters who steal the show. The robots R2-D2 and C-3PO certainly have the best lines; a high-tech Laurel and Hardy, they move from one fine mess to another, complaining all the way. The series is graced with a supporting cast of all manner of visually imaginative aliens, from Yoda, whose wrinkled face is remarkably lifelike, to Jabba the Hutt, a terrifying mass of protoplasm.

In the end, though, both the popularity and the major aesthetic achievement of the Star Wars series is its successful evolution from sword-and-sorcery space opera to resonant myth. Through the skillful collaboration of many people—writers Leigh BRACKETT and Lawrence Kasdan and directors Irvin Kershner and Richard Marquand—Lucas's vision has been triumphantly created on the screen, depicting an epic of such engaging magnitude that it has become a contemporary myth.

B.K.G.

STARMAN (1984).
Directed by John Carpenter; screenplay by Bruce A. Evans and Raynold Gideon; photographed by Donald M. Morgan; music by Jack Nitzche. With Jeff Bridges, Karen Allen, Charles Martin Smith, Richard Jaeckel, Robert Phalen, Tony Edwards. 115 minutes. Color.

Starman seems a calculated combination of that sense of wonder associated with Steven SPIELBERG's films and the parable of the alien as stranger in a strange land—

a perhaps deliberate departure by its director, John CAR-PENTER, who here eschewed the violence, action, and fright typical of his early work in favor of a more gentle, even romantic approach.

An alien being (Jeff Bridges) arrives in remote Wisconsin and takes the physical form of the heroine's dead husband. After the woman (Karen Allen) recovers from her initial shock, the two develop a close relationship, made more intense as they flee from nasty State Department officials who've discovered the alien's presence. The movie ends with the extraterrestrial's rescue at a predetermined rendezvous point while, as in CLOSE ENCOUNTERS OF THE THIRD KIND (1977), everyone gazes skyward in awe at the mother ship.

The film's compound of science-fiction formulas offers mixed results. On the one hand, it shows great strength in its depiction of the two main characters and their deepening relationship. (Bridges in particular gives one of the best performances of his career as the alien who suddenly finds himself in a human body.) On the other hand, the narrative conflict is unsatisfyingly simplistic, in large part because the pursuing government agents are too one-dimensional to generate much interest. Despite its shortcomings, however, the film proved popular enough to inspire a weekly TV series of the same name, which ran during the 1985–86 season.

B.K.G.

STARSHIP INVASIONS (1977). *Directed by Ed Hunt; screenplay by Ed Hunt; photographed by Mark Irwin; music by Gil Melle. With Robert Vaughn, Christopher Lee, Daniel Pilon, Tiiu Leek, Helen Shaver. 89 minutes. Color.*

Filmed in and around Toronto, *Starship Invasions* is a modest-budget UFO adventure in which evil aliens of the Legion of the Winged Serpent, led by Christopher Lee, unleash a "suicide ray" on the people of Earth. Peaceful aliens, assisted by UFO expert Robert Vaughn, battle to defeat the invaders. Warren Keillor's special effects are impressive despite having been produced without high-tech equipment.

K.R.D.

STASHEFF, CHRISTOPHER (1944–). American science-fiction and fantasy writer. Stasheff began his career with *The Warlock in Spite of Himself* (1969). Set on the planet Gramarye, the book grafts SF to fantasy as it describes galactic agent Rod Gallowglass's attempts to protect this medieval planet from totalitarian forces. Stasheff's later work, with the exception of *A Wizard in Bedlam* (1979), consists of sequels to his first novel; most are unimportant, with the minor exception of *The Warlock Unlocked* (1982), which shows the author's growing preoccupation with Catholicism.

OTHER WORKS: *King Kobold* (1971; revised 1984); *Escape Velocity* (1983); *The Warlock Enraged* (1985); *The Warlock Is Missing* (1986).

M.M.W.

THE STEPFORD WIVES (1975). *Directed by Bryan Forbes; screenplay by William Goldman; adapted from the novel by Ira Levin; photographed by Owen Roziman; music by Michael Small. With Katharine Ross, Paula Prentiss, Peter Masterson, Patrick O'Neal, Nanette Newman, Tina Louise. 114 minutes. Color.*

When a married couple moves to a Connecticut suburb, the wife (Katharine Ross) discovers that the leader of the local Men's Society, a former Disneyland technician, is manufacturing perfect physical replicas of the community's wives, which behave like stereotypical housewives, concerned only with cooking, cleaning, child care, and husband coddling. When she attempts some consciousness raising among these model drudges, the film develops a chilling paranoia reminiscent of INVASION OF THE BODY SNATCHERS (1955) and another Ira LEVIN novel turned into film, ROSEMARY'S BABY (1968).

Like Rosemary, the character played by Ross suspects that strange things are going on. Despite her foreboding and finally her efforts to escape, she too is replaced by an android. As it turns out, all the husbands of Stepford have conspired to exchange their real wives for robot simulacra. The final image of the wives in the supermarket is a chilling ballet of zombies. The film was followed by two made-for-TV sequels.

M.T.W.

STEPHENSON, ANDREW M[ICHAEL] (1946–). British author born in Venezuela. Stephenson, who earned a bachelor's degree in electrical and electronic engineering in 1969 and has worked as a design engineer, started in science fiction, like Harry HARRISON, as an illustrator.

His first story, "Holding Action," was published in *Astounding* in 1971. His first novel, *Nightwatch* (1977), was set on the moon and dealt with thinking machines and their creator. *The Wall of Years* (1980), his second novel, brought together time travel and parallel worlds, and sent a twenty-first-century protagonist into the ninth century to protect the future against possible destruction. It was a promising beginning, but Stephenson has not been prolific and has been inactive in the field recently.

J.E.G.

STERLING, BRUCE (1954–). American science-fiction writer who became a major spokesman for the CYBERPUNK literary movement of the 1980s and be-

came known, through the pronouncements in his flyer *Cheap Truth* and by his own work—particularly as editor of *Mirrorshades: The Cyberpunk Anthology*—as "the chairman." Sterling was born in Brownsville, Texas, and earned a bachelor's degree in journalism from the University of Texas at Austin, where he still lives. His first story, "Man-Made Self," was published in *Lone Star Universe* (1976) after he had attended a Clarion SF Writers Workshop, followed by the publication of his first novel, *Involution Ocean* (1977).

Sterling's affiliation with cyberpunk was predated by his identification with another, larger group of writers who have been attempting to review and reanimate the traditional conventions of the genre. Scientific advancement, artificial environments, genetic and surgical modification of humans, alien contact, and human colonization of the solar system all play their roles in his short stories and novels, but in his hands this material is the stuff of astonishing futures and unique societies. *Involution Ocean,* for instance, features the planet Nullaqua, a sinister world so inherently confusing that his characters escape through using drugs.

But as unusual as his setting may be, Sterling is even more startling in his portrayal of humanity's future. Like John VARLEY and William GIBSON, he can convince his readers that tomorrow's humanity will not be simply more of the same. Confronted with challenges and technological developments impossible to predict, Sterling tells us, people *must* change. *The Artificial Kid* (1980) is a study in how control of the environment and the ability to extend life has dramatically transformed the species. The elderly of this world can't keep up with the pace of change and the young have trouble holding onto any belief when the next day may bring a new and utterly different truth. People are, therefore, caught between the need to adjust to a world in constant flux and the necessity to find some stable system of values so that they can go on with their daily lives. Only a few, including the eponymous hero, are willing to take the essential steps that will spring them from such a trap.

Schismatrix (1985) depicts an even more disordered world. Based on a society first presented in "The Swarm" (1982), the novel describes the struggle between two factions who have radically different views of how humanity should develop. The Mechanists believe that people should be surgically enhanced, often by implanting marvelous new prosthetics. The Shapers are convinced that mankind's future depends on genetic engineering. The result is an amazing number of new human species, called "clades," each of which holds its own variation of the Mechanist or Shaper beliefs, which in turn throw off a spectrum of cults. Not surprisingly, Brian W. ALDISS has called the book's concern "not Future Shock, but Future Blitzkrieg."

S.H.G.

STERNBACH, RICK (1951–   ).   American science-fiction and astronomical artist. Sternbach was the first illustrator since Chesley BONESTELL to use classical astronomical art in SF illustration and was largely responsible for creating a niche in the genre for it. Although a skilled user of the airbrush, he does not depend on it alone for effects. His work has appeared on the covers and in the interiors of magazines such as GALAXY, ANALOG, THE MAGAZINE OF FANTASY AND SCIENCE FICTION, *Astronomy Magazine*, and *If*. He has worked extensively for Del Rey/Ballantine Books, but he has also painted covers for DAW Books, Berkley, Fawcett, and Pocket Books.

In 1978 Sternbach joined Carl SAGAN's PBS series, *Cosmos*, as Assistant Art Director; in 1980 he received an Emmy award for his contributions to the show. He has also been nominated four times for the Hugo award, winning twice for Best Professional Artist (1977 and 1978). In 1976, while at the World SF Convention in Kansas City, Sternbach helped found the Association of Science Fiction and Fantasy Artists (ASFA), which was formed to spread information to SF artists on matters such as copyright law, art techniques, contracts, and convention art shows. He was one of the founders in 1983 of the International Association of Astronomical Artists (IAAA). Sternbach is currently working as the illustrator for STAR TREK: *The Next Generation*.

J.G.

STEVENS, FRANCIS (Pseudonym of Gertrude Barrows Bennett) (1884–1939?).   American science-fantasy writer for the PULP MAGAZINES of 1917–1923, often compared with A. MERRITT, although her first novel preceded all but a few Merritt short stories. Stevens, widowed in 1910, took up secretarial work to support a daughter, and then, when her father died, started writing fiction to take care of her ailing mother. She stopped writing and returned to work as a secretary when her mother died.

Her fiction, however, belies her apparent lack of artistic commitment: it was of excellent quality for the period, and three of her novels, *The Heads of Cerberus* (1919/1952), *Claimed!* (1920/1966), and *The Citadel of Fear* (1918/1970), were reprinted in book form. Three of her novels and three of her seven short stories also were reprinted in *Famous Fantastic Mysteries* and *Fantastic Novels* between 1940 and 1950.

The Citadel of Fear takes place in a Merrittlike lost city, Tlapallan, in Mexico, but is characterized by greater realism and humor than Merritt's work; the evil in the ancient city eventually threatens the American countryside. *The Heads of Cerberus* offers a Dust of Purgatory that transports people into an alternate-world Philadelphia for the sake of political and social satire.

Claimed! deals with a carved box found on a Pacific island that a supernatural being from the past attempts to reclaim.

OTHER WORKS: "The Nightmare" (1917); "Serapion" (1920); "Sunfire" (1923).

J.E.G.

STEVENSON, ROBERT LOUIS (1850–1894).

British writer of adventure stories, also a noted essayist and children's poet. Stevenson's classic dual-personality tale *The Strange Case of Dr. Jekyll and Mr. Hyde* (1886) has become a synonymous illustration of schizophrenia as well as a deep influence on the psychological theme in science fiction. A tormented work, *Jekyll and Hyde* grew out of Stevenson's early youth in Edinburgh, during which he became obsessed by a long series of sequential nightmares in which he led a horrific double life. These dreams only ceased when he was given a powerful opiate by a doctor. In modern times, when the control or change of personality by drugs is taken for granted, Stevenson's ideas have become far less fantastic, but this book remains the clearest prototype of all stories of transformation and drug dependency. The original draft (which the author scrapped) had Jekyll simply disguising himself as the evil Hyde and thus omitted the allegory, whereas the final, published draft set the story firmly in the laboratory and the realms of SF. Stevenson's theme of dualism and the doppelgänger is found in many of his shorter tales, notably "Markheim" (1886), in which the ghostly stranger is revealed to be the murderer's good conscience, and "Olalla" (1885), another fine study of a diseased mind.

OTHER WORK: *The Merry Men, and Other Tales and Fables* (1887).

R.D.

STEWART, GEORGE R[IPPEY] (1895–1980).

American writer of mainstream fiction and English professor at the University of California from 1942 to 1962; his *Earth Abides* (1949) won the first International Fantasy Award in 1951 and became a classic of ecological science fiction. Ecology also figures in Stewart's *Storm* (1941) and *Fire* (1948), which, though not otherwise SF, are distinguished by their narrative viewpoint: the catastrophic event itself. *Earth Abides*, however, is more overtly SF, describing as it does a holocaust, the almost total elimination of the human species by a deadly virus. Isherwood Williams (known subsequently as Ish) misses the plague because he is on a mountain-climbing trip (and perhaps because he suffers a rattlesnake bite). He makes his way back to the San Francisco area, helps restore a bit of civilization among the few survivors, and goes on an epic journey of discovery across the United

States. The novel raises serious questions about the cultural transmission of values and history as the survivors decide what to preserve and under what conditions survival itself is worthwhile.

H.L.P.

STILSON, CHARLES B. (?–?).

American writer who wrote in the first two decades of the twentieth century for Frank Munsey's magazines. All three novels of Stilson's trilogy (*Polaris of the Snows*, 1915; *Minos of the Sardanes*, 1916; and *Polaris and the Immortals*, 1917) were published first by *All-Story* and reissued in the mid-1960s as paperback books. The trilogy concerns a lost world in the Antarctic and the adventures of Polaris, a young man who tries to learn what lies in the North. His actions and words echo those of the more popular heroes of Edgar Rice BURROUGHS, particularly Tarzan and John Carter.

S.H.G.

STOCKTON, FRANK R. (Professional name of Francis Richard Stockton) (1834–1902).

American short story writer, novelist, and editor (for *Scribner's Magazine*). Stockton is best known for his short tale "The Lady or the Tiger?" (1882) and his novels *The Great War Syndicate* (1889) and *The Great Stone of Sandis* (1898). His numerous short stories and four novels combine humor with fantasy and science fiction.

N.H.

STOKER, BRAM (Professional name of Abraham Stoker) (1847–1912).

Irish author famed for the classic vampire novel *Dracula* (1897), which has been filmed over a hundred times and is the primary source for the image of the vampire in modern popular culture, including its use in science fiction. Where the figure of the vampire appears, as in Richard MATHESON's *I Am Legend* or Frederic BROWN's "Blood," it ultimately derives from *Dracula*. Stoker actually wrote as a sideline, devoting much of his time after 1877 to managing the career of the great actor Henry Irving. *Dracula* is a vivid horror novel, and certainly the definitive treatment of the vampire theme. Stoker's other work is sharply inferior; indeed it reads like something dashed off by a harried acting manager in his spare time, although there are some effective stories in *Dracula's Guest* (1914).

OTHER WORKS: *Under the Sunset* (1882); *The Mystery of the Sea* (1902); *The Jewel of the Seven Stars* (1903); *The Lady of the Shroud* (1909); *The Lair of the White Worm* (1911).

D.S.

STOVER, LEON E. (1929–).

American anthropologist, editor, and writer. Stover taught one of the earliest courses in science fiction (at the Illinois Institute of Technology) and published a critical study (*La Science-Fiction américaine: essai d'anthropologie culturelle*, 1972) based on his lectures. He has edited an SF anthology with Willis E. McNelly (*Above the Human Landscape*, 1972) and another with Harry Harrison (*Apeman, Spaceman: Anthropological Science Fiction*, (1968), and collaborated with Harrison on a lost Atlantis story (*Stonehenge*, 1972). Stover was the first chairman of the John W. Campbell Memorial Award committee.

S.H.G.

STRANGE INVADERS (1983).

Directed by Michael Laughlin; screenplay by William Condon and Michael Laughlin; photographed by Louis Horvath; music by John Addison. With Paul LeMat, Nancy Allen, Diana Scarwid, Michael Lerner, Louise Fletcher, Wallace Shawn, Fiona Lewis, Kenneth Tobey, June Lockhart, Charles Lane, Lulu Sylbert. 94 minutes. Color.

Strange Invaders is a sophisticated tribute to 1950s science-fiction movies, successful as both an involving thriller on its own terms and a spoof of the iconography of the fifties films, particularly Invaders from Mars (1953); Kenneth Tobey, a popular actor of the 1950s, is wittily cast as an alien.

When his ex-wife leaves their daughter with him and then vanishes, a college professor (Paul LeMat) becomes involved in a plot by aliens who took over a small town in 1958 and have been living there ever since. The government, assisting the aliens, also becomes involved.

Though showing an affection for and an understanding of its predecessors, *Strange Invaders* never merely copies their effects. The aliens turn out to be harmless, here only to study us. The departure of the alien impersonators, who literally shed their human faces as they go, is surprisingly poignant. The film is also highlighted by some of the most beautiful SPECIAL EFFECTS of the 1980s, created by John Muto, Robert Skotak, and Private Stock Effects, Inc. The first unmasking of an alien is unnervingly realistic.

The film's exhilarating mix of spoof and suspense puzzled audiences of the 1980s, unaccustomed as they were to intelligent movies about alien invasion. But *Strange Invaders* is likely to find its audience in years to come.

B.W.

STRETE, CRAIG [KEE] (1950–).

American writer and editor (for European publishers) who writes impassioned short stories that usually deal with social rather than technological themes. Strete makes extensive use of his Native American background in his stories, which most frequently deal with the pressure on minority groups to conform to the world of the white European male. In "Bleeding Man" (1974), for example, people are literally assimilated into the system as suppliers of blood. In "When They Find You" (1977) the colonization of other planets is viewed from the perspective of the victims it creates.

However, as powerful as Strete's themes may be, his stories are equally remarkable for their language and style. Frequently mythic in material and tone, such stories as "Time Deer" (1974) and "Why Has the Virgin Mary Never Entered the Wigwam of Standing Bear?" (1976) combine legend with science fiction in a style filled with haunting rhythmic patterns. In a genre dedicated to describing the present by looking to the future, Strete adds a historical point of view that rarely fails to startle readers into thought.

OTHER WORKS: *The Bleeding Man and Other Science Fiction Stories* (collection, 1977); *If All Else Fails* (collection, 1980; expanded edition of *Als Al het Andere Faalt*, Amsterdam, 1976); *Dreams That Burn in the Night* (collection, 1982).

S.H.G.

STRUGATSKY, ARKADY (1925–) and BORIS (1933–).

Russian brothers and science-fiction writers, arguably the Soviet Union's most eminent practitioners of the genre. The brothers Strugatsky, who have always written as a team, were educated as a linguist and a computer expert, respectively. Their first book was published in 1957; by 1986 they had published more than twenty books, many widely translated.

Their work began with the Noon, the Twenty-second Century cycle of novels (so called from the title of the collection of linked stories published in 1962). They returned to the same space-time continuum in their later works: *An Inhabited Island* (*The Prisoners of Power*, 1971), *The Kid* (*The Space Mowgli*, 1973), *The Guy from Hell* (1974), *A Beetle in the Anthill* (1980), and *Waves Dampen Wind* (1986). Appearing at first like an ideal utopian future, the setting's internal problems, tragic mistakes, and moral quests gradually become apparent.

The Strugatskys' other novels are connected by the central moral dilemma of interference in the development of less advanced planets and the quandary of means versus ends. In *Escape Attempt* (1962) and *Hard to Be a God* (1964), as well as some of the novels in the Noon cycle, questions are raised about the moral obligations of a highly civilized space race to interfere with underdeveloped planets, and those questions are analyzed on many levels. The means versus ends issue is brought to its logical conclusion—the realization that there are many possible ends—partly in *Roadside Picnic* (1972), which was filmed as *Stalker* (1981), and more completely in the later *A Billion Years to the End of the World* (*Def-*

initely Maybe, 1977).

The authors' gift for satire is manifested in light, humorous fairy tales, such as *Monday Begins at Saturday* (1965), and complex, bitter attacks on philistine consumers in *The Century's Objects of Prey* (*The Final Circle of Paradise*, 1965) and *The Second Martian Invasion* (1967). Their most complex work to date is a multileveled philosophical parable with a Kafkaesque plot, *The Snail on the Slope* (1966–1968).

V.G.

STURGEON, THEODORE (Born Edward Hamilton Waldo) (1918–1985).

American writer. Sturgeon held several transient jobs before settling into his writing career. Although he wrote some fiction (mostly hackwork) in other genres, his creative talents were almost exclusively focused on science fiction and fantasy, including some work for radio and TV. He was always a serious, often impassioned writer who did much to reveal the potential of SF and fantasy to dramatize human problems in quasi-allegorical form. The great majority of his stories feature alienated protagonists whose suffering is eventually healed by extraordinary—sometimes overtly miraculous—means. He was the most affectively powerful of all the recruits who helped shape John W. CAMPBELL's GOLDEN AGE, and though famed as a man who introduced sex into magazine SF, he has not been given due credit for introducing *love* into pulp SF, treating it earnestly and seriously.

Sturgeon's early stories, more fantasy than SF, are collected in *Without Sorcery* (1948; abridged as *Not without Sorcery*), *E Pluribus Unicorn* (1953), *Caviar* (1955), and *A Way Home* (1955; revised as *Thunder and Roses*). The psi boom of the 1950s provided him with the imaginative vocabulary to develop his characteristic themes in the SF field, and his first novel, *The Dreaming Jewels* (1950; also known as *The Synthetic Man*) is the story of a boy who runs away to join a circus and gradually acquires control of his latent superhumanity. This theme is dramatically sophisticated in the classic *More Than Human* (1953), in which a group of freak children combine their disparate powers into a collaborative gestalt.

In both stories much attention is paid to the matter of moral education, which remained a key theme in Sturgeon's stories of burgeoning superhumanity. The most spectacular of his accounts of transcendental evolution is *The Cosmic Rape* (1958), whose shorter magazine version, "To Marry Medusa," has also been reprinted in *The Joyous Invasions* (1965). Here an alien hive mind tries to absorb humankind, but having put human beings truly in touch with one another for the first time, it cannot cope with the power of the being thus created.

Sturgeon broke further new ground with his thoughtful utopian novel *Venus Plus X* (1960), which skeptically

Theodore Sturgeon

analyzes the possibility of an ideal society founded on physiologically reformed sexual politics. After this, however, his career went into something of a decline as he apparently grappled unsuccessfully with writer's block. He published a handful of new stories some years later, including the award-winning "Slow Sculpture" (1970), but most of these works give the impression of being unfinished would-be novels saved from abortion by makeshift conclusions. The collections of his stories issued in the 1970s and 1980s tend to recombine old materials or rescue relatively minor unreprinted works, although they are by no means uninteresting.

His last completed novel, the theological fantasy *Godbody* (1986), remained unpublished for many years until after his death. His last stories, notably "If All Men Were Brothers, Would You Let One Marry Your Sister" (1967) and "Why Dolphins Don't Bite" (1980), often frame desperate pleas for moral tolerance, offering speculative apologias for such taboo behaviors as incest and cannibalism. In this respect they echo his fascinating psychoanalytical melodrama *Some of Your Blood* (1961), about the tribulations of a young vampire. An SF short story award in Sturgeon's honor has been established at the University of Kansas, where his manuscripts and papers have been deposited.

OTHER WORKS: *A Touch of Strange* (collection, 1958); *Aliens 4* (collection, 1959); *Beyond* (collection, 1960); *Sturgeon in Orbit* (collection, 1964); *. . . And My Fear Is Great and Baby Is Three* (collection, 1965); *Starshine* (collection, 1966); *Sturgeon Is Alive and Well* (collection, 1971); *The Worlds of Theodore Sturgeon* (collection, 1972); *To Here and the Easel* (collection,

1973); *Case and the Dreamer* (collection, 1973); *Visions and Venturers* (collection, 1978); *Maturity* (collection, 1979); *The Golden Helix* (collection, 1979); *The Stars Are the Styx* (collection, 1979); *Slow Sculpture* (collection, 1982); *Alien Cargo* (collection, 1984).

B.S.

SUCHARITKUL, SOMTOW [PAPINIAN] (1953–).

Thai author and musical composer, educated in Britain, resident in Hollywood; adept at the depiction of bizarre, alien cultures. Most of Sucharitkul's work, often space opera of the gaudiest sort, is indeed bizarre, but the gaudiness is an ironic mask for satiric concerns. He achieved prominence in the late 1970s with his Mallworld and Inquestor series of short stories in ISAAC ASIMOV'S SCIENCE FICTION MAGAZINE. The Mallworld stories are uproarious comedies of tacky consumerism about a shopping mall in space which also have moments of real drama. The Inquestor series is an elaborate attempt, in the author's words, to create a universe "of extreme cruelty and beauty" in which the utopia-destroying Inquestors play inscrutable games with human destiny. Both series have spawned books, but Sucharitkul's first published novel was *Starship and Haiku* (1981), a beautifully restrained tale of a death-worshiping, postholocaust future; it remains among his finest works.

Sucharitkul's strengths include a splendid lyricism, sensitive characterizations, and outrageous inventiveness, but he can also be flashy and self-indulgent. Already enormously prolific, he is still in a formative stage, and may well turn out to be a superstar of the 1990s.

OTHER WORKS: *Mallworld* (1981; revised 1984); *Light on the Sound* (1982; revised as *The Dawning Shadow: Light on the Sound*, 1986); *The Throne of Madness* (1983; revised as *The Dawning Shadow: The Throne of Madness*, 1986); *Fire from the Wine Dark Sea* (1983); *The Utopia Hunters* (1984); *Vampire Junction* (1984, as S. P. Somtow); *The Darkling Wind* (1985); *The Alien Swordmaster* (1985); *The Fallen Country* (1986); *The Shattered Horse* (1986, as S. P. Somtow).

D.S.

SUMMERS, LEO RAMON (1925–1985).

American illustrator who did most of his work for GALAXY and *Astounding*/ANALOG, although some of his art appeared in AMAZING and *Fantastic* when he was the art director for Ziff-Davis (1952–1956). Summers's humorous drawing style is sketchy and almost cartoonish, with light, loose lines. While at Ziff-Davis he engineered the change of the company's magazines from pulp format to digest size. Although he produced a few *Fantastic* covers, most of his work is magazine interiors.

J.G.

SUPERGIRL (1984).

Directed by Jeannot Szwarc; screenplay by David Odell; photographed by Alan Hume; music by Jerry Goldsmith. With Helen Slater, Faye Dunaway, Hart Bochner, Brenda Vaccaro, Peter Cook, Marc McClure, Maureen Teefy, Peter O'Toole, Mia Farrow, Simon Ward. 114 minutes. Color.

Made by the same producers as the SUPERMAN films, *Supergirl* pleased few, perhaps because the approach its makers took differs so much from that of the Superman films. Certainly, *Supergirl* is less spectacular, centering on a romantic rivalry rather than the fate of the world. Also, it treats the well-established mythology from the comics cavalierly.

Kara, Superman's cousin (Helen Slater), has to come to Earth, where she (unlike Clark Kent) *magically* becomes Supergirl, battling a carnival mentalist who has acquired the magical object Supergirl seeks.

Presumably the makers felt this movie would appeal mostly to teenage girls and so relied on emotional elements rather than logic. The beginning of the film is foolish and it alienated many; by the time *Supergirl* becomes a pleasant action comedy in the second half, most have given up on it.

B.W.

——————— SUPERMAN ———————

One of the most popular comic-book features of all time, *Superman* presents a hero who was rocketed from his home planet, Krypton, as an infant and raised on Earth, where he found he had superhuman powers: the ability to fly, the strength of a hundred men, and nearly total invulnerability.

Superman was the brainchild of two young science-fiction fans living in Cleveland, writer Jerome Siegel and artist Joseph Shuster. He was not the first character they had created who possessed extraordinary abilities. The January 1933 issue of their fanzine *Science Fiction* offered a villain with incredible mental powers in a story entitled "The Reign of the Superman."

They later decided to collaborate on a comic strip involving a heroic Superman. "We were in the depths of the great Depression. The world was full of cruel injustices, and in Europe war seemed imminent. I wondered what *I* would do if I could make things better," Siegel was once quoted as saying. He postulated the idea of a "a character like Samson, Hercules and all the strong men I ever heard tell of rolled into one."

Siegel and Shuster spent five years looking for a publisher for *Superman*. They wanted it to be a newspaper comic strip but were continually rejected by syndicates. The breakthrough came when editor Sheldon Mayer liked the idea enough to have it shown to Harry Donenfield, president of the company that eventually became known as DC Comics. Mayer described his enthusiasm for the

Superman in the comics

strip, comparing it with other favorite stories—*The Scarlet Pimpernel, Zorro,* and *The Desert Song,* wherein the mystery man and his alter ego are in effect two distinct characters "to be played off against each other." Mayer said, "The Scarlet Pimpernel's alter ego was scared of the sight of blood, a hopeless dandy; no one would have suspected he was a hero. The same goes for *Superman.* Give the audience an opportunity to say, 'Boy, isn't the bad guy gonna get it when the sissy turns into a hero,' and they'll love you for it!"

The audience indeed couldn't get enough of Superman. His debut in the June 1938 *Action Comics* No. 1 was a success and prompted the launch of a title devoted solely to his adventures the following year. The comics introduced the paradox of Superman's secret identity: a timid Clark Kent, he tried in vain to garner the attention of his reporter colleague Lois Lane. But Lois had eyes only for her flying hero and despised Clark for his cowardice.

Months after *Superman*'s first appearance, *The Adventures of Superman,* a radio program broadcast three times a week, debuted on the Mutual Network, then on ABC. Producer Robert Maxwell cast Clayton "Bud" Collyer in the title role. Collyer became so important to the program that the writers had to concoct a unique way to replace him during his two-week vacation. They invented Kryptonite, a substance so deadly that Superman could barely talk while exposed to it. All faithful listeners heard was the sound of their helpless hero moaning . . .

until Collyer returned. The series also added the character of Jimmy Olsen, cub reporter, to the supporting cast.

A newspaper strip for the McClure Syndicate began in 1939. The strip's art chores were inherited three years later by Wayne Boring, who continued to draw it until it ceased publication in 1967.

Between 1941 and 1943, seventeen animated cartoons featuring Superman were produced by Max and Dave Fleischer, whose Fleischer Studios had enjoyed previous success with characters such as Betty Boop, Koko the Clown, and Popeye. Paramount Pictures, the studio's distributor, had suggested that they do a series of Superman cartoons, but the Fleischers refused, citing the high cost of realistic animation and varied special effects. When Paramount pressed them, the Fleischers invented a budget that was four times their normal production cost: $100,000. To their surprise, Paramount agreed. To keep the feel of both the strip and the radio show, the Fleischers hired Joe Shuster to draw elaborate model sheets and Bud Collyer to provide Superman's voice. Fleischer Studios did the first nine cartoons. They were taken over in 1943 by Paramount and renamed Famous Studios; that organization produced the last eight cartoons.

Because of their unusually high budgets, the Fleischers were able to create enormously elaborate animation. The process of rotoscoping—tracing drawings over live-action film of actors—was used to simulate motion as accurately as possible. Ominous shadows, always difficult to animate well, loomed everywhere, and the cartoons rivaled the work of the Fleischers' chief competitor, Walt Disney; they remain staples of animation festivals throughout the country.

Kirk Alyn played the Man of Steel, often doing his own stunts, in two fifteen-chapter Columbia movie serials, *Superman* (1948) and *Atom Man vs. Superman* (1950). To show Superman in flight, the producers used an animated figure of the Man of Steel.

George Reeves played the lead in the feature film *Superman and the Mole Men* (1951). He went on to appear in the 104 episodes of the television series *The Adventures of Superman* from 1951 to 1957. The show is distinctive for having some of its episodes filmed in color, a rarity for the 1950s, largely through the foresight of its executive producer, DC editor Whitney Ellsworth.

In 1966 Superman was animated for television by Filmation, in *The New Adventures of Superman.* The animation was simple, often stiff, as a result of the restrictive budgets of television production. Many shortcuts had to be taken to produce the cartoons quickly and cheaply, and unfortunately the corner cutting showed. The same sequence of Clark changing into his Superman outfit was used over and over again. In one episode, Superman's *S* emblem appears on his chest backward (perhaps because one sequence of drawings was "flopped," or reversed, to create another set). But for all that, the series remained as close to the comics as possible. Luthor, Brainiac, and Mr. Mxyzptlk appear very much like their comic-book counterparts, Lois Lane keeps the pillbox hat she wore in so many issues of the magazine, and Jimmy Olsen sports his ubiquitous bow tie.

In 1973 Hanna-Barbera produced *Super Friends*, an animated series featuring Superman, Batman, and other DC heroes. This show had to comply with strict new network guidelines regarding the portrayal of violence, so the plots are a good deal "softer" than their forerunners. The series introduced a pair of alien teenagers, another pair of Earthling kids, and their inevitable pets, a dog and a creature that resembles an otherworldly chimp. After many title changes, the show was still running in 1986 as *The Super Powers Show*.

In 1978 Christopher Reeve played the Man of Steel in the first of three big-budget films produced by Alexander and Ilya Salkind. *Superman the Movie* was directed by Richard Donner, with a screenplay by Mario Puzo. Gene Hackman played Superman's nefarious enemy, Lex Luthor, and Marlon Brando portrayed the Man of Steel's Kryptonian father, Jor-El. Richard Lester directed both *Superman II* (1980) and *Superman III* (1983), the latter featuring Richard Pryor as a bumbling, would-be bad guy, and Annette O'Toole as Clark Kent's hometown sweetheart, Lana Lang. The first two films were well received by critics and managed to capture the grandeur and nobility of the character's Kryptonian roots, and Christopher Reeve portrayed the Man of Steel as down-to-earth, human, and likable. The third film in the series, however, could not unite its disparate plot and stylistic elements, part small-town romance, part James Bondian scheme to take over the world, part Richard Pryor farce. Another sequel, *Superman IV: the Quest for Peace*, was released in 1987. A well-intentioned tale of Superman's efforts to rid the globe of nuclear weapons, it failed to impress critics or audiences and quickly faded from theaters.

Superman, in all its forms, did a great deal to popularize far-flung science-fiction ideas, among them extraterrestrial civilizations, space travel, and enhanced human capabilities. The comic book's editors, particularly Mort Weisinger and later Julius Schwartz, themselves longtime SF fans, worked hard to give *Superman* at least a pseudoscientific background, positing, for example, that Earth's gravity is less than that of the Man of Steel's home planet, Krypton, thereby explaining his ability to fly. Under the tutelage of Weisinger and Schwartz, no SF theme went unexplored.

The book continues to do well today. Over the years artists such as Curt Swan, Murphy Anderson, Kurt Schaffenberger, and Al Plastino did much to crystallize the clean, crisp style of the feature.

In 1986 slipping sales led to a revamping and restyling of the Superman legend. A six-issue miniseries, *The Man*

George Reeves as television's Man of Steel

of Steel, written and drawn by John Byrne, became one of the largest-selling comic books of the past fifteen years. Superman himself has been downscaled somewhat. He no longer possesses the power to move planets, and his strength and the optimum ability of his various powers have been lessened. Further, in this revisionist version of the legend, Superman's adoptive parents, Ma and Pa Kent, are still alive. There are no other survivors of planet Krypton: no Supergirl; no superdog, Krypto; no Super-Monkey. Young Clark never became Superboy, the Boy of Steel. Superman's secret identity is no longer the subject of intrigue. It is not generally assumed by the public that he *has* one. While by no means macho, Clark is no longer "meek" or "mild-mannered"; he keeps Nautilus equipment in his apartment to explain his muscles.

This effort has been made to make the character fit the mold of current comic-book buyers' tastes in adventure heroes. It guarantees that Superman will continue to endure in his readers' imaginations.

Superman (1978).   *Directed by Richard Donner; screenplay by Mario Puzo; photographed by Geoffrey Unsworth; music by John Williams. With Christopher Reeve, Margot Kidder, Marlon Brando, Gene Hackman, Ned Beatty, Jackie Cooper, Marc McClure, Glenn Ford, Valerie Perrine, Phyllis Thaxter, Jeff East, Trevor Howard, Susannah York. 143 minutes. Color.*

Superman II (1980).   *Directed by Richard Lester; screenplay by Mario Puzo; photographed by Bob Paynter; music by John Williams. With Christopher Reeve, Margot Kidder, Gene Hackman, Ned Beatty, Jackie Cooper, Valerie Perrine, Susannah York, Clifton James, E. G. Marshall, Marc McClure, Terence Stamp, Sarah Douglas, Jack O'Halloran. 127 minutes. Color.*

Superman III (1983).   *Directed by Richard Les-*

ter; screenplay by David and Leslie Newman; photographed by Robert Paynter; music by John Williams. With Christopher Reeve, Richard Pryor, Annette O'Toole, Jackie Cooper, Marc McClure, Annie Ross, Pamela Stephenson, Robert Vaughn, Margot Kidder. 123 minutes. Color.

Superman IV: the Quest for Peace (1987). Directed by Sidney J. Furie; screenplay by Lawrence Konner and Mark Rosenthal; photographed by Ernest Day; music by John Williams. With Christopher Reeve, Gene Hackman, Margot Kidder, Jon Cryer, Mariel Hemingway, Jackie Cooper, Marc McClure, Mark Pillow. 89 minutes. Color.

J.T.C.

SUPERMEN

Supermen are featured in profusion in ancient mythologies, but it was only in the wake of Charles Darwin that writers again began to imagine the emergence of superhumans in our midst. British scientific romance produced an abundance of such images; early examples, such as H. G. WELLS's Food of the Gods (1904) and J. D. BERESFORD's The Hampdenshire Wonder (1911), laid the groundwork for such novels as Odd John (1934) by Olaf STAPLEDON and The Young Men Are Coming! (1937) by M. P. SHIEL, which reflect postwar disillusionment with contemporary humankind. The French writer Alfred Jarry treated the idea mockingly in The Supermale (1902), but The New Adam (1924), by his compatriot Noelle Roger, regards the advent of a hyperrational superman as a threat of which humanity must beware. This theme was popularized in the science-fiction pulps in such tales as Seeds of Life (1931) by John TAINE and The Intelligence Gigantic (1933) by John Russell FEARN. American writers, though, also produced stories sympathetic to the position of isolated supermen in the human world: Gladiator (1930) by Philip WYLIE and The New Adam (1936) by Stanley G. WEINBAUM.

The readiness of SF writers and readers to identify with persecuted supermen was soon displayed in lavish measure, first by A. E. VAN VOGT in Slan (1940) and many other novels, and later by writers such as Zenna HENDERSON and Wilmar H. SHIRAS. A new stereotype of the superman was provided in the 1940s by Duke University parapsychologist J. B. Rhine, whose notion that anyone might be harboring latent "psi powers" became the warrant for countless wish fulfillment fantasies as well as more thoughtful stories about individuals and whole societies adapting to the acquisition of these capabilities. Alfred BESTER's The Demolished Man (1953) and Poul ANDERSON's Brain Wave (1954) are examples. The enthusiasm of SF writers for the idea of metamorphosis into superhumanity extended to take in more striking transcendence, as in More Than Human (1953) by Theodore STURGEON and Childhood's End (1953) by Arthur C. CLARKE. Although the 1950s psi boom is now long gone, interest in emerging superhumanity remains a central concern in the work of several leading writers, including Robert SILVERBERG, the late Frank HERBERT, and Ian WATSON.

B.S.

SUPERPOWERS

One of the basic themes of science fiction is the human development of superpowers—understandably so, since the essential subject of much SF is change, and the creation or evolution of extraordinary physical or mental powers can create significant change for those who possess them or those who must cope with them. Authors have considered such questions as What powers would confer true superiority? How would such powers reveal themselves, and what advantages or disadvantages would they involve? How would individuals and society as a whole respond to the possession of such powers? How would others react to those who have such powers? What kind of world would the presence of these extraordinary powers create?

Before World War II individuals with a wide range of unusual powers—SUPERMAN, Doc Savage, Tarzan, the Shadow—were protagonists in popular fiction, not just in SF. Usually they were portrayed as heroes, physically as well as mentally superior, who used their special talents to fight crime or evil in general. Such multipowered figures who righted wrongs or worked for good also figured in the SF of the period. E. E. "Doc" SMITH's heroic Lensmen were typical, although to be sure their enemies, agents of the evil Boskone, were almost as powerful.

A few writers, mostly in the mainstream, such as J. D. BERESFORD in The Hampdenshire Wonder (1911), Philip WYLIE in Gladiator (1930), and W. Olaf STAPLEDON in Odd John (1935), presented such people as the tragic victims of society, inevitably destroyed by envy or hatred. Occasionally, however, writers such as Stanley G. WEINBAUM in "The Adaptive Ultimate" (1935) presented them as potential tyrants.

Concern about human distrust, or hatred, of difference or superiority continued in postwar SF: Judith MERRIL's "That Only a Mother" (1948) shows fathers killing their defective though talented children; Wilmar H. SHIRAS's "In Hiding" (1948; expanded into Children of the Atom, 1953) reveals superior children learning to hide their abilities from adult society; Algis BUDRYS's "Nobody Bothers Gus" (1955) offers the suggestion that superpowers would evolve with the natural protection of going unnoticed.

In Frank M. ROBINSON's The Power (1956; filmed 1967), the hero hunts a villain with superpowers, including the ability to make others perceive him differently, and in the end develops his own special abilities. The tyrannical aspect of superpowers reached its ultimate expression in Jerome BIXBY's "It's a *Good* Life" (1953), wherein a child's omnipotence releases upon a group of people unfettered, amoral childish desires.

The question of society organizing itself against superpowers or the individuals who possess them is the concern of A. E. VAN VOGT's *Slan* (1940) and James BLISH's *Jack of Eagles* (1951), in which the respective heroes engage in almost continuous conflict with the society around them and with antagonists who possess the same powers. In Theodore STURGEON's *More Than Human* (1953) the group of talented individuals who form a gestalt superman are all social outcasts because of their special abilities. In Arthur C. CLARKE's *Childhood's End* (1953) the strange children who evolve from humanity to join the Overmind must be protected by aliens, and the children are so inhuman that when they depart they destroy the Earth and everything on it.

Earlier writers, too, had considered the drawbacks of special talents: H. G. WELLS's *The Invisible Man* (1897) expresses the idea that invisibility has major drawbacks, and his "The Story of Davidson's Eyes" (1895) deals with a man who gets nothing but trouble out of an accident that enables him to see what is happening on the other side of the world. Immortality, in works from H. Rider HAGGARD's *She* (1886) through Aldous HUXLEY's *After Many a Summer Dies the Swan* (1939) to James E. GUNN's *The Immortals* (1962), often exacts a payment. Stories of telepathy, best illustrated by Robert SILVERBERG's *Dying Inside* (1972), often emphasize the loneliness of the person who can read minds and sometimes the unpleasantness, agony, or even insanity involved in sharing other people's thoughts or being unable to shut them out. In fact, the point of many such stories is not only that every new development has disadvantages but that humanity may be better off without superpowers.

Other authors have dealt with societies in which superpowers have been integrated; the implicit moral of most SF is that, since change will occur whatever we do, we must learn to live with it. In *The Demolished Man* (1953) and *The Stars My Destination* (1956), Alfred BESTER described societies in which telepathy and teleportation have become as commonplace as the telephone and the airplane. A. E. van Vogt's *The World of Null-A* (1945/1948) deals with a man of undiscovered superpowers in a society that has institutionalized Alfred Korzybski's non-Aristotelian (or null-A) thinking, which gives exceptional mental abilities to those who master it. In *Dune* (1963–64/1965) and its sequels Frank HERBERT showed a galactic empire coping with an array of strange talents developed through drugs, environment, the banning of computers, and genetic manipulation. But Herbert also revealed the difficulties involved, including the terrible burden of precognition and the danger to humanity of its search for messiahs.

In recent fiction about superpowers, computers play an increasingly central role, often bestowing power on those who can work with them most effectively: William GIBSON's CYBERPUNK classic *Neuromancer* (1984) was the first of a group of such works that show the consequences of superpowers not in the lives of the characters, who cope with their unpleasant environment as best they can, but in the gritty, amoral underworld the computers and their sometime masters, the great international corporations, create or allow to exist.

S.E.G.

SWANWICK, MICHAEL [JURGEN] (1950–).
American science-fiction writer who has made a steady climb to notice since the publication of his first story, "The Feast of St. Janis," in *New Dimensions II* in 1980. That story and "Ginungagap" were finalists for the Nebula Award in 1981. The following year "Mummer Kiss" was a Nebula Award finalist and "The Man Who Met Picasso" was a finalist for the World Fantasy Award.

Two stories published in 1984—"Trojan Horse" and "Marrow Death"—were Nebula finalists, as were "The Gods of Mars" (with Gardner DOZOIS and Jack DANN) and "Dogfight" (with William GIBSON) for 1985. That was the year his first novel, *In the Drift*, an alternate-history story in which the Three Mile Island reactor melted down and created a death zone known as the Drift, was published as a Terry Carr Ace Special. His second novel, *Vacuum Flowers*, was a Nebula finalist for 1987. Up to that time he had been identified primarily with the "humanist" school of SF, but *Vacuum Flowers*, with its plug-in personalities and colonized asteroids, was greeted as quintessential CYBERPUNK.

Swanwick has been published in *Omni*, *Penthouse*, and *Triquarterly* in addition to the usual SF magazines. Born in Schenectady, New York, he lives in Philadelphia and in 1988 was at work on a third novel and a collection of short stories.

J.E.G.

SWIFT, JONATHAN (1667–1745).   British poet,
satirist, and Anglican cleric. Swift's satire of science anticipated science fiction's technique of extrapolating experimental discoveries into unknown worlds in order to understand present reality more clearly, and his social criticism has transcended the controversial issues of his time and become a high water mark of literary satire. He is justly famous for his acerbic attacks on religion (*A Tale of a Tub*, 1704), learning (*The Battle of the Books*, 1704), and economic exploitation (*A Modest Proposal*, 1729). Swift's magnum opus, however, is *Gulliver's Travels* (1726), a voyage to imaginary lands that prefigured and ultimately led to the development of SF.

In Book 3, "The Voyage to Laputa," *Gulliver's Trav-*

els brilliantly exposes the insanity of a science that does not serve humanity. Few modern readers will fail to see the connection between Swift's "Flying Island," in which scientists (SF's first mad scientists) threaten harried inhabitants with annihilation, and the more contemporary fears of the postatomic age (typified in *Dr. Strangelove*). Swift satirized the very instruments and theories of eighteenth-century scientists by making them the vehicles for his caricatures: the microscope was represented by the Lilliputian view; the telescope by the Brobdingnagian view; Isaac Newton's mathematics and gravitational theories by the scientists of Laputa; and the ideal of Reason by the Houyhnhnms.

M.T.W.

T

TAINE, JOHN (Pseudonym of Eric Temple Bell) (1883–1960).

American author of fantastic novels and short stories who, under his real name, was an eminent mathematician and teacher—professor of mathematics at the California Institute of Technology, president of the Mathematical Association of America, and a research mathematician, author of mathematical tests, and science popularizer.

About half of Taine's science-fantasy adventure novels were published as original books; the other half appeared first in PULP MAGAZINES. His first novel, *The Purple Sapphire* (1924), is a fantasy about a lost world; most of his science fiction, however, concerns technological disasters in which teams of oddly mixed characters seek out the causes of the disaster, sometimes, as in *The Time Stream* (1931/1946), traveling in time. Another Taine novel, *Before the Dawn* (1934), shows viewers in the present following the adventures of a dinosaur. Much of Taine's work deals with evolutionary possibilities: *Seeds of Life* (1931/1951) is an important early superman novel based on the notion of radiation speeding up evolution, an idea used as well in *The Iron Star* (1930). *The Crystal Horde* (1930/1952) also concerns evolution, in this case of living crystals.

Taine's style is direct and readable. His resolutions are often tentative, with occasional intimations of tragedy or regret, as when explorers in *The Forbidden Garden* (1947), another evolutionary novel, speculate on whether their germ cells have been affected by their stay in radioactive surroundings.

OTHER WORKS: *Quayle's Invention* (1927); *The Gold Tooth* (1927); *Green Fire* (1928); *The Greatest Adventure* (1929); *The Cosmic Geoids and One Other* (1949); *G.O.G. 666* (1954).

R.H.W.

TARANTULA (1955).

Directed by Jack Arnold; screenplay by Robert M. Fresco and Martin Berkeley; adapted from the episode "No Food for Thought" by Robert M. Fresco for Science Fiction Theatre; *photographed by George Robinson. With John Agar, Mara Corday, Leo G. Carroll, Nestor Paiva, Ross Elliott, Clint Eastwood. 80 minutes. Black and white.*

To increase food supplies for a hungry world, scientists working in desert isolation produce a nutrient that grows animals to enormous proportions but proves to cause acromegaly in human beings. When one of the scientists, who had experimented on himself, goes insane and injects head scientist Leo G. Carroll, a spider escapes. Continually growing, it menaces all and sundry until it is finally destroyed by Air Corps pilot Clint Eastwood.

Constructed as a mystery, this exciting and suspenseful "big bug" film, like many of director Jack ARNOLD's science-fiction movies, is set in the southwestern desert. The giant arachnid—a real spider, photographically enlarged—is generally convincing, and Carroll gives a creditable performance as the scientist accidentally responsible for the dire happenings. Clifford Stine and David S. Horsley provided the special effects.

B.W.

————— TELEVISION —————

Television was part of science fiction long before science fiction became part of television. In 1898, in "From the 'London Times' of 1904," Mark TWAIN described the "telelectroscope," and even earlier, in 1882, Albert Robida's *The Twentieth Century*, published in France, anticipated a future society permeated by what the author-illustrator called the "telephonoscope." Since he had no concept of broadcasting, Robida forecast, in effect, *cable* television. But he was right on the mark about its social impact, as the dominant medium of news and entertainment, and as a profound influence on cultural values.

Hugo GERNSBACK, father of the science-fiction magazine, coined the word *television* in 1909 in his popular-science magazine *Modern Electrics* (he also coined the phrase *science fiction* in the first issue of *Science Wonder Stories* in 1929, but nothing quite as prophetic as Robida's work appeared in early magazine SF, although Gernsback's own 1911 novel, *Ralph 124C 41+*, predicted television as well as radar, night baseball, and dozens of other technological marvels. Some later stories, such as Stanley G. WEINBAUM's "A Martian Odyssey" (1934), refer to television programs in passing, but television as a social phenomenon was rarely touched on in the classics of the 1930s.

In what passed for SF film, the medium was strictly a novelty—used, for example, as *machina ex dei* to trap

Companion comic book to TV's *Captain Video*

the villain in *The Phantom Empire* (1935) and to reveal a pleading Dale Arden to FLASH GORDON (and an endangered Flash to Dale) in that 1936 serial. Telescreens, used for communication, were actually more common than television in magazine science-fiction and movie serials alike. By the 1940s, however, social awareness had set in—Henry KUTTNER's "The Proud Robot" (1943), for example, is placed against a background of commercial rivalry between TV and movies, and even earlier, Theodore STURGEON's first SF story, "Ether Breather" (1939), dealt with creatures inhabiting the ether who play havoc with commercial TV.

By 1949 commercial television was a reality—Gernsback, again, had broadcast the first television program in 1928 over his radio station WRNY (he also issued the first television magazine, *Television*, that same year—but transcontinental broadcasting would not start for another two years). One of the earliest programs was SF: *Captain Video* (1949–1953), soon followed by *Space Cadet* (1950–1956). Both were juvenile, with small budgets, but *Space Cadet*—based on an idea by Robert A. HEINLEIN and with Willy LEY as technical adviser—was by far the better of the two. Most other programs of the 1950s, such as *The Adventures of Superman*

(1953–1957), *Space Patrol* (1954–55), and *Rocky Jones* (1955–56) were also juvenile and usually scientifically illiterate as well. An exception was *Tales of Tomorrow* (1952–1954), an anthology series that included adaptations of work by Heinlein, Weinbaum, Leinster, Cyril M. KORNBLUTH, William TENN, and other noted science-fiction writers. *Science Fiction Theater* (1955–1957), while striving for the same sort of relative dignity, suffered from a lack of real SF input—its stories were an outsider's idea of the genre. Oddly enough, all of these overlapped with RADIO's *Dimension X* and *X Minus One*, broadcast off and on between 1949 and 1957, in which the dramatization of SF may have reached its highest point. *One Step Beyond* (1959–1961) and *Thriller* (1960–1962) were almost entirely fantasy, and *Batman* (1966–1968) was a juvenile series derived from the comic book but played for camp.

Still regarded as the two greatest SF TV series of all time are Rod SERLING's THE TWILIGHT ZONE (1959–1964) and Gene RODDENBERRY's STAR TREK (1966–1969). Strictly speaking, Serling's program was as much fantasy and allegory as SF (Serling's 1970–72 *Night Gallery* was mostly occult, but broadcast an occasional excellent SF adaptation such as Kornbluth's "The Little Black Bag"). It also served as an outlet for the sort of social criticism rigorously avoided by commercial TV. Richard MATHESON, in such episodes as "Nightmare at 20,000 Feet" (a "gremlin" attacks an airliner) and "Third from the Sun" (a family flees threatened atomic war on its planet for the "safe" haven of what turns out to be Earth), typified the thematic concerns of the series. Charles Beaumont was the other best-known contributor, but Serling himself set the tone with his wry, ironic introductions and episodes, and he paid his sources the ultimate tribute of respecting their words and visions enough to try to replicate their impact on the screen.

Star Trek, by contrast, was meant to be hard-core SF, full of alien worlds and scientific wonders. It wasn't quite that—it wasn't "*Wagon Train* to the stars," as Roddenberry tried to sell it to a reluctant network, either. The settings and ideas that once seemed sophisticated may now seem quaint, but Roddenberry's series did indeed introduce a mass audience to the universe of science fiction, and helped pave the way for STAR WARS and the revolution in SF film that followed (including the tremendously popular *Star Trek* films themselves), though its spectacular success and influence came in syndication. While it attracted the talent of Harlan ELLISON, Theodore STURGEON, Norman SPINRAD, and other SF writers, their contributions were ultimately less important than the spirit of the series, expressed in the relationship among Kirk, Spock, and the other members of the *Enterprise* crew, and in the continuing theme (despite the Klingons) of the brotherhood of intelligent life and a bright and hopeful future for humanity. Its successful 1987 sequel, *Star Trek: The New Generation*, even

Alien from *The Outer Limits*

made peace with the Klingons.

Leslie Stevens's *The Outer Limits* (1963–1965) was another anthology series in the tradition of *Twilight Zone*. Despite some outstanding episodes, such as Ellison's "Demon with a Glass Hand," it was mostly a monster mash. Quinn Martin's *The Invaders* (1967–68) had an intriguing premise (aliens imitating humans and attempting to do away with Roy Thinnes, the only man who has caught on to what is happening), but could find no viable variations upon its chase format. *The Immortal* (1970–71), adapted from James GUNN's 1962 *The Immortals,* also was played as a series of chases (including endless car chases) and lasted only a season. *The Starlost* (1973), a syndicated series about a generation starship, was so compromised in production that creator and screenwriter Harlan Ellison disowned it with a derisive pseudonym, Cordwainer Bird. Irwin ALLEN was responsible for several series, the most successful being LOST IN SPACE (1965–1968), which involved a middle-class family stranded on another planet and had more charm than intelligence. Lacking in both were such other Allen efforts as VOYAGE TO THE BOTTOM OF THE SEA (1964–1968), *The Time Tunnel* (1966–67), and LAND OF THE GIANTS (1968–1970), and Gerry Anderson's *U.F.O.* (1969–70) and SPACE 1999 (1975–1977)—marked down, as one wag put it, from 2001.

The last two, oddly enough, were British productions, and the British have traditionally done better with SF adaptations than the U.S., notably with *The Avengers* (1962–1963 and 1966–1969, of which the 1966–68 years, in which Diana Rigg played Mrs. Emma Peel, were the most popular), which had SF episodes; *The Prisoner* (1968, only seventeen episodes), which was as much paranoia as science fiction; the incredibly long-lasting DOCTOR WHO (1963–   ), which started life as a children's show and became a cult series with many adults; and the special series: *A for Andromeda* (1961) and *The Andromeda Breakthrough* (1962) written by Norman Jones and cosmologist (and SF writer) Fred HOYLE; and Nigel Kneale's highly praised QUATERMASS series (*The Quatermass Xperiment,* 1953, *Quatermass II,* 1957, and *Quatermass and the Pit,* 1958, all of which were turned into films).

Some of the most successful SF TV series have been situation comedies such as Jack Chertok's MY FAVORITE MARTIAN (1963–1966), starring Ray Walston, and Dale McRaven's MORK AND MINDY (1978–1982), which introduced Robin Williams. Harve Bennett's *The Six Million Dollar Man* (1973–1978), which had an SF premise (the bionic man) but was played for adventure, was a top draw at its time slot (but mostly for a juvenile audience), spawned *The Bionic Woman* (1976), and featured, for a time, a Bionic Boy. For some reason robots haven't done as well on the tube as aliens or bionically altered people: Chertok's *My Living Doll* (1964–65) was a failure. More spectacular have been the failures of programs inspired by the success of *Star Wars,* such as John Dykstra's BATTLESTAR GALACTICA (1978–79) and Richard Caffey's BUCK ROGERS (1979–1981), which imitated the special effects of George LUCAS without creating any real *sense* of SF. Subsequent failures, such as that of Kenneth Johnson's *V* (1983–84), which was more successful in book form than on the screen, might have soured the medium, at least for big-budget SF.

The ideal format for SF on television would seem to be the anthology show, allowing, as it does, the presentation of a new *idea* each week. In 1985 three attempts were made to bring it back to television: an hour-long *Twilight Zone,* featuring two or more different stories each show, a half-hour refilming of *Alfred Hitchcock Presents,* and Steven SPIELBERG's half-hour *Amazing Stories.* None of them was successful enough to gain a TV-sized audience, demonstrating the truth that while SF thrives on change, viewers want to tune in each week to familiar faces and situations. And *that* may mean that *Star Trek* and its successor, with their continuing cast but changing challenges, are as close to science fiction as television is going to get.

                                                                                  J.J.P.

TEMPLE, WILLIAM F[REDERICK] (1914–   ).

British author whose interest in science fiction developed in his native England under the influence of Arthur C. CLARKE, John WYNDHAM, and John CHRISTOPHER; like them, he tried to expand the traditional boundaries of the genre, particularly in what he called "the third dimension" of character. Temple's characters are better drawn than those in many works of the time, and his plots are often ingenious, as in his first, and most successful, novel, *The Four-Sided Triangle* (1939/1949), in which a disappointed suitor creates a duplicate of his beloved in a matter copier. Because she is an exact duplicate, however, she also chooses the other man, and the resulting confusion is handled with deftness and humor. The novel was filmed in 1953. Temple also wrote ninety-three short stories published in magazines and collections.

OTHER WORKS: *Martin Magnus, Planet Rover* (1955); *Martin Magnus on Mars* (1956); *The Automated Goliath* (1962); *The Three Suns of Amara* (1962); *Battle on Venus* (1963); *Shoot at the Moon* (1966); *The Fleshpots of Sansato* (1968).

R.H.W.

TENN, WILLIAM (Pseudonym of Philip Klass) (1920–).

American author and academic. Tenn was a prolific writer of science-fiction short stories during the 1950s, particularly for *Galaxy* but has written little since the early 1960s. He became a professor of English at Pennsylvania State University in 1966. His stories are often deftly satiric, and he was particularly adept at exploring the ironic possibilities of time travel plots. Almost all his short fiction is assembled in six volumes: *Of All Possible Worlds* (1955), *The Human Angle* (1956), *Time in Advance* (1958), *The Seven Sexes* (1968), *The Square Root of Man* (1968), and *The Wooden Star* (1968). His longer works are a comic short novel about a man transported back to the world of Greek mythology, *A Lamp for Medusa* ("Medusa Was a Lady," 1951/1968), and a novel about humans living like mice in the dwellings of giant alien invaders, *Of Men and Monsters* (1968). He also edited an early theme anthology, *Children of Wonder* (1953).

Tenn's strength as a writer lies in the sensitivity that allowed him to identify and dramatize the pathetic as well as the comic aspects of his ironic situations, giving stories such as "Down among the Dead Men" (1954) and "Time Waits for Winthrop" (1957) an unusually poignant dimension.

B.S.

THE 10TH VICTIM (*La Decima Vittima; La Dixième Victime*) (1965).

Directed by Elio Petri; screenplay by Ennio Flajano, Tonino Guerra, Giorgio Salvioni, and Elio Petri; adapted from the short story "Seventh Victim" by Robert Sheckley; photographed by Gianni Di Venanzo; music by Pietro Piccioni. With Marcello Mastroianni, Ursula Andress, Elsa Martinelli, *Salvo Randone, Massimo Serato. 92 minutes. Color.*

In the twenty first century war has been outlawed, and violent passions have been sublimated by the immensely popular Big Hunt, in which volunteers are randomly selected to be alternate murderers and victims; the tenth victim grants the killer great fame and fortune. As her tenth victim, Caroline (Ursula Andress) has been assigned laconic Marcello (Marcello Mastroianni), who's only up to his sixth kill. While Marcello tries to outwit Caroline, the two fall in love.

This Italian-French production has some fresh moments and witty ideas but is largely an aimless comedy-drama. Despite the premise, it has little narrative drive, and the ending, even both "surprise" climaxes, is predictable. The drab English dubbing also makes the film less than compelling. Andress is beautiful but little more; however, Mastroianni, one of the world's great actors, is a perfect figure for audience identification: smart but not a genius, wary and attractive. The art direction by Piero Poletto is excellent. As are most Continental science-fiction films, *The 10th Victim* is intended for adults, but it is more admirable for what it attempts than for what it achieves.

B.W.

THE TERMINAL MAN (1974).

Directed by Mike Hodges; screenplay by Mike Hodges;, adapted from the novel by Michael Crichton; photographed by Richard H. Kline; music by Johann Sebastian Bach (as conducted by Glenn Gould). With George Segal, Joan Hackett, Richard Dysart, Michael C. Gwynne, Donald Moffat, Jill Clayburgh, Matt Clark, Ian Wolfe. 104 minutes. Color.

The protagonist of *The Terminal Man* (George Segal) has a pathological fear of machines and is prone to violent rages. A tiny computer terminal, designed to ease the rages by stimulation of other parts of the brain, is placed in his head. It backfires by "demanding" the rages in order to bring on the stimulation, and Segal becomes a homicidal maniac.

Michael CRICHTON's straightforward novel was pretentiously adapted to the screen by Mike Hodges (later to film FLASH GORDON, 1980). The music of Johann Sebastian Bach serves as the score, and the sets and costumes are almost entirely black and white. The cast is good, and the film boasts a few effective scenes, but Hodges's style is at odds with the material, and the film is ponderous and off the mark.

B.W.

THE TERMINATOR (1984).

Directed by James Cameron; screenplay by James Cameron and Gale Anne Hurd; photographed by Adam Greenberg. With Arnold Schwarzenegger, Linda Hamilton, Paul Win-

field. 105 minutes. Color.

The Terminator is a pulpy thriller with a punch. Arnold Schwarzenegger plays a laconic superman from the twenty-first century shipped back to the 1980s in order to assassinate Linda Hamilton, who otherwise will be the progenitor of a line of heroes who will eventually dominate the future.

This is a film about force, about masculine strength and feminine endurance. Schwarzenegger's performance is its most notable aspect; he emerges as Nietzsche's superman brought to life, a creature of almost godlike, invincible power. Yet even with Schwarzenegger's participation, the film is strikingly feminist; its message is that women can beat intense odds, that even faced with a force as mighty as Schwarzenegger (a being who can destroy police stations with three blasts of his supernatural weapons) women can ultimately triumph over masculine might.

If a film is judged by the number of its imitators, *The Terminator* is probably the most important science-fiction film of the 1980s. Yet unlike its successors, *The Terminator* manages to reach deep into the viewer's soul. Schwarzenegger has subsequently made such entertaining, minor films as *Predator* (1987); Cameron later directed ALIENS (1986), which continues his analysis of the nature of feminine power.

M.M.W.

TESTAMENT (1983). *Directed by Lynne Littman; screenplay by John Sacret Young; adapted from the story "The Last Testament" by Carol Amen; photographed by Steven Poster; music by James Horner. With Jane Alexander, Ross Harris, Roxana Zal, Lukas Haas, Philip Anglim, Lilia Skala, Leon Ames, Lurene Tuttle, Rebecca De Mornay, Kevin Costner, Mako, William Devane. 89 minutes. Color.*

The mother of three children (Jane Alexander) sees her husband (William Devane) off to San Francisco just before the outbreak of nuclear war. The small northern California city in which she lives is cut off from the outside world; the citizens try to get along, but unseen radiation increasingly takes its toll. The story focuses on Alexander and the gradual deaths of those around her.

Testament met with mixed reaction; some found it sanctimonious and sentimental, populated with stereotypes; others objected to its point of view—that it hardly matters who started the war. But more were affected by its low-key, unsensational approach to the concept of nuclear destruction; instead of the graphic depiction of millions dying, as in THE DAY AFTER (1983), *Testament* offers an examination of the deaths of individuals. Made for PBS-TV, the film received theatrical bookings first, eventually reaching a wider audience than most such cautionary tales.

Although it does have some aspects of a standard television movie, the film's reliance on ordinary events brought the impact of the horrors of nuclear war home to some who may have rarely considered the idea before.

B.W.

TEVIS, WALTER [STONE] (1928–1984). American mainstream author and college professor. Born in San Francisco, Tevis earned an M.A. from the University of Kentucky in 1956 and an M.F.A. from the University of Iowa in 1961. He taught English at Ohio University until his last years, when he returned to full-time writing.

Best known for his novel *The Hustler* (1959), filmed with Paul Newman in the role of the pool hustler on the make, and its later sequel, *The Color of Money* (1984), also filmed with Newman as Fast Eddie grown older and wiser, Tevis was a science-fiction writer from the first, with a half-dozen stories published in SF magazines, mostly GALAXY, in the late 1950s and as many SF novels (three) as mainstream.

Tevis's best-known SF novel, *The Man Who Fell to Earth* (1963, filmed in 1976—see THE MAN WHO FELL TO EARTH—by Nicolas Roeg with David Bowie as the alien who comes to Earth with advanced technology to save his dying planet) emphasized the growing isolation of the alien and his descent into alcoholism even though his attempt to solve his problem, by amassing vast amounts of wealth, is apparently successful. By focusing on the character of Thomas Jerome Newton, Tevis emphasized mainstream virtues at the expense of the SF reader's interest in the larger situation. To be overly concerned about Newton's fate seemed to many readers sentimental in the face of his planet's and his family's plight.

Tevis wrote in 1981 that he sometimes felt alienated and that, in writing about alienated characters, from actual aliens to pool players and robots, he was writing disguised autobiography. His second SF novel, *Mockingbird* (1980), was less successful than his first, and more derivative in its views of a dehumanized future U.S. through the eyes of a robot with human aspirations. *The Steps of the Sun* (1984), his third SF novel, deals with Ben Belson's attempts to restore the position of a poverty-stricken U.S. by discoveries in space, and his difficulties, like Newton's, in sharing his solutions; like *The Man Who Fell to Earth*, however, it is more about the soul of its protagonist.

Tevis also published a collection of his short science fiction in *Far from Home* (1983).

J.E.G.

THEATER

One critic of theater has suggested that science fiction and live drama are inherently incompatible, that SF relies on the reader's imaginative power or the illusions that can be produced technically for film or television. An alternate theory is that all live theatrical productions have become an elite art form, with rising costs automatically eliminating mass audiences, and that because sophisticated SF requires an audience educated to certain protocols and conventions, SF theater is restricted to a small percentage of that elite who support contemporary theater. For whatever reasons, it's clear that SF in the theater has not kept pace with the explosion in popularity of SF film, television, and even print in the last seventy years.

Dramatizations of SF concepts for live theatrical performance are at least as old as modern SF itself. By far the most successful have been written directly as plays, in most cases by those who also wrote SF in narrative form, and, with a few notable exceptions, in a comic tone. However, the best-known SF play of all time, *Rossum's Universal Robots (R.U.R.)* (1921) by the Czech Karel CAPEK, is grimly serious. It gave the world a new word (*robot*, actually coined by Capek's brother Josef) and a new concept, the artificially created worker-machine, which have captured the imaginations of countless SF readers and writers ever since. Isaac ASIMOV's debt to Capek is obvious. Capek wrote seven other plays as well as numerous novels, but none had achieved the fame or had the influence of *R.U.R.*

Also in 1921, in Britain, another world-famous playwright, the Irishman George Bernard Shaw, gave the world his "metabiological pentateuch," *Back to Methuselah,* consisting of the five plays "In the Beginning," "The Gospel of the Brothers Barnabas," "The Thing Happens," "Tragedy of an Elderly Gentleman," and "As Far As Thought Can Reach." The premises of this comic work (based on a creative misunderstanding of Jean-Baptiste Lamarck, an early evolutionist later overshadowed by Charles Darwin) are that the human species hasn't finished evolving and that we can choose the direction of evolution if we wish. Arthur C. CLARKE paid tribute to Shaw's influence on his thought by having characters in *Childhood's End* (1953) produce *Back to Methuselah* during the Golden Age.

Over the years other mainstream playwrights (like mainstream novelists) have toyed with SF occasionally and with mixed success. Thornton Wilder's *The Skin of Our Teeth* (1942), which won the Pulitzer Prize in 1943, is noticeably similar in conception to *Back to Methuselah.* One critic has interpreted Eugène Ionesco's *The Chairs* (1952) as SF because a character in the play mentions that Paris ceased to exist 400,000 years ago, but little in that play or other absurdist drama seems to fit the general conception of what SF means to the public or to fans. Gore VIDAL's *Visit to a Small Planet* (1957), the story of an alien visitor who comes to Earth to enjoy war games, is unusual in that it was originally a TV play, subsequently enjoyed nearly a year's run on Broadway, and later became a film. Howard Ashman's musical *The*

Little Shop of Horrors (1982), based on the 1960 Roger CORMAN film (see LITTLE SHOP OF HORRORS), enjoyed a run Off Broadway, continues in dinner-theater productions around the country, and was successfully readapted for film in 1986. Edward Albee's *Seascape* (1974, about chatting dinosaurs and evolution) also won a Pulitzer, and his *The Man Who Had Three Arms* (1981–82) uses a fantastic premise in a Kafkaesque fashion.

In recent years the most prolific SF author to write for the stage in the United States is Ray BRADBURY, who has also written for film and television. Since the early 1960s Bradbury has invested his own funds in his theatrical productions (all adaptations of his own stories) in the Los Angeles area with considerable local acclaim if not great financial return. His plays have been received moderately well in Chicago in Off-Loop theaters but have been produced in New York with less success. (In the introduction to one volume of his plays, Bradbury mentioned works by Shaw, suggesting direct influence.) Bradbury's best dramatizations (such as "The Veldt" (1950) and "To the Chicago Abyss" (1963)) treat his preoccupation with the dark side of human nature, the generation gap, and the destructive influence of social and technological change on human culture. Among Bradbury's projects is transforming his novel *Fahrenheit 451* (1953) into a musical.

In Britain in the 1970s and 1980s, Ken Campbell and Chris Langham of the Science Fiction Theatre of Liverpool have adapted a number of well-known SF works, again to mixed reviews. Douglas ADAMS has also written for their company. Only marginally SF, the London production of Richard O'Brien's *The Rocky Horror Show* (1978–79) became a cult favorite among SF fans after it was made into the film *The Rocky Horror Picture Show* (1975) and distributed in the United States.

In recent years in the United States, regional theater in cities such as Chicago, Miami, Minneapolis, San Francisco, and Boston have attempted original SF plays and adaptations of SF novels and short stories. Among the most ambitious was Stuart Gordon's Organic Theater production in Chicago (1983) of Joe HALDEMAN's own adaptation of his Hugo-winning *The Forever War* (1974); the script tried to capture and compress the epic scope of the novel within the time-bound medium of the stage, but the central theme of endless war took second place to the sensational aspect of the dominance of homosexuality in the future. Gordon had earlier written *Warp* (1971), an original SF play that ran for over a year in Chicago but closed after just one disastrous week in New York. In October 1986 Boston's Colonial Theater presented an adaptation of J. R. R. Tolkien's Lord of the Rings trilogy, using puppets three to seven feet tall as well as four actors. The script was originally written in French for a Montreal repertory company.

If one accepts one definition of SF as literature which explores the impact of science and technology on human affairs, some plays may claim to be science *fiction* even though they are firmly based on science *facts,* and they would surely have been regarded as SF in an earlier age. For example, Russian playwright Vladimir Gubaryev's *Sarcophagus: A Tragedy* (1986, translated into English by Michael Glenny 1986), a direct response to the nuclear accident at Chernobyl, tells the story of the doctors who try to cope with the horror of radiation sickness. Although it has played in several other Soviet republics, it seems likely to be produced in London and Tokyo before it will be seen in Moscow.

Some fan groups have attempted to fill the SF theater gap, to the delight of other fans. One of the most successful has been the Moebius Theater, an amateur company formed in 1976 under the direction of Michael Blake. It has performed original material (written by Blake and others in the group and much influenced by the improvisational method of Chicago's Second City Troupe) at SF conventions in eight states in the Midwest in the last ten years and (in Off-Loop Chicago) for a professional run in 1982. Although the group has not formally disbanded, Blake left in 1985, and it remains unclear whether the company will continue without his strong leadership.

Nevertheless, SF in theater persists, if only because it is nurtured by SF fans. The 1986 Worldcon in Atlanta featured a well-received humorous skit (untitled) in the opening ceremonies written by Tom Fuller, who also played the narrator. In less than a hour and using only three characters, Fuller dramatized the entire history of SF in the twentieth century with a stagy self-consciousness that spoofed both theatrical and SF conventions (in both senses of the word). Like Blake of the Moebius Theater, Fuller reveals an understanding that one need not be solemn to make serious points.

The wedding of science fiction to the theater may not be a marriage made in Heaven, but the mutual attraction between the two continues to inspire writers to seek the form and its eager, if limited, audience.

E.A.H.

THEM! (1954).
Directed by Gordon Douglas; screenplay by Ted Sherdemann; adapted from the short story by George Worthington Yates; photographed by Sid Hickox; music by Bronislau Kaper. With Edmund Gwenn, James Whitmore, James Arness. 83 minutes. Black and white.

Them! is one of the first, and best, science-fiction movies of the early 1950s depicting giant monsters wreaking havoc on American cities as a result of nuclear testing. Although oversized scorpions, tarantulas, and praying mantises would follow, the giant ants of *Them!* mark the first instance of this insect motif in SF cinema. Ably directed by Gordon Douglas, the film constructs a taut narrative with little that is digressive.

Two policemen discover a child wandering in the desert in a state of shock and upon further investigation come upon a strangely wrecked trailer. An FBI agent is called in, and he concludes that ants have mutated into giants as a result of nuclear tests. The ants are destroyed, except for one queen, who has escaped to the sewer system of Los Angeles, where she lays her eggs. Much of the latter part of the film is devoted to the search-and-destroy procedure by which the army wipes out the large nest of ants below the city.

Like many other SF films of the period, *Them!* is often considered a metaphor for Cold War paranoia. According to this view, the unemotional, undifferentiated society of the ants represents the American fear of invasion by faceless hordes of unemotional Communists; the building of the ants' lair beneath the city suggests the threat of infiltration and subversion that pervaded the era. Finally, though, it is the tight story line, eerily expressive sound track, and excellent special effects by Ralph Ayers that make the film thoroughly enjoyable as a solid, conventional monster movie.

B.K.G.

THESE ARE THE DAMNED (*The Damned*) (1961).
Directed by Joseph Losey; screenplay by Evan Jones; adapted from the novel The Children of Light *by H. L. Lawrence; photographed by Arthur Grant; music by James Bernard. With MacDonald Carey, Shirley Ann Field, Viveca Lindfors, Alexander Knox, Oliver Reed, Rachel Clay. 96 minutes. Black and white.*

The Damned, as this film was called in Britain, was made there by Joseph Losey, an American expatriate, but release was delayed by the distributor, who clearly uncertain about possible public reaction to Losey's attempted indictment of the moral failings of the Western military-industrial alliance. It was cut to 87 minutes for British release and edited even more—down to 77 minutes—for its American release.

The story tells of the visit in the small boat by an American (MacDonald Carey) to an English coastal town, where he becomes involved with the sister (Shirley Ann Field) of the leader of a motorcycle gang (Oliver Reed) and a scientist in charge of a secret project at a nearby military base (Alexander Knox). The scientist is entrusted with educating a group of radioactive children, who were contaminated during their mothers' pregnancies. Somehow the children survived the radiation with only their body temperatures lowered, and the scientist hopes they will provide the key to surviving nuclear war. In their attempt to free the children from their subterranean prison, Carey and Field are fatally contaminated. The makers of this film never decided whether it was science fiction, suspense, romance, or motorcycle gang violence, but the imagery, such as the final scene of a vulture-like helicopter above the boat carrying the dying hero and heroine, is often effective in creating or sustaining a mood.

W.L.

THE THING (1951). *Directed by Christian Nyby; screenplay by Charles Lederer; adapted from the short story "Who Goes There?" by John W. Campbell, Jr.; photographed by Russell Harlan; music by Dimitri Tiomkin. With Kenneth Tobey, Margaret Sheridan, Robert Cornthwaite, Douglas Spencer, James Arness, Dewey Martin. 86 minutes. Black and white. Alternate title:* The Thing from Another World.

THE THING (1982). *Directed by John Carpenter; screenplay by Bill Lancaster; adapted from the short story by John W. Campbell, Jr.; photographed by Dean Cundy; music by Ennio Morricone. With Kurt Russell, A. Wilford Brimley, T. K. Carter, David Clennon, Keith David, Richard Dysart, Charles Hallahan. 109 minutes. Color.*

Incubating the alien's progeny in *The Thing* (1951)

A touchstone film of the genre, the first version of *The Thing* is a controversial movie that has been both praised and condemned. On the one hand, it has been viewed as a paradigm of the cinema's debasing treatment of science fiction and, on the other, as an effectively atmospheric monster movie that established the tone and many conventions of the genre. That the film accommodates both positions is an indication of its importance and complexity, hidden behind an apparently simple surface.

The plot is indeed rather straightforward. A group of military men is dispatched to the Arctic to investigate a strange fluctuation in the magnetic field, and they discover a spacecraft buried in the ice. When they try to dislodge it, the ship is accidentally destroyed, but the alien pilot is found embedded in a block of ice. They bring the ice block back to the base, where it thaws, reviving the alien, who proceeds to kill a number of the men in its vampiric need for human blood and the desire to multiply itself. Some of the scientists want to communicate with the Thing, but the military personnel are convinced of the necessity to destroy it. In the final confrontation the alien is electrocuted by the military men.

Those who view this film as an unfortunate example of cinema's tendency to simplify SF literature point out the considerable and significant changes in the film from John W. CAMPBELL, Jr.'s story. Campbell's alien shape shifter is changed into a grunting, inarticulate monster (James Arness)—a "super carrot," in the vivid phrase of Scotty, the film's journalist. Unlike Campell's creature, who merely seeks to survive, the film's Thing seems unnecessarily aggressive, and it stretches to the snapping point one's willing suspension of disbelief to accept the idea that such a vegetable Frankenstein could have invented the technology for interplanetary travel.

In addition, critics of the film compare it negatively

with the other important early SF movies of the decade, DESTINATION MOON (1950) and THE DAY THE EARTH STOOD STILL (1951), because it lacks both the former's scientific realism and the latter's openness to alien encounters. Instead, they say, it serves as the unhappy model for the proliferation of bug-eyed monsters and xenophobia that would characterize so many later 1950s SF movies. Certainly the scientist's desire to communicate with the Thing is depicted as futile and foolish, as he is summarily knocked aside by the creature. The film fittingly ends with the journalist speaking by radio to the world, and directly to the audience, warning us all to "keep watching the skies."

On the positive side, those who admire the film see in it the virtues of a genre movie pared of all irrelevancies. For example, the debate between reason and action, mind and body, represented by the conflict between the scientists and the military, is a staple convention of the SF film. In *The Thing* the conflict is made prominent by the setting in the barren Arctic, where there are no secondary characters and nothing in the mise-en-scène but that which is central to the conflict. The movie also establishes a wonderful atmosphere of menace that is maintained from start to finish. Although the film's direction is credited to Christian Nyby, it clearly bears the stamp of its producer, Howard Hawks, in its fast-paced, overlapping dialogue and its depiction of an isolated group of professionals intent on doing their job.

The second version of *The Thing*, directed by John CARPENTER, is actually not a remake because it bypasses the Hawks-Nyby film and returns to Campbell's original story. It is most significant that Carpenter retained Campbell's idea of an alien that has the ability to duplicate the appearance of any biological organism. But while this faithfulness to its source promises a more sophisticated treatment, it also makes the film aesthetically inferior to its predecessor. For all the advances in special-effects technology since 1951 and the director's narrative skill, this film is a surprising disappointment.

Carpenter allowed so much screen time for the monster's various transformations that Rob Bottin's special effects, while certainly impressive, swamp the human characters and change a potentially powerful drama of paranoia and perceptual uncertainty into little more than a spectacle of visual tricks. The final scene, in which only two men are left alive, each guardedly watching the other out of fear that *he* might be the alien, is an effective image of distrust. Unfortunately, though, it comes too late: it is hard to care about the human characters when all along they have taken a backseat to the special effects.

B.K.G.

Raymond Massey in *Things to Come*

THINGS TO COME (1936)   *Directed by William Cameron Menzies; screenplay by H. G. Wells; photographed by Georges Perinal; music by Arthur Bliss. With Raymond Massey, Edward Chapman, Ralph Richardson, Margueretta Scott, Cedric Hardwicke, Sophie Stewart, Ann Todd, Derrick deMarney, John Clements. 113 minutes. Black and white. Alternate title:* The Shape of Things to Come.

Since its release, *Things to Come* has continued to generate controversy. For years many science-fiction readers and writers considered it the only good SF film, largely because it deals effectively with ideas; for this strength they credited H. G. WELLS's intimate involvement with Alexander Korda's production; many film critics, however, blamed Wells for the film's shortcomings and attacked his "shoddy pamphleteering." Nevertheless, the film has been praised for its "choreography of matter" and its concern with consistent design—virtues it shares with that classic of the SF cinema 2001: A SPACE ODYSSEY (1968).

Things to Come encompasses a century of future history, from 1936 to 2036, beginning with the destruction of civilization in a world war. The survivors are rescued from misery and despotism by an organization of airmen, engineers, and technocrats calling itself Wings over the World, which organizes the building of a new and more humane world civilization. At the end, as this civilization readies its first manned Moon shot, reactionary elements try to prevent the launching of the astronauts (a man and a woman).

It is difficult for the modern viewer to see *Things to Come* as it was originally intended: surviving television prints, butchered to fit commerical slots, run from 88 to 93 minutes; the first American release ran 100 minutes, the first British version 113 minutes, the original 130

minutes. In addition, other elements of the film seem dated. To audiences weaned on high-tech special effects, Ned Mann's model work comes off as creaky, and World War II, though chillingly prophesied, seems stagy and obvious today, as does the film's simplistic pacifism. The air attack on England, however, is imaginatively depicted.

Nevertheless, despite lapses, the drama of this first significant SF sound film rises to admirable heights in the opening third, with its convincing picture of civilization in ruins, fighting plagues and living under warlords. The final third, with its clean white surfaces, crystalline shafts of light, and spacious plazas, still presents a plausible vision of a future city, and the pitting of social concerns against a space program is genuinely prophetic. The film's closing scene is its most memorable, as Raymond Massey, standing against a starry sky, exhorts humanity to continue to explore and understand the universe.

Things to Come is perhaps more rewarding to viewers who can bring to it some awareness of Wells and his ideas, for it captures a mood of looking ahead and presents ideas that are common currency in SF. It may be a worthy failure overall, but it is filled with memorable visuals, striking design, and a vibrant wedding of sound and image. An accurate assessment waits for a complete version and the kind of restoration recently bestowed on Fritz LANG's METROPOLIS (1926).

G.Z.

THIS ISLAND EARTH (1955).   *Directed by Joseph M. Newman (some climactic scenes directed by Jack Arnold); screenplay by Franklin Coen and Edward G. O'Callaghan; adapted from the novel by*

Raymond F. Jones; photographed by Clifford Stine; music by Herman Stine. With Jeff Morrow, Rex Reason, Faith Domergue, Lance Fuller, Russell Johnson, Douglas Spencer, Robert Nichols, Regis Parton, Eddie Parker. 86 minutes. Color.

Science-fiction spectacles in the 1950s were rare, apart from George PAL's productions; *This Island Earth* was Universal-International's only space epic. Based on a novel by Raymond F. Jones, the film inverts Jones's message: instead of his point that humanity should be welcomed into the congress of the planets, the film perhaps inadvertently suggests that space is very dangerous and we should stay home. The aliens, including their "Mutant" slaves, have enlarged heads; too much intelligence, obviously, is not good for you, and everyone in space is fighting. Earth is not just an island in this film, it's a shelter.

The first half of the movie is an SF mystery, engrossing and well structured. Scientist Rex Reason is recruited by mysterious Exeter (Jeff Morrow), who asks him to join other nuclear scientists at a remote estate. Odd events occur, so Reason and Faith Domergue try to escape, but their plane is swallowed by a flying saucer. It turns out that Exeter and his companions, from the planet Metaluna, need the assistance of Earth's scientists in defending their world against enemy Zahgons. But their effort is to no avail: the atomic shield around Metaluna is breached at the film's climax, and the planet turns into a miniature sun. After returning Reason and Domergue to Earth, Exeter, the sole survivor of Metaluna, crashes into the sea in his blazing flying saucer.

Many of the special effects in *This Island Earth*, under the direction of David S. Horsley and cinematographer Clifford Stine, are outstanding. Some of the model work looks like what it is, but even the least effective shots have a scale and grandeur uncommon in SF films until the mid-1970s. In vivid Technicolor, the film is entertaining on the level of spectacle alone.

During this period, insecure about the appeal of the genre, Universal wanted a monster in every SF film. Here it is the strange insectoid creature called the Mutant. Nothing like it appears in Jones's novel, but the nightmarish creation has a cockeyed splendor that makes it one of the best-remembered creatures of the 1950s. The design is credited to Bud Westmore.

The filmmakers' intent was only to give audiences a thrilling spectacle; in that they succeeded. The brainwashing (never shown) by Metalunans of uncooperative scientists certainly reflects Cold War tensions, but this detail is only a function of the plot; the film is hardly an allegory or a satire.

Joseph M. Newman was a standard studio director with no special abilities; however, he had purchased the novel and, failing in an attempt to mount it as an independent production, brought the property to Universal and saw the film to completion. Under his direction

Morrow gives an admirable performance as Exeter, sympathetic to his captives but loyal to Metaluna.

This Island Earth can be marked as one of the very last in the early wave of 1950s SF movies; until this point SF films were made for adults, but from 1956 on they were increasingly aimed at teenagers, their biggest audience.

B.W.

THOMAS, TED [THEODORE L.] (1900–).

American writer and attorney who has written more than forty-five short stories under his own name and eight (constituting the Patent Attorney series) as Leonard Lockhard. The Lockhard stories spoof government red tape and future inventions. Many of the stories written as Ted Thomas are noteworthy for their attempts at realism, particularly those that deal with near future space exploration: "The Far Look" (1957), "Satellite Passage" (1959), and "Lunar Landing" (1965). Thomas has also written a series of stories about the Weather Control Board, a group much like Rudyard Kipling's Aerial Board of Control, which governs the world because of its ability to manipulate the weather. Such stories as "The Weatherman" (1964) and "The Weather on the Sun" (1970) follow the board as it handles both rebellions and natural crises.

Thomas has written two novels in collaboration with Kate Wilhelm. *The Clone* (1968) describes not a clone but a blob of matter that assimilates anything it comes in contact with; *The Year of the Cloud* (1968) is a disaster novel. Both works concern threats to humanity and display believable plots and effective characterizations.

S.H.G.

THREADS (1984). *Directed by Mick Jackson; screenplay by Barry Hines, With Karen Meagher, Reece Dinsdale, Rita May, Nicholas Lane, Victoria O'Keefe. 110 minutes. Color.*

THE DAY AFTER (1983) focused on the university town of Lawrence, Kansas, after a nuclear holocaust; *Threads*, as if in response, was a made-for-television British film that focuses, more narrowly, on a pair of working-class families in Sheffield, England, in the same circumstance. Even grimmer and more harrowing than *The Day After*, *Threads* did not get the same coverage or stir up the same debate—possibly because *The Day After* got there the year before.

J.E.G.

THX-1138 (1970). *Directed by George Lucas; screenplay by George Lucas and Walter Murch; photographed by Dave Meyers and Albert Kihn; music*

by Lalo Schifrin. With Donald Pleasence, Robert Duvall, Don Pedro Colley, Maggie McOmie, Ian Wolfe, Marshall Efron. 88 minutes. Color.

THX-1138 is the first feature-length science-fiction film directed by George LUCAS, who seven years later would make the blockbuster epic STAR WARS. Based on a twenty-minute film Lucas had made five years earlier as a student in the Film Department of UCLA, the movie brings together a variety of SF gambits. Although this lengthier version reveals some narrative problems—a result in part of its being considerably reedited by Warner Bros. after its completion—*THX-1138* clearly marked Lucas as an important new director.

The details of this ironic utopia are for the most part derivative, as is the narrative. Elements of Yevgeny ZA-MYATIN's *We* (1924), Aldous HUXLEY's *Brave New World* (1933), George ORWELL's *1984,* and other works can be found in its story of one man (Robert Duvall) in a future society who, after engaging in an illicit love affair, seeks to escape from his constraining world. But it is Lucas's frequently original imagery that gives *THX-1138* its value and power as a work of SF.

The film was cleverly shot in the underground tunnels of San Francisco's then unfinished Bay Area Rapid Transit system, suggesting the extent to which its society is both repressive and oppressive. Lucas's all-white detention area, with its walls, ceiling, and floor seeming to stretch into infinity, is both visually compelling and a loaded metaphor for the invisible constraints of ideology. The sterile atmosphere of the detention area informs the design of the entire society, and better than any film before it, *THX-1138* visually captures the frightening coldness and efficiency so skillfully invoked in the opening pages of *Brave New World*. Thus, while the film offers little that is new dramatically, its visual imagination inevitably established it as a cult favorite.

B.K.G.

TIME AFTER TIME (1979). *Directed by Nicholas Meyer; screenplay by Nicholas Meyer; photographed by Paul Lohmann; music by Miklos Rozsa. With Malcolm McDowell, Mary Steenburgen, David Warner, Charles Cioffi, Kent Williams, Adonia Katsaros, Patti D'Arbanville. 112 minutes. Color.*

The premise of *Time after Time* is amusingly ingenious; apart from Mary Steenburgen's charming performance, in fact, the idea is the most memorable element of this predictably structured film. In 1893, H. G. WELLS himself (Malcolm McDowell) has no sooner demonstrated his time machine to friends then one of them, Dr. Stevenson (David Warner), flees into the future in it—for he is none other than Jack the Ripper. Wells follows, to the San Francisco of 1979. Stevenson continues his murders while Wells contends with a very real future and tries to stop Stevenson. Those who know the

life of the real Wells can predict the otherwise surprising ending.

Plunking Wells himself down in a science-fiction movie is a cheeky conceit, helped immeasurably by McDowell's affectionate performance. The prophet of free love is confronted not just with the future but with a woman whose 1979 ideas about sex are far in advance of Wells's own. But the film also wearily has Wells confront the most outré elements of 1979 in standard innocent-abroad style. This aspect is more interesting, however, than the depiction of Jack the Ripper (although Warner is fine) as a sensation-loving libertine—he must have been very different in reality. The film was financially unsuccessful and scorned by many influential critics.

B.W.

TIME BANDITS (1982). *Directed by Terry Gilliam; screenplay by Michael Palin and Terry Gilliam; photographed by Peter Biziou; music by Mike Moran; additional songs and material by George Harrison. With John Cleese, Sean Connery, Shelley Duvall, Katherine Helmond, Ian Holm, Michael Palin, David Rappoport, Ralph Richardson, Peter Vaughan, David Warner, Craig Warnock. 116 minutes. Color.*

This British film is a delightful compound of satire and fantasy, an amusing moral allegory employing time travel and Christian mythology as unifying motifs. At first glance the film's episodic nature and irreverent spoofing suggest a number of sketches in the Monty Python mode—not surprising, given the participation of Terry Gilliam, Michael Palin, and John Cleese. Indeed some reviewers treated *Time Bandits* as merely another variation on *Monty Python and the Holy Grail* (1975), although *Time Bandits* is far more mature and focused.

The plot centers on the adventures of a band of six midgets who rebel against working for the "supreme being" (they claim to have designed the shrubbery in Eden). After stealing the "map" of time, they have set off in search of plunder and an easy life. But they accidentally acquire a conscience in the person of a strong-willed and imaginative boy, played effectively by Craig Warnock. The film follows the adventures of this essential seven as they roam backward through time, looting and fleeing, unaware that they are being manipulated by the Prince of Darkness, played somewhat broadly by David Warner.

The first two sequences, dealing with Napoleon's invasion of Italy in 1796 and Robin Hood's grim and dirty Middle Ages, are played purely in the Monty Python style. Napoleon (Michael Palin) is a cynical buffoon avenging himself on the world because of his shortness of stature, and Robin Hood (John Cleese) is a politician fronting for a band of cutthroats in a seedy and amoral world.

The irony becomes richer and more mature, however, in sequences dealing with ancient Greece, where Sean Connery does a sardonic turn as an opportunistic warrior who gains a hero image and becomes king; in the "time of legend," in which Katherine Helmond is charmingly vacuous as an ogre's wife; and at the Palace of Ultimate Darkness, where Ralph Richardson, playing a fussy but benevolent God (in a conservative business suit), arrives to save the boy and the six time bandits from destruction at the hands of the Devil. Throughout these adventures only the innocence and resolution of the boy protagonist appear to save the bandits from their incompetence and folly. Indeed, aside from the Supreme Being, the boy is the only true moral character in the film, a point underscored by an ironic twist to the happy ending, wherein his materialistic and uncaring parents are destroyed by their own greed.

In the final analysis Gilliam's film moves swiftly, displaying impressive special effects and bravura performances and a determined antisentimental treatment of its theme. It must surely rank as one of the superior time travel movies.

E.L.C.

THE TIME MACHINE (1960). *Directed by George Pal; screenplay by David Duncan; adapted from the novel by H. G. Wells; photographed by Paul C. Vogel; music by Russell Garcia. With Rod Taylor, Yvette Mimieux, Sebastian Cabot, Whit Bissel, Alan Young, Tom Helmore. 103 minutes. Color.*

The Time Machine, considered by some to be the best of the more recent H. G. WELLS adaptations, is a good but flawed film. The story of the man who builds a time machine and travels into the far future, only to find humanity split into the peaceful but mindless Eloi and the cannibalistic Morlocks, is vividly presented, as is the Time Traveler's romance with a woman of the future, Weena (Yvette Mimieux). But many of Wells's ideas have been tinkered with, to the detriment of the film. The split between the Eloi and the Morlocks, for example, is presented not as a class division but as the result of nuclear wars, during which a portion of humanity learned to live underground. Into this future comes Wells's Time Traveler (Rod Taylor), a man from the 1890s searching for an answer to the failure of history. He is properly heroic, attempting to save Weena from the Morlocks; what he cannot fight, however, is the great gulf of time that separates them, and in the end he is forced to flee to his own age.

The film's greatest flaw is that it fails to climb the Wellsian heights, leaving out what many consider the most significant aspect of the original story: the Time Traveler's journey to the last moments on Earth. It has been reported that George PAL did indeed film such a sequence but was ordered by the studio to leave it out.

Still, the novelty of time travel is well presented, and Taylor makes a good Time Traveler. Mimieux is excellent as Weena, although her ability to speak English strains credibility. The Victorian period sets are charming, especially the time machine itself—a wonderful conceit of metal and crystal whose motion through time is brilliantly depicted. Despite its resemblance to the worst of California, the land of the Eloi is genuinely chilling.

If the missing sequence does exist, perhaps audiences may yet see a restored version of the film as Pal planned it; the definitive adaptation of *The Time Machine,* however, still awaits the ambitious filmmaker.

G.Z.

———— TIME TRAVEL ————

Time travel, the ability of individuals or objects to move back and forth in time, has had a long history in science fiction. Some critics insist that travel in time is impossible and therefore a fantasy concept inappropriate in SF, but most authors refuse to be deterred by such narrow legalisms.

Stories about time travel, like SF itself, were not written until Western civilization developed the concept of a future (and a past) that was different from the present; that concept originated with the Industrial and Scientific revolutions. The earliest method of fictional time travel was to fall asleep for a dozen or a hundred years, as in Washington Irving's "Rip Van Winkle" (1819), Edward BELLAMY's *Looking Backward* (1888), and H. G. WELLS's *When the Sleeper Wakes* (1899). The first use of sleeping away the years may have been in Louis-Sébastien Mercier's *Memoirs of the Year Two Thousand Five Hundred* (1771).

A recent variation is to be frozen after death and restored to life in the future. Other methods have been to project one's mind or spirit into someone else's consciousness in another time; to experience another time in a dream, as in Jack LONDON's *Before Adam* (1906) and Wells's "A Dream of Armageddon" (1901); to be projected by some accident, as in Isaac ASIMOV's *Pebble in the Sky* (1950) and Robert A. HEINLEIN's *Farnham's Freehold* (1964); or to experience the time dilation effect of near speed-of-light space travel, as in L. Ron HUBBARD's *Return to Tomorrow* (1950/1954).

The most liberating influence on time travel stories, however, was H. G. Wells's *The Time Machine* (1895), which allowed the protagonist mechanical control over the process as well as a return to the present to bring back his story and assess the consequences of the present on the future. In that novella Wells described a time machine for the first time (his Time Traveler even demonstrates a model) and provided the standard rationale for mechanical time travel describing time as a fourth dimension in which people can travel as they do in the other three. In the past half century time machines have become the method of choice.

Authors transport their characters to the future usually to comment on contemporary society; time travel offers a vivid method for tracing today's problems to their final, sometimes horrible, ends, as in *The Time Machine*. Time travel into the past allows authors to describe how the individual or collective present became what it is, or to compare the past to the present, sometimes for satiric or comic purposes, as in Mark TWAIN's *A Connecticut Yankee in King Arthur's Court* (1889).

Other SF authors have used time travel to create exotic settings and rationales for adventure. Frequently their works feature centuries-spanning battles, as one side or another endeavors to disrupt or maintain the historic status quo. Jack WILLIAMSON's *The Legion of Time* (1938) is the earliest major example of this type.

Most time travel plots have elements of both social criticism and adventure, as indeed *The Time Machine* does. Stories by Poul ANDERSON, Richard C. MEREDITH, and Nicholas Yermakov (writing as Simon Hawke) involve soldiers fighting battles in time and never knowing the reason for the combat or even who commands them. All they know is that if they lose just one battle their society disappears. Perhaps the best example is Fritz LEIBER's Hugo-winning *The Big Time* (1958/1961).

The technical description of time travel in such stories is not usually the core of the work, although authors such as Philip K. DICK and Robert A. Heinlein, in his solipsistic "By His Bootstraps" (1941) and "All You Zombies" (1959), have used time travel to speculate about the nature of reality. The most important use of time travel has been to explore the impact it has on the individual or society. In Asimov's *The End of Eternity* (1955), time travel deals with the way attempts to create a better future produced a closed, repressive society. Michael MOORCOCK's *Behold the Man* (1966) provides a time traveler with the answer to his lack of faith when he becomes Jesus.

Other writers, following Twain's example, have used time travel to create humor. A major novel of this type is L. Sprague DE CAMP's *Lest Darkness Fall* (1939/1941), in which an updated Connecticut Yankee gets transported to sixth-century Rome and tries to stop the coming of the Dark Ages. Other authors have used the paradoxes of time travel, as in William TENN's "Brooklyn Project" (1948), Ray BRADBURY's "A Sound of Thunder" (1952), Alfred BESTER's "The Men Who Murdered Mohammed" (1958), and the film BACK TO THE FUTURE (1985). Still others have had machines or visitors from the future aggravate the present, as in Henry KUTTNER and C. L. MOORE's "Twonky" (1942), "When the Bough Breaks" (1944), and "Vintage Season" (1946), William Tenn's "Child's Play" (1947), or Cyril M. KORNBLUTH's "The Little Black Bag" (1950); or they have brought the past to the present, as in T. L. SHERRED's "E for Effort" (1947).

Perhaps the most memorable humorous time travel work is Harry HARRISON's *The Technicolor Time Machine* (1967), in which a film producer goes into the past for location shots.

Dinosaurs, tourism, one's ancestors, and animal collecting have been frequent topics for time travel stories, as have notions of modern superiority or the persistence of civilizations or the human species itself. Not all time travel stories are satiric, but they offer excellent opportunities for writers to slip their literary knives into deserving victims.

Time travel, with its conventions, tends to date stories today and is used to comment on the conventions or the genre, as in the film *Time after Time* (1979), in which H. G. Wells chases Jack the Ripper into the present. Moreover, contemporary methods for creating believable futures have diminished the need to use time travel as a narrative device, and depictions of time travel now often deal with the inherent problems of the process, such as Ian WATSON's "The Very Slow Time Machine" (1978). Nevertheless, time travel is a device the SF writers have not yet exhausted for original plots.

S.E.G./J.E.G.

TIPTREE, JAMES, JR. (Pseudonym of Alice Bradley Sheldon) (1915–1987).

American writer and psychologist who became a noted, though elusive, science-fiction writer in her fifties; she also wrote as Raccoona Sheldon.

Sheldon's childhood exposure to a diversity of cultural beliefs, values, and taboos, particularly with regard to the "natural roles" of women, while traveling in Africa, India, and Southeast Asia with her explorer-parents influenced her fiction. Sheldon studied graphic arts and painting at a number of colleges, had several exhibitions of her paintings, served in World War II as the first woman Army Air Force intelligence officer, operated a small private business, and eventually joined the newly chartered Central Intelligence Agency. Three years later she left the CIA and in her late forties returned to college for a Ph.D. in experimental psychology. Several years after receiving this degree she abandoned college teaching to write SF short stories full time, although she used her male pseudonym to conceal her identity even from such insightful critics as Theodore Sturgeon and Robert Silverberg.

Sheldon's first SF story was published in 1968. Her fiction was recognized almost immediately for its skilled use of language, its intricate plots ("start from the end," she wrote once, "and preferably 5000 feet underground on a dark day and then *Don't tell them*"), and the psychological depth of her characters. Many of her early stories—such as "The Women Men Don't See" (1973) and her 1976 novella "Houston, Houston, Do You Read?" which won both Nebula and Hugo awards that year—

Alice Sheldon, better known as James Tiptree, Jr.

concerned the psychological and physical exploitation of women. She also won a Nebula Award in 1973 for "Love Is the Plan, the Plan Is Death," a story about alien reproduction told entirely from an alien viewpoint, and in 1977 for "The Screwfly Solution," in which aliens, in order to eliminate the human species, reinforce men's natural brutality toward women. She received a Hugo in 1974 for the novella "The Girl Who Was Plugged In," about a rejected girl who finds brief happiness wired into a female android.

When Sheldon's real identity was finally revealed in 1977, the "radical feminist" element of her work received even more attention. In a larger sense, however, her focus has always been on all sentient beings as victims of their societies and environments: her characters are almost always individuals unable to cope with an indifferent, even malevolent, universe.

In Sheldon's first novel, *Up the Walls of the World* (1978), she shifted to characters trying to overcome their victimization. The absurdist black humor of her earlier work was replaced by something more positive: a celebration of diversity as the necessary first step in character development.

In her last works Sheldon turned often to interstellar settings, as in her 1986 *Locus* poll winner "The Only Neat Thing to Do," while through her prose style, always artful, she struggled to establish a new lexicon for human responsiveness: for example, creating new meanings for such common words as *green* and *go*. Sheldon's final novel, *Brightness Falls from the Air* (1985), is an even more intricate account of an isolated, frail group of beings, naked under the onslaught of a passing nova front, who manage to defeat the forces of greed and destructiveness

that threaten them and their alien friends. The protagonists' triumph against both enemies and time itself can be seen as Sheldon's most positive response to the basic background of entropy (the slow and certain death of everything) that has been the central theme of all her SF writing. These were her only two novels; in 1987 she shot her ailing husband and then killed herself.

OTHER WORKS: *Ten Thousand Light-Years from Home* (collection, 1973); *Warm Worlds and Otherwise* (collection, 1975); *Star-Songs of an Old Primate* (collection, 1978); *Out of the Everywhere and Other Extraordinary Visions* (collection, 1981); *The Starry Rift* (collection, 1986); *Byte Beautiful: Eight Science Fiction Stories* (collection, 1986).

A.J.F.

TOM CORBETT, SPACE CADET (1950–1956).
Directed by George Gould and Ralph Ward; written by Alfred Bester and others. With Frankie Thomas, Jan Merlin, Al Markhim. 15–30-minute episodes, three times a week and on Saturdays. Black-and-white television and radio series.

A group of cadets in a twenty-fourth-century space academy train to protect Venus, Earth, Mars, and Jupiter, and undergo various adventures in the process. The series, more scientifically accurate than *Captain Video* (1949–1956) or SPACE PATROL (also 1950–56)—probably because of the influence of Willy Ley, who served as technical adviser—produced numerous spin-offs, including eight Grosset & Dunlap novels, twelve comic books, two RCA records, and a Field Enterprises newspaper strip drawn by Ray Bailey.

J.C.

THE TRANS-ATLANTIC TUNNEL (*The Tunnel*) (1935).
Directed by Maurice Elvey; screenplay by Clemence Dane and L. du Garde Peach; adapted from the novel Der Tunnel *by Bernhard Kellerman; photographed by Günther Krampf; music by Louis Levy. With Richard Dix, Leslie Banks, Madge Evans, Helen Vinson, C. Aubrey Smith, Basil Sydney, Henry Oscar, Cyril Raymond, Walter Huston, George Arliss. 70 minutes. Black and white.*

A dedicated American engineer (Richard Dix) and his British counterpart (Leslie Banks) mastermind the construction of a tunnel between Great Britain and the United States despite financial and personal hardships. The American's wife (Madge Evans) goes blind tending injured tunnel workers and his son is killed during construction. The U.S. president (Walter Huston) and British prime minister (George Arliss) meet at the middle when the tunnel is complete.

A rare example of a science-fiction film with too much emphasis on the characters, *The Trans-Atlantic Tunnel* is at its liveliest depicting the mammoth machines digging the spectacular tunnel. The special effects, by J. Whithead, B. Guidobaldi, and A. Stroppa, include breathtaking scenes of tunnel disaster and sabotage that were lifted from the 1933 German version, *Der Tunnel*. However, the story's overreliance on personal rivalry, financial manipulation, and politics tends to be distracting. Performances are generally very good.

Along with *F.P. 1* (1933), *Gold* (1934), and THINGS TO COME (1936), the various versions of *The Tunnel* were, with few exceptions, the most spectacular examples of sound SF cinema until the late 1970s.

B.W.

TREMAINE, F[REDERICK] ORLIN (1899–1956).

American editor and occasional author. Tremaine, who became editor of *Astounding Stories* in 1933, when the magazine was bought by Street & Smith, was a major influence on the transition from the Harry Bates pulp-adventure style to John W. CAMPBELL's idea-oriented emphasis, which led to science fiction's so-called GOLDEN AGE.

Tremaine was thirty-four when he became *Astounding*'s editor, only six years older than Campbell when Tremaine hired him as his successor in December of 1937. But Tremaine was an experienced editor, having worked for *Smart Set*, *True Story*, and the Clayton chain from whom *Astounding* was purchased. He marked the change by emphasizing ideas, particularly unusual ones, and instituted a practice of including one such story in every issue, which he labeled a "thought variant." He also recruited such established authors as E. E "Doc" SMITH, Murray LEINSTER, Jack WILLIAMSON, and Campbell, whose more sensitively written mood stories of philosophy and psychology, under the name of Don A. Stuart, Tremaine not only published but encouraged him to write to the exclusion of his earlier space epics. He also attracted such new authors as L. Sprague DE CAMP and Eric Frank RUSSELL.

Astounding was a thriving enterprise, clearly the leading magazine in the field and set on the path toward the Golden Age, when Tremaine hired Campbell as his successor and moved up to direct a group of Street & Smith magazines. That would last less than a year: Tremaine soon left to create a publishing firm of his own, including in 1940–41 an SF magazine titled *Comet Stories*, whose short and unspectacular career (in spite of the publication of a Doc Smith short story) suggests that success in the field required a timely combination of editorial vision, authors inspired by that vision, and publishing resources.

Tremaine wrote a handful of SF stories himself, all but one ("The Upper Level Road" as Warner Van Lorne) after he had turned *Astounding* over to Campbell.

J.E.G.

A TRIP TO THE MOON (*Le Voyage dans la Lune*) (Silent, 1902).

Directed by Georges Méliès. With George Méliès, Victor Andre, Bleuette Bernon, Depierre, Farjaux, the Corps de Ballet of the Théâtre du Châtelet, and acrobats of the Folies-Bergère. 14 minutes. Hand colored.

A Trip to the Moon was the world's first science-fiction epic. Today it may seem like a quaint, brief farce, combining scenes from two SF novels of director Georges MÉLIÈS's time, Jules VERNE's *From the Earth to the Moon* (1865) and H. G. WELLS's *The First Men in the Moon* (1901), showing prancing ballerinas helping load a group of explorers into a giant cardboard cannon and firing a shell that lands in the right eye of the meringuelike face of the man in the Moon. On the Moon the explorers discover giant mushrooms and acrobatic Selenites, who explode when struck. Safely returning to the Earth in their projectile, they fall into the sea and observe the wonders of ocean life. But in a time when most films ran only a minute or so, this work's one-reel length was monumental. Not only did it fulfill its intention of demonstrating the magic possible in the cinema but it revealed the natural affinity of film and SF—and, like numerous films to follow, rejected SF's serious ideas in favor of special effects.

Méliès brought to cinema the full repertoire of the stage magician that he was, but he never advanced beyond illustrating his stories with a series of dynamic tableaux.

W.L.

TRON (1982).

Directed by Steven Lisberger; screenplay by Steven Lisberger and Bonnie MacBird; photographed by Bruce Logan; music by Wendy Carlos. With Bruce Boxleitner, Jeff Bridges, Cindy Morgan, David Warner, Barnard Hughes. 96 minutes. Color.

When Flynn, a software engineer (Jeff Bridges), tries to locate a file in the memory bank of the Master Control Program, the MCP—which has become powerful enough to transform matter from the real world into elements of the computer system—transports Flynn into the system, forcing him to become a video gladiator. Tron, a program designed to monitor system access, joins forces with Flynn to fight electronic warriors and overthrow the MCP.

Tron is a variation on the motif of computer as character, which has continued to gain popularity as a science-fiction film convention. Not only is *Tron* a man versus machine story, reminiscent of the conflict with HAL in 2001: A SPACE ODYSSEY (1968), but it also elevates the human-created software to "hero" status, indicating that technology is neither good nor evil but is under human control. However, in *Tron* this moral takes second place to the overwhelming but splendid abstract geometrical constructions of the special effects.

Called an "Alice in Computerland" fantasy, the film is a mesmerizing visualization of the electronic civilization inside a mainframe computer. Just as FANTASTIC VOYAGE (1966) took us on a journey through the human brain, *Tron* treats us to a tour of the imaginary brain of the computer. The production itself underscores the computer-world theme, using a combination of computer-generated special effects and Disney Studio's traditional animation processes to create high-tech landscapes of grids and mazes.

As a film, however, *Tron* is deficient in plot, drama, and clarity, failing to involve the viewers emotionally, although we may occasionally wonder if we have created a microcosmos beneath our fingertips.

D.P.V.

TRUMBULL, DOUGLAS (1942–). American SPECIAL EFFECTS technician and occasional film director. Educated as a designer and illustrator, Trumbull began his career in films on a short subject, *Lifeline in Space,* made for the U.S. Air Force; his work on the Cinerama short *To The Moon and Beyond* caught the attention of Stanley KUBRICK, and Trumbull was hired as one of five effects directors on Kubrick's 2001: A SPACE ODYSSEY (1968). The following year, he worked on the effects for Robert WISE's THE ANDROMEDA STRAIN. Trumbull's penchant for solving problems in new ways—he developed the "slit-scan" process, among others—rapidly made him the most sought-after special effects director in the United States. In 1972 SILENT RUNNING was released; Trumbull not only supervised the effects but produced and directed the film as well. He also supervised the effects for CLOSE ENCOUNTERS OF THE THIRD KIND (1977), STAR TREK: *The Motion Picture* (1979), and BLADE RUNNER (1982). In 1983 his second film as director, BRAINSTORM, was released after a troubled production history, but, as with *Silent Running,* it was unsuccessful financially and critically. Even before that, Trumbull had begun working on Showscan, his new process in which movies are projected at sixty frames per second rather than the usual twenty-four, increasing clarity and a feeling of reality.

"The biggest problem with special effects today," Trumbull has said, "particularly in dealing with science fiction, is not to project the future, but to avoid reflecting the present." His dazzling, inventive effects accomplish this goal, but as a director Trumbull has yet to prove himself; despite his obvious interest in emotional material, his directorial work is largely uninventive and dry.

B.W.

TUBB, E[DWIN] C[HARLES] (1919–). British writer of science fiction whose volume of production

may be matched only by the number of his pseudonyms, among them Volsted Gridban, Charles Grey, Alan Guthrie, George Holt, Gill Hunt, Alan (also Allen) Innes, Gregory Kern, Nigel Lloyd, Arthur Maclean, Carl Maddox, Brian Shaw, Roy Sheldon, Edward Thomson, Ken Wainwright, Douglas West, and Frank Winnard. Indeed, since his first story ("No Short Cut") was sold to NEW WORLDS in 1951, he has employed more than sixty names.

Tubb's science fiction is most often of the action-adventure kind, and his wide popularity is founded on his ability to tell a story well and quickly. His heroes are usually models of masculinity, good with their fists and attractive to women, epitomizing a single-minded devotion to the task at hand and the direct approach to human and alien relationships alike.

The ultimate Tubb hero is Earl Dumarest, a grim, humorless man in search of the planet Earth who lives out a continuing series of adventures in the far future. Dumarest is constantly threatened by the Cyclan, modified humans who are collectively linked to a grotesque computer. The series of novels (*The Winds of Gath,* 1967; *Derai,* 1968; *Toyman,* 1969; *Kalin,* 1969; *The Jester at Scar,* 1970; *Lallia,* 1971; *Technos,* 1972; *Veruchia,* 1973; *Mayenne,* 1973; *Jondelle,* 1973; *Zenya,* 1974; *Eloise,* 1975; *Eye of the Zodiac,* 1975; *Jack of Swords,* 1976; *Spectrum of a Forgotten Sun,* 1976; *Haven of Darkness,* 1977; *Prison of Night,* 1977; *Incident on Ath,* 1978; *The Quillian Sector, 1978; Web of Sand,* 1979; *Iduna's Universe,* 1979; *The Terra Data,* 1980; *Earth Is Heaven,* 1982; *Melome,* 1983; and *Angado,* 1984) that details Dumarest's adventures are noteworthy for the variety of worlds and landscapes Tubb creates.

Under the name of Gregory Kern, Tubb has also written a second, ongoing, series of novels (*Galaxy of the Lost,* 1973; *Slave Ship from Sergan,* 1973; *Monster of Metelaze,* 1973; *Enemy within the Skull,* 1974; *Jewel of Jarhen,* 1974; *Seetee Alert!,* 1974; *The Gholan Gate,* 1974; *The Eater of Worlds,* 1974; *Earth Enslaved,* 1974; *Planet of Dread,* 1974; *Spawn of Laban,* 1974; *The Genetic Buccaneer,* 1974; *A World Aflame,* 1974; *The Ghosts of Epidoris,* 1975; *Mimics of Dephene,* 1975; *Beyond the Galactic Lens,* 1975; *Das Kosmiche Duelle,* 1976; and *Galactiad,* 1983) which features Cap Kennedy, a super-secret galactic agent who is ever ready to fight the forces of evil. Less imaginative than the Dumarest series in both its setting and plot twists, these stories nevertheless contain all the ingredients to please lovers of SPACE OPERA.

Tubb is, moreover, a master at handling the conventional material of SF. His use of a generation starship in *The Space-Born* (1956) and cybernetics in *Enterprise 2115* (1954; reprinted as *The Mechanical Monarch,* 1958) are as good as any to be found in the genre. And his novelizations of a number of scripts from the television series SPACE 1999 (*Breakaway,* 1975; *Collision Course,*

1975; *Alien Seed,* 1976; *Rogue Planet,* 1976; and *Earthfall,* 1977) have the flavor of old-fashioned pulp SF that many readers still find enjoyable.

OTHER WORKS: *Saturn Patrol* (1951); *Planetfall* (1951); *Argentis* (1952); *Alien Impact* (1952); *Atom War on Mars* (1952); *Alien Universe* (1952); *Reverse Universe* (1952); *The Mutants Rebel* (1953); *Venusian Adventure* (1953); *Planetoid Disposals Ltd.* (1953); *De Bracy's Drug* (1953); *Fugitive of Time* (1953); *The Wall* (1953); *Dynasty of Doom* (1953); *Tormented City* (1953); *Space Hunger* (1953); *I Fight for Mars* (1953); *Alien Life* (1954); *The Living World* (1954); *World at Bay* (1954); *The Metal Eater* (1954); *Journey to Mars* (1954); *Menace from the Past* (1954); *City of No Return* (1954); *The Stellar Legion* (1954); *The Hell Planet* (1954); *The Resurrected Man* (1954); *The Extra Man* (1954); *The Hand of Havoc* (1954); *Alien Dust* (1955); *Touch of Evil* (1959); *Moon Base* (1964); *Ten from Tomorrow* (collection, 1966); *Death Is a Dream* (1967); *C.O.D. Mars* (1968); *S.T.A.R. Flight* (1969); *Escape into Space* (1969); *Century of the Manikin* (1972); *A Scatter of Stardust* (collection, 1972); *Atilus the Slave* (1975); *Atilus the Gladiator* (1975); *The Primitive* (1977); *Gladiator* (1978); *Stellar Assignment* (1979); *Death Wears a White Face* (1979); *The Luck Machine* (1980); *Pawn of the Omphalos* (1980); *The Coming Event* (1982); *Stardeath* (1983); *Symbol of Terra* (1985).

S.H.G.

TUCKER, GEORGE (1775–1861).

American essayist, biographer, economist, historian, philosopher, and congressman who wrote two satiric science-fiction novels much in the spirit of Jonathan SWIFT's *Gulliver's Travels* (1726). *A Voyage to the Moon* (1827, as Joseph Atterly) introduced the concept of antigravity and described the first scientifically plausible spaceship. *A Century Hence, Or a Romance of 1941* (an epistolary romance, unpublished until 1977) anticipated such important issues as overpopulation, women's rights, international politics, and Russian expansionism.

N.H.

TUCKER, [ARTHUR] WILSON ["BOB"] (1914–   ).

American writer and celebrated science-fiction fan. Since his initial sale in 1941 to *Super Science Stories,* Tucker has published more than a score of books, equally divided between the SF and mystery-suspense genres, most with a strong midwestern flavor. He did not finish grade school and is entirely self-educated. Before his retirement he worked as a motion picture projectionist and stage electrician.

Tucker's straightforward brand of SF is understated and compact, neatly dramatizing issues as big as Armageddon with small casts, often deployed in his native

Illinois under "Mr. Lincoln's Wonderful Sky." His favorite SF plot device is temporal dislocation, through either immortality (*The Time Masters,* 1953) or time travel (*The Lincoln Hunters,* 1968). In *The Year of the Quiet Sun* (1970), a retroactive winner of the Campbell Memorial Award in 1976, a biblical archaeologist travels to the future in an age of race war and confronts problems from his own past. These and other similar works express Tucker's strong interest in history.

In the realm of SF fandom, Tucker is a legend, having been continuously active since 1931 as a writer and raconteur. Fans know him as the originator of "Tuckerization," the naming of fictional characters after SF personalities. In 1970 Tucker won the Hugo for best fan writer and in 1948 and 1967 was Fan Guest of Honor at the World SF Convention.

NOTABLE OTHER WORKS: *The Long, Loud Silence* (1952); *Wild Talent/Man from Tomorrow* (1954); *The Science Fiction Sub-Treasury* (1954); *Time Bomb* (1955); *Ice and Iron* (1974).

S.L.M.

TURNER, GEORGE [REGINALD] (1916–   ).

Australian writer and critic. Born in Melbourne, Turner served for six years in the Australian Imperial Forces in World War II. His fiction, consisting of three science-fiction novels (and a half-dozen others, plus a handful of short stories), is concerned with the ethics of survival. The novels—*Beloved Son* (1978), *Vaneglory* (1981), and *Yesterday's Men* (1983)—are all set in the same post-holocaust world of the twenty-first century but do not form a trilogy. Called the Ethical Culture series, they are based on similar assumptions about forthcoming events: the Collapse of 1992 caused by incautious genetic manipulation and subsequent nuclear bombings leads to a new world developed around the Ethic of Non-Interference. But new tinkering emerges along with new problems, particularly the dangers of romanticism and utopianism.

Turner came to SF writing late, having first made his name as a critic in the Australian fanzine *Science Fiction Commentary.* Since 1970 he has reviewed science fiction for the Melbourne *Age.* He has contributed articles to critical collections and won the Miles Franklin Award in 1963, the Commonwealth Literary Fund Award in 1968, and the Ditmar Award in 1984.

J.E.G.

TURTLEDOVE, HARRY [NORMAN] (1949–   ).

American writer of science fiction and fantasy whose first fantasy novels and short stories appeared under the pseudonym Eric Iverson. A history professor, Turtledove has successfully transferred his historical knowledge to his fiction. After the publication in 1979 of two sword-

and-sorcery novels, *Wereblood* and *Werenight*, Turtledove achieved significant success beginning in 1987 with the publication of a four-part fantasy series (*The Misplaced Legion, An Emperor for the Legion, The Legion of Videssos,* and *Swords of the Legion*) and his first SF novel, *Agent of Byzantium.* Two more SF novels, *Non-Interference* and *A Different Flesh,* were published in 1988.

Turtledove's science fiction has been published mostly in ANALOG, where he has had a remarkable record of publication (eight stories in 1985, five in 1986, and a three-part serial, *The Report on Bilbeis IV,* and another story in 1987). He cites as inspiration the fiction of Poul ANDERSON and L. Sprague DE CAMP. In addition to his science fiction, Turtledove has published an academic work, *The Chronicle of Theophanes: An English Translation of* anni mundi 6095–6305 (A.D. 602–813).

J.E.G.

TUTTLE, LISA (1952–   ).   American writer and columnist married for a time to British writer Christopher PRIEST. Tuttle frequently combines horror and science fiction in her fiction to produce powerful and memorable tales (for example, "Sangre," 1977; "The House Lord," 1978; "In the Arcade," 1979, and "Sun City," 1980). In "Changelings" (1976) she created a credible future world in which people are controlled by surgical procedures that modify their behavior. Children are used to spy on their parents, and adults live in constant fear of their offspring.

Tuttle has also written sensitive stories that combine SF, fantasy, and horror to highlight human problems in self-esteem and socialization (for example, "Stranger in the House," 1972; "The Hollow Man," 1979; "Bug House," 1980; and "Flying to Byzantium," 1985). "The Family Monkey" (1977) is a study in personal relationships as the human characters first rescue an alien and then turn it into a servant until its own race returns for it.

Tuttle's first novel, *Windhaven* (1982), was a collaboration with George R. R. MARTIN, who has become one of her biggest boosters. It describes a colony of humans who created their own feudal civilization after their ancestors were wrecked on an alien planet. In *Familiar Spirits* (1983), a solo novel, Tuttle once again created rounded characters in vivid—and terrifying—situations. She has also published a collection, *A Spaceship Built of Stone and Other Stories* (1987).

S.H.G.

TWAIN, MARK (Pseudonym of Samuel Langhorne Clemens) (1835–1910).   American writer who, like many other authors of the nineteenth century, as Bruce Franklin has demonstrated in *Future Perfect*

(1966), frequently wrote science fiction.

Twain's most important foray into the still developing genre was *A Connecticut Yankee in King Arthur's Court* (1889). He was handicapped by his lack of a convincing method for his pragmatic, problem-solving protagonist to reach King Arthur's time (Hank Morgan gets knocked out with a crowbar and finds himself in A.D. 528, and he is restored to his own time when Merlin puts him to sleep), but Twain's naturalistic method of depicting the *ordinariness* of the Age of Chivalry prefigures the later techniques of such authors as Robert A. HEINLEIN, for all that the satirically idealized Arthurian England of the book is decidedly nonhistorical. The story is SF, however, not so much because it concerns time travel but because it considers the various ways in which industrialization will change society, as Morgan turns Camelot into a modern industrial power and then destroys it through megalomania. A great work in its own right, this novel had a significant impact on subsequent time travel stories: L. Sprague DE CAMP's *Lest Darkness Fall* (1941), for example, is a deliberate attempt to restate realistically the theme that a man from the present might use his superior knowledge to alter the past.

Numerous Twain stories have fantastic elements. "From the *London Times* of 1904" (1898) deals pessimistically with the social impact of television. Two posthumously published fragments, "The Great Dark" (written 1898, published 1962) and "3000 Years among the Microbes" (written 1905, published in part 1923, complete edition published 1966), explore fantastic realms beneath the microscope. Among his short stories are a number of utopias, dystopias, and fantasies. Certainly in Twain's time change was in the air, and many writers were examining its impact on human existence. But Twain himself was concerned with invention (the story of his ill-fated financial involvement in the attempt to create a typesetting machine has often been told) and with the process of change in the world around him. His life encompassed the transformation of America from frontier settlements to industrialized cities, and that evolution, and the discrepancies between the American dream and its reality, might be considered his most important literary theme, whether in *Life on the Mississippi* (1883) and *Huckleberry Finn* (1885), or in his SF.

D.S.

20 MILLION MILES TO EARTH (1957).   *Directed by Nathan Juran; screenplay by Bob Williams and Christopher Knopf; photographed by Irving Lippman and Carlos Ventigmilia; music supervised by Mischa Bakaleinikoff. With William Hopper, Joan Taylor, Frank Puglia, John Zaremba, Thomas Browne Henry, Tito Vuolo, Jan Arvan, Arthur Space, Ray Harryhausen. 84 minutes. Black and white.*

An American spaceship returning from Venus (hence

the film's title) crashes into the sea off Italy. A small Venusian animal escapes and begins growing rapidly; captured, it escapes again in Rome, wreaking scenic destruction before being killed in the Colosseum.

This, the last of their black-and-white films, is among the best liked from producer Charles H. Schneer and stop-motion expert Ray HARRYHAUSEN, but it is valued entirely for Harryhausen's effects. The direction is pedestrian and the script unimaginative, but the interestingly designed creature is fluid and dramatic in motion, brought to life by some of Harryhausen's best work. However, a comparison with KING KONG (1933) demonstrates that whereas Willis O'BRIEN was a genius, Ray Harryhausen, always striving for realism rather than personality, is a highly skilled craftsman. Kong was a character in his own right; the creature here is only a big animal.

B.W.

THE 27TH DAY (1957).   *Directed by William Asher; screenplay by John Mantley; adapted from the novel by John Mantley; photographed by Henry Freulich; music supervised by Mischa Bakaleinikoff. With Gene Barry, Valerie French, George Voskovec, Azenath Janti, Marie Tsien, Stefan Schnabel, Arnold Moss, Frederick Ledebur, Paul Birch. 74 minutes. Black and white.*

Kidnapped by a dignified alien, people from several countries are given capsules that can (by unclear methods) evaporate every human being on Earth; though needing a home, the aliens hope that humanity can decipher a puzzle about the capsules before wiping itself out. Just before a fiendish Communist can kill the entire West, it is found that the capsules can kill only "every enemy of peace and freedom" in the world. This done, the alien and his race are invited to live on Earth.

The 27th Day is naively anti-Communist, though made with conviction and commitment. The idea that all sociopolitical problems of humanity would be solved by the elimination of a relatively few people is so unsophisticated as to be breathtaking.

B.W.

20,000 LEAGUES UNDER THE SEA (1954).
Directed by Richard Fleischer; screenplay by Earl Felton; adapted from the novel by Jules Verne; photographed by Franz Planer; music by Paul J. Smith. With James Mason, Kirk Douglas, Paul Lukas, Peter Lorre, Robert J. Wilke, Carleton Young, Ted de Corsia, Percy Helton. 127 minutes. Color.

Walt Disney's elaborate production of *20,000 Leagues under the Sea* was immensely popular; among other side effects, it established Jules VERNE as an author whose

works could be successfully filmed. The film is so vivid and memorable that its plot, not overly faithful to that of Verne, became the plot of the novel in the minds of people the world over. The first atomic submarine was named *Nautilus*, ostensibly after the sub in Verne's novel—but only the film mentions atomic power.

In 1868, after a series of mysterious ship disasters, three men fall into the hands of Captain Nemo, a militant pacifist with his own submarine (James Mason). After many adventures, including a brine-soaked battle with a giant squid, the three escape and Nemo goes down with his submarine (and up in a mushroom cloud).

Leagues is a splendid family adventure film, produced on a lavish scale with exciting special effects and handsome photography. The *Nautilus* is a masterpiece of design (by Harper Goff), fish shaped and thoroughly nineteenth century, complete with pipe organ, on which the brooding Nemo plays the music of Bach. The film has some drawbacks: it lacks a central character, and the humor, mostly centering on Kirk Douglas, is childish. Despite these weaknesses, though, this is arguably the best film based on a Verne novel.

B.W.

TWILIGHT ZONE (1959–1964).   *Directed by Mitchell Leisen, John Brahm, Richard Donner, Robert Florey, Jacques Tourneur, Ida Lupino, and others; written by Rod Serling, Richard Matheson, Charles Beaumont, George Clayton Johnson, Manly Wade Wellman, Ray Bradbury, Earl Hamner, Jr., and others; photographed by George T. Clemens and Robert W. Pittack; music by Van Cleave, Jerry Goldsmith, Laurindo Almeida, Bernard Herrmann, and others. 30 or 60 minutes. Black and white.*
TWILIGHT ZONE (1985–1987).   *Directed by Wes Craven, David Steinberg, Gerd Oswald, Noel Black, and others; written by Gerrit Graham, Rockne S. O'Bannon, Harlan Ellison, Martin Pasko, and others. 60 minutes. Color.*
TWILIGHT ZONE—THE MOVIE (1983).   *Directed by John Landis, Steven Spielberg, Joe Dante, and George Miller; screenplay by John Landis, George Clayton Johnson, Richard Matheson, and Melissa Mathison; photographed by Steven Larner, Allen Daviau, and John Hora; music by Jerry Goldsmith. With Vic Morrow, Scatman Crothers, Bill Quinn, Selma Diamond, Kathleen Quinlan, Jeremy Licht, Keven McCarthy, Dan Ackroyd, Albert Brooks. 105 minutes. Color.*

The original *Twilight Zone* television series, unlike the earlier SCIENCE FICTION THEATRE, was not always science fiction; some shows were SF, some horror, some comedy, some social commentary, some fantasy. But the range and diversity suggests one of the show's primary appeals: you never knew exactly what you were going to get. The hallmark of creator and host Rod SER-LING's best work for *Twilight Zone* was the fantastic return to a happier past, but he rarely couched this theme in purely science-fictional terms: "Walking Distance" (1959), "A Stop at Willoughby" (1960), "One Hundred Yards over the Rim" (1961), and "In Praise of Pip" (1963) are all more readily categorizable as fantasy than as SF.

One of the more obvious inspirations for *Twilight Zone* writers was the Frank Capra fantasy *It's a Wonderful Life* (1946); another touchstone, *Dead of Night* (1946), was horror fantasy. The Capra film's themes of the sanctity of life and the importance of loved ones, as well as such plot elements as guardian angels and miraculous rescues from suicide, surface again and again in shows such as "Mr. Bevis" (1960) and "The Changing of the Guard" and "Cavendar Is Coming" (both 1962), all by Serling, and "Person or Persons Unknown" (1962) and "Printer's Devil" (1963), by Charles Beaumont. Beaumont wrote several of the most unforgettable *Twilight Zones*, including "Shadow Play" (1961), with its *Dead of Night*–like nightmare-within-nightmare story structure; and "The Jungle" (1961), in which a voodoo hex turns a big city into a jungle.

Nevertheless, science fiction was frequently represented in the series, and in an era when little SF was televised, and virtually none of it was for adults, *Twilight Zone* episodes were an oasis in a vast wasteland for SF fans, who tuned in to get the latest story with its traditional twist at the end. A number of episodes were adapted from published stories, such as Lewis Padgett's "What You Need" (1945), Jerome BIXBY's "It's a *Good* Life" (1953), Damon KNIGHT's "To Serve Man" (1950), and Ray BRADBURY's "I Sing the Body Electric" (1969).

Other SF episodes were written especially for the series, such as Earl Hamner, Jr.'s "Stopover in a Quiet Town" (1964), in which a couple awakens, haunted by a child's laughter, in a desolate town from which they try to escape by train, only to find themselves continually returning. At the end they are revealed to be the kidnapped playthings of a gigantic alien child. At the end of the famous "The Eye of the Beholder" (1960), by Rod Serling, the bandages of a surgical patient are unwrapped to reveal a beautiful woman, but the surgeons, pig-faced mutants, recoil in horror. But the show's scope was limited by its almost nonexistent special effects budget, as witness the final scene of Richard MATHESON's "The Invaders" (1961), in which tiny aliens, who turn out to be Earth astronauts, are represented by windup toys.

The show's popularity in syndication led eventually to a 1983 feature film and a second, hour-long television series. The quality of the series varied to say the least. With its new format—several new stories in each installment—it was possible to see three terrible *Twilight Zones* in one night. At least three memorable stories, however, have been added to the canon: "A Matter of Minutes" (1986), "Cold Reading" (1986), and "The

Tracy Stratford and friend in the *Twilight Zone* episode "Little Girl Lost"

Burning Man" (1985). "A Matter of Minutes," scripted by Rockne S. O'Bannon from Theodore STURGEON's "Yesterday Was Monday" (1941) is a witty behind-the-scenes look at time that demonstrates how each minute of our waking and sleeping lives is created for us by crack teams of time workers. In "Cold Reading" Dick Shawn, a radio show writer dissatisfied with phony sound effects, magically gets the real thing, but the recording room is overrun with monkeys, macaws, and so forth. And Ray Bradbury contributed, with typical lyric wit, "The Burning Man," about a sinister supernatural hitchhiker.

The movie that came between the two series was at once more and less than both. The quality of the unexpected in the series was lost in the film: three of the four story segments were remakes. Steven SPIELBERG directed an untitled remake of George Clayton JOHNSON's 1962 "Kick the Can"; Joe DANTE, a remake of "It's a *Good* Life"; George Miller, a remake of Richard Matheson's "Nightmare at 20,000 Feet" (1963). John Landis contributed the only original material, including notably a sharp, spooky-charming, mood-setting introduction featuring Dan Ackroyd and Albert Brooks. Fortunately for viewers, Matheson had a hand in all three remakes and Johnson in one, and the directors all seem to have taken readily to the short story–film form. The new "Kick the Can" segment especially benefits from the presence of *Twilight Zone* veterans. A tale of rest home residents offered the gift of youth, it suggests, through their differing reactions, the mixed blessing such a second-time-around gift might be. Like *Twilight Zone* itself.

D.W.

THE TWO-CULTURES DEBATE

Fundamental disagreements between the literary culture and the scientific culture about the quality and direction of life, even the purpose of life, were the subject of a 1959 Rede lecture at Cambridge, "The Two Cultures" (published as *The Two Cultures and the Scientific Revolution*), by physicist and novelist C. P. Snow. The lecture set off a debate in which members of the two cultures squared off across the Western world, but it was only the culmination of a disagreement that began with the origins of science and the beginnings of the Industrial Revolution, that existed in science fiction since its beginnings, and that would be continued afterwards between "NEW WAVE" and "Old Wave" science fiction and between representatives of the two cultures down to the present.

In his lecture Snow described that critical division: "I believe the intellectual life of the whole of western society is increasingly split into two polar groups . . . literary intellectuals at one pole—at the other scientists. . . . The non-scientists have a rooted impression that the scientists are shallowly optimistic, unaware of man's condition. On the other hand, the scientists believe that the literary intellectuals are totally lacking in foresight, peculiarly unconcerned with their brother man, in a deep sense anti-intellectual, anxious to restrict both art and thought to the existential moment."

Snow was trying to bridge the gap, partly by reforming the curriculum of the English schools to include the sciences as a significant part of its studies, but he predicted trouble doing so because of the tendency "to let our social forms crystalise . . . the more we iron out economic inequalities." The privileged control the curriculum of education, Snow went on to say, and thus there is little hope for a balance between the liberal arts and the sciences.

He pointed to the literary response to the Industrial Revolution and the unwillingness of a writer of high class to see that "the hideous back-streets, the smoking chimneys, the internal price" were not a permanent consequence of industrialization. Instead the educated elite insisted that poverty and poor living conditions resulted from humanity selling its soul to science and technology, that if people had been content with living within the limits of a "natural" state all would have been well. Snow, however, argued that science and technology held the only answers to the problems of the poor.

One reason for the literati's lack of interest in advancing the Industrial Revolution, Snow suggested, was that it was the one hope the poor of the world had, but that hope threatened to reshape society and put all people on a more equal footing. It was one thing, he said, to choose poverty for oneself, particularly if one had wealth and decided to "do a modern Walden." But no one had the right to choose poverty for others. He insisted that "with singular unanimity, in any country where they have had the chance, the poor have walked off the land into the factories as fast as the factories could take them."

The reaction from the literary culture was immediate: Snow was attacking the very root of modern letters and suggesting that inhumane motives might lie beneath. F. R. Leavis, the noted Milton scholar and the heir to the critical theories of Matthew Arnold ("the best that is known and thought . . ."), struck back in the Richmond Lecture, also at Cambridge, titled "Two Cultures? The Significance of C. P. Snow" (published in *An Essay on Sir Charles Snow's Rede Lecture*, 1963). Leavis claimed that Snow confused the social condition with the individual condition, and that it is with the individual that education is most concerned. Snow failed to see the consequences for the individual of American industrialization typified in "the human emptiness: emptiness and boredom craving alcohol." Industrialization had created a working class with leisure, but the modern worker had no ability "to use his leisure in any but essentially passive ways." In addition to claiming that Snow was "utterly without a glimmer of what creative literature is, or why it matters," he revealed his ultimate vision of the good life: "Who will assert that the average member of a modern society is more fully human, or more alive, than a Bushman, an Indian peasant, or a member of one of those poignantly surviving primitive peoples, with their marvellous art and skills and vital intelligence?"

Such arguments go back to the beginnings of science itself. As early as the onset of the Industrial Revolution in eighteenth-century England, the debate over the benefits of scientific and technological change was already raging. Does the future of humanity lie with its scientific and technological discoveries or with traditional humanistic values that reached their peak in pre-Christian Athens and from which time they have gradually declined? Is science a pathway to a new Golden Age or another detour that will lead humanity even farther from the Garden of Eden? Is the race in danger of having its heart (and soul) replaced with soulless machines? And, most importantly, has our society evolved in separate cultures: the world of science and the world of letters?

Jonathan SWIFT supplied one answer in Gulliver's third voyage, to the air-borne island of Laputa (*Gulliver's*

Travels, 1772). The tale was a savage attack upon England's scientific Royal Society (which had been created in response to Sir Francis Bacon's "The New Atlantis" and its House of Salomon), and particularly Sir Isaac Newton. Swift described the hare-brained scientists in Laputa as "projectors" who had led the country to disaster while they ignored more common-sense and humane answers to the people's misery. Scientists, the story said, posed a danger because their quest for "improvements" upon nature distracted people from human concerns.

Yet many of Swift's contemporaries did not share his views. The poet James Thompson in "A Poem Sacred to the Memory of Sir Isaac Newton" (1772) called Newton "beloved of Heaven" and said that he "saw the finished university of things in all its order, magnitude, and parts. . . ."

The debate continued in the nineteenth century with Matthew Arnold and Thomas Henry Huxley. Huxley, champion of Darwin's evolutionary theories and H. G. WELLS's college biology teacher, had proposed an increase in the science taught in English universities. Arnold disagreed in "Literature and Science" (1882, also, interestingly enough, the Rede lecture at Cambridge): science should play a role in education, but the knowledge of science is simply knowledge and fails to address the central concerns of the human mind and heart. Scientists can't relate the information they uncover to those questions most important to a society's being. Only poetry and eloquence can do that, for they are the result of "the criticism of life by gifted men, alive and active with extraordinary power." They transcend "facts," he said, and deal with "truth."

Huxley, on the other hand, maintained in "Science and Culture" (1880) that "We cannot know the best thoughts and sayings of the Greeks unless we know what they thought about natural phenomena. We cannot fully appreciate their criticism of life unless we understand the extent to which that criticism was affected by scientific conceptions." He acknowledged the importance of a literary education but belittled the notion that it should so dominate the curriculum that no room can be found for significant education in the sciences. As he put it: "Every Englishman has, in his native tongue, an almost perfect instrument of literary expression; and, in his own literature, models of every kind of literary excellence. If an Englishman cannot get literary culture out of his Bible, his Shakespeare, his Milton, neither, in my belief, will the profoundest study of Homer and Sophocles, Virgil and Horace, give it to him."

This debate about the essence of education spilled over into literary theory when authors such as H. G. Wells and Henry James entered the fray. These former admirers of each other's work argued over the nature and goals of literature. Wells characterized the state of the English novel (in his *Experiment in Autobiography,*

1934) as something "produced in an atmosphere of security for the entertainment of secure people who like to feel established and safe for good." Moreover, the chief end of the novel had become "character-interest" rather than "adjustment-interest" because the literati were dedicated to maintaining the *status quo.* They had no real desire to create permanent changes for the underprivileged but only preached about the advantages of poverty for the soul and the innate nobility of the primitive life.

For his part James was distressed at the propagandistic nature of Wells's later works. He believed that Wells had sacrificed art to exhortation and in the process wrote sermons addressed to the most materialistic side of humanity. Such a change in the writer of *Kipps* and *A Modern Utopia* was lamentable because Wells had shown such great promise.

Given the involvement of Swift and Wells in the debate between the relative merits of the liberal arts as opposed to those of the sciences and the appearance of the same arguments in such works as Mary SHELLEY's *Frankenstein: Or, The Modern Prometheus* (1818), it was inevitable that as science fiction appeared upon the literary scene these arguments would become a significant source for the genre's themes. Indeed, fifty years before Snow's lectures, E. M. FORSTER's "The Machine Stops" (1909), reacting to what Forster called "one of the earlier heavens of H. G. Wells," showed machines reinforcing the worst aspects of humanity and people becoming little more than insects dependent on the machines for their lives and even their ideas. David H. KELLER in "The Revolt of the Pedestrians" (1928) agreed: labor-saving devices cater to humanity's natural dislike of work, and what isn't used—like legs in this story—will atrophy.

On the other hand, some SF writers saw the new technology as an unparalleled opportunity for the human race to transcend limitations that could never have been overcome before. John W. CAMPBELL in "Twilight" (1934), whose situation is almost identical with that of "The Machine Stops," saw the machine as an acceptable successor to biological humans. Capable of lifespans far beyond our own, the machines could take the essential human characteristic, curiosity, to the stars. Isaac ASIMOV's vision of the benefits of machines was more earthbound in "The Evitable Conflict" (1949) but possibly more controversial. He suggested that by putting control of economic and political institutions into the hands of machines, humanity would finally be freed from the natural and the artificial forces that have controlled its destiny until now.

Between the extremes of Forster and Asimov lie the majority of SF writers, although most write stories that tend to favor one side of the debate over the other. Jack WILLIAMSON's "With Folded Hands" (1947), Harlan ELLISON's " 'Repent, Harlequin!' Said the Ticktockman"

(1964), Damon KNIGHT's "Masks" (1968), and Theodore STURGEON's "Slow Sculpture" (1970) are notable in their support of the literary culture, or in their opposition to the machine. Robert A. HEINLEIN's "Universe" (1941), James GUNN's "The Listeners" (1968), and Edward BRYANT's "Particle Theory" (1977) argue for a beneficial relationship between humanity and its technology.

A third group of stories—including some written by authors just mentioned—has attempted a synthesis. Brian W. ALDISS's "Working in the Spaceship Yards" (1969), Robert SHECKLEY's "Can You Feel Anything When I Do This?" (1969), and Gregory BENFORD's "Exposures" (1981) each contribute a vision of how the two cultures are ultimately part of a single culture.

The debate will continue because the issues remain. The British NEW WAVE of the 1960s reacted to the optimism of Asimov and Heinlein with science fiction that centered on individuals as victims of their industrialized societies or of an incomprehensible or hostile universe. American writers responded with works in the late 1960s and the 1970s that used the New Wave's stylistic innovations to show how humanity's future was unavoidably linked to its technology. And in the 1980s new writers created what has been called CYBERPUNK, a form that takes for granted that, for good or for ill, humans will become an extension of the machines they have invented, or the machines, an extension of human will. Science fiction is, after all, the unique medium for this dispute because it shares features of both cultures: the subject matter of its stories is change, usually brought about by science or technology, and much of that fiction deals with the impact of the scientific culture upon humanity. But it can only be dealt with in a literary way, and its methods of exploring those changes come from and continue to depend upon the literary tradition.

Occasional fan resentment of "literary" writing may be traced to fandom's traditional allegiance to the scientific culture and its resentment of the other culture's symbols. Some literary dismissals of science fiction for its lack of "literary" values can derive from traditional SF's cultural emblems and attitudes. Increasingly, however, innovation and tradition are coming together in SF. Uneasy though this marriage may at times become, from the more perfect union emerge the most frequent and fruitful treatments of the "Two-Cultures Debate," and the best hope for its resolution.

S.H.G.

2001: A SPACE ODYSSEY (1968).   *Directed by Stanley Kubrick; screenplay by Stanley Kubrick and Arthur C. Clarke; adapted from "The Sentinel" by Arthur C. Clarke and the simultaneously released novel* 2001: A Space Odyssey *by Clarke; photographed by Geoffrey Unsworth and John Alcott; music by Richard Strauss, Aram Khachaturian, Johann Strauss,*

Gyorgy Ligeti. With Keir Dullea, Gary Lockwood, William Sylvester, Douglas Rain. 141 minutes. Color.
2010 (1984).   *Directed by Peter Hyams; screenplay by Peter Hyams; adapted from the novel* 2010: Odyssey Two *by Arthur C. Clarke; photographed by Peter Hyams; music by David Shire. With Roy Scheider, John Lithgow, Helen Mirren, Bob Balaban, Keir Dullea, James McEachin, Elya Baskin, Douglas Rain. 116 minutes. Color.*

What many believe to be the greatest science-fiction film of all time appeared in 1968: *2001: A Space Odyssey* showed what scientific accuracy and realism could do for the visual images of written SF, in this case the work of Arthur C. CLARKE, the great prophetic regionalist of our solar system. As with THINGS TO COME (1936), much of this film's success can be attributed to the fact that an SF writer worked on the screenplay. Clarke went H. G. WELLS one better and wrote an original novel, to be released with the film, while working on the screenplay.

The film is divided into three parts. In the first our prehuman ancestors discover a black monolith and are affected by it in some mysterious way, after which they learn to use tools. The second part of the film takes place in the year 2001: Heywood Floyd (William Sylvester) goes to the Moon, where another monolith has been discovered. As he and other scientists examine the monolith, it emits a powerful signal toward Jupiter. The film's last section takes place aboard the spaceship *Discovery*, en route to Jupiter. The ship is controlled by HAL 9000, an advanced computer, which gets into a series of altercations with astronauts David Bowman (Keir Dullea) and Frank Poole (Gary Lockwood). HAL kills Poole and the astronauts who are still in hibernation for the voyage, but Bowman manages to shut the computer down. Near Jupiter, Bowman confronts a third monolith and is drawn into a strange vortex. Forces beyond his understanding transform him into a superchild (the Starchild) and return him to the vicinity of Earth for unexplained reasons.

This already abstruse plot hides yet another story, which presents human evolution as a nurturing effort undertaken by a high alien civilization in Earth's remote past. The first monolith stimulates mental development among our prehuman ancestors; the second sends an alarm signal to the monolith circling Jupiter to announce that the species has developed space travel; the signal deliberately lures a human expedition to the giant planet, where Bowman becomes a sample for the investigation by the aliens.

What we see in *2001* does not clearly suggest what in fact happens. Director Stanley KUBRICK cut the film by some seventeen minutes after audience previews, sacrificing some connective tissue, several small details, and Clarke's narration at the beginning, which would have oriented many viewers and produced a more immediate audience understanding—a necessary feature of good SF, and especially Clarke's fiction.

Nevertheless, the sense of mystery gained is not entirely out of place; the film's overwhelming visual impact kept audiences watching, and the mystery sent them in search of explanations. Clarke's original narrative marches visually, in typically majestic, reflective step, with nearly complete technical and scientific accuracy, for which Kubrick spared no expense. Clarke's love for the natural wonders of the universe and his sense of the preciousness of intelligent life shine through the film.

The sequel, *2010*, was expected to be little more than a footnote to Kubrick's film, but Peter Hyams's streamlined version of Clarke's new novel turned out better than the usual Hollywood sequel and may stand more than one viewing despite serious flaws.

Nine years after the events of the first film, Dr. Heywood Floyd (Roy Scheider) joins a Russian expedition to Jupiter. *Discovery*'s orbit around the giant planet is decaying. An American expedition will not be ready in time, so Floyd, Dr. Chandra (Bob Balaban), and Walter Curnow (John Lithgow) are put into hibernation aboard the Soviet spaceship *Leonov*. Floyd's mission is to reactivate HAL and save *Discovery*'s store of data, which might reveal what happened to its crew.

Arriving at Jupiter, Floyd's team and the crew of the *Leonov* discover that the black monolith is multiplying itself. It eats up Jupiter and kindles it into a second Sun, turning our solar system into a double star and making Jupiter's moons more hospitable. The *Leonov*, with an assist from *Discovery*'s engines, escapes from Jupiter's gravitational field just as the new sun erupts into existence.

Both this film and the new novel find interesting ways back into the story of *2001*. HAL's death in the Kubrick film now takes on an element of classic tragedy. As HAL is reactivated by his mentor and friend, Dr. Chandra, we feel the enormity of what was done to this rational mind, and by extension to all reason. When HAL is told what he must do to help the return of the *Leonov*, he exhibits self-sacrifice, based on an understanding of the truth. This is one of Clarke's great themes, and it survives in the new film.

Sadly, although *2010*'s SPECIAL EFFECTS are often outstanding, the film's technical blunders become more prominent during a second viewing: whereas Kubrick gave us the factual silence of space, for example, Hyams gives us engine roars, explosions, crackles, and pops. In addition, the script provides no sense of the characters' inner life.

A serious criticism of both films is that they are better enjoyed by those familiar with the novels. The sequel explains itself much more than does *2001*, but Kubrick's is the superior achievement—perhaps because it preserves a sense of mystery and evokes a visceral response to the wonders of the universe.

G.Z.

THE TWONKY (1953).

Directed by Arch Oboler; screenplay by Arch Oboler; adapted from the short story by Lewis Padgett (Henry Kuttner); photographed by Joseph Biroc; music by Jack Meakin. With Hans Conried, Billy Lynn, Janet Warren, Gloria Blondell, Ed Max. 72 minutes. Black and white.

A typical suburban man (Hans Conried) finds his life disrupted when a "twonky" takes over his television set. The set serves him in many ways—a spirit from the future—but is tyrannical in others (it censors his reading, for instance). Finally he destroys it rather than have it destroy him (as in the story).

Based on a short story by Henry KUTTNER, one of the masters of the form in science fiction, *The Twonky* is a catastrophe. Labored and coy, the film lumbers where it should sprint. Arch Oboler added heavy-handed satire, and instead of being dangerous, the TV set is merely whimsical.

B.W.

U

THE ULTIMATE WARRIOR (1975).

Directed by Robert Clouse; screenplay by Robert Clouse; photographed by Gerald Hirschfield; music by Gil Mellé. With Max von Sydow, Yul Brynner, Joanna Miles, William Smith, Richard Kelton, Stephen McHattie, Darrell Zwerling. 94 minutes. Color.

This postholocaust film's bleak future is a result of ecological rather than atomic catastrophe, and is slightly unusual for being set in a devastated New York. Yul Brynner is a warrior for hire who assists Max von Sydow, head of a peaceful community, against evil gangs, at last fleeing the city with a pregnant woman (Joanna Miles) and seeds intended for new crops. Despite a good cast, conventional writing and directing, plus a heavy emphasis on action rather than story or characterization, make this film forgettable. It was, in fact, barely released.

B.W.

UNDERSEA KINGDOM (1936).

Directed by B. Reeves Eason and Joseph Kane; screenplay by John Rathmell, Maurice Geraghty, Oliver Drake, and Tracy Knight; photographed by William Nobles and Edgar Lyons; music by Arthur Kay and Jacques Aubran. With Ray "Crash" Corrigan, Lois Wilde, Monte Blue, William Farnum, C. Montague Shaw, Smiley Burnette, Lon Chaney, Jr. 230 minutes (serial verison), 100 minutes (feature version). Black and white. Alternate title: Sharad of Atlantis.

One of the marvelously awful science-fiction serials

that entertained American youths in the depths of the Depression was *Undersea Kingdom:* Republic Pictures discovers Atlantis, or, as Professor Norton (C. Montague Shaw) puts it: "Unless my calculations are wrong, we've come across the lost continent of Atlantis!" The Atlanteans have perfected television and called it reflectoplate, and they can create artificial earthquakes ("Start the earthquake!"). There is lots of good action and bad dialogue as Crash Corrigan, more or less playing himself, takes on the evil Unga Khan (Monte Blue) and his robots, also known as Volkites. A typical premature declaration: "That's the end of Crash Corrigan!"

D.W.

THE UNIVERSE

The word *universe* is most often used to stand for "all that is." Alternatively, it can mean "all of which we know." The distinction between these two meanings is an important one for science fiction. In the former sense the universe is the setting within which a story takes place. The latter definition implies that there may exist realms other than those familiar to the character or reader, possibly with alien characteristics or strange rules of operation.

The huge volume presently encompassed by astronomy—containing all the stars and galaxies observed through the most powerful telescopes—is sometimes referred to as the *cosmos* or the *metagalaxy*. It is defined by three spacial dimensions, the flow of time, and a set of relationships between objects and events. These relationships, or physical laws, control the behavior of matter and energy within space and time.

Cosmic space appears to occupy a volume roughly 30 billion light-years across and seems to have been expanding ever since an early explosive or inflationary event commonly called the Big Bang, about 15 to 25 billion years ago. However, the initial image brought to mind—of a simple bubble enlarging in emptiness—is misleading. There is no "central" point in this expansion. Or rather, *all* points appear to be central. And the deeper into the distance one peers, the farther back one looks into *time*. Light from the most distant quasars was emitted up to 13 billion years ago, when the cosmos was much, much smaller. Back then apparently space was a realm of exploding galaxies and star-devouring black holes.

Even the bubble's *shape* is a matter of some debate. Physicists believe that space is curved in a dimension higher than our customary three. If the curvature is positive (spherical), the universe is closed and gravity will eventually slow the expansion and bring about a collapse of all matter. If the curvature is negative, the expansion will continue forever, long past the eventual extinction of all the stars. This would lead to the slow, inevitable

"heat death" of the universe.

Recent evidence suggests that the distribution of matter in the cosmos is far from uniform. Galaxies clump in clusters, then in superclusters. These accumulations appear to lie on the rims of huge vacancies, as if all visible matter condensed at the edges of vast bubbles left over from the early moments of the Big Bang.

Scale (bigness) is the most obvious attribute of the "universe." It has also been the topic of many science-fiction stories. Johannes KEPLER's "Somnium" (1634), inspired by the revolutionary new view of the heavens announced by Nicolaus Copernicus, is just one example of an early tale that, by taking its hero, Duracotus, to the Moon, greatly expanded the realm within which fictional characters could operate, at last separating the definition of *world* from that of *universe*. And yet these early stories deal only with the Solar System, as if the planetary orbits encompassed all that could rationally be considered.

This hesitancy on issues of scale began to fade in the twentieth century, as the discoveries of Harlow Shapley and Edwin P. Hubble "expanded" the galaxy. David LINDSAY's *A Voyage to Arcturus* (1920) broke the Solar System barrier, as did E. E. SMITH's *The Skylark of Space* (1928/1946), offering readers a taste of galaxywide vistas.

At the other end of scale, Fitz-James O'BRIEN's "The Diamond Lens" (1858) has its protagonist fall for a feminine creature found living in a drop of water. "The Girl in the Golden Atom" (1919), by Ray CUMMINGS, deals with the since discredited idea that electrons moving around atomic nuclei might actually be planets orbiting their own suns. In "Surface Tension" (1932) James BLISH showed a clan of humans reduced to the size of rotifers and paramecia, whose cosmos consists of a small puddle. Theodore STURGEON's "Microcosmic God" (1941) also deals with a universe in miniature. Greg BEAR's *Blood Music* (1985) proposes intelligent life on the level of a single human cell, which achieves the ability to think and act independently with amazing results.

Many tales have been written about the hero who learns that the universe possesses scale beyond his or her dreams, including Samuel Johnson's *Rasselas* (1759), about a young man who goes forth from a tranquil Abyssinian valley to discover the wide world. Daniel F. GALOUYE's *Dark Universe* (1961) was a prototype for the story about an underground community that has forgotten the surface world. *Universe* (1941) by Robert A. HEINLEIN, *Starship* (1958) by Brian W. ALDISS, and *Captive Universe* (1969) by Harry HARRISON also concern "discovery" of scale. In each the protagonist—an unsophisticated descendant of nearly forgotten astronauts—at first believes a mammoth colony ship to be the entire universe.

The incredible scale of the visible cosmos appears to intimidate most writers. Nearly all space fiction has restricted itself to the Earth's galaxy (the Milky Way) or at most a few neighboring galaxies. Time scales in stories generally involve years, decades, or at most millennia. This is understandable, given the difficulty of portraying human characters and their problems and emotions on a stage 30 billion light-years across.

Nonetheless, a number of authors have dared these vistas. In *Last and First Men* (1930) Olaf STAPLEDON traced the future of humanity over a span of more than a billion years while restricting his canvas to the Solar System. His *Starmaker* (1937) is even bolder, taking readers on a tour of many levels and realms of thinking life. *Cities in Flight* (1970) by James BLISH presents a feel for vast times and distances, concluding with the end of the universe. Piers ANTHONY's *Macroscope* (1969) sends its characters exploring the universe using the planet Neptune as a spaceship. In *Tau Zero* (1970) by Poul ANDERSON an accelerated starship of humans comes so close to the speed of light that they outlast the final collapse of the metagalaxy, escape through a subsequent Big Bang, and live to colonize an entirely new universe.

Truly cosmic scale has been portrayed in a few stories. In his series beginning with *In the Ocean of Night* (1977), Gregory BENFORD dealt with the explosive jets found at the cores of galaxies, eventually describing how life might survive the ultimate heat death of the universe. David BRIN's story "Bubbles" (1987) is set amid the supercluster strings that surround vast intergalactic voids in space.

The discovery of a larger scale to things also figures into a great many stories about *parallel* continua (see Alternate Worlds). A number of theoretical physicists give some credence to the possibility of parallel realities through the Many Worlds hypothesis. These theories form the background of Frederik POHL's *The Coming of the Quantum Cats* (1985). In Keith LAUMER's *Worlds of the Imperium* (1962) and Richard C. MEREDITH's *At the Narrow Passage* (1973), the number of separate continua (or overlapping universes) is small enough to be conquerable by crosstime powers. Robert SHECKLEY's collection *Store of Infinity* (1960) features stories that explore the implications of multiple worlds. Larry NIVEN's "All the Myriad Ways" (1973) hauntingly proposes that the mesh of parallel reality might be so fine as to prevent any chance of orderly crosstime travel.

In fact, much fantasy appears to be based on the premise that the universe contains other accessible universes in which "the rules" are different, allowing magical or pseudomagical powers. L. Sprague DE CAMP and Fletcher PRATT collaborated on a series, beginning with *The Incomplete Enchanter* (1940/1942), which humorously explores "scientific" access to magical realms. Marion Zimmer BRADLEY's *Darkover Landfall* (1972) and its sequels propose a single planet where physical law can be modified.

Time is as basic a feature of our universe as are spacial

Illustration by Virgil Finlay

dimensions. Travel in time is a common SF theme (see Time Travel). However, the truly cosmic scale of time is much less often explored. In *The Weapon Shops of Isher* (1942), A. E. VAN VOGT turned an unwilling time traveler into the proximate cause of the Big Bang itself. George ZEBROWSKI's *Macrolife* (1979) reaches its climax at the end of our universe. In *Timescape* (1981) Gregory Benford explored in a much more scientifically convincing way the perennial idea of changing reality by communicating through time.

Spacial dimension and time help define what we call the universe. But at least as important are the relationships called physical laws, which astronomers assume to be constant (or nearly so) across our cosmos. In *Gateway* (1977) and its sequels, Frederik Pohl explored many of these relations, which "coincidentally" allow the existence of human life. Rudy RUCKER's *White Light* (1980) considers the scaling effects of pure mathematics itself.

Because the term *universe* can apply to subjective reality—what the individual perceives—as well as objective reality—what we call the real world—SF writers have often tackled the question How real is real? Philip K. DICK wrote quite often on this theme, most notably in *The Martian Time Slip* (1964) and *Ubik* (1969), as did Fritz LEIBER in *The Sinful Ones* (1953), Stanisław LEM in *Solaris* (1961, translated into English 1970) and Christopher PRIEST in *The Inverted World* (1974). M. K. Joseph's *The Hole within the Zero* (1967) combines many of the themes covered in this discussion by merging the subjective and the objective when an expedition encounters probabilistic reality at the "edge" of the universe.

The universe itself can also be personalized—made a character in the story. This has been accomplished either by emphasizing the implacability of its merciless laws, as in Tom GODWIN's "The Cold Equations" (1954), or by dealing directly in matters theological, as in James Blish's series of novels beginning with *A Case of Conscience* (1958) and Frank HERBERT's *Destination Void* (1966). Gregory Benford dealt with the trap of omniscience and immortality in "Time's Rub" (1985).

One last interpretation of the word *universe* must be mentioned—that of the self-consistent world model in which an author sets a series of mutually connected stories (see Series). Readers of SF demand that series writers not change rules or premises midway through a story cycle. Still, there is great variety of settings for such works, from the gritty extrapolation of Poul Anderson's Polesotechnic League through Anne McCAFFREY's soft science Pern to Raymond E. Feist's magical Midkemia. In the best such extended exercises, the reader is given a well-wrought future or alternate reality that is both entertaining and honestly thought provoking.

Science fiction on "universal" themes has proved a challenging subgenre that often generates the field's most memorable work. Nowhere else is it more forcefully shown how literature and science jointly alter each other and are altered as humanity's range of knowledge slowly grows and evolves.

G.D.B.

UTLEY, STEVEN (1948–   ).

American writer, prolific and respected author of sometimes startling short fiction and poetry. Utley was one of the most important (and occasionally controversial) young science-fiction authors of the 1970s. In 1980 he all but stopped writing in order to devote most of his creative energies to other endeavors, including cartooning. His work appeared frequently in magazines and anthologies; with George W. Proctor he edited *Lone Star Universe: Speculative Fiction from Texas* (1976). His best-known stories include "Getting Away" (1976), in which escape from a horrid future is only imaginary; "Upstart" (1977), in which space hero stereotypes are shown to be ridiculous; and, with Howard Waldrop, the Nebula Award nominee "Custer's Last Jump" (1976), in which the Sioux defeat the 7th Cavalry (and the 505th Balloon Infantry) by utilizing armed monoplanes.

B.D.

—— UTOPIAS AND DYSTOPIAS ——

Utopia is an imaginary country invented by Thomas MORE in order that it could be compared and contrasted with sixteenth-century England to dramatize the failings of English sociopolitical organization. More's Utopia is not really an ideal society, because many of its attributes serve a satiric purpose, but the word was eventually coopted as a generic title for images of social perfection, as if it were derived from the Greek *eutopos* ("better place") rather than *outopos* ("nowhere"). Attempts to design ideal societies had, of course, been made long before More's time—classical versions include Plato's *Republic*. The majority of such projects, however, are undercut in some measure by an element of satire, and even the classical utopias shelter an ironic suspicion that humans are ill fitted for life in an earthly paradise.

At the end of the eighteenth century the philosophers of the Enlightenment—particularly those in France—popularized the idea of progress: the notion that human society is subject to a gradual evolutionary improvement. From this time on images of ideal societies tended to be located in future time rather than remote places, and utopian fantasy entered a phase that Frank Manuel in *Utopias and Utopian Thought* (1966) has called "euchronian." The idea of building utopia as a political project inspired many of the political—particularly socialist—movements of the late eighteenth and nineteenth centuries and became the animating force in many attempted revolutions.

Nations that actually had revolutions—America and France—tended to retain euchronian optimism with greater conviction than those that did not—including Britain. America produced many more utopian works of fiction in the nineteenth century than Britain did, ranging from Mary Griffith's *Three Hundred Years Hence* (1836) to the enormously successful *Looking Backward, 2000–1887* (1888) by Edward BELLAMY. British images of ideal society were detached at an early stage from the idea of technological progress, often remaining conservatively allied with nostalgia for an imagined agrarian paradise. Samuel Butler's *Erewhon* (1972) satirizes science and is disenchanted with machinery; Richard Jeffries's *After London* (1885) and W. H. Hudson's *A Crystal Age* (1887) look forward to futures in which civilization has been mercifully obliterated.

British writers contemplating technological advancement found the idea threatening rather than seductive; many developed the thesis that technological miracles might gradually "dehumanize" the social order, that a mechanization of the human world might drive out tender feelings and simple delights. Such anxieties can be seen in the earliest dystopian fantasies: images of worlds worse than ours and into which we are in danger of delivering ourselves by our pursuit of the ends of vulgar materialism. Early examples include H. C. Marriott Watson's

Erchomenon (1879) and Walter Besant's *The Inner House* (1888). British literature of this period did produce one striking image of the world transformed for the better by a new power source, Edward BULWER-LYTTON's *The Coming Race* (1871), but this is more an occult romance than a euchronian anticipation, and in its fashion it anticipated much later works that tie the idea of utopia to the notion of a new Enlightenment of mental or spiritual evolution, as in William Dean Howells's *A Traveler from Altruria* (1872) in the United States.

Once the building of utopia became a hypothetical political project, utopians began to disagree among themselves about the character of the state that was to be constructed by future people. Edward Bellamy's image of a regimented leisure society was by no means to everyone's taste, and *Looking Backward* called forth many replies in kind, including William Morris's *News from Nowhere* (1890). These alternate visions of the socialist millennium helped illustrate the differences between Bellamy's materialistic American socialism, Morris's romantic British socialism, and the Marxist tradition (whose ideals are best represented in the utopian chapter of Anatole France's *The White Stone*, 1905).

These disagreements as to what the good life really might be like, and what kind of political organization would permit its flourishing, led to another shift in the characteristic mode of utopian thought. In Manuel's terminology, the euchronian phase gave way to a "eupsychian" phase, in which utopian speculators began to pay much more attention to "theories of happiness," so that their adventures in imaginary political economy became intimately entangled with psychological speculations about human needs and desires. At a crude level this shift can easily be seen in many of the early dystopian novels, in which materialistic progress is often linked to spiritual decay and there is a strong emphasis on the necessity of religious faith and ideals as instruments of temporal or transcendental salvation. Two good examples are Ignatius Donnelly's *Caesar's Column* (1890), the most striking of the early American dystopias, and the British work *Lord of the World* (1907) by Robert Hugh Benson.

After the turn of the century dystopian fantasies began to be produced as instruments of political propaganda, arguing against political creeds by extrapolating them into nightmare future states. Anticapitalist dystopias include *The Iron Heel* (1907) by Jack LONDON, *The Air Trust* (1915) by George Allan ENGLAND, and *Useless Hands* (1920) by Claude Farrere. Antisocialist dystopias include *The Unknown Tomorrow* (1910) by William le Queux, *Crucible Island* (1919) by Conde B. Pallen, and *Anthem* (1938) by Ayn RAND. A later political climate was to produce antifascist dystopias such as *Land under England* (1935) by Joseph O'Neill.

Dystopian alarmism and competition between alternative utopias combined to make utopian optimism seem very precarious. The naive form of the philosophy of progress that considered social evolution to be necessarily improving was discarded, and it was accepted that the building of a better world would be a hard struggle whose success was by no means guaranteed. The future came to be seen as a spectrum of alternative worlds, any one of which might come into being, and would-be utopians acquired a sense of urgency in regard to setting the world on the right path *now*, lest the way forward be lost.

This new way of thinking is reflected strongly in the work of the last great utopian writer to emerge in Britain: H. G. WELLS. Wells was well aware of the hazards facing humanity—the temptations that might seduce history onto a road to Hell. He tried as hard as he could, though, to soothe the anxieties raised in such stories of his own as *The Time Machine* (1895), "A Story of the Days to Come" (1897), and *When the Sleeper Wakes* (1899), countering them with prescriptions for social renewal, set out first in his nonfictional *Anticipations* (1901) and later in such fantasies as *A Modern Utopia* (1905) and *Men Like Gods* (1923). But for all his determination, Wells seemed always to lack faith in the kind of evolutionary socialism he preached. Some of his utopian fantasies are fantasies indeed, imagining miraculous metamorphoses of society—as in *The Food of the Gods* (1904) and *In the Days of the Comet* (1906)—and in more realistic works he frequently proposed that the contemporary world would have to be torn apart by warfare on an unprecedented scale before a new order could be constructed; *The World Set Free* (1914) and *The Shape of Things to Come* (1933) both adopt this assumption.

In the United States the search for an earthly paradise free from the temptations of technology and civilization led authors such as Herman Melville and R. L. Stevenson to Polynesia, Henry David Thoreau to *Walden* (1857), various groups to experiments with back-to-the-soil communities such as Brook Farm (1841–1847), and religions such as the Mormons, the Mennonites, the Shakers, and the Doukhobors to their several solutions. They were overtaken, however, by a growth and a faith in technology as the means to a better existence.

In America optimism was much easier to sustain, and the increasing rapidity of technological progress was a source of inspiration to many, not least to the immigrant popularizer of science, Hugo GERNSBACK, who serialized his own utopian romance, *Ralph 124C 41+* (1911), in *Modern Electrics* and went on to invent "scientifiction" as a didactic instrument of propaganda to help pave the way to an automated wonderland of wealth and opportunity. The tone of the editorial material in the early science-fiction pulp magazines was determinedly optimistic, but the tone of their fiction never quite measured up to its presumed mission. It was not just that Gernsback reprinted H. G. Wells's more anxious works alongside exuberant celebrations of progress by Jules VERNE and such German writers as Otfrid von Hanstein; the American writers he recruited often introduced anxieties about the way things were going as well. Notable among them was David H. KELLER, who was perennially worried about the annihilation of ordinary human values in a high-tech future. Indeed some of the most memorable stories from the early SF pulps are images of humanity become hopelessly decadent as a result of being made too comfortable by technology; examples include "City of the Living Dead" (1930) by Laurence Manning and Fletcher Pratt and "Twilight" (1934) by John W. CAMPBELL, Jr.

This link between the "utopia of comforts" and the prospect of decadence and degeneracy had been noted by Wells in his image of the Eloi in *The Time Machine,* and it was taken up by many dissenters from his utopian crusade. E. M. FORSTER used the perspective in "The Machine Stops" (1909), and it became central to the argument of seriously intended utopian satires such as Muriel Jaeger's *The Question Mark* (1926) and Aldous HUXLEY's *Brave New World* (1932)—which remains even today the ultimate indictment of the leisure society. For many writers the link between civilization and corruption seemed so clear that they could find hope for the future only in a complete abandonment of technology and a return to Rousseauistic noble savagery—we find such a proposition in J. Leslie Mitchell's *Gay Hunter* (1934) and tacitly in S. Fowler WRIGHT's collection of dystopian stories *The New Gods Lead* (1932). Even in America, David H. Keller could rejoice in the destruction of civilization in "The Metal Doom" (1932), and the most massive utopian fantasy of the 1940s was Austin Tappan Wright's *Islandia* (1942), which is heavy with nostalgia for a simpler way of life. The notion of recovering lost satisfactions by technological retreat is also to be found in more ironic and romantic fantasies, including John GLOAG's *The New Pleasure* (1933) and James HILTON's *Lost Horizon* (1933).

In Britain the loss of faith in the direction of history that was so powerfully assisted by World War I was brought to its culmination by World War II, and the most nightmarish images of future dystopia were produced there during and after the war: *The Riddle of the Tower* (1944) by J. D. BERESFORD and Esme Wynne-Tyson, *Ape and Essence* (1949) by Aldous Huxley, and *Nineteen Eighty-four* (1949) by George ORWELL. The only non-British work that compares in intensity with these is Yevgeny ZAMYATIN's remarkable *We* (1924), the product of postrevolutionary disenchantment in the USSR. Writers such as H. G. Wells, who had tried to keep alive a flickering flame of optimism, found it extinguished by the war; Wells's last book was the despairing *Mind at the End of Its Tether* (1945), and the British writer who had ranged farther in time and space than any other in search of hope for the future, Olaf STAPLEDON, ultimately found it impossible to balance optimism against pessimism when he tried to measure them out in such works

as *Darkness and the Light* (1942) and *The Flames* (1947). Images of saner and safer futures became increasingly tied to the idea that a new and superior race must displace *Homo sapiens,* perhaps by means of some marvelous evolutionary leap.

American writers too moved gradually toward this conclusion. Utopian thought in the eupsychian vein supposes that a sane society can only be constructed from the clay of sane individuals and that the seeds of utopia can be brought to flower through the psychological transformation of individuals. At the crudest level this supposition gives rise to such works as B. F. Skinner's behaviorist utopia *Walden Two* (1948), but a far more sophisticated version can be found in Gerald Heard's *Doppelgängers* (1947), which looks forward to "the psychological revolution." In Heard's manifesto, though, the revolution that begins in scientific psychology ends in a mystical acquisition of superhumanity, a wishful fantasy that is reflected promiscuously in the magazine SF of this period.

The optimism of the SF of the late 1940s and the 1950s is largely detached from technological progress per se and associated instead with the evolution of psi powers, as popularized by J. B. Rhine. The idea that the blossoming of these latent powers would pave the way for the establishment of utopia can be found in Henry KUTTNER's Baldy series, Wilmar H. SHIRAS's *Children of the Atom* (1953), and George O. SMITH's *Highways in Hiding* (1956), although the most dramatic fantasies of the New Enlightenment are Theodore STURGEON's *More Than Human* (1953), Alfred BESTER's *The Demolished Man* (1953), and Poul ANDERSON's *Brain Wave* (1954). With this notion of eupsychian transcendence always at hand as a reservoir of optimism, SF writers cheerfully began to produce in profusion images of future society made dreadful by technological advance. American dystopianism flourished in such works as *Player Piano* (1952) by Kurt VONNEGUT, Jr., *The Space Merchants* (1953) by Frederik POHL and Cyril M. KORNBLUTH, and *Fahrenheit 451* (1953) by Ray BRADBURY. Some of these works do end on a note of authentic despair, but the vast majority of the run-of-the-mill examples balance their horrific vision with images of transcendence (via evolving superhumanity) or escape (via spaceships). The spaceship often functions in SF of this period as a kind of safety valve by which dystopian pressure can be cathartically released; we see this in *The Space Merchants,* in Isaac ASIMOV's *The End of Eternity* (1955), and in James GUNN's *The Joy Makers* (1961).

The dystopian currents in SF became much stronger in the 1960s, when alarmism about overpopulation and pollution gave rise to many horrific images of the future, including Harry HARRISON's *Make Room! Make Room!* (1966), John BRUNNER's *Stand on Zanzibar* (1968), and Robert SILVERBERG's *The World Inside* (1971). In the 1950's the blame for dystopian futures was usually attributed to the political masters of society, who were often charged with "distorting" society by the single-minded pursuit of inappropriate ends. The dystopias of the 1960s and 1970s, however, generally set forth a deeper pessimism, in which the good intentions of politicians and parties are simply impotent to hold back or control those social processes that produce misery and frustration. In many stories of this period the world seems perversely determined to become a kind of Hell, and the black irony of this insistence is savored in a species of dystopian fantasy that is almost surreal, exemplified by such works as *Nova Express* (1964) by William Burroughs and *Moderan* (1971) by David R. BUNCH. A grimmer and more realistic version of the same ironic consciousness can be found in Thomas M. DISCH's *334* (1972).

In the face of this trend, attempts to use SF as a medium of utopian planning have been few and far from confident. Increasing attention to the injustices of sexual politics has led a number of feminist writers (not all female) to speculate about societies in which patriarchal oppression has been overcome. An early example is Theodore STURGEON's *Venus Plus X* (1960), and writers who have taken a consistent interest in sexual politics include Joanna RUSS and Samuel R. DELANY. It seems, though, that the only genuine ideal societies portrayed in such works are all-female worlds from which oppressive maleness has conveniently been banished—a kind of wishful thinking first embodied in Charlotte Perkins Gilman's *Herland* (1915). The Bellamyesque tradition of American socialist thought was reintroduced into SF by Mack REYNOLDS in *Looking Backward from the Year 2000* (1973), but when he extrapolated this line of thought through a series of novels with a similar setting, Reynolds eventually fell prey to the old arguments about decadence and degeneracy in the leisure society, to which he gave pessimistic rein in *After Utopia* (1977).

A much more careful consideration of utopian ideals was undertaken by Ursula K. LE GUIN in *The Dispossessed* (1974), tellingly subtitled "An Ambiguous Utopia." The drift of Le Guin's argument here, though, is that social equality is likely to be sustained only by circumstances of relative deprivation; this and subsequent works, including *Always Coming Home* (1986), assert that the good life is to be sought in eupsychian terms and tacitly accept that the quest is easier in societies that have largely abandoned mechanical means of production. This supposition can be found in several versions of contemporary social philosophy, including the works of E. F. Schumacher, whose advocacy of technology on "a human scale" is elaborated in Ernest Callenbach's utopian fantasy *Ecotopia* (1975).

The force of this idea has become so considerable in recent times that even diehard apologists for technological advance have begun to construct utopian images in which the operative technology is hidden from view and left largely to its own devices, allowing the human population to enjoy a life-style that reproduces those aspects of primitive society we find attractive without the concomitant disadvantages. A naive version of this philosophy can be found in Ray F. NELSON's *Then Beggars Could Ride* (1976), but a more striking argument tending in this direction is presented in recent work by Arthur C. CLARKE, culminating in *The Songs of Distant Earth* (1986). This is one of the very few novels which propose that a society is conceivable wherein ordinary human beings, untransformed by any psychic miracle, can selectively enjoy the benefits of the technological cornucopia without becoming either dehumanized or degenerate; significantly, this society is placed on another world and has been created from scratch, without the burdens that humans inherit from their history.

The history of utopian and dystopian images in modern imaginative fiction reflects a gradual but massive loss of faith in the idea of progress. No one, it seems, now believes that technological advancement goes hand in hand with moral advancement, and it appears highly likely to most people that the correlation is negative. This conclusion is largely a loss of faith in human nature; our fictions suggest that we consider ourselves ill fitted to be utopians, because we are greedy, lazy, and power hungry. We do not trust ourselves to use machinery, or the wealth created by it, wisely. It is a particularly telling observation that modern SF writers have little difficulty imagining that alien beings might be much better fitted by nature for happy and peaceful existence than we. It is, in a way, ironic that the proliferation of modern SF has taken place in the context of an abandonment of the mythology of progress that so inspired its American founding father, Hugo Gernsback. For this reason science fiction has become something very different from what he imagined, possessed of an ideological ambivalence that has added greatly to its fascination.

B.S.

V

VALIGURSKY, ED[WARD I.] (1926–   ). American illustrator best known for his skillfully wrought "gadget art." Valigursky was trained at the Art Institute of Chicago, the American Academy of Arts, and the Art Institute of Pittsburgh. He painted realistic covers for AMAZING STORIES, *Fantastic,* and paperback book publishers such as Ace, Ballantine, Pyramid, Dell, Berkley, and Pocket Books, as well as non-science-fiction covers for *Mechanics Illustrated.* He was also an associate art director for Ziff-Davis and art director for Quinn publications. His best-remembered works appeared on Ace

Double books, such as Robert SILVERBERG'S *The 13th Immortal, The Changeling Worlds* by H. Ken BULMER, Clifford D. SIMAK'S *City,* and Ivar Jorgenson's *Starhaven.* Valigursky's robots, like those of his contemporary Mel HUNTER, are his trademark; they are vivid and grimly menacing. His gunmetal gray spaceships are some of the most graceful ever painted, with swept-back wings and needle-sharp bows. Although his paintings show lapses in scientific accuracy, they are marked by a photographic realism.

J.G.

VALLEJO, BORIS (1948–　).

American fantasy and science-fiction artist. Born in Lima, Peru, Vallejo came to the United States in 1964 and soon began to earn a living as a freelance artist. In 1971 he sold a painting to Marvel Comics, which published it on the cover of *Eerie* in July of that year. He painted a number of additional covers for Marvel, but is best known for his work on *The Savage Sword of Conan;* indeed, many aficionados consider Vallejo's Conan the definitive portrayal of Robert E. HOWARD's massive hero.

Vallejo, who signs his work simply *Boris,* is almost exclusively a cover painter, for such publishers as DAW Books, Del Rey/Ballantine, and Pocket Books. His super-realistic and highly dramatic style is similar to that of Frank FRAZETTA, especially in his use of dominant central figures against nebulous backgrounds. Like Frazetta, he has often used himself as a model. Unlike Frazetta, however, Vallejo is as adept at illustrating high-tech science-fiction machinery as barbarian maidens. Although he has never done interior illustrations, the sketches published in his book *The Fantastic Art of Boris Vallejo* (1978) show a fine handling of pen-and-ink.

J.G.

THE VALLEY OF GWANGI (1969).

Directed by Jim O'Connolly; screenplay by William E. Bast, additional material by Julian More; photographed by Erwin Hillier; music by Jerome Moross. With James Franciscus, Gila Golan, Richard Carlson, Laurence Naismith, Freda Jackson, Gustavo Rojo. 95 minutes. Color.

Between KING KONG (1933) and MIGHTY JOE YOUNG (1949), pioneer stop-motion animator Willis O'BRIEN began several uncompleted projects; one was *Gwangi,* for which he wrote the screen story. Several years after his death, Ray HARRYHAUSEN—once O'Brien's protégé—filmed the old idea.

In Mexico in 1910, cowboys from a circus follow the trail of a stolen *eohippus* back to the valley of its origin and find the valley populated by other prehistoric creatures, including a fifteen-foot *allosaurus* they dub Gwangi. They capture Gwangi and exhibit him in a bullring, but

he escapes, menacing the town before dying in a blazing cathedral.

Despite bland performances by the leading actors and unexciting direction, *The Valley of Gwangi* is novel and amusing, and features some of Harryhausen's finest animation. Released in a period when escapist films were scorned, it met with no reception at all but in recent years has been recognized as one of Harryhausen's better works.

B.W.

VAN SCYOC, SYDNEY J[OYCE] (1939–　).

American writer who sets most of her science fiction on the Earth in the near future. Van Scyoc writes social SF with an emphasis on the effects of change on human characters. Frequently, it is advanced technology that significantly alters human behavior in her work, as in "Pollony Undiverted" (1963), "One Man's Dream" (1964), and "Visit to Cleveland General" (1969). Even her first novel, *Saltflower* (1971), despite its fascinating story of a dying alien race that seeds the Earth in the hope of continuing the species, centers on human social behavior.

In perhaps her strongest novel to date, *Assignment: Nor'Dyren* (1976), Van Scyoc's use of aliens to comment on human values is most clear. The Earth, in this near future world, has become a dystopia full of comfortable unemployed people who have allowed the government to gain control over every phase of their lives. One of its inhabitants, Tollan Bailey, travels to the planet Nor'Dyren, where humanlike aliens are floundering because of their society's rigid structure. As Bailey attempts to understand and help them, Van Scyoc suggests her vision of the perfect society: a world in which individuals are free to explore all styles of life and expression.

Alien contact and human values are also at the heart of *Starmother* (1976) and *Cloudcry* (1977), both of which highlight a fine ability to describe both alien and human perceptions and emotions. Most recently Van Scyoc has been writing novels that form the Darkchild series (*Darkchild,* 1982; *Bluesong,* 1983; *Starsilk,* 1984). These works credibly describe aliens whose relationships to human characters occasion haunting, poetic scenes.

OTHER WORKS: *Sunwaifs* (1981); *Daughters of the Sun-Stone* (1985, made up of *Darkchild, Bluesong,* and *Starsilk*).

S.H.G.

VAN VOGT, A[LFRED] E[LTON] (1912–　).

Canadian-born American writer. Van Vogt began to write science fiction for John W. CAMPBELL's *Astounding* in 1939 and became a prominent figure of Campbell's GOLDEN AGE. Some of his early work was done in collaboration with his first wife, E. Mayne HULL (1905–

1975). His first story, "Black Destroyer" (1939; subsequently built into *The Voyage of the Space Beagle*, 1950), features the first of many memorable alien beings involved in a contest for survival with human explorers. His first novel, *Slan* (1940/1947; revised 1951), introduces what was to become his foremost preoccupation: its central character has latent superhuman powers that explode into awesome potency under the pressure of harassment and threat. This key image recurs constantly in van Vogt's work, providing his tense plots with spectacular climaxes.

He is much given to convoluted and tangled story lines—his natural imaginative fertility is supplemented by the technique of binding several distinct short pieces into what he calls "fix-up" novels—and these usually require resolutions that are literary analogues of Alexander's cutting of the Gordian knot. Critics of his work charge him with failing to make sense in deploying his complex and disparate materials, but enthusiasts love the grandiosity of his schemes and the panache of his imaginative flourishes.

Van Vogt played a key role in helping to develop the Galactic Empire scenario, which in turn played a key role in liberating the imaginative potential of American SF. His stories collected as the novel *The Weapon Shops of Isher* (1941–1942–1949/1951) and its sequel *The Weapon Makers* (1943/1946; revised 1952) feature an imperial government on the Earth opposed by the Libertarian Weapon Shops. Another collection novel, *Empire of the Atom* (1946–1947/1956), and its sequel *The Wizard of Linn* (1950/1962) transpose aspects of the history of the Roman Empire into a future galactic culture somewhat after the fashion of Isaac Asimov's Foundation series. *The World of Null-A* (1945/1948) and *The Pawns of Null-A* (1948–1949/1956; also known as *The Players of Null-A*)—his most celebrated, confusing, and effective work of the Golden Age period—similarly expand their action to a grand galactic scale, this time pitting a stultified and militaristic political order against a superhuman champion of "non-Aristotelian logic."

The imaginative inspiration for these novels came from Alfred Korzybski's theory of general semantics, the first of several pseudoscientific vogues in which Campbell and his disciples were to become interested. Van Vogt was later recruited to the cause of the most notorious of these adventures in scientific unorthodoxy, L. Ron Hubbard's Dianetics, which promised to show how people can take control of their supposed latent superhumanity after the fashion of so many van Vogtian heroes.

After a long hiatus in his career, van Vogt returned to SF writing in the late 1960s and published fairly prolifically in the 1970s. His most important works of this period are *The Battle of Forever* (1971), whose typically superhuman hero matures in baroque far future settings, and *The Anarchistic Colossus* (1977), which further develops his interest in hypothetical Libertarian social

A. E. van Vogt

systems. In many of his later novels, including the third Null-A novel, *Null-A Three* (1985), he was content to provide ritual reenactments of his standard themes, but he continued to develop new hypotheses, including some ideas about female psychology, displayed in *The Secret Galactics* (1974, also known as *Earth Factor X*) and elsewhere. Despite the flamboyance of his work, he is not a careless writer; van Vogt's power lies in conjuring up striking and powerful images, which have captivated many fans and influenced many later writers, most obviously Charles L. HARNESS and Ian Wallace.

NOTABLE OTHER WORKS: *The Book of Ptath* (1943/1947); *Out of the Unknown* (with E. Mayne Hull, 1948); *Masters of Time* (1950; includes "Recruiting Station," 1942, also known as *Earth's Last Fortress*); *The House That Stood Still* (1950, also known as *The Mating Cry* and *The Undercover Aliens*); *The Mixed Men* (1952); *Destination: Universe!* (1952); *Away and Beyond* (1952); *The Universe Maker* ("The Shadow Men" 1949/1953); *The Mind Cage* (1957); *The War against the Rull* (1959); *Siege of the Unseen* ("The Chronicler" 1946/1959, also known as *The Three Eyes of Evil*); *The Beast* (1963, also known as *Moonbeast*); *The Twisted Men* (1964); *Rogue Ship* (1965); *The Winged Man* (with E. Mayne Hull, 1944/1966); *The Silkie* (1969); *Quest for the Future* (1970); *Children of Tomorrow* (1970); *More Than Superhuman* (1971); *The Darkness on Diamondia* (1972); *The Book of van Vogt* (collection, 1972, also known as *Lost: Fifty Suns*); *Future*

Glitter (1973, also known as *Tyranopolis*); *The Man with a Thousand Names* (1974); *Supermind* (1977); *Pendulum* (1978); *Renaissance* (1979); *Cosmic Encounter* (1980); *Computerworld* (1983, also known as *Computer Eye*).

B.S.

VANCE, JACK (1916–).

American writer of science fiction, fantasy, and mysteries, known for his prose style and for fanciful and exotic settings. Vance has received the Hugo and Nebula awards for his SF and the Mystery Writers of America's Edgar Award for *The Man in the Cage* (1960).

Born John Holbrook Vance and raised in the San Francisco Bay area, he attended the University of California, Berkeley, served in the merchant marine, and began publishing in the pulp magazines after World War II. Vance's first markets were the pulps, primarily *Thrilling Wonder* and *Startling,* to which he sold adventure tales with titles such as "The World-Thinker" (1945; his first sale), "Planet of the Black Dust" (1946), and "Phalid's Fate" (1946), featuring space pirates, interplanetary agents, and well-drawn aliens. In 1948 he created his first series character, the canny, middle-aged, impecunious Magnus Ridolph. In the Ridolph stories and such efforts as "I'll Build Your Dream Castle" (1947) and "The Potters of Firsk" (1950), Vance perfected his portrayal of trickery, horse trading, verbal fencing, and other subtle forms of aggression.

By the time his first book, *The Dying Earth* (1950), was published, Vance's literary personality was fully formed. Consisting of six connected stories of the far future, it combines fairy tale, fable, and romantic adventure conventions with an elegant verbal surface and treats the themes of megalomania, exploitation, perception and reality, and decadence and renewal. Despite its initial appearance as a newsstand-distributed, digest-sized paperback, it was the first of several Vance works to gain classic status and has been reprinted often since 1962.

After 1950 Vance wrote more in the longer forms—novelette, novella, "complete in this issue" novel. While he still produced adventure stories, he nearly always put on the work his own stamp—stylish prose, vivid settings, strikingly alien cultures of human and nonhuman origin. These traits, apparent even in the often hastily written Ridolph stories, reappear in more polished form in such long works as *Son of the Tree* (1951/1964), *Big Planet* (1952/1957), and *The Houses of Iszm* (1954/1964). There are, in addition, short stories by Vance that significantly expand or depart from pulp conventions, for example, "Noise" (1952), "The Devil on Salvation Bluff" (1955), and "The Men Return" (1957), all of which play games with perception and reality.

Alongside these adventures and exotica, Vance was developing a social vision. In addition to the passing satiric thrusts of *Big Planet* (1952/1957) and "Abercrombie Station" (1952; as Part 1 of *Monsters in Orbit,* 1956), there are extended investigations of the social implications of telekinesis in "Telek" (1952) and immortality in *To Live Forever* (1956). What might have been universal gifts are restricted to small elites, either in a deliberate attempt to form an oligarchy ("Telek") or because of the limits imposed by the finite resources of a single world (*To Live Forever*). These fundamentals—exploitation, the nature of authentic freedom, the problem of limits—are thematic constants in Vance's work from the Ridolph stories through the Lyonesse novels.

Between 1956 and 1969 Vance published fifteen volumes of new SF and fantasy, four books of short fiction, and eight mystery novels under his own name and three pseudonyms (Adam Wade, Peter Held, Ellery Queen). He received awards and nominations and saw his earlier magazine work reprinted. While he continued to produce notable single works—the award winners *The Dragon Masters* (1962/1963) and *The Last Castle* (1966/1967), *The Languages of Pao* (1957/1958), *The Blue World* (1964/1966), *Emphyrio* (1969)—the bulk of his SF and fantasy appeared in series. The Oikumene of the Demon Princes series, the Dying Earth, the planets Durdane and Tschai provided ample intellectual and aesthetic elbowroom for the by now familiar range of Vancean motifs and themes: revenge and detective story in the Demon Princes, the search for identity and independence in Durdane, exotic adventure in Tschai, trickery and ironic comedy in the Dying Earth. In the 1970s and 1980s Vance added the Gaean Reach and Alastor Cluster and the lost lands of Lyonesse as settings for his SF and fantasy respectively.

Vance's reputation as a stylist and his gift for the colorful and exotic earned him a following in the 1950s that by the 1970s had developed into a minifandom, with the occasional appearance of fanzines and the foundation of a small press, Underwood-Miller, to reprint his work in hardcover. Eventually academic attention followed, resulting in a scattering of journal articles and at least two books. The consensus of fans and critics is that Vance is a writerly writer, deserving of more attention than he has received from the mass SF audience. There is also a growing recognition of the importance of the *content* of his fiction and the fact that he is more than a spinner of elegant entertainments, that his fascination with odd social arrangements and legal systems, with space pirates and slavers, and with obsessed, oddly sympathetic villains adds up to a coherent vision of human possibilities in a universe of infinite variety.

OTHER WORKS: *The Five Gold Bands* (1950; reprinted as *The Space Pirate*, 1953); *Slaves of the Klau* (1952/1958; retitled *Gold and Iron,* 1982); *Vandals of the Void* (1953); *The Star King* (1963/1964); *Future Tense* (collection, 1964; retitled *Dust of Far Suns,* 1981); *The*

Killing Machine (1964); *Space Opera* (1965); *The World Between and Other Stories* (collection, 1965); *Brains of the Earth* (1966; retitled *Nopalgarth*, 1980); *The Many Worlds of Magnus Ridolph* (collection, 1966; expanded as *The Complete Magnus Ridolph*, 1980); *Eyes of the Overworld* (1966); *The Palace of Love* (1966/1967); *City of the Chasch* (1968); *Eight Fantasms and Magics* (collection, 1969); *Servants of the Wankh* (1969); *The Dirdir* (1969); *The Pnume* (1970); *The Faceless Man* (1971/1973, also known as *The Anome*); *The Brave Free Men* (1972/1973); *Trullion: Alastor 2262* (1972/1973); *The Asutra* (1973); *The Gray Prince* (1974); *Marune: Alastor 933* (1975); *Showboat World* (1975); *Maske: Thaery* (1976); *Wyst: Alastor 1716* (1978); *Green Magic* (collection, 1979); *The Face* (1979); *Galactic Effectuator* (1981); *The Book of Dreams* (1981); *Lost Moons* (collection, 1982); *The Narrow Land* (collection, 1982); *Lyonesse* (1983); *The Green Pearl* (1985); *The Dark Side of the Moon* (collection, 1986); *The Augmented Agent* (collection, 1986); *Araminta Station* (1987).

R.F.L.

John Varley

VARLEY, JOHN [HERBERT] (1947–).

American science-fiction writer; the outstanding new author of the 1970s, as his two Nebula Awards, three Hugo Awards, and the French Prix Apollo attest. Born in Texas and now living in Oregon, Varley became a full-time free-lance writer in 1973, on the basis of short stories alone. His first novel was not published until 1978.

Varley specializes in fascinating future worlds that have either altered radically from present-day Earth because of some cataclysmic event or stand on the verge of a great discovery. In his short fiction, particularly the stories collected in *The Persistence of Vision* (1978; published in Britain as *In the Hall of the Martian Kings*), he excels at depicting daily life in the future, skillfully incorporating the details of startling scientific advances that have become the stuff of everyday life. A number of the stories, for instance, deal with cloning, which has become so easy that people store clones against the need for organ transplants or, in the case of death, total replacement complete with frequently updated memories.

The Ophiuchi Hotline (1978), Varley's first novel, may still be his best. The background events that it describes in some detail lie behind many of his stories: some 550 years before the book begins, humanity was exiled from Earth by unidentified aliens, who have reserved the planet for whales and dolphins. What was left of the human race had to make do with the other planets of the Solar System and their satellites. Then, about 150 years after the loss of Earth, radio signals (which become known as the Ophiuchi Hotline) began to be received. Those signals contained scientific information far in advance of human science. Although humanity has understood only a tenth of that information, what it has been able to use has created enormous changes in human lives, including the ability to record the contents of human brains, procedures for gene manipulation, methods for mining black holes, and the process of cloning. Humanity may be exiled, but the radio signals have allowed it to grow and develop, though in ways that present-day humans might find bizarre, even offensive. Varley explores these changes and shows how our moral and ethical attitudes are a product of the state of our technology, while his characters attempt to discover the source of the radio signals.

The trilogy comprising *Titan* (1979), *Wizard* (1980), and *Demon* (1984) enhanced Varley's popularity although it exhibited no particular advance in artistry or in his future history. By placing the action of these novels almost entirely on a sentient satellite of Saturn, the nearly omnipotent but possibly insane Gaea, Varley allowed himself the virtually unlimited scope of fantasy while grounding his imagination in the ecological details of a strange new world. As in *The Ophiuchi Hotline*, the novels in this series are narrated largely from the viewpoint of a woman, in this case Cirocco Jones, a NASA spaceship pilot and adventurer sent, with a few companions, to explore this new phenomenon. Jones first discovers and explores Gaea, then reluctantly serves it, and finally battles Gaea's growing madness.

Millennium (1983), which fell between the second and third novels in the trilogy, is an expansion of a 1977 short story, "Air Raid," for which Varley also wrote a screenplay for a film that did not get produced. Varley still seems strongest at the shorter lengths in which he

first excelled: his first Hugo and Nebula Award winner
was "Persistence of Vision" (1978), a novella about a
disease that leaves many children blind and deaf; a man
enters a community of such children and, as in H. G.
Wells's "The Country of the Blind" (1904), discovers
that his eyesight may be a handicap. Two other notable
short works are "The Pusher," which won a Hugo in
1982, and "Press Enter," a novella that won a Hugo and
a Nebula in 1985.

OTHER WORKS: *The Barbie Murders and Other Stories* (collection, 1980); *Blue Champagne* (collection,
1986).

S.H.G.

VERCORS (Pseudonym of Jean Bruller)
(1902–   ).   French painter and writer better known
in the mainstream as the author of *The Silence of the
Sea* (*Le Silence de la mer*, 1942), a classic war resistance novel. Vercors has often used science-fiction themes
and imagery. *You Shall Know Them* (*Les Animaux
dénaturés*, 1952) is about the discovery of a missing
link and the ensuing ethical conflict. *The Insurgents*
(1957) features a quest for immortality, and *Sylva* (1961)
treads a strong allegorical line, as a vixen turns into a
woman and then back again. An unprolific but poetic
author, Vercors has been inactive since the 1960s.

M.J.

VERNE, JULES [GABRIEL] (1828–1905).
French author of sixty-four novels who, with H. G. Wells,
stands as one of the recognized founders of modern
science fiction. Verne was from an early age fascinated
by the sea, a major influence on his work, and as a
teenager once attempted to run away to sea. Declining
to pursue a legal career in his father's footsteps, he embarked on a literary one. Alexandre Dumas was a major
influence and model during the unpromising early years
when Verne turned out verse, opera librettos, and unremarkable dramas. He began publishing popular travel
articles in magazines around 1857; in 1863 the publisher
Pierre-Jules Hetzel encouraged him to fictionalize these
pieces for a new educational magazine for the young.
The association between the two men was to last until
Verne's death and is responsible for a major body of
imaginative fiction.

Although Verne wrote within the existing confines of
popular literature, his talent was in basing his romances
on a groundwork of actual fact, ensuring plausibility for
all his extrapolations of scientific progress, geographic
travails, and rough-hewn heroes and ambivalent mad
scientists. Some of the *voyages extraordinaires* initially
serialized by Hetzel in his *Magazine d'éducation et de
récréation* and later published in book form do not qualify as SF, including what is possibly Verne's most famous

Jules Verne

novel, *Around the World in Eighty Days* (1873). Several posthumous novels and short stories credited to Verne
were written or edited by his son Michel Jules-Verne.

Verne's first romance, *Five Weeks in a Balloon* (1863),
was essentially a rumbustious geographic adventure, but
his next book, *Journey to the Center of the Earth* (1864),
introduced fascinating speculative concepts as three protagonists lead an expedition into the heart of an Icelandic
volcano that takes them to a lighted cavern world at the
Earth's core. *From the Earth to the Moon* (1865) is a
striking example of early hard SF, detailing with great
precision the preparations and scientific premises (still
mostly correct, apart from the deadly effect of acceler-
ation on the passengers) for a voyage to the Moon. Its
sequel, *Around the Moon* (1870), is more fanciful, a
tale about survival in space and the group's eventual
return to the Earth.

Twenty Thousand Leagues under the Sea (1870)
introduced Captain Nemo and his supersubmarine *Nautilus*. They returned in *The Mysterious Island* (1874–
75). Nemo, a lone, anarchist figure at odds with warring
humanity, remains one of Verne's most memorable characters and was a harbinger of the increasing darkness of
the writer's later work, in which the magic attraction of
science fades in its continuous confrontation with the
dark side of humankind. In *Hector Servadac* (1877) a
group of disparate personalities is stolen away from the

Earth's surface by a passing comet to face conflict and adversity; *The Begum's Fortune* (1878), *The Purchase of the North Pole* (1889), and *The Castle of the Carpathians* (1892) witness the souring of Verne's love affair with scientific wonder.

Other notable Verne novels in the genre include *The Clipper of the Clouds* (1886) and its sequel *The Master of the World* (1904), both featuring the archetypal mad inventor Robur; *The Floating Island* (1895); *An Antarctic Mystery* (1897), a rationalist sequel to Edgar Allan Poe's *Arthur Gordon Pym;* and *The Village in the Tree Tops* (1901).

Verne's posthumous SF novels are *The Chase of the Golden Meteor* (1908); *The Secret of Wilhelm Storitz* (1910), about invisibility; *The Barsac Mission* (1914); and a collection of short stories, *Yesterday and Tomorrow* (1910).

M.J.

VIAN, BORIS (1920–1959).

French writer whose bittersweet blend of pataphysics and surrealism influenced the NEW WAVE movement of the 1960s and spawned a cult following. Vian helped introduce American science fiction into France after World War II and translated the work of A. E. VAN VOGT among others. Also active as a playwright, poet, songwriter, jazz musician, and author of thrillers, he is now principally remembered for a gently humorous series of five fantasy-impregnated novels: *Vercoquin et le Plancton* (1946); *Froth on the Daydream* (*L'Ecume des jours,* 1947), about the survival of love under an authoritarian regime; *L'Automne à Pékin* (1947), a desert utopia; *L'Herbe rouge* (1950), a time travel story; and *Heartsnatcher* (*L'Arrache-Coeur,* 1953). It was only after his early death from a heart attack that his books became popular.

M.J.

VIDAL, GORE (1925–   ).

American writer best known for his historical novels and essays on politics and culture as well as several fine works that make use of science-fiction conventions, such as the novels *Messiah* (1954), *Kalki* (1978), and *Duluth* (1983) and the play *Visit to a Small Planet* (1956). Vidal's satire and wit are the common ingredients of all his work, so most SF readers find his SF stronger in its satire than in its science fiction. He is more in the tradition of Petronius and Juvenal than that of Isaac Asimov and Robert A. Heinlein.

Messiah is an early apocalyptic novel about the appearance of a new religious messiah. *Visit to a Small Planet* uses the SF plot convention of alien invasion; however, destructive human feelings are the play's concern. *Kalki* is an end-of-the-world novel whose real target is the destructiveness of some utopian religious

communities. *Duluth* also, while containing many SF conventions, is ultimately a satire on middle American values.

OTHER WORKS: *Myra Breckinridge* (1968); *Myron* (1974); *Creation* (1981).

C.B.

VIDEODROME (1982).

Directed by David Cronenberg; screenplay by David Cronenberg; photographed by Mark Irwin; music by Howard Shore. With James Woods, Sonya Smits, Deborah Harry, Peter Dvorsky, Les Carlson, Jack Creley. 89 minutes. Color.

Videodrome is a McLuhanesque technological science-fiction horror film about the medium of television and its effects on the viewer. An opportunistic television producer (James Woods) grows fascinated, then obsessed with, then hypnotized by a sadistic-erotic TV program entitled *Videodrome* emanating from a mysterious pirate station. His fantasies, stimulated by the show, grow increasingly out of control and clearly represent the consciousness of the typical male viewer as shaped by contemporary television's emphasis on violence, sex, and spectacle.

The film becomes a formal tour de force as fantasy merges with exterior reality to the point that the viewer of the film, like director and scriptwriter David CRONENBERG's character, cannot separate the two. This narrative style formally articulates the degree to which we are all programmed by the media—a theme strikingly visualized by the newly evolved orifice in the producer's stomach for receiving video software, an image of biological fear that is also typical of Cronenberg's other work.

B.K.G.

VILLAGE OF THE DAMNED (1960).

Directed by Wolf Rilla; screenplay by Wolf Rilla, Sterling Silliphant, and George Barclay; adapted from the novel The Midwich Cuckoos *by John Wyndham; photographed by Geoffrey Faithful; music by Ron Goodwin. With George Sanders, Barbara Shelley, Martin Stephens, Michael Gwynn, Laurence Naismith. 77 minutes. Black and white.*

John WYNDHAM's *The Midwich Cuckoos* was a quietly effective English-style catastrophe novel when it was published in 1957, almost the last of Wyndham's follow-ups to the success of *The Day of the Triffids* (1951) in seeking a broader audience for science fiction. The film is remarkably faithful to the novel's story about the inhabitants of an English village falling simultaneously asleep; nine months later the women give birth to remarkable children, apparently as an attempt at alien takeover.

The film menace, as in the novel, gathers quiet strength as the children develop. They are distinguished in the film by eyes that glow when they use their power of influencing the will of others; they also are linked telepathically so that whatever one learns, they all know. The children have such great potential that they may become the future rulers of humanity, and only with regret, and difficulty, do the adults finally bring themselves to destroy them lest humanity lose its free will and indeed its humanity.

J.E.G.

VINCENT, HARL (Pseudonym of Harold Vincent Schoepflin) (1893–1968). American pulp science-fiction writer, a prolific and very popular contributor of stories to AMAZING, *Astounding,* and other magazines from 1928 to 1942. After a hiatus of some twenty years, Vincent began writing again in the 1960s, when he produced, among other works, *The Doomsday Planet* (1966); like much of his other work, this is an interplanetary travel novel.

J.H.

Joan D. Vinge

VINGE, JOAN [CAROL] D[ENNISON] (1948–). American writer. Born in Baltimore, Vinge got a bachelor's degree in anthropology from San Diego State University and worked for a year as a salvage archaeologist. She began writing science fiction in 1973, the year after she married fellow writer (and professor of mathematics) Vernor Vinge. Her first story, "Tin Soldier," was published in 1974 in *Orbit 14;* her first novel, *The Outcasts of Heaven Belt,* in 1978; and her major novel, *The Snow Queen,* in 1980. She is now married to SF editor Jim Frenkel.

Vinge has said that she tends "to write anthropological science fiction, with an emphasis on the interaction of different cultures (human and alien), and of individual people to their surroundings. The importance of communication across barriers of alienness often becomes a theme in my work." That theme is embodied in "View from a Height," a short story that, along with "Fireship," was a finalist for the Hugo Award in 1979 ("Eyes of Amber" won the Hugo in 1978). Emmylou, the heroine of "View," is headed on a one-way journey of observation out of the Solar System. Her isolation doesn't much bother her, because she was born without natural immunities and has always been cut off from the rest of humanity. However, she learns that a cure for her condition has been discovered back on Earth and that this fact has been deleted from the information being relayed to her.

The Snow Queen, based on Hans Christian Andersen's fairy tale but owing more to Robert Graves's *The White Goddess,* won the Hugo Award for 1980. On an alien planet exploited by a distant power and cut off periodically from contact with the rest of the galaxy, a

Winter Queen has survived beyond her normal life span by slaughtering the gentle, immortal Mers, an alien species and one of the legacies from an earlier human civilization. She is committed to technology even to the extent of sabotaging her exiled clone's natural succession to the throne. That clone, the Summer Queen, raised in an isolated community close to nature, eventually deposes her "mother" and unites her ecological concerns with an appreciation for technology that suggests a promising synthesis.

Vinge is best in creating feeling, suffering characters, and the minor characters in *The Snow Queen* sometimes seem more real than the major ones. One of them, BZ Gundhalinu, who in *Snow Queen* was tortured by a criminal gang, is the protagonist of the sequel, *World's End* (1984), in which the snow-and-castles fantasy atmosphere of the planet Tiamat gives way to the swamp-and-desert SF wilderness of World's End, where the hero undergoes similar torments, though here they are mental.

Much of Vinge's writing in the 1980s was devoted to the novelization of screenplays, for which she seems to have a special aptitude: *Return of the Jedi Storybook* (1983), *The Dune Storybook* (1984), *Ladyhawke* (1985), *Mad Max: Beyond Thunderdome* (1985), *Return to Oz* (1985), and *Santa Claus* (1985). The first two novelizations were for children, as was her novel *Psion* (1982).

Vinge has published three collections of short stories: *Fireship* (1978; as *Fireship, and Mother and Child,* 1981), *Eyes of Amber and Other Stories* (1979), and *Phoenix in the Ashes* (1985).

J.E.G.

VINGE, VERNOR [STEFFEN] (1944–). American science-fiction writer and professor of mathematics at San Diego State University. Vinge earned his Ph.D. from the University of California, San Diego, in 1971. His first story, "Apartness," was published in 1965; his first novel, *Grimm's World,* appeared in 1969; and he published only a handful of stories and another novel in the 1970s. In the 1980s, however, the pace and success of his writing picked up markedly.

Vinge is known for his craftsmanship in exploring the consequences of change and in the presentation of characters—usually distinguished by remarkable intellectual powers—faced with social dislocation. In *The Witling* (1976), for example, one of the protagonists is a genius who suffers from arrested emotional development. The world on which she lives pairs a medieval technology with psi abilities; she must cope with the love of a man she considers her inferior (he cannot teleport) and a plot by her fellow citizens to exploit two off-worlders stranded on the planet; she is as much an outcast on her own world as the strangers and must face the impossible task of finding some measure of peace and happiness.

Melancholy in tone, if not downright bleak, Vinge's novels rarely offer a complete resolution of the problems confronting his characters. In *True Names* (1981), for example, an unimaginative and oppressive bureaucracy is still intact at the end of the book, although several characters have managed to live meaningfully in spite of it.

Vinge, formerly married to the writer Joan VINGE, attracted increased notice from critics, fellow writers, and readers in the 1980s not only with *True Names* and *The Peace War* (1984), about a galactic civilization that has learned to use the technology of stasis fields in a variety of applications, including weapons and prisons, but also with *Marooned in Realtime* (1986), the sequel to *The Peace War* (they were published in a combined edition in 1986 as *Across Realtime*) and the reprinting of *Grimm's World* as *Tatja Grimm's World* (1987).

S.H.G.

VISIT TO A SMALL PLANET (1960). *Directed by Norman Taurog; screenplay by Edmund Beloin and Henry Garson; adapted from the teleplay by Gore Vidal; photographed by Loyal Griggs; music by Leigh Harline. With Jerry Lewis, Joan Blackman, Fred Clark, John Williams, Jerome Cowan, Gale Gordon, Lee Patrick. 85 minutes. Black and white.*

In 1955 Gore VIDAL's TV play *A Visit to a Small Planet* starred Cyril Ritchard as Kreton, an arrogant, impish alien who comes to study humanity, then decides on a whim to destroy the Earth. He's revealed at the climax to be a child and is taken home by his elders. Two years later Vidal expanded the play into a popular Broadway production, also starring Ritchard, and used the story as a

forum for satiric comments on American beliefs.

When the work was adapted as a film in 1960, virtually all Vidal's satire was shunted aside in favor of slapstick geared to its star, Jerry Lewis, who became simply an alien version of "That Kid," his usual screen persona. As comedy of this type, the film is pleasant enough, but there's too much talk and the charcters are uninteresting.

B.W.

VOLTAIRE (Pseudonym of François-Marie Arouet) (1694–1778). French historian and author, and one of the leading figures of the French Enlightenment, whose plays and philosophical writings are characterized by liberalism, skepticism, and common sense. Voltaire's satiric story "Micromegas" (1750) presented the first interplanetary voyage in fiction: a visit to Saturn and the Earth by a traveler from the star Sirius. Also significant in the history of science fiction is Voltaire's picaresque satire *Candide* (1759), in which the utopian Eldorado is described.

N.H.

VON HARBOU, THEA (1888–1954). German writer, married to film director Fritz LANG from 1924 to 1933, who coauthored Lang's screenplays and wrote the novels that provided the scenarios for his two science-fiction films, the futuristic masterpiece METROPOLIS (1927) and WOMAN IN THE MOON (*Die Frau im Mond,* 1928).

J.H.

VONNEGUT, KURT, JR. (1922–). American mainstream author who served in the U.S. Army during World War II and survived the firebombing of Dresden in February 1945, a traumatic experience that later provided the setting for his antiwar classic *Slaughterhouse-Five* (1969). After three years as a General Electric research laboratory publicist, an experience that served as the basis for his first novel, *Player Piano* (1952), Vonnegut became a full-time writer in 1950, turning out stories for slick and science-fiction magazines.

Vonnegut's early novels were published as SF, but when the novel *Cat's Cradle* (1963) appeared, he made the decision to bring out future works without the SF designation, and he has since been published as a mainstream novelist. His work, however, eludes easy categorization. He was never exclusively an SF writer, but SF motifs have remained a staple in many of his short stories and most of his novels. He has developed his own unique, metaphoric universe as well as a distinctive, colloquial, and digressive style of black humor and satire.

His satire has targeted almost every aspect of present-day American life, only reserving a corner of nostalgia for the communal small-town life-style of a bygone Midwest. More basically his writings reflect a pessimistic view of humanity's ability to cope with the kind of civilization it has created. We need illusion to make sense of a meaningless world, Vonnegut tells us, but some illusions are more harmful than others, and technology seems to generate particularly harmful ones.

The exposure of illusory ideas generally provides both the plot and the comedy of Vonnegut's fiction, and his SF devices are often the metaphoric extension of this exposure. His characters may serve a similar function, sometimes suggested by their emblematic names (Paul Proteus, Malachi Constant). They also may reappear in novel after novel, as does the pathetically unsuccessful SF writer Kilgore Trout, whose visions are larger than his ability to convey them.

Player Piano, later described by Vonnegut as a "rip-off from *Brave New World*," does not differ significantly from other 1950s SF. It pictures a future high-tech dystopia but intimates that the destruction of technology is no way out. *The Sirens of Titan* (1959), which attacks the concept of causality and the confusion of luck with God's will, reveals human history as a trivial incident manipulated by the alien Tralfamadorians to further an equally trivial scheme. In *Cat's Cradle*, remarkable for its creation of a complete island society, the fake religion of Bokonon seems harmless compared with the disastrous consequences of a certain line of scientific thinking. In the complex unraveling of time traveler Billy Pilgrim's wartime trauma in *Slaughterhouse-Five*, time itself fades into illusion. The holocaust and postholocaust scenarios of *Slapstick* (1976), *Deadeye Dick* (1983), and *Galapagos* (1985) offer variants of a more general theme: the incompatibility of the intellectual aspirations and the emotional needs of humankind. In *Galapagos* a survival-fit species finally evolves from human stock without the oversized brains that make us dangerous to ourselves, but that species—the reader discovers—is no longer human.

OTHER WORKS: *Canary in a Cat House* (collection, 1961); *Mother Night* (1962); *God Bless You, Mr. Rosewater* (1965); *Welcome to the Monkey House* (collection, 1968); *Breakfast of Champions* (1973); *Wampeters, Foma, and Granfalloons* (nonfiction, 1975); *Jailbird* (1979).

J.H.

VOYAGE TO THE BOTTOM OF THE SEA (1961).

Directed by Irwin Allen; screenplay by Irwin Allen and Charles Bennett; photographed by Winton Hoch and John Lamb; music by Paul Sawtell and Bert Shefter. With Walter Pidgeon, Robert Sterling, Peter Lorre, Joan Fontaine, Barbara Eden, Michael Ansara, Frankie Avalon. 105 minutes. Color.

The Van Allen radiation belt has been ignited and threatens the world with incineration; a scientist responsible for the building of the nuclear-powered *Seaview* is commissioned by the United Nations to commandeer a crew for a special mission: to fire a Polaris missile into an undersea trench in the hope that it will cause the radiation belt to explode outward.

This film is an obvious variation on Jules VERNE's *20,000 Leagues under the Sea* (1873), from the futuristic submarine to the obligatory giant squid. Scientific fact is blithely ignored, while preposterous theories provide the basis for the plot. The Van Allen belt bursts into flame, although in reality there is insufficient oxygen at its altitude to maintain combustion; the fiery phenomenon causes icebergs to sink rather than to melt. In his novelization of the movie in 1961, Theodore STURGEON attempted, with little success, to explain these scientific impossibilities.

Of a fine cast, Walter Pidgeon, as the loud and domineering Admiral Nelson, is the only one having fun; the other actors are wasted in stereotyped roles. The film, alas, is not rescued by its special effects, which range from outstanding to mediocre.

Nevertheless, *Voyage* was a box-office success, enabling Irwin ALLEN to create a companion television series in 1964. With Richard Basehart and David Hedison, it ran for four seasons, utilizing the movie's sets and much of its excellent undersea footage.

M.T.W.

WALDROP, HOWARD (1946–).

American writer whose science fiction is filled with images of contemporary popular culture: monster films of the 1950s ("All about Strange Monsters of the Recent Past," 1980), rock-and-roll stars and comedians ("Save a Place in the Lifeboat for Me," 1976), and bad SF movies ("Dr. Hudson's Secret Gorilla," 1978) have all found their way into Waldrop's short stories. "The Ugly Chicken" (1980), winner of a Nebula Award, is a fine mix of the comic and tragic in the form of a journal kept by an ornithologist searching for dodoes in Mississippi. Waldrop obviously enjoys writing these pieces, but sometimes he so indulges his sense of whimsy that the stories seem more like private jokes than communications between author and readers. His recent fiction, however, particularly "The Lions Are Asleep Tonight" (1986), which received honorable mention for the Theodore Sturgeon Memorial Award, suggests that he can deal with serious subject matter in a disciplined style. Some of his stories have been collected in *Howard, Who?* (1986) and *All about*

Strange Monsters of the Recent Past (1987).

Waldrop's first novel, *The Texas-Israeli War: 1999* (1974), was a collaboration with Jake Saunders. Originally the short story "A Voice and Bitter Weeping" (1974), the novel describes how Texans attempt to protect their oil (1973 was the year of the oil embargo) from the rest of the United States by hiring mercenaries from Israel. *Them Bones* (1984), a solo novel, mixes time travel with adventure as a confused band of archaeologists tries to make sense of a burial mound filled with anachronisms. In this case Waldrop manages to control his sense of the absurd, and if the novel adds little to the time travel theme, it still gives the reader several hours of pure entertainment.

S.H.G.

WALLACE, F[LOYD] L. (?–?).

American writer most active in the 1950s and a regular contributor to the SF magazines. Wallace's first work to appear was "Hideaway" (1951), but he may be best known for "Big Ancestor" (1954), a story which suggests that humankind descended from alien rats. His novella "Worlds in Balance" (1953) saw separate publication in Australia in 1955, but his only published novel is *Address: Centauri* (1955), based on his novella "Accidental Flight" (1952), which portrays the first volunteers for interstellar flight as crippled and handicapped. Wallace was a competent and reliable writer not afraid to experiment with new ideas.

M.A.

WAR

The many possibilities for extraordinary change in the conduct and consequences of wars have always provided abundant but limited material for futuristic fiction. These tales of the Next Great War, *der Zukunftskrieg, la guerre de l'avenir,* as they used to be called, evolved in exact phase with the rise and fall in popular enthusiasm for international conflict. The first main period of their publication coincided with the spread of aggressive nationalism in nineteenth-century Europe and with the arms race that followed in the wake of John Ericsson's *Monitor* and the quite unexpected events of the Franco-German War of 1870. Before the 1870s the few stories of future warfare that appeared were entirely taken up with political possibilities: the glorious British conquest of Europe, for instance, in *The Reign of George VI, 1900–1925* (anonymous, 1763) and the many anti-French plays and invasion stories of the Napoleonic period. Comparable American stories dealt with a future civil war, among them Beverly Tucker's *The Partisan Leader* (1856) and Edmund Ruffin's *Anticipations of the Future* (1860). And then, in the May 1871 issue of *Blackwood's Magazine,* the story of the war to come found its appropriate form in "The Battle of Dorking," the famous short story by George Tomkyns CHESNEY, a former officer in the Bengal Engineers and later a member of Parliament. His after-the-disaster narrative techniques offered a working model to all those—journalists, colonels, admirals, politicians—who had much to say about the future of their nations.

For nearly fifty years, before the unexpected realities of the First World War changed everything, Chesney's story set the style for a minor publishing industry that found support and profit in a widespread and largely innocent interest in coming wars. These stories projected the best or the worst that could conceivably happen to a nation. In the United States, for instance, the argument in favor of a bigger navy was the source of Samuel Barton's *The Battle of the Swash* (1888) and of the lamentable disasters related by Henry Grattan Donnelly in *The Stricken Nation* (1889). The main market for future war tales, however, was in Europe. The three major powers fought out "the coming war" in pamphlets and short stories, and then in the 1890s in full-scale illustrated stories in the new illustrated press. Some became classics of their kind: the first illustrated anticipations in Albert Robida's *La Guerre au XXme siècle* (1888), Erskine Childers's *The Riddle of the Sands* (1903), and P. G. Wodehouse's *The Swoop* (1909). The most inventive and plausible stories came from H. G. WELLS: a celebrated anticipation of tank warfare in "The Land Ironclads" (1903), an accurate forecast of air bombardment in *The War in the Air* (1908), and the first account of atomic warfare in *The World Set Free* (1914). The account of the Martian invasion in *The War of the Worlds* (1898) is outstanding for its imaginative treatment of possible military technologies.

After the First World War this all changed. The glory departed from the old hurrah literature, and the earnest stories that appeared between and at the beginning of the two world wars were filled with warnings of the disasters to come, as in L. Ron HUBBARD's *Final Blackout* (1940). After Hiroshima the doomsday story became the dominant mode: as the perpetual warfare state projected in George ORWELL's *Nineteen Eighty-four* (1949), the postdisaster community first described in Aldous HUXLEY's *Ape and Essence* (1948), the moment of truth in Stanley KUBRICK's film DR. STRANGELOVE (1964), or the real thing in Frank HERBERT's *The Dragon in the Sea* (1956). The last forty years have seen the publication of some of the most original and effective stories in the genre: Bernard WOLFE's *Limbo* (1952), Cyril M. KORNBLUTH's *The Syndic* (1953), Robert Shafer's *The Conquered Place* (1955), Nevil SHUTE's *On the Beach* (1957), Hans Helmut Kirst's *Keiner Kommt Davon* (1957), and Walter M. MILLER, Jr.'s *A Canticle for Leibowitz* (1960). In recent years a carefully doctored version of the future war theme has proved most profitable for the American entertainment industry in the incidental battles of the STAR TREK series and the extraordinary success of the STAR WARS productions.

I.F.C.

WAR GAMES (1983). *Directed by John Badham; screenplay by Lawrence Lasker and Walter F. Parkes; photographed by William Fraker; music by Arthur B. Rubinstein. With Matthew Broderick, Ally Sheedy, Dabney Coleman, John Wood, Barry Corbin, Juanin Clay. 113 minutes. Color.*

David, a seventeen-year-old computer hacker (Matthew Broderick), is able to tap into various data bases from his home computer, accomplishing such feats as reserving airline tickets and changing the grades on his record in the school's computer. Thinking they have accessed a video-game company's computer system, David, watched by his friend Jennifer (Ally Sheedy), starts to play an interactive game called Global Thermonuclear War. He has actually tapped into WOPR, a supercomputer at NORAD known as "Joshua" that has been programmed to determine all possible actions and responses in a nuclear war and has the newly conferred ability to launch nuclear missiles. Joshua, unable to distinguish between game and reality, brings the world to the brink of war. The film's crucial question is Can Joshua, an artificial intelligence, learn that in some games (and situations) there can be no winners before causing a nuclear holocaust?

The responsible use of computer technology is the primary issue dealt with in this modern initiation tale. While Joshua, like HAL in 2001: A SPACE ODYSSEY (1968), has humanlike qualities, indicating intelligence and emotion, the limitations of its artificial intelligence are apparent. It is the combination of David's irresponsible use of technology and the NORAD officials' overreliance on technology that starts the countdown to global destruction. The resolution of the crisis marks the initiation of David and the NORAD officials into the computer age.

War Games reflects current societal fears of computer technology and nuclear holocaust. It shows the mundane side of technology as we see David impressing Jennifer with his clever, if morally questionable, use of the home computer. In contrast, as the camera tours the immense war room at NORAD, we see the potential power of the supercomputer. As the crisis builds, the film underscores the threat by moving from the vast to the specific. The sight of the giant video screen silently tracking the paths of launched missiles over the world is horrifying, as is the sound of the relentless, dispassionate voice reporting the status of the situation and the countdown in progress. Shifting to the pathos of the individual human situation, the camera shows us David and Jennifer by a peaceful sea under a silent night sky,

waiting helplessly for the end of life.

The film is supenseful and highly entertaining. Whereas TRON (1982) deals with the fear of computer technology by creating a highly fanciful imaginary world, *War Games* presents a convincing, realistic scenario for its computer-as-character motif. This is not an example of technology out of control, as in DEMON SEED (1977), but a technology given too much control. In a nice twist, as a final antiwar statement, the film asks why if even a machine can learn the meaning of the no-winner war humanity can't.

D.P.V.

WAR-GODS OF THE DEEP (City under the Sea) (1965). *Directed by Jacques Tourneur; screenplay by Charles Bennett, Louis M. Heyward, and David Whittaker; adapted from the poem "The City in the Sea" and the story "A Descent into the Maelström" by Edgar Allan Poe; photographed by Stephen Dade and John Lamb; music by Stanley Black. With Vincent Price, David Tomlinson, Tab Hunter, Susan Hart, John Le Mesurier. 85 minutes. Color.*

Jacques Tourneur's last film takes little more than an incident from Edgar Allan POE's story and a mood from his poem. This tale of smugglers and fish-men-monsters operating out of the sunken city of Lyonesse owes as much to the Atlantis and Dr. Syn stories as it does to Poe. Generally regarded as minor Tourneur, the film nevertheless manages, at least in the above-the-sea scenes, to create a chilly atmosphere, half Poe and half *I Walked with a Zombie.*

D.W.

WAR OF THE WORLDS (1953). *Directed by Byron Haskin; screenplay by Barre Lyndon; adapted from the novel by H. G. Wells; photographed by George Barnes; music by Leith Stevens. With Gene Barry, Ann Robinson, Les Tremayne, Lewis Martin, Robert Cornthwaite. 85 minutes. Color.*

War of the Worlds, the third of producer George PAL's significant science-fiction films, is noteworthy less as a successful cinematic treatment of H. G. WELLS's vision than as one of the few American SF movies of the period to depict an all-out attack by aliens (a feature more characteristic of Japanese SF movies) and therefore as a work revealing the zeitgeist of its time. Just as Wells's novel may be read as the nightmarish unleashing of guilt upon an imperialist society, the film may be understood on one level as articulating the more contemporary fear of being invaded by cold-blooded Communists.

The movie retains the basics of Wells's plot, although it does make some significant changes, including altering the time and location from England in 1890 to contemporary California and adding a typical Hollywood love interest.

A meteor lands in a small southern California town, and when several people attempt to investigate they are disintegrated by a death ray. Similar meteors land elsewhere around the globe, and soon the Martian war machines (Wells's carefully described tripod machines are here replaced by more conventional looking flying saucers, a revision apparently prompted more by financial than by thematic or even topical reasons) launch their orchestrated assault. Terrestrial (that is to say, American) military weaponry, even including an atomic bomb, detonated as a last resort, proves completely ineffective against the Martian rays, which disintegrate both humans and hardware.

The film's scientist-hero, Gene Barry, like everyone else, is helpless against the alien onslaught. But taking refuge in a deserted house near one of the Martian landing sites with Ann Robinson, he begins to learn from her the values of family and emotional commitment, as opposed to the cool intellect of his science and, by extension, the detached reason of the Martians. In the climax, as defeat for Earth seems certain, Barry and Robinson gather with other survivors in a church. While everyone is "praying for a miracle," the Martians burst through the church walls and then suddenly die—as a result, we learn, of infection by terrestrial bacteria. Thus the world is saved not by nature but by a literal deus ex machina, since—as Cedric Hardwicke's voice-over makes clear—it was God who put the microbes on the Earth in the first place.

Although the reason for the failure of the Martian invasion is the same in both film and novel, the church location and the prayer are the film's inventions. By invoking faith rather than biology, therefore, the movie is more conservative in its vision than is Wells's shocking subversion of comfortable British society. At the same time, however, the film strays from convention by depicting the military as impotent. It is this tension between its embrace of traditional values and its questioning of military technology, as well as the elaborate depiction of an alien attack, that gives the film its lasting interest.

B.K.G.

WATERLOO, STANLEY (1846–1913).

American writer noted for the seminal novel of anthropological science fiction, *The Story of Ab* (1897), wherein Waterloo, through the eponymous caveman Ab, showed humankind's rise from savagery through the discovery and mastery of the necessities of life. This novel set the standard for all other such works, which include Jack LONDON's *Before Adam* (1906) and most recently Jean M. AUEL's Earth's Children series. Waterloo wrote another caveman story, "Christmas 200,000 B.C.," in *The Wolf's Long Howl* (1899) and also used the topic as the starting point for *A Son of the Ages* (1914), in which, via reincarnation and racial memory, we are able to

follow the successive lives of the caveman Scar through significant episodes in history, including the sinking of Atlantis. Waterloo's only other novel associated with SF is *Armageddon* (1898), which falls into the future war category so popular at the end of the nineteenth century. Other stories in *The Wolf's Long Howl* are of interest, especially "Love and a Triangle," with its endeavors to communicate with Martian intelligences.

M.A.

WATKINS, PETER (1935–).

British filmmaker, known for his political consciousness, who has made a series of powerful and unique films mixing documentary techniques with fictional scenarios. Watkins joined the BBC in 1963 and there made his first two professional films, *Culloden* (1964) and the controversial *The War Game* (1965), a thoroughly convincing "documentary" account of the results of a nuclear attack on Great Britain. Its uncompromising treatment, as well as the resulting exposure of government civil defense policy as hopelessly unrealistic, earned the film an Academy Award for best documentary but caused it to be banned by the BBC, which had sponsored it. Watkins promptly resigned; he has steadfastly continued in his documentary approach to fictional but politically loaded material even though he has found it increasingly difficult to obtain financial backing for his projects. *Privilege* (1967), *The Gladiators* (1969), and *Punishment Park* (1970) all translate contemporary political issues into Orwellian science-fiction stories of social control and media manipulation. Since 1978 Watkins has been involved in a number of biographical films about artists and composers as well as becoming an international media activist.

OTHER WORK: *The Trap* (1975).

B.K.G.

WATSON, IAN (1943–).

British writer and prolific member of the post–NEW WAVE generation. Born in Northumberland, Watson read English at Oxford University and lectured in English in Tanzania and Tokyo before returning to teach future studies at Birmingham Polytechnic. He is now a full-time writer.

All Watson's writings explore what he calls "the relationship between reality and consciousness," and he has found a wide variety of means by which to treat this theme, from linguistics to UFO mythology. His writing is dense and essentially cerebral, and there is a strong transcendental strain to all his work, including his critical articles on such writers as Philip K. DICK and Ursula K. LE GUIN.

Watson's first novel, *The Embedding* (1973), established him as a brilliant speculative writer. Using three intertwining plots, all concerned with the ability of LAN-

Ian Watson

GUAGE to create various realities, it links intellectual and scientific discourse with a desire for spiritual and physical transcendence. This combination, presented in either hopeful or despairing terms, is at the core of almost all his work. In *The Jonah Kit* (1975), for example, whales are the key to escape to another continuum; in *The Martian Inca* (1977), the key is a viral activator in the soil of Mars. The catalysts in *Alien Embassy* (1977) and *The Miracle Visitors* (1978) are, respectively, a method of out-of-body travel and the phenomenon of UFO experiences. Watson often presents outlandish concepts in a carefully objective scientific discourse.

With *God's World* (1979), Watson began to rewrite traditional science-fiction themes, deliberately working with such conventional hardware as exploration ships. Although he called *The Gardens of Delight* (1980) his first fantasy novel, it's as much SF as the others, describing the landing of a starship probe on a planet transformed by some Power into an exact living reproduction of the famous Hieronymus Bosch triptych. Another novel of transformations, it uses alchemy as its "science." Indeed, Watson has always played his conceptual games with wit and humor, and he continued to do so in *Deathhunter* (1981), a near future thriller of ideas full of ontological speculations and sociological extrapolations.

If Watson is widely praised as a writer of ideas, he is sometimes criticized for his characterizations, because his characters always seem to be at the service of their text's concepts. In his recent trilogy *The Book of the River* (1984), *The Book of the Stars* (1984), and *The Book of Being* (1985), however, he has created in the

narrator, Yaleen, a delightfully human and complex figure. This trilogy is possibly Watson's most popular work yet.

Watson's short fiction, collected in *The Very Slow Time Machine* (1979) and *Slow Birds and Other Stories* (1981), shares with his novels both imaginative vigor and speculative daring. His shorter pieces often use conventional SF images for powerful allegorical effect, as in "Slow Birds," where Cruise missiles disrupt the pastoral lives of people in another dimension. His satiric hatchet job on Margaret Thatcher in "Mistress of Cold" is an effective reminder that his work has always had a political dimension. Watson continues to provoke his readers with new work whose intellectual daring remains dazzling.

OTHER WORKS: *Under Heaven's Bridge* (with *Michael Bishop*, 1980); *Chekhov's Journey* (1983); *Converts* (1984); *Queen Magic, King Magic* (1986); *Evil Water* (collection, 1987).

D.B.

WEINBAUM, STANLEY G[RAUMAN] (1902–1935).

American writer of science fiction. Weinbaum, educated as a chemical engineer, became one of the novas of the SF cosmos, blazing up spectacularly with sprightly, well-written stories about believable alien creatures and dying of throat cancer fifteen months after the publication of his first story, the well-remembered and often anthologized "A Martian Odyssey" (1934). His characters include Tweel, a funny ostrichlike remnant of Martian civilization; Professor Manderpootz, who creates useless inventions; and the immortals, who dominate the "weeds" of *The Black Flame* (1948).

Before Weinbaum, aliens were usually modeled after H. G. WELLS's tentacled menaces. But Weinbaum's aliens are warm and often humorous albeit truly alien, and yet believable because their differences come out of their altered environments and different but workable systems of logic: there is the silicon beast on Mars, whose only function is to ingest sand and excrete glassy bricks, and Tweel, who communicates complex concepts to a stranded astronaut using half a dozen English words, although the human is baffled by him.

By contrast, *The New Adam* (1939/1948) offers a human who is completely alien to his world, a superbeing with two brains (like A. E. VAN VOGT's Gosseyn in *The World of Null-A*, 1948). This novel stresses the futility of all knowledge and suggests that intellectual supremacy can be its own destruction. Similarly, the hero of *The Black Flame* is initially rejected by both the immortals and the common people because he comes from a thousand-year past.

OTHER WORKS: *The Dark Other* (1950); *The Best of Stanley G. Weinbaum* (collection, 1974).

R.H.W.

WEIRD SCIENCE (1985).

WEIRD SCIENCE (1985). *Directed by John Hughes; screenplay by John Hughes; photographed by Matthew F. Leonetti; music by Ira Newborn. With Anthony Michael Hall, Kelly Le Brock, Ilan Mitchell-Smith, Bill Paxton, Suzanne Snyder, Judie Aronson. 94 minutes. Color.*

During a lightning storm, with the power from a nearby computer center and their home computer, Gary (Anthony Michael Hall) and Wyatt (Ilan Mitchell-Smith), two teenagers, miraculously create Lisa, the incarnation of their perfect woman. She is a composite of feminine images from the marketplace (*Playboy* and others) with a mind jejune enough to captivate her bumbling creators. Their mishaps are climaxed by a teenager's dream: a wild party and the discovery of two real girls who like them for themselves.

In *Weird Science* John Hughes was obviously looking for laughs more than for the possible Frankenstein and Cinderella themes that he playfully advanced. Using the public's ambivalence toward computer technology (magic versus science) as a base, Hughes created his own version of Mary Wollstonecraft SHELLEY's much abused theme: two teenagers, embarked on the rites of puberty, imagine more than they know what to do with. While the plot is outlandish, the acting labored, and the special effects more light than heat, this film is at times an amusing attempt to elevate the nerd in all of us. Unfortunately this kids-in-heat movie is more conventional than weird.

M.T.W.

WEISINGER, MORT[IMER] (1915–).

WEISINGER, MORT[IMER] (1915–). American editor and author. Born in Manhattan and educated at New York University, Weisinger is best remembered as the long-time editor of SUPERMAN comics, but his early efforts were in the science-fiction fan and magazine field. After selling a few stories to AMAZING and *Wonder Stories* in the mid-1930s and editing several early fan magazines, the twenty-one-year-old Weisinger talked himself into a position as editor at Standard Publications just before that pulp chain group bought *Wonder Stories* in 1936 and renamed it *Thrilling Wonder Stories*. *Startling Stories* was soon added, and in 1939 Weisinger created *Captain Future*.

Weisinger's contribution to the SF magazine field was the quest for the new and unusual. In its pursuit, he initiated the editorial practice, later perfected by John W. CAMPBELL, of suggesting ideas to his writers and commissioning stories, sometimes built around covers, as well as the development of story series, the predecessor of the later trilogy. Those covers, in keeping with the editorial aims of the "Thrilling" group, were often garish and juvenile, usually featuring a "bug-eyed monster," but the magazines also published much fiction of merit.

In 1941 Weisinger was named editor of the two-year-old *Superman* comic magazine, and, after service in World War II and a period of article writing, returned to the magazine and later the editorial direction of all DC Comics. Weisinger, later succeeded by his one-time fanzine colleague and partner in the first SF literary agency, Julius Schwartz, contributed a series of new ideas to the magazine's writers, many of whom he recruited from among SF writers, including Edmond HAMILTON, Otto BINDER, H. L. GOLD, and Alfred BESTER.

After his retirement, Weisinger made a triumphal return to article writing and to other non-fiction works such as his persistent seller, *1001 Valuable Things You Can Get for Free*.

J.E.G.

WELLMAN, MANLEY WADE (1903–1986).

WELLMAN, MANLEY WADE (1903–1986). American writer, journalist, and college instructor. Born in Angola, Wellman earned bachelor's degrees from Wichita University and Columbia. He worked for newspapers in Wichita and in the 1960s taught creative writing at the University of North Carolina. For most of his life, however, he was a full-time writer of a variety of books, articles, and stories, with more than seventy-five volumes to his credit. He was best known among science-fiction and fantasy readers for a series of stories about a wandering singer of ballads, with a guitar with silver strings, who gets involved in a series of confrontations with supernatural evil, collected in *Who Fears the Devil?* (1963).

Wellman's connection with the PULP MAGAZINES began with a *Weird Tales* story in 1927; his first science-fiction contribution was "When Planets Clashed" in *Wonder Stories Quarterly* (1931). He published eleven SF novels, beginning with *The Invading Asteroid* in 1932 and concluding with *The Beyonders* in 1977, and two collections of SF short stories, *Worse Things Waiting* (1973) and *Lonely Vigils* (1981). None of these works has withstood the passage of time as well as his fantasies, although *Twice in Time*, about an alternate history in which a contemporary man goes back to become Leonardo da Vinci, is still of interest, as is a series of witty Sherlock Holmes pastiches, which united Holmes with Doyle's other major character, Professor Challenger, in H. G. WELLS's London, written with Wellman's son Wade and brought together as a novel titled *Sherlock Holmes's War of the Worlds* (1975).

Between 1947 and 1971 Wellman wrote thirty-five juvenile novels, mostly historical. He also wrote a series of non-fiction books on history, particularly of the North Carolina area. In his later years he brought back Minstrel John in a series of novels: *The Old Gods Waken* (1979), *After Dark* (1980), *The Lost and the Lurking* (1981), *The Hanging Stones* (1982), and *The Voice from the Mountain* (1984).

Wellman won an Ellery Queen award in 1946 and was awarded the H. P. Lovecraft Award of the World

Fantasy Convention in 1975.

NOTABLE OTHER WORKS: *Sojarr of Titan* (1949); *The Beasts from Beyond* (1950); *The Devil's Planet* (1951); *Giants from Eternity* (1959); *The Dark Destroyers* (1959); *Island in the Sky* (1961); *The Solar Invasion* (1968).

J.E.G.

WELLS, H[ERBERT] G[EORGE] (1866–1946).

British author considered by many the father of science fiction. Wells's career overlapped that of Jules VERNE (1828–1905); Verne was still alive when Wells was producing his finest tales and almost all his works of SF, which were then called scientific romances, including *The Time Machine* (1895) and *The War of the Worlds* (1898). Wells was a better writer than Verne, owning almost all the gifts a novelist can possess; in fifty years he produced some 150 titles, and most of his SF books and stories have never been out of print.

Wells grew up in poverty; his father had been a gardener, his mother a lady's maid, but before he was born his parents had sunk their small resources in an unsuccessful crockery shop, which was saved from bankruptcy by his father's earnings as a professional cricket player. At ten or eleven, however, a fall disabled his father, and several years later the shop fell on hard times. His mother was forced once again to take up service, and his father found, as Wells described it, "a small, inexpensive cottage." About his early days, Wells went on to say, "Further education for the writer seemed impossible. There was some trouble in finding him employment, an unhandy boy preoccupied with reading." After time as a draper's apprentice, a "pupil-teacher" in an elementary school, a chemist's apprentice, and again as a draper, "he prayed to have his indentures cancelled, and became a sort of pupil-teacher. In the interval between these attempts to begin life he took refuge in the housekeeper's room with his mother."

Wells escaped by a combination of luck and genius, winning a scholarship to the Royal College of Science, Kensington, where he studied biology under the great T. H. Huxley and took his degree in zoology. When he was twenty-one, an accident on the football field destroyed one kidney and made him a semi-invalid for a while, giving him the opportunity and the incentive to write for a living, which made him a fortune, an international reputation as a prophet (an early futurist) that led him to hobnob with the world's political great, and notoriety for his unconventional attitudes and his reputation as a lady's man.

He was successful from the start with short stories, articles, and humorous sketches. His fame spread swiftly throughout the world after the publication of *The Time Machine*, and even the miseries of his early life were turned to good account in such novels as *Kipps* (1905), *Tono-Bungay* (1909), and *The History of Mr. Polly*

H. G. Wells

(1910). These sagas of ordinary people in turn-of-the-century England belong to the best tradition of Charles Dickens and would have assured Wells's fame even if he had never trafficked with Martians.

Wells is considered the father of modern SF not only because he made it popular—Verne did that before him with his *voyages extraordinaires*—but because, as did Jonathan Swift, he made ideas the center of his work and originated or definitively adapted most of the ideas that became the subject matter of later writers down to the present, focused his work on the nature and fate of the human species, and established the tone of pessimistic irony that has become traditional with literary SF ever since.

The Time Machine, still Wells's masterpiece, originated the idea of mechanical time travel used by hundreds of writers since and concerns the evolution of humanity, with its Morlocks and Eloi, and the fate of Earth itself. *The Island of Dr. Moreau* (1896) presents early speculations about vivisection and forced evolution. *The Invisible Man* (1897) not only pioneered the concept of manmade invisibility but considers its drawbacks as well. *When the Sleeper Wakes* (1899) uses an old device for arriving in the future—long sleep—but that future, a kind of technological tyranny, inspired hundreds of other works, including Yevgeny ZAMYATIN's *We* (1924), Aldous HUXLEY's *Brave New World* (1932), and George ORWELL's *Nineteen Eighty-four* (1949). *The First Men in the Moon* (1901) was not the first story about Moon travel (it had been preceded by one almost seventeen centuries before), or even the first to use antigravity as a motive force, but it was one of the earliest speculations about the problems of overspecialization.

After 1901 Wells's success and his political and social interests led him to write novels of contemporary life and money-making encyclopedias such as his *Outline of History* (1920), and when he turned to SF topics, they developed along propaganda lines in such works as *The Food of the Gods* (1904), *A Modern Utopia* (1905), *In the Days of the Comet* (1906), *The War in the Air* (1908), and *The World Set Free* (1914), which includes an early prediction of the atomic bomb and was credited by Leo Szilard with giving him the idea for what turned out to be the Manhattan Project.

The War of the Worlds may have had a greater impact than any of Wells's other novels, precipitating a nationwide panic when a 1938 radio version was broadcast by Orson Welles's *Mercury Theater of the Air* (which itself was dramatized on television in 1975 as *The Night That Panicked America*). The novel was the first to deal seriously with alien invasion. Unlike his predecessors or his later imitators, Wells made his monsters plausible and motivated, with their logical plan of conquest and their weapons—poison gas and heat rays—a vision not only of World War I but possibly of World War III. He also is guilty of creating the myth (Steven SPIELBERG's CLOSE ENCOUNTERS OF THE THIRD KIND, 1977, was an exception) that aliens must be horrible, which resulted in a host of pulp magazine covers featuring BEMs (bug-eyed monsters).

After a decline following his death, Wells's literary reputation has regained some of its earlier standing, particularly for his scientific romances, resulting in the formation of an H. G. Wells Society in Britain, a 1986 international conference on his work, and dozens of new books and biographies, as well as continuing reprintings of his SF works. His work has often been filmed, sometimes foolishly, sometimes well. The most effective dramatization he did himself, the script for THINGS TO COME (1936), which although badly dated remains one of the most important SF films ever made; the best Hollywood adaptations were produced by George PAL: THE WAR OF THE WORLDS (1953) and particularly THE TIME MACHINE (1960), which Pal also directed.

OTHER WORKS: *The Short Stories of H. G. Wells* (collection, 1927); *The Scientific Romances of H. G. Wells* (collection, 1933).

A.C.C.

Illustration by Wesso for John W. Campbell, Jr.'s "The Voice of the Void" (*Amazing Stories Quarterly*, Summer 1930)

his contemporaries. Still, of the pulp magazine artists, Wesso was second only to Paul in his use of grand space and scale. A familiar Wesso image is the gigantic spacecraft, usually cylindrical or spherical, dotted with hundreds of portholes. His works are often scientifically inaccurate, and he generally portrayed space as any color but black. One of his most famous covers was for E. E. "Doc" SMITH's *Skylark Three* (AMAZING STORIES, August 1930); he also painted covers and did interior black-and-white illustrations for pulp writers such as Miles J. Brewer, Thomas Calvert McClary, Arthur J. Burks, and Jack WILLIAMSON. Wesso worked primarily for the Clayton-run *Astounding Stories of Super-Science*, for which he painted all thirty-four covers. He also produced covers for *Amazing Stories*, *Startling Stories*, and *Thrilling Wonder Stories*.

J.G.

WESSO[LOWSKI, HANS WALDEMAR] (1894–?). American illustrator, one of the Big Four of the 1930s (with Frank R. PAUL, Howard V. BROWN, and Leo MOREY). Wesso learned his craft at the Berlin Royal Academy, but in spite of his classical training he often produced the same type of crude, garish cover as

WEST, WALLACE [GEORGE] (1900–1980). American writer and lawyer. A popular contributor to the pulp magazines since the publication of "Loup-Garou" (1927), West acquired a stronger reputation in the weird fiction field than in science fiction, although he wrote highly original stories for the pulps in the 1930s, such as "The Phantom Dictator" (1935), which looks at the power of the media, and returned with equal inventiveness though less storytelling skill in the 1950s. His first book was *The Bird of Time* (1959), a rather lighthearted interplanetary tale. *Lords of Atlantis* (1952/1960) describes a prehistory when Martians colonized the Mediterranean basin. *River of Time* (1963) is a rather routine tale of time manipulation, but *Time Lockers* (1956/1964) features the more fascinating concept of a bank in which time can be deposited and withdrawn.

OTHER WORKS: *The Memory Bank* (1951/1961); *Outposts in Space* (1962); *The Everlasting Exiles* (1967).

M.A.

WESTWORLD (1973).

Directed by Michael Crichton; screenplay by Michael Crichton; photographed by Gene Polito; music by Fred Karlin. With Yul Brynner, Richard Benjamin, James Brolin, Alan Oppenheimer, Dick Van Patten, Linda Scott, Victoria Shaw. 88 minutes. Color.

FUTUREWORLD (1976).

Directed by Richard T. Heffron; screenplay by Mayo Simon and George Schenck; photographed by Howard Schwartz and Gene Polito; music by Fred Karlin. With Peter Fonda, Blythe Danner, Arthur Hill, Yul Brynner, John Ryan, Stuart Margolin. 104 minutes. Color.

Michael CRICHTON, author of *The Andromeda Strain*, made his directing debut with *Westworld*, a science-fiction melodrama about a futuristic amusement park. Delos is a Disneyland-like complex of three past eras (Westworld, Romanworld, and Medievalworld) in which high-rolling tourists get their vicarious thrills. Two of the guests (Richard Benjamin and James Brolin) choose Westworld to realize their fantasies of virility by shooting gunfighters, robbing the bank, and sleeping with the local dance hall girls, who are, like the other townspeople, robots. The robots, however, develop a glitch and rampage through Westworld, killing the tourists and destroying the park.

Yul Brynner gives an excellent performance as a gunslinging robot in this cinematic thriller. The audience can't help cheering on the revenge of the robots as fantasy changes to reality in this playground for grown-ups.

Futureworld was produced as a sequel to the highly successful *Westworld*. Following the Westworld disaster, the park at Delos has been closed, reconstructed, and reopened. The park authorities invite journalists (Peter Fonda and Blythe Danner) to tour Delos, verifying its safeness. The journalists, however, discover a plot to replace world leaders with robotic replicas.

The major appeal of *Futureworld* is in its visualization of the new park attractions. Use of NASA facilities helped to provide incredible spaceflight simulations as well as a panoply of other cinematic wizardry. Unfortunately,

the human-versus-machine theme, revivified in *Westworld*, is trivialized again in *Futureworld*.

M.T.W.

WHALE, JAMES (1889–1957).

British film director who worked exclusively in Hollywood, best known today for his eccentric, witty horror thrillers of the 1930s; although he made only four such films (one of which was not fantastic), his reputation rests on firm foundations. Three of Whale's films—FRANKENSTEIN (1931), THE INVISIBLE MAN (1933), and *The Bride of Frankenstein* (1935)—are masterpieces, not just great science-fiction-horror films but superb movies by any standards.

Whale made many other films but no others in the genre for which he is now best known; he codirected *Hell's Angels* (1930) with Howard Hughes as well as several romances and light comedies for Universal, but his only other film shown today is the stylish *Show Boat* (1936).

Whale's visual style is Germanic, with low camera angles, deep shadows (sometimes painted on the sets), and, later, considerable camera movement. It is not for his visual style, however, but for his quirky wit that Whale and his films are known today. There are only traces of humor in *Frankenstein*, mostly centering on Fritz (Dwight Frye), Frankenstein's assistant: for instance, before ascending a gnarled stone staircase, Fritz fastidiously pulls up his sock. Frankenstein's harrumphing father (Frederick Kerr), allegedly German but clearly a standard British type, provides what other humor *Frankenstein* offers, although the film is a fine thriller.

It was with *The Old Dark House* (1932) that Whale's visual style and sense of humor became more baroque. *The Invisible Man* continued in this vein, particularly in the early scenes before the title character (Claude Rains) whips off his bandages to reveal nothing whatsoever. The later portions of the film are more serious, and it ends with genuine poignancy.

Whale's finest film, which some regard as the best horror movie ever made, is *The Bride of Frankenstein*. He had resisted Universal's pleas to do a sequel to the first film but finally found a way to satisfy himself and the studio as well: he made a comedy or, as Whale himself termed it, "a hoot." This bizarre movie, one of the few genuinely unique Hollywood films, was not successful, and when the administration changed at Universal, Whale fell out of favor.

His last released film came out in 1941. A moderately wealthy man, Whale spent the rest of his life quietly, never summoning enough interest in the many projects offered him to return to directing. In 1956 his health began to decline, and on May 29, 1957, he committed suicide. Ironically, in that year his classic horror films were being rediscovered on television.

B.W.

Cover illustration by Whelan for Asimov's *Foundation and Earth*

WHELAN, MICHAEL (1950–   ).   American il-
lustrator, seven-time Hugo Award winner (1980–1986—
he withdrew his name from competition in 1987); and
easily the most sought-after science-fiction and fantasy
artist of the 1980s. Whelan trained at San Jose State
University and Los Angeles's Art Center College of Design, but he developed the hard-edged realism that appears in his work primarily while working as a medical
illustrator. He burst on the genre in the mid-1970s and
by 1980 was doing cover illustrations for virtually all the
major paperback book publishers, particularly Ace, DAW,
and Ballantine/Del Rey. While fully capable of painting
the most intricate technological machinery, Whelan seems
most comfortable concentrating on people and landscapes and, unlike many other artists, seems equally at
ease with SF, fantasy, and horror. The standard Whelan
cover, as far as it exists, consists of one or two figures
in the lower center of the painting with a vast, complex,
and thoroughly believable world in the background; he
shares this major characteristic with Frank Kelly FREAS.

An artist with a sense of humor, Whelan occasionally
uses his (and his wife's) face in his paintings; the cover
of Alan Dean FOSTER's *With Friends Like These* (1977)
is a good example. Some of his best-known works are
on the covers of Anne McCAFFREY's *The White Dragon*,
Friday by Robert A. HEINLEIN, Stephen KING's *Firestarter*,
Larry NIVEN's *The Integral Trees*, and *Chanur's Venture*
by C. J. CHERRYH. An excellent collection of his work
appears in *Wonderworks*, edited by Kelly and Polly
Freas (1978).

J.G.

WHEN DINOSAURS RULED THE EARTH
(1971).   *Directed by Val Guest; screenplay by Val
Guest; photographed by Dick Bush; music by Mario
Nascimbene. With Victoria Vetri, Robin Hawdon, Patrick Allen, Drewe Henley, Sean Caffrey, Magda Kon-
opka, Billy Cornelius. 100 minutes. Color.*

This was Hammer Films' follow-up to ONE MILLION
YEARS B.C. (1966), with the initial story by no other than
J. G. BALLARD (credited as J.B. on U.S. prints); however,
Ballard's fanciful plot was discarded in favor of a mis-
guided "realistic" approach.

In prehistoric times a young woman (Victoria Vetri),
cast out from her tribe, is befriended by a dinosaur mother
and newly hatched baby. At the climax the Moon is
explosively born out of the Earth.

The acting is adequate, although there is no dialogue
per se. Jim Danforth, a superlative American stop-motion
animator and matte artist, created the special effects.
Unfortunately, the film was poorly received, and Danforth, whose stop-motion work is among the best ever
done, has rarely had the opportunity to show his abilities
again.

B.W.

WHEN WORLDS COLLIDE (1951).   *Directed
by Rudolph Mate; screenplay by Sydney Boehm;
adapted from the novel by Edwin Balmer and Philip
Wylie; photographed by John F. Seitz and W. Howard
Greene; music by Leith Stevens. With Richard Derr,
Barbara Rush, Peter Hanson, John Hoyt, Larry Keat-
ing, Judith Ames, Jim Congdon, Kirk Alyn, Kip (Stuart)
Whitman, Paul Frees. 83 minutes. Color.*

Two wandering planets enter the Solar System; one
will pass near the Earth resulting in worldwide catastrophe; the second will strike the planet. Because the first
will go into an Earthlike orbit, a huge "Space Ark" is
hastily built in the hope of reaching it, and lottery-
selected survivors migrate to the new world as the Earth
is destroyed.

After George PAL's independently produced success
DESTINATION MOON (1950), Paramount hired him to film
the novel by Edwin BALMER and Philip WYLIE, long planned
for production. The film rights had been purchased by
Cecil B. De Mille in the 1930s, and another script was
prepared in the late 1940s. Although the resulting film
is not Pal's best, burdened with inadequate performers
and a very low budget, it's workmanlike and fast paced.
A shot of Times Square being flooded is impressive, but
Gordon Jennings and Harry Barndollar's scant special
effects are notable more for ambition than for results,
and there is no shot of the actual destruction of the Earth.
Chesley BONESTELL, whose spectacular paintings grace
Destination Moon, served as technical adviser and illustrator.

B.W.

WHITE, JAMES (1928–   ).   Irish writer of well-wrought traditional science-fiction tales. Over the years White has built·a large and enthusiastic audience for his Sector General series, which concerns a fully realized interspecies hospital on the Rim of the Galaxy. His fascinating cast of characters and his belief in the basic decency of all intelligent life-forms have seen him through six Sector General books over the past quarter century.

The success of Sector General should not imply, however, that White has only one arrow in his quiver. *Lifeboat* (1972) is an outstanding melodrama, *All Judgement Fled* (1968) is an engrossing first-contact novel, and "Tableau" (1958) is one of the field's more memorable antiwar stories.

OTHER WORKS: *The Secret Visitors* (1957); *Second Ending* (1962); *Hospital Station* (1962); *Star Surgeon* (1963); *Deadly Litter* (1964); *Escape Orbit* (1965); *The Watch Below* (1966); *The Aliens among Us* (1969); *Major Operation* (1971); *Tomorrow Is Too Far* (1971); *The Dream Millennium* (1974); *Monsters and Medics* (1977); *Underkill (1979, British edition only); Ambulance Ship* (1979); *Future Past* (1982); *Sector General* (1983); *Star Healer* (1985); *Code Blue—Emergency* (1987).

M.R.

WHITE, TED [THEODORE EDWIN] (1938–   ). American writer and editor who first achieved prominence in the 1950s as an articulate fan; his prolific and forceful commentary on literary politics within SF, informed by personal observation going back to his teens, has been a notable constant in White's career.

White's own SF displays a studied control of adventure story structure, sometimes employed to unconventional ends: his major novel, the phantasmagoric *By Furies Possessed* (1970), subverts genre clichés about alien parasites to achieve emotionally intense effects. A juvenile, *Secret of the Marauder Satellite* (1967), was widely praised for credible detail and characterization. White's editorial career includes a resourceful tenure, from 1968 to 1978, as editor of the impoverished AMAZING STORIES and *Fantastic,* during which time both magazines regained much standing in the field. In 1979–80 he served as editor of the slick SF-and-comics magazine *Heavy Metal,* and in 1985–86 he designed and was editorial director of the "multimedia SF magazine" *Stardate.*

OTHER WORKS: *Invasion from 2500* (with Terry Carr under the joint pseudonym Norman Edwards, 1964); *Android Avenger* (1965); *Phoenix Prime* (1966); *The Sorceress of Qar* (1966); *The Jewels of Elsewhen* (1967); *Lost in Space* (novelization, as Ron Archer, with Dave Van Arnam, 1967); *Captain America: The Great Gold Steal* (novelization, 1968); *Sideslip* (with Dave Van Arnam, 1968); *The Spawn of the Death Machine* (1968);

No Time Like Tomorrow (1969); *Trouble on Project Ceres* (1971); *Star Wolf!* (1971); *The Best from Amazing Stories* (editor, 1973); *The Best from Fantastic* (editor, 1973); *Forbidden World* (with David F. Bischoff, 1977).

P.N.H.

WILCOX, [CLEO EL]DON (1905–   ).   American writer and artist, one of the more talented contributors to the Ziff-Davis science-fiction PULP MAGAZINES AMAZING STORIES and *Fantastic Adventures* under the editorship of Raymond A. PALMER. Wilcox, born in Lucas, Kansas, was a graduate of the University of Kansas with an M.A. in sociology, which he subsequently taught for three years. He turned to writing as a break from teaching and soon found himself selling regularly to Palmer. His first sale was "The Pit of Death" (1939), but his most important story is "The Voyage That Lasted 600 Years" (1940), one of the earliest stories on the theme of the generation starship, suggested to Wilcox by his sociological studies. Another popular Wilcox story was "The Whispering Gorilla" (1940), which lent itself to a sequel, "The Return of the Whispering Gorilla" (1943), written by David Vern (under the pseudonym David V. Reed). (These two stories were later published in England as *The Whispering Gorilla,* 1950, credited solely to Vern.)

Wilcox has used the pen names Miles Shelton, Cleo Eldon, Max Overton, and Buzz-Bolt Atomcracker. He has written little SF since the 1950s, although he did several scripts for the *Captain Video* television series. He has written books for young people, edited newspapers, and taught creative writing. He now lives in retirement in Florida.

M.A.

WILD IN THE STREETS (1968).   Directed by Barry Shear; screenplay by Robert Thom; photographed by Richard Moore; music by Barry Mann and Cynthia Weil. With Christopher Jones, Shelley Winters, Diane Varsi, Hal Holbrook. 96 minutes. Color.

After the voting age is lowered to fourteen, a rock star (Christopher Jones) becomes president of the United States in this film which, despite its heavy "hippie" topicality, has proved remarkably prescient about both American culture and science-fiction film. The story is set in motion by a greedy senatorial candidate (Hal Holbrook), whose attempt to manipulate young voters by enlisting their rock-star-hero in his campaign backfires when the rock star appropriates his fans' support for himself. Once elected president, the rock star institutes policies mandating that adults over thirty-five be confined to concentration camps, where they are kept docile by LSD.

In 1968 the suggestions that the media could be so easily manipulated and that a rock star could exercise real political power must have seemed far less likely than they do today. Moreover, in combining rock music with a science-fiction premise, *Wild in the Streets* pointed toward the blending of music video visual techniques, rock-star actors, and narrative-related rock film scores that characterize contemporary SF film.

B.L.

WILHELM, KATE (Née Gertrude Meredith) (1928–).

American writer who has helped bring a new power of characterization to the science-fiction genre; now married to Damon KNIGHT, with whom she has codirected the Milford SF Writers Conference. Wilhelm has also taught at various Clarion Workshops.

Even in her early novels, based on standard SF themes, Wilhelm displayed both her concern for character development and her interest in the moral problems raised by technological advances. In the works she has published since the appearance of *Margaret and I* in 1971, however, she has developed her talent for complex characterization and moral exploration to ever greater heights. Moreover, she is equally adept at the novel and shorter fiction; indeed, some of her finest work is in the novella form.

What initially sets Wilhelm's fiction apart from much genre writing is its apparent ordinariness. Her stories almost always begin quietly, in a commonplace setting, after which the uncommon makes itself felt in the lives of her characters. In "The Planners" (1968), for example, the fact that the protagonist continually fantasizes about his fellow workers and friends is not made clear right away, yet it eventually stands as an ethical comment on his research on both monkeys and human beings, and its effects. "April Fool's Day Forever" (1970) deals with immortality and its cost in human creativity from the point of view of an artist who has chosen to remain mortal. In fact, Wilhelm's complex handling of narrative point of view is mostly responsible for the depth of her characterizations.

This propensity is especially true of her major novels. In *The Clewiston Test* (1976) the protagonist is isolated by a car accident but in that isolation learns to question all aspects of her life, including her research. *Where Late the Sweet Birds Sang* (1977), critically praised as one of the best treatments of cloning in SF, shows both sides of the problem by presenting stories from both the natural and cloned humans' points of view. In the more recent *Juniper Time* (1979), the children of astronauts must confront a technologically devastated world, which can no longer support the dreams of their parents. And this is finally the core of Wilhelm's SF: a refusal of the easy technological optimism of much conventional SF but also a refusal of the easy despair of the antitechnological view.

NOTABLE OTHER WORKS: *The Mile-Long Spaceship* (1963); *More Bitter Than Death* (1963); *The Clone* (with Ted Thomas, 1965); *The Nevermore Affair* (1966); *The Killer Thing* (1967); *The Downstairs Room* (1968); *Let the Fire Fall* (1969); *Year of the Cloud* (with Ted Thomas, 1970); *Abyss* (1971); *City of Cain* (1974); *The Infinity Box* (1975); *Fault Lines* (1977); *Somerset Dreams and Other Fictions* (collection, 1978); *Huysman's Pets* (1986).

D.B.

WILLIAMS, PAUL O[SBORNE] (1935–).

American writer. A professor of literature at Principia College in Elsah, Illinois, and an authority on midwestern history, Williams is known in the genre for his Pelbar Cycle, a series of seven novels set in a postholocaust America, primarily in the Midwest. Like Edgar PANGBORN, whose *Davy* and related science-fiction works the Pelbar Cycle somewhat resembles, Williams is a cautious optimist, but he has a greater sympathy toward traditional religious values.

Beginning with *The Breaking of Northwall* (1981) and ending with *The Sword of Forebearance* (1985), the cycle develops the theme of reconciliation and reunion among rival peoples of the Heart (Mississippi) River region. These include the ossified city cultures of the Pelbar themselves and the nomadic tribal societies of the Sentani and Shumai, traditionally hostile to each other, which must find common cause against an invasion of barbarians from the East. While the familiar postholocaust theme of the revival of technology recurs in such developments as the reinvention of the steamboat, the rediscovery of the Bible is an equal challenge to the culture of Pelbar, which centers on a matriarchal religion. Nor does the worldview of the technocratic past, represented by descendants of the people from before the Time of Fire found in an ancient shelter, offer an answer for the future. Rather it is the opening of trade, of contacts between communities, and the development of mutual sympathy and understanding that make possible any revival of true civilization. Williams's protagonists are usually dissidents in their own communities who perceive the need for more universal values and thus act as catalysts for change.

J.J.P.

WILLIAMS, WALTER JON (1953–).

American author. Williams was born in Minnesota but earned a bachelor's degree in English and history from the University of New Mexico in 1975. He took up fiction writing with a series of five historical novels under the name of John Williams before turning to science fiction with *Ambassador of Progress* in 1984. His best-known novel, *Hardwired* (1986), with its giant corporations and their orbital headquarters, falls into the CYBERPUNK category, but it develops a character of its own.

OTHER WORKS: *Knight Moves* (1985); *Voice of the Whirlwind* (1987); *The Crown Jewels* (1987); *House of Shards* (1988).

J.E.G.

WILLIAMSON, JACK (1908–   ). American science-fiction writer and university professor of English. Williamson has been an active writer in more decades than any other SF author, beginning with his first published story, "The Metal Man," in the December 1928 issue of AMAZING STORIES. In 1976 he received the Grand Master Nebula Award from the SCIENCE FICTION WRITERS OF AMERICA.

Before 1945 Williamson wrote traditional SPACE OPERA; early space epics such as the Legion of Space trilogy (1934/1947, 1936/1950, 1939/1950) and *The Legion of Time* (1938/1952) made him a favorite of fan readers, and he was one of the authors whose work was often reprinted by postwar fan publishers. His *Golden Blood* (*Weird Tales*, 1933/1964) and *Darker Than You Think* (*Unknown*, 1940/1948) established his credentials as a writer of fantasy adventure.

Williamson's work after 1945, in particular "With Folded Hands" (1947) and its sequel *The Humanoids* (1949), revealed his developing concern for characterization and his focus on the sociological and psychological impact of technological change. One of his major themes, evident in many variations throughout his writing, is the American frontier—a fascination born of his lifelong residency in New Mexico, with its rugged land and climate. He has described SF as a variation on the epic, with the conquest of space as its central metaphor. *The Reefs of Space* (with Frederik POHL, 1964) developed out of his interest in Walter Prescott Webb's complex historical theory of the American frontier.

Williamson's long struggle for success as a free-lance writer and for psychological understanding is recounted in his autobiography, *Wonder's Child* (1984), which also describes the development of SF from an isolated pulp magazine field to a broadly accepted publishing phenomenon. In addition, it discusses his contacts and relationships with other SF editors and writers, including a period in California from 1940 to 1941 in which he was associated with The Mañana Literary Society organized by Robert A. HEINLEIN, which included almost every SF writer in the Los Angeles area.

In the late 1940s Williamson turned to the academic world, earning his M.A. in English from Eastern New Mexico University in his then hometown of Portales and his Ph.D. from the University of Colorado. His dissertation was published as *H. G. Wells: Critic of Progress* (1973); he also edited *Science Fiction: Education for Tomorrow* (1980). He taught at Eastern New Mexico until his retirement in 1977. While there he taught one of the earliest science-fiction courses. Upon his retire-

Jack Williamson

ment he was named a distinguished professor, a lecture series was endowed in his honor, and in 1982 the university opened its Jack Williamson SF Library, a permanent collection of Williamson materials.

During World War II, at the suggestion of *Astounding* editor John W. CAMPBELL, Williamson assumed a new persona as Will Stewart and produced a series of stories and a novel about asteroid miners who discover contraterrene (or C.T.) asteroids; this fiction was collected as *Seetee Ship* (1942–43/1951), followed by the novel *Seetee Shock* (1949/1950). Its publication as books earned him an assignment to create and write scripts for a *New York Sunday News* comic strip, "Beyond Mars," from 1952 to 1955.

In the early 1950s Williamson wrote a series of stories later collected in *The Trial of Terra* (1951, 1952, 1961/1962) in which he invented the word *psionics* to describe a potential science of psychic powers, with the *psion* as the elemental unit of mental energy. In 1951, in *Dragon's Island*, he also invented the term *genetic engineering*.

In the 1950s, as a way of overcoming writer's block, he began a series of collaborations, first with James E. GUNN on *Star Bridge* (1955), then in a continuing relationship with Frederik Pohl, beginning in 1954 with *Undersea Quest*. He returned to full-time writing after his university retirement, producing sequels to his most famous early work, the Legion trilogy and *The Humanoids*, in *The Queen of the Legion* (1983) and *The*

Humanoid Touch (1980), as well as such new novels as *Brother to Demons, Brother to Gods* (1979), *Manseed* (1982), *Lifeburst* (1984), and *Firechild* (1986).

OTHER WORKS: *The Green Girl* (1950); *Dome around America* (1955); *Undersea Fleet* (with Frederik Pohl, 1956); *Undersea City* (with Pohl, 1958); *The Reign of Wizardry* (1964); *Starchild* (with Pohl, 1965); *Bright New Universe* (1967); *Trapped in Space* (1968); *The Pandora Effect* (1969); *Rogue Star* (with Pohl, 1969); *People Machines* (1971); *The Moon Children* (1972); *The Early Williamson* (collection, 1975); *The Power of Blackness* (1976); *The Best of Jack Williamson* (collection, 1978); *The Alien Intelligence* (1980); *The Birth of a New Republic* (with Miles J. Breuer, 1981); *Wall around a Star* (with Pohl, 1983); *Land's End* (with Pohl, 1987); *Deadfall* (sequel to *Lifeburst*, 1988).

H.L.P.

WILLIS, CONNIE [CONSTANCE E.] (1945–).
American writer of science fiction, fantasy, and supernatural fiction who has emerged as one of science fiction's most talented short story writers. Willis won two Nebulas in 1982 and a Hugo in 1983 and has continued to produce stories on unusual topics with remarkable skill, some of which are collected in *Fire Watch* (1985).

In the title story of this collection, a Nebula winner, Willis developed one of her major themes, the complications of time travel: the story depicts a historical researcher who returns to the time of the London blitz, becomes involved in an effort to save a cathedral, and ends up learning more about himself than about history. In her other Nebula winner, "A Letter from the Clearys," a young woman tries to save her sanity in a paranoid postholocaust world. "The Sidon in the Mirror" (1983), a Nebula finalist, tells the story of a mining colony on the surface of a burned-out star through the personnel of a bordello that caters to the miners' destructive and self-destructive urges.

Willis's first novel, *Water Witch* (with Cynthia Felice, 1982), is an amusing story about a con artist on a planet with a water shortage. Her second novel, *Lincoln's Dreams* (1987), however, returned to her preoccupation with time travel, in this case with a young woman who dreams the nightmares of Robert E. Lee so compellingly that she and others experience the Civil War as historic personages.

H.M.Z.

WILSON, COLIN [HENRY] (1931–). Brit-
ish writer and self-taught philosopher whose obsession with humanity's entrapment in triviality and consequent alienation from freedom and ecstasy pervades his work. Born in Leicester, the son of a factory worker, Wilson was aware from an early age of what he called the "veg-

etable mediocrity" of his working-class background. A series of menial jobs, a stint in the Royal Air Force, and an unhappy marriage increased his sense of alienation and his own motivation for significant action.

His first book, *The Outsider* (1956), presents the thesis of a common difference in a small group of people that makes them outsiders to the rest of society, which is sick. This thesis, and its corollary that humanity *should* be vital, aware, and visionary, form the basis for all Wilson's writing, whether philosophical, factual, or fictional. His novels are fictional presentations of his philosophical concepts. Style, plot, and characterization, although competent, are always subordinate to ideas.

Wilson's few science-fiction novels have gained a cult following that has kept them continually in print. He admired the "Lovecraft tradition," and *The Mind Parasites* (1967) unabashedly exploits H. P. LOVECRAFT's Cthulhu mythos, projecting a future discovery that the Tsathogguans, microscopic parasites, have infected humanity's best minds, ensuring mediocrity; they kill their hosts rather than risk discovery. A group of outsiders successfully frees itself from infection and immediately experiences immense freedom, joy, and visionary unity. In *The Philosopher's Stone* (1969) Wilson speculated that insertion of a special alloy into the brain's frontal lobes can alchemically transform the outsider into someone with "an infinite appetite for life," for whom life is "endlessly rich, infinitely desirable." Having observed not only that the triviality of everyday events saps one's energy but also that certain individuals cause the same fatiguing effect, Wilson wrote *The Space Vampires* (1976) to dramatize the concept. Recently filmed and reprinted as *Lifeforce* (1985), this novel posits the discovery of a derelict spaceship whose inhabitants feed on the life force of others. As do his other SF novels, this one ends with an increase in the awareness, energy, joy, and capability of the protagonists.

Wilson's optimistic conviction that a higher reality of "pure *meaning*" exists phenomenologically—that some portion of humanity already lives it through occult experiences, "peak experiences" as described by psychologist Abraham Maslow, or visionary knowledge transcending the "triviality of everydayness"—continues to attract a hard core of readers.

NOTABLE OTHER WORKS: *The Strange Genius of David Lindsay* (1970); *Tree by Tolkien* (1973); *The Return of the Lloigor* (1974); *Science Fiction as Existentialism* (1978); *Necronomicon* (1978); *Starseekers* (1980); *Poltergeist!* (1981); *The Essential Colin Wilson* (collection, 1985); *Lord of the Underworld* (1986).

J.E.B.

WILSON, F[RANCIS] PAUL (1946–). Amer-
ican writer who is also a practicing physician, composer, and musician. One of the last young writers edited by

F. Paul Wilson

John W. CAMPBELL, Jr., Wilson won the first libertarian Prometheus Award for his second novel, *Wheels within Wheels* (1979). Like his first novel, *Healer* (1976), and his third, *An Enemy of the State* (1980), it deals with the LaNague Federation and Peter LaNague, an immortal psychiatric healer who protects humanity against aliens and other dangers in the inhabited worlds. As an existential hero, LaNague is, like characters in the works of Albert Camus, one of Wilson's early influences, beyond good and evil. Wilson also has combined science-fiction elements with horror in such works as *The Keep* (1981) and *The Tomb* (1984). His work is mostly concerned with philosophical issues and social trends.

H.L.P.

WILSON, RICHARD (1920–1987).   American writer, reporter, and news bureau agent, one of the talented FUTURIANS who, along with Frederik POHL, Cyril M. KORNBLUTH, Damon KNIGHT, Donald A. WOLLHEIM, and others, did so much to advance science fiction beginning in the 1940s. Although Wilson did not achieve the fame of the others, he was still a competent writer. His stories are frequently in a lighthearted vein, occasionally satiric, always smoothly composed and delivered. His first sale was "Murder from Mars" (1940), but he did not begin to write regularly for the magazines until the 1950s; before his death in 1987 he produced a large and readable body of work.

Wilson's stories are collected in *Those Idiots from Earth* (1957) and *Time Out for Tomorrow* (1962), which

perhaps best reflect his general level of work. A collection of later stories is needed to include his Nebula Award–winning "Mother to the World" (1968), a more poignant story than usual for Wilson. Wilson's novels, like so many of his stories, are also lighthearted; they include *The Girls from Planet 5* (1955) and *30-Day Wonder* (1960), both depicting comic alien invasions, and perhaps his best, *And Then the Town Took Off* (1958/ 1960; published in Britain as "Super City," 1959), wherein the town of Superior, Ohio, secedes from the Earth, to hover 12,000 feet above it. Unlike the other Futurians, Wilson did not use a host of pseudonyms, but a couple of his stories were published under the names Ivar Towers and Edward Halibut.

M.A.

WILSON, ROBERT ANTON (1932–   ).   American writer. Wilson's first novel, *Illuminatus!* (1975), a collaboration with Robert Shea, is still his masterpiece, a witty dissection of the conspiratorial mind. *Illuminatus!* is a playful novel, but beneath the play is an exhaustive analysis of the paranoid mentality, through the medium of a cosmic war between the forces of anarchy (Discordians) and order (Erisians). Wilson's later novels continue, in a less developed way, the themes of *Illuminatus!* The historical fantasy *Masks of the Illuminati* (1981) almost equals *Illuminatus!* in its sinister power, but the trilogy *Schroedinger's Cat* (1979–1981; a revised and expanded version of *The Sex Magicians*, 1973) devolves into Joycean meaninglessness. Wilson's other novels are not science fiction.

M.M.W.

WISE, ROBERT (1914–   ).   American film editor and director who made important science-fiction movies in the 1950s and 1970s. Known primarily for his wide-ranging commercial reliability and his versatility, Wise began his career as a film editor. He quickly established a reputation by editing Orson Welles's monumental *Citizen Kane* (1941), a film noted for its bravura style, to which the editing contributes significantly. Later, for the same studio, RKO, Wise directed two horror classics for producer Val Lewton, *The Curse of the Cat People* (1944) and *The Body Snatcher* (1945). He would return to the horror genre years later with *The Haunting* (1963), a superbly crafted work of Gothic menace. His later films fall into a variety of genres, and beginning with *West Side Story* (1961) Wise generally seemed to sacrifice a sense of personal style for commercial success.

His first venture into SF remains one of the best examples of the genre in the 1950s. THE DAY THE EARTH STOOD STILL (1951), based on Harry BATES's "Farewell to the Master," avoids the xenophobia characteristic of so many Eisenhower-era SF movies, depicting the alien with a sense of wonder closer to the more contemporary sensibility of Steven SPIELBERG. Wise's later SF films are well wrought but less memorable. THE ANDROMEDA STRAIN (1971) is interesting in its concern for scientific plausibility, but STAR TREK: *The Motion Picture* (1979) was for many disappointing because of its respectful but ponderous approach.

B.K.G.

WODHAMS, JACK (1931–   ).   Australian author and postal worker, born in England. Wodhams, primarily a short story writer, made his first sale, "There Is a Crooked Man," to *Astounding* in 1967 and has contributed steadily since then to U.S., Australian, and British publications, and the small press field. His style, which seems particularly appropriate for his customary U.S. outlet, *Astounding*, is a novel idea, sometimes of the "dangerous invention" category, carried forward irresistibly by dialogue, with little description or analysis. His only novel published in the United States, *The Authentic Touch* (1971), is a humorous account of a vacation resort planet and the bewilderment of civilized vacationers presented with authentic re-creations of past history. Wodhams's novels *Looking for Blucher* (1980), hallucinatory adventures held together by a story frame, and *Ryn* (1982), about reincarnation and an infant remembering a previous life as an adult, and the collection *Future War* (1982) were published in Australia.

R.S.C.

WOLFE, BERNARD (1915–1985).   American mainstream writer. Despite a few magazine and anthology appearances, Wolfe is essentially a one-book author in science fiction. But what a book! *Limbo* (1952), which J. G. BALLARD has called the greatest American SF novel, is one of the most trenchant satires in SF or any other genre. Set a generation or so after World War III, it depicts a world in the thrall of an insane ideology called Immob, which prescribes voluntary amputation of the limbs as a literal form of disarmament. Both the former United States and the former Soviet Union have adopted Immob, and its sacred book, *Dodge the Steamroller!*, is as ubiquitous as the Little Red Book in Mao's China. But it seems everyone has misunderstood the absurdist intent of the author, Dr. Martine, who deserted World War III for a remote island and returns to civilization to witness the ideological insanity of his unintended handiwork. Ironic, witty, filled with puns as well as action, Wolfe's novel also adopted typographical trickery from the mainstream avant-garde resembling that of Alfred BESTER in *The Demolished Man*, also published in 1952, and *The Stars My Destination* (1956).

J.J.P.

Gene Wolfe

WOLFE, GENE [RODMAN] (1931–   ).   American writer considered one of the finest prose stylists in contemporary science fiction. Born in Brooklyn, Wolfe grew up in Texas, studying science and engineering at Texas A & M University, the University of Houston, and, after a stint in the U.S. Army, Miami University. Since 1972 he has been senior editor of *Plant Engineering*, a trade magazine. From the time one of his early stories appeared in *Orbit 2*, Wolfe has been recognized as a "writer's writer," a creator of complex, ambiguous, beautifully wrought fiction.

His first novel, *Operation ARES* (1970), gave few hints of the subtleties of his later fiction, although certain scenes reveal his ability to create atmosphere. But "The Island of Dr. Death and Other Stories" (1970) established him as a major voice. Two later stories, "The Death of Dr. Island" (1973) and "The Doctor of Death Island" (1978), form a triptych on the themes of isolation and confinement, all realized in strict SF terms. In these stories, as in the three linked novellas of *The Fifth Head of Cerberus* (1972), Wolfe used an imaginative yet oblique style that challenges the reader to perceive standard SF landscapes in a fresh manner. *The Fifth Head of Cerberus*, with its explorations of cloning, anthropology, alien encounter, settlement, and various technologies, also investigates the nature of the narrative act and the narrator's place within it. Two works in particular stand out among Wolfe's other short fictions: "Seven American Nights" (1978), a phantasmagoric diary of a young Iranian's journey through the twenty-first-century ruins of a decayed United States, and "Alien Stones" (1972), a marvelously ambiguous treatment of the alien artifact theme. In all Wolfe's works, even the minor pieces, the sure hand of the artist and the craftsman is evident.

In the mid-1970s Wolfe published two non-SF books: *Peace,* a superbly evocative book of memory, transforms the common SF theme of time travel into a metaphor for the inner workings of the mind, reliving, and rewriting, his life; *The Devil in a Forest* is a juvenile fantasy set in the Middle Ages. Both reflect the best qualities of Wolfe's prose style.

In 1980 Wolfe published *The Shadow of the Torturer* (1980), the first volume of his tetralogy The Book of the New Sun. A dramatic departure, it took its place immediately in the front rank of SF epics. Set millions of years in the future, on a "dying Earth" (the homage to Jack VANCE, among many others, is deliberate throughout), it and the following volumes, *The Claw of the Conciliator* (1981), *The Sword of the Lictor* (1981), and *The Citadel of the Autarch* (1983), are the "memoirs" of Severian, once an apprentice torturer, now the ruler of Urth. In its play with and examination of all the conventions of large-scale science fantasy, its incredible largess with the ancient gift of story itself, and its complex literary self-referentiality, The Book of the New Sun has set the standards by which all such works should be judged.

Since completing this vast work, Wolfe has published a few collections of shorter fiction; one strange novel of contemporary political fantasy, *Free Live Free* (1984); and the first volume of a new historical fantasy series, *Soldier of the Mist* (1986), set in preclassical Greece at the time of the Persian War. Typically, he has presented himself with a marvelous narrative problem by choosing a narrator who can only remember the day that has just passed as he writes; in solving this problem Wolfe has found new ways to bring a conventional background to mysterious and glowing life.

OTHER WORKS: *Gene Wolfe's Book of Days* (1981); *The Castle of the Otter* (1983); *The Wolfe Archipelago* (1983); *Plan(e)t Engineering* (1984); *The Urth of the New Sun* (1987).

D.B.

WOLLHEIM, DONALD A[LLEN] (1914–   ).

American editor, publisher, and author as well as noted science-fiction fan and collector. Wollheim's career has paralleled the rise and acceptance of SF, a field that he helped shape in each of his associations.

Wollheim's early reading of SF led to the publication of his first SF story, "The Man from Ariel" (1934), in Hugo GERNSBACK's *Wonder Stories,* and he has continued to write and publish throughout his varied career, accumulating a total of eighteen novels and two collections of stories. His experience in trying to collect payment for his story from Gernsback led him to contact other fans and writers, and launched a fateful career as one of fandom's most active and vociferous members, opposing Gernsback's Science Fiction League and advocating a more openly futuristic, even political, fan stance. Wollheim and his cohorts later formed the FU-

TURIANS, the renowned group of fans-turned-authors that lasted from 1938 to 1945; out of it came the writers, editors, agents, and publishers who would change the face of SF in the 1950s and later. As a fan Wollheim coproduced the semiprofessional magazine *Fanciful Tales* (1936) as well as the long-running *The Phantagraph* (1934–1946), selections from which were later published as *Operation: Phantasy* (1967).

Wollheim's opportunity to edit professionally came in 1941, when he joined Albing Publications to edit the short-lived *Stirring Science Stories* (1941–42) and *Cosmic Stories* (1941); working virtually without a budget, he depended largely on the charity of his fellow Futurians, who provided their work free of charge. That exposure led to his joining Ace Magazines, where he learned the editorial craft from 1942 to 1947. Of equal or greater importance was his editing of the first paperback SF anthology, *The Pocket Book of Science Fiction* (1943), which was of tremendous significance to the development and recognition of the field, as well as Viking's *Portable Novels of Science* (1945).

From 1947 to 1952 Wollheim moved to Avon Books and edited the eighteen-volume *Avon Fantasy Reader* (1947–1952) and the three-volume *Avon Science Fiction Reader* (1951–52), paperback anthologies in digest magazine format, as well as other magazines and anthologies. In 1952 he returned to Ace and, with publisher A. A. Wyn, launched Ace paperbacks, including the innovation of the Ace Double, two books bound back to back. Ace became the major paperback publisher of SF, and Wollheim remained there until 1971, becoming vice-president in 1967. During this period he brought into paperback most of the leading SF writers of the 1950s as well as discovered some of the major names of the 1960s, among them Samuel R. DELANY, Ursula K. LE GUIN, and Roger ZELAZNY. He got the work of Andre NORTON, Philip K. DICK, and Gordon R. DICKSON into paperback, resurrected the work of Edgar Rice BURROUGHS, and in 1965 created a storm by bringing into print in America an unauthorized but legal paperback edition of J. R. R. Tolkien's Lord of the Rings. Wollheim assembled a number of useful anthologies for Ace. In 1965 he launched, with Terry CARR (who had joined Ace as associate editor in 1964), the annual World's Best Science Fiction (1965–1971), as well as the Ace Specials.

In 1971 Wollheim left Ace to establish his own independent publishing company specializing in SF, DAW Books. This has been a highly successful venture, introducing many new writers, including C. J. CHERRYH, Tanith LEE, and Brian M. STABLEFORD. Wollheim also renewed his Annual World's Best SF (with Art Saha, 1972–   ). He retired from direct involvement in the company in 1986 because of ill health.

Wollheim wrote many short stories, some of them collected in *Two Dozen Dragon Eggs* (1969) and *The*

Donald A. Wollheim

Men from Ariel (1982), and a series of early juveniles, as David Grinnell, for Winston Adventures in SF, beginning with *The Secret of Saturn's Rings* (1954), as well as the Mike Mars series for Doubleday, beginning with *Mike Mars, Astronaut* (1961), which follows Mars's career through the various stages of the space program. In addition to the Grinnell pseudonym, Wollheim has written under the names Millard Verne Gordon, Martin Pearson, Lawrence Woods, W. Malcolm White, Wallace Baird Halleck, Graham Conway, and Zachary Good, as well as a number of communal pen names shared with fellow Futurians in their early days.

Wollheim offered his own perceptions of the development of modern SF and its characteristics in *The Universe Makers* (1971).

M.A.

WOMAN IN THE MOON (Die Frau im mond) (Silent, 1929).

Directed by Fritz Lang; screenplay by Fritz Lang and Thea von Harbou; adapted from the novel Die Frau im mond *by Thea von Harbou; photographed by Kurt Courant and Otto Kanturek; music by Willy Schmidt-Gentner. With Gerda Maurus, Willy Fritsch, Gustav von Wangenheim, Klaus Pohl, Fritz Rasp, Gustl Stark-Gstettenbauer. 97 minutes. Black and white. Alternate title:* By Rocket to the Moon.

The first rocket is launched to the Moon, which has an atmosphere as well as plenty of gold; greed and jealousy result in some deaths. Fritz LANG's painstaking attempt at realism is compromised by flat characters and trite personal clashes; the film is ponderously slow, making it difficult viewing for most audiences today.

But this was the first serious space travel movie ever made and the only one for more than twenty years; it is handsomely designed, and the special effects by Konstantin Tschetwerikoff and Oskar Fischinger are impressive. Given the limits of then current knowledge, it is still one of the most accurate depictions of lunar travel. It also has the distinction of having invented the prelaunch countdown; Lang added it for simple dramatic tension.

B.W.

—————— WOMEN ——————

Science fiction traditionally has been considered a literature for men and boys: men wrote it and boys read it. The truth behind this tradition can be verified over most of the history of SF by inspecting any table of contents or readership survey. It would not make sense then to have an entry in an SF encyclopedia about men, but the topic of women and SF is worth considering.

Actually women have been a part of SF since its beginnings, but their role until recent times was relatively minor, with a few exceptions. Science-fiction writers often pride themselves on exploring alternatives or assumptions counter to what is normally accepted; in fact, however, they have usually reflected the deeply rooted beliefs of their societies. Male and female writers alike often wrote of worlds vastly different from our own in which women still pursued, without questioning, only traditional roles as wives and mothers. Mary Wollstonecraft SHELLEY's novel *Frankenstein* (1818) may be the first true work of SF because it reflects an awareness of new scientific discoveries at the dawn of the Industrial Age and anticipated the methods of H. G. WELLS. Shelley's place in the pantheon of SF writers seems secure, but other women writers, now forgotten, also contributed to fantastic literature during the nineteenth century. Marie Corelli, Rhoda Broughton, Sara Coleridge, and Jane Loudon, among others, produced works bordering on SF, often influenced in mood and setting by Gothic literature. Mary Bradley Lane's *Mizora* (1890) was an early all-female utopia.

Yet the two major nineteenth-century figures in science fiction, Jules VERNE and H. G. Wells, paid little attention to female characters in their work. Verne's characters are nineteenth-century men, essentially unchanged by exciting adventures, strange new devices, or the discovery of other worlds. Wells was very much interested in the rights of women, but this concern is largely absent from his SF (although not from some of his "utopian" works). The most memorable female character in his classic works of SF may be Weena in *The Time Machine* (1895), one of the childlike and helpless

Eloi of a far future Earth.

The early twentieth century saw the publication of two significant works by women, Charlotte Perkins Gilman's *Herland* (1915) and Francis Stevens's *The Heads of Cerberus* (1919). In *Herland* Gilman, a once famous early feminist who has been neglected until recently, depicted in clean, readable prose an altruistic, female society. Sexuality, however, is absent from this utopia; it remained for later writers to deal openly and sympathetically with lesbianism. Stevens (whose actual name was Gertrude Barrows) may have been the first SF writer to use, in *The Heads of Cerberus,* the concept of parallel worlds.

In the 1930s C. L. MOORE began to publish stories in the pulp magazines; because of her use of initials, these stories were assumed by some readers to be the work of a man. Moore showed that she could write from a male point of view in her Northwest Smith stories about a future adventurer, but she also wrote fantasies with a strong, sword-wielding heroine, Jirel of Joiry. Among her most notable works is the novella "No Woman Born" (1944), one of the earliest thoughtful treatments of the cyborg. After her marriage to Henry KUTTNER, most of her work was written in collaboration with her husband, some of it under the joint pseudonym Lewis Padgett.

Among the love interests, scientists' daughters, and scantily clad stock female characters that populate SF works of the 1930s and 1940s, there are a few intriguing women in stories by men, but they seem to reflect some ambivalence on the part of their creators. In Lester DEL REY's classic story "Helen O'Loy" (1938), a man builds a female robot and programs her to be the perfect wife: Helen, the robot, even decides to die with her inventor, although her robot body makes her virtually immortal. (A similar idea appeared later in Ira LEVIN's *The Stepford Wives*, 1972, in which all the men in a town decide that androids would make better wives than real women.) Isaac ASIMOV, in his "robot" stories of the 1940s and 1950s, depicted one of SF's major female characters, Dr. Susan Calvin. Asimov was clearly sympathetic to this brilliant robotics expert and drew her as an admirable character. Yet Calvin also prefers robots to people and has never married; the scientific realm in these stories remains predominantly male.

During the 1940s and early 1950s, more women began to write and publish SF, yet their work, though often of high quality, did not change the direction of the field as a whole or influence men to alter their usual treatment of female characters. Leigh BRACKETT became a popular writer of space opera, although some consider her novel of a future Amishlike society, *The Long Tomorrow* (1955), her best work. Marion Zimmer BRADLEY's writing, first published in 1954, is also marked by colorful settings and adventure, although she began to explore women's roles in her later fiction, most notably her Darkover series.

Andre NORTON, often unfairly neglected because most of her work is for younger readers, also began to publish during the 1950s; her novels feature vivid description, strong feeling for her characters, and detailed descriptions of alien ways and settings. Judith MERRIL's first story, "That Only a Mother," a tale of a nuclear war's aftermath seen through the eyes of a woman, appeared in *Astounding* in 1948. So did Wilmar H. SHIRAS's "In Hiding," which later became part of her novel *Children of the Atom* (1953), a story about mutant children whose parents were exposed to radioactivity while working in a nuclear power plant. Katherine MACLEAN specialized in the rigorous hard SF story; Margaret ST. CLAIR (who also wrote under the name Idris Seabright) published sharp and elegant SF and fantasy often containing a dark side.

The 1950s saw another development in SF that accurately reflected the attitudes of that time. Many stories of the period, often written by women, feature passive or addle-brained female characters who solve problems inadvertently or through ineptitude. These stories show women primarily as child rearers, consumers, or wives trying to hold their families together after atomic war or other disasters. Such stories, some of which might be read as veiled criticisms of the lives many women led at the time, were written by Mildred Clingerman, Alice Eleanor Jones, Ann Warren Griffith, and others. Zenna HENDERSON became popular during the 1950s for her series of stories about the People, gentle humanlike aliens with extrasensory powers; some readers found these tales moving and warm, while others criticized them for being overly sentimental—a charge often leveled at work by women.

In contrast, one of SF's most popular writers, Robert A. HEINLEIN, showed women in a wide variety of roles. His novels and stories, even those dating from the 1940s and 1950s, are filled with women and girls who join the army, pilot spaceships, study mathematics, or are physicians and engineers. His work represents an advance over earlier stories; Heinlein's female characters are capable of intellectual activities and courageous deeds. They often end up, however in a subordinate position to an even more competent male, a situation they tend to welcome.

The early 1960s saw the growing prominence of women writers in the field. Perhaps not coincidentally, writers and readers were then questioning the assumptions and the style of much SF. Several British writers, publishing in the magazine NEW WORLDS, experimented with literary forms and subject matter. Many American writers were also influenced by this development, and Judith MERRIL, already a force in the field with her series of annual anthologies that reprinted the best SF of the year, did much to popularize these new trends. Women were beginning to emerge as major writers who would affect SF as a whole, and many were influenced by the growing feminist movement.

(left to right) C. J. Cherryh, Lee Killough, Susan Schwartz, Joanna Russ

Among the writers who first came to prominence during the 1960s were Hilary Bailey, Josephine Saxton, Phyllis GOTLIEB, Carol EMSHWILLER, Kit Reed, Sonya Dorman, Naomi Mitchison, and Pamela Zoline, who used a homemaker-heroine in her experimental story "The Heat Death of the Universe" (1967). Joanna RUSS wrote a series of stories and a novel, *Picnic on Paradise* (1968), featuring a heroine named Alyx, who is strong and anything but traditional. Kate WILHELM's stories and novels are notable for their realism, smooth style, skillful use of traditional SF elements, and questions about the presuppositions of science and technology. Ann MCCAFFREY, who had been writing since the 1950s, became the first woman to win both the Hugo and Nebula awards; her work, including *The Ship Who Sang* (1969) and her widely popular Dragonriders of Pern series, is romantic in tone but also marked by the prominence of female characters. Rosel George Brown dealt with an interstellar heroine in *Sibyl Sue Blue* (1966).

The 1960s also brought about franker treatments of sexuality in a literature that had often shied away from the subject. For some writers this simply added the role of woman as sex object to the more traditional ones of housewife, child raiser, damsel in distress, and scientist's daughter. Advances in the depiction of sex often meant only that the hero was free to go to bed with the heroine. In John NORMAN's Gor series, for example, begun with *Tarnsman of Gor* (1966), the author argued explicitly that women are only happy when they are dominated sadomasochistically—hardly an advance in the treatment of female characters.

In 1969 Ursula K. LE GUIN's *The Left Hand of Darkness* was published and hailed as a significant work by a major writer; the book won both Hugo and Nebula awards. This classic story of the Gethenians, a people who are genderless except during their monthly fertile season, when each becomes either male or female with

no way of knowing which sex "he" will be, raises questions about our cultural assumptions. By the end of the 1960s it was clear that women could look to a variety of other women writers as models for or influences on their own science fiction.

The 1970s brought about the full flowering of many female talents, several of them affected by the issues the women's movement was raising. Joanna Russ's award-winning story "When It Changed" (1972) and her novel *The Female Man* (1975) are both explicitly feminist works that feature the intriguing and often appealing all-female world of Whileaway. Ursula K. Le Guin's utopian novel *The Dispossessed* was published in 1974, and two years later Kate Wilhelm won a Hugo for *Where Late the Sweet Birds Sang* and also published *The Clewiston Test*, a novel about a female research scientist who fears how her discovery might be used. Vonda N. MCINTYRE won both Hugo and Nebula awards for her novel *Dreamsnake* (1978), a story of a healer traveling through a postnuclear landscape. Suzy McKee CHARNAS depicted a society where women are treated as cattle in *Walk to the End of the World* (1974), then followed it with a tale of an all-female society in *Motherlines* (1978). C. J. CHERRYH, noted for her detailed backgrounds and careful research, began to publish the first of her many novels. And the reading public learned that the acclaimed James TIPTREE, Jr., assumed to be a man with some sympathy for feminism, was in fact the retired psychologist Alice B. Sheldon.

Important SF by women outside the genre's circles includes Marge PIERCY's *Woman on the Edge of Time* (1976), Cecelia Holland's *Floating Worlds* (1976), Doris LESSING's *The Memoirs of a Survivor* (1975), Sally Miller Gearhart's *The Wanderground* (1978), Anna Kavan's *Ice* (1970), Monique Wittig's *Les Guérillères* (1971), and the striking fantastic fiction of Angela Carter. Pamela SARGENT reprinted short fiction by women in the an-

(left to right) Pamela Sargent, Margaret St. Clair, Lisa Tuttle, Connie Willis

thology *Women of Wonder* (1975), which proved popular enough to bring about two sequels, *More Women of Wonder* (1976) and *The New Women of Wonder* (1978). Vonda N. McIntyre and Susan Janice Anderson published original feminist SF by women and men in *Aurora: Beyond Equality* (1976); among the stories is Tiptree's controversial tale of male astronauts trapped on an all-female future Earth, "Houston, Houston, Do You Read?" Other anthologies of SF by women are Robert SILVERBERG's *The Crystal Ship* (1976), Virginia KIDD's *Millennial Women* (1978), and Alice Laurance's *Cassandra Rising* (1978); Sam MOSKOWITZ edited a collection of early utopian fiction entitled *When Women Rule* (1972), and Jessica A. SALMONSON published *Amazons!* (1979), an anthology featuring strong female characters.

Among other writers who began to publish during this decade were Doris PISERCHIA, Elizabeth A. LYNN, Marta RANDALL, Lisa TUTTLE, Grania Davis, Tanith LEE, Phyllis EISENSTEIN, Suzette Haden ELGIN, and Chelsea Quinn YARBRO. At the end of the decade, Octavia E. BUTLER, one of the few black writers of SF, combined SF and the historical experience of black people in her novels *Kindred* (1979) and *Wild Seed* (1980).

At the beginning of the 1980s, women still represented a minority in the field, but they were no longer a minor voice. Julian May, who had published no SF since her short story "Dune Roller" in 1953, came out with a novel, *The Many-Colored Land* (1980), the first in her Tales of Pliocene Exile series. Writers such as James Tiptree, Jr., Suzy McKee Charnas, Kate Wilhelm, Joanna Russ, Octavia E. Butler, Connie WILLIS, C. J. Cherryh, and Nancy Kress were to win a number of awards for their work; Andre Norton was given a Grand Master Nebula (for a body of work) in 1984; she was the first woman to be so honored. Anne McCaffrey, Marion Zimmer Bradley, and Ursula K. Le Guin became known to a much wider audience, while the percentage of female

SF readers and fans continued to increase. Joan D. VINGE won the Hugo Award for her novel *The Snow Queen* (1980), which shows the effect a black hole used as a gateway to other worlds might have on the culture of a distant planet. The book also draws on myth and fairy tales, thus making it a good example of the form known as science fantasy. Many women writers, among them Tanith Lee, Elizabeth A. Lynn, Marion Zimmer Bradley, Marta Randall, Chelsea Quinn Yarbro, and C. J. Cherryh, moved easily between writing SF and writing fantasy.

In spite of the growing diversity of women writers, the impression remained in some circles that women's writing, in addition to revealing a perceived gift for deeper characterization, is actually closer to fantasy and rarely draws on the hard sciences for material—a charge that might come as a surprise to readers of C. J. Cherryh, Katherine MacLEAN, some of the work of Janet Morris and Joan D. Vinge or, more recently, Susan SHWARTZ. In fact, the number of women who are writing, and the forms they use, make it impossible to generalize about their work as a whole. A necessarily incomplete list of women now writing SF would include Kim Antieau, Jayge CARR, Jo Clayton, Juanita COULSON, Diane Duane, Zoë Fairbairns, Cynthia Felice, Karen Joy Fowler, Leigh Kennedy, Lee KILLOUGH, Jacqueline LICHTENBERG, Jean Lorrah, Ardath Mayhar, Ann Maxwell, R. M. Meluch, Raylyn Moore, Barbara Paul, Diana L. Paxson, Rachel Pollack, Jody Scott, S. C. Sykes, Sydney J. VAN SCYOC, Sharon Webb, Cherry Wilder, and M. K. Wren. Fantasy writers of interest are Esther Friesner, Mary Gentle, Lisa Goldstein, Sharon Green, Barbara Hambly, Diana Wynne Jones, Phyllis Ann Karr, Katherine Kurtz, R. A. MacAvoy, Patricia A. McKILLIP, Robin McKinley, Meredith Pierce, Jessica A. Salmonson, Elizabeth Scarborough, and Nancy Springer; some of these have also written work that borders on SF. Among those who have written SF for younger readers are Virginia Hamilton, Jean Karl, A. M. Lightner,

Jan Mark, Louise Lawrence, Madeline L'ENGLE, and Jane Yolen. Two interesting collections of work by women, *Space of Her Own* (1984), edited by Shawna McCarthy, and *Despatches from the Frontiers of the Female Mind* (1985), edited by Jen Green and Sarah Lefanu, have also recently seen print. Notable too is Jeffrey M. Elliot's *Kindred Spirits* (1984), the first anthology of SF on gay and lesbian themes, which includes stories by women.

Although many male SF writers leave much to be desired in their treatment of female characters, several have attempted to go beyond stock characterizations. Works by men notable for their treatment of women include Philip WYLIE's *The Disappearance* (1951), in which both men and women suddenly find themselves in a world populated only by their own sex; Theodore STURGEON's *Venus Plus X* (1960), which depicts a world of hermaphrodites; and John WYNDHAM's "Consider Her Ways" (1956), which shows an all-female society and is told from the point of view of a twentieth-century woman. James H. Schmitz and Fritz LEIBER have also written sensitively about women. Among recent writers, Samuel R. DELANY and John VARLEY have clearly been influenced by the women's movement. It is no longer possible for writers to assume that traditional roles will necessarily persist in future societies.

At present women writers as a group are not ignored within science fiction, yet two recent developments show that another battle might be brewing. One is the growing conservatism of our culture as a whole, which has led to questions about what the goals of the women's movement should now be. Another, within the field, is the sudden, striking popularity of a kind of SF and a group of talented writers perhaps unfairly lumped together under the term CYBERPUNKS. This diverse and inventive band share a streetwise sensibility, a fascination with computers and technology of all kinds, a clean, forceful "tough guy" style, and a taste for bizarre future extrapolations; they also have in common the fact that, except for the witty writer Pat Cadigan, they are all male. Science fiction has always reflected the culture at large; in this age of increasing militarization, macho posturing, and second thoughts about the possibility or desirability of truly egalitarian societies, it is perhaps not surprising—although it is disheartening—that a largely male-dominated new form of SF that has all the infatuation with technology characteristic of much past work is being hailed as the forerunner of future SF.

Three recent works by women are notable in this context. Joan SLONCZEWSKI's *The Door into Ocean* (1986) draws on the author's training as a biologist to depict a pacifistic female society and a more aggressive masculine culture. Ursula K. Le Guin's *Always Coming Home* (1985) models its future world on tribal societies of the past; Le Guin has stated that she finds much modern SF "hard, gray, martial, and threatening." Margaret Atwood, in *The Handmaid's Tale* (1986), writes of a future

world in which women have no legal rights and are assigned rigid roles—and makes us believe that many women would assist in their own repression. All these novels raise questions about the role of women and emphasize the fact that, in both SF and the real world, women and men are still far from true equality.

P.S.

THE WORLD THE FLESH AND THE DEVIL (1959). *Directed by Ranald MacDougall; screenplay by Ranald MacDougall; loosely adapted from the novel* The Purple Cloud *by M. P. Shiel; photographed by Harold J. Marzorati; music by Miklos Rozsa. With Harry Belafonte, Inger Stevens, Mel Ferrer. 95 minutes. Black and white.*

Earnest, skillfully made, and well acted, *The World the Flesh and the Devil* was severely compromised by the introduction of irrelevant ideas and a refusal to treat some of its elements with logic.

A black miner (Harry Belafonte), trapped by a cave-in, emerges to find all of humanity dead, killed by radioactive sodium in the air. He goes into nearby Manhattan and sets up housekeeping. A young (white) woman (Inger Stevens) turns up, and shortly thereafter, a white man (Mel Ferrer). Sexual and racial tensions arise, and the two men stalk each other with guns but resolve their difficulties at the optimistic climax.

The filmmakers' intent was allegory rather than science fiction, but they also stressed believability; alas, allegory and credibility here work against each other—there are no bodies visible, for instance, and live birds are seen at the end—so the film is difficult to accept as either allegorical or realistic. The racial element, though nobly intended, is under the circumstances intrusive and unlikely.

However, the scenes of Belafonte alone in a real and deserted Manhattan, filmed with great difficulty, have an undeniable power, creating a sense of desolation and loss that no other end-of-the-world film has approached.

B.W.

WORLD SF. International organization of science-fiction professionals. The concept for World SF—an international organization not limited to writers, but including SF professionals of all kinds—came from a writers' convention promoted by Harry HARRISON in Dublin in 1976. The group's efforts have been focused on improving relationships between the SF communities of the Western and Socialist countries and improving and promoting translations, for which reason its annual awards, the Karels (named for the Czech science-fiction writer Karel CAPEK), are given to the best translators. The group meets annually, most often in Europe. Its first five presidents were Harrison (Ireland), Frederik POHL (U.S.A.),

Brian W. ALDISS (England), Sam LUNDWALL (Sweden), and Gianfranco Viviani (Italy).

E.A.H.

WRIGHT, S[YDNEY] FOWLER (1874–1965).

British writer. Wright made his first career as an accountant but involved himself with the Empire Poetry League and took charge of its publishing activities, issuing his extravagant futuristic fantasy *The Amphibians* (1924; combined with a sequel as *The World Below*, 1929) from the league's Merton Press. He founded his own publishing company to issue his translation of Dante's *Inferno* and his catastrophe story *Deluge* (1927), which became a best-seller. This was quickly followed by *The Island of Captain Sparrow* (1928). Wright's other SF novels include a trilogy whose heroine experiences other lives in the distant past and future: *Dream, or the Simian Maid* (1931), *The Vengeance of Gwa* (1935, as Anthony Wingrave), and *Spiders' War* (1954); and a future war trilogy: *Prelude in Prague* (1935), *Four Days War* (1936), and *Megiddo's Ridge* (1937). His short fiction, collected in *The New Gods Lead* (1932; expanded as *The Throne of Saturn*, 1949), is striking in its condemnation of social and technological trends.

OTHER WORKS: *Dawn* (1927); *The Bell Street Murders* (1931, as Sydney Fowler); *Beyond the Rim* (1932); *Power* (1933); *The Adventure of the Blue Room* (1945, as Sydney Fowler).

B.S.

WU, WILLIAM F. (1951–   ).

American writer whose stories include gentle fantasies, rollicking high-tech adventures, war-gaming fiction, and hard science fiction; all his fiction, however, is notable for its fluid use of language and its sensitive, unstereotypical characterizations. A 1974 graduate of the Clarion Science Fiction Writers Workshop, Wu has published works in fields as diverse as literary criticism, fantasy, horror, and SF. His short story "Wong's Lost and Found Emporium" (1983) was a nominee for the World Fantasy, Nebula, and Hugo awards in 1984, and his story "Hong's Bluff" (1985) was a nominee for the Nebula and the Hugo in 1986. In addition to his solo work, he has collaborated with Rob Chilson on a series of stories that began appearing in *Analog* in 1985. His nonfiction book *The Yellow Peril: Chinese Americans in American Fiction, 1850–1940* (1982) was a nominee for the Thorpe Menn Award in 1983. His first novel, *MasterPlay*, a story of war gaming and future justice, was published in 1987.

B.D.

WYLIE, PHILIP [GORDON] (1902–1971).

American writer who held a variety of government, publishing, and screenwriting jobs but produced science-fiction novels as well as other writing, including scathing analyses of American morality, such as the World War II best-seller *Generation of Vipers* (1942). During his lifetime Wylie was considered a major author even though he aimed at a popular audience.

Wylie decided early to write fact or fiction honestly and clearly, with a genuine respect for the broad popular audience he sought. Because of his literary connections, he published SF novels in nongenre markets while others faced the more restricted SF magazines. From *Gladiator* (1930) to *The End of the Dream* (1972), he produced ten SF novels.

Wylie's first three SF novels, *Gladiator, The Murderer Invisible* (1931), and *The Savage Gentleman* (1932), were social criticism; in each an outsider—by basic nature, capability, or upbringing—confronts the flaws in society. The gladiator, Hugo Banner, is a genetically produced superman (the comic-book hero SUPERMAN was inspired by the novel) who looks critically at such human follies as the stock market, fraternity parties, and football games. William Carpenter, a wronged scientist who finds a means to achieve invisibility in order to exact revenge, goes on to wreak mayhem. The savage gentleman, who has been educated far from humankind, is a variation on the Tarzan theme.

Wylie's most widely known SF novel, written in collaboration with Edwin BALMER, is *When Worlds Collide* (1933), in which a gas-giant planet destroys the Earth and a few parties escape in hastily built spaceships to an Earthlike satellite. Wylie and Balmer wrote a sequel, *After Worlds Collide* (1934), in which the various groups settle the new planet and squabble about forms of government. WHEN WORLDS COLLIDE was filmed by George PAL in 1951.

Wylie's cleverest novel, *The Disappearance* (1951), depicts a world-line split in which women and men suddenly find themselves in separate worlds; Wylie used this plot device to examine the roles of the sexes in contemporary America. After several nuclear catastrophe novels, Wylie's last, *The End of the Dream* (1972), describes an environmental apocalypse in which pollution and mutated ocean leeches wreak awful havoc. It is symptomatic of Wylie's writing that, to the moment of his death, he was seeking to improve humanity by exposing its foolishness to a broad audience.

OTHER WORKS: *Finnley Wrenn: A Novel in a New Manner* (1934); *Tomorrow* (1954); *Triumph* (1963).

P.B.

WYNDHAM, JOHN (Pseudonym of John Wyndham Parkes Lucas Beynon Harris) (1903–1969).

British writer who made a breakthrough into best-sellerdom with *The Day of the Triffids* (1951) and followed it with three other highly successful science-fiction novels, which together established him as one of the most widely read SF writers in the English-speaking world.

Wyndham was born in the English Midlands and started writing short stories in 1925; he had his first SF sale, as John Beynon Harris, in 1931: "Worlds to Barter" for *Wonder Stories*. In the 1930s and 1940s he published pulp magazine stories not noticeably more effective or successful than those of many other writers, mostly in the United States, under various pseudonyms. It was not until 1951 that he found his voice, and his fame, as Wyndham.

The Day of the Triffids, a novel of British bravery in the face of dual catastrophes—near universal blindness induced by a meteor shower and the spread of mobile killer plants (the triffids of the title)—greatly appealed to a generation of Britons accustomed to the reality and mythology of the blitz. It appealed, too, to an overseas audience as an effective revival of the genre in which British writers since H. G. WELLS had been notably successful: the catastrophe novel used as an opportunity to explore characters under extreme stress. It would launch a new tradition of such novels, particularly in Britain but spreading to the United States as well. A film version (see THE DAY OF THE TRIFFIDS) appeared in 1963.

Another Wyndham catastrophe novel followed: *The Kraken Wakes* (1953; published in the United States as *Out of the Deeps*). In 1955 came the very different, and much underestimated, *The Chrysalids* (published in the United States as *Re-Birth*), an early and effective exploration of mutants in a postholocaust society. A fourth major title is *The Midwich Cuckoos* (1957, alternate title *Village of the Damned*, filmed 1960; a sequel, *Children of the Damned*, was released in 1963). In it an eerie race of half-alien children is born to the women of an English village.

Wyndham's novels and short story collections, among them *Jizzle* (1954) and *The Seeds of Time* (1956), were in their day read much more widely in the United Kingdom and Australia than were those of other SF authors; they continue to be well known there, perhaps because they were successfully promoted as thrillers, not SF. Wyndham's books also were acceptable to those who might never have read the work of Isaac ASIMOV or Robert A. HEINLEIN, following as they did the grand tradition of H. G. Wells.

OTHER WORKS: *The Secret People* (1935); *Planet Plane* (1936, as John Beynon); *Stowaway to Mars* (1953); *The Outward Urge* (with Lucas Parkes, 1959); *Trouble with Lichen* (1960); *Consider Her Ways, and Others* (collection, 1961).

E.J.

X

X—THE MAN WITH X-RAY EYES (1963).
Directed by Roger Corman; screenplay by Robert Dillon and Ray Russell; photographed by Floyd Crosby; music by Les Baxter. With Ray Milland, Diana Van Der Vlis, Harold J. Stone, John Hoyt, Don Rickles, John Dierkes. 80 minutes. Color.

This atypical film from Roger CORMAN is one of his most interesting; although hampered by a budget far too low for the undertaking and a story line that fails to exploit thoroughly the possibilities of X-ray vision, *X—The Man with X-Ray Eyes* is intelligent and largely unsensational.

Dr. Xavier (Ray Milland), irritated that funds for his experiments to improve human vision have been cut off, administers his eyedrops to himself and finds he can see through cloth and paper. Obsessed with determining the limits of this new vision, he continues to take the drugs. When he accidentally causes the death of a colleague, he goes into hiding at a carnival. His X-ray vision becomes so powerful that he fears he can see to the center of the universe, all the way to God, and rips out his eyes.

Unlike Corman's other genre films, *X* is neither a horror film nor a monster movie but science-fiction melodrama. The basic plot is hackneyed—scientist experiments on self, things go wrong—but Corman's swift pace and Milland's good performance, as well as some philosophical speculation, make it well above average for its period. Some of the characters are standard types, but Xavier himself is unusually complex, neither the tortured victim of his own experiments nor a megalomaniac; his obsession with wanting to see more and more is a metaphor for scientific inquiry, and Corman and his writers do not judge Xavier for his desires, only for his obsession.

It's unfortunate that the special effects in the film are woefully inadequate, only barely suggesting the idea of X-ray vision. The film was more highly regarded at its initial release than it is now, but in time it will doubtless regain a measure of its initial fame.

B.W.

X THE UNKNOWN (1957).
Directed by Leslie Norman and Joseph Walton; screenplay by Jimmy Sangster; photographed by Gerald Gibbs; music by James Bernard. With Dean Jagger, Leo McKern, William Lucas, Edward Chapman, John Harvey, Anthony Newley, Ian MacNaughton, Michael Ripper. 78 minutes. Black and white.

This overlooked film is one of the best of the second-rank science-fiction films of the 1950s, although it is based on an unlikely premise. Throughout it is low key, realistic, well acted, enthusiastically ghoulish, and suspenseful. It is notable for being the first genre screenplay of Jimmy Sangster, who soon became famous for his series of screenplays for Hammer Films.

A creature from the center of the Earth emerges from a fissure in Scotland and seeks out radioactive material for sustenance; it is so radioactive itself that it dissolves passersby. It is disappointingly revealed as a vast living sheet of mud, and the ending is pointlessly inconclusive.

B.W.

Y

YARBRO, CHELSEA QUINN (1942–   ).

American writer, best known for her historical-fantasy novels about a vampire, Le Comte de Saint-Germain, who does more good than harm as he survives into various centuries. Born in Berkeley, California, where she still lives, Yarbro attended San Francisco State College and managed the Mirthmakers Children's Theatre, for which she also wrote plays. She has also been a cartographer, composer, and card and palm reader, as well as secretary of the SCIENCE FICTION WRITERS OF AMERICA, and has written suspense, occult, mystery, and children's fiction.

Yarbro's first science-fiction story, "The Posture of Prophecy," was published in *If* in 1969. Her first two novels, a suspense thriller and a dystopian SF work titled *Time of the Fourth Horseman*, were published in 1976. The latter, in which an attempt to control population by bringing back childhood diseases precipitates a greater catastrophe, set the tone for much of her science fiction, a tone captured in the title of her first collection, *Cautionary Tales* (1978). That year saw the publication as well of her second novel, *False Dawn* (which also deals with a world ravaged by disease), and her first Saint-Germain vampire novel, *Hotel Transylvania: A Novel of Forbidden Love.*

Yarbro's fantasies, on which most of her success has been built and which represent the largest part of her production, allow her greater opportunity for the color and romance that seem to be her particular specialties. All her fiction has to do, as she has written, "with some aspect of love and survival," and even her science fiction is used for the occasions it offers to place suitable characters under extreme stress. But where her SF is dark and its settings grim, her fantasies are almost operatic in their bright backdrops, large gestures, and grand moments.

"Music," Yarbro has written, "very much influenced me, not only as subject matter, but structurally as well,"

and as James TIPTREE, Jr., wrote in the introduction to *Cautionary Tales*, Yarbro likes to put characters in moments of confrontation that feel like grand opera duets. She celebrates the power of love, even love unrequited, as a positive force, and observes the love of power. She has even written stories based on opera, such as "Un Bel Di," which structures an encounter between alien races on *Madame Butterfly*.

NOTABLE OTHER WORKS: *On Saint Hubert's Thing* (collection, 1982); *Hyacinths* (1983); *Nomads* (novelization, 1984); *Signs and Portents* (collection, 1984).

J.E.G.

YEP, LAURENCE [MICHAEL] (1948–   ).

American writer of science fiction and children's stories, with a Ph.D. in English from the State University of New York, Buffalo. Yep's greatest success has been in the area of children's literature, most notably his novels about Chinese-Americans in San Francisco, for which he has received a number of awards. Nevertheless, he has produced a small but promising body of science fiction, distinguished by a sensitive use of language, imaginatively detailed descriptions of alien landscapes and civilizations, and an interest in serious themes. Much of his SF reflects, however indirectly, his own childhood sense of alienation. His first SF novel, *Sweetwater* (1973), is a juvenile about the conflict between traditional values and the need to survive by changing. He continued this theme with his first adult novel, *Seademons* (1977), wherein aliens teach human beings the importance of living harmoniously with their environment. Yep has also written *Shadow Lord* (1985), a novel in the STAR TREK series, and a few SF short stories.

S.H.G.

YOUNG, ROBERT F[RANKLIN] (1915–1986).

American who worked as an inspector in a nonferrous foundry; prolific writer of science-fiction and fantasy short stories since his first sale, "The Black Deep Thou Wingest" (1953). Young is better remembered for his short, flippant vignettes, often stinging satires on American society, than for his longer, more sensitive tales. Some of the best from his first decade of writing were collected as *The Worlds of Robert F. Young* (1965) and *A Glass of Stars* (1968), but a good selection of his later works is wanting. His most successful story was "Little Dog Gone" (1964), a Hugo nominee, but perhaps his best story is "To Fell a Tree" (1959), about a man's attempts on an alien world to cut down a vast tree that is home for a native dryad. This story was later redeveloped for his short novel *The Last Yggdrasill* (1982). A time travel adventure in prehistory, "When Time Was New" (1964), also formed the basis of a later novel, *Eridahn* (1983). His most serious novel-length work,

Starfinder (1980), concerns an organic space-time ship, the *Spacewhale*. Here Young explored the relationships among the captain, John Starfinder, the ship, and a young woman, Ciely Bleu, and developed an intriguing series of hieroglyphs to portray telepathic communication.

OTHER WORK: *The Vizier's Second Daughter* (1985).

M.A.

Z

ZAHN, TIMOTHY (1951–). American science-fiction writer who came into prominence in the mid-1980s, with three books published in 1985 and three more in 1986. Zahn's short fiction, however, particularly that published in ANALOG, was the first to attract notice for the puzzles it poses for its characters and readers alike. Born in Chicago, he earned a master's degree in physics from the University of Illinois, Urbana, where he now lives; he has been a full-time writer since 1980.

Zahn has written that the first duty of a writer of SF, or of any fiction, is to entertain. And since the appearance in ANALOG of his first story, "Ernie" (1979), he has had little trouble constructing entertaining stories, many of which take the form of challenges to the reader to solve a specific problem before the characters do. In "Hollow Victory" (1981), for instance, two humans must understand the nature of an alien disease using the limited set of clues available to them (and to the readers). Zahn is equally proficient, however, at adventure stories in which humans confront challenges as they explore space ("Cascade Point," 1983, winner of a Hugo Award), are contacted by aliens ("Dark Thoughts at Noon," 1982), or learn to adjust to changes within their own societies ("The Final Report on the Lifeline Experiment," 1983).

Zahn's novels stress action and frequently involve galactic empires (*Cobra*, 1985; *Spinneret*, 1985). *The Blackcollar* (1983) may remind readers of Robert A. HEINLEIN's *Starship Troopers* (1959) without Heinlein's lectures on government and citizenship. His novels rarely involve adventure to the exclusion of thought, however. In *A Coming of Age* (1985), for example, Zahn combines a mystery story with a fascinating portrait of a world on which all children have telekinetic powers until the onset of puberty. The mystery is engrossing, but of equal interest is his compelling study of a young girl who is rapidly approaching the loss of her powers. For Zahn this combination of entertainment and deeper meaning represents his definition of the SF writer's responsibility.

OTHER WORKS: *Cascade Point* (collection, 1986); *The Backlash Mission* (1986); *Cobra Strike* (1986); *Triplet* (1987).

S.H.G.

ZAMYATIN, YEVGENY [IVANOVICH] (1884–1937). Russian naval engineer and author who first embraced the Bolshevik Revolution but was vilified and silenced by Party orthodoxy in the late 1920s. Zamyatin sought and received permission from Stalin to leave the Soviet Union after the publication in an émigré journal of his great dystopia, *We* (1924).

We is based on the author's perceptions of what Soviet Communism was soon to become: people are numbers, individuality is abolished, sex is arranged by coupons, and the hero, after an illicit love affair, develops an "incurable condition," a soul, for which he undergoes an operation—the surgical removal of his imagination.

The novel was influential on the dystopias of the 1930s and 1940s. Influenced by the utopian and dystopian novels of H. G. WELLS, *We*, in company with Wells's works, marked the shift from the traditional notion of political change to the modern utopia or dystopia based on scientific and technological change. *We*, a major work of fiction and a major contribution to utopian thought, influenced, in turn, such later writers as Aldous HUXLEY and George ORWELL, particularly Orwell's *Nineteen Eighty-four* (1949). It is, however, more futuristic than Orwell's work: Zamyatin's Unique State of twelve centuries hence incorporates space travel and robots.

We was written in 1920 and published in English translation in 1924. Publication in the Soviet Union will finally become a reality in this age of *glasnost:* the novel is scheduled to appear in the magazine *Znamia* ("Banner").

D.S.

ZEBROWSKI, GEORGE (1945–). American science-fiction writer, editor, and critic. Born in Villach, Austria, the child of Poles who had been kidnapped by Germans as slave labor while still in their teens, Zebrowski spent part of his early life in Italy and England before he and his family arrived in the United States.

This early experience, along with Zebrowski's study of philosophy at the State University of New York, Binghamton, is reflected in his fiction, particularly his first novel, *The Omega Point* (1972), the story of a man whose home world was destroyed before his birth and who continues to fight his universe's old enemies. Zebrowski has been a full-time writer ever since; he also edited the *SFWA Bulletin* from 1970 to 1975 and again beginning in 1983, served as editor of Crown Books' SF reprint series, and edited more than half a dozen anthologies, including three volumes of Nebula Award Stories and a semiannual volume, *Synergy*.

A sense of displacement and the search for a cosmic vision characterize much of Zebrowski's writing, including the novel for which he is best known, *Macrolife* (1979). This book begins with a future Earth moving toward destruction, depicts the society of mobile space habitats in which the survivors live, and concludes with the ultimate fate of the universe.

Zebrowski's two novels for young adults also display his ability to develop a complex technological background and scientifically sophisticated ideas. In *Sunspacer* (1984) a teenage boy leaves the Earth to attend college in a space habitat and eventually joins the space dwellers. *The Stars Will Speak* (1985) tells of a teenage girl who leaves her space habitat to study with those on the Earth who are trying to decode a message from an alien civilization.

Unlike some writers known for their cosmic scope, such as Olaf STAPLEDON, Zebrowski shows an equal command of the shorter forms; his short stories are cogent and sharply written. "Heathen God" (1971), his fourth story and the first nominated for a Nebula Award, is about a priest's encounter with an alien who might be God; it displays the author's penchant for intellectual adventure. "Starcrossed" (1973) relates the erotic imaginings of a cyborg-piloted spaceship; "The Cliometricon" (1975), with its nameless narrator who explores various historical possibilities on a screen, comments on the alternate-history theme. "The Word Sweep" (1979) describes a future in which words materialize into objects. "The Eichmann Variations" (1984), told from the point of view of the infamous war criminal, and "General Jaruzelski at the Zoo" (1987), an allegory about Poland's relationship with the Soviet Union, are literarily sophisticated and surrealistic, with sharp social and political commentary, while in "Gödel's Doom" (1985) a change in a central mathematical theorem alters reality.

What unites these otherwise dissimilar stories, and indeed all Zebrowski's work, is the author's willingness to tackle difficult themes, new and genuinely original ideas, and the human reaction to a wide variety of unique situations and dilemmas, and his ability to write about them in his distinctive, carefully wrought, and often poetic prose style. He writes hard SF with literary intent.

OTHER WORKS: *The Star Web* (1975); *Ashes and Stars* (1977); *The Monadic Universe and Other Stories* (collection, 1977).

                                                                                                    J.M.E.

ZELAZNY, ROGER (1937–   ).

American science-fiction and fantasy writer who rose quickly in the mid-1960s to a front-rank position in the field with both readers and critics and has remained there since. Born in Cleveland, Ohio, Zelazny attended Western Reserve University and Columbia University, where he earned an M.A. in English. He worked as an interviewer for the Social Security Administration before becoming a full-time writer in 1969. His earliest writings, marked by frequent allusions to literature and mythology and constructed around internal conflicts motivated by religious

Roger Zelazny

and psychological themes, are vivid, fast paced, and skillfully written. Along with Harlan ELLISON and Samuel R. DELANY, he sometimes is considered, because of his concern with literary style, one of the leading members of the American NEW WAVE.

Zelazny's writings characteristically feature religious backgrounds and themes, and his protagonists tend to be both active and intensely contemplative. The hero of *This Immortal* (1966), his first novel, which won a Hugo Award, must keep himself alive while touring a ruined Earth and at the same time come to terms with his own motivations: is he controlled by decisions he made in the past, or is he free to act anew?

Zelazny's characterizations resonate with allusions to myth and literature. Gallinger, the hero of his SFWA Hall of Fame novelette "A Rose for Ecclesiastes" (1963), thinks of himself as a tragic Hamletlike figure and at first sees parallels to *Hamlet* in his own experience. The story ends, however, not with a corpse-littered stage but with images of rebirth.

Zelazny's early work shows special delight in stretching the limits of SF storytelling. *The Immortal*, with its wry superman, was followed by the very different mood of *The Dream Master* (1966), published originally as the Nebula Award–winning novella "He Who Shapes" (1965). It features Zelazny's only truly tragic hero, a "neuroparticipation" therapist who rearranges the dreams of his patients and eventually surrenders to the madness of one of them. "A Rose for Ecclesiastes" and "The Doors of His Face, the Lamps of His Mouth" (winner of the 1965 Nebula Award) pay homage to the pulp magazine SF written about an inhabited Mars and a watery Venus.

Lord of Light (1967 Hugo winner) is probably Zelazny's finest novel. It describes a planet colonized by refugees from India who are tyrannized by a few of their fellow citizens who have assumed the guise and powers of the Hindu gods. Instead of easing his readers into the strange setting and unfamiliar mythology, Zelazny began the story in the middle, centuries after the initial landing; that the reader can absorb—and care to absorb—the complexities of the plot and setting is a tribute to the author's storytelling ability.

Lord of Light was followed by the moving *Isle of the Dead* (1969), in which the protagonist discovers that he is the embodiment of an alien god's will. Notable later works include *Doorways in the Sand* (1976), a lighthearted SF mystery that is probably Zelazny's most accessible novel and is one of his two personal favorites (the other is *Lord of Light*); *Eye of Cat* (1982), which draws on American Indian mythology; and the deceptively casual fantasy stories in *Dilvish, the Damned* and *The Changing Land* (both 1981).

In 1970, with the Amber series, Zelazny turned his attention to fantasy, although it is a form of fantasy in which the magic is as circumscribed as science. The first Amber series comprises five novels: *Nine Princes in Amber* (1970), *The Guns of Avalon* (1972), *Sign of the Unicorn* (1975), *The Hand of Oberon* (1976), and *The Courts of Chaos* (1978). The parallel worlds that radiate from Amber ("the one, true world") have the feel of magic, but the series can also be considered alternate-world SF. It has provided Zelazny with a broad canvas on which to depict a man's discovery of the ambiguities of his personal responsibilities while he struggles to keep his world from absorption into the Chaos from which it was born. Readers, who have made the books Zelazny's most persistently popular, generally ignore the novels' serious content and focus instead on the romance and adventure of Amber's superpowered royal family. Zelazny has extended the Amber series with another five-part series, in which he has continued the adventures of the son of the hero of the earlier books.

Whether writing straight science fiction or fantasy tinged with SF, Zelazny remains one of the most fascinating and consistently interesting writers in the genre. His work is distinguished by a willingness to try new ideas and styles.

OTHER WORKS: *Four for Tomorrow* (collection, 1967); *Nebula Award Stories Three* (editor, 1968); *Creatures of Light and Darkness* (1969); *Damnation Alley* (1969); *The Doors of His Face, the Lamps of His Mouth, and Other Stories* (collection, 1971); *Jack of Shadows* (1971); *Today We Choose Faces* (1973); *To Die in Italbar* (1973); *Bridge of Ashes* (1976); *Deus Irae* (with Philip K. Dick, 1976); *My Name Is Legion* (collection, 1976); *The Illustrated Roger Zelazny* (collection, 1978); *Roadmarks* (1979); *The Last Defender of Camelot* (collection, 1980); *Changeling* (1980); *Coils* (with Fred Saberhagen, 1980); *Madwand* (1981); *A Rhapsody of Amber* (1981); *Unicorn Variations* (collection, 1983); *Trumps of Doom* (1985); *Blood of Amber* (1986); *Signs of Chaos*.

J.S.

CHECKLIST OF MOVIE
AND TELEVISION ENTRIES

The Abominable Snowman of the Himalayas
The Absent-Minded Professor
The Adventures of Buckaroo Banzai
Aelita
Alien
Aliens
Allen, Irwin
Alphaville
Alraune
Altered States
The Amazing Colossal Man
Android
The Andromeda Strain
The Angry Red Planet
Animal Farm
Arnold, Jack
Attack of the Crab Monsters
Attack of the 50-Foot Woman
Back to the Future
Barbarella
Battle beyond the Stars
Battle for the Planet of the Apes
Battlestar Galactica
The Beast from 20,000 Fathoms
Beast with a Million Eyes
Beneath the Planet of the Apes
Berkeley Square
The Birds
The Black Hole
The Black Scorpion
Blade Runner
The Blob
Blue Thunder
A Boy and His Dog
The Boys from Brazil
The Brain from Planet Arous
Brainstorm
Brazil
Bride of Frankenstein
Bride of the Monster
The Brother from Another Planet
Buck Rogers
Capricorn One
Carlson, Richard
Carpenter, John
Cat-Women of the Moon
Charly
Children of the Damned
The China Syndrome
The Clan of the Cave Bear

A Clockwork Orange
Close Encounters of the Third Kind
Cocoon
The Colossus of New York
Colossus: The Forbin Project
The Conquest of Space
Conquest of the Planet of the Apes
Corman, Roger
The Cosmic Monster
Crabbe, Buster
Crack in the World
The Crawling Eye
Creature from the Black Lagoon
Creature from the Haunted Sea
The Creature Walks among Us
Creature with the Atom Brain
Cronenberg, David
The Curse of Frankenstein
Damnation Alley
Dante, Joe
Dark Star
The Day After
The Day of the Triffids
The Day the Earth Caught Fire
The Day the Earth Stood Still
The Day the World Ended
The Deadly Mantis
Demon Seed
Destination Moon
Devil Doll
Devil Girl from Mars
Dr. Cyclops
Dr. Jekyll and Mr. Hyde on Film
Dr. Strangelove
Doctor Who
Doctor X
Donovan's Brain
Dune
E.T.: The Extra-Terrestrial
Earth vs. the Flying Saucers
The Empire Strikes Back
Enemy Mine
Escape from New York
Escape from the Planet of the Apes
The Evil of Frankenstein
The Fabulous World of Jules Verne
Fahrenheit 451
Fail Safe
Fantastic Planet
Fantastic Voyage
Film

The Final Countdown
First Man into Space
First Men in the Moon
Five
Flash Gordon
The Fly
Forbidden Planet
Four-Sided Triangle
Frankenstein on Film
From the Earth to the Moon
Futureworld
The Ghost of Frankenstein
The Giant Behemoth
Glen and Randa
Godzilla, King of the Monsters
Gorgo
Hangar 18
Harryhausen, Ray
Haskin, Byron
Heartbeeps
The Hitch-Hiker's Guide to the Galaxy
Homunculus
The Horror of Frankenstein
House of Dracula
House of Frankenstein
I Married a Monster from Outer Space
Iceman
I'll Never Forget You
The Illustrated Man
The Immortal
The Incredible Shrinking Man
The Incredible Shrinking Woman
Innerspace
Invaders from Mars
Invasion of the Body Snatchers
Invasion U.S.A.
The Invisible Boy
The Invisible Man
The Invisible Ray
Island of Dr. Moreau
Island of Lost Souls
It Came from beneath the Sea
It Came from Outer Space
It Conquered the World
It! The Terror from beyond Space
La Jetée
Journey to the Center of the Earth
Journey to the Seventh Planet
Just Imagine

ILLUSTRATION CREDITS AND ACKNOWLEDGMENTS